FROM DEAD TO WORSE

Also by Charlaine Harris

SOOKIE STACKHOUSE

Dead Until Dark

Living Dead in Dallas

Club Dead

Dead to the World

Dead as a Doornail

Definitely Dead

All Together Dead

From Dead to Worse

Dead and Gone

HARPER CONNELLY

Grave Sight

Grave Surprise

An Ice Cold Grave

Grave Secret

FROM DEAD TO WORSE

CHARLAINE HARRIS

First published in Great Britain in 2008 by
Gollancz
An imprint of the Orion Publishing Group
Orion House, 5 Upper St Martin's Lane, London WC2H 9EA
An Hachette UK Company

This edition published in Great Britain in 2009 by
Gollancz

7 9 10 8

A CIP catalogue record for this book
is available from the British Library

ISBN 978 0 575 08396 7

Printed and bound in the UK by
CPI Mackays, Chatham ME5 8TD

The Orion Publishing Group's policy is to use papers that are natural, renewable and recyclable products and made from wood grown in sustainable forests. The logging and manufacturing processes are expected to conform to the environmental regulations of the country of origin.

www.orionbooks.co.uk

Though she can't walk or see quite as well as she used to, my mother, Jean Harris, remains the most complete person I have ever met. She's been the bulwark of my existence, the foundation I was built on, and the best mother a woman could have.

ACKNOWLEDGMENTS

A tip of the hat to Anastasia Luettecke, who was a perfectionist in supplying me with Octavia's Latin. And thanks to Murv Sellars for being the go-between. As always, I owe a great debt of thanks to Toni L. P. Kelner and Dana Cameron for their valuable comments and the gift of their time. My one and only minion, Debi Murray, assisted me with her encyclopedic knowledge of the Sookie universe. The group of enthusiastic readers known as Charlaine's Charlatans gave me moral (and morale) support, and I hope this book will serve as their reward.

If this was The Lord of the Rings *and I had a smart British* voice like Cate Blanchett, I could tell you the background of the events of that fall in a really suspenseful way. And you'd be straining to hear the rest.

But what happened in my little corner of northwest Louisiana wasn't an epic story. The vampire war was more of the nature of a small-country takeover, and the Were war was like a border skirmish. Even in the annals of supernatural America—I guess they exist somewhere—they were minor chapters . . . unless you were actively involved in the takeovers and skirmishes.

Then they became pretty damn major.

And everything was due to Katrina, the disaster that just kept on spreading grief, woe, and permanent change in its wake.

Before Hurricane Katrina, Louisiana had a flourishing vampire community. In fact, the vampire population of New Orleans had burgeoned, making it the place to go if you wanted to see vampires; and lots of Americans did. The undead jazz clubs, featuring musicians no one had seen playing in public in decades, were special draws. Vamp strip clubs, vamp psychics, vamp sex acts; secret and not-so-secret places where you could get bitten and have an orgasm on the spot: all this was available in southern Louisiana.

In the northern part of the state . . . not so much. I live in the northern part in a small town called Bon Temps. But even in my area, where vamps are relatively thin on the ground, the undead were making economic and social strides.

All in all, vampire business in the Pelican State was booming. But then came the death of the King of Arkansas while his wife, the Queen of Louisiana, was entertaining him soon after their wedding. Since the corpse vanished and all the witnesses—except me—were supernaturals, human law took no notice. But the other vampires did, and the queen, Sophie-Anne Leclerq, landed in a very dicey legal position. Then came Katrina, which wiped out the financial base of Sophie-Anne's empire. Still, the queen was floundering back from those disasters, when another one followed hard on their heels. Sophie-Anne and some of her strongest adherents—and me, Sookie Stackhouse, telepath and human—were caught in a terrible explosion in Rhodes, the destruction of the vampire hotel called the Pyramid of Gizeh. A splinter group of the Fellowship of the Sun claimed responsibility, and while the leaders of that anti-vampire "church" decried the hate crime, everyone knew that the Fellowship was hardly agonizing over those who were terribly wounded in the blast, much less over the (finally, absolutely) dead vampires or the humans who served them.

Sophie-Anne lost her legs, several members of her entourage, and her dearest companion. Her life was saved by her half-demon lawyer, Mr. Cataliades. But her recuperation time was going to be lengthy, and she was in a position of terrible vulnerability.

What part did I play in all this?

I'd helped save lives after the pyramid went down, and I was terrified I was now on the radar of people who might want me to spend my time in their service, using my telepathy for their purposes. Some of those purposes were good, and I wouldn't mind lending a hand in rescue services from time to time, but I wanted to keep my life to myself. I was alive; my boyfriend, Quinn, was alive; and the vampires most important to me had survived, too. As far as the troubles Sophie-Anne faced, the political consequences of the attack and the fact that supernatural groups were circling the weakened state of Louisiana like hyenas around a dying gazelle . . . I didn't think about it at all.

I had other stuff on my mind, personal stuff. I'm not used to thinking much further than the end of my fingertips; that's my only excuse. Not only was I not thinking about the vampire situation, there was another supernatural situation I didn't ponder that turned out to be just as crucial to my future.

Close to Bon Temps, in Shreveport, there's a Were pack whose ranks are swollen by the men and women from Barksdale Air Force Base. During the past year, this Were pack had become sharply divided between two factions. I'd learned in American History what Abraham Lincoln, quoting the Bible, had to say about houses divided.

To assume that these two situations would work themselves out, to fail to foresee that their resolution would involve me, well . . . that was where I was almost fatally blind. I'm telepathic, not psychic. Vampire minds are big relaxing blanks to me. Weres are difficult to read, though not impossible. That's my only excuse for being unaware of the trouble brewing all around me.

What was I so busy thinking about? Weddings—and my missing boyfriend.

Chapter 1

I was making a neat arrangement of liquor bottles on the folding table behind the portable bar when Halleigh Robinson rushed up, her normally sweet face flushed and tear-streaked. Since she was supposed to be getting married within an hour and was still wearing blue jeans and a T-shirt, she got my immediate attention.

"Sookie!" she said, rounding the bar to grab my arm. "You have to help me."

I'd already helped her by putting on my bartending clothes instead of the pretty dress I'd planned on wearing. "Sure," I said, imagining Halleigh wanted me to make her a special drink— though if I'd listened in to her thoughts, I'd have known differently already. However, I was trying to be on my best behavior, and I was shielding like crazy. Being telepathic is no picnic, especially at a high-tension event like a double wedding. I'd expected to be a guest instead of a bartender. But the caterer's bartender had been in a car wreck on her way over from Shreveport, and Sam, who'd been unhired when E(E)E had insisted on using their own bartender, was abruptly hired again.

I was a little disappointed to be on the working side of the bar, but you had to oblige the bride on her special day. "What can I do for you?" I asked.

"I need you to be my bridesmaid," she said.

"Ah . . . what?"

"Tiffany fainted after Mr. Cumberland took the first round of pictures. She's on her way to the hospital."

It was an hour before the wedding, and the photographer had been trying to get a number of group shots out of the way. The bridesmaids and the groomsmen were already togged out. Halleigh should have been getting into her wedding finery, but instead here she was in jeans and curlers, no makeup, and a tear-streaked face.

Who could resist that?

"You're the right size," she said. "And Tiffany is probably just about to have her appendix out. So, can you try on the dress?"

I glanced at Sam, my boss.

Sam smiled at me and nodded. "Go on, Sook. We don't officially open for business until after the wedding."

So I followed Halleigh into Belle Rive, the Bellefleur mansion, recently restored to something like its antebellum glory. The wooden floors gleamed, the harp by the stairs shone with gilt, the silverware displayed on the big sideboard in the dining room glowed with polishing. There were servers in white coats buzzing around everywhere, the E(E)E logo on their tunics done in an elaborate black script. Extreme(ly Elegant) Events had become the premier upscale caterer in the United States. I felt a stab in my heart when I noticed the logo, because my missing guy worked for the supernatural branch of E(E)E. I didn't have long to feel the ache, though, because Halleigh was dragging me up the stairs at a relentless pace.

The first bedroom at the top was full of youngish women in gold-colored dresses, all fussing around Halleigh's soon-to-be sister-in-law, Portia Bellefleur. Halleigh zoomed past that door to enter the second room on the left. It was equally full of younger women, but these were in midnight blue chiffon. The room was in chaos, with the bridesmaids' civilian clothes piled here and there. There was a makeup and hair station over by the west wall, staffed by a stoic woman in a pink smock, curling rod in her hand.

Halleigh tossed introductions through the air like paper pellets. "Gals, this is Sookie Stackhouse. Sookie, this is my sister Fay, my cousin Kelly, my best friend Sarah, my other best friend Dana. And here's the dress. It's an eight."

I was amazed that Halleigh had had the presence of mind to divest Tiffany of the bridesmaid dress before her departure for the hospital. Brides are ruthless. In a matter of minutes, I was stripped down to the essentials. I was glad I'd worn nice underwear, since there wasn't any time for modesty. How embarrassing it would have been to be in granny panties with holes! The dress was lined, so I didn't need a slip, another stroke of luck.

There was a spare pair of thigh-highs, which I pulled on, and then the dress went over my head. Sometimes I wear a ten—in fact, most of the time—so I was holding my breath while Fay zipped it up.

If I didn't breathe a lot, it would be okay.

"Super!" one of the other women (Dana?) said with great happiness. "Now the shoes."

"Oh, God," I said when I saw them. They were very high heels dyed to match the midnight blue dress, and I slid my feet into them, anticipating pain. Kelly (maybe) buckled the straps, and I stood up. All of us held our breath as I took a step, then another. They were about half a size too small. It was an important half.

"I can get through the wedding," I said, and they all clapped.

"Over here then," said Pink Smock, and I sat in her chair and had more makeup reapplied over my own and my hair redone while the real bridesmaids and Halleigh's mother assisted Halleigh into her dress. Pink Smock had a lot of hair to work with. I've only had light trims in the past three years, I guess, and it's way down past my shoulder blades now. My roommate, Amelia, had put some highlights in, and that had turned out real good. I was blonder than ever.

I examined myself in the full-length mirror, and it seemed impossible I could have been so transformed in twenty minutes. From working barmaid in a white ruffled tux shirt and black trousers to bridesmaid in a midnight blue dress—and three inches taller, to boot.

Hey, I looked *great.* The dress was a super color for me, the skirt was gently A-line, the short sleeves weren't too tight, and it wasn't low cut enough to look slutty. With my boobs, the slut factor kicks in if I'm not careful.

I was yanked out of self-admiration by the practical Dana, who said, "Listen, here's the drill." From that moment on, I listened and nodded. I examined a little diagram. I nodded some more. Dana was one organized gal. If I ever invaded a small country, this was the woman I wanted on my side.

By the time we made our way carefully down the stairs (long skirts and high heels, not a good combination), I was fully briefed and ready for my first trip down the aisle as a bridesmaid.

Most girls have done this a couple of times before they reach twenty-six, but Tara Thornton, the only friend I had close enough to ask me, had up and eloped while I was out of town.

The other wedding party was assembled downstairs when we descended. Portia's group would precede Halleigh's. The two grooms and their groomsmen were already outside if all was going smoothly, because now it was five minutes until liftoff.

Portia Bellefleur and her bridesmaids averaged seven years older than Halleigh's posse. Portia was the big sister of Andy Bellefleur, Bon Temps police detective and Halleigh's groom. Portia's dress was a little over-the-top—it was covered with pearls and so much lace and sequins I thought it could stand by itself—but then, it was Portia's big day and she could wear whatever she damn well pleased. All Portia's bridesmaids were wearing gold.

The bridesmaids' bouquets all matched—white and dark

blue and yellow. Coordinated with the dark blue of Halleigh's bridesmaid selection, the result was very pretty.

The wedding planner, a thin nervous woman with a big cloud of dark curly hair, counted heads almost audibly. When she was satisfied everyone she needed was present and accounted for, she flung open the double doors to the huge brick patio. We could see the crowd, backs to us, seated on the lawn in two sections of white folding chairs, with a strip of red carpet running between the two sides. They were facing the platform where the priest stood at an altar decked in cloth and gleaming candlesticks. To the right of the priest, Portia's groom, Glen Vick, was waiting, facing the house. And, therefore, us. He looked very, very nervous, but he was smiling. His groomsmen were already in position flanking him.

Portia's golden bridesmaids stepped out onto the patio, and one by one they began their march down the aisle through the manicured garden. The scent of wedding flowers made the night sweet. And the Belle Rive roses were blooming, even in October.

Finally, to a huge swell of music, Portia crossed the patio to the end of the carpet, the wedding coordinator (with some effort) lifting the train of Portia's dress so it wouldn't drag on the bricks.

At the priest's nod, everyone stood and faced the rear so they could see Portia's triumphal march. She'd waited years for this.

After Portia's safe arrival at the altar, it was our party's turn. Halleigh gave each one of us an air kiss on the cheek as we stepped past her out onto the patio. She even included me, which was sweet of her. The wedding coordinator sent us off one by one, to stand reflecting our designated groomsman up front. Mine was a Bellefleur cousin from Monroe who was quite startled to see me coming instead of Tiffany. I walked at the slow pace Dana had emphasized and held my bouquet in my clasped hands at the desired angle. I'd been watching the other maids like a hawk. I wanted to get this right.

All the faces were turned to me, and I was so nervous I forgot to block. The thoughts of the crowd rushed at me in a gush of unwanted communication. *Looks so pretty... What happened to Tiffany...? Wow, what a rack.... Hurry it up, I need a drink.... What the hell am I doing here? She drags me to every dog fight in the parish.... I love wedding cake.*

A photographer stepped in front of me and took a picture. It was someone I knew, a pretty werewolf named Maria-Star Cooper. She was the assistant of Al Cumberland, a well-known photographer based in Shreveport. I smiled at Maria-Star and she took another shot. I continued down the carpet, held on to my smile, and pushed away all the racket in my head.

After a moment I noticed there were blank spots in the crowd, which signaled the presence of vampires. Glen had requested a night wedding specifically so he could invite some of his more important vampire clients. I'd been sure Portia truly loved him when she agreed to that, because Portia didn't like bloodsuckers at all. In fact, they gave her the creeps.

I kind of liked vampires in general, because their brains were closed to me. Being in their company was oddly restful. Okay, a strain in other ways, but at least my brain could relax.

Finally, I arrived at my designated spot. I'd watched Portia and Glen's attendants arrange themselves in an inverted V, with a space at the front for the nuptial couple. Our group was doing the same thing. I'd nailed it, and I exhaled in relief. Since I wasn't taking the place of the maid of honor, my work was over. All I had to do was stand still and look attentive, and I thought I could do that.

The music swelled to a second crescendo, and the priest gave his signal again. The crowd rose and turned to look at the second bride. Halleigh began moving slowly toward us. She looked absolutely radiant. Halleigh had selected a much simpler dress than Portia's, and she looked very young and very sweet. She was at least five years younger than Andy, maybe more. Halleigh's dad, as tanned and fit as his wife, stepped out to take Halleigh's arm when she drew abreast; since Portia had come down the aisle alone (her father was long dead), it had been decided Halleigh would, too.

After I'd had my fill of Halleigh's smile, I looked over the crowd who'd rotated to follow the bride's progress.

There were so many familiar faces: teachers from the elementary school where Halleigh taught, members of the police department where Andy worked, the friends of old Mrs. Caroline Bellefleur who were still alive and tottering, Portia's fellow lawyers and other people who worked in the justice system, and Glen Vick's clients and other accountants. Almost every chair was occupied.

There were a few black faces to be seen, and a few brown faces, but most of the wedding guests were middle-class

Caucasians. The palest faces in the crowd were the vampires', of course. One of them I knew well. Bill Compton, my neighbor and former lover, was sitting about halfway back, wearing a tuxedo and looking very handsome. Bill managed to seem at home in whatever he chose to wear. Beside him sat his human girlfriend, Selah Pumphrey, a real estate agent from Clarice. She was wearing a burgundy gown that set off her dark hair. There were perhaps five vamps I didn't recognize. I assumed they were clients of Glen's. Though Glen didn't know it, there were several other attendees who were more (and less) than human.

My boss, Sam, was a rare true shapeshifter who could become any animal. The photographer was a werewolf like his assistant. To all the regular wedding guests, he looked like a well-rounded, rather short African-American male wearing a nice suit and carrying a big camera. But Al turned into a wolf at the full moon just like Maria-Star. There were a few other Weres in the crowd, though only one I knew—Amanda, a red-haired woman in her late thirties who owned a bar in Shreveport called the Hair of the Dog. Maybe Glen's firm handled the bar's books.

And there was one werepanther, Calvin Norris. Calvin had brought a date, I was glad to see, though I was less than thrilled after I identified her as Tanya Grissom. Blech. What was she doing back in town? And why had Calvin been on the guest list? I liked him, but I couldn't figure out the connection.

While I'd been scanning the crowd for familiar faces, Halleigh had assumed her position by Andy, and now all the bridesmaids and groomsmen had to face forward to listen to the service.

Since I didn't have a big emotional investment in this proceeding, I found myself mentally wandering while Father Kempton Littrell, the Episcopal priest who ordinarily came to the little Bon Temps church once every two weeks, conducted the service. The lights that had been set up to illuminate the garden glinted off Father Littrell's glasses and bleached some of the color out of his face. He looked almost like a vampire.

Things proceeded pretty much on the standard plan. Boy, it was lucky I was used to standing up at the bar, because this was a lot of standing, and in high heels, too. I seldom wore heels, much less three-inch ones. It felt strange being five foot nine. I tried not to shift around, possessed my soul with patience.

Now Glen was putting the ring on Portia's finger, and Portia looked almost pretty as she looked down at their clasped hands. She'd never be one of my favorite people—nor I hers—but I wished her well. Glen was bony and had darkish receding hair and major glasses. If you called central casting and ordered an "accountant type," they'd send you Glen. But I could tell directly from his brain that he loved Portia, and she loved him.

I let myself shift a bit, put my weight a little more on my right leg.

Then Father Littrell started all over again on Halleigh and Andy. I kept my smile pasted to my face (no problem there; I did it all the time at the bar) and watched Halleigh become Mrs. Andrew Bellefleur. I was lucky. Episcopalian weddings can be long, but the two couples had opted for having the shorter form of the service.

At last the music swelled to triumphant strains, and the newlyweds exited to the house. The wedding party trailed after them in reverse order. On my way down the aisle, I felt genuinely happy and a weensy bit proud. I'd helped Halleigh in her time of need... and very soon I was going to get to take these shoes off.

From his chair, Bill caught my eye and silently put his hand over his heart. It was a romantic and totally unexpected gesture, and for a moment I softened toward him. I very nearly smiled, though Selah was right there by his side. Just in time, I reminded myself that Bill was a no-good rat bastard, and I swept on my painful way. Sam was standing a couple of yards past the last row of chairs, wearing a white tux shirt like the one I'd had on and black dress pants. Relaxed and at ease, that was Sam. Even his tangled halo of strawberry blond hair somehow fit in.

I flashed him a genuine smile, and he grinned back. He gave me a thumbs-up, and though shifter brains are hard to read, I could tell he approved of the way I looked and the way I'd conducted myself. His bright blue eyes never left me. He's been my boss for five years, and we've gotten along great for the most part. He'd been pretty upset when I'd started dating a vampire, but he'd gotten over it.

I needed to get to work, and pronto. I caught up with Dana. "When can we change?" I asked.

"Oh, we have pictures to do yet," Dana said cheerfully. Her

husband had come up to put his arm around her. He was holding their baby, a tiny thing swaddled in sex-neutral yellow.

"Surely I won't be needed for those," I said. "You-all took a lot of pictures earlier, right? Before what's-her-name got sick."

"Tiffany. Yes, but there'll be more."

I seriously doubted the family would want me in them, though my absence would unbalance the symmetry in the group pictures. I found Al Cumberland.

"Yes," he said, snapping away at the brides and grooms as they beamed at each other. "I do need some shots. You got to stay in costume."

"Crap," I said, because my feet hurt.

"Listen, Sookie, the best I can do is to shoot your group first. Andy, Halleigh! That is... Mrs. Bellefleur! If you-all will come this way, let's get your pictures done."

Portia Bellefleur Vick looked a little astonished that her group wasn't going first, but she had way too many people to greet to really get riled. While Maria-Star snapped away at the touching scene, a distant relative wheeled old Miss Caroline up to Portia, and Portia bent to kiss her grandmother. Portia and Andy had lived with Miss Caroline for years, after their own parents had passed away. Miss Caroline's poor health had delayed the weddings at least twice. The original plan had been for last spring, and it had been a rush job because Miss Caroline was failing. She'd had a heart attack and then recovered. After that, she'd broken her hip. I had to say, for someone who'd survived two major health disasters, Miss Caroline looked... Well, to tell the truth, she looked just like a very old lady who'd had a heart attack and a broken hip. She was all dressed up in a beige silk suit. She even had on some makeup, and her snow-white hair was arranged à la Lauren Bacall. She'd been a beauty in her day, an autocrat her entire life, and a famous cook until the recent past.

Caroline Bellefleur was in her seventh heaven this night. She'd married off both her grandchildren, she was getting plenty of tribute, and Belle Rive was looking spectacular, thanks to the vampire who was staring at her with an absolutely unreadable face.

Bill Compton had discovered he was the Bellefleurs' ancestor, and he had anonymously given Miss Caroline a whacking big bunch of money. She'd enjoyed spending it so much, and she had had no idea it had come from a vampire. She'd thought it a legacy from a distant relative. I thought it was kind of ironic that the Bellefleurs would just as soon have spit on Bill as thanked him. But he was part of the family, and I was glad he'd found a way to attend.

I took a deep breath, banished Bill's dark gaze from my consciousness, and smiled at the camera. I occupied my designated space in the pictures to balance out the wedding party, dodged the googly-eyed cousin, and finally hotfooted it up the stairs to change into my bartender's rig.

There was no one up here, and it was a relief to be in the room by myself.

I shimmied out of the dress, hung it up, and sat on a stool to unbuckle the straps of the painful shoes.

There was a little sound at the door, and I looked up,

startled. Bill was standing just inside the room, his hands in his pockets, his skin glowing gently. His fangs were out.

"Trying to change here," I said tartly. No point in making a big show of modesty. He'd seen every inch of me.

"You didn't tell them," he said.

"Huh?" Then my brain caught up. Bill meant that I hadn't told the Bellefleurs that he was their ancestor. "No, of course not," I said. "You asked me not to."

"I thought, in your anger, you might give them the information."

I gave him an incredulous look. "No, some of us actually have honor," I said. He looked away for a minute. "By the way, your face healed real well."

During the Fellowship of the Sun bombing in Rhodes, Bill's face had been exposed to the sun with really stomach-churning results.

"I slept for six days," he said. "When I finally got up, it was mostly healed. And as for your dig about my failing in honor, I haven't any defense . . . except that when Sophie-Anne told me to pursue you . . . I was reluctant, Sookie. At first, I didn't want to even pretend to have a permanent relationship with a human woman. I thought it degraded me. I only came into the bar to identify you when I couldn't put it off any longer. And that evening didn't turn out like I'd planned. I went outside with the drainers, and things happened. When you were the one who came to my aid, I decided it was fate. I did what I had been told to do by my queen. In so doing, I fell into a trap I couldn't escape. I still can't."

The trap of LUUUUVVVV, I thought sarcastically. But he was too serious, too calm, to mock. I was simply defending my own heart with the weapon of bitchiness.

"You got you a girlfriend," I said. "You go on back to Selah." I looked down to make sure I'd gotten the little strap on the second sandal unlatched. I worked the shoe off. When I glanced back up, Bill's dark eyes were fixed on me.

"I would give anything to lie with you again," he said.

I froze, my hands in the act of rolling the thigh-high hose off my left leg.

Okay, that pretty much stunned me on several different levels. First, the biblical "lie with." Second, my astonishment that he considered me such a memorable bed partner.

Maybe he only remembered the virgins.

"I don't want to fool with you tonight, and Sam's waiting on me down there to help him tend bar," I said roughly. "You go on." I stood and turned my back to him while I pulled on my pants and my shirt, tucking the shirt in. Then it was time for the black running shoes. After a quick check in the mirror to make sure I still had on some lipstick, I faced the doorway.

He was gone.

I went down the wide stairs and out the patio doors into the garden, relieved to be resuming my more accustomed place behind a bar. My feet still hurt. So did the sore spot in my heart labeled Bill Compton.

Sam gave me a smiling glance as I scurried into place. Miss Caroline had vetoed our request to leave a tip jar out, but bar patrons had already stuffed a few bills into an empty highball glass, and I intended to let that stay in position.

"You looked real pretty in the dress," Sam said as he mixed a rum and Coke. I handed a beer across the bar and smiled at the older man who'd come to fetch it. He gave me a huge tip, and I glanced down to see that in my hurry to get downstairs I'd skipped a button. I was showing a little extra cleavage. I was momentarily embarrassed, but it wasn't a slutty button, just a "Hey, I've got boobs" button. So I let it be.

"Thanks," I said, hoping Sam hadn't noticed this quick evaluation. "I hope I did everything right."

"Of course you did," Sam said, as if the possibility of me blowing my new role had never crossed his mind. This is why he's the greatest boss I've ever had.

"Well, good evening," said a slightly nasal voice, and I looked up from the wine I was pouring to see that Tanya Grissom was taking up space and breathing air that could be better used by almost anyone else. Her escort, Calvin, was nowhere in sight.

"Hey, Tanya," Sam said. "How you doing? It's been a while."

"Well, I had to tie up some loose ends in Mississippi," Tanya said. "But I'm back here visiting, and I wondered if you needed any part-time help, Sam."

I pressed my mouth shut and kept my hands busy. Tanya stepped to the side nearest Sam when an elderly lady asked me for some tonic water with a wedge of lime. I handed it to her so quickly she looked astonished, and then I took care of Sam's next customer. I could hear from Sam's brain that he was pleased to see Tanya. Men can be idiots, right? To be fair, I did know some things about her that Sam didn't.

Selah Pumphrey was next in line, and I could only be amazed at my luck. However, Bill's girlfriend just asked for a rum and Coke.

"Sure," I said, trying not to sound relieved, and began putting the drink together.

"I heard him," Selah said very quietly.

"Heard who?" I asked, distracted by my effort to listen to what Tanya and Sam were saying—either with my ears or with my brain.

"I heard Bill when he was talking to you earlier." When I didn't speak, she continued, "I snuck up the stairs after him."

"Then he knows you were there," I said absently, and handed her the drink. Her eyes flared wide at me for a second—alarmed, angry? She stalked off. If wishes could kill, I would be lifeless on the ground.

Tanya began to turn away from Sam as if her body was thinking of leaving, but her head was still talking to my boss. Finally, her whole self went back to her date. I looked after her, thinking dark thoughts.

"Well, that's good news," Sam said with a smile. "Tanya's available for a while."

I bit back my urge to tell him that Tanya had made it quite clear she was available. "Oh, yeah, great," I said. There were so many people I liked. Why were two of the women I really didn't care for at this wedding tonight? Well, at least my feet were practically whimpering with pleasure at getting out of the too-small heels.

I smiled and made drinks and cleared away empty bottles and went to Sam's truck to unload more stock. I opened beers and poured wine and mopped up spills until I felt like a perpetual-motion machine.

The vampire clients arrived at the bar in a cluster. I uncorked one bottle of Royalty Blended, a premium blend of synthetic blood and the real blood of actual European royalty. It had to be refrigerated, of course, and it was a very special treat for Glen's clients, a treat he'd personally arranged. (The only vampire drink that exceeded Royalty Blended in price was the nearly pure Royalty, which contained only a trace of preservatives.) Sam lined up the wineglasses. Then he told me to pour it out. I was extraspecial careful not to spill a drop. Sam handed each glass to its recipient. The vampires, including Bill, all tipped very heavily, big smiles on their faces as they lifted their glasses in a toast to the newlyweds.

After a sip of the dark fluid in the wineglasses, their fangs ran out to prove their enjoyment. Some of the human guests looked a smidge uneasy at this expression of appreciation, but Glen was right there smiling and nodding. He knew enough about vampires not to offer to shake hands. I noticed the new Mrs. Vick was not hobnobbing with the undead guests, though she made one pass through the cluster with a strained smile fixed on her face.

When one of the vampires came back for a glass of ordinary TrueBlood, I handed him the warm drink. "Thank you," he said, tipping me yet again. While he had his billfold open, I saw a Nevada driver's license. I'm familiar with a wide variety of licenses from carding kids at the bar; he'd come far for this wedding. I really looked at him for the first time. When he knew he'd caught my attention, he put his hands together and bowed slightly. Since I'd been reading a mystery set in Thailand, I knew this was a *wai*, a courteous greeting practiced by Buddhists—or maybe just Thai people in general? Anyway, he meant to be polite. After a brief hesitation, I put down the rag in my hand and copied his movement. The vampire looked pleased.

"I call myself Jonathan," he said. "Americans can't pronounce my real name."

There might have been a touch of arrogance and contempt there, but I couldn't blame him.

"I'm Sookie Stackhouse," I said.

Jonathan was a smallish man, maybe five foot eight, with the light copper coloring and dusky black hair of his country. He was really handsome. His nose was small and broad, his lips plump. His brown eyes were topped with absolutely straight black brows. His skin was so fine I couldn't detect any pores. He had that little shine vampires have.

"This is your husband?" he asked, picking up his glass of blood and tilting his head in Sam's direction. Sam was busy mixing a piña colada for one of the bridesmaids.

"No, sir, he's my boss."

Just then, Terry Bellefleur, second cousin to Portia and Andy, lurched up to ask for another beer. I was real fond of

Terry, but he was a bad drunk, and I thought he was well on his way to achieving that condition. Though the Vietnam vet wanted to stand and talk about the president's policy on the current war, I walked him over to another family member, a distant cousin from Baton Rouge, and made sure the man was going to keep an eye on Terry and prevent him from driving off in his pickup.

The vampire Jonathan was keeping an eye on *me* while I did this, and I wasn't sure why. But I didn't observe anything aggressive or lustful in his stance or demeanor, and his fangs were in. It seemed safe to disregard him and take care of business. If there was some reason Jonathan wanted to talk to me, I'd find out about it sooner or later. Later was fine.

As I fetched a case of Cokes from Sam's truck, my attention was caught by a man standing alone in the shadows cast by the big live oak on the west side of the lawn. He was tall, slim, and impeccably dressed in a suit that was obviously very expensive. The man stepped forward a little and I could see his face, could realize he was returning my gaze. My first impression was that he was a lovely creature and not a man at all. Whatever he was, human wasn't part of it. Though he had some age on him, he was extremely handsome, and his hair, still pale gold, was as long as mine. He wore it pulled back neatly. He was slightly withered, like a delicious apple that had been in the crisper too long, but his back was absolutely straight and he wore no glasses. He did carry a cane, a very simple black one with a gold head.

When he stepped out of the shadows, the vampires turned

as a group to look. After a moment they slightly inclined their heads. He returned the acknowledgment. They kept their distance, as if he was dangerous or awesome.

This episode was very strange, but I didn't have time to think about it. Everyone wanted one last free drink. The reception was winding down, and people were filtering to the front of the house for the leave-taking of the happy couples. Halleigh and Portia had disappeared upstairs to change into their going-away outfits. The E(E)E staff had been vigilant about clearing up empty cups and the little plates that had held cake and finger food, so the garden looked relatively neat.

Now that we weren't busy, Sam let me know he had something on his mind. "Sookie, am I getting the wrong idea, or do you dislike Tanya?"

"I do have something against Tanya," I said. "I'm just not sure I should tell you about it. You clearly like her." You'd think I'd been sampling the bourbon. Or truth serum.

"If you don't like to work with her, I want to hear the reason," he said. "You're my friend. I respect your opinion."

This was very pleasant to hear.

"Tanya is pretty," I said. "She's bright and able." Those were the good things.

"And?"

"And she came here as a spy," I said. "The Pelts sent her, trying to find out if I had anything to do with the disappearance of their daughter Debbie. You remember when they came to the bar?"

"Yes," said Sam. In the illumination that had been strung

up all around the garden, he looked both brightly lit and darkly shadowed. "You did have something to do with it?"

"Everything," I said sadly. "But it was self-defense."

"I know it must have been." He'd taken my hand. My own jerked in surprise. "I know you," he said, and didn't let go.

Sam's faith made me feel a little warm glow inside. I'd worked for Sam a long time now, and his good opinion meant a lot to me. I felt almost choked up, and I had to clear my throat. "So, I wasn't happy to see Tanya," I continued. "I didn't trust her from the start, and when I found out why she'd come to Bon Temps, I got really down on her. I don't know if she still gets paid by the Pelts. Plus, tonight she's here with Calvin, and she's got no business hitting on you." My tone was a lot angrier than I'd intended.

"Oh." Sam looked disconcerted.

"But if you want to go out with her, go ahead," I said, trying to lighten up. "I mean—she can't be all bad. And I guess she thought she was doing the right thing, coming to help find information on a missing shifter." That sounded pretty good and might even be the truth. "I don't have to like who you date," I added, just to make it clear I understood I had no claim on him.

"Yeah, but I feel better if you do," he said.

"Same here," I agreed, to my own surprise.

Chapter 2

We began packing up in a quiet and unobtrusive way, since there were still lingering guests.

"As along as we're talking about dates, what happened to Quinn?" he asked as we worked. "You've been moping ever since you got back from Rhodes."

"Well, I told you he got hurt pretty bad in the bombing." Quinn's branch of E(E)E staged special events for the supe community: vampire hierarchal weddings, Were coming of age parties, packleader contests, and the like. That was why Quinn had been in the Pyramid of Gizeh when the Fellowship did its dirty deed.

The FotS people were anti-vampire, but they had no idea that vampires were just the visible, public tip of the iceberg in the supernatural world. No one knew this; or at least only a few people like me, though more and more were in on the big secret. I was sure the Fellowship fanatics would hate werewolves or shapeshifters like Sam just as much as they hated vampires . . . if they knew they existed. That time might come soon.

"Yeah, but I would have thought . . ."

"I know, I would have thought Quinn and I were all set, too," I said, and if my voice was dreary, well, thinking about my missing weretiger made me feel that way. "I kept thinking I'd hear from him. But not a word."

"You still got his sister's car?" Frannie Quinn had loaned me her car so I could get home after the Rhodes disaster.

"No, it vanished one night when Amelia and I were both at work. I called and left a voice mail on his cell to say it had been taken, but I never heard back."

"Sookie, I'm sorry," Sam said. He knew that was inadequate, but what could he say?

"Yeah, me, too," I said, trying not to sound too depressed. It was an effort to keep from retreading tired mental ground. I knew Quinn didn't blame me in any way for his injuries. I'd seen him in the hospital in Rhodes before I'd left, and he'd been in the care of his sister, Fran, who didn't seem to hate me at that point. No blame, no hate—why no communication?

It was like the ground had opened to swallow him up. I threw up my hands and tried to think of something else. Keeping busy was the best remedy when I was worried. We began to shift some of our things to Sam's truck, parked about a block away. He carried most of the heavier stuff. Sam is not a big guy, but he's really strong, as all shifters are.

By ten thirty we were almost finished. From the cheers at the front of the house, I knew that the brides had descended the staircase in their honeymoon clothes, thrown their bouquets, and departed. Portia and Glen were going to San Francisco, and Halleigh and Andy were going to Jamaica to some resort. I couldn't help but know.

Sam told me I could leave. "I'll get Dawson to help me unload at the bar," he said. Since Dawson, who'd been standing in for Sam at Merlotte's Bar tonight, was built like a boulder, I agreed that was a good plan.

When we divided the tips, I got about three hundred dollars. It had been a lucrative evening. I tucked the money in my pants pocket. It made a big roll, since it was mostly ones. I was glad we were in Bon Temps instead of a big city, or I'd worry that someone would hit me on the head before I got to my car.

"Well, night, Sam," I said, and checked my pocket for my car keys. I hadn't bothered with bringing a purse. As I went down the slope of the backyard to the sidewalk, I patted my hair self-consciously. I'd been able to stop the pink smock lady from putting it on top of my head, so she'd done it puffy and curly and sort of Farrah Fawcett. I felt silly.

There were cars going by, most of them wedding guests taking their departure. There was some regular Saturday night traffic. The line of vehicles parked against the curb stretched for a very long way down the street, so all traffic was moving slowly.

I'd illegally parked with the driver's side against the curb, not usually a big deal in our little town.

I bent to unlock my car door, and I heard a noise behind me. In a single movement, I palmed my keys and clenched my fist, wheeled, and hit as hard as I could. The keys gave my fist quite a core, and the man behind me staggered across the sidewalk to land on his butt on the slope of the lawn.

"I mean you no harm," said Jonathan.

It isn't easy to look dignified and nonthreatening when you have blood running from one corner of your mouth and you're sitting on your ass, but the Asian vampire managed it.

"You surprised me," I said, which was a gross understatement.

"I can see that," he said, and got easily to his feet. He brought out a handkerchief and patted his mouth.

I wasn't going to apologize. People who sneak up on me when I'm alone at night, well, they deserve what they get. But I reconsidered. Vampires move quietly. "I'm sorry I assumed the worst," I said, which was sort of a compromise. "I should have identified you."

"No, it would have been too late by then," Jonathan said. "A woman alone must defend herself."

"I appreciate your understanding," I said carefully. I glanced behind him, tried not to register anything on my face. Since I hear so many startling things from people's brains, I'm used to doing that. I looked directly at Jonathan. "Did you... Why were you here?"

"I'm passing through Louisiana, and I came to the wedding

as a guest of Hamilton Tharp," he said. "I'm staying in Area Five, with the permission of Eric Northman."

I had no idea who Hamilton Tharp was—presumably some buddy of the Bellefleurs'. But I knew Eric Northman quite well. (In fact, at one time I'd known him from his head to his toes, and all points in between.) Eric was the sheriff of Area Five, a large chunk of northern Louisiana. We were tied together in a complex way, which most days I resented like hell.

"Actually, what I was asking you was—why did you approach me just now?" I waited, keys still clutched in my hand. I'd go for his eyes, I decided. Even vampires are vulnerable there.

"I was curious," Jonathan said finally. His hands were folded in front of him. I was developing a strong dislike for the vamp.

"Why?"

"I heard a little at Fangtasia about the blond woman Eric values so highly. Eric has such a hard nose that it didn't seem likely any human woman could interest him."

"So how'd you know I was going to be here, at this wedding, tonight?"

His eyes flickered. He hadn't expected me to persist in questioning. He had expected to be able to calm me, maybe at this moment was trying to coerce me with his glamour. But that just didn't work on me.

"The young woman who works for Eric, his child Pam, mentioned it," he said.

Liar, liar, pants on fire, I thought. I hadn't talked to Pam in a couple of weeks, and our last conversation hadn't been girlish chatter about my social and work schedule. She'd been recovering from the wounds she'd sustained in Rhodes. Her recovery, and Eric's, and the queen's, had been the sole topic of our conversation.

"Of course," I said. "Well, good evening. I need to be leaving." I unlocked the door and carefully slid inside, trying to keep my eyes fixed on Jonathan so I'd be ready for a sudden move. He stood as still as a statue, inclining his head to me after I started the car and pulled off. At the next stop sign, I buckled my seat belt. I hadn't wanted to pin myself down while he was so close. I locked the car doors, and I looked all around me. No vampires in sight. I thought, *That was really, really weird.* In fact, I should probably call Eric and relate the incident to him.

You know what the weirdest part was? The withered man with the long blond hair had been standing in the shadows behind the vampire the whole time. Our eyes had even met once. His beautiful face had been quite unreadable. But I'd known he didn't want me to acknowledge his presence. I hadn't read his mind—I couldn't—but I'd known this nonetheless.

And weirdest of all, Jonathan hadn't known he was there. Given the acute sense of smell that all vampires possessed, Jonathan's ignorance was simply extraordinary.

I was still mulling over the strange little episode when I turned off Hummingbird Road and onto the long driveway through the woods that led back to my old house. The core of the house had been built more than a hundred and sixty years before, but of course very little of the original structure remained. It had been added to, remodeled, and reroofed a score of times over the course of the decades. A two-room farmhouse to begin with, it was now much larger, but it remained a very ordinary home.

Tonight the house looked peaceful in the glow of the outside security light that Amelia Broadway, my housemate, had left on for me. Amelia's car was parked in back, and I pulled alongside it. I kept my keys out in case she'd gone upstairs for the night. She'd left the screen door unlatched, and I latched it behind me. I unlocked the back door and relocked it. We were hell on security, Amelia and I, especially at night.

A little to my surprise, Amelia was sitting at the kitchen table, waiting for me. We'd developed a routine after weeks of living together, and generally Amelia would have retired upstairs by this time. She had her own TV, her cell phone, and her laptop up there, and she'd gotten a library card, so she had plenty to read. Plus, she had her spell work, which I didn't ask questions about. Ever. Amelia is a witch.

"How'd it go?" she asked, stirring her tea as if she had to create a tiny whirlpool.

"Well, they got married. No one pulled a Jane Eyre. Glen's vampire customers behaved themselves, and Miss Caroline was gracious all over the place. But I had to stand in for one of the bridesmaids."

"Oh, wow! Tell me."

So I did, and we shared a few laughs. I thought of telling

Amelia about the beautiful man, but I didn't. What could I say? "He looked at me"? I did tell her about Jonathan from Nevada.

"What do you think he really wanted?" Amelia said.

"I can't imagine." I shrugged.

"You need to find out. Especially since you'd never heard of the guy whose guest he said he was."

"I'm going to call Eric—if not tonight, then tomorrow night."

"Too bad you didn't buy a copy of that database Bill is peddling. I saw an ad for it on the Internet yesterday, on a vampire site." This might seem like a sudden change of subject, but Bill's database contained pictures and/or biographies of all the vampires he'd been able to locate all over the world, and a few he'd just heard about. Bill's little CD was making more money for his boss, the queen, than I could ever have imagined. But you had to be a vampire to purchase a copy, and they had ways of checking.

"Well, since Bill is charging five hundred dollars a pop, and impersonating a vampire is a dangerous risk . . ." I said.

Amelia waved her hand. "It'd be worth it," she said.

Amelia is a lot more sophisticated than I am . . . at least in some ways. She grew up in New Orleans, and she'd lived there most of her life. Now she was living with me because she'd made a giant mistake. She'd needed to leave New Orleans after her inexperience had caused a magical catastrophe. It was lucky she'd departed when she had, because Katrina followed soon after. Since the hurricane, her tenant was living in the top-floor apartment of Amelia's house. Amelia's own apartment on the bottom floor had sustained some damage. She wasn't charging the tenant rent because he was overseeing the repair of the house.

And here came the reason Amelia wasn't moving back to New Orleans any time soon. Bob padded into the kitchen to say hello, rubbing himself affectionately against my legs.

"Hey, my little honey bunny," I said, picking up the long-haired black-and-white cat. "How's my precious? I wuv him!"

"I'm gonna barf," Amelia said. But I knew that she talked just as disgustingly to Bob when I wasn't around.

"Any progress?" I said, raising my head from Bob's fur. He'd had a bath this afternoon—I could tell from his fluffy factor.

"No," she said, her voice flat with discouragement. "I worked on him for an hour today, and I only gave him a lizard tail. Took everything I had to get it changed back."

Bob was really a guy, that is, a man. A sort of nerdy-looking man with dark hair and glasses, though Amelia had confided he had some outstanding attributes that weren't apparent when he was dressed for the street. Amelia wasn't supposed to be practicing transformational magic when she turned Bob into a cat; they were having what must have been very adventurous sex. I'd never had the nerve to ask her what she'd been trying to do. It was clear that it was something pretty exotic.

"The deal is," Amelia said suddenly, and I went on the alert. The real reason she'd stayed up to see me was about to be revealed. Amelia was a very clear broadcaster, so I picked it right up from her brain. But I let her go on and speak, because people *really* don't like it if you tell them they don't have to actually speak to you, especially when the topic is something they've had to build up to. "My dad is going to be in Shreveport tomorrow, and he wants to come by Bon Temps to see me," she said in a rush. "It'll be him and his chauffeur, Marley. He wants to come for supper."

The next day would be Sunday. Merlotte's would be open only in the afternoon, but I wasn't scheduled to work anyway, I saw with a glance at my calendar. "So I'll just go out," I said. "I could go visit JB and Tara. No big."

"Please be here," she said, and her face was naked with pleading. She didn't spell out why. But I could read the reason easy enough. Amelia had a very conflicted relationship with her dad; in fact, she'd taken her mother's last name, Broadway, though in part that was because her father was so well-known. Copley Carmichael had lots of political clout and he was rich, though I didn't know how Katrina had affected his income. Carmichael owned huge lumberyards and was a builder, and Katrina might have wiped out his businesses. On the other hand, the whole area needed lumber and rebuilding.

"What time's he coming?" I asked.

"Five."

"Does the chauffeur eat at the same table as him?" I'd never dealt with employees. We just had the one table here in the kitchen. I sure wasn't going to make the man sit on the back steps.

"Oh, God," she said. This had clearly never occurred to her. "What will we do about Marley?"

"That's what I'm asking you." I may have sounded a little too patient.

"Listen," Amelia said. "You don't know my dad. You don't know how he is."

I knew from Amelia's brain that her feelings about her father were really mixed. It was very difficult to pick through the love, fear, and anxiety to get to Amelia's true basic attitude. I knew few rich people, and even fewer rich people who employed full-time chauffeurs.

This visit was going to be interesting.

I said good night to Amelia and went to bed, and though there was a lot to think about, my body was tired and I was soon asleep.

Sunday was another beautiful day. I thought of the newlyweds, safely launched on their new lives, and I thought of old Miss Caroline, who was enjoying the company of a couple of her cousins (youngsters in their sixties) by way of watchdogs and companions. When Portia and Glen returned, the cousins would go back to their more humble home, probably with some relief. Halleigh and Andy would move into their own small house.

I wondered about Jonathan and the beautiful withered man.

I reminded myself to call Eric the next night when he was up.

I thought about Bill's unexpected words.

For the millionth time, I speculated about Quinn's silence.

But before I could get too broody, I was caught up in Hurricane Amelia.

There are lots of things I've come to enjoy, even love, about Amelia. She's straightforward, enthusiastic, and talented. She knows all about the supernatural world, and my place in it. She thinks my weird "talent" is really cool. I can talk to her about anything. She's never going to react with disgust or horror. On the other hand, Amelia is impulsive and headstrong, but you have to take people like they are. I've really enjoyed having Amelia living with me.

On the practical side, she's a decent cook, she's careful about keeping our property separate, and God knows she's tidy. What Amelia really does well is *clean.* She cleans when she's bored, she cleans when she's nervous, and she cleans when she feels guilty. I am no slouch in the housekeeping department, but Amelia is world-class. The day she had a near-miss auto accident, she cleaned my living room furniture, upholstery and all. When her tenant called her to tell her the roof had to be replaced, she went down to EZ Rent and brought home a machine to polish and buff the wooden floors upstairs *and* downstairs.

When I got up at nine, Amelia was already deep in a cleaning frenzy because of her father's impending visit. By the time I left for church at about ten forty-five, Amelia was on her hands and knees in the downstairs hall bathroom, which admittedly is very old-fashioned looking with its tiny octagonal black-and-white tiles and a huge old claw-footed bathtub; but (thanks to my brother, Jason) it has a more modern toilet. This was the bathroom Amelia used, since there wasn't one upstairs. I had a small, private one off my bedroom, added in the fifties. In my house, you could see several major decorating trends over the past few decades all in one building.

"You really think it was that dirty?" I said, standing in the doorway. I was talking to Amelia's rump.

She raised her head and passed a rubber-gloved hand over her forehead to push her short hair out of the way.

"No, it wasn't bad, but I want it to be great."

"My house is just an old house, Amelia. I don't think it can look great." There was no point in my apologizing for the age and wear of the house and its furnishings. This was the best I could do, and I loved it.

"This is a wonderful old home, Sookie," Amelia said fiercely. "But I have to be busy."

"Okay," I said. "Well, I'm going to church. I'll be home by twelve thirty."

"Can you go to the store after church? The list is on the counter."

I agreed, glad to have something to do that would keep me out of the house longer.

The morning felt more like March (March in the south, that is) than October. When I got out of my car at the Methodist church, I raised my face to the slight breeze. There was a touch of winter in the air, a little taste of it. The windows in the modest church were open. When we sang, our combined voices floated out over the grass and trees. But I saw some leaves blow past as the pastor preached.

Frankly, I don't always listen to the sermon. Sometimes the

hour in church is just a time to think, a time to consider where my life is going. But at least those thoughts are in a context. And when you watch leaves falling off trees, your context gets pretty narrow.

Today I listened. Reverend Collins talked about giving God the things that were due him while giving Caesar the things due *him.* That seemed like an April fifteenth type sermon to me, and I caught myself wondering if Reverend Collins paid his taxes quarterly. But after a while, I figured he was talking about the laws we break all the time without feeling guilty—like the speed limit, or sticking a letter in with some presents in a box you're mailing at the post office, without paying the extra postage.

I smiled at Reverend Collins on my way out of the church. He always looks a little troubled when he sees me.

I said hello to Maxine Fortenberry and her husband, Ed, as I reached the parking lot. Maxine was large and formidable, and Ed was so shy and quiet he was almost invisible. Their son, Hoyt, was my brother Jason's best friend. Hoyt was standing behind his mother. He was wearing a nice suit, and his hair had been trimmed. Interesting signs.

"Sugar, you give me a hug!" Maxine said, and of course I did. Maxine had been a good friend to my grandmother, though she was more the age my dad would have been. I smiled at Ed and gave Hoyt a little wave.

"You're looking nice," I told him, and he smiled. I didn't think I'd ever seen Hoyt smile like that, and I glanced at Maxine. She was grinning.

"Hoyt, he's dating that Holly you work with," Maxine said. "She's got a little one, and that's a thing to think about, but he's always liked kids."

"I didn't know," I said. I really had been out of it lately. "That's just great, Hoyt. Holly's a real nice girl."

I wasn't sure I would have put it quite that way if I'd had time to think, so maybe it was lucky I didn't. There were some big positives about Holly (devoted to her son, Cody; loyal to her friends; a competent worker). She'd been divorced for several years, so Hoyt wasn't a rebound. I wondered if Holly had told Hoyt she was a Wiccan. Nope, she hadn't, or Maxine wouldn't be smiling so broadly.

"We're meeting her for lunch at the Sizzler," she said, referring to the steakhouse up by the interstate. "Holly's not much of a churchgoer, but we're working on getting her to come with us and bring Cody. We better get moving if we're gonna be on time."

"Way to go, Hoyt," I said, patting his arm as he went by me. He gave me a pleased look.

Everyone was getting married or falling in love. I was happy for them. Happy, happy, happy. I pasted a smile on my face and went to Piggly Wiggly. I fished Amelia's list out of my purse. It was pretty long, but I was sure there'd be additions by now. I called her on my cell phone, and she had already thought of three more items to add, so I was some little while in the store.

My arms were weighed down with plastic bags as I struggled up the steps to the back porch. Amelia shot out to the car to grab the other bags. "Where have you been?" she asked, as if she'd been standing by the door tapping her toe.

I looked at my watch. "I got out of church and went to the store," I said defensively. "It's only one."

Amelia passed me again, heavily laden. She shook her head in exasperation as she went by, making a noise that could only be described as "Urrrrrgh."

The rest of the afternoon was like that, as though Amelia were getting ready for the date of her life.

I'm not a bad cook, but Amelia would let me do only the most menial chores in fixing the dinner. I got to chop onions and tomatoes. Oh, yeah, she let me wash the preparation dishes. I'd always wondered if she could do the dishes like the fairy godmothers in *Sleeping Beauty*, but she just snorted when I brought it up.

The house was spanky clean, and though I tried not to mind, I noticed that Amelia had even given the floor of my bedroom a once-over. As a rule, we didn't go into each other's space.

"Sorry I went in your room," Amelia said suddenly, and I jumped—me, the telepath. Amelia had beaten me at my own game. "It was one of those crazy impulses I get. I was vacuuming, and I just thought I'd get your floor, too. And before I thought about it, I was done. I put your slippers up under your bed."

"Okay," I said, trying to sound neutral.

"Hey, I *am* sorry."

I nodded and went back to drying the dishes and putting

them away. The menu, as decided by Amelia, was tossed green salad with tomatoes and slivered carrots, lasagna, hot garlic bread, and steamed fresh mixed vegetables. I don't know diddly-squat about steamed vegetables, but I had prepared all the raw materials—the zucchini, bell peppers, mushrooms, cauliflower. Late in the afternoon, I was deemed capable of tossing the salad, and I got to put the cloth and the little bouquet of flowers on the table and arrange the place settings. Four place settings.

I'd offered to take Mr. Marley into the living room with me, where we could eat on TV trays, but you would have thought I'd offered to wash his feet, Amelia was so horrified.

"No, you're sticking with me," she said.

"You gotta talk to your dad," I said. "At some point, I'm leaving the room."

She took a deep breath and let it out. "Okay, I'm a grown-up," she muttered.

"Scaredy-cat," I said.

"You haven't met him yet."

Amelia hurried upstairs at four fifteen to get ready. I was sitting in the living room reading a library book when I heard a car on the gravel driveway. I glanced at the clock on the mantel. It was four forty-eight. I yelled up the staircase and stood to look out the window. The afternoon was drawing to a close, but since we hadn't reverted to standard time yet, it was easy to see the Lincoln Town Car parked in front. A man with clipped dark hair, wearing a business suit, got out of the driver's seat. This must be Marley. He wasn't wearing a chauffeur's hat, somewhat to my disappointment. He opened a rear door. Out stepped Copley Carmichael.

Amelia's dad wasn't very tall, and he had short thick gray hair that looked like a really good carpet, dense and smooth and expertly cut. He was very tan, and his eyebrows were still dark. No glasses. No lips. Well, he did have lips, but they were really thin, so his mouth looked like a trap.

Mr. Carmichael looked around him as if he were doing a tax assessment.

I heard Amelia clattering down the stairs behind me as I watched the man in my front yard complete his survey. Marley the chauffeur was looking right at the house. He'd spotted my face at the window.

"Marley's sort of new," Amelia said. "He's been with my dad for just two years."

"Your dad's always had a driver?"

"Yeah. Marley's a bodyguard, too," Amelia said casually, as if everyone's dad had a bodyguard.

They were walking up the gravel sidewalk now, not even looking at its neat border of ilex. Up the wooden steps. Across the front porch. Knocking.

I thought of all the scary creatures that had been in my house: Weres, shifters, vampires, even a demon or two. Why should I be worried about this man? I straightened my spine, chilled my anxious brain, and went to the front door, though Amelia almost beat me to it. After all, this was my house.

I put my hand on the knob, and I got my smile ready before I opened the door.

"Please come in," I said, and Marley opened the screen door for Mr. Carmichael, who came in and hugged his daughter but not before he'd cast another comprehensive look around the living room.

He was as clear a broadcaster as his daughter.

He was thinking this looked mighty shabby for a daughter of his. . . . Pretty girl Amelia was living with . . . Wondered if Amelia was having sex with her . . . The girl was probably no better than she should be. . . . No police record, though she had dated a vampire and had a wild brother . . .

Of course a rich and powerful man like Copley Carmichael would have his daughter's new housemate investigated. Such a procedure had simply never occurred to me, like so many things the rich did.

I took a deep breath. "I'm Sookie Stackhouse," I said politely. "You must be Mr. Carmichael. And this is?" After shaking Mr. Carmichael's hand, I extended mine to Marley.

For a second, I thought I'd caught Amelia's dad off-footed. But he recovered in record time.

"This is Tyrese Marley," Mr. Carmichael said smoothly.

The chauffeur shook my hand gently, as if he didn't want to break my bones, and then he nodded to Amelia. "Miss Amelia," he said, and Amelia looked angry, as if she was going to tell him to cut the "Miss," but then she reconsidered. All these thoughts, pinging back and forth . . . It was enough to keep me distracted.

Tyrese Marley was a very, very light-skinned African-American. He was far from black; his skin was more the color of old ivory. His eyes were bright hazel. Though his hair was black, it wasn't curly, and it had a red cast. Marley was a man you'd always look at twice.

"I'll take the car back to town and get some gas," he said to his boss. "While you spend time with Miss Amelia. When you want me back?"

Mr. Carmichael looked down at his watch. "A couple of hours."

"You're welcome to stay for supper," I said, managing a very neutral tone. I wanted what made everyone feel comfortable.

"I have a few errands I need to run," Tyrese Marley said with no inflection. "Thanks for the invitation. I'll see you later." He left.

Okay, end of my attempt at democracy.

Tyrese couldn't have known how much I would have preferred going into town rather than staying in the house. I braced myself and began the social necessities. "Can I get you a glass of wine, Mr. Carmichael, or something else to drink? What about you, Amelia?"

"Call me Cope," he said, smiling. It was way too much like a shark's grin to warm my heart. "Sure, a glass of whatever's open. You, baby?"

"Some of the white," she said, and I heard her telling her dad to be seated as I went to the kitchen.

I served the wine and added it to the tray with our hors d'oeuvres: crackers, a warm Brie spread, and apricot jam mixed with hot peppers. We had some cute little knives that looked good with the tray, and Amelia had gotten cocktail napkins for the drinks.

Cope had a good appetite, and he enjoyed the Brie. He sipped the wine, which was an Arkansas label, and nodded politely. Well, at least he didn't spit it out. I seldom drink, and I'm no kind of wine connoisseur. In fact, I'm not a connoisseur of anything at all. But I enjoyed the wine, sip by sip.

"Amelia, tell me what you're doing with your time while you're waiting for your home to be repaired," Cope said, which I thought was a reasonable opening.

I started to tell him that for starters, she wasn't screwing around with me, but I thought that might be a little too direct. I tried very hard not to read his thoughts, but I swear, with him and his daughter in the same room, it was like listening to a television broadcast.

"I've done some filing for one of the local insurance agents. And I'm working part-time at Merlotte's Bar," Amelia said. "I serve drinks and the occasional chicken basket."

"Is the bar work interesting?" Cope didn't sound sarcastic, I'll give him that. But, of course, I was sure he'd had Sam researched, too.

"It's not bad," she said with a slight smile. That was a lot of restraint for Amelia, so I checked into her brain to see that she was squeezing herself into a conversational girdle. "I get good tips."

Her father nodded. "You, Miss Stackhouse?" Cope asked politely.

He knew everything about me but the shade of fingernail polish I was wearing, and I was sure he'd add that to my file if he could. "I work at Merlotte's full-time," I said, just as if he didn't know that. "I've been there for years."

"You have family in the area?"

"Oh, yes, we've been here forever," I said. "Or as close to forever as Americans get. But our family's dwindled down. It's just me and my brother now."

"Older brother? Younger?"

"Older," I said. "Married, real recently."

"So maybe there'll be other little Stackhouses," he said, trying to sound like he thought that would be a good thing.

I nodded as if the possibility pleased me, too. I didn't like my brother's wife much, and I thought it was entirely possible that any kids they had would be pretty rotten. In fact, one was on the way right now, if Crystal didn't miscarry again. My brother was a werepanther (bitten, not born), and his wife was a born . . . a pure . . . werepanther, that is. Being raised in the little werepanther community of Hotshot was not an easy thing, and would be even harder for kids who weren't pure.

"Dad, can I get you some more wine?" Amelia was out of her chair like a shot, and she sped on her way to the kitchen with the half-empty wineglass. Good, quality alone time with Amelia's dad.

"Sookie," Cope said, "you've been very kind to let my daughter live with you all this time."

"Amelia pays rent," I said. "She buys half the groceries. She pays her way."

"Nonetheless, I wish you'd let me give you something for your trouble."

"What Amelia gives me on rent is enough. After all, she's paid for some improvements to the property, too."

His face sharpened then, as if he was on the scent of something big. Did he think I'd talked Amelia into putting a pool in the backyard?

"She got a window air conditioner put in her bedroom upstairs," I said. "And she got an extra phone line for the computer. And I think she got a throw rug and some curtains for her room, too."

"She lives upstairs?"

"Yes," I said, surprised he didn't somehow know already. Perhaps there were a few things his intelligence net hadn't scooped up. "I live down here, she lives up there, and we share the kitchen and living room, though I think Amelia's got a TV upstairs, too. Hey, Amelia!" I called.

"Yeah?" Her voice floated down the hall from the kitchen.

"You still got that little TV up there?"

"Yeah, I hooked it up to the cable."

"Just wondered."

I smiled at Cope, indicating the conversational ball was in his court. He was thinking of several things to ask me, and he was thinking of the best way to approach me to get the most information. A name popped to the surface in the whirlpool of his thoughts, and it took everything I had to keep a polite expression.

"The first tenant Amelia had in the house on Chloe—she was your cousin, right?" Cope said.

"Hadley. Yes." I kept my face calm as I nodded. "Did you know her?"

"I know her husband," he said, and smiled.

Chapter 3

I knew Amelia had returned and was standing by the wing-back chair where her father sat, and I knew she was frozen in place. I knew I didn't breathe for a second.

"I never met him," I said. I felt as if I'd been walking in a jungle and fallen into a concealed pit. I was sure glad I was the only telepath in the house. I hadn't told anyone, anyone at all, about what I'd found in Hadley's lockbox when I'd cleaned it out that day at a bank in New Orleans. "They'd been divorced for a while before Hadley died."

"You should take the time to meet him someday. He's an interesting man," Cope said, as if he wasn't aware he was dropping a bombshell on me. Of course he was waiting for my reaction. He'd hoped I hadn't known about the marriage at all, that I'd be taken completely by surprise. "He's a skilled carpenter. I'd love to track him down and hire him again."

The chair he was sitting on had been upholstered in a cream-colored material with lots of tiny blue flowers on green arching stems embroidered on it. It was still pretty, if faded. I concentrated on the pattern of the chair so I wouldn't show Copley Carmichael how very angry I was.

"He doesn't mean anything to me, no matter how interesting he is," I said in a voice so level you could've played pool on it. "Their marriage was over and done. As I'm sure you know, Hadley had another partner at the time she died." Was murdered. But the government hadn't gotten around to taking much notice of vampire deaths unless those deaths were caused by humans. Vampires did most of their own self-policing.

"I'd think you'd want to see the baby, though," Copley said.

Thank God I picked this out of Copley's head a second or two before he actually spoke the words. Even knowing what he was going to say, I felt his oh-so-casual remark hit me like a blow to the stomach. But I didn't want to give him the satisfaction of letting him see that. "My cousin Hadley was wild. She used drugs and people. She wasn't the most stable person in the world. She was really pretty, and she had a way about her, so she always had admirers." There, I'd said everything pro and con about my cousin Hadley. And I hadn't said the word "baby." *What baby?*

"How'd your family feel when she became a vampire?" Cope said.

Hadley's change was a matter of public record. "Turned" vampires were supposed to register when they entered their altered state of being. They had to name their maker. It was a kind of governmental vampire birth control. You can bet the Bureau of Vampire Affairs would come down like a ton of bricks on a vampire who made too many other little vampires. Hadley had been turned by Sophie-Anne Leclerq herself.

Amelia had put her father's wineglass down within his reach and resumed her seat on the sofa beside me. "Dad, Hadley lived upstairs from me for two years," she said. "Of course we knew she was a vampire. For goodness sake, I thought you'd want to tell me all the hometown news."

God bless Amelia. I was having a hard time holding myself together, and only years of doing that very thing when I telepathically overheard something awful was keeping me glued.

"I need to check on the food. Excuse me," I murmured, and rose and left the room. I hoped I didn't scurry. I tried to walk normally. But once in the kitchen, I kept on going out the back door and across the back porch, out the screen door and into the yard.

If I thought I'd hear Hadley's ghostly voice telling me what to do, I was disappointed. Vampires don't leave ghosts, at least as far as I know. Some vampires believe they don't possess souls. I don't know. That's up to God. And here I was babbling to myself, because I didn't want to think about Hadley's baby, about the fact that I hadn't known about the child.

Maybe it was just Copley's way. Maybe he always wanted to demonstrate the extent of his knowledge, as a way of showing his power to the people he dealt with.

I had to go back in there for Amelia's sake. I braced myself, put my smile back on—though I knew it was a creepy, nervous smile—and back I went. I perched by Amelia and beamed at both of them. They looked at me expectantly, and I realized a conversational lull had fallen.

"Oh," said Cope suddenly. "Amelia, I forgot to tell you. Someone called the house for you last week, someone I didn't know."

"Her name?"

"Oh, let me think. Mrs. Beech wrote it down. Ophelia? Octavia? Octavia Fant. That was it. Unusual."

I thought Amelia was going to faint. She turned a funny color and she braced her hand against the arm of the couch. "You're sure?" she asked.

"Yes, I'm sure. I gave her your cell phone number, and I told her you were living in Bon Temps."

"Thanks, Dad," Amelia croaked. "Ah, I'll bet supper's done; let me go check."

"Didn't Sookie just look at the food?" He wore the broad tolerant smile a man wears when he thinks women are being silly.

"Oh, sure, but it's in the end stage," I said while Amelia shot out of the room as swiftly as I'd just done. "It would be awful if it burned. Amelia worked so hard."

"Do you know this Ms. Fant?" Cope asked.

"No, I can't say as I do."

"Amelia looked almost scared. No one's trying to hurt my girl, right?"

He was a different man when he said that, and one I could

almost like. No matter what else he was, Cope didn't want anyone hurting his daughter. Anyone except him, that is.

"I don't think so." I knew who Octavia Fant was because Amelia's brain had just told me, but she herself hadn't spoken it out loud, so it wasn't a thing I could share. Sometimes the things I hear out loud and the things I hear in my head become really tangled and confused—one of the reasons why I have a reputation for being borderline crazy. "You're a contractor, Mr. Carmichael?"

"Cope, please. Yes, among other things."

"I guess your business must be booming right now," I said.

"If my company was twice as big, we couldn't keep up with the jobs there are to do," he said. "But I hated to see New Orleans all torn up."

Oddly enough, I believed him.

Supper went smoothly enough. If Amelia's father was disconcerted at eating in the kitchen, he didn't give a sign of it. Since he was a builder, he noticed that the kitchen portion of the house was new and I had to tell him about the fire, but that could have happened to anyone, right? I left out the part about the arsonist.

Cope seemed to enjoy his food and complimented Amelia, who was mighty pleased. He had another glass of wine with his meal, but no more than that, and he ate moderately, too. He and Amelia talked about friends of the family and some relatives, and I was left alone to think. Believe me, I had a lot of thinking to do.

Hadley's marriage license and divorce decree had been in

her lockbox at her bank when I'd opened it after her death. The box had contained some family things—a few pictures, her mother's obituary, several pieces of jewelry. There'd also been a lock of fine hair, dark and wispy, with a bit of Scotch tape to keep it together. It had been placed in a little envelope. I'd wondered when I'd noticed how fine the hair was. But there hadn't been a birth certificate or any other scrap of evidence that Hadley had had a baby.

Up until now, I'd had no clearly defined reason to contact Hadley's former husband. I hadn't even known he existed until I'd opened her lockbox. He wasn't mentioned in her will. I'd never met him. He hadn't shown up while I was in New Orleans.

Why hadn't she mentioned the child in her will? Surely any parent would do that. And though she'd named Mr. Cataliades and me as the joint executors, she hadn't told either of us—well, she hadn't told me—that she had relinquished her rights to her child, either.

"Sookie, would you pass the butter?" Amelia asked, and I could tell from her tone it wasn't the first time she'd spoken to me.

"Of course," I said. "Can I get either of you any more water or another glass of wine?"

They both declined.

After supper, I volunteered to do the dishes. Amelia accepted my offer after a brief pause. She and her father had to have some time alone, even if Amelia didn't relish the prospect.

I washed and dried and put away the dishes in relative peace.

I wiped down the counters and whipped the tablecloth off the table and popped it into the washer on the enclosed back porch. I went into my room and read for a while, though I didn't take in much of what was happening on the page. Finally, I laid the book aside and got a box out of my underwear drawer. This box contained everything I'd retrieved from Hadley's lockbox. I checked the name on the marriage certificate. On impulse, I called information.

"I need a listing for a Remy Savoy," I said.

"What city?"

"New Orleans."

"That number's been disconnected."

"Try Metairie."

"No, ma'am."

"Okay, thanks."

Of course, a lot of people had moved since Katrina, and a lot of those moves were permanent. People who had fled the hurricane had no reason to come back, in many cases. There was nowhere to live and no job to go to, in all too many cases.

I wondered how to search for Hadley's ex-husband.

A very unwelcome solution crept into my head. Bill Compton was a computer whiz. Maybe he could track down this Remy Savoy, find out where he was now, discover if the child was with him.

I rolled the idea around in my head like a mouthful of doubtful wine. Given our exchange of the night before at the wedding, I could not imagine myself approaching Bill to ask for a favor, though he'd be the right man for the job.

A wave of longing for Quinn almost took me to my knees. Quinn was a smart and well-traveled man, and he would surely have a good piece of advice for me. If I ever saw him again.

I shook myself. I could just hear a car pulling into the parking area by the sidewalk at the front of the house. Tyrese Marley was returning for Cope. I straightened my back and left my room, my smile fixed firmly on my face.

The front door was open, and Tyrese was standing in it, pretty much filling it up from side to side. He was a big man. Cope was leaning over to give his daughter a peck on the cheek, which she accepted without a hint of a smile. Bob the cat came through the door and sat down beside her. The cat was looking up at Amelia's father with his wide-eyed stare.

"You have a cat, Amelia? I thought you hated cats."

Bob switched his gaze to Amelia. Nothing can stare like a cat.

"Dad! That was years ago! This is Bob. He's great." Amelia picked up the black-and-white cat and held him to her chest. Bob looked smug and began purring.

"Hmmm. Well, I'll be calling you. Please take care. I hate to think about you being up here at the other end of the state."

"It's just a few hours' ride away," Amelia said, sounding all of seventeen.

"True," he said, trying for rueful but charming. He missed by a foot or two. "Sookie, thanks for the evening," he called over his daughter's shoulder.

Marley had gone to Merlotte's to see if he could scope out any information on me, I heard clearly from his brain. He'd picked up quite a few odds and ends. He'd talked to Arlene, which was bad, and to our current cook and our busboy, which was good. Plus assorted bar patrons. He'd have a mixed report to convey.

The moment the car pulled away, Amelia collapsed onto the sofa with relief. "Thank God he's gone," she said. "Now do you see what I mean?"

"Yeah," I said. I sat beside her. "He's a mover and a shaker, isn't he?"

"Always has been," she said. "He's trying to maintain a relationship, but our ideas don't match."

"Your dad loves you."

"He does. But he loves power and control, too."

That was putting it conservatively.

"And he doesn't know you have your own form of power."

"No, he doesn't believe in it at all," Amelia said. "He'll tell you he's a devout Catholic, but that's not the truth."

"In a way, that's good," I said. "If he believed in your witch power, he'd try to make you do all kinds of things for him. You wouldn't want to do some of them, I bet." I could have bitten my tongue, but Amelia didn't take offense.

"You're right," she said. "I wouldn't want to help him advance his agenda. He's capable of doing that without my assistance. If he'd just leave me alone, I'd be content. He's always trying to improve my life, on his terms. I'm really doing okay."

"Who was that who had called you in New Orleans?" Though I knew, I had to pretend. "Fant, her name was?"

Amelia shuddered. "Octavia Fant is my mentor," she said. "She's the reason I left New Orleans. I figured my coven would do something awful to me when they found out about Bob. She's the head of my coven. Or what's left of it. If anything's left of it."

"Ooops."

"Yeah, no shit. I'm going to have to pay the price now."

"You think she'll come up here?"

"I'm only surprised she's not here already."

Despite her expressed fear, Amelia had been worried sick about the welfare of her mentor after Katrina. She had made a huge effort to track the woman, though she didn't want Octavia to find *her.*

Amelia feared being discovered, especially with Bob still in his cat form. She'd told me that her dabbling in transformational magic would be considered all the more reprehensible because she was still an intern, or something along those lines . . . a step above novice, anyway. Amelia didn't discuss the witch infrastructure.

"You didn't think of telling your father not to reveal your location?"

"Asking him to do that would have made him so curious he'd have torn up my entire life to find out why I'd asked. I never thought Octavia would call him, since she knows how I feel about him."

Which was, to say the least, conflicted.

"I have something to tell you that I forgot," Amelia said abruptly. "Speaking of phone calls, Eric called you."

"When?"

"Ah, last night. Before you got home. You were so full of

news when you got here, I just forgot to tell you. Plus, you'd said you were going to call him anyway. And I was really upset about my dad coming. I'm sorry, Sookie. I promise I'll write a note next time."

This was not the first time Amelia had neglected to tell me about a caller. I wasn't pleased, but it was water under the bridge, and our day had been stressful enough. I hoped Eric had found out about the money the queen owed me for my services in Rhodes. I hadn't gotten a check yet, and I hated to bug her since she'd been hurt so badly. I went to the phone in my room to call Fangtasia, which should be in full blast. The club was open every night except Monday.

"Fangtasia, the bar with a bite," Clancy said.

Oh, great. My least favorite vampire. I phrased my request carefully. "Clancy, it's Sookie. Eric asked me to return his call."

There was a moment of silence. I was willing to bet that Clancy was trying to figure out if he could block my access to Eric. He decided he couldn't. "One moment," he said. A brief pause while I listened to "Strangers in the Night." Then Eric picked up the phone.

"Hello?" he said.

"I'm sorry I didn't call you back before now. I just got your message. Did you call about my money?"

A moment of silence. "No, about something else entirely. Will you go out with me tomorrow night?"

I stared at the telephone. I couldn't manage a coherent thought. Finally I said, "Eric, I'm dating Quinn."

"And how long has it been since you've seen him?"

"Since Rhodes."

"How long has it been since you heard from him?"

"Since Rhodes." My voice was wooden. I was unwilling to talk to Eric about this, but we had shared blood often enough to have a much stronger tie than I liked. In fact, I loathed our bond, one we'd been compelled to forge. But when I heard his voice, I felt content. When I was with him, I felt beautiful and happy. And there was nothing I could do about it.

"I think you can give me one evening," Eric said. "It doesn't sound as though Quinn has you booked."

"That was mean."

"It's Quinn who's cruel, promising you he'd be here and then not keeping his word." There was a dark element in Eric's voice, an undertone of anger.

"Do you know what's happened to him?" I asked. "Do you know where he is?"

There was a significant silence. "No," Eric said very gently. "I don't know. But there is someone in town who wants to meet you. I promised I would arrange it. I'd like to take you to Shreveport myself."

So this wasn't a *date* date.

"You mean that guy Jonathan? He came to the wedding and introduced himself. I've got to say, I didn't much care for the guy. No offense, if he's a friend of yours."

"Jonathan? What Jonathan?"

"I'm talking about the Asian guy; he's maybe Thai? He was at the Bellefleur wedding last night. He said he wanted to see me because he was staying in Shreveport and he'd heard a lot about me. He said he'd checked in with you, like a good little visiting vampire."

"I don't know him," Eric said. His voice was much sharper. "I'll ask here at Fangtasia to see if anyone has seen him. And I'll prompt the queen about your money, though she is . . . not herself. Now, will you please do what I'm asking you to do?"

I made a face at the telephone. "I guess," I said. "Who'm I meeting? And where?"

"I'll have to let the 'who' remain a mystery," Eric said. "As to where, we'll go to dinner at a nice restaurant. The kind you'd call casual dressy."

"You don't eat. What will you do?"

"I'll introduce you and stay as long as you need me to."

A crowded restaurant should be all right. "Okay," I said, not very graciously. "I'll get off work about six or six thirty."

"I'll be there to pick you up at seven."

"Give me till seven thirty. I need to change." I knew I sounded grumpy, and that was exactly how I felt. I hated the big mystery around this meeting.

"You'll feel better when you see me," he said. Dammit, he was absolutely right.

Chapter 4

I checked my Word of the Day calendar while I was waiting for my hair-straightening iron to heat up. "Epicene." Huh.

Since I didn't know what restaurant we were going to, and I didn't know who we'd meet there, I picked my most comfortable option and wore a sky blue silk T-shirt that Amelia had said was too big for her, and some black dress slacks with black heels. I don't wear a lot of jewelry, so a gold chain and some little gold earrings did the decorating for me. I'd had a tough day at work, but I was too curious about the evening ahead to feel tired.

Eric was on time, and I felt (surprise) a rush of pleasure when I saw him. I don't think that was entirely due to the blood bond between us. I think any heterosexual woman would feel a rush of pleasure at the sight of Eric. He was a tall man and must have been seen as a giant in his time. He was built to swing a heavy sword to hew down his enemies. Eric's golden blond hair sprang back like a lion's mane from a bold forehead. There was nothing *epicene* about Eric, nothing ethereally beautiful, either. He was all male.

Eric bent to kiss me on the cheek. I felt warm and safe. This was the effect Eric had on me now that we'd swapped blood more than three times. The blood sharing hadn't been for pleasure but a necessity—at least I'd thought so—every time, but the price I paid was steep. We were bonded now, and when he was near, I was absurdly happy. I tried to enjoy the sensation, but knowing it wasn't completely natural made that hard to do.

Since Eric had come in his Corvette, I was extra glad I'd worn pants. Getting into and out of a Corvette modestly was a very difficult procedure if you were wearing a dress. I made small talk on the way to Shreveport, but Eric was uncharacteristically silent. I tried to question him about Jonathan, the mysterious vampire at the wedding, but Eric said, "We'll talk about that later. You haven't seen him again, have you?"

"No," I said. "Should I expect to?"

Eric shook his head. There was an uncomfortable pause. From the way he was gripping the wheel, I could tell that Eric was building up to saying something he didn't want to say.

"I'm glad for your sake that it appears Andre didn't survive the bombing," he said.

The queen's dearest child, Andre, had died in the bombing in Rhodes. But it hadn't been the bomb that had killed him.

Quinn and I knew what had done the deed: a big splinter of wood that Quinn had driven into Andre's heart while the vampire lay disabled. Quinn had killed Andre for my sake, because he knew Andre had plans for me that made me sick with fear.

"I'm sure the queen will miss him," I said carefully.

Eric shot me a sharp glance. "The queen is distraught," he said. "And her healing will take months more. What I was beginning to say . . ." His voice trailed off.

This wasn't like Eric. "What?" I demanded.

"You saved my life," he said. I'd turned to look at him, but he was looking straight ahead at the road. "You saved my life, and Pam's, too."

I shifted uncomfortably. "Yeah, well." Miss Articulate. The silence lengthened until I felt I had to say something else. "We do have the blood tie thing going."

Eric didn't respond for a stretch of time. "That's not why you came to wake me, first of all, the day the hotel blew up," he said. "But we won't talk further about this now. You have a big evening ahead."

Yes, boss, I said snippily, but only to myself.

We were in a part of Shreveport I didn't know too well. It was definitely out of the main shopping area, with which I was fairly familiar. We were in a neighborhood where the houses were large and the lawns were groomed. The businesses were small and pricey . . . what retailers called "boutiques." We pulled into a group of such shops. It was arranged in an L, and the restaurant was at the rear of the L. It was called Les Deux Poissons. There were maybe eight cars parked there, and each one of them represented my yearly income. I looked down at my clothes, feeling suddenly uneasy.

"Don't worry, you're beautiful," Eric said quietly. He leaned over to unbuckle my seat belt (to my astonishment), and as he straightened he kissed me again, this time on the mouth. His bright blue eyes blazed out of his white face. He looked as if a whole story was on the tip of his tongue. But then he swallowed it back and unfolded himself from the car to walk around to my side to open the door for me. Maybe I wasn't the only one this blood bond worked on, huh?

From his tension I realized that some major event was coming at me fast, and I began to be afraid. Eric took my hand as we walked across to the restaurant, and he ran his thumb absently across my palm. I was surprised to find out there was a direct line from my palm to my, my, hootchie.

We stepped into the foyer, where there was a little fountain and a screen that blocked the view of the diners. The woman standing at the podium was beautiful and black, her hair shaved very close to her skull. She wore a draped dress of orange and brown and the highest heels I had ever seen. She might as well have been wearing toe shoes. I looked at her closely, and I sampled the signature of her brain, and I found she was human. She smiled brilliantly at Eric and had the sense to give me a share of that smile.

"A party of two?" she said.

"We're meeting someone," Eric said.

"Oh, the gentleman…"

"Yes."

"Right this way, please." Her smile replaced by a look almost of envy, she turned and walked gracefully into the depths of the restaurant. Eric gestured for me to follow her. The interior was fairly dark, and candles flickered on the tables, which were covered with snowy white cloths and elaborately folded napkins.

My eyes were on the hostess's back, so when she came to a halt, I didn't immediately recognize that she'd stopped at the table where we were to sit. She stepped aside. Seated facing me was the lovely man who'd been at the wedding two nights before.

The hostess spun on her high heel, touched the back of the chair to the man's right to indicate I should sit there, and told us our server would be with us. The man rose to pull out my chair and hold it for me. I glanced back at Eric. He gave me a reassuring nod. I slipped in front of the chair and the man pushed it forward with perfect timing.

Eric didn't sit. I wanted him to explain what was happening, but he didn't speak. He looked almost sad.

The beautiful man was looking at me intently. "Child," he said to get my attention. Then he pushed back his long, fine golden hair. None of the other diners were positioned to see what he was showing me.

His ear was pointed. He was a fairy.

I knew two other fairies. But they avoided vampires at all costs, because the smell of a fairy was as intoxicating to a vampire as honey is to a bear. According to a vampire who was particularly gifted in the scent sense, I had a trace of fairy blood.

"Okay," I said, to let him know the ears had registered.

"Sookie, this is Niall Brigant," Eric said. He pronounced it "Nye-all." "He's going to talk to you over supper. I'll be outside if you need me." He inclined his head stiffly to the fairy and then he was gone.

I watched Eric walk away, and I was bowled over with a rush of anxiety. Then I felt a hand on top of my own. I turned to meet the eyes of the fairy.

"As he said, my name is Niall." His voice was light, sexless, resonant. His eyes were green, the deepest green you can imagine. In the flickering candlelight, the color hardly mattered—it was the depth you noticed. His hand on mine was light as a feather but very warm.

"Who are you?" I asked, and I wasn't asking him to repeat his name.

"I'm your great-grandfather," Niall Brigant said.

"Oh, *shit*," I said, and covered my mouth with my hand. "Sorry, I just . . ." I shook my head. "Great-grandpa?" I said, trying out the concept. Niall Brigant winced delicately. On a real man, the gesture would have looked effeminate, but on Niall it didn't.

Lots of kids in our neck of the woods call their grandfathers "Papaw." I'd *love* to see his reaction to that. The idea helped me recover my scattered sense of self.

"Please explain," I said very politely. The waiter came to inquire after our drink orders and recite the specials of the day.

Niall ordered a bottle of wine and told him we would have the salmon. He did not consult me. High-handed.

The young man nodded vigorously. "Great choice," he said. He was a Were, and though I would have expected him to be curious about Niall (who after all was a supernatural being not often encountered), I seemed to be of more interest. I attributed that to the waiter's youth and my boobs.

See, here's the weird thing about meeting my self-proclaimed relative: I never doubted his truthfulness. This was my true great-grandfather, and the knowledge just clicked into place as if it fit into a puzzle.

"I'll tell you all about it," Niall said. Very slowly, telegraphing his intention, he leaned over to kiss my cheek. His mouth and eyes crinkled as his facial muscles moved to frame the kiss. The fine cobweb of wrinkles did not in any way detract from his beauty; he was like very old silk or a crackled painting by an ancient master.

This was a big night for getting kissed.

"When I was still young, perhaps five or six hundred years ago, I used to wander among the humans," Niall said. "And every now and then, as a male will, I'd see a human woman I found appealing."

I glanced around so I wouldn't be staring at him every second, and I noticed a strange thing: no one was looking at us but our waiter. I mean, not even a casual glance strayed our way. And no human brains in the room were even registering our presence. My great-grandfather paused while I did this, and resumed speaking when I'd finished evaluating the situation.

"I saw such a woman in the woods one day, and her name was Einin. She thought I was an angel." He was silent for a moment. "She was delicious," he said. "She was lively, and happy, and simple." Niall's eyes were fixed on my face. I wondered if he thought I was like Einin: simple. "I was young enough to be infatuated, young enough to be able to ignore the inevitable end of our connection as she aged and I did not. But Einin got pregnant, which was a shock. Fairies and humans don't cross-breed often. Einin gave birth to twins, which is quite common among the fae. Einin and both boys lived through the birthing, which in those times was far from certain. She called our older son Fintan. The second was Dermot."

The waiter brought our wine, and I was jerked out of the spell Niall's voice had laid on me. It was like we'd been sitting around a campfire in the woods listening to an ancient legend, and then snap! We were in a modern restaurant in Shreveport, Louisiana, and there were other people around who had no idea what was going on. I automatically lifted my glass and took a sip of wine. I felt I was entitled.

"Fintan the Half Fairy was your paternal grandfather, Sookie," Niall said.

"No. I know who my grandfather was." My voice was shaking a little, I noticed, but it was still very quiet. "My grandfather was Mitchell Stackhouse and he married Adele Hale. My father was Corbett Hale Stackhouse, and he and my mom died in a flash flood when I was a little girl. Then I was raised by my grandmother Adele." Though I remembered the vampire in

Mississippi who'd told me he detected a trace of fairy blood in my veins, and I believed this was my great-grandfather, I just couldn't adjust my inner picture of my family.

"What was your grandmother like?" Niall asked.

"She raised me when she didn't have to," I said. "She took me and Jason into her home, and she worked hard to raise us right. We learned everything from her. She loved us. She had two children herself and buried them both, and that must have about killed her, but still she was strong for us."

"She was beautiful when she was young," Niall said. His green eyes lingered on my face as if he were trying to find some trace of her beauty in her granddaughter.

"I guess," I said uncertainly. You don't think about your grandmother in terms of beauty, at least in the normal way of things.

"I saw her after Fintan made her pregnant," Niall said. "She was lovely. Her husband had told her he could not give her children. He'd had mumps at the wrong time. That's a disease, isn't it?" I nodded. "She met Fintan one day when she was beating a rug out on the clothesline, in back of the house where you now live. He asked her for a drink of water. He was smitten on the spot. She wanted children so badly, and he promised her he could give them to her."

"You said fairies and people weren't usually fertile when they crossbreed."

"But Fintan was only half fairy. And he already knew that he was able to give a woman a child." Niall's mouth quirked.

"The first woman he loved died in childbirth, but your grandmother and her son were more fortunate, and then two years later she was able to carry Fintan's daughter to completion."

"He raped her," I said, almost hoping it was so. My grandmother had been the most true-blue woman I'd ever met. I couldn't picture her cheating anyone out of anything, particularly since she'd promised in front of God to be faithful to my grandfather.

"No, he did not. She wanted children, though she didn't want to be unfaithful to her husband. Fintan didn't care about the feelings of others, and he wanted her desperately," Niall said. "But he was never violent. He would not have raped her. However, my son could talk a woman into anything, even into something against her moral judgment. . . . And if she was very beautiful, so was he."

I tried to see the woman she must have been, in the grandmother I'd known. And I just couldn't.

"What was your father like, my grandson?" Niall asked.

"He was a handsome guy," I said. "He was a hard worker. He was a good dad."

Niall smiled slightly. "How did your mother feel about him?"

That question cut sharply into my warm memories of my father. "She, ah, she was really devoted to him." Maybe at the expense of her children.

"She was obsessed?" Niall's voice was not judgmental but certain, as if he knew my answer.

"Real possessive," I admitted. "Though I was only seven when they died, even I could see that. I guess I thought it was normal. She really wanted to give him all her attention. Sometimes Jason and I were in the way. And she was really jealous, I remember." I tried to look amused, as if my mother being so jealous of my father was a charming quirk.

"It was the fairy in him that made her hold on so strongly," Niall said. "It takes some humans that way. She saw the supernatural in him, and it enthralled her. Tell me, was she a good mother?"

"She tried hard," I whispered.

She had tried. My mother had known how to be a good mother theoretically. She knew how a good mother acted toward her children. She'd made herself go through all the motions. But all her true love had been saved for my father, who'd been bemused by the intensity of her passion. I could see that now, as an adult. As a child, I'd been confused and hurt.

The red-haired Were brought our salad and set it down in front of us. He wanted to ask us if we needed anything else, but he was too scared. He'd picked up on the atmosphere at the table.

"Why did you decide now to come meet me?" I asked. "How long have you known about me?" I put my napkin in my lap and sat there holding the fork. I should take a bite. Wasting was not part of the way I'd been raised. By my grandmother. Who'd had sex with a half fairy (who'd wandered into the yard like a stray dog). Enough sex over enough time to produce two children.

"I've known about your family for the past sixty years, give or take. But my son Fintan forbade me seeing any of you."

He carefully put a bit of tomato into his mouth, held it there, thought about it, chewed it. He ate the way I would if I was visiting an Indian or Nicaraguan restaurant.

"What changed?" I said, but I figured it out. "So your son is dead now."

"Yes," he said, and put down the fork. "Fintan is dead. After all, he was half human. And he'd lived for seven hundred years."

Was I supposed to have an opinion about this? I felt so numb, as though Niall had shot Novocain into my emotional center. I probably should ask how my—my *grandfather* had come to die, but I couldn't bring myself to do it.

"So you decided to come tell me about this—why?" I was proud of how calm I sounded.

"I'm old, even for my kind. I would like to know you. I can't atone for the way your life has been shaped by the heritage Fintan gave you. But I will try to make your life a little easier, if you'll permit me."

"Can you take the telepathy away?" I asked. A wild hope, not unmixed with fear, flared in me like a sunspot.

"You are asking if I can remove something from the fiber of your being," Niall said. "No, I can't do that."

I slumped in my chair. "Thought I'd ask," I said, fighting away tears. "Do I get three wishes, or is that with genies?"

Niall regarded me with no humor at all. "You wouldn't want to meet a genie," he said. "And I'm not a figure of fun. I am a prince."

"Sorry," I said. "I'm having a little trouble coping with all this . . . Great-grandfather." I didn't remember my human great-grandfathers. My grandfathers—okay, I guess one of them hadn't truly been my grandfather—hadn't looked or acted a thing like this beautiful creature. My grandfather Stackhouse died sixteen years ago, and my mother's parents had died before I was into my teens. So I'd known my grandmother Adele much better than any of the others, actually much better than I'd known my true parents.

"Hey," I said. "How come Eric fetched me for you? You're fairy, after all. Vampires go nuts when they smell fairies."

In fact, most vampires lost their self-control when they were around fairies. Only a very disciplined vampire could behave when a fairy got within smelling distance. My fairy godmother, Claudine, was terrified of being anywhere around a bloodsucker.

"I can suppress my essence," Niall said. "They can see me but not smell me. It's a convenient magic. I can keep humans from even noticing me, as you have observed."

The way he said this let me know that he was not only very old and very powerful, but he was also very proud. "Did you send Claudine to me?" I said.

"Yes. I hope she's been of use. Only people of part-fae blood can have such a relationship with a fairy. I knew you needed her."

"Oh, yes, she's saved my life," I said. "She's been wonderful." She'd even taken me shopping. "Are all fairies as nice as Claudine, or as beautiful as her brother?"

Claude, male stripper and now entrepreneur, was as handsome as a man could get, and he had the personality of a self-absorbed turnip.

"Dear one," Niall said, "we are all beautiful to humans; but some fairies are very nasty indeed."

Okay, here came the downside. I had a strong feeling that finding out I had a great-grandfather who was a full-blooded fairy was supposed to be good news, from Niall's point of view—but that it wasn't a completely iced cupcake. Now I would get the bad news.

"You went many years without being found," Niall said, "in part because that was what Fintan wanted."

"But he watched me?" I almost felt warmth in my heart at hearing that.

"My son was remorseful that he'd condemned two children to the half-in, half-out existence he'd experienced as a fairy who wasn't truly a fairy. I'm afraid the others of our race weren't kind to him." My great-grandfather's gaze was steady. "I did my best to defend him, but it wasn't enough. Fintan also found he wasn't human enough to pass as human, at least not for more than a short time."

"You don't look like this normally?" I asked, very curious.

"No." And just for a split second, I saw an almost blinding light, with Niall in the middle of it, beautiful and perfect. No wonder Einin had thought he was an angel.

"Claudine said she was working her way up," I said. "What does that mean?" I was floundering through this conversation. I felt like I'd been knocked down to my knees by all this information, and I was struggling to get to my emotional feet. I wasn't having a very successful time doing it.

"She shouldn't have told you that," Niall said. He debated with himself for a second or two before continuing. "Shifters are humans with a genetic twist, vampires are dead humans transformed into something different, but the fae have only a basic shape in common with humans. There are many kinds of fae—from the grotesque, like goblins, to the beautiful, like us." He said this quite unself-consciously.

"Are there angels?"

"Angels are yet another form, and one which has undergone an almost complete transformation, physical and moral. It can take hundreds of years to become an angel."

Poor Claudine.

"But enough about this," Niall said. "I want to know about you. My son kept me from your father and your aunt, and then from their children. His death came too late for me to know your cousin Hadley. But now I can see you and touch you." Which, incidentally, Niall was doing in a way that wasn't exactly human: if his hand wasn't holding mine, it was placed flat against my shoulder, or my back. This wasn't exactly the way humans related, but it wasn't hurting me. I wasn't as freaked out as I might have been, since I'd noticed Claudine was very touchy-feely, too. Since I couldn't get telepathic vibes from fairies, this much contact was tolerable. With a regular human being, I'd be bombarded with thoughts, since touch increased my sensitivity to telepathic contact.

"Did Fintan have any other children or grandchildren?" I asked. It would be nice to have more family.

"We'll talk of that later," Niall said, which sent up an immediate red flag. "Now that you know me a little," he said, "please tell me what I can do for you."

"Why should you do anything for me?" I said. We'd had the genie conversation. I wasn't going to revisit that.

"I can tell that your life has been hard. Now that I am allowed to see you, let me help you in some way."

"You sent me Claudine. She's been a big help," I repeated. Without the crutch of my sixth sense, I was having trouble understanding my great-grandfather's emotional and mental set. Was he grieving for his son? What had their relationship really been? Had Fintan thought he was doing us all a good deed in keeping his dad away from the Stackhouses all these years? Was Niall evil, or did he have bad intentions toward me? He could have done something awful to me from afar without going to the trouble of meeting me and paying for an expensive dinner.

"You wouldn't want to explain any more, huh?"

Niall shook his head, his hair brushing his shoulders like strands of gold and silver spun out to incredible fineness.

I had an idea. "Can you find my boyfriend?" I asked hopefully.

"You have a man? Besides the vampire?"

"Eric is not my man, but since I've had his blood a few times, and he's had mine . . ."

"That's why I approached you through him. You have a tie to him."

"Yes."

"I have known Eric Northman for a long time. I thought you would come if he asked you to. Did I do wrong?"

I was startled at this appeal. "No, sir," I said. "I don't think I'd have come if he hadn't told me it was okay. He wouldn't have brought me if he hadn't trusted you. . . . At least, I don't think so."

"Do you want me to kill him? End the tie?"

"No!" I said, getting kind of excited in a bad way. "No!"

A few people actually glanced at us for the first time, hearing my agitation despite my great-grandfather's *don't-look* influence.

"The other boyfriend," Niall said, and took another bite of his salmon. "Who is he and when did he vanish?"

"Quinn the weretiger," I said. "He's been gone since the explosion in Rhodes. He was hurt, but I saw him afterward."

"I heard about the Pyramid," Niall said. "You were there?"

I told him about it, and my newly discovered great-grandfather listened with a refreshing lack of judgment. He was neither horrified nor appalled, and he didn't feel sorry for me. I really liked that.

While I talked, I had a chance to regroup my emotions. "You know what?" I said when there was a natural pause. "Don't look for Quinn. He knows where I am, and he's got my number." *In more ways than one,* I thought sourly. "He'll show up when he feels like he can, I guess. Or not."

"But that leaves me with nothing to do as a gift for you," my great-grandfather said.

"Just give me a raincheck," I said, smiling, and then had to explain the term to him. "Something'll come up. Am I . . . Can

I talk about you? To my friends?" I asked. "No, I guess not." I couldn't imagine telling my friend Tara that I had a new great-grandfather who was a fairy. Amelia might be more understanding.

"I want to keep our relationship a secret," he said. "I am so glad to know you finally, and I want to know you better." He laid his hand against my cheek. "But I have powerful enemies, and I wouldn't want them to think of harming you to get at me."

I nodded. I understood. But it was kind of deflating to have a brand-new relative and be forbidden to talk about him. Niall's hand left my cheek to drift down to my own hand.

"What about Jason?" I asked. "Are you gonna talk to him, too?"

"Jason," he said, his face showing distaste. "Somehow the essential spark passed Jason by. I know he is made of the same material as you, but in him the blood has only shown itself in his ability to attract lovers, which after all is not much recommendation. He wouldn't understand or appreciate our connection."

Great-grandfather sounded pretty snotty when he said that. I started to say something in Jason's defense, but then I closed my mouth. I had to admit to my most secret self that Niall was almost certainly right. Jason would be full of demands, and he would talk.

"How often are you going to be around?" I said instead, striving hard to sound nonchalant. I knew I was expressing myself clumsily, but I didn't know how else to establish some framework for this new and awkward relationship.

"I'll try to visit you like any other relative would," he said.

I tried hard to picture that. Niall and I eating at the Hamburger Palace? Sharing a pew at church on a Sunday? I didn't think so.

"I feel like there's a lot you're not telling me," I said bluntly.

"Then we'll have something to talk about next time," he said, and one sea green eye winked at me. Okay, that was unexpected. He handed me a business card, another thing I didn't anticipate. It said simply, "Niall Brigant," with a telephone number centered beneath. "You can reach me at that number any time. Someone will answer."

"Thanks," I said. "I guess you know my phone number?" He nodded. I'd thought he was ready to leave, but he lingered. He seemed as reluctant to part as I was. "So," I began, clearing my throat. "What do you do all day?" I can't tell you how strange and neat it felt to be with a family member. I only had Jason, and he wasn't exactly a close brother, the kind you told everything to. I could count on him in a pinch, but hanging out together? Not going to happen.

My great-grandfather answered my question, but when I tried to recall it afterward, I couldn't come up with anything specific. I guess he did secret fairy-prince stuff. He did tell me he had part ownership in a bank or two, a company that made lawn furniture, and—and this seemed odd to me—a company that created and tested experimental medicine.

I looked at him doubtfully. "Medicine for humans," I said, to be sure I understood.

"Yes. For the most part," he responded. "But a few of the chemists make special things for us."

"For the fae."

He nodded, fine corn-silk hair falling around his face as his head moved. "There is so much iron now," he said. "I don't know if you realize that we are very sensitive to iron? And yet if we wear gloves every moment, we're too conspicuous in today's world." I looked at his right hand as it lay over mine on the white tablecloth. I extracted my fingers, stroked his skin. It felt oddly smooth.

"It's like an invisible glove," I said.

"Exactly." He nodded. "One of their formulas. But enough about me."

Just when it was getting interesting, I thought. But I could see that my great-grandfather had no real reason to trust me with all his secrets yet.

Niall asked me about my job, and my boss, and my routine, like a real great-grandfather would. Though he clearly didn't like the idea of his great-granddaughter working, the bar part of it didn't seem to disturb him. As I've said, Niall wasn't easy to read. His thoughts were his own as far as I was concerned; but I did notice that every now and then he stopped himself from speaking.

Eventually, dinner got eaten, and I glanced at my watch, astounded at how many hours had passed. I needed to go. I had to work the next day. I excused myself, thanking my great-grandfather (it still made me shiver, thinking of him that way) for the meal and very hesitantly leaning forward to kiss his cheek as he'd kissed mine. He seemed to hold his breath while I did so, and his skin felt soft and lustrous as a silky plum under my lips. Even though he could look like a human, he didn't feel like one.

He stood when I left, but he remained at the table—to take care of the bill, I assumed. I went outside without registering anything my eyes saw along the way. Eric was waiting for me in the parking lot. He'd had some TrueBlood while he was waiting, and he'd been reading in the car, which was parked under a light.

I was exhausted.

I didn't realize how nerve-wracking my dinner with Niall had been until I was out of his presence. Though I'd been sitting in a comfortable chair the whole meal, I was as tired as if we'd been talking while we were running.

Niall had been able to mask the fairy odor from Eric in the restaurant, but I saw from the flare of Eric's nostrils that the intoxicating scent clung to me. Eric's eyes closed in ecstasy, and he actually licked his lips. I felt like a T-bone just out of reach of a hungry dog.

"Snap out of it," I said. I wasn't in the mood.

With a huge effort, Eric reined himself in. "When you smell like that," he said, "I just want to fuck you and bite you and rub myself all over you."

That was pretty comprehensive, and I won't say I didn't have a second (split evenly between lust and fear) of picturing such activity. But I had larger issues to think about.

"Hold your horses," I said. "What do you know about fairies? Aside from how they taste?"

Eric looked at me with clearer eyes. "They're lovely, male

and female both. Incredibly tough and ferocious. They aren't immortal, but they live a very long time unless something happens to them. You can kill them with iron, for example. There are other ways to kill them, but it's hard work. They like to keep to themselves for the most part. They like moderate climates. I don't know what they eat or drink when they're by themselves. They sample the food of other cultures; I've even seen a fairy try blood. They have a higher opinion of themselves than they have any right to. When they give their word, they keep it." He thought for a moment. "They have different magics. They can't all do the same things. And they are very magical. It's their essence. They have no gods but their own race, for they've often been mistaken for gods. In fact, some of them have taken on the attributes of a deity."

I gaped at him. "What do you mean?"

"Well, I don't mean they're *holy*," Eric said. "I mean that the fairies who inhabit the woods identify with the woods so strongly that to hurt one is to hurt the other. So they've suffered a great drop in numbers. Obviously, we vampires are not going to be up on fairy politics and survival issues, since we are so dangerous to them... simply because we find them intoxicating."

I'd never thought to ask Claudine about any of this. For one thing, she didn't seem to enjoy talking about being a fairy, and when she popped up, it was usually when I was in trouble and therefore sadly self-absorbed. For another thing, I'd imagined there were maybe a small handful of fairies left in the world, but Eric was telling me there once were as many fairies as there were vampires, though the fairy race was on the wane.

In sharp contrast, vampires—at least in America—were definitely on the increase. There were three bills wending their way through Congress dealing with vampire immigration. America had the distinction (along with Canada, Japan, Norway, Sweden, England, and Germany) of being a country that had responded to the Great Revelation with relative calm.

The night of the carefully orchestrated Great Revelation, vampires all over the world had appeared on television, radio, in person, whatever the best means of communication in the area might be, to tell the human population, "Hey! We actually exist. But we're not life threatening! The new Japanese synthetic blood satisfies our nutritional requirements."

The six years since then had been one big learning curve.

Tonight I'd added a huge amount to my store of supernatural lore.

"So the vampires have the upper hand," I said.

"We're not at war," Eric said. "We haven't been at war for centuries."

"So in the past the vampires and the fairies have fought each other? I mean, like, pitched battles?"

"Yes," Eric said. "And if it came to that again, the first one I'd take out is Niall."

"Why?"

"He's very powerful in the fairy world. He is very magical. If he's sincere in his desire to take you under his wing, you're both very lucky and very unlucky." Eric started the car and we pulled out of the parking lot. I hadn't seen Niall come out of the restaurant. Maybe he'd just poofed out of the dining room. I hoped he'd paid our bill first.

"I guess I have to ask you to explain that," I said. But I had a feeling I didn't really want to know the answer.

"There were thousands of fairies in the United States once," Eric said. "Now there are only hundreds. But the ones that are left are very determined survivors. And not all of those are friends of the prince's."

"Oh, good. I needed another supernatural group who dislikes me," I muttered.

We drove through the night in silence, wending our way back to the interstate that would carry us east to Bon Temps. Eric seemed heavily thoughtful. I also had plenty of food for thought; more than I'd eaten at supper, that was for sure.

I found that on the whole, I felt cautiously happy. It was good to have a kind of belated great-grandfather. Niall seemed genuinely anxious to establish a relationship with me. I still had a heap of questions to ask, but they could wait until we knew each other better.

Eric's Corvette could go pretty damn fast, and Eric wasn't exactly sticking to the speed limit on the interstate. I wasn't awfully surprised when I saw the blinking lights coming up behind us. I was only astonished the cop car could catch up with Eric.

"A-hum," I said, and Eric cursed in a language that probably hadn't been spoken out loud in centuries. But even the sheriff of Area Five has to obey human laws these days, or at least he has to pretend to. Eric pulled over to the shoulder.

"With a vanity plate like BLDSKR, what do you expect?" I asked, not so secretly enjoying the moment. I saw the dark shape of the trooper emerging from the car behind us, walking up with something in his hand—clipboard, flashlight?

I looked harder. I reached out. A snarled mass of aggression and fear met my inner ear.

"Were! There's something wrong," I said, and Eric's big hand shoved me down into the floorboard, which would have provided a little more concealment if the car had been anything other than a Corvette.

Then the patrolman came up to the window and tried to shoot me.

Chapter 5

Eric had turned to fill the window and block the rest of the car from the shooter's aim, and he got it in the neck. For an awful moment, Eric slumped back in the seat, his face blank and dark blood flowing sluggishly down his white skin. I screamed as if noise would protect me, and the gun pointed at me as the gunman leaned into the car to aim past Eric.

But he'd been a fool to do that. Eric's hand clamped on the man's wrist, and Eric began squeezing. The "patrolman" started doing a little shrieking of his own, flailing uselessly at Eric with his empty hand. The gun fell on top of me. I'm just lucky it didn't discharge when it fell. I don't know much about handguns, but this one was big and lethal-looking, and I scrambled to an upright position and aimed it at the shooter.

He froze in place, half in and half out of the window. Eric

had already broken his arm and had kept a tight grip. The fool should have been more afraid of the vampire who had a hold on him than the waitress who hardly knew how to fire the gun, but the gun commanded his attention.

I was sure I would have heard if the highway patrol had decided to start shooting speeders instead of ticketing them.

"Who are you?" I said, and no one could blame me if my voice wasn't too steady. "Who sent you?"

"They told me to," the Were gasped. Now that I had time to notice details, I could see he wasn't wearing a proper highway patrol uniform. It was the right color, and the hat was right, but the pants weren't uniform pants.

"They, who?" I asked.

Eric's fangs clamped into the Were's shoulder. Despite his wound, Eric was pulling the faux patrolman into the car inch by inch. It seemed only fair that Eric got some blood since he'd lost so much of his own. The assassin began crying.

"Don't let him turn me into one of them," he appealed to me.

"You should be so lucky," I said, not because I actually thought it was so darn great to be a vampire but because I was sure Eric had something much worse in mind.

I got out of the car because there was no point in trying to get Eric to release the Were. He wouldn't listen to me with the bloodlust on him so strong. My bond to Eric was the crucial factor in this decision. I was happy that he was enjoying himself, getting the blood he needed. I was furious that someone had tried to hurt him. Since both of these feelings would not normally be colors in my emotional palette, I knew what was to blame.

Plus, the inside of the Corvette had gotten unpleasantly crowded, what with me, Eric, and most of the Were.

Miraculously, no cars passed while I trotted along the shoulder to our attacker's vehicle, which (not so much to my surprise) turned out to be a plain white car with an illegal flashing attachment. I turned out the car's lights and, by punching or disconnecting every wire and button I could find, managed to kill the flashers, too. Now we were not nearly so conspicuous. Eric had shut down the Corvette's lights moments into the encounter.

I looked over the inside of the white car quickly but didn't see an envelope marked "Revelation of who hired me, in case I get caught." I needed a clue. There should at least have been a phone number on a scrap of paper, a phone number I could look up in a reverse directory. If I knew how to do such a thing. Rats. I trudged back to Eric's car, noticing in the lights of a passing semi that there weren't any legs sticking out of the driver's window anymore, which rendered the Corvette a lot less conspicuous. But we needed to get out of there.

I peered into the Corvette and found it empty. The only reminder of what had just happened was a smear of blood on Eric's seat, and I pulled a tissue out of my purse, spat on it, and rubbed the drying blood off; not a very elegant solution, but practical.

Suddenly, Eric was beside me, and I had to stifle a shriek. He was still excited by the unexpected attack, and he pinned me against the side of the car, holding my head at the correct angle for a kiss. I felt a lurch of desire and came very close to saying, "What the hell, take me now, you big Viking." It was not only the blood bond inclining me to accept his tacit offer, but my memory of how wonderful Eric was in bed. But I thought of Quinn and detached myself from Eric's mouth with a great effort.

For a second, I didn't think he was going to let go, but he did. "Let me see," I said in an unsteady voice, and pulled his shirt collar aside to look at the bullet wound. Eric had almost finished healing, but of course his shirt was still wet with blood.

"What was that about?" he asked. "Was that an enemy of yours?"

"I have no idea."

"He shot at you," Eric said, as if I was just a wee bit slow. "He wanted you first."

"But what if he did that to hurt you? What if he would have blamed my death on you?" I was so tired of being the object of plots that I suspected I was trying to *will* Eric into being the target. Another idea struck me, and I veered into it. "And how'd they find us?"

"Someone who knew we'd be driving back to Bon Temps tonight," Eric said. "Someone who knew what car I was in."

"It couldn't have been Niall," I said, and then rethought my flash of loyalty to my brand-new, self-proclaimed great-grandfather. After all, he might have been lying the whole time we were at the table. How would I know? I couldn't get in his head. The ignorance of my position felt strange to me.

But I didn't believe Niall had been lying.

"I don't think it was the fairy, either," Eric said. "But we'd better talk about it on the road. This isn't a good place for us to linger."

He was right about that. I didn't know where he'd put the body, and I realized that I didn't really care. A year ago it would have torn me up, leaving a body behind as we sped away along the interstate. Now I was just glad it was him and not me who was lying in the woods.

I was a terrible Christian and a decent survivalist.

As we drove through the dark, I pondered the chasm yawning right in front of me, waiting for me to take that extra step. I felt stranded on that brink. I found it harder and harder to stick to what was right, when what was expedient made better sense. Really, my brain told me ruthlessly, didn't I understand that Quinn had dumped me? Wouldn't he have gotten in touch if he still considered us a couple? Hadn't I always had a soft spot for Eric, who made love like a train thundering into a tunnel? Didn't I have beaucoup evidence that Eric could defend me better than anyone I knew?

I could hardly summon the energy to be shocked at myself.

If you find yourself considering who to take for a lover because of his ability to defend you, you're getting pretty close to selecting a mate because you think he has desirable traits to pass along to future generations. And if there'd been a chance I could have had Eric's child (a thought that made me shiver), he would have been at the top of the list, a list I hadn't even known I'd been compiling. I pictured myself as a female peacock looking for the male peacock with the prettiest display of tail, or a wolf waiting for the leader (strongest, smartest, bravest) of the pack to mount her.

Okay, I'd yucked myself out. I was a human woman. I tried to be a good woman. I had to find Quinn because I had committed myself to him . . . sort of.

No, no quibbling!

"What are you thinking about, Sookie?" Eric asked out of the darkness. "Your face has had thoughts rippling across it too fast to follow."

The fact that he could see me—not only in the dark, but while he was supposed to be watching the road—was exasperating and scary. And proof of his superiority, my inner cavewoman said.

"Eric, just get me home. I'm in emotional overload."

He didn't speak again. Maybe he was being wise, or maybe the healing was painful.

"We need to talk about this again," he said when he pulled into my driveway. He parked in front of the house, turned to me as much as he could in the little car. "Sookie, I'm hurting. . . . Can I . . ." He leaned over, brushed his fingers over my neck.

At the very idea, my body betrayed me. A throbbing started down low, and that was just wrong. A person shouldn't get excited at the idea of being bitten. That's bad, right? I clenched my fists so tightly my fingernails made my palms hurt.

Now that I could see him better, now that the interior of the car was illuminated with the harsh glare of the security light, I realized that Eric was even paler than usual. As I watched, the bullet began exiting the wound, and he leaned back against his seat, his eyes shut. Millimeter by millimeter, the bullet was extruded until it dropped into my waiting hand. I remembered Eric getting me to suck out a bullet in his arm. Ha! What a fraud he'd been. The bullet would've come out on its own. My indignation made me feel more like myself.

"I think you can make it home," I said, though I felt an almost irresistible urge to lean over to him and offer my neck or my wrist. I gritted my teeth and got out of the car. "You can stop at Merlotte's and get bottled blood if you really need some."

"You're hard-hearted," Eric said, but he didn't sound truly angry or affronted.

"I am," I said, and I smiled at him. "You be careful, you hear?"

"Of course," he said. "And I'm not stopping for any policemen."

I made myself march into the house without looking back. When I was inside the front door and had shut it firmly behind me, I felt an immediate relief. Thank goodness. I'd wondered if I was going to turn around at every step I took away from him. This blood tie thing was really irritating. If I wasn't careful and vigilant, I was going to do something I'd regret.

"I am woman, hear me roar," I said.

"Gosh, what prompted that?" Amelia asked, and I jumped. She was coming down the hall from the kitchen in her nightgown and matching robe, peach with cream-colored lace trim. Everything of Amelia's was nice. She'd never sneer at anyone else's shopping habits, but she'd never wear anything from Wal-Mart, either.

"I've had a trying evening," I said. I looked down at myself. Only a little blood on the blue silk T-shirt. I'd have to soak it. "How have things gone here?"

"Octavia called me," Amelia said, and though she was trying to keep her voice steady, I could feel the anxiety coming off her in waves.

"Your mentor." I wasn't at my brightest.

"Yep, the one and only." She bent down to pick up Bob, who always seemed to be around if Amelia was upset. She held him to her chest and buried her face in his fur. "She had heard, of course. Even after Katrina and all the changes it made in her life, she has to bring up *the mistake*." (That was what Amelia called it—the mistake.)

"I wonder what Bob calls it," I said.

Amelia looked over Bob's head at me, and I knew instantly I'd said a tactless thing. "Sorry," I said. "I wasn't thinking. But maybe it's not too realistic to think you can get out of this without being called to account, huh?"

"You're right," she said. She didn't seem too happy about my rightness, but at least she said it. "I did wrong. I attempted something I shouldn't have, and Bob paid the price."

Wow, when Amelia decided to confess, she went whole hog.

"I'm going to have to take my licks," she said. "Maybe they'll take away my magic practice for a year. Maybe longer."

"Oh. That seems harsh," I said. In my fantasy, her mentor just scolded Amelia in front of a room full of magicians and sorcerers and witches or what-have-you, and then they transformed Bob back. He promptly forgave Amelia and told her he loved her. Since he forgave her, the rest of the assemblage did, too, and Amelia and Bob came back to my house and lived here together . . . for a good long while. (I wasn't too specific about that part.)

"That's the mildest punishment possible," Amelia said.

"Oh."

"You don't want to know the other possible sentences." She was right. I didn't. "Well, what mysterious errand did Eric take you on?" Amelia asked.

Amelia couldn't have tipped off anyone to our destination or route; she hadn't known where we were going. "Oh, ah, he just wanted to take me to a new restaurant in Shreveport. It had a French name. It was pretty nice."

"So, this was like a date?" I could tell she was wondering what place Quinn played in my relationship with Eric.

"Oh, no, not a date," I said, sounding unconvincing even to myself. "No guy-girl action going on. Just, you know, hanging out." Kissing. Getting shot.

"He sure is handsome," Amelia said.

"Yeah, no doubt about it. I've met some toothsome guys. Remember Claude?" I'd shown Amelia the poster that had arrived in the mail two weeks before, a blowup of the romance novel cover for which Claude had posed. She'd been impressed—what woman wouldn't be?

"Ah, I went to watch Claude strip last week." Amelia couldn't meet my eyes.

"And you didn't take me!" Claude was a very disagreeable person, especially when contrasted with his sister, Claudine, but he was beyond gorgeous. He was in the Brad Pitt stratosphere of male beauty. Of course, he was gay. Wouldn't you know it? "You went while I was at work?"

"I thought you wouldn't approve of my going," she said, ducking her head. "I mean, since you're friends with his sister. I went with Tara. JB was working. Are you mad?"

"Nah. I don't care." My friend Tara owned a dress shop, and her new husband, JB, worked at a women's exercise center. "I would like to see Claude trying to act like he was enjoying himself."

"I think he was having a good time," she said. "There's no one Claude loves better than Claude, right? So all these women looking at him and admiring him . . . He's not into women, but he's sure into being admired."

"True. Let's go see him together sometime."

"Okay," she said, and I could tell she was quite cheerful again. "Now, tell me what you ordered at this new fancy restaurant." So I told her. But all the while I was wishing I didn't have to keep silent about my great-grandfather. I wanted so badly to tell Amelia about Niall: how he looked, what he'd said, that I had a whole history I hadn't known. And it would take me a while to process what my grandmother had endured, to alter my picture of her in light of the facts I'd learned. And

I had to rethink my unpleasant memories of my mother, too. She'd fallen for my dad like a ton of bricks, and she'd had his kids because she loved him . . . only to find that she didn't want to share him with them, especially with me, another female. At least, this was my new insight.

"There was more stuff," I said, a yawn splitting my jaw in two. It was very late. "But I've got to get to bed. I get any phone calls or anything?"

"That Were from Shreveport called. He wanted to talk to you, and I told him you were out for the evening and he should call you on your cell. He asked if he could meet up with you, but I said I didn't know where you were."

"Alcide," I said. "I wonder what he wanted." I figured I'd call him tomorrow.

"And some girl called. Said she'd been a waitress at Merlotte's before, and she'd seen you at the wedding last night."

"Tanya?"

"Yeah, that was her name."

"What did she want?"

"Don't know. She said she'd call back tomorrow or see you at the bar."

"Crap. I hope Sam didn't hire her to fill in or something."

"I thought I was the fill-in bargirl."

"Yeah, unless someone's quit. I warn you, Sam likes her."

"You don't?"

"She's a treacherous bitch."

"Gosh, tell me what you really think."

"No kidding, Amelia, she took a job at Merlotte's so she could spy on me for the Pelts."

"Oh, *that's* the one. Well, she won't spy on you again. I'll take steps."

That was a scarier thought than working with Tanya. Amelia was a strong and skillful witch, don't get me wrong, but she was also prone to attempt things beyond her experience level. Hence Bob.

"Check with me first, please," I said, and Amelia looked surprised.

"Well, sure," she said. "Now, I'm off to bed."

She made her way up the steps with Bob in her arms, and I went to my small bathroom to remove my makeup and put on my own nightgown. Amelia hadn't noticed the speckles of blood on the shirt, and I put it in the sink to soak.

What a day it had been. I'd spent time with Eric, who always rattled my chain, and I'd found a living relative, though not a human one. I'd learned a lot of stuff about my family, most of it unpleasant. I'd eaten in a fancy restaurant, though I could hardly recall the food. And finally, I'd been shot at.

When I crawled into bed, I said my prayers, trying to put Quinn at the top of the list. I thought the excitement of discovering a great-grandfather would keep me awake that night, but sleep claimed me right when I was in the middle of asking God to help me find my way through the moral morass of being party to a killing.

Chapter 6

There was a knock on the front door the next morning about an hour before I wanted to wake up. I heard it only because Bob had come into my room and jumped on my bed, where he wasn't supposed to be, settling into the space behind my knees while I lay on my side. He purred loudly, and I reached down to scratch behind his ears. I loved cats. That didn't stop me from liking dogs, too, and only the fact that I was gone so much kept me from getting a puppy. Terry Bellefleur had offered me one, but I'd wavered until his pups were gone. I wondered if Bob would mind a kitten companion. Would Amelia get jealous if I bought a female cat? I had to smile even as I snuggled deeper into the bed.

But I wasn't truly asleep, and I did hear the knock.

I muttered a few words about the person at the door, and I slid on my slippers and threw on my thin blue cotton bathrobe.

The morning had a hint of chill, reminding me that despite the mild and sunny days, this was October. There were Halloweens when even a sweater was too warm, and there were Halloweens when you had to wear a light coat when you did your trick-or-treating.

I looked through the peephole and saw an elderly black woman with a halo of white hair. She was light-skinned and her features were narrow and sharp: nose, lips, eyes. She was wearing magenta lipstick and a yellow pantsuit. But she didn't seem armed or dangerous. This just goes to show how misleading first appearances can be. I opened the door.

"Young lady, I'm here to see Amelia Broadway," the woman informed me in very precisely pronounced English.

"Please come in," I said, because this was an older woman and I'd been brought up to revere old people. "Have a seat." I indicated the couch. "I'll go up and get Amelia."

I noticed she didn't apologize for getting me out of bed or for showing up unannounced. I climbed the stairs with a grim feeling that Amelia wasn't going to enjoy this message.

I so seldom went up to the second floor that it surprised me to see how nice Amelia had made it look. Since the upper bedrooms had only had basic furniture in them, she'd turned the one to the right, the larger one, into her bedroom. The one to the left was her sitting room. It held her television, an easy chair and ottoman, a small computer desk and her computer, and a plant or two. The bedroom, which I believed had been built for a generation of Stackhouses that had sired three boys in quick succession, had only a small closet, but Amelia had bought rolling clothes racks from somewhere on the Internet and assembled them handily. Then she'd bought a tri-fold screen at an auction and repainted it and arranged it in front of the racks to camouflage them. Her bright bedspread and the old table she'd repainted to serve as her makeup table added to the color that jumped out from the white-painted walls. Amid all this cheer was one dismal witch.

Amelia was sitting up in bed, her short hair mashed into strange shapes. "Who is that I hear downstairs?" she asked in a very hushed voice.

"Older black lady, light-skinned? Sharp way about her?"

"Omigod," Amelia breathed, and slumped back against her dozen or so pillows. "It's Octavia."

"Well, you come down and have a word with her. I can't entertain her."

Amelia snarled at me, but she accepted the inevitable. She got out of bed and pulled off her nightgown. She pulled on a bra and panties and some jeans, and she extracted a sweater from a drawer.

I went down to tell Octavia Fant that Amelia was coming. Amelia would have to walk right past her to get to the bathroom, since there was only the one staircase, but at least I could smooth the way.

"Can I get you some coffee?" I asked. The older woman was busy looking around the room with her bright brown eyes.

"If you have some tea, I'd like a cup," Octavia Fant said.

"Yes, ma'am, we have some," I said, relieved that Amelia had insisted on buying it. I had no idea what kind it was, and I hoped it was in a bag, because I'd never made hot tea in my life.

"Good," she said, and that was that.

"Amelia's on her way down," I said, trying to think of some graceful way to add, "And she's going to have to hurry through the room to pee and brush her teeth, so pretend you don't see her." I abandoned that lost cause and fled to the kitchen.

I retrieved Amelia's tea from one of her designated shelves, and while the water was getting hot, I got down two cups and saucers and put them on a tray. I added the sugar bowl and a tiny pitcher with milk and two spoons. *Napkins!* I thought, and wished I had some cloth ones instead of regular paper. (This was how Octavia Fant made me feel, without her using a bit of magic on me.) I heard the water running in the hall bathroom just as I put a handful of cookies on a plate and added that to the assemblage. I didn't have any flowers or a little vase, which was the only other thing I thought of that I could've added. I picked up the tray and made my way slowly down the hall to the living room.

I set the tray down on the coffee table in front of Ms. Fant. She looked up at me with her piercing eyes and gave me a curt nod of thanks. I realized that I could not read her mind. I'd been holding off, waiting for a moment when I could really give her her proper due, but she knew how to block me out. I'd never met a human who could do that. For a second I felt almost irritated. Then I remembered who and what she was, and I scooted off to my room to make my bed and visit my own little bathroom. I passed Amelia in the hall, and she gave me a scared look.

Sorry, Amelia, I thought, as I closed my bedroom door firmly. *You're on your own.*

I didn't have to be at work until the evening, so I put on some old jeans and a Fangtasia T-shirt ("The Bar with a Bite"). Pam had given it to me when the bar first started selling them. I slid my feet into some Crocs and went into the kitchen to fix my own beverage, coffee. I made some toast and got the local paper I'd grabbed when I'd answered the door. Rolling the rubber band off, I glanced at the front page. The school board had met, the local Wal-Mart had donated generously to the Boys and Girls Club's after-school program, and the state legislature had voted to recognize vampire-human marriages. Well, well. No one had thought that bill would ever pass.

I flipped open the paper to read the obituaries. First the local deaths—no one I knew, good. Then the area deaths—oh, *no.*

MARIA-STAR COOPER, read the heading. The item said only, "Maria-Star Cooper, 25, a resident of Shreveport, died unexpectedly at her home yesterday. Cooper, a photographer, is survived by her mother and father, Matthew and Stella Cooper of Minden, and three brothers. Arrangements are pending."

I felt suddenly out of breath and sank into the straight-back chair with a feeling of total disbelief. Maria-Star and I hadn't exactly been friends, but I'd liked her well enough, and she and Alcide Herveaux, a major figure in the Shreveport Were pack, had been going together for months. Poor Alcide! His first girlfriend had died violently, and now this.

The phone rang and I jumped. I grabbed it up with a terrible feeling of disaster. "Hello?" I said cautiously, as if the phone could spit at me.

"Sookie," said Alcide. He had a deep voice, and now it was husky with tears.

"I'm so sorry," I said. "I just read the paper." There was nothing else to say. Now I knew why he'd called the night before.

"She was murdered," Alcide said.

"Oh, my God."

"Sookie, it was only the beginning. On the off chance that Furnan is after you, too, I want you to stay alert."

"Too late," I said after a moment given to absorbing this awful news. "Someone tried to kill me last night."

Alcide held the phone away from him and howled. Hearing this, in the middle of the day, over the telephone . . . Even then, it was frightening.

Trouble within the Shreveport pack had been brewing for a while. Even I, separated from Were politics, had known that. Patrick Furnan, the leader of the Long Tooth pack, had gotten his office by killing Alcide's father in combat. The victory had been legal—well, Were legal—but there had been a few not-so-legal plays along the way. Alcide—strong, young, prosperous, and packing a grudge—had always been a threat to Furnan, at least in Furnan's mind.

This was a tense topic, since Weres were secret from the human population, not out in the open like vampires. The day was coming, and coming soon, when the shifter population would step forward. I'd heard them speak of it over and over.

But that hadn't happened yet, and it wouldn't be good if the first knowledge the humans had of the Weres was of bodies turning up all over the place.

"Someone will be over there right away," Alcide said.

"Absolutely not. I have to go to work tonight, and I'm so utterly on the edge of this thing that I'm sure they won't try again. But I do need to know how the guy knew where and when to find me."

"Tell Amanda the circumstances," Alcide said, his voice thick with anger, and then Amanda came on. Hard to believe that when I'd seen her at the wedding we'd both been so cheerful.

"Tell me," she said crisply, and I knew this was no time to argue. I told her the story as tersely as possible (leaving out Niall, and Eric's name, and most other details), and she was silent for a few seconds after I'd finished speaking.

"Since he was taken out, that's one less we have to worry about," she said, sounding simply relieved. "I wish you'd known who he was."

"Sorry," I said a bit acidly. "I was thinking about the gun, not his ID. How come you-all can have a war with as few people as you have?" The Shreveport pack couldn't number over thirty.

"Reinforcements from other territories."

"Why would anyone do that?" Why join in a war that wasn't yours? What was the point of losing your own people when it was the other pack's dispute?

"There are perks to backing the winning side," Amanda said. "Listen, you still got that witch living with you?"

"I do."

"Then there's something you can do to help."

"Okay," I said, though I didn't recall offering. "What would that be?"

"You need to ask your witch friend if she'll go to Maria-Star's apartment and get some kind of reading on what happened there. Is that possible? We want to know the Weres involved."

"It's possible, but I don't know if she'll do it."

"Ask her now, please."

"Ah . . . let me call you back. She's got a visitor."

Before I went out to the living room, I made a call. I didn't want to leave this message on the answering machine at Fangtasia, which wouldn't be open yet, so I called Pam's cell, something I'd never done before. As it rang, I found myself wondering if it was in the coffin with her. That was an eerie thing to picture. I didn't know if Pam actually slept in a coffin or not, but if she did . . . I shuddered. Of course, the phone went to voice mail, and I said, "Pam, I've found out why Eric and I were pulled over last night, or at least I think so. There's a Were war brewing, and I think I was the target. Someone sold us out to Patrick Furnan. And I didn't tell anyone where I was going." That was a problem Eric and I had been too shaken to discuss the night before. How had anyone, anyone at all, known where we'd be last night? That we'd be driving back from Shreveport.

Amelia and Octavia were in the middle of a discussion, but neither of them looked as angry or upset as I'd feared.

"I hate to intrude," I said as both pairs of eyes turned to

me. Octavia's eyes were brown, Amelia's bright blue, but at the moment they were eerily alike in expression.

"Yes?" Octavia was clearly queen of the situation.

Any witch worth her salt would know about Weres. I condensed the issues of the Were war down to a few sentences, told them about the attack the night before on the interstate, and explained Amanda's request.

"Is this something you should get involved with, Amelia?" Octavia asked, her voice making it quite clear there was only one answer she should give.

"Oh, I think so," Amelia said. She smiled. "Can't have someone shooting at my roomie. I'll help Amanda."

Octavia couldn't have been more shocked if Amelia had spat a watermelon seed on her pants. "Amelia! You're trying things beyond your ability! This will lead to terrible trouble! Look what you've already done to poor Bob Jessup."

Oh, boy, I hadn't known Amelia that long, but I already knew that was a poor way to get her to comply with your wishes. If Amelia was proud of anything, it was her witchy ability. Challenging her expertise was a sure way to rattle her. On the other hand, Bob was a major fuckup.

"Can you change him back?" I asked the older witch.

Octavia looked at me sharply. "Of course," she said.

"Then why don't you do it, and we can go from there?" I said.

Octavia looked very startled, and I knew I shouldn't have gotten up in her face like that. On the other hand, if she wanted to show Amelia that her magic was more powerful, here was her chance. Bob the cat was sitting in Amelia's lap, looking unconcerned. Octavia reached in her pocket and pulled out a pill container filled with what looked like marijuana; but I guess any dried herb pretty much looks the same, and I haven't ever actually handled marijuana, so I'm no judge. Anyway, Octavia took a pinch of this dried green stuff and reached out to let the bits drop on the cat's fur. Bob didn't seem to mind.

Amelia's face was a picture as she watched Octavia casting a spell, which seemed to consist of some Latin, a few motions, and the aforementioned herb. Finally, Octavia uttered what must have been the esoteric equivalent of "Allakazam!" and pointed at the cat.

Nothing happened.

Octavia repeated the phrase even more forcefully. Again with the finger pointing.

And again with the no results.

"You know what I think?" I said. No one seemed to want to know, but it was my house. "I wonder if Bob was always a cat, and for some reason he was temporarily human. That's why you can't change him back. Maybe he's in his true form right now."

"That's ridiculous," the older witch snapped. She was some kind of put out at her failure. Amelia was trying hard to suppress a grin.

"If you're so sure after this that Amelia's incompetent, which I happen to know she isn't, you might want to consider coming to see Maria-Star's apartment with us," I said. "Make sure Amelia doesn't get into any trouble."

Amelia looked indignant for a second, but she seemed to see my plan, and she added her entreaty to mine.

"Very well. I'll come along," Octavia said grandly.

I couldn't see into the old witch's mind, but I'd worked at a bar long enough to know a lonely person when I saw one.

I got the address from Amanda, who told me Dawson was guarding the place until we arrived. I knew him and liked him, since he'd helped me out before. He owned a local motorcycle repair shop a couple of miles out of Bon Temps, and he sometimes ran Merlotte's for Sam. Dawson didn't run with a pack, and the news that he was pitching in with Alcide's rebel faction was significant.

I can't say the drive to the outskirts of Shreveport was a bonding experience for the three of us, but I did fill Octavia in on the background of the pack troubles. And I explained my own involvement. "When the contest for packmaster was taking place," I said, "Alcide wanted me there as a human lie detector. I actually did catch the other guy cheating, which was good. But after that, it became a fight to the death, and Patrick Furnan was stronger. He killed Jackson Herveaux."

"I guess they covered up the death?" The old witch seemed neither shocked nor surprised.

"Yes, they put the body out at an isolated farm he owned, knowing no one would look there for a while. The wounds on the body weren't recognizable by the time he was found."

"Has Patrick Furnan been a good leader?"

"I really don't know," I admitted. "Alcide has always seemed to have a discontented group around him, and they're the ones I know best in the pack, so I guess I'm on Alcide's side."

"Did you ever consider that you could just step aside? Let the best Were win?"

"No," I said honestly. "I would have been just as glad if Alcide hadn't called me and told me about the pack troubles. But now that I know, I'll help him if I can. Not that I'm an angel or anything. But Patrick Furnan hates me, and it's only smart to help his enemy, point number one. And I liked Maria-Star, point number two. And someone tried to kill me last night, someone who may have been hired by Furnan, point number three."

Octavia nodded. She was sure no wussy old lady.

Maria-Star had lived in a rather dated apartment building on Highway 3 between Benton and Shreveport. It was a small complex, just two buildings side by side facing a parking lot, right there on the highway. The buildings backed onto a field, and the adjacent businesses were day businesses: an insurance agency and a dentist's office.

Each of the two red brick buildings was divided into four apartments. I noticed a familiar battered pickup truck in front of the building on the right, and I parked by it. These apartments were enclosed; you went in the common entrance into a hall, and there was a door on either side of the stairway to the second floor. Maria-Star had lived on the ground-floor left apartment. This was easy to spot, because Dawson was propped against the wall beside her door.

I introduced him to the two witches as "Dawson" because I didn't know his first name. Dawson was a supersized man. I'd bet you could crack pecans on his biceps. He had dark brown hair beginning to show just a little gray, and a neatly trimmed mustache. I'd known who he was all my life, but I'd never known him well. Dawson was probably seven or eight years older than me, and he'd married early. And divorced early, too. His son, who lived with the mother, was quite a football player for Clarice High School. Dawson looked tougher than any guy I'd ever met. I don't know if it was the very dark eyes, or the grim face, or simply the size of him.

There was crime scene tape across the apartment doorway. My eyes welled up when I saw it. Maria-Star had died violently in this space only hours before. Dawson produced a set of keys (Alcide's?) and unlocked the door, and we ducked under the tape to enter.

And we all stood frozen in silence, appalled at the state of the little living room. My way was blocked by an overturned occasional table with a big gash marring the wood. My eyes flickered over the irregular dark stains on the walls until my brain told me the stains were blood.

The smell was faint but unpleasant. I began to breathe shallowly so I wouldn't get sick.

"Now, what do you want us to do?" Octavia asked.

"I thought you'd do an ectoplasmic reconstruction, like Amelia did before," I said.

"Amelia did an ectoplasmic reconstruction?" Octavia had dropped the haughty tone and sounded genuinely surprised and admiring. "I've never seen one."

Amelia nodded modestly. "With Terry and Bob and Patsy," she said. "It worked great. We had a big area to cover."

"Then I'm sure we can do one here," Octavia said. She looked interested and excited. It was like her face had woken up. I realized that what I'd seen before had been her depressed face. And I was getting enough from her head (now that she wasn't concentrating on keeping me out) to let me know that Octavia had spent a month after Katrina wondering where her next meal would come from, where she'd lay her head from night to night. Now she lived with family, though I didn't get a clean picture.

"I brought the stuff with me," Amelia said. Her brain was radiating pride and relief. She might yet get out from under the Bob contretemps without paying a huge price.

Dawson stood leaning against the wall, listening with apparent interest. Since he was a Were, it was hard to read his thoughts, but he was definitely relaxed.

I envied him. It wasn't possible for me to be at ease in this terrible little apartment, which almost echoed with the violence done in its walls. I was scared to sit on the love seat or the armchair, both upholstered in blue and white checks. The carpet was a darker blue, and the paint was white. Everything matched. The apartment was a little dull for my taste. But it had been neat and clean and carefully arranged, and less than twenty-four hours ago it had been a home.

I could see through to the bedroom, where the covers were thrown back. This was the only sign of disorder in the bedroom or the kitchen. The living room had been the center of the violence.

For lack of a better place to park myself, I went to lean against the bare wall beside Dawson.

I didn't think the motorcycle repairman and I had ever had a long conversation, though he'd gotten shot in my defense a few months before. I'd heard that *the law* (in this case, Andy Bellefleur and his fellow detective Alcee Beck) suspected more took place at Dawson's shop than motorcycle repairs, but they'd never caught Dawson doing anything illegal. Dawson also hired out as a bodyguard from time to time, or maybe he volunteered his services. He was certainly suited to the job.

"Were you friends?" Dawson rumbled, nodding his head at the bloodiest spot on the floor, the spot where Maria-Star had died.

"We were more like friendly acquaintances," I said, not wanting to claim more grief than my due. "I saw her at a wedding a couple of nights ago." I started to say she'd been fine then, but that would have been stupid. You don't sicken before you're murdered.

"When was the last time anyone talked to Maria-Star?" Amelia asked Dawson. "I need to establish some time limits."

"Eleven last night," he said. "Phone call from Alcide. He was out of town, with witnesses. Neighbor heard a big to-do from in here about thirty minutes after that, called the police." That was a long speech for Dawson. Amelia went back to her preparations, and Octavia read a thin book that Amelia had extracted from her little backpack.

"Have you ever watched one of these before?" Dawson said to me.

"Yeah, in New Orleans. I gather this is kind of rare and hard to do. Amelia's really good."

"She's livin' with you?"

I nodded.

"That's what I heard," he said. We were quiet for a moment. Dawson was proving to be a restful companion as well as a handy hunk of muscle.

There was some gesturing, and there was some chanting, with Octavia following her onetime student. Octavia might never have done an ectoplasmic reconstruction, but the longer the ritual went on the more power reverberated in the small room, until my fingernails seemed to hum with it. Dawson didn't exactly look frightened, but he was definitely on the alert as the pressure of the magic built. He uncrossed his arms and stood up straight, and I did, too.

Though I knew what to expect, it was still startling to me when Maria-Star appeared in the room with us. Beside me, I felt Dawson jerk with surprise. Maria-Star was painting her toenails. Her long dark hair was gathered into a ponytail on top of her head. She was sitting on the carpet in front of the television, a sheet of newspaper spread carefully under her foot. The magically re-created image had the same watery look I'd seen in a previous reconstruction, when I'd observed my cousin Hadley during her last few hours on earth. Maria-Star wasn't exactly in color. She was like an image filled with glistening gel. Because the apartment was no longer in the same order it had been when she'd sat in that spot, the effect was odd. She was sitting right in the middle of the overturned coffee table.

We didn't have long to wait. Maria-Star finished her toenails and sat watching the television set (now dark and dead) while she waited for them to dry. She did a few leg exercises while she waited. Then she gathered up the polish and the little spacers she'd had between her toes and folded the paper. She rose and went into the bathroom. Since the actual bathroom door was now half-closed, the watery Maria-Star had to walk through it. From our angle, Dawson and I couldn't see inside, but Amelia, whose hands were extended in a kind of sustaining gesture, gave a little shrug as if to say Maria-Star was not doing anything important. Ectoplasmic peeing, maybe.

In a few minutes, the young woman appeared again, this time in her nightgown. She went into the bedroom and turned back the bed. Suddenly, her head turned toward the door.

It was like watching a pantomime. Clearly Maria-Star had heard a sound at her door, and the sound was unexpected. I didn't know if she was hearing the doorbell, a knocking, or someone trying to pick the lock.

Her alert posture turned to alarm, even panic. She went back into the living room and picked up her cell phone—we saw it appear when she touched it—and punched a couple of numbers. Calling someone on speed dial. But before the phone could even have rung on the other end, the door exploded inward and a man was on her, a half wolf, half man. He showed up because he was a living thing, but he was clearer when he was close to Maria-Star, the focus of the spell. He pinned

Maria-Star to the floor and bit her deeply on her shoulder. Her mouth opened wide, and you could tell she was screaming and she was fighting like a Were, but he'd caught her totally by surprise and her arms were pinned down. Gleaming lines indicated blood running down from the bite.

Dawson gripped my shoulder, a growl rising from his throat. I didn't know if he was furious at the attack on Maria-Star, excited by the action and the impression of flowing blood, or all of the above.

A second Were was right behind the first. He was in his human form. He had a knife in his right hand. He plunged it into Maria-Star's torso, withdrew it, reared back, and plunged it in again. As the knife rose and fell, it cast blood drops on the walls. We could see the blood drops, so there must be ectoplasm (or whatever it really is) in blood, too.

I hadn't known the first man. This guy, I recognized. He was Cal Myers, a henchman of Furnan's and a police detective on the Shreveport force.

The blitz attack had taken only seconds. The moment Maria-Star was clearly mortally wounded, they were out the door, closing it behind them. I was shocked by the sudden and dreadful cruelty of the murder, and I felt my breath coming faster. Maria-Star, glistening and almost clear, lay there before us for a moment in the middle of the wreckage, gleaming blood splotches on her shirt and on the floor around her, and then she just winked out of existence, because she had died in that moment.

We all stood in appalled silence. The witches were silent, their arms dropping down by their sides as if they were puppets whose strings had been cut. Octavia was crying, tears running down her creased cheeks. Amelia looked as though she were thinking of throwing up. I was shivering in reaction, and even Dawson looked nauseated.

"I didn't know the first guy since he'd only half changed," Dawson said. "The second one looked familiar. He's a cop, right? In Shreveport?"

"Cal Myers. Better call Alcide," I said when I thought my voice would work. "And Alcide needs to send these ladies something for their trouble, when he gets his own sorted out." I figured Alcide might not think of that since he was mourning for Maria-Star, but the witches had done this work with no mention of recompense. They deserved to be rewarded for their effort. It had cost them dearly: both of them had folded onto the love seat.

"If you ladies can manage," Dawson said, "we better get our asses out of here. No telling when the police'll be back. The crime lab finished just five minutes before you got here."

While the witches gathered their energy and all their paraphernalia, I talked to Dawson. "You said Alcide's got a good alibi?"

Dawson nodded. "He got a phone call from Maria-Star's neighbor. She called Alcide right after she called the police, when she heard all the ruckus. Granted, the call was to his cell phone, but he answered right away and she could hear the sounds of the hotel bar behind the conversation. Plus, he was in the bar with people he'd just met who swore he was there when he found out she'd been killed. They aren't likely to forget."

"I guess the police are trying to find a motive." That was what they did on the TV shows.

"She didn't have enemies," Dawson said.

"Now what?" Amelia said. She and Octavia were on their feet, but they were clearly drained. Dawson shepherded us out of the apartment and relocked it.

"Thanks for coming, ladies," Dawson told Amelia and Octavia. He turned to me. "Sookie, could you come with me, explain to Alcide what we just saw? Can Amelia drive Miss Fant back?"

"Ah. Sure. If she's not too tired."

Amelia said she thought she could manage. We'd come in my car, so I tossed her the keys. "You okay driving?" I asked, just to reassure myself.

She nodded. "I'll take it slow."

I was scrambling into Dawson's truck when I realized that this step dragged me even further into the Were war. Then I figured, *Patrick Furnan already tried to kill me. Can't get any worse.*

Chapter 7

Dawson's pickup, a Dodge Ram, although battered on the out-side, was orderly within. It wasn't a new vehicle by any means—probably five years old—but it was very well-maintained both under the hood and in the cab.

"You're not a member of the pack, Dawson, right?"

"It's Tray. Tray Dawson."

"Oh, I'm sorry."

Dawson shrugged, as if to say *No big deal.* "I never was a good pack animal," he said. "I couldn't keep in line. I couldn't follow the chain of command."

"So why are you joining in this fight?" I said.

"Patrick Furnan tried to put me out of business," Dawson said.

"Why'd he do that?"

"Aren't that many other motorcycle repair shops in the area, especially since Furnan bought the Harley-Davidson dealership in Shreveport," Tray explained. "That so-and-so's greedy. He wants it all for himself. He doesn't care who goes broke. When he realized I was sticking with my shop, he sent a couple of his guys down to see me. They beat me up, busted up the shop."

"They must have been really good," I said. It was hard to believe anyone could best Tray Dawson. "Did you call the police?"

"No. The cops in Bon Temps aren't that crazy about me anyway. But I threw in with Alcide."

Detective Cal Myers, obviously, was not above doing Furnan's dirty work. It was Myers who'd collaborated with Furnan in cheating in the packmaster contest. But I was truly shocked that he would go as far as murdering Maria-Star, whose only sin was being loved by Alcide. We'd seen it with our own eyes, though.

"What's the deal with you and the police in Bon Temps?" I asked, as long as we were talking about law enforcement.

He laughed. "I used to be a cop; did you know that?"

"No," I said, genuinely surprised. "No kidding?"

"For real," he said. "I was on the force in New Orleans. But I didn't like the politics, and my captain was a real bastard, pardon me."

I nodded gravely. It had been a long time since someone had apologized for using bad language within my hearing. "So, something happened?"

"Yeah, eventually things came to a head. The captain accused me of taking some money this scuzzbag had left lying on a table when we arrested him in his home." Tray shook his head in disgust. "I had to quit then. I liked the job."

"What did you like about it?"

"No two days were alike. Yeah, sure, we got in the cars and patrolled. That was the same. But every time we got out something different would happen."

I nodded. I could understand that. Every day at the bar was a little different, too, though probably not as different as Tray's days had been in the patrol car.

We drove in silence for a while. I could tell Tray was thinking about the odds of Alcide overcoming Furnan in the struggle for dominance. He was thinking Alcide was a lucky guy to have dated Maria-Star and me, and all the luckier since that bitch Debbie Pelt had vanished. Good riddance, Tray thought.

"Now I get to ask you a question," Tray said.

"Only fair."

"You have something to do with Debbie disappearing?"

I took a deep breath. "Yeah. Self-defense."

"Good for you. Someone needed to do it."

We were quiet again for at least ten minutes. Not to drag the past into the present too much, but Alcide had broken up with Debbie Pelt before I met him. Then he dated me a little. Debbie decided I was an enemy, and she tried to kill me. I got her first. I'd come to terms with it . . . as much as you ever do. However, it had been impossible for Alcide to ever look at me again in the same way, and who could blame him? He'd found Maria-Star, and that was a good thing.

Had been a good thing.

I felt tears well up in my eyes and looked out the window. We'd passed the racetrack and the turnoff to Pierre Bossier Mall, and we went a couple more exits before Tray turned the truck onto the off ramp.

We meandered through a modest neighborhood for a while, Tray checking his rearview mirror so often that even I realized he was watching for anyone following us. Tray suddenly turned into a driveway and pulled around to the back of one of the slightly larger homes, which was demurely clad in white siding. We parked under a porte cochere in the back, along with another pickup. There was a small Nissan parked off to the side. There were a couple of motorcycles, too, and Tray gave them a glance of professional interest.

"Whose place?" I was a little hesitant about asking yet another question, but after all, I did want to know where I was.

"Amanda's," he said. He waited for me to precede him, and I went up the three steps leading up to the back door and rang the bell.

"Who's there?" asked a muffled voice.

"Sookie and Dawson," I said.

The door opened cautiously, the entrance blocked by Amanda so we couldn't see past her. I don't know much about handguns, but she had a big revolver in her hand pointed steadily at my chest. This was the second time in two days I'd had a gun pointed at me. Suddenly, I felt very cold and a little dizzy.

"Okay," Amanda said after looking us over sharply.

Alcide was standing behind the door, a shotgun at the ready. He'd stepped out into view as we came in, and when his own senses had checked us out, he stood down. He put the shotgun on the kitchen counter and sat at the kitchen table.

"I'm sorry about Maria-Star, Alcide," I said, forcing the words through stiff lips. Having guns aimed at you is just plain terrifying, especially at close range.

"I haven't gotten it yet," he said, his voice flat and even. I decided he was saying that the impact of her death hadn't hit him. "We were thinking about moving in together. It would have saved her life."

There wasn't any point in wallowing in what-might-have-been. That was only another way to torture yourself. What had actually happened was bad enough.

"We know who did it," Dawson said, and a shiver ran through the room. There were more Weres in the house—I could sense them now—and they had all become alert at Tray Dawson's words.

"What? How?" Without my seeing the movement, Alcide was on his feet.

"She got her witch friends to do a reconstruction," Tray said, nodding in my direction. "I watched. It was two guys. One I'd never seen, so Furnan's brought in some wolves from outside. The second was Cal Myers."

Alcide's big hands were clenched in fists. He didn't seem to know where to start speaking, he had so many reactions. "Furnan's hired help," Alcide said, finally picking a jumping-in point. "So we're within our rights to kill on sight. We'll snatch one of the bastards and make him talk. We can't bring a hostage here; someone would notice. Tray, where?"

"Hair of the Dog," he answered.

Amanda wasn't too crazy about that idea. She owned that bar, and using it as an execution or torture site didn't appeal to her. She opened her mouth to protest. Alcide faced her and snarled, his face twisting into something that wasn't quite Alcide. She cowered and nodded her assent.

Alcide raised his voice even more for his next pronouncement. "Cal Myers is Kill on Sight."

"But he's a pack member, and members get trials," Amanda said, and then cowered, correctly anticipating Alcide's wordless roar of rage.

"You haven't asked me about the man who tried to kill me," I said. I wanted to defuse the situation, if that was possible.

As furious as he was, Alcide was still too decent to remind me that I'd lived and Maria-Star hadn't, or that he'd loved Maria-Star much more than he'd ever cared about me. Both thoughts crossed his mind, though.

"He was a Were," I said. "About five foot ten, in his twenties. He was clean-shaven. He had brown hair and blue eyes and a big birthmark on his neck."

"Oh," said Amanda. "That sounds like what's-his-name, the brand-new mechanic at Furnan's shop. Hired last week. Lucky Owens. Ha! Who were you with?"

"I was with Eric Northman," I said.

There was a long, not entirely friendly silence. Weres and vampires are natural rivals, if not out-and-out enemies.

"So, the guy's dead?" Tray asked practically, and I nodded.

"How'd he approach you?" Alcide asked in a voice that was more rational.

"That's an interesting question," I said. "I was on the interstate driving home from Shreveport with Eric. We'd been to a restaurant here."

"So who would know where you were and who you were with?" Amanda said while Alcide frowned down at the floor, deep in thought.

"Or that you'd have to return home along the interstate last night." Tray was really rising in my opinion; he was right in there with the practical and pertinent ideas.

"I only told my roommate I was going out to dinner, not where," I said. "We met someone there, but we can leave him out. Eric knew, because he was acting as chauffeur. But I know Eric and the other man didn't tip anyone off."

"How can you be so sure?" Tray asked.

"Eric got shot protecting me," I said. "And the person he took me to meet was a relative."

Amanda and Tray didn't realize how small my family was, so they didn't get how momentous that statement was. But Alcide, who knew more about me, glared. "You're making this up," he said.

"No, I'm not." I stared back. I knew this was a terrible day for Alcide, but I didn't have to explain my life to him. But I had a sudden thought. "You know, the waiter—he was a Were." That would explain a lot.

"What's the name of the restaurant?"

"Les Deux Poissons." My accent wasn't good, but the Weres nodded.

"Kendall works there," Alcide said. "Kendall Kent. Long

reddish hair?" I nodded, and he looked sad. "I thought Kendall would come around to our side. We had a beer together a couple of times."

"That's Jack Kent's oldest. All he would have had to do was place a phone call," Amanda said. "Maybe he didn't know . . ."

"Not an excuse," Tray said. His deep voice reverberated in the little kitchen. "Kendall has to know who Sookie is, from the packmaster contest. She's a friend of the pack. Instead of telling Alcide she was in our territory and should be protected, he called Furnan and told him where Sookie was, maybe let him know when she started home. Made it easy for Lucky to lie in wait."

I wanted to protest that there was no certainty that it had happened like that, but when I thought about it, it had to have been exactly that way or in some manner very close to it. Just to be sure I was remembering correctly, I called Amelia and asked her if she'd told any callers where I was the night before.

"No," she said. "I heard from Octavia, who didn't know you. I got a call from that werepanther boy I met at your brother's wedding. Believe me, you didn't come up in that conversation. Alcide called, real upset. Tanya. I told her nothing."

"Thanks, roomie," I said. "You recovering?"

"Yeah, I'm feeling better, and Octavia left to go back to the family she's been staying with in Monroe."

"Okay, see you when I get back."

"You going to make it back in time for work?"

"Yeah, I *have* to make it to work." Since I'd spent that week in Rhodes, I have to be careful to stick to the schedule for a while, otherwise the other waitresses would get up in my face about Sam giving me all the breaks. I hung up. "She told no one," I said.

"So you—and Eric—had a leisurely dinner at an expensive restaurant, with another man."

I looked at him incredulously. This was so far off the point. I concentrated. I'd never poked a mental probe into such turmoil. Alcide was feeling grief for Maria-Star, guilt because he hadn't protected her, anger that I'd been drawn into the conflict, and above all, eagerness to knock some skulls. As the cherry on top of all that, Alcide—irrationally—hated that I'd been out with Eric.

I tried to keep my mouth shut out of respect for his loss; I was no stranger to mixed emotions myself. But I found I'd become abruptly and completely tired of him. "Okay," I said. "Fight your own battles. I came when you asked me to. I helped you when you asked me to, both at the battle for packleader and today, at expense and emotional grief to myself. Screw you, Alcide. Maybe Furnan is the better Were." I spun on my heel and caught the look Tray Dawson was giving Alcide while I marched out of the kitchen, down the steps, and into the carport. If there'd been a can, I would've kicked it.

"I'll take you home," Tray said, appearing at my side, and I marched over to the side of the truck, grateful that he was giving me the wherewithal to leave. When I'd stormed out, I hadn't been thinking about what would happen next. It's the ruin of a good exit when you have to go back and look in the phone book for a cab company.

I'd believed Alcide truly loathed me after the Debbie debacle. Apparently the loathing was not total.

"Kind of ironic, isn't it?" I said after a silent spell. "I almost got shot last night because Patrick Furnan thought that would upset Alcide. Until ten minutes ago, I would have sworn that wasn't true."

Tray looked like he would rather be cutting up onions than dealing with this conversation. After another pause, he said, "Alcide's acting like a butthead, but he's got a lot on his plate."

"I understand that," I said, and shut my mouth before I said one more word.

As it turned out, I *was* on time to go to work that night. I was so upset while I was changing clothes that I almost split my black pants, I yanked them on so hard. I brushed my hair with such unnecessary vigor that it crackled.

"Men are incomprehensible assholes," I said to Amelia.

"No shit," she said. "When I was searching for Bob today, I found a female cat in the woods with kittens. And guess what? They were all black-and-white."

I really had no idea what to say.

"So to hell with the promise I made him, right? I'm going to have fun. He can go have sex; I can have sex. And if he vomits on my bedspread again, I'll get after him with the broom."

I was trying not to look directly at Amelia. "I don't blame you," I said, trying to keep my voice steady. It was nice to be on the verge of laughter instead of wanting to smack someone. I grabbed up my purse, checked my ponytail in the mirror in the hall bathroom, and exited out the back door to drive to Merlotte's.

I felt tired before I even walked through the employees' door, not a good way to start my shift.

I didn't see Sam when I stowed my purse in the deep desk drawer we all used. When I came out of the hall that accessed the two public bathrooms, Sam's office, the storeroom, and the kitchen (though the kitchen door was kept locked from the inside, most of the time), I found Sam behind the bar. I gave him a wave as I tied on the white apron I'd pulled from the stack of dozens. I slid my order pad and a pencil into a pocket, looked around to find Arlene, whom I'd be replacing, and scanned the tables in our section.

My heart sank. No peaceful evening for me. Some asses in Fellowship of the Sun T-shirts were sitting at one of the tables. The Fellowship was a radical organization that believed (a) vampires were sinful by nature, almost demons, and (b) they should be executed. The Fellowship "preachers" wouldn't say so publicly, but the Fellowship advocated the total eradication of the undead. I'd heard there was even a little primer to advise members of how that could be carried out. After the Rhodes bombing they'd become bolder in their hatred.

The FotS group was growing as Americans struggled to come to terms with something they couldn't understand—and as hundreds of vampires streamed into the country that had given them the most favorable reception of all the nations on earth. Since a few heavily Catholic and Muslim countries had adopted a policy of killing vampires on sight, the U.S. had begun accepting vampires as refugees from religious or political persecution, and the backlash against this policy was violent. I'd recently seen a bumper sticker that read, "I'll say vamps are alive when you pry my cold dead fingers from my ripped-out throat."

I regarded the FotS as intolerant and ignorant, and I despised those who belonged to its ranks. But I was used to keeping my mouth shut on the topic at the bar, the same way I was used to avoiding discussions on abortion or gun control or gays in the military.

Of course, the FotS guys were probably Arlene's buddies. My weak-minded ex-friend had fallen hook, line, and sinker for the pseudo religion that the FotS propagated.

Arlene curtly briefed me on the tables as she headed out the back door, her face set hard against me. As I watched her go, I wondered how her kids were. I used to babysit them a lot. They probably hated me now, if they listened to their mother.

I shook off my melancholy, because Sam didn't pay me to be moody. I made the rounds of the customers, refreshed drinks, made sure everyone had enough food, brought a clean fork for a woman who'd dropped hers, supplied extra napkins to the table where Catfish Hennessy was eating chicken strips, and exchanged cheerful words with the guys seated at the bar. I treated the FotS table just like I treated everyone else, and they didn't seem to be paying me any special attention, which was just fine with me. I had every expectation that they'd leave with no trouble . . . until Pam walked in.

Pam is white as a sheet of paper and looks just like Alice

in Wonderland would look if she'd grown up to become a vampire. In fact, this evening Pam even had a blue band restraining her straight fair hair, and she was wearing a dress instead of her usual pants set. She was lovely—even if she looked like a vampire cast in an episode of *Leave It to Beaver.* Her dress had little puff sleeves with white trim, and her collar had white trim, too. The tiny buttons down the front of her bodice were white, to match the polka dots on the skirt. No hose, I noticed, but any hose she bought would look bizarre since the rest of her skin was so pale.

"Hey, Pam," I said as she made a beeline for me.

"Sookie," she said warmly, and gave me a kiss as light as a snowflake. Her lips felt cool on my cheek.

"What's up?" I asked. Pam usually worked at Fangtasia in the evening.

"I have a date," she said. "Do you think I look good?" She spun around.

"Oh, sure," I said. "You always look good, Pam." That was only the truth. Though Pam's clothing choices were often ultra-conservative and strangely dated, that didn't mean they didn't become her. She had a kind of sweet-but-lethal charm. "Who's the lucky guy?"

She looked as arch as a vampire over two hundred years old can look. "Who says it's a guy?" she said.

"Oh, right." I glanced around. "Who's the lucky person?"

Just then my roomie walked in. Amelia was wearing a beautiful pair of black linen pants and heels with an off-white sweater and a pair of amber and tortoiseshell earrings. She looked conservative, too, but in a more modern way. Amelia strode over to us, smiled at Pam, and said, "Had a drink yet?"

Pam smiled in a way I'd never seen her smile before. It was . . . coy. "No, waiting for you."

They sat at the bar and Sam served them. Soon they were chatting away, and when their drinks were gone, they got up to leave.

When they passed me on their way out, Amelia said, "I'll see you when I see you"—her way of telling me she might not be home tonight.

"Okay, you two have fun," I said. Their departure was followed by more than one pair of male eyes. If corneas steamed up like glasses do, all the guys in the bar would be seeing blurry.

I made the round of my tables again, fetching new beers for one, leaving the bill at another, until I reached the table with the two guys wearing the FotS shirts. They were still watching the door as though they expected Pam to jump back inside and scream, "BOO!"

"Did I just see what I thought I saw?" one of the men asked me. He was in his thirties, clean-shaven, brown-haired, just another guy. The other man was someone I would have eyed with caution if we'd been in an elevator alone. He was thin, had a beard fringe along his jaw, was decorated with a few tattoos that looked like home jobs to me—jail tats—and he was carrying a knife strapped to his ankle, a thing that hadn't been too hard for me to spot once I'd heard in his mind that he was armed.

"What do you think you just saw?" I asked sweetly. Brown Hair thought I was a bit simple. But that was a good camouflage, and it meant that Arlene hadn't sunk to telling all and sundry about my little peculiarities. No one in Bon Temps (if you asked them outside of church on Sunday) would have said telepathy was possible. If you'd asked them outside of Merlotte's on a Saturday night, they might have said there was something to it.

"I think I saw a vamp come in here, just like she had a right. And I think I saw a woman acting happy to walk out with her. I swear to God, I cannot believe it." He looked at me as if I was sure to share his outrage. Jail Tat nodded vigorously.

"I'm sorry—you see two women walking out of a bar together, and that bothers you? I don't understand your problem with that." Of course I did, but you have to play it out sometimes.

"Sookie!" Sam was calling me.

"Can I get you gentlemen anything else?" I asked, since Sam was undoubtedly trying to call me back to my senses.

They were both looking at me oddly now, having correctly deduced that I was not exactly down with their program.

"I guess we're ready to leave," said Jail Tat, clearly hoping I'd be made to suffer for driving paying customers away. "You got our check ready?" I'd *had* their check ready, and I laid it down on the table in between them. They each glanced at it, slapped a ten on top, and shoved their chairs back.

"I'll be back with your change in just a second," I said, and turned.

"No change," said Brown Hair, though his tone was surly and he didn't seem genuinely thrilled with my service.

"Jerks," I muttered as I went to the cash register at the bar.

Sam said, "Sookie, you have to suck it up."

I was so surprised that I stared at Sam. We were both behind the bar, and Sam was mixing a vodka collins. Sam continued quietly, keeping his eyes on his hands, "You have to serve them like they were anybody else."

It wasn't too often that Sam treated me like an employee rather than a trusted associate. It hurt; the more so when I realized he was right. Though I'd been polite on the surface, I would have (and should have) swallowed their last remarks with no comment—if it hadn't been for the FotS T-shirts. Merlotte's wasn't my business. It was Sam's. If customers didn't come back, he'd suffer the consequences. Eventually, if he had to let barmaids go, I would, too.

"I'm sorry," I said, though it wasn't easy to manage saying it. I smiled brightly at Sam and went off to do an unnecessary round of my tables, one that probably crossed the line from attentive and into irritating. But if I went into the employees' bathroom or the public ladies' room, I'd end up crying, because it hurt to be admonished and it hurt to be wrong; but most of all, it hurt to be put in my place.

When we closed that night, I left as quickly and quietly as possible. I knew I was going to have to get over being hurt, but I preferred to do my healing in my own home. I didn't want to have any "little talks" with Sam—or anyone else, for that matter. Holly was looking at me with way too much curiosity.

So I scooted out to the parking lot with my purse, my apron still on. Tray was leaning against my car. I jumped before I could stop myself.

"You running scared?" he asked.

"No, I'm running upset," I said. "What are you doing here?"

"I'm going to follow you home," he said. "Amelia there?"

"No, she's out on a date."

"Then I'm definitely checking out the house," the big man said, and climbed into his truck to follow me out Hummingbird Road.

There wasn't any reason to object that I could see. In fact, it made me feel good to have someone with me, someone I pretty much trusted.

My house was just as I'd left it, or rather, as Amelia had left it. The outside security lights had come on automatically, and she'd left the light over the sink on in the kitchen as well as the back porch light. Keys in hand, I crossed to the kitchen door.

Tray's big hand gripped my arm when I started to twist the doorknob.

"There's no one there," I said, having checked in my own way. "And it's warded by Amelia."

"You stay here while I look around," he said gently. I nodded and let him in. After a few seconds' silence, he opened the door to tell me I could come into the kitchen. I was ready to follow him through the house for the rest of his search, but he said, "I'd sure like a glass of Coke, if you got any."

He'd deflected me perfectly from following him by appealing to my hospitality. My grandmother would have hit me with a fly swatter if I hadn't gotten Tray a Coke right then.

By the time he arrived back in the kitchen and pronounced

the house clear of intruders, the icy Coke was sitting in a glass on the table, and there was a meatloaf sandwich sitting by it. With a folded napkin.

Without a word, Tray sat down and put the napkin in his lap and ate the sandwich and drank the Coke. I sat opposite him with my own drink.

"I hear your man has vanished," Tray said when he'd patted his lips with the napkin.

I nodded.

"What do you think happened to him?"

I explained the circumstances. "So I haven't heard a word from him," I concluded. This story was sounding almost automatic, like I ought to tape it.

"That's bad" was all he said. Somehow it made me feel better, this quiet, undramatic discussion of a very touchy subject. After a minute of thoughtful silence, Tray said, "I hope you find him soon."

"Thanks. I'm real anxious to know how he's doing." That was a huge understatement.

"Well, I'd better be getting on," he said. "If you get nervous in the night, you call me. I can be here in ten minutes. It's no good, you being alone out here with the war starting."

I had a mental image of tanks coming down my driveway.

"How bad do you think it could get?" I asked.

"My dad told me in the last war, which was when his daddy was little, the pack in Shreveport got into it with the pack in Monroe. The Shreveport pack was about forty then, counting the halfies." Halfies was the common term for Weres who'd become wolves by being bitten. They could only turn into a kind of wolf-man, never achieving the perfect wolf form that born Weres thought was vastly superior. "But the Monroe pack had a bunch of college kids in it, so it come up to forty, forty-five, too. At the end of the fighting, both packs were halved."

I thought of the Weres I knew. "I hope it stops now," I said.

"It ain't gonna," Tray said practically. "They've tasted blood, and killing Alcide's girl instead of trying for Alcide was a cowardly way to open the fight. Them trying to get you, too; that only made it worse. You don't have a drop of Were blood. You're a friend of the pack. That should make you untouchable, not a target. And this afternoon, Alcide found Christine Larrabee dead."

I was shocked all over again. Christine Larrabee was—had been—the widow of one of the previous packleaders. She had a high standing in the Were community, and she'd rather reluctantly endorsed Jackson Herveaux for packleader. Now she had gotten a delayed payback.

"He's not going after any men?" I finally managed to speak.

Tray's face was dark with contempt. "Naw," the Were said. "The only way I can read it is, Furnan wants to set Alcide's temper off. He wants everyone to be on a hair trigger, while Furnan himself stays cool and collected. He's about got what he wants, too. Between grief and the personal insult, Alcide is aimed to go off like a shotgun. He needs to be more like a sniper rifle."

"Isn't Furnan's strategy real . . . unusual?"

"Yes," Tray said heavily. "I don't know what's gotten into

him. Apparently, he don't want to face Alcide in personal combat. He don't want to just beat Alcide. He's aiming to kill Alcide and all Alcide's people, as far as I can tell. A few of the Weres, the ones with little kids, they already repledged themselves to him. They're too scared of what he'd do to their kids, after the attacks against women." The Were stood. "Thanks for the food. I've got to go feed my dogs. You lock up good after me, you hear? And where's your cell phone?"

I handed it to him, and with surprisingly neat movements for such large hands, Tray programmed his cell phone number into my directory. Then he left with a casual wave of his hand. He had a small neat house by his repair shop, and I was really relieved to find he'd timed the journey from there to here at only ten minutes. I locked the door behind him, and I checked the kitchen windows. Sure enough, Amelia had left one open at some point during the mild afternoon. After that discovery, I felt compelled to check every window in the house, even the ones upstairs.

After that was done and I felt as secure as I was going to feel, I turned on the television and sat in front of it, not really seeing what was happening on the screen. I had a lot to think about.

Months ago, I'd gone to the packmaster contest at Alcide's request to watch for trickery. It was my bad luck that my presence had been noticed and my discovery of Furnan's treachery had been public. It griped me that I'd been drawn into this fight, which was none of my own. In fact, bottom line: knowing Alcide had brought me nothing but grief.

I was almost relieved to feel a head of anger building at this injustice, but my better self urged me to squash it in the bud. It wasn't Alcide's fault that Debbie Pelt had been such a murderous bitch, and it wasn't Alcide's fault that Patrick Furnan had decided to cheat in the contest. Likewise, Alcide wasn't responsible for Furnan's bloodthirsty and uncharacteristic approach to consolidating his pack. I wondered if this behavior was even remotely wolflike.

I figured it was just Patrick Furnan–like.

The telephone rang, and I jumped about a mile. "Hello?" I said, unhappy at how frightened I sounded.

"The Were Herveaux called me," Eric said. "He confirms that he's at war with his packmaster."

"Yeah," I said. "You needed confirmation from Alcide? My message wasn't enough?"

"I'd thought of an alternative to the theory that you were attacked in a strike against Alcide. I'm sure Niall must have mentioned that he has enemies."

"Uh-huh."

"I wondered if one of those enemies had acted very swiftly. If the Weres have spies, so may the fairies."

I pondered that. "So, in wanting to meet me, he almost caused my death."

"But he had the wisdom to ask me to escort you to and from Shreveport."

"So he saved my life, even though he risked it."

Silence.

"Actually," I said, leaping to firmer emotional ground, "you saved my life, and I'm grateful." I half expected Eric to ask me just how grateful I was, to refer to the kissing... but still he didn't speak.

Just as I was about to blurt out something stupid to break the silence, the vampire said, "I'll only interfere in the Were war to defend our interests. Or to defend you."

My turn for a silent spell. "All right," I said weakly.

"If you see trouble coming, if they try to draw you in further, call me immediately," Eric told me. "I believe the assassin truly was sent by the packmaster. Certainly he was a Were."

"Some of Alcide's people recognized the description. The guy, Lucky somebody, had just been taken on by Furnan as a mechanic."

"Strange that he'd entrust such an errand to someone he hardly knew."

"Since the guy turned out to be so unlucky."

Eric actually snorted. Then he said, "I won't talk to Niall of this any further. Of course, I told him what occurred."

I had a moment's ridiculous pang because Niall hadn't rushed to my side or called to ask if I was okay. I'd only met him once, and now I was sad he wasn't acting like my nursemaid.

"All right, Eric, thanks," I said, and hung up as he was saying good-bye. I should have asked him about my money again, but I was too dispirited; besides, it wasn't Eric's problem.

I was jumpy the whole time I was getting ready for bed, but nothing happened to make me more anxious. I reminded myself about fifty times that Amelia had warded the house. The wards would work whether she was in the house or not.

I had some good locks on the doors.

I was tired.

Finally, I slept, but I woke up more than once, listening for an assassin.

Chapter 8

I got up with heavy eyes the next day. I felt groggy and my head hurt. I had what amounted to an emotional hangover. Something had to change. I couldn't spend another night like this. I wondered if I should call Alcide and see if he'd, ah, gone to the mattresses with his soldiers. Maybe they'd let me have a corner? But the very idea of having to do that to feel safe made me angry.

I couldn't stop the thought from going through my head—*If Quinn were here, I could stay in my own home without fear.* And for a moment, I wasn't just worried about my missing wounded boyfriend, I was mad at him.

I was ready to be mad at *someone.* There was too much loose emotion hanging around.

Well, this was the beginning of a very special day, huh?

No Amelia. I had to assume she'd spent the night with Pam. I didn't have any problem with their having a relationship. I simply wanted Amelia to be around because I was lonely and scared. Her absence left a little blank spot in my landscape.

At least the air was cooler this morning. You could feel clearly that fall was on the way, was already in the ground waiting to leap up and claim the leaves and grass and flowers. I put on a sweater over my nightgown and went out on the front porch to drink my first cup of coffee. I listened to the birds for a while; they weren't as noisy as they were in the spring, but their songs and discussions let me know that nothing unusual was in the woods this morning. I finished my coffee and tried to plan out my day, but I kept running up against a mental roadblock. It was hard to make plans when you suspected someone might try to kill you. If I could tear myself away from the issue of my possibly impending death, I needed to vacuum the downstairs, do a load of my laundry, and go to the library. If I survived those chores, I had to go to work.

I wondered where Quinn was.

I wondered when I'd hear from my new great-grandfather again.

I wondered if any more Weres had died during the night.

I wondered when my phone would ring.

Since nothing happened on my front porch, I dragged myself inside and did my usual morning get-ready routine. When I looked at the mirror, I was sorry I'd troubled. I didn't look rested and refreshed. I looked like a worried person who hadn't gotten any sleep. I dabbed some concealer beneath my eyes and put on a little extra eye shadow and blush to give my face some color. Then I decided I looked like a clown and rubbed most of it off. After feeding Bob and scolding him for the litter of kittens, I checked all my locks again and hopped in the car to go to the library.

The Renard Parish library, Bon Temps branch, is not a large building. Our librarian graduated from Louisiana Tech in Ruston, and she is a super lady in her late thirties named Barbara Beck. Her husband, Alcee, is a detective on the Bon Temps force, and I really hope Barbara doesn't know what he's up to. Alcee Beck is a tough man who does good things . . . sometimes. He also does quite a few bad things. Alcee was lucky when he got Barbara to marry him, and he knows it.

Barbara's the only full-time employee of the branch library, and I wasn't surprised to find her by herself when I pushed open the heavy door. She was shelving books. Barbara dressed in what I thought of as comfortable chic, meaning she picked out knits in bright colors and wore matching shoes. She favored chunky, bold jewelry, too.

"Good morning, Sookie," she said, smiling her big smile.

"Barbara," I said, trying to smile back. She noticed I wasn't my usual self, but she kept her thoughts to herself. Not really, of course, since I have my little disability, but she didn't say anything out loud. I put the books I was returning on the appropriate desk, and I began looking at the shelves of new arrivals. Most of them were some permutation on self-help. Going by how popular these books were and how often they were checked out, everyone in Bon Temps should have become perfect by now.

I grabbed up two new romances and a couple of mysteries, and even a science fiction, which I rarely read. (I guess I thought my reality was crazier than anything a science fiction writer could dream up.) While I was looking at the jacket of a book by an author I'd never read, I heard a thunk in the background and knew someone had come in the back door of the library. I didn't pay attention; some people habitually used the back door.

Barbara made a little noise, and I looked up. The man behind her was huge, at least six foot six, and whip thin. He had a big knife, and he was holding it to Barbara's throat. For a second I thought he was a robber, and I wondered who would ever think of robbing a library. For the overdue-book money?

"Don't scream," he hissed through long sharp teeth. I froze. Barbara was in some space beyond fear. She was way into terror. But I could hear another active brain in the building.

Someone else was coming in the back door very quietly.

"Detective Beck will kill you for hurting his wife," I said very loudly. And I said it with absolute certainty. "Kiss your ass good-bye."

"I don't know who that is and I don't care," the tall man said.

"You better care, muthafucker," said Alcee Beck, who'd stepped up behind him silently. He put his gun to the man's head. "Now, you let go of my wife and you drop that knife."

But Sharp Teeth wasn't about to do that. He spun, pushed Barbara at Alcee, and ran right toward me, knife raised.

I threw a Nora Roberts hardback at him, whacking him

upside his head. I extended my foot. Blinded by the impact of the book, Sharp Teeth tripped over the foot, just as I'd hoped.

He fell on his own knife, which I *hadn't* planned.

The library fell abruptly silent except for Barbara's gasping breath. Alcee Beck and I stared down at the creeping pool of blood coming out from under the man.

"Ah-oh," I said.

"Wellllll . . . shit," said Alcee Beck. "Where'd you learn to throw like that, Sookie Stackhouse?"

"Softball," I said, which was the literal truth.

As you can imagine, I was late to work that afternoon. I was even more tired than I had been to start with, but I was thinking that I might live through the day. So far, two times in a row, fate had intervened to prevent my assassination. I had to assume that Sharp Teeth had been sent to kill me and had botched it, just as the fake highway patrolman had done. Maybe my luck wouldn't hold a third time; but there was a chance it would. What were the odds that another vampire would take a bullet for me, or that, by sheer accident, Alcee Beck would drop off his wife's lunch that she'd left at home on the kitchen counter? Slim, right? But I'd beaten those odds twice.

No matter what the police were officially assuming (since I didn't know the guy and no one could say I did—and he'd seized Barbara, not me), Alcee Beck now had me in his sights. He was really good at reading situations, and he had seen that Sharp Teeth was focused on me. Barbara had been a means to get my attention. Alcee would never forgive me for that, even if it hadn't been my fault. Plus, I'd thrown that book with suspicious force and accuracy.

In his place, I would probably feel the same way.

So now I was at Merlotte's, going through the motions in a weary way, wondering where to go and what to do and why Patrick Furnan had gone nuts. And where had all these strangers come from? I hadn't known the Were who'd broken down Maria-Star's door. Eric had been shot by a guy who'd worked at Patrick Furnan's dealership only a few days. I'd never seen Sharp Teeth before, and he was an unforgettable kind of guy.

The whole situation made no sense at all.

Suddenly I had an idea. I asked Sam if I could make a phone call since my tables were quiet, and he nodded. He'd been giving me those narrow looks all evening, looks that meant he was going to pin me down and talk to me soon, but for now I had a breather. So I went into Sam's office, looked in his Shreveport phone book to get the listing for Patrick Furnan's home, and I called him.

"Hello?"

I recognized the voice.

"Patrick Furnan?" I said, just to be sure.

"Speaking."

"Why are you trying to kill me?"

"What? Who is this?"

"Oh, come on. It's Sookie Stackhouse. Why are you doing this?"

There was a long pause.

"Are you trying to trap me?" he asked.

"How? You think I got the phone tapped? I want to know why. I never did anything to you. I'm not even dating Alcide. But you're trying to off me like I am powerful. You killed poor Maria-Star. You killed Christine Larrabee. What's with this? I'm not important."

Patrick Furnan said slowly, "You really believe it's me doing this? Killing female pack members? Trying to kill you?"

"Sure I do."

"It's not me. I read about Maria-Star. Christine Larrabee is dead?" He sounded almost frightened.

"Yes," I said, and my voice was as uncertain as his. "And someone's tried to kill me twice. I'm afraid some totally innocent person is going to get caught in the cross fire. And of course, I don't want to die."

Furnan said, "My wife disappeared yesterday." His voice was ragged with grief and fear. And anger. "Alcide's got her, and that fucker is going to pay."

"Alcide wouldn't do that," I said. (Well, I was pretty sure Alcide wouldn't do that.) "You're saying you *didn't* order the hits on Maria-Star and Christine? And me?"

"No, why would I go for the women? We never want to kill pure-blooded female Weres. Except maybe Amanda," Furnan added tactlessly. "If we're going to kill someone, it'd be the men."

"I think you and Alcide need to have a sit-down. He doesn't have your wife. He thinks you've gone crazy, attacking women."

There was a long silence. Furnan said, "I think you're right about that sit-down, unless you made up this whole thing to get me into a position where Alcide can kill me."

"I just want to live to see the next week myself."

"I'll agree to meet with Alcide if you'll be there and if you'll swear to tell each of us what the other is thinking. You're a friend of the pack, *all* the pack. You can help us now."

Patrick Furnan was so anxious to find his wife he was even willing to believe in me.

I thought of the deaths that had already taken place. I thought of the deaths that were to come, perhaps including my own. I wondered what the hell was going on. "I'll do it if you and Alcide will sit down unarmed," I said. "If what I suspect is true, you have a common enemy who's trying to get you two to kill each other off."

"If that black-haired bastard will agree to it, I'll give it a shot," said Furnan. "If Alcide has my wife, not a hair on her body better be disturbed, and he better bring her with him. Or I swear to God I'll dismember him."

"I understand. I'll make sure he understands, too. We'll be getting back with you," I promised, and I hoped with all my heart that I was telling the truth.

Chapter 9

It was the middle of the same night and I was about to walk into danger. It was my own damn fault. Through a swift series of phone calls, Alcide and Furnan had worked out where to meet. I'd envisioned them sitting down across a table, their lieutenants right behind them, and working this whole situation out. Mrs. Furnan would appear and the couple would reunite. Everyone would be content, or at least less hostile. I would be nowhere around.

Yet here I was at an abandoned office center in Shreveport, the same one where the contest for packmaster had taken place. At least Sam was with me. It was dark and cool and the wind was lifting my hair from my shoulders. I shifted from foot to foot, anxious to get this over with. Though he was not as fidgety as I was, I could tell Sam felt the same way.

It was my fault he was here. When he'd become so curious about what was brewing with the Weres, I'd had to tell him. After all, if someone came through the door of Merlotte's trying to shoot me down, Sam at least deserved to know why his bar was full of holes. I'd argued bitterly with him when he'd told me he was coming with me, but here we both were.

Maybe I'm lying to myself. Maybe I simply wanted a friend with me, someone definitely on my side. Maybe I was just scared. Actually, no "maybe" about that at all.

The night was brisk, and we were both wearing waterproof jackets with hoods. Not that we needed the hoods, but if it got any colder, we might be grateful for them. The abandoned office park stretched around us in gloomy silence. We stood in the loading bay of a firm that had accepted big shipments of something. The large metal pull-down doors where the trucks had been unloaded looked like big shiny eyes in the gleam of the remaining security lights.

Actually, there were lots of big shiny eyes around tonight. The Sharks and the Jets were negotiating. Oh, excuse me, the Furnan Weres and the Herveaux Weres. The two sides of the pack might come to an understanding, and they might not. And right smack dab in the middle stood Sam the Shapeshifter and Sookie the Telepath.

As I felt the hard red throbbing of Were brains approaching from both north and south, I turned to Sam and said from the bottom of my heart, "I should never have let you come with me. I should never have opened my mouth."

"You've gotten into the habit of not telling me things,

Sookie. I want you to tell me what's going on with you. Especially if there's danger." Sam's red gold hair blew around his head in the sharp little breeze wafting between the buildings. I felt his difference more strongly than I ever had. Sam is a rare true shapeshifter. He can change into anything. He prefers the form of a dog, because dogs are familiar and friendly and people don't shoot at them too often. I looked into his blue eyes and saw the wildness in them. "They're here," he said, raising his nose to the breeze.

Then the two groups were standing about ten feet away on either side of us, and it was time to concentrate.

I recognized the faces of a few of the Furnan wolves, who were more numerous. Cal Myers, the police detective, was among them. It took some kind of nerve for Furnan to bring Cal along when he was proclaiming his innocence. I also recognized the teenage girl Furnan had taken as part of his victory celebration after Jackson Herveaux's defeat. She looked a million years older tonight.

Alcide's group included auburn-haired Amanda, who nodded at me, her face serious, and some werewolves I'd seen at the Hair of the Dog the night Quinn and I had visited the bar. The scrawny girl who'd worn the red leather bustier that night was standing right behind Alcide, and she was both intensely excited and deeply scared. To my surprise, Dawson was there. He wasn't as much of a lone wolf as he'd painted himself to be.

Alcide and Furnan stepped away from their packs.

This was the agreed-on format for the parley, or sit-down, or whatever you wanted to call it: I would stand between Furnan and Alcide. Each Were leader would grip one of my hands. I would be the human lie detector while they talked. I had sworn to tell each one if the other lied, at least to the best of my ability. I could read minds, but minds can be deceptive and tricky or just dense. I'd never done anything exactly like this, and I prayed my ability would be extra precise tonight and that I would use it wisely, so I could help to end this life taking.

Alcide approached me stiffly, his face harsh in the hard glare of the security lighting. For the first time, I noticed that he looked thinner and older. There was a little gray in the black hair that hadn't been there when his father had been alive. Patrick Furnan, too, didn't look well. He'd always had a tendency to porkiness, and now he looked as though he'd gained a good fifteen or twenty pounds. Being packmaster hadn't been good to him. And the shock of the abduction of his wife had laid its mark on his face.

I did something that I never imagined I would do. I held out my right hand to him. He took it, and the flood of his ideas washed through me instantly. Even his twisty Were brain was easy to read because he was so focused. I held out my left hand to Alcide, and he grasped it too tightly. For a long minute, I felt inundated. Then, with a huge effort, I channeled them into a stream so I wouldn't be overwhelmed. It would be easy for them to lie out loud, but it's not so easy to lie inside your own head. Not consistently. I closed my eyes. A flip of the coin had given Alcide the first question.

"Patrick, why did you kill my woman?" The words sounded

like they were cutting up Alcide's throat. "She was pure Were, and she was as gentle as a Were can be."

"I never ordered any of my people to kill any of yours," Patrick Furnan said. He sounded so tired he could hardly stand up, and his thoughts were proceeding in much the same way: slowly, wearily, on a track he'd worn in his own brain. He was easier to read than Alcide. He meant what he said.

Alcide was listening with great attention, and he said next, "Did you tell anyone not in your pack to kill Maria-Star and Sookie and Mrs. Larrabee?"

"I never gave orders to kill any of you, ever," Furnan said.

"He believes that," I said.

Unfortunately, Furnan wouldn't shut up. "I hate you," he said, sounding just as tired as he had before. "I would be glad if a truck hit you. But I didn't kill anyone."

"He believes that, too," I said, maybe a little dryly.

Alcide demanded, "How can you claim to be innocent with Cal Myers standing with your pack? He stabbed Maria-Star to death."

Furnan looked confused. "Cal wasn't there," he said.

"He believes what he says," I told Alcide. I turned my face to Furnan. "Cal was there, and he murdered Maria-Star." Though I dared not lose focus, I heard the whispering start all around Cal Myers, saw the rest of the Furnan Weres step away from him.

It was Furnan's turn to ask a question.

"My wife," he said, and his voice cracked. "Why her?"

"I didn't take Libby," Alcide said. "I would never abduct a woman, especially a Were woman with young. I would never order anyone else to do it."

He believed that. "Alcide didn't do it himself, and he didn't order it done." But Alcide hated Patrick Furnan with a great ferocity. Furnan hadn't needed to kill Jackson Herveaux at the climax of the contest, but he had. Better to start his leadership with the elimination of his rival. Jackson would never have submitted to his rule, and would have been a thorn in his side for years. I was getting thoughts from both sides, wafts of ideas so strong it burned in my head, and I said, "Calm down, both of you." I could feel Sam behind me, his warmth, the touch of his mind, and I said, "Sam, don't touch me, okay?"

He understood, and he moved away.

"Neither of you killed any of the people who have died. And neither of you ordered it done. As far as I can tell."

Alcide said, "Give us Cal Myers to question."

"Then where is my wife?" Furnan growled.

"Dead and gone," said a clear voice. "And I'm ready to take her place. Cal is mine."

We all looked up, because the voice had come from the flat roof of the building. There were four Weres up there, and the brunette female who'd spoken was closest to the edge. She had a sense of the dramatic, I'll give her that. Female Weres have power and status but they're not packleader . . . ever. This woman was clearly large and in charge, though she was maybe five foot two. She had prepared to change; that is to say, she was naked. Or maybe she just wanted Alcide and Furnan to see what they could be getting. Which was a lot, both in quantity and in quality.

"Priscilla," said Furnan.

It seemed like such an unlikely name for the Were that I felt myself actually smile, which was a bad idea under the circumstances.

"You know her," Alcide said to Furnan. "Is this part of your plan?"

"No," I answered for him. My mind careened through the thoughts I could read and latched on to one thread in particular. "Furnan, Cal is her creature," I said. "He's betrayed you."

"I thought if I picked off a few key bitches, you two would kill each other off," Priscilla said. "Too bad it didn't work."

"Who is this?" Alcide asked Furnan again.

"She's the mate of Arthur Hebert, a packleader from St. Catherine Parish." St. Catherine was way south, just east of New Orleans. It had been hit hard by Katrina.

"Arthur is dead. We don't have a home anymore," Priscilla Hebert said. "We want yours."

Well, that was clear enough.

"Cal, why have you done this?" Furnan asked his lieutenant. Cal should have gotten up on the roof while he was able. The Furnan wolves and the Herveaux wolves had formed a circle around him.

"Cal's my brother," Priscilla called. "You better not touch a hair on his body." There was an edge of desperation to her voice that hadn't been there before. Cal looked up at his sister unhappily. He realized what a fix he was in, and I was pretty sure he wanted her to shut up. That would be his last thought.

Furnan's arm was suddenly out of its sleeve and covered with hair. With huge force, he swung at his former cohort, eviscerating the Were. Alcide's clawed hand took off the back of Cal's head as the traitor fell to the ground. Cal's blood sprayed over me in an arc. At my back, Sam was humming with the energy of his oncoming change, triggered by the tension, the smell of blood, and my involuntary yelp.

Priscilla Hebert roared in rage and anguish. With inhuman grace, she leaped from the top of the building to the parking lot, followed by her henchmen (henchwolves?).

The war had begun.

Sam and I had worked ourselves into the middle of the Shreveport wolves. As Priscilla's pack began closing in from each side, Sam said, "I'm going to change, Sookie."

I couldn't see what use a collie would be in this situation, but I said, "Okay, boss." He grinned at me in a lopsided way, stripped off his clothes, and bent over. All around us the Weres were doing the same. The chill night air was full of the gloppy sound, the sound of hard things moving through thick, sticky liquid, that characterizes the transformation from man to animal. Huge wolves straightened and shook themselves all around me; I recognized the wolf forms of Alcide and Furnan. I tried counting the wolves in our suddenly reunited pack, but they were milling around, positioning themselves for the coming battle, and there was no way to keep track of them.

I turned to Sam to give him a pat and found myself standing beside a lion.

"Sam," I said in a whisper, and he roared.

Everyone froze in place for a long moment. The Shreveport wolves were just as scared as the St. Catherine's wolves at first, but then they seemed to realize that Sam was on their side, and yips of excitement echoed between the empty buildings.

Then the fighting started.

Sam tried to surround me, which was impossible, but it was a gallant attempt. As an unarmed human, I was basically helpless in this struggle. It was a very unpleasant feeling—in fact, a terrifying feeling.

I was the frailest thing on site.

Sam was magnificent. His huge paws flashed, and when he hit a wolf square on, that wolf went *down.* I danced around like a demented elf, trying to stay out the way. I couldn't watch everything that was going on. Clusters of St. Catherine wolves made for Furnan, Alcide, and Sam, while individual battles went on around us. I realized that these clusters had been charged with taking down the leaders, and I knew that a lot of planning had gone into this. Priscilla Hebert hadn't allowed for getting her brother out quickly enough, but that wasn't slowing her down any.

No one seemed to be too concerned with me, since I posed no threat. But there was every chance I'd get knocked down by the snarling combatants and be hurt as severely as I would if I had been the target. Priscilla, now a gray wolf, targeted Sam. I guess she wanted to prove she had more balls than anyone by going for the biggest and most dangerous target. But Amanda was biting at Priscilla's hind legs as Priscilla worked her way through the melee. Priscilla responded by turning her head to bare her teeth at the smaller wolf. Amanda danced away, and then when Priscilla turned to resume her progress, Amanda darted back to bite the leg again. Since Amanda's bite was powerful enough to break bone, this was more than an annoyance, and Priscilla rounded on her in full display. Before I could even think *Oh no,* Priscilla seized Amanda in her iron jaws and broke her neck.

While I stood staring in horror, Priscilla dropped Amanda's body on the ground and wheeled to leap onto Sam's back. He shook and shook but she had sunk her fangs into his neck and she would not be dislodged.

Something in me snapped as surely as the bones in Amanda's neck. I lost any sense I might have had, and I launched myself in the air as if I were a wolf, too. To keep from sliding off the heaving mass of animals, I wound my arms in the fur around Priscilla's neck, and I wound my legs around Priscilla's middle, and I tightened my arms until I was just about hugging myself. Priscilla didn't want to let go of Sam, so she flung herself from side to side to knock me loose. But I was clinging to her like a homicidal monkey.

Finally, she had to let go of his neck to deal with me. I squeezed and squeezed harder, and she tried to bite me, but she couldn't reach around properly since I was on her back. She was able to curve enough to graze my leg with her fangs, but she couldn't hold on. The pain hardly registered. I tightened my grip even more though my arms were aching like hell. If I let go one little bit, I would join Amanda.

Though all of this took place so quickly it was hard to believe, I felt as if I'd been trying to kill this woman/wolf for eternity. I wasn't really thinking, "Die, die," in my head; I just wanted her to *stop what she was doing*, and she wouldn't, dammit. Then there was another ear-shattering roar, and huge teeth flashed an inch away from my arms. I understood I should let go, and the second my arms loosened, I tumbled off the wolf, rolling over the pavement to land in a heap a few feet away.

There was a sort of *pop!* and Claudine was standing over me. She was in a tank top and pajama bottoms and she had a case of bedhead. From between her striped legs I saw the lion bite the wolf's head nearly off, then spit her out in a fastidious way. Then he turned to survey the parking lot, evaluating the next threat.

One of the wolves leaped at Claudine. She proved she was completely awake. While the animal was in midair her hands clamped on its ears. She swung him, using his own momentum. Claudine flung the huge wolf with the ease of a frat boy tossing a beer can, and the wolf smacked against the loading dock with a sound that seemed quite final. The speed of this attack and its conclusion was absolutely incredible.

Claudine didn't move from her straddling stance, and I was smart enough to stay put. Actually, I was exhausted, frightened, and a little bloody, though only the red spatter on my leg seemed to be my own. Fighting takes such a short time, yet it uses up the body's reserves with amazing speed. At least, that's the way it works with humans. Claudine looked pretty sparky.

"Bring it on, fur-ass!" she shrieked, beckoning with both hands to a Were who was slinking up on her from behind. She'd twisted around without moving her legs, a maneuver that would be impossible for a mundane human body. The Were launched and got exactly the same treatment as its packmate. As far as I could tell, Claudine wasn't even breathing heavy. Her eyes were wider and more intent than usual, and she held her body in a loose crouch, clearly ready for action.

There was more roaring, and barking, and growling, and shrieks of pain, and rending noises that didn't bear thinking about. But after maybe five more minutes of battle, the noise died down.

Claudine had not even glanced down at me during this time because she was guarding my body. When she did, she winced. So I looked pretty bad.

"I was late," she said, shifting her feet so she was standing on one side of me. She reached down and I seized her hand. In a flash, I was on my feet. I hugged her. Not only did I want to, I needed to. Claudine always smelled so wonderful, and her body was curiously firmer to the touch than human flesh. She seemed happy to hug me back, and we clung together for a long moment while I regained my equilibrium.

Then I raised my head to look around, dreading what I would see. The fallen lay in heaps of fur around us. The dark stains on the pavement were not from oil drips. Here and there a bedraggled wolf nosed through the corpses, looking for some-one in particular. The lion was crouched a couple of yards away, panting. Blood streaked his fur. There was an open wound on his shoulder, the one caused by Priscilla. There was another bite on his back.

I didn't know what to do first. "Thanks, Claudine," I said, and kissed her cheek.

"I can't always make it," Claudine cautioned me. "Don't count on an automatic rescue."

"Am I wearing some kind of fairy Life Alert button? How'd you know to come?" I could tell she wasn't going to answer. "Anyway, I sure appreciate this rescue. Hey, I guess you know I met my great-grandfather." I was babbling. I was so glad to be alive.

She bowed her head. "The prince is my grandfather," she said.

"Oh," I said. "So, we're like cousins?"

She looked down at me, her eyes clear and dark and calm. She didn't look like a woman who'd just killed two wolves as quick as you could snap your fingers. "Yes," she said. "I guess we are."

"So what do you call him? Granddaddy? Popsy?"

"I call him 'my lord.' "

"Oh."

She stepped away to check out the wolves she'd disposed of (I was pretty sure they were still dead), so I went over to the lion. I crouched beside him and put my arm around his neck. He rumbled. Automatically, I scratched the top of his head and behind his ears, just like I did with Bob. The rumble intensified.

"Sam," I said. "Thanks so much. I owe you my life. How bad are your wounds? What can I do about them?"

Sam sighed. He laid his head on the ground.

"You're tired?"

Then the air around him got hyper, and I pulled away from him. I knew what was coming. After a few moments, the body that lay beside me was human, not animal. I ran my eyes over Sam anxiously and I saw that he still had the wounds, but they were much smaller than they'd been on his lion form. All shape-shifters are great at healing. It says a lot about the way my life had changed that it didn't seem significant to me that Sam was buck naked. I had kind of gone beyond that now—which was good, since there were bare bodies all around me. The corpses were changing back, as well as the injured wolves.

It had been easier to look at the bodies in wolf form.

Cal Myers and his sister, Priscilla, were dead, of course, as were the two Weres Claudine had dispatched. Amanda was dead. The skinny girl I'd met in the Hair of the Dog was alive, though severely wounded in the upper thigh. I recognized Amanda's bartender, too; he seemed unscathed. Tray Dawson was cradling an arm that looked broken.

Patrick Furnan lay in the middle of a ring of the dead and wounded, all of them Priscilla's wolves. With some difficulty, I picked my way through broken, bloody bodies. I could feel all the eyes, wolf and human, focus on me as I squatted by him. I put my fingers on his neck and got nothing. I checked his wrist. I even put my hand against his chest. No movement.

"Gone," I said, and those remaining in wolf form began to howl. Far more disturbing were the howls coming from the throats of the Weres in human form.

Alcide staggered over to me. He appeared to be more or less intact, though streaks of blood matted his chest hair. He passed the slain Priscilla, kicking her corpse as he went by. He knelt for a moment by Patrick Furnan, dipping his head as though he was bowing to the corpse. Then he rose to his feet. He looked dark, savage, and resolute.

"I am the leader of this pack!" he said in a voice of absolute certainty. The scene became eerily quiet as the surviving wolves absorbed that.

"You need to leave now," Claudine said very quietly right behind me. I jumped like a rabbit. I'd been mesmerized by the beauty of Alcide, by the primitive wildness rolling off him.

"What? Why?"

"They're going to celebrate their victory and the ascension of a new packmaster," she said.

The skinny girl clenched her hands together and brought them down on the skull of a fallen—but still twitching—enemy. The bones broke with a nasty crunch. All around me the defeated Weres were being executed, at least those who were severely wounded. A small cluster of three scrambled to kneel in front of Alcide, their heads tilted back. Two of them were women. One was an adolescent male. They were offering Alcide their throats in surrender. Alcide was very excited. All over. I remembered the way Patrick Furnan had celebrated when he got the packmaster job. I didn't know if Alcide was going to fuck the hostages or kill them. I took in my breath to exclaim. I don't know what I would've said, but Sam's grimy hand clapped over my mouth. I rolled my eyes to glare at him, both angry and agitated, and he shook his head vehemently. He held my gaze for a long moment to make sure I would stay silent, and then he removed his hand. He put his arm around my waist and turned me abruptly away from the scene. Claudine took the rear guard as Sam marched me rapidly away. I kept my eyes forward.

I tried not to listen to the noises.

Chapter 10

Sam had some extra clothes in his truck, and he pulled them on matter-of-factly. Claudine said, "I have to get back to bed," as if she'd been awoken to let the cat out or go to the bathroom, and then *pop!* she was gone.

"I'll drive," I offered, because Sam was wounded.

He handed me his keys.

We started out in silence. It was an effort to remember the route to get back to the interstate to return to Bon Temps because I was still shocked on several different levels.

"That's a normal reaction to battle," Sam said. "The surge of lust."

I carefully didn't look at Sam's lap to see if he was having his own surge. "Yeah, I know that. I've been in a few fights now. A few too many."

"Plus, Alcide did ascend to the packmaster position." Another reason to feel "happy."

"But he did this whole battle thing because Maria-Star died." So he should have been too depressed to think about celebrating the death of his enemy, was my point.

"He did this *whole battle thing* because he was threatened," Sam said. "It's really stupid of Alcide and Furnan that they didn't sit down and talk before it came to this point. They could have figured out what was happening much earlier. If you hadn't persuaded them, they'd still be getting picked off and they'd have started an all-out war. They'd have done most of Priscilla Hebert's work for her."

I was sick of the Weres, their aggression and stubbornness. "Sam, you went through all of this because of me. I feel terrible about that. I would have died if it wasn't for you. I owe you big-time. And I'm so sorry."

"Keeping you alive," Sam said, "is important to me." He closed his eyes and slept the rest of the way back to his trailer. He limped up the steps unaided, and his door shut firmly. Feeling a little forlorn and not a little depressed, I got in my own car and drove home, wondering how to fit what had happened that night into the rest of my life.

Amelia and Pam were sitting in the kitchen. Amelia had made some tea, and Pam was working on a piece of embroidery. Her hands flew as the needle pierced the fabric, and I didn't know what was most astonishing: her skill or her choice of pastimes.

"What have you and Sam been up to?" Amelia asked with

a big smile. "You look like you've been rode hard and put away wet."

Then she looked more closely and said, "What happened, Sookie?"

Even Pam put down her embroidery and gave me her most serious face. "You smell," she said. "You smell of blood and war."

I looked down at myself and registered what a mess I was. My clothes were bloody, torn, and dirty, and my leg ached. It was first aid time, and I couldn't have had better care from Nurse Amelia and Nurse Pam. Pam was a little excited by the wound, but she restrained herself like a good vampire. I knew she'd tell Eric everything, but I just couldn't find it in me to care. Amelia said a healing spell over my leg. Healing wasn't her strongest suit, she told me modestly, but the spell helped a bit. My leg did stop throbbing.

"Aren't you worried?" Amelia asked. "This is from a Were. What if you caught it?"

"It's harder to catch than almost any communicable disease," I said, since I'd asked almost every werecreature I'd met about the chances of their condition being transmitted by bite. After all, they have doctors, too. And researchers. "Most people have to be bitten several times, all over their body, to get it, and even then it's not for sure." It's not like the flu or the common cold. Plus, if you cleaned the wound soon afterward, your chances dropped considerably even from that. I'd poured a bottle of water over my leg before I'd gotten in the car. "So I'm not worried, but I *am* sore, and I think I might have a scar."

"Eric won't be happy," Pam said with an anticipatory smile.

"You endangered yourself because of the Weres. You know he holds them in low esteem."

"Yeah, yeah, yeah," I said, not caring one little bit. "He can go fly a kite."

Pam brightened. "I'll tell him that," she said.

"Why do you like to tease him so much?" I asked, realizing I was almost sluggish with weariness.

"I've never had this much ammunition to tease him with," she answered, and then she and Amelia were out of my room, and I was blessedly alone and in my own bed and alive, and then I was asleep.

The shower I took the next morning was a sublime experience. In the list of Great Showers I've Had, this one ranked at least number 4. (The best shower was the one I'd shared with Eric, and I couldn't even think of that one without shivering all over.) I scoured myself clean. My leg looked good, and though I was even more sore from pulling muscles I didn't use too much, I felt a disaster had been averted and that evil had been vanquished, at least in a gray sort of way.

As I stood under the pounding hot water, rinsing my hair, I thought about Priscilla Hebert. In my brief glimpse into her world, she'd been at least trying to find a place for her disenfranchised pack, and she'd done the research to find a weak area where she could establish a foothold. Maybe if she'd come to Patrick Furnan as a supplicant, he would have been glad to give a home to her pack. But he would never have surrendered leadership. He'd killed Jackson Herveaux to attain it, so he sure wouldn't have agreed to any kind of co-op arrangement with Priscilla—even if wolf society would permit that, which was doubtful, especially given her status as a rare female packleader.

Well, she wasn't one anymore.

Theoretically, I admired her attempt to reestablish her wolves in a new home. Since I'd met Priscilla in the flesh, I could only be glad she hadn't succeeded.

Clean and refreshed, I dried my hair and put on my makeup. I was working the day shift, so I had to be at Merlotte's at eleven. I pulled on the usual uniform of black pants and white shirt, decided to leave my hair loose for once, and tied my black Reeboks.

I decided I felt pretty good, all things considered.

A lot of people were dead, and a lot of grief was hanging around the events of last night, but at least the encroaching pack had been defeated and now the Shreveport area should be peaceful for a while. The war was over in a very short time. And the Weres hadn't been exposed to the rest of the world, though that was a step they'd have to take soon. The longer the vampires were public, the more likely it became that someone would out the Weres.

I added that fact to the giant box full of things that were not my problem.

The scrape on my leg, whether due to its nature or because of Amelia's ministrations, was already scabbed over. There were bruises on my arms and legs, but my uniform covered them. It was feasible to wear long sleeves today, because it was actually cool. In fact, a jacket would have been nice, and I regretted not having thrown one on as I drove to work. Amelia hadn't been stirring when I left, and I had no idea if Pam was in my secret vampire hidey-hole in the spare bedroom. Hey, not my concern!

As I drove, I was adding to the list of things I shouldn't have to worry about or consider. But I came to a dead halt when I got to work. When I saw my boss, a lot of thoughts came crowding in that I hadn't anticipated. Not that Sam looked beaten up or anything. He looked pretty much as usual when I stopped in his office to drop my purse in its usual drawer. In fact, the brawl seemed to have invigorated him. Maybe it had felt good to change into something more aggressive than a collie. Maybe he'd enjoyed kicking some werewolf butt. Ripping open some werewolf stomachs . . . breaking some werewolf spines.

Okay, well—whose life had been saved by the aforesaid ripping and breaking? My thoughts cleared up in a hurry. Impulsively, I bent to give him a kiss on the cheek. I smelled the smell that was Sam: aftershave, the woods, something wild yet familiar.

"How are you feeling?" he asked, as if I always kissed him hello.

"Better than I thought I would," I said. "You?"

"A little achy, but I'll do."

Holly stuck her head in. "Hey, Sookie, Sam." She came in to deposit her own purse.

"Holly, I hear you and Hoyt are an item," I said, and I hoped I looked smiling and pleased.

"Yeah, we're hitting it off okay," she said, trying for nonchalance. "He's really good with Cody, and his family's real nice." Despite her aggressively dyed spiky black hair and her heavy makeup, there was something wistful and vulnerable about Holly's face.

It was easy for me to say, "I hope it works out." Holly looked very pleased. She knew as well as I did that if she married Hoyt she'd be for all intents and purposes my sister-in-law, since the bond between Jason and Hoyt was so strong.

Then Sam began telling us about a problem he was having with one of his beer distributors, and Holly and I tied on our aprons, and our working day began. I stuck my head through the hatch to wave at the kitchen staff. The current cook at Merlotte's was an ex-army guy named Carson. Short-order cooks come and go. Carson was one of the better ones. He'd mastered burgers Lafayette right away (hamburgers steeped in a former cook's special sauce), and he got the chicken strips and fries done exactly right, and he didn't have tantrums or try to stab the busboy. He showed up on time and left the kitchen clean at the end of his shift, and that was such a huge thing Sam would have forgiven Carson a lot of weirdness.

We were light on customers, so Holly and I were getting the drinks and Sam was on the phone in his office when Tanya Grissom came in the front door. The short, curvy woman looked as pretty and healthy as a milkmaid. Tanya went light on the makeup and heavy on the self-assurance.

"Where's Sam?" she asked. Her little mouth curved up in a smile. I smiled back just as insincerely. Bitch.

"Office," I said, as if I always knew exactly where Sam was.

"That woman there," Holly said, pausing on her way to the serving hatch. "That gal is a deep well."

"Why do you say that?"

"She's living out at Hotshot, rooming with some of the women out there," Holly said. Of all the regular citizens of Bon Temps, Holly was one of the few who knew that there were such creatures as Weres and shifters. I didn't know if she'd discovered that the residents of Hotshot were werepanthers, but she knew they were inbred and strange, because that was a byword in Renard Parish. And she considered Tanya (a werefox) guilty by association, or at least *suspicious* by association.

I had a stab of genuine anxiety. I thought, *Tanya and Sam could change together. Sam would enjoy that. He could even change into a fox himself, if he wanted to.*

It was a huge effort to smile at my customers after I'd had that idea. I was ashamed when I realized I should be happy to see someone interested in Sam, someone who could appreciate his true nature. It didn't say much for me that I wasn't happy at all. But she wasn't good enough for him, and I'd warned him about her.

Tanya returned from the hallway leading to Sam's office and went out the front door, not looking as confident as she'd gone in. I smiled at her back. Ha! Sam came out to pull beers. He didn't seem nearly as cheerful.

That wiped the smile off my face. While I served Sheriff Bud Dearborn and Alcee Beck their lunch (Alcee glowering at me all the while), I worried about that. I decided to take a peek in Sam's head, because I was getting better at aiming my talent in certain ways. It was also easier to block it off and keep it out of my everyday activities now that I'd bonded with Eric, though I hated to admit that. It's not nice to flit around in someone else's thoughts, but I've always been able to do it, and it was just second nature.

I know that's a lame excuse. But I was used to knowing, not to wondering. Shifters are harder to read than regular people, and Sam was hard even for a shifter, but I got that he was frustrated, uncertain, and thoughtful.

Then I was horrified at my own audacity and lack of manners. Sam had risked his life for me the night before. He had *saved my life.* And here I was, rummaging around in his head like a kid in a box full of toys. Shame made my cheeks flush, and I lost the thread of what the gal at my table was saying until she asked me gently if I felt all right. I snapped out of it and focused and took her order for chili and crackers and a glass of sweet tea. Her friend, a woman in her fifties, asked for a hamburger Lafayette and a side salad. I got her choice of dressing and beer, and shot off to the hatch to turn in the order. I nodded at the tap when I stood by Sam, and he handed me the beer a second later. I was too rattled to talk to him. He shot me a curious glance.

I was glad to leave the bar when my shift was up. Holly and I turned over to Arlene and Danielle, and grabbed our purses. We emerged into near-darkness. The security lights were already on. It was going to rain later, and clouds obscured the stars. We could hear Carrie Underwood singing on the jukebox, faintly. She wanted Jesus to take the wheel. That seemed like a real good idea.

We stood by our cars for a moment in the parking lot. The wind was blowing, and it was downright chilly.

"I know Jason is Hoyt's best friend," Holly said. Her voice sounded uncertain, and though her face was hard to decipher, I knew she wasn't sure I'd want to hear what she was going to say. "I've always liked Hoyt. He was a good guy in high school. I guess—I hope you don't really get mad at me—I guess what stopped me from dating him earlier was his being so tight with Jason."

I didn't know how to respond. "You don't like Jason," I said finally.

"Oh, sure, I like Jason. Who doesn't? But is he good for Hoyt? Can Hoyt be happy if that cord between them is weaker? 'Cause I can't think about getting closer to Hoyt unless I believe he can stick with me the way he's always stuck with Jason. You can see what I mean."

"Yes," I said. "I love my brother. But I know Jason isn't really in the habit of thinking about the welfare of other people." And that was putting it mildly.

Holly said, "I like you. I don't want to hurt your feelings. But I figured you'd know, anyway."

"Yeah, I kinda did," I said. "I like you, too, Holly. You're a good mother. You've worked hard to take care of your kid. You're on good terms with your ex. But what about Danielle? I would've said you were as tight with her as Hoyt is with Jason." Danielle was another divorced mother, and she and Holly had been thick as thieves since they were in first grade. Danielle had more of a support system than Holly. Danielle's mother and father were still hale and were very glad to help out with her two kids. Danielle had been going with a guy for some time now, too.

"I would never have said anything could come between Danielle and me, Sookie." Holly pulled on her Windbreaker and fished for her keys in the depths of her purse. "But her and me, we've parted ways a little bit. We still see each other for lunch sometimes, and our kids still play together." Holly sighed heavily. "I don't know. When I got interested in something other than the world here in Bon Temps, the world we grew up in, Danielle started thinking there was something a little wrong with that, with my curiosity. When I decided to become a Wiccan, she hated that, still does hate it. If she knew about the Weres, if she knew what had happened to me . . ." A shapeshifting witch had tried to force Eric to give her a piece of his financial enterprises. She'd forced all the local witches she could round up into helping her, including an unwilling Holly. "That whole thing changed me," Holly said now.

"It does, doesn't it? Dealing with the supes."

"Yeah. But they're part of our world. Someday everyone will know that. Someday . . . the whole world will be different."

I blinked. This was unexpected. "What do you mean?"

"When they all come out," Holly said, surprised at my lack of insight. "When they all come out and admit their existence. Everyone, everyone in the world, will have to adjust. But some people won't want to. Maybe there'll be a backlash. Wars maybe. Maybe the Weres will fight all the other shifters, or maybe the humans will attack the Weres and the vampires.

Or the vampires—you know they don't like the wolves worth a durn—they'll wait until some fine night, and then they'll kill them all and get the humans to say thank you."

She had a touch of the poet in her, did Holly. And she was quite a visionary, in a doom-ridden way. I'd had no idea Holly was that deep, and I was again ashamed of myself. Mind readers shouldn't be taken by surprise like that. I'd tried so hard to stay out of people's minds that I was missing important cues.

"All of that, or none of that," I said. "Maybe people will just accept it. Not in every country. I mean, when you think of what happened to the vampires in eastern Europe and some of South America . . ."

"The pope never sorted that one out," Holly commented.

I nodded. "Kind of hard to know what to say, I guess." Most churches had had (excuse me) a hell of a time deciding on a scriptural and theological policy toward the undead. The Were announcement would sure add another wrinkle to that. They were definitely alive, no doubt about it. . . . But they had almost too much life, as opposed to already having died once.

I shifted my feet. I hadn't intended on standing out here and solving the world's problems and speculating on the future. I was still tired from the night before. "I'll see you, Holly. Maybe you and me and Amelia can go to the movies in Clarice some night?"

"Sure," she said, a little surprised. "That Amelia, she doesn't think much of my craft, but at least we can talk the talk a little."

Too late, I had a conviction the threesome wouldn't work out, but what the hell. We could give it a try.

I drove home wondering if anyone would be there waiting

for me. The answer came when I parked beside Pam's car at the back door. Pam drove a conservative car, of course, a Toyota with a Fangtasia bumper sticker. I was only surprised it wasn't a minivan.

Pam and Amelia were watching a DVD in the living room. They were sitting on the couch but not exactly twined around each other. Bob was curled up in my recliner. There was a bowl of popcorn on Amelia's lap and a bottle of TrueBlood in Pam's hand. I stepped around so I could see what they were watching. *Underworld.* Hmmm.

"Kate Beckinsale is hot," Amelia said. "Hey, how was work?"

"Okay," I said. "Pam, how come you have two evenings off in a row?"

"I deserve it," Pam said. "I haven't had time off in two years. Eric agreed I was due. How do you think I would look in that black outfit?"

"Oh, as good as Beckinsale," Amelia said, and turned her head to smile at Pam. They were at the ooey-gooey stage. Considering my own complete lack of ooey, I didn't want to be around.

"Did Eric find out any more about that Jonathan guy?" I asked.

"I don't know. Why don't you call him yourself?" Pam said with a complete lack of concern.

"Right, you're off duty," I muttered, and stomped back to my room, grumpy and a little ashamed of myself. I punched in the number for Fangtasia without even having to look it up. So not good. And it was on speed dial on my cell phone. Geez. Not something I wanted to ponder just at the moment.

The phone rang, and I put my dreary musing aside. You had to be on your game when you talked to Eric.

"Fangtasia, the bar with a bite. This is Lizbet." One of the fangbangers. I scrounged around my mental closet, trying to put a face with the name. Okay—tall, very round and proud of it, moon face, gorgeous brown hair.

"Lizbet, this is Sookie Stackhouse," I said.

"Oh, hi," she said, sounding startled and impressed.

"Um . . . hi. Listen, could I speak to Eric, please?"

"I'll see if the master is available," Lizbet breathed, trying to sound reverent and all mysterious.

"Master," my ass.

The fangbangers were men and women who loved vampires so much they wanted to be around them every minute the vampires were awake. Jobs at places like Fangtasia were bread and butter to these people, and the opportunity to get bitten was regarded as close to sacred. The fangbanger code required them to be *honored* if some bloodsucker wanted to sample them; and if they died of it, well, that was just about an honor, too. Behind all the pathos and tangled sexuality of the typical fangbanger was the underlying hope that some vampire would think the fangbanger was "worthy" of being turned into a vampire. Like you had to pass a character test.

"Thanks, Lizbet," I said.

Lizbet set the phone down with a thud and went off looking for Eric. I couldn't have made her happier.

"Yes," said Eric after about five minutes.

"Busy, were you?"

"Ah . . . having supper."

I wrinkled my nose. "Well, hope you had enough," I said with a total lack of sincerity. "Listen, did you find out anything about that Jonathan?"

"Have you seen him again?" Eric asked sharply.

"Ah, no. I was just wondering."

"If you see him, I need to know immediately."

"Okay, got that. What have you learned?"

"He's been seen other places," Eric said. "He even came here one night when I was away. Pam's at your house, right?"

I had a sinking feeling in my gut. Maybe Pam wasn't sleeping with Amelia out of sheer attraction. Maybe she'd combined business with a great cover story, and she was staying with Amelia to keep an eye on me. *Damn vampires,* I thought angrily, because that scenario was entirely too close to an incident in my recent past that had hurt me incredibly.

I wasn't going to ask. Knowing would be worse than suspecting.

"Yes," I said between stiff lips. "She's here."

"Good," Eric said with some satisfaction. "If he appears again, I know she can take care of it. Not that that's why she's there," he added unconvincingly. The obvious afterthought was Eric's attempt at pacifying what he could tell were my upset feelings; it sure didn't arise from any feeling of guilt.

I scowled at my closet door. "Are you gonna give me any real information on why you're so jumpy about this guy?"

"You haven't seen the queen since Rhodes," Eric said.

This was not going to be a good conversation. "No," I said. "What's the deal with her legs?"

"They're growing back," Eric said after a brief hesitation.

I wondered if the feet were growing right out of her stumps, or if the legs would grow out and then the feet would appear at the end of the process. "That's good, right?" I said. Having legs had to be a good thing.

"It hurts very much," Eric said, "when you lose parts and they grow back. It'll take a while. She's very . . . She's incapacitated." He said the last word very slowly, as if it was a word he knew but had never said aloud.

I thought about what he was telling me, both on the surface and beneath. Conversations with Eric were seldom single-layered.

"She's not well enough to be in charge," I said in conclusion. "Then who is?"

"The sheriffs have been running things," Eric said. "Gervaise perished in the bombing, of course; that leaves me, Cleo, and Arla Yvonne. It would have been clearer if Andre had survived." I felt a twinge of panic and guilt. I could have saved Andre. I'd feared and loathed him, and I hadn't. I'd let him be killed.

Eric was silent for a minute, and I wondered if he was picking up on the fear and guilt. It would be very bad if he ever learned that Quinn had killed Andre for my sake. Eric continued, "Andre could have held the center because he was so established as the queen's right hand. If one of her minions had to die, I wish I could have picked Sigebert, who's all muscles and no brains. At least Sigebert's there to guard her body, though Andre could have done that and guarded her territory as well."

I'd never heard Eric so chatty about vampire affairs. I was beginning to have an awful creeping feeling that I knew where he was headed.

"You expect some kind of takeover," I said, and felt my heart plummet. Not again. "You think Jonathan was a scout."

"Watch out, or I'll begin to think you can read my mind." Though Eric's tone was light as a marshmallow, his meaning was a sharp blade hidden inside.

"That's impossible," I said, and if he thought I was lying, he didn't challenge me. Eric seemed to be regretting telling me so much. The rest of our talk was very brief. He told me again to call him at the first sight of Jonathan, and I assured him I'd be glad to.

After I'd hung up, I didn't feel quite as sleepy. In honor of the chilly night I pulled on my fleecy pajama bottoms, white with pink sheep, and a white T-shirt. I unearthed my map of Louisiana and found a pencil. I sketched in the areas I knew. I was piecing my knowledge together from bits of conversations that had taken place in my presence. Eric had Area Five. The queen had had Area One, which was New Orleans and vicinity. That made sense. But in between, there was a jumble. The finally deceased Gervaise had had the area including Baton Rouge, and that was where the queen had been living since Katrina damaged her New Orleans properties so heavily. So that should have been Area Two, due to its prominence. But it was called Area Four. Very lightly, I traced a line that I could erase, and would, after I'd looked at it for a bit.

I mined my head for other bits of information. Five, at the top of the state, stretched nearly all the way across. Eric was richer and more powerful than I'd thought. Below him, and fairly even in territory, were Cleo Babbitt's Area Three and Arla Yvonne's Area Two. A swoop down to the Gulf from the southwesternmost corner of Mississippi marked off the large areas formerly held by Gervaise and the queen, Four and One respectively. I could only imagine what vampiric political contortions had led to the numbering and arrangement.

I looked at the map for a few long minutes before I erased all the light lines I'd drawn. I glanced at the clock. Nearly an hour had passed since my conversation with Eric. In a melancholy mood, I brushed my teeth and washed my face. After I climbed into bed and said my prayers, I lay there awake for quite a while. I was pondering the undeniable truth that the most powerful vampire in the state of Louisiana, at this very point in time, was Eric Northman, my blood-bonded, once-upon-a-time lover. Eric had said in my hearing that he didn't want to be king, didn't want to take over new territory; and since I'd figured out the extent of his territory right now, the size of it made that assertion a little more likely.

I believed I knew Eric a little, maybe as much as a human can know a vampire, which doesn't mean my knowledge was profound. I didn't believe he wanted to take over the state, or he would have done so. I did think his power meant there was a giant target pinned to his back. I needed to try to sleep. I glanced at the clock again. An hour and a half since I'd talked to Eric.

Bill glided into my room quite silently.

"What's up?" I asked, trying to keep my voice very quiet, very calm, though every nerve in my body had started shrieking.

"I'm uneasy," he said in his cool voice, and I almost laughed. "Pam had to leave for Fangtasia. She called me to take her place here."

"Why?"

He sat in the chair in the corner. It was pretty dark in my room, but the curtains weren't drawn completely shut and I got some illumination from the yard's security light. There was a night-light in the bathroom, too, and I could make out the contours of his body and the blur of his face. Bill had a little glow, like all vampires do in my eyes.

"Pam couldn't get Cleo on the phone," he said. "Eric left the club to run an errand, and Pam couldn't raise him, either. But I got his voice mail; I'm sure he'll call back. It's Cleo not answering that's the rub."

"Pam and Cleo are friends?"

"No, not at all," he said, matter-of-factly. "But Pam should be able to talk to her at her all-night grocery. Cleo always answers."

"Why was Pam trying to reach her?" I asked.

"They call each other every night," Bill said. "Then Cleo calls Arla Yvonne. They have a chain. It should not be broken, not in these days." Bill stood up with a speed that I couldn't follow. "Listen!" he whispered, his voice as light on my ear as a moth wing. "Do you hear?"

I didn't hear jack shit. I held still under the covers, wishing passionately that this whole thing would just go away. Weres, vampires, trouble, strife... But no such luck. "What do you hear?" I asked, trying to be as quiet as Bill was being, an effort doomed in the attempt.

"Someone's coming," he said.

And then I heard a knock on the front door. It was a very quiet knock.

I threw back the covers and got up. I couldn't find my slippers because I was so rattled. I started for the bedroom door on my bare feet. The night was chilly, and I hadn't turned on the heat yet; my soles pressed coldly against the polished wood of the floor.

"I'll answer the door," Bill said, and he was ahead of me without my having seen him move.

"Jesus Christ, Shepherd of Judea," I muttered, and followed him. I wondered where Amelia was: asleep upstairs or on the living room couch? I hoped she was only asleep. I was so spooked by that time that I imagined she might be dead.

Bill glided silently through the dark house, down the hall, to the living room (which still smelled like popcorn), to the front door, and then he looked through the peephole, which for some reason I found funny. I had to slap a hand over my mouth to keep from giggling.

No one shot Bill through the peephole. No one tried to batter the door down. No one screamed.

The continuing silence was breaking me out in goose bumps. I didn't even see Bill move. His cool voice came from right beside my ear. "It is a very young woman. Her hair is dyed white or blond, and it's very short and dark at the roots. She's skinny. She's human. She's scared."

She wasn't the only one.

I tried like hell to think who my middle-of-the-night caller could be. Suddenly I thought I might know. "Frannie," I breathed. "Quinn's sister. Maybe."

"Let me in," a girl's voice said. "Oh, *please* let me in."

It was just like a ghost story I'd read once. Every hair on my arms stood up.

"I have to tell you what's happened to Quinn," Frannie said, and that decided me on the spot.

"Open the door," I said to Bill in my normal voice. "We have to let her in."

"She's human," Bill said, as if to say, "How much trouble can she be?" He unlocked the front door.

I won't say Frannie tumbled in, but she sure didn't waste any time getting through the door and slamming it behind her. I hadn't had a good first impression of Frannie, who was long on the aggression and attitude and short on the charm, but I'd come to know her a fraction better as she sat at Quinn's bedside in the hospital after the explosion. She'd had a hard life, and she loved her brother.

"What's happened?" I asked sharply as Frannie stumbled to the nearest chair and sat down.

"You *would* have a vampire here," she said. "Can I have a glass of water? Then I'll try to do what Quinn wants."

I hurried to the kitchen and got her a drink. I turned on the light in the kitchen, but even when I came back to the living room, we kept it dark.

"Where's your car?" Bill asked.

"It broke down about a mile back," she said. "But I couldn't wait with it. I called a tow truck and left the keys in the ignition. I hope to God they get it off the road and out of sight."

"Tell me *right now* what's happening," I said.

"Short or long version?"

"Short."

"Some vampires from Vegas are coming to take over Louisiana."

It was a showstopper.

Chapter 11

Bill's voice was very fierce. "Where, when, how many?"

"They've taken out some of the sheriffs already," Frannie said, and I could tell there was just a hint of enjoyment at getting to deliver this momentous news. "Smaller forces are taking out the weaker ones while a larger force gathers to surround Fangtasia to deal with Eric."

Bill was on his cell phone before the words had finished leaving Frannie's mouth, and I was left gaping at him. I had come so late to the realization of how weak Louisiana's situation was that it seemed to me for a second that I had brought this about by thinking of it.

"How did this happen?" I asked the girl. "How did Quinn get involved? How is he? Did he send you here?"

"*Of course* he sent me here," she said, as if I were the stupidest person she'd ever met. "He knows you're tied to that vampire Eric, so that makes you part of the target. The Vegas vamps sent someone to have a look at you, even."

Jonathan.

"I mean, they were evaluating Eric's assets, and you were considered part of that."

"Why was this Quinn's problem?" I asked, which may not have been the clearest way to put it, but she got my meaning.

"Our mother, our goddamned screwed-up, screw-up *mother*," Frannie said bitterly. "You know she got captured and raped by some hunters, right? In Colorado. Like a hundred years ago." Actually, it had been maybe nineteen years ago, because that was how Frannie had been conceived.

"And Quinn rescued her and killed them all, though he was just a kid, and he went in debt to the local vampires to get them to help him clean up the scene and get his mom away."

I knew Quinn's mother's sad history. I was nodding frantically by now, because I wanted to get to something I hadn't heard yet.

"Okay, well, my mom was pregnant with me after the rape," Frannie said, glaring at me defiantly. "So she had me, but she was never right in the head, and growing up with her was kinda hard, right? Quinn was working off his debt in the pits." (Think *Gladiator* with wereanimals.) "She never got right in the head," Frannie repeated. "And she's kept getting worse."

"I get that," I said, trying to keep my voice level. Bill seemed on the verge of thumping Frannie to speed up her narrative, but I shook my head.

"Okay, so she was in a nice place that Quinn was paying

for outside Las Vegas, the only assisted-living center in America where you can send people like my mom." The Deranged Weretiger Nursing Home? "But Mom got loose, and she killed some tourist and took her clothes and caught a ride into Vegas and picked up a man. She killed him, too. She robbed him and took his money and gambled until we caught up with her." Frannie paused and took a deep breath. "Quinn was still healing from Rhodes, and this about killed him."

"Oh, no." But I had a feeling I hadn't heard the bottom line on this incident yet.

"Yeah, what's worse, right? The escape, or the killing?"

Probably the tourists had had an opinion on that.

I vaguely noticed that Amelia had entered the room, and I also realized that she didn't seem startled to see Bill. So she'd been awake when Bill had taken Pam's place. Amelia hadn't met Frannie before, but she didn't interrupt the flow.

"Anyway, there's a huge vampire cartel in Vegas, because the pickings are so rich," Frannie told us. "They tracked down Mom before the police could catch her. They cleaned up after her *again.* Turns out that Whispering Palms, the place that lost her, had alerted all the supes in the area to be on the lookout. By the time I got to the casino where they'd grabbed Mom, the vamps were telling Quinn that they'd taken care of everything and now there was more debt for him to work off. He said he was coming off a bad injury and he couldn't go back in the pits. They offered to take me on as a blood donor or a whore for visiting vamps instead, and he just about took out the one who said that."

Of course. I exchanged a glance with Bill. The offer to "employ" Frannie had been designed to make anything else look better.

"Then they said they knew of a really weak kingdom that was just about up for grabs, and they meant Louisiana. Quinn told 'em they could get it for free if the King of Nevada would just marry Sophie-Anne, her being in no position to argue. But it turned out the king was right there. He said he detested cripples and no way would he marry a vampire who'd killed her previous husband, no matter how sweet her kingdom was, even with Arkansas thrown in." Sophie-Anne was the titular head of Arkansas as well as Louisiana since she'd been found innocent of her husband's (the King of Arkansas's) murder in a vampire court. Sophie-Anne hadn't had a chance to consolidate her claim, because of the bombing. But I was sure it was on her to-do list, right after her legs grew back.

Bill flipped his phone open again and began punching in numbers. Whoever he called, he didn't get an answer. His dark eyes were blazing. He was absolutely revved up. He leaned over to pick up a sword he'd left propped against the couch. Yep, he'd come fully armed. I didn't keep items like that in my toolshed.

"They'll want to take us out quietly and quickly so the human news media won't catch on. They'll concoct a story to explain why familiar vampires have been replaced with strange ones," Bill said. "You, girl—what part does your brother have to play in this?"

"They made him tell them how many people you-all had

and share what else he knew about the situation in Lousiana," Frannie said. To make matters perfect, she began to cry. "He didn't want to. He tried to bargain with them, but they had him where they wanted him." Now Frannie looked about ten years older than she was. "He tried to call Sookie a million times, but they were watching him, and he was scared he'd be leading them right to her. But they found out anyway. Once he knew what they were going to do, he took a big risk—for both of us—and sent me on ahead. I was glad I'd got a friend to get my car back from you."

"One of you should have called me, written me, something." Despite our current crisis, I couldn't stop myself from expressing my bitterness.

"He couldn't let you know how bad it was. He said he knew you'd try to get him out of it somehow, but there was no way out."

"Well, sure I would have tried to get him out of it," I said. "That's what you do when someone's in trouble."

Bill was silent but I felt his eyes on me. I'd rescued Bill when he'd been in trouble. Sometimes I was sorry I had.

"Your brother, why is he with them now?" Bill asked sharply. "He's given them information. They are vampires. What do they need with him?"

"They're bringing him with them so he can negotiate with the supe community, specifically the Weres," Frannie said, sounding suddenly like Miss Corporate Secretary. I felt sort of sorry for Frannie. As the product of a union between a human and a weretiger, she had no special powers to give her an edge or to provide her with a bargaining chip. Her face was streaked with smeared mascara and her nails were chewed down to the quick. She was a mess.

And this was no time to be worried about Frannie, because the vampires of Vegas were taking over the state.

"What had we better do?" I asked. "Amelia, have you checked the house wards? Do they include our cars?" Amelia nodded briskly. "Bill, you've called Fangtasia and all the other sheriffs?"

Bill nodded. "No answer from Cleo. Arla Yvonne answered, and she had already gotten wind of the attack. She said she was going to ground and would try to work her way up to Shreveport. She has six of her nest with her. Since Gervaise met his end, his vampires have been tending the queen, and Booth Crimmons has been their lieutenant. Booth says he was out tonight and his child, Audrey, who was left with the queen and Sigebert, doesn't answer. Even the deputy that Sophie-Anne sent to Little Rock is not responding."

We were all silent for a moment. The idea that Sophie-Anne might be finally dead was almost unimaginable.

Bill shook himself visibly. "So," he continued, "we might stay here, or we might find another place for you three. When I'm sure you're safe, I have to get to Eric as soon as I can. He'll need every pair of hands tonight if he's to survive."

Some of the other sheriffs were surely dead. Eric might die tonight. The full realization smacked me in the face with the force of a huge gloved hand. I sucked in a jagged breath and fought to stay on my feet. I just couldn't think about that.

"We'll be fine," Amelia said stoutly. "I'm sure you're a great fighter, Bill, but we aren't defenseless."

With all due respect to Amelia's witchcraft ability, we were so defenseless; at least against vampires.

Bill spun away from us and stared down the hall at the back door. He'd heard something that hadn't reached our human ears. But a second later, I heard a familiar voice.

"Bill, let me in. The sooner, the better!"

"It's Eric," Bill said with great satisfaction. Moving so fast he was a blur, he went to the rear of the house. Sure enough, Eric was outside, and something in me relaxed. He was alive. I noticed that he was hardly his usual tidy self. His T-shirt was torn, and he was barefoot.

"I was cut off from the club," he said as he and Bill came up the hall to join us. "My house was no good, not by myself. I couldn't reach anyone else. I got your message, Bill. So, Sookie, I'm here to ask for your hospitality."

"Of course," I said automatically, though I really should have thought about it. "But maybe we should go to—" I was about to suggest we cut across the graveyard and go to Bill's house, which was larger and would have more facilities for vampires, when trouble erupted from another source. We hadn't been paying any attention to Frannie since she'd finished her story, and the slump she'd experienced once her dramatic news had been delivered had allowed her to think of the potential for disaster we faced.

"I gotta get out of here," Frannie said. "Quinn told me to stay here, but you guys are..." Her voice was rising and she was on her feet and every muscle in her neck stood out in sharp relief as her head whipped around in her agitation.

"Frannie," Bill said. He put his white hands on each side of Frannie's face. He looked into the girl's eyes. Frannie fell silent. "You stay here, you stupid girl, and do what Sookie tells you to do."

"Okay," Frannie said in a calm voice.

"Thanks," I said. Amelia was looking at Bill in a shocked kind of way. I guess she'd never seen a vamp use his whammy before. "I'm going to get my shotgun," I said to no one, but before I could move, Eric turned to the closet by the front door. He reached in and extricated the Benelli. He turned to hand it to me with a bemused expression. Our eyes met.

Eric had remembered where I kept the shotgun. He'd learned that when he'd stayed with me while his memory was lost.

When I could look away, I saw Amelia was looking self-consciously thoughtful. Even in my short experience of living with Amelia, I had learned that this was not a look I liked. It meant she was about to make a point, and it was a point I wouldn't care for.

"Are we getting all excited about nothing?" she asked rhetorically. "Maybe we're panicking for no good reason."

Bill looked at Amelia as if she'd turned into a baboon. Frannie looked totally unconcerned.

"After all," Amelia said, wearing a small, superior smile, "why would anyone come after *us* at all? Or more specifically *you*, Sookie. Because I don't suppose vampires would come after *me*. But that aside, why would they come here? You're not an essential part of the vampire defense system. What would give them a good reason to want to kill or capture you?"

Eric had been making a circuit of the doors and windows. He finished as Amelia was winding up her speech. "What's happened?" he asked.

I said, "Amelia is explaining to me why there's no rational reason the vampires would come after me in their attempt to conquer the state."

"Of course they'll come," Eric said, barely glancing at Amelia. He examined Frannie for a minute, nodded in approval, and then stood to the side of a living room window to look out. "Sookie's got a blood tie to me. And now I am here."

"Yeah," Amelia said heavily. "Thanks a lot, Eric, for making a beeline for this house."

"Amelia. Are you not a witch with much power?"

"Yes, I am," she said cautiously.

"Isn't your father a wealthy man with a lot of influence in the state? Isn't your mentor a great witch?"

Who had been doing some research on the Internet? Eric and Copley Carmichael had something in common.

"Yeah," Amelia said. "Okay, they'd be happy if they could corral us. But still, if Eric hadn't come here, I don't think we'd need to worry about physical injury."

"You're wondering if we're actually in danger?" I said. "Vampires, excited, bloodlust?"

"We won't be any use if we're not alive."

"Accidents happen," I said, and Bill snorted. I'd never heard him make such an ordinary sound, and I looked at him. Bill was enjoying the prospect of a good fight. His fangs were out. Frannie was staring at him, but her expression didn't change. If there'd been the slightest chance she'd stay calm and cooperative, I might have asked Bill to bring her out of the artificial state. I loved having Frannie still and quiet—but I hated her loss of free will.

"Why did Pam leave?" I asked.

"She can be of more value at Fangtasia. The others have gone to the club, and she can tell me if they are sealed in it or not. It was stupid of me to call them all and tell them to gather; I should have told them to scatter." From the way he looked now, it wasn't a mistake Eric would ever make again.

Bill stood close to a window, listening to the sounds of the night. He looked at Eric and shook his head. No one there yet.

Eric's phone rang. He listened for a minute, said, "Good fortune to you," and hung up.

"Most of the others are in the club," he told Bill, who nodded.

"Where is Claudine?" Bill asked me.

"I have no idea." How come Claudine came sometimes when I was in trouble and didn't come at others? Was I just wearing her out? "But I don't think she'll come, because you guys are here. There's no point in her showing up to defend me if you and Eric can't keep your fangs off of her."

Bill stiffened. His sharp ears had picked up something. He turned and exchanged a long glance with Eric. "Not the company I'd have chosen," Bill said in his cool voice. "But we'll make a good showing. I do regret the women." And he looked at me, his deep dark eyes full of some intense emotion. Love? Sorrow? Without a hint or two from his silent brain, I couldn't tell.

"We're not in our graves yet," Eric said, just as coolly.

Now I too could hear the cars coming down the driveway. Amelia made an involuntary sound of fear, and Frannie's eyes got even wider, though she stayed in her chair as if paralyzed. Eric and Bill sank into themselves.

The cars stopped out front, and there were the sounds of doors opening and shutting, someone walking up to the house.

There was a brisk knock—not on the door, but on one of the porch uprights.

I moved toward it slowly. Bill gripped my arm and stepped in front of me. "Who is there?" he called, and immediately shifted us three feet away.

He'd expected someone to fire through the door.

That didn't happen.

"It is I, the vampire Victor Madden," said a cheerful voice.

Okay, unexpected. And especially to Eric, who closed his eyes briefly. Victor Madden's identity and presence had told Eric volumes, and I didn't know what he'd read in those volumes.

"Do you know him?" I whispered to Bill.

Bill said, "Yes. I've met him." But he didn't add any details and stood lost in an inner debate. I've never wanted more intensely to know what someone was thinking than I did at that moment. The silence was getting to me.

"Friend or foe?" I called.

Victor laughed. It was a real good laugh—genial, an "I'm laughing with you, not at you" kind of chortle. "That's an excellent question," he said, "and one only you can answer. Do I have the honor of talking to Sookie Stackhouse, famed telepath?"

"You have the honor of talking to Sookie Stackhouse,

barmaid," I said frostily. And I heard a sort of throaty ruffling noise, a vocalization of an animal. A large animal.

My heart sank into my bare feet.

"The wards will hold," Amelia was saying to herself in a rapid whisper. "The wards will hold; the wards will hold." Bill was gazing at me with his dark eyes, thoughts flickering across his face in rapid succession. Frannie was looking vague and detached, but her eyes were fixed on the door. She'd heard the sound, too.

"Quinn's out there with them," I whispered to Amelia, since she was the only one in the room who hadn't figured that out.

Amelia said, "He's on *their* side?"

"They've got his mom," I reminded her. But I felt sick inside.

"But we've got his sister," Amelia said.

Eric looked as thoughtful as Bill. In fact, they were looking at each other now, and I could believe they were having a whole dialogue without speaking a word.

All this thoughtfulness wasn't good. It meant they hadn't decided which way they were going to jump.

"May we come in?" asked the charming voice. "Or may we treat with one of you face-to-face? You seem to have quite a few safeguards on the house."

Amelia pumped her arm and said, "Yes!" She grinned at me.

Nothing wrong with a little deserved self-congratulation, though the timing of it might be a bit off. I smiled back at her, though I felt my cheeks would crack.

Eric seemed to gather himself, and after one long last look at each other, he and Bill relaxed. Eric turned to me, kissed me on the lips very lightly, and looked at my face for a long moment. "He'll spare you," Eric said, and I understood he wasn't really talking to me but to himself. "You're too unique to waste."

And then he opened the door.

Chapter 12

Since the lights were still off in the living room and the secu- rity light was on outside, from inside the house we could see pretty well. The vampire standing by himself in the front yard was not particularly tall, but he was a striking man. He was wearing a business suit. His hair was short and curly, and though the light wasn't good for making such a determination, I thought it was black. He stood with an attitude, like a *GQ* model.

Eric was pretty much blocking the doorway, so that was all I could tell. It seemed tacky to go to the window and stare.

"Eric Northman," said Victor Madden. "I haven't seen you in a few decades."

"You've been working hard in the desert," Eric said neutrally.

"Yes, business has been booming. There are some things

I want to discuss with you—rather urgent things, I'm afraid. May I come in?"

"How many are with you?" Eric asked.

"Ten," I whispered at Eric's back. "Nine vamps and Quinn." If a human brain left a buzzing hole in my inner consciousness, a vampire brain left an empty one. All I had to do was count the holes.

"Four companions are with me," Victor said, sounding absolutely truthful and frank.

"I think you've lost your counting ability," Eric said. "I believe there are nine vampires there, and one shifter."

Victor's silhouette realigned as his hand twitched. "No use trying to pull the wool over your eyes, old sport."

"Old sport?" muttered Amelia.

"Let them step out of the woods so I can see," Eric called.

Amelia and Bill and I abandoned being discreet and went to the windows to watch. One by one, the vampires of Las Vegas came out of the trees. Since they were at the edges of the darkness I couldn't see most of them very well, but I noticed a statuesque woman with lots of brown hair and a man no taller than me who sported a neat beard and an earring.

The last to emerge from the woods was the tiger. I was sure Quinn had shifted into his animal form because he didn't want to look at me face-to-face. I felt horribly sorry for him. I figured that however ripped up inside I was, his insides had to be like hamburger meat.

"I see a few familiar faces," Eric said. "Are they all under your charge?"

This had a meaning that I didn't understand.

"Yes," Victor said very firmly.

This meant something to Eric. He stood back from the doorway, and the the rest of us turned to look at him. "Sookie," Eric said, "it's not for me to invite him in. This is your house." Eric turned to Amelia. "Is your ward specific?" he asked. "Will the ward let in him only?"

"Yes," she said. I wished she sounded more certain. "He has to be invited in by someone the ward accepts, like Sookie."

Bob the cat strolled to the open doorway. He sat in the exact middle of the threshold, his tail wrapped around his paws, and surveyed the newcomer steadily. Victor laughed a little when Bob first appeared, but that died away after a second.

"This is not just a cat," Victor said.

"No," I said, loud enough for Victor to hear me. "Neither is the one out there." The tiger made a chuffing sound, which I'd read was supposed to be friendly. I guess it was as close as Quinn could come to telling me he was sorry about the whole damn thing. Or maybe not. I came to stand right behind Bob. He raised his head to look at me, and then strolled off with as much indifference as he'd arrived. Cats.

Victor Madden approached the front porch. Evidently the wards would not let him cross the boards, and he waited at the foot of the steps. Amelia flipped on the front porch lights, and Victor blinked in the sudden glare. He was a very attractive man, if not exactly handsome. His eyes were big and brown, and his jaw was decided. He had beautiful teeth displayed in a jaw-cracking smile. He looked at me very carefully.

"Reports of your attractions were not exaggerated," he said, which took me a minute to decipher. I was too scared to be at my most intelligent. I made out Jonathan the spy among the vampires in the yard.

"Uh-huh," I said, unimpressed. "You alone can come in."

"I'm delighted," he said, bowing. He took a cautious step up and looked relieved. After that he crossed the porch so smoothly that all of a sudden he was right in front of me, his pocket handkerchief—I swear to God, a snowy white pocket handkerchief—almost touching my white T-shirt. It was all I could do to keep from flinching, but I managed to hold very still. I met his eyes and felt the pressure behind them. He was trying his mind tricks to see what might work on me.

Not much would, in my experience. After I'd let him establish that, I moved back to give him room to enter.

Victor stood quite still just inside the door. He gave everyone in the room a very cautious look, though his smile never faded. When he spotted Bill, the smile actually brightened. "Ah, Compton," he said, and though I expected he'd follow up with a more illuminating remark, that didn't happen. He gave Amelia a thorough scrutiny. "The source of the magic," he muttered, and inclined his head to her. Frannie got a quicker evaluation. When Victor recognized her, he looked, for one second, severely displeased.

I should have hidden her. I simply hadn't thought about it. Now the Las Vegas group knew that Quinn had sent his sister ahead to warn us. I wondered if we'd survive this.

If we lived until daytime, we three humans could leave in

a car, and if the cars were disabled, well, we had cell phones and could call for a pickup. But there was no telling what other day-walking helpers the vampires of Las Vegas had . . . besides Quinn. And as far as Eric and Bill being able to fight their way through the line of vampires outside: they could try. I didn't know how far they'd get.

"Please have a seat," I said, though I sounded about as welcoming as a church lady forced to entertain an atheist. We all moved to the couch and the chairs. We left Frannie where she was. It would be better to maintain every bit of calm we could manage. The tension in the room was almost palpable as it was.

I switched on some lamps and asked the vampires if they would like a drink. They all looked surprised. Only Victor accepted. After a nod from me, Amelia went to the kitchen to heat up some TrueBlood. Eric and Bill were on the couch, Victor had taken the easy chair, and I perched on the edge of the recliner, my hands clenched in my lap. There was a long silence while Victor selected his opening line.

"Your queen is dead, Viking," he said.

Eric's head jerked. Amelia, entering, stopped in her tracks for a second before carrying the glass of TrueBlood to Victor. He accepted it with a little bow. Amelia stared down at him, and I noticed her hand was hidden in the folds of her robe. Just as I drew in breath to tell her not to be crazy, she moved away from him and came to stand by me.

Eric said, "I had guessed that was the case. How many of the sheriffs?" I had to hand it to him. You couldn't tell how he felt from his voice.

Victor made a show of consulting his memory. "Let me see. Oh, yes! All of them."

I pressed my lips together hard so no sound would escape. Amelia pulled out the straight-backed chair we keep to one side of the hearth. She set it close to me and sank down on it like she was a bag of sand. Now that she was sitting, I could see she had a knife clutched in her hand, the filleting knife from the kitchen. It was real sharp.

"What of their people?" Bill asked. Bill was doing the clean-slate imitation, too.

"There are a few alive. A dark young man named Rasul . . . a few servitors of Arla Yvonne. Cleo Babbitt's crew died with her even after an offer of surrender, and Sigebert seems to have perished with Sophie-Anne."

"Fangtasia?" Eric had saved this for last because he could hardly bear to speak of it. I wanted to go over to him and put my arms around him, but he wouldn't appreciate that at all. It would look weak.

There was a long silence while Victor took a swallow of the TrueBlood.

Then he said, "Eric, your people are all in the club. They have not surrendered. They say they won't until they hear from you. We're ready to burn it down. One of your minions escaped, and she—we think it is a female—is taking out any of my people stupid enough to get separated from the others."

Yay, *Pam*! I bent my head to hide an involuntary smile. Amelia grinned at me. Even Eric looked pleased, just for a split second. Bill's face didn't alter a bit.

"Why am I alive, of all the sheriffs?" Eric asked—the four-hundred-pound question.

"Because you're the most efficient, the most productive, and the most practical." Victor had the answer ready at his lips. "And you have one of the biggest moneymakers living in your area and working for you." He nodded toward Bill. "Our king would like to leave you in position, if you will swear loyalty to him."

"I suppose I know what will happen if I refuse."

"My people in Shreveport are ready with the torches," Victor said with his cheerful smile. "Actually, with more modern devices, but you get the point. And, of course, we can take care of your little group here. You are certainly fond of diversity, Eric. I trail you here thinking to find you with your elite vampires, and we find you in this odd company."

I didn't even think about bristling. We were an odd company, no doubt about it. I also noticed the rest of us didn't get a vote. This all rested on the question of how proud Eric was.

In the silence, I wondered how long Eric would ponder his decision. If he didn't cave, we'd all die. That would be Victor's way of "taking care" of us, despite Eric's out-loud thought about me being too valuable to kill. I didn't think Victor gave a fig for my "value," much less Amelia's. Even if we overwhelmed Victor (and between Bill and Eric that could probably be managed), the rest of the vampires outside had only to set this house on fire as they were threatening to do Fangtasia, and we'd be gone. They might not be able to come in without an invitation, but we certainly had to get out.

My eyes met Amelia's. Her brain was pinging with fear,

though she was making a supreme effort to keep her spine stiff. If she called Copley, he would bargain for her life, and he had the wherewithal to bargain effectively. If the Las Vegas crew was hungry enough to invade Louisiana, then they were hungry enough to accept a bribe for the life of the daughter of Copley Carmichael. And surely Frannie would be okay, since her brother was right outside? Surely they would spare Frannie to keep Quinn complaisant? Victor had already pointed out that Bill had skills they needed, because his computer database had proved lucrative. So Eric and I were the most expendable.

I thought about Sam, wished I could call him and talk to him for just a minute. But I wouldn't drag him into this for the world, because that would mean his sure death. I closed my eyes and said good-bye to him.

There was a sound outside the door, and it took me a moment to interpret it as a tiger's noise. Quinn wanted in.

Eric looked at me, and I shook my head. This was bad enough without throwing Quinn into the mix. Amelia whispered, "Sookie," and pressed her hand against me. It was the hand with the knife.

"Don't," I said. "It won't do any good." I hoped Victor didn't realize what her intent was.

Eric's eyes were wide and fixed on the future. They blazed blue in the long silence.

Then something unexpected happened. Frannie snapped out of the trance, and she opened her mouth and began to scream. When the first shriek ripped out of her mouth, the door began to thud. In about five seconds Quinn splintered my door by throwing his four hundred and fifty pounds against it. Frannie scrambled to her feet and ran for it, seizing the knob and yanking it open before Victor could grab her, though he missed her by half an inch.

Quinn bounded into the house so quickly he knocked his sister down. He stood over her, roaring at all of us.

To his credit Victor showed no fear. He said, "Quinn, listen to me."

After a second, Quinn shut up. It was always hard to say how much humanity was left in the animal form of a shifter. I'd had evidence the Weres understood me perfectly, and I'd communicated with Quinn before when he was a tiger; he'd definitely comprehended. But hearing Frannie scream had uncorked his rage and he didn't seem to know where to aim it. While Victor was paying attention to Quinn, I fished a card out of my pocket.

I hated the thought of using my great-grandfather's Get Out of Jail Free card so soon ("Love ya, Gramps—rescue me!"), and I hated the thought of bringing him without warning into a room full of vampires. But if ever there was a time for fairy intervention, that time would be now, and I might have left it too late. I had my cell phone in my pajama pocket. I pulled it out surreptitiously and flipped it open, wishing I'd put him on speed dial. I looked down, checking the number, and began to press the buttons. Victor was talking to Quinn, trying to persuade him that Frannie was not being hurt.

Did I not do everything right? Did I not wait until I was sure I needed him before I called? Had I not been so clever to have the card on me, to have the phone with me?

Sometimes, when you do everything right, it still turns out all wrong.

Just as the call went through, a quick hand reached around, plucked the phone from my hand, and dashed it against the wall.

"We can't bring him in," Eric said in my ear, "or a war will start that will kill all of us."

I think he meant all of *him*, because I was pretty sure I would be okay if Great-grandpa started a war to keep me that way, but there was no help for it now. I looked at Eric with something very close to hatred.

"There's no one you can call who would help you in this situation," Victor Madden said complacently. But then he looked a little less pleased with himself, as if he was having second thoughts. "Unless there is something I don't know about you," he added.

"There is much you don't know about Sookie," Bill said. It was the first time he'd spoken since Madden had entered. "Know this: I will die for her. If you harm her, I'll kill you." Bill turned his dark eyes on Eric. "Can you say the same?"

Eric plainly wouldn't, which put him behind in the "Who Loves Sookie More?" stakes. At the moment, that wasn't so relevant. "You must also know this," Eric said to Victor. "Even more pertinently, if anything happens to her, forces you can't imagine will be set into motion."

Victor looked deeply thoughtful. "Of course, that could be an idle threat," he said. "But somehow, I believe you are serious. If you're referring to this tiger, though, I don't think he'll kill us all for her, since we have his mother and his sister in our grasp. The tiger already has a lot to answer for, since I see his sister here."

Amelia had moved over to put her arm around Frannie, both to sooth her and to include herself in the tiger's circle of protection. She looked at me, thinking very clearly, *Should I try some magic? Maybe a stasis spell?*

It was very clever of Amelia to think of communicating this way with me, and I thought about her offer furiously. The stasis spell would hold everything exactly as it was. But I didn't know if her spell could encompass the vampires waiting outside, and I couldn't see the situation would be much improved if she froze only all of us in the room except for herself. Could she be specific about whom the spell affected? I wished that Amelia were telepathic, too, and I'd never wished that on anyone before. As things lay, there was just too much I didn't know. Reluctantly I shook my head.

"This is ridiculous," Victor said. His impatience was calculated. "Eric, this is the bottom line and my last offer. Do you accept my king's takeover of Louisiana and Arkansas, or do you want to fight to the death?"

There was another, shorter pause.

"I accept the sovereignty of your king," Eric said, his voice flat.

"Bill Compton?" Victor asked.

Bill looked at me, his dark eyes dwelling on my face. "I accept," he said.

And just like that, Louisiana had a new king, and the old regime was gone.

Chapter 13

I felt the tension whoosh out of me like the air out of a punc-tured tire.

Eric said, "Victor, call your people off. I want to hear you tell them."

Victor, beaming harder than ever, whipped a tiny cell phone from his pocket and called someone named Delilah to give her his orders. Eric used his own cell to phone Fangtasia. Eric told Clancy about the change in leadership.

"Don't forget to tell Pam," Eric said very clearly, "lest she kill off a few more of Victor's people."

There was an awkward pause. Everyone was wondering what came next.

Now that I was pretty sure I was going to live, I hoped Quinn would change back to his human form so I could talk to him. There was a lot to talk about. I wasn't sure I had a right to feel this, but I felt betrayed.

I don't think the world is about me. I could see he'd been forced into this situation.

There was always a lot of forcing around vampires.

As I saw it, this was the second time his mother had set Quinn up, quite inadvertently, to take her fall with the vamps. I got that she wasn't responsible; truly, I did. She'd never wanted to be raped, and she hadn't chosen to become mentally ill. I'd never met the woman and probably never would, but she was surely a loose cannon. Quinn had done what he could. He'd sent his sister ahead to warn us, though I wasn't exactly sure that had ended up helping so very much.

But points for trying.

Now, as I watched the tiger nuzzle Frannie, I knew I'd made mistakes all the way down the line with Quinn. And I felt the anger of betrayal; no matter how I reasoned with myself, the image of seeing my boyfriend on the side of vampires I had to regard as enemies had lit a fire in me. I shook myself, looking around the room.

Amelia had made a dash for the bathroom as soon as she could decently let go of Frannie, who was still crying. I suspected the tension had been too much for my witchy roommate, and sounds from the hall bathroom confirmed that. Eric was still on the phone with Clancy, pretending to be busy while he absorbed the huge change in his circumstances. I couldn't read his mind, but I knew that. He walked down the hall, maybe wanting some privacy to reassess his future.

Victor had gone outside to talk to his cohorts, and I heard one of them say, "Yeah! *Yes!*" as if his team had scored a winning goal, which I supposed was the case.

As for me, I felt a little weak in the knees, and my thoughts were in such a tumult they could scarcely be called thoughts. Bill's arm went around me, and he lowered me to the chair Eric had vacated. I felt his cool lips brush my cheek. I would have to possess a heart of stone not to be affected by his little speech to Victor—I hadn't forgotten it, no matter how terrifying the night had been—and my heart is not made of stone.

Bill knelt by my feet, his white face turned up to me. "I hope someday you'll turn to me," he said. "I'll never force myself or my company on you." And he got up and walked outside to meet his new vampire kin.

Okey-dokey.

God bless me; the night wasn't over yet.

I trudged back to my bedroom and pushed the door open, intending to wash my face or brush my teeth or make some stab at smoothing my hair, because I thought it might make me feel a little less trampled.

Eric was sitting on my bed, his face buried in his hands.

He looked up at me as I entered, and he looked shocked. Well, no wonder, what with the very thorough takeover and traumatic changing of the guard.

"Sitting here on your bed, smelling your scent," he said in a voice so low I had to strain to hear it. "Sookie . . . I remember everything."

"Oh, *hell*," I said, and went in the bathroom and shut the

door. I brushed my hair and my teeth and scrubbed my face, but I had to come out. I was being as cowardly as Quinn if I didn't face the vampire.

Eric started talking the minute I emerged. "I can't believe I—"

"Yeah, yeah, I know, loved a mere human, made all those promises, was as sweet as pie and wanted to stay with me forever," I muttered. Surely there was a shortcut we could take through this scene.

"I can't believe I felt something so strongly and was so happy for the first time in hundreds of years," Eric said with some dignity. "Give me some credit for that, too."

I rubbed my forehead. It was the middle of the night, I'd thought I was going to die, the man I'd been thinking of as my boyfriend had just turned my whole picture of him upside down. Though now "his" vamps were on the same side as "my" vamps, I'd emotionally aligned myself with the vampires of Louisiana, even if some of them had been terrifying in the extreme. Could Victor Madden and his crew be any less scary? I thought not. This very night they'd killed quite a few vamps I'd known and liked.

Coming on top of all these events, I didn't think I could cope with an Eric who'd just had a revelation.

"Can we talk about this some other time, if we have to talk about it?" I asked.

"Yes," he said after a long pause. "Yes. This isn't the right moment."

"I don't know that any time will be right for this conversation."

"But we're going to have it," Eric said.

"Eric . . . oh, okay." I made an "erase" movement with my hand. "I'm glad the new regime wants to keep you on."

"It would hurt you if I died."

"Yeah, we're blood bound, yadda yadda yadda."

"Not because of the bond."

"Okay, you're right. It would hurt me if you died. Also I would have died, too, most likely, so it wouldn't have hurt for long. Now can you please scoot?"

"Oh, yes," he said with a return of the old Eric flare. "I'll *scoot* for now, but I'm going to see you later. And rest assured, my lover, we'll come to an understanding. As for the vampires of Las Vegas, they'll be well-suited to running another state that relies heavily on tourism. The King of Nevada is a powerful man, and Victor is not one you can take lightly. Victor is ruthless, but he won't destroy something he may be able to use. He's very good at reining in his temper."

"So you're not really that unhappy with the takeover?" I couldn't keep the shock out of my voice.

"It's happened," Eric said. "There's no goal to be met in being 'unhappy' now. I can't bring anyone back to life, and I can't defeat Nevada by myself. I won't ask my people to die in a futile attempt."

I just couldn't match Eric's pragmatism. I could see his points, and in fact when I'd had some rest, I might agree with him. But not here, not now; he seemed way too cold for me. Of course, he'd had a few hundred years to get that way, and maybe he'd had to go through this process many times.

What a bleak prospect.

Eric paused on his way out the door to bend down to kiss me on the cheek. This was another evening for collecting kisses. "I'm sorry about the tiger," he said, and that was the final cap to the night as far as I was concerned. I sat slumped in the little chair in the bedroom corner until I was sure everyone was out of the house. When only one warm brain remained, Amelia's, I peered out of my room to get a visual. Yep, everyone else was gone.

"Amelia?" I called.

"Yeah," she answered, and I went to find her. She was in the living room, and she was as exhausted as I was.

"Are you going to be able to sleep?" I asked.

"I don't know. I'm going to try." She shook her head. "This changes everything."

"Which this?" Amazingly, she understood me.

"Oh, the vampire takeover. My dad had lots of dealings with the New Orleans vampires. He was going to be working for Sophie-Anne, repairing her headquarters in New Orleans. All her other properties, too. I better call him and tell him. He's going to want to get in there early with the new guy."

In her own way Amelia was being as practical as Eric. I felt out of tune with the whole world. I couldn't think of anyone I could call who would feel the least bit mournful over the loss of Sophie-Anne, Arla Yvonne, Cleo... And the list went on. It made me wonder, for the first time, if vampires might not get inured to loss. Look at all the life that passed them by and then vanished. Generation after generation went to their graves, while still the undead lived on. And on.

Well, this tired human—who would eventually pass on—needed some sleep in the worst possible way. If there was another hostile takeover tonight, it would have to proceed without me. I locked the doors all over again, called up the stairs to Amelia to tell her good night, and crawled back into my bed. I lay awake for at least thirty minutes, because my muscles twitched just when I was about to drift off. I would start up into full wakefulness, thinking someone was coming in the room to warn me about a great disaster.

But finally even the twitching couldn't keep me awake any longer. I fell into a heavy sleep. When I woke, the sun was up and shining in the window, and Quinn was sitting in the chair in the corner where I'd slumped the night before while I was trying to deal with Eric.

This was an unpleasant trend. I didn't want a lot of guys popping in and out of my bedroom. I wanted one who would stay.

"Who let you in?" I asked, propping myself up on one elbow. He looked good for someone who hadn't gotten much sleep. He was a very large man with a very smooth head and huge purple eyes. I had always loved the way he looked.

"Amelia," he said. "I know I shouldn't have come in; I should have waited until you were up. You might not want me in the house."

I went in the bathroom to give myself a minute, another

ploy that was getting all too familiar. When I came out, a little neater and more awake than when I'd entered, Quinn had a mug of coffee for me. I took a sip and instantly felt better able to cope with whatever was coming. But not in my bedroom.

"Kitchen," I said, and we went to the room that had always been the heart of the house. It had been dated when the fire had gotten it. Now I had a brand-new kitchen, but I still missed the old one. The table where my family had eaten for years had been replaced with a modern one, and the new chairs were lots more comfortable than the old ones, but regret still caught at me every now and then when I thought of what had been lost.

I had an ominous feeling that "regret" was going to be the theme of the day. During my troubled sleep, apparently I'd absorbed a dose of the practicality that had seemed so sad to me the night before. To stave off the conversation we were going to have to have, I stepped to the back door and looked to see that Amelia's car was gone. At least we were alone.

I sat down opposite the man I'd hoped to love.

"Babe, you look like someone just told you I was dead," Quinn said.

"Might as well have," I said, because I had to plow into this and look to neither the right nor the left. He flinched.

"Sookie, what could I have done?" he asked. "What could I have done?" There was an edge of anger in his voice.

"What can *I* do?" I asked in return, because I had no answer for him.

"I sent Frannie! I tried to warn you!"

"Too little, too late," I said. I second-guessed myself immediately: Was I being too hard, unfair, ungrateful? "If you'd called me weeks ago, even once, I might feel different. But I guess you were too busy trying to find your mother."

"So you're breaking up with me because of my mother," he said. He sounded bitter and I didn't blame him.

"Yes," I said after a moment's inner testing of my own resolve. "I think I am. It's not your mom as much as her whole situation. Your mother will always have to come first as long as she's alive, because she's so damaged. I've got sympathy for that, believe me. And I'm sorry that you and Frannie have a hard row to hoe. I know all about hard rows."

Quinn was looking down into his coffee mug, his face drawn with anger and weariness. This was probably the worst possible moment to be having this showdown, and yet it had to be done. I hurt too bad to let it last any longer.

"Yet, knowing all this, and knowing I care for you, you don't want to see me anymore," Quinn said, biting each word out. "You don't want to try to make it work."

"I care for you, too, and I had hoped we'd have a lot more," I said. "But last night was just too much for me. Remember, I had to find out your past from someone else? I think maybe you didn't tell me about it from the start because you knew it would be an issue. Not your pit fighting—I don't care about that. But your mom and Frannie... Well, they're your family. They're... dependent. They have to have you. They'll always come first." I stopped for a moment, biting the inside of my cheek. This was the hardest part. "I want to be first. I know that's selfish, and maybe unattainable, and maybe shallow. But

I just want to come first with someone. If that's wrong of me, so be it. I'll be wrong. But that's the way I feel."

"Then there's nothing left to talk about," Quinn said after a moment's thought. He looked at me bleakly. I couldn't disagree. His big hands flat on the table, he pushed to his feet and left.

I felt like a bad person. I felt miserable and bereft. I felt like a selfish bitch.

But I let him walk out the door.

Chapter 14

While I was getting ready for work—yes, even after a night like the one I'd had, I had to go to work—there was a knock at the front door. I'd heard something big coming down the driveway, so I'd tied my shoes hastily.

The FedEx truck was not a frequent visitor at my house, and the thin woman who hopped out was a stranger. I opened the battered front door with some difficulty. It was never going to be the same after Quinn's entrance the night before. I made a mental note to call the Lowe's in Clarice to ask about a replacement. Maybe Jason would help me hang it. The FedEx lady gave a long look at the door's splintered condition when I finally got it open.

"You want to sign for this?" she said as she held out a package, tactfully not commenting.

"Sure." I accepted the box, a little puzzled. It had come from Fangtasia. Huh. As soon as the truck had wheeled back out to Hummingbird Road, I opened the package. It was a red cell phone. It was programmed to my number. There was a note with it. "Sorry about the other one, lover," it read. Signed with a big "E." There was a charger included. And a car charger, too. And a notice that my first six months' bill had been paid.

With a kind of bemused feeling, I heard another truck coming. I didn't even bother to move from the front porch. The new arrival was from the Shreveport Home Depot. It was a new front door, very pretty, with a two-man crew to install it. All charges had been taken care of.

I wondered if Eric would clean out my dryer vent.

I got to Merlotte's early so I could have a talk with Sam. But his office door was shut, and I could hear voices inside. Though not unheard of, the closed door was rare. I was instantly concerned and curious. I could read Sam's familiar mental signature, and there was another one that I had encountered before. I heard a scrape of chair legs inside, and I hastily stepped into the storeroom before the door opened.

Tanya Grissom walked by.

I waited for a couple of beats, then decided my business was so urgent I had to risk a conversation with Sam, though he might not be in the mood for it. My boss was still in his creaky wooden rolling chair, his feet propped on the desk. His hair was even more of a mess than usual. He looked like he had a reddish halo. He also looked thoughtful and preoccupied, but when I said I needed to tell him some things, he nodded and asked me to shut the door.

"Do you know what happened last night?" I asked.

"I hear there was a hostile takeover," Sam said. He tilted back on the springs of his rolling chair, and they squeaked in an irritating way. I was definitely balancing on a thin edge today, so I had to bite my lip to keep from snapping at him.

"Yeah, you might say that." A hostile takeover was pretty much a perfect way to put it. I told him what had happened at my house.

Sam looked troubled. "I don't ever interfere in vamp business," he said. "The two-natured and vamps don't mix well. I'm really sorry you got pulled into that, Sookie. That asshole Eric." He looked like there was more he wanted to say, but he pressed his lips together.

"Do you know anything about the King of Nevada?" I asked.

"I know he has a publishing empire," Sam said promptly. "And he has at least one casino and some restaurants. He's also the ultimate owner of a management company that handles vampire entertainers. You know, the Elvis Undead Revue with all-vamp Elvis tribute artists, which is pretty funny when you think about it, and some great dance groups." We both knew that the real Elvis was still around but rarely in any shape to perform. "If there had to be a takeover of a tourist state, Felipe de Castro is the right vampire for the job. He'll make sure New Orleans gets rebuilt like it ought to be, because he'll want the revenue."

"Felipe de Castro . . . That sounds exotic," I said.

"I haven't met him, but I understand he's very, ah, charismatic," Sam said. "I wonder if he'll be coming to Louisiana to live or if this Victor Madden will be his agent here. Either way, it won't affect the bar. But there's no doubt it'll affect you, Sookie." Sam uncrossed his legs and sat up straight in his chair, which shrieked in protest. "I wish there was some way to get you out of the vampire loop."

"The night I met Bill, if I'd known what I know now, I wonder if I'd have done anything different," I said. "Maybe I would've let the Rattrays have him." I'd rescued Bill from a sleazy couple who turned out to be not only sleazy, but murderers. They were vampire drainers, people who lured vampires to spots where the vamps could be subdued with silver chains and drained of blood, which sold for big bucks on the black market. Drainers lived hazardous lives. The Rattrays had paid the full price.

"You don't mean that," Sam said. He rocked in the chair again (*squeak! squeak!*) and rose to his feet. "You would never do that."

It felt really pleasant to hear something nice about myself, especially after the morning's conversation with Quinn. I was tempted to talk to Sam about that, too, but he was edging toward the door. Time to go to work, for both of us. I got up, too. We went out and began the usual motions. My mind was hardly on it, though.

To revive my flagging spirits, I tried to think of some bright point in the future, something to look forward to. I couldn't come up with anything. For a long, bleak moment I stood by the bar, my hand on my order pad, trying not to step over the edge into the chasm of depression. Then I slapped myself on the cheek. *Idiot! I have a house, and friends, and a job. I'm luckier than millions of people on the planet. Things will look up.*

For a while, that worked. I smiled at everyone, and if that smile was brittle, by God, it was still a smile.

After an hour or two, Jason came into the bar with his wife, Crystal. Crystal was looking sullen and slightly pregnant, and Jason was looking... Well, he had that hard look about him, the mean look he got sometimes when he'd been disappointed.

"What's up?" I asked.

"Oh, not much," Jason said expansively. "You bring us a couple beers?"

"Sure," I said, thinking he'd never ordered for Crystal before. Crystal was a pretty woman several years younger than Jason. She was a werepanther, but she wasn't a very good one, mostly because of all the inbreeding in the Hotshot community. Crystal had a hard time changing if it wasn't the full moon, and she had miscarried at least twice that I knew of. I pitied her losses, the more so because I knew the panther community considered her weak. Now Crystal was pregnant a third time. That pregnancy had maybe been the only reason Calvin had let her marry Jason, who was bitten, not born. That is, he'd become a panther by being repeatedly bitten—by a jealous male who wanted Crystal for himself. Jason couldn't change into a real panther but into a sort of half-beast, half-man version. He enjoyed it.

I brought them their beers along with two frosted mugs

and waited to see if they were going to place a food order. I wondered about Crystal drinking, but decided it wasn't my business.

"I'd like me a cheeseburger with fries," Jason said. No surprise there.

"What about you, Crystal?" I asked, trying to sound friendly. After all, this was my sister-in-law.

"Oh, *I* don't have enough money to eat," she said.

I had no idea what to say. I looked at Jason inquiringly, and he gave me a shrug. This shrug said (to his sister), "I've done something stupid and wrong but I'm not going to back down, because I'm a stubborn shit."

"Crystal, I'll be glad to stand you lunch," I said very quietly. "What would you like?"

She glared at her husband. "I'd like the same, Sookie."

I wrote her order down on a separate slip and strode to the hatch to turn them in. I had been ready to get angry, and Jason had lit a match and thrown it on my temper. The whole story was clear in their heads, and as I came to understand what was going on, I was sick of both of them.

Crystal and Jason had settled into Jason's house, but almost every day Crystal rode out to Hotshot, her comfort zone, where she didn't have to pretend anything. She was used to being surrounded by her kin, and she especially missed her sister and her sister's babies. Tanya Grissom was renting a room from Crystal's sister, the room Crystal had lived in until she married Jason. Crystal and Tanya had become instant buddies. Since Tanya's favorite occupation was shopping, Crystal had gone along for the ride several times. In fact, she'd spent all the money Jason had given her for household expenses. She'd done this two paychecks in a row, despite multiple scenes and promises.

Now Jason refused to give her any more money. He was doing all the grocery shopping and picking up any dry cleaning, paying every bill himself. He'd told Crystal if she wanted any money of her own, she had to get a job. The unskilled and pregnant Crystal had not succeeded in finding one, so she didn't have a dime.

Jason was trying to make a point, but by humiliating his wife in public he was making the wrong point entirely. What an idiot my brother could be.

What I could do about this situation? Well . . . nothing. They had to work it out themselves. I was looking at two stunted people who'd never grown up, and I wasn't optimistic about their chances.

With a deep twinge of unease, I remembered their unusual wedding vows; at least, they'd seemed odd to me, though I supposed they were the Hotshot norm. As Jason's closest living relative, I'd had to promise to take the punishment if Jason misbehaved, just as her uncle Calvin had promised the same on Crystal's behalf. I'd been pretty damn rash to make that promise.

When I carried their plates to their table, I saw that the two were in the jaw-clenching, looking-anywhere-but-at-each-other stage of quarreling. I put the plates down carefully, got them a bottle of Heinz ketchup, and skedaddled. I'd interfered enough by buying Crystal lunch.

There was a person involved in this I *could* approach, and I promised myself then and there that I would. All my anger and unhappiness focused on Tanya Grissom. I really wanted to do something awful to that woman. What the hell was she hanging around for, sniffing around Sam? What was her goal in drawing Crystal into this spending spiral? (And I didn't think for a second it was by chance that Tanya's newest big buddy was my sister-in-law.) Was Tanya trying to irritate me to death? It was like having a horsefly buzzing around and lighting occasionally . . . but never quite close enough to swat. While I went about my job on autopilot, I pondered what I could do to get her out of my orbit. For the first time in my life, I wondered if I could forcibly pin another person down to read her mind. It wouldn't be so easy, since Tanya was a wereanimal, but I would find out what was driving her. And I had the conviction that information would save me a lot of heartache . . . a lot.

While I plotted and schemed and fumed, Crystal and Jason silently ate their food, and Jason pointedly paid his own bill, while I took care of Crystal's. They left, and I wondered what their evening would be like. I was glad I wasn't going to be a party to it.

From behind the bar Sam had observed all this, and he asked me in a low voice, "What's up with those two?"

"They're having the newlywed blues," I said. "Severe adjustment problems."

He looked troubled. "Don't let them drag you into it," he said, and then looked like he regretted opening his mouth. "Sorry, don't mean to give you unwanted advice," he said.

Something prickled at the corners of my eyes. Sam was giving me advice because he cared about me. In my overwrought state, that was cause for sentimental tears. "That's okay, boss," I said, trying to sound perky and carefree. I spun on my heel and went to patrol my tables. Sheriff Bud Dearborn was sitting in my section, which was unusual. Normally he'd pick a seat somewhere else if he knew I was working. Bud had a basket of onion rings in front of him, liberally doused with ketchup, and he was reading a Shreveport paper. The lead story was POLICE SEARCH FOR SIX, and I stopped to ask Bud if I could have his paper when he was through with it.

He looked at me suspiciously. His little eyes in his mashed-in face scanned me as if he suspected he'd find a bloody cleaver hanging from my belt. "Sure, Sookie," he said after a long moment. "You got any of these missing people stowed away at your house?"

I beamed at him, anxiety transforming my smile into the bright grin of someone who wasn't all there mentally. "No, Bud, I just want to find out what's going on in the world. I'm behind on the news."

Bud said, "I'll leave it on the table," and he began reading again. I think he would have pinned Jimmy Hoffa on me if he could have figured a way to make it stick. Not that he necessarily thought I was a murderer, but he thought I was fishy and maybe involved in things that he didn't want happening in his parish. Bud Dearborn and Alcee Beck had that conviction in common, especially since the death of the man in the library. Luckily for me, the man had turned out to have a record as long as my arm; and not only a record, but one for violent crimes.

Though Alcee knew I'd acted in self-defense, he'd never trust me . . . and neither would Bud Dearborn.

When Bud had finished his beer and his onion rings and departed to rain terror on the evildoers of Renard Parish, I took his paper over to the bar and read the story with Sam looking over my shoulder. I had deliberately stayed away from the news after the bloodbath at the empty office park. I'd been sure the Were community couldn't cover up something so big; all they could do was muddy the trail the police would surely be following. That proved to be the case.

> After more than twenty-four hours, police remain baffled in their search for six missing Shreveport citizens. Hampering them is their inability to discover anyone who saw any of the missing people after ten o'clock on Wednesday night.
>
> "We can't find anything they had in common," said Detective Willie Cromwell.
>
> Among the missing is a Shreveport police detective, Cal Myers; Amanda Whatley, owner of a bar in the central Shreveport area; Patrick Furnan, owner of the local Harley-Davidson dealership, and his wife, Libby; Christine Larrabee, widow of John Larrabee, retired school superintendent; and Julio Martinez, an airman from Barksdale Air Force Base. Neighbors of the Furnans say they hadn't seen Libby Furnan for a day prior to Patrick Furnan's disappearance, and Christine Larrabee's cousin says she had not been able to contact Larrabee by phone for three days, so police specu-

late that the two women may have met with foul play prior to the disappearance of the others.

The disappearance of Detective Cal Myers has the force on edge. His partner, Detective Mike Loughlin, said, "Myers was one of the newly promoted detectives, and we hadn't had time to get to know each other well. I have no idea what could have happened to him." Myers, 29, had been with the Shreveport force for seven years. He was not married.

"If they are all dead, you would think at least one body would have turned up by now," Detective Cromwell said yesterday. "We have searched all their residences and businesses for clues, and so far we have come up with nothing."

To add to the mystery, on Monday another Shreveport area resident was murdered. Maria-Star Cooper, photographer's assistant, was slain in her apartment on Highway 3. "The apartment was like a butcher shop," said Cooper's landlord, among the first on the scene. No suspects have been reported in the slaying. "Everyone loved Maria-Star," said her mother, Anita Cooper. "She was so talented and pretty."

Police do not yet know if Cooper's death is related to the disappearances.

In other news, Don Dominica, owner of Don's RV Park, reported the absence of the owners of three RVs parked on his property for a week. "I'm not sure how many people were in each trailer," he said. "They all arrived together and rented the spaces for a month. The name on the rental is Priscilla Hebert. I think at least six people were in each RV. They all seemed pretty normal to me."

Asked if all their belongings were still in place, Dominica replied, "I don't know; I haven't been checking. I ain't got time for that. But I haven't seen hide nor hair of them for days."

Other residents of the RV park had not met the newcomers. "They kept to themselves," said a neighbor.

Police Chief Parfit Graham said, "I'm sure we'll solve these crimes. The right piece of information will surface. In the meantime, if anyone has knowledge of the whereabouts of any of these people, call the Tipster Hotline."

I considered it. I imagined the phone call. "All of these people died as a result of the werewolf war," I would say. "They were all Weres, and a displaced and hungry pack from south Louisiana decided the dissension in the ranks in Shreveport created an opening for them."

I didn't think I'd get much of a hearing.

"So they haven't found the site yet," Sam said very quietly.

"I guess that really was a good place for the meeting."

"Sooner or later, though . . ."

"Yeah. I wonder what's left?"

"Alcide's crew's had plenty of time now," Sam said. "So, not much. They probably burned the bodies somewhere out in the sticks. Or buried them on someone's land."

I shuddered. Thank God I hadn't had to be part of that; and at least I really *didn't* know where the bodies were buried. After checking my tables and serving some more drinks, I went back to the paper and flipped it open to the obituaries. Reading down the column headed "State Deaths," I got an awful shock.

> SOPHIE-ANNE LECLERQ, prominent businesswoman, residing in Baton Rouge since Katrina, died of Sino-AIDS in her home. Leclerq, a vampire, had extensive holdings in New Orleans and in many places in the state. Sources close to Leclerq say she had lived in Louisiana for a hundred years or more.

I'd never seen an obituary for a vampire. This one was a complete fabrication. Sophie-Anne had not had Sino-AIDS, the only disease that could cross from humans to vampires. Sophie-Anne had probably had an acute attack of Mr. Stake. Sino-AIDS was dreaded among vampires, of course, despite the fact that it was hard to communicate. At least it provided a palatable explanation for the human business community as to why Sophie-Anne's holdings were being managed by another vampire, and it was an explanation that no one would question too closely, especially since there was no body to refute the claim. To get it in today's paper, someone must have called it in directly after she'd been killed, perhaps even before she was dead. Ugh. I shivered.

I wondered what had really happened to Sigebert, Sophie-Anne's devoted bodyguard. Victor had implied Sigebert had perished along with the queen, but he hadn't definitely said so. I couldn't believe the bodyguard could still be alive. He would never have let anyone get close enough to kill Sophie-Anne.

Sigebert had been at her side for so many years, hundreds upon hundreds, that I didn't think he could have survived her loss.

I left the newspaper open to the obituaries and placed it on Sam's desk, figuring the bar was too busy a place to talk about it even if we had the time. We'd had an influx of customers. I was running my feet off serving them and pocketing some good tips, too. But after the week I'd had, it was not only hard to feel normally happy about the money, it was also impossible to feel normally cheerful about being at work. I just did my best to smile and respond when I was spoken to.

By the time I got off work, I didn't want to talk to anyone about anything.

But of course, I didn't get my druthers.

There were two women waiting in the front yard at my house, and they both radiated anger. One, I already knew: Frannie Quinn. The woman with her had to be Quinn's mother. In the harsh glare of the security light I had a good look at the woman whose life had been such a disaster. I realized no one had ever told me her name. She was still pretty, but in a Goth sort of way that wasn't kind to her age. She was in her forties; her face was gaunt, her eyes shadowed. She had dark hair with more than a touch of gray, and she was very tall and thin. Frannie was wearing a tank top that showed her bra, and tight jeans, and boots. Her mother was wearing pretty much the same outfit but in different colors. I guessed Frannie had charge of dressing her mother.

I parked beside them, because I had no intention of inviting them in. I got out of my car reluctantly.

"You bitch," Frannie said passionately. Her young face was rigid with anger. "How could you do that to my brother? He did so much for you!"

That was one way to look at it. "Frannie," I said, keeping my voice as calm and level as I could, "what happens between Quinn and me is really not any of your business."

The front door opened, and Amelia stepped out on the porch. "Sookie, you need me?" she asked, and I smelled magic around her.

"I'm coming in, in just a second," I said clearly, but didn't tell her to go back inside. Mrs. Quinn was a pureblood weretiger, and Frannie was half; they were both stronger than me.

Mrs. Quinn stepped forward and looked at me quizzically. "You're the one John loved," she said. "You're the one who broke up with him."

"Yes, ma'am. It just wasn't going to work out."

"They say I have to go back to that place in the desert," she said. "Where they store all the crazy Weres."

No shit. "Oh, do they?" I said, to make it clear I had nothing to do with it.

"Yes," she said, and lapsed into silence, which was kind of a big relief.

Frannie, however, had not done with me. "I loaned you my car," she said. "I came to warn you."

"And I thank you," I said. My heart sank. I couldn't think of any magic words to lessen the pain in the air. "Believe me, I wish things had worked out different." Lame but true.

"What's wrong with my brother?" Frannie asked. "He's handsome; he loves you; he's got money. *He's a great guy.* What's wrong with you that you don't want him?"

The bald answer—that I really admired Quinn but didn't want to play second fiddle to his family's needs—was simply unspeakable for two reasons: it was unnecessarily hurtful, and I might be seriously injured as a result. Mrs. Quinn might not be compos mentis, but she was listening with growing agitation. If she changed to her tiger form, I had no idea what would happen. She might run off into the woods, or she might attack. All this zoomed through my mind in little pictures. I had to say something.

"Frannie," I said very slowly and deliberately because I had no idea what I was going to follow that up with. "There's nothing wrong with your brother at all. I think he's the greatest. But we just have too many strikes against us as a couple. I want him to have the best chance at making a match with some lucky, lucky woman. So I cut him loose. Believe me, I'm hurting, too." This was mostly true, which helped. But I hoped Amelia had her fingertips primed to deliver some good magic. And I hoped she got the spell right. Just in case, I began shifting away from Frannie and her mother.

Frannie was teetering on the brink of action, and her mother was looking increasingly restless. Amelia had eased forward to the edge of the porch. The smell of magic intensified. For a long moment, the night seemed to catch its breath.

And then Frannie turned away. "Come on, Mama," she said, and the two women got into Frannie's car. I took advantage of the moment to run up on the porch. Amelia and I stood shoulder to shoulder wordlessly until Frannie started up the car and drove away.

"Well," Amelia said. "So, you broke up with him, I'm gathering."

"Yeah." I was exhausted. "He had too much baggage." Then I winced. "Gosh, I never thought I'd catch myself saying that. Especially considering my own."

"He had his mama." Amelia was on a perceptive roll that night.

"Yeah, he had his mama. Listen, thanks for coming out of the house and risking a mauling."

"What are roommates for?" Amelia gave me a light hug and said, "You look like you need to have a bowl of soup and go to bed."

"Yeah," I said. "That sounds about right."

Chapter 15

I slept very late the next day. And I slept like a stone. I didn't dream. I didn't toss or turn. I didn't get up to pee. When I woke up, it was close to noon, so it was good I didn't have to be at Merlotte's until evening.

I could hear voices in the living room. This was the downside of having a roommate. There was someone there when you woke up, and sometimes that person had company. However, Amelia was very good about making enough coffee for me when she got up earlier. That prospect got me out of bed.

I had to get dressed since we had company; besides, the other voice sounded masculine. I did a little brisk grooming in the bathroom and threw off my nightgown. I put on a bra and a T-shirt and some khakis. Good enough. I made a beeline for the kitchen and found that Amelia had indeed made a big pot of coffee. And she'd left a mug ready for me. Oh, great. I poured, and popped some sourdough bread in the toaster. The back porch door slammed, and I turned in surprise to see Tyrese Marley enter with an armful of firewood.

"Where do you keep your wood after you bring it in?" he asked.

"I have a rack by the fireplace in the living room." He'd been splitting the wood Jason had cut and stacked by the toolshed the spring before. "That's really nice of you," I said, floundering. "Um, have you had any coffee, or some toast? Or . . ." I glanced at the clock. "What about a ham or meatloaf sandwich?"

"Food sounds good," he said, striding down the hall as though the wood weighed nothing.

So the guest in the living room was Copley Carmichael. Why Amelia's dad was here, I had no clue. I scrambled to assemble a couple of sandwiches, poured some water, and put two kinds of chips by his plate so Marley could pick what he wanted. Then I sat down at the table myself and finally got to drink my coffee and eat my toast. I still had some of my grandmother's plum jam to spread on it, and I tried not to be melancholy every time I used it. No point in letting good jam go to waste. She would have certainly looked at it that way.

Marley returned and sat down opposite me with no sign of discomfort. I relaxed myself.

"I appreciate the work," I said after he'd had a bite of his food.

"I got nothing else to do while he talks to Amelia," Marley said. "Plus, if she's still here all winter, he'll be glad if she can have a fire. Who cut that wood for you and didn't split it?"

"My brother," I said.

"Humph," Marley said, and settled into eating.

I finished my toast, poured myself a second mug of coffee, and asked Marley if he needed anything.

"I'm good, thank you," he said, and opened the bag of barbecue potato chips.

I excused myself to take a shower. It was definitely cooler today, and I got a long-sleeved T-shirt out of a drawer I hadn't opened in months. It was Halloween weather. It was past time to buy a pumpkin and some candy . . . not that I got many trick-or-treaters. For the first time in days, I felt normal: that is to say, comfortably happy with myself and my world. There was a lot to grieve about, and I would, but I wasn't walking around expecting a smack in the face.

Of course, the minute I thought that, I began to brood on bad things. I realized I hadn't heard anything from the Shreveport vampires, and then I wondered why I thought I should or would. This period of adjustment from one regime to another had to be full of tension and negotiation, and it was best to leave them to it. I hadn't heard from the Weres of Shreveport, either. Since the investigation into the disappearance of all those people was still active, that was a good thing.

And since I'd just broken up with my boyfriend, that meant (theoretically) I was footloose and fancy-free. I put on eye makeup as a gesture toward my freedom. And then I added some lipstick. It was hard to feel adventurous, actually. I hadn't wanted to be fancy-free.

As I finished making my bed, Amelia knocked at my door.

"Come on in," I said, folding my nightgown and putting it in the drawer. "What's up?"

"Well, my father has a favor to ask you," she said.

I could feel my face settle into grim lines. Of course, there had to be something Copley wanted if he'd driven up from New Orleans to talk to his daughter. And I could imagine what that request was.

"Go on," I said, crossing my arms over my chest.

"Oh, Sookie, your body language is already saying no!"

"Ignore my body and speak your piece."

She heaved a big sigh to indicate how reluctant she was to drag me into her dad's stuff. But I could tell she was tickled pink that he'd asked her to help him. "Well, since I told him about the Vegas vampire takeover, he wants to reestablish his business link with the vampires. He wants an introduction. He was hoping you could, like, broker that."

"I don't even know Felipe de Castro."

"No, but you know that Victor. And he looks like he's got his eyes on his own advancement."

"You know him as well as I do," I pointed out.

"Maybe, but what's more important is that he knows who you are, and I'm just the other woman in the room," Amelia said, and I could see her point—though I hated it. "I mean, he knows who I am, who my dad is, but he really noticed you."

"Oh, Amelia," I moaned, and for just a moment felt like kicking her.

"I know you won't like this, but he said he was ready to pay, like, a finder's fee," Amelia muttered, looking embarrassed.

I waved my hands in front of me to fan that thought away. I was not going to let my friend's father pay me money to make a phone call or whatever I had to do. At that moment I knew I'd decided I had to do this for Amelia's sake.

We went to the living room to talk face-to-face with Copley.

He greeted me with far more enthusiasm than he'd shown on his previous visit. He fixed his gaze on me, did the whole "I'm focused on you" thing. I regarded him with a skeptical eye. Since he was no fool, he picked up on that immediately.

"I'm sorry, Miss Stackhouse, for intruding here so soon after my last visit," he said, laying on the smarm. "But things in New Orleans are so desperate. We're trying to rebuild to bring the jobs back in. This connection is really important to me, and I employ a lot of people."

One, I didn't think Copley Carmichael was hurting for business even without the contracts for rebuilding the vampire properties. Two, I didn't for a minute think his sole motivation was the improvement of the damaged city; but after a moment of looking into his head, I was willing to concede that accounted for at least a fraction of his urgency.

Also, Marley had split the wood for the winter and carried a load in. That counted for more with me than any appeal based on emotion.

"I'll call Fangtasia tonight," I said. "I'll see what they say. That's the limit of my involvement."

"Miss Stackhouse, I'm indeed indebted," he said. "What can I do for you?"

"Your chauffeur already did it," I said. "If he could finish splitting that oak, that would be a great favor." I'm not a very good wood splitter, and I know because I've tried. Three or four logs done, and I'm wiped out.

"That's what he's been doing?" Copley did a good job of looking astonished. I wasn't sure if it was genuine or not. "Well, how enterprising of Marley."

Amelia was smiling and trying not to let her dad notice it. "Okay, then we're settled," she said briskly. "Dad, can I fix you a sandwich or soup? We have some chips or some potato salad."

"Sounds good," he said, since he was still trying to be just plain folks.

"Marley and I have already eaten," I said casually, and added, "I need to run to town, Amelia. You need anything?"

"I could use some stamps," she said. "You going by the post office?"

I shrugged. "It's on the way. Bye, Mr. Carmichael."

"Call me Cope, please, Sookie."

I'd just known he was going to say that. Next he was going to try being courtly. Sure enough, he smiled at me with exactly the right blend of admiration and respect.

I got my purse and headed out the back door. Marley was still working on the woodpile in his shirtsleeves. I hoped that had been his very own idea. I hoped he got a raise.

I didn't really have anything to do in town. But I had wanted to dodge any further conversation with Amelia's dad. I stopped by the store and got some more paper towels, bread, and tuna, and I stopped by the Sonic and got an Oreo Blast. Oh, I was a bad girl, no doubt about it. I was sitting in my car working on the Blast when I spied an interesting couple two cars away. They hadn't noticed me, apparently, because Tanya and Arlene were talking steadily. The two were in Tanya's Mustang. Arlene's hair was newly colored, so it was flaming red to the roots, caught up at the back in a banana clip. My former friend was wearing a tiger-print knit top, all I could see of her ensemble. Tanya was wearing a pretty lime green blouse and a dark brown sweater. And she was listening intently.

I tried to believe they were talking about something other than me. I mean, I try not to be too paranoid. But when you see your ex-buddy talking to your known enemy, you have to at least entertain the possibility that the topic of you has come up in an unflattering way.

It wasn't so much that they didn't like me. I've known people all my life who didn't like me. I've known exactly why and how much they didn't like me. That's really unpleasant, as you can well imagine. What bothered me was that I thought Arlene and Tanya were moving into the realm of actually doing something to me.

I wondered what I could find out. If I moved closer, they'd definitely notice me, but I wasn't sure I could "hear" them from where I was. I bent over like I was fiddling with my CD player, and I focused on them. I tried to mentally skip over or plow through the people in the intervening cars to reach them, which wasn't an easy task.

Finally, the familiar pattern of Arlene helped me to home in. The first impression I got was one of pleasure. Arlene was enjoying herself immensely, since she had the undivided attention of a fairly new audience and she was getting to talk about her new boyfriend's convictions about the need to kill all vampires and maybe people who collaborated with them. Arlene had no hard convictions that she'd formed for herself, but she was great at adopting other people's if they suited her emotionally.

When Tanya had an especially strong surge of exasperation, I zoomed in on her thought pattern. I was in. I remained in my half-concealed position, my hand moving every now and then over the CDs in my little car folder, while I tried to pick out everything I could.

Tanya was still in the pay of the Pelts: Sandra Pelt, specifically. And gradually I came to understand that Tanya had been sent here to do anything she could to make me miserable.

Sandra Pelt was the sister of Debbie Pelt, whom I'd shot to death in my kitchen. (After she'd tried to kill *me.* Several times. Let me point that out.)

Dammit. I was sick to death of the issue of Debbie Pelt. The woman had been a bane to me alive. She had been as malicious and vindictive as her little sister, Sandra. I'd suffered over her death, felt guilty, felt remorseful, felt like I had a huge *C* for "Cain" on my forehead. Killing a vampire is bad enough, but the corpse goes away and they're sort of... erased. Killing another human being changes you forever.

That's how it ought to be.

But it's possible to grow sick of that feeling, tired of that albatross around your emotional neck. And I'd grown both sick and tired of Debbie Pelt. Then her sister and her parents had begun giving me grief, had had me kidnapped. The tables had turned, and I'd held them in my power. In return for me letting them go, they'd agreed to leave me alone. Sandra had promised to stay away until her parents died. I had to wonder if the elder Pelts were still among the living.

I started up my car and began cruising around Bon Temps, waving at familiar faces in almost every vehicle I passed. I had no idea what to do. I stopped at the little town park and got out of my car. I began to stroll, my hands jammed in my pockets. My head was all in a snarl.

I remembered the night I'd confessed to my first lover, Bill, that my great-uncle had molested me when I'd been a child. Bill had taken my story so to heart that he had arranged for a visitor to drop by my great-uncle's house. Lo and behold, my uncle had died from a fall down the stairs. I'd been furious at Bill for taking over my own past. But I couldn't deny that having my great-uncle dead had felt good. That profound relief had made me feel complicit in the assassination.

When I'd been trying to find survivors in the twisted debris of the Pyramid of Gizeh, I'd found someone still living, a vampire who wanted to keep me firmly under his control for the queen's benefit. Andre had been terribly wounded, but he would have lived if an injured Quinn hadn't crawled over and snuffed Andre out. I'd walked away without stopping Quinn or saving Andre, and that had made me several degrees more guilty of Andre's death than of my great-uncle's.

I strode through the empty park, kicking at the stray leaves that came my way. I was struggling with a sick temptation. I had only to say the word to any of many members of the supernatural community, and Tanya would be dead. Or I could set my sights on the source and have Sandra taken out. And again—what a relief her departure from the world would be.

I just couldn't do it.

But I couldn't live with Tanya nipping at my heels, either. She'd done her best to ruin my brother's already shaky relationship with his wife. That was just wrong.

I finally thought of the right person to consult. And she lived with me, so that was convenient.

When I got back to my house, Amelia's dad and his obliging chauffeur had departed. Amelia was in the kitchen, washing dishes.

"Amelia," I said, and she jumped. "Sorry," I apologized. "I should've walked heavier."

"I was hoping that my dad and I understood each other a little better," she confessed. "But I don't think that's really true. He just needs me to do something for him now and then."

"Well, at least we got the firewood split."

She laughed a little and dried off her hands. "You look like you have something big to say."

"I want to clear the decks before I tell you this long story. I'm doing your dad a favor, but I'm really doing it for you," I said. "I'll call Fangtasia for your father no matter what, because you're my roommate and that'll make you happy. So that's a done deal. Now I'm going to tell you about a terrible thing I did."

Amelia sat at the table and I sat opposite her, just like Marley and I had done earlier. "This sounds interesting," she said. "I'm ready. Bring it on."

I told Amelia all about it: Debbie Pelt, Alcide, Sandra Pelt and her parents, their vow that Sandra would never bother me again while they lived. What they had on me and how I felt about it. Tanya Grissom, spy and sneak and saboteur of my brother's marriage.

"Whoa," she said when I'd finished. She thought for a minute. "Okay, first off, let's check on Mr. and Mrs. Pelt." We used the computer I'd brought back from Hadley's apartment in New Orleans. It took all of five minutes to discover that Gordon and Barbara Pelt had died two weeks before when they'd attempted to make a left turn into a gas station only to be hit broadside by a tractor trailer.

We looked at each other, our noses wrinkled. "Ewww," Amelia said. "Bad way to go."

"I wonder if she even waited till they were in the ground before she activated the Aggravate Sookie to Death plan," I said.

"This bitch isn't going to let up. You sure Debbie Pelt was adopted? Because this totally vindictive attitude seems to run in that family."

"They must have really bonded," I said. "In fact, I got the impression that Debbie was more of a sister to Sandra than she was a daughter to her parents."

Amelia nodded thoughtfully. "A little pathology going on there," she said. "Well, let me think about what I can do. I don't do death magic. And you've said you don't want Tanya and Sandra to die, so I'm taking you at your word."

"Good," I said briefly. "And, uh, I'm willing to pay for this, of course."

"Poo," Amelia said. "You were willing to take me in when I needed to get out of town. You've put up with me all this time."

"Well, you do pay rent," I pointed out.

"Yeah, enough to cover my part of the utilities. And you put up with me, and you don't seem to be all up in arms about the Bob situation. So believe me, I'm really glad to do this for you. I've just got to figure out what I'm actually going to do. Do you mind if I consult with Octavia?"

"No, not at all," I said, trying not to show that I was relieved at the idea of the older witch offering her expertise. "You got it, right? Got that she was at loose ends? Out of money?"

"Yeah," Amelia said. "And I don't know how to give her some without offering offense. This is a good way to do it. I understand that she's stuck in a random corner of the living room in the house of the niece she's staying with. She told me that—more or less—but I don't know what I can do about it."

"I'll think about it," I promised. "If she really, really needs to move out of her niece's, she could stay in my extra bedroom for a little while." That wasn't an offer that delighted me, but the old witch had seemed pretty miserable. She'd been entertained by going on the little jaunt to poor Maria-Star's apartment, which had been a ghastly sight.

"We'll try to come up with something long-term," Amelia said. "I'm going to go give her a call."

"Okay. Let me know what you-all come up with. I got to get ready for work."

There weren't too many houses between mine and Merlotte's, but all of them had ghosts hanging from trees, inflated plastic pumpkins in the yard, and a real pumpkin or two sitting on the front porch. The Prescotts had a sheaf of corn, a bale of hay, and some ornamental squash and pumpkins arranged artfully on the front lawn. I made a mental memo to tell Lorinda Prescott how attractive it was when next I saw her at Wal-Mart or the post office.

By the time I got to work, it was dark. I got out my cell phone to call Fangtasia before I went inside.

"Fangtasia, the bar with a bite. Come into Shreveport's premier vampire bar, where the undead do their drinking every single night," said a recording. "For bar hours, press one. To schedule a private party, press two. To speak to a live human or a dead vampire, press three. And know this: prank calls are not tolerated. We will find you."

I was sure the voice was Pam's. She'd sounded remarkably bored. I pressed three.

"Fangtasia, where all your undead dreams come true," said one of the fangbangers. "This is Elvira. How may I direct you?"

Elvira, my ass. "This is Sookie Stackhouse. I need to speak with Eric," I said.

"Could Clancy help you?" Elvira asked.

"No."

Elvira seemed stumped.

"The master is very busy," she said, as if that would be hard for a human like me to understand.

Elvira was definitely a newbie. Or maybe I was getting kind of arrogant. I was irritated with "Elvira." "Listen," I said, trying to sound pleasant. "You get Eric on the phone in two minutes or he'll be mighty unhappy with you."

"*Well,*" Elvira said. "You don't have to be a bitch about it."

"Evidently I do."

"I'm putting you on hold," Elvira said viciously. I glanced at the employee door of the bar. I needed to hustle.

Click. "This is Eric," he said. "Is this my former lover?"

Okay, even that made things inside me thud and shiver in excitement. "Yeah, yeah, yeah," I said, proud of how unshaken I sounded. "Listen, Eric, for what it's worth, I had a visit today from a New Orleans bigwig named Copley Carmichael. He'd been involved with Sophie-Anne in some business negotiations about rebuilding the headquarters. He wants to establish a relationship with the new regime." I took a deep breath. "Are you okay?" I asked, negating in one plaintive question all my cultivated indifference.

"Yes," he said, his voice intensely personal. "Yes, I am... coping with this. We are very, very lucky we were in a position to... We're very lucky."

I let out my breath very softly so he wouldn't pick up on it. Of course, he would anyway. I can't say I'd been on pins and needles wondering how things were going with the vampires, but I hadn't been resting very easy, either. "Okay, very good," I said briskly. "Now, about Copley. Is there anyone around who'd like to hook up with him about the construction stuff?"

"Is he in the area?"

"I don't know. He was here this morning. I can ask."

"The vampire I am working with now would probably be the right woman for him to approach. She could meet him at your bar or here at Fangtasia."

"Okay. I'm sure he'd do either one."

"Let me know. He needs to call here to set up an appointment. He should ask for Sandy."

I laughed. "Sandy, huh?"

"Yes," he said, sounding grim enough to sober me in a hurry. "She is not a bit funny, Sookie."

"Okay, okay, I get it. Let me call his daughter, she'll call him, he'll call Fangtasia, it'll all get set up, and I've done my favor for him."

"This is Amelia's father?"

"Yes. He's a jerk," I said. "But he's her dad, and I guess he knows his building stuff."

"I lay in front of your fire and talked to you about your life," he said.

Okay, way out of left field. "Uh. Yeah. We did that."

"I remember our shower together."

"We did that, too."

"We did so many things."

"Ah . . . yeah. Okay."

"In fact, if I didn't have so much to do here in Shreveport, I would be tempted to visit you all by myself to remind you how much you enjoyed those things."

"If memory serves," I said sharply, "you kind of enjoyed them, too."

"Oh, yes."

"Eric, I really need to go. I got to get to work." Or spontaneously combust, whichever came first.

"Good-bye." He could make even that sound sexy.

"Good-bye." I didn't.

It took me a second to gather my thoughts back together. I was remembering things I'd tried hard to forget. The days Eric had stayed with me—well, the nights—we'd done a lot of talking and a lot of sexing. And it had been wonderful. The companionship. The sex. The laughing. The sex. The conversations. The . . . well.

Somehow going in to serve beers seemed drab, all of a sudden.

But that was my job, and I owed it to Sam to show up and work. I trudged in, stowed my purse, and nodded to Sam as I tapped Holly on the shoulder to tell her I was here to take over. We switched shifts for the change and convenience but mostly because the night tips were higher. Holly was glad to see me because she had a date that night with Hoyt. They were going to a movie and dinner in Shreveport. She'd gotten a teenager to babysit Cody. She was telling me this as I was getting it from her contented brain, and I had to work hard not to get confused. That showed me how rattled I'd been by my conversation with Eric.

I was really busy for about thirty minutes, making sure everyone was well-supplied with drinks and food. I caught a moment to call Amelia soon after that to relay Eric's message, and she told me that she'd call her dad the minute she hung up. "Thanks, Sook," she said. "Again, you're a great roomie."

I hoped she'd think of that when she and Octavia were devising a magical solution to my Tanya problem.

Claudine came into Merlotte's that evening, raising male pulses as she sauntered to the bar. She was wearing a green silk blouse, black pants, and black high-heeled boots. That made her at least six foot one, I estimated. To my amazement, her twin brother, Claude, trailed in after her. The racing pulses spread to the opposite sex with the speed of wildfire. Claude, whose hair was as black as Claudine's, though not as long, was as lovely a hunk as ever posed in a Calvin Klein ad. Claude was wearing a masculine version of Claudine's outfit, and he'd tied his hair back with a leather thong. He was also wearing very "guy" boots. Since he stripped at a club in Monroe on ladies' night, Claude knew exactly how to smile at women, though he wasn't interested in them. I take that back. He was interested in how much money they had in their purses.

The twins had never come in together; in fact, I didn't recall Claude setting foot in Merlotte's before. He had his own place to run, his own fish to fry.

Of course I went over to say hi, and I got a comprehensive hug from Claudine. To my amazement, Claude followed suit. I figured he was playing to the audience, which was pretty much the whole bar. Even Sam was goggling; together, the fairy twins were overwhelming.

We stood at the bar with me sandwiched between them, each with an arm around me, and I heard brains light up all around the room with little fantasies, some of which startled even me, and I've seen the most bizarre things people can imagine. Yep, it's all there for lucky me to see in living color.

"We bring you greetings from our grandfather," Claude

said. His voice was so quiet and liquid that I was sure no one else would be able to hear it. Possibly Sam could, but he was always good for discretion.

"He wonders why you haven't called," Claudine said, "especially considering the events of the other night, in Shreveport."

"Well, that was over with," I said, surprised. "Why tell him about something that had already turned out okay? You were there. But I did try to call him the other night."

"It rang once," Claudine murmured.

"However, a certain person broke my phone so I couldn't complete the call. He told me it was the wrong thing to do, that it would start a war. I lived through that, too. So that was okay."

"You need to talk to Niall, tell him the whole story," Claudine said. She smiled across the room at Catfish Hennessy, who put his beer mug down on the table so hard that it slopped over. "Now that Niall's made himself known to you, he wants you to confide in him."

"Why can't he pick up the phone like everyone else in the world?"

"He doesn't spend all his time in this world," Claude said. "There are still places for only our kind."

"Very small places," Claudine said longingly. "But very special."

I was glad to have kin, and I was always glad to see Claudine, who was literally my lifesaver. But the two sibs together were a little overpowering, overwhelming—and when they stood so close with me crowded between them (even Sam was having a visual from that), their sweet smell, the smell that made them so intoxicating to vampires, was drowning my poor nose.

"Look," Claude said, mildly amused. "I think we have company."

Arlene was sidling nearer, looking at Claude as if she'd spied a whole plate of barbecue and onion rings. "Who's your friend, Sookie?" she asked.

"This is Claude," I said. "He's my distant cousin."

"Well, Claude, nice to meet ya," Arlene said.

She had some nerve, considering the way she felt about me now and how she'd treated me since she'd started going to the Fellowship of the Sun services.

Claude looked massively uninterested. He nodded.

Arlene had expected more, and after a moment of silence, she pretended to hear someone from one of her tables calling her. "Gotta go get a pitcher!" she said brightly, and bustled off. I saw her bend over a table, talking very seriously to a couple of guys I didn't know.

"It's always good to see you two, but I *am* at work," I said. "So, did you just come to tell me my . . . that Niall wants to know why I called once and hung up?"

"And never called thereafter to explain," Claudine said. She bent down to kiss my cheek. "Please call him tonight when you get off work."

"Okay," I said. "I still wish he'd called me himself to ask." Messengers were all well and good, but the phone was quicker. And I'd like to hear his voice. No matter where my great-grandfather might be, he could wink back into this world to call if he really was that taxed about my safety.

I thought he could, anyway.

Of course, I didn't know what being a fairy prince entailed. Write that down under "problems I know I'll never face."

After another round of hugs and kisses, the twins sauntered out of the bar, and many wistful eyes followed them on their progress out the door.

"Hoo, Sookie, you got some hot friends!" Catfish Hennessy called, and there was a general tide of agreement.

"I've seen that guy at a club in Monroe. Doesn't he strip?" said a nurse named Debi Murray who worked at the hospital in nearby Clarice. She was sitting with a couple of other nurses.

"Yeah," I said. "He owns the club, too."

"Looks *and* loot," said one of the other nurses. Her name was Beverly something. "I'm taking my daughter next ladies' night. She just broke up with a real loser."

"Well . . ." I debated explaining that Claude wouldn't be interested in anyone's daughter, then decided that wasn't my responsibility. "Have a good time," I said instead.

Since I'd taken time out with my sort-of cousins, I had to hustle to sweeten everyone up. Though they hadn't had my attention during the visit, they had had the entertainment of the twins, so no one was really miffed.

Toward the end of my shift, Copley Carmichael walked in.

He looked funny alone. I assumed Marley was waiting in the car.

In his beautiful suit and with his expensive haircut, he didn't exactly fit in, but I got to give him credit: he acted like he came into places like Merlotte's all the time. I happened to be standing by Sam, who was mixing a bourbon and Coke for one of my tables. I explained to Sam who the stranger was.

I delivered the drink and nodded at an empty table. Mr. Carmichael took the hint and settled in.

"Hey! Can I get you a drink, Mr. Carmichael?" I said.

"Please get me a single malt scotch," he said. "Whatever you've got will be fine. I'm meeting someone here, Sookie, thanks to your phone call. You just tell me the next time you need anything, and I'll do everything in my power to make it happen."

"Not necessary, Mr. Carmichael."

"Please, call me Cope."

"Um-hmmm. Okay, let me get your scotch."

I didn't know a single malt scotch from a hole in the ground, but Sam did, of course, and he gave me a shining clean glass with a very respectable shot of it. I serve liquor, but I seldom drink it. Most folks around here drink the real obvious stuff: beer, bourbon and Coke, gin and tonic, Jack Daniel's.

I set the drink and cocktail napkin on the table in front of Mr. Carmichael, and I returned with a little bowl of snack mix.

Then I left him alone, because I had other people to tend to. But I kept track of him. I noticed Sam was keeping a careful eye on Amelia's dad, too. But everyone else was too involved in their own conversations and their own drinking to give much mind to the stranger, one not nearly as interesting as Claude and Claudine.

In a moment when I wasn't looking, a vampire joined Cope. I don't think anyone else knew what she was. She was a real recent vamp, by which I mean she'd died in the past fifty years, and she had prematurely silver hair that was cut in a modest chin-length style. She was small, maybe five foot two, and she was round and firm in all the right places. She was wearing little silver-rimmed glasses that were sheer affectation, because I'd never met a vampire whose eyesight wasn't absolutely perfect and in fact sharper than any human's.

"Can I get you some blood?" I asked.

Her eyes were like lasers. Once she was really giving you her attention, you were sorry.

"You're the woman Sookie," she said.

I didn't see any need to affirm what she was so sure of. I waited.

"A glass of TrueBlood, please," she said. "Quite warm. And I'd like to meet your boss, if you would fetch him."

Like Sam was a bone. Nonetheless, she was a customer and I was a barmaid. So I heated a TrueBlood for her and told Sam he was wanted.

"I'll be there in a minute," he said, because he was getting a tray of drinks ready for Arlene.

I nodded and took the blood over to the vampire.

"Thank you," she said civilly. "I'm Sandy Sechrest, the new area rep for the King of Louisiana."

I had no idea where Sandy had grown up, but it had been in the United States and had not been in the south. "Pleased to meet you," I said, but not with a whole lot of enthusiasm. Area rep? Wasn't that what sheriffs were, among their other functions? What did that mean for Eric?

At that moment Sam came to the table, and I left because I didn't want to look inquisitive. Besides, I could probably pick it up from his brain later if Sam chose not to tell me what the new vampire wanted. He was good at blocking, but he had to make a special effort to do it.

The three engaged in a conversation for a couple of minutes, then Sam excused himself to get back behind the bar.

I glanced at the vampire and the mogul from time to time in case they needed something more to drink, but neither of them indicated a thirst. They were talking very seriously, and both of them were adept at maintaining a poker face. I didn't care enough to try to latch onto Mr. Carmichael's thoughts, and of course Sandy Sechrest was a blank to me.

The rest of the night was the usual stuff. I didn't even notice when the new king's rep and Mr. Carmichael left. Then it was time to close everything out and get my tables ready for Terry Bellefleur to come in and clean early in the morning. By the time I really looked around me, everyone was gone but Sam and me.

"Hey, you through?" he said.

"Yeah," I said after another look around.

"You got a minute?"

I always had a minute for Sam.

Chapter 16

He sat in the chair behind his desk and tilted it back at the usual dangerous angle. I sat in one of the chairs in front of the desk, the one with the most padding in the seat. Most of the lights in the building were out except the one that stayed on over the bar area and the one in Sam's office. The building rang with silence after the cacophony of voices rising over the jukebox and the sounds of cooking, washing, footsteps.

"That Sandy Sechrest," he said. "She's got a whole new job."

"Yeah? What the king's rep supposed to do?"

"Well, as far as I can tell, she'll travel the state pretty much constantly, seeing if the citizens have problems with any vampires, seeing if the sheriffs have everything in order and under control in their own fiefs, and reporting in to the king. She's like an undead troubleshooter."

"Oh." I thought that over. I couldn't see that the job would detract from Eric's. If Eric was okay, his crew would be okay. Other than that, I didn't care what the vampires did. "So, she decided to meet you because . . . ?"

"She understood I had associations in the regional supernatural community," Sam said dryly. "She wanted me to know she was available to consult in the event 'problems arose.' I have her business card." He held it up. I don't know if I expected it to drip with blood or what, but it was only a regular business card.

"Okay." I shrugged.

"What did Claudine and her brother want?" Sam asked.

I was feeling very bad about concealing my new great-grandfather from Sam, but Niall had told me to keep him a secret. "She hadn't heard from me since the fight in Shreveport," I said. "She just wanted to check up, and she got Claude to come with her."

Sam looked at me a little sharply but he didn't comment. "Maybe," he said after a minute, "this will be a long era of peace. Maybe we can just work in the bar and nothing will happen in the supe community. I'm hoping so, because the time is coming closer and closer when the Weres are going to go public."

"You think it's soon?" I had no idea how America would react to the news that vampires were not the only things out there in the night. "You think all the other shifters will announce the same night?"

"We'll have to," Sam said. "We're talking on our website about it."

Sam did have a life that was unknown to me. That sparked

a thought. I hesitated, then plowed ahead. There were too many questions in my own life. I wanted to get at least some of them answered.

"How'd you come to settle here?" I asked.

"I'd passed through the area," he said. "I was in the army for four years."

"You were?" I couldn't believe I hadn't known that.

"Yeah," he said. "I didn't know what I wanted to do in my life, so I joined when I was eighteen. My mom cried and my dad swore since I'd been accepted to a college, but I'd made up my mind. I was about the stubbornest teenager on the planet."

"Where'd you grow up?"

"At least partly in Wright, Texas," he said. "Outside of Fort Worth. Way outside of Fort Worth. It wasn't any bigger than Bon Temps. We moved around all during my childhood, though, because my dad was in the service himself. He got out when I was about fourteen, and my mom's family was in Wright, so that's where we went."

"Was it hard settling down after moving so much?" I'd never lived anywhere but Bon Temps.

"It was great," he said. "I was so ready to stay in one place. I hadn't realized how hard it would be to find my own niche in a group of kids who'd grown up together, but I was able to take care of myself. I played baseball and basketball, so I found my place. Then I joined the army. Go figure."

I was fascinated. "Are your mom and dad still in Wright?" I asked. "It must have been hard for him in the military, with him being a shifter." Since Sam was a shapeshifter, I knew without him having to tell me that he was the first-born child of pure-blooded shapeshifters.

"Yeah, the full moons were a bitch. There was an herbal drink his Irish grandmother used to make. He learned how to make it himself. It was foul beyond belief, but he drank it on full moons when he had to be on duty and had to be seen all night, and that helped him maintain. . . . But you didn't want to be around him the next day. Dad passed away about six years ago, left me a chunk of money. I'd always liked this area, and this bar was up for sale. It seemed like a good way to invest the money."

"And your mom?"

"She's still in Wright. She married again about two years after Dad died. He's a good enough guy. He's regular." Not a shifter or any kind of supernatural. "So there's a limit to how close I can get to him," Sam said.

"Your mom's a full-blood. Surely he suspects."

"He's willfully blind, I think. She has to go out for her evening run, she says, or she's spending the night with her sister in Waco, or she's driving over to visit me, or some other excuse."

"Must be hard to maintain."

"I would never try to do that. I almost married a regular girl once, while I was in the service. But I just couldn't marry someone and keep that big a secret. It saves my sanity, having someone to talk to about it, Sookie." He smiled at me, and I appreciated the trust he was showing. "If the Weres announce, then we'll all go public. It'll be a great burden off me."

We both knew there would be new problems to face, but there wasn't any need to talk about future trouble. Trouble always came at its own pace.

"You got any sisters or brothers?" I asked.

"One of each. My sister is married with two kids, and my brother is still single. He's a great guy." Sam was smiling and his face looked more relaxed than I'd ever seen. "Craig's getting married in the spring, he says," Sam went on. "Maybe you can go to the wedding with me."

I was so astonished I didn't know what to say, and I was very flattered and pleased. "That sounds like fun. Tell me when you know the date," I said. Sam and I had gone out, once, and it had been very pleasant; but it was in the midst of my problems with Bill and the evening had never been repeated.

Sam nodded casually, and the little jolt of tension that had run through me evaporated. After all, this was *Sam*, my boss, and come to think of it, also one of my best friends. He'd clicked into that slot during the past year. I got up. I had my purse, and I pulled on my jacket.

"Did you get an invitation for the Fangtasia Halloween party this year?" he asked.

"No. After the last party they invited me to, they might not want me to come back," I said. "Besides, with all the recent losses, I don't know if Eric'll feel like celebrating."

"You think we ought to have a Halloween party at Merlotte's?" he asked.

"Maybe not with candy and stuff like that," I said, thinking hard. "Maybe a goodie bag for each customer, with dry roasted peanuts? Or a bowl of orange popcorn on each table? And some decorations?"

Sam looked in the direction of the bar as if he could see through the walls. "That sounds good. Make a thing of it." Ordinarily we only decorated for Christmas, and that only after Thanksgiving, at Sam's insistence.

I waved good night and left the bar, leaving Sam to check that everything was locked tight.

The night had a cold bite to it. This would be one of the Halloweens that really felt like the Halloweens I'd seen in children's books.

In the center of the parking lot, his face turned up to the sliver of moon, his eyes closed, stood my great-grandfather. His pale hair hung down his back like a thick curtain. His myriad of fine creases were invisible in the moonlight, or else he'd divested himself of them. He was carrying his cane, and once again he was wearing a suit, a black suit. There was a heavy ring on his right hand, the hand gripping the cane.

He was the most beautiful being I'd ever seen.

He didn't look remotely like a human grandfather. Human grandfathers wore gimme caps from the John Deere place and overalls. They took you fishing. They let you ride on their tractors. They groused at you for being too pampered and then they bought you candy. As for human great-grandfathers, most of us hardly got to know ours.

I became aware of Sam standing by my side.

"Who is that?" he breathed.

"That's my, ah, my great-granddad," I said. He was right there in front of me. I had to explain.

"Oh," he said, his voice was full of amazement.

"I just found out," I said apologetically.

Niall stopped soaking up the moonlight and his eyes opened. "My great-granddaughter," he said, as if my presence in the Merlotte's parking lot was a pleasant surprise. "Who is your friend?"

"Niall, this is Sam Merlotte, who owns this bar," I said.

Sam extended his hand cautiously, and after a good look at it, Niall touched it with his own. I could feel Sam give a slight jerk, as if my great-grandfather had had a buzzer in his hand.

"Great-granddaughter," Niall said, "I hear you were in danger in the fracas between the werewolves."

"Yes, but Sam was with me, and then Claudine came," I said, feeling oddly defensive. "I didn't know there was going to be a fracas, as you put it, when I went. I was trying to be a peacemaker. We were ambushed."

"Yes, that's what Claudine reported," he said. "I understand the bitch is dead?"

By which he meant Priscilla. "Yes, sir," I said. "The bitch is dead."

"And then you were in danger again one night later?"

I was beginning to feel definitely guilty of something. "Well, that's not actually my norm," I said. "It just happened that the vampires of Louisiana got overrun by the vampires of Nevada."

Niall seemed only mildly interested. "But you went as far as dialing the number I left you."

"Ah, yes, sir, I was pretty scared. But then Eric knocked the phone out of my hand because he thought if you came into the equation, there'd be an out-and-out war. As it turned out, I guess that was for the best, because he surrendered to Victor Madden." I was still a little angry about it, though, even after Eric's gift of the replacement phone.

"Ahhh."

I couldn't make head nor tail of that noncommittal sound. This might be the downside of having a great-grandfather on site. I'd been called on the carpet. It was a feeling I hadn't had since I was a young teen and Gran had found out I'd skipped taking out the trash and folding the laundry. I didn't like the feeling now any more than I'd liked it then.

"I love your courage," Niall said unexpectedly. "But you are very frail—mortal, breakable, and short-lived. I don't want to lose you just when I finally became able to speak to you."

"I don't know what to say," I muttered.

"You don't want me to stop you from doing anything. You won't change. How can I protect you?"

"I don't think you can, not a hundred percent."

"Then what use am I to you?"

"You don't have to be of use to me," I said, surprised. He didn't seem to have the emotional set I had. I didn't know how to explain it to him. "It's enough for me—it's wonderful—just knowing you exist. That you care about me. That I have living family, no matter how distant and different. And you don't think I'm weird or crazy or embarrassing."

"Embarrassing?" He looked puzzled. "You're far more interesting than most humans."

"Thank you for not thinking I'm defective," I said.

"Other humans think you're *defective*?" Niall sounded genuinely outraged.

"They can't be comfortable sometimes," Sam said unexpectedly. "Knowing she can read their minds."

"But you, shapeshifter?"

"I think she's great," Sam said. And I could tell he was absolutely sincere.

My back straightened. I felt a flush of pride. In the emotional warmth of the moment, I almost told my great-grandfather about the big problem I'd uncovered today, to prove I could share. But I had a pretty good feeling that his solution to the Sandra Pelt–Tanya Grissom Axis of Evil would be to cause their deaths in a macabre way. My sort-of cousin Claudine might be trying to become an angel, a being I associated with Christianity, but Niall Brigant was definitely from another ethos entirely. I suspected his outlook was, "I'll take your eye ahead of time, just in case you want mine." Well, maybe not that preemptive, but close.

"There is nothing I can do for you?" He sounded almost plaintive.

"I'd really like it if you'd just come spend some time with me at the house, when you have some to spare. I'd like to cook you supper. If you want to do that?" It made me feel shy, offering him something I wasn't sure he'd value.

He looked at me with glowing eyes. I could not read his face, and though his body was shaped like a human body, he was not. He was a complete puzzle to me. Maybe he was exasperated or bored or repulsed by my suggestion.

Finally Niall said, "Yes. I'll do that. I'll tell you ahead of time, of course. In the meantime, if you need anything of me, call the number. Don't let anyone dissuade you if you think I can be of help. I will have words with Eric. He's been useful to me in the past, but he can't second-guess me with you."

"Has he known I was your kin for very long?" I held my breath, waiting for the answer.

Niall had turned to go. Now he turned back a little, so I saw his face in profile. "No," he said. "I had to know him better, first. I told him only before he brought you to meet me. He wouldn't help me until I told him why I wanted you."

And then he was gone. It was like he'd walked through a door we couldn't see, and for all I knew, that was exactly what he'd done.

"Okay," Sam said after a long moment. "Okay, that was really . . . different."

"Are you all right with all this?" I waved a hand toward the spot where Niall had been standing. Probably. Unless what we'd seen had been some astral projection or something.

"It's not my place to be okay with it. It's your thing," Sam said.

"I want to love him," I said. "He's so beautiful and he seems to care so much, but he's really, really . . ."

"Scary," Sam finished.

"Yeah."

"And he approached you through Eric?"

Since apparently my great-grandfather thought it was okay if Sam knew about him, I told Sam about my first meeting with Niall.

"Hmmm. Well, I don't know what to make of that. Vampires and fairies don't interact, because of the vampire tendency to eat fairies."

"Niall can mask his scent," I explained proudly.

Sam looked overloaded with information. "That's another thing I've never heard of. I hope Jason doesn't know about this?"

"Oh, God, no."

"You know he'd be jealous and that would make him mad at you."

"Since I know Niall and he doesn't?"

"Yep. Envy would just eat Jason up."

"I know Jason's not the world's most generous person," I began, to be cut off when Sam snorted. "Okay," I said, "he's selfish. But he's still my brother anyway, and I have to stick by him. But maybe it's better if I never tell him. Still, Niall didn't have any problem showing himself to *you*, after telling me to keep him a secret."

"I'm guessing he did some checking up," Sam said mildly. He hugged me, which was a welcome surprise. I felt like I needed a hug after Niall's drop-in. I hugged Sam back. He felt warm, and comforting, and human.

But neither of us was 100 percent human.

In the next instant, I thought, *We are, too.* We had more in common with humans than with the other part of us. We lived like humans; we would die like humans. Since I knew Sam pretty well, I knew he wanted a family and someone to love and a future that contained all the things plain humans want: prosperity, good health, descendants, laughter. Sam didn't want to be a leader of any pack, and I didn't want to be princess of anybody—not that any pureblood fairy would ever think I was anything other than a lowly by-product of their own wonderfulness. That was one of the big differences between Jason and me. Jason would spend his life wishing he was more supernatural than he was; I had spent mine wishing I was less, if my telepathy was indeed supernatural.

Sam kissed me on the cheek, and then after a moment's hesitation, he turned to go into his trailer, walking through the gate in the carefully trimmed hedge and up the steps to the little deck he'd built outside his door. When he'd inserted the key, he turned to smile at me.

"Some night, huh?"

"Yeah," I said. "Some night."

Sam watched while I got in my car, made a pressing gesture to remind me to lock my car doors, waited while I complied, and then went into his trailer. I drove home preoccupied with deep questions and shallow ones, and it was lucky there wasn't any traffic on the road.

Chapter 17

Amelia and Octavia were sitting at the kitchen table the next day when I shambled out. Amelia had used up all the coffee, but at least she'd washed the pot and it took only a few minutes to make myself a much-needed cup. Amelia and her mentor kept a tactful conversation going while I bumbled around getting some cereal, adding some sweetener, pouring milk over it. I hunched over the bowl because I didn't want to dribble milk down my tank top. And by the way, it was getting too cold to wear a tank top around the house. I pulled on a cheap jacket made of sweats material and was able to finish my coffee and cereal in comfort.

"What's up, you two?" I asked, signaling I was ready to interact with the rest of the world.

"Amelia told me about your problem," Octavia said. "And about your very kind offer."

Ah-oh. What offer?

I nodded wisely, as if I had a clue.

"I'll be so glad to be out of my niece's house, you have no idea," the older woman said earnestly. "Janesha has three little ones, including one toddler, and a boyfriend that comes and goes. I'm sleeping on the living room couch, and when the kids get up in the morning, they come in and turn on the cartoons. Whether or not I'm up. It's their house, of course, and I've been there for weeks, so they've lost the sense that I'm company."

I gathered that Octavia was going to be sleeping in the bedroom opposite me or in the extra one upstairs. I was voting for the one upstairs.

"And you know, now that I'm older, I need quicker access to a bathroom." She looked at me with that humorous deprecation people show when they're admitting to a passage-of-time condition. "So downstairs would be wonderful, especially since my knees are arthritic. Did I tell you Janesha's apartment is upstairs?"

"No," I said through numb lips. Geez, this had happened so fast.

"Now, about your problem. I'm not a black witch at all, but you need to get these young women out of your life, both Ms. Pelt's agent and Ms. Pelt herself."

I nodded vigorously.

"So," Amelia said, unable to keep quiet any longer, "we've come up with a plan."

"I'm all ears," I said, and poured myself a second cup of coffee. I needed it.

"The simplest way to get rid of Tanya, of course, is to tell your friend Calvin Norris what she's doing," Octavia said.

I gaped at her. "Ah, that seems likely to result in some pretty bad things happening to Tanya," I said.

"Isn't that what you want?" Octavia looked innocent in a real sly way.

"Well, yeah, but I don't want her to die. I mean, I don't want anything she can't get over to happen to her. I just want her away and not coming back."

Amelia said, " 'Away and not coming back' sounds pretty final to me."

It sounded that way to me, too. "I'll rephrase. I want her to be off somewhere living her life but far away from me," I said. "Is that clear enough?" I wasn't trying to sound sharp; I just wanted to express myself.

"Yes, young lady, I think we can understand that," said Octavia with frost in her voice.

"I don't want there to be any misunderstanding here," I said. "There's a lot at stake. I think Calvin kind of likes Tanya. On the other hand, I bet he could scare her pretty effectively."

"Enough to get her to leave forever?"

"You'd have to demonstrate that you were telling the truth," Amelia said. "About her sabotaging you."

"What do you have in mind?" I asked.

"Okay, here's what we think," Amelia said, and just like that, Phase One was in place. It turned out to be something I could have thought of myself, but the witches' help made the planning run much more smoothly.

I called Calvin at home, and asked him to stop by when he had a minute to spare around lunchtime. He sounded surprised to hear from me, but he agreed to come.

He got a further surprise when he came into the kitchen and found Amelia and Octavia there. Calvin, the leader of the werepanthers who lived in the little community of Hotshot, had met Amelia several times before, but Octavia was new to him. He respected her immediately because he was able to sense her power. That was a big help.

Calvin was probably in his midforties, strong and solid, sure of himself. His hair was graying, but he was straight as an arrow in posture, and he possessed a huge calm that couldn't fail to impress. He'd been interested in me for a while, and I'd only been sorry I couldn't feel the same way. He was a good man.

"What's up, Sookie?" he said after he'd turned down the offer of cookies or tea or Coke.

I took a deep breath. "I don't like to be a tale-teller, Calvin, but we have a problem," I said.

"Tanya," he said immediately.

"Yeah," I said, not bothering to hide my relief.

"She's a sly one," he said, and I was sorry to hear an element of admiration in his voice.

"She's a spy," Amelia said. Amelia could cut right to the chase.

"Who for?" Calvin tilted his head to one side, unsurprised and curious.

I told him an edited version of the story, a story I was extremely sick of repeating. Calvin needed to know that the

Pelts had a big beef with me, that Sandra would hound me to my grave, that Tanya had been planted as a gadfly.

Calvin stretched out his legs while he listened, his arms crossed over his chest. He was wearing brand-new jeans and a plaid shirt. He smelled like fresh-cut trees.

"You want to put a spell on her?" he asked Amelia when I'd finished.

"We do," she said. "But we need you to get her here."

"What would the effect be? Would it hurt her?"

"She'd lose interest in doing harm to Sookie and all her family. She wouldn't want to obey Sandra Pelt anymore. It wouldn't hurt her physically at all."

"Would this change her mentally?"

"No," Octavia said. "But it's not as sure a spell as the one that would make her not want to be here anymore. If we cast that one, she'd leave here, and she wouldn't want to come back."

Calvin mulled this over. "I kind of like that ole girl," he said. "She's a live one. I've been pretty concerned over the trouble she's causing Crystal and Jason, though, and I've been wondering what steps to take about Crystal's crazy spending. I guess this kind of brings the issue front and center."

"You like her?" I said. I wanted all cards on the table.

"I said that."

"No, I mean, you *like* her."

"Well, her and me, we've had some good times now and then."

"You don't want her to go away," I said. "You want to try the other thing."

"That's about the size of it. You're right: she can't stay and keep on going like she is. She either changes her ways, or she leaves." He looked unhappy about that. "You working today, Sookie?"

I looked at the wall calendar. "No, it's my day off." I'd have two days in a row off.

"I'll get aholt of her and bring her by tonight. That give you ladies enough time?"

The two witches looked at each other and consulted silently.

"Yes, that will be fine," Octavia said.

"I'll get her here by seven," Calvin said.

This was moving with unexpected smoothness.

"Thanks, Calvin," I said. "This is really helpful."

"This'll kill a lot of birds with one stone, if it works," Calvin said. "Of course, if it don't work, you two ladies won't be my favorite people." His voice was completely matter-of-fact.

The two witches didn't look happy.

Calvin eyed Bob, who happened to stroll into the room. "Hello, brother," Calvin said to the cat. He gave Amelia a narrowed-eye look. "Seems to me like your magic don't work all the time."

Amelia looked guilty and offended simultaneously. "We'll get this to work," she said, tight-lipped. "You just see."

"I aim to."

I spent the rest of the day doing my laundry, redoing my nails, changing my sheets—all those tasks you save up for your day off. I went by the library to swap books and absolutely nothing happened. One of Barbara Beck's part-time assistants was on duty, which was good. I didn't want to experience the horror of the attack all over again, as I surely would in every encounter with Barbara for a long time to come. I noticed the stain was gone from the library floor.

After that, I went to the grocery store. No Weres attacked, no vampires rose. No one tried to kill me or anyone I knew. No secret relatives revealed themselves, and not a soul tried to involve me in his or her problems, marital or otherwise.

I was practically reeking with normality by the time I got home.

Tonight was my cooking night, and I'd decided to fix pork chops. I have a favorite homemade breading mix that I make in a huge batch, so I soaked the chops in milk and then dredged them with the mix so they were ready for the oven. I fixed baked apples stuffed with raisins and cinnamon and butter and popped them in to bake and I flavored some canned green beans and some canned corn and put them on low heat. After a while, I opened the oven to put in the meat. I thought about making biscuits, but there seemed to be more than enough calories on board.

While I cooked, the witches were doing stuff in the living room. They seemed to be having a good old time. I could hear Octavia's voice, which sounded very much like it was in teaching mode. Every now and then, Amelia would ask a question.

I did a lot of muttering to myself while I cooked. I hoped this magical procedure worked, and I was grateful to the witches for being so willing to help. But I was feeling a little sideswiped on the domestic front. My brief mention to Amelia that Octavia could stay with us for a little while had been a spur of the moment thing. (I could tell I was going to have to be more careful in conversations with my roomie from now on.) Octavia hadn't said she'd be in my house for a weekend, or a month, or any measure of time. That scared me.

I could have cornered Amelia and told her, "You didn't ask me if Octavia could stay *right now at this moment*, and it's my house," I supposed. But I *did* have a free room, and Octavia *did* need someplace to stay. It was a little late to discover that I wasn't entirely happy at having a third person in the house—a third person I barely knew.

Maybe I could find a job for Octavia, because regular earnings would allow the older woman her independence and she'd move out of here. I wondered about the state of her house in New Orleans. I assumed it was unlivable. For all the power she had, I guess even Octavia couldn't undo the damage a hurricane had done. After her references to stairs and increased bathroom needs, I'd revised her age upward, but she still didn't seem any older than, say, sixty-three. That was practically a spring chicken, these days.

I called Octavia and Amelia to the table at six o'clock. I had the table set and the iced tea poured, but I let them serve their own plates from the stove. Not elegant, but it did save on dishes.

We didn't talk a lot as we ate. All three of us were thinking about the evening to come. As much as I disliked her, I was a little worried about Tanya.

I felt funny about the idea of altering someone, but the bottom line was, I needed Tanya off my back and out of my life and the lives of those around me. Or I needed her to get a new attitude about what she was doing in Bon Temps. I couldn't see any way around those facts. In line with my new practicality, I'd realized that if I had to choose between continuing my life with Tanya's interference or continuing my life with Tanya altered, there was no contest.

I cleared the plates away. Normally, if one of us cooked, the other did the dishes, but the two women had magical preparations to make. It was just as well; I wanted to keep busy.

We heard the gravel crunching under the wheels of a truck at 7:05.

When we'd asked him to have her here at seven, I hadn't realized he'd bring her as a parcel.

Calvin carried Tanya in over his shoulder. Tanya was compact, but no featherweight. Calvin was definitely working, but his breathing was nice and even and he hadn't broken a sweat. Tanya's hands and ankles were bound, but I noticed he'd wrapped a scarf under the rope so she wouldn't get chafed. And (thank God) she was gagged, but with a jaunty red bandanna. Yes, the head werepanther definitely had a thing for Tanya.

Of course, she was mad as a disturbed rattler, wriggling and twisting and glaring. She tried to kick Calvin, and he slapped her on her butt. "You stop that now," he said, but not as if he was particularly upset. "You've done wrong; you got to take your medicine."

He'd come in the front door, and now he dumped Tanya on the couch.

The witches had drawn some things in chalk on the floor of the living room, a process that hadn't found much favor with me. Amelia had assured me she could clean it all up, and since she was a champion cleaner, I'd let them proceed.

There were various piles of things (I really didn't want to look too closely) set around in bowls. Octavia lit the material in one bowl and carried it over to Tanya. She wafted the smoke toward Tanya with her hand. I took an extra step back, and Calvin, who was standing behind the couch and holding Tanya by the shoulders, turned his head. Tanya held her breath as long as she could.

After breathing the smoke, she relaxed.

"She needs to be sitting there," Octavia said, pointing to an area circled by chalky symbols. Calvin plonked Tanya down on a straight-backed chair in the middle. She stayed put, thanks to the mysterious smoke.

Octavia started chanting in a language I didn't understand. Amelia's spells had always been in Latin, or at least a primitive form of it (she'd told me that), but I thought Octavia was more diverse. She was speaking something that sounded entirely different.

I'd been very nervous about this ritual, but it turned out to be pretty boring unless you were one of the participants. I wished I could open the windows to get the smell of the smoke out of the house, and I was glad Amelia had thought to take the batteries out of the smoke detectors. Tanya was clearly feeling something, but I wasn't sure it was the removal of the Pelt effect.

"Tanya Grissom," Octavia said, "yank the roots of evil out of your soul and remove yourself from the influence of those who would use you for evil ends." Octavia made several gestures over

Tanya while holding a curious item that looked awfully like a human bone wound around with a vine. I tried not to wonder where she'd gotten the bone.

Tanya squealed beneath her gag, and her back arched alarmingly. Then she relaxed.

Amelia made a gesture, and Calvin bent over to untie the red bandanna that had made Tanya look like a small bandit. He pulled another handkerchief, a clean white one, out of Tanya's mouth. She'd definitely been abducted with affection and consideration.

"I can't believe you're doing this to me!" Tanya shrieked the second her mouth would work. "I can't believe you kidnapped me like a caveman, you big jerk!" If her hands had been free, Calvin would have taken a pummeling. "And what the hell is up with this smoke? Sookie, are you trying to burn your house down? Hey, woman, would you get that crap out of my face?" Tanya batted at the vine-wrapped bone with her bound hands.

"I'm Octavia Fant."

"Well, goody, Octavia Fant. Get me out of these ropes!"

Octavia and Amelia exchanged glances.

Tanya appealed to me. "Sookie, tell these nuts to let me go! Calvin, I was halfway interested in you before you tied me up and dumped me here! What did you think you were doing?"

"Saving your life," Calvin said. "You ain't gonna run now, are you? We got some talking to do."

"Okay," Tanya said slowly, as she realized (I could hear her) that something serious was afoot. "What's all this about?"

"Sandra Pelt," I said.

"Yeah, I know Sandra. What about her?"

"What's your connection?" Amelia asked.

"What's your interest, Amy?" Tanya countered.

"Amelia," I corrected, sitting on the big ottoman in front of Tanya. "And you need to answer this question."

Tanya gave me a sharp look—she had a repertoire of them—and said, "I used to have a cousin who was adopted by the Pelts, and Sandra was my cousin's adopted sister."

"Do you have a close friendship with Sandra?" I said.

"No, not especially. I haven't seen her in a while."

"You didn't make a bargain with her recently?"

"No, Sandra and I don't see each other too much."

"What do you think of her?" Octavia asked.

"I think she's a double-barreled bitch. But I sort of admire her," Tanya said. "If Sandra wants something, she goes after it." She shrugged. "She's kind of extreme for my taste."

"So if she told you to ruin someone's life, you wouldn't do it?" Octavia was eyeing Tanya intently.

"I got better fish to fry than that," Tanya said. "She can go around ruining lives on her own, if she wants to do it so bad."

"You wouldn't be a part of that?"

"No," Tanya said. She was sincere, I could tell. In fact, she was beginning to get anxious at our line of questioning. "Ah, have I done something bad to somebody?"

"I think you got in a little over your head," Calvin said. "These nice ladies have intervened. Amelia and Miss Octavia are, ah, wise women. And you know Sookie already."

"Yeah, I know Sookie." Tanya gave me a sour look. "She won't make friends with me no matter what I do."

Well, yeah, I didn't want you close enough to stab me in the back, I thought, but I didn't say anything.

"Tanya, you've taken my sister-in-law shopping a little too much lately," I said.

Tanya burst into laughter. "Too much retail therapy for the pregnant bride?" she said. But then she looked puzzled. "Yeah, it does seem like we went to the mall in Monroe too many times for my checkbook. Where'd I get the money? I don't even like shopping that much. Why'd I do that?"

"You're not going to do it anymore," Calvin said.

"You don't tell me what I'm going to do, Calvin Norris!" Tanya shot back. "I won't go shopping because I don't want to go, not because you tell me not to."

Calvin looked relieved.

Amelia and Octavia looked relieved.

We all nodded simultaneously. This was Tanya, all right. And she seemed to be minus the destructive guidance of Sandra Pelt. I didn't know if Sandra had whipped up some witchcraft of her own, or if she'd just offered Tanya a lot of money and talked her into thinking Debbie's death was my fault, but the witches appeared to have been successful in excising the tainted Sandra portion of Tanya's character.

I felt oddly deflated at this easy—easy to me, that is—removal of a real thorn in my side. I found myself wishing we could abduct Sandra Pelt and reprogram her, too. I didn't think she'd be as easy to convert. There had been some big pathology going on in the Pelt family.

The witches were happy. Calvin was pleased. I was relieved. Calvin told Tanya he was going to take her back to Hotshot. The somewhat-puzzled Tanya made her departure with a lot more dignity than her entrance. She didn't understand why she'd been in my house and she didn't seem to remember what the witches had done. But she also didn't seem upset about that confusion in her memory.

The best of all possible worlds.

Maybe Jason and Crystal could work things out now that Tanya's pernicious influence was gone. After all, Crystal had really wanted to marry Jason, and she had seemed genuinely pleased that she was pregnant again. Why she was so discontented now . . . I simply didn't get it.

I could add her to the long list of people I didn't understand.

While the witches cleaned up the living room with the windows open—though it was a chilly night, I wanted to get rid of the lingering smell of the herbs—I sprawled on my bed with a book. I found I wasn't focused enough to read. Finally, I decided to go outside, and I threw on a hoody and called to Amelia to let her know. I sat in one of the wooden chairs Amelia and I had bought at Wal-Mart at end-of-summer clearance-sale prices, and I admired the matching table with its umbrella all over again. I reminded myself to take the umbrella down and cover the furniture for the winter. Then I leaned back and let go of my thoughts.

For a while it was nice to simply be outside, smelling the

trees and the ground, hearing a whip-poor-will give its enigmatic call from the surrounding woods. The security light made me feel safe, though I knew that was an illusion. If there's light, you can just see what's coming for you a little more clearly.

Bill stepped out of the woods and strolled silently over to the yard set. He sat in one of the other chairs.

We didn't speak for several moments. I didn't feel the surge of anguish I'd felt over the past few months when he was around. He barely disturbed the fall night with his presence, he was so much a part of it.

"Selah has moved to Little Rock," he said.

"How come?"

"She got a position with a large firm," he said. "It was what she told me she wanted. They specialize in vampire properties."

"She hooked on vamps?"

"I believe so. Not my doing."

"Weren't you her first?" Maybe I sounded a little bitter. He'd been my first, in every way.

"Don't," he said, and turned his face toward me. It was radiantly pale. "No," he said finally. "I was not her first. And I always knew it was the vampire in me that attracted her, not the person who was a vampire."

I understood what he was saying. When I'd learned he'd been ordered to ingratiate himself with me, I'd felt it was the telepath in me that had gotten his attention, not the woman who was the telepath. "What goes around, comes around," I said.

"I never cared about her," he said. "Or very little." He shrugged. "There've been so many like her."

"I'm not sure how you think this is going to make me feel."

"I'm only telling you the truth. There has been only one you." And then he got up and walked back into the woods, human slow, letting me watch him leave.

Apparently Bill was conducting a kind of stealth campaign to win back my regard. I wondered if he dreamed I could love him again. I still felt pain when I thought of the night I'd learned the truth. I figured my regard would be the outer limits of what he could hope to earn. Trust, love? I couldn't see that happening.

I sat outside for a few more minutes, thinking about the evening I'd just had. One enemy agent down. The enemy herself to go. Then I thought of the police search for the missing people, all Weres, in Shreveport. I wondered when they'd give up.

Surely I wouldn't have to deal with Were politics again any time soon; the survivors would be absorbed in setting their house in order.

I hoped Alcide was enjoying being the leader, and I wondered if he'd succeeded in creating yet another little purebred Were the night of the takeover. I wondered who had taken the Furnan children.

As long as I was speculating, I wondered where Felipe de Castro had established his headquarters in Louisiana or if he'd stayed in Vegas. I wondered if anyone had told Bubba that Louisiana was under a new regime, and I wondered if I'd ever see him again. He had one of the most famous faces in the world, but his head had been sadly addled by being brought over at the last possible second by a vampire working in the morgue in Memphis. Bubba had not weathered Katrina well; he'd gotten cut off from the other New Orleans vampires and had had to subsist on rats and small animals (left-behind pet cats, I suspected) until he'd been rescued one night by a search party of Baton Rouge vamps. The last I'd heard, they'd had to send him out of state for rest and recuperation. Maybe he'd wind up in Vegas. He'd always done well in Vegas, when he was alive.

Suddenly, I realized I was stiff with sitting so long, and the night had grown uncomfortably cold. My jacket wasn't doing the job. It was time to go inside and go to bed. The rest of the house was dark, and I figured Octavia and Amelia were exhausted by their witch work.

I heaved myself up from the chair, let the umbrella down, and opened the toolshed door, leaning the umbrella against a bench where the man I'd thought was my grandfather had made repairs. I shut the toolshed door, feeling I was shutting summer inside.

Chapter 18

After a quiet and peaceful Monday off, I went in Tuesday to work the lunch shift. When I'd left home, Amelia had been painting a chest of drawers she'd found at the local junk store. Octavia had been trimming the dead heads off the roses. She'd said they needed pruning back for the winter, and I'd told her to have at it. My grandmother had been the rose person in our household, and she hadn't let me lay a finger on them unless they needed spraying for aphids. That had been one of my jobs.

Jason came into Merlotte's for lunch with a bunch of his coworkers. They put two tables together and formed a cluster of happy men. Cooler weather and no big storms made for happy parish road crews. Jason seemed almost overly animated, his brain a jumble of leaping thoughts. Maybe having the pernicious influence of Tanya erased had already made a difference.

But I made a real effort to stay out of his head, because after all, he was my brother.

When I carried a big tray of Cokes and tea over to the table, Jason said, "Crystal says hey."

"How's she feeling today?" I asked, to show proper concern, and Jason made a circle of his forefinger and thumb. I served the last mug of tea, careful to put it down evenly so it wouldn't spill, and I asked Dove Beck, a cousin of Alcee's, if he wanted any extra lemon.

"No, thanks," he said politely. Dove, who'd gotten married the day after graduation, was a whole different kettle of fish from Alcee. At thirty, he was younger, and as far as I could tell—and I could tell pretty far—he didn't have that inner core of anger that the detective did. I'd gone to school with one of Dove's sisters.

"How's Angela?" I asked him, and he smiled.

"She married Maurice Kershaw," he said. "They got a little boy, cutest kid in the world. Angela's a new woman—she don't smoke or drink, and she's in church when the doors open."

"I'm glad to hear that. Tell her I asked," I said, and began taking orders. I heard Jason telling his buddies about a fence he was going to build, but I didn't have time to pay attention.

Jason lingered after the other men were going out to their vehicles. "Sook, would you run by and check on Crystal when you get off?"

"Sure, but won't you be leaving work then?"

"I got to go over to Clarice and pick up some chain-link. Crystal wants us to fence in some of the backyard for the baby. So it'll have a safe place to play."

I was surprised that Crystal was showing that much foresight and maternal instinct. Maybe having the baby would change her. I thought about Angela Kershaw and her little boy.

I didn't want to count up how many girls younger than me had been married for years and had babies—or just had the babies. I told myself envy was a sin, and I worked hard, smiling and nodding to everyone. Luckily, it was a busy day. During the afternoon lull, Sam asked me to help him take inventory in the storeroom while Holly covered the bar and the floor. We only had our two resident alcoholics to serve, so Holly was not going to have to work very hard. Since I was very nervous with Sam's Blackberry, he entered the totals while I counted, and I had to climb up on a stepladder and then back down about fifty times, counting and dusting. We bought our cleaning supplies in bulk. We counted all those, too. Sam was just a counting fool today.

The storeroom doesn't have any windows, so it got pretty warm in there while we were working. I was glad to get out of its stuffy confines when Sam was finally satisfied. I pulled a spiderweb out of his hair as I went by on my way to the bathroom, where I scrubbed my hands and carefully wiped my face, checking my ponytail (as best I could) for any spiderwebs I might have picked up myself.

As I left the bar, I was so looking forward to getting in the shower that I almost turned left to go home. Just in time, I remembered I'd promised to look in on Crystal, so I turned right instead.

Jason lived in my parents' house, and he'd kept it up very nicely. My brother was a house-proud kind of guy. He didn't mind spending his free time on painting, mowing, and basic repairs, a side of him I always found a bit surprising. He'd recently painted the outside a buff color and the trim a glowing white, and the little house looked very spruce. There was a driveway that made a U shape in front. He'd added a branch that led to the porte cochere in back of the house, but I pulled up to the front steps. I stuffed my car keys in my pocket and crossed the porch. I turned the knob because I planned on sticking my head in the door and calling to Crystal, since I was family. The front door was unlocked, as most front doors were during the daytime. The family room was empty.

"Hey, Crystal, it's Sookie!" I called, though I tried to keep my voice subdued so I wouldn't startle her if she were napping.

I heard a muffled sound, a moan. It came from the biggest bedroom, the one my parents had used, which lay across the family room and to my right.

Oh, shit, she's miscarrying again, I thought, and dashed to the closed door. I flung it open so hard it bounced off the wall, but I didn't pay a bit of attention, because bouncing on the bed were Crystal and Dove Beck.

I was so shocked, so angry, and so distraught that as they stopped what they were doing and stared up at me, I said the worst thing I could think of. "No wonder you lose all your babies." I spun on my heel and marched out of the house. I was so outraged I couldn't even get in the car. It was really unfortunate that Calvin pulled up behind me and leaped from his truck almost before it stopped.

"My God, what's wrong?" he said. "Is Crystal okay?"

"Why don't you ask her that?" I said nastily, and climbed into my car only to sit there shaking. Calvin ran into the house as if he had to put out a fire, and I guess that was about the size of it.

"Jason, *dammit*," I yelled, thumping my fist on my steering wheel. I should have taken the time to listen to Jason's brain. He'd known good and well that since he had business in Clarice, Dove and Crystal would probably take the opportunity to have a tryst. He'd planned on me being dutiful and dropping by. It was just too big a coincidence that Calvin had shown up. He must have also told Calvin to check on Crystal. So there was no deniability, and no chance of hushing this up—not since Calvin and I both knew. I had been right to worry about the terms of the marriage, and now I had something entirely new to worry about.

Plus, I was ashamed. I was ashamed of the behavior of everyone involved. In my code of conduct, which doesn't really make me a very good Christian at all, what single people do in caring relationships is their own business. Even in a more casual relationship—well, if the people respect one another, okay. But a couple who's promised to be faithful, who's pledged that publicly, are governed by a whole different set of rules, in my world.

Not in Crystal's world, or Dove's world, apparently.

Calvin came back down the steps looking years older than he had when he'd bounded up them. He stopped by my car. He wore an expression twin to mine—disillusion, disappointment, disgust. Lots of *dis*es there.

"I'll be in touch," he said. "We got to have the ceremony now."

Crystal came out on the porch wrapped in a leopard-print bathrobe, and rather than endure her speaking to me I started the car and left as quickly as I could. I drove home in a daze. When I came in the back door, Amelia was chopping up something on the old cutting board, the one that had survived the fire with only scorch marks. She turned to speak to me and had opened her mouth when she saw my face. I shook my head at her, warning her not to talk, and I went straight into my room.

This would have been a good day for me to be living by myself again.

I sat in my room in the little chair in the corner, the one that had seated so many visitors lately. Bob was curled up in a ball on my bed, a place he was expressly forbidden to sleep. Someone had opened my door during the day. I thought about chewing Amelia out about that, then discarded the idea when I saw a pile of clean and folded underwear lying on top of my dresser.

"Bob," I said, and the cat unfolded and leaped to his feet in one fluid movement. He stood on my bed, staring at me with wide golden eyes. "Get the hell out of here," I said. With immense dignity Bob leaped down from the bed and stalked to the door. I opened it a few inches and he went out, managing to leave the impression that he was doing this of his own free will. I shut the door behind him.

I love cats. I just wanted to be by myself.

The phone rang, and I stood up to answer it.

"Tomorrow night," Calvin said. "Wear something comfortable. Seven o'clock." He sounded sad and tired.

"Okay," I said, and we both hung up. I sat there a while longer. Whatever this ceremony consisted of, did I have to be a participant? Yeah, I did. Unlike Crystal, I kept my promises. I'd had to stand up for Jason at his wedding, as his closest relative, as a surrogate to take his punishment if he was unfaithful to his new wife. Calvin had stood up for Crystal. And now look what we'd come to.

I didn't know what was going to happen, but I knew it was going to be awful. Though the werepanthers understood the necessity for breeding each available pure male panther to each available pure female panther (the only way to produce purebred baby panthers), they also believed once the breeding had been given a chance, any partnerships formed should be monogamous. If you didn't want to take that vow, you didn't form a partnership or marry. This was the way they ran their community. Crystal would have absorbed these rules from birth, and Jason had learned them from Calvin before the wedding.

Jason didn't call, and I was glad. I wondered what was happening at his house, but only in a dull kind of way. When had Crystal met Dove Beck? Did Dove's wife know about this? I wasn't surprised that Crystal had cheated on Jason, but I was a little astonished at her choice.

I decided that Crystal had wanted to make her betrayal as emphatic as it could possibly be. She was saying, "I'll have sex with someone else while I'm carrying your child. And he'll be older than you, and a different race from you, and he'll even work for you!" Twisting the knife in deeper with every layer.

If this was retaliation for the damn cheeseburger, I'd say she'd gotten a steak-size vengeance.

Because I didn't want to seem like I was sulking, I came out for supper, which was lowly and comforting tuna noodle casserole with peas and onions. After stacking the dishes for Octavia to take care of, I retreated back to my room. The two witches were practically tiptoeing up and down the hall because they were so anxious not to disturb me, though of course they were dying to ask me what the problem was.

But they didn't; God bless them. I really couldn't have explained. I was too mortified.

I said about a million prayers before I went to sleep that night, but none of them ended up making me feel any better.

I went to work the next day because I had to. Staying home wouldn't have made me feel any better. I was profoundly glad Jason didn't come into Merlotte's, because I would have thrown a mug at him if he had.

Sam eyed me carefully several times and finally he drew me behind the bar with him. "Tell me what's happening," he said.

Tears flooded my eyes, and I was within an ace of making a real scene. I squatted down hastily, as if I'd dropped something on the floor, and I said, "Sam, please don't ask me. I'm too upset to talk about it." Suddenly, I realized it would be a big comfort to tell Sam, but I just couldn't, not in the crowded bar.

"Hey, you know I'm here if you need me." His face was serious. He patted my shoulder.

I was so lucky to have him for a boss.

His gesture reminded me that I had lots of friends who would not dishonor themselves as Crystal had done. Jason had dishonored himself, too, by forcing Calvin and me to witness her cheap betrayal. I had so many friends who would not do such a thing! It was a trick of fate that the one who would was my own brother.

This thought made me feel better and stronger.

I actually had a backbone by the time I got home. No one else was there. I hesitated, wondering whether I could call Tara or beg Sam to take an hour off, or even call Bill to go with me to Hotshot . . . but that was just weakness talking. This was something I had to do by myself. Calvin had warned me to wear something comfortable and not to dress up, and my Merlotte's outfit was certainly both those things. But it seemed wrong to wear my work clothes to an event like this. There might be blood. I didn't know what to anticipate. I pulled on yoga pants and an old gray sweatshirt. I made sure my hair was pulled back. I looked like I was dressed to clean out my closets.

On the drive to Hotshot, I turned up the radio and sang at the top of my lungs to keep myself from thinking. I harmonized with Evanescence and agreed with the Dixie Chicks that I wasn't going to back down . . . a good spine-stiffening song to listen to.

I reached Hotshot well before seven. I'd last been out here at Jason and Crystal's wedding, where I'd danced with Quinn. That visit of Quinn's had been the only time he and I had been intimate. In hindsight, I regretted having taken that step. It had been a mistake. I'd been banking on a future that never came to pass. I'd jumped the gun. I hoped I'd never make that mistake again.

I parked, as I had the night of Jason's wedding, by the side of the road. There weren't nearly as many cars here tonight as there had been then, when many plain human people had been guests. But there were a few extra vehicles. I recognized Jason's truck. The others belonged to the few werepanthers who didn't live in Hotshot.

A little crowd had already assembled in the backyard of Calvin's house. People made way for me until I'd gotten to the center of the gathering and found Crystal, Jason, and Calvin. I saw some familiar faces. A middle-aged panther named Maryelizabeth nodded to me. I saw her daughter nearby. The girl, whose name I couldn't remember, was by no means the only underage observer. I got that creepy feeling that raised the hairs on my arms, the way I did every time I tried to picture everyday life in Hotshot.

Calvin was staring down at his boots, and he didn't look up. Jason didn't meet my eyes, either. Only Crystal was upright and defiant, her dark eyes catching mine, daring me to stare her down. I did dare, and after a moment she dropped her gaze to somewhere in the middle distance.

Maryelizabeth had a tattered old book in her hand, and she opened it to a page she'd marked with a torn piece of newspaper. The community seemed to still and settle. This was the purpose for which they'd assembled.

"We people of the fang and claw are here because one of us broke her vows," Maryelizabeth read. "At the marriage of

Crystal and Jason, werepanthers of this community, they each promised to remain true to their marriage vows, both in the way of the cat and the way of the human. Crystal's surrogate was her uncle Calvin, and Jason's was his sister, Sookie."

I was aware of the eyes of all the assembled community moving from Calvin to me. A lot of those eyes were golden yellow. Inbreeding in Hotshot had produced some slightly alarming results.

"Now that Crystal has broken her vows, a fact witnessed by the surrogates, her uncle has offered to take the punishment since Crystal is pregnant."

This was going to be even nastier than I'd suspected.

"Since Calvin takes Crystal's place, Sookie, do you choose to take Jason's place?"

Oh, *crap.* I looked at Calvin and I knew my whole face was asking him if there was any way out of this. And his whole face told me no. He actually looked sorry for me.

I would never forgive my brother—or Crystal—for this.

"Sookie," Maryelizabeth prompted.

"What would I have to do?" I said, and if I sounded sullen and grudging and angry, I thought I had a good reason.

Maryelizabeth opened the book again and read the answer. "We exist by our wits and our claws, and if faith is broken, a claw is broken," she said.

I stared at her, trying to make sense of that.

"Either you or Jason has to break Calvin's finger," she said simply. "In fact, since Crystal broke the faith completely, you have to break two, at least. More would be better. Jason gets to pick, I guess."

More would be better. Jesus Christ, Shepherd of Judea. I tried to be dispassionate. Who could cause the most damage to my friend Calvin? My brother, no doubt about it. If I was a true friend to Calvin, I would do this. Could I bring myself to? And then it was taken out of my hands.

Jason said, "I didn't think it would happen this way, Sookie." He sounded simultaneously angry, confused, and defensive. "If Calvin stands in for Crystal, I want Sookie to stand in for me," he told Maryelizabeth. I never thought I could hate my own brother, but at that moment I found out it was possible.

"So be it," said Maryelizabeth.

I tried to boost myself up mentally. After all, this wasn't maybe quite as bad as I'd anticipated. I'd pictured Calvin being whipped or having to whip Crystal. Or we might have had to do some awful thing involving knives; that would have been way worse.

I tried to believe this might not be so bad right up until the time two of the males carried out a pair of concrete blocks and put them on top of the picnic table.

And then Maryelizabeth produced a brick. She held it out to me.

I began to shake my head involuntarily because I felt a heavy twinge in my stomach. Nausea did flip-flops in my belly. Looking at the common red brick, I began to have an idea what this was going to cost me.

Calvin stepped forward and took my hand. He leaned over to talk very close to my ear. "Darlin'," he said, "you have to do this. I accepted this, when I stood up for her when she married.

And I knew what she was. And you know Jason. This might easily have been the other way 'round. I might be about to do this to you. And you don't heal as well. This is better. And it has to be. Our people require this." He straightened and looked me right in the eyes. His own were golden, utterly strange, and quite steady.

I pinched my lips together, and I made myself nod. Calvin gave me a bracing look and took his place by the table. He put his hand on the concrete blocks. With no further ado, Maryelizabeth handed me the brick. The rest of the panthers waited patiently for me to perform the punishment. The vampires would have dressed this all up with a special wardrobe and probably an extraspecial fancy brick from an old temple or something, but not the panthers. It was just a damn brick. I held it with both hands gripping one long side.

After I'd looked at it for a long minute, I said to Jason. "I don't want to talk to you again. Ever." I faced Crystal. "I hope you enjoyed it, bitch," I said, and I turned as quick as I could and brought the brick down on Calvin's hand.

Chapter 19

Amelia and Octavia hovered around for two days before they decided leaving me alone was the best policy. Reading their anxious thoughts just made me surlier, because I didn't want to accept comfort. I should suffer for what I'd done, and that meant I couldn't accept any easing of my misery. So I gloomed and sulked and brooded and rained my grim mood all over my house.

My brother came into the bar once, and I turned my back on him. Dove Beck didn't choose to drink at Merlotte's, which was a good thing, though he was the least guilty of the bunch as far as I was concerned—though that didn't make him any clean Gene. When Alcee Beck came in, it was clear his brother had confided in him, because Alcee looked even angrier than usual, and he met my eyes every chance he got, just to let me know he was my equal.

Thank God, Calvin didn't show. I couldn't have stood it. I heard enough talk around the bar from his coworkers at Norcross about the accident he'd had while he was working on his truck at home.

Most unexpectedly, on the third night Eric walked into Merlotte's. I took one look at him and suddenly my throat seemed to ease and I felt tears well up in my eyes. But Eric walked through as though he owned the place, and he went into the hall to Sam's office. Moments later Sam stuck his head out and beckoned to me.

After I walked in, I didn't expect Sam to shut the office door.

"What's wrong?" Sam asked me. He'd been trying to find out for days, and I'd been fending off his well-meant queries.

Eric was standing to one side, his arms crossed over his chest. He made a gesture with one hand that said, "Tell us; we're waiting." Despite his brusqueness, his presence relaxed the big knot inside me, the one that had kept the words locked in my stomach.

"I broke Calvin Norris's hand into bits," I said. "With a brick."

"Then he was . . . He stood up for your sister-in-law at the wedding," Sam said, figuring it out quickly. Eric looked blank. The vampires know something about the wereanimals—they have to—but the vamps think they are far superior, so they don't make an effort to learn specifics about the rituals and rhythms of being a were.

"She had to break his hand, which represents his claws in

panther form," Sam explained impatiently. "She stood up for Jason." And then Sam and Eric exchanged a look that scared me in its complete agreement. Neither of them liked Jason one little bit.

Sam looked from me to Eric as if he expected Eric to do something to make me feel better. "I don't belong to him," I said sharply, since all this was making me feel handled in a major way. "Did you think Eric coming would make me all happy and carefree?"

"No," Sam said, sounding a little angry himself. "But I hoped it would help you talk about whatever was wrong."

"What's wrong," I said very quietly. "Okay, what's wrong is that my brother arranged for Calvin and me to check on Crystal, who's about four months pregnant, and he fixed it so we'd get there at about the same time. And when we checked, we found Crystal in bed with Dove Beck. As Jason knew we would."

Eric said, "And for this, you had to break the werepanther's fingers." He might have been asking if I'd had to wear chicken bones and turn around three times, it was so obvious he was inquiring into the quaint customs of a primitive tribe.

"Yes, Eric, that's what I had to do," I said grimly. "I had to break my friend's fingers with a brick in front of a crowd."

For the first time Eric seemed to realize that he'd taken the wrong approach. Sam was looking at him in total exasperation. "And I thought you'd be such a big help," he said.

"I have a few things going in Shreveport," Eric answered with a shade of defensiveness. "Including hosting the new king."

Sam muttered something that sounded suspiciously like, "Fucking vampires."

This was totally unfair. I'd expected tons of sympathy when I finally confessed the reason for my bad mood. But now Sam and Eric were so wrapped up in being irritated with each other that neither one of them was giving me a moment's thought. "Well, thanks, guys," I said. "This has been a lot of fun. Eric, big help there—I appreciate the kind words." And I left in what my grandmother called high dudgeon. I stomped back out into the bar and waited on tables so grimly that some people were scared to call me over to order more drinks.

I decided to clean the surfaces behind the bar, because Sam was still in his office with Eric . . . though possibly Eric had left out the back door. I scrubbed and polished and pulled some beers for Holly, and I straightened everything so meticulously that Sam might have a wee problem finding things. Just for a week or two.

Then Sam came out to take his place, looked at the counter in mute displeasure, and jerked his head to indicate I should get the hell out from behind the bar. My bad mood was catching.

You know how it is sometimes, when someone really tries to cheer you up? When you just decide that by golly, nothing in the world is going to make you feel better? Sam had thrown Eric at me like he was throwing a happy pill, yet he was aggravated that I hadn't swallowed it. Instead of being grateful that Sam was fond enough of me to call Eric, I was mad at him for his assumption.

I was in a totally black mood.

Quinn was gone. I'd banished him. Stupid mistake or wise decision? Verdict still out.

Lots of Weres were dead in Shreveport because of Priscilla, and I'd watched some of them die. Believe me, that sticks with you.

More than a few vampires were dead, too, including some I'd known fairly well.

My brother was a devious manipulative bastard.

My great-grandfather wasn't ever going to take me fishing.

Okay, now I was getting silly. Suddenly, I smiled, because I was picturing the prince of the fairies in old denim overalls and a Bon Temps Hawks baseball cap, carrying a can of worms and a couple of fishing poles.

I caught Sam's eye as I cleared a table of plates. I winked at him.

He turned away, shaking his head, but I caught a hint of a smile at the corners of his mouth.

And just like that, my bad mood was officially over. My common sense kicked in. There was no point in lashing myself over the Hotshot incident any longer. I'd had to do what I'd had to do. Calvin understood that better than I did. My brother was an asshole, and Crystal was a whore. These were facts I had to deal with. Granted, they were both unhappy people who were acting out because they were married to the wrong spouse, but they were also both chronologically adults, and I couldn't fix their marriage any more than I'd been able to prevent it.

The Weres had dealt with their own problems in their own way, and I'd done my best to help them. Vampires, ditto . . . sort of.

Okay. Not *all* better, but enough better.

When I got off work, I wasn't completely annoyed to find Eric waiting by my car. He seemed to be enjoying the night, standing all by himself in the cold. I was shivering myself because I hadn't brought a heavy jacket. My Windbreaker wasn't enough.

"It's been nice to be by myself for a while," Eric said unexpectedly.

"I guess at Fangtasia you're always surrounded," I said.

"Always surrounded by people wanting things," he said.

"But you enjoy that, right? Being the big kahuna?"

Eric looked like he was mulling that over. "Yes, I like that. I like being the boss. I don't like being . . . overseen. Is that a word? I'll be glad when Felipe de Castro and his minion Sandy take their departure. Victor will stay to take over New Orleans."

Eric was *sharing.* This was almost unprecedented. This was like a normal give-and-take between equals.

"What's the new king like?" Cold as I was, I couldn't resist keeping the conversation going.

"He's handsome, ruthless, and clever," Eric said.

"Like you." I could have slapped myself.

Eric nodded after a moment. "But more so," Eric said grimly. "I'll have to keep very alert to stay ahead of him."

"How gratifying to hear you say so," said an accented voice.

This was definitely an *Oh, shit!* moment. (An OSM, as I called them to myself.) A gorgeous man stepped out from the trees, and I blinked as I took him in. As Eric bowed, I scanned

Felipe de Castro from his gleaming shoes to his bold face. As I bowed, too, belatedly, I realized that Eric hadn't been exaggerating when he said the new king was handsome. Felipe de Castro was a Latin male who threw Jimmy Smits into the shade, and I am a big admirer of Mr. Smits. Though perhaps five foot ten or so, Castro carried himself with such importance and straight posture that you couldn't think of him as short—rather, he made other men look too tall. His dark thick hair was clipped close to his head, and he had a mustache and chin strip. He had caramel skin and dark eyes, strong arched eyebrows, a bold nose. The king wore a cape—no kidding, a real full-length black cape. I'll tell you how impressive he was; I didn't even think of giggling. Other than the cape, he seemed dressed for a night that might include flamenco dancing, with a white shirt, black vest, and black dress slacks. One of Castro's ears was pierced, and there was a dark stone in it. The overhead security light didn't let me get a better idea of what it might be. Ruby? Emerald?

I'd straightened up and I was staring again. But when I glanced at Eric, I saw he was still bowing. Ah-oh. Well, I wasn't one of his subjects and I wasn't going to do that again. It had gone against my Americanness to do it once.

"Hi, I'm Sookie Stackhouse," I said, since the silence was getting awkward. I automatically held out my hand, remembered vamps didn't shake, and snatched it back. "Excuse me," I said.

The king inclined his head. "Miss Stackhouse," he said, his accent strumming my name delightfully. ("Meees Stekhuss.")

"Yes, sir. I'm sorry to meet you and run, but it's really cold out here and I need to get home." I beamed at him, my lunatic beam I give when I'm really nervous. "Good-bye, Eric," I babbled, and stood on tiptoe to kiss him on the cheek. "Give me a call when you have a minute. Unless you need me to stay, for some crazy reason?"

"No, lover, you need to go home and get into the warmth," Eric said, clasping both my hands in his. "I'll call you when my work permits."

When he let go of me, I did an awkward sort of dip in the king's direction (American! Not used to bowing!) and hopped into my car before either vampire could change his mind about my departure. I felt like a coward—a very relieved coward—as I backed out of my space and drove out of the parking lot. But I was already debating the wisdom of my departure as I turned onto Hummingbird Road.

I was worried about Eric. This was a fairly new phenomenon, one that made me very uneasy, and it had started the night of the coup. Worrying about Eric was like worrying about the well-being of a rock or a tornado. When had I ever had to worry about him before? He was one of the most powerful vampires I'd ever met. But Sophie-Anne had been even more powerful and protected by the huge warrior Sigebert, and look what had happened to her. I felt abruptly, acutely miserable. What was wrong with me?

I had a terrible idea. Maybe I was worried simply because Eric was worried? Miserable because Eric was miserable? Could I receive his emotions this strongly and from this great a distance? Should I turn around and find out what was happening? If the king was being cruel to Eric, I couldn't possibly be of any assistance. I had to pull over to the side of the road. I couldn't drive anymore.

I'd never had a panic attack, but I thought I was having one now. I was paralyzed with indecision; again, not one of my usual characteristics. Struggling with myself, trying to think clearly, I realized I had to turn back whether I wanted to or not. It was an obligation I couldn't ignore, not because I was bonded to Eric, but because I liked him.

I turned the wheel and did a U-turn in the middle of Hummingbird Road. Since I'd seen only two cars since I'd left the bar, the maneuver was no big traffic violation. I drove back a lot faster than I'd left, and when I got to Merlotte's, I found that the customer parking lot was completely empty. I parked in front and pulled my old softball bat out from under the seat. My grandmother had given it to me for my sixteenth birthday. It was a very good bat, though it had seen better days. I crept around the building, taking advantage of the bushes that grew at the foundation for cover. Nandinas. I hate nandinas. They're straggly and ugly and leggy, and I'm allergic to them. Though I was covered with a Windbreaker, pants, and socks, the minute I began threading my way among the plants, my nose began to run.

I peeked around the corner very cautiously.

I was so shocked I couldn't believe what I was seeing.

Sigebert, the queen's bodyguard, had *not* been killed in the coup. No, sirree, he was still among the undead. And he was here in the Merlotte's parking lot, and he was having a lot of fun with the new king, Felipe de Castro, and with Eric, and with Sam, who had been swept up in the net probably by simply leaving his bar to walk to his trailer.

I took a deep breath—a deep but *silent* breath—and made myself analyze what I was seeing. Sigebert was a mountain of a man, and he'd been the queen's muscle for centuries. His brother, Wybert, had died in the queen's service, and I was sure Sigebert had been a target of the Nevada vamps; they'd left their mark on him. Vampires heal fast, but Sigebert had been wounded badly enough that even days after he'd fought, he was still visibly damaged. There was a huge cut across his forehead and a horrible-looking mark just above where I thought his heart would be. His clothes were ripped and stained and filthy. Maybe the Nevada vamps thought he'd disintegrated when in fact he'd managed to get away and hide. *Not important,* I told myself.

The important part was that he'd succeeded in binding both Eric and Felipe de Castro with silver chains. How? *Not important,* I told myself again. Maybe this tendency to mentally wander was coming from Eric, who was looking much more battered than the king. Of course, Sigebert would see Eric as a traitor.

Eric was bleeding from the head and his arm was clearly broken. Castro was bleeding sluggishly from the mouth, so Sigebert had maybe stomped on him. Eric and Castro were both lying on the ground, and in the harsh security light they both looked whiter than snow. Sam had been tied to the bumper of his own truck somehow, and he wasn't damaged at all, at least so far. Thank God.

I tried to figure out how I could conquer Sigebert with my aluminum softball bat, but I didn't come up with any good ideas. If I rushed him, he'd just laugh. Even as grievously wounded as he was, he was still a vampire and I was no match for him unless I had a great idea. So I watched, and I waited, but in the end I couldn't stand to see him hurting Eric anymore; believe me, when a vampire kicks you, you get plenty hurt. Plus, Sigebert was having a great time with the big knife he had brought.

The biggest weapon at my disposal? Okay, that would be my car. I felt a little pang of regret, because it was the best car I'd ever had, and Tara had sold it to me for a dollar when she'd gotten a newer one. But it was the only thing I could think of that would make a dent in Sigebert.

So back I crept, praying that Sigebert would be so absorbed in his torture that he wouldn't notice the sound of the car door. I laid my head on the steering wheel and thought as hard as I've ever thought. I considered the parking lot and its topography, and I thought about the location of the bound vampires, and I took a deep breath and turned the key. I started around the building, wishing my car could creep through the damn nandina bushes like I had, and I swung wide to allow room to charge, and my lights caught Sigebert, and I hit the accelerator and went straight at him. He tried to get out of the way, but he was none too bright and I'd caught him with his pants down (literally—I really didn't like to think about his next torture plan) and I hit him very hard, and up he bounced, to land on the roof of the car with a huge thud.

I screamed and braked, because this was as far as my plan had gone. He slid down the back of the car, leaving a horrible sheet of dark blood, and disappeared from view. Scared he'd pop up in the rearview mirror, I threw the car into reverse and hit the pedal again. *Bump. Bump.* I yanked the gear stick into park and leaped out, bat in hand, to find Sigebert's legs and most of his torso were wedged under the car. I dashed over to Eric and began fumbling with the silver chain, while he stared at me with his eyes wide. Castro was cursing in Spanish, fluently and fluidly, and Sam was saying, "Hurry, Sookie, hurry!" which really didn't help my powers of concentration.

I gave up on the damn chains and got the big knife and cut Sam free so he could help. The knife came close enough to his skin to make him yelp a time or two, but I was really doing the best I could, and he didn't bleed. To give him credit, he made it over to Castro in record time and began freeing him while I ran back to Eric, laying the knife on the ground beside us as I worked. Now that I had at least one ally who had the use of his hands and legs, I was able to concentrate, and I got Eric's legs unbound (at least now he could run away—I guess that was my thinking) and then, more slowly, his arms and hands. The silver had been wound around him many times, and Sigebert had made sure it touched Eric's hands. They looked ghastly. Castro had suffered even more from the chains because Sigebert had divested him of his beautiful cape and most of his shirt.

I was unwinding the last strand when Eric shoved me as hard as he could, grabbed the knife, and leaped to his feet so swiftly I saw only a blur. Then he was on Sigebert, who had actually lifted the car to release his own trapped legs. He'd begun dragging himself out from under, and in another minute he would have been ambulatory.

Did I mention it was a big knife? And it must have been sharp, too, because Eric landed by Sigebert, said, "Go to your maker," and cut off the warrior vampire's head.

"Oh," I said shakily, and sat down abruptly on the cold parking lot gravel. "Oh, wow." We all remained where we were, panting, for a good five minutes. Then Sam straightened up from the side of Felipe de Castro and offered him a hand. The vampire took it, and when he was upright, he introduced himself to Sam, who automatically introduced himself right back.

"Miss Stackhouse," the king said, "I am in your debt."

Damn straight.

"It's okay," I said in a voice that wasn't nearly as level as it should be.

"Thank you," he said. "If your car is too damaged to repair, I will be very glad to buy you another one."

"Oh, thanks," I said with absolute sincerity, as I stood up. "I'll try to drive it home tonight. I don't know how I can explain the damage. Do you think the body shop would believe I ran over an alligator?" That did happen occasionally. Was it weird that I was worried about the car insurance?

"Dawson would look at it for you," Sam said. His voice was as odd as mine. He, too, had thought he was going to die. "I know he's a motorcycle repairman, but I bet he could fix your car. He works on his own all the time."

"Do what is necessary," said Castro grandly. "I will pay.

Eric, would you care to explain what just happened?" His voice was considerably more acerbic.

"You should ask your crew to explain," Eric retorted, with some justification. "Didn't they tell you Sigebert, the queen's bodyguard, was dead? Yet here he is."

"An excellent point." Castro looked down at the crumbling body. "So that was the legendary Sigebert. He's gone to join his brother, Wybert." He sounded quite pleased.

I hadn't known the brothers were famous among the vampires, but they'd certainly been unique. Their mountainous physiques, their broken and primitive English, their utter devotion to the woman who'd turned them centuries before—sure, any right-minded vampire would love that story. I sagged where I stood, and Eric, moving faster than I could see, picked me up. It was a very Scarlett and Rhett moment, spoiled only by the fact that there were two other guys there, we were in a humdrum parking lot, and I was unhappy about the damage to my car. Plus not a little shocked.

"How'd he get the jump on three strong guys like you-all?" I asked. I didn't worry about Eric holding me. It made me feel tiny, not a feeling I got to enjoy all that often.

There was a moment of general embarrassment.

"I was standing with my back to the woods," Castro explained. "He had the chains arranged for throwing. . . . Your word is almost the same. *Lazo.*"

"Lasso," Sam said.

"Ah, lasso. The first one, he threw around me, and of course, the shock was great. Before Eric could land on him, he had

Eric as well. The pain from the silver... very quickly we were bound. When this one"—he nodded toward Sam—"came to our aid, Sigebert knocked him unconscious and got rope from the back of Sam's truck and tied him up."

"We were too involved in our discussion to be wary," Eric said. He sounded pretty grim, and I didn't blame him. But I decided to keep my mouth shut.

"Ironic, eh, that we needed a human girl to rescue us," the king said blithely, the very idea that I'd decided not to voice.

"Yes, very amusing," Eric said in a dreadfully unamused voice. "Why did you return, Sookie?"

"I felt your, ah, anger at being attacked." For "anger" read "despair."

The new king looked very interested. "A blood bond. How interesting."

"No, not really," I said. "Sam, I wonder if you'd mind driving me home. I don't know where you gentlemen left your cars, or if you flew. I *do* wonder how Sigebert knew where to find you."

Felipe de Castro and Eric shared almost identical expressions of deep thought.

"We'll find out," Eric said, and set me down. "And then heads are going to roll." Eric was good at setting heads to rolling. It was one of his favorite things. I was willing to put my money on Castro sharing that predilection, because the king was looking positively gleeful in anticipation.

Sam fished his keys out of his pocket without a word, and I climbed into the truck with him. We left the two vampires involved in a deep conversation. Sigebert's corpse, still partially under my poor car, was almost gone, leaving a dark greasy residue on the gravel of the parking lot. The good thing about vampires—no corpse disposal.

"I'll call Dawson tonight," Sam said unexpectedly.

"Oh, Sam, thank you," I said. "I'm so glad you were there."

"It's the parking lot of my *bar*," he said, and it might have been my own guilty reaction, but I thought I detected some reproach. I suddenly came to the full realization that Sam had walked into a situation in his own backyard, a situation he had no stake or interest in, and that he'd almost died as a result. And why had Eric been in the parking lot back of Merlotte's? To talk to me. And then Felipe de Castro had followed to talk to Eric . . . though I wasn't sure why. But the point was, them being there at all was my fault.

"Oh, Sam," I said, almost in tears, "I'm so sorry. I didn't know Eric would wait for me, and I sure didn't know the king would follow him. I still don't know why he was there. I'm so sorry," I said again. I would say it a hundred times if it would take that tone out of Sam's voice.

"It's not your fault," he said. "I asked Eric to come here in the first place. It's their fault. I don't know how we can pry you loose from them."

"This was bad, but somehow you're not taking it like I thought you would."

"I just want to be left in peace," he said unexpectedly. "I don't want to get involved in supernatural politics. I don't want to have to take sides in Were shit. I'm not a Were. I'm a shapeshifter, and shifters don't organize. We're too different. I hate vampire politics even more than Were politics."

"You're mad at me."

"No!" He seemed to be struggling with what he wanted to say. "I don't want that for you, either! Weren't you happier before?"

"You mean before I knew any vampires; before I knew about the rest of the world that lies outside the boundaries?"

Sam nodded.

"In some ways. It was nice to have a clear path before me," I said. "I do get really sick of the politics and the battles. But my life wasn't any prize, Sam. Every day was a struggle just to act like I was a regular human, like I didn't know all the things I know about other humans. The cheating and infidelity, the little acts of dishonesty, the unkindness. The really severe judgments people pass on each other. Their lack of charity. When you know all that, it's hard to keep going sometimes. Knowing about the supernatural world puts all that in a different perspective. I don't know why. People aren't any better or worse than the supernaturals, but they're not all there is, either."

"I guess I understand," Sam said, though he sounded a little doubtful.

"Plus," I said very quietly, "it's nice to be valued for the very thing that makes regular people think I'm just a crazy girl."

"Definitely understand that," Sam said. "But there's a price."

"Oh, no doubt about it."

"You willing to pay?"

"So far."

We chugged up my driveway. No lights on. The witchy duo had gone to bed, or else they were out partying or casting spells.

"In the morning, I'll call Dawson," Sam said. "He'll check out your car, make sure you can drive it, or he'll get it towed to his place. Think you can get a ride to work?"

"I'm sure I can," I said. "Amelia can bring me in."

Sam walked me to the back door like he was bringing me home from a date. The porch light was on, which was thoughtful of Amelia. Sam put his arms around me, which was a surprise, and then he just snugged his head in close to mine, and we stood there enjoying each other's warmth for a long moment.

"We survived the Were war," he said. "You made it through the vampire coup. Now we lived through the attack of the berserk bodyguard. I hope we keep up our record."

"Now you're scaring me," I said as I remembered all the other things I'd survived. I should be dead, no doubt about it.

His warm lips brushed my cheek. "Maybe that's a good thing," he said, and turned to go back to his truck.

I watched him climb in and reverse, and then I unlocked the back door and went to my room. After all the adrenaline and the fear and the accelerated pace of life (and death) in the parking lot of Merlotte's, my own room seemed very quiet and clean and secure. I'd done my best to kill someone tonight. It was only by chance Sigebert had survived my attempt at vehicular homicide. Twice. I couldn't help but notice that I wasn't feeling remorseful. This was surely a flaw, but at the moment I just didn't care. There were definitely parts of my character I didn't approve of, and maybe from time to time I had moments when I didn't like myself much. But I got through each day as it came to me, and so far I'd survived everything life had thrown at me. I could only hope that the survival was worth the price I'd paid.

Chapter 20

To my relief, I woke up in an empty house. Neither Amelia's nor Octavia's throbbing heads were under my roof. I lay in bed and reveled in the knowledge. Maybe the next time I had a whole day off, I could spend it completely alone. That didn't seem a likely occurrence, but a girl can dream. After I planned my day (call Sam to find out about my car, pay some bills, go to work), I got into the shower and really scrubbed. I used as much hot water as I wanted. I painted my toenails and my fingernails, and I pulled on a pair of sweatpants and a T-shirt and went in to make some coffee. The kitchen was spanking clean; God bless Amelia.

The coffee was great, the toast delicious spread with blueberry jam. Even my taste buds were happy. After I cleaned up from breakfast, I was practically singing with the pleasure of solitude. I went back to my room to make my bed and put on my makeup.

Of course, that was when the knock came at the back door, nearly making me jump out of my skin. I stepped into some shoes and went to answer it.

Tray Dawson was there, and he was smiling. "Sookie, your car is doing fine," he said. "I had to do a little replacing here and there, and it's the first time I ever had to scrape vampire ash off an undercarriage, but you're good to go."

"Oh, thanks! Can you come in?"

"Just for a minute," he said. "You got a Coke in the refrigerator?"

"I sure do." I brought him a Coke, asked if he wanted some cookies or a peanut butter sandwich to go with it, and when he'd turned that down, I excused myself to finish my makeup. I'd figured Dawson would run me to the car, but he'd driven it over to my place, as it turned out, so I'd need to give him a ride instead.

I had my checkbook out and my pen in hand when I sat at the table opposite the big man and asked him how much I owed him.

"Not a dime," Dawson said. "The new guy paid for it."

"The new king?"

"Yeah, he called me in the middle of the night last night. Told me the story, more or less, and asked me if I could look at the car first thing in the morning. I was awake when he called, so it didn't make me no nevermind. I got over to Merlotte's this morning, told Sam he wasted a phone call since I already knew all about it. I followed him while he drove the car out to my place, and we put it up on the rack and had a good look."

This was a long speech for Dawson. I put my checkbook back in my purse and listened, silently asking him if he wanted more Coke by pointing at his glass. He shook his head, letting me know he was satisfied. "We had to tighten up a few things, replace your windshield fluid reservoir. I knew just where another car like yours was at Rusty's Salvage, and it didn't take no time to do the job."

I could only thank him again. I drove Dawson out to his repair shop. Since the last time I'd driven by, he'd trimmed up the front yard of his home, a modest but tidy frame house that stood next door to the big shop. Dawson had also put all the bits and pieces of motorcycles under cover somewhere, instead of having them strewn around in a handy but unattractive spread. And his pickup was clean.

As Dawson slid out of the car, I said, "I'm so grateful. I know cars aren't your specialty and I do appreciate your working on mine." Repairman to the underworld, that was Tray Dawson.

"Well, I did it because I wanted to," Dawson said, and then he paused. "But if you could see your way to it, I'd sure like it if you'd put in a word for me with your friend Amelia."

"I don't have much influence over Amelia," I said. "But I'll be glad to tell her what a sterling character you are."

He smiled very broadly: no suppression there. I didn't think I'd ever seen Dawson crack such a grin. "She sure looks healthy," he said, and since I had no idea what Dawson's criteria for admiration were, that was a big clue.

"You call her up, I'll give a reference," I said.

"It's a deal."

We parted happy, and he loped across the newly neat yard to his shop. I didn't know if Dawson would be to Amelia's taste or not, but I'd do my best to persuade her to give him a chance.

As I drove home, I listened to the car for any strange noise. It purred away.

Amelia and Octavia came in as I was leaving for work.

"How are you feeling?" Amelia said with a knowing air.

"Fine," I said automatically. Then I understood she thought I hadn't come home the night before. She thought I'd been having a good time with someone. "Hey, you remember Tray Dawson, right? You met him at Maria-Star's apartment."

"Sure."

"He's going to call you. Be sweet."

I left her grinning after me as I got into my car.

For once, work was boring and normal. Terry was substituting since Sam hated to work on Sunday afternoons. Merlotte's was having a calm day. We opened late on Sunday and we closed early, so I was ready to start home by seven. No one showed up in the parking lot, and I was able to walk directly to my car without being accosted for a long, weird conversation or being attacked.

The next morning I had errands to run in town. I was short on cash, so I drove to the ATM, waving at Tara Thornton du Rone. Tara smiled and waved back. Marriage was suiting her, and I hoped she and JB were having a happier time of it than my brother and his wife. As I drove away from the bank, to my astonishment I spotted Alcide Herveaux coming out of the offices of Sid Matt Lancaster, an ancient and renowned lawyer. I pulled into Sid Matt's parking lot, and Alcide came over to talk to me.

I should have driven on, hoping he hadn't noticed me.

The conversation was awkward. Alcide had had a lot to deal with, in all fairness. His girlfriend was dead, brutally murdered. Several other members of his pack were also dead. He'd had a huge cover-up to arrange. But he was now the leader of the pack, and he had gotten to celebrate his victory in the traditional way. In hindsight, I suspect he was fairly embarrassed at having sex with a young woman in public, especially so soon after his girlfriend's death. This was quite a bundle of emotions I was reading in his head, and he was flushed when he came to my car window.

"Sookie, I haven't had a chance to thank you for all your help that night. It's lucky for us your boss decided to come with you."

Yeah, since you wouldn't have saved my life and he did, I'm glad, too. "No problem, Alcide," I said, my voice wonderfully even and calm. I was going to have a good day, dammit. "Have things settled down in Shreveport?"

"The police don't seem to have a clue," he said, glancing around to make sure no one else was within hearing distance. "They haven't found the site yet, and there's been a lot of rain. We're hoping sooner rather than later they'll cut back on their investigation."

"You-all still planning the big announcement?"

"It'll have to be soon. The heads of other packs in the area have been in contact with me. We don't have a meeting of all the leaders like the vampires do, mostly because they have one leader for each state and we have a hell of a lot of packleaders. Looks like we'll all elect a representative from the packleaders, one from each state, and those representatives will go to a national meeting."

"That sounds like a step in the right direction."

"Also, we might ask other wereanimals if they want to come in with us. Like, Sam could belong to my pack in an auxiliary way, though he's not a Were. And it would be good if the lone wolves, like Dawson, came to some of the pack parties . . . came out howling with us or something."

"Dawson seems to like his life the way it is," I said. "And you'll have to talk to Sam, not me, about whether he wants to associate with you-all formally."

"Sure. You seem to have a lot of influence with him. Just thought I'd mention it."

I didn't see it that way. Sam had a lot of influence over me, but whether I had any over him . . . I was dubious. Alcide began making the little shifts in stance that told me as clearly as his brain had that he was about to go his way on whatever business had brought him to Bon Temps.

"Alcide," I said, seized by an impulse, "I do have a question."

He said, "Sure."

"Who's taking care of the Furnan children?"

He looked at me, then away. "Libby's sister. She's got three of her own, but she said she was glad to take them in. There's enough money for their upbringing. When it comes time for them to go to college, we'll see what we can do for the boy."

"For the boy?"

"He's pack."

If I'd had a brick in my hand, I wouldn't have minded using it on Alcide. Good God almighty. I took a deep breath. To give him credit, the sex of the child wasn't the issue at all. It was his pure blood.

"There may be enough insurance money for the girl to go, too," Alcide said, since he was no fool. "The aunt wasn't too clear about that, but she knows we'll help."

"And she knows who 'we' is?"

He shook his head. "We told her it was a secret society, like the Masons, that Furnan belonged to."

There didn't seem to be anything left to say.

"Good luck," I said. He'd already had a fair share of that, no matter what you thought about the two dead women that had been his girlfriends. After all, he himself had survived to achieve his father's goal.

"Thank you, and thanks again for your part in that luck. You're still a friend of the pack," he said very seriously. His beautiful green eyes lingered on my face. "And you're one of my favorite women in the world," he added unexpectedly.

"That's a real nice compliment, Alcide," I said, and drove away. I was glad I'd talked to him. Alcide had grown up a lot in the past few weeks. All in all, he was changing into a man I admired much more than I had the old one.

I'd never forget the blood and the screaming of the horrific night in the abandoned office park in Shreveport, but I began to feel that some good had come out of it.

When I returned home, I found that Octavia and Amelia were in the front yard, raking. This was a delightful discovery. I hated raking worse than anything in the world, but if I didn't go over the yard once or twice during the fall, the pine needle buildup was dreadful.

I had been thanking people all day long. I parked in the back and came out the front.

"Do you bag these up or burn them?" Amelia called.

"Oh, I burn 'em when there's not a burn ban on," I said. "It's so nice of you both to think of doing this." I wasn't aiming to gush—but having your very least favorite chore done for you was really quite a treat.

"I need the exercise," Octavia said. "We went to the mall in Monroe yesterday, so I did get some walking in."

I thought Amelia treated Octavia more like a grandmother than a teacher.

"Did Tray call?" I asked.

"He sure did." Amelia smiled broadly.

"He thought you were fine-looking."

Octavia laughed. "Amelia, you're a femme fatale."

She looked happy and said, "I think he's an interesting guy."

"A bit older than you," I said, just so she'd know.

Amelia shrugged. "I don't care. I'm ready to date. I think Pam and I are more buddies than honeys. And since I found that litter of kittens, I'm open for guy business."

"You really think Bob made a choice? Wouldn't that have been, like, instinct?" I said.

Just then, the cat in question wandered across the yard, curious to see why we were all standing out in the open when there was a perfectly good couch and a few beds in the house.

Octavia gave a gusty sigh. "Oh, hell," she muttered. She straightened and held her hands out. *"Potestas mea te in formam veram tuam commutabit natura ips reaffirmet Incantationes praeviae deletae sunt,"* she said.

The cat blinked up at Octavia. Then it made a peculiar noise, a kind of cry I'd never heard come out of a cat's throat before. Suddenly the air around him was thick and dense and cloudy and full of sparks. The cat shrieked again. Amelia was staring at the animal with her mouth wide open. Octavia looked resigned and a little sad.

The cat writhed on the fading grass, and suddenly it had a human leg.

"God almighty!" I said, and clapped a hand over my mouth.

Now it had two legs, two hairy legs, and then it had a penis, and then it began to be a man all over, shrieking all the while. After a horrible two minutes, the witch Bob Jessup lay on the lawn, shaking all over but entirely human again. After another minute, he stopped shrieking and just twitched. Not an improvement, really, but easier on the eardrums.

Then he lunged to his feet, leaped onto Amelia, and made a determined effort to choke her to death.

I grabbed his shoulders to pull him off of her, and Octavia said, "You don't want me to use magic on you again, right?"

That proved a very effective threat. Bob let go of Amelia and stood panting in the cold air. "I can't believe you did that to me!" he said. "I can't believe I spent the last few months as a cat!"

"How do you feel?" I asked. "Are you weak? Do you need help into the house? Would you like some clothes?"

He looked down at himself vaguely. He hadn't worn clothes in a while, but suddenly he turned red, very nearly all over. "Yes," he said stiffly. "Yes, I would like some clothes."

"Come with me," I said. The dusk was coming on as I led Bob into the house. Bob was a smallish guy, and I thought a pair of my sweats might fit him. No, Amelia was a little taller, and a clothes donation from her would be only fair. I spotted the basket full of folded clothes on the stairs where Amelia had left it to carry up the next time she went to her room. Lo and behold, there was an old blue sweatshirt and a pair of black sweat pants. I handed the clothes to Bob wordlessly, and he pulled them on with trembling fingers. I flipped through the stack and found a pair of socks that were plain white. He sat down on the couch to pull them on. That was as far as I could go toward clothing him. His feet were larger than mine or Amelia's, so shoes were out.

Bob wrapped his arms around himself like he feared he was going to disappear. His dark hair was clinging to his skull. He blinked, and I wondered what had happened to his glasses. I hoped Amelia had stored them somewhere.

"Bob, can I get you a drink?" I asked.

"Yes, please," he said. He seemed to be having a bit of trouble getting his mouth to form the words. His hand moved up to his mouth in a curious gesture, and I realized it was just like my cat Tina's movement when she had raised her paw to lick it before she used it to groom herself. Bob realized what he was doing and lowered his hand abruptly.

I thought about bringing him milk in a bowl but decided that would be insulting. I brought him some iced tea instead. He gulped it but made a face.

"Sorry," I said. "I should have asked if you like tea."

"I do like tea," he said, and stared at the glass as if he'd just connected tea with the liquid he'd had in his mouth. "I'm just not used to it anymore."

Okay, I know this is really awful, but I actually opened my mouth to ask him if he wanted some kibble. Amelia had a bag of 9Lives on the back porch shelf. I bit the inside of my mouth, hard. "What about a sandwich?" I asked. I had no idea what to talk to Bob about. Mice?

"Sure," he said. He didn't seem to know what he wanted to do next.

So I made him a peanut butter and jelly, and a ham and pickle on whole wheat with mustard. He ate them both, chewing very slowly and carefully. Then he said, "Excuse me," and got up to find the bathroom. He shut the door behind him, and stayed in there for a long time.

Amelia and Octavia had come in by the time Bob emerged.

"I'm so sorry," Amelia said.

"Me, too," Octavia said. She looked older and smaller.

"You knew all along how to change him?" I tried to keep my voice level and nonjudgmental. "Your failed attempt was a fraud?"

Octavia nodded. "I was scared if you didn't need me, I wouldn't get to visit anymore. I'd have to go stay all day at my niece's. It's so much nicer here. I would have said something soon, because my conscience was bothering me something awful, especially since I'm living here." She shook her gray head from side to side. "I'm a bad woman for letting Bob be a cat for extra days."

Amelia was shocked. Obviously, her teacher's fall from grace was an amazing development to Amelia, clearly overshadowing her own guilt about what she'd done to Bob in the first place. Amelia was definitely a live-in-the-moment kind of person.

Bob came out of the bathroom. He marched up to us. "I want to go back to my place in New Orleans," Bob said. "Where the hell are we? How did I get here?"

Amelia's face lost all its animation. Octavia looked grim. I quietly left the room. It was going to be very unpleasant, the two women telling Bob about Katrina. I didn't want to be around while he tried to process that terrible news on top of everything else he was trying to handle.

I wondered where Bob had lived, if his house or apartment was still standing, if his possessions were somehow intact. If his family was alive. I heard Octavia's voice rising and falling, and then I heard a terrible silence.

Chapter 21

The next day I took Bob to Wal-Mart to purchase some clothes. Amelia had pressed some money into Bob's hand, and the young man had accepted it because he had no choice. He could hardly wait to get away from Amelia. And I couldn't say as how I blamed him.

As we drove to town, Bob kept blinking around him in a stunned way. When we entered the store, he went to the nearest aisle and rubbed his head against the corner. I smiled brightly at Marcia Albanese, a wealthy older woman who was on the school board. I hadn't seen her since she'd given Halleigh a wedding shower.

"Who's your friend?" Marcia asked. She was both naturally social and curious. She didn't ask about the head rubbing, which endeared her to me forever.

"Marcia, this is Bob Jessup, a visitor from out of town," I said, and wished I'd prepared a story. Bob nodded at Marcia with wide eyes and held out his hand. At least he didn't poke her with his head and demand to have his ears scratched. Marcia shook hands and told Bob she was pleased to meet him.

"Thanks, nice to meet you, too," Bob said. Oh, good, he sounded really normal.

"Are you going to be in Bon Temps long, Bob?" Marcia said.

"Oh, God, no," he said. "Excuse me, I have to buy some shoes." And he walked off (very smoothly and sinuously) to the men's shoe aisles. He was wearing a pair of flip-flops Amelia had donated, bright green ones that weren't quite big enough.

Marcia was clearly taken aback, but I really couldn't think of a good explanation. "See you later," I said, and followed in his wake. Bob got some sneakers, some socks, two pairs of pants, two T-shirts, and a jacket, plus some underwear. I asked Bob what he'd like to eat, and he asked me if I could make salmon croquettes.

"I sure can," I said, relieved he'd asked for something so easy, and got the cans of salmon I'd need. He also wanted chocolate pudding, and that was easy enough, too. He left the other menu selections up to me.

We had an early supper that night before I had to leave for work, and Bob seemed really pleased with the croquettes and the pudding. He looked much better, too, since he'd showered and put on his new clothes. He was even speaking to Amelia. I gathered from their conversation that she'd taken him through the websites about Katrina and its survivors, and he'd been in contact with the Red Cross. The family he'd grown up in, his aunt's, had lived in Bay Saint Louis, in southern Mississippi, and we all knew what had happened there.

"What will you do now?" I asked, since I figured he'd had a while to think about it now.

"I've got to go see," he said. "I want to try to find out what happened to my apartment in New Orleans, but my family is more important. And I've got to think of something to tell them, to explain where I've been and why I haven't been in touch."

We were all silent, because that was a puzzler.

"You could tell 'em you were enchanted by an evil witch," Amelia said glumly.

Bob snorted. "They might believe it," he said. "They know I'm not a normal person. But I don't think they'd be able to swallow that it lasted so long. Maybe I'll tell them that I lost my memory. Or that I went to Vegas and got married."

"You contacted them regularly, before Katrina?" I said.

He shrugged. "Every couple of weeks," he said. "I didn't think of us as close. But I would definitely have tried after Katrina. I love them." He looked away for a minute.

We kicked around ideas for a while, but there really wasn't a credible reason he would have been out of touch for so long. Amelia said she was going to buy Bob a bus ticket to Hattiesburg and he would try to find a ride from there into the most affected area so he could track down his people.

Amelia was clearing her conscience by spending money on Bob. I had no issue with that. She should be doing so; and I hoped Bob would find his folks, or at least discover what had happened to them, where they were living now.

Before I left for work, I stood in the doorway of the kitchen for a minute or two, looking at the three of them. I tried to see in Bob what Amelia had seen, the element that had attracted her so powerfully. Bob was thin and not particularly tall, and his inky hair naturally lay flat to his skull. Amelia had unearthed his glasses, and they were black-rimmed and thick. I'd seen every inch of Bob, and I realized Mother Nature had been generous to him in the man-bits department, but surely that wasn't enough to explain Amelia's ardent sexcapades with this guy.

Then Bob laughed, the first time he'd laughed since he'd become human again, and I got it. Bob had white, even teeth and great lips, and when he smiled, there was a kind of sardonic, intellectual sexiness about him.

Mystery solved.

When I got home, he would be gone, so I said good-bye to Bob, thinking I'd never see him again, unless he decided to return to Bon Temps to get revenge on Amelia.

As I drove into town, I wondered if we could get a real cat. After all, we had the litter box and the cat food. I'd ask Amelia and Octavia in a couple of days. That would surely give them time to stop being so antsy about Bob's cat-dom.

Alcide Herveaux was sitting at the bar talking with Sam when I came into the main room ready for work. Odd, him turning up again. I stopped for a second, and then made my feet move again. I managed a nod, and waved to Holly to tell her I was taking over. She held up a finger, indicating she was taking care of one customer's bill, and then she'd be out of there. I got a hello from one woman and a howdy from another man, and I felt instantly comfortable. This was my place, my home away from home.

Jasper Voss wanted another rum and Coke, Catfish wanted a pitcher of beer for himself and his wife and another couple, and one of our alcoholics, Jane Bodehouse, was ready to eat something. She said she didn't care what it was, so I got her the chicken tender basket. Getting Jane to eat at all was a real problem, and I hoped she'd down at least half of the basket. Jane was sitting at the other end of the bar from Alcide, and Sam jerked his head sideways to indicate I should join them. I turned Jane's order in and then I reluctantly went over to them. I leaned on the end of the bar.

"Sookie," Alcide said, nodding to me. "I came to say thank you to Sam."

"Good," I said bluntly.

Alcide nodded, not meeting my eyes.

After a moment the new packleader said, "Now no one will dare to try to encroach. If Priscilla hadn't attacked at the moment she picked, with us all together and aware of the danger we faced as a group, she could have kept us divided and kept picking us off until we'd killed each other."

"So she went crazy and you got lucky," I said.

"We came together because of your talent," Alcide said. "And you'll always be a friend of the pack. So is Sam. Ask us to do a service for you, any time, any place, and we'll be there." He nodded to Sam, put some money on the bar, and left.

Sam said, "Nice to have a favor stashed in the bank, huh?"

I had to smile back. "Yeah, that's a good feeling." In fact, I felt full of good cheer all of a sudden. When I looked at the door, I found out why. Eric was coming in, with Pam beside him. They sat at one of my tables, and I went over, consumed with curiosity. Also exasperation. Couldn't they stay away?

They both ordered TrueBlood, and after I served Jane Bodehouse her chicken basket and Sam warmed up the bottles, I was headed back to their table. Their presence wouldn't have rocked any boats if Arlene and her buddies hadn't been in the bar that night.

They were sneering together in an unmistakable way as I put the bottles in front of Eric and Pam, and I had a hard time maintaining my waitress calm as I asked the two if they wanted mugs with that.

"The bottle will be fine," Eric said. "I may need it to smash some skulls."

If I had been feeling Eric's good cheer, Eric was feeling my anxiety.

"No, no, no," I said almost in a whisper. I knew they could hear me. "Let's have peace. We've had enough war and killing."

"Yes," Pam agreed. "We can save the killing for later."

"I'm happy to see both of you, but I'm having a busy evening," I said. "Are you-all just out barhopping to get new ideas for Fangtasia, or can I do something for you?"

"We can do something for you," Pam said. She smiled at the two guys in the Fellowship of the Sun T-shirts, and since she was a wee bit angry, her fangs were showing. I hoped the sight would subdue them, but since they were assholes without a lick of sense, it inflamed their zeal. Pam downed the blood and licked her lips.

"Pam," I said between my teeth. "For goodness' sake, stop making it worse."

Pam gave me a flirty smile, simply so she'd hit all the buttons.

Eric said, "Pam," and immediately all the provocation disappeared, though Pam looked a little disappointed. But she sat up straighter, put her hands in her lap, and crossed her legs at the ankle. No one could have looked more innocent or demure.

"Thank you," Eric said. "Dear one—that's you, Sookie—you so impressed Felipe de Castro that he has given us permission to offer you our formal protection. This is a decision only made by the king, you understand, and it's a binding contract. You rendered him such service that he felt this was the only way to repay you."

"So, this is a big deal?"

"Yes, my lover, it is a very big deal. That means when you call us for help, we are obliged to come and risk our lives for yours. This is not a promise vampires make very often, since we grow more and more jealous of our lives the longer we live. You'd think it would be the other way around."

"Every now and then you'll find someone who wants to meet the sun after a long life," Pam said, as if she wanted to set the record straight.

"Yes," Eric said, frowning. "Every now and then. But he offers you a real honor, Sookie."

"I'm real obliged to you for bringing the news, Eric, Pam."

"Of course, I'd hoped your beautiful roommate would come in," Pam said. She leered at me. So maybe her hanging around Amelia hadn't been entirely Eric's idea.

I laughed out loud. "Well, she's got a lot to think about tonight," I said.

I'd been thinking so hard about the vampire protection that I hadn't noticed the approach of the shorter of the FotS adherants. Now he pushed past me in such a way that he rammed my shoulder, deliberately knocking me to the side. I staggered before I managed to regain my balance. Not everyone noticed, but a few of the bar patrons did. Sam had started around the bar and Eric was already on his feet when I turned and brought my tray down on the asshole's head with all the strength I could muster.

He did a little bit of staggering himself.

Those that had noticed the bit of aggravation began applauding. "Good for you, Sookie," Catfish called. "Hey, jerkoff, leave the waitresses alone."

Arlene was flushed and angry, and she almost exploded then and there. Sam stepped up to her and murmured something in her ear. She flushed even redder and glared at him, but she kept her mouth shut. The taller FotS guy came to his pal's aid and they left the bar. Neither of them spoke (I wasn't sure Shorty *could* speak), but they might as well have had "You haven't seen the last of us" tattooed on their foreheads.

I could see where the vampires' protection and my friend of the pack status might come in handy.

Eric and Pam finished their drinks and sat long enough to prove they weren't skedaddling because they felt unwelcome and weren't leaving in pursuit of the Fellowship fans. Eric tipped me a twenty and blew me a kiss as he went out the door—so did Pam—earning me an extra-special glare from my former BFF Arlene.

I worked too hard the rest of the night to think about any of the interesting things that had happened that day. After the patrons all left, even Jane Bodehouse (her son came to get her), we put out the Halloween decorations. Sam had gotten a little pumpkin for each table and painted a face on each one. I was filled with admiration, because the faces were really clever, and some of them looked like bar patrons. In fact, one looked a lot like my dear brother.

"I had no idea you could do this," I said, and he looked pleased.

"It was fun," he said, and hung a long strand of fall leaves—of course, they were actually made of cloth—around the bar mirror and among some of the bottles. I tacked up a life-size cardboard skeleton with little rivets at the joints so it could be positioned. I arranged this one so it was clearly dancing. We couldn't have any depressing skeletons at the bar. We had to have happy ones.

Even Arlene unbent a little because this was something different and fun to do, though we had to stay a bit later to do it.

I was ready to go home and go to bed when I said good night to Sam and Arlene. Arlene didn't answer, but she didn't throw me the look of disgust she usually awarded me, either.

Naturally, my day wasn't over.

My great-grandfather was sitting on my front porch when

I got to the house. It was very strange to see him in the front porch swing, in the odd combination of night and light that the security lamp and the dark hour combined to create. I wished for one moment that I was as beautiful as he was, and then I had to smile at myself.

I parked my car in the front and got out. Tried to walk quietly going up the steps so I wouldn't wake Amelia, whose bedroom overlooked the front. The house was dark, so I was sure they were in bed, unless they'd been delayed at the bus station when they delivered Bob.

"Great-grandfather," I said. "I'm glad to see you."

"You're tired, Sookie."

"Well, I just got off work." I wondered if he ever got tired himself. I couldn't imagine a fairy prince splitting wood or trying to find a leak in his water line.

"I wanted to see you," he said. "Have you thought of anything I can do for you?" He sounded mighty hopeful.

What a night this was for people giving me positive feedback. Why didn't I have more nights like this?

I thought for a minute. The Weres had made peace, in their own way. Quinn had been found. The vampires had settled into a new regime. The Fellowship fanatics had left the bar with a minimum of trouble. Bob was a man again. I didn't suppose Niall wanted to offer Octavia a room in his own house, wherever that might be. For all I knew, he had a house in a babbling brook or under a live oak somewhere deep in the woods.

"There is something I want," I said, surprised I hadn't thought of it before.

"What is it?" he asked, sounding quite pleased.

"I want to know the whereabouts of a man named Remy Savoy. He may have left New Orleans during Katrina. He may have a little child with him." I gave my great-grandfather Savoy's last known address.

Niall looked confident. "I'll find him for you, Sookie."

"I'd sure appreciate it."

"Nothing else? Nothing more?"

"I have to say . . . this sounds mighty ungracious . . . but I can't help but wonder why you seem to want to do something for me so badly."

"Why would I not? You are my only living kin."

"But you seem to have been content without me for the first twenty-seven years of my life."

"My son would not let me come near you."

"You told me that, but I don't get it. Why? He didn't make an appearance to let me know he cared anything about me. He never showed himself to me, or . . ." Played Scrabble with me, sent me a graduation present, rented a limousine for me to go to the prom, bought me a pretty dress, took me in his arms on the many occasions when I'd cried (growing up isn't easy for a telepath). He hadn't saved me from being molested by my great-uncle, or rescued my parents, one of whom was his son, when they drowned in a flash flood, or stopped a vampire from setting my house on fire while I was sleeping inside. All this guarding and watching my alleged grandfather Fintan had allegedly done had not paid off in any tangible way for me; and if it had paid off intangibly, I didn't know about it.

Would even worse things have happened? Hard to imagine.

I supposed my grandfather could have been fighting off hordes of slavering demons outside my bedroom window every night, but I couldn't feel grateful if I didn't know about it.

Niall looked upset, which was an expression I'd never seen him wear before. "There are things I can't tell you," he finally said. "When I can make myself speak of them, I will."

"Okay," I said dryly. "But this isn't exactly the give-and-take thing I wanted to have with my great-grandfather, I got to say. This is me telling you everything, and you telling me nothing."

"This may not be what you wanted, but it's what I can give," Niall said with some stiffness. "I do love you, and I had hoped that would be what mattered."

"I'm glad to hear you love me," I said very slowly, because I didn't want to risk seeing him walk away from Demanding Sookie. "But acting like it would be even better."

"I don't act as though I love you?"

"You vanish and reappear when it suits you. All your offers of help aren't help of the practical kind, like the stuff most grandfathers—or great-grandfathers—do. They fix their granddaughter's car with their own hands, or they offer to help with her college tuition, or they mow her lawn so she doesn't have to. Or they take her hunting. You're not going to do that."

"No," he said. "I'm not." A ghost of a smile crossed his face. "You wouldn't want to go hunting with me."

Okay, I wasn't going to think about that too closely. "So, I don't have any idea of how we're supposed to be together. You're outside my frame of reference."

"I understand," he said seriously. "All the great-grandfathers you know are human, and that I am not. You're not what I expected, either."

"Yeah, I got that." Did I even know any other great-grandfathers? Among friends my own age, even grandfathers were not a sure thing, much less great-grandfathers. But the ones I'd met were all 100 percent human. "I hope I'm not a disappointment," I said.

"No," he said slowly. "A surprise. Not a disappointment. I'm as poor at predicting your actions and reactions as you are at predicting mine. We'll have to work through this slowly." I found myself wondering again why he wasn't more interested in Jason, whose name activated an ache deep inside me. Someday soon I was going to have to talk to my brother, but I couldn't face the idea now. I almost asked Niall to check on Jason, but then I changed my mind and kept silent. Niall eyed my face.

"You don't want to tell me something, Sookie. I worry when you do that. But my love is sincere and deep, and I'll find Remy Savoy for you." He kissed me on the cheek. "You smell like my kin," he said approvingly.

And he poofed.

So, another mysterious conversation with my mysterious great-grandfather had been concluded by him on his own terms. Again. I sighed, fished my keys out of my purse, and unlocked the front door. The house was quiet and dark, and I made my way through the living room and into the hall with as little noise as I could make. I turned on my bedside lamp and performed my nightly routine, curtains closed against the morning sun that would try to wake me in a few short hours.

Had I been an ungrateful bitch to my great-grandfather? When I reviewed what I'd said, I wondered if I'd sounded demanding and whiney. In a more optimistic interpretation, I thought I might have sounded like a stand-up woman, the kind people shouldn't mess with, the kind of woman who speaks her mind.

I turned on the heat before I got into bed. Octavia and Amelia hadn't complained, but it had definitely been chilly the past few mornings. The stale smell that always comes when the heat is used the first time filled the air, and I wrinkled my nose as I snuggled under the sheet and the blanket. Then the *whoosh* noise lulled me into sleep.

I'd been hearing voices for some time before I realized they were outside my door. I blinked, saw it was day, and shut my eyes again. Back to sleep. The voices continued, and I could tell they were arguing. I cracked open one eye to peer at the digital clock on the bedside table. It was nine thirty. Gack. Since the voices wouldn't shut up or go away, I reluctantly opened both eyes at one time, absorbed the fact that the day was not bright, and sat up, pushing the covers back. I moved to the window to the left of the bed and looked out. Gray and rainy. As I stood there, drops began to hit the glass; it was going to be that kind of day.

I went to the bathroom and heard the voices outside hush

now that I was clearly up and stirring. I threw open the door to find my two housemates standing right outside, which was no big surprise.

"We didn't know if we should wake you," Octavia said. She looked anxious.

"But I thought we ought to, because a message from a magical source is clearly important," Amelia said. She appeared to have said it many times in the past few minutes, from the expression on Octavia's face.

"What message?" I asked, deciding to ignore the argument part of this conversation.

"This one," Octavia said, handing me a large buff envelope. It was made of heavy paper, like a super-fancy wedding invitation. My name was on the outside. No address, just my name. Furthermore, it was sealed with wax. The imprint in the wax was the head of a unicorn.

"Okey-dokey," I said. This was going to be an unusual letter.

I walked into the kitchen to get a cup of coffee and a knife, in that order, both the witches trailing behind me like a Greek chorus. Having poured the coffee and pulled out a chair to sit at the table, I slid the knife under the seal and detached it gently. I opened the flap and pulled out a card. On the card was a handwritten address: 1245 Bienville, Red Ditch, Louisiana. That was all.

"What does it mean?" Octavia said. She and Amelia were naturally standing right behind me so they could get a good view.

"It's the location of someone I've been searching for," I said, which was not exactly the truth but close enough.

"Where's Red Ditch?" Octavia said. "I've never heard of it." Amelia was already fetching the Louisiana map from the drawer under the telephone. She looked up the town, running her finger down the columns of names.

"It's not too far," she said. "See?" She put her finger on a tiny dot about an hour and a half's drive southeast of Bon Temps.

I drank my coffee as fast as I could and scrambled into some jeans. I slapped a little makeup on and brushed my hair and headed out the front door to my car, map in hand.

Octavia and Amelia followed me out, dying to know what I was going to do and what significance the message had for me. But they were just going to have to wonder, at least for right now. I wondered why I was in such a hurry to do this. It wasn't like he was going to vanish, unless Remy Savoy was a fairy, too. I thought that highly unlikely.

I had to be back for the evening shift, but I had plenty of time.

I drove with the radio on, and this morning I was in a country-and-western kind of mood. Travis Tritt and Carrie Underwood accompanied me, and by the time I drove into Red Ditch, I was feeling my roots. There was even less to Red Ditch than there was to Bon Temps, and that's saying something.

I figured it would be easy to find Bienville Street, and I was right. It was the kind of street you can find anywhere in America. The houses were small, neat, boxy, with room for one car in the carport and a small yard. In the case of 1245, the backyard was fenced in and I could see a lively little black dog running around. There wasn't a doghouse, so the pooch was an indoor-outdoor animal. Everything was neat, but not obsessively so. The bushes around the house were trimmed and the yard was raked. I drove by a couple of times, and then I wondered what I was going to do. How would I find out what I wanted to know?

There was a pickup truck parked in the garage, so Savoy was probably at home. I took a deep breath, parked across from the house, and tried to send my extra ability hunting. But in a neighborhood full of the thoughts of the living people in these houses, it was hard. I thought I was getting two brain signatures from the house I was watching, but it was hard to be absolutely sure.

"Fuck it," I said, and got out of the car. I popped my keys in my jacket pocket and went up the sidewalk to the front door. I knocked.

"Hold on, son," said a man's voice inside, and I heard a child's voice say, "Daddy, me! I get it!"

"No, Hunter," the man said, and the door opened. He was looking at me through a screen door. He unhooked it and pushed it open when he saw I was a woman. "Hi," he said. "Can I help you?"

I looked down at the child who wiggled past him to look up at me. He was maybe four years old. He had dark hair and eyes. He was the spitting image of Hadley. Then I looked at the man again. Something in his face had changed during my protracted silence.

"Who are you?" he said in an entirely different voice.

"I'm Sookie Stackhouse," I said. I couldn't think of any artful way to do this. "I'm Hadley's cousin. I just found out where you were."

"You can't have any claim on him," said the man, keeping a very tight rein on his voice.

"Of course not," I said, surprised. "I just want to meet him. I don't have much family."

There was another significant pause. He was weighing my words and my demeanor and he was deciding whether to slam the door or let me in.

"Daddy, she's pretty," said the boy, and that seemed to tip the balance in my favor.

"Come on in," Hadley's ex-husband said.

I looked around the small living room, which had a couch and a recliner, a television and a bookcase full of DVDs and children's books, and a scattering of toys.

"I worked Saturday, so I have today off," he said, in case I imagined he was unemployed. "Oh, I'm Remy Savoy. I guess you knew that."

I nodded.

"This is Hunter," he said, and the child got a case of the shys. He hid behind his father's legs and peeked around at me. "Please sit down," Remy added.

I shoved a newspaper to one end of the couch and sat, trying not to stare at the man or the child. My cousin Hadley had been very striking, and she'd married a good-looking man. It was hard to peg down what left that impression. His nose was big, his jaw stuck out a little, and his eyes were a little wide-spaced. But the sum of all this was a man most women would look at twice. His hair was that medium shade between blond and brown, and it was thick and layered, the back hanging over his collar. He was wearing a flannel shirt unbuttoned over a white Hanes T-shirt. Jeans. No shoes. A dimple in his chin.

Hunter was wearing corduroy pants and a sweatshirt with a big football on the front. His clothes were brand-new, unlike his dad's.

I'd finished looking at them before Remy'd finished looking at me. He didn't think I had any trace of Hadley in my face. My body was plumper and my coloring was lighter and I wasn't as hard. He thought I looked like I didn't have a lot of money. He thought I was pretty, like his son did. But he didn't trust me.

"How long has it been since you heard from her?" I asked.

"I haven't heard from Hadley since a few months after he was born," Remy said. He was used to that, but there was sadness in his thoughts, too.

Hunter was sitting on the floor, playing with some trucks. He loaded some Duplos into the back of a dump truck, which backed up to a fire engine very slowly, guided by Hunter's small hands. To the astonishment of the Duplo man sitting in the cab of the fire engines, the dump truck let go of its load all over the fire engine. Hunter got a big kick out of this, and he said, "Daddy, look!"

"I see it, son." Remy looked at me intently. "Why are you here?" he asked, deciding to get right to the point.

"I only found out there might be a baby a couple of weeks ago," I said. "Wasn't any point in tracking you down until I heard that."

"I never met her family," he said. "How'd you know she was married? Did she tell you?" Then, reluctantly, he said, "Is she okay?"

"No," I said very quietly. I didn't want Hunter to become interested. The boy was loading all the Duplos back into the dump truck. "She's been dead since before Katrina."

I could hear the shock detonate like a little bomb in his head. "She was already a vamp, I heard," he said uncertainly, his voice wavering. "That kind of dead?"

"No. I mean really, finally."

"What happened?"

"She was attacked by another vampire," I said. "He was jealous of Hadley's relationship with her, ah, her . . ."

"Girlfriend?" No mistaking the bitterness in her ex-husband's voice and in his head.

"Yeah."

"That was a shocker," he said, but in his head all the shock had worn off. There was only a grim resignation, a loss of pride.

"I didn't know about any of this until after she passed."

"You're her cousin? I remember her telling me she had two. . . . You got a brother, right?"

"Yes," I said.

"You knew she had been married to me?"

"I found out when I cleaned out her safe-deposit box a few weeks ago. I didn't know there had been a son. I apologize for that." I wasn't sure why I was apologizing or how I could have known, but I was sorry I hadn't even considered the fact that Hadley and her husband might have had a child. Hadley had been a little older than me, and I guessed Remy was probably thirty or thereabouts.

"You look fine," he said suddenly, and I flushed, understanding him instantly.

"Hadley told you I had a disability." I looked away from him, at the boy, who jumped to his feet, announced he had to go to the bathroom, and dashed out of the room. I couldn't help but smile.

"Yeah, she said something. . . . She said you had a hard time of it in school," he said tactfully. Hadley had told him I was crazy as hell. He was seeing no signs of it, and he wondered why Hadley had thought so. But he glanced in the direction the child had gone, and I knew he was thinking he had to be careful since Hunter was in the house, he had to be alert for any signs of this instability—though Hadley had never specified what form of craziness I had.

"That's true," I said. "I had a hard time of it. Hadley wasn't any big help. But her mom, my aunt Linda, was a great woman before the cancer got her. She was real kind to me, always. And we had some good moments now and then."

"I could say the same. We did have some good moments," Remy said. His forearms were braced on his knees and his big hands, scarred and battered, hung down. He was a man who knew what hard work was.

There was a sound at the front door and a woman came in without bothering to knock. "Hey, baby," she said, smiling at Remy. When she noticed me, her smile faltered and faded away.

"Kristen, this is a relative of my ex-wife's," Remy said, and there wasn't any haste or apology in his voice.

Kristen had long brown hair and big brown eyes and she was maybe twenty-five. She was wearing khakis and a polo shirt with a logo on the chest, a laughing duck. The legend above the duck read, "Jerry's Detailing." "Nice to meet you," Kristen said insincerely. "I'm Kristen Duchesne, Remy's girlfriend."

"Pleased to meet you," I said, more honestly. "Sookie Stackhouse."

"You didn't offer this woman a drink, Remy! Sookie, can I get you a Coke or a Sprite?"

She knew what was in the refrigerator. I wondered if she lived here. Well, none of my business, as long as she was good to Hadley's son.

"No, thanks," I said. "I've got to be going in a minute." I made a little production out of looking at my watch. "I got to go to work this evening."

"Oh, where is that?" Kristen asked. She was a little more relaxed.

"Merlotte's. It's a bar in Bon Temps," I said. "About eighty miles from here."

"Sure, that's where your wife was from," Kristen said, glancing at Remy.

Remy said, "Sookie came with some news, I'm afraid." His hands twisted together, though his voice was steady. "Hadley is dead."

Kristen inhaled sharply but she had to keep her comment

to herself because Hunter dashed back into the room. "Daddy, I washed my hands!" he shouted, and his father smiled at him.

"Good for you, son," he said, and ruffled the boy's dark hair. "Say hello to Kristen."

"Hey, Kristen," Hunter said without much interest.

I stood. I wished I had a business card to leave. This seemed odd and wrong, to just walk out. But Kristen's presence was oddly inhibiting. She picked up Hunter and slung him on her hip. He was quite a load for her, but she made a point of making it look easy and habitual, though it wasn't. But she did like the little boy; I could see it in her head.

"Kristen likes me," Hunter said, and I looked at him sharply.

"Sure I do," Kristen said, and laughed.

Remy was looking from Hunter to me with a troubled face, a face that was just beginning to look worried.

I wondered how to explain our relationship to Hunter. I was pretty close to being his aunt, as we reckon things here. Kids don't care about second cousins.

"Aunt Sookie," Hunter said, testing the words. "I got an aunt?"

I took a deep breath. *Yes, you do, Hunter,* I thought.

"I never had one before."

"You got one now," I told him, and I looked into Remy's eyes. They were frightened. He hadn't spelled it out to himself yet, but he knew.

There was something I had to say to him, regardless of Kristen's presence. I could feel her confusion and her sense that something was going on without her knowledge. But I didn't have the space on my agenda to worry about Kristen, too. Hunter was the important person.

"You're gonna need me," I told Remy. "When he gets a little older, you're gonna need to talk. My number's in the book, and I'm not going anywhere. You understand?"

Kristen said, "What's going on? Why are we getting so serious?"

"Don't worry, Kris," Remy said gently. "Just family stuff."

Kristen lowered a wriggling Hunter to the floor. "Uh-huh," she said, in the tone of someone who knows full well she's having the wool pulled over her eyes.

"Stackhouse," I reminded Remy. "Don't put it off till too late, when he's already miserable."

"I understand," he said. He looked miserable himself, and I didn't blame him.

"I've got to go," I said again, to reassure Kristen.

"Aunt Sookie, you going?" Hunter asked. He wasn't quite ready to hug me yet, but he thought about it. He liked me. "You coming back?"

"Sometime, Hunter," I said. "Maybe your dad will bring you to visit me someday."

I shook Kristen's hand, shook Remy's, which they both thought was odd, and opened the door. As I put one foot on the steps, Hunter said silently, *Bye, Aunt Sookie.*

Bye, Hunter, I said right back.

DEAD UNTIL DARK

CHARLAINE HARRIS

First published in Great Britain in 2004 by
Little, Brown

This edition published in Great Britain in 2009 by
Gollancz
An imprint of the Orion Publishing Group
Orion House, 5 Upper St Martin's Lane, London WC2H 9EA
An Hachette UK Company

A CIP catalogue record for this book
is available from the British Library

ISBN 978 0 575 08936 5

10 12 14 16 18 19 17 15 13 11

Printed and bound in the UK by CPI Mackays,
Chatham ME5 8TD

www.orionbooks.co.uk

DEAD UNTIL DARK

Also by Charlaine Harris

SOOKIE STACKHOUSE

Dead Until Dark

Living Dead in Dallas

Club Dead

Dead to the World

Dead as a Doornail

Definitely Dead

All Together Dead

From Dead to Worse

Dead and Gone

HARPER CONNELLY

Grave Sight

Grave Surprise

An Ice Cold Grave

Grave Secret

My thanks and appreciation go to the people
who thought this book
was a good idea –
Dean James, Toni L. P. Kelner
and
Gary and Susan Nowlin

Chapter 1

I'd been waiting for the vampire for years when he walked into the bar.

Ever since vampires came out of the coffin (as they laughingly put it) four years ago, I'd hoped one would come to Bon Temps. We had all the other minorities in our little town – why not the newest, the legally recognized undead? But rural northern Louisiana wasn't too tempting to vampires, apparently; on the other hand, New Orleans was a real center for them – the whole Anne Rice thing, right?

It's not that long a drive from Bon Temps to New Orleans, and everyone who came into the bar said that if you threw a rock on a street corner you'd hit one. Though you better not.

But I was waiting for my own vampire.

You can tell I don't get out much. And it's not because I'm not pretty. I am. I'm blond and blue-eyed and twenty-five, and my legs are strong and my bosom is substantial, and I have a waspy waistline. I look good in the warm-weather waitress outfit Sam picked for us: black shorts, white T, white socks, black Nikes.

But I have a disability. That's how I try to think of it.

The bar patrons just say I'm crazy.

Either way, the result is that I almost never have a date. So little treats count a lot with me.

And he sat at one of my tables – the vampire.

I knew immediately what he was. It amazed me when no one else turned around to stare. They couldn't tell! But to me, his skin had a little glow, and I just knew.

I could have danced with joy, and in fact I did do a little step right there by the bar. Sam Merlotte, my boss, looked up from the drink he was mixing and gave me a tiny smile. I grabbed my tray and pad and went over to the vampire's table. I hoped that my lipstick was still even and my ponytail was still neat. I'm kind of tense, and I could feel my smile yanking the corners of my mouth up.

He seemed lost in thought, and I had a chance to give him a good once-over before he looked up. He was a little under six feet, I estimated. He had thick brown hair, combed straight back and brushing his collar, and his long sideburns seemed curiously old-fashioned. He was pale, of course; hey, he was dead, if you believed the old tales. The politically correct theory, the one the vamps themselves publicly backed, had it that this guy was the victim of a virus that left him apparently dead for a couple of days and thereafter allergic to sunlight, silver, and garlic. The details depended on which newspaper you read. They were all full of vampire stuff these days.

Anyway, his lips were lovely, sharply sculpted, and he had arched dark brows. His nose swooped down right out of that arch, like a prince's in a Byzantine mosaic. When he finally looked up, I saw his eyes were even darker than his hair, and the whites were incredibly white.

'What can I get you?' I asked, happy almost beyond words.

He raised his eyebrows. 'Do you have the bottled synthetic blood?' he asked.

'No, I'm so sorry! Sam's got some on order. Should be in next week.'

'Then red wine, please,' he said, and his voice was cool and clear, like a stream over smooth stones. I laughed out loud. It was too perfect.

'Don't mind Sookie, mister, she's crazy,' came a familiar voice from the booth against the wall. All my happiness deflated, though I could feel the smile still straining my lips. The vampire was staring at me, watching the life go out of my face.

'I'll get your wine right away,' I said, and strode off, not even looking at Mack Rattray's smug face. He was there almost every night, he and his wife Denise. I called them the Rat Couple. They'd done their best to make me miserable since they'd moved into the rent trailer at Four Tracks Corner. I had hoped that they'd blow out of Bon Temps as suddenly as they'd blown in.

When they'd first come into Merlotte's, I'd very rudely listened in to their thoughts – I know, pretty low-class of me. But I get bored like everyone else, and though I spend most of my time blocking out the thoughts of other people that try to pass through my brain, sometimes I just give in. So I knew some things about the Rattrays that maybe no one else did. For one thing, I knew they'd been in jail, though I didn't know why. For another, I'd read the nasty thoughts Mack Rattray had entertained about yours truly. And then I'd heard in Denise's thoughts that she'd abandoned a baby she'd had two years before, a baby that wasn't Mack's.

And they didn't tip, either.

Sam poured a glass of the house red wine, looking over at the vampire's table as he put it on my tray.

When Sam looked back at me, I could tell he too knew our new customer was undead. Sam's eyes are Paul Newman blue, as opposed to my own hazy blue gray. Sam is blond, too, but his hair is wiry and his blond is almost a sort of hot red gold. He is always a little sunburned, and though he looks slight in his clothes, I have seen him unload trucks with his shirt off, and he has plenty of upper body strength. I never listen to Sam's thoughts. He's my boss. I've had to quit jobs before because I found out things I didn't want to know about my boss.

But Sam didn't comment, he just gave me the wine. I checked the glass to make sure it was sparkly clean and made my way back to the vampire's table.

'Your wine, sir,' I said ceremoniously and placed it carefully on the table exactly in front of him. He looked at me again, and I stared into his lovely eyes while I had the chance. 'Enjoy,' I said proudly. Behind me, Mack Rattray yelled, 'Hey, Sookie! We need another pitcher of beer here!' I sighed and turned to take the empty pitcher from the Rats' table. Denise was in fine form tonight, I noticed, wearing a halter top and short shorts, her mess of brown hair floofing around her head in fashionable tangles. Denise wasn't truly pretty, but she was so flashy and confident that it took awhile to figure that out.

A little while later, to my dismay, I saw the Rattrays had moved over to the vampire's table. They were talking at him. I couldn't see that he was responding a lot, but he wasn't leaving either.

'Look at that!' I said disgustedly to Arlene, my fellow

waitress. Arlene is redheaded and freckled and ten years older than me, and she's been married four times. She has two kids, and from time to time, I think she considers me her third.

'New guy, huh?' she said with small interest. Arlene is currently dating Rene Lenier, and though I can't see the attraction, she seems pretty satisfied. I think Rene was her second husband.

'Oh, he's a vampire,' I said, just having to share my delight with someone.

'Really? Here? Well, just think,' she said, smiling a little to show she appreciated my pleasure. 'He can't be too bright, though, honey, if he's with the Rats. On the other hand, Denise is giving him quite a show.'

I figured it out after Arlene made it plain to me; she's much better at sizing up sexual situations than I am due to her experience and my lack.

The vampire was hungry. I'd always heard that the synthetic blood the Japanese had developed kept vampires up to par as far as nutrition, but didn't really satisfy their hunger, which was why there were 'Unfortunate Incidents' from time to time. (That was the vampire euphemism for the bloody slaying of a human.) And here was Denise Rattray, stroking her throat, turning her neck from side to side . . . what a *bitch*.

My brother, Jason, came into the bar, then, and sauntered over to give me a hug. He knows that women like a man who's good to his family and also kind to the disabled, so hugging me is a double whammy of recommendation. Not that Jason needs many more points than he has just by being himself. He's handsome. He can sure be mean, too, but most women seem quite willing to overlook that.

'Hey, sis, how's Gran?'

'She's okay, about the same. Come by to see.'

'I will. Who's loose tonight?'

'Look for yourself.' I noticed that when Jason began to glance around there was a flutter of female hands to hair, blouses, lips.

'Hey. I see DeeAnne. She free?'

'She's here with a trucker from Hammond. He's in the bathroom. Watch it.'

Jason grinned at me, and I marvelled that other women could not see the selfishness of that smile. Even Arlene tucked in her T-shirt when Jason came in, and after four husbands she should have known a little about evaluating men. The other waitress I worked with, Dawn, tossed her hair and straightened her back to make her boobs stand out. Jason gave her an amiable wave. She pretended to sneer. She's on the outs with Jason, but she still wants him to notice her.

I got really busy – everyone came to Merlotte's on Saturday night for some portion of the evening – so I lost track of my vampire for a while. When I next had a moment to check on him, he was talking to Denise. Mack was looking at him with an expression so avid that I became worried.

I went closer to the table, staring at Mack. Finally, I let down my guard and listened.

Mack and Denise had been in jail for vampire draining.

Deeply upset, I nevertheless automatically carried a pitcher of beer and some glasses to a raucous table of four. Since vampire blood was supposed to temporarily relieve symptoms of illness and increase sexual potency, kind of like prednisone and Viagra rolled into one, there was a huge black market for genuine, undiluted vampire blood. Where there's a market there are suppliers; in this case, I'd just learned, the scummy Rat Couple. They'd formerly trapped vampires and drained them, selling the little vials of blood for as much as $200 apiece. It had been the drug of choice for at least two years now. Some buyers went crazy after drinking pure vampire blood, but that didn't slow the market any.

The drained vampire didn't last long, as a rule. The drainers left the vampires staked or simply dumped them out in the open. When the sun came up, that was all she wrote. From time to time, you read about the tables being turned when the vampire managed to get free. Then you got your dead drainers.

Now my vampire was getting up and leaving with the Rats. Mack met my eyes, and I saw him looking distinctly startled at the expression on my face. He turned away, shrugging me off like everyone else.

That made me mad. Really mad.

What should I do? While I struggled with myself, they were out the door. Would the vampire believe me if I ran after them, told him? No one else did. Or if by chance they did, they hated and feared me for reading the thoughts concealed in people's brains. Arlene had begged me to read her fourth husband's mind when he'd come in to pick her up one night because she was pretty certain he was thinking of leaving her and the kids, but I wouldn't because I wanted to keep the one friend I had. And even Arlene hadn't been able to ask me directly because that would be admitting I had this gift, this curse. People couldn't admit it. They had to think I was crazy. Which sometimes I almost was!

So I dithered, confused and frightened and angry, and then I knew I just had to act. I was goaded by the look Mack had given me – as if I was negligible.

I slid down the bar to Jason, where he was sweeping DeeAnne off her feet. She didn't take much sweeping, popular opinion had it. The trucker from Hammond was glowering from her other side.

'Jason,' I said urgently. He turned to give me a warning glare. 'Listen, is that chain still in the back of the pickup?'

'Never leave home without it,' he said lazily, his eyes scanning my face for signs of trouble. 'You going to fight, Sookie?'

I smiled at him, so used to grinning that it was easy. 'I sure hope not,' I said cheerfully.

'Hey, you need help?' After all, he was my brother.

'No, thanks,' I said, trying to sound reassuring. And I slipped over to Arlene. 'Listen, I got to leave a little early. My tables are pretty thin, can you cover for me?' I didn't think I'd ever asked Arlene such a thing, though I'd covered for her many times. She, too, offered me help. 'That's okay,' I said. 'I'll be back in if I can. If you clean my area, I'll do your trailer.'

Arlene nodded her red mane enthusiastically.

I pointed to the employee door, to myself, and made my fingers walk, to tell Sam where I was going.

He nodded. He didn't look happy.

So out the back door I went, trying to make my feet quiet on the gravel. The employee parking lot is at the rear of the bar, through a door leading into the storeroom. The cook's car was there, and Arlene's, Dawn's, and mine. To my right, the east, Sam's pickup was sitting in front of his trailer.

I went out of the gravelled employee parking area onto the blacktop that surfaced the much larger customer lot to the west of the bar. Woods surrounded the clearing in which Merlotte's stood, and the edges of the parking lot were mostly gravel. Sam kept it well lit, and the surrealistic glare of the high, parking lot lights made everything look strange.

I saw the Rat Couple's dented red sports car, so I knew they were close.

I found Jason's truck at last. It was black with custom aqua and pink swirls on the sides. He sure did love to be noticed. I pulled myself up by the tailgate and rummaged around in the bed for his chain, a thick length of links that he carried in case of a fight. I looped it and carried it pressed to my body so it wouldn't chink.

I thought a second. The only halfway private spot to which the Rattrays could have lured the vampire was the end of the parking lot where the trees actually overhung the cars. So I crept in that direction, trying to move fast and low.

I paused every few seconds and listened. Soon I heard a groan and the faint sounds of voices. I snaked between the cars, and I spotted them right where I'd figured they'd be. The vampire was down on the ground on his back, his face contorted in agony, and the gleam of chains crisscrossed his wrists and ran down to his ankles. Silver. There were two little vials of blood already on the ground beside Denise's feet, and as I watched, she fixed a new Vacutainer to the needle. The tourniquet above his elbow dug cruelly into his arm.

Their backs were to me, and the vampire hadn't seen me yet. I loosened the coiled chain so a good three feet of it swung free. Who to attack first? They were both small and vicious.

I remembered Mack's contemptuous dismissal and the fact that he never left me a tip. Mack first.

I'd never actually been in a fight before. Somehow I was positively looking forward to it.

I leapt out from behind a pickup and swung the chain. It thwacked across Mack's back as he knelt beside his victim. He screamed and jumped up. After a glance, Denise set about getting the third Vacutainer plugged. Mack's hand dipped down to his boot and came up shining. I gulped. He had a knife in his hand.

'Uh-oh,' I said, and grinned at him.

'You crazy bitch!' he screamed. He sounded like he was looking forward to using the knife. I was too involved to keep my mental guard up, and I had a clear flash of what Mack wanted to do to me. It drove me really crazy. I went for him with every intention of hurting him as badly as I could. But he was ready for me and jumped forward with the knife while I was swinging the chain. He sliced at my arm and just missed it. The chain, on its recoil, wrapped around his skinny neck like a lover. Mack's yell of triumph turned into a gurgle. He dropped the knife and clawed at the links with both hands. Losing air, he dropped to his knees on the rough pavement, yanking the chain from my hand.

Well, there went Jason' s chain. I swooped down and scooped up Mack's knife, holding it like I knew how to use it. Denise had been lunging forward, looking like a redneck witch in the lines and shadows of the security lights.

She stopped in her tracks when she saw I had Mack's

knife. She cursed and railed and said terrible things. I waited till she'd run down to say, 'Get. Out. Now.'

Denise stared holes of hate in my head. She tried to scoop up the vials of blood, but I hissed at her to leave them alone. So she pulled Mack to his feet. He was still making choking, gurgling sounds and holding the chain. Denise kind of dragged him along to their car and shoved him in through the passenger's side. Yanking some keys from her pocket Denise threw herself in the driver's seat.

As I heard the engine roar into life, suddenly I realized that the Rats now had another weapon. Faster than I've ever moved, I ran to the vampire's head and panted, 'Push with your feet!' I grabbed him under the arms and yanked back with all my might, and he caught on and braced his feet and shoved. We were just inside the tree line when the red car came roaring down at us. Denise missed us by less than a yard when she had to swerve to avoid hitting a pine. Then I heard the big motor of the Rats' car receding in the distance.

'Oh, wow,' I breathed, and knelt by the vampire because my knees wouldn't hold me up any more. I breathed heavily for just a minute, trying to get hold of myself. The vampire moved a little, and I looked over. To my horror, I saw wisps of smoke coming up from his wrists where the silver touched them.

'Oh, you poor thing,' I said, angry at myself for not caring for him instantly. Still trying to catch my breath, I began to unwind the thin bands of silver, which all seemed to be part of one very long chain. 'Poor baby,' I whispered, never thinking until later how incongruous that sounded. I have agile fingers, and I released his wrists pretty quickly. I wondered how the Rats had distracted him while they got into position to put them on, and I could feel myself reddening as I pictured it.

The vampire cradled his arms to his chest while I worked on the silver wrapped around his legs. His ankles had fared better since the drainers hadn't troubled to pull up his jeans legs and put the silver against his bare skin.

'I'm sorry I didn't get here faster,' I said apologetically. 'You'll feel better in a minute, right? Do you want me to leave?'

'No.'

That made me feel pretty good until he added, 'They might come back, and I can't fight yet.' His cool voice was uneven, but I couldn't exactly say I'd heard him panting.

I made a sour face at him, and while he was recovering, I took a few precautions. I sat with my back to him, giving him some privacy. I know how unpleasant it is to be stared at when you're hurting. I hunkered down on the pavement, keeping watch on the parking lot. Several cars left, and others came in, but none came down to our end by the woods. By the movement of the air around me, I knew when the vampire had sat up.

He didn't speak right away. I turned my head to the left to look at him. He was closer than I'd thought. His big dark eyes looked into mine. His fangs had retracted; I was a little disappointed about that.

'Thank you,' he said stiffly.

So he wasn't thrilled about being rescued by a woman. Typical guy.

Since he was being so ungracious, I felt I could do something rude, too, and I listened to him, opening my mind completely.

And I heard . . . nothing.

'Oh,' I said, hearing the shock in my own voice, hardly knowing what I was saying. 'I *can't hear you.*'

'Thank you!' the vampire said, moving his lips exaggeratedly.

'No, no . . . I can hear you speak, but . . .' and in my excitement, I did something I ordinarily would never do, because it was pushy, and personal, and revealed I was disabled. I turned fully to him and put my hands on both sides of his white face, and I looked at him intently. I focused with all my energy. *Nothing.* It was like having to listen to the radio all the time, to stations you didn't get to select, and then suddenly tuning in to a wavelength you couldn't receive.

It was heaven.

His eyes were getting wider and darker, though he was holding absolutely still.

'Oh, excuse me,' I said with a gasp of embarrassment. I snatched my hands away and resumed staring at the parking lot. I began babbling about Mack and Denise, all the time thinking how marvelous it would be to have a companion I could not hear unless he chose to speak out loud. How beautiful his silence was.

'. . . so I figured I better come out here to see how you were,' I concluded, and had no idea what I'd been saying.

'You came out here to rescue me. It was brave,' he said in a voice so seductive it would have shivered DeeAnne right out of her red nylon panties.

'Now you cut that out,' I said tartly, coming right down to earth with a thud.

He looked astonished for a whole second before his face returned to its white smoothness.

'Aren't you afraid to be alone with a hungry vampire?' he

asked, something arch and yet dangerous running beneath the words.

'Nope.'

'Are you assuming that since you came to my rescue that you're safe, that I harbor an ounce of sentimental feeling after all these years? Vampires often turn on those who trust them. We don't have human values, you know.'

'A lot of humans turn on those who trust them,' I pointed out. I can be practical. 'I'm not a total fool.' I held out my arm and turned my neck. While he'd been recovering, I'd been wrapping the Rats' chains around my neck and arms.

He shivered visibly.

'But there's a juicy artery in your groin,' he said after a pause to regroup, his voice as slithery as a snake on a slide

'Don't you talk dirty,' I told him. 'I won't listen to that.'

Once again we looked at each other in silence. I was afraid I'd never see him again; after all, his first visit to Merlotte's hadn't exactly been a success. So I was trying to absorb every detail I could; I would treasure this encounter and rehash it for a long, long time. It was rare, a prize. I wanted to touch his skin again. I couldn't remember how it felt. But that would be going beyond some boundary of manners, and also maybe start him going on the seductive crap again.

'Would you like to drink the blood they collected?' he asked unexpectedly. 'It would be a way for me to show my gratitude.' He gestured at the stoppered vials lying on the blacktop. 'My blood is supposed to improve your sex life and your health.'

'I'm healthy as a horse,' I told him honestly. 'And I have no sex life to speak of. You do what you want with it.'

'You could sell it,' he suggested, but I thought he was just waiting to see what I'd say about that.

'I wouldn't touch it,' I said, insulted.

'You're different,' he said. 'What are you?' He seemed to be going through a list of possibilities in his head from the way he was looking at me. To my pleasure, I could not hear a one of them.

'Well. I'm Sookie Stackhouse, and I'm a waitress,' I told him. 'What's your name?' I thought I could at least ask that without being presuming.

'Bill,' he said.

Before I could stop myself, I rocked back onto my butt with laughter. 'The vampire Bill!' I said. 'I thought it might be Antoine, or Basil, or Langford! Bill!' I hadn't laughed so hard in a long time. 'Well, see ya, Bill. I got to get back to work.' I could feel the tense grin snap back into place when I thought of Merlotte's. I put my hand on Bill's shoulder and pushed up. It was rock hard, and I was on my feet so fast I had to stop myself from stumbling. I examined my socks to make sure their cuffs were exactly even, and I looked up and down my outfit to check for wear and tear during the fight with the Rats. I dusted off my bottom since I'd been sitting on the dirty pavement and gave Bill a wave as I started off across the parking lot.

It had been a stimulating evening, one with a lot of food for thought. I felt almost as cheerful as my smile when I considered it.

But Jason was going to be mighty angry about the chain.

After work that night, I drove home, which is only about four miles south from the bar. Jason had been gone (and so had DeeAnne) when I got back to work, and that had been another good thing. I was reviewing the evening as I drove to my grandmother's house, where I lived. It's right before Tall Pines cemetery, which lies off a narrow two-lane parish road. My great-great-great grandfather had started the house, and he'd had ideas about privacy, so to reach it you had to turn off the parish road into the driveway, go through some woods, and then you arrived at the clearing in which the house stood.

It's sure not any historic landmark, since most of the oldest parts have been ripped down and replaced over the years, and of course it's got electricity and plumbing and insulation, all that good modern stuff. But it still has a tin roof that gleams blindingly on sunny days. When the roof needed to be replaced, I wanted to put regular roofing tiles on it, but my grandmother said no. Though I was paying, it's her house; so naturally, tin it was.

Historical or not, I'd lived in this house since I was about seven, and I'd visited it often before then, so I loved it. It was just a big old family home, too big for Granny and me, I guess. It had a broad front covered by a screened-in porch, and it was painted white, Granny being a traditionalist all the way. I went through the big living room, strewn with battered furniture arranged to suit us, and down the hall to the first bedroom on the left, the biggest.

Adele Hale Stackhouse, my grandmother, was propped up in her high bed, about a million pillows padding her skinny shoulders. She was wearing a long-sleeved cotton nightgown even in the warmth of this spring night, and her bedside lamp was still on. There was a book propped in her lap.

'Hey,' I said.

'Hi, honey.'

My grandmother is very small and very old, but her hair is still thick, and so white it almost has the very faintest of green tinges. She wears it kind of rolled against her neck during the day, but at night it's loose or braided. I looked at the cover of her book.

'You reading Danielle Steel again?'

'Oh, that woman can sure tell a story.' My grandmother's great pleasures were reading Danielle Steel, watching her soap operas (which she called her 'stories') and attending meetings of the myriad clubs she'd belonged to all her adult life, it seemed. Her favorites were the Descendants of the Glorious Dead and the Bon Temps Gardening Society.

'Guess what happened tonight?' I asked her.

'What? You got a date?'

'No,' I said, working to keep a smile on my face. 'A vampire came into the bar.'

'Ooh, did he have fangs?'

I'd seen them glisten in the parking lot lights when the Rats were draining him, but there was no need to describe that to Gran. 'Sure, but they were retracted.'

'A vampire right here in Bon Temps.' Granny was as pleased as punch. 'Did he bite anybody in the bar?'

'Oh, no, Gran! He just sat and had a glass of red wine. Well, he ordered it, but he didn't drink it. I think he just wanted some company.'

'Wonder where he stays.'

'He wouldn't be too likely to tell anyone that.'

'No,' Gran said, thinking about it a moment. 'I guess not. Did you like him?'

Now that was kind of a hard question. I mulled it over. 'I don't know. He was real interesting,' I said cautiously.

'I'd surely love to meet him.' I wasn't surprised Gran said this because she enjoyed new things almost as much as I did. She wasn't one of those reactionaries who'd decided vampires were damned right off the bat. 'But I better go to sleep now. I was just waiting for you to come home before I turned out my light.'

I bent over to give Gran a kiss, and said, 'Night night.'

I half-closed her door on my way out and heard the click of the lamp as she turned it off. My cat, Tina, came from wherever she'd been sleeping to rub against my legs, and I picked her up and cuddled her for a while before putting her out for the night. I glanced at the clock. It was almost two o'clock, and my bed was calling me.

My room was right across the hall from Gran's. When I first used this room, after my folks had died, Gran had moved my bedroom furniture from their house so I'd feel more homey. And here it was still, the single bed and vanity in white-painted wood, the small chest of drawers.

I turned on my own light and shut the door and began taking off my clothes. I had at least five pairs of black shorts and many, many white T-shirts, since those tended to get stained so easily. No telling how many pairs of white socks were rolled up in my drawer. So I didn't have to do the wash tonight. I was too tired for a shower. I did brush my teeth and wash the makeup off my face, slap on some moisturizer, and take the band out of my hair.

I crawled into bed in my favorite Mickey Mouse sleep T-shirt, which came almost to my knees. I turned on my side, like I always do, and I relished the silence of the room. Almost everyone's brain is turned off in the wee hours of the night, and the vibrations are gone, the intrusions do not have to be repelled. With such peace, I only had time to think of the vampire's dark eyes, and then I fell into the deep sleep of exhaustion.

By lunchtime the next day I was in my folding aluminum chaise out in the front yard, getting browner by the second. I was in my favorite white strapless two-piece, and it was a little roomier than last summer, so I was pleased as punch.

Then I heard a vehicle coming down the drive, and Jason's black truck with its pink and aqua blazons pulled up to within a yard of my feet.

Jason climbed down – did I mention the truck sports those high tires? – to stalk toward me. He was wearing his usual work clothes, a khaki shirt and pants, and he had his sheathed knife clipped to his belt, like most of the county road workers did. Just by the way he walked, I knew he was in a huff.

I put my dark glasses on.

'Why didn't you tell me you beat up the Rattrays last night?' My brother threw himself into the aluminum yard chair by my chaise. 'Where's Gran?' he asked belatedly.

'Hanging out the laundry,' I said. Gran used the dryer in a pinch, but she really liked hanging the wet clothes out in the sun. Of course the clothesline was in the backyard, where clotheslines should be. 'She's fixing country-fried steak and sweet potatoes and green beans she put up last year, for lunch,' I added, knowing that would distract Jason a little bit. I hoped Gran stayed out back. I didn't want her to hear this conversation. 'Keep your voice low,' I reminded him.

'Rene Lenier couldn't wait till I got to work this morning to tell me all about it. He was over to the Rattrays' trailer last night to buy him some weed, and Denise drove up like she wanted to kill someone. Rene said he liked to have gotten killed, she was so mad. It took both Rene and Denise to get Mack into the trailer, and then they took him to the hospital in Monroe.' Jason glared at me accusingly.

'Did Rene tell you that Mack came after me with a knife?' I asked, deciding attacking was the best way of handling this. I could tell Jason's pique was due in large part to the fact that he had heard about this from someone else.

'If Denise told Rene, he didn't mention it to me,' Jason said slowly, and I saw his handsome face darken with rage. 'He came after you with a knife?'

'So I had to defend myself,' I said, as if it were matter-of-fact. 'And he took your chain.' This was all true, if a little skewed.

'I came in to tell you,' I continued, 'but by the time I got back in the bar, you were gone with DeeAnne, and since I was fine, it just didn't seem worth tracking you down. I knew you'd feel obliged to go after him if I told you about the knife,' I added diplomatically. There was a lot more truth in that, since Jason dearly loves a fight.

'What the hell were you doing out there anyway?' he asked, but he had relaxed, and I knew he was accepting this.

'Did you know that, in addition to selling drugs, the Rats are vampire drainers?'

Now he was fascinated. 'No . . . so?'

'Well, one of my customers last night was a vampire, and they were draining him out in Merlotte's parking lot! I couldn't have that.'

'There's a vampire here in Bon Temps?'

'Yep. Even if you don't want a vampire for your best

friend, you can't let trash like the Rats drain them. It's not like siphoning gas out of a car. And they would have left him out in the woods to die.' Though the Rats hadn't told me their intentions, that was my bet. Even if they'd put him under cover so he could survive the day, a drained vampire took at least twenty years to recover, at least that's what one had said on *Oprah*. And that's if another vampire took care of him.

'The vampire was in the bar when I was there?' Jason asked, dazzled.

'Uh-huh. The dark-haired guy sitting with the Rats.'

Jason grinned at my epithet for the Rattrays. But he hadn't let go of the night before, yet. 'How'd you know he was a vampire?' he asked, but when he looked at me, I could tell he was wishing he had bitten his tongue.

'I just knew,' I said in my flattest voice.

'Right.' And we shared a whole unspoken conversation.

'Homulka doesn't have a vampire,' Jason said thoughtfully. He tilted his face back to catch the sun, and I knew we were off dangerous ground.

'True,' I agreed. Homulka was the town Bon Temps loved to hate. We'd been rivals in football, basketball, and historical significance for generations.

'Neither does Roedale,' Gran said from behind us, and Jason and I both jumped. I give Jason credit, he jumps up and gives Gran a hug everytime he sees her.

'Gran, you got enough food in the oven for me?'

'You and two others,' Gran said. Our grandmother smiled up at Jason. She was not blind to his faults (or mine), but she loved him. 'I just got a phone call from Everlee Mason. She was telling me you hooked up with DeeAnne last night.'

'Boy oh boy, can't do anything in this town without getting caught,' Jason said, but he wasn't really angry.

'That DeeAnne,' Gran said warningly as we all started into the house, 'she's been pregnant one time I know of. You just take care she doesn't have one of yours, you'll be paying the rest of your life. 'Course, that may be the only way I get great-grandchildren!'

Gran had the food ready on the table, so after Jason hung up his hat we sat down and said grace. Then Gran and Jason began gossiping with each other (though they called it 'catching up') about people in our little town and parish. My brother worked for the state, supervising road crews. It seemed to me like Jason's day consisted of driving around in a state pickup, clocking off work, and then driving around all night in his own pickup. Rene was on one of the work crews Jason oversaw, and they'd been to high school together. They hung around with Hoyt Fortenberry a lot.

'Sookie, I had to replace the hot water heater in the house,' Jason said suddenly. He lives in my parents' old house, the one we'd been living in when they died in a flash flood. We lived with Gran after that, but when Jason got through his two years of college and went to work for the state, he moved back into the house, which on paper is half mine.

'You need any money on that?' I asked.

'Naw, I got it.'

We both make salaries, but we also have a little income from a fund established when an oil well was sunk on my parents' property. It played out in a few years, but my parents and then Gran made sure the money was invested. It saved Jason and me a lot of struggle, that padding. I don't know how Gran could have raised us if it hadn't been for that money. She was determined not to sell any land, but her own income is not much more than social security. That's one reason I don't get an apartment. If I get groceries when I'm living with her, that's reasonable, to her; but if I buy groceries and bring them to her house and leave them on her table and go home to my house, that's charity and that makes her mad.

'What kind did you get?' I asked, just to show interest.

He was dying to tell me; Jason's an appliance freak, and he wanted to describe his comparison shopping for a new water heater in detail. I listened with as much attention as I could muster.

And then he interrupted himself. 'Hey Sook, you remember Maudette Pickens?'

'Sure,' I said, surprised. 'We graduated in the same class.'

'Somebody killed Maudette in her apartment last night.'

Gran and I were riveted. 'When?' Gran asked, puzzled that she hadn't heard already.

'They just found her this very morning in her bedroom. Her boss tried to call her to find out why she hadn't shown up for work yesterday and today and got no answer, so he rode over and got the manager up, and they unlocked the place. You know she had the apartment across from DeeAnne's?' Bon Temps had only one bona fide apartment complex, a three-building, two-story U-shaped grouping, so we knew exactly where he meant.

'She got killed there?' I felt ill. I remembered Maudette clearly. Maudette had had a heavy jaw and a square bottom, pretty black hair and husky shoulders. Maudette had been a plodder, never bright or ambitious. I thought I recalled her working at the Grabbit Kwik, a gas station/convenience store.

'Yeah, she'd been working there for at least a year, I guess,' Jason confirmed.

'How was it done?' My grandmother had that squinched, give-it-to-me-quick look with which nice people ask for bad news.

'She had some vampire bites on her – uh – inner thighs,' my brother said, looking down at his plate. 'But that wasn't what killed her. She was strangled. DeeAnne told me Maudette liked to go to that vampire bar in Shreveport when she had a couple of days off, so maybe that's where she got the bites. Might not have been *Sookie's* vampire.'

'Maudette was a fang-banger?' I felt queasy, imagining slow, chunky Maudette draped in the exotic black dresses fang-bangers affected.

'What's that?' asked Gran. She must have missed *Sally-Jessy* the day the phenomenon was explored.

'Men and women that hang around with vampires and enjoy being bitten. Vampire groupies. They don't last too long, I think, because they want to be bitten too much, and sooner or later they get that one bite too many.'

'But a bite didn't kill Maudette.' Gran wanted to be sure she had it straight.

'Nope, strangling.' Jason had begun finishing his lunch.

'Don't you always get gas at the Grabbit?' I asked.

'Sure. So do a lot of people.'

'And didn't you hang around with Maudette some?' Gran asked.

'Well, in a way of speaking,' Jason said cautiously.

I took that to mean he'd bedded Maudette when he couldn't find anyone else.

'I hope the sheriff doesn't want to talk to you,' Gran

said, shaking her head as if indicating 'no' would make it less likely.

'What?' Jason was turning red, looking defensive.

'You see Maudette in the store all the time when you get your gas, you so-to-speak date her, then she winds up dead in an apartment you're familiar with,' I summarized. It wasn't much, but it was something, and there were so few mysterious homicides in Bon Temps that I thought every stone would be turned in its investigation.

'I ain't the only one who fills the bill. Plenty of other guys get their gas there, and all of them know Maudette.'

'Yeah, but in what sense?' Gran asked bluntly. 'She wasn't a prostitute, was she? So she will have talked about who she saw.'

'She just liked to have a good time, she wasn't a pro.' It was good of Jason to defend Maudette, considering what I knew of his selfish character. I began to think a little better of my big brother. 'She was kinda lonely, I guess,' he added.

Jason looked at both of us, then, and saw we were surprised and touched.

'Speaking of prostitutes,' he said hastily, 'there's one in Monroe specializes in vampires. She keeps a guy standing by with a stake in case one gets carried away. She drinks synthetic blood to keep her blood supply up.'

That was a pretty definite change of subject, so Gran and I tried to think of a question we could ask without being indecent.

'Wonder how much she charges?' I ventured, and when Jason told us the figure he'd heard, we both gasped.

Once we got off the topic of Maudette's murder, lunch went about as usual, with Jason looking at his watch and exclaiming that he had to leave just when it was time to do the dishes.

But Gran's mind was still running on vampires, I found out. She came into my room later, when I was putting on my makeup to go to work.

'How old you reckon the vampire is, the one you met?'

'I have no idea, Gran.' I was putting on my mascara looking wide-eyed and trying to hold still so I wouldn't poke myself in the eye, so my voice came out funny, as if I was trying out for a horror movie.

'Do you suppose . . . he might remember the War?'

I didn't need to ask which war. After all, Gran was a charter member of the Descendants of the Glorious Dead.

'Could be,' I said, turning my face from side to side to make sure my blush was even.

'You think he might come to talk to us about it? We could have a special meeting.'

'At night,' I reminded her.

'Oh. Yes, it'd have to be.' The Descendants usually met at noon at the library and brought a bag lunch.

I thought about it. It would be plain rude to suggest to the vampire that he ought to speak to Gran's club because I'd saved his blood from Drainers, but maybe he would offer if I gave a little hint? I didn't like to, but I'd do it for Gran. 'I'll ask him the next time he comes in,' I promised.

'At least he could come talk to me and maybe I could tape his recollections?' Gran said. I could hear her mind clicking as she thought of what a coup that would be for her. 'It would be so interesting to the other club members,' she said piously.

I stifled an impulse to laugh. 'I'll suggest it to him,' I said. 'We'll see.'

When I left, Gran was clearly counting her chickens.

I hadn't thought of Rene Lenier going to Sam with the story of the parking lot fight. Rene'd been a busy bee, though. When I got to work that afternoon, I assumed the agitation I felt in the air was due to Maudette's murder. I found out different.

Sam hustled me into the storeroom the minute I came in. He was hopping with anger. He reamed me up one side and down the other.

Sam had never been mad with me before, and soon I was on the edge of tears.

'And if you think a customer isn't safe, you tell me, and I'll deal with it, not you,' he was saying for the sixth time, when I finally realized that Sam had been scared for me.

I caught that rolling off him before I clamped down firmly on 'hearing' Sam. Listening in to your boss led to disaster.

It had never occurred to me to ask Sam – or anyone else – for help.

'And if you think someone is being harmed in our parking lot, your next move is to call the police, not step out there yourself like a vigilante,' Sam huffed. His fair complexion, always ruddy, was redder than ever, and his wiry golden hair looked as if he hadn't combed it.

'Okay,' I said, trying to keep my voice even and my eyes wide open so the tears wouldn't roll out. 'Are you gonna fire me?'

'No! No!' he exclaimed, apparently even angrier. 'I don't want to lose you!' He gripped my shoulders and gave me a little shake. Then he stood looking at me with wide, crackling blue eyes, and I felt a surge of heat rushing out from him. Touching accelerates my disability, makes it imperative that I hear the person touching. I stared right into his eyes for a long moment, then I remembered myself, and I jumped back as his hands dropped away.

I whirled and left the storeroom, spooked.

I'd learned a couple of disconcerting things. Sam desired me; and I couldn't hear his thoughts as clearly as I could other people's. I'd had waves of impressions of how he was feeling, but not thoughts. More like wearing a mood ring than getting a fax.

So, what did I do about either piece of information?

Absolutely nothing.

I'd never looked on Sam as a beddable man before – or at least not beddable by me – for a lot of reasons. But the simplest one was that I never looked at anyone that way, not because I don't have hormones – boy, do I have hormones – but they are constantly tamped down because sex, for me, is a disaster. Can you imagine knowing everything your sex partner is thinking? Right. Along the order of 'Gosh, look at that mole . . . her butt is a little big . . . wish she'd move to the right a little . . . why doesn't she take the hint and . . .?' You get the idea. It's chilling to the emotions, believe me. And during sex, there is simply no way to keep a mental guard up.

Another reason is that I like Sam for a boss, and I like my job, which gets me out and keeps me active and earning so I won't turn into the recluse my grandmother fears I'll become. Working in an office is hard for me, and college was simply impossible because of the grim concentration necessary. It just drained me.

So, right now, I wanted to mull over the rush of desire I'd felt from him. It wasn't like he'd made me a verbal proposition or thrown me down on the storeroom floor. I'd felt his feelings, and I could ignore them if I chose. I appreciated the delicacy of this, and wondered if Sam had touched me on purpose, if he actually knew what I was.

I took care not be alone with him, but I have to admit I was pretty shaken that night.

The next two nights were better. We fell back into our comfortable relationship. I was relieved. I was disappointed. I was also run off my feet since Maudette's murder sparked a business boom at Merlotte's. All sorts of rumors were buzzing around Bon Temps, and the Shreveport news team did a little piece on Maudette Pickens' grisly death. Though I didn't attend her funeral, my grandmother did, and she said the church was jam-packed. Poor lumpy Maudette, with her bitten thighs, was more interesting in death than she'd ever been in life.

I was about to have two days off, and I was worried I'd miss connecting with the vampire, Bill. I needed to relay my grandmother's request. He hadn't returned to the bar, and I began to wonder if he would.

Mack and Denise hadn't been back in Merlotte's either, but Rene Lenier and Hoyt Fortenberry made sure I knew they'd threatened me with horrible things. I can't say I was seriously alarmed. Criminal trash like the Rats roamed the highways and trailer parks of America, not smart enough or moral enough to settle down to productive living. They never made a positive mark on the world, or amounted to a hill of beans, to my way of thinking. I shrugged off Rene's warnings.

But he sure enjoyed relaying them. Rene Lenier was small like Sam, but where Sam was ruddy and blond, Rene was swarthy and had a bushy headful of rough, black hair threaded with gray. Rene often came by the bar to drink a beer and visit with Arlene because (as he was fond of telling anyone in the bar) she was his favorite ex-wife. He had three. Hoyt Fortenberry was more of a cipher than Rene. He was neither dark nor fair, neither big nor little. He always seemed cheerful and always tipped decent. He admired my brother Jason far beyond what Jason deserved, in my opinion.

I was glad Rene and Hoyt weren't there the night the vampire returned.

He sat at the same table.

Now that the vampire was actually in front of me, I felt a little shy. I found I'd forgotten the almost imperceptible glow of his skin. I'd exaggerated his height and the clear-cut lines of his mouth.

'What can I get you?' I asked.

He looked up at me. I had forgotten, too, the depth of his eyes. He didn't smile or blink; he was so immobile. For the second time, I relaxed into his silence. When I let down my guard, I could feel my face relax. It was as good as getting a massage (I am guessing).

'What are you?' he asked me. It was the second time he'd wanted to know.

'I'm a waitress,' I said, again deliberately misunderstanding him. I could feel my smile snap back into place again. My little bit of peace vanished.

'Red wine,' he ordered, and if he was disappointed I couldn't tell by his voice.

'Sure,' I said. 'The synthetic blood should come in on the truck tomorrow. Listen, could I talk to you after work? I have a favor to ask you.'

'Of course. I'm in your debt.' And he sure didn't sound happy about it.

'Not a favor for me!' I was getting miffed myself. 'For my grandmother. If you'll be up – well, I guess you will be – when I get off work at one-thirty, would you very much mind meeting me at the employee door at the back of the bar?' I nodded toward it, and my ponytail bounced around my shoulders. His eyes followed the movement of my hair.

'I'd be delighted.'

I didn't know if he was displaying the courtesy Gran insisted was the standard in bygone times, or if he was plain old mocking me.

I resisted the temptation to stick out my tongue at him or blow a raspberry. I spun on my heel and marched back to the bar. When I brought him his wine, he tipped me 20 percent. Soon after that, I looked over at his table only to realize he'd vanished. I wondered if he'd keep his word.

Arlene and Dawn left before I was ready to go, for one reason and another; mostly because all the napkin holders in my area proved to be half-empty. As I retrieved my purse from the locked cabinet in Sam's office, where I stow it while I work, I called good-bye to my boss. I could hear him clanking around in the men's room, probably trying to fix the leaky toilet. I stepped into the ladies' room for a second to check my hair and makeup.

When I stepped outside I noticed that Sam had already switched off the customer parking lot lights. Only the security light on the electricity pole in front of his trailer illuminated the employee parking lot. To the amusement of Arlene and Dawn, Sam had put in a yard and planted boxwood in front of his trailer, and they were constantly teasing him about the neat line of his hedge.

I thought it was pretty.

As usual, Sam's truck was parked in front of his trailer so my car was the only one left in the lot.

I stretched, looking from side to side. No Bill. I was surprised at how disappointed I was. I had really expected him to be courteous, even if his heart (did he have one?) wasn't in it.

Maybe, I thought with a smile, he'd jump out of a tree, or appear with a poof! in front of me draped in a red-lined black cape. But nothing happened. So I trudged over to my car.

I'd hoped for a surprise, but not the one I got.

Mack Rattray jumped out from behind my car and in one stride got close enough to clip me in the jaw. He didn't hold back one little bit, and I went down onto the gravel like a sack of cement. I let out a yell when I went down, but the ground knocked all the air out of me and some skin off of me, and I was silent and breathless and helpless. Then I saw Denise, saw her swing back her heavy boot, had just enough warning to roll into a ball before the Rattrays began kicking me.

The pain was immediate, intense, and unrelenting. I threw my arms over my face instinctively, taking the beating on my forearms, legs, and my back.

I think I was sure, during the first few blows, that they'd stop and hiss warnings and curses at me and leave. But I remember the exact moment I realized that they intended to kill me.

I could lie there passively and take a beating, but I would not lie there and be killed.

The next time a leg came close I lunged and grabbed it and held on for my life. I was trying to bite, trying to at least mark one of them. I wasn't even sure whose leg I had.

Then, from behind me, I heard a growl. Oh, no, they've brought a dog, I thought. The growl was definitely hostile. If I'd had any leeway with my emotions, the hair would have stood up on my scalp.

I took one more kick to the spine, and then the beating stopped.

The last kick had done something dreadful to me. I could hear my own breathing, stertorous, and a strange bubbling sound that seemed to be coming from my own lungs.

'What the hell is that?' Mack Rattray asked, and he sounded absolutely terrified.

I heard the growl again, closer, right behind me. And from another direction, I heard a sort of snarl. Denise began wailing, Mack was cursing. Denise yanked her leg from my grasp, which had grown very weak. My arms flopped to the ground. They seemed to be beyond my control. Though my vision was cloudy, I could see that my right arm was broken. My face felt wet. I was scared to continue evaluating my injuries.

Mack began screaming, and then Denise, and there seemed to be all kinds of activity going on around me, but I couldn't move. My only view was my broken arm and my battered knees and the darkness under my car.

Some time later there was silence. Behind me, the dog whined. A cold nose poked my ear, and a warm tongue licked it. I tried to raise my hand to pet the dog that had undoubtedly saved my life, but I couldn't. I could hear myself sigh. It seemed to come from a long way away.

Facing the fact, I said, 'I'm dying.' It began to seem more and more real to me. The toads and crickets that had been making the most of the night had fallen silent at all the activity and noise in the parking lot, so my little voice came out clearly and fell into the darkness. Oddly enough, soon after that I heard two voices.

Then a pair of knees covered in bloody blue jeans came into my view. The vampire Bill leaned over so I could look into his face. There was blood smeared on his mouth, and his fangs were out, glistening white against his lower lip. I tried to smile at him, but my face wasn't working right.

'I'm going to pick you up,' Bill said. He sounded calm.

'I'll die if you do,' I whispered.

He looked me over carefully. 'Not just yet,' he said, after this evaluation. Oddly enough, this made me feel better; no telling how many injuries he'd seen in his lifetime, I figured.

'This will hurt,' he warned me.

It was hard to imagine anything that wouldn't.

His arms slid under me before I had time to get afraid. I screamed, but it was a weak effort.

'Quick,' said a voice urgently.

'We're going back in the woods out of sight,' Bill said, cradling my body to him as if it weighed nothing.

Was he going to bury me back there, out of sight? After he'd just rescued me from the Rats? I almost didn't care.

It was only a small relief when he laid me down on a carpet of pine needles in the darkness of the woods. In the distance, I could see the glow of the light in the parking lot. I felt my hair trickling blood, and I felt the pain of my broken arm and the agony of deep bruises, but what was most frightening was what I didn't feel.

I didn't feel my legs.

My abdomen felt full, heavy. The phrase 'internal bleeding' lodged in my thoughts, such as they were.

'You will die unless you do as I say,' Bill told me.

'Sorry, don't want to be a vampire,' I said, and my voice was weak and thready.

'No, you won't be,' he said more gently. 'You'll heal. Quickly. I have a cure. But you have to be willing.'

'Then trot out the cure,' I whispered. 'I'm going.' I could feel the pull the grayness was exerting on me.

In the little part of my mind that was still receiving signals from the world, I heard Bill grunt as if he'd been hurt. Then something was pressed up against my mouth.

'Drink,' he said.

I tried to stick out my tongue, managed. He was bleeding, squeezing to encourage the flow of blood from his wrist into my mouth. I gagged. But I wanted to live. I forced myself to swallow. And swallow again.

Suddenly the blood tasted good, salty, the stuff of life. My unbroken arm rose, my hand clamped the vampire's wrist to my mouth. I felt better with every swallow. And after a minute, I drifted off to sleep.

When I woke up, I was still in the woods, still lying on the ground. Someone was stretched out beside me; it was the vampire. I could see his glow. I could feel his tongue moving on my head. He was licking my head wound. I could hardly begrudge him.

'Do I taste different from other people?' I asked.

'Yes,' he said in a thick voice. 'What are you?'

It was the third time he'd asked. Third time's the charm, Gran always said.

'Hey, I'm not dead,' I said. I suddenly remembered I'd

expected to check out for good. I wiggled my arm, the one that had been broken. It was weak, but it wasn't flopping any longer. I could feel my legs, and I wiggled them, too. I breathed in and out experimentally and was pleased with the resulting mild ache. I struggled to sit up. That proved to be quite an effort, but not an impossibility. It was like my first fever-free day after I'd had pneumonia as a kid. Feeble but blissful. I was aware I'd survived something awful.

Before I finished straightening, he'd put his arms under me and cradled me to him. He leaned back against a tree. I felt very comfortable sitting on his lap, my head against his chest.

'What I am, is telepathic,' I said. 'I can hear people's thoughts.'

'Even mine?' He sounded merely curious.

'No. That's why I like you so much,' I said, floating on a sea of pinkish well-being. I couldn't seem to be bothered with camouflaging my thoughts.

I felt his chest rumble as he laughed. The laugh was a little rusty.

'I can't hear you at all,' I blathered on, my voice dreamy. 'You have no idea how peaceful that is. After a lifetime of blah, blah, blah, to hear . . . nothing.'

'How do you manage going out with men? With men your age, their only thought is still surely how to get you into bed.'

'Well, I don't. Manage. And frankly, at any age, I think their goal is get a woman in bed. I don't date. Everyone thinks I'm crazy, you know, because I can't tell them the truth; which is, that I'm driven crazy by all these thoughts, all these heads. I had a few dates when I started working at the bar, guys who hadn't heard about me. But it was the same as always. You can't concentrate on being comfortable with a guy, or getting a head of steam up, when you can hear they're wondering if you dye your hair, or thinking that your butt's not pretty, or imagining what your boobs look like.'

Suddenly I felt more alert, and I realized how much of myself I was revealing to this creature.

'Excuse me,' I said. 'I didn't mean to burden you with my problems. Thank you for saving me from the Rats.'

'It was my fault they had a chance to get you at all,' he said. I could tell there was rage just under the calm surface of his voice. 'If I had had the courtesy to be on time, it would not have happened. So I owed you some of my blood. I owed you the healing.'

'Are they dead?' To my embarrassment, my voice sounded squeaky.

'Oh, yes.'

I gulped. I couldn't regret that the world was rid of the Rats. But I had to look this straight in the face, I couldn't dodge the realization that I was sitting in the lap of a murderer. Yet I was quite happy to sit there, his arms around me.

'I should worry about this, but I'm not,' I said, before I knew what I was going to say. I felt that lusty laugh again.

'Sookie, why did you want to talk to me tonight?'

I had to think back hard. Though I was miraculously recovered from the beating physically, I felt a little hazy mentally.

'My grandmother is real anxious to know how old you are,' I said hesitantly. I didn't know how personal a question that was to a vampire. The vampire in question was stroking my back as though he were soothing a kitten.

'I was made vampire in 1870, when I was thirty human years old.' I looked up; his glowing face was expressionless, his eyes pits of blackness in the dark woods.

'Did you fight in the War?'

'Yes.'

'I have the feeling you're gonna get mad. But it would make her and her club so happy if you'd tell them a little bit about the War, about what it was really like.'

'Club?'

'She belongs to Descendants of the Glorious Dead.'

'Glorious dead.' The vampire's voice was unreadable, but I could tell, sure enough, he wasn't happy.

'Listen, you wouldn't have to tell them about the maggots and the infections and the starvation,' I said. 'They have their own picture of the War, and though they're not stupid people – they've lived through other wars – they would like to know more about the way people lived then, and uniforms and troop movements.'

'Clean things.'

I took a deep breath. 'Yep.'

'Would it make you happy if I did this?'

'What difference does that make? It would make Gran happy, and since you're in Bon Temps and seem to want to live around here, it would be a good public relations move for you.'

'Would it make you happy?'

He was not a guy you could evade. 'Well, yes.'

'Then I'll do it.'

'Gran says to please eat before you come,' I said.

Again I heard the rumbling laugh, deeper this time.

'I'm looking forward to meeting her now. Can I call on you some night?'

'Ah. Sure. I work my last night tomorrow night, and the day after I'm off for two days, so Thursday would be a good night.' I lifted my arm to look at my watch. It was running, but the glass was covered with dried blood. 'Oh, yuck,' I said, wetting my finger in my mouth and cleaning the watch face off with spit. I pressed the button that illuminated the hands, and gasped when I saw what time it was.

'Oh, gosh, I got to get home. I hope Gran went to sleep.'

'She must worry about you being out so late at night by yourself,' Bill observed. He sounded disapproving. Maybe he was thinking of Maudette? I had a moment of deep unease, wondering if in fact Bill had known her, if she'd invited him to come home with her. But I rejected the idea because I was stubbornly unwilling to dwell on the odd, awful, nature of Maudette's life and death; I didn't want that horror to cast a shadow on my little bit of happiness.

'It's part of my job,' I said tartly. 'Can't be helped. I don't work nights all the time, anyway. But when I can, I do.'

'Why?' The vampire gave me a shove up to my feet, and then he rose easily from the ground.

'Better tips. Harder work. No time to think.'

'But night is more dangerous,' he said disapprovingly.

He ought to know. 'Now don't you go sounding like my grandmother,' I chided him mildly. We had almost reached the parking lot.

'I'm older than your grandmother,' he reminded me. That brought the conversation up short.

After I stepped out of the woods, I stood staring. The parking lot was as serene and untouched as if nothing had ever happened there, as if I hadn't been nearly beaten to death on that patch of gravel only an hour before, as if the Rats hadn't met their bloody end.

The lights in the bar and in Sam's trailer were off.

The gravel was wet, but not bloody.

My purse was sitting on the hood of my car.

'And what about the dog?' I said.

I turned to look at my savior.

He wasn't there.

Chapter 2

I got up very late the next morning, which was not too surprising. Gran had been asleep when I got home, to my relief, and I was able to climb into my bed without waking her.

I was drinking a cup of coffee at the kitchen table and Gran was cleaning out the pantry when the phone rang. Gran eased her bottom up onto the stool by the counter, her normal chatting perch, to answer it.

'*Hel*-lo,' she said. For some reason, she always sounded put out, as if a phone call were the last thing on earth she wanted. I knew for a fact that wasn't the case.

'Hey, Everlee. No, sitting here talking to Sookie, she just got up. No, I haven't heard any news today. No, no one called me yet. What? What tornado? Last night was clear. Four Tracks Corner? It did? No! No, it did not! Really? Both of 'em? Um, um, um. What did Mike Spencer say?'

Mike Spencer was our parish coroner. I began to have a creepy feeling. I finished my coffee and poured myself another cup. I thought I was going to need it.

Gran hung up a minute later. 'Sookie, you are not going to believe what has happened!'

I was willing to bet I would believe it.

'What?' I asked, trying not to look guilty.

'No matter how smooth the weather looked last night, a tornado must have touched down at Four Tracks Corner! It turned over that rent trailer in the clearing there. The couple that was staying in it, they both got killed, trapped under the trailer somehow and crushed to a pulp. Mike says he hasn't seen anything like it.'

'Is he sending the bodies for autopsy?'

'Well, I think he has to, though the cause of death seems clear enough, according to Stella. The trailer is over on its side, their car is halfway on top of it, and trees are pulled up in the yard.'

'My God,' I whispered, thinking of the strength necessary to accomplish the staging of that scene.

'Honey, you didn't tell me if your friend the vampire came in last night?'

I jumped in a guilty way until I realized that in Gran's mind, she'd changed subjects. She'd been asking me if I'd seen Bill every day, and now, at last, I could tell her yes – but not with a light heart.

Predictably, Gran was excited out of her gourd. She fluttered around the kitchen as if Prince Charles were the expected guest.

'Tomorrow night. Now what time's he coming?' she asked.

'After dark. That's as close as I can get.'

'We're on daylight saving time, so that'll be pretty late.' Gran considered. 'Good, we'll have time to eat supper and clear it away beforehand. And we'll have all day tomorrow to clean the house. I haven't cleaned that area rug in a year, I bet!'

'Gran, we're talking about a guy who sleeps in the ground all day,' I reminded her. 'I don't think he'd ever look at the rug.'

'Well, if I'm not doing it for him, then I'm doing it for me, so I can feel proud,' Gran said unanswerably. 'Besides, young lady, how do you know where he sleeps?'

'Good question, Gran. I don't. But he has to keep out of the light and he has to keep safe, so that's my guess.'

Nothing would prevent my grandmother from going into a house-proud frenzy, I realized very shortly. While I was getting ready for work, she went to the grocery and rented a rug cleaner and set to cleaning.

On my way to Merlotte's, I detoured north a bit and drove by the Four Tracks Corner. It was a crossroads as old as human habitation of the area. Now formalized by road signs and pavement, local lore said it was the intersection of two hunting trails. Sooner or later, there would be ranch-style houses and strip malls lining the roads, I guessed, but for now it was woods and the hunting was still good, according to Jason.

Since there was nothing to prevent me, I drove down the rutted path that led to the clearing where the Rattrays' rented trailer had stood. I stopped my car and stared out the windshield, appalled. The trailer, a very small and old one, lay crushed ten feet behind its original location. The Rattrays' dented red car was still resting on one end of the accordian-pleated mobile home. Bushes and debris were littered around the clearing, and the woods behind the trailer showed signs of a great force passing through; branches snapped off, the top of one pine hanging down by a thread of bark. There were clothes up in the branches, and even a roast pan.

I got out slowly and looked around me. The damage was simply incredible, especially since I knew it hadn't been caused by a tornado; Bill the vampire had staged this scene to account for the deaths of the Rattrays.

An old Jeep bumped its way down the ruts to come to a stop by me.

'Well, Sookie Stackhouse!' called Mike Spencer. 'What you doing here, girl? Ain't you got work to go to?'

'Yes, sir. I knew the Rat – the Rattrays. This is just an awful thing.' I thought that was sufficiently ambiguous. I could see now that the sheriff was with Mike.

'An awful thing. Yes, well. I did hear,' Sheriff Bud Dearborn said as climbed down out of the Jeep, 'that you and Mack and Denise didn't exactly see eye to eye in the parking lot of Merlotte's, last week.'

I felt a cold chill somewhere around the region of my liver as the two men ranged themselves in front of me.

Mike Spencer was the funeral director of one of Bon Temps' two funeral homes. As Mike was always quick and definite in pointing out, anyone who wanted could be buried by Spencer and Sons Funeral Home; but only white people seemed to want to. Likewise, only people of color chose to be buried at Sweet Rest. Mike himself was a heavy middle-aged man with hair and mustache the color of weak tea, and a fondness for cowboy boots and string ties that he could not wear when he was on duty at Spencer and Sons. He was wearing them now.

Sheriff Dearborn, who had the reputation of being a good man, was a little older than Mike, but fit and tough from his thick gray hair to his heavy shoes. The sheriff had a mashed-in face and quick brown eyes. He had been a good friend of my father's.

'Yes, sir, we had us a disagreement,' I said frankly in my down-homiest voice.

'You want to tell me about it?' The sheriff pulled out a Marlboro and lit it with a plain, metal lighter.

And I made a mistake. I should have just told him. I was supposed to be crazy, and some thought me simple, too. But for the life of me, I could see no reason to explain myself to Bud Dearborn. No reason, except good sense.

'Why?' I asked.

His small brown eyes were suddenly sharp, and the amiable air vanished.

'Sookie,' he said, with a world of disappointment in his voice. I didn't believe in it for a minute.

'I didn't do this,' I said, waving my hand at the destruction.

'No, you didn't,' he agreed. 'But just the same, they die the week after they have a fight with someone, I feel I should ask questions.'

I was reconsidering staring him down. It would feel good, but I didn't think feeling good was worth it. It was becoming apparent to me that a reputation for simplicity could be handy.

I may be uneducated and unworldly, but I'm not stupid or unread.

'Well, they were hurting my friend,' I confessed, hanging my head and eyeing my shoes.

'Would that be this vampire that's living at the old Compton house?' Mike Spencer and Bud Dearborn exchanged glances.

'Yes, sir.' I was surprised to hear where Bill was living,

but they didn't know that. From years of deliberately not reacting to things I heard that I didn't want to know, I have good facial control. The old Compton house was right across the fields from us, on the same side of the road. Between our houses lay only the woods and the cemetery. How handy for Bill, I thought, and smiled.

'Sookie Stackhouse, your granny is letting you associate with that vampire?' Spencer said unwisely.

'You can sure talk to her about that,' I suggested maliciously, hardly able to wait to hear what Gran would say when someone suggested she wasn't taking care of me. 'You know, the Rattrays were trying to drain Bill.'

'So the vampire was being drained by the Rattrays? And you stopped them?' interrupted the sheriff.

'Yes,' I said and tried to look resolute.

'Vampire draining is illegal,' he mused.

'Isn't it murder, to kill a vampire that hasn't attacked you?' I asked.

I may have pushed the naivete a little too hard.

'You know damn good and well it is, though I don't agree with that law. It is a law, and I will uphold it,' the sheriff said stiffly.

'So the vampire just let them leave, without threatening vengeance? Saying anything like he wished they were dead?' Mike Spencer was being stupid.

'That's right.' I smiled at both of them and then looked at my watch. I remembered the blood on its face, my blood, beaten out of me by the Rattrays. I had to look through that blood to read the time.

'Excuse me, I have to get to work,' I said. 'Good-bye, Mr. Spencer, Sheriff.'

'Good-bye, Sookie,' Sheriff Dearborn said. He looked

like he had more to ask me, but couldn't think of how to put it. I could tell he wasn't totally happy with the look of the scene, and I doubted any tornado had shown up on radar anywhere. Nonetheless, there was the trailer, there was the car, there were the trees, and the Rattrays had been dead under them. What could you decide but that the tornado had killed them? I guessed the bodies had been sent for an autopsy, and I wondered how much could be told by such a procedure under the circumstances.

The human mind is an amazing thing. Sheriff Dearborn must have known that vampires are very strong. But he just couldn't imagine how strong one could be: strong enough to turn over a trailor, crush it. It was even hard for me to comprehend, and I knew good and well that no tornado had touched down at Four Corners.

The whole bar was humming with the news of the deaths. Maudette's murder had taken a backseat to Denise and Mack's demises. I caught Sam eyeing me a couple of times and I thought about the night before and wondered how much he knew. But I was scared to ask in case he hadn't seen anything. I knew there were things that had happened the night before that I hadn't yet explained to my own satisfaction, but I was so grateful to be alive that I put off thinking of them.

I'd never smiled so hard while I toted drinks, I'd never made change so briskly, I'd never gotten orders so exactly. Even ol' bushy-haired Rene didn't slow me down, though he insisted on dragging me into his long-winded conversations every time I came near the table he was sharing with Hoyt and a couple of other cronies.

Rene played the role of crazy Cajun some of the time, though any Cajun accent he might assume was faked. His folks had let their heritage fade. Every woman he'd married had been hard-living and wild. His brief hitch with Arlene had been when she was young and childless, and she'd told me that from time to time she'd done things then that curled her hair to think about now. She'd grown up since then, but Rene hadn't. Arlene was sure fond of him, to my amazement.

Everyone in the bar was excited that night because of the unusual happenings in Bon Temps. A woman had been murdered, and it was a mystery; usually murders in Bon Temps are easily solved. And a couple had died violently by a freak of nature. I attributed what happened next to that excitement. This is a neighborhood bar, with a few out of towners who pass through on a regular basis, and I've never had much problem with unwanted attention. But that night one of the men at a table next to Rene and Hoyt's, a heavy blond man with a broad, red face, slid his hand up the leg of my shorts when I was bringing their beer.

That doesn't fly at Merlotte's.

I thought of bringing the tray down on his head when I felt the hand removed. I felt someone standing right behind me. I turned my head and saw Rene, who had left his chair without my even realizing it. I followed his arm down and saw that his hand was gripping the blond's and squeezing. The blond's red face was turning a mottled mixture.

'Hey, man, let go!' the blond protested. 'I didn't mean nothing.'

'You don't touch anyone who works here. That's the rule.' Rene might be short and slim, but anyone there would have put his money on our local boy over the beefier visitor.

'Okay, okay.'

'Apologize to the lady.'

'To Crazy Sookie?' His voice was incredulous. He must have been here before.

Rene's hand must have tightened. I saw tears spring into the blond's eyes.

'I'm sorry, Sookie, okay?'

I nodded as regally as I could. Rene let go of the man's hand abruptly and jerked his thumb to tell the guy to take a hike. The blond lost no time throwing himself out the door. His companion followed.

'Rene, you should have let me handle that myself,' I said to him very quietly when it seemed the patrons had resumed their conversations. We'd given the gossip mill enough grist for at least a couple of days. 'But I appreciate you standing up for me.'

'I don't want no one messing with Arlene's friend,' Rene said matter-of-factly. 'Merlotte's is a nice place, we all want to keep it nice. 'Sides, sometimes you remind me of Cindy, you know?'

Cindy was Rene's sister. She'd moved to Baton Rouge a year or two ago. Cindy was blond and blue-eyed: beyond that I couldn't think of a similarity. But it didn't seem polite to say so. 'You see Cindy much?' I asked. Hoyt and the other man at the table were exchanging Shreveport Captains scores and statistics.

'Every so now and then,' Rene said, shaking his head as if to say he'd like it to be more often. 'She works in a hospital cafeteria.'

I patted him on the shoulder. 'I gotta go work.'

When I reached the bar to get my next order, Sam raised his eyebrows at me. I widened my eyes to show how amazed

I was at Rene's intervention, and Sam shrugged slightly, as if to say there was no accounting for human behavior.

But when I went behind the bar to get some more napkins, I noticed he'd pulled out the baseball bat he kept below the till for emergencies.

Gran kept me busy all the next day. She dusted and vacuumed and mopped, and I scrubbed the bathrooms – did vampires even need to use the bathroom? I wondered, as I chugged the toilet brush around the bowl. Gran had me vacuum the cat hair off the sofa. I emptied all the trash cans. I polished all the tables. I wiped down the washer and the dryer, for goodness sake.

When Gran urged me to get in the shower and change my clothes, I realized that she regarded Bill the vampire as my date. That made me feel a little odd. One, Gran was so desperate for me to have a social life that even a vampire was eligible for my attention; two, that I had some feelings that backed up that idea; three, that Bill might accurately read all this; four, could vampires even do it like humans?

I showered and put on my makeup and wore a dress, since I knew Gran would have a fit if I didn't. It was a little blue cotton-knit dress with tiny daisies all over it, and it was tighter than Gran liked and shorter than Jason deemed proper in his sister. I'd heard that the first time I'd worn it. I put my little yellow ball earrings in and wore my hair pulled up and back with a yellow banana clip holding it loosely.

Gran gave me one odd look, which I was at a loss to interpret. I could have found out easily enough by listening in, but that was a terrible thing to do to the person you lived with, so I was careful not to. She herself was wearing a skirt and blouse that she often wore to the Descendants of the Glorious Dead meetings, not quite good enough for church, but not plain enough for everyday wear.

I was sweeping the front porch, which we'd forgotten, when he came. He made a vampire entrance; one minute he wasn't there, and the next he was, standing at the bottom of the steps and looking up at me.

I grinned. 'Didn't scare me,' I said.

He looked a little embarrassed. 'It's just a habit,' he said, 'appearing like that. I don't make much noise.'

I opened the door. 'Come on in,' I invited, and he came up the steps, looking around.

'I remember this,' he said. 'It wasn't so big, though.'

'You remember this house? Gran's gonna love it.' I preceded him into the living room, calling Gran as I went.

She came into the living room very much on her dignity, and I realized for the first time she'd taken great pains with her thick white hair, which was smooth and orderly for a change, wrapped around her head in a complicated coil. She had on lipstick, too.

Bill proved as adept at social tactics as my grandmother. They greeted, thanked each other, complimented, and finally Bill ended up sitting on the couch and, after carrying out a tray with three glasses of peach tea, my Gran sat in the easy chair, making it clear I was to perch by Bill. There was no way to get out of this without being even more obvious, so I sat by him, but scooted forward to the edge, as if I might hop up at any moment to get him a refill on his, the ritual glass of iced tea.

He politely touched his lips to the edge of the glass and then set it down. Gran and I took big nervous swallows of ours.

Gran picked an unfortunate opening topic. She said, 'I guess you heard about the strange tornado.'

'Tell me,' Bill said, his cool voice as smooth as silk. I didn't dare look at him, but sat with my hands folded and my eyes fixed to them.

So Gran told him about the freak tornado and the deaths of the Rats. She told him the whole thing seemed pretty awful, but cut-and-dried, and at that I thought Bill relaxed just a millimeter.

'I went by yesterday on my way to work,' I said, without raising my gaze. 'By the trailer.'

'Did you find it looked as you expected?' Bill asked, only curiosity in his voice.

'No,' I said. 'It wasn't anything I could have expected. I was really . . . amazed.'

'Sookie, you've seen tornado damage before,' Gran said, surprised.

I changed the subject. 'Bill, where'd you get your shirt? It looks nice.' He was wearing khaki Dockers and a green-and-brown striped golfing shirt, polished loafers, and thin, brown socks.

'Dillard's,' he said, and I tried to imagine him at the mall in Monroe, perhaps, other people turning to look at this exotic creature with his glowing skin and beautiful eyes. Where would he get the money to pay with? How did he wash his clothes? Did he go into his coffin naked? Did he have a car or did he just float wherever he wanted to go?

Gran was pleased with the normality of Bill's shopping habits. It gave me another pang of pain, observing how glad she was to see my supposed suitor in her living room, even if (according to popular literature) he was a victim of a virus that made him seem dead.

Gran plunged into questioning Bill. He answered her with courtesy and apparent goodwill. Okay, he was a *polite* dead man.

'And your people were from this area?' Gran inquired.

'My father's people were Comptons, my mother's people Loudermilks,' Bill said readily. He seemed quite relaxed.

'There are lots of Loudermilks left,' Gran said happily. 'But I'm afraid old Mr. Jessie Compton died last year.'

'I know,' Bill said easily. 'That's why I came back. The land reverted to me, and since things have changed in our culture toward people of my particular persuasion, I decided to claim it.'

'Did you know the Stackhouses? Sookie says you have a long history.' I thought Gran had put it well. I smiled at my hands.

'I remember Jonas Stackhouse,' Bill said, to Gran's delight. 'My folks were here when Bon Temps was just a hole in the road at the edge of the frontier. Jonas Stackhouse moved here with his wife and his four children when I was a young man of sixteen. Isn't this the house he built, at least in part?'

I noticed that when Bill was thinking of the past, his voice took on a different cadence and vocabulary. I wondered how many changes in slang and tone his English had taken on through the past century.

Of course, Gran was in genealogical hog heaven. She wanted to know all about Jonas, her husband's great-great-great-great-grandfather. 'Did he own slaves?' she asked.

'Ma'am, if I remember correctly, he had a house slave and a yard slave. The house slave was a woman of middle age and the yard slave a very big young man, very strong, named Minas. But the Stackhouses mostly worked their own fields, as did my folks.'

'Oh, that is exactly the kind of thing my little group would love to hear! Did Sookie tell you . . .' Gran and Bill, after much polite do-si-doing, set a date for Bill to address a night meeting of the Descendants.

'And now, if you'll excuse Sookie and me, maybe we'll take a walk. It's a lovely night.' Slowly, so I could see it coming, he reached over and took my hand, rising and pulling me to my feet, too. His hand was cold and hard and smooth. Bill wasn't quite asking Gran's permission, but not quite not, either.

'Oh, you two go on,' my grandmother said, fluttering with happiness. 'I have so many things to look up. You'll have to tell me all the local names you remember from when you were . . .' and here Gran ran down, not wanting to say something wounding.

'Resident here in Bon Temps,' I supplied helpfully.

'Of course,' the vampire said, and I could tell from the compression of his lips that he was trying not to smile.

Somehow we were at the door, and I knew that Bill had lifted me and moved me quickly. I smiled, genuinely. I like the unexpected.

'We'll be back in a while,' I said to Gran. I didn't think she'd noticed my odd transition, since she was gathering up our tea glasses.

'Oh, you two don't hurry on my account,' she said. 'I'll be just fine.'

Outside, the frogs and toads and bugs were singing their nightly rural opera. Bill kept my hand as we strolled out into the yard, full of the smell of new-mown grass and budding things. My cat, Tina, came out of the shadows and asked to be tickled, and I bent over and scratched her head. To my surprise, the cat rubbed against Bill's legs, an activity he did nothing to discourage.

'You like this animal?' he asked, his voice neutral.

'It's my cat,' I said. 'Her name is Tina, and I like her a lot.'

Without comment, Bill stood still, waiting until Tina went on her way into the darkness outside the porch light.

'Would you like to sit in the swing or the lawn chairs, or would you like to walk?' I asked, since I felt I was now the hostess.

'Oh, let's walk for a while. I need to stretch my legs.'

Somehow this statement unsettled me a little, but I began moving down the long driveway in the direction of the two-lane parish road that ran in front of both our homes.

'Did the trailer upset you?'

I tried to think how to put it.

'I feel very . . . hmmm. Fragile. When I think about the trailer.'

'You knew I was strong.'

I tilted my head from side to side, considering. 'Yes, but I didn't realize the full extent of your strength,' I told him. 'Or your imagination.'

'Over the years, we get good at hiding what we've done.'

'So. I guess you've killed a bunch of people.'

'Some.' Deal with it, his voice implied.

I clasped both hands behind my back. 'Were you hungrier right after you became a vampire? How did that happen?'

He hadn't expected that. He looked at me. I could feel his eyes on me even though we were now in the dark. The woods were close around us. Our feet crunched on the gravel.

'As to how I became a vampire, that's too long a story for now,' he said. 'But yes, when I was younger – a few times – I killed by accident. I was never sure when I'd get to eat again, you understand? We were always hunted, naturally, and there was no such thing as artificial blood. And there were not as many people then. But I had been a good man when I was alive – I mean, before I caught the virus. So I tried to be civilized about it, select bad people as my victims, never feed on children. I managed never to kill a child, at least. It's so different now. I can go to the all-night clinic in any city and get some synthetic blood, though it's disgusting. Or I can pay a whore and get enough blood to keep going for a couple of days. Or I can glamor someone, so they'll let me bite them for love and then forget all about it. And I don't need so much now.'

'Or you can meet a girl who gets head injuries,' I said.

'Oh, you were the dessert. The Rattrays were the meal.'

Deal with it.

'Whoa,' I said, feeling breathless. 'Give me a minute.'

And he did. Not one man in a million would have allowed me that time without speaking. I opened my mind, let my guards down completely, relaxed. His silence washed over me. I stood, closed my eyes, breathed out the relief that was too profound for words.

'Are you happy now?' he asked, just as if he could tell.

'Yes,' I breathed. At that moment I felt that no matter what this creature beside me had done, this peace was priceless after a lifetime of the yammering of other minds inside my own.

'You feel good to me, too,' he said, surprising me.

'How so?' I asked, dreamy and slow.

'No fear, no hurry, no condemnation. I don't have to use my glamor to make you hold still, to have a conversation with you.'

'Glamor?'

'Like hypnotism,' he explained. 'All vampires use it, to some extent or another. Because to feed, until the new synthetic blood was developed, we had to persuade people we were harmless . . . or assure them they hadn't seen us at all . . . or delude them into thinking they'd seen something else.'

'Does it work on me?'

'Of course,' he said, sounding shocked.

'Okay, do it.'

'Look at me.'

'It's dark.'

'No matter. Look at my face.' And he stepped in front of me, his hands resting lightly on my shoulders, and looked down at me. I could see the faint shine of his skin and eyes, and I peered up at him, wondering if I'd begin to squawk like a chicken or take my clothes off.

But what happened was . . . nothing. I felt only the nearly druglike relaxation of being with him.

'Can you feel my influence?' he asked. He sounded a little breathless.

'Not a bit, I'm sorry,' I said humbly. 'I just see you glow.'

'You can see that?' I'd surprised him again.

'Sure. Can't everyone?'

'No. This is strange, Sookie.'

'If you say so. Can I see you levitate?'

'Right here?' Bill sounded amused.

'Sure, why not? Unless there's a reason?'

'No, none at all.' And he let go of my arms and began to rise.

I breathed a sigh of pure rapture. He floated up in the dark, gleaming like white marble in the moonlight. When he was about two feet off the ground, he began hovering. I thought he was smiling down at me.

'Can all of you do that?' I asked.

'Can you sing?'

'Nope, can't carry a tune.'

'Well, we can't all do the same things, either.' Bill came down slowly and landed on the ground without a thump. 'Most humans are squeamish about vampires. You don't seem to be,' he commented.

I shrugged. Who was I to be squeamish about something out of the ordinary? He seemed to understand because, after a pause, during which we'd resumed walking, Bill said, 'Has it always been hard for you?'

'Yes, always.' I couldn't say otherwise, though I didn't want to whine. 'When I was very small, that was worst, because I didn't know how to put up my guard, and I heard thoughts I wasn't supposed to hear, of course, and I repeated them like a child will. My parents didn't know what to do about me. It embarrassed my father in particular. My mother finally took me to a child psychologist, who knew exactly what I was, but she just couldn't accept it and kept trying to tell my folks I was reading their body language and was very observant, so I had good reason to imagine I heard people's thoughts. Of course, she couldn't admit I was literally *hearing people's thoughts* because that just didn't fit into her world.

'And I did poorly in school because it was so hard for me to concentrate when so few others were. But when there was testing, I would test very high because the other kids were concentrating on their own papers . . . that gave me a little leeway. Sometimes my folks thought I was lazy for not doing well on everyday work. Sometimes the teachers thought I had a learning disability; oh, you wouldn't believe the theories. I must have had my eyes and ears tested every two months, seemed like, and brain scans . . . gosh. My poor folks paid through the nose. But they never could accept the simple truth. At least outwardly, you know?'

'But they knew inside.'

'Yes. Once, when my dad was trying to decide whether to back a man who wanted to open an auto parts store, he asked me to sit with him when the man came to the house. After the man left, my dad took me outside and looked away and said, 'Sookie, is he telling the truth?' It was the strangest moment.'

'How old were you?'

'I must've been less than seven 'cause they died when I was in the second grade.'

'How?'

'Flash flood. Caught them on the bridge west of here.'

Bill didn't comment. Of course, he'd seen deaths piled upon deaths.

'Was the man lying?' he asked after a few seconds had gone by.

'Oh, yes. He planned to take Daddy's money and run.'

'You have a gift.'

'Gift. Right.' I could feel the corners of my mouth pull down.

'It makes you different from other humans.'

'You're telling me.' We walked for a moment in silence. 'So you don't consider yourself human at all?'

'I haven't for a long time.'

'Do you really believe you've lost your soul?' That was what the Catholic Church was preaching about vampires.

'I have no way of knowing,' Bill said, almost casually. It was apparent that he'd brooded over it so often it was quite a commonplace thought to him. 'Personally, I think not. There is something in me that isn't cruel, not murderous, even after all these years. Though I can be both.'

'It's not your fault you were infected with a virus.'

Bill snorted, even managing to sound elegant doing that. 'There have been theories as long as there have been vampires. Maybe that one is true.' Then he looked as if he was sorry he'd said that. 'If what makes a vampire is a virus,' he went on in a more offhand manner, 'it's a selective one.'

'How do you become a vampire?' I'd read all kinds of stuff, but this would be straight from the horse's mouth.

'I would have to drain you, at one sitting or over two or three days, to the point of your death, then give you my blood. You would lie like a corpse for about forty-eight hours, sometimes as long as three days, then rise and walk at night. And you would be hungry.'

The way he said 'hungry' made me shiver.

'No other way?'

'Other vampires have told me humans they habitually bite, day after day, can become vampires quite unexpectedly. But that requires consecutive, deep, feedings. Others, under the same conditions, merely become anemic. Then again, when people are near to death for some other reason, a car accident or a drug overdose, perhaps, the process can go . . . badly wrong.'

I was getting the creepies. 'Time to change the subject. What do you plan on doing with the Compton land?'

'I plan on living there, as long as I can. I'm tired of drifting from city to city. I grew up in the country. Now that I have a legal right to exist, and I can go to Monroe or Shreveport or New Orleans for synthetic blood or prostitutes who specialize in our kind, I want to stay here. At least see if it's possible. I've been roaming for decades.'

'What kind of shape is the house in?'

'Pretty bad,' he admitted. 'I've been trying to clean it out. That I can do at night. But I need workmen to get some repairs done. I'm not bad at carpentry, but I don't know a thing about electricity.'

Of course, he wouldn't.

'It seems to me the house may need rewiring,' Bill continued, sounding for all the world like any other anxious homeowner.

'Do you have a phone?'

'Sure,' he said, surprised.

'So what's the problem with the workmen?'

'It's hard to get in touch with them at night, hard to get them to meet with me so I can explain what needs doing. They're scared, or they think it's a prank call.' Frustration was evident in Bill's voice, though his face was turned away from me.

I laughed. 'If you want, I'll call them,' I offered. 'They know me. Even though everyone thinks I'm crazy, they know I'm honest.'

'That would be a great favor,' Bill said, after some hesitation. 'They could work during the day, after I'd met with them to discuss the job and the cost.'

'What an inconvenience, not being able to get out in the day,' I said thoughtlessly. I'd never really considered it before.

Bill's voice was dry. 'It certainly is.'

'And having to hide your resting place,' I blundered on.

When I felt the quality of Bill's silence, I apologized.

'I'm sorry,' I said. If it hadn't been so dark, he would have seen me turn red.

'A vampire's daytime resting place is his most closely guarded secret,' Bill said stiffly.

'I apologize.'

'I accept,' he said, after a bad little moment. We reached the road and looked up and down it as if we expected a taxi. I could see him clearly by the moonlight, now that we were out of the trees. He could see me, too. He looked me up and down.

'Your dress is the color of your eyes.'

'Thank you.' I sure couldn't see him that clearly.

'Not a lot of it, though.'

'Excuse me?'

'It's hard for me to get used to young ladies with so few clothes on,' Bill said.

'You've had a few decades to get used to it,' I said tartly. 'Come on, Bill! Dresses have been short for forty years now!'

'I liked long skirts,' he said nostalgically. 'I liked the underthings women wore. The petticoats.'

I made a rude noise.

'Do you even have a petticoat?' he asked.

'I have a very pretty beige nylon slip with lace,' I said indignantly. 'If you were a human guy, I'd say you were angling for me to talk about my underwear!'

He laughed, that deep, unused chuckle that affected me so strongly. 'Do you have that slip on, Sookie?'

I stuck out my tongue at him because I knew he could

see me. I edged the skirt of my dress up, revealing the lace of the slip and a couple more inches of tanned me.

'Happy?' I asked.

'You have pretty legs, but I still like long dresses better.'

'You're stubborn,' I told him.

'That's what my wife always told me.'

'You were married.'

'Yes, I became a vampire when I was thirty. I had a wife and I had five living children. My sister, Sarah, lived with us. She never wed. Her young man was killed in the war.'

'The Civil War.'

'Yes. I came back from the battlefield. I was one of the lucky ones. At least I thought so at the time.'

'You fought for the Confederacy,' I said wonderingly. 'If you still had your uniform and wore it to the club, the ladies would faint with joy.'

'I hadn't much of a uniform by the end of the war,' he said grimly. 'We were in rags and starving.' He seemed to shake himself. 'It had no meaning for me after I became vampire,' Bill said, his voice once again chilly and remote.

'I've brought up something that upset you,' I said. 'I am sorry. What should we talk about?' We turned and began to stroll back down the driveway toward the house.

'Your life,' he said. 'Tell me what you do when you get up in the morning.'

'I get out of bed. Then I make it up right away. I eat breakfast. Toast, sometimes cereal, sometimes eggs, and coffee – and I brush my teeth and shower and dress. Sometimes I shave my legs, you know. If it's a workday, I go in to work. If I don't go in until night, I might go shopping, or take Gran to the store, or rent a movie to watch, or sunbathe. And I read a lot. I'm lucky Gran is still spry. She does the wash and the ironing and most of the cooking.'

'What about young men?'

'Oh, I told you about that. It's just impossible.'

'So what will you do, Sookie?' he asked gently.

'Grow old and die.' My voice was short. He'd touched on my sensitive area once too often.

To my surprise, Bill reached over and took my hand. Now that we'd made each other a little angry, touched some sore spots, the air seemed somehow clearer. In the quiet night, a breeze wafted my hair around my face.

'Take the clip out?' Bill asked.

No reason not to. I reclaimed my hand and reached up to open the clip. I shook my head to loosen my hair. I stuck the clip in his pocket, since I hadn't any. As if it was the most normal thing in the world, Bill began running his fingers through my hair, spreading it out on my shoulders.

I touched his sideburns, since apparently touching was okay. 'They're long,' I observed.

'That was the fashion,' he said. 'It's lucky for me I didn't wear a beard as so many men did, or I'd have it for eternity.'

'You never have to shave?'

'No, luckily I had just shaven.' He seemed fascinated with my hair. 'In the moonlight, it looks silver.' he said very quietly.

'Ah. What do you like to do?'

I could see a shadow of a smile in the darkness.

'I like to read, too.' He thought. 'I like the movies . . . of course, I've followed their whole inception. I like the company of people who lead ordinary lives. Sometimes I crave the company of other vampires, though most of them lead very different lives from mine.'

We walked in silence for a moment.

'Do you like television?'

'Sometimes,' he confessed. 'For a while I taped soap operas and watched them at night when I thought I might be forgetting what it was like to be human. After a while I stopped, because from the examples I saw on those shows, forgetting humanity was a good thing.' I laughed.

We walked into the circle of light around the house. I had half-expected Gran to be on the porch swing waiting for us, but she wasn't. And only one dim bulb glowed in the living room. Really, Gran, I thought, exasperated. This was just like being brought home from a first date by a new man. I actually caught myself wondering if Bill would try to kiss me or not. With his views on long dresses, he would probably think it was out of line. But as stupid as kissing a vampire might seem, I realized that was what I really wanted to do, more than anything.

I got a tight feeling in my chest, a bitterness, at another thing I was denied. And I thought, Why not?

I stopped him by pulling gently on his hand. I stretched up and lay my lips on his shining cheek. I inhaled the scent of him, ordinary but faintly salty. He was wearing a trace of cologne.

I felt him shudder. He turned his head so his lips touched mine. After a moment, I reached to circle his neck with my arms. His kiss deepened, and I parted my lips. I'd never been kissed like this. It went on and on until I thought the whole world was involved in this kiss in the vampire's mouth on mine. I could feel my breathing speeding up, and I began to want other things to happen.

Suddenly Bill pulled back. He looked shaken, which pleased me no end. 'Good night, Sookie,' he said, stroking my hair one last time.

'Good night, Bill,' I said. I sounded pretty quavery myself 'I'll try to call some electricians tomorrow. I'll let you know what they say.'

'Come by the house tomorrow night – if you're off work?'

'Yes,' I said. I was still trying to gather myself.

'See you then. Thanks, Sookie.' And he turned away to walk through the woods back over to his place. Once he reached the darkness, he was invisible.

I stood staring like a fool, until I shook myself and went inside to go to bed.

I spent an indecent amount of time lying awake in bed wondering if the undead could actually do – it. Also, I wondered if it would be possible to have a frank discussion with Bill about that. Sometimes he seemed very old-fashioned, sometimes he seemed as normal as the guy next door. Well, not really, but pretty normal.

It seemed both wonderful and pathetic to me that the one creature I'd met in years that I'd want to have sex with was actually not human. My telepathy limited my options severely. I could have had sex just to have it, sure; but I had waited to have sex I could actually enjoy.

What if we did it, and after all these years I discovered I had no talent for it? Or maybe it wouldn't feel good. Maybe all the books and movies exaggerated. Arlene, too, who never seemed to understand that her sex life was not something I wanted to hear about.

I finally got to sleep, to have long, dark dreams.

The next morning, between fielding Gran's questions about my walk with Bill and our future plans, I made some phone calls. I found two electricians, a plumber, and some other service people who gave me phone numbers where they could be reached at night and made sure they understood that a phone call from Bill Compton was not a prank.

Finally, I was lying out in the sun turning toasty when Gran carried the phone out to me.

'It's your boss,' she said. Gran liked Sam, and he must have said something to make her happy because she was grinning like a Cheshire cat.

'Hi, Sam,' I said, maybe not sounding too glad because I knew something had gone wrong at work.

'Dawn didn't make it in, cher,' he said.

'Oh . . . *hell*,' I said, knowing I'd have to go in. 'I kind of have plans, Sam.' That was a first. 'When do you need me?'

'Could you just come in from five to nine? That would help out a lot.'

'Am I gonna get another full day off?'

'What about Dawn splitting a shift with you another night?'

I made a rude noise, and Gran stood there with a stern face. I knew I'd get a lecture later. 'Oh, all right,' I said grudgingly. 'See you at five.'

'Thanks, Sookie,' he said. 'I knew I could count on you.'

I tried to feel good about that. It seemed like a boring virtue. You can always count on Sookie to step in and help because she doesn't have a life!

Of course, it would be fine to get to Bill's after nine. He'd be up all night, anyway.

Work had never seemed so slow. I had trouble concentrating enough to keep my guard intact because I was always thinking about Bill. It was lucky there weren't many customers, or I would have heard unwanted thoughts galore. As it was, I found out Arlene's period was late, and she was scared she was pregnant, and before I could stop myself I gave her a hug. She stared at me searchingly and then turned red in the face.

'Did you read my mind, Sookie?' she asked, warning written in her voice. Arlene was one of the few people who simply acknowledged my ability without trying to explain it or categorizing me as a freak for possessing such an ability. She also didn't talk about it often or in any normal voice, I'd noticed.

'Sorry, I didn't mean to,' I apologized. 'I'm just not focused today.'

'All right, then. You stay out from now on, though.' And Arlene, her flaming curls bobbing around her cheeks, shook her finger in my face.

I felt like crying. 'Sorry,' I said again and strode off into the storeroom to collect myself. I had to pull my face straight and hold in those tears.

I heard the door open behind me.

'Hey, I said I was sorry, Arlene!' I snapped, wanting to be left alone. Sometimes Arlene confused telepathy with psychic talent. I was scared she'd ask me if she was really pregnant. She'd be better off buying an early home pregnancy kit.

'Sookie.' It was Sam. He turned me around with a hand on my shoulder. 'What's wrong?'

His voice was gentle and pushed me much closer to tears.

'You should sound mean so I won't cry!' I said.

He laughed, not a big laugh, a small one. He put an arm around me.

'What's the matter?' He wasn't going to give up and go away.

'Oh, I . . .' and I stopped dead. I'd never, ever explicitly discussed my problem (that's how I thought of it) with Sam or anyone else. Everyone in Bon Temps knew the rumors about why I was strange, but no one seemed to realize that I had to listen to their mental clatter nonstop, whether I wanted to or not – every day, the yammer yammer yammer . . .

'Did you hear something that bothered you?' His voice was quiet and matter-of-fact. He touched the middle of my forehead, to indicate he knew exactly how I could 'hear.'

'Yes.'

'Can't help it, can you?'

'Nope.'

'Hate it, don't you, cher?'

'Oh, yes.'

'Not your fault then, is it?'

'I try not to listen, but I can't always keep my guard up.' I felt a tear I hadn't been able to quell start trickling down my cheek.

'Is that how you do it? How do you keep your guard up, Sookie?'

He sounded really interested, not as though he thought I was a basket case. I looked up, not very far, into Sam's prominent, brilliant blue eyes.

'I just . . . it's hard to describe unless you can do it . . . I pull up a fence – no, not a fence, it's like I'm snapping together steel plates – between my brain and all others.'

'You have to hold the plates up?'

'Yes. It takes a lot of concentration. It's like dividing my mind all the time. That's why people think I'm crazy. Half my brain is trying to keep the steel plates up, and the other half might be taking drink orders, so sometimes there's not a lot left over for coherent conversation.' What a gush of relief I was feeling, just being able to talk about it.

'Do you hear words or just get impressions?'

'Depends on who I'm listening to. And their state. If they're drunk, or really disturbed, it's just pictures, impressions, intentions. If they're sober and sane it's words and some pictures.'

'The vampire says you can't hear him.'

The idea of Bill and Sam having a conversation about me made me feel very peculiar. 'That's true,' I admitted.

'Is that relaxing to you?'

'Oh, *yes*.' I meant it from my heart.

'Can you hear me, Sookie?'

'I don't want to try!' I said hastily. I moved to the door of the storeroom and stood with my hand on the knob. I pulled a tissue from my shorts pocket and patted the tear track off my cheek. 'I'll have to quit if I read your mind, Sam! I like you, I like it here.'

'Just try it sometime, Sookie,' he said casually, turning to open a carton of whiskey with the razor-edged box cutter he kept in his pocket. 'Don't worry about me. You have a job as long as you want one.'

I wiped down a table Jason had spilled salt on. He'd been in earlier to eat a hamburger and fries and down a couple of beers.

I was turning over Sam's offer in my mind.

I wouldn't try to listen to him today. He was ready for me. I'd wait when he was busy doing something else. I'd just sort of slip in and give him a listen. He'd invited me which was absolutely unique.

It was kind of nice to be invited.

I repaired my makeup and brushed my hair. I'd worn it

loose, since Bill had seemed to like that, and a darn nuisance it had been all evening. It was just about time to go, so I retrieved my purse from its drawer in Sam's office.

The Compton house, like Gran's, was set back from the road. It was a bit more visible from the parish road than hers, and it had a view of the cemetery, which her house didn't. This was due (at least in part) to the Compton house's higher setting. It was on top of a knoll and it was fully two-storied. Gran's house had a couple of spare bedrooms upstairs, and an attic, but it was more like half a top story.

At one point in the family's long history, the Comptons had had a very nice house. Even in the dark, it had a certain graciousness. But I knew in the daylight you could see the pillars were peeling, the wood siding was crooked, and the yard was simply a jungle. In the humid warmth of Louisiana, yard growth could get out of hand mighty quick, and old Mr. Compton had not been one to hire someone to do his yard work. When he'd gotten too feeble, it had simply gone undone.

The circular drive hadn't gotten fresh gravel in many years, and my car lurched to the front door. I saw that the house was all lit up, and I began to realize that the evening would not go like last evening. There was another car parked in front of the house, a Lincoln Continental, white with a dark blue top. A blue-on-white bumper sticker read VAMPIRES SUCK. A red and yellow one stated HONK IF YOU'RE A BLOOD DONOR! The vanity plate read, simply, FANGS 1.

If Bill already had company, maybe I should just go on home.

But I had been invited and was expected. Hesitantly, I raised my hand and knocked.

The door was opened by a female vampire.

She glowed like crazy. She was at least five feet eleven and black. She was wearing spandex. An exercise bra in flamingo pink and matching calf-length leggings, with a man's white dress shirt flung on unbuttoned, constituted the vampire's ensemble.

I thought she looked cheap as hell and most likely absolutely mouthwatering from a male point of view.

'Hey, little human chick,' the vampire purred.

And all of a sudden I realized I was in danger. Bill had warned me repeatedly that not all vampires were like him, and he had moments when he was not so nice, himself. I couldn't read this creature's mind, but I could hear cruelty in her voice.

Maybe she had hurt Bill. Maybe she was his lover.

All of this passed through my mind in a rush, but none of it showed on my face. I've had years of experience in controlling my face. I could feel my bright smile snap on protectively, my spine straightened, and I said cheerfully, 'Hi! I was supposed to drop by tonight and give Bill some information. Is he available?'

The female vampire laughed at me, which was nothing I wasn't used to. My smile notched up a degree brighter. This critter radiated danger the way a light bulb gives off heat.

'This little human gal here says she has some information for you, Bill!' she yelled over her (slim, brown, beautiful) shoulder.

I tried not to let relief show in any way.

'You wanna see this little thing? Or shall I just give her a love bite?'

Over my dead body, I thought furiously, and then realized it might be just that.

I didn't hear Bill speak, but the vampire stood back, and I stepped into the old house. Running wouldn't do any good; this vamp could undoubtedly bring me down before I'd gone five steps. And I hadn't laid eyes on Bill, and I couldn't be sure he was all right until I saw him. I'd brave this out and hope for the best. I'm pretty good at doing that.

The big front room was crammed with dark old furniture and people. No, not people, I realized after I'd looked carefully; two people, and two more strange vampires.

The two vampires were both male and white. One had a buzz cut and tattoos on every visible inch of his skin. The other was even taller than the woman, maybe six foot four, with a head of long rippling dark hair and a magnificent build.

The humans were less impressive. The woman was blond and plump, thirty-five or older. She was wearing maybe a pound too much makeup. She looked as worn as an old boot. The man was another story. He was lovely, the prettiest man I'd ever seen. He couldn't have been more than twenty-one. He was swarthy, maybe Hispanic, small and fine-boned. He wore denim cut-offs and nothing else. Except for makeup. I took that in my stride, but I didn't find it appealing.

Then Bill moved and I saw him, standing in the shadows of the dark hall leading from the living room to the back of the house. I looked at him, trying to get my bearings in this unexpected situation. To my dismay, he didn't look at all reassuring. His face was very still, absolutely impenetrable. Though I couldn't believe I was even thinking it, it would have been great at that point to have had a peek into his mind.

'Well, we can have a wonderful evening now,' the long-haired male vampire said. He sounded delighted. 'Is this a little friend of yours, Bill? She's so fresh.'

I thought of a few choice words I'd learned from Jason.

'If you'll just excuse me and Bill a minute,' I said very politely, as if this was a perfectly normal evening, 'I've been arranging for workmen for the house.' I tried to sound businesslike and impersonal, though wearing shorts and a T-shirt and Nikes does not inspire professional respect. But I hoped I conveyed the impression that nice people I encountered in the course of my working day could not possibly hold any threat of danger.

'And we heard Bill was on a diet of synthetic blood only,' said the tattooed vampire. 'Guess we heard wrong, Diane.'

The female vampire cocked her head and gave me a long look. 'I'm not so sure. She looks like a virgin to me.'

I didn't think Diane was talking hymens.

I took a few casual steps toward Bill, hoping like hell he would defend me if worst came to worst, but finding myself not absolutely sure. I was still smiling, hoping he would speak, would move.

And then he did. 'Sookie is mine,' he said, and his voice was so cold and smooth it wouldn't have made a ripple in the water if it had been a stone.

I looked at him sharply, but I had enough brains to keep my mouth shut.

'How good you been taking care of our Bill?' Diane asked.

'None of your fucking business,' I answered, using one of Jason's words and still smiling. I said I had a temper.

There was a sharp little pause. Everyone, human and vampire, seemed to examine me closely enough to count the hairs on my arms. Then the tall male began to rock with laughter and the others followed suit. While they were yukking it up, I moved a few feet closer to Bill. His dark eyes were fixed on me – he wasn't laughing – and I got the distinct feeling he wished, just as much as I did, that I could read his mind.

He was in some danger, I could tell. And if he was, then I was.

'You have a funny smile,' said the tall male thoughtfully. I'd liked him better when he was laughing.

'Oh, Malcolm,' said Diane. 'All human women look funny to you.'

Malcolm pulled the human male to him and gave him a long kiss. I began to feel a little sick. That kind of stuff is private. 'This is true,' Malcolm said, pulling away after a moment, to the small man's apparent disappointment. 'But there is something rare about this one. Maybe she has rich blood.'

'Aw,' said the blond woman, in a voice that could blister paint, 'that's just crazy Sookie Stackhouse.'

I looked at the woman with more attention. I recognized her at last, when I mentally erased a few miles of hard road and half the makeup. Janella Lennox had worked at Merlotte's for two weeks until Sam had fired her. She'd moved to Monroe, Arlene had told me.

The male vampire with the tattoos put his arm around Janella and rubbed her breasts. I could feel the blood drain out of my face. I was disgusted. It got worse. Janella, as lost to decency as the vampire, put her hand on his crotch and massaged.

At least I saw clearly that vampires can sure have sex.

I was less than excited about that knowledge at the moment.

Malcolm was watching me, and I'd showed my distaste.

'She's innocent,' he said to Bill, with a smile full of anticipation.

'She's mine,' Bill said again. This time his voice was more intense. If he'd been a rattlesnake his warning could not have been clearer.

'Now, Bill, you can't tell me you've been getting everything you need from that little thing,' Diane said. 'You look pale and droopy. She ain't been taking good care of you.'

I inched a little closer to Bill.

'Here,' offered Diane, whom I was beginning to hate, 'have a taste of Liam's woman or Malcolm's pretty boy, Jerry.'

Janella didn't react to being offered around, maybe because she was too busy unzipping Liam's jeans, but Malcolm's beautiful boyfriend, Jerry, slithered willingly over to Bill. I smiled as though my jaws were going to crack as he wrapped his arms around Bill, nuzzled Bill's neck, rubbed his chest against Bill's shirt.

The strain in my vampire's face was terrible to see. His fangs slid out. I saw them fully extended for the first time. The synthetic blood was not answering all Bill's needs, all right.

Jerry began licking a spot at the base of Bill's neck. Keeping my guard up was proving to be more than I could handle. Since three present were vampires, whose thoughts I couldn't hear, and Janella was fully occupied, that left Jerry. I listened and gagged.

Bill, shaking with temptation, was actually bending to sink his fangs into Jerry's neck when I said, 'No! He has the Sino-virus!'

As if released from a spell, Bill looked at me over Jerry's shoulder. He was breathing heavily, but his fangs retracted. I took advantage of the moment by taking more steps. I was within a yard of Bill, now.

'Sino-AIDS,' I said.

Alcoholic and heavily drugged victims affected vampires temporarily, and some of them were said to enjoy that buzz; but the blood of a human with full-blown AIDS didn't, nor did sexually transmitted diseases, or any other bugs that plagued humans.

Except Sino-AIDS. Even Sino-AIDS didn't kill vampires as surely as the AIDS virus killed humans, but it left the undead very weak for nearly a month, during which time it was comparatively easy to catch and stake them. And every now and then, if a vampire fed from an infected human more than once, the vampire actually died – redied? – without being staked. Still rare in the United States, Sino-AIDS was gaining a foothold around ports like New Orleans, with sailors and other travelers from many countries passing through the city in a partying mood.

All the vampires were frozen, staring at Jerry as if he were death in disguise; and for them, perhaps, he was.

The beautiful young man took me completely by surprise. He turned and leapt on me. He was no vampire, but he was strong, evidently only in the earliest stages of the virus, and he knocked me against the wall to my left. He circled my throat with one hand and lifted the other to punch me in the face. My arms were still coming up to defend myself when Jerry's hand was seized, and his body froze.

'Let go of her throat,' Bill said in such a terrifying voice that I was scared myself. By now, the scares were just piling up so quickly I didn't think I'd ever feel safe again. But Jerry' s fingers didn't relax, and I made a little whimpering sound without wanting to at all. I slewed my eyes sideways, and when I looked at Jerry's gray face, I realized that Bill was holding his hand, Malcolm was gripping his legs, and Jerry was so frightened he couldn't grasp what was wanted of him.

The room began to get fuzzy, and voices buzzed in and out. Jerry's mind was beating against mine. I was helpless to hold him out. His mind was clouded with visions of the lover who had passed the virus to Jerry, a lover who had left him for a vampire, a lover Jerry himself had murdered in a fit of jealous rage. Jerry was seeing his death coming from the vampires he had wanted to kill, and he was not satisfied that he had extracted enough vengeance with the vampires he had already infected.

I could see Diane's face over Jerry's shoulder, and she was smiling.

Bill broke Jerry's wrist.

He screamed and collapsed on the floor. The blood began surging into my head again, and I almost fainted. Malcolm picked Jerry up and carried him over to the couch as casually as if Jerry were a rolled-up rug. But Malcolm's face was not as casual. I knew Jerry would be lucky if he died quickly.

Bill stepped in front of me, taking Jerry's place. His fingers, the fingers that had just broken Jerry's wrist, massaged my neck as gently as my grandmother's would have done. He put a finger across my lips to make sure I knew to keep silent.

Then, his arm around me, he turned to face the other vampires.

'This has all been very entertaining,' Liam said. His voice was as cool as if Janella wasn't giving him a truly intimate massage there on the couch. He hadn't troubled himself to budge during the whole incident. He had newly visible tattoos I could never in this world have imagined. I was sick to my stomach. 'But I think we should be driving back to Monroe. We have to have a little talk with Jerry when he wakes up, right, Malcolm?'

Malcolm heaved the unconscious Jerry over his shoulder and nodded at Liam. Diane looked disappointed.

'But fellas,' she protested. 'We haven't found out how this little gal knew.'

The two male vampires simultaneously switched their gaze to me. Quite casually, Liam took a second off to reach a climax. Yep, vampires could do it, all right. After a little sigh of completion, he said, 'Thanks, Janella. That's a good question, Malcolm. As usual, our Diane has cut to the quick.' And the three visiting vampires laughed as if that was a very good joke, but I thought it was a scary one.

'You can't speak yet, can you, sweetheart?' Bill gave my shoulder a squeeze as he asked, as if I couldn't get the hint.

I shook my head.

'I could probably make her talk,' Diane offered.

'Diane, you forget,' Bill said gently.

'Oh, yeah. She's yours,' Diane said. But she didn't sound cowed or convinced.

'We'll have to visit some other time,' Bill said, and his voice made it clear the others had to leave or fight him.

Liam stood, zipped up his pants, gestured to his human woman. 'Out, Janella, we're being evicted.' The tattoos rippled across his heavy arms as he stretched. Janella ran her hands along his ribs as if she just couldn't get enough of him, and he swatted her away as lightly as if she'd been a fly. She looked vexed, but not mortified as I would have been. This was not new treatment for Janella.

Malcolm picked up Jerry and carried him out the front door without a word. If drinking from Jerry had given him the virus, Malcolm was not yet impaired. Diane went last, slinging a purse over her shoulder and casting a bright-eyed glance behind her.

'I'll leave you two lovebirds on your own, then. It's been fun, honey,' she said lightly, and she slammed the door behind her.

The minute I heard the car start up outside, I fainted.

I'd never done so in my life, and I hoped never to again but I felt I had some excuse.

I seemed to spend a lot of time around Bill unconscious. That was a crucial thought, and I knew it deserved a lot of pondering, but not just at that moment. When I came to, everything I'd seen and heard rushed back, and I gagged for real. Immediately Bill bent me over the edge of the couch. But I managed to keep my food down, maybe because there wasn't much in my stomach.

'Do vampires act like that?' I whispered. My throat was sore and bruised where Jerry had squeezed it. 'They were horrible.'

'I tried to catch you at the bar when I found out you weren't at home,' Bill said. His voice was empty. 'But you'd left.'

Though I knew it wouldn't help a thing, I began crying.

I was sure Jerry was dead by now, and I felt I should have done something about that, but I couldn't have kept silent when he was about to infect Bill. So many things about this short episode had upset me so deeply that I didn't know where to begin being upset. In maybe fifteen minutes I'd been in fear of my life, in fear for Bill's life (well – existence), made to witness sex acts that should be strictly private, seen my potential sweetie in the throes of blood lust (emphasis on lust), and nearly been choked to death by a diseased hustler.

On second thought, I gave myself full permission to cry. I sat up and wept and mopped my face with a handkerchief Bill handed me. My curiosity about why a vampire would need a handkerchief was just a little flicker of normality, drenched by the flood of my nervous tears.

Bill had enough sense not to put his arms around me. He sat on the floor, and had the grace to keep his eyes averted while I mopped myself dry.

'When vampires live in nests,' he said suddenly, 'they often become more cruel because they egg each other on. They see others like themselves constantly, and so they are reminded of how far from being human they are. They become laws unto themselves. Vampires like me, who live alone, are a little better reminded of their former humanity.'

I listened to his soft voice, going slowly through his thoughts as he made an attempt to explain the unexplainable to me.

'Sookie, our life is seducing and taking and has been for centuries, for some of us. Synthetic blood and grudging human acceptance isn't going to change that overnight – or over a decade. Diane and Liam and Malcolm have been together for fifty years.'

'How sweet,' I said, and my voice held something I'd never heard from myself before: bitterness. 'Their golden wedding anniversary.'

'Can you forget about this?' Bill asked. His huge dark eyes came closer and closer. His mouth was about two inches from mine.

'I don't know.' The words jerked out of me. 'Do you know, I didn't know if you could do it?'

His eyebrows rose interrogatively. 'Do . . . ?'

'Get –' and I stopped, trying to think of a pleasant way to put it. I'd seen more crudity this evening than I'd seen in my lifetime, and I didn't want to add to it. 'An erection,' I said, avoiding his eyes.

'You know better now.' He sounded like he was trying not to be amused. 'We can have sex, but we can't make children or have them. Doesn't it make you feel better, that Diane can't have a baby?'

My fuses blew. I opened my eyes and looked at him steadily. 'Don't – you – laugh – at – me.'

'Oh, Sookie,' he said, and his hand rose to touch my cheek.

I dodged his hand and struggled to my feet. He didn't help me, which was a good thing, but he sat on the floor watching me with a still, unreadable face. Bill's fangs had retracted, but I knew he was still suffering from hunger. Too bad.

My purse was on the floor by the front door. I wasn't walking very steadily, but I was walking. I pulled the list of electricians out of a pocket and lay it on a table.

'I have to go.'

He was in front of me suddenly. He'd done one of those vampire things again. 'Can I kiss you good-bye?' he asked, his hands down at his sides, making it so obvious he wouldn't touch me until I said green light.

'No,' I said vehemently. 'I can't stand it after them.'

'I'll come see you.'

'Yes. Maybe.'

He reached past me to open the door, but I thought he was reaching for me, and I flinched.

I spun on my heel and almost ran to my car, tears blurring my vision again. I was glad the drive home was so short.

Chapter 3

The phone was ringing. I pulled my pillow over my head. Surely Gran would get it? As the irritating noise persisted, I realized Gran must be gone shopping or outside working in the yard. I began squirming to the bed table, not happy but resigned. With the headache and regrets of someone who has a terrible hangover (though mine was emotional rather than alcohol induced) I stretched out a shaky hand and grabbed the receiver.

'Yes?' I asked. It didn't come out quite right. I cleared my throat and tried again. 'Hello?'

'Sookie?'

'Um-hum. Sam?'

'Yeah. Listen, cher, do me a favor?'

'What?' I was due to work today anyway, and I didn't want to hold down Dawn's shift and mine, too.

'Go by Dawn's place, and see what she's up to, would you? She won't answer her phone, and she hasn't come in. The delivery truck just pulled up, and I got to tell these guys where to put stuff.'

'Now? You want me to go now?' My old bed had never held on to me harder.

'Could you?' For the first time, he seemed to grasp my unusual mood. I had never refused Sam anything.

'I guess so,' I said, feeling tired all over again at the very idea. I wasn't too crazy about Dawn, and she wasn't too crazy about me. She was convinced I'd read her mind and told Jason something she'd been thinking about him, which had cause him to break up with her. If I took that kind of interest in Jason's romances, I'd never have time to eat or sleep.

I showered and pulled on my work clothes, moving sluggishly. All my bounce had gone flat, like soda with the top left off. I ate cereal and brushed my teeth and told Gran where I was going when I tracked her down; she'd been outside planting petunias in a tub by the back door. She didn't seem to understand exactly what I meant, but smiled and waved anyway. Gran was getting a little more deaf every week, but I realized that was no great wonder since she was seventy-eight. It was marvelous that she was so strong and healthy, and her brain was sound as a bell.

As I went on my unwelcome errand, I thought about how hard it must have been for Gran to raise two more children after she'd already raised her own. My father, her son, had died when I was seven and Jason ten. When I'd been twenty-three, Gran's daughter, my Aunt Linda, had died of uterine cancer. Aunt Linda's girl, Hadley, had vanished into the same subculture that had spawned the Rattrays even before Aunt Linda had passed away, and to this day we didn't know if Hadley realizes her mother is dead. That was a lot of grief to get through, yet Gran had always been strong for us.

I peered through my windshield at the three small duplexes on one side of Berry Street, a run-down block or two that ran behind the oldest part of downtown Bon Temps. Dawn lived in one of them. I spotted her car, a green compact, in the driveway of one of the better-kept houses, and pulled in behind it. Dawn had already put a hanging basket of begonias by her front door, but they looked dry. I knocked.

I waited for a minute or two. I knocked again.

'Sookie, you need some help?' The voice sounded familiar. I turned around and shielded my eyes from the morning sun. Rene Lenier was standing by his pickup, parked across the street at one of the small frame houses that populated the rest of the neighborhood.

'Well,' I began, not sure if I needed help or not, or if I did that Rene could supply it. 'Have you seen Dawn? She didn't come to work today, and she never called in yesterday. Sam asked me to stop by.'

'Sam should come do his own dirty work,' Rene said, which perversely made me defend my boss.

'Truck came in, had to he unloaded.' I turned and knocked again. 'Dawn,' I yelled. 'Come let me in.' I looked down at the concrete porch. The pine pollen had begun falling two days ago. Dawn's porch was solid yellow. Mine were the only footprints. My scalp began to prickle.

I barely registered the fact that Rene stood awkwardly by the door to his pickup, unsure whether to stay or go.

Dawn's duplex was a one-story, quite small, and the door to the other half was just feet away from Dawn's. Its little driveway was empty, and there were no curtains at the windows. It looked as though Dawn was temporarily out of a neighbor. Dawn had been proud enough to hang curtains, white with dark gold flowers. They were drawn, but the fabric was thin and unlined, and Dawn hadn't shut the cheap one-inch aluminum blinds. I peered in and discovered the living room held only some flea-market furniture. A coffee mug sat on the table by a lumpy recliner and an old couch covered with a hand-crocheted afghan was pushed against the wall.

'I think I'll go around back,' I called to Rene. He started across the street as though I'd given him a signal, and I stepped off the front porch. My feet brushed the dusty grass, yellow with pine pollen, and I knew I'd have to dust off my shoes and maybe change my socks before work. During pine pollen season, everything turns yellow. Cars, plants, roofs, windows, all are powdered with a golden haze. The ponds and pools of rainwater have yellow scum around the edges.

Dawn's bathroom window was so discreetly high that I couldn't see in. She'd lowered the blinds in the bedroom, but hadn't closed them tightly. I could see a little through the slats. Dawn was in bed on her back. The bedclothes were tossed around wildly. Her legs were spraddled. Her face was swollen and discolored, and her tongue protruded from her mouth. There were flies crawling on it.

I could hear Rene coming up behind me.

'Go call the police,' I said.

'What you say, Sookie? You see her?'

'Go *call the police!*'

'Okay, okay!' Rene beat a hasty retreat.

Some female solidarity had made me not want Rene to see Dawn like that, without Dawn's consent. And my fellow waitress was far beyond consenting.

I stood with my back to the window, horribly tempted

to look again in the futile hope I'd made a mistake the first time. Staring at the duplex next door to Dawn's, maybe a scant six feet away, I wondered how its tenants could have avoided hearing Dawn's death, which had been violent.

Here came Rene again. His weatherbeaten face was puckered into an expression of deep concern, and his bright brown eyes looked suspiciously shiney.

'Would you call Sam, too?' I asked. Without a word, he turned and trudged back to his place. He was being mighty good. Despite his tendency to gossip, Rene had always been one to help where he saw a need. I remembered him coming out to the house to help Jason hang Gran's porch swing, a random memory of a day far different from this.

The duplex next door was just like Dawn's, so I was looking directly at its bedroom window. Now a face appeared, and the window was raised. A tousled head poked out. 'What you doing, Sookie Stackhouse?' asked a slow, deep, male voice. I peered at him for a minute, finally placing the face, while trying not to look too closely at the fine, bare chest underneath.

'JB?'

'Sure thing.'

I'd gone to high school with JB du Rone. In fact, some of my few dates had been with JB, who was lovely but so simple that he didn't care if I read his mind or not. Even under today's circumstances, I could appreciate JB's beauty. When your hormones have been held in check as long as mine, it doesn't take much to set them off. I heaved a sigh at the sight of JB's muscular arms and pectorals.

'What you doing out here?' he asked again.

'Something bad seems to have happened to Dawn,' I

said, not knowing if I should tell him or not. 'My boss sent me here to look for her when she didn't come to work.'

'She in there?' JB simply scrambled out of the window. He had some shorts on, cut-offs.

'Please don't look,' I asked, holding up my hand and without warning I began crying. I was doing that a lot lately, too. 'She looks so awful, JB.'

'Aw, honey,' he said, and bless his country heart, he put an arm around me and patted me on the shoulder. If there was a female around who needed comforting, by God, that was a priority to JB du Rone.

'Dawn liked 'em rough,' he said consolingly, as if that would explain everything.

It might to some people, but not to unworldly me.

'What, rough?' I asked, hoping I had a tissue in my shorts pocket.

I looked up at JB to see him turn a little red.

'Honey, she liked . . . aw, Sookie, you don't need to hear this.'

I had a widespread reputation for virtue, which I found somewhat ironic. At the moment, it was inconvenient.

'You can tell me, I worked with her,' I said, and JB nodded solemnly, as if that made sense.

'Well, honey, she liked men to – like, bite and hit her.' JB looked weirded out by this preference of Dawn's. I must have made a face because he said, 'I know, I can't understand why some people like that, either.' JB, never one to ignore an opportunity to make hay, put both arms around me and kept up the patting, but it seemed to concentrate on the middle of my back (checking to see if I was wearing a bra) and then quite a bit lower (JB liked firm rear ends, I remembered.)

A lot of questions hovered on the edge of my tongue, but they remained shut inside my mouth. The police got there, in the persons of Kenya Jones and Kevin Prior. When the town police chief had partnered Kenya and Kevin, he'd been indulging his sense of humor, the town figured, for Kenya was at least five foot eleven, the color of bitter chocolate, and built to weather hurricanes. Kevin possibly made it up to five foot eight, had freckles over every visible inch of his pale body, and had the narrow, fatless build of a runner. Oddly enough, the two Ks got along very well, though they'd had some memorable quarrels.

Now they both looked like cops.

'What's this about, Miss Stackhouse?' Kenya asked. 'Rene says something happened to Dawn Green?' She'd scanned JB while she talked, and Kevin was looking at the ground all around us. I had no idea why, but I was sure there was a good police reason.

'My boss sent me here to find out why Dawn missed work yesterday and hadn't shown up today,' I said. 'I knocked on her door, and she didn't answer, but her car was here. I was worried about her, so I started around the house looking in the windows, and she's in there.' I pointed behind them, and the two officers turned to look at the window. Then they looked at each other and nodded as if they'd had a whole conversation. While Kenya went over to the window, Kevin went around to the back door.

JB had forgotten to pat while he watched the officers work. In fact, his mouth was a little open, revealing perfect teeth. He wanted to go look through the window more than anything, but he couldn't shoulder past Kenya, who pretty much took up whatever space was available.

I didn't want my own thoughts any more. I relaxed,

dropping my guard, and listened to the thoughts of others. Out of the clamor, I picked one thread and concentrated on it.

Kenya Jones turned back to stare through us without seeing us. She was thinking of everything she and Kevin needed to do to keep the investigation as textbook perfect as Bon Temps patrol officers could. She was thinking she'd heard bad things about Dawn and her liking for rough sex. She was thinking that it was no surprise Dawn had met a bad end, though she felt sorry for anyone who ended up with flies crawling on her face. Kenya was thinking she was sorry she'd eaten that extra doughnut that morning at the Nut Hut because it might come back up and that would shame her as a black woman police officer.

I tuned in to another channel.

JB was thinking about Dawn getting killed during rough sex just a few feet away from him, and while it was awful it was also a little exciting and Sookie was still built wonderful. He wished he could screw her right now. She was so sweet and nice. He was pushing away the humiliation he'd felt when Dawn had wanted him to hit her, and he couldn't, and it was an old humiliation.

I switched.

Kevin came around the corner thinking that he and Kenya better not botch any evidence and that he was glad no one knew he'd ever slept with Dawn Green. He was furious that someone had killed a woman he knew, and he was hoping it wasn't a black man because that would make his relationship with Kenya even more tense.

I switched.

Rene Lenier was wishing someone would come and get the body out of the house. He was hoping no one knew he'd slept with Dawn Green. I couldn't spell out his thoughts exactly, they were very black and snarled. Some people I can't get a clear reading on. He was very agitated.

Sam came hurrying toward me, slowing down when he saw JB was touching me. I could not read Sam's thoughts. I could feel his emotions (right now a mix of worry, concern, and anger) but I could not spell out one single thought. This was so fascinating and unexpected that I stepped out of JB's embrace, wanting to go up to Sam and grab his arms and look into his eyes and really probe around in his head. I remembered when he'd touched me, and I'd shied away. Now he *felt* me in his head and though he kept on walking toward me, his mind flinched back. Despite his invitation to me, he hadn't known I would see he was different from others: I picked up on that until he shut me down.

I'd never felt anything like it. It was like an iron door slamming. In my face.

I'd been on the point of reaching out to him instinctively, but my hand dropped to my side. Sam deliberately looked at Kevin, not at me.

'What's happening, Officer?' Sam asked.

'We're going to break into this house, Mr. Merlotte, unless you have a master key.'

Why would Sam have a key?

'He's my landlord,' JB said in my ear, and I jumped.

'He is?' I asked stupidly.

'He owns all three duplexes.'

Sam had been fishing in his pocket, and now he came up with a bunch of keys. He flipped through them expertly, stopping at one and singling it out, getting it off the ring and handing it to Kevin.

'This fits front and back?' Kevin asked. Sam nodded. He still wasn't looking at me.

Kevin went to the back door of the duplex, out of sight, and we were all so quiet we could hear the key turn in the lock. Then he was in the bedroom with the dead woman, and we could see his face twist when the smell hit him. Holding one hand across his mouth and nose, he bent over the body and put his fingers on her neck. He looked out the window then and shook his head at his partner. Kenya nodded and headed out to the street to use the radio in the patrol car.

'Listen, Sookie, how about going to dinner with me tonight?' JB asked. 'This has been tough on you, and you need some fun to make up for it.'

'Thanks, JB.' I was very conscious of Sam listening. 'It's really nice of you to ask. But I have a feeling I'm going to be working extra hours today.'

For just a second, JB's handsome face was blank. Then comprehension filtered in. 'Yeah, Sam's gotta hire someone else,' he observed. 'I got a cousin in Springhill needs a job. Maybe I'll give her a call. We could live right next door to each other, now.'

I smiled at him, though I am sure it was a very weak smile, as I stood shoulder to shoulder with the man I'd worked with for two years.

'I'm sorry, Sookie,' he said quietly.

'For what?' My own voice was just as low. Was he going to acknowledge what had passed between us – or rather, failed to pass?

'For sending you to check on Dawn. I should have come myself. I was sure she was just shacked up with someone new and needed a reminder that she was supposed to be working. The last time I had to come get her, she yelled at me so much I just didn't want to deal with it again. So like a coward, I sent you, and you had to find her like that.'

'You're full of surprises, Sam.'

He didn't turn to look at me or make any reply. But his fingers folded around mine. For a long moment, we stood in the sun with people buzzing around us, holding hands. His palm was hot and dry, and his fingers were strong. I felt I had truly connected with another human. But then his grip loosened, and Sam stepped over to talk with the detective, who was emerging from his car, and JB began asking me how Dawn had looked, and the world fell back into its same old groove.

The contrast was cruel. I felt tired all over again, and remembered the night before in more detail than I wanted to. The world seemed a bad and terrible place, all its denizens suspect, and I the lamb wandering through the valley of death with a bell around my neck. I stomped over to my car and opened the door, sank sideways into the seat. I'd be standing plenty today; I'd sit while I could.

JB followed me. Now that he'd rediscovered me, he could not be detached. I remembered when Gran had had high hopes for some permanent relationship between us, when I'd been in high school. But talking to JB, even reading his mind, was as interesting as a kindergarten primer was to an adult reader. It was one of God's jokes that such a dumb mind had been put in such an eloquent body.

He knelt before me and took my hand. I found myself hoping that some smart rich lady would come along and marry JB and take care of him and enjoy what he had to offer. She would be getting a bargain.

'Where are you working now?' I asked him, just to distract myself.

'My dad's warehouse,' he said.

That was the job of last resort, the one JB always returned to when he got fired from other jobs for doing something lamebrained, or for not showing up, or for offending some supervisor mortally. JB's dad ran an auto parts store.

'How are your folks doing?'

'Oh, fine. Sookie, we should do something together.'

Don't tempt me, I thought.

Someday my hormones were going to get the better of me and I'd do something I'd regret; and I could do worse than do it with JB. But I would hold out and hope for something better. 'Thanks, honey,' I said. 'Maybe we will. But I'm kind of upset right now.'

'Are you in love with that vampire?' he asked directly.

'Where did you hear that?'

'Dawn said so.' JB's face clouded as he remembered Dawn was dead. What Dawn had said, I found on scanning JB's mind, was 'That new vampire is interested in Sookie Stackhouse. I'd be better for him. He needs a woman who can take some rough treatment. Sookie would scream if he touched her.'

It was pointless being mad at a dead person, but briefly I indulged myself by doing just that.

Then the detective was walking toward us, and JB got to his feet and moved away.

The detective took JB's position, squatting on the ground in front of me. I must look in bad shape.

'Miss Stackhouse?' he asked. He was using that quiet intense voice many professionals adopt in a crisis. 'I'm Andy Bellefleur.' The Bellefleurs had been around Bon Temps as long as there'd been a Bon Temps, so I wasn't amused at a man being 'beautiful flower.' In fact, I felt sorry for whoever thought it was amusing as I looked down at the block of muscle that was Detective Bellefleur. This particular family member had graduated before Jason, and I'd been one class behind his sister Portia.

He'd been placing me, too. 'Your brother doing okay?' he asked, his voice still quiet, not quite as neutral. It sounded like he'd had a run-in or two with Jason.

'The little I see of him, he's doing fine,' I answered.

'And your grandmother?'

I smiled. 'She's out planting flowers this morning.'

'That's wonderful,' he said, doing that sincere head shake that's supposed to indicate admiring amazement. 'Now, I understand that you work at Merlotte's?'

'Yes.'

'And so did Dawn Green?'

'Yes.'

'When was the last time you saw Dawn?'

'Two days ago. At work.' I already felt exhausted. Without shifting my feet from the ground or my arm from the steering wheel, I lay my head sideways on the headrest of the driver's seat.

'Did you talk to her then?'

I tried to remember. 'I don't think so.'

'Were you close to Miss Green?'

'No.'

'And why did you come here today?'

I explained about working for Dawn yesterday, about Sam's phone call this morning.

'Did Mr. Merlotte tell you why he didn't want to come here himself?'

'Yes, a truck was there to unload. Sam has to show the guys where to put the boxes.' Sam also did a lot of the unloading himself, half the time, to speed up the process.

'Do you think Mr. Merlotte had any relationship with Dawn?'

'He was her boss.'

'No, outside work.'

'Nope.'

'You sound pretty positive.'

'I am.'

'Do you have a relationship with Sam?'

'No.'

'Then how are you so sure?'

Good question. Because from time to time I'd heard thoughts that indicated that if she didn't hate Sam, Dawn sure as hell wasn't real fond of him? Not too smart a thing to tell the detective.

'Sam keeps everything real professional at the bar,' I said. It sounded lame, even to me. It just happened to be the truth.

'Did you know anything about Dawn's personal life?'

'No.'

'You weren't friendly?'

'Not particularly.' My thoughts drifted as the detective bent his head in thought. At least that was what it looked like.

'Why is that?'

'I guess we didn't have anything in common.'

'Like what? Give me an example.'

I sighed heavily, blowing my lips out in exasperation. If we didn't have anything in common, how could I give him an example?

'Okay?' I said slowly. 'Dawn had a real active social life, and she liked to be with men. She wasn't so crazy about spending time with women. Her family is from Monroe, so she didn't have family ties here. She drank, and I don't. I read a lot, and she didn't. That enough?'

Andy Bellefleur scanned my face to see if I was giving him attitude. He must have been reassured by what he saw.

'So, you two didn't ever see each other after working hours?'

'That's correct.'

'Doesn't it seem strange to you that Sam Merlotte asked you to check on Dawn, then?'

'No, not at all,' I said stoutly. At least, it didn't seem strange now, after Sam's description of Dawn's tantrum. 'This is on my way to the bar, and I don't have children like Arlene, the other waitress on our shift. So it would be easier for me.' That was pretty sound, I thought. If I said Dawn had screamed at Sam the last time he'd been here, that would give exactly the wrong impression.

'What did you do after work two days ago, Sookie?'

'I didn't come to work. I had the day off.'

'And your plan for that day was –?'

'I sunbathed and helped Gran clean house, and we had company.'

'Who would that be?'

'That would be Bill Compton.'

'The vampire.'

'Right.'

'How late was Mr. Compton at your house?'

'I don't know. Maybe midnight or one.'

'How did he seem to you?'

'He seemed fine.'

'Edgy? Irritated?'

'No.'

'Miss Stackhouse, we need to talk to you more at the station house. This is going to take awhile, here, as you can see.'

'Okay, I guess.'

'Can you come in a couple of hours?'

I looked at my wristwatch. 'If Sam doesn't need me to work.'

'You know, Miss Stackhouse, this really takes precedence over working at a bar.'

Okay, I was pissed off. Not because he thought murder investigations were more important than getting to work on time; I agreed with him, there. It was his unspoken prejudice against my particular job.

'You may not think my job amounts to much, but it's one I'm good at, and I like it. I am as worthy of respect as your sister, the lawyer, Andy Bellefleur, and don't you forget it. I am not stupid, and I am not a slut.'

The detective turned red, slowly and unattractively. 'I apologize,' Andy said stiffly. He was still trying to deny the old connection, the shared high school, the knowledge of each other's family. He was thinking he should have been a detective in another town, where he could treat people the way he thought a police officer should.

'No, you'll be a better detective here if you can get over that attitude,' I told him. His gray eyes flared wide in shock, and I was childishly glad I'd rocked him, though I was sure I would pay for it sooner or later. I always did when I gave people a peek at my disability.

Mostly, people couldn't get away from me fast enough when I'd given them a taste of mind reading, but Andy

Bellefleur was fascinated. 'It's true, then,' he breathed, as if we were somewhere alone instead of sitting in the driveway of a rundown duplex in rural Louisiana.

'No, forget it,' I said quickly. 'I can just tell sometimes by the way people look what they're thinking.'

He deliberately thought about unbuttoning my blouse. But I was wary now, back to my normal state of barricaded seige, and I did no more than smile brightly. I could tell I wasn't fooling him, though.

'When you're ready for me, you come to the bar. We can talk in the storeroom or Sam's office,' I said firmly and swung my legs into the car.

The bar was buzzing when I got there. Sam had called Terry Bellefleur, Andy's second cousin if I recalled correctly, in to watch the bar while he talked to the police at Dawn's place. Terry had had a bad war in Vietnam, and he existed narrowly on government disability of some kind. He'd been wounded, captured, held prisoner for two years, and now his thoughts were most often so scary that I was extra special careful when I was around him. Terry had a hard life, and acting normal was even harder for him than it was for me. Terry didn't drink, thank God.

Today I gave him a light kiss on the cheek while I got my tray and scrubbed my hands. Through the window into the little kitchen I could see Lafayette Reynold, the cook, flipping burgers and sinking a basket of fries into hot oil. Merlotte's serves a few sandwiches, and that's all. Sam doesn't want to run a restaurant, but a bar with some food available.

'What was that for, not that I'm not honored,' Terry said. He'd raised his eyebrows. Terry was redhaired, though when he needed a shave, I could tell his whiskers were gray. Terry spent a lot of time outside, but his skin never exactly tanned. It got a rough, reddened look, which made the scars on his left cheek stand out more clearly. That didn't seem to bother Terry. Arlene had been to bed with Terry one night when she'd been drinking, and she'd confided in me that Terry had many scars even worse than the one on his cheek.

'Just for being here,' I said.

'It true about Dawn?'

Lafayette put two plates on the serving hatch. He winked at me with a sweep of his thick, false lashes. Lafayette wears a lot of makeup. I was so used to him I never thought of it any more, but now his eye shadow brought the boy, Jerry, to my mind. I'd let him go with the three vampires without protest. That had probably been wrong, but realistic. I couldn't have stopped them from taking him. I couldn't have gotten the police to catch up with them in time. He was dying anyway, and he was taking as many vampires and humans with him as he could; and he was already a killer himself. I told my conscience this would be the last talk we'd have about Jerry.

'Arlene, burgers up,' Terry called, jerking me back into the here and now. Arlene came over to grab the plates. She gave me a look that said she was going to pump me dry at the first chance she got. Charlsie Tooten was working, too. She filled in when one of the regular women got sick or just didn't show. I hoped Charlsie would take Dawn's place full-time. I'd always liked her.

'Yeah, Dawn's dead,' I told Terry. He didn't seem to mind my long pause.

'What happened to her?'

'I don't know, but it wasn't peaceful.' I'd seen blood on the sheets, not a lot, but some.

'Maudette,' Terry said, and I instantly understood.

'Maybe,' I said. It sure was possible that whoever had done in Dawn was the same person who'd killed Maudette.

Of course, everyone in Renard Parish came in that day, if not for lunch, then for an afternoon cup of coffee or a beer. If they couldn't make their work schedule bend around that they waited until they clocked out and came in on their way home. Two young women in our town murdered in one month? You bet people wanted to talk.

Sam returned about two, with heat radiating off his body and sweat trickling down his face from standing out in the shadeless yard at the crime scene. He told me that Andy Bellefleur had said he was coming to talk to me again soon.

'I don't know why,' I said, maybe a tad sullenly. 'I never hung around with Dawn. What happened to her, did they tell you?'

'Someone strangled her after beating on her a little,' Sam said. 'But she had some old tooth marks, too. Like Maudette.'

'There are lots of vampires, Sam,' I said, answering his unspoken comment.

'Sookie.' His voice was so serious and quiet. It made me remember how he'd held my hand at Dawn's house, and then I remembered how he'd shut me out of his mind, known I was probing, known how to keep me out. 'Honey, Bill is a good guy, for a vampire, but he's just not human.'

'Honey, neither are you,' I said, very quietly but very sharply. And I turned my back on Sam, not exactly wanting to admit why I was so angry with him, but wanting him to know it nonetheless.

I worked like a demon. Whatever her faults, Dawn had

been efficient, and Charlsie just couldn't keep up with the pace. She was willing, and I was sure she'd catch up with the rhythm of the bar, but for tonight, Arlene and I had to take up the slack.

I earned a ton of money in tips that evening and on into the night when people found out I'd actually discovered the body. I just kept my face solemn and got through it, not wanting to offend customers who just wanted to know what everyone else in town wanted to know.

On my way home, I allowed myself to relax a little. I was exhausted. The last thing I expected to see, after I turned into the little drive through the woods that led to our house, was Bill Compton. He was leaning against a pine tree waiting for me. I drove past him a little, almost deciding to ignore him. But then I stopped.

He opened my door. Without looking him in the eyes, I got out. He seemed comfortable in the night, in a way I never could be. There were too many childhood taboos about the night and the darkness and things that went bump.

Come to think of it, Bill was one of those things. No wonder he felt at ease.

'Are you going to look at your feet all night, or are you going to talk to me?' he asked in a voice that was just above a whisper.

'Something happened you should know about.'

'Tell me.' He was trying to do something to me: I could feel his power hovering around me, but I batted it away. He sighed.

'I can't stand up,' I said wearily. 'Let's sit on the ground or something. My feet are tired.'

In answer, he picked me up and set me on the hood of

the car. Then he stood in front of me, his arms crossed, very obviously waiting.

'Tell me.'

'Dawn was murdered. Just like Maudette Pickens.'

'Dawn?'

Suddenly I felt a little better. 'The other waitress at the bar.'

'The redheaded one, the one who's been married so often?'

I felt a lot better. 'No, the dark-haired one, the one who kept bumping into your chair with her hips to get you to notice her.'

'Oh, that one. She came to my house.'

'Dawn? When?'

'After you left the other night. The night the other vampires were there. She's lucky she missed them. She was very confident of her ability to handle anything.'

I looked up at him. 'Why is she so lucky? Wouldn't you have protected her?'

Bill's eyes were totally dark in the moonlight. 'I don't think so,' he said.

'You are . . .'

'I'm a vampire, Sookie. I don't think like you. I don't care about people automatically.'

'You protected me.'

'You're different.'

'Yeah? I'm a waitress, like Dawn. I come from a plain family, like Maudette. What's so different?'

I was in a sudden rage. I knew what was coming.

His cool finger touched the middle of my forehead. 'Different,' he said. 'You're not like us. But you're not like them, either.'

I felt a flare of rage so intense it was almost divine. I hauled off and hit him, an insane thing to do. It was like hitting a Brink's armored truck. In a flash, he had me off the car and pinned to him, my arms bound to my sides by one of his arms.

'No!' I screamed. I kicked and fought, but I might as well have saved the energy. Finally I sagged against him.

My breathing was ragged, and so was his. But I didn't think it was for the same reason.

'Why did you think I needed to know about Dawn?' He sounded so reasonable, you'd think the struggle hadn't happened.

'Well, Mr. Lord of Darkness,' I said furiously, 'Maudette had old bite marks on her thighs, and the police told Sam that Dawn had bite marks, too.'

If silence can be characterized, his was thoughtful. While he was mulling, or whatever vampires do, his embrace loosened. One hand began rubbing my back absently, as if I was a puppy who had whimpered.

'You imply they didn't die from these bites.'

'No. From strangulation.'

'Not a vampire, then.' His tone put it beyond question.

'Why not?'

'If a vampire had been feeding from these women, they would have been drained instead of strangled. They wouldn't have been wasted like that.'

Just when I was beginning to be comfortable with Bill, he'd say something so cold, so vampirey, I had to start all over again.

'Then,' I said wearily, 'either you have a crafty vampire with great self-control, or you have someone who's determined to kill women who've been with vampires.'

'Hmmm.'

I didn't feel very good about either of those choices.

'Do you think I'd do that?' he asked.

The question was unexpected. I wriggled in his pinioning embrace to look up at him.

'You've taken great care to point out how heartless you are,' I reminded him. 'What do you really want me to believe?'

And it was so wonderful not to know. I almost smiled.

'I could have killed them, but I wouldn't do it here, or now,' Bill said. He had no color in the moonlight except for the dark pools of his eyes and the dark arches of his brows. 'This is where I want to stay. I want a home.'

A vampire, yearning for home.

Bill read my face. 'Don't pity me, Sookie. That would be a mistake.' He seemed willing me to stare into his eyes.

'Bill, you can't glamor me, or whatever you do. You can't enchant me into pulling my T-shirt down for you to bite me, you can't convince me you weren't ever here, you can't do any of your usual stuff. You have to be regular with me, or just force me.'

'No,' he said, his mouth almost on mine. 'I won't force you.'

I fought the urge to kiss him. But at least I knew it was my very own urge, not a manufactured one.

'So, if it wasn't you,' I said, struggling to keep on course, 'then Maudette and Dawn knew another vampire. Maudette went to the vampire bar in Shreveport. Maybe Dawn did too. Will you take me there?'

'Why?' he asked, sounding no more than curious.

I just couldn't explain being in danger to someone who

was so used to being beyond it. At least at night. 'I'm not sure Andy Bellefleur will go to the trouble,' I lied.

'There are still Bellefleurs here,' he said, and there was something different in his voice. His arms hardened around me to the point of pain.

'Yes,' I said. 'Lots of them. Andy is a police detective. His sister, Portia, is a lawyer. His cousin Terry is a veteran and a bartender. He substitutes for Sam. There are lots of others.'

'Bellefleur . . .'

I was getting crushed.

'Bill,' I said, my voice squeaky with panic.

He loosened his grip immediately. 'Excuse me,' he said formally.

'I have to go to bed,' I said. 'I'm really tired, Bill.'

He set me down on the gravel with scarcely a bump. He looked down at me.

'You told those other vampires that I belonged to you,' I said.

'Yes.'

'What exactly did that mean?'

'That means that if they try to feed on you, I'll kill them,' he said. 'It means you are my human.'

'I have to say I'm glad you did that, but I'm not really sure what being your human entails,' I said cautiously. 'And I don't recall being asked if that was okay with me.'

'Whatever it is, it's probably better than partying with Malcolm, Liam, and Diane.'

He wasn't going to answer me directly.

'Are you going to take me to the bar?'

'What's your next night off?'

'Two nights from now.'

'Then, at sunset. I'll drive.'

'You have a car?'

'How do you think I get places?' There might have been a smile on his shining face. He turned to melt into the woods. Over his shoulder he said, 'Sookie. Do me proud.'

I was left standing with my mouth open.

Do him proud indeed.

Chapter 4

Half the patrons of Merlotte's thought Bill had had a hand in the markings on the women's bodies. The other 50 percent thought that some of the vampires from bigger towns or cities had bitten Maudette and Dawn when they were out barhopping, and they deserved what they got if they wanted to go to bed with vampires. Some thought the girls had been strangled by a vampire, some thought they had just continued their promiscuous ways into disaster.

But everyone who came into Merlotte's was worried that some other woman would be killed, too. I couldn't count the times I was told to be careful, told to watch my friend Bill Compton, told to lock my doors and not let anyone in my house . . . As if those were things I wouldn't do, normally.

Jason came in for both commiseration and suspicion as a man who'd 'dated' both women. He came by the house one day and held forth for a whole hour, while Gran and I tried to encourage him to keep going with his work like an innocent man would. But for the first time in my memory, my handsome brother was really worried. I wasn't exactly glad he was in trouble, but I wasn't exactly sorry, either. I know that was small and petty of me.

I am not perfect.

I am so not-perfect that despite the deaths of two women I knew, I spent a substantial amount of time wondering what Bill meant about doing him proud. I had no idea what constituted appropriate dress for visiting a vampire bar. I wasn't about to dress in some kind of stupid costume, as I'd heard some bar visitors did.

I sure didn't know anyone to ask.

I wasn't tall enough or bony enough to dress in the sort of spandex outfit the vampire Diane had worn.

Finally I pulled a dress from the back of my closet, one I'd had little occasion to wear. It was a Nice Date dress, if you wanted the personal interest of whoever was your escort. It was cut square and low in the neck and it was sleeveless. It was tight and white. The fabric was thinly scattered with bright red flowers with long green stems. My tan glowed and my boobs showed. I wore red enamel earrings and red high-heeled screw-me shoes. I had a little red straw purse. I put on light makeup and wore my wavy hair loose down my back.

Gran's eyes opened wide when I came out of my room.

'Honey, you look beautiful,' she said. 'Aren't you going to be a little cold in that dress?'

I grinned. 'No, ma'am, I don't think so. It's pretty warm outside.'

'Wouldn't you like to wear a nice white sweater over that?'

'No, I don't think so.' I laughed. I had pushed the other vampires far enough back in my mind to where looking sexy was okay again. I was pretty excited about having a date, though I had kind of asked Bill myself and it was more of a fact-finding mission. That, too, I tried to forget, so I could just enjoy myself.

Sam called me to tell me my paycheck was ready. He asked if I'd come in and pick it up, which I usually did if I wasn't going to work the next day.

I drove to Merlotte's feeling a little anxious at walking in dressed up.

But when I came in the door, I got the tribute of a moment of stunned silence. Sam's back was to me, but Lafayette was looking through the hatch and Rene and JB were at the bar. Unfortunately, so was my brother, Jason, whose eyes opened wide when he turned to see what Rene was staring at.

'You lookin' good, girl!' called Lafayette enthusiastically. 'Where you get that dress?'

'Oh, I've had this old thing forever,' I said mockingly, and he laughed.

Sam turned to see what Lafayette was gawking at, and his eyes got wide, too.

'God almighty,' he breathed. I walked over to ask for my check, feeling very self-conscious.

'Come in the office, Sookie,' he said, and I followed him to his small cubicle by the storeroom. Rene gave me a half-hug on my way by him, and JB kissed my cheek.

Sam rummaged through the piles of paper on top of his desk, and finally came up with my check. He didn't hand it to me, though.

'Are you going somewhere special?' Sam asked, almost unwillingly.

'I have a date,' I said, trying to sound matter-of-fact.

'You look great,' Sam said, and I saw him swallow. His eyes were hot.

'Thank you. Um, Sam, can I have my check?'

'Sure.' He handed it to me, and I popped it in my purse.

'Good-bye, then.'

'Good-bye.' But instead of indicating I should leave, Sam stepped over and smelled me. He put his face close to my neck and inhaled. His brilliant blue eyes closed briefly, as if to evaluate my odor. He exhaled gently, his breath hot on my bare skin.

I stepped out of the door and left the bar, puzzled and interested in Sam's behavior.

When I got home a strange car was parked in front of the house. It was a black Cadillac, and it shone like glass. Bill's. Where did they get the money to buy these cars? Shaking my head, I went up the steps to the porch and walked in. Bill turned to the door expectantly; he was sitting on the couch talking to Gran, who was perched on one arm of an old overstuffed chair.

When he saw me, I was sure I'd overdone it, and he was really angry. His face went quite still. His eyes flared. His fingers curved as if he were scooping something up with them.

'Is this all right?' I asked anxiously. I felt the blood surge up into my cheeks.

'Yes,' he said finally. But his pause had been long enough to anger my grandmother.

'Anyone with a brain in his head has got to admit that Sookie is one of the prettiest girls around,' she said, her voice friendly on the surface but steel underneath.

'Oh, yes,' he agreed, but there was a curious lack of inflection in his voice.

Well, screw him. I'd tried my best. I stiffened my back, and said, 'Shall we go, then?'

'Yes,' he said again, and stood. 'Good-bye, Mrs. Stackhouse. It was a pleasure seeing you again.'

'Well, you two have a good time,' she said, mollified. 'Drive careful, Bill, and don't drink too much.'

He raised an eyebrow. 'No, ma'am.'

Gran let that sail right on past.

Bill held my car door open as I got in, a carefully calculated series of maneuvers to keep as much of me as possible in the dress. He shut the door and got in on the driver's side. I wondered who had taught him to drive a car. Henry Ford, probably.

'I'm sorry I'm not dressed correctly,' I said, looking straight ahead of me.

We'd been going slowly on the bumpy driveway through the woods. The car lurched to a halt.

'Who said that?' Bill asked, his voice very gentle.

'You looked at me as though I'd done something wrong,' I snapped.

'I'm just doubting my ability to get you in and out without having to kill someone who wants you.'

'You're being sarcastic.' I still wouldn't look.

His hand gripped the back of my neck, forced me to turn to him.

'Do I look like I am?' he asked.

His dark eyes were wide and unblinking.

'Ah . . . no,' I admitted.

'Then accept what I say.'

The ride to Shreveport was mostly silent, but not uncomfortably so. Bill played tapes most of the way. He was partial to Kenny G.

Fangtasia, the vampire bar, was located in a suburban shopping area of Shreveport, close to a Sam's and a Toys 'R' Us. It was in a shopping strip, which was all closed down at this hour except for the bar. The name of the place was spelled out in jazzy red neon above the door, and the facade was painted steel gray, a red door providing color contrast. Whoever owned the place must have thought gray was less obvious than black because the interior was decorated in the same colors.

I was carded at the door by a vampire. Of course, she recognized Bill as one of her own kind and acknowledged him with a cool nod, but she scanned me intently. Chalky pale, as all Caucasian vampires are, she was eerily striking in her long black dress with its trailing sleeves. I wondered if the overdone 'vampire' look was her own inclination, or if she'd just adopted it because the human patrons thought it appropriate.

'I haven't been carded in years,' I said, fishing in my red purse for my driver's license. We were standing in a little boxy entrance hall.

'I can no longer tell human ages, and we must be very careful we serve no minors. In any capacity,' she said with what was probably meant to be a genial smile. She cast a sideways look at Bill, her eyes flicking up and down him with an offensive interest. Offensive to me, at least.

'I haven't seen you in a few months,' she said to him, her voice as cool and sweet as his could be.

'I'm mainstreaming,' he explained, and she nodded.

'What were you telling her?' I whispered as we walked down the short hall and through the red double doors into the main room.

'That I'm trying to live among humans.'

I wanted to hear more, but then I got my first comprehensive look at Fangtasia's interior. Everything was in gray, black, and red. The walls were lined with framed pictures of every movie vampire who had shown fangs on the silver screen, from Bela Lugosi to George Hamilton to Gary Oldman, from famous to obscure. The lighting was dim, of course, nothing unusual about that; what was unusual was the clientele. And the posted signs.

The bar was full. The human clients were divided among vampire groupies and tourists. The groupies (fang-bangers, they were called) were dressed in their best finery. It ranged from the traditional capes and tuxes for the men to many Morticia Adams ripoffs among the females. The clothes ranged from reproductions of those worn by Brad Pitt and Tom Cruise in *Interview with the Vampire* to some modern outfits that I thought were influenced by *The Hunger.* Some of the fang-bangers were wearing false fangs, some had painted trickles of blood from the corners of their mouths or puncture marks on their necks. They were extraordinary, and extraordinarily pathetic.

The tourists looked like tourists anywhere, maybe more adventurous than most. But to enter into the spirit of the bar, they were nearly all dressed in black like the fang-bangers. Maybe it was part of a tour package? 'Bring some black for your exciting visit to a real vampire bar! Follow the rules, and you'll be fine, catching a glimpse of this exotic underworld.'

Strewn among this human assortment, like real jewels in a bin of rhinestones, were the vampires, perhaps fifteen of them. They mostly favored dark clothes, too.

I stood in the middle of the floor, looking around me

with interest and amazement and some distaste, and Bill whispered, 'You look like a white candle in a coal mine.'

I laughed, and we strolled through the scattered tables to the bar. It was the only bar I'd ever seen that had a case of warmed bottled blood on display. Bill, naturally, ordered one and I took a deep breath and ordered a gin and tonic. The bartender smiled at me, showing me that his fangs had shot out a little at the pleasure of serving me. I tried to smile back and look modest at the same time. He was an American Indian, with long coal black straight hair and a craggy nose, a straight line of a mouth, and a whippy build.

'How's it going, Bill?' the bartender asked. 'Long time, no see. This your meal for the night?' He nodded toward me as he put our drinks on the bar before us.

'This is my friend Sookie. She has some questions to ask.'

'Anything, beautiful woman,' said the bartender, smiling once again. I liked him better when his mouth was the straight line.

'Have you seen this woman, or this one, in the bar?' I asked, drawing the newspaper photos of Maudette and Dawn from my purse. 'Or this man?' With a jolt of misgiving, I pulled out my brother's picture.

'Yes to the women, no to the man, though he looks delicious,' said the bartender, smiling at me again. 'Your brother, perhaps?'

'Yes.'

'What possibilities,' he whispered.

It was lucky I'd had extensive practice in face control. 'Do you remember who the women hung around with?'

'That's something I wouldn't know,' he replied quickly,

his face closing down. 'That's something we don't notice, here. You won't, either.'

'Thank you,' I said politely, realizing I'd broken a bar rule. It was dangerous to ask who left with whom, evidently. 'I appreciate your taking the time.'

He looked at me consideringly. 'That one,' he said, poking a finger at Dawn's picture, 'she wanted to die.'

'How do you know?'

'Everyone who comes here does, to one extent or another,' he said so matter-of-factly I could tell he took that for granted. 'That is what we are. Death.'

I shuddered. Bill's hand on my arm drew me away to a just-vacated booth. Underscoring the Indian's pronouncement, at regular intervals wall placards proclaimed, 'No biting on premises.' 'No lingering in the parking lot.' 'Conduct your personal business elsewhere.' 'Your patronage is appreciated. Proceed at your own risk.'

Bill took the top off the bottle with one finger and took a sip. I tried not to look, failed. Of course he saw my face, and he shook his head.

'This is the reality, Sookie,' he said. 'I need it to live.'

There were red stains between his teeth.

'Of course,' I said, trying to match the matter-of-fact tone of the bartender. I took a deep breath. 'Do you suppose I want to die, since I came here with you?'

'I think you want to find out why other people are dying,' he said. But I wasn't sure that was what he really believed.

I didn't think Bill had yet realized that his personal position was precarious. I sipped my drink, felt the blossoming warmth of the gin spread through me.

A fang-banger approached the booth. I was half-hidden

by Bill, but still, they'd all seen me enter with him. She was frizzy-haired and bony, with glasses that she stuffed in a purse as she walked over. She bent across the table to get her mouth about two inches from Bill.

'Hi, dangerous,' she said in what she hoped was a seductive voice. She tapped Bill's bottled blood with a fingernail painted scarlet. 'I have the real stuff.' She stroked her neck to make sure he got the point.

I took a deep breath to control my temper. I had invited Bill to this place; he hadn't invited me. I could not comment on what he chose to do here, though I had a surprisingly vivid mental image of leaving a slap mark on this hussy's pale, freckled cheek. I held absolutely still so I wouldn't give Bill any cues about what I wanted.

'I have a companion,' Bill said gently.

'She doesn't have any puncture marks on her neck,' the girl observed, acknowledging my presence with a contemptuous look. She might as well have said 'Chicken!' and flapped her arms like wings. I wondered if steam was visibly coming out of my ears.

'I have a companion,' Bill said again, his voice not so gentle this time.

'You don't know what you're missing,' she said, her big pale eyes flashing with offense.

'Yes, I do,' he said.

She recoiled as if I'd actually done the slapping, and stomped off to her table.

To my disgust, she was only the first of four. These people, men and women, wanted to be intimate with a vampire, and they weren't shy about it.

Bill handled all of them with calm aplomb.

'You're not talking,' he said, after a man of forty had left his eyes actually tearing up at Bill's rejection.

'There's nothing for me to say,' I replied, with great self-control.

'You could have sent them on their way. Do you want me to leave you? Is there someone else here who catches your fancy? Long Shadow, there at the bar, would love to spend time with you, I can tell.'

'Oh, for God's sake, no!' I wouldn't have felt safe with any of the other vampires in the bar, would have been terrified they were like Liam or Diane. Bill had turned his dark eyes to me and seemed to be waiting for me to say something else. 'I do have to ask them if they've seen Dawn and Maudette in here, though.'

'Do you want me with you?'

'Please,' I said, and sounded more frightened than I'd wanted to. I'd meant to ask like it would be a casual pleasure to have his company.

'The vampire over there is handsome; he has scanned you twice,' he said. I almost wondered if he was doing a little tongue biting himself.

'You're teasing me,' I said uncertainly after a moment.

The vampire he'd indicated was handsome, in fact, radiant; blond and blue-eyed, tall and broad shouldered. He was wearing boots, jeans, and a vest. Period. Kind of like the guys on the cover of romance books. He scared me to death.

'His name is Eric,' said Bill.

'How old is he?'

'Very. He's the oldest thing in this bar.'

'Is he mean?'

'We're all mean, Sookie. We're all very strong and very violent.'

'Not you,' I said. I saw his face close in on itself. 'You want to live mainstream. You're not gonna do antisocial stuff.'

'Just when I think you're too naive to walk around alone you say something shrewd,' he said, with a short laugh. 'All right, we'll go talk to Eric.'

Eric, who, it was true, had glanced my way once or twice, was sitting with a female vampire who was just as lovely as he. They'd already repelled several advances by humans. In fact, one lovelorn young man had already crawled across the floor and kissed the female's boot. She'd stared down at him and kicked him in the shoulder. You could tell it had been an effort for her not to kick him in the face. Tourists flinched, and a couple got up and left hurriedly, but the fang-bangers seemed to take this scene for granted.

At our approach, Eric looked up and scowled until he realized who the intruders were.

'Bill,' he said, nodding. Vampires didn't seem to shake hands.

Instead of walking right up to the table, Bill stood a careful distance away, and since he was gripping my arm above my elbow, I had to stop, too. This seemed to be the courteous distance with this set.

'Who's your friend?' asked the female. Though Eric had a slight accent, this woman talked pure American, and her round face and sweet features would have done credit to a milkmaid. She smiled, and her fangs ran out, kind of ruining the image.

'Hi, I'm Sookie Stackhouse,' I said politely.

'Aren't you sweet,' Eric observed, and I hoped he was thinking of my character.

'Not especially,' I said.

Eric stared at me in surprise for a moment. Then he laughed, and the female did, too.

'Sookie, this is Pam and I am Eric,' the blond vampire said. Bill and Pam gave each other the vampire nod.

There was a pause. I would have spoken, but Bill squeezed my arm.

'My friend Sookie would like to ask a couple of questions,' Bill said.

The seated vampires exchanged bored glances.

Pam said, 'Like how long are our fangs, and what kind of coffin do we sleep in?' Her voice was laced with contempt, and you could tell those were tourist questions that she hated.

'No, ma'am,' I said. I hoped Bill wouldn't pinch my arm off. I thought I was being calm and courteous.

She stared at me with amazement.

What the hell was so startling? I was getting a little tired of this. Before Bill could give me any more painful hints, I opened my purse and took out the pictures. 'I'd like to know if you've seen either of these women in this bar.' I wasn't getting Jason's picture out in front of this female. It would've been like putting a bowl of milk in front of a cat.

They looked at the pictures. Bill's face was blank. Eric looked up. 'I have been with this one,' he said coolly, tapping Dawn's picture. 'She liked pain.'

Pam was surprised Eric had answered me, I could tell by her eyebrows. She seemed somehow obligated to follow his example. 'I have seen both of them. I have never been with them. This one,' she flicked her finger at Maudette's picture, 'was a pathetic creature.'

'Thank you very much, that's all of your time I need to

take,' I said, and tried to turn to leave. But Bill still held my arm imprisoned.

'Bill, are you quite attached to your friend?' Eric asked.

It took a second for the meaning to sink in. Eric the Hunk was asking if I could be borrowed.

'She is mine,' Bill said, but he wasn't roaring it as he had to the nasty vampires from Monroe. Nonetheless, he sounded pretty darn firm.

Eric inclined his golden head, but he gave me the onceover again. At least he started with my face.

Bill seemed to relax. He bowed to Eric, somehow including Pam in the gesture, backed away for two steps, finally permitting me to turn my back to the couple.

'Gee whiz, what was that about?' I asked in a furious whisper. I'd have a big bruise the next day.

'They're older than I am by centuries,' Bill said, looking very vampirey.

'Is that the pecking order? By age?'

'Pecking order,' Bill said thoughtfully. 'That's not a bad way to put it.' He almost laughed. I could tell by the way his lip twitched.

'If you had been interested, I would have been obliged to let you go with Eric,' he said, after we'd resumed our seats and had a belt from our drinks.

'No,' I said sharply.

'Why didn't you say anything when the fang-bangers came to our table trying to seduce me away from you?'

We weren't operating on the same wave level. Maybe social nuances weren't something vampires cared about. I was going to have to explain something that couldn't really bear much explaining.

I made a very unladylike sound out of sheer exasperation.

'Okay,' I said sharply. 'Listen up, Bill! When you came to my house, I had to invite you. When you came here with me, I had to invite you. You haven't asked me out. Lurking in my driveway doesn't count, and asking me to stop by your house and leave a list of contractors doesn't count. So it's always been me asking you. How can I tell you that you have to stay with me, if you want to go? If those girls will let you suck their blood – or that guy, for that matter – then I don't feel I have a right to stand in your way!'

'Eric is much better looking than I am,' Bill said. 'He is more powerful, and I understand sex with him is unforgettable. He is so old he only needs to take a sip to maintain his strength. He almost never kills any more. So, as vampires go, he's a good guy. You could still go with him. He is still looking at you. He would try his glamor on you if you were not with me.'

'I don't want to go with Eric,' I said stubbornly.

'I don't want to go with any of the fang-bangers,' he said. We sat in silence for a minute or two.

'So we're all right,' I said obscurely.

'Yes.'

We took a few moments more, thinking this over.

'Want another drink?' he asked.

'Yes, unless you need to get back.'

'No, this is fine.'

He went to the bar. Eric's friend Pam left, and Eric appeared to be counting my eyelashes. I tried to keep my gaze on my hands, to indicate modesty. I felt power tweaks kind of flow over me and had an uneasy feeling Eric was trying to influence me. I risked a quick peek, and sure enough he was looking at me expectantly. Was I supposed to pull off my dress? Bark like a dog? Kick Bill in the shins? Shit.

Bill came back with our drinks.

'He's gonna know I'm not normal,' I said grimly. Bill didn't seem to need an explanation.

'He's breaking the rules just attempting to glamorize you after I've told him you're mine,' Bill said. He sounded pretty pissed off. His voice didn't get hotter and hotter like mine would have, but colder and colder.

'You seem to be telling everyone that,' I muttered. Without doing anything about it, I added silently.

'It's vampire tradition,' Bill explained again. 'If I pronounce you mine, no one else can try to feed on you.'

'Feed on me, that's a delightful phrase,' I said sharply, and Bill actually had an expression of exasperation for all of two seconds.

'I'm protecting you,' he said, his voice not quite as neutral as usual.

'Had it occurred to you that I –'

And I stopped short. I closed my eyes. I counted to ten.

When I ventured a look at Bill, his eyes were fixed on my face, unblinking. I could practically hear the gears mesh.

'You – don't need protection?' he guessed softly. 'You are protecting – me?'

I didn't say anything. I can do that.

But he took the back of my skull in his hand. He turned my head to him as though I were a puppet. (This was getting to be an annoying habit of his.) He looked so hard into my eyes that I thought I had tunnels burned into my brain.

I pursed my lips and blew into his face. 'Boo,' I said. I was very uncomfortable. I glanced at the people in the bar, letting my guard down, listening.

'Boring,' I told him. 'These people are boring.'

'Are they, Sookie? What are they thinking?' It was a relief to hear his voice, no matter that his voice was a little odd.

'Sex, sex, sex.' And that was true. Every single person in that bar had sex on the brain. Even the tourists, who mostly weren't thinking about having sex with the vampires themselves, but were thinking about the fang-bangers having sex with the vampires.

'What are you thinking about, Sookie?'

'Not sex,' I answered promptly and truthfully. I'd just gotten an unpleasant shock.

'Is that so?'

'I was thinking about the chances of us getting out of here without any trouble.'

'Why were you thinking about that?'

'Because one of the tourists is a cop in disguise, and he just went to the bathroom, and he knows that a vampire is in there, sucking on the neck of a fang-banger. He's already called the police on his little radio.'

'Out,' he said smoothly, and we were out of the booth swiftly and moving for the door. Pam had vanished, but as we passed Eric's table, Bill gave him some sign. Just as smoothly, Eric eased from his seat and rose to his magnificent height, his stride so much longer than ours that he passed out the door first, taking the arm of the bouncer and propelling her outside with us.

As we were about to go out the door, I remembered the bartender, Long Shadow, had answered my questions willingly, so I turned and jabbed my finger in the direction of the door, unmistakably telling him to leave. He looked as alarmed as a vampire can look, and as Bill yanked me through the double doors, he was throwing down his towel.

Outside, Eric was waiting by his car – a Corvette, naturally.

'There's going to be a raid,' Bill said.

'How do you know?'

Bill stuck on that one.

'Me,' I said, getting him off the hook.

Eric's wide blue eyes shone even in the gloom of the parking lot. I was going to have to explain.

'I read a policeman's mind,' I muttered. I snuck a look to see how Eric was taking this, and he was staring at me the same way the Monroe vampires had. Thoughtful. Hungry.

'That's interesting,' he said. 'I had a psychic once. It was incredible.'

'Did the psychic think so?' My voice was tarter than I'd meant it to be.

I could hear Bill's indrawn breath.

Eric laughed. 'For a while,' he answered ambiguously.

We heard sirens in the distance, and without further words Eric and the bouncer slid into his car and were gone into the night, the car seeming quieter than others' cars, somehow. Bill and I buckled up hastily, and we were leaving the parking lot by one exit just as the police were coming in by another. They had their vampire van with them, a special prisoner transport with silver bars. It was driven by two cops who were of the fanged persuasion, and they sprang out of their van and reached the club door with a speed that rendered them just blurs on my human vision.

We had driven a few blocks when suddenly Bill pulled into the parking lot of yet another darkened strip mall.

'What–?' I began, but got no further. Bill had unclipped

my seat belt, moved the seat back, and grabbed me before I had finished my sentence. Frightened that he was angry, I pushed against him at first, but I might as well have been heaving against a tree. Then his mouth located mine, and I knew what he was.

Oh, boy, could he kiss. We might have problems communicating on some levels, but this wasn't one of them. We had a great time for maybe five minutes. I felt all the right things moving through my body in waves. Despite the awkwardness of being in the front seat of a car, I managed to be comfortable, mostly because he was so strong and considerate. I nipped his skin with my teeth. He made a sound like a growl.

'Sookie!' His voice was ragged.

I moved away from him, maybe half an inch.

'If you do that any more I'll have you whether you want to be had or not,' he said, and I could tell he meant it.

'You don't want to,' I said finally, trying not to make it a question.

'Oh, yes, I want to,' and he grabbed my hand and showed me.

Suddenly, there was a bright rotating light beside us.

'The police,' I said. I could see a figure get out of the patrol car and start toward Bill's window. 'Don't let him know you're a vampire, Bill,' I said hastily, fearing fallout from the Fangtasia raid. Though most police forces loved having vampires join them on the job, there was a lot of prejudice against vampires on the street, especially as part of a mixed couple.

The policeman's heavy hand rapped on the window.

Bill turned on the motor, hit the button that lowered the window. But he was silent, and I realized his fangs had not retracted. If he opened his mouth, it would be really obvious he was a vampire.

'Hello, officer,' I said.

'Good evening,' the man said, politely enough. He bent to look in the window. 'You two know all the shops here are closed, right?'

'Yes, sir.'

'Now, I can tell you been messing around a little, and I got nothing against that, but you two need to go home and do this kind of thing.'

'We will.' I nodded eagerly, and Bill managed a stiff inclination of his head.

'We're raiding a bar a few blocks back,' the patrolman said casually. I could see only a little of his face, but he seemed burly and middle-aged. 'You two coming from there, by any chance?'

'No,' I said.

'Vampire bar,' the cop remarked.

'Nope. Not us.'

'Let me just shine this light on your neck, miss, if you don't mind.'

'Not at all.'

And by golly, he shone that old flashlight on my neck and then on Bill's.

'Okay, just checking. You two move on now.'

'Yes, we will.'

Bill's nod was even more curt. While the patrolman waited, I slid back over to my side and clipped my seat belt, and Bill put the car in gear and backed up.

Bill was just infuriated. All the way home he kept a sullen (I guess) silence, whereas I was inclined to view the whole thing as funny.

I was cheerful at finding Bill wasn't indifferent to my personal attractions, such as they were. I began to hope that someday he would want to kiss me again, maybe longer and harder, and maybe even – we could go further? I was trying not to get my hopes up. Actually, there was a thing or two that Bill didn't know about me, that no one knew, and I was very careful to try to keep my expectations modest.

When he got me back to Gran's, he came around and opened my door, which made me raise my eyebrows; but I am not one to stop a courteous act. I assumed Bill did realize I had functioning arms and the mental ability to figure out the door-opening mechanism. When I stepped out, he backed up.

I was hurt. He didn't want to kiss me again; he was regretting our earlier episode. Probably pining after that damn Pam. Or maybe even Long Shadow. I was beginning to see that the ability to have sex for several centuries leaves room for lots of experimentation. Would a telepath be so bad to add to his list?

I kind of hunched my shoulders together and wrapped my arms across my chest.

'Are you cold?' Bill asked instantly, putting his arm around me. But it was the physical equivalent of a coat, he seemed to be trying to stay as far away from me as the arm made possible.

'I am sorry I have pestered you. I won't ask you for any more,' I said, keeping my voice even. Even as I spoke I realized that Gran hadn't set up a date for Bill to speak to the Descendants, but she and Bill would just have to work that out.

He stood still. Finally he said, 'You – are – incredibly –

naive.' And he didn't even add that codicil about shrewdness, like he had earlier.

'Well,' I said blankly. 'I am?'

'Or maybe one of God's fools,' he said, and that sounded a lot less pleasant, like Quasimodo or something.

'I guess,' I said tartly, 'you'll just have to find out.'

'It had better be me that finds out,' he said darkly, which I didn't understand at all. He walked me up to the door, and I was sure hoping for another kiss, but he gave me a little peck on the forehead. 'Good night, Sookie,' he whispered.

I rested my cheek against his for a moment. 'Thanks for taking me,' I said, and moved away quickly before he thought I was asking for something else. 'I'm not calling you again.' And before I could lose my determination, I slipped into the dark house and shut the door in Bill's face.

Chapter 5

I certainly had a lot to think about the next couple of days. For someone who was always hoarding new things to keep from being bored, I'd stored enough up to last me for weeks. The people in Fangtasia, alone, were food for examination, to say nothing of the vampires. From longing to meet one vampire, now I'd met more than I cared to know.

A lot of men from Bon Temps and the surrounding area had been called in to the police station to answer a few questions about Dawn Green and her habits. Embarrassingly enough, Detective Bellefleur took to hanging around the bar on his off-hours, never drinking more alcohol than one beer, but observing everything that took place around him. Since Merlotte's was not exactly a hotbed of illegal activity, no one minded too much once they got used to Andy being there.

He always seemed to pick a table in my section. And he began to play a silent game with me. When I came to his table, he'd be thinking something provocative, trying to get me to say something. He didn't seem to understand how indecent that was. The provocation was the point, not the insult. He just wanted me to read his mind again. I couldn't figure out why.

Then, maybe the fifth or sixth time I had to get him something, I guess it was a Diet Coke, he pictured me cavorting with my brother. I was so nervous when I went to the table (knowing to expect something, but not knowing exactly what) that I was beyond getting angry and into the realm of tears. It reminded me of the less sophisticated tormenting I'd taken when I was in grade school.

Andy had looked up with an expectant face, and when he saw tears an amazing range of things ran across his face in quick succession: triumph, chagrin, then scalding shame.

I poured the damn Coke down his shirt.

I walked right past the bar and out the back door.

'What's the matter?' Sam asked sharply. He was right on my heels.

I shook my head, not wanting to explain, and pulled an aging tissue out of my shorts pocket to mop my eyes with.

'Has he been saying ugly things to you?' Sam asked, his voice lower and angrier.

'He's been thinking them,' I said helplessly, 'to get a rise out of me. He knows.'

'Son of a bitch,' Sam said, which almost shocked me back to normal. Sam didn't curse.

Once I started crying, it seemed like I couldn't stop. I was getting my crying time done for a number of little unhappinesses.

'Just go on back in,' I said, embarrassed at my waterworks. 'I'll be okay in just a minute.'

I heard the back door of the bar open and shut. I figured Sam had taken me at my word. But instead, Andy Bellefleur said, 'I apologize, Sookie.'

'That's Miss Stackhouse to you, Andy Bellefleur,' I said. 'It seems to me like you better be out finding who killed Maudette and Dawn instead of playing nasty mind games with me.'

I turned around and looked at the policeman. He was looking horribly embarrassed. I thought he was sincere in his shame.

Sam was swinging his arms, full of the energy of anger.

'Bellefleur, sit in someone else's area if you come back,' he said, but his voice held a lot of suppressed violence.

Andy looked at Sam. He was twice as thick in the body, taller by two inches. But I would have put my money on Sam at that moment, and it seemed Andy didn't want to risk the challenge either, if only from good sense. He just nodded and walked across the parking lot to his car. The sun glinted on the blond highlights in his brown hair.

'Sookie, I'm sorry,' Sam said.

'Not your fault.'

'Do you want to take some time off? We're not so busy today.'

'Nope. I'll finish my shift.' Charlsie Tooten was getting into the swing of things, but I wouldn't feel good about leaving. It was Arlene's day off.

We went back into the bar, and though several people looked at us curiously as we entered, no one asked us what had happened. There was only one couple sitting in my area, and they were busy eating and had glasses full of liquid, so they wouldn't be needing me. I began putting up wine-glasses. Sam leaned against the workspace beside me.

'Is it true that Bill Compton is going to speak to the Descendants of the Glorious Dead tonight?'

'According to my grandmother.'

'Are you going?'

'I hadn't planned on it.' I didn't want to see Bill until he called me and made an appointment to see me.

Sam didn't say anything else then, but later in the afternoon, as I was retrieving my purse from his office, he came in and fiddled with some papers on his desk. I'd pulled out my brush and was trying to get a tangle out of my ponytail. From the way Sam dithered around, it seemed apparent that he wanted to talk to me, and I felt a wave of exasperation at the indirection men seemed to take.

Like Andy Bellefleur. He could just have asked me about my disability, instead of playing games with me.

Like Bill. He could just have stated his intentions, instead of this strange hot-cold thing.

'So?' I said, more sharply than I'd intended.

He flushed under my gaze.

'I wondered if you'd like to go to the Descendants meeting with me and have a cup of coffee afterward.'

I was flabbergasted. My brush stopped in midswoop. A number of things ran through my mind, the feel of his hand when I'd held it in front of Dawn Green's duplex, the wall I'd met in his mind, the unwisdom of dating your boss.

'Sure,' I said, after a notable pause.

He seemed to exhale. 'Good. Then I'll pick you up at your house at seven-twenty or so. The meeting starts at seven-thirty.'

'Okay. I'll see you then.'

Afraid I'd do something peculiar if I stayed longer, I grabbed my purse and strode out to my car. I couldn't decide whether to giggle with glee or groan at my own idiocy.

It was five-forty-five by the time I got home. Gran already had supper on the table since she had to leave early to carry refreshments to the Descendants meeting, which was held at the Community Building.

'Wonder if he could have come if we'd had it in the fellowship hall of Good Faith Baptist?' Gran said out of the blue. But I didn't have a problem latching on to her train of thought.

'Oh, I think so,' I said. 'I think that idea about vampires being scared of religious items isn't true. But I haven't asked him.'

'They do have a big cross hung up in there,' Gran went on.

'I'll be at the meeting after all,' I said. 'I'm going with Sam Merlotte.'

'Your boss, Sam?' Gran was very surprised.

'Yes, ma'am.'

'Hmmm. Well, well.' Gran began smiling while she put the plates on the table. I was trying to think of what to wear while we ate our sandwiches and fruit salad. Gran was excited about the meeting, about listening to Bill and introducing him to her friends, and now she was in outer space somewhere (probably around Venus) since I actually had a date. With a human.

'We'll be going out afterward,' I said, 'so I guess I'll get home maybe an hour after the meeting's over.' There weren't that many places to have coffee in Bon Temps. And those restaurants weren't exactly places you'd want to linger.

'Okay, honey. You just take your time.' Gran was already dressed, and after supper I helped her load up the cookie trays and the big coffee urn she'd bought for just such events. Gran had pulled her car around to the back door, which saved us a lot of steps. She was happy as she could be and fussed and chattered the whole time we were loading. This was her kind of night.

I shed my waitress clothes and got into the shower lickety-split. While I soaped up, I tried to think of what to wear. Nothing black and white, that was for sure; I had gotten pretty sick of the Merlotte's waitress colors. I shaved my legs again, didn't have time to wash my hair and dry it, but I'd done it the night before. I flung open my closet and stared. Sam had seen the white flowered dress. The denim jumper wasn't nice enough for Gran's friends. Finally I yanked out some khaki slacks and a bronze silk blouse with short sleeves. I had brown leather sandals and a brown leather belt that would look good. I hung a chain around my neck, stuck in some big gold earrings and I was ready. As if he'd timed it, Sam rang the doorbell.

There was a moment of awkwardness as I opened the door.

'You're welcome to come in, but I think we just have time –'

'I'd like to sit and visit, but I think we just have time –'

We both laughed.

I locked the door and pulled it to, and Sam hurried to open the door of his pickup. I was glad I'd worn pants, as I pictured trying to get up in the high cab in one of my shorter skirts.

'Need a boost?' he asked hopefully.

'I think I got it,' I said, trying not to smile.

We were silent on the way to the Community Building, which was in the older part of Bon Temps; the part that predated the War. The structure was not antebellum, but there had actually been a building on that site that had gotten destroyed during the War, though no one seemed to have a record of what it had been.

The Descendants of the Glorious Dead were a mixed bunch. There were some very old, very fragile members, and some not quite so old and very lively members, and there were even a scattering of middle-aged men and women. But there were no young members, which Gran had often lamented, with many significant glances at me.

Mr. Sterling Norris, a longtime friend of my grandmother's and the mayor of Bon Temps, was the greeter that night, and he stood at the door shaking hands and having a little conversation with everyone who entered.

'Miss Sookie, you look prettier every day,' Mr. Norris said. 'And Sam, we haven't seen you in a coon's age! Sookie, is it true this vampire is a friend of yours?'

'Yes, sir.'

'Can you say for sure that we're all safe?'

'Yes, I'm sure you are. He's a very nice . . . person.' Being? Entity? If you like the living dead, he's pretty neat?

'If you say so,' Mr. Norris said dubiously. 'In my time, such a thing was just a fairy tale.'

'Oh, Mr. Norris, it's still your time,' I said with the cheerful smile expected of me, and he laughed and motioned us on in, which was what was expected of him. Sam took my hand and sort of steered me to the next to last row of metal chairs, and I waved at my grandmother as we took our seats. It was just time for the meeting to start, and the room held maybe forty people, quite a gathering for Bon Temps. But Bill wasn't there.

Just then the president of Descendants, a massive, solid

woman by the name of Maxine Fortenberry, came to the podium.

'Good evening! Good evening!' she boomed. 'Our guest of honor has just called to say he's having car trouble and will be a few minutes late. So let's go on and have our business meeting while we're waiting for him.'

The group settled down, and we got through all the boring stuff, Sam sitting beside me with his arms crossed over his chest, his right leg crossed over the left at the ankle. I was being especially careful to keep my mind guarded and face smiling, and I was a little deflated when Sam leaned slightly to me and whispered, 'It's okay to relax.'

'I thought I was,' I whispered back.

'I don't think you know how.'

I raised my eyebrows at him. I was going to have a few things to say to Mr. Merlotte after the meeting.

Just then Bill came in, and there was a moment of sheer silence as those who hadn't seen him before adjusted to his presence. If you've never been in the company of a vampire before, it's a thing you really have to get used to. Under the fluorescent lighting, Bill really looked much more unhuman than he did under the dim lighting in Merlotte's, or the equally dim lighting in his own home. There was no way he could pass for a regular guy. His pallor was very marked, of course, and the deep pools of his eyes looked darker and colder. He was wearing a lightweight medium-blue suit, and I was willing to bet that had been Gran's advice. He looked great. The dominant line of the arch of his eyebrow, the curve of his bold nose, the chiseled lips, the white hands with their long fingers and carefully trimmed nails . . . He was having an exchange with the president, and she was charmed out of her support hose by Bill's close-lipped smile.

I didn't know if Bill was casting a glamor over the whole room, or if these people were just predisposed to be interested, but the whole group hushed expectantly.

Then Bill saw me. I swear his eyebrows twitched. He gave me a little bow, and I nodded back, finding no smile in me to give him. Even in the crowd, I stood at the edge of the deep pool of his silence.

Mrs. Fortenberry introduced Bill, but I don't remember what she said or how she skirted the fact that Bill was a different kind of creature.

Then Bill began speaking. He had notes, I saw with some surprise. Beside me, Sam leaned forward, his eyes fixed on Bill's face.

'. . . we didn't have any blankets and very little food,' Bill was saying calmly. 'There were many deserters.'

That was not a favorite fact of the Descendants, but a few of them were nodding in agreement. This account must match what they'd learned in their studies.

An ancient man in the first row raised his hand.

'Sir, did you by chance know my great-grandfather, Tolliver Humphries?'

'Yes,' Bill said, after a moment. His face was unreadable. 'Tolliver was my friend.'

And just for a moment, there was something so tragic in his voice that I had to close my eyes.

'What was he like?' quavered the old man.

'Well, he was foolhardy, which led to his death,' said Bill with a wry smile. 'He was brave. He never made a cent in his life that he didn't waste.'

'How did he die? Were you there?'

'Yes, I was there,' said Bill wearily. 'I saw him get shot by a Northern sniper in the woods about twenty miles from here. He was slow because he was starved. We all were. About the middle of the morning, a cold morning, Tolliver saw a boy in our troop get shot as he lay in poor cover in the middle of a field. The boy was not dead, but painfully wounded. But he could call to us, and he did, all morning. He called to us to help him. He knew he would die if someone didn't.'

The whole room had grown so silent you could hear a pin drop.

'He screamed and he moaned. I almost shot him myself, to shut him up, because I knew to venture out to rescue him was suicide. But I could not quite bring myself to kill him. That would be murder, not war, I told myself. But later I wished I had shot him, for Tolliver was less able than I to withstand the boy's pleading. After two hours of it, he told me he planned to try to rescue the boy. I argued with him. But Tolliver told me that God wanted him to attempt it. He had been praying as we lay in the woods.

'Though I told Tolliver that God did not wish him to waste his life foolishly – that he had a wife and children praying for his safe return at home – Tolliver asked me to divert the enemy while he attempted the boy's rescue. He ran out into the field like it was a spring day and he was well rested. And he got as far as the wounded boy. But then a shot rang out, and Tolliver fell dead. And, after a time, the boy began screaming for help again.'

'What happened to him?' asked Mrs. Fortenberry, her voice as quiet as she could manage to make it.

'He lived,' Bill said, and there was tone to his voice that

sent shivers down my spine. 'He survived the day, and we were able to retrieve him that night.'

Somehow those people had come alive again as Bill spoke, and for the old man in the front row there was a memory to cherish, a memory that said much about his ancestor's character.

I don't think anyone who'd come to the meeting that night was prepared for the impact of hearing about the Civil War from a survivor. They were enthralled; they were shattered.

When Bill had answered the last question, there was thunderous applause, or at least it was as thunderous as forty people could make it. Even Sam, not Bill's biggest fan, managed to put his hands together.

Everyone wanted to have a personal word with Bill afterward except me and Sam. While the reluctant guest speaker was surrounded by Descendants, Sam and I sneaked out to Sam's pickup. We went to the Crawdad Diner, a real dive that happened to have very good food. I wasn't hungry, but Sam had key lime pie with his coffee.

'That was interesting,' Sam said cautiously.

'Bill's speech? Yes,' I said, just as cautiously.

'Do you have feelings for him?'

After all the indirection, Sam had decided to storm the main gate.

'Yes,' I said.

'Sookie,' Sam said, 'you have no future with him.'

'On the other hand, he's been around a while. I expect he'll be around for another few hundred years.'

'You never know what's going to happen to a vampire.'

I couldn't argue with that. But, as I pointed out to Sam, I couldn't know what was going to happen to me, a human, either.

We wrangled back and forth like this for too long. Finally, exasperated, I said, 'What's it to you, Sam?'

His ruddy skin flushed. His bright blue eyes met mine. 'I like you, Sookie. As friend or maybe something else sometime . . .'

Huh?

'I just hate to see you take a wrong turn.'

I looked at him. I could feel my skeptical face forming, eyebrows drawn together, the corner of my mouth tugging up.

'Sure,' I said, my voice matching my face.

'I've always liked you.'

'So much that you had to wait till someone else showed an interest, before you mentioned it to me?'

'I deserve that.' He seemed to be turning something over in his mind, something he wanted to say, but hadn't the resolution.

Whatever it was, he couldn't come out with it, apparently.

'Let's go,' I suggested. It would be hard to turn the conversation back to neutral ground, I figured. I might as well go home.

It was a funny ride back. Sam always seemed on the verge of speaking, and then he'd shake his head and keep silent. I was so aggravated I wanted to swat him.

We got home later than I'd thought. Gran's light was on, but the rest of the house was dark. I didn't see her car, so I figured she'd parked in back to unload the leftovers right into the kitchen. The porch light was on for me.

Sam walked around and opened the pickup door, and I stepped down. But in the shadow, my foot missed the running board, and I just sort of tumbled out. Sam caught me. First his hands gripped my arms to steady me, then they just slid around me. And he kissed me.

I assumed it was going to be a little good-night peck, but his mouth just kind of lingered. It was really more than pleasant, but suddenly my inner censor said, 'This is the boss.'

I gently disengaged. He was immediately aware that I was backing off, and gently slid his hands down my arms until he was just holding hands with me. We went to the door, not speaking.

'I had a good time,' I said, softly. I didn't want to wake Gran, and I didn't want to sound bouncy.

'I did too. Again sometime?'

'We'll see,' I said. I really didn't know how I felt about Sam.

I waited to hear his truck turn around before I switched off the porch light and went into the house. I was unbuttoning my blouse as I walked, tired and ready for bed.

Something was wrong.

I stopped in the middle of the living room. I looked around me.

Everything looked all right, didn't it?

Yes. Everything was in its proper place.

It was the smell.

It was a sort of penny smell.

A coppery smell, sharp and salty.

The smell of blood.

It was down here with me, not upstairs where the guest bedrooms sat in neat solitude.

'Gran?' I called. I hated the quavering in my voice.

I made myself move, I made myself go to the door of her

room. It was pristine. I began switching on lights as I went through the house.

My room was just as I'd left it.

The bathroom was empty.

The washroom was empty.

I switched on the last light. The kitchen was . . .

I screamed, over and over. My hands were fluttering uselessly in the air, trembling more with each scream. I heard a crash behind me, but couldn't be concerned. Then big hands gripped me and moved me, and a big body was between me and what I'd seen on the kitchen floor. I didn't recognize Bill, but he picked me up and moved me to the living room where I couldn't see any more.

'Sookie,' he said harshly. 'Shut up! This isn't any good!' If he'd been kind to me, I'd have kept on shrieking.

'Sorry,' I said, still out of my mind. 'I am acting like that boy.'

He stared at me blankly.

'The one in your story,' I said numbly.

'We have to call the police.'

'Sure.'

'We have to dial the phone.'

'Wait. How did you come here?'

'Your grandmother gave me a ride home, but I insisted on coming with her first and helping her unload the car.'

'So why are you still here?'

'I was waiting for you.'

'So, did you see who killed her?'

'No. I went home, across the cemetery, to change.'

He was wearing blue jeans and Grateful Dead T-shirt, and suddenly I began to giggle.

'That's priceless,' I said, doubling over with the laughter.

And I was crying, just as suddenly. I picked up the phone and dialled 911.

Andy Bellefleur was there in five minutes.

Jason came as soon as I reached him. I tried to call him at four or five different places, and finally reached him at Merlotte's. Terry Bellefleur was bartending for Sam that night, and when he'd gotten back from telling Jason to come to his grandmother's house, I asked Terry if he'd call Sam and tell him I had troubles and couldn't work for a few days.

Terry must have called Sam right away because Sam was at my house within thirty minutes, still wearing the clothes he'd worn to the meeting that night. At the sight of him I looked down, remembering unbuttoning my blouse as I walked through the living room, a fact I'd completely lost track of; but I was decent. It dawned on me that Bill must have set me to rights. I might find that embarrassing later, but at the moment I was just grateful.

So Jason came in, and when I told him Gran was dead, and dead by violence, he just looked at me. There seemed to be nothing going on behind his eyes. It was as if someone had erased his capacity for absorbing new facts. Then what I'd said sank in, and my brother sank to his knees right where he stood, and I knelt in front of him. He put his arms around me and lay his head on my shoulder, and we just stayed there for a while. We were all that was left.

Bill and Sam were out in the front yard sitting in lawn chairs, out of the way of the police. Soon Jason and I were asked to go out on the porch, at least, and we opted to sit outside, too. It was a mild evening, and I sat facing the house, all lit up like a birthday cake, and the people that came and went from it like ants who'd been allowed at the party. All this industry surrounding the tissue that had been my grandmother.

'What happened?' Jason asked finally.

'I came in from the meeting,' I said very slowly. 'After Sam pulled off in his truck. I knew something was wrong. I looked in every room.' This was the story of How I Found Grandmother Dead, the official version. 'And when I got to the kitchen I saw her.'

Jason turned his head very slowly so his eyes met mine.

'Tell me.'

I shook my head silently. But it was his right to know. 'She was beaten up, but she had tried to fight back, I think. Whoever did this cut her up some. And then strangled her, it looked like.'

I could not even look at my brother's face. 'It was my fault.' My voice was nothing more than a whisper.

'How do you figure that?' Jason said, sounding nothing more than dull and sluggish.

'I figure someone came to kill me like they killed Maudette and Dawn, but Gran was here instead.'

I could see the idea percolate in Jason's brain.

'I was supposed to be home tonight while she was at the meeting, but Sam asked me to go at the last minute. My car was here like it would be normally because we went in Sam's truck. Gran had parked her car around back while she was unloading, so it wouldn't look like she was here, just me. She had given Bill a ride home, but he helped her unload and went to change clothes. After he left, whoever it was . . . got her.'

'How do we know it wasn't Bill?' Jason asked, as though Bill wasn't sitting right there beside him.

'How do we know it wasn't anyone?' I said, exasperated at my brother's slow wits. 'It could be anyone, anyone we know. I don't think it was Bill. I don't think Bill killed Maudette and Dawn. And I do think whoever killed Maudette and Dawn killed Grandmother.'

'Did you know,' Jason said, his voice too loud, 'that Grandmother left you this house all by yourself?'

It was like he'd thrown a bucket of cold water in my face. I saw Sam wince, too. Bill's eyes got darker and chillier.

'No. I just always assumed you and I would share like we did on the other one.' Our parents' house, the one Jason lived in now.

'She left you all the land, too.'

'Why are you saying this?' I was going to cry again, just when I'd been sure I was dry of tears now.

'She wasn't fair!' he was yelling. 'It wasn't fair, and now she can't set it right!'

I began to shake. Bill pulled me out of the chair and began walking with me up and down the yard. Sam sat in front of Jason and began talking to him earnestly, his voice low and intense.

Bill's arm was around me, but I couldn't stop shaking.

'Did he mean that?' I asked, not expecting Bill to answer.

'No,' he said. I looked up, surprised.

'No, he couldn't help your grandmother, and he couldn't handle the idea of someone lying in wait for you and killing her instead. So he had to get angry about something. And instead of getting angry with you for not getting killed, he's angry about things. I wouldn't let it worry me.'

'I think it's pretty amazing that you're saying this,' I told him bluntly.

'Oh, I took some night school courses in psychology,' said Bill Compton, vampire.

And, I couldn't help thinking, hunters always study their prey. 'Why would Gran leave me all this, and not Jason?'

'Maybe you'll find out later,' he said, and that seemed fine to me.

Then Andy Bellefleur came out of the house and stood on the steps, looking up at the sky as if there were clues written on it.

'Compton,' he called sharply.

'No,' I said, and my voice came out as a growl.

I could feel Bill look down at me with the slight surprise that was a big reaction, coming from him.

'Now it's gonna happen,' I said furiously.

'You *were* protecting me,' he said. 'You thought the police would suspect me of killing those two women. That's why you wanted to be sure they were accessible to other vampires. Now you think this Bellefleur will try to blame your grandmother's death on me.'

'Yes.'

He took a deep breath. We were in the dark, by the trees that lined the yard. Andy bellowed Bill's name again.

'Sookie,' Bill said gently, 'I am sure you were the intended victim, as sure as you are.'

It was kind of a shock to hear someone else say it.

'And I didn't kill them. So if the killer was the same as their killer, then I didn't do it, and he will see that. Even if he is a Bellefleur.'

We began walking back into the light. I wanted none of this to be. I wanted the lights and the people to vanish, all of them, Bill, too. I wanted to be alone in the house with my grandmother, and I wanted her to look happy, as she had the last time I'd seen her.

It was futile and childish, but I could wish it nonetheless. I was lost in that dream, so lost I didn't see harm coming until it was too late.

My brother, Jason, stepped in front of me and slapped me in the face.

It was so unexpected and so painful that I lost my balance and staggered to the side, landing hard on one knee.

Jason seemed to be coming after me again, but Bill was suddenly in front of me, crouched, and his fangs were out and he was scary as hell. Sam tackled Jason and brought him down, and he may have whacked Jason's face against the ground once for good measure.

Andy Bellefleur was stunned at this unexpected display of violence. But after a second he stepped in between our two little groups on the lawn. He looked at Bill and swallowed, but he said in a steady voice, 'Compton, back off. He won't hit her again.'

Bill was taking deep breaths, trying to control his hunger for Jason's blood. I couldn't read his thoughts, but I could read his body language.

I couldn't exactly read Sam's thoughts, but I could tell he was very angry.

Jason was sobbing. His thoughts were a confused and tangled blue mess.

And Andy Bellefleur didn't like any of us and wished he could lock every freaking one of us up for some reason or another.

I pushed myself wearily to my feet and touched the painful spot of my cheek, using that to distract me from the pain in my heart, the dreadful grief that rolled over me.

I thought this night would never end.

The funeral was the largest ever held in Renard Parish. The minister said so. Under a brilliant early summer sky, my grandmother was buried beside my mother and father in our family plot in the ancient cemetery between the Comptons' house and Gran's house.

Jason had been right. It was my house, now. The house and the twenty acres surrounding it were mine, as were the mineral rights. Gran's money, what there was, had been divided fairly between us, and Gran had stipulated that I give Jason my half of the home our parents had lived in, if I wanted to retain full rights to her house. That was easy to do, and I didn't want any money from Jason for that half, though my lawyer looked dubious when I told him that. Jason would just blow his top if I mentioned paying me for my half; the fact that I was part-owner had never been more than a fantasy to him. Yet Gran leaving her house to me outright had come as a big shock. She had understood him better than I had.

It was lucky I had income other than from the bar, I thought heavily, trying to concentrate on something besides her loss. Paying taxes on the land and house, plus the upkeep of the house, which Gran had assumed at least partially, would really stretch my income.

'I guess you'll want to move,' Maxine Fortenberry said when she was cleaning the kitchen. Maxine had brought over devilled eggs and ham salad, and she was trying to be extra helpful by scrubbing.

'No,' I said, surprised.

'But honey, with it happening right here . . .' Maxine's heavy face creased with concern.

'I have far more good memories of this kitchen than bad ones,' I explained.

'Oh, what a good way to look at it,' she said, surprised. 'Sookie, you really are smarter than anyone gives you credit for being.'

'Gosh, thanks, Mrs. Fortenberry,' I said, and if she heard the dry tone in my voice she didn't react. Maybe that was wise.

'Is your friend coming to the funeral?' The kitchen was very warm. Bulky, square Maxine was blotting her face with a dishtowel. The spot where Gran had fallen had been scrubbed by her friends, God bless them.

'My friend. Oh, Bill? No, he can't.'

She looked at me blankly.

'We're having it in the daytime, of course.'

She still didn't comprehend.

'He can't come out.'

'Oh, of course!' She gave herself a light tap on the temple to indicate she was knocking sense into her head. 'Silly me. Would he really fry?'

'Well, he says he would.'

'You know, I'm so glad he gave that talk at the club, that has really made such a difference in making him part of the community.'

I nodded, abstracted.

'There's really a lot of feeling about the murders, Sookie. There's really a lot of talk about vampires, about how they're responsible for these deaths.'

I looked at her with narrowed eyes.

'Don't you go all mad on me, Sookie Stackhouse! Since Bill was so sweet about telling those fascinating stories at the Descendants meeting, most people don't think he could do those awful things that were done to those women.' I wondered what stories were making the rounds, and I shuddered to think. 'But he's had some visitors that people didn't much like the looks of.'

I wondered if she meant Malcolm, Liam, and Diane. I hadn't much liked their looks either, and I resisted the automatic impulse to defend them.

'Vampires are just as different among themselves as humans are,' I said.

'That's what I told Andy Bellefleur,' she said, nodding vehemently. 'I said to Andy, you should go after some of those others, the ones that don't want to learn how to live with us, not like Bill Compton, who's really making an effort to settle in. He was telling me at the funeral home that he'd gotten his kitchen finished, finally.'

I could only stare at her. I tried to think of what Bill might make in his kitchen. Why would he need one?

But none of the distractions worked, and finally I just realized that for a while I was going to be crying every whip-stitch. And I did.

At the funeral Jason stood beside me, apparently over his surge of anger at me, apparently back in his right mind. He didn't touch me or talk to me, but he didn't hit me, either. I felt very alone. But then I realized as I looked out over the hillside that the whole town was grieving with me. There were cars as far as I could see on the narrow drives through the cemetery, there were hundreds of dark-clad folks around the funeral-home tent. Sam was there in a suit (looking quite unlike himself), and Arlene, standing by Rene, was wearing a flowered Sunday dress. Lafayette stood at the very back of the crowd, along with Terry Bellefleur and Charlsie Tooten; the bar must be closed! And all Gran's friends, all, the ones who could still walk. Mr. Norris wept openly, a snowy white handkerchief held up to his eyes. Maxine's heavy face was set in graven lines of sadness. While the minister said what he had to, while Jason and I sat alone in the family area in the uneven folding chairs, I felt something in me detach and fly up, up into the blue brilliance: and I knew that whatever had happened to my grandmother, now she was at home.

The rest of the day went by in a blur, thank God. I didn't want to remember it, didn't want to even know it was happening. But one moment stood out.

Jason and I were standing by the dining room table in Gran's house, some temporary truce between us. We greeted the mourners, most of whom did their best not to stare at the bruise on my cheek.

We glided through it, Jason thinking that he would go home and have a drink after, and he wouldn't have to see me for a while and then it would be all right, and me thinking almost exactly the same thing. Except for the drink.

A well-meaning woman came up to us, the sort of woman who has thought over every ramification of a situation that was none of her business to start with.

'I am so sorry for you kids,' she said, and I looked at her; for the life of me I couldn't remember her name. She was a Methodist. She had three grown children. But her name ran right out the other side of my head.

'You know it was so sad seeing you two there alone today, it made me remember your mother and father so much,' she said, her face creasing into a mask of sympathy that I knew was automatic. I glanced at Jason, looked back to the woman, nodded.

'Yes,' I said. But I heard her thought before she spoke, and I began to blanch.

'But where was Adele's brother today, your great uncle? Surely he's still living?'

'We're not in touch,' I said, and my tone would have discouraged anyone more sensitive than this lady.

'But her only brother! Surely you . . .' and her voice died away as our combined stare finally sank home.

Several other people had commented briefly on our Uncle Bartlett's absence, but we had given the 'this is family business' signals that cut them right off. This woman – what was her name? – just hadn't been as quick to read them. She'd brought a taco salad, and I planned to throw it right into the garbage when she'd left.

'We do have to tell him,' Jason said quietly after she left. I put my guard up, I had no desire to know what he was thinking.

'You call him,' I said.

'All right.'

And that was all we said to each other for the rest of the day.

Chapter 6

I stayed at home for three days after the funeral. It was too long; I needed to go back to work. But I kept thinking of things I just had to do, or so I told myself. I cleaned out Gran's room. Arlene happened to drop by, and I asked her for help, because I just couldn't be in there alone with my grandmother's things, all so familiar and imbued with her personal odor of Johnson's baby powder and Campho-Phenique.

So my friend Arlene helped me pack everything up to take to the disaster relief agency. There'd been tornadoes in northern Arkansas the past few days, and surely some person who had lost everything could use all the clothes. Gran had been smaller and thinner than I, and besides that her tastes were very different, so I wanted nothing of hers except the jewelry. She'd never worn much, but what she wore was real and precious to me.

It was amazing what Gran had managed to pack into her room. I didn't even want to think about what she'd stored in the attic: that would be dealt with later, in the fall, when the attic was bearably cool and I'd time to think.

I probably threw away more than I should have, but it

made me feel efficient and strong to be doing this, and I did a drastic job of it. Arlene folded and packed, only putting aside papers and photographs, letters and bills and cancelled checks. My grandmother had never used a credit card in her life and never bought anything on time, God bless her, which made the winding-up much easier.

Arlene asked about Gran's car. It was five years old and had very little mileage. 'Will you sell yours and keep hers?' she asked. 'Yours is newer, but it's small.'

'I hadn't thought,' I said. And I found I couldn't think of it; that cleaning out the bedroom was the extent of what I could do that day.

At the end of the afternoon, the bedroom was empty of Gran. Arlene and I turned the mattress and I remade the bed out of habit. It was an old four-poster in the rice pattern. I had always thought her bedroom set was beautiful, and it occurred to me that now it was mine. I could move into the bigger bedroom and have a private bath instead of using the one in the hall.

Suddenly, that was exactly what I wanted to do. The furniture I'd been using in my bedroom had been moved over here from my parents' house when they'd died, and it was kids' furniture; overly feminine, sort of reminiscent of Barbies and sleepovers.

Not that I'd ever had many sleepovers, or been to many.

Nope, nope, nope, I wasn't going to fall into that old pit. I was what I was, and I had a life, and I could enjoy things; the little treats that kept me going.

'I might move in here,' I told Arlene as she taped a box shut.

'Isn't that a little soon?' she asked. She flushed red when she realized she'd sounded critical.

'It would be easier to be in here than be across the hall thinking about the room being empty,' I said. Arlene thought that through, crouched beside the cardboard box with the roll of tape in her hand.

'I can see that,' she agreed, with a nod of her flaming red head.

We loaded the cardboard boxes into Arlene's car. She had kindly agreed to drop them by the collection center on her way home, and I gratefully accepted the offer. I didn't want anyone to look at me knowingly, with pity, when I gave away my grandmother's clothes and shoes and nightgowns. When Arlene left, I hugged her and gave her a kiss on the cheek, and she stared at me. That was outside the bounds our friendship had had up till now. She bent her head to mine and we very gently bumped foreheads.

'You crazy girl,' she said, affection in her voice. 'You come see us, now. Lisa's been wanting you to baby-sit again.'

'You tell her Aunt Sookie said hi to her, and to Coby, too.'

'I will.' And Arlene sauntered off to her car, her flaming hair puffing in a waving mass above her head, her full body making her waitress outfit look like one big promise.

All my energy drained away as Arlene's car bumped down the driveway through the trees. I felt a million years old, alone and lonely. This was the way it was going to be from now on.

I didn't feel hungry, but the clock told me it was time to eat. I went into the kitchen and pulled one of the many Tupperware containers from the refrigerator. It held turkey and grape salad, and I liked it, but I sat there at the table just picking at it with a fork. I gave up, returning it to the icebox and going to the bathroom for a much-needed shower. The corners of closets are always dusty, and even a housekeeper as good as my grandmother had been had not been able to defeat that dust.

The shower felt wonderful. The hot water seemed to steam out some of my misery, and I shampooed my hair and scrubbed every inch of skin, shaving my legs and armpits. After I climbed out, I plucked my eyebrows and put on skin lotion and deodorant and a spray to untangle my hair and anything else I could lay my hands on. With my hair trailing down my back in a cascade of wet snarls, I pulled on my nightshirt, a white one with Tweety Bird on the front, and I got my comb. I'd sit in front of the television to have something to watch while I got my hair combed out, always a tedious process.

My little burst of purpose expired, and I felt almost numb.

The doorbell rang just as I was trailing into the living room with my comb in one hand and a towel in the other.

I looked through the peephole. Bill was waiting patiently on the porch.

I let him in without feeling either glad or sorry to see him.

He took me in with some surprise: the nightshirt, the wet hair, the bare feet. No makeup.

'Come in,' I said.

'Are you sure?'

'Yes.'

And he came in, looking around him as he always did. 'What are you doing?' he asked, seeing the pile of things I'd put to one side because I thought friends of Gran's might want them: Mr. Norris might be pleased to get the framed picture of his mother and Gran's mother together, for example.

'I cleaned out the bedroom today,' I said. 'I think I'll move into it.' Then I couldn't think of anything else to say. He turned to look at me carefully.

'Let me comb out your hair,' he said.

I nodded indifferently. Bill sat on the flowered couch and indicated the old ottoman positioned in front of it. I sat down obediently, and he scooted forward a little, framing me with his thighs. Starting at the crown of my head, he began teasing the tangles out of my hair.

As always, his mental silence was a treat. Each time, it was like putting the first foot into a cool pool of water when I'd been on a long, dusty hike on a hot day.

As a bonus, Bill's long fingers seemed adept at dealing with the thick mane of my hair. I sat with my eyes closed, gradually becoming tranquil. I could feel the slight movements of his body behind me as he worked with the comb. I could almost hear his heart beating, I thought, and then realized how strange an idea that was. His heart, after all, didn't.

'I used to do this for my sister, Sarah,' he murmured quietly, as if he knew how peaceful I'd gotten and was trying not to break my mood. 'She had hair darker than yours, even longer. She'd never cut it. When we were children, and my mother was busy, she'd have me work on Sarah's hair.'

'Was Sarah younger than you, or older?' I asked in a slow, drugged voice.

'She was younger. She was three years younger.'

'Did you have other brothers or sisters?'

'My mother lost two in childbirth,' he said slowly, as if

he could barely remember. 'I lost my brother, Robert, when he was twelve and I was eleven. He caught a fever, and it killed him. Now they would pump him full of penicillin, and he would be all right. But they couldn't then. Sarah survived the war, she and my mother, though my father died while I was soldiering; he had what I've learned since was a stroke. My wife was living with my family then, and my children . . .'

'Oh, Bill,' I said sadly, almost in a whisper, for he had lost so much.

'Don't, Sookie,' he said, and his voice had regained its cold clarity.

He worked on in silence for a while, until I could tell the comb was running free through my hair. He picked up the white towel I'd tossed on the arm of the couch and began to pat my hair dry, and as it dried he ran his fingers through it to give it body.

'Mmmm,' I said, and as I heard it, it was no longer the sound of someone being soothed.

I could feel his cool fingers lifting the hair away from my neck and then I felt his mouth just at the nape. I couldn't speak or move. I exhaled slowly, trying not to make another sound. His lips moved to my ear, and he caught the lobe of it between his teeth. Then his tongue darted in. His arms came around me, crossing over my chest, pulling me back against him.

And for a miracle I only heard what his body was saying, not those niggling things from minds that only foul up moments like this. His body was saying something very simple.

He lifted me as easily as I'd rotate an infant. He turned me so I was facing him on his lap, my legs on either side of his. I put my arms around him and bent a little to kiss him. It went on and on, but after a while Bill settled into a rhythm with his tongue, a rhythm even someone as inexperienced as I could identify. The nightshirt slid up to the tops of my thighs. My hands began to rub his arms helplessly. Strangely, I thought of a pan of caramels my grandmother had put on the stove for a candy recipe, and I thought of the melted, warm sweet goldenness of them.

He stood up with me still wrapped around him. 'Where?' he asked.

And I pointed to my grandmother's former room. He carried me in as we were, my legs locked around him, my head on his shoulder, and he lay me on the clean bed. He stood by the bed and in the moonlight coming in the unshaded windows, I saw him undress, quickly and neatly. Though I was getting great pleasure from watching him, I knew I had to do the same; but still a little embarrassed, I just drew off the nightshirt and tossed it onto the floor.

I stared at him. I'd never seen anything so beautiful or so scary in my life.

'Oh, Bill,' I said anxiously, when he was beside me in the bed, 'I don't want to disappoint you.'

'That's not possible,' he whispered. His eyes looked at my body as if it were a drink of water on a desert dune.

'I don't know much,' I confessed, my voice barely audible.

'Don't worry. I know a lot.' His hands began drifting over me, touching me in places I'd never been touched. I jerked with surprise, then opened myself to him.

'Will this be different from doing it with a regular guy?' I asked.

'Oh, yes.'

I looked up at him questioningly.

'It'll be better,' he said in my ear, and I felt a twinge of pure excitement.

A little shyly, I reached down to touch him, and he made a very human sound. After a moment, the sound became deeper.

'Now?' I asked, my voice ragged and shaking.

'Oh, yes,' he said, and then he was on top of me.

A moment later he found out the true extent of my inexperience.

'You should have told me,' he said, but very gently. He held himself still with an almost palpable effort.

'Oh, please don't stop!' I begged, thinking that the top would fly off my head, something drastic would happen, if he didn't go on with it.

'I have no intention of stopping,' he promised a little grimly. 'Sookie . . . this will hurt.'

In answer, I raised myself. He made an incoherent noise and pushed into me.

I held my breath. I bit my lip. Ow, ow, ow.

'Darling,' Bill said. No one had ever called me that. 'How are you?' Vampire or not, he was trembling with the effort of holding back.

'Okay,' I said inadequately. I was over the sting, and I'd lose my courage if we didn't proceed. 'Now,' I said, and I bit him hard on the shoulder.

He gasped, and jerked, and he began moving in earnest. At first I was dazed, but I began to catch on and keep up. He found my response very exciting, and I began to feel that something was just around the corner, so to speak – something very big and good. I said, 'Oh, please, Bill, please!' and dug my nails in his hips, almost there, almost there, and then a small shift in our alignment allowed him to press even more directly against me and almost before I could gather myself I was flying, flying, seeing white with gold streaks. I felt Bill's teeth against my neck, and I said, 'Yes!' I felt his fangs penetrate, but it was a small pain, an exciting pain, and as he came inside me I felt him draw on the little wound.

We lay there for a long time, from time to time trembling with little aftershocks. I would never forget his taste and smell as long as I lived, I would never forget the feel of him inside me this first time – my first time, ever – I would never forget the pleasure.

Finally Bill moved to lie beside me, propped on one elbow, and he put his hand over my stomach.

'I am the first.'

'Yes.'

'Oh, Sookie.' He bent to kiss me, his lips tracing the line of my throat.

'You could tell I don't know much,' I said shyly. 'But was that all right for you? I mean, about on a par with other women at least? I'll get better.'

'You can get more skilled, Sookie, but you can't get any better.' He kissed me on the cheek. 'You're wonderful.'

'Will I be sore?'

'I know you'll think this is odd, but I don't remember. The only virgin I was ever with was my wife, and that was a century and a half ago . . . yes, I recall, you will be very sore. We won't be able to make love again, for a day or two.'

'Your blood heals,' I observed after a little pause, feeling my cheeks redden.

In the moonlight, I could see him shift, to look at me more directly. 'So it does,' he said. 'Would you like that?'

'Sure. Wouldn't you?'

'Yes,' he breathed, and bit his own arm.

It was so sudden that I cried out, but he casually rubbed a finger in his own blood, and then before I could tense up he slid that finger up inside me. He began moving it very gently, and in a moment, sure enough, the pain was gone.

'Thanks,' I said. 'I'm better now.'

But he didn't remove his finger.

'Oh,' I said. 'Would you like to do it again so soon? Can you do that?' And as his finger kept up its motion, I began to hope so.

'Look and see,' he offered, a hint of amusement in his sweet dark voice.

I whispered, hardly recognizing myself, 'Tell me what you want me to do.'

And he did.

I went back to work the next day. No matter what Bill's healing powers were, I was a little uncomfortable, but boy, did I feel powerful. It was a totally new feeling for me. It was hard not to feel – well, cocky is surely the wrong word – maybe incredibly smug is closer.

Of course, there were the same old problems at the bar – the cacophony of voices, the buzzing of them, the persistence. But somehow I seemed better able to tone them down, to tamp them into a pocket. It was easier to keep my guard up, and I felt consequently more relaxed. Or maybe since I was more relaxed – boy, was I more relaxed – it was easier to guard? I don't know. But I felt better, and I was able to accept the condolences of the patrons with calm instead of tears.

Jason came in at lunch and had a couple of beers with his

hamburger, which wasn't his normal regimen. He usually didn't drink during the work day. I knew he'd get mad if I said anything directly, so I just asked him if everything was okay.

'The chief had me in again today,' he said in a low voice. He looked around to make sure no one else was listening, but the bar was sparsely filled that day since the Rotary Club was meeting at the Community Building.

'What is he asking you?' My voice was equally low.

'How often I'd seen Maudette, did I always get my gas at the place she worked. . . . Over and over and over, like I hadn't answered those questions seventy-five times. My boss is at the end of his patience, Sookie, and I don't blame him. I been gone from work at least two days, maybe three, with all the trips I been making down to the police station.'

'Maybe you better get a lawyer,' I said uneasily.

'That's what Rene said.'

Then Rene Lenier and I saw eye to eye.

'What about Sid Matt Lancaster?' Sidney Matthew Lancaster, native son and a whiskey sour drinker, had the reputation of being the most aggressive trial lawyer in the parish. I liked him because he always treated me with respect when I served him in the bar.

'He might be my best bet.' Jason looked as petulant and grim as a lovely person can. We exchanged a glance. We both knew Gran's lawyer was too old to handle the case if Jason was ever, God forbid, arrested.

Jason was far too self-absorbed to notice anything different about me, but I'd worn a white golf shirt (instead of my usual round-necked T-shirt) for the protection of its collar. Arlene was not as unaware as my brother. She'd been eyeing me all morning, and by the time the three o'clock lull hit, she was pretty sure she'd got me figured out.

'Girl,' she said, 'you been having fun?'

I turned red as a beet. 'Having fun' made my relationship with Bill lighter than it was, but it was accurate as far as it went. I didn't know whether to take the high road and say, 'No, making love,' or keep my mouth shut, or tell Arlene it was none of her business, or just shout, 'Yes!'

'Oh, Sookie, who is the man?'

Uh-oh. 'Um, well, he's not . . .'

'Not local? You dating one of those servicemen from Bossier City?'

'No,' I said hesitantly.

'Sam? I've seen him looking at you.'

'No.'

'Who, then?'

I was acting like I was ashamed. Straighten your spine, Sookie Stackhouse, I told myself sternly. Pay the piper.

'Bill,' I said, hoping against hope that she'd just say, 'Oh, yeah.'

'Bill,' Arlene said blankly. I noticed Sam had drifted up and was listening. So was Charlsie Tooten. Even Lafayette stuck his head through the hatch.

'Bill,' I said, trying to sound firm. 'You know. Bill.'

'Bill Auberjunois?'

'No.'

'Bill . . . ?'

'Bill Compton,' Sam said flatly, just as I opened my mouth to say the same thing. 'Vampire Bill.'

Arlene was flabbergasted, Charlsie Tooten immediately gave a little shriek, and Lafayette about dropped his bottom jaw.

'Honey, couldn't you just date a regular human fella?' Arlene asked when she got her voice back.

'A regular human fella didn't ask me out.' I could feel the color fix in my cheeks. I stood there with my back straight, feeling defiant and looking it, I'm sure.

'But, sweetie,' Charlsie Tooten fluted in her babyish voice, 'honey . . . Bill's, ah, got that virus.'

'I know that,' I said, hearing the distinct edge in my voice.

'I thought you were going to say you were dating a black, but you've gone one better, ain't you, girl?' Lafayette said, picking at his fingernail polish.

Sam didn't say anything. He just stood leaning against the bar, and there was a white line around his mouth as if he were biting his cheek inside.

I stared at them all in turn, forcing them to either swallow this or spit it out.

Arlene got through it first. 'All right, then. He better treat you good, or we'll get our stakes out!'

They were all able to laugh at that, albeit weakly.

'And you'll save a lot on groceries!' Lafayette pointed out.

But then in one step Sam ruined it all, that tentative acceptance, by suddenly moving to stand beside me and pull the collar of my shirt down.

You could have cut the silence of my friends with a knife.

'Oh, shit,' Lafayette said, very softly.

I looked right into Sam's eyes, thinking I'd never forgive him for doing this to me.

'Don't you touch my clothes,' I told him, stepping away from him and pulling the collar back straight. 'Don't tend to my personal life.'

'I'm scared for you, I'm worried about you,' he said, as Arlene and Charlsie hastily found other things to do.

'No you're not, or not entirely. You're mad as hell. Well listen, buddy. You *never got in line*.'

And I stalked away to wipe down the Formica on one of the tables. Then I collected all the salt shakers and refilled them. Then I checked the pepper shakers and the bottles of hot peppers on each table and booth, the Tabasco sauce, too. I just kept working and kept my eyes in front of me, and gradually, the atmosphere cooled down.

Sam was back in his office doing paperwork or something, I didn't care what, as long as he kept his opinions to himself. I still felt like he'd ripped the curtain off a private area of my life when he'd exposed my neck, and I hadn't forgiven him. But Arlene and Charlsie had found make-work, as I'd done, and by the time the after-work crowd began trickling in, we were once again fairly comfortable with one another.

Arlene came into the women's room with me. 'Listen, Sookie, I got to ask. Are vampires all everyone says they are, in the lover department?'

I just smiled.

Bill came into the bar that evening, just after dark. I'd worked late since one of the evening waitresses had had car trouble. One minute he wasn't there, and the next minute he was, slowing down so I could see him coming. If Bill had any doubts about making our relationship public, he didn't show them. He lifted my hand and kissed it in a gesture that performed by anyone else would have seemed phony as hell. I felt the touch of his lips on the back of my hand all the way down to my toes, and I knew he could tell that.

'How are you this evening?' he whispered, and I shivered.

'A little . . .' I found I couldn't get the words out.

'You can tell me later,' he suggested. 'When are you through?'

'Just as soon as Susie gets here.'

'Come to my house.'

'Okay.' I smiled up at him, feeling radiant and light-headed.

And Bill smiled back, though since my nearness had affected him, his fangs were showing, and maybe to anyone else but me the effect was a little – unsettling.

He bent to kiss me, just a light touch on the cheek, and he turned to leave. But just at that moment, the evening went all to hell.

Malcolm and Diane came in, flinging the door open as if they were making a grand entrance, and of course, they were. I wondered where Liam was. Probably parking the car. It was too much to hope they'd left him at home.

Folks in Bon Temps were getting accustomed to Bill, but the flamboyant Malcolm and the equally flamboyant Diane caused quite a stir. My first thought was that this wasn't going to help people get used to Bill and me.

Malcolm was wearing leather pants and a kind of chain-mail shirt. He looked like something on the cover of a rock album. Diane was wearing a one-piece lime green bodysuit spun out of Lycra or some other very thin, stretchy cloth. I was sure I could count her pubic hairs if I so desired. Blacks didn't come into Merlotte's much, but if any black was absolutely safe there, it was Diane. I saw Lafayette goggling through the hatch in open admiration, spiced by a dollop of fear.

The two vampires shrieked with feigned surprise when

they saw Bill, like demented drunks. As far as I could tell, Bill was not happy about their presence, but he seemed to handle their invasion calmly, as he did almost everything.

Malcolm kissed Bill on the mouth, and so did Diane. It was hard to tell which greeting was more offensive to the customers in the bar. Bill had better show distaste, and quick, I thought, if he wanted to stay in good with the human inhabitants of Bon Temps.

Bill, who was no fool, took a step back and put his arm around me, dissociating himself from the vampires and aligning himself with the humans.

'So your little waitress is still alive,' Diane said, and her clear voice was audible through the whole bar. 'Isn't that amazing.'

'Her grandmother was murdered last week,' Bill said quietly, trying to subdue Diane's desire to make a scene.

Her gorgeous lunatic brown eyes fixed on me, and I felt cold.

'Is that right?' she said and laughed.

That was it. No one would forgive her now. If Bill had been trying to find a way to entrench himself, this would be the scenario I would write. On the other hand, the disgust I could feel massing from the humans in the bar could backlash and wash over Bill as well as the renegades.

Of course . . . to Diane and her friends, Bill was the renegade.

'When's someone going to kill you, baby?' She ran a fingernail under my chin, and I knocked her hand away.

She would have been on me if Malcolm hadn't grabbed her hand, lazily, almost effortlessly. But I saw the strain show in the way he was standing.

'Bill,' he said conversationally, as if he wasn't exerting every muscle he had to keep Diane still, 'I hear this town is losing its unskilled service personnel at a terrible rate. And a little bird in Shreveport tells me you and your friend here were at Fangtasia asking questions about what vampire the murdered fang-bangers might have been with.

'You know that's for us to know, no one else,' Malcolm continued, and all of a sudden his face was so serious it was truly terrifying. 'Some of us don't want to go to – baseball – games and . . .' (here he was searching his memory for something disgustingly human, I could tell) 'barbecues! We are Vampire!' He invested the word with majesty, with glamor, and I could tell a lot of the people in the bar were falling under his spell. Malcolm was intelligent enough to want to erase the bad impression he knew Diane had made, all the while showering contempt on those of us it had been made on.

I stomped on his instep with every ounce of weight I could muster. He showed his fangs at me. The people in the bar blinked and shook themselves.

'Why don't you just get outta here, mister,' Rene said. He was slouched at the bar with his elbows flanking a beer.

There was moment when things hung in the balance, when the bar could have turned into a bloodbath. None of my fellow humans seemed to quite comprehend how strong vampires were, or how ruthless. Bill had moved in front of me, a fact registered by every citizen in Merlotte's.

'Well, if we're not wanted . . .' Malcolm said. His thick-muscled masculinity warred with the fluting voice he suddenly affected. 'These good people would like to eat meat, Diane, and do human things. By themselves. Or with our former friend Bill.'

'I think the little waitress would like to do a very human thing with Bill,' Diane began, when Malcolm caught her by the arm and propelled her from the room before she could cause more damage.

The entire bar seemed to shudder collectively when they were out the door, and I thought I better leave, even though Susie hadn't shown up yet. Bill waited for me outside; when I asked him why, he said he wanted to be sure they'd really left.

I followed Bill to his house, thinking we'd gotten off relatively lightly from the vampire visitation. I wondered why Diane and Malcolm had come; it seemed odd to me that they would be cruising so far from home and decide, on a whim, to drop in Merlotte's. Since they were making no real effort at assimilation, maybe they wanted to scotch Bill's prospects.

The Compton house was visibly different from the last time I'd been in, the sickening evening I'd met the other vampires.

The contractors were really coming through for Bill, whether because they were scared not to or because he was paying well, I didn't know. Maybe both. The living room was getting a new ceiling and the new wallpaper was white with a delicate flowered pattern. The hardwood floors had been cleaned, and they shone as they must have originally. Bill led me to the kitchen. It was sparse, naturally, but bright and cheerful and had a brand-new refrigerator full of bottled synthetic blood (yuck).

The downstairs bathroom was opulent.

As far as I knew, Bill never used the bathroom; at least for the primary human function. I stared around me in amazement.

The space for this grand bathroom had been achieved by including what had formerly been the pantry and about half the old kitchen.

'I like to shower,' he said, pointing to a clear shower stall in one corner. It was big enough for two grownups and maybe a dwarf or two. 'And I like to lie in warm water.' He indicated the centerpiece of the room, a huge sort of tub surrounded by an indoor deck of cedar, with steps on two sides. There were potted plants arranged all around it. The room was as close to being in the middle of a very luxurious jungle as you could get in northern Louisiana.

'What is that?' I asked, awed.

'It's a portable spa,' Bill said proudly. 'It has jets you can adjust individually so each person can get the right force of water. It's a hot tub,' he simplified.

'It has seats,' I said, looking in. The interior was decorated around the top with green and blue tiles. There were fancy controls on the outside.

Bill turned them, and water began to surge.

'Maybe we can bathe together?' Bill suggested.

I felt my cheeks flame, and my heart began to pound a little faster.

'Maybe now?' Bill's fingers tugging at my shirt where it was tucked into my black shorts.

'Oh, well . . . maybe.' I couldn't seem to look at him straight when I thought of how this – okay, man – had seen more of me than I'd ever let anyone see, including my doctor.

'Have you missed me?' he asked, his hands unbuttoning my shorts and peeling them down.

'Yes,' I said promptly because I knew that to be true.

He laughed, even as he knelt to untie my Nikes. 'What did you miss most, Sookie?'

'I missed your silence,' I said without thinking at all.

He looked up. His fingers paused in the act of pulling the end of the bow to loosen it.

'My silence,' he said.

'Not being able to hear your thoughts. You just can't imagine, Bill, how wonderful that is.'

'I was thinking you'd say something else.'

'Well, I missed that, too.'

'Tell me about it,' he invited, pulling my socks off and running his fingers up my thigh, tugging off the panties and shorts.

'Bill! I'm embarrassed,' I protested.

'Sookie, don't be embarrassed with me. Least of anyone, with me.' He was standing now, divesting me of my shirt and reaching behind me to unsnap my bra, running his hands over the marks the straps had made on my skin, turning his attention to my breasts. He toed off his sandals at some point.

'I'll try,' I said, looking at my own toes.

'Undress me.'

Now that I could do. I unbuttoned his shirt briskly and eased it out of his pants and off his shoulders. I unbuckled his belt and began to work on the waist button of his slacks. It was stiff, and I had quite a job.

I thought I was going to cry if the button didn't cooperate more. I felt clumsy and inept.

He took my hands and led them up to his chest. 'Slow, Sookie, slow,' he said, and his voice had gone soft and shivery. I could feel myself relaxing almost inch by inch, and I began to stroke his chest as he'd stroked mine, twining the curly hair around my fingers and gently pinching his flat nipples. His hand went behind my head and pressed gently.

I hadn't known men liked that, but Bill sure did, so I paid equal attention to the other one. While I was doing that, my hands resumed work on the damn button, and this time it came undone with ease. I began pushing down his pants, sliding my fingers inside his Jockeys.

He helped me down into the spa, the water frothing around our legs.

'Shall I bathe you first?' he asked.

'No,' I said breathlessly. 'Give me the soap.'

Chapter 7

The next night Bill and I had an unsettling conversation. We were in his bed, his huge bed with the carved headboard and a brand-new Restonic mattress. His sheets were flowered like his wallpaper, and I remember wondering if he liked flowers printed on his possessions because he couldn't see the real thing, at least as they were meant to be seen . . . in the daylight.

Bill was lying on his side, looking down at me. We'd been to the movies; Bill was crazy about movies with aliens, maybe having some kindred feeling for space creatures. It had been a real shoot-'em-up, with almost all the aliens being ugly, creepy, bent on killing. He'd fumed about that while he'd taken me out to eat, and then back to his place. I'd been glad when he'd suggested testing the new bed.

I was the first to lie on it with him.

He was looking at me, as he liked to do, I was learning. Maybe he was listening to my heart pounding, since he could hear things I couldn't, or maybe he was watching my pulse throb, because he could see things I couldn't, too. Our conversation had strayed from the movie we'd seen to the nearing parish elections (Bill was going to try to register to vote, absentee ballot), and then to our childhoods. I was realizing that Bill was trying desperately to remember what it had been like to be a regular person.

'Did you ever play "show me yours" with your brother?' he asked. 'They now say that's normal, but I will never forget my mother beating the tarnation out of my brother Robert after she found him in the bushes with Sarah.'

'No,' I said, trying to sound casual, but my face tightened, and I could feel the clenching of fear in my stomach.

'You're not telling the truth.'

'Yes, I am.' I kept my eyes fixed on his chin, hoping to think of some way to change the topic. But Bill was nothing if not persistent.

'Not your brother, then. Who?'

'I don't want to talk about this.' My hands contracted into fists, and I could feel myself begin to shut down.

But Bill hated being evaded. He was used to people telling him whatever he wanted to know because he was used to using his glamor to get his way.

'Tell me, Sookie.' His voice was coaxing, his eyes big pools of curiosity. He ran his thumbnail down my stomach, and I shivered.

'I had a . . . funny uncle,' I said, feeling the familiar tight smile stretch my lips.

He raised his dark arched brows. He hadn't heard the phrase.

I said as distantly as I could manage, 'That's an adult male relative who molests his . . . the children in the family.'

His eyes began to burn. He swallowed; I could see his Adam's apple move. I grinned at him. My hands were pulling my hair back from my face. I couldn't stop it.

'And someone did this to you? How old were you?'

'Oh, it started when I was real little,' and I could feel my breathing begin to speed up, my heart beat faster, the panicky traits that always came back when I remembered. My knees drew up and pressed together. 'I guess I was five,' I babbled, talking faster and faster, 'I know you can tell, he never actually, ah, screwed me, but he did other stuff,' and now my hands were shaking in front of my eyes where I held them to shield them from Bill's gaze. 'And the worst thing, Bill, the worst thing,' I went on, just unable to stop, 'is that every time he came to visit, I always knew what he was going to do because I could read his mind! And there wasn't anything I could do to stop it!' I clamped my hands over my mouth to make myself shut up. I wasn't supposed to talk about it. I rolled over onto my stomach to conceal myself, and held my body absolutely rigid.

After a long time, I felt Bill's cool hand on my shoulder. It lay there, comforting.

'This was before your parents died?' he said in his usual calm voice. I still couldn't look at him.

'Yes.'

'You told your mama? She did nothing?'

'No. She thought I was dirty minded, or that I'd found some book at the library that taught me something she didn't feel I was ready to know.' I could remember her face, framed in hair about two shades darker than my medium blond. Her face pinched with distaste. She had come from a very conservative family, and any public display of affection or any mention of a subject she thought indecent was flatly discouraged.

'I wonder that she and my father seemed happy,' I told my vampire. 'They were so different.' Then I saw how ludicrous my saying that was. I rolled over to my side. 'As if we aren't,' I told Bill, and tried to smile. Bill's face was quite still, but I could see a muscle in his neck jumping.

'Did you tell your father?'

'Yes, right before he died. I was too embarrassed to talk to him about it when I was younger; and Mother didn't believe me. But I couldn't stand it anymore, knowing I was going to see my great-uncle Bartlett at least two weekends out of every month when he drove up to visit.'

'He still lives?'

'Uncle Bartlett? Oh, sure. He's Gran's brother, and Gran was my dad's mother. My uncle lives in Shreveport. But when Jason and I went to live with Gran, after my parents died, the first time Uncle Bartlett came to her house I hid. When she found me and asked me why, I told her. And she believed me.' I felt the relief of that day all over again, the beautiful sound of my grandmother's voice promising me I'd never have to see her brother again, that he would never never come to the house.

And he hadn't. She had cut off her own brother to protect me. He'd tried with Gran's daughter, Linda, too, when she was a small girl, but my grandmother had buried the incident in her own mind, dismissed it as something misunderstood. She had told me that she'd never left her brother alone with Linda at any time after that, had almost quit inviting him to her home, while not quite letting herself believe that he'd touched her little girl's privates.

'So he's a Stackhouse, too?'

'Oh, no. See, Gran became a Stackhouse when she married, but she was a Hale before.' I wondered at having to spell this out for Bill. He was sure Southern enough, even if he was a vampire, to keep track of a simple family relationship like that.

Bill looked distant, miles away. I had put him off with my grim nasty little story, and I had chilled my own blood, that was for sure.

'Here, I'll leave,' I said and slid out of bed, bending to retrieve my clothes. Quicker than I could see, he was off the bed and taking the clothes from my hands.

'Don't leave me now,' he said. 'Stay.'

'I'm a weepy ol' thing tonight.' Two tears trickled down my cheeks, and I smiled at him.

His fingers wiped the tears from my face, and his tongue traced their marks.

'Stay with me till dawn,' he said.

'But you have to get in your hidey hole by then.'

'My what?'

'Wherever you spend the day. I don't want to know where it is!' I held up my hands to emphasize that. 'But don't you have to get in there before it's even a little light?'

'Oh,' he said, 'I'll know. I can feel it coming.'

'So you can't oversleep?'

'No.'

'All right. Will you let me get some sleep?'

'Of course I will,' he said with a gentlemanly bow, only a little off mark because he was naked. 'In a little while.' Then, as I lay down on the bed and held out my arms to him, he said, 'Eventually.'

*

Sure enough, in the morning I was in the bed by myself. I lay there for a little, thinking. I'd had little niggling thoughts from time to time, but for the first time the flaws in my relationship with the vampire hopped out of their own hidey hole and took over my brain.

I would never see Bill in the sunlight. I would never fix his breakfast, never meet him for lunch. (He could bear to watch me eat food, though he wasn't thrilled by the process, and I always had to brush my teeth afterward very thoroughly, which was a good habit anyway.)

I could never have a child by Bill, which was nice at least when you thought of not having to practice birth control, but . . .

I'd never call Bill at the office to ask him to stop on the way home for some milk. He'd never join the Rotary, or give a career speech at the high school, or coach Little League Baseball.

He'd never go to church with me.

And I knew that now, while I lay here awake – listening to the birds chirping their morning sounds and the trucks beginning to rumble down the road while all over Bon Temps people were getting up and putting on the coffee and fetching their papers and planning their day – that the creature I loved was lying somewhere in a hole underground, to all intents and purposes dead until dark.

I was so down by then that I had to think of an upside, while I cleaned up a little in the bathroom and dressed.

He seemed to genuinely care for me. It was kind of nice, but unsettling, not to know exactly how much.

Sex with him was absolutely great. I had never dreamed it would be that wonderful.

No one would mess with me while I was Bill's girlfriend.

Any hands that had patted me in unwanted caresses were kept in their owner's laps, now. And if the person who'd killed my grandmother had killed her because she'd walked in on him while he was waiting for me, he wouldn't get another try at me.

And I could relax with Bill, a luxury so precious I could not put a value on it. My mind could range at will, and I would not learn anything he didn't tell me.

There was that.

It was in this kind of contemplative mood that I came down Bill's steps to my car.

To my amazement, Jason was there sitting in his pickup.

This was not exactly a happy moment. I trudged over to his window.

'I see it's true,' he said. He handed me a Styrofoam cup of coffee from the Grabbit Quik. 'Get in the truck with me.'

I climbed in, pleased by the coffee but cautious overall. I put my guard up immediately. It slipped back into place slowly and painfully, like wiggling back into a girdle that was too tight in the first place.

'I can't say nothing,' he told me. 'Not after the way I lived my life these past few years. As near as I can tell, he's your first, isn't he?'

I nodded.

'He treat you good?'

I nodded again.

'I got something to tell you.'

'Okay.'

'Uncle Bartlett got killed last night.'

I stared at him, the steam from the coffee rising between us as I pried the lid off the cup. 'He's dead,' I said, trying to understand it. I'd worked hard never to think of him, and here I thought of him, and the next thing I heard, he was dead.

'Yep.'

'Wow.' I looked out the window at the rosy light on the horizon. I felt a surge of – freedom. The only one who remembered besides me, the only one who'd enjoyed it, who insisted to the end that I had initiated and continued the sick activities he thought were so gratifying . . . he was *dead*. I took a deep breath.

'I hope he's in hell,' I said. 'I hope every time he thinks of what he did to me, a demon pokes him in the butt with a pitchfork.'

'God, Sookie!'

'He never messed with you.'

'Damn straight!'

'Implying what?'

'Nothing, Sookie! But he never bothered anyone but you that I know of!'

'Bullshit. He molested Aunt Linda, too.'

Jason's face went blank with shock. I'd finally gotten through to my brother. 'Gran told you that?'

'Yes.'

'She never said anything to me.'

'Gran knew it was hard for you, not seeing him again when she could tell you loved him. But she couldn't let you be alone with him, because she couldn't be a hundred per-cent sure girls were all he wanted.'

'I've seen him the past couple of years.'

'You have?' This was news to me. It would have been news to Gran, too.

'Sookie, he was an old man. He was so sick. He had

prostate trouble, and he was feeble, and he had to use a walker.'

'That probably slowed him down chasing the five-year-olds.'

'Get over it!'

'Right! Like I could!'

We glared at each other over the width of the truck seat. 'So what happened to him?' I asked finally, reluctantly.

'A burglar broke into his house last night.'

'Yeah? And?'

'And broke his neck. Threw him down the stairs.'

'Okay. So I know. Now I'm going home. I gotta shower and get ready for work.'

'That's all you're saying?'

'What else is there to say?'

'Don't want to know about the funeral?'

'No.'

'Don't want to know about his will?'

'No.'

He threw up his hands. 'All right,' he said, as if he'd been arguing a point very hard with me and realized that I was intractable.

'What else? Anything?' I asked.

'No. Just your great-uncle dying. I thought that was enough.'

'Actually, you're right,' I said, opening the truck door and sliding out. 'That was enough.' I raised my cup to him. 'Thanks for the coffee, brother.'

It wasn't till I got to work that it clicked.

I was drying a glass and really not thinking about Uncle Bartlett, and suddenly my fingers lost all strength.

'Jesus Christ, Shepherd of Judea,' I said, looking down at the broken slivers of glass at my feet. 'Bill had him killed.'

I don't know why I was so sure I was right; but I was, the minute the idea crossed my mind. Maybe I had heard Bill dialing the phone when I was half-asleep. Maybe the expression on Bill's face when I'd finished telling him about Uncle Bartlett had rung a silent warning bell.

I wondered if Bill would pay the other vampire in money or if he'd repay him in kind.

I got through work in a frozen state. I couldn't talk to anyone about what I was thinking, couldn't even say I was sick without someone asking me what was wrong. So I didn't speak at all, I just worked. I tuned out everything except the next order I had to fill. I drove home trying to feel just as frozen, but I had to face facts when I was alone.

I freaked out.

I had known, really I had, that Bill certainly had killed a human or two in his long, long, life. When he'd been a young vampire, when he'd needed lots of blood, before he'd gained control of his needs sufficiently to exist on a gulp here, a mouthful there, without actually killing anyone he drank from . . . he'd told me himself there'd been a death or two along the way. And he'd killed the Rattrays. But they'd have done me in that night in back of Merlotte's, without a doubt, if Bill hadn't intervened. I was naturally inclined to excuse him those deaths.

How was the murder of Uncle Bartlett different? He'd harmed me, too, dreadfully, made my already difficult childhood a true nightmare. Hadn't I been relieved, even pleased, to hear he'd been found dead? Didn't my horror at

Bill's intervention reek of hypocrisy of the worst sort?

Yes. No?

Tired and incredibly confused, I sat on my front steps and waited in the darkness, my arms wrapped around my knees. The crickets were singing in the tall grass when he came, arriving so quietly and quickly I didn't hear him. One minute I was alone with the night, and the next, Bill was sitting on the steps beside me.

'What do you want to do tonight, Sookie?' His arm went around me.

'Oh, Bill.' My voice was heavy with despair.

His arm dropped. I didn't look up at his face, couldn't have seen it through the darkness, anyway.

'You should not have done it.'

He didn't bother with denying it at least.

'I am glad he's dead, Bill. But I can't . . .'

'Do you think I would ever hurt you, Sookie?' His voice was quiet and rustling, like feet through dry grass.

'No. Oddly enough, I don't think you would hurt me, even if you were really mad at me.'

'Then . . . ?'

'It's like dating the Godfather, Bill. I'm scared to say anything around you now. I'm not used to my problems being solved that way.'

'I love you.'

He'd never said it before, and I might almost have imagined it now, his voice was so low and whispery.

'Do you, Bill?' I didn't raise my face, kept my forehead pressed against my knees.

'Yes, I do.'

'Then you have to let my life get lived, Bill, you can't alter it for me.'

'You wanted me to alter it when the Rattrays were beating you.'

'Point taken. But I can't have you trying to fine-tune my day-to-day life. I'm gonna get mad at people, people are gonna get mad at me. I can't worry about them being killed. I can't live like that, honey. You see what I'm saying?'

'Honey?' he repeated.

'I love you,' I said. 'I don't know why, but I do. I want to call you all those gooshy words you use when you love someone, no matter how stupid it sounds since you're a vampire. I want to tell you you're my baby, that I'll love you till we're old and gray – though that's not gonna happen. That I know you'll always be true to me – hey, that's not gonna happen either. I keep running up against a brick wall when I try to tell you I love you, Bill.' I fell silent. I was all cried out.

'This crisis came sooner than I thought it would,' Bill said from the darkness. The crickets had resumed their chorus, and I listened to them for a long moment.

'Yeah.'

'What now, Sookie?'

'I have to have a little time.'

'Before . . . ?'

'Before I decide if the love is worth the misery.'

'Sookie, if you knew how different you taste, how much I want to protect you . . .'

I could tell from Bill's voice that these were very tender feelings he was sharing with me. 'Oddly enough,' I said, 'that's what I feel about you. But I have to live here, and I have to live with myself, and I have to think about some rules we gotta get clear between us.'

'So what do we do now?'

'I think. You go do whatever you were doing before we met.'

'Trying to figure out if I could live mainstream. Trying to think of who I'd feed on, if I could stop drinking that damn synthetic blood.'

'I know you'll – feed on someone else besides me.' I was trying very hard to keep my voice level. 'Please, not anyone here, not anyone I have to see. I couldn't bear it. It's not fair of me to ask, but I'm asking.'

'If you won't date anyone else, won't bed anyone else.'

'I won't.' That seemed an easy enough promise to make. 'Will you mind if I come into the bar?'

'No. I'm not telling anyone we're apart. I'm not talking about it.'

He leaned over, I could feel the pressure on my arm as his body pressed against it.

'Kiss me,' he said.

I lifted my head and turned, and our lips met. It was blue fire, not orange-and-red flames, not that kind of heat: blue fire. After a second, his arms went around me. After another, my arms went around him. I began to feel boneless, limp. With a gasp, I pulled away.

'Oh, we can't, Bill.'

I heard his breath draw in. 'Of course not, if we're separating,' he said quietly, but he didn't sound like he thought I meant it. 'We should definitely not be kissing. Still less should I want to throw you back on the porch and fuck you till you faint.'

My knees were actually shaking. His deliberately crude language, coming out in that cold sweet voice, made the longing inside me surge even higher. It took everything I had, every little scrap of self-control, to push myself up and go in the house.

But I did it.

In the following week, I began to craft a life without Gran and without Bill. I worked nights and worked hard. I was extra careful, for the first time in my life, about locks and security. There was a murderer out there, and I no longer had my powerful protector. I considered getting a dog, but couldn't decide what kind I wanted. My cat, Tina, was only protection in the sense that she always reacted when someone came very near the house.

I got calls from Gran's lawyer from time to time, informing me about the progress of winding up her estate. I got calls from Bartlett's lawyer. My great-uncle had left me twenty thousand dollars, a great sum for him. I almost turned down the legacy. But I thought again. I gave the money to the local mental health center, earmarking it for the treatment of children who were victims of molestation and rape.

They were glad to get it.

I took vitamins, loads of them, because I was a little anemic. I drank lots of fluids and ate lots of protein.

And I ate as much garlic as I wanted, something Bill hadn't been able to tolerate. He said it came out through my pores, even, when I had garlic bread with spaghetti and meat sauce one night.

I slept and slept and slept. Staying up nights after a work shift had me rest-deprived.

After three days I felt restored, physically. In fact, it seemed to me that I was a little stronger than I had been.

I began to take in what was happening around me.

The first thing I noticed was that local folks were really pissed off at the vampires who nested in Monroe. Diane, Liam, and Malcolm had been touring bars in the area, apparently trying to make it impossible for other vampires who wanted to mainstream. They'd been behaving outrageously, offensively. The three vampires made the escapades of the Louisiana Tech students look bland.

They didn't seem to ever imagine they were endangering themselves. The freedom of being out of the coffin had gone to their heads. The right to legally exist had withdrawn all their constraints, all their prudence and caution. Malcolm nipped at a bartender in Bogaloosas. Diane danced naked in Farmerville. Liam dated an underage girl in Shongaloo, and her mother, too. He took blood from both. He didn't erase the memory of either.

Rene was talking to Mike Spencer, the funeral director, in Merlotte's one Thursday night, and they hushed when I got near. Naturally, that caught my attention. So I read Mike's mind. A group of local men were thinking of burning out the Monroe vampires.

I didn't know what to do. The three were, if not exactly friends of Bill, at least sort of coreligionists. But I loathed Malcolm, Diane, and Liam just as much as anyone else. On the other hand; and boy – there always was another hand, wasn't there? – it just went against my grain to know ahead of the fact about premeditated murders and just sit on my hands.

Maybe this was all liquor talking. Just to check, I dipped into the minds of the people around me. To my dismay, many of them were thinking about torching the vampire's nest. But I couldn't track down the origin of the idea. It felt as though the poison had flowed from one mind and infected others.

There wasn't any proof, any proof at all, that Maudette and Dawn and my grandmother had been killed by a vampire. In fact, rumor had it that the coroner's report might show evidence against that. But the three vampires were behaving in such a way that people wanted to blame them for something, wanted to get rid of them, and since Maudette and Dawn were both vampire-bitten and habitués of vampire bars, well, folks just cobbled that together to pound out a conviction.

Bill came in the seventh night I'd been alone. He appeared at his table quite suddenly. He wasn't by himself. There was a boy with him, a boy who looked maybe fifteen. He was a vampire, too.

'Sookie, this is Harlen Ives from Minneapolis,' Bill said, as if this were an ordinary introduction.

'Harlen,' I said, and nodded. 'Pleased to meet you.'

'Sookie.' He bobbed his head at me, too.

'Harlen is in transit from Minnesota to New Orleans,' Bill said, sounding positively chatty.

'I'm going on vacation,' Harlen said. 'I've been wanting to visit New Orleans for years. It's just a mecca for us, you know.'

'Oh . . . right,' I said, trying to sound matter of fact.

'There's this number you can call,' Harlen informed me. 'You can stay with an actual resident, or you can rent a . . .'

'Coffin?' I asked brightly.

'Well, yes.'

'How nice for you,' I said, smiling for all I was worth. 'What can I get you? I believe Sam has restocked the blood, Bill, if you'd like some? It's flavored A neg, or we've got the O positive.'

'Oh, A negative, I think,' Bill said, after he and Harlen had a silent communication.

'Coming right up!' I stomped back to the cooler behind the bar and pulled out two A negs, popped the tops, and carted them back on a tray. I smiled the whole time, just like I used to.

'Are you all right, Sookie?' Bill asked in a more natural voice after I'd plonked their drinks down in front of them.

'Of course, Bill,' I said cheerily. I wanted to break the bottle over Bill's head. Harlen, indeed. Overnight stay. Right.

'Harlen would like to drive over to visit Malcolm, later,' Bill said, when I came to take the empties and ask if they wanted a refill.

'I'm sure Malcolm would love to meet Harlen,' I said trying not to sound as bitchy as I felt.

'Oh, meeting Bill has just been super,' Harlen said, smiling at me, showing fangs. Harlen knew how to do bitch, all right. 'But Malcolm is absolutely a legend.'

'Watch out,' I said to Bill. I wanted to tell him how much peril the three nesting vampires had put themselves into, but I didn't think it'd come to a head just yet. And I didn't want to spell it out because Harlen was sitting there, batting his baby blues at me and looking like a teen sex symbol. 'Nobody's too happy with those three, right now,' I added, after a moment. It was not an effectual warning.

Bill just looked at me, puzzled, and I spun on my heel and walked away.

I came to regret that moment, regret it bitterly.

After Bill and Harlen had left, the bar buzzed even harder

with the kind of talk I'd heard from Rene and Mike Spencer. It seemed to me like someone had been lighting fire, keeping the anger level stoked up. But for the life of me I couldn't discover who it was, though I did some random listening, both mental and physical. Jason came into the bar, and we said hello, but not much more. He hadn't forgiven me for my reaction to Uncle Bartlett's death.

He'd get over it. At least he wasn't thinking about burning anything, except maybe creating some heat in Liz Barrett's bed. Liz, even younger than me, had curly short brown hair and big brown eyes and an unexpectedly no-nonsense air about her that made me think Jason might have met his match. After I'd said good-bye to them after their pitcher of beer was empty, I realized that the anger level in the bar had escalated, that the men were really serious about doing something.

I began to be more than anxious.

As the evening wore on, the activity in the bar grew more and more frenetic. Less women, more men. More table-hopping. More drinking. Men were standing, instead of sitting. It was hard to pin down, since there wasn't any big meeting, really. It was by word-of-mouth, whispered from ear to ear. No one jumped on the bar and screamed, 'Whatta ya say, boys? Are we gonna put up with those monsters in our midst? To the castle!' or anything like that. It was just that, after a time, they all began drifting out, standing in huddled groups out in the parking lot. I looked out one of the windows at them, shaking my head. This wasn't good.

Sam was uneasy, too.

'What do you think?' I asked him, and I realized this was

the first time I'd spoken to him all evening, other than 'Pass the pitcher,' or 'Give me another margarita.'

'I think we've got a mob,' he said. 'But they'll hardly go over to Monroe now. The vampires'll be up and about until dawn.'

'Where is their house, Sam?'

'I understand it's on the outskirts of Monroe on the west side – in other words, closest to us,' he told me. 'I don't know for sure.'

I drove home after closing, half hoping I'd see Bill lurking in my driveway so I could tell him what was afoot.

But I didn't see him, and I wouldn't go to his house. After a long hesitation, I dialed his number, but got only his answering machine. I left a message. I had no idea what the three nesting vampires' phone was listed under, if they had a phone at all.

As I pulled off my shoes and removed my jewelry – all silver, take that, Bill! – I remember worrying, but I wasn't worrying enough. I went to bed and quickly to sleep in the bedroom that was now mine. The moonlight streamed in the open shades, making strange shadows on the floor. But I only stared at them for a few minutes. Bill didn't wake me that night, returning my call.

But the phone did ring, early in the morning, after daylight.

'What?' I asked, dazed, the receiver pressed to my ear. I peered at the clock. It was seven-thirty.

'They burned the vampires' house,' Jason said. 'I hope yours wasn't in it.'

'What?' I asked again, but my voice was panicked now.

'They burned the vampires' house outside of Monroe.

After sunrise. It's on Callista Street, west of Archer.'

I remembered Bill saying he might take Harlen over there. Had he stayed?

'No.' I said it definitely.

'Yes.'

'I have to go,' I said, hanging up the phone.

It smoldered in the bright sunlight. Wisps of smoke trailed up into the blue sky. Charred wood looked like alligator skin. Fire trucks and law enforcement cars were parked helter-skelter on the lawn of the two-story house. A group of the curious stood behind yellow tape.

The remains of four coffins sat side by side on the scorched grass. There was a body bag, too. I began to walk toward them, but for the longest time they seemed to be no closer; it was like one of those dreams where you can never reach your goal.

Someone grabbed my arm and tried to stop me. I can't remember what I said, but I remember a horrified face. I trudged on through the debris, inhaling the smell of burned things, wet charred things, a smell that wouldn't leave me the rest of my life.

I reached the first coffin and looked in. What was left of the lid was open to the light. The sun was coming up; any moment now it would kiss the dreadful thing resting on soggy, white silk lining.

Was it Bill? There was no way to tell. The corpse was disintegrating bit by bit even as I watched. Tiny fragments flaked off and blew into the breeze, or disappeared in a tiny puff of smoke where the sun's rays began to touch the body.

Each coffin held a similar horror.

Sam was standing by me.

'Can you call this murder, Sam?'

He shook his head. 'I just don't know, Sookie. Legally, killing the vampires is murder. But you'd have to prove arson first, though I don't think that'd be very hard.' We could both smell gasoline. There were men buzzing around the house, climbing here and there, yelling to each other. It didn't appear to me that these men were conducting any serious crime-scene investigation.

'But this body here, Sookie.' Sam pointed to the body bag on the grass. 'This was a real human, and they have to investigate. I don't think any member of that mob ever realized there might be a human in there, ever considered anything besides what they did.'

'So why are you here, Sam?'

'For you,' he said simply.

'I won't know if it's Bill all day, Sam.'

'Yes, I know.'

'What am I supposed to do all day? How can I wait?'

'Maybe some drugs,' he suggested. 'What about sleeping pills or something?'

'I don't have anything like that,' I said. 'I've never had trouble sleeping.'

This conversation was getting odder and odder, but I don't think I could have said anything else.

A big man was in front of me, the local law. He was sweating in the morning heat, and he looked like he'd been up for hours. Maybe he'd been on the night shift and had to stay on when the fire started.

When men I knew had started the fire.

'Did you know these people, miss?'

'Yes, I did. I'd met them.'

'Can you identify the remains?'

'Who could identify that?' I asked incredulously.

The bodies were almost gone now, featureless and disintegrating.

He looked sick. 'Yes, ma'am. But the person.'

'I'll look,' I said before I had time to think. The habit of being helpful was mighty hard to break.

As if he could tell I was about to change my mind, the big man knelt on the singed grass and unzipped the bag. The sooty face inside was that of a girl I'd never met. I thanked God.

'I don't know her,' I said, and felt my knees give. Sam caught me before I was on the ground, and I had to lean against him.

'Poor girl,' I whispered. 'Sam, I don't know what to do.'

The law took part of my time that day. They wanted to know everything I knew about the vampires who had owned the house, and I told them, but it didn't amount to much. Malcolm, Diane, Liam. Where they'd come from, their age, why they'd settled in Monroe, who their lawyers were; how would I know anything like that? I'd never even been to their house before.

When my questioner, whoever he was, found out that I'd met them through Bill, he wanted to know where Bill was, how he could contact him.

'He may be right there,' I said, pointing to the fourth coffin. 'I won't know till dark.' My hand rose of its own volition and covered my mouth.

Just then one of the firemen started to laugh, and his companion, too. 'Southern fried vampires!' the shorter one hooted to the man who was questioning me. 'We got us some Southern fried vampires here!'

He didn't think it was so damn funny when I kicked

him. Sam pulled me off and the man who'd been questioning me grabbed the fireman I'd attacked. I was screaming like a banshee and would have gone for him again if Sam had let go.

But he didn't. He dragged me toward my car, his hands just as strong as bands of iron. I had a sudden vision of how ashamed my grandmother would have been to see me screaming at a public servant, to see me physically attack someone. The idea pricked my crazy hostility like a needle puncturing a balloon. I let Sam shove me into the passenger's seat, and when he started the car and began backing away, I let him drive me home while I sat in utter silence.

We got to my house all too soon. It was only ten o'clock in the morning. Since it was daylight savings time I had at least ten plus hours to wait.

Sam made some phone calls while I sat on the couch staring ahead of me. Five minutes had passed when he came back into the living room.

'Come on, Sookie,' he said briskly. 'These blinds are filthy.'

'What?'

'The blinds. How could you have let them go like this?'

'What?'

'We're going to clean. Get a bucket and some ammonia and some rags. Make some coffee.'

Moving slowly and cautiously, afraid I might dry up and blow away like the bodies in the coffins, I did as he bid me.

Sam had the curtains down on the living-room windows by the time I got back with the bucket and rags.

'Where's the washing machine?'

'Back there, off the kitchen,' I said, pointing.

Sam went back to the washroom with an armful of

curtains. Gran had washed those not a month ago, for Bill's visit. I didn't say a word.

I lowered one of the blinds, closed it, and began washing. When the blinds were clean, we polished the windows themselves. It began raining about the middle of the morning. We couldn't get the outside. Sam got the long-handled dust mop and got the spider webs out of the corners of the high ceiling, and I wiped down the baseboards. He took down the mirror over the mantel, dusted the parts that we couldn't normally reach, and then we cleaned the mirror and rehung it. I cleaned the old marble fireplace till there wasn't a trace of winter's fire left. I got a pretty screen and put it over the fireplace, one painted with magnolia blossoms. I cleaned the television screen and had Sam lift it so I could dust underneath. I put all the movies back in their own boxes and labeled what I'd taped. I took all the cushions off the couch and vacuumed up the debris that had collected beneath them, finding a dollar and five cents in change. I vacuumed the carpet and used the dust mop on the wood floors.

We moved into the dining room and polished everything that could be polished. When the wood of the table and chairs was gleaming, Sam asked me how long it'd been since I'd done Gran's silver.

I hadn't ever polished Gran's silver. We opened the buffet to find that, yes, it certainly needed it. So into the kitchen we carried it, and we found the silver polish, and we polished away. The radio was on, but I gradually realized that Sam was turning it off every time the news began.

We cleaned all day. It rained all day. Sam only spoke to me to direct me to the next task.

I worked very hard. So did he.

By the time the light was growing dim, I had the cleanest house in Renard Parish.

Sam said, 'I'm going now, Sookie. I think you want to be alone.'

'Yes,' I said. 'I want to thank you some time, but I can't thank you now. You saved me today.'

I felt his lips on my forehead and then a minute later I heard the door slam. I sat at the table while the darkness began to fill the kitchen. When I almost could not see, I went outside. I took my big flashlight.

It didn't matter that it was still raining. I had on a sleeveless denim dress and a pair of sandals, what I'd pulled on that morning after Jason had called me.

I stood in the pouring warm rain, my hair plastered to my skull and my dress clinging wetly to my skin. I turned left to the woods and began to make my way through them, slowly and carefully at first. As Sam's calming influence began to evaporate, I began to run, tearing my cheeks on branches, scratching my legs on thorny vines. I came out of the woods and began to dash through the cemetery, the beam of the flashlight bobbing before me. I had thought I was going to the house on the other side, the Compton house: but then I knew Bill must be here, somewhere in this six acres of bones and stones. I stood in the center of the oldest part of the graveyard, surrounded by monuments and modest tombstones, in the company of the dead.

I screamed, 'Bill Compton! Come out now!'

I turned in circles, looking around in the near-blackness, knowing even if I couldn't see him, Bill would be able to see me, if he could see anything – if he wasn't one of those blackened, flaking atrocities I'd seen in the front yard of the house outside Monroe.

No sound. No movement except the falling of the gentle drenching rain.

'Bill! Bill! Come out!'

I felt, rather than heard, movement to my right. I turned the beam of the flashlight in that direction. The ground was buckling. As I watched, a white hand shot up from the red soil. The dirt began to heave and crumble. A figure climbed out of the ground.

'Bill?'

It moved toward me. Covered with red streaks, his hair full of dirt, Bill took a hesitant step in my direction.

I couldn't even go to him.

'Sookie,' he said, very close to me, 'why are you here?' For once, he sounded disoriented and uncertain.

I had to tell him, but I couldn't open my mouth.

'Sweetheart?'

I went down like a stone. I was abruptly on my knees in the sodden grass.

'What happened while I slept?' He was kneeling by me, bare and streaming with rain.

'You don't have clothes on,' I murmured.

'They'd just get dirty," he said sensibly. 'When I'm going to sleep in the soil, I take them off.'

'Oh. Sure.'

'Now you have to tell me.'

'You have to not hate me.'

'What have you done?'

'Oh my God, it wasn't me! But I could have warned you more, I could have grabbed you and made you listen. I tried to call you, Bill!'

'What has happened?'

I put one hand on either side of his face, touching his

skin, realizing how much I would have lost, how much I might yet lose.

'They're dead, Bill, the vampires from Monroe. And someone else with them.'

'Harlen,' he said tonelessly. 'Harlen stayed over last night, he and Diane really hit it off.' He waited for me to finish, his eyes fixed on mine.

'They were burned.'

'On purpose.'

'Yes.'

He squatted beside me in the rain, in the dark, his face not visible to me. The flashlight was gripped in my hand, and all my strength had ebbed away. I could feel his anger.

I could feel his cruelty.

I could feel his hunger.

He had never been more completely vampire. There wasn't anything human in him.

He turned his face to the sky and howled.

I thought he might kill someone, the rage rolling off him was so great. And the nearest person was me.

As I comprehended my own danger, Bill gripped my upper arms. He pulled me to him, slowly. There was no point in struggling, in fact I sensed that would only excite Bill more. Bill held me about an inch from him, I could almost smell his skin, and I could feel the turmoil in him, I could taste his rage.

Directing that energy in another way might save me. I leaned that inch, put my mouth on his chest. I licked the rain off, rubbed my cheek against his nipple, pressed myself against him.

The next moment his teeth grazed my shoulder, and his

body, hard and rigid and ready, shoved me so forcefully I was suddenly on my back in the mud. He slid directly into me as if he were trying to reach through me to the soil. I shrieked, and he growled in response, as though we were truly mud people, primitives from caves. My hands, gripping the flesh of his back, felt the rain pelting down and the blood under my nails, and his relentless movement. I thought I would be plowed into this mud, into my grave. His fangs sank into my neck.

Suddenly I came. Bill howled as he reached his own completion, and he collapsed on me, his fangs pulling out and his tongue cleaning the puncture marks.

I had thought he might kill me without even meaning to.

My muscles would not obey me, even if I had known what I wanted to do. Bill scooped me up. He took me to his house, pushing open the door and carrying me straight through into the large bathroom. Laying me gently on the carpet, where I spread mud and rainwater and a little streak of blood, Bill turned on the warm water in the spa, and when it was full he put me in and then got in himself. We sat on the seats, our legs trailing out in the warm frothing water that became discolored quickly.

Bill's eyes were staring miles away.

'All dead?' he said, his voice nearly inaudible.

'All dead, and a human girl, too,' I said quietly.

'What have you been doing all day?'

'Cleaning. Sam made me clean my house.'

'Sam,' Bill said thoughtfully. 'Tell me, Sookie. Can you read Sam's mind?'

'No,' I confessed, suddenly exhausted. I submerged my head, and when I came up, Bill had gotten the shampoo bottle. He soaped my hair and rinsed it, combed it as he had the first time we'd made love.

'Bill, I'm sorry about your friends,' I said, so exhausted I could hardly get the words out. 'And I am so glad you are alive.' I slid my arms around his neck and lay my head on his shoulder. It was hard as a rock. I remember Bill drying me off with a big white towel, and I remember thinking how soft the pillow was, and I remember him sliding into bed beside me and putting his arm around me. Then I fell into sleep.

In the small hours of the morning, I woke halfway to hear someone moving around the room. I must have been dreaming, and it must have been bad, because I woke with my heart racing. 'Bill?' I asked, and I could hear the fear in my voice.

'What's wrong?' he asked, and I felt the bed indent as he sat on the edge.

'Are you all right?'

'Yes, I was just out walking.'

'No one's out there?'

'No, sweetheart.' I could hear the sound of cloth moving over skin, and then he was under the sheets with me.

'Oh, Bill, that could have been you in one of those coffins,' I said, the agony still fresh in my mind.

'Sookie, did you ever think that could have been you in the body bag? What if they come here, to burn this house, at dawn?'

'You have to come to my house! They won't burn my house. You can be safe with me,' I said earnestly.

'Sookie, listen: because of me you could die.'

'What would I lose?' I asked, hearing the passion in my voice. 'I've had the best time since I met you, the best time of my life!'

'If I die, go to Sam.'

'Passing me along already?'

'Never,' he said, and his smooth voice was cold. 'Never.' I felt his hands grip my shoulders; he was on one elbow beside me. He scooted a little closer, and I could feel the cool length of his body.

'Listen, Bill,' I said. 'I'm not educated, but I'm not stupid. I'm not real experienced or worldly, either, but I don't think I'm naive.' I hoped he wasn't smiling in the dark. 'I can make them accept you. I can.'

'If anyone can, you will,' he said. 'I want to enter you again.'

'You mean–? Oh, yeah. I see what you mean.' He'd taken my hand and guided it down to him. 'I'd like that, too.' And I sure would, if I could survive it after the pounding I'd taken in the graveyard. Bill had been so angry that now I felt battered. But I could also feel that liquidy warm feeling running through me, that restless excitement to which Bill had addicted me. 'Honey,' I said, caressing him up and down his length, 'honey.' I kissed him, felt his tongue in my mouth. I touched his fangs with my own tongue. 'Can you do it without biting?' I whispered.

'Yes. It's just like a grand finale when I taste your blood.'

'Would it be almost as good without?'

'It can never be as good without, but I don't want to weaken you.'

'If you wouldn't mind,' I said tentatively. 'It took me a few days to feel up to par.'

'I've been selfish . . . you're just so good.'

'If I'm strong, it'll be even better,' I suggested.

'Show me how strong you are,' he said teasingly.

'Lie on your back. I'm not real sure how this works, but

I know other people do it.' I straddled him, heard his breathing quicken. I was glad the room was dark and outside the rain was still pouring. A flash of lightening showed me his eyes, glowing. I carefully maneuvered into what I hoped was the correct position, and guided him inside me. I had great faith in instinct, and sure enough it didn't play me false.

Chapter 8

Together again, my doubts at least temporarily drenched by the fear I'd felt when I'd thought I might have lost him, Bill and I settled into an uneasy routine.

If I worked nights, I would go over to Bill's house when I finished, and usually I spent the rest of the night there. If I worked days, Bill would come to my house after sunset, and we would watch TV, or go to the movies, or play Scrabble. I had to have every third night off, or Bill had to refrain from biting those nights; otherwise I began to feel weak and draggy. And there was the danger, if Bill fed on me too much . . . I kept chugging vitamins and iron until Bill complained about the flavor. Then I cut back on the iron.

When I slept at night, Bill would go do other stuff. Sometimes he read, sometimes he wandered the night; sometimes he'd go out and do my yard work under the illumination of the security lights.

If he ever took blood from anyone else, he kept it secret, and he did it far from Bon Temps, which was what I had asked.

I say this routine was uneasy because it seemed to me that we were waiting. The burning of the Monroe nest had enraged Bill and (I think) frightened him. To be so powerful when awake and so helpless when asleep had to be galling.

Both of us were wondering if public feeling against vampires would abate now that the worst troublemakers in the area were dead.

Though Bill didn't say anything directly, I knew from the course our conversation took from time to time that he was worried about my safety with the murderer of Dawn, Maudette, and my grandmother still at large.

If the men of Bon Temps and the surrounding towns thought burning out the Monroe vampires would set their minds at ease about the murders, they were wrong. Autopsy reports from the three victims finally proved they had their full complement of blood when they were killed. Furthermore, the bite marks on Maudette and Dawn had not only looked old, they were proved to be old. The cause of their deaths was strangulation. Maudette and Dawn had had sex before they'd died. And afterward.

Arlene and Charlsie and I were cautious about things like going out into the parking lot by ourselves, making sure our homes were still locked tight before we entered them, trying to notice what cars were around us as we drove. But it's hard to keep careful that way, a real strain on the nerves, and I am sure we all lapsed back into our sloppy ways. Maybe it was more excusable for Arlene and Charlsie, since they lived with other people, unlike the first two victims; Arlene with her kids (and Rene Lenier, off and on), and Charlsie with her husband, Ralph.

I was the only one who lived alone.

Jason came into the bar almost every night, and he made a point of talking to me every time. I realized he was trying to heal whatever breach lay between us, and I responded as much as I could. But Jason was drinking more, too, and his bed had as many occupants as a public toilet, though he seemed to have real feelings for Liz Barrett. We worked cautiously together on settling the business of Gran's estate and Uncle Bartlett's, though he had more to do with that than I. Uncle Bartlett had left Jason everything but my legacy.

Jason told me one night when he'd had an extra beer that he'd been back to the police station twice more, and it was driving him crazy. He'd talked to Sid Matt Lancaster, finally, and Sid Matt had advised Jason not to go to the police station any more unless Sid Matt went with him.

'How come they keep hauling you in?' I asked Jason. 'There must be something you haven't told me. Andy Bellefleur hasn't kept after anybody else, and I know Dawn and Maudette both weren't too picky about who came home with them.'

Jason looked mortified. I'd never seen my beautiful older brother look as embarrassed.

'Movies,' he mumbled.

I bent closer to be sure I'd heard him right. 'Movies?' I said, incredulously.

'Shhh,' he hissed, looking guilty as hell. 'We made movies.'

I guess I was just as embarrassed as Jason. Sisters and brothers don't need to know everything about each other. 'And you gave them a copy,' I said tentatively, trying to figure out just how dumb Jason had been.

He looked off in another direction, his hazy blue eyes romantically shiny with tears.

'Moron,' I said. 'Even allowing for the fact that you couldn't know how this was gonna come to public light what's gonna happen when you decide to get married? What if one of your ex-flames mails a copy of your little tango to your bride-to-be?'

'Thanks for kicking me when I'm down, Sis.'

I took a deep breath. 'Okay, okay. You've quit making these little videos, right?'

He nodded emphatically. I didn't believe him.

'And you told Sid Matt all about it, right?'

He nodded less firmly.

'And you think that's why Andy is on your case so much?'

'Yeah,' Jason said morosely.

'So, if they test your semen and it isn't a match for what was inside Maudette and Dawn, you're clear.' By now, I was as shifty-faced as my brother. We had never talked about semen samples before.

'That's what Sid Matt says. I just don't trust that stuff.'

My brother didn't trust the most reliable scientific evidence that could be presented in a court. 'You think Andy's going to fake the results?'

'No, Andy's okay. He's just doing his job. I just don't know about that DNA stuff.'

'Moron,' I said, and turned away to get another pitcher of beer for four guys from Ruston, college students on a big night out in the boonies. I could only hope Sid Matt Lancaster was good at persuasion.

I spoke to Jason once more before he left Merlotte's. 'Can you help me?' he asked, turning up to me a face I hardly recognized. I was standing by his table, and his date for the night had gone to the ladies' room.

My brother had never asked me for help before.

'How?'

'Can't you just read the minds of the men who come in here and find out if one of them did it?'

'That's not as easy as it sounds, Jason,' I said slowly, thinking as I went along. 'For one thing, the man would have to be thinking of his crime while he sat here, at the exact moment I listened in. For another thing, I can't always read clear thoughts. Some people, it's just like listening to a radio, I can hear every little thing. Other people, I just get a mass of feelings, not spelled out; it's like hearing someone talk in their sleep, see? You can hear they're talking, you can tell if they're upset or happy, but you can't hear the exact words. And then other times, I can hear a thought, but I can't trace it to its source if the room is crowded.'

Jason was staring at me. It was the first time we had talked openly about my disability.

'How do you stop from going crazy?' he asked, shaking his head in amazement.

I was about to try to explain putting up my guard, but Liz Barrett returned to the table, newly lipsticked and fluffed. I watched Jason resume his woman-hunting persona like shrugging on a heavy coat, and I regretted not getting to talk to him more when he was by himself.

That night, as the staff got ready to leave, Arlene asked me if I could baby-sit for her the next evening. It would be an off-day for both of us, and she wanted to go to Shreveport with Rene to see a movie and go out to eat.

'Sure!' I said. 'I haven't kept the kids in a while.'

Suddenly Arlene's face froze. She half-turned to me, opened her mouth, thought the better of speaking, then thought again. 'Will . . . ah . . . will Bill be there?'

'Yes, we'd planned on watching a movie. I was going to stop by the video rental place, tomorrow morning. But I'll get something for the kids to watch instead.' Abruptly, I caught her meaning. 'Whoa. You mean you don't want to leave the kids with me if Bill's gonna be there?' I could feel my eyes narrow to slits and my voice drop down to its angry register.

'Sookie,' she began helplessly, 'honey, I love you. But you can't understand, you're not a mother. I can't leave my kids with a vampire. I just can't.'

'No matter that I'm there, and I love your kids, too? No matter that Bill would never in a million years harm a child.' I slung my purse over my shoulder and stalked out the back door, leaving Arlene standing there looking torn. By golly, she ought to be upset!

I was a little calmer by the time I turned onto the road to go home, but I was still riled up. I was worried about Jason, miffed at Arlene, and almost permanently frosted at Sam, who was pretending these days that I was a mere acquaintance. I debated whether to just go home rather than going to Bill's, decided that was a good idea.

It was a measure of how much he worried about me that Bill was at my house about fifteen minutes after I should have been at his.

'You didn't come, you didn't call,' he said quietly when I answered the door.

'I'm in a temper,' I said. 'A bad one.'

Wisely he kept his distance.

'I apologize for making you worry,' I said after a moment. 'I won't do that again.' I strode away from him, toward the kitchen. He followed behind, or at least I presumed he did. Bill was so quiet you never knew until you looked.

He leaned against the door frame as I stood in the middle of the kitchen floor, wondering why I'd come in the room, feeling a rising tide of anger. I was getting pissed off all over again. I really wanted to throw something, damage something. This was not the way I'd been brought up, to give way to destructive impulses like that. I contained it, screwing my eyes shut, clenching my fists.

'I'm gonna dig a hole,' I said, and I marched out the back door. I opened the door to the tool shed, removed the shovel, and stomped to the back of the yard. There was a patch back there where nothing ever grew, I don't know why. I sunk the shovel in, pushed it with my foot, came up with a hunk of soil. I kept on going. The pile of dirt grew as the hole deepened.

'I have excellent arm and shoulder muscles,' I said, resting against the shovel and panting.

Bill was sitting in a lawn chair watching. He didn't say anything.

I resumed digging.

Finally, I had a really nice hole.

'Were you going to bury anything?' Bill asked, when he could tell I was done.

'No.' I looked down at the cavity in the ground. 'I'm going to plant a tree.'

'What kind?'

'A live oak,' I said off the top of my head.

'Where can you get one?'

'At the Garden Center. I'll go sometime this week.'

'They take a long time to grow.'

'What difference would that make to you?' I snapped. I put the shovel up in the shed, then leaned against it, suddenly exhausted.

Bill made as if to pick me up.

'I am a *grown woman*,' I snarled. 'I can walk into the house on my own.'

'Have I done something to you?' Bill asked. There was very little loving in his voice, and I was brought up short. I had indulged myself enough.

'I apologize,' I said. 'Again.'

'What has made you so angry?'

I just couldn't tell him about Arlene.

'What do you do when you get mad, Bill?'

'I tear up a tree,' he said. 'Sometimes I hurt someone.'

Digging a hole didn't seem so bad. It had been sort of constructive. But I was still wired – it was just more of a subdued buzz than a high-frequency whine. I cast around restlessly for something to affect.

Bill seemed adept at reading the symptoms. 'Make love,' he suggested. 'Make love with me.'

'I'm not in the right mood for love.'

'Let me try to persuade you.'

It turned out he could.

At least it wore off the excess energy of anger, but I still had a residue of sadness that sex couldn't cure. Arlene had hurt my feelings. I stared into space while Bill braided my hair, a pastime that he apparently found soothing.

Every now and then I felt like I was Bill's doll.

'Jason was in the bar tonight,' I said.

'What did he want?'

Bill was too clever by far, sometimes, at reading people.

'He appealed to my mind-reading powers. He wanted me to scan the minds of the men who came into the bar until I found out who the murderer was.'

'Except for a few dozen flaws, that's not a bad idea.'

'You think?'

'Both your brother and I will be regarded with less suspicion if the murderer is in jail. And you'll be safe.'

'That's true, but I don't know how to go about it. It would be hard, and painful, and boring, to wade through all that stuff trying to find a little bit of information, a flash of thought.'

'Not any more painful or hard than being suspected of murder. You're just accustomed to keeping your gift locked up.'

'Do you think so?' I began to turn to look at his face, but he held me still so he could finish braiding. I'd never seen keeping out of people's minds as selfish, but in this case I supposed it was. I would have to invade a lot of privacy. 'A detective,' I murmured, trying to see myself in a better light than just nosey.

'Sookie,' Bill said, and something in his voice made me take notice. 'Eric has told me to bring you to Shreveport again.'

It took me a second to remember who Eric was. 'Oh, the big Viking vampire?'

'The very old vampire,' Bill said precisely.

'You mean, he ordered you to bring me there?' I didn't like the sound of this at all. I'd been sitting on the side of the bed, Bill behind me, and now I turned to look in his face. This time he didn't stop me. I stared at Bill, seeing something in his face that I'd never seen before. 'You *have* to do this,' I said, appalled. I could not imagine someone giving Bill an order. 'But honey, I don't want to go see Eric.'

I could see that made no difference.

'What is he, the Godfather of vampires?' I asked, angry

and incredulous. 'Did he give you an offer you couldn't refuse?'

'He is older than me. More to the point, he is stronger.'

'Nobody's stronger than you,' I said stoutly.

'I wish you were right.'

'So is he the head of Vampire Region Ten, or something?'

'Yes. Something like that.'

Bill was always closemouthed about how vampires controlled their own affairs. That had been fine with me, until now.

'What does he want? What will happen if I don't go?'

Bill just sidestepped the first question. 'He'll send someone – several someones – to get you.'

'Other vampires.'

'Yes.' Bill's eyes were opaque, shining with his difference, brown and rich.

I tried to think this through. I wasn't used to being ordered around. I wasn't used to no choices at all. It took my thick skull several minutes to evaluate the situation.

'So, you'd feel obliged to fight them?'

'Of course. You are mine.'

There was that 'mine' again. It seemed he really meant it. I sure felt like whining, but I knew it wouldn't do any good.

'I guess I have to go,' I said, trying not to sound bitter. 'This is just plain old blackmail.'

'Sookie, vampires *aren't like humans*. Eric is using the best means to achieve his goal, which is getting you to Shreveport.' He didn't have to spell all this out; I understood it.

'Well, I understand it now, but I hate it. I'm between a rock and hard place! What does he want me for, anyway?'

An obvious answer popped right into my mind, and I looked at Bill, horrified. 'Oh, no, I won't do that!'

'He won't have sex with you or bite you, not without killing me.' Bill's glowing face lost all vestiges of familiarity and became utterly alien.

'And he knows that,' I said tentatively, 'so there must be another reason he wants me in Shreveport.'

'Yes,' Bill agreed, 'but I don't know what it is.'

'Well, if it doesn't have to do with my physical charms, or the unusual quality of my blood, it must have to do with my . . . little quirk.'

'Your gift.'

'Right,' I said, sarcasm dripping from my voice. 'My precious gift.' All the anger I thought I'd eased off my shoulders came back to sit like a four-hundred-pound gorilla. And I was scared to death. I wondered how Bill felt. I was even scared to ask that.

'When?' I asked instead.

'Tomorrow night.'

'I guess this is the downside of nontraditional dating.' I stared over Bill's shoulder at the pattern of the wallpaper my grandmother had chosen ten years ago. I promised myself that if I got through this, I would repaper.

'I love you.' His voice was just a whisper.

This wasn't Bill's fault. 'I love you, too,' I said. I had to stop myself from begging, Please don't let the bad vampire hurt me, please don't let the vampire rape me. If I was between a rock and a hard place, Bill was doubly so. I couldn't even begin to estimate the self-control he was employing. Unless he really was calm? Could a vampire face pain and this form of helplessness without some inner turmoil?

I searched his face, the familiar clear lines and white

matte complexion, the dark arches of his brows and proud line of his nose. I observed that Bill's fangs were only slightly extended, and rage and lust ran them full out.

'Tonight,' he said. 'Sookie . . .' His hands began urging me, to lie beside him.

'What?'

'Tonight, I think, you should drink from me.'

I made a face. 'Ick! Don't you need all your strength for tomorrow night? I'm not hurt.'

'How have you felt since you drank from me? Since I put my blood inside you?'

I mulled it over. 'Good,' I admitted.

'Have you been sick?'

'No, but then I almost never am.'

'Have you had more energy?'

'When you weren't taking it back!' I said tartly, but I could feel my lips curve up in a little smile.

'Have you been stronger?'

'I – yes, I guess I have.' I realized for the first time how extraordinary it was that I'd carried in a new chair, by myself, the week before.

'Has it been easier to control your power?'

'Yes, I did notice that.' I'd written it off to increased relaxation.

'If you drink from me tonight, tomorrow night you will have more resources.'

'But you'll be weaker.'

'If you don't take much, I'll recoup during the day when I sleep. And I may have to find someone else to drink from tomorrow night before we go.'

My face filled with hurt. Suspecting he was doing it and knowing were sure two different things.

'Sookie, this is for us. No sex with anyone else, I promise you.'

'You really think all this is necessary.'

'Maybe necessary. At least helpful. And we need all the help we can get.'

'Oh, all right. How do we do this?' I had only the haziest recollection of the night of the beating, and I was glad of it.

He looked at me quizzically. I had the impression he was amused. 'Aren't you excited, Sookie?'

'At drinking blood from you? Excuse me, that's not my turn-on.'

He shook his head, as if that was beyond his understanding. 'I forget,' he said simply. 'I forget how it is to be otherwise. Would you prefer neck, wrist, groin?'

'Not groin,' I said hastily. 'I don't know, Bill. Yuck. Whichever.'

'Neck,' he said. 'Lie on top of me, Sookie.'

'That's like sex.'

'It's the easiest way.'

So I straddled him and gently let myself down. This felt very peculiar. This was a position we used for lovemaking and nothing else.

'Bite, Sookie,' he whispered.

'I can't do that!' I protested.

'Bite, or I'll have to use a knife.'

'My teeth aren't sharp like yours.'

'They're sharp enough.'

'I'll hurt you.'

He laughed silently. I could feel his chest moving beneath me.

'Damn.' I breathed, and steeling myself, I bit his neck. I

did a good job because there was no sense prolonging this. I tasted the metallic blood in my mouth. Bill groaned softly, and his hands brushed my back and continued down. His fingers found me.

I gave a gasp of shock.

'Drink,' he said raggedly, and I sucked hard. He groaned, louder, deeper, and I felt him pressing against me. A little ripple of madness went through me, and I attached myself to him like a barnacle, and he entered me, began moving, his hands now gripping my hip bones. I drank and saw visions, visions all with a background of darkness, of white things coming up from the ground and going hunting, the thrill of the run through the woods, the prey panting ahead and the excitement of its fear; pursuit, legs pumping, hearing the thrumming of blood through the veins of the pursued . . .

Bill made a noise deep in his chest and convulsed inside me. I raised my head from his neck, and a wave of dark delight carried me out to sea.

This was pretty exotic stuff for a telepathic barmaid from northern Louisiana.

Chapter 9

I was getting ready by sunset the next day. Bill had said he was going to feed somewhere before we went, and as upset as the idea made me, I had to agree it made sense. He was right about how I'd feel after my little informal vitamin supplement the night before, too. I felt super. I felt very strong, very alert, very quick-witted, and oddly enough, I also felt very pretty.

What would I wear for my own little interview with a vampire? I didn't want to look like I was trying to be sexy, but I didn't want to make a fool of myself by wearing a shapeless gunnysack, either. Blue jeans seemed to be the answer, as they so often are. I put on white sandals and a pale blue scoop-neck tee. I hadn't worn it since I'd started seeing Bill because it exposed his fang marks. But Bill's 'ownership' of me, I figured, could not be too strongly reinforced tonight. Remembering the cop last time checking my neck. I tucked a scarf in my purse. I thought again and added a silver necklace. I brushed my hair, which seemed at least three shades lighter, and let it ripple down my back.

Just when I was really having to struggle with picturing Bill with somebody else, he knocked. I opened the door and we stood looking at each other for a minute. His lips had more color than normal, so he'd done it. I bit my own lips to keep from saying anything.

'You did change,' he said first.

'You think anyone else'll be able to tell?' I hoped not.

'I don't know.' He held out his hand, and we walked to his car. He opened my door, and I brushed by him to climb in. I stiffened.

'What's wrong?' he asked, after a moment.

'Nothing,' I said, trying to keep my voice even, and I sat in the passenger's seat and stared straight ahead of me.

I told myself I might as well be mad at the cow who had given him his hamburger. But somehow the simile just didn't work.

'You smell different,' I said after we'd been on the highway for a few minutes. We drove for a few minutes in silence.

'Now you know how I will feel if Eric touches you,' he told me. 'But I think I'll feel worse because Eric will enjoy touching you, and I didn't much enjoy my feeding.'

I figured that wasn't totally, strictly, true: I know I always enjoy eating even if I'm not served my favorite food. But I appreciated the sentiment.

We didn't talk much. We were both worried about what was ahead of us. All too soon, we were parking at Fangtasia again, but this time in the back. As Bill held open the car door, I had to fight an impulse to cling to the seat and refuse to get out. Once I made myself emerge, I had another struggle involving my intense desire to hide behind Bill. I gave a kind of gasp, took his arm, and we walked to the door like we were going to a party we were anticipating with pleasure.

Bill looked down at me with approval.

I fought an urge to scowl at him.

He knocked on the metal door with FANGTASIA stencilled on it. We were in a service and delivery alley that ran behind all the stores in the little strip mall. There were several other cars parked back there, Eric's sporty red convertible among them. All the vehicles were high-priced.

You won't find a vampire in a Ford Fiesta.

Bill knocked, three quick, two spaced apart. The Secret Vampire Knock, I guess. Maybe I'd get to learn the Secret Handshake.

The beautiful blond vampire opened the door, the female who'd been at the table with Eric when I'd been to the bar before. She stood back without speaking to let us enter.

If Bill had been human, he would have protested at how tightly I was holding his hand.

The female was in front of us more quickly than my eyes could follow, and I started. Bill wasn't surprised at all, naturally. She led us through a storeroom disconcertingly similar to Merlotte's and into a little corridor. We went through the door on our right.

Eric was in the small room, his presence dominating it. Bill didn't exactly kneel to kiss his ring, but he did nod kind of deep. There was another vampire in the room, the bartender, Long Shadow; he was in fine form tonight, in a skinny-strap tee and weight-lifting pants, all in deep green.

'Bill, Sookie,' Eric greeted us. 'Bill, you and Sookie know Long Shadow. Sookie, you remember Pam.' Pam was the blond female. 'And this is Bruce.'

Bruce was a human, the most frightened human I'd ever seen. I had considerable sympathy with that. Middle-aged and paunchy, Bruce had thinning dark hair that curved in stiff waves across his scalp. He was jowly and small-mouthed. He was wearing a nice suit, beige, with a white shirt and a brown-and-navy patterned tie. He was sweating heavily. He was in a straight chair across the desk from Eric. Naturally, Eric was in the power chair. Pam and Long Shadow were standing against the wall across from Eric, by the door. Bill took his place beside them, but as I moved to join him, Eric spoke again.

'Sookie, listen to Bruce.'

I stood staring at Bruce for a second, waiting for him to speak, until I understood what Eric meant.

'What exactly am I listening for?' I asked, knowing my voice was sharp.

'Someone has embezzled about sixty thousand dollars from us,' Eric explained.

Boy, somebody had a death wish.

'And rather than put all our human employees to death or torture, we thought perhaps you would look into their minds and tell us who it was.'

He said 'death or torture' as calmly as I said, 'Bud or Old Milwaukee.'

'And then what will you do?' I asked.

Eric seemed surprised.

'Whoever it is will give our money back,' he said simply.

'And then?'

His big blue eyes narrowed as he stared at me.

'Why, if we can produce proof of the crime, we'll turn the culprit over to the police,' he said smoothly.

Liar, liar, pants on fire. 'I'll make a deal, Eric,' I said, not bothering to smile. Winsome did not count with Eric, and he was far from any desire to jump my bones. At the moment.

He smiled, indulgently. 'What would that be, Sookie?'

'If you really do turn the guilty person over to the police I'll do this for you again, whenever you want.'

Eric cocked an eyebrow.

'Yeah, I know I'd probably have to anyway. But isn't it better if I come willing, if we have good faith with each other?' I broke into a sweat. I could not believe I was bargaining with a vampire.

Eric actually seemed to be thinking that over. And suddenly, I was in his thoughts. He was thinking he could make me do what he wanted, anywhere, anytime, just by threatening Bill or some human I loved. But he wanted to mainstream, to keep as legal as he could, to keep his relations with humans aboveboard, or at least as aboveboard as vampire-human dealings could be. He didn't want to kill anyone if he didn't have to.

It was like suddenly being plunged into a pit of snakes, cold snakes, lethal snakes. It was only a flash, a slice of his mind, sort of, but it left me facing a whole new reality.

'Besides,' I said quickly, before he could see I'd been inside his head, 'how sure are you that the thief is a human?'

Pam and Long Shadow both moved suddenly, but Eric flooded the room with his presence, commanding them to be still.

'That's an interesting idea,' he said. 'Pam and Long Shadow are my partners in this bar, and if none of the humans is guilty, I guess we'll have to look at them.'

'Just a thought,' I said meekly, and Eric looked at me

with the glacial blue eyes of a being who hardly remembers what humanity was like.

'Start now, with this man,' he commanded.

I knelt by Bruce's chair, trying to decide how to proceed. I'd never tried to formalize something that was pretty chancy. Touching would help; direct contact clarified the transmission, so to speak. I took Bruce's hand, found that too personal (and too sweaty) and pushed back his coat cuff. I took hold of his wrist. I looked into his small eyes.

I didn't take the money, who took it, what crazy fool would put us in danger like this, what will Lillian do if they kill me, and Bobby and Heather, why did I work for vampires anyway, it's sheer greed, and I'm paying for it, God I'll never work for these things again how can this crazy woman find out who took the fucking money why doesn't she let go of me what is she is she a vampire, too, or some kind of demon her eyes are so strange I should have found out earlier that the money was missing and found out who took it before I even said anything to Eric . . .

'Did you take the money?' I breathed, though I was sure I already knew the answer.

'No,' Bruce groaned, sweat running down his face, and his thoughts, his reaction to the question, confirmed what I'd heard already.

'Do you know who did?'

'I wish.'

I stood, turned to Eric, shook my head. 'Not this guy,' I said.

Pam escorted poor Bruce out, brought the next interrogee.

My subject was a barmaid, dressed in trailing black with lots of cleavage on display, her ragged strawberry blond hair straggling down her back. Of course, working at Fangtasia would be a dream job for a fang-banger, and this gal had the scars to prove she enjoyed her perks. She was confident enough to grin at Eric, foolish enough to take the wooden chair with some confidence, even crossing her legs like Sharon Stone – she hoped. She was surprised to see a strange vampire and a new woman in the room, and not pleased by my presence, though Bill made her lick her lips.

'Hey, sweetie,' she said to Eric, and I decided she must have no imagination at all.

'Ginger, answer this woman's questions,' Eric said. His voice was like a stone wall, flat and implacable.

Ginger seemed to understand for the first time that this was a time to be serious. She crossed her ankles this time, sat with her hands on the tops of her thighs, and assumed a stern face. 'Yes, master,' she said, and I thought I was going to barf.

She waved an imperious hand at me, as if to say, 'Begin fellow vampire server.' I reached down for her wrist, and she flung my hand away. 'Don't touch me,' she said, almost hissing.

It was such an extreme reaction that the vampires tensed up, and I could feel that crackling the air in the room.

'Pam, hold Ginger still,' Eric commanded, and Pam appeared silently behind Ginger's chair, leaning over and putting her hands on Ginger's upper arms. You could tell Ginger struggled some because her head moved around, but Pam held her upper body in a grip that kept the girl's body absolutely immobile.

My fingers circled her wrist. 'Did you take the money?' I asked, staring into Ginger's flat brown eyes.

She screamed, then, long and loud. She began to curse

me. I listened to the chaos in the girl's tiny brain. It was like trying to walk over a bombed site.

'She knows who did,' I said to Eric. Ginger fell silent then, though she was sobbing. 'She can't say the name,' I told the blond vampire. 'He has bitten her.' I touched the scars on Ginger's neck as if that needed more illustration. 'It's some kind of compulsion,' I reported, after I'd tried again. 'She can't even picture him.'

'Hypnosis,' Pam commented. Her proximity to the frightened girl had made Pam's fangs run out. 'A strong vampire.'

'Bring in her closest friend,' I suggested.

Ginger was shaking like a leaf by then with thoughts she was compelled not to think pressing her from their locked closet.

'Should she stay, or go?' Pam asked me directly.

'She should go. It'll only scare someone else.'

I was so into this, so into openly using my strange ability, that I didn't look at Bill. I felt that somehow if I looked at him, it would weaken me. I knew where he was, that he and Long Shadow had not moved since the questioning had begun.

Pam hauled the trembling Ginger away. I don't know what she did with the barmaid, but she returned with another waitress in the same kind of clothes. This woman's name was Belinda, and she was older and wiser. Belinda had brown hair, glasses, and the sexiest pouting mouth I'd ever seen.

'Belinda, what vampire has Ginger been seeing?' Eric asked smoothly once Belinda was seated, and I was touching her. The waitress had enough sense to accept the process quietly, enough intelligence to realize she had to be honest.

'Anyone that would have her,' Belinda said bluntly.

I saw an image in Belinda's mind, but she had to think the name.

'Which one from here?' I asked suddenly, and then I had the name. My eyes sought his corner before I could open my mouth, and then he was on me, Long Shadow, vaulting over the chair holding Belinda to land on top of me as I crouched in front of her. I was bowled over backward into Eric's desk, and only my upflung arms saved me from his teeth sinking into my throat and ripping it out. He bit my forearm savagely, and I screamed; at least I tried to, but with so little air left from the impact it was more like an alarmed choking noise.

I was only conscious of the heavy figure on top of me and the pain of my arm, my own fear. I hadn't been frightened that the Rats were going to kill me until almost too late, but I understood that to keep his name from leaving my lips, Long Shadow was ready to kill me instantly, and when I heard the awful noise and felt his body press even harder on me I didn't have any idea what it meant. I'd been able to see his eyes over the top of my arm. They were wide, brown, crazed, icy. Suddenly they dulled and seemed to almost flatten. Blood gushed out of Long Shadow's mouth, bathing my arm. It flowed into my open mouth, and I gagged. His teeth relaxed, and his face fell in on itself. It began to wrinkle. His eyes turned into gelatinous pools. Handfuls of his thick black hair fell on my face.

I was shocked beyond moving. Hands gripped my shoulders and began pulling me out from under the decaying corpse. I pushed with my feet to scrabble back faster.

There wasn't an odor, but there was gunk, black and streaky, and the absolute horror and disgust of watching

Long Shadow deconstruct with incredible speed. There was a stake sticking out of his back. Eric stood watching, as we all were, but he had a mallet in his hand. Bill was behind me, having pulled me out from under Long Shadow. Pam was standing by the door, her hand gripping Belinda's arm. The waitress looked as rocky as I must have.

Even the gunk began to vanish in smoke. We all stood frozen until the last wisp was gone. The carpet had a kind of scorched mark on it.

'You'll have to get you an area rug,' I said, completely out of the blue. Honest to God, I couldn't stand the silence any more.

'Your mouth is bloody,' Eric said. All the vampires had fully extended fangs. They'd gotten pretty excited.

'He bled onto me.'

'Did any go down your throat?'

'Probably. What does that mean?'

'That remains to be seen,' Pam said. Her voice was dark and husky. She was eyeing Belinda in a way that would have made me distinctly nervous, but Belinda seemed to be preening, incredibly. 'Usually,' Pam went on, her eyes on Belinda's pouty lips, 'we drink from humans, not the other way around.'

Eric was looking at me with interest, the same kind of interest that Pam had in Belinda. 'How do things look to you now, Sookie?' he asked in such a smooth voice you'd never think he'd just executed an old friend.

How *did* things look to me now? Brighter. Sounds were clearer, and I could hear better. I wanted to turn and look at Bill, but I was scared to take my eyes off Eric.

'Well, I guess Bill and me'll go now,' I said, as if no other process was possible. 'I did that for you, Eric, and now we get to go. No retaliation for Ginger and Belinda and Bruce, okay? We agreed.' I started toward the door with an assurance I was far from feeling. 'I'll just bet you need to go see how the bar is doing, huh? Who's mixing the drinks, tonight?'

'We got a substitute,' Eric said absently, his eyes never leaving my neck. 'You smell different, Sookie,' he murmured, taking a step closer.

'Well, remember now, Eric, we had a deal,' I reminded him, my smile broad and tense, my voice snapping with good cheer. 'Bill and I are going home now, aren't we?' I risked a glance behind me at Bill. My heart sank. His eyes were open wide, unblinking, his lips drawn back in a silent snarl to expose his extended fangs. His pupils were dilated enormously. He was staring at Eric.

'Pam, get out of the way,' I said, quietly but sharply. Once Pam was distracted from her own blood lust, she evaluated the situation in one glance. She swung open the office door and propelled Belinda through it, stood beside it to usher us out. 'Call Ginger,' I suggested, and the sense of what I was saying penetrated Pam's fog of desire. 'Ginger,' she called hoarsely, and the blond girl stumbled from a door down the hall. 'Eric wants you,' Pam told her. Ginger's face lit up like she had a date with David Duchovny, and she was in the room and rubbing against Eric almost as fast as a vampire could have. As if he'd woken from a spell, Eric looked down at Ginger when she ran her hands up his chest. As he bent to kiss her, Eric looked at me over her head. 'I'll see you again,' he said, and I pulled Bill out the door as quick as a wink. Bill didn't want to go. It was like trying to tow a log. But once we were out in the hall he seemed to be a little more aware of the need to get out of there, and we hurried from Fangtasia and got into Bill's car.

I looked down at myself. I was bloodstained and wrinkled, and I smelled funny. Yuck. I looked over at Bill to share my disgust with him, but he was looking at me in an unmistakable way.

'No,' I said forcefully. 'You start this car and get out of here before anything else happens, Bill Compton. I tell you flat, I'm not in the mood.'

He scooted across the seat toward me, his arms scooping me up before I could say anything else. Then his mouth was on mine, and after a second his tongue began licking the blood from my face.

I was really scared. I was also really angry. I grabbed his ears and pulled his head away from mine using every ounce of strength I possessed, which happened to be more than I thought I had.

His eyes were still like caves with ghosts dwelling in their depths.

'Bill!' I shrieked. I shook him. 'Snap out of it!'

Slowly, his personality seeped back into his eyes. He drew a shuddering sigh. He kissed me lightly on the lips.

'Okay, can we go home now?' I asked, ashamed that my voice was so quavery.

'Sure,' he said, sounding none too steady himself.

'Was that like sharks scenting blood?' I asked, after a fifteen-minute silent drive that almost had us out of Shreveport.

'Good analogy.'

He didn't need to apologize. He'd been doing what nature dictated, as least as natural as vampires got. He didn't bother to. I would kind of liked to have heard an apology.

'So, am I in trouble?' I asked finally. It was two in the morning, and I found the question didn't bother me as much as it should have.

'Eric will hold you to your word,' Bill said. 'As to whether he will leave you alone personally, I don't know. I wish . . .' but his voice trailed off. It was the first time I'd heard Bill wish for anything.

'Sixty thousand dollars isn't a lot of money to a vampire, surely,' I observed. 'You all seem to have plenty of money.'

'Vampires rob their victims, of course,' Bill said matter-of-factly. 'Early on, we take the money from the corpse. Later, when we're more experienced, we can exert enough control to persuade a human to give us money willingly, then forget it's been done. Some of us hire money managers, some of us go into real estate, some of us live on the interest from our investments. Eric and Pam went in together on the bar. Eric put up most of the money, Pam the rest. They had known Long Shadow for a hundred years, and they hired him to be bartender. He betrayed them.'

'Why would he steal from them?'

'He must have had some venture he needed the capital for,' Bill said absently. 'And he was in a mainstreaming position. He couldn't just go out and kill a bank manager after hypnotizing him and persuading the man to give him the money. So he took it from Eric.'

'Wouldn't Eric have loaned it to him?'

'If Long Shadow hadn't been too proud to ask, yes,' Bill said.

We had another long silence. Finally I said, 'I always think of vampires as smarter than humans, but they're not, huh?'

'Not always,' he agreed.

When we reached the outskirts of Bon Temps, I asked Bill to drop me off at home. He looked sideways at me, but didn't say anything. Maybe vampires were smarter than humans, after all.

Chapter 10

The next day, when I was getting ready for work, I realized I was definitely off vampires for a while. Even Bill.

I was ready to remind myself I was a human.

The trouble was, I had to notice that I was a changed human.

It wasn't anything major. After the first infusion of Bill's blood on the night the Rats had beaten me, I'd felt healed, healthy, stronger. But not markedly different. Maybe more – well, sexier.

After my second draft of Bill's blood, I'd felt really strong, and I'd been braver because I'd had more confidence. I felt more secure in my sexuality and its power. It seemed apparent I was handling my disability with more aplomb and capability.

I'd had Long Shadow's blood by accident. The next morning, looking in the mirror, my teeth were whiter and sharper. My hair looked lighter and livelier, and my eyes were brighter. I looked like a poster girl for good hygiene, or some healthy cause like taking vitamins or drinking milk. The savage bite on my arm (Long Shadow's last bite on this earth, I realized) was not completely healed, but it was well on its way.

Then my purse spilled as I picked it up, and my change rolled under the couch. I held up the end of the couch with one hand while with the other I retrieved the coins.

Whoa.

I straightened and took a deep breath. At least the sunlight didn't hurt my eyes, and I didn't want to bite everyone I saw. I'd enjoyed my breakfast toast, rather than longing for tomato juice. I wasn't turning into a vampire. Maybe I was sort of an enhanced human?

Life had sure been simpler when I hadn't dated.

When I got to Merlotte's, everything was ready except for slicing the lemons and limes. We served the fruit both with mixed drinks and with tea, and I got out the cutting board and a sharp knife. Lafayette was tying on his apron as I got the lemons from the big refrigerator.

'You highlighted your hair, Sookie?'

I shook my head. Under the enveloping white apron, Lafayette was a symphony of color; he was wearing a fuschia thin-strap tee, dark purple jeans, red thong sandals, and he had sort of raspberry eye shadow on.

'It sure looks lighter,' he said skeptically, raising his own plucked brows.

'I've been out in the sun a lot,' I assured him. Dawn had never gotten along with Lafayette, whether because he was black or because he was gay, I didn't know . . . maybe both. Arlene and Charlsie just accepted the cook, but didn't go out of their ways to be friendly. But I'd always kind of liked Lafayette because he conducted what had to be a tough life with verve and grace.

I looked down at the cutting board. All the lemons had been quartered. All the limes had been sliced. My hand was holding the knife, and it was wet with juices. I had done it without knowing it. In about thirty seconds. I closed my eyes. My God.

When I opened them, Lafayette was staring from my face to my hands.

'Tell me I didn't just see that, girlfriend,' he suggested.

'You didn't,' I said. My voice was cool and level, I was surprised to note. 'Excuse me, I got to put these away.' I put the fruit in separate containers in the big cooler behind the bar where Sam kept the beer. When I shut the door, Sam was standing there, his arms crossed across his chest. He didn't look happy.

'Are you all right?' he asked. His bright blue eyes scanned me up and down. 'You do something to your hair?' he said uncertainly.

I laughed. I realized that my guard had slid into place easily, that it didn't have to be a painful process. 'Been out in the sun,' I said.

'What happened to your arm?'

I looked down at my right forearm. I'd covered the bite with a bandage.

'Dog bit me.'

'Had it had its shots?'

'Sure.'

I looked up at Sam, not too far, and it seemed to me his wiry, curly, red-blond hair snapped with energy. It seemed to me I could hear his heart beating. I could feel his uncertainty, his desire. My body responded instantly. I focussed on his thin lips, and the rich smell of his aftershave filled my lungs. He moved two inches closer. I could feel the breath going in and out of his lungs. I knew his penis was stiffening.

Then Charlsie Tooten came in the front door and slammed it behind her. We both took a step away from each other. Thank God for Charlsie, I thought. Plump, dumb, good-natured, and hardworking, Charlsie was a dream employee. Married to Ralph, her high school sweetheart, who worked at one of the chicken processing plants, Charlsie had a girl in the eleventh grade and a married daughter. Charlsie loved to work at the bar so she could get out and see people, and she had a knack for dealing with drunks that got them out the door without a fight.

'Hi, you two!' she called cheerfully. Her dark brown hair (L'Oreal, Lafayette said) was pulled back dramatically to hang from the crown of her head in a cascade of ringlets. Her blouse was spotless and the pockets of her shorts gaped since the contents were too packed. Charlsie was wearing sheer black support hose and Keds, and her artificial nails were a sort of burgundy red.

'That girl of mine is expecting. Just call me Grandma!' she said, and I could tell Charlsie was happy as a clam. I gave her the expected hug, and Sam patted her on the shoulder. We were both glad to see her.

'When is the baby due?' I asked, and Charlsie was off and running. I didn't have to say anything for the next five minutes. Then Arlene trailed in, makeup inexpertly covering the hickeys on her neck, and she listened to everything all over again. Once my eyes met Sam's, and after a little moment, we looked away simultaneously.

Then we began serving the lunchtime crowd, and the incident was over.

Most people didn't drink much at lunchtime, maybe a

beer or a glass of wine. A hefty proportion just had iced tea or water. The lunch crowd consisted of people who happened to be close to Merlotte's when the lunch hour came, people who were regulars and thought of it naturally, and the local alcoholics for whom their lunchtime drink was maybe the third or fourth. As I began to take orders, I remembered my brother's plea.

I listened in all day, and it was gruelling. I'd never spent the day listening; I'd never let my guard down for so long. Maybe it wasn't as painful as it had been; maybe I felt cooler about what I was hearing. Sheriff Bud Dearborn was sitting at a table with the mayor, my grandmother's friend Sterling Norris. Mr. Norris patted me on the shoulder, standing up to do so, and I realized it was the first time I'd seen him since Gran's funeral.

'How are you doing, Sookie?' he asked in a sympathetic voice. He was looking poorly, himself.

'Just great, Mr. Norris. Yourself?'

'I'm an old man, Sookie,' he said with an uncertain smile. He didn't even wait for me to protest. 'These murders are wearing me down. We haven't had a murder in Bon Temps since Darryl Mayhew shot Sue Mayhew. And there wasn't no mystery about that.'

'That was . . . what? Six years ago?' I asked the sheriff, just to keep standing there. Mr. Norris was feeling so sad at seeing me because he was thinking my brother was going to be arrested for murder, for killing Maudette Pickens, and the mayor reckoned that meant Jason had most likely also killed Gran. I ducked my head to hide my eyes.

'I guess so. Let's see, I remember we were dressed up for Jean-Anne's dance recital . . . so that was . . . yes, you're right, Sookie, six years ago.' The sheriff nodded at me with approval. 'Jason been in today?' he asked casually, as if it were a mere afterthought.

'No, haven't seen him,' I said. The sheriff told me he wanted iced tea and a hamburger; and he was thinking of the time he'd caught Jason with his Jean-Anne, making out like crazy in the bed of Jason's pickup truck.

Oh, Lord. He was thinking Jean-Anne was lucky she hadn't been strangled. And then he had a clear thought that cut me to the quick: Sheriff Dearborn thought, These girls are all bottom-feeders, anyway.

I could read his thought in its context because the sheriff happened to be an easy scan. I could feel the nuances of the idea. He was thinking, 'Low-skill jobs, no college, screwing vampires . . . bottom of the barrel.'

Hurt and angry didn't begin to describe how I felt at this assessment.

I went from table to table automatically, fetching drinks and sandwiches and clearing up the remainders, working as hard as I usually did, with that awful smile stretching my face. I talked to twenty people I knew, most of whom had thoughts as innocent as the day is long. Most customers were thinking of work, or tasks they had to get done at home, or some little problem they needed to solve, like getting the Sears repairman to come work on the dishwasher or getting the house clean for weekend company.

Arlene was relieved her period had started.

Charlsie was immersed in pink glowing reflections on her shot at immortality, her grandchild. She was praying earnestly for an easy pregnancy and safe delivery for her daughter.

Lafayette was thinking that working with me was getting spooky.

Policeman Kevin Pryor was wondering what his partner Kenya was doing on her day off. He himself was helping his mother clean out the tool shed and hating every minute of it.

I heard many comments, both aloud and unspoken, about my hair and complexion and the bandage on my arm. I seemed more desirable to more men, and one woman. Some of the guys who'd gone on the vampire burning expedition were thinking they didn't have a chance with me because of my vampire sympathies, and they were regretting their impulsive act. I marked their identities in my mind. I wasn't going to forget they could have killed my Bill, even though at the moment the rest of the vampire community was low on my list of favorite things.

Andy Bellefleur and his sister, Portia, were having lunch together, something they did at least once every week. Portia was a female version of Andy: medium height, blocky build, determined mouth and jaw. The resemblance between brother and sister favored Andy, not Portia. She was a very competent lawyer, I'd heard. I might have suggested her to Jason when he was thinking he'd need an attorney, if she'd not been female . . . and I'd been thinking about Portia's welfare more than Jason's.

Today the lawyer was feeling inwardly depressed because she was educated and made good money, but never had a date. That was her inner preoccupation.

Andy was disgusted with my continued association with Bill Compton, interested in my improved appearance, and curious about how vampires had sex. He also was feeling sorry he was probably going to arrest Jason. He was thinking that the case against Jason was not much stronger than that against several other men, but Jason was the one who looked the most scared, which meant he had something to hide. And there were the videos, which showed Jason having sex – not exactly regular, garden-variety sex – with Maudette and Dawn.

I stared at Andy while I processed his thoughts, which made him uneasy. Andy really did know what I was capable of. 'Sookie, you going to get that beer?' he asked finally, waving a broad hand in the air to make sure he had my attention.

'Sure, Andy,' I said absently, and got one out of the cooler. 'You need any more tea, Portia?'

'No, thanks, Sookie,' Portia said politely, patting her mouth with her paper napkin. Portia was remembering high school, when she would have sold her soul for a date with the gorgeous Jason Stackhouse. She was wondering what Jason was doing now, if he had a thought in his head that would interest her – maybe his body would be worth the sacrifice of intellectual companionship? So Portia hadn't seen the tapes, didn't know of their existence; Andy was being a good cop.

I tried to picture Portia with Jason, and I couldn't help smiling. That would be an experience for both of them. I wished, not for the first time, that I could plant ideas as well as reap them.

By the end of my shift, I'd learned – nothing. Except that the videos my brother had so unwisely made featured mild bondage, which caused Andy to think of the ligature marks around the victims' necks.

So, taken as a whole, letting my head open for my brother had been a futile exercise. All I'd heard tended to make me worry more and didn't supply any additional information that might help his cause.

A different crowd would come in tonight. I had never come to Merlotte's just for fun. Should I come in tonight? What would Bill do? Did I want to see him?

I felt friendless. There was no one I could talk to about Bill, no one who wouldn't be halfway shocked I was seeing him in the first place. How could I tell Arlene I was blue because Bill's vampire buddies were terrifying and ruthless, that one of them had bitten me the night before, bled into my mouth, been staked on top of me? This was not the kind of problem Arlene was equipped to handle.

I couldn't think of anyone who was.

I couldn't recall anyone dating a vampire who wasn't an indiscriminate vampire groupie, a fang-banger who would go with just any bloodsucker.

By the time I left work, my enhanced physical appearance no longer had the power to make me confident. I felt like a freak.

I puttered around the house, took a short nap, watered Gran's flowers. Toward dusk, I ate something I'd nuked in the microwave. Wavering up until the last moment about going out, I finally put on a red shirt and white slacks and some jewelry and drove back to Merlotte's.

It felt very strange entering as a customer. Sam was back behind the bar, and his eyebrows went up as he marked my entrance. Three waitresses I knew by sight were working tonight, and a different cook was grilling hamburgers, I saw through the serving hatch.

Jason was at the bar. For a wonder, the stool next to him was empty, and I eased onto it.

He turned to me with his face set for a new woman: mouth loose and smiling, eyes bright and wide. When he saw it was me, his expression underwent a comical change.

'What the hell are you doing here, Sookie?' he asked, his voice indignant.

'You'd think you weren't glad to see me,' I remarked. When Sam paused in front of me, I asked him for a bourbon and coke, without meeting his eyes. 'I did what you told me to do, and so far nothing,' I whispered to my brother. 'I came in here tonight to try some more people.'

'Thanks, Sookie,' he said, after a long pause. 'I guess I didn't realize what I was asking. Hey, is something different about your hair?'

He even paid for my drink when Sam slid it in front of me.

We didn't seem to have much to talk about, which was actually okay, since I was trying to listen to the other customers. There were a few strangers, and I scanned them first, to see if they were possible suspects. It didn't seem they were, I decided reluctantly. One was thinking hard about how much he missed his wife, and the subtext was that he was faithful to her. One was thinking about it being his first time here, and the drinks were good. Another was just concentrating on sitting up straight and hoping he could drive back to the motel.

I'd had another drink.

Jason and I had been swapping conjectures about how much the lawyer's fees would be when Gran's estate was settled. He glanced at the doorway and said, 'Uh-oh.'

'What?' I asked, not turning to see what he was looking at.

'Sis, the boyfriend's here. And he's not alone.'

My first idea was that Bill had brought one of his fellow vampires with him, which would have been upsetting and unwise. But when I turned, I realized why Jason had sounded so angry. Bill was with a human girl. He had a grip on her arm, she was coming on to him like a whore, and his eyes were scanning the crowd. I decided he was looking for my reaction.

I got off the barstool and decided another thing.

I was drunk. I seldom drank at all, and two bourbon and cokes consumed within minutes had made me, if not knee-walking drunk, at least tipsy.

Bill's eyes met mine. He hadn't really expected to find me here. I couldn't read his mind as I had Eric's for an awful moment, but I could read his body language.

'Hey, Vampire Bill!' Jason's friend Hoyt called. Bill nodded politely in Hoyt's direction, but began to steer the girl – tiny, dark – in my direction.

I had no idea what to do.

'Sis, what's his game?' Jason said. He was working up a head of steam. 'That gal's a fang-banger from Monroe. I knew her when she liked humans.'

I still had no idea what to do. My hurt was overwhelming, but my pride kept trying to contain it. I had to add a dash of guilt to that emotional stew. I hadn't been where Bill had expected me to be, and I hadn't left him a note. Then again – on the other hand (my fifth or sixth) – I'd had a lot of shocks the night before at the command performance in Shreveport; and only my association with him had obliged me to go to *that* shindig.

My warring impulses held me still. I wanted to pitch myself on her and beat the shit out of her, but I hadn't been brought up to brawl in barrooms. (I also wanted to beat the shit out of Bill, but I might as well go bang my head on the wall for the all the damage it would do him.) Then, too, I wanted to burst into tears because my feelings were hurt – but that would be weak. The best option was not to show anything because Jason was ready to launch into Bill, and all it needed was some action from me to squeeze his trigger.

Too much conflict on top of too much alcohol.

While I was enumerating all these options, Bill had approached, wending his way through the tables, with the woman in tow. I noticed the room was quieter. Instead of watching, I was being watched.

I could feel my eyes well with tears while my hands fisted. Great. The worst of both responses.

'Sookie,' Bill said, 'this is what Eric dropped off at my doorstep.'

I could hardly understand what he was saying.

'So?' I said furiously. I looked right into the girl's eyes. They were big and dark and excited. I kept my own lids wide apart, knowing if I blinked the tears would flow.

'As a reward,' Bill said. I couldn't understand how he felt about this.

'Free *beverage*?' I said, and couldn't believe how venomous my voice sounded.

Jason put his hand on my shoulder. 'Steady, girl,' he said, his voice as low and mean as mine. 'He ain't worth it.'

I didn't know what Bill wasn't worth, but I was about to find out. It was almost exhilarating to have no idea what I was about to do, after a lifetime of control.

Bill was regarding me with sharp attention. Under the fluorescents over the bar, he looked remarkably white. He hadn't fed from her. And his fangs were retracted.

'Come outside and talk,' he said.

'With her?' I was almost growling.

'No,' he said. 'With me. I have to send her back.'

The distaste in his voice influenced me, and I followed Bill outside, keeping my head up and not meeting any eyes. He kept ahold of the girl's arm, and she was practically walking on her toes to keep up. I didn't know Jason was coming with us until I turned to see him behind me as we passed into the parking lot. Outside, people were coming and going, but it was marginally better than the crowded bar.

'Hi,' the girl said chattily. 'My name's Desiree. I think I've met you before, Jason.'

'What are you doing here, Desiree?' Jason asked, his voice quiet. You could almost believe he was calm.

'Eric sent me over here to Bon Temps as a reward for Bill,' she said coyly, looking at Bill from the corners of her eyes. 'But he seems less than thrilled. I don't know why. I'm practically a special vintage.'

'Eric?' Jason asked me.

'A vampire from Shreveport. Bar owner. Head honcho.'

'He left her on my doorstep,' Bill told me. 'I didn't ask for her.'

'What are you going to do?'

'Send her back,' he said impatiently. 'You and I have to talk.'

I gulped. I felt my fingers uncurl.

'She needs a ride back to Monroe?' Jason asked.

Bill looked surprised. 'Yes. Are you offering? I need to talk to your sister.'

'Sure,' Jason said, all geniality. I was instantly suspicious.

'I can't believe you're refusing me,' Desiree said, looking up at Bill and pouting. 'No one has ever turned me down before.'

'Of course I am grateful, and I'm sure you are, as you put it, a special vintage,' Bill said politely. 'But I have my own wine cellar.'

Little Desiree stared at him blankly for a second before comprehension slowly lit her brown eyes. 'This woman yours?' she asked, jerking her head at me.

'She is.'

Jason shifted nervously at Bill's flat statement.

Desiree gave me a good looking over. 'She's got funny eyes,' she finally pronounced.

'She's my sister,' Jason said.

'Oh. I'm sorry. You're much more . . . normal.' Desiree gave Jason the up-and-down, and seemed more pleased with what she saw. 'Hey, what's your last name?'

Jason took her hand and began leading her toward his pickup. 'Stackhouse,' he was saying, giving her the full eye treatment, as they walked away. 'Maybe on the way home, you can tell me a little about what you do . . .'

I turned back to Bill, wondering what Jason's motive was for this generous act, and met Bill's gaze. It was like walking into a brick wall.

'So, you want to talk?' I asked harshly.

'Not here. Come home with me.'

I scuffed the gravel with my shoe. 'Not your house.'

'Then yours.'

'No.'

He raised his arched brows. 'Where then?'

Good question.

'My folks' pond.' Since Jason was going to be giving Miss Dark and Tiny a ride home, he wouldn't be there.

'I'll follow you,' he said briefly, and we parted to go to our respective cars.

The property where I'd spent my first few years was to the west of Bon Temps. I turned down the familiar gravel driveway and parked at the house, a modest ranch that Jason kept up pretty well. Bill emerged from his car as I slid from mine, and I motioned him to follow me. We went around the house and down the slope, following a path set with big paving stones. In a minute we were at the pond, man-made, that my dad had put in our backyard and stocked, anticipating fishing with his son in that water for years.

There was a kind of patio overlooking the water, and on one of the metal chairs was a folded blanket. Without asking me, Bill picked it up and shook it out, spreading it on the grass downslope from the patio. I sat on it reluctantly, thinking the blanket wasn't safe for the same reasons meeting him in either home wasn't safe. When I was close to Bill, what I thought about was being even closer to him.

I hugged my knees to me and stared off across the water. There was a security light on the other side of the pond, and I could see it reflected in the still water. Bill lay on his back next to me. I could feel his eyes on my face. He laced his fingers together across his ribs, ostentatiously keeping his hands to himself.

'Last night frightened you,' he said neutrally.

'Weren't you just a little scared?' I asked, more quietly than I'd thought I would.

'For you. A little for myself.'

I wanted to lie on my stomach but worried about getting that close to him. When I saw his skin glow in the moonlight, I yearned to touch him.

'It scared me that Eric can control our lives while we're a couple.'

'Do you not want to be a couple anymore?'

The pain in my chest was so bad I put my hand over it, pressing the area above my breast.

'Sookie?' He was kneeling by me, an arm around me.

I couldn't answer. I had no breath.

'Do you love me?' he asked.

I nodded.

'Why do you talk of leaving me?'

The pain made its way out through my eyes in the form of tears.

'I'm too scared of the other vampires and the way they are. What will he ask me to do next? He'll try to make me do something else. He'll tell me he'll kill you otherwise. Or he'll threaten Jason. And he can do it.'

Bill's voice was as quiet as the sound of a cricket in the grass. A month ago, I might not have been able to hear it. 'Don't cry,' he told me. 'Sookie, I have to tell you unwelcome facts.'

The only welcome thing he could have told me at that point was that Eric was dead.

'Eric is intrigued by you now. He can tell you have mental powers that most humans don't have, or ignore if they know they possess them. He anticipates your blood is rich and sweet.' Bill's voice got hoarse when he said that, and I shivered. 'And you're beautiful. You're even more beautiful now. He doesn't realize you have had our blood three times.'

'You know that Long Shadow bled onto me?'

'Yes. I saw.'

'Is there anything magic about three times?'

He laughed, that low, rumbly, rusty laugh. 'No. But the more vampire blood you drink, the more desirable you become to our kind, and actually, more desirable to anyone. And Desiree thought she was a vintage! I wonder what vampire said that to her.'

'One that wanted to get in her pants,' I said flatly, and he laughed again. I loved to hear him laugh.

'With all this telling me how lovely I am, are you saying that Eric, like, lusts for me?'

'Yes.'

'What's to stop him from taking me? You say he's stronger than you.'

'Courtesy and custom, first of all.'

I didn't snort, but I came close.

'Don't discount that. We're all observant of custom, we vampires. We have to live together for centuries.'

'Anything else?'

'I am not as strong as Eric, but I'm not a new vampire. He might get badly hurt in a fight with me, or I might even win if I got lucky.'

'Anything else?'

'Maybe,' Bill said carefully, 'you yourself.'

'How so?'

'If you can be valuable to him otherwise, he may leave you alone if he knows that is your sincere wish.'

'But I don't want to be valuable to him! I don't want to ever see him again!'

'You promised Eric you'd help him again,' Bill reminded me.

'If he turned the thief over to the police,' I said. 'And what did Eric do? He staked him!'

'Possibly saving your life in the process.'

'Well, I found his thief!'

'Sookie, you don't know much about the world.'

I stared at him, surprised. 'I guess that's so.'

'Things don't turn out . . . even.' Bill stared out into the darkness. 'Even I think sometimes I don't know much, anymore.' Another gloomy pause. 'I have only once before seen one vampire stake another. Eric is going beyond the limits of our world.'

'So, he's not too likely to take much notice of that custom and courtesy you were bragging about earlier.'

'Pam may keep him to the old ways.'

'What is she to him?'

'He made her. That is, he made her vampire, centuries ago. She comes back to him from time to time and helps him do whatever he is doing at the moment. Eric's always been something of a rogue, and the older he gets the more willful he gets.' Calling Eric willful seemed a huge understatement to me.

'So, have we talked our way around in circles?' I asked. Bill seemed to be considering. 'Yes,' he confirmed, a tinge of regret in his voice. 'You don't like associating with vampires other than myself, and I have told you we have no choice.'

'How about this Desiree thing?'

'He had someone drop her off on my doorstep, hoping I would be pleased he'd sent me a pretty gift. Also, it would test my devotion to you if I drank from her. Perhaps he poisoned her blood somehow, and her blood would have weakened me. Maybe she would just have been a crack in my armor.' He shrugged. 'Did you think I had a date?'

'Yes.' I felt my face harden, thinking about Bill walking in with the girl.

'You weren't at home. I had to come find you.' His tone wasn't accusatory, but it wasn't happy, either.

'I was trying to help Jason out by listening. And I was still upset from last night.'

'Are we all right now?'

'No, but we're as all right as we can get,' I said. 'I guess no matter who I cared for, it wouldn't always go smooth. But I hadn't counted on obstacles this drastic. There's no way you can ever outrank Eric, I guess, since age is the criterion.'

'No,' said Bill. 'Not outrank . . .' and he suddenly looked thoughtful. 'Though there may be something I can do along those lines. I don't want to – it goes against my nature – but we would be more secure.'

I let him think.

'Yes,' he concluded, ending his long brood. He didn't offer to explain, and I didn't ask.

'I love you,' he said, as if that was the bottom line to whatever course of action he was considering. His face loomed over me, luminous and beautiful in the half-darkness.

'I feel the same about you,' I said, and put my hands against his chest so he wouldn't tempt me. 'But we have too much against us right now. If we can pry Eric off our backs, that would help. And another thing, we have to stop this murder investigation. That would be a second big piece of trouble off our backs. This murderer has the deaths of your friends to answer for, and the deaths of Maudette and Dawn to answer for.' I paused, took a deep breath. 'And the death of my grandmother.' I blinked back tears. I'd gotten adjusted to Gran not being in the house when I came home, and I was getting used to not talking to her and sharing my day with her, but every now and then I had a stab of grief so acute it robbed me of breath.

'Why do you think the same killer is responsible for the Monroe vampires being burned?'

'I think it was the murderer who planted this idea, this vigilante thing, in the men in the bar that night. I think it was the murderer who went from group to group, egging the guys on. I've lived here all my life, and I've never seen people around here act that way. There's got to be a reason they did this time.'

'He agitated them? Fomented the burning?'

'Yes.'

'Listening hasn't turned up anything?'

'No,' I admitted glumly. 'But that's not to say tomorrow will be the same.'

'You're an optimist, Sookie.'

'Yes, I am. I have to be.' I patted his cheek, thinking how my optimism had been justified since he had entered my life.

'You keep on listening, since you think it may be fruitful,' he said. 'I'll work on something else, for now. I'll see you tomorrow evening at your place, okay? I may . . . no, let me explain then.'

'All right.' I was curious, but Bill obviously wasn't ready to talk.

On my way home, following the taillights of Bill's car as far as my driveway, I thought of how much more frightening the past few weeks would have been if I hadn't had the security of Bill's presence. As I went cautiously down the driveway, I found myself wishing Bill hadn't felt he had to go home to make some necessary phone calls. The few nights we'd spent apart, I wouldn't say I'd been exactly writhing with fear, but I'd been very jumpy and anxious. At the house by myself, I spent lots of time going from locked window to locked door, and I wasn't used to living that way. I felt disheartened at the thought of the night ahead.

Before I got out of my car, I scanned the yard, glad I'd remembered to turn on the security lights before I left for the bar. Nothing was moving. Usually Tina came running when I'd been gone, anxious to get in the house for some cat kibble, but tonight she must be hunting in the woods.

I separated my house key from the bunch on my key ring. I dashed from the car to the front door, inserted and twisted the key in record time, and slammed and locked the door behind me. This was no way to live, I thought, shaking my head in dismay; and just as I completed that idea, something hit the front door with a thud. I shrieked before I could stop myself.

I ran for the portable phone by the couch. I punched in Bill's number as I went around the room pulling down the shades. What if the line was busy? He'd said he was going home to use the phone!

But I caught him just as he walked in the door. He sounded breathless as he picked up the receiver. 'Yes?' he said. He always sounded suspicious.

'Bill,' I gasped, 'there's someone outside!'

He crashed the phone down. A vampire of action.

He was there in two minutes. Looking out into the yard from a slightly lifted blind, I glimpsed him coming into the yard from the woods, moving with a speed and silence a human could never equal. The relief of seeing him was overwhelming. For a second I felt ashamed at calling Bill to rescue me: I should have handled the situation myself. Then I thought, Why? When you know a practically invincible being who professes to adore you, someone so hard to kill it's next to impossible, someone preternaturally strong, that's who you're gonna call.

Bill investigated the yard and the woods, moving with a sure, silent grace. Finally he came lightly up the steps. He bent over something on the front porch. The angle was too acute, and I couldn't tell what it was. When he straightened, he had something in his hands, and he looked absolutely . . . expressionless.

This was very bad.

I went reluctantly to the front door and unlocked it. I pushed out the screen door.

Bill was holding the body of my cat.

'Tina?' I said, hearing my voice quaver and not caring at all. 'Is she dead?'

Bill nodded, one little jerk of his head.

'What – how?'

'Strangled, I think.'

I could feel my face crumple. Bill had to stand there holding the corpse while I cried my eyes out.

'I never got that live oak,' I said, having calmed a little. I didn't sound very steady. 'We can put her in that hole.' So around to the backyard we went, poor Bill holding Tina, trying to look comfortable about it, and me trying not to dissolve again. Bill knelt and lay the little bundle of black fur at the bottom of my excavation. I fetched the shovel and began to fill it in, but the sight of the first dirt hitting Tina's fur undid me all over again. Silently, Bill took the shovel from my hands. I turned my back, and he finished the awful job.

'Come inside,' he said gently when it was finished.

We went in the house, having to walk around to the front because I hadn't yet unlocked the back.

Bill patted me and comforted me, though I knew he hadn't ever been crazy about Tina. 'God bless you, Bill,' I whispered. I tightened my arms around him ferociously, in a sudden convulsion of fear that he, too, would be taken from me. When I'd gotten the sobs reduced to hiccups, I looked up, hoping I hadn't made him uncomfortable with my flood of emotion.

Bill was furious. He was staring at the wall over my shoulder, and his eyes were glowing. He was the most frightening thing I'd ever seen in my life.

'Did you find anything out in the yard?' I asked.

'No. I found traces of his presence. Some footprints, a lingering scent. Nothing you could bring into court as proof,' he went on, reading my mind.

'Would you mind staying here until you have to go to . . . get away from the sun?'

'Of course.' He stared at me. He'd fully intended to do that whether or not I agreed, I could tell.

'If you still need to make phone calls, just make them here. I don't care.' I meant if they were on my phone bill.

'I have a calling card,' he said, once again astonishing me. Who would have thought?

I washed my face and took a Tylenol before I put on my nightgown, sadder than I'd been since Gran had been killed, and sadder in different way. The death of a pet is naturally not in the same category as the death of a family member, I chided myself, but it didn't seem to affect my misery. I went through all the reasoning I was capable of and came no closer to any truth except the fact that I'd fed and brushed and loved Tina for four years, and I would miss her.

Chapter 11

My nerves were raw the next day. When I got to work and told Arlene what had happened, she gave me a hard hug, and said, 'I'd like to kill the bastard that did that to poor Tina!' Somehow, that made me feel a lot better. Charlsie was just as sympathetic, if more concerned with the shock to me rather than the agonized demise of my cat. Sam just looked grim. He thought I should call the sheriff, or Andy Bellefleur, and tell one of them what had happened. I finally did call Bud Dearborn.

'Usually these things go in cycles,' Bud rumbled. 'Ain't nobody else reported a pet missing or dead, though. I'm afraid it sounds like some kind a personal thing, Sookie. That vampire friend of yours, he like cats?'

I closed my eyes and breathed deeply. I was using the phone in Sam's office, and he was sitting behind the desk figuring out his next liquor order.

'Bill was at home when whoever killed Tina threw her on my porch,' I said as calmly as I could. 'I called him directly afterward, and he answered the phone.' Sam looked up quizzically, and I rolled my eyes to let him know my opinion of the sheriff's suspicions.

'And he told you the cat was strangled,' Bud went on ponderously.

'Yes.'

'Do you have the ligature?'

'No. I didn't even see what it was.'

'What did you do with the kitty?'

'We buried her.'

'Was that your idea or Mr. Compton's?'

'Mine.' What else would we have done with Tina?

'We may come dig your kitty up. If we had had the ligature and the cat, maybe we could see if the method of strangulation matched the method used in killing Dawn and Maudette,' Bud explained ponderously.

'I'm sorry. I didn't think about that.'

'Well, it don't matter much. Without the ligature.'

'Okay, good-bye.' I hung up, probably applying a little more pressure than the receiver required. Sam's eyebrows lifted.

'Bud is a jerk,' I told him.

'Bud's not a bad policeman,' Sam said quietly. 'None of us here are used to murders that are this sick.'

'You're right,' I admitted, after a moment. 'I wasn't being fair. He just kept saying "ligature" like he was proud he'd learned a new word. I'm sorry I got mad at him.'

'You don't have to be perfect, Sookie.'

'You mean I get to screw up and be less than understanding and forgiving, from time to time? Thanks, boss.' I smiled at him, feeling the wry twist to my lips, and got up off the edge of his desk where I'd been propped to make my phone call. I stretched. It wasn't until I saw the way

Sam's eyes drank in that stretch that I became self-conscious again. 'Back to work!' I said briskly and strode out of the room, trying to make sure there wasn't a hint of sway to my hips.

'Would you keep the kids for a couple of hours this evening?' Arlene asked, a little shyly. I remembered the last time we'd talked about my keeping her kids, and I remembered the offense I'd taken at her reluctance to leave her kids with a vampire. I hadn't been thinking like a mother would think. Now, Arlene was trying to apologize.

'I'd be glad to.' I waited to see if Arlene would mention Bill again, but she didn't. 'When to when?'

'Well, Rene and I are gonna go to the movies in Monroe,' she said. 'Say, six-thirty?'

'Sure. Will they have had supper?'

'Oh, yeah, I'll feed 'em. They'll be excited to see their aunt Sookie.'

'I look forward to it.'

'Thanks,' Arlene said. She paused, almost said something else, then appeared to think again. 'See you at six-thirty.'

I got home about five, most of the way driving against the sun, which was glaring like it was staring me down. I changed to a blue-and-green knit short set, brushed my hair and secured it with a banana clip. I had a sandwich, sitting uneasily by myself at the kitchen table. The house felt big and empty, and I was glad to see Rene drive up with Coby and Lisa.

'Arlene's having trouble with one of her artificial nails,' he explained, looking embarrassed at having to relay this feminine problem. 'And Coby and Lisa were raring to get over here.' I noticed Rene was still in his work clothes – heavy boots, knife, hat, and all. Arlene wasn't going to let him take her anywhere until he showered and changed.

Coby was eight and Lisa was five, and they were hanging all over me like big earrings when Rene bent to kiss them good-bye. His affection for the kids gave Rene a big gold star in my book, and I smiled at him approvingly. I took the kids' hands to lead them back to the kitchen for some ice cream.

'We'll see you about ten-thirty, eleven,' he said. 'If that's all right.' He put his hand on the doorknob.

'Sure,' I agreed. I opened my mouth to offer to keep the kids for the night, as I'd done on previous occasions, but then I thought of Tina's limp body. I decided that tonight they'd better not stay. I raced the kids to the kitchen, and a minute or two later I heard Rene's old pickup rattling down the driveway.

I picked up Lisa. 'I can hardly lift you anymore, girl, you're getting so big! And you, Coby, you shaving yet?' We sat at the table for a good thirty minutes while the children ate ice cream and rattled off their list of achievements since we'd last visited.

Then Lisa wanted to read to me, so I got out a coloring book with the color and number words printed inside, and she read those to me with some pride. Coby, of course, had to prove he could read much better, and then they wanted to watch a favorite show. Before I knew it, it was dark.

'My friend is coming over tonight,' I told them. 'His name is Bill.'

'Mama told us you had a special friend,' Coby said. 'I better like him. He better be nice to you.'

'Oh, he is,' I assured the boy, who had straightened and

thrust out his chest, ready to defend me if my special friend wasn't nice enough in Coby's estimation.

'Does he send you flowers?' Lisa asked romantically.

'No, not yet. Maybe you can kind of hint I'd like some?'

'Ooo. Yeah, I can do that.'

'Has he asked you to marry him?

'Well, no. But I haven't asked him, either.'

Naturally, Bill picked that moment to knock.

'I have company,' I said, smiling, when I answered the door.

'I can hear,' he said.

I took his hand and led him into the kitchen.

'Bill, this is Coby and this young woman is Lisa,' I said formally.

'Good, I've been wanting to meet you,' Bill said, to my surprise. 'Lisa and Coby, is it all right with you if I keep company with your aunt Sookie?'

They eyed him thoughtfully. 'She isn't really our aunt,' Coby said, testing the waters. 'She's our mom's good friend.'

'Is that right?'

'Yes, and she says you don't send her flowers,' Lisa said. For once, her little voice was crystal clear. I was so glad to realize that Lisa had gotten over her little problem with her *r*s. Really.

Bill looked sideways at me. I shrugged. 'Well, they asked me,' I said helplessly.

'Hmmm,' he said thoughtfully. 'I'll have to mend my ways, Lisa. Thank you for pointing that out to me. When is Aunt Sookie's birthday, do you know?'

I could feel my face flushing. 'Bill,' I said sharply. 'Cut it out.'

'Do you know, Coby?' Bill asked the boy.

Coby shook his head, regretfully. 'But I know it's in the summer because the last time Mama took Sookie to lunch in Shreveport for her birthday, it was summertime. We stayed with Rene.'

'You're smart to remember that, Coby,' Bill told him.

'I'm smarter than that! Guess what I learned in school the other day.' And Coby was off and running.

Lisa eyed Bill with great attention the whole time Coby spoke, and when Coby was finished, she said, 'You look real white, Bill.'

'Yes,' he said, 'that's my normal complexion.'

The kids exchanged glances. I could tell they were deciding that 'normal complexion' was an illness, and it wouldn't be too polite to ask more questions. Every now and then children show a certain tactfulness.

Bill, initially a little stiff, began to get more and more flexible as the evening wore on. I was ready to admit I was tired by nine, but he was still going strong with the kids when Arlene and Rene came by to pick them up at eleven.

I'd just introduced my friends to Bill, who shook their hands in an absolutely normal way, when another caller arrived.

A handsome vampire with thick black hair combed into an improbable wavy style strolled up out of the woods as Arlene was bundling the kids into the truck, and Rene and Bill were chatting. Bill waved a casual hand at the vampire, and he raised one in return, joining Bill and Rene as if he'd been expected.

From the front porch swing, I watched Bill introduce the two, and the vampire and Rene shook hands. Rene was gaping at the newcomer, and I could tell he felt he'd recognized him. Bill looked meaningfully at Rene and shook his head, and Rene's mouth closed on whatever comment he'd been going to make.

The newcomer was husky, taller than Bill, and he wore old jeans and an 'I Visited Graceland' T-shirt. His heavy boots were worn at the heel. He carried a squirt bottle of synthetic blood in one hand and took a swig from time to time. Mr. Social Skills.

Maybe I'd been cued by Rene's reaction, but the more I looked at the vampire, the more familiar he seemed. I tried mentally warming up the skin tone, adding a few lines, making him stand straighter and investing his face with some liveliness.

Oh my God.

It was the man from Memphis.

Rene turned to go, and Bill began steering the newcomer up to me. From ten feet away, the vampire called, 'Hey, Bill tells me someone killed your cat!' He had a heavy Southern accent.

Bill closed his eyes for a second, and I just nodded speechlessly.

'Well, I'm sorry about that. I like cats,' the tall vampire said, and I clearly got the idea he didn't mean he liked to stroke their fur. I hoped the kids weren't picking up on that, but Arlene's horrified face appeared in the truck window. All the good will Bill had established had probably just gone down the drain.

Rene shook his head behind the vampire's back and climbed into the driver's seat, calling a good-bye as he started up the engine. He stuck his head out the window for a long last look at the newcomer. He must have said something to Arlene because she appeared at her window again, staring for all she was worth. I saw her mouth drop open in shock as she looked harder at the creature standing beside Bill. Her head disappeared into the truck, and I heard a screech as the truck pulled away.

'Sookie,' Bill said warningly, 'this is *Bubba*.'

'Bubba,' I repeated, not quite trusting my ears.

'Yep, Bubba,' the vampire said cheerfully, goodwill radiating from his fearsome smile. 'That's me. Pleased to meetcha.'

I shook hands with him, making myself smile back. Good God Almighty, I never thought I'd be shaking hands with *him*. But he'd sure changed for the worse.

'Bubba, would you mind waiting here on the porch? Let me explain our arrangement to Sookie.'

'That's all right with me,' Bubba said casually. He settled on the swing, as happy and brainless as a clam.

We went into the living room, but not before I'd noticed that when Bubba had made his appearance, much of the night noise – bugs, frogs – had simply stopped. 'I had hoped to explain this to you before Bubba got here,' Bill whispered. 'But I couldn't.'

I said, 'Is that who I think it is?'

'Yes. So now you know at least some of the sighting stories are true. But *don't* call him by his name. Call him Bubba! Something went wrong when he came over – from human to vampire – maybe it was all the chemicals in his blood.'

'But he was really dead, wasn't he?'

'Not . . . quite. One of us was a morgue attendant and a big fan, and he could detect the tiny spark still left, so he brought him over, in a hurried manner.'

'Brought him over?'

'Made him vampire,' Bill explained. 'But that was a mistake. He's never been the same from what my friends tell me. He's as smart as a tree trunk, so to make a living he does odd jobs for the rest of us. We can't have him out in public, you can see that.'

I nodded, my mouth hanging open. Of course not. 'Geez,' I murmured, stunned at the royalty in my yard.

'So remember how stupid he is, and how impulsive . . . don't spend time alone with him, and don't ever call him anything but Bubba. Also, he likes pets, as he told you, and a diet of their blood hasn't made him any the more reliable. Now, as to why I brought him here . . .'

I stood with my arms across my chest, waiting for Bill's explanation with some interest.

'Sweetheart, I have to go out of town for a while,' Bill said.

The unexpectedness of this completely disconcerted me.

'What . . . why? No, wait. I don't need to know.' I waved my hands in front of me, shooing away any implication that Bill was obligated to tell me his business.

'I'll tell you when I get back,' he said firmly.

'So where does your friend – Bubba – come in?' Though I had a nasty feeling I already knew.

'Bubba is going to watch you while I'm gone,' Bill said stiffly.

I raised my eyebrows.

'All right. He's not long on . . .' Bill cast around. '. . . anything,' he finally admitted. 'But he's strong, and he'll do what I tell him, and he'll make sure no one breaks into your house.'

'He'll stay out in the woods?'

'Oh, yes,' Bill said emphatically. 'He's not even supposed

to come up and speak to you. At dark, he'll just find a place from which he can see the house, and he'll watch all night.'

I'd have to remember to close my blinds. The idea of the dim vampire peering in my windows was not edifying.

'You really think this is necessary?' I asked helplessly. 'You know, I don't remember you asking me.'

Bill sort of heaved, his version of taking a deep breath. 'Sweetheart,' he began in an overly patient voice, 'I am trying very hard to get used to the way women want to be treated now. But it isn't natural to me, especially when I fear you are in danger. I'm trying to give myself peace of mind while I'm gone. I wish I didn't have to go, and it isn't what I want to do, but what I have to do, for us.'

I eyed him. 'I hear you,' I said finally. 'I'm not crazy about this, but I am afraid at night, and I guess . . . well, okay.'

Frankly, I don't think it mattered a damn whether I consented or not. After all, how could I make Bubba leave if he didn't want to go? Even the law enforcement people in our little town didn't have the equipment to deal with vampires, and if they were faced with this particular vampire, they'd just stand and gape for long enough for him to tear them apart. I appreciated Bill's concern, and I figured I better have the good grace to thank him. I gave him a little hug.

'Well, if you have to go off, you just be careful while you're gone,' I said, trying not to sound forlorn. 'Do you have a place to stay?'

'Yes. I'll be in New Orleans. There was a room open at the Blood in the Quarter.'

I'd read an article about this hotel, the first in the world that catered exclusively to vampires. It promised complete security, and so far it had delivered. It was right smack dab in the middle of the French Quarter, too. And at dusk it was absolutely surrounded by fang-bangers and tourists waiting for the vampires to come out.

I began to feel envious. Trying not to look like a wistful puppy who's being pushed back in the door when its owners leave, I yanked my smile back into place. 'Well, you have a good time,' I said brightly. 'Got your packing done? The drive should take a few hours, and it's already dark.'

'The car is ready.' I understood for the first time that he had delayed leaving to spend time with me and Arlene's kids. 'I had better leave.' He hesitated, seemed to be searching for the right words. Then he held out his hands to me. I took them, and he pulled a little, just exerted a tiny pressure. I moved into his embrace. I rubbed my face against his shirt. My arms circled him, pressed him into me.

'I'll miss you,' he said. His voice was just a breath in the air, but I heard him. I felt him kiss the top of my head, and then he stepped away from me and out the front door. I heard his voice on the front porch as he gave Bubba some last minute directions, and I heard the squeak of the swing as Bubba got up.

I didn't look out the window until I heard Bill's car going down the driveway. Then I saw Bubba sauntering into the woods. I told myself, as I took my shower, that Bill must trust Bubba since he'd left him guarding me. But I still wasn't sure who I was more afraid of: the murderer Bubba was watching for, or Bubba himself.

At work the next day, Arlene asked me why the vampire

had been at my house. I wasn't surprised that she'd brought it up.

'Well, Bill had to go out of town, and he worries, you know . . .' I was hoping to let it drop at that. But Charlsie had drifted up (we weren't at all busy: the Chamber of Commerce was having a lunch and speaker at Fins and Hooves, and the Ladies' Prayers and Potatoes group were topping their baked potatoes at old Mrs. Bellefleur's huge house). 'You mean,' Charlsie said with starry eyes, 'that your man got you a personal bodyguard?'

I nodded reluctantly. You could put it that way.

'That's so romantic,' Charlsie sighed.

You could look at it that way.

'But you should see him,' Arlene told Charlsie, having held her tongue as long as she could. 'He's exactly like—!'

'Oh, no, not when you talk to him,' I interrupted. 'He's not at all the same.' That was true. 'And he really doesn't like it when he hears that name.'

'Oh,' said Arlene in a hushed voice, as if Bubba could be listening in the broad daylight.

'I do feel safer with Bubba in the woods,' I said, which was more or less true.

'Oh, he doesn't stay in the house?' Charlsie asked, clearly a little disappointed.

'God, no!' I said, then mentally apologized to God for taking his name in vain. I was having to do that a lot lately. 'No, Bubba stays in the woods at night, watching the house.'

'Was that true about the cats?' Arlene looked squeamish.

'He was just joking. Not a great sense of humor, huh?' I was lying through my teeth. I certainly believed Bubba enjoyed a snack of cat blood.

Arlene shook her head, unconvinced. It was time to change the subject. 'Did you and Rene have fun on your evening out?' I asked.

'Rene was so good last night, wasn't he?' she said, her cheeks pink.

A much-married woman, blushing. 'You tell me.' Arlene enjoyed a little ribald teasing.

'Oh, you! What I mean, he was real polite to Bill and even that Bubba.'

'Any reason why he wouldn't be?'

'He has kind of a problem with vampires, Sookie.' Arlene shook her head. 'I know, I do, too,' she confessed when I looked at her with raised eyebrows. 'But Rene really has some prejudice. Cindy dated a vampire for a while, and that just made Rene awful upset.'

'Cindy okay?' I had a great interest in the health of someone who'd dated a vamp.

'I haven't seen her,' Arlene admitted, 'but Rene goes to visit every other week or so. She's doing well, she's back on the right track. She has a job in a hospital cafeteria.'

Sam, who'd been standing behind the bar loading the refrigerator with bottled blood, said, 'Maybe Cindy would like to move back home. Lindsey Krause quit the other shift because she's moving to Little Rock.'

That certainly focussed our attention. Merlotte's was becoming seriously understaffed. For some reason, low-level service jobs had dropped in popularity in the last couple of months.

'You interviewed anyone else?' Arlene asked.

'I'll have to go through the files,' Sam said wearily. I knew that Arlene and I were the only barmaids, waitresses, servers, whatever you wanted to call us, that Sam had hung on to for more then two years. No, that wasn't true; there was Susanne Mitchell, on the other shift. Sam spent lots of time hiring and occasionally firing. 'Sookie, would you have a look through the file, see if there's anyone there you know has moved, anyone already got a job, anyone you really recommend? That would save me some time.'

'Sure,' I said. I remembered Arlene doing the same thing a couple of years ago when Dawn had been hired. We had more ties to the community than Sam, who never seemed to join anything. Sam had been in Bon Temps for six years now, and I had never met anyone who seemed to know about Sam's life prior to his buying the bar here.

I settled down at Sam's desk with the thick file of applications. After a few minutes, I could tell I was really making a difference. I had three piles: moved, employed elsewhere, good material. Then I added a fourth and fifth stack: a pile for people I couldn't work with because I couldn't stand them, and a pile for the dead. The first form on the fifth pile had been filled out by a girl who'd died in a car accident last Christmas, and I felt sorry for her folks all over again when I saw her name at the top of the form. The other application was headed 'Maudette Pickens.'

Maudette had applied for a job with Sam three months before her death. I guess working at Grabbit Kwik was pretty uninspiring. When I glanced over the filled-in blanks and noticed how poor Maudette's handwriting and spelling had been, it made me feel pitiful all over again. I tried to imagine my brother thinking of having sex with this woman – and filming it – was a worthwhile way to spend his time, and I marvelled at Jason's strange mentality. I hadn't seen him since he'd driven off with Desiree. I hoped he'd gotten home in one piece. That gal was a real handful. I wished he'd settle down with Liz Barrett: she had enough backbone to hold him up, too.

Whenever I thought about my brother lately, it was to worry. If only he hadn't known Maudette and Dawn so well! Lots of men knew them both, apparently, both casually and carnally. They'd both been vampire bitten. Dawn had liked rough sex, and I didn't know Maudette's proclivities. Lots of men got gas and coffee at the Grabbit Kwik, and lots of men came in to get a drink here, too. But only my stupid brother had recorded sex with Dawn and Maudette on film.

I stared at the big plastic cup on Sam's desk, which had been full of iced tea. 'The Big Kwencher from Grabbit Kwik' was written in neon orange on the side of the green cup. Sam knew them both, too. Dawn had worked for him, Maudette had applied for a job here.

Sam sure didn't like *me* dating a vampire. Maybe he didn't like *anyone* dating a vampire.

Sam walked in just then, and I jumped like I'd been doing something bad. And I had, in my book. Thinking evil of a friend was a bad thing to do.

'Which is the good pile?' he asked, but he gave me a puzzled look.

I handed him a short stack of maybe ten applications. 'This gal, Amy Burley,' I said, indicating the one on top, 'has experience, she's only subbing at the Good Times Bar, and Charlsie used to work with her there. So you could check with Charlsie first.'

'Thanks, Sookie. This'll save me some trouble.'

I nodded curtly in acknowledgment.

'Are you all right?' he asked. 'You seem kind of distant today.'

I looked at him closely. He looked just like he always did. But his mind was closed to me. How could he do that? The only other mind completely closed to me was Bill's, because of his vampire state. But Sam was sure no vampire.

'Just missing Bill,' I said deliberately. Would he lecture me about the evils of dating a vampire?

Sam said, 'It's daytime. He couldn't very well be here.'

'Of course not,' I said stiffly, and was about to add, 'He's out of town.' Then I asked myself if that was a smart thing to do when I had even a hint of suspicion in my heart about my boss. I left the office so abruptly that Sam stared after me in astonishment.

When I saw Arlene and Sam having a long conversation later that day, their sidelong glances told me clearly that I was the topic. Sam went back to his office looking more worried than ever. But we didn't have any more chitchat the rest of the day.

Going home that evening was hard because I knew I'd be alone until morning. When I'd been alone other evenings, I'd had the reassurance that Bill was just a phone call away. Now he wasn't. I tried to feel good about being guarded once it was dark and Bubba crawled out of whatever hole he'd slept in, but I didn't manage it.

I called Jason, but he wasn't home. I called Merlotte's, thinking he might be there, but Terry Bellefleur answered the phone and said Jason hadn't been in.

I wondered what Sam was doing tonight. I wondered why he never seemed to date much. It wasn't for want of offers, I'd been able to observe many times.

Dawn had been especially aggressive.

That evening I couldn't think of anything that pleased me.

I began wondering if Bubba was the hitman – hitvampire? – Bill had called when he wanted Uncle Bartlett bumped off. I wondered why Bill had chosen such a dimwitted creature to guard me.

Every book I picked up seemed wrong, somehow. Every television show I tried to watch seemed completely ridiculous. I tried to read my *Time* and became incensed at the determination to commit suicide that possessed so many nations. I pitched the magazine across the room.

My mind scrabbled around like a squirrel trying to get out of a cage. It couldn't light on anything or be comfortable anywhere.

When the phone rang, I jumped a foot.

'Hello?' I said harshly.

'Jason's here now,' Terry Bellefleur said. 'He wants to buy you a drink.'

I thought uneasily about going out to the car, now that it was dark; about coming home to an empty house, at least a house I would have to hope was empty. Then I scolded myself because, after all, there would be someone watching the house, someone very strong, if very brainless.

'Okay, I'll be there in a minute,' I said.

Terry simply hung up. Mr. Chatterbox.

I pulled on a denim skirt and a yellow T-shirt and, looking both ways, crossed the yard to my car. I'd left on every outside light, and I unlocked my car and scooted inside quick as a wink. Once inside the car, I relocked my door.

This was sure no way to live.

*

I automatically parked in the employee lot when I got to Merlotte's. There was a dog pawing around the Dumpster, and I patted him on the head when I went in. We had to call the pound about once a week to come get some stray or dumped dogs, so many of them pregnant it just made me sick.

Terry was behind the bar.

'Hey,' I said, looking around. 'Where's Jason?'

'He ain't here,' Terry said. 'I haven't seen him this evening. I told you so on the phone.'

I gaped at him. 'But you called me after that and said he had come in.'

'No, I didn't.'

We stared at each other. Terry was having one of his bad nights, I could tell. His head was writhing around on the inside with the snakes of his army service and his battle with alcohol and drugs. On the outside, you could see he was flushed and sweating despite the air conditioning, and his movements were jerky and clumsy. Poor Terry.

'You really didn't?' I asked, in as neutral a tone as possible.

'Said so, didn't I?' His voice was belligerent.

I hoped none of the bar patrons gave Terry trouble tonight.

I backed out with a conciliatory smile.

The dog was still at the back door. He whined when he saw me.

'Are you hungry, fella?' I asked. He came right up to me, without the cringing I'd come to expect from strays. As he moved more into the light, I saw that this dog had been recently abandoned, if his glossy coat was any indicator. He was a collie, at least mostly. I started to step into the kitchen to ask whoever was cooking if they had any scraps for this guy, but then I had a better idea.

'I know bad ol' Bubba is at the house, but maybe you could come in the house with me,' I said in that baby voice I use with animals when I think nobody's listening. 'Can you pee outside, so we don't make a mess in the house? Hmmm, boy?'

As if he'd understood me, the collie marked the corner of the Dumpster.

'Good fella! Come for a ride?' I opened my car door, hoping he wouldn't get the seats too dirty. The dog hesitated. 'Come on, sugar, I'll give you something good to eat when we get to my place, okay?' Bribery was not necessarily a bad thing.

After a couple more looks and a thorough sniffing of my hands, the dog jumped onto the passenger seat and sat looking out the windshield like he'd committed himself to this adventure.

I told him I appreciated it, and I tickled his ears. We set off, and the dog made it clear he was used to riding.

'Now, when we get to the house, buddy,' I told the collie firmly, 'we're gonna make tracks for the front door, okay? There's an ogre in the woods who'd just love to eat you up.'

The dog gave an excited yip.

'Well, he's not gonna get a chance,' I soothed him. It sure was nice to have something to talk to. It was even nice he couldn't talk back, at least for the moment. And I didn't have to keep my guard up because he wasn't human. Relaxing. 'We're gonna hurry.'

'Woof,' agreed my companion.

'I got to call you something,' I said. 'How about . . . Buffy?'

The dog growled.

'Okay. Rover?'

Whine.

'Don't like that either. Hmmm.' We turned into my driveway.

'Maybe you already have a name?' I asked. 'Let me check your neck.' After I turned off the engine, I ran my fingers through the thick hair. Not even a flea collar. 'Someone's been taking bad care of you, sweetie,' I said. 'But not anymore. I'll be a good mama.' With that last inanity, I got my house key ready and opened my door. In a flash, the dog pushed past me and stood in the yard, looking around him alertly. He sniffed the air, and a growl rose in his throat.

'It's just the good vampire, sugar, the one that's guarding the house. You come on inside.' With some constant coaxing, I got the dog to come into the house. I locked the door behind us instantly.

The dog padded all around the living room, sniffing and peering. After watching him for a minute to be sure he wasn't going to chew on anything or lift his leg, I went to the kitchen to find something for him to eat. I filled a big bowl with water. I got another plastic bowl Gran had kept lettuce in, and I put the remains of Tina's cat food and some leftover taco meat in it. I figured if you'd been starving, that would be acceptable. The dog finally worked his way back to the kitchen and headed for the bowls. He sniffed at the food and raised his head to give me a long look.

'I'm sorry. I don't have any dog food. That's the best I could come up with. If you want to stay with me, I'll get some Kibbles 'N Bits.' The dog stared at me for a few more seconds, then bent his head to the bowl. He ate a little meat, took a drink, and looked up at me expectantly.

'Can I call you Rex?'

A little growl.

'What about Dean?' I asked. 'Dean's a nice name.' A pleasant guy who helped me at a Shreveport bookstore was named Dean. His eyes looked kind of like this collie's, observant and intelligent. And Dean was a little different; I'd never met a dog named Dean. 'I'll bet you're smarter than Bubba,' I said thoughtfully, and the dog gave his short, sharp bark.

'Well, come on, Dean, let's get ready for bed,' I said, quite enjoying having something to talk to. The dog padded after me into the bedroom, checking out all the furniture very thoroughly. I pulled off the skirt and tee, put them away, and stepped out of my panties and unhooked my bra. The dog watched me with great attention while I pulled out a clean nightgown and went into the bathroom to shower. When I stepped out, clean and soothed, Dean was sitting in the doorway, his head cocked to one side.

'That's to get clean, people like to have showers,' I told him. 'I know dogs don't. I guess it's a human thing.' I brushed my teeth and pulled on my nightgown. 'You ready for sleep, Dean?'

In answer, he jumped up on the bed, turned in a circle, and lay down.

'Hey! Wait a minute!' I'd certainly talked myself into that one. Gran would have a fit if she could know a dog was on her bed. Gran had believed animals were fine as long as they spent the night outside. Humans inside, animals outside, had been her rule. Well, now I had a vampire outside and a collie on my bed.

I said, 'You get down!' and pointed at the rug.

The collie, slowly, reluctantly, descended from the bed. He eyed me reproachfully as he sat on the rug.

'You stay there,' I said sternly and got in the bed. I was very tired, and not nearly so nervous now that the dog was here; though what help I expected him to be in case of an intruder, I didn't know, since he didn't know me well enough to be loyal to me. But I would accept any comfort I could find, and I began to relax into sleep. Just as I was drifting off, I felt the bed indent under the weight of the collie. A narrow tongue gave my cheek a swipe. The dog settled close to me. I turned over and patted him. It was sort of nice having him here.

The next thing I knew, it was dawn. I could hear the birds going to town outside, chirping up a storm, and it felt wonderful to be snuggled in bed. I could feel the warmth of the dog through my nightgown; I must have gotten hot during the night and thrown off the sheet. I drowsily patted the animal's head and began to stroke his fur, my fingers running idly through the thick hair. He wriggled even closer, sniffed my face, put his arm around me.

His *arm*?

I was off the bed and shrieking in one move.

In my bed, Sam propped himself on his elbows, sunny side up, and looked at me with some amusement.

'Oh, ohmyGod! Sam, how'd you get here? What are you doing? Where's Dean?' I covered my face with my hands and turned my back, but I'd certainly seen all there was to see of Sam.

'Woof,' said Sam, from a human throat, and the truth stomped over me in combat boots.

I whirled back to face him, so angry I felt like I was going to blow a gasket.

'You watched me undress last night, you . . . you . . . damn dog!'

'Sookie,' he said, persuasively. 'Listen to me.'

Another thought struck me. 'Oh, Sam. Bill will kill you.' I sat on the slipper chair in the corner by the bathroom door. I put my elbows on my knees and hung my head. 'Oh, no,' I said. 'No, no, no.'

He was kneeling in front of me. The wiry red-gold hair of his head was duplicated on his chest and trailed in a line down to . . . I shut my eyes again.

'Sookie, I was worried when Arlene told me you were going to be alone,' Sam began.

'Didn't she tell you about Bubba?'

'Bubba?'

'This vampire Bill left watching the house.'

'Oh. Yeah, she said he reminded her of some singer.'

'Well, his name is Bubba. He likes to drain animals for fun.'

I had the satisfaction of seeing (through my fingers) Sam turn pale.

'Well, isn't it lucky you let me in, then,' he said finally.

Suddenly recalled to his guise of the night before, I said, 'What are you, Sam?'

'I'm a shapeshifter. I thought it was time you knew.'

'Did you have to do it quite like that?'

'Actually,' he said, embarrassed, 'I had planned on waking up and getting out before you opened your eyes. I just overslept. Running around on all fours kind of tires you out.'

'I thought people just changed into wolves.'

'Nope. I can change into anything.'

I was so interested I dropped my hands and tried to just

stare at his face. 'How often?' I asked. 'Do you get to pick?'

'I have to at the full moon,' he explained. 'Other times, I have to will it; it's harder and it takes longer. I turn into whatever animal I saw before I changed. So I keep a dog book open to a picture of a collie on my coffee table. Collies are big, but non-threatening.'

'So, you could be a bird?'

'Yeah, but flying is hard. I'm always scared I'm going to get fried on a power line, or fly into a window.'

'Why? Why did you want me to know?'

'You seemed to handle Bill being a vampire really well. In fact, you seemed to enjoy it. So I thought I would see if you could handle my . . . condition.'

'But what you are,' I said abruptly, off on a mental tangent, 'can't be explained by a virus! I mean, you utterly change!'

He didn't say anything. He just looked at me, the eyes now blue, but just as intelligent and observant.

'Being a shapeshifter is definitely supernatural. If that is, then other things can be. So . . .' I said, slowly, carefully, 'Bill hasn't got a virus at all. Being a vampire, it really can't be explained by an allergy to silver or garlic or sunlight . . . that's just so much bullshit the vampires are spreading around, propaganda, you might say . . . so they can be more easily accepted, as sufferers from a terrible disease. But really they're . . . they're really . . .'

I dashed into the bathroom and threw up. Luckily, I made it to the toilet.

'Yeah,' Sam said from the doorway, his voice sad. 'I'm sorry, Sookie. But Bill doesn't just have a virus. He's really, really dead.'

*

I washed my face and brushed my teeth twice. I sat down on the edge of the bed, feeling too tired to go further. Sam sat beside me. He put his arm around me comfortingly, and after a moment I nestled closer, laying my cheek in the hollow of his neck.

'You know, once I was listening to NPR,' I said, completely at random. 'They were broadcasting a piece about cryogenics, about how lots of people are opting to just freeze their head because it's so much cheaper than getting your whole body frozen.'

'Ummm?'

'Guess what song they played for the closing?'

'What, Sookie?'

'Put Your Head on My Shoulder.'

Sam made a choking noise, then doubled over with laughter.

'Listen, Sam,' I said, when he'd calmed down. 'I hear what you're telling me, but I have to work this out with Bill. I love Bill. I am loyal to him. And he isn't here to give his point of view.'

'Oh, this isn't about me trying to woo you away from Bill. Though that would be great.' And Sam smiled his rare and brilliant smile. He seemed much more relaxed with me now that I knew his secret.

'Then what is it about?'

'This is about keeping you alive until the murderer is caught.'

'So that's why you woke up naked in my bed? For my protection?'

He had the grace to look ashamed. 'Well, maybe I could have planned it better. But I did think you needed someone with you, since Arlene told me Bill was out of town. I knew you wouldn't let me spend the night here as a human.'

'Will you rest easy now that you know Bubba is watching the house at night?'

'Vampires are strong, and ferocious,' Sam conceded. 'I guess this Bubba owes Bill something, or he wouldn't be doing him a favor. Vampires aren't big on doing each other favors. They have a lot of structure in their world.'

I should have paid more attention to what Sam was saying, but I was thinking I'd better not explain about Bubba's origins.

'If there's you, and Bill, I guess there must be lots of other things outside of nature,' I said, realizing what a treasure trove of thought awaited me. Since I'd met Bill, I hadn't felt so much need to hoard neat things up for future contemplation, but it never hurt to be prepared. 'You'll have to tell me sometime.' Big Foot? The Loch Ness Monster? I'd always believed in the Loch Ness monster.

'Well, I guess I better be getting back home,' Sam said. He looked at me hopefully. He was still naked.

'Yes, I think you better. But – oh, dang it – you . . . oh, hell.' I stomped upstairs to look for some clothes. It seemed to me Jason had a couple of things in an upstairs closet he kept here for some emergency.

Sure enough, there was a pair of blue jeans and a work shirt in the first upstairs bedroom. It was already hot up there, under the tin roof, because the upstairs was on a separate thermostat. I came back down, grateful to feel the cool conditioned air.

'Here,' I said, handing Sam the clothes. 'I hope they fit well enough.' He looked as though he wanted to start our conversation back up, but I was too aware now that I was clad in a thin nylon nightgown and he was clad in nothing at all.

'On with the clothes,' I said firmly. 'And you get dressed out in the living room.' I shooed him out and shut the door behind him. I thought it would be insulting to lock the door, so I didn't. I did get dressed in record time, pulling on clean underwear and the denim skirt and yellow shirt I'd had on the night before. I dabbed on my makeup, put on some earrings, and brushed my hair up into a ponytail, putting a yellow scrunchy over the elastic band. My morale rose as I looked in the mirror. My smile turned into a frown when I thought I heard a truck pulling into the front yard.

I came out of the bedroom like I'd been fired from a cannon, hoping like hell Sam was dressed and hiding. He'd done one better. He'd changed back into a dog. The clothes were scattered on the floor, and I swept them up and stuffed them into the closet in the hall.

'Good boy!' I said enthusiastically and scratched behind his ears. Dean responded by sticking his cold black nose up my skirt. 'Now you cut that out,' I said, and looked through the front window. 'It's Andy Bellefleur,' I told the dog.

Andy jumped out of his Dodge Ram, stretched for a long second, and headed for my front door. I opened it, Dean by my side.

I eyed Andy quizzically. 'You look like you been up all night long, Andy. Can I make you some coffee?'

The dog stirred restlessly beside me.

'That would be great,' he said. 'Can I come in?'

'Sure.' I stood aside. Dean growled.

'You got a good guard dog, there. Here, fella Come here.'

Andy squatted to hold out a hand to the collie, whom I simply could not think of as Sam. Dean sniffed Andy's hand, but wouldn't give it a lick. Instead, he kept between me and Andy.

'Come on back to the kitchen,' I said, and Andy stood and followed me. I had the coffee on in a jiffy and put some bread in the toaster. Assembling the cream and sugar and spoons and mugs took a few more minutes, but then I had to face why Andy was here. His face was drawn; he looked ten years older than I knew him to be. This was no courtesy call.

'Sookie, were you here last night? You didn't work?'

'No, I didn't. I was here except for a quick trip in to Merlotte's.'

'Was Bill here any of that time?'

'No, he's in New Orleans. He's staying in that new hotel in the French Quarter, the one just for vampires.'

'You're sure that's where he is.'

'Yes.' I could feel my face tighten. The bad thing was coming.

'I've been up all night,' Andy said.

'Yes.'

'I've just come from another crime scene.'

'Yes.' I went into his mind. 'Amy Burley?' I stared at his eyes, trying to make sure. 'Amy who worked at the Good Times Bar?' The name at the top of yesterday's pile of prospective barmaids, the name I'd left for Sam. I looked down at the dog. He lay on the floor with his muzzle between his paws, looking as sad and stunned as I felt. He whined pathetically.

Andy's brown eyes were boring a hole in me. 'How'd you know?'

'Cut the crap, Andy, you know I can read minds. I feel awful. Poor Amy. Was it like the others?'

'Yes,' he said. 'Yes, it was like the others. But the puncture marks were fresher.'

I thought of the night Bill and I had had to go to Shreveport to answer Eric's summons. Had Amy given Bill blood that night? I couldn't even count how many days ago that had been, my schedule had been so thrown off by all the strange and terrible events of the past few weeks.

I sat down heavily in a wooden kitchen chair, shaking my head absently for a few minutes, amazed at the turn my life had taken.

Amy Burley's life had no more turns to take. I shook the odd spell of apathy off, rose and poured the coffee.

'Bill hasn't been here since the night before last,' I said.

'And you were here all night?'

'Yes, I was. My dog can tell you,' and I smiled down at Dean, who whined at being noticed. He came over to lay his fuzzy head on my knees while I drank my coffee. I smoothed his ears.

'Did you hear from your brother?'

'No, but I got a funny phone call, from someone who said he was at Merlotte's.' After the words left my mouth I realized the caller must have been Sam, luring me over to Merlotte's so he could maneuver himself into accompanying me home. Dean yawned, a big jaw-cracking yawn that let us see every one of his white sharp teeth.

I wished I'd kept my mouth shut.

But now I had to explain the whole thing to Andy, who was slumped only half-awake in my kitchen chair, his plaid shirt wrinkled and blotched with coffee stains, his khakis shapeless through long wear. Andy was longing for bed the way a horse longs for his own stall.

'You need to get some rest,' I said gently. There was something sad about Andy Bellefleur, something daunted.

'It's these murders,' he said, his voice unsteady from exhaustion. 'These poor women. And they were all the same in so many ways.'

'Uneducated, blue-collar women who worked in bars? Didn't mind having a vampire lover from time to time?'

He nodded, his eyes drooping shut.

'Women just like me, in other words.'

His eyes opened then. He was aghast at his error. 'Sookie . . .'

'I understand, Andy,' I said. 'In some respects, we are all alike, and if you accept the attack on my grandmother as intended for me, well, I guess then I'm the only survivor.'

I wondered who the murderer had left to kill. Was I the only one alive who met his criteria? That was the scariest thought I'd had all day.

Andy was practically nodding over his coffee cup.

'Why don't you go lie down in the other bedroom?' I suggested quietly. 'You have to have some sleep. You're not safe to drive, I wouldn't think.'

'That's kind of you,' Andy said, his voice dragging. He sounded a little surprised, like kindness wasn't something he expected from me. 'But I have to get home, set my alarm. I can sleep for maybe three hours.'

'I promise I'll wake you up,' I said. I didn't want Andy sleeping in my house, but I didn't want him to have a wreck on the way to his house, either. Old Mrs. Bellefleur would never forgive me, and probably Portia wouldn't either. 'You come lie down in this room.' I led him to my old bedroom. My single bed was neatly made up. 'You just lie down on top of the bed, and I'll set the alarm.' I did, while he watched. 'Now, get a little sleep. I have one errand to run, and I'll be right back.' Andy didn't offer any more resistance, but sat heavily on the bed even as I shut the door.

The dog had been padding after me while I got Andy situated, and now I said to him, in a quite different tone, 'You go get dressed right *now*!'

Andy stuck his head out the bedroom door. 'Sookie, who are you talking to?'

'The dog,' I answered instantly. 'He always gets his collar, and I put it on every day.'

'Why do you ever take it off?'

'It jingles at night, keeps me up. You go to bed, now.'

'All right.' Looking satisfied at my explanation, Andy shut the door again.

I retrieved Jason's clothes from the closet, put them on the couch in front of the dog, and sat with my back turned. But I realized I could see in the mirror over the mantel.

The air grew hazy around the collie, seemed to hum and vibrate with energy, and then the form began to change within that electric concentration. When the haze cleared, there was Sam kneeling on the floor, buck-naked. Wow, what a bottom. I had to make myself close my eyes, tell myself repeatedly that I had not been unfaithful to Bill. Bill's butt, I told myself staunchly, was every bit as neat.

'I'm ready,' Sam's voice said, so close behind me that I jumped. I stood up quickly and turned to face him, and found his face about six inches from mine.

'Sookie,' he said hopefully, his hand landing on my shoulder, rubbing and caressing it.

I was angry because half of me wanted to respond.

'Listen here, buddy, you could have told me about yourself any time in the past few years. We've known each other what, four years? Or even more! And yet, Sam, despite the fact that I see you almost daily, you wait until Bill is interested in me, before you even . . .' and unable to think how to finish, I threw my hands up in the air.

Sam drew back, which was a good thing.

'I didn't see what was in front of me until I thought it might be taken away,' he said, his voice quiet.

I had nothing to say to that. 'Time to go home,' I told him. 'And we better get you there without anyone seeing you. I mean it.'

This was chancy enough without some mischievous person like Rene seeing Sam in my car in the early morning and drawing wrong conclusions. And passing them on to Bill.

So off we went, Sam hunched down in the backseat. I pulled cautiously behind Merlotte's. There was a truck there; black, with pink and aqua flames down the sides. Jason's.

'Uh-oh,' I said.

'What?' Sam's voice was somewhat muffled by his position.

'Let me go look,' I said, beginning to be anxious. Why would Jason park over here in the employees' parking area? And it seemed to me there was a shape in the truck.

I opened my door. I waited for the sound to alert the figure in the truck. I watched for evidence of movement. When nothing happened, I began to walk across the gravel, as frightened as I'd ever been in the light of day.

When I got closer to the window, I could see that the figure inside was Jason. He was slumped behind the wheel.

I could see that his shirt was stained, that his chin was resting on his chest, that his hands were limp on the seat on either side of him, that the mark on his handsome face was a long red scratch. I could see a videotape resting on the truck dashboard, unlabelled.

'Sam,' I said, hating the fear in my voice. 'Please come here.'

Quicker than I could believe, Sam was beside me, then reaching past me to unlatch the truck door. Since the truck had apparently been sitting there for several hours – there was dew on its hood – with the windows closed, in the early summer, the smell that rolled out was pretty strong and compounded of at least three elements: blood, sex, and liquor.

'Call the ambulance!' I said urgently as Sam reached in to feel for Jason's pulse. Sam looked at me doubtfully. 'Are you sure you want to do that?' he asked.

'Of course! He's unconscious!'

'Wait, Sookie. Think about this.'

And I might have reconsidered in just a minute, but at that moment Arlene pulled up in her beat-up blue Ford, and Sam sighed and went into his trailer to phone.

I was so naive. That's what comes of being a law-abiding citizen for nearly every day of my life.

I rode with Jason to the tiny local hospital, oblivious to the police looking very carefully at Jason's truck, blind to the squad car following the ambulance, totally trusting when the emergency room doctor sent me home, telling me he'd call me when Jason regained consciousness. The doctor told me, eyeing me curiously, that Jason was apparently sleeping off the effects of alcohol or drugs. But Jason had never drunk that much before, and Jason didn't use drugs:

our cousin Hadley's descent into the life of the streets had made a profound impression on both of us. I told the doctor all that, and he listened, and he shooed me off.

Not knowing what to think, I went home to find that Andy Bellefleur had been roused by his pager. He'd left me a note telling me that, and nothing else. Later on, I found that he'd actually been in the hospital while I was there, and waited until I was gone out of consideration for me before he'd handcuffed Jason to the bed.

Chapter 12

Sam came to give me the news about eleven o'clock. 'They're going to arrest Jason as soon as he comes to, Sookie, which looks like being soon.' Sam didn't tell me how he came to know this, and I didn't ask.

I stared at him, tears running down my face. Any other day, I might have thought of how plain I look when I cry, but today was not a day I cared about my outsides. I was all in a knot, frightened for Jason, sad about Amy Burley, full of anger the police were making such a stupid mistake, and underneath it all, missing my Bill.

'They think it looks like Amy Burley put up a fight. They think he got drunk after he killed her.'

'Thanks, Sam, for warning me.' My voice came from way faraway. 'You better go to work, now.'

After Sam had seen that I needed to be alone, I called information and got the number of Blood in the Quarter. I punched in the numbers, feeling somehow I was doing a bad thing, but I couldn't think how or why.

'Bloooooood . . . in the Quarter,' announced a deep voice dramatically. 'Your coffin away from home.'

Geez. 'Good morning. This is Sookie Stackhouse calling from Bon Temps,' I said politely. 'I need to leave a message for Bill Compton. He's a guest there.'

'Fang or human?'

'Ah . . . fang.'

'Just one minute, please.'

The deep voice came back on the line after a moment. 'What is the message, madam?'

That gave me pause.

'Please tell Mr. Compton that . . . my brother has been arrested, and I would appreciate it if he could come home as soon as his business is completed.'

'I have that down.' The sound of scribbling. 'And your name again?'

'Stackhouse. Sookie Stackhouse.'

'All right, miss. I'll see to it that he gets your message.'

'Thanks.'

And that was the only action I could think of to take, until I realized it would be much more practical to call Sid Matt Lancaster. He did his best to sound appalled to hear Jason was going to be arrested, said he'd hurry over to the hospital as soon as he got out of court that afternoon, and that he'd report back to me.

I drove back to the hospital to see if they'd let me sit with Jason until he became conscious. They wouldn't. I wondered if he was already conscious, and they weren't telling me. I saw Andy Bellefleur at the other end of the hall, and he turned and walked the other way.

Damn coward.

I went home because I couldn't think of anything to do. I realized it wasn't a workday for me anyway, and that was a good thing, though I didn't really care too much at that point. It occurred to me that I wasn't handling this as well as I ought, that I had been much steadier when Gran had died.

But that had been a finite situation. We would bury Gran, her killer would be arrested, we would go on. If the police seriously believed that Jason had killed Gran in addition to the other women, then the world was such a bad and chancy place that I wanted no part of it.

But I realized, as I sat and looked in front of me that long, long afternoon, that it was naivete like that that had led to Jason's arrest. If I'd just gotten him into Sam's trailer and cleaned him up, hidden the film until I found out what it contained, above all not called the ambulance . . . that had been what Sam had been thinking when he'd looked at me so doubtfully. However, Arlene's arrival had kind of wiped out my options.

I thought the phone would start ringing as soon as people heard.

But no one called.

They didn't know what to say.

Sid Matt Lancaster came about four-thirty.

Without any preliminary, he told me, 'They've arrested him. For first-degree murder.'

I closed my eyes. When I opened them, Sid was regarding me with a shrewd expression on his mild face. His conservative black-framed glasses magnified his muddy brown eyes, and his jowls and sharp nose made him look a little like a bloodhound.

'What does he say?' I asked.

'He says that he was with Amy last night.'

I sighed.

'He says they went to bed together, that he had been

with Amy before. He says he hadn't seen Amy in a long time, that the last time they were together Amy was acting jealous about the other women he was seeing, really angry. So he was surprised when she approached him last night in Good Times. Jason says Amy acted funny all night, like she had an agenda he didn't know about. He remembers having sex with her, he remembers them lying in bed having a drink afterward, then he remembers nothing until he woke up in the hospital.'

'He was set up,' I said firmly, thinking I sounded exactly like a bad made-for-TV movie.

'Of course.' Sid Matt's eyes were as steady and assured as if he'd been at Amy Burley's place last night.

Hell, maybe he had.

'Listen, Sid Matt.' I leaned forward and made him meet my eyes. 'Even if I could somehow believe that Jason had killed Amy, and Dawn, and Maudette, I could never believe he would raise his finger to hurt my grandmother.'

'All right, then.' Sid Matt prepared to meet my thoughts, fair and square, his entire body proclaimed it. 'Miss Sookie, let's just assume for a minute that Jason did have some kind of involvement in those deaths. Perhaps, the police might think, your friend Bill Compton killed your grandmother since she was keeping you two apart.'

I tried to give the appearance of considering this piece of idiocy. 'Well, Sid Matt, my grandmother liked Bill, and she was pleased I was seeing him.'

Until he put his game face back on, I saw stark disbelief in the lawyer's eyes. He wouldn't be at all happy if his daughter was seeing a vampire. He couldn't imagine a responsible parent being anything but appalled. And he couldn't imagine trying to convince a jury that my grandmother had been pleased I was dating a guy who wasn't even alive, and furthermore was over a hundred years older than me.

Those were Sid Matt's thoughts.

'Have you met Bill?' I asked.

He was taken aback. 'No,' he admitted. 'You know, Miss Sookie, I'm not for this vampire stuff. I think it's taking a chink out of a wall we should keep built up, a wall between us and the so-called virus-infected. I think God intended that wall to be there, and I for one will hold up my section.'

'The problem with that, Sid Matt, is that I personally was created straddling that wall.' After a lifetime of keeping my mouth shut about my 'gift,' I found that if it would help Jason, I'd shake it in anybody's face.

'Well,' Sid Matt said bravely, pushing his glasses up on the bridge of his sharp nose, 'I am sure the Good Lord gave you this problem I've heard about for a reason. You have to learn how to use it for his glory.'

No one had ever quite put it that way. That was an idea to chew over when I had time.

'I've made us stray from the subject, I'm afraid, and I know your time is valuable.' I gathered my thoughts. 'I want Jason out on bail. There is nothing but circumstantial evidence tying him to Amy's murder, am I right?'

'He's admitted to being with the victim right before the murder, and the videotape, one of the cops hinted to me pretty strongly, shows your brother having sex with the victim. The time and date on the film indicate it was made in the hours before her death, if not minutes.'

Damn Jason's peculiar bedroom preferences. 'Jason doesn't drink much at all. He smelled of liquor in the truck. I think it was just spilled over him. I think a test will prove that. Maybe Amy gave him some narcotic in the drink she fixed him.'

'Why would she do that?'

'Because, like so many women, she was mad at Jason because she wanted him so much. My brother is able to date almost anyone he wants. No, I'm using that euphemism.'

Sid Matt looked surprised I knew the word.

'He could go to bed with almost anyone he wanted. A dream life, most guys would think.' Weariness descended on me like fog. 'Now there he sits in the jail.'

'You think another man did this to him? Framed him for this murder?'

'Yes, I do.' I leaned forward, trying to persuade this skeptical lawyer by the force of my own belief. 'Someone envious of him. Someone who knows his schedule, who kills these women when Jason's off work. Someone who knows Jason had had sex with these gals. Someone who knows he likes to make tapes.'

'Could be almost anyone,' Jason's lawyer said practically.

'Yep,' I said sadly. 'Even if Jason was nice enough to keep quiet about exactly who he'd been with, all anyone'd have to do is see who he left a bar with at closing time. Just being observant, maybe having asked about the tapes on a visit to his house . . .' My brother might be somewhat immoral, but I didn't think he'd show those videos to anyone else. He might tell another man that he liked to make the videos, though. 'So this man, whoever he is, made some kind of deal with Amy, knowing she was mad at Jason. Maybe he told her he was going to play a practical joke on Jason or something.'

'Your brother's never been arrested before,' Sid Matt observed.

'No.' Though it had been a near thing, a couple of times, to hear Jason tell it.

'No record, upstanding member of the community, steady job. There may be a chance I can get him out on bail. But if he runs, you'll lose everything.'

It truly had never occurred to me that Jason might skip bail. I didn't know anything about arranging for bail, and I didn't know what I'd have to do, but I wanted Jason out of that jail. Somehow, staying in jail until the legal processes had been gone through before the trial . . . somehow, that would make him look guiltier.

'You find out about it and let me know what I have to do,' I said. 'In the meantime, can I go see him?'

'He'd rather you didn't,' Sid Matt said.

That hurt dreadfully. 'Why?' I asked, trying really hard not to tear up again.

'He's ashamed,' said the lawyer.

The thought of Jason feeling shame was fascinating.

'So,' I said, trying to move along, suddenly tired of this unsatisfactory meeting. 'You'll call me when I can actually do something?'

Sid Matt nodded, his jowls trembling slightly with the movement. I made him uneasy. He sure was glad to be leaving me.

The lawyer drove off in his pickup, clapping a cowboy hat on his head when he was still in sight.

When it was full dark, I went out to check on Bubba. He was sitting under a pin oak, bottles of blood lined up beside him, empties on one side, fulls on the other.

I had a flashlight, and though I knew Bubba was there, it was still a shock to see him in the beam of light. I shook my head. Something really had gone wrong when Bubba 'came over,' no doubt about it. I was sincerely glad I couldn't read Bubba's thoughts. His eyes were crazy as hell.

'Hey, sugar,' he said, his Southern accent as thick as syrup. 'How you doing? You come to keep me company?'

'I just wanted to make sure you were comfortable,' I said.

'Well, I could think of places I'd be more comfortable, but since you're Bill's girl, I ain't about to talk about them.'

'Good,' I said firmly.

'Any cats around here? I'm getting mighty tired of this bottled stuff.'

'No cats. I'm sure Bill will be back soon, and then you can go home.' I started back toward the house, not feeling comfortable enough in Bubba's presence to prolong the conversation, if you could call it that. I wondered what thoughts Bubba had during his long watchful nights; I wondered if he remembered his past.

'What about that dog?' he called after me.

'He went home,' I called back over my shoulder.

'Too bad,' Bubba said to himself, so softly I almost didn't hear him.

I got ready for bed. I watched television. I ate some ice cream, and I even chopped up a Heath Bar for a topping. None of my usual comfort things seemed to work tonight. My brother was in jail, my boyfriend was in New Orleans, my grandmother was dead, and someone had murdered my cat. I felt lonely and sorry for myself all the way around.

Sometimes you just have to roll in it.

Bill didn't return my call.

That added fuel to the flame of my misery. He'd probably found some accommodating whore in New Orleans, or some fang-banger, like the ones who hung around Blood in the Quarter every night, hoping for a vampire 'date.'

If I were a drinking woman, I would have gotten drunk. If I'd been a casual woman, I would have called lovely JB du Rone and had sex with him. But I'm not anything so dramatic or drastic, so I just ate ice cream and watched old movies on TV. By an eerie coincidence, *Blue Hawaii* was on.

I finally went to bed about midnight.

A shriek outside my bedroom window woke me up. I sat up straight in bed. I heard thumps, and thuds, and finally a voice I was sure was Bubba's shouting, 'Come back here, sucker!'

When I hadn't heard anything in a couple of minutes, I pulled on a bathrobe and went to the front door. The yard, lit by the security light, was empty. Then I glimpsed movement to the left, and when I stuck my head out the door, I saw Bubba, trudging back to his hideout.

'What happened?' I called softly.

Bubba changed direction and slouched over to the porch.

'Sure enough, some sumbitch, scuse me, was sneaking around the house,' Bubba said. His brown eyes were glowing, and he looked more like his former self. 'I heard him minutes before he got here, and I thought I'd catch ahold of him. But he cut through the woods to the road, and he had a truck parked there.'

'Did you get a look?'

'Not enough of one to describe him,' Bubba said shamefacedly. 'He was driving a pickup, but I couldn't even tell what color it was. Dark.'

'You saved me, though,' I said, hoping my very real gratitude showed in my voice. I felt a swell of love for Bill, who had arranged my protection. Even Bubba looked better than he had before. 'Thanks, Bubba.'

'Aw, think nothing of it,' he said graciously, and for that moment he stood up straight, kind of tossed his head back, had that sleepy smile on his face . . . it *was* him, and I'd opened my mouth to say his name, when Bill's warning came back to shut my mouth.

Jason made bail the next day.

It cost a fortune. I signed what Sid Matt told me to, though mostly the collateral was Jason's house and truck and his fishing boat. If Jason had ever been arrested before, even for jaywalking, I don't think he would have been permitted to post bond.

I was standing on the courthouse steps wearing my horrible, sober, navy blue suit in the heat of the late morning. Sweat trickled down my face and ran between my lips in that nasty way that makes you want to go jump in the shower. Jason stopped in front of me. I hadn't been sure he would speak. His face was years older. Real trouble had come to sit on his shoulder, real trouble that would not go away or ease up, like grief did.

'I can't talk to you about this,' he said, so softly I could barely hear him. 'You know it wasn't me. I've never been violent beyond a fight or two in a parking lot over some woman.'

I touched his shoulder, let my hand drop when he didn't respond. 'I never thought it was you. I never will. I'm sorry I was fool enough to call 911 yesterday. If I'd realized that wasn't your blood, I'd have taken you into Sam's trailer and cleaned you up and burned the tape. I was just so scared that was your blood.' And I felt my eyes fill. This was no time to cry, though, and I tightened up all over, feeling my face tense. Jason's mind was a mess, like a mental pigsty. In it bubbled an unhealthy brew compounded of regrets, shame at his sexual habits being made public, guilt that he didn't feel worse about Amy being killed, horror that anyone in the town would think he'd killed his own grandmother while lying in wait for his sister.

'We'll get through this,' I said helplessly.

'We'll get through this,' he repeated, trying to make his voice sound strong and assured. But I thought it would be awhile, a long while, before Jason's assurance, that golden certainty that had made him irresistible, returned to his posture and his face and his speech.

Maybe it never would.

We parted there, at the courthouse. We had nothing more to say.

I sat in the bar all day, looking at the men who came in, reading their minds. Not one of them was thinking of how he'd killed four women and gotten away with it so far. At lunchtime Hoyt and Rene walked in the door and walked back out when they saw me sitting. Too embarrassing for them, I guess.

Finally, Sam made me leave. He said I was so creepy that I was driving away any customers who might give me useful information.

I trudged out the door and into the glaring sun. It was about to set. I thought about Bubba, about Bill, about all those creatures that were coming out of their deep sleep to walk the surface of the earth.

I stopped at the Grabbit Kwik to buy some milk for my morning cereal. The new clerk was a kid with pimples and a huge Adam's apple, who stared at me eagerly as if he was trying to make a print in his head of how I looked, the sister of a murderer. I could tell he could hardly wait for me to leave the store so he could use the phone to call his girlfriend. He was wishing he could see the puncture marks on my neck. He was wondering if there was any way he could find out how vampires did it.

This was the kind of trash I had to listen to, day in, day out. No matter how hard I concentrated on something else, no matter how high I kept my guard, how broad I kept my smile, it seeped through.

I reached home just when it was getting dark. After putting away the milk and taking off my suit, I put on a pair of shorts and a black Garth Brooks T-shirt and tried to think of some goal for the evening. I couldn't settle down enough to read; and I needed to go to the library and change my books anyway, which would be a real ordeal under the circumstances. Nothing on TV was good, at least tonight. I thought I might watch *Braveheart* again: Mel Gibson in a kilt is always a mood raiser. But it was just too bloody for my frame of mind. I couldn't bear for that gal get her throat cut again, even though I knew when to cover my eyes.

I'd gone into the bathroom to wash off my sweaty makeup when, over the sound of the running water. I thought I heard a yowl outside.

I turned the faucets off. I stood still, almost feeling my antenna twitch, I was listening so intently. What . . .? Water from my wet face trickled onto my T-shirt.

No sound. No sound at all.

I crept toward the front door because it was closest to Bubba's watch point in the woods.

I opened the door a little. I yelled, 'Bubba?'

No answer.

I tried again.

It seemed to me even the locusts and toads were holding their breaths. The night was so silent it might hold anything. Something was prowling out there, in the darkness.

I tried to think, but my heart was hammering so hard it interfered with the process.

Call the police, first.

I found that was not an option. The phone was dead.

So I could either wait in this house for trouble to come to me, or I could go out into the woods.

That was a tough one. I bit into my lower lip while I went around the house turning out the lamps, trying to map out a course of action. The house provided some protection: locks, walls, nooks, and crannies. But I knew any really determined person could get in, and then I would be trapped.

Okay. How could I get outside without being seen? I turned off the outside lights, for a start. The back door was closer to the woods, so that was the better choice. I knew the woods pretty well. I should be able to hide in them until daylight. I could go over to Bill's house, maybe; surely his phone was working, and I had a key.

Or I could try to get to my car and start it. But that pinned me down to a particular place for particular seconds.

No, the woods seemed the better choice to me.

In one of my pockets I tucked Bill's key and a pocketknife of my grandfather's that Gran had kept in the living-room table drawer, handy for opening packages. I tucked a tiny flashlight in the other pocket. Gran kept an old rifle in the coat closet by the front door. It had been my dad's when he was little, and she mostly had used it for shooting snakes; well, I had me a snake to shoot. I hated the damn rifle, hated the thought of using it, but now seemed to be the time.

It wasn't there.

I could hardly believe my senses. I felt all through the closet.

He'd been in my house!

But it hadn't been broken into.

Someone I'd invited in. Who'd been here? I tried to list them all as I went to the back door, my sneakers retied so they wouldn't have any spare shoelaces to step on. I skinned my hair into a ponytail sloppily, almost one handed, so it wouldn't get in my face, and twisted a rubber band around it. But all the time I thought about the stolen rifle.

Who'd been in my house? Bill, Jason, Arlene, Rene, the kids, Andy Bellefleur, Sam, Sid Matt; I was sure I'd left them all alone for a minute or two, perhaps long enough to stick the rifle outside to retrieve later.

Then I remembered the day of the funeral. Almost everyone I knew had been in and out of the house when Gran had died, and I couldn't remember if I'd seen the rifle since then. But it would have been hard to have casually strolled out of the crowded, busy house with a rifle. And if it had vanished then, I thought I would have noticed its absence by now. In fact, I was almost sure I would have.

I had to shove that aside now and concentrate on outwitting whatever was out there in the dark.

I opened the back door. I duckwalked out, keeping as low as I could, and gently eased the door nearly shut behind me. Rather than use the steps, I straightened one leg and tapped the ground while squatting on the porch; I shifted my weight to it, pulled the other leg behind me. I crouched again. This was a lot like playing hide and seek with Jason in the woods when we were kids.

I prayed I was not playing hide and seek with Jason again.

I used the tub full of flowers that Gran had planted as cover first, then I crept to her car, my second goal. I looked up in the sky. The moon was huge, and since the night was clear the stars were out. The air was heavy with humidity, and it was still hot. My arms were slick with sweat in minutes.

Next step, from the car to the mimosa tree.

I wasn't as quiet this time. I tripped over a stump and hit the ground hard. I bit the inside of my mouth to keep from crying out. Pain shot through my leg and hip, and I knew the edges of the ragged stump had scraped my thigh pretty severely. Why hadn't I come out and sawed that stump off clean? Gran had asked Jason to do it, but he'd never found the time.

I heard, sensed, movement. Throwing caution to the winds, I leaped up and dashed for the trees. Someone crashed through the edge of the woods to my right and headed for me. But I knew where I was going, and in a vault that amazed me, I'd seized the low branch of our favorite childhood climbing tree and pulled myself up. If I lived until the next day, I'd have severely strained muscles, but it would be worth it. I balanced on the branch, trying to keep my breathing quiet, when I wanted to pant and groan like a dog dreaming.

I wished this were a dream. Yet here I undeniably was, Sookie Stackhouse, waitress and mind reader, sitting on a branch in the woods in the dead of night, armed with nothing more than a pocket knife.

Movement below me; a man glided through the woods.

He had a length of cord hanging from one wrist. Oh, Jesus. Though the moon was almost full, his head shyed stubbornly in the shadow of the tree, and I couldn't tell who it was. He passed underneath without seeing me.

When he was out of sight, I breathed again. As quietly as I could, I scrambled down. I began working my way through the woods to the road. It would take awhile, but if I could get to the road maybe I could flag someone down. Then I thought of how seldom the road got traveled; it might be better to work my way across the cemetery to Bill's house. I thought of the cemetery at night, of the murderer looking for me, and I shivered all over.

Being even more scared was pointless. I had to concentrate on the here and now. I watched every foot placement, moving slowly. A fall would be noisy in this undergrowth, and he'd be on me in a minute.

I found the dead cat about ten yards south east of my perching tree. The cat's throat was a gaping wound. I couldn't even tell what color its fur had been in the bleaching effect of the moonlight, but the dark splotches around the little corpse were surely blood. After five more feet of stealthy movement, I found Bubba. He was unconscious or dead. With a vampire it was hard to tell the difference. But with no stake through his heart, and his head still on, I could hope he was only unconscious.

Someone had brought Bubba a drugged cat, I figured.

Someone who had known Bubba was guarding me and had heard of Bubba's penchant for draining cats.

I heard a crackle behind me. The snap of a twig. I glided into the shadow of the nearest large tree. I was mad, mad and scared, and I wondered if I would die this night.

I might not have the rifle, but I had a built-in tool. I closed my eyes and reached out with my mind.

Dark tangle, red, black. Hate.

I flinched. But this was necessary, this was my only protection. I let down every shred of defense.

Into my head poured images that made me sick, made me terrified. Dawn, asking someone to punch her, then finding out that he'd got one of her hose in his hand, was stretching it between his fingers, preparing to tighten it around her neck. A flash of Maudette, naked and begging. A woman I'd never seen, her bare back to me, bruises and welts covering it. Then my grandmother – my grandmother – in our familiar kitchen, angry and fighting for her life.

I was paralyzed by the shock of it, the horror of it. Whose thoughts were these? I had an image of Arlene's kids, playing on my living room floor; I saw myself, and I didn't look like the person I saw in my own mirror. I had huge holes in my neck, and I was lewd; I had a knowing leer on my face, and I patted the inside of my thigh suggestively.

I was in the mind of Rene Lenier. This was how Rene saw me.

Rene was mad.

Now I knew why I'd never been able to read his thoughts explicitly; he kept them in a secret hole, a place in his mind he kept hidden and separate from his conscious self.

He was seeing an outline behind a tree now and wondering if it looked like the outline of a woman.

He was seeing me.

I bolted and ran west toward the cemetery. I couldn't

listen to his head anymore, because my own head was focused so fixedly on running, dodging the obstacles of trees, bushes, fallen limbs, a little gully where rain had collected. My strong legs pumped, my arms swung, and my breath sounded like the wheezing of a bagpipe.

I broke from the woods and was in the cemetery. The oldest portion of the graveyard was farther north toward Bill's house, and it had the best places of concealment. I bounded over headstones, the modern kind, set almost flush with the ground, no good for hiding. I leaped over Gran's grave, the earth still raw, no stone yet. Her killer followed me. I turned to look, to see how close he was, like a fool, and in the moonlight I saw Rene's rough head of hair clearly as he gained on me.

I ran down into the gentle bowl the cemetery formed, then began sprinting up the other side. When I thought there were enough large headstones and statues between me and Rene, I dodged behind a tall granite column topped with a cross. I remained standing, flattening myself against the cold hardness of the stone. I clamped a hand across my own mouth to silence my sobbing effort to get air in my lungs. I made myself calm enough to try to listen to Rene; but his thoughts were not even coherent enough to decipher, except the rage he felt. Then a clear concept presented itself.

'Your sister,' I yelled. 'Is Cindy still alive, Rene?'

'Bitch!' he screamed, and I knew in that second that the first woman to die had been Rene's sister, the one who liked vampires, the one he was supposedly still visiting from time to time, according to Arlene. Rene had killed Cindy, his waitress sister, while she was still wearing her pink-and-white hospital cafeteria uniform. He'd strangled her with her apron strings. And he'd had sex with her, after she was dead. She'd sunk so low, she wouldn't mind her own brother, he'd thought, as much as he was capable of thinking. Anyone who'd let a vampire do that deserved to die. And he'd hidden her body from shame. The others weren't his flesh and blood; it had been all right to let them lie.

I'd gotten sucked down into Rene's sick interior like a twig dragged down by a whirlpool, and it made me stagger. When I came back into my own head, he was on me. He hit me in the face as hard as he could, and he expected me to go down. The blow broke my nose and hurt so bad I almost blanked out, but I didn't collapse. I hit him back. My lack of experience made my blow ineffectual. I just thumped him in the ribs, and he grunted, but in the next instant he retaliated.

His fist broke my collarbone. But I didn't fall.

He hadn't known how strong I was. In the moonlight, his face was shocked when I fought back, and I thanked the vampire blood I'd taken. I thought of my brave grandmother, and I launched myself at him, grabbing him by the ears and attempting to hit his head against the granite column. His hands shot up to grip my forearms, and he tried to pull me away so I'd loose my grip. Finally he succeeded, but I could tell from his eyes he was surprised and more on guard. I tried to knee him, but he anticipated me, twisting just far enough away to dodge me. While I was off-balance, he pushed, and I hit the ground with a teeth-chattering thud.

Then he was straddling me. But he'd dropped the cord in our struggle, and while he held my neck with one hand, he was groping with the other for his method of choice. My right arm was pinned, but my left was free, and I struck and clawed at him. He had to ignore this, had to look for the strangling cord because that was part of his ritual. My scrabbling hand encountered a familiar shape.

Rene, in his work clothes, was still wearing his knife on his belt. I yanked the snap open and pulled the knife from its sheath, and while he was still thinking, 'I should have taken that off,' I sank the knife into the soft flesh of his waist, angling up. And I pulled it out.

He screamed, then.

He staggered to his feet, twisting his upper torso sideways, trying with both hands to stanch the blood that was pouring from the wound.

I scuttered backward, getting up, trying to put distance between myself and man who was a monster just as surely as Bill was.

Rene screamed, 'Aw, Jesus, woman! What you done to me? Oh, God, it hurts!'

That was rich.

He was scared now, frightened of discovery, of an end to his games, of an end to his vengeance.

'Girls like you deserve to die,' he snarled. 'I can feel you in my head, you freak!'

'Who's the freak around here?' I hissed. 'Die, you bastard.'

I didn't know I had it in me. I stood by the headstone in a crouch, the bloody knife still clutched in my hand, waiting for him to charge me again.

He staggered in circles, and I watched, my face stony. I closed my mind to him, to his feeling his death crawl up behind him. I stood ready to knife him a second time when he fell to the ground. When I was sure he couldn't move, I went to Bill's house, but I didn't run. I told myself it was because I couldn't: but I'm not sure. I kept seeing my grandmother, encapsuled in Rene's memory forever, fighting for her life in her own house.

I fished Bill's key out of my pocket, almost amazed it was still there.

I turned it somehow, staggered into the big living room, felt for the phone. My fingers touched the buttons, managed to figure out which was the nine and where the one was. I pushed the numbers hard enough to make them beep, and then, without warning, I checked out of consciousness.

I knew I was in the hospital: I was surrounded by the clean smell of hospital sheets.

The next thing I knew was that I hurt all over.

And someone was in the room with me. I opened my eyes, not without effort.

Andy Bellefleur. His square face was even more fatigued than the last time I'd seen him.

'Can you hear me?' he said.

I nodded, just a tiny movement, but even that sent a wave of pain through my head.

'We got him,' he said, and then he proceeded to tell me a lot more, but I fell back asleep.

It was daylight when I woke again, and this time, I seemed to be much more alert.

Someone in the room.

'Who's here?' I said, and my voice came out in a painful rasp.

Kevin rose from the chair in the corner, rolling a crossword puzzle magazine and sticking it into his uniform pocket.

'Where's Kenya?' I whispered.

He grinned at me unexpectedly. 'She was here for a couple of hours,' he explained. 'She'll be back soon. I spelled her for lunch.'

His thin face and body formed one lean line of approval. 'You are one tough lady,' he told me.

'I don't feel tough,' I managed.

'You got hurt,' he told me as if I didn't know that.

'Rene.'

'We found him out in the cemetery,' Kevin assured me. 'You stuck him pretty good. But he was still conscious, and he told us he'd been trying to kill you.'

'Good.'

'He was real sorry he hadn't finished the job. I can't believe he spilled the beans like that, but he was some kind of hurting and he was some kind of scared, by the time we got to him. He told us the whole thing was your fault because you wouldn't just lie down to die like the others. He said it must run in your genes, because your grandmother . . .' Here Kevin stopped short, aware that he was on upsetting ground.

'She fought, too,' I whispered.

Kenya came in then, massive, impassive, and holding a steaming Styrofoam cup of coffee.

'She's awake,' Kevin said, beaming at his partner.

'Good.' Kenya sounded less overjoyed about it. 'She say what happened? Maybe we should call Andy.'

'Yeah, that's what he said to do. But he's just been asleep four hours.'

'The man said call.'

Kevin shrugged, went to the phone at the side of the bed. I eased off into a doze as I heard him speaking, but I could hear him murmur with Kenya as they waited. He was talking about his hunting dogs. Kenya, I guess, was listening.

Andy came in, I could feel his thoughts, the pattern of his brain. His solid presence came to roost by my bed. I opened my eyes as he was bending to look at me. We exchanged a long stare.

Two pairs of feet in regulation shoes moved out into the hall.

'He's still alive,' Andy said abruptly. 'And he won't stop talking.'

I made the briefest motion of my head, indicating a nod, I hoped.

'He says this goes back to his sister, who was seeing a vampire. She evidently got so low on blood that Rene thought she'd turn into a vamp herself if he didn't stop her. He gave her an ultimatum, one evening in her apartment. She talked back, said she wouldn't give up her lover. She was tying her apron around her, getting ready to go to work as they were arguing. He yanked it off her, strangled her . . . did other stuff.'

Andy looked a little sick.

'I know,' I whispered.

'It seems to me,' Andy began again, 'that somehow he decided he'd feel justified in doing that horrible thing if he convinced himself that everyone in his sister's situation deserved to die. In fact, the murders here are very similar to two in Shreveport that haven't been solved up until now, and we're expecting Rene to touch on those while he's rambling along. If he makes it.'

I could feel my lips pressing together in horrified sympathy for those other poor women.

'Can you tell me what happened to you?' Andy asked quietly. 'Go slow, take your time, and keep your voice down to a whisper. Your throat is badly bruised.'

I had figured that out for myself, thanks very much. I murmured my account of the evening, and I didn't leave anything out. Andy had switched on a little tape recorder after asking me if that was all right. He placed it on the pillow close to my mouth when I indicated the device was okay with me, so he'd have the whole story.

'Mr. Compton still out of town?' he asked me, after I'd finished.

'New Orleans,' I whispered, barely able to speak.

'We'll look in Rene's house for the rifle, now that we know it's yours. It'll be a nice piece of corroborative evidence.'

Then a gleaming young woman in white came into the room, looked at my face, and told Andy he'd have to come back some other time.

He nodded at me, gave me an awkward pat on the hand, and left. He gave the doctor a backward glance of admiration. She was sure worth admiring, but she was also wearing a wedding ring, so Andy was once again too late.

She thought he seemed too serious and grim.

I didn't want to hear this.

But I didn't have enough energy to keep everyone out of my head.

'Miss Stackhouse, how are you feeling?' the young woman asked a little too loudly. She was brunette and lean, with wide brown eyes and a full mouth.

'Like hell,' I whispered.

'I can imagine,' she said, nodding repeatedly while looking me over. I somehow didn't think she could. I was willing to bet she'd never been beaten up by a multiple murderer in a graveyard.

'You just lost your grandmother, too, didn't you?' she asked sympathetically. I nodded, just a fraction of an inch.

'My husband died about six months ago,' she said. 'I know about grief. It's tough being brave, isn't it?'

Well, well, well. I let my expression ask a question.

'He had cancer,' she explained. I tried to look my condolences without moving anything, which was nearly impossible.

'Well,' she said, standing upright, returning to her brisk manner, 'Miss Stackhouse, you're sure gonna live. You have a broken collarbone, and two broken ribs, and a broken nose.'

Shepherd of Judea! No wonder I felt bad.

'Your face and neck are severely bruised. Of course, you could tell your throat was hurt.'

I was trying to imagine what I looked like. Good thing I didn't have a mirror handy.

'And you have lots of relatively minor bruises and cuts on your legs and arms.' She smiled. 'Your stomach is fine, and your feet!'

Hohoho. Very funny.

'I have prescribed pain medication for you, so when you start feeling bad, just ring for the nurse.'

A visitor stuck his head in the door behind her. She turned blocking my view, and said, 'Hello?'

'This Sookie's room?'

'Yes, I was just finishing her examination. You can come in.' The doctor (whose name was Sonntag, by her nameplate) looked questioningly at me to get my permission, and I managed a tiny 'Sure.'

JB du Rone drifted to my bedside, looking as lovely as the cover model on a romance novel. His tawny hair gleamed under the fluorescent lights, his eyes were just the same color, and his sleeveless shirt showed muscle definition that might have been chiseled with a – well, with a chisel. He was looking down at me, and Dr. Sonntag was drinking him in.

'Hey, Sookie, you feelin' all right?' he asked. He lay a finger gently on my cheek. He kissed an unbruised spot on my forehead.

'Thanks,' I whispered. 'I'll be okay. Meet my doctor.'

JB turned his wide eyes on Dr. Sonntag, who practically tripped over her own feet to introduce herself.

'Doctors weren't this pretty when I was getting my shots,' JB said sincerely and simply.

'You haven't been to a doctor since you were a kid?' Dr. Sonntag said, amazed.

'I never get sick.' He beamed at her. 'Strong as an ox.'

And the brain of one. But Dr. Sonntag probably had smarts enough for two.

She couldn't think of any reason for lingering, though she cast a wistful glance over her shoulder as she left.

JB bent down to me and said earnestly, 'Can I bring you anything, Sookie? Nabs or something?'

The thought of trying to eat crackers made tears come to my eyes. 'No thanks,' I breathed. 'The doctor's a widow.'

You could change subjects on JB without him wondering why.

'Wow,' he said, impressed. 'She's smart and single.'

I wiggled my eyebrows in a significant way.

'You think I oughtta ask her out?' JB looked as thoughtful as it was possible for him to be. 'That might be a good idea.' He smiled down at me. 'Long as *you* won't date me, Sookie. You're always number one to me. You just crook your little finger, and I'll come running.'

What a sweet guy. I didn't believe in his devotion for a minute, but I did believe he knew how to make a woman feel good, even if she was as sure as I was that I looked breathtakingly bad. I felt pretty bad, too. Where were those pain pills? I tried to smile at JB.

'You're hurting,' he said. 'I'll send the nurse down here.'

Oh, good. The reach to the little button had seemed longer and longer as I tried to get my arm to move.

He kissed me again as he left and said, 'I'll go track that doctor of yours down, Sookie. I better ask her some more questions about your recovery.'

After the nurse injected some stuff into my IV drip, I was just looking forward to feeling no pain when the door opened again.

My brother came in. He stood by my bed for a long time, staring at my face. He said finally, heavily, 'I talked to the doctor for a minute before she left for the cafeteria with JB. She told me what-all was wrong with you.' He walked away from me, took a turn around the room, came back. More staring. 'You look like hell.'

'Thanks,' I whispered.

'Oh, yeah, your throat. I forgot.'

He started to pat me, thought the better of it.

'Listen, Sis, I gotta say thank you, but it's got me down that you stood in for me when it came time to fight.'

If I could have, I'd have kicked him.

Stood in for him, hell.

'I owe you big, Sis. I was so dumb, thinking Rene was a good friend.'

Betrayed. He felt betrayed.

Then Arlene came in, to make things just peachy keen.

She was a mess. Her hair was in a red tangle, she had no makeup, and her clothes were chosen at random. I'd never seen Arlene without her hair curled and her makeup loud and bright.

She looked down at me – boy, would I be glad when I could stand up again – and for a second her face was hard as granite, but when she really took in my face, she began to crumble.

'I was so mad at you, I didn't believe it, but now that I'm seeing you and what he did . . . oh, Sookie, can you ever forgive me?'

Geez, I wanted her out of here. I tried to telegraph this to Jason, and for once I got through, because he put an arm around her shoulders and led her out. Arlene was sobbing before she reached the door. 'I didn't know . . .' she said, barely coherent. 'I just didn't know!'

'Hell, neither did I,' Jason said heavily.

I took a nap after trying to ingest some delicious green gelatin.

My big excitement of the afternoon was walking to the bathroom, more or less by myself. I sat in the chair for ten minutes, after which I was more than ready to get back in bed. I looked in the mirror concealed in the rolling table and was very sorry I had.

I was running a little temperature, just enough to make me shivery and tender-skinned. My face was blue and gray and my nose was swollen double. My right eye was puffy and almost closed. I shuddered, and even that hurt. My legs . . . oh, hell, I didn't even want to check. I lay back very carefully and wanted this day to be over. Probably four days from now I'd feel just great. Work! When could I go back to work?

A little knock at the door distracted me. Another damn visitor. Well, this was someone I didn't know. An older lady with blue hair and red-framed glasses wheeled in a cart. She was wearing the yellow smock the hospital volunteers called Sunshine Ladies had to don when they were working.

The cart was covered with flowers for the patients in this wing.

'I'm delivering you a load of best wishes!' the lady said cheerfully.

I smiled, but the effect must have been ghastly because her own cheer wavered a little.

'These are for you,' she said, lifting a potted plant decorated with a red ribbon. 'Here's the card, honey. Let's see, these are for you, too . . .' This was an arrangement of cut flowers, featuring pink rosebuds and pink carnations and white baby's breath. She plucked the card from that bowl too. Surveying the cart, she said, 'Now, aren't you the lucky one! Here are some more for you!!'

The focus of the third floral tribute was a bizarre red flower I'd never seen before, surrounded by a host of other, more familiar blooms. I looked at this one doubtfully. The Sunshine Lady dutifully presented me with the card from the plastic prongs.

After she'd smiled her way out of the room, I opened the little envelopes. It was easier to move when I was in a better mood, I noticed wryly.

The potted plant was from Sam and 'all your coworkers at Merlotte's' read the card, but it was written in Sam's handwriting. I touched the glossy leaves and wondered where I'd put it when I took it home. The cut flowers were from Sid Matt Lancaster and Elva Deene Lancaster – pooey. The arrangement centered with the peculiar red blossom (I decided that somehow the flower looked almost obscene, like a lady's private part) was definitely the most interesting of the three. I opened the card with some curiosity. It bore only a signature, 'Eric.'

That was all I needed. How the hell had he heard I was in the hospital? Why hadn't I heard from Bill?

After some delicious red gelatin for supper, I focused on the television for a couple of hours, since I hadn't anything to read, even if my eyes had been up to it. My bruises grew more charming every hour, and I felt weary to my bones, despite the fact that I'd only walked once to the bathroom and twice around my room. I switched off the television and turned onto my side. I fell asleep, and in my dreams the pain from my body seeped in and made me have nightmares. I ran in my dreams, ran through the cemetery, afraid for my life, falling over stones; into open graves, encountering all the people I knew who lay there: my father and mother, my grandmother, Maudette Pickens, Dawn Green, even a childhood friend who'd been killed in a hunting accident. I was looking for a particular headstone; if I found it, I was home free. They would all go back into their graves and leave me alone. I ran from this one to that one, putting my hand on each one, hoping it would be the right stone. I whimpered.

'Sweetheart, you're safe,' came a familiar cool voice.

'Bill,' I muttered. I turned to face a stone I hadn't yet touched. When I lay my fingers on it, they traced the letters 'William Erasmus Compton.' As if I'd been dashed with cold water, my eyes flew open, I drew in a breath to scream, and my throat gave a great throb of pain. I choked on the extra air, and the pain of the coughing, which pretty much hurt every single thing I'd broken, completed my awakening. A hand slipped under my cheek, the cool fingers feeling wonderfully good against my hot skin. I tried not to whimper, but a little noise made its way through my teeth.

'Turn to the light, darling,' Bill said, his voice very light and casual.

I'd been sleeping with my back to the light the nurse had left on, the one in the bathroom. Now I rolled obediently to my back and looked up at my vampire.

Bill hissed.

'I'll kill him,' he said, with a simple certainty that chilled me to the bone.

There was enough tension in the room to send a fleet of the nervous running for their tranquilizers.

'Hi, Bill,' I croaked. 'Glad to see you, too. Where you been so long? Thanks for returning all my calls.'

That brought him up short. He blinked. I could feel him making an effort to calm himself.

'Sookie,' he said. 'I didn't call because I wanted to tell you in person what has happened.' I couldn't read the expression on his face. If I'd had to take a shot, I would've said he looked proud of himself.

He paused, scanned all visible portions of me.

'This doesn't hurt,' I croaked obligingly, extending my hand to him. He kissed that, lingered over it in a way that sent a faint tingle through my body. Believe me, a faint tingle was more than I'd thought I was capable of.

'Tell me what has been done to you,' he commanded.

'Then lean down so I can whisper. This really hurts.'

He pulled a chair close to the bed, lowered the bed rail,

and lay his chin on his folded arms. His face was maybe four inches from mine.

'Your nose is broken,' he observed.

I rolled my eyes. 'Glad you spotted that,' I whispered. 'I'll tell the doctor when she comes in.'

His gaze narrowed. 'Stop trying to deflect me.'

'Okay. Nose broken, two ribs, a collarbone.'

But Bill wanted to examine me all over, and he pulled the sheet down. My mortification was complete. Of course, I was wearing an awful hospital gown, in itself a downer, and I hadn't bathed properly, and my face was several different shades, and my hair hadn't been brushed.

'I want to take you home,' he announced, after he'd run his hands all over and minutely examined each scrape and cut. The Vampire Physician.

I motioned with my hand to make him bend down. 'No,' I breathed. I pointed to the drip bag. He eyed it with some suspicion, but of course he had to know what one was.

'I can take it out,' he said.

I shook my head vehemently.

'You don't want me to take care of you?'

I puffed out my breath in exasperation, which hurt like hell.

I made a writing motion with my hand, and Bill searched the drawers until he found a notepad. Oddly enough, he had a pen. I wrote, 'They'll let me out of the hospital tomorrow if my fever doesn't go high.'

'Who'll take you home?' he asked. He was standing by the bed again, and looking down at me with stern disapproval, like a teacher whose best pupil happens to be chronically tardy.

'I'll get them to call Jason, or Charlsie Tooten,' I wrote. If things had been different, I would have written Arlene's name automatically.

'I'll be there at dark,' he said.

I looked up into his pale face, the clear whites of his eyes almost shining in the gloomy room.

'I'll heal you,' he offered. 'Let me give you some blood.'

I remembered the way my hair had lightened, remembered that I was almost twice as strong as I'd ever been. I shook my head.

'Why not?' he said, as if he'd offered me a drink of water when I was thirsty and I'd said no. I thought maybe I'd hurt his feelings.

I took his hand and guided it to my mouth. I kissed the palm gently. I held the hand to my better cheek.

'People notice I am changing,' I wrote, after a moment. 'I notice I am changing.'

He bowed his head for a moment, and then looked at me sadly.

'You know what happened?' I wrote.

'Bubba told me part of it,' he said, and his face grew scary as he mentioned the half-witted vampire. 'Sam told me the rest, and I went to the police department and read the police reports.'

'Andy let you do that?' I scribbled.

'No one knew I was there,' he said carelessly.

I tried to imagine that, and it gave me the creeps.

I gave him a disapproving look.

'Tell me what happened in New Orleans,' I wrote. I was beginning to feel sleepy again.

'You will have to know a little about us,' he said hesitantly.

'Woo woo, secret vampire stuff!!' I croaked.

It was his turn to give me disapproving.

'We're a little organized,' he told me. 'I was trying to think of ways to keep us safe from Eric.' Involuntarily, I looked at the red flower arrangement.

'I knew if I were an official, like Eric, it would be much more difficult for him to interfere with my private life.'

I looked encouraging, or at least I tried to.

'So I attended the regional meeting, and though I have never been involved in our politics, I ran for an office. And through some concentrated lobbying, I won!'

This was absolutely amazing. Bill was a *union rep*? I wondered about the concentrated lobbying, too. Did that mean Bill had killed all the opposition? Or that he'd bought the voters a bottle of A positive apiece?

'What is your job?' I wrote slowly, imagining Bill sitting in a meeting. I tried to look proud, which seemed to be what Bill was looking for.

'I'm the Fifth Area investigator,' he said. 'I'll tell you what that means when you're home. I don't want to wear you out.'

I nodded, beaming at him. I sure hoped he didn't take it into his head to ask me who all the flowers were from. I wondered if I had to write Eric a thank-you note. I wondered why my mind was going off on all these tangents. Must be the pain medication.

I gestured to Bill to draw close. He did, his face resting on the bed next to mine. 'Don't kill Rene,' I whispered.

He looked cold, colder, coldest.

'I may have already done the job. He's in intensive care. But even if he lives, there's been enough murder. Let the law do it. I don't want any more witchhunts coming after you. I want us to have peace.' It was becoming very difficult to talk. I took his hand in both of mine, held it again to my least-bruised cheek. Suddenly, how much I had missed him became a solid lump lodged in my chest, and I held out my arms. He sat carefully on the edge of the bed, and leaning toward me, he carefully, carefully, slid his arms under me and pulled me up to him, a fraction of an inch at a time, to give me time to tell him if it hurt.

'I won't kill him,' Bill said finally, into my ear.

'Sweetheart,' I breathed, knowing his sharp hearing could pick it up. 'I missed you.' I heard his quick sigh, and his arms tightened a little, his hands began their gentle stroking down my back. 'I wonder how quickly you can heal,' he said, 'without my help?'

'Oh, I'll try to hurry,' I whispered. 'I'll bet I surprise the doctor as it is.'

A collie trotted down the corridor, looked in the open door, said, 'Rowwf,' and trotted away. Astonished, Bill turned to glance out into the corridor. Oh, yeah, it was the full moon, tonight – I could see it out of the window. I could see something else, too. A white face appeared out of the blackness and floated between me and the moon. It was a handsome face, framed by long golden hair. Eric the Vampire grinned at me and gradually disappeared from my view. He was flying.

'Soon we'll be back to normal,' Bill said, laying me down gently so he could switch out the light in the bathroom. He glowed in the dark.

'Right,' I whispered. 'Yeah. Back to normal.'

LIVING DEAD IN DALLAS

Also by Charlaine Harris

SOOKIE STACKHOUSE

Dead Until Dark

Living Dead in Dallas

Club Dead

Dead to the World

Dead as a Doornail

Definitely Dead

All Together Dead

From Dead to Worse

Dead and Gone

HARPER CONNELLY

Grave Sight

Grave Surprise

An Ice Cold Grave

Grave Secret

LIVING DEAD IN DALLAS

CHARLAINE HARRIS

First published in Great Britain in 2004 by
Little, Brown

This edition published in Great Britain in 2009 by
Gollancz
An imprint of the Orion Publishing Group
Orion House, 5 Upper St Martin's Lane, London WC2H 9EA
An Hachette UK Company

A CIP catalogue record for this book
is available from the British Library

ISBN 978 0 575 08938 9

7 9 10 8 6

Printed and bound in the UK by
CPI Mackays, Chatham ME5 8TD

www.orionbooks.co.uk

This book is dedicated to all the people who told me they enjoyed DEAD UNTIL DARK.
Thanks for the encouragement.

Acknowledgments

My thanks go to Patsy Asher of Remember the Alibi in San Antonio, Texas; Chloe Green of Dallas; and the helpful cyber-friends I've made on DorothyL, who answered all my questions promptly and enthusiastically. I have the greatest job in the world.

Chapter 1

Andy Bellefleur was as drunk as a skunk. This wasn't normal for Andy – believe me, I know all the drunks in Bon Temps. Working at Sam Merlotte's bar for several years has pretty much introduced me to all of them. But Andy Bellefleur, native son and detective on Bon Temps's small police force, had never been drunk in Merlotte's before. I was mighty curious as to why tonight was an exception.

Andy and I aren't friends by any stretch of the imagination, so I couldn't ask him outright. But other means were open to me, and I decided to use them. Though I try to limit employing my disability, or gift, or whatever you want to call it, to find out things that might have an effect on me or mine, sometimes sheer curiosity wins out.

I let down my mental guard and read Andy's mind. I was sorry.

Andy had had to arrest a man that morning for kidnapping. He'd taken his ten-year-old neighbor to a place in the woods and raped her. The girl was in the hospital, and the man was in jail, but the damage that had been dealt was irreparable. I felt weepy and sad. It was a crime that touched too closely on my own past. I liked Andy a little better for his depression.

'Andy Bellefleur, give me your keys,' I said. His broad face turned up to me, showing very little comprehension. After a long pause while my meaning filtered through to his addled brain, Andy fumbled in the pocket of his khakis and handed me his heavy key ring. I put another bourbon-and-Coke on the bar in front of him. 'My treat,' I said, and went to the phone at the end of the bar to call Portia, Andy's sister. The Bellefleur siblings lived in a decaying large white two-story antebellum, formerly quite a showplace, on the prettiest street in the nicest area of Bon Temps. On Magnolia Creek Road, all the homes faced the strip of park through which ran the stream, crossed here and there by decorative bridges for foot traffic only; a road ran on both sides. There were a few other old homes on Magnolia Creek Road, but they were all in better repair than the Bellefleur place, Belle Rive. Belle Rive was just too much for Portia, a lawyer, and Andy, a cop, to maintain, since the money to support such a home and its grounds was long since gone. But their grandmother, Caroline, stubbornly refused to sell.

Portia answered on the second ring.

'Portia, this is Sookie Stackhouse,' I said, having to raise my voice over the background noise in the bar.

'You must be at work.'

'Yes. Andy's here, and he's three sheets to the wind. I took his keys. Can you come get him?'

'Andy had too much to drink? That's rare. Sure, I'll be there in ten minutes,' she promised, and hung up.

'You're a sweet girl, Sookie,' Andy volunteered unexpectedly.

He'd finished the drink I'd poured for him. I swept the glass out of sight and hoped he wouldn't ask for more. 'Thanks, Andy,' I said. 'You're okay, yourself.'

'Where's . . . boyfriend?'

'Right here,' said a cool voice, and Bill Compton appeared just behind Andy. I smiled at him over Andy's drooping head. Bill was about five foot ten, with dark brown hair and eyes. He had the broad shoulders and hard muscular arms of a man who's done manual labor for years. Bill had worked a farm with his father, and then for himself, before he'd gone to be a soldier in the war. That would be the Civil War.

'Hey, V. B.!' called Charlsie Tooten's husband, Micah. Bill raised a casual hand to return the greeting, and my brother, Jason, said, 'Evening, Vampire Bill,' in a perfectly polite way. Jason, who had not exactly welcomed Bill into our little family circle, had turned over a whole new leaf. I was sort of mentally holding my breath, waiting to see if his improved attitude was permanent.

'Bill, you're okay for a bloodsucker,' Andy said judiciously, rotating on his bar stool so he could face Bill. I upgraded my opinion of Andy's drunkenness, since he had never otherwise been enthusiastic about the acceptance of vampires into America's mainstream society.

'Thanks,' Bill said dryly. 'You're not too bad for a Bellefleur.' He leaned across the bar to give me a kiss. His lips were as cool as his voice. You had to get used to it. Like when you laid your head on his chest, and you didn't hear a heartbeat inside. 'Evening, sweetheart,' he said in his low voice. I slid a glass of the Japanese-developed synthetic B negative across the bar, and he knocked it back and licked his lips. He looked pinker almost immediately.

'How'd your meeting go, honey?' I asked. Bill had been in Shreveport the better part of the night.

'I'll tell you later.'

I hoped his work-related story was less distressing than Andy's. 'Okay. I'd appreciate it if you'd help Portia get Andy to her car. Here she comes now,' I said, nodding toward the door.

For once; Portia was not wearing the skirt, blouse, jacket, hose, and low-heeled pumps that constituted her professional uniform. She'd changed to blue jeans and a ragged Sophie Newcomb sweatshirt. Portia was built as squarely as her brother, but she had long, thick, chestnut hair. Keeping it beautifully tended was Portia's one signal that she hadn't given up yet. She plowed single-mindedly through the rowdy crowd.

'Well, he's soused, all right,' she said, evaluating her brother. Portia was trying to ignore Bill, who made her very uneasy. 'It doesn't happen often, but if he decides to tie one on, he does a good job.'

'Portia, Bill can carry him to your car,' I said. Andy was taller than Portia and thick in body, clearly too much of a burden for his sister.

'I think I can handle him,' she told me firmly, still not looking toward Bill, who raised his eyebrows at me.

So I let her get one arm around him and try to hoist him off the stool. Andy stayed perched. Portia glanced around for Sam Merlotte, the bar owner, who was small and wiry in appearance but very strong. 'Sam's bartending at an anniversary party at the country club,' I said. 'Better let Bill help.'

'All right,' the lawyer said stiffly, her eyes on the polished wood of the bar. 'Thanks very much.'

Bill had Andy up and moving toward the door in seconds, in spite of Andy's legs tending to turn to jelly. Micah Tooten jumped up to open the door, so Bill was able to sweep Andy right out into the parking lot.

'Thanks, Sookie,' Portia said. 'Is his bar tab settled up?'

I nodded.

'Okay,' she said, slapping her hand on the bar to signal she was out of there. She had to listen to a chorus of well-meant advice as she followed Bill out the front door of Merlotte's.

That was how Detective Andy Bellefleur's old Buick came to sit in the parking lot at Merlotte's all night and into the next day. The Buick had certainly been empty when Andy had gotten out to enter the bar, he would later swear. He'd also testify that he'd had been so preoccupied by his internal turmoil that he'd forgotten to lock the car.

At some point between eight o'clock, when Andy had arrived at Merlotte's, and ten the next morning, when I arrived to help open the bar, Andy's car acquired a new passenger.

This one would cause considerable embarrassment for the policeman.

This one was dead.

I shouldn't have been there at all. I'd worked the late shift the night before, and I should've worked the late shift again that night. But Bill had asked me if I could switch with one of my coworkers, because he needed me to accompany him to Shreveport, and Sam hadn't objected. I'd asked my friend Arlene if she'd work my shift. She was due a day off, but she always wanted to earn the better tips we got at night, and she agreed to come in at five that afternoon.

By all rights, Andy should've collected his car that morning, but he'd been too hung over to fool with getting Portia to run him over to Merlotte's, which was out of the way to the police station. She'd told him she would pick him up at work at noon, and they'd eat lunch at the bar. Then he could retrieve his car.

So the Buick, with its silent passenger, waited for discovery far longer than it should have.

I'd gotten about six hours' sleep the night before, so I was feeling pretty good. Dating a vampire can be hard on your equilibrium if you're truly a daytime person, like me. I'd helped close the bar, and left for home with Bill by one o'clock. We'd gotten in Bill's hot tub together, then done other things, but I'd gotten to bed by a little after two, and I didn't get up until almost nine. Bill had long been in the ground by then.

I drank lots of water and orange juice and took a multivitamin and iron supplement for breakfast, which was my regimen since Bill had come into my life and brought (along with love, adventure, and excitement) the constant threat of anemia. The weather was getting cooler, thank God, and I sat on Bill's front porch wearing a cardigan and the black slacks we wore to work at Merlotte's when it was too cool for shorts. My white golf shirt had MERLOTTE'S BAR embroidered on the left breast.

As I skimmed the morning paper, with one part of my mind I was recording the fact that the grass was definitely not growing as fast. Some of the leaves appeared to be beginning to turn. The high school football stadium might be just about tolerable this coming Friday night.

The summer just hates to let go in Louisiana, even northern Louisiana. Fall begins in a very halfhearted way, as though it might quit at any minute and revert to the stifling heat of July. But I was on the alert, and I could spot traces of fall this morning. Fall and winter meant longer nights, more time with Bill, more hours of sleep.

So I was cheerful when I went to work. When I saw the Buick sitting all by its lonesome in front of the bar, I remembered Andy's surprising binge the night before. I have to confess, I smiled when I thought of how he'd be feeling today. Just as I was about to drive around in back and park with the other employees, I noticed that Andy's rear passenger door was open just a little bit. That would make his dome light stay on, surely? And his battery would run down. And he'd be angry, and have to come in the bar to call the tow truck, or ask someone to jump him . . . so I put my car in park and slid out, leaving it running. That turned out to be an optimistic error.

I shoved the door to, but it would only give an inch. So I pressed my body to it, thinking it would latch and I could be on my way. Again, the door would not click shut. Impatiently, I yanked it all the way open to find out what was in the way. A wave of smell gusted out into the parking lot, a dreadful smell. Dismay clutched at my throat, because the smell was not unknown to me. I peered into the backseat of the car, my hand covering my mouth, though that hardly helped with the smell.

'Oh, man,' I whispered. 'Oh, shit.' Lafayette, the cook for one shift at Merlotte's, had been shoved into the backseat. He was naked. It was Lafayette's thin brown foot, its toenails painted a deep crimson, that had kept the door from shutting, and it was Lafayette's corpse that smelled to high heaven.

I backed away hastily, then scrambled into my car and drove around back behind the bar, blowing my horn. Sam came running out of the employee door, an apron tied around his waist. I turned off my car and was out of it so quick I hardly realized I'd done it, and I wrapped myself around Sam like a static-filled sock.

'What is it?' Sam's voice said in my ear. I leaned back to look at him, not having to gaze up too much since Sam is a smallish man. His reddish gold hair was gleaming in the morning sun. He has true-blue eyes, and they were wide with apprehension.

'It's Lafayette,' I said, and began crying. That was ridiculous and silly and no help at all, but I couldn't help it. 'He's dead, in Andy Bellefleur's car.'

Sam's arms tightened behind my back and drew me into his body once more. 'Sookie, I'm sorry you saw it,' he said. 'We'll call the police. Poor Lafayette.'

Being a cook at Merlotte's does not exactly call for any extraordinary culinary skill, since Sam just offers a few sandwiches and fries, so there's a high turnover. But Lafayette had lasted longer than most, to my surprise. Lafayette had been gay, flamboyantly gay, makeup-and-long-fingernails gay. People in northern Louisiana are less tolerant of that than New Orleans people, and I expect Lafayette, a man of color, had had a doubly hard time of it. Despite – or because of – his difficulties, he was cheerful, entertainingly mischievous, clever, and actually a good cook. He had a special sauce he steeped hamburgers in, and people asked for Burgers Lafayette pretty regular.

'Did he have family here?' I asked Sam. We eased apart self-consciously and went into the building, to Sam's office.

'He had a cousin,' Sam said, as his fingers punched 9-1-1. 'Please come to Merlotte's on Hummingbird Road,' he told the dispatcher. 'There's a dead man in a car here. Yes, in the parking lot, in the front of the place. Oh, and you might want to alert Andy Bellefleur. It's his car.'

I could hear the squawk on the other end of the line from where I stood.

Danielle Gray and Holly Cleary, the two waitresses on the morning shift, came through the back door laughing. Both divorced women in their midtwenties, Danielle and Holly were lifelong friends who seemed to be quite happy working their jobs as long as they were together. Holly had a five-year-old son who was at kindergarten, and Danielle had a seven-year-old daughter and a boy too young for school, who stayed with Danielle's mother while Danielle was at Merlotte's. I would never be any closer to the two women – who, after all, were around my age – because they were careful to be sufficient unto themselves.

'What's the matter?' Danielle asked when she saw my face. Her own, narrow and freckled, became instantly worried.

'Why's Andy's car out front?' Holly asked. She'd dated Andy Bellefleur for a while, I recalled. Holly had short blond hair that hung around her face like wilted daisy petals, and the prettiest skin I'd ever seen. 'He spend the night in it?'

'No,' I said, 'but someone else did.'

'Who?'

'Lafayette's in it.'

'Andy let a black queer sleep in his car?' This was Holly, who was the blunt straightforward one.

'What happened to him?' This was Danielle, who was the smarter of the two.

'We don't know,' Sam said. 'The police are on the way.'

'You mean,' Danielle said, slowly and carefully, 'that he's dead.'

'Yes,' I told her. 'That's exactly what we mean.'

'Well, we're set to open in an hour.' Holly's hands settled on her round hips. 'What are we gonna do about that? If the police let us open, who's gonna cook for us? People come in, they'll want lunch.'

'We better get ready, just in case,' Sam said. 'Though I'm thinking we won't get to open until sometime this afternoon.' He went into his office to begin calling substitute cooks.

It felt strange to be going about the opening routine, just as if Lafayette were going to mince in any minute with a story about some party he'd been to, the way he had a few days before. The sirens came shrieking down the county road that ran in front of Merlotte's. Cars crunched across Sam's gravel parking lot. By the time we had the chairs down, the tables set, and extra silverware rolled in napkins and ready to replace used settings, the police came in.

Merlotte's is out of the city limits, so the parish sheriff, Bud Dearborn, would be in charge. Bud Dearborn, who'd been a good friend of my father's, was gray-haired now. He had a mashed-in face, like a human Pekinese, and opaque brown eyes. As he came in the front door of the bar, I noticed Bud was wearing heavy boots and his Saints cap. He must have been called in from working on his farm. With Bud was Alcee Beck, the only African American detective on the parish force. Alcee was so black that his white shirt gleamed in contrast. His tie was knotted precisely, and his suit was absolutely correct. His shoes were polished and shining.

Bud and Alcee, between them, ran the parish . . . at least some of the more important elements that kept it functional. Mike Spencer, funeral home director and parish coroner, had a heavy hand in local affairs, too, and he was a good friend of Bud's. I was willing to bet Mike was already out in the parking lot, pronouncing poor Lafayette dead.

Bud Spencer said, 'Who found the body?'

'I did.' Bud and Alcee changed course slightly and headed toward me.

'Sam, can we borrow your office?' Bud asked. Without waiting for Sam's response, he jerked his head to indicate I should go in.

'Sure, go right ahead,' my boss said dryly. 'Sookie, you okay?'

'Fine, Sam.' I wasn't sure that was true, but there wasn't anything Sam could do about it without getting into trouble, and all to no avail. Though Bud gestured to me to sit down, I shook my head as he and Alcee settled themselves in the office chairs. Bud, of course, took Sam's big chair, while Alcee made do with the better extra chair, the one with a little padding left.

'Tell us about the last time you saw Lafayette alive,' Bud suggested.

I thought about it.

'He wasn't working last night,' I said. 'Anthony was working, Anthony Bolivar.'

'Who is that?' Alcee's broad forehead wrinkled. 'Don't recognize the name.'

'He's a friend of Bill's. He was passing through, and he needed a job. He had the experience.' He'd worked in a diner during the Great Depression.

'You mean the short-order cook at Merlotte's is a *vampire?*'

'So?' I asked. I could feel my mouth setting stubborn, and my brows drawing in, and I knew my face was getting mad. I was trying hard not to read their minds trying hard to stay completely out of this, but it wasn't easy. Bud Dearborn was average, but Alcee projected his thoughts like a lighthouse sends a signal. Right now he was beaming disgust and fear.

In the months before I'd met Bill, and found that he treasured that disability of mine – my gift, as he saw it – I'd done my best to pretend to myself and everyone else that I couldn't really 'read' minds. But since Bill had liberated me from the little prison I'd built for myself I'd been practicing and experimenting, with Bill's encouragement. For him, I had put into words the things I'd been feeling for years. Some people sent a clear, strong message, like Alcee. Most people were more off-and-on, like Bud Dearborn. It depended a lot on how strong their emotions were, how clear-headed they were, what the weather was, for all I knew. Some people were murky as hell, and it was almost impossible to tell what they were thinking. I could get a reading of their moods, maybe, but that was all.

I had admitted that if I was touching people while I tried to read their thoughts, it made the picture clearer – like getting cable, after having only an antenna. And I'd found that if I 'sent' a person relaxing images, I could flow through his brain like water.

There was nothing I wanted less than to flow through Alcee Beck's mind. But absolutely involuntarily I was getting a full picture of Alcee's deeply superstitious reaction to finding out there was a vampire working at Merlotte's, his revulsion on discovering I was the woman he'd heard about who was dating a vampire, his deep conviction that the openly gay Lafayette had been a disgrace to the black community. Alcee figured someone must have it in for

Andy Bellefleur, to have parked a gay black man's carcass in Andy's car. Alcee was wondering if Lafayette had had AIDS, if the virus could have seeped into Andy's car seat somehow and survived there. He'd sell the car, if it were his.

If I'd touched Alcee, I would have known his phone number and his wife's bra size.

Bud Dearborn was looking at me funny. 'Did you say something?' I asked.

'Yeah. I was wondering if you had seen Lafayette in here during the evening. Did he come in to have a drink?'

'I never saw him here.' Come to think of it, I'd never seen Lafayette have a drink. For the first time, I realized that though the lunch crowd was mixed, the night bar patrons were almost exclusively white.

'Where did he spend his social time?'

'I have no idea.' All Lafayette's stories were told with the names changed to protect the innocent. Well, actually, the guilty.

'When did you see him last?'

'Dead, in the car.'

Bud shook his head in exasperation. 'Alive, Sookie.'

'Hmmm. I guess . . . three days ago. He was still here when I got here to work my shift, and we said hello to each other. Oh, he told me about a party he'd been to.' I tried to recall his exact words. 'He said he'd been to a house where there were all kinds of sex hijinks going on.'

The two men gaped at me.

'Well, that's what he said! I don't know how much truth was in it.' I could just see Lafayette's face as he'd told me about it, the coy way he kept putting his finger across his lips to indicate he wasn't telling me any names or places.

'Didn't you think someone should know about that?' Bud Dearborn looked stunned.

'It was a private party. Why should I tell anyone about it?'

But that kind of party shouldn't happen in their parish. Both men were glaring at me. Through compressed lips, Bud said, 'Did Lafayette tell you anything about drugs being used at this get-together?'

'No, I don't remember anything like that.'

'Was this party at the home of someone white, or someone black?'

'White,' I said, and then wished I'd pled ignorance. But Lafayette had been really impressed by the home – though not because it was large or fancy. Why had he been so impressed? I wasn't too sure what would constitute impressive for Lafayette, who had grown up poor and stayed that way, but I was sure he'd been talking about the home of someone white, because he'd said, 'All the pictures on the walls, they all white as lilies and smiling like alligators.' I didn't offer that comment to the police, and they didn't ask further.

When I'd left Sam's office, after explaining why Andy's car had been in the parking lot in the first place, I went back to stand behind the bar. I didn't want to watch the activity out in the parking lot, and there weren't any customers to wait on because the police had the entrances to the lot blocked off.

Sam was rearranging the bottles behind the bar, dusting as he went, and Holly and Danielle had plunked themselves down at a table in the smoking section so Danielle could have a cigarette.

'How was it?' Sam asked.

'Not much to it. They didn't like hearing about Anthony working here, and they didn't like what I told them about the party Lafayette was bragging about the other day. Did you hear him telling me? The orgy thing?'

'Yeah, he said something to me about that, too. Must have been a big evening for him. If it really happened.'

'You think Lafayette made it up?'

'I don't think there are too many biracial, bisexual parties in Bon Temps,' he said.

'But that's just because no one invited you to one,' I said pointedly. I wondered if I really knew at all what went on in our little town. Of all the people in Bon Temps, I should be the one to know the ins and the outs, since all that information was more or less readily available to me, if I chose to dig for it. 'At least, I assume that's the case?'

'That's the case,' Sam said, smiling at me a little as he dusted a bottle of whiskey.

'I guess my invitation got lost in the mail, too.'

'You think Lafayette came back here last night to talk more to you or me about this party?'

I shrugged. 'He may have just arranged to meet someone in the parking lot. After all, everyone knows where Merlotte's is. Had he gotten his paycheck?' It was the end of the week, when Sam normally paid us.

'No. Maybe he'd come in for that, but I'd have given it to him at work the next day. Today.'

'I wonder who invited Lafayette to that party.'

'Good question.'

'You don't reckon he'd have been dumb enough to try to blackmail anyone, do you?'

Sam rubbed the-fake wood of the bar with a clean rag. The bar was already shining, but he liked to keep his hands busy, I'd noticed. 'I don't think so,' he said, after he'd thought it over. 'No, they sure asked the wrong person. You know how indiscreet Lafayette was. Not only did he tell us that he went to such a party – and I'm betting he wasn't supposed to – he might have wanted to build more on it than the other, ah, participants, would feel comfortable with.'

'Like, keep in contact with the people at the party? Give them a sly wink in public?'

'Something like that.'

'I guess if you have sex with someone, or watch them having sex, you feel pretty much like you're their equal.' I said this doubtfully, having limited experience in that area, but Sam was nodding.

'Lafayette wanted to be accepted for what he was more than anything else,' he said, and I had to agree.

Chapter 2

We reopened at four-thirty, by which time we were all as bored as we could possibly be. I was ashamed of that, since after all, we were there because a man we knew had died, but it was undeniable that after straightening up the storeroom, cleaning out Sam's office, and playing several hands of bourre (Sam won five dollars and change) we were all ready to see someone new. When Terry Bellefleur, Andy's cousin and a frequent substitute barman or cook at Merlotte's, came through the back door, he was a welcome sight.

I guess Terry was in his late fifties. A Vietnam vet, he'd been a prisoner of war for a year and a half. Terry had some obvious facial scarring, and my friend Arlene told me that the scars on his body were even more drastic. Terry was redheaded, though he was graying a little more each month, it seemed like.

I'd always been fond of Terry, who bent over backward to be kind to me – except when he was in one of his black moods. Everyone knew not to cross Terry Bellefleur when he was in one of his moods. Terry's dark days were inevitably preceded by nightmares of the worst kind, as his neighbors testified. They could hear Terry hollering on the nightmare nights.

I never, never read Terry's mind.

Terry looked okay today. His shoulders were relaxed, and his eyes didn't dart from side to side. 'You okay, sweet thing?' he asked, patting my arm sympathetically.

'Thanks, Terry, I'm fine. Just sorry about Lafayette.'

'Yeah, he wasn't too bad.' From Terry, that was high praise. 'Did his job, always showed up on time. Cleaned the kitchen good. Never a bad word.' Functioning on that level was Terry's highest ambition. 'And then he dies in Andy's Buick.'

'I'm afraid Andy's car is kind of . . .' I groped for the blandest term.

'It's cleanable,' he said. Terry was anxious to close that subject.

'Did he tell you what had happened to Lafayette?'

'Andy says it looks like his neck was broken. And there was some, ah, evidence that he'd been . . . messed with.' Terry's brown eyes flickered away, revealing his discomfort. 'Messed with' meant something violent and sexual to Terry.

'Oh. Gosh, how awful.' Danielle and Holly had come up behind me, and Sam, with another sack of garbage he'd cleaned out of his office, paused on his way to the Dumpster out back.

'He didn't look that . . . I mean, the car didn't look that . . .'

'Stained?'

'Right.'

'Andy thinks he was killed somewhere else.'

'Yuck,' said Holly. 'Don't talk about it. That's too much for me.'

Terry looked over my shoulder at the two women. He had no great love for either Holly or Danielle, though I didn't know why and had made no effort to learn. I tried to leave people privacy, especially now that I had better control over my own ability. I heard the two moving away, after Terry had kept his gaze trained on them for a few seconds.

'Portia came and got Andy last night?' he asked.

'Yes, I called her. He couldn't drive. Though I'm betting he wishes I'd let him, now.' I was just never going to be number one on Andy Bellefleur's popularity list.

'She have trouble getting him to her car?'

'Bill helped her.'

'Vampire Bill? Your boyfriend?'

'Uh-huh.'

'I hope he didn't scare her,' Terry said, as if he didn't remember I was still there.

I could feel my face squinching up. 'There's no reason on earth why Bill would ever scare Portia Bellefleur,' I said, and something about the way I said it penetrated Terry's fog of private thought.

'Portia ain't as tough as everyone thinks she is,' Terry told me. 'You, on the other hand, are a sweet little éclair on the outside and a pit bull on the inside.'

'I don't know whether I should feel flattered, or whether I should sock you in the nose.'

'There you go. How many women – or men, for that matter – would say such a thing to a crazy man like me?' And Terry smiled, as a ghost would smile. I hadn't known how conscious of his reputation Terry was, until now.

I stood on tiptoe to give him a kiss on the scarred cheek, to show him I wasn't scared of him. As I sank back to my heels, I realized that wasn't exactly true. Under some circumstances, not only would I be quite wary of this damaged man, but I might become very frightened indeed.

Terry tied the strings of one of the white cook's aprons and began to open up the kitchen. The rest of us got back into the work mode. I wouldn't have long to wait tables, since I was getting off at six tonight to get ready to drive to Shreveport with Bill. I hated for Sam to pay me for the time I'd spent lollygagging around Merlotte's today, waiting to work; but straightening the storeroom and cleaning out Sam's office had to count for something.

As soon as the police opened up the parking lot, people began streaming in, in as heavy a flow as a small town like Bon Temps ever gets. Andy and Portia were among the first in, and I saw Terry look out the hatch from the kitchen at his cousins. They waved at him, and he raised a spatula to acknowledge their greeting. I wondered how close a cousin Terry actually was. He wasn't a first cousin, I was sure. Of course, here you could call someone your cousin or your aunt or your uncle with little or no blood relation at all. After my mother and father had died in a flash flood that swept their car off a bridge, my mother's best friend tried to come by my Gran's every week or two with a little present for me; and I'd called her Aunt Patty my whole life.

I answered all the customers' questions if I had time, and served hamburgers and salads and chicken breast strips – and beer – until I felt dazed. When I glanced at the clock, it was time for me to go. In the ladies' room I found my replacement, my friend Arlene. Arlene's flaming red hair (two shades redder this month) was arranged in an elaborate cluster of curls on the back of her head, and her tight pants let the world know she'd lost seven pounds. Arlene had been married four times, and she was on the lookout for number five.

We talked about the murder for a couple of minutes, and I briefed her on the status of my tables, before I grabbed my purse from Sam's office and scooted out the back door. It wasn't quite dark when I pulled up to my house, which is a quarter mile back in the woods off a seldom-traveled parish road. It's an old house, parts of it dating back a hundred and forty-plus years, but it's been altered and added onto so often we don't count it as an antebellum house. It's just an old farmhouse, anyway. My grandmother, Adele Hale Stackhouse, left me this house, and I treasured it. Bill had spoken of me moving into his place, which sat on a hill just across the cemetery from my home, but I was reluctant to leave my own turf.

I yanked off my waitress outfit and opened my closet. If we were going over to Shreveport on vampire business, Bill would want me to dress up a little. I couldn't quite figure that out, since he didn't want anyone else making a pass at me, but he always wanted me to look extra pretty when we were going to Fangtasia, a vampire-owned bar catering mainly to tourists.

Men.

I couldn't make up my mind, so I hopped in the shower. Thinking about Fangtasia always made me tense. The vampires who owned it were part of the vampire power structure, and once they'd discovered my unique talent, I'd become a desirable acquisition to them. Only Bill's determined entry into the vampire self-governing system had kept me safe; that is, living where I wanted to live, working at my chosen job. But in return for that safety, I was still obliged to show up when I was summoned, and to put my telepathy to use for them. Milder measures than their former choices (torture and terror) were what 'mainstreaming' vampires needed. The hot water immediately made me feel better, and I relaxed as it beat on my back.

'Shall I join you?'

'Shit, Bill!' My heart pounding a mile a minute, I leaned against the shower wall for support.

'Sorry, sweetheart. Didn't you hear the bathroom door opening?'

'No, dammit. Why can't you just call "Honey, I'm home," or something?'

'Sorry,' he said again, not sounding very sincere. 'Do you need someone to scrub your back?'

'No, thank you,' I hissed. 'I'm not in the back-scrubbing kind of mood.'

Bill grinned (so I could see his fangs were retracted) and pulled the shower curtain closed.

When I came out of the bathroom, towel wrapped around me more or less modestly, he was stretched out on my bed, his shoes neatly lined up on the little rug by the night table. Bill was wearing a dark blue long-sleeved shirt and khakis, with socks that matched the shirt and polished loafers. His dark brown hair was brushed straight back, and his long sideburns looked retro.

Well, they were, but more retro than most people could ever have imagined.

He has high arched brows and a high-bridged nose. His mouth is the kind you see on Greek statues, at least the ones I've seen in pictures. He died a few years after the end of the Civil War (or the War of Northern Aggression, as my grandmother always called it).

'What's the agenda for tonight?' I asked. 'Business, or pleasure?'

'Being with you is always pleasure,' Bill said.

'We're going to Shreveport for what reason?' I asked, since I know a dodgy answer when I hear one.

'We were summoned.'

'By?'

'Eric, of course.'

Now that Bill had run for, and accepted, a position as Area 5 investigator, he was at Eric's beck and call – and under Eric's protection. That meant, Bill had explained, that anyone attacking Bill would also have to deal with Eric, and it meant that Bill's possessions were sacred to Eric. Which included me. I wasn't thrilled to be numbered among Bill's possessions, but it was better than some of the alternatives.

I made a face in the mirror.

'Sookie, you made a deal with Eric.'

'Yeah,' I admitted, 'I did.'

'So you must stick by it.'

'I plan on it.'

'Wear those tight blue jeans that lace up the sides,' Bill suggested.

They weren't denim at all, but some kind of stretchy stuff. Bill just loved me in those jeans, which came down low. More than once, I had wondered if Bill had some kind of Britney Spears fantasy thing going on. Since I was fully aware that I looked good in the jeans, I pulled them on, and a dark blue-and-white-checked short-sleeved shirt that buttoned up the front and stopped about two inches below my bra. Just to exhibit a little independence (after all, he'd better remember I was my own woman) I brushed my hair into a ponytail high up on my head. I pinned a blue bow over the elastic band and slapped on a little makeup. Bill glanced at his watch once or twice, but I took my time. If he was so all-fired concerned about how I was going to impress his vampire friends, he could just wait for me.

Once we were in the car and on our way west to Shreveport, Bill said, 'I started a new business venture today.'

Frankly, I'd been wondering where Bill's money came from. He never seemed rich: he never seemed poor. But he never worked, either; unless it was on the nights we weren't together.

I was uneasily aware that any vampire worth his salt could become wealthy; after all, when you can control the minds of humans to some extent, it's not that difficult to persuade them to part with money or stock tips or investment opportunities. And until vampires gained the legal right to exist, they hadn't had to pay taxes, see. Even the U.S. government had to admit it couldn't tax the dead. But if you gave them rights, Congress had figured, and gave them the vote, then you could obligate them into paying taxes.

When the Japanese had perfected the synthetic blood that actually enabled vampires to 'live' without drinking human blood, it had been possible for vampires to come out of the coffin. 'See, we don't have to victimize mankind to exist,' they could say. 'We are not a threat.'

But I knew Bill's big thrill was when he drank from me. He might have a pretty steady diet of LifeFlow (the most popular marketing name for the synthetic blood) but nipping my neck was incomparably better. He could drink some bottled A positive in front of a whole bar full of people, but if he planned on a mouthful of Sookie Stackhouse, we had better by golly be in private, the effect was that different. Bill didn't get any kind of erotic thrill from a wineglass of LifeFlow.

'So what's this new business?' I asked.

'I bought the strip mall by the highway, the one where LaLaurie's is.'

'Who owned that?'

'The Bellefleurs originally owned the land. They let Sid Matt Lancaster do a development deal for them.'

Sid Matt Lancaster had acted as my brother's lawyer before. He'd been around for donkey's years and had way more clout than Portia.

'That's good for the Bellefleurs. They've been trying to sell that for a couple of years. They need the cash, bad. You bought the land and the strip mall? How big a parcel of land is that?'

'Just an acre, but it's in a good location,' Bill said, in a businesslike voice that I'd never heard before.

'That same strip's got LaLaurie's, and a hair salon, and Tara's Togs?' Aside from the country club, LaLaurie's was the only restaurant with any pretensions in the Bon Temps area. It was where you took your wife for your twenty-fifth wedding anniversary, or your boss when you wanted a promotion, or a date you really, really wanted to impress. But it didn't make a lot of money, I'd heard.

I have no inkling of how to run a business, or manage business dealings, having been just a step or two ahead of poor all my life. If my parents hadn't had the good fortune to find a little oil on their land and save all the money from it before the oil ran out, Jason and Gran and I would've had a hand-to-mouth time of it. At least twice, we had been close to selling my parents' place, just to keep up Gran's house and taxes, while she raised the two of us.

'So, how does that work? You own the building that houses those three businesses, and they pay you rent?'

Bill nodded. 'So now, if you want to get something done to your hair, go to Clip and Curl.'

I'd only been to a hairdresser once in my life. If the ends got ragged, I usually went over to Arlene's trailer and she trimmed them evenly. 'Do you think my hair needs something done to it?' I asked uncertainly.

'No, it's beautiful.' Bill was reassuringly positive. 'But if you should want to go, they have, ah, manicures, and hair-care products.' He said 'hair-care products' as if it were in a foreign language. I stifled a smile.

'And,' he continued, 'take anyone you want to LaLaurie's, and you won't have to pay.'

I turned in my seat to stare at him.

'And Tara knows that if you come in, she will put any clothes you buy on my account.'

I could feel my temper creak and give way. Bill, unfortunately, could not. 'So, in other words,' I said, proud of the evenness of my voice, 'they know to indulge the boss's fancy woman.'

Bill seemed to realize he'd made a mistake. 'Oh Sookie,' he began, but I wasn't having any of it. My pride had risen up and whopped me in the face. I don't lose my temper a lot, but when I do, I make a good job of it.

'Why can't you just send me some damn flowers, like anyone else's boyfriend? Or some candy. I like candy. Just buy me a Hallmark card, why don't you? Or a kitten or a scarf!'

'I meant to give you something,' he said cautiously.

'You've made me feel like a kept woman. And you've certainly given the people who work at those businesses the impression I am.'

As far as I could tell in the dim dashboard light, Bill looked like he was trying to figure out the difference. We were just past the turnoff to Mimosa Lake, and I could see the deep woods on the lake side of the road in Bill's headlights.

To my complete surprise, the car coughed and stopped dead. I took it as a sign.

Bill would've locked the doors if he'd known what I was going to do, because he certainly looked startled when I scrambled out of the car and marched over to the woods by the road.

'Sookie, get back in here right now!' Bill was mad now, by God. Well, it had taken him long enough.

I shot him the bird as I stepped into the woods.

I knew if Bill wanted me in the car, I'd be in the car, since Bill's about twenty times stronger and faster than me. After a few seconds in the darkness, I almost wished he'd catch up with me. But then my pride gave a twitch, and I knew I'd done the right thing. Bill seemed to be a little confused about the nature of our relationship, and I wanted him to get it straight in his head. He could just take his sorry ass to Shreveport and explain my absence to his superior, Eric. By golly, that'd show him.

'Sookie,' Bill called from the road, 'I'm going to go to the nearest service station to get a mechanic.'

'Good luck,' I muttered under my breath. A service station with a full-time mechanic; open at night? Bill was thinking of the fifties, or some other era.

'You're acting like a child, Sookie,' Bill said. 'I could come to get you, but I'm not going to waste the time. When you're calm, come get in the car and lock it. I'm going now.' Bill had his pride, too.

To my mingled relief and concern, I heard the faint footfalls along the road that meant Bill was running at vampire speed. He'd really left.

He probably thought *he* was teaching *me* a lesson. When it was just the opposite. I told myself that several times. After all, he'd be back in a few minutes. I was sure. All I had to do was be sure I didn't stumble far enough through the woods to fall into the lake.

It was *really dark* in the pines. Though the moon was not full, it was a cloudless night, and the shadows in the trees were pitch black in contrast with the cool remote glow of the open spaces.

I made my way back to the road, then took a deep breath and began marching back toward Bon Temps, the opposite direction from Bill. I wondered how many miles we'd put between us and Bon Temps before Bill had begun our conversation. Not so very many, I reassured myself, and patted myself on the back that I was wearing sneakers, not high-heeled sandals. I hadn't brought a sweater, and the exposed skin between my cropped top and my low-cut blue jeans felt goose-pimply. I began to run down the shoulder in an easy jog. There weren't any streetlights, so I would have been in bad shape if it weren't for the moonlight.

Just about the time I recalled that there was someone out there who'd murdered Lafayette, I heard footsteps in the woods parallel to my own path.

When I stopped, the movement in the trees did also.

I'd rather know now. 'Okay, who's there?' I called. 'If you're going to eat me, let's just get it over with.'

A woman stepped out of the woods. With her was a razorback, a feral hog. Its tusks gleamed from the shadows. In her left hand she carried a sort of stick or wand, with a tuft of something on its end.

'Great,' I whispered to myself. 'Just great.' The woman was as scary as the razorback. I was sure she wasn't a vampire, because I could feel the activity in her mind; but she was sure some supernatural being, so she didn't send a clear signal. I could snatch the tenor of her thoughts anyway. She was amused.

That couldn't be good.

I hoped the razorback was feeling friendly. They were very rarely seen around Bon Temps, though every now and then a hunter would spot one; even more rarely bring one down. That was a picture-in-the-paper occasion. This hog smelled, an awful and distinctive odor.

I wasn't sure which to address. After all, the razorback might not be a true animal at all, but a shapeshifter. That was one thing I'd learned in the past few months. If vampires, so long thought of as thrilling fiction, actually did exist, so did other things that we'd regarded as equally exciting fiction.

I was really nervous, so I smiled.

She had long snarled hair, an indeterminate dark in the uncertain light, and she was wearing almost nothing. She had a kind of shift on, but it was short and ragged and stained. She was barefoot. She smiled back at me. Rather than scream, I grinned even more brightly.

'I have no intention of eating you,' she said.

'Glad to hear it. What about your friend?'

'Oh, the hog.' As if she'd just noticed it, the woman reached over and scratched the razorback's neck, like I would a friendly dog's. The ferocious tusks bobbed up and down. 'She'll do what I tell her,' the woman said casually. I didn't need a translator to understand the threat. I tried to look equally casual as I glanced around the open space where I stood, hoping to locate a tree that I could climb if I had to. But all the trunks close enough for me to reach in time were bare of branches; they were the loblolly pines grown by the millions in our neck of the woods, for their lumber. The branches start about fifteen feet up.

I realized what I should've thought of sooner; Bill's car stopping there was no accident, and maybe even the fight we'd had was no coincidence.

'You wanted to talk to me about something?' I asked her, and in turning to her I found she'd come several feet closer. I could see her face a little better now, and I was in no wise reassured. There was a stain around her mouth, and when it opened as she spoke, I could see the teeth had dark margins; Miss Mysterious had been eating a raw mammal. 'I see you've already had supper,' I said nervously, and then could've slapped myself.

'Mmmm,' she said. 'You are Bill's pet?'

'Yes,' I said. I objected to the terminology, but I wasn't in much position to take a stand. 'He would be really awfully upset if anything happened to me.'

'As if a vampire's anger is anything to me,' she said offhandedly.

'Excuse me, ma'am, but what are you? If you don't mind me asking.'

She smiled again, and I shuddered. 'Not at all. I'm a maenad.'

That was something Greek. I didn't know exactly what, but it was wild, female, and lived in nature, if my impressions were correct.

'That's very interesting,' I said, grinning for all I was worth. 'And you are out here tonight because . . .?'

'I need a message taken to Eric Northman,' she said, moving closer. This time I could see her do it. The hog snuffled along at her side as if she were tied to the woman. The smell was indescribable. I could see the little brushy tail of the razorback – it was switching back and forth in a brisk, impatient sort of way.

'What's the message?' I glanced up at her – and whirled to run as quickly as I could. If I hadn't ingested some vampire blood at the beginning of the summer, I couldn't have turned in time, and I would've taken the blow on my face and chest instead of my back. It felt exactly as though someone very strong had swung a heavy rake and the points had caught in my skin, gone deeper, and torn their way across my back.

I couldn't keep to my feet, but pitched forward and landed on my stomach. I heard her laughing behind me, and the hog snuffling, and then I registered the fact that she had gone. I lay there crying for a minute or two. I was trying not to shriek, and I found myself panting like a woman in labor, attempting to master the pain. My back hurt like hell.

I was mad, too, with the little energy I could spare. I was just a living bulletin board to that bitch, that maenad, whatever the hell she was. As I crawled, over twigs and rough ground, pine needles and dust, I grew angrier and angrier. I was shaking all over from the pain and the rage, dragging myself along, until I didn't feel I was worth killing, I was such a mess. I'd begun the crawl back to the car, trying to head back to the likeliest spot for Bill to find me, but when I was almost there I had second thoughts about staying out in the open.

I'd been assuming the road meant help – but of course, it didn't. I'd found out a few minutes before that not everyone met by chance was in a helping kind of mood. What if I met up with something else, something hungry? The smell of my blood might be attracting a predator at this very moment; a shark is said to be able to detect the tiniest particles of blood in the water, and a vampire is surely the shark's land equivalent.

So I crawled inside the tree line, instead of staying out beside the road where I'd be visible. This didn't seem like a very dignified or meaningful place to die. This was no Alamo, or Thermopylae. This was just a spot in the vegetation by a road in northern Louisiana. I was probably lying in poison ivy. I would probably not live long enough to break out, though.

I expected every second that the pain would begin to abate, but it only increased. I couldn't prevent the tears from coursing down my cheeks. I managed not to sob out loud, so I wouldn't attract any more attention, but it was impossible to keep completely still.

I was concentrating so desperately on maintaining my silence that I almost missed Bill. He was pacing along the road looking into the woods, and I could tell by the way he was walking that he was alert to danger. Bill knew something was wrong.

'Bill,' I whispered, but with his vampire hearing, it was like a shout.

He was instantly still, his eyes scanning the shadows. 'I'm here,' I said, and swallowed back a sob. 'Watch out.' I might be a living booby trap.

In the moonlight, I could see that his face was clean of emotion, but I knew he was weighing the odds, just as I was. One of us had to move, and I realized if I came out into the moon glow, at least Bill could see more clearly if anything attacked.

I stuck my hands out, gripped the grass, and pulled. I couldn't even get up to my knees, so this progress was my best speed. I pushed a little with my feet, though even that use of my back muscles was excruciating. I didn't want to look at Bill while I moved toward him, because I didn't want to soften at the sight of his rage. It was an almost palpable thing.

'What did this to you, Sookie?' he asked softly.

'Get me in the car. Please, get me out of here,' I said, doing my best to hold myself together. 'If I make a lot of noise, she might come back.' I shivered all over at the thought. 'Take me to Eric,' I said, trying to keep my voice even. 'She said this was a message for Eric Northman.'

Bill squatted beside me. 'I have to lift you,' he told me.

Oh, no. I started to say, 'There must be some other way,' but I knew there wasn't. Bill knew better than to hesitate. Before I could anticipate the pain to its full extent, he scooted an arm under me and applied his other hand to my crotch, and in an instant he had me dangling across his shoulder.

I screamed out loud. I tried not to sob after that, so Bill could listen for an attack, but I didn't manage that very well. Bill began to run along the road, back to the car. It was running already, its engine idling smoothly. Bill flung open the back door and tried to feed me gently but quickly onto the backseat of the Cadillac. It was impossible not to cause me more pain by doing this, but he made the attempt.

'It was her,' I said, when I could say anything coherent. 'It was her who made the car stop and made me get out.' I was keeping an open mind about whether she'd caused the fight to begin with.

'We'll talk about it in a little while,' he said. He sped toward Shreveport, at the highest speed he could, while I clawed at the upholstery in an attempt to keep control over myself.

All I remember about that ride was that it was at least two years long.

Bill got me to the back door of Fangtasia somehow, and kicked it to get attention.

'What?' Pam sounded hostile. She was a pretty blond vampire I'd met a couple of times before, a sensible sort of individual with considerable business acumen. 'Oh, Bill. What's happened? Oh, yum, she's bleeding.'

'Get Eric,' Bill said.

'He's been waiting in here,' she began, but Bill strode right by her with me bouncing on his shoulder like a bag of bloody game. I was so out of it by that time that I wouldn't have cared if he'd carried me onto the dance floor of the bar out front, but instead, Bill blew into Eric's office laden with me and rage.

'This is on your account,' Bill snarled, and I moaned as he shook me as though he were drawing Eric's attention to me. I hardly see how Eric could have been looking anywhere else, since I was a full-grown female and probably the only bleeding woman in his office.

I would have loved to faint, to pass right out. But I didn't. I just sagged over Bill's shoulder and hurt. 'Go to hell,' I mumbled.

'What, my darling?'

'Go to *hell*.'

'We must lay her on her stomach on the couch,' Eric said. 'Here, let me . . .' I felt another pair of hands grip my legs, Bill sort of turned underneath me, and together they deposited me carefully on the broad couch that Eric had just bought for his office. It had that new smell, and it was leather. I was glad, staring at it from the distance of half an inch, that he hadn't gotten cloth upholstery. 'Pam, call the doctor.' I heard footsteps leave the room, and Eric crouched down to look into my face. It was quite a crouch, because Eric, tall and broad, looks exactly like what he is, a former Viking.

'What has happened to you?' he asked.

I glared at him, so incensed I could hardly speak. 'I am a message to you,' I said, almost in a whisper. 'This woman in the woods made Bill's car stop, and maybe even made us argue, and then she came up to me with this hog.'

'A *pig*?' Eric could not have been more astonished if I'd said she had a canary up her nose.

'Oink, oink. Razorback. Wild pig. And she said she wanted to send you a message, and I turned in time to keep her from getting my face, but she got my back, and then she left.'

'Your face. She would have gotten your face,' Bill said. I saw his hands clenching by his thighs, and the back of him as he began pacing around the office. 'Eric, her cuts are not so deep. What's wrong with her?'

'Sookie,' Eric said gently, 'what did this woman look like?'

His face was right by mine, his thick golden hair almost touching my face.

'She looked nuts, I'll tell you how she looked. And she called you Eric Northman.'

'That's the last name I use for human dealings,' he said. 'By looking nuts, you mean she looked . . . how?'

'Her clothes were all ragged and she had blood around her mouth and in her teeth, like she'd just eaten something raw. She was carrying this kind of wand thing, with something on the end of it. Her hair was long and tangled . . . look, speaking of hair, my hair is getting stuck to my back.' I gasped.

'Yes, I see.' Eric began trying to separate my long hair from my wounds, where blood was acting as an adherent as it thickened.

Pam came in then, with the doctor. If I had hoped Eric meant a regular doctor, like a stethoscope and tongue depressor kind of person, I was once again doomed to disappointment. This doctor was a dwarf, who hardly had to bend over to look me in the eyes. Bill hovered, vibrating with tension, while the small woman examined my wounds. She was wearing a pair of white pants and a tunic, just like doctors at the hospital; well, just like doctors used to, before they started wearing that green color, or blue, or whatever crazy print came their way. Her face was full of her nose, and her skin was olive. Her hair was golden brown and coarse, incredibly thick and wavy. She wore it dipped fairly short. She put me in mind of a hobbit. Maybe she *was* a hobbit. My understanding of reality had taken several raps to the head in the past few months.

'What kind of doctor are you?' I asked, though it took some time for me to collect myself enough.

'The healing kind,' she said in a surprisingly deep voice. 'You have been poisoned.'

'So that's why I keeping thinking I'm gonna die,' I muttered.

'You will, quite soon,' she said.

'Thanks a lot, Doc. What can you do about that?'

'We don't have a lot of choices. You've been poisoned. Have you ever heard of Komodo dragons? Their mouths are teeming with bacteria. Well, maenad wounds have the same toxic level. After a dragon has bitten you, the creature tracks you for hours, waiting for the bacteria to kill you. For maenads, the delayed death adds to the fun. For Komodo dragons, who knows?'

Thanks for the National Geographic side trip, Doc. 'What can you do?' I asked, through gritted teeth.

'I can close the exterior wounds. But your bloodstream has been compromised, and your blood must be removed and replaced. That is a job for the vampires.' The good doctor seemed positively jolly at the prospect of everyone working together. On me.

She turned to the gathered vamps. 'If only one of you takes the poisoned blood, that one will be pretty miserable. It's the element of magic that the maenad imparts. The Komodo dragon bite would be no problem for you guys.' She laughed heartily.

I hated her. Tears streamed down my face from the pain.

'So,' she continued, 'when I'm finished, each of you take a turn, removing just a little. Then we'll give her a transfusion.'

'Of human blood,' I said, wanting to make that perfectly clear. I'd had to have Bill's blood once to survive massive injuries and once to survive an examination of sorts, and I'd had another vampire's blood by accident, unlikely as that sounds. I'd been able to see changes in me after that blood ingestion, changes I didn't want to amplify by taking another dose. Vampire blood was the drug of choice among the wealthy now, and as far as I was concerned, they could have it.

'If Eric can pull some strings and get the human blood,' the dwarf said. 'At least half the transfusion can be synthetic. I'm Dr. Ludwig, by the way.'

'I can get the blood, and we owe her the healing,' I heard Eric say, to my relief. I would have given a lot to see Bill's face, at that moment. 'What is your type, Sookie?' Eric asked.

'O positive,' I said, glad my blood was so common.

'That shouldn't be a problem,' Eric said. 'Can you take care of that, Pam?'

Again, a sense of movement in the room. Dr. Ludwig bent forward and began licking my back. I shrieked.

'She's the doctor, Sookie,' Bill said. 'She will heal you this way.'

'But she'll get poisoned,' I said, trying to think of an objection that wouldn't sound homophobic and sizist. Truly, I didn't want anyone licking my back, female dwarf or large male vampire.

'She is the healer,' Eric said, in a rebuking kind of way. 'You must accept her treatment.'

'Oh, all right,' I said, not even caring how sullen I sounded. 'By the way, I haven't heard an "I'm sorry" from you yet.' My sense of grievance had overwhelmed my sense of self-preservation.

'I am sorry that the maenad picked on you.'

I glared at him. 'Not enough,' I said. I was trying hard to hang on to this conversation.

'Angelic Sookie, vision of love and beauty, I am prostrate that the wicked evil maenad violated your smooth and voluptuous body, in an attempt to deliver a message to me.'

'That's more like it.' I would have taken more satisfaction in Eric's words if I hadn't been jabbed with pain just then. (The doctor's treatment was not exactly comfortable.) Apologies had better be either heartfelt or elaborate, and since Eric didn't have a heart to feel (or at least I hadn't noticed it so far) he might as well distract me with words.

'I take it the message means that she's going to war with you?' I asked, trying to ignore the activities of Dr. Ludwig. I was sweating all over. The pain in my back was excruciating. I could feel tears trickling down my face. The room seemed to have acquired a yellow haze; everything looked sickly.

Eric looked surprised. 'Not exactly,' he said cautiously. 'Pam?'

'It's on the way,' she said. 'This is bad.'

'Start,' Bill said urgently. 'She's changing color.'

I wondered, almost idly, what color I'd become. I couldn't hold my head off the couch anymore, as I'd been trying to do to look a little more alert. I laid my cheek on the leather, and immediately my sweat bound me to the surface. The burning sensation that radiated through my body from the claw marks on my back grew more intense, and I shrieked because I just couldn't help it. The dwarf leaped from the couch and bent to examine my eyes.

She shook her head. 'Yes, if there's to be any hope,' she said, but she sounded very far away to me. She had a syringe in her hand. The last thing I registered was Eric's face moving closer, and it seemed to me he winked.

Chapter 3

I opened my eyes with great reluctance. I felt that I'd been sleeping in a car, or that I'd taken a nap in a straight-back chair; I'd definitely dozed off somewhere inappropriate and uncomfortable. I felt groggy, and I ached all over. Pam was sitting on the floor a yard away, her wide blue eyes fixed on me.

'It worked,' she commented. 'Dr. Ludwig was right.'

'Great.'

'Yes, it would have been a pity to lose you before we'd gotten a chance to get some good out of you,' she said with shocking practicality. 'There are many other humans associated with us the maenad could have picked, and those humans are far more expendable.'

'Thanks for the warm fuzzies, Pam,' I muttered. I felt the last degree of nasty, as if I'd been dipped in a vat of sweat and then rolled in the dust. Even my teeth felt scummy.

'You're welcome,' she said, and she almost smiled. So Pam had a sense of humor, not something vampires were noted for. You never saw vampire stand-up comedians, and human jokes just left vampires cold, ha-ha. (Some of *their* humor could give you nightmares for a week.)

'What happened?'

Pam relaced her fingers around her knee. 'We did as Dr. Ludwig said. Bill, Eric, Chow, and I all took a turn, and when you were almost dry we began the transfusion.'

I thought about that for a minute, glad I'd checked out of consciousness before I could experience the procedure. Bill always took blood when we were making love, so I associated it with the height of erotic activity. To have 'donated' to so many people would have been extremely embarrassing to me if I'd been there for it, so to speak. 'Who's Chow?' I asked.

'See if you can sit up,' Pam advised. 'Chow is our new bartender. He is quite a draw.'

'Oh?'

'Tattoos,' Pam said, sounding almost human for a moment. 'He's tall for an Asian, and he has a wonderful set of . . . tattoos.'

I tried to look like I cared. I pushed up, feeling a certain tenderness that made me very cautious. It was like my back was covered with wounds that had just healed, wounds that might break open again if I weren't careful. And that, Pam told me, was exactly the case.

Also, I had no shirt on. Or anything else. Above the waist. Below, my jeans were still intact, though remarkably nasty.

'Your shirt was so ragged we had to tear it off,' Pam said, smiling openly. 'We took turns holding you on our laps. You were much admired. Bill was furious.'

'Go to hell' was all I could think of to say.

'Well, as to that, who knows?' Pam shrugged. 'I meant to pay you a compliment. You must be a modest woman.'

She got up and opened a closet door. There were shirts hanging inside; an extra store for Eric, I assumed. Pam pulled one off a hanger and tossed it to me. I reached up to catch it and had to admit that movement was comparatively easy.

'Pam; is there a shower here?' I hated to pull the pristine white shirt over my grimy self.

'Yes, in the storeroom. By the employees' bathroom.'

It was extremely basic, but it was a shower with soap and a towel. You had to step right out into the storeroom, which was probably just fine with the vampires, since modesty is not a big issue with them. When Pam agreed to guard the door, I enlisted her help in pulling off the jeans and shucking my shoes and socks. She enjoyed the process a little too much.

It was the best shower I'd ever had.

I had to move slowly and carefully. I found I was as shaky as though I'd passed through a grave illness, like pneumonia or a virulent strain of the flu. And I guess I had. Pam opened the door enough to pass me some underwear, which was a pleasant surprise, at least until I dried myself and prepared to struggle into it. The underpants were so tiny and lacy they hardly deserved to be called panties. At least they were white. I knew I was better when I caught myself wishing I could see how I looked in a mirror. The underpants and the white shirt were the only garments I could bear to put on. I came out barefoot, to find that Pam had rolled up the jeans and everything else and stuffed them in a plastic bag so I could get them home to the wash. My tan looked extremely brown against the white of the snowy shirt. I walked very slowly back to Eric's office and fished in my purse for my brush. As I began to try to work through the tangles, Bill came in and took the brush from my hand.

'Let me do that, darling,' he said tenderly. 'How are you? Slide off the shirt, so I can check your back.' I did anxiously hoping there weren't cameras in the office – though from Pam's account, I might as well relax.

'How does it look?' I asked him over my shoulder.

Bill said briefly, 'There will be marks.'

'I figured.' Better on my back than on my front. And being scarred was better than being dead.

I slipped the shirt back on, and Bill began working on my hair, a favorite thing for him. I grew tired very quickly and sat in Eric's chair while Bill stood behind me.

'So why did the maenad pick me?'

'She would have been waiting for the first vampire to come through. That I had you with me – so much easier to hurt – that was a bonus.'

'Did she cause our fight?'

'No, I think that was just chance. I still don't understand why you got so angry.'

'I'm too tired to explain, Bill. We'll talk about it tomorrow, okay?'

Eric came in, along with a vampire I knew must be Chow. Right away I could see why Chow would bring in customers. He was the first Asian vampire I'd seen, and he was extremely handsome. He was also covered – at least the parts I could see – with that intricate tattooing that I'd heard members of the Yakuza favored. Whether Chow had been a gangster when he was human or not, he was certainly sinister now. Pam slid through the door after another minute had passed, saying, 'All locked up. Dr. Ludwig left, too.'

So Fangtasia had closed its doors for the night. It must be two in the morning, then. Bill continued to brush my hair, and I sat in the office chair with my hands on my thighs, acutely conscious of my inadequate clothing. Though, come to think of it, Eric was so tall his shirt covered as much of me as some of my short sets. I guess it was the French-cut bikini panties underneath that made me so embarrassed. Also, no bra. Since God was generous with me in the bosom department, there's no mistaking when I leave off a bra.

But no matter if my clothes showed more of me than I wanted, no matter if all of these people had seen even more of my boobs than they could discern now, I had to mind my manners.

'Thank you all for saving my life,' I said. I didn't succeed in sounding warm, but I hope they could tell I was sincere.

'It was truly my pleasure,' said Chow, with an unmistakable leer in his voice. He had a trace of an accent, but I don't have enough experience with the different characteristics of the many strains of Asians to tell you where he came from originally. I am sure 'Chow' was not his complete name, either, but it was all the other vampires called him. 'It would have been perfect, without the poison.'

I could feel Bill tense behind me. He laid his hands on my shoulders, and I reached up to put my fingers over his.

Eric said, 'It was worth ingesting the poison.' He held his fingers to his lips and kissed them, as if praising the bouquet of my blood. Ick.

Pam smiled. 'Any time, Sookie.'

Oh, just fantastic. 'You, too, Bill,' I said, leaning my head back against him.

'It was my privilege,' he said, controlling his temper with an effort.

'You two had a fight before Sookie's encounter with the maenad?' Eric asked. 'Is that what I heard Sookie say?'

'That's our business,' I snapped, and the three vampires smiled at each other. I didn't like that one bit. 'By the way, why did you want us to come over here tonight, anyway?' I asked, hoping to get off of the topic of Bill and me.

'You remember your promise to me, Sookie? That you would use your mental ability to help me out, as long as I let the humans involved live?'

'Of course I remember.' I am not one to forget a promise, especially one made to a vampire.

'Since Bill has been appointed investigator of Area 5, we have not had a lot of mysteries. But Area 6, in Texas, has need of your special asset. So we have loaned you out.'

I realized I'd been rented, like a chainsaw or backhoe. I wondered if the vampires of Dallas had had to put down a deposit against damage.

'I won't go without Bill.' I looked Eric steadily in the eye. Bill's fingers gave me a little squeeze, so I knew I'd said the right thing.

'He'll be there. We drove a hard bargain,' Eric said, smiling broadly. The effect was really disconcerting, because he was happy about something, and his fangs were out. 'We were afraid they might keep you, or kill you, so an escort was part of our deal all along. And who better than Bill? If anything should render Bill incapable of guarding you, we will send another escort right out. And the vampires of Dallas have agreed to providing a car and chauffeur, lodgings and meals, and of course, a nice fee. Bill will get a percentage of that.'

When I'd be doing the work? 'You must work out your financial arrangement with Bill,' Eric said smoothly. 'I am sure he will at least recompense you for your time away from your bar job.'

Had Ann Landers ever covered 'When Your Date Becomes Your Manager'?

'Why a maenad?' I asked, startling all of them. I hoped I was pronouncing the word correctly. 'Naiads are water and dryads are trees, right? So why a maenad, out there in the woods? Weren't maenads just women driven mad by the god Bacchus?'

'Sookie, you have unexpected depths,' Eric said, after an appreciable pause. I didn't tell him I'd learned that from reading a mystery. Let him think I read ancient Greek literature in the original language. It couldn't hurt.

Chow said, 'The god entered some women so completely that they became immortal, or very close to it. Bacchus was the god of the grape, of course, so bars are very interesting to maenads. In fact, so interesting that they don't like other creatures of the darkness becoming involved. Maenads consider that the violence sparked by the consumption of alcohol belongs to them; that's what they feed off, now that no one formally worships their god. And they are attracted to pride.'

That rang a chime. Hadn't Bill and I both been feeling our pride, tonight?

'We had only heard rumors one was in the area,' Eric said. 'Until Bill brought you in.'

'So what was she warning you of? What does she want?'

'Tribute,' Pam said. 'We think.'

'What kind?'

Pam shrugged. It seemed that was the only answer I was going to get.

'Or what?' I asked. Again with the stares. I gave a deep sigh of exasperation. 'What's she gonna do if you don't pay her tribute?'

'Send her madness.' Bill sounded worried.

'Into the bar? Merlotte's?' Though there were plenty of bars in the area.

The vampires eyed each other.

'Or into one of us,' Chow said. 'It has happened. The Halloween massacre of 1876, in St. Petersburg.'

They all nodded solemnly. 'I was there,' Eric said. 'It took twenty of us to clean up. And we had to stake Gregory, it took all of us to do that. The maenad, Phryne, received tribute after that, you can be sure.'

For the vampires to stake one of their own, things had to be pretty serious. Eric had staked a vampire who had stolen from him, and Bill had told me Eric had had to pay a severe penalty. Who to, Bill hadn't said, and I hadn't asked. There were some things I could live quite well without knowing.

'So you'll give a tribute to this maenad?'

They were exchanging thoughts on this, I could tell. 'Yes,' Eric said. 'It is better if we do.'

'I guess maenads are pretty hard to kill,' Bill said, a question in his voice.

Eric shuddered. 'Oh, yes,' he said. 'Oh, yes.'

During our ride back to Bon Temps, Bill and I were silent. I had a lot of questions about the evening, but I was tired from my bones out to my skin.

'Sam should know about this,' I said, as we stopped at my house.

Bill came around to open my door. 'Why, Sookie?' He took my hand to pull me from the car, knowing that I could barely walk.

'Because . . .' and then I stopped dead. Bill knew Sam was supernatural, but I didn't want to remind him. Sam owned a bar, and we had been closer to Bon Temps than Shreveport when the maenad had interfered.

'He owns a bar, but he should be all right,' Bill said reasonably. 'Besides, the maenad said the message was for Eric.'

That was true.

'You think too much about Sam to suit me,' Bill said, and I gaped up at him.

'You're jealous?' Bill was very wary when other vampires seemed to be admiring me, but I'd assumed that was just territorial. I didn't know how to feel about this new development. I'd never had anyone feel jealous of my attentions before.

Bill didn't answer, in a very snitty way.

'Hmmm,' I said thoughtfully. 'Well, well, well.' I was smiling to myself as Bill helped me up the steps and through the old house, into my room; the room my grandmother had slept in for so many years. Now the walls were painted pale yellow, the woodwork was off-white, the curtains were off-white with bright flowers scattered over them. The bed had a matching cover.

I went into the bathroom for a moment to brush my teeth and take care of necessities, and came out still in Eric's shirt.

'Take it off,' Bill said.

'Look, Bill, normally I'd be hot to trot, but tonight –'

'I just hate to see you in his shirt.'

Well, well, *well*. I could get used to this. On the other hand, if he carried it to extremes, it could be a nuisance.

'Oh, all right,' I said, making a sigh he could hear from yards away. 'I guess I'll just have to take this ole shirt off.' I unbuttoned it slowly, knowing Bill's eyes were watching my hands move down the buttons, pulling the shirt apart a little more each time. Finally, I doffed it and stood there in Pam's white underwear.

'Oh,' Bill breathed, and that was tribute enough for me. Maenads be damned, just seeing Bill's face made me feel like a goddess.

Maybe I'd go to Foxy Femme Lingerie in Ruston my next day off. Or maybe Bill's newly acquired clothing store carried lingerie?

Explaining to Sam that I needed to go to Dallas wasn't easy. Sam had been wonderful to me when I'd lost my grandmother, and I counted him as a good friend, a great boss, and (every now and then) a sexual fantasy. I just told Sam that I was taking a little vacation; God knows, I'd never asked for one before. But he pretty much had figured out what the deal was. Sam didn't like it. His brilliant blue eyes looked hot and his face stony, and even his red-blond hair seemed to sizzle. Though he practically muzzled himself to keep from saying so, Sam obviously thought Bill should not have agreed to my going. But Sam didn't know all the circumstances of my dealings with the vampires, just as only Bill, of the vampires I knew, realized that Sam was a shapeshifter. And I tried not to remind Bill. I didn't want Bill thinking about Sam any more than he already did. Bill might decide Sam was an enemy, and I definitely didn't want Bill to do that. Bill is a really bad enemy to have.

I am good at keeping secrets and keeping my face blank, after years of reading unwanted items out of peoples' minds. But I have to confess that compartmentalizing Bill and Sam took a lot of energy.

Sam had leaned back in his chair after he'd agreed to give me the time off, his wiry build hidden by a big kingfisher-blue Merlotte's Bar tee shirt. His jeans were old but clean, and his boots were heavy-soled and ancient. I was sitting on the edge of the visitor's chair in front of Sam's desk, the office door shut behind me. I knew no one could be standing outside the door listening; after all, the bar was as noisy as usual, with the jukebox wailing a zydeco tune and the bellowing of people who'd had a few drinks. But still, when you talked about something like the maenad, you wanted to lower your voice, and I leaned across the desk.

Sam automatically mimicked my posture, and I put my hand on his arm and said in a whisper, 'Sam, there's a maenad out by the Shreveport road.' Sam's face went blank for a long second before he whooped with laughter.

Sam didn't get over his convulsions for at least three minutes, during which time I got pretty mad. 'I'm sorry,' he kept saying, and off he'd go again. You know how irritating that can be when you're the one who triggered it? He came around the desk, still trying to smother his chuckles. I stood because he was standing, but I was fuming. He grasped my shoulders. 'I'm sorry, Sookie,' he repeated. 'I've never seen one, but I've heard they're nasty. Why does this concern you? The maenad, that is.'

'Because she's not happy, as you would know if you could see the scars on my back,' I snapped, and his face changed then, by golly.

'You were hurt? How did this happen?'

So I told him, trying to leave some of the drama out of it, and toning down the healing process employed by the vampires of Shreveport. He still wanted to see the scars. I turned around, and he pulled up my tee shirt, not past bra strap level. He didn't make a sound, but I felt a touch on my back, and after a second I realized Sam had kissed my skin. I shivered. He pulled the tee shirt over my scars and turned me around.

'I'm very sorry,' he said, with complete sincerity. He wasn't laughing now, wasn't even close to it. He was awful close to me. I could practically feel the heat radiating from his skin, electricity crackling through the small fine hairs on his arms.

I took a deep breath. 'I'm worried she'll turn her attention to you,' I explained. 'What do maenads want as tribute, Sam?'

'My mother used to tell my father that they love a proud man,' he said, and for a moment I thought he was still teasing me. But I looked at his face, and he was not. 'Maenads love nothing more than to tear a proud man down to size. Literally.'

'Yuck,' I said. 'Anything else satisfy them?'

'Large game. Bears, tigers, so on.'

'Hard to find a tiger in Louisiana. Maybe you could find a bear, but how'd you get it to the maenad's territory?' I pondered this for a while, but didn't come to any answer. 'I assume she'd want it alive,' I said, a question in my voice.

Sam, who seemed to have been watching me instead of thinking over the problem, nodded, and then he leaned forward and kissed me.

I should have seen it coming.

He was so warm after Bill, whose body never got up to warm. Tepid, maybe. Sam's lips actually felt hot, and his tongue, too. The kiss was deep, intense, unexpected; like the excitement you feel when someone gives you a present you didn't know you wanted. His arms were around me, mine were around him, and we were giving it everything we had, until I came back to earth.

I pulled away a little, and he slowly raised his head from mine.

'I do need to get out of town for a little while,' I said.

'Sorry, Sookie, but I've been wanting to do that for years.'

There were a lot of ways I could go from that statement, but I ratcheted up my determination and took the high road. 'Sam, you know I am . . .'

'In love with Bill,' he finished my sentence.

I wasn't completely sure I was in love with Bill, but I loved him, and I had committed myself to him. So to simplify the matter, I nodded in agreement.

I couldn't read Sam's thoughts clearly, because he was a supernatural being. But I would have been a dunce, a telepathic null, not to feel the waves of frustration and longing that rolled off of him.

'The point I was trying to make,' I said, after a minute, during which time we disentangled and stepped away from each other, 'is that if this maenad takes a special interest in bars, this is a bar run by someone who is not exactly run-of-the-mill human, like Eric's bar in Shreveport. So you better watch out.'

Sam seemed to take heart that I was warning him, seemed to get some hope from it. 'Thanks for telling me, Sookie. The next time I change, I'll be careful in the woods.'

I hadn't even thought of Sam encountering the maenad

in his shapeshifting adventures, and I had to sit down abruptly as I pictured that.

'Oh, no,' I told him emphatically. 'Don't change at all.'

'It's full moon in four days,' Sam said, after a glance at the calendar. 'I'll have to. I've already got Terry scheduled to work for me that night.'

'What do you tell him?'

'I tell him I have a date. He hasn't looked at the calendar to figure out that every time I ask him to work, it's a full moon.'

'That's something. Did the police come back any more about Lafayette?'

'No.' Sam shook his head. 'And I hired a friend of Lafayette's, Khan.'

'As in Sher Khan?'

'As in Chaka Khan.'

'Okay, but can he cook?'

'He's been fired from the Shrimp Boat.'

'What for?'

'Artistic temperament, I gather.' Sam's voice was dry.

'Won't need much of that around here,' I observed, my hand on the doorknob. I was glad Sam and I had had a conversation, just to ease down from our tense and unprecedented situation. We had never embraced each other at work. In fact, we'd only kissed once, when Sam brought me home after our single date months before. Sam was my boss, and starting something with your boss is always a bad idea. Starting something with your boss when your boyfriend is a vampire is another bad idea, possibly a fatal idea. Sam needed to find a woman. Quickly.

When I'm nervous, I smile. I was beaming when I said, 'Back to work,' and stepped through the door, shutting it behind me. I had a muddle of feelings about everything that had happened in Sam's office, but I pushed it all away, and prepared to hustle some drinks.

There was nothing unusual about the crowd that night in Merlotte's. My brother's friend Hoyt Fortenberry was drinking with some of his cronies. Kevin Prior, whom I was more accustomed to seeing in uniform, was sitting with Hoyt, but Kevin was not having a happy evening. He looked as though he'd rather be in his patrol car with his partner, Kenya. My brother, Jason, came in with his more and more frequent arm decoration, Liz Barrett. Liz always acted glad to see me, but she never tried to ingratiate herself, which earned her high points in my book. My grandmother would have been glad to know Jason was dating Liz so often. Jason had played the scene for years, until the scene was pretty darned tired of Jason. After all, there is a finite pool of women in Bon Temps and its surrounding area, and Jason had fished that pool for years. He needed to restock.

Besides, Liz seemed willing to ignore Jason's little brushes with the law.

'Baby sis!' he said in greeting. 'Bring me and Liz a Seven-and-Seven apiece, would you?'

'Glad to,' I said, smiling. Carried away on a wave of optimism, I listened in to Liz for a moment; she was hoping that very soon Jason would pop the question. The sooner the better, she thought, because she was pretty sure she was pregnant.

Good thing I've had years of concealing what I was thinking. I brought them each a drink, carefully shielding myself from any other stray thoughts I might catch, and tried to think what I should do. That's one of the worst things about being telepathic; things people are thinking, not talking about, are things other people (like me) really don't want to know. Or shouldn't want to know. I've heard enough secrets to choke a camel, and believe me, not a one of them was to my advantage in any way.

If Liz was pregnant, the last thing she needed was a drink, no matter who the baby's daddy was.

I watched her carefully, and she took a tiny sip from her glass. She wrapped her hand around it to partially hide it from public view. She and Jason chatted for a minute, then Hoyt called out to him, and Jason swung around on the bar stool to face his high school buddy. Liz stared down at her drink, as if she'd really like to gulp it in one swallow. I handed her a similar glass of plain 7UP and whisked the mived drink away.

Liz's big round brown eyes gazed up at me in astonishment. 'Not for you,' I said very quietly. Liz's olive complexion turned as white as it could. 'You have good sense,' I said. I was struggling to explain why I'd intervened, when it was against my personal policy to act on what I learned in such a surreptitious way. 'You have good sense, you can do this right.'

Jason turned back around then, and I got a call for another pitcher from one of my tables. As I moved out from behind the bar to answer the summons, I noticed Portia Bellefleur in the doorway. Portia peered around the dark bar as though she were searching for someone. To my astonishment, that someone turned out to be me.

'Sookie, do you have a minute?' she asked.

I could count the personal conversations I'd had with Portia on one hand, almost on one finger, and I couldn't imagine what was on her mind.

'Sit over there,' I said, nodding at an empty table in my area. 'I'll be with you in a minute.'

'Oh, all right. And I'd better order a glass of wine, I guess. Merlot.'

'I'll have it right there.' I poured her glass carefully, and put it on a tray. After checking visually to make sure all my customers looked content, I carried the tray over to Portia's table and sat opposite her. I perched on the edge of the chair, so anyone who ran out of a drink could see I was fixing to hop up in just a second.

'What can I do for you?' I reached up to check that my ponytail was secure and smiled at Portia.

She seemed intent on her wineglass. She turned it with her fingers, took a sip, positioned it on the exact center of the coaster. 'I have a favor to ask you,' she said.

No shit, Sherlock. Since I'd never had a casual conversation with Portia longer than two sentences, it was obvious she needed something from me.

'Let me guess. You were sent here by your brother to ask me to listen in on people's thoughts when they're in the bar, so I can find out about this orgy thing Lafayette went to.' Like I hadn't seen that coming.

Portia looked embarrassed, but determined. 'He would never have asked you if he wasn't in serious trouble, Sookie.'

'He would never have asked me because he doesn't like me. Though I've never been anything but nice to him his whole life! But now, it's okay to ask me for help, because he really needs me.'

Portia's fair complexion was turning a deep unbecoming red. I knew it wasn't very pleasant of me to take out her brother's problems on her, but she had, after all, agreed to be the messenger. You know what happens to messengers.

That made me think of my own messenger role the night before, and I wondered if I should be feeling lucky today.

'I wasn't for this,' she muttered. It hurt her pride, to ask a favor of a barmaid; a Stackhouse, to boot.

Nobody liked me having a 'gift.' No one wanted me to use it on her. But everyone wanted me to find out something to her advantage, no matter how I felt about sifting through the thoughts (mostly unpleasant and irrelevant) of bar patrons to glean pertinent information.

'You'd probably forgotten that just recently Andy arrested my brother for murder?' Of course he'd had to let Jason go, but still.

If Portia had turned any redder she'd have lit a fire. 'Just forget it, then,' she said, scraping together all her dignity. 'We don't need help from a freak like you, anyway.'

I had touched her at the quick, because Portia had always been courteous, if not warm.

'Listen to me, Portia Bellefleur. I'll listen a little. Not for you or your brother, but because I liked Lafayette. He was a friend of mine, and he was always sweeter to me than you or Andy.'

'I don't like you.'

'I don't care.'

'Darling, is there a problem?' asked a cool voice from behind me.

Bill. I reached with my mind, and felt the relaxing empty space right behind me. Other minds just buzzed like bees in a jar, but Bill's was like a globe filled with air. It was wonderful. Portia stood up so abruptly that her chair almost went over backwards. She was frightened of even being close to Bill, like he was a venomous snake or something.

'Portia was just asking me for a favor,' I said slowly, aware for the first time that our little trio was attracting a certain amount of attention from the crowd.

'In return for the many kind things the Bellefleurs have done for you?' Bill asked. Portia snapped. She whirled around to stalk out of the bar. Bill watched her leave with the oddest expression of satisfaction.

'Now I have to find out what that was about,' I said, and leaned back against him. His arms circled me and drew me back closer to him. It was like being cuddled by a tree.

'The vampires in Dallas have made their arrangements,' Bill said. 'Can you leave tomorrow evening?'

'What about you?'

'I can travel in my coffin, if you're willing to make sure I'm unloaded at the airport. Then we'll have all night to find out what it is the Dallas vampires want us to do.'

'So I'll have to take you to the airport in a hearse?'

'No, sweetheart. Just get yourself there. There's a transportation service that does that kind of thing.'

'Just takes vampires places in daytime?'

'Yes, they're licensed and bonded.'

I'd have to think about that for a while. 'Want a bottle? Sam has some on the heater.'

'Yes, please, I'd like some O positive.'

My blood type. How sweet. I smiled at Bill, not my strained normal grin, but a true smile from my heart. I was so lucky to have him, no matter how many problems we had as a couple. I couldn't believe I'd kissed someone else, and I blotted out that idea as soon as it skittered across my mind.

Bill smiled back, maybe not the most reassuring sight, since he was happy to see me. 'How soon can you get off?' he asked, leaning closer.

I glanced down at my watch. 'Thirty minutes,' I promised.

'I'll be waiting for you.' He sat at the table Portia had vacated, and I brought him the blood, *tout de suite.*

Kevin drifted over to talk to him, ended up sitting down at the table. I was near enough only twice to catch fragments of the conversation; they were talking about the types of crimes we had in our small town, and the price of gas, and who would win the next sheriff's election. It was so normal! I beamed with pride. When Bill had first started coming into Merlotte's, the atmosphere had been on the strained side. Now, people came and went casually, speaking to Bill or only nodding, but not making a big issue of it either way. There were enough legal issues facing vampires without the social issues involved, too.

As Bill drove me home that night, he seemed to be in an excited mood. I couldn't account for that until I figured out that he was pleased about his visit to Dallas.

'Got itchy feet?' I asked, curious and not too pleased about his sudden case of travel lust.

'I have traveled for years. Staying in Bon Temps these months has been wonderful,' he said as he reached over to pat my hand, 'but naturally I like to visit with others of my own kind, and the vampires of Shreveport have too much power over me. I can't relax when I'm with them.'

'Were vampires this organized before you went public?' I tried not to ask questions about vampire society, because I was never sure how Bill would react, but I was really curious.

'Not in the same way,' he said evasively. I knew that was the best answer I'd get from him, but I sighed a little anyway. Mr. Mystery. Vampires still kept limits clearly drawn. No doctor could examine them, no vampires could be required to join the armed forces. In returned for these legal concessions, Americans had demanded that vampires who were doctors and nurses – and there were more than a few – had to hang up their stethoscopes, because humans were too leery of a blood-drinking health care professional. Even though, as far as humans knew, vampirism was an extreme allergic reaction to a combination of various things, including garlic and sunlight.

Though I was a human – albeit a weird one – I knew better. I'd been a lot happier when I believed Bill had some classifiable illness. Now, I knew that creatures we'd shoved off into the realm of myth and legend had a nasty habit of proving themselves real. Take the maenad. Who'd have believed an ancient Greek legend would be strolling through the woods of northern Louisiana?

Maybe there really *were* fairies at the bottom of the garden, a phrase I remembered from a song my grandmother had sung when she hung out the clothes on the line.

'Sookie?' Bill's voice was gently persistent.

'What?'

'You were thinking mighty hard about something.'

'Yes, just wondering about the future,' I said vaguely. 'And the flight. You'll have to fill me in on all the arrangements, and when I have to be at the airport. And what clothes should I take?'

Bill began to turn that over in his head as we pulled up in the driveway in front of my old house, and I knew he would take my request seriously. It was one of the many good things about him.

'Before you pack, though,' he said, his dark eyes solemn under the arch of his brows, 'there is something else we have to discuss.'

'What?' I was standing in the middle of my bedroom floor, staring in the open closet door, when his words registered.

'Relaxation techniques.'

I swung around to face him, my hands on my hips. 'What on earth are you talking about?'

'This.' He scooped me up in the classic Rhett Butler carrying stance, and though I was wearing slacks rather than a long red – negligee? gown? – Bill managed to make me feel like I was as beautiful, as unforgettable, as Scarlett O'Hara. He didn't have to traipse up any stairs, either; the bed was very close. Most evenings, Bill took things very slow, so slow I thought I would start screaming before we came to the point, so to speak. But tonight, excited by the trip, by the imminent excursion, Bill's speed had greatly accelerated. We reached the end of the tunnel together, and as we lay together during the little aftershocks following successful love, I wondered what the vampires of Dallas would make of our association.

I'd only been to Dallas once, on a senior trip to Six Flags, and it hadn't been a wonderful time for me. I'd been clumsy at protecting my mind from the thoughts eternally broadcasting from other brains, I'd been unprepared for the unexpected pairing of my best friend, Marianne, and a classmate named Dennis Engelbright, and I'd never been away from home before.

This would be different, I told myself sternly. I was going at the request of the vampires of Dallas; was that glamorous, or what? I was needed because of my unique skills. I should focus on not calling my quirks a disability. I had learned how to control my telepathy, at least to have much more precision and predictability. I had my own man. No one would abandon me.

Still, I have to admit that before I went to sleep, I cried a few tears for the misery that had been my lot.

Chapter 4

It was as hot as the six shades of hell in Dallas, especially on the pavement at the airport. Our brief few days of fall had relapsed back into summer. Torch-hot gusts of air bearing all the sounds and smells of the Dallas–Fort Worth airport – the workings of small vehicles and airplanes, their fuel and their cargo – seemed to accumulate around the foot of the ramp from the cargo bay of the plane I'd been waiting for. I'd flown a regular commercial flight, but Bill had had to be shipped specially.

I was flapping my suit jacket, trying to keep my underarms dry, when the Catholic priest approached me.

Initially, I was so respectful of his collar that I didn't object to his approach, even though I didn't really want to talk to anyone. I had just emerged from one totally new experience, and I had several more such hurdles ahead of me.

'Can I be of some service to you? I couldn't help but notice your situation,' the small man said. He was soberly clothed in clerical black, and he sounded chock-full of sympathy. Furthermore, he had the confidence of someone used to approaching strangers and being received politely. He had what I thought was sort of an unusual haircut for a priest, though; his brown hair was longish, and tangled, and he had a mustache, too. But I only noticed this vaguely.

'My situation?' I asked, not really paying attention to his words. I'd just glimpsed the polished wood coffin at the edge of the cargo hold. Bill was such a traditionalist; metal would have been more practical for travel. The uniformed attendants were rolling it to the head of the ramp, so they must have put wheels under it somehow. They'd promised Bill it would get to its destination without a scratch. And the armed guards behind me were insurance that no fanatic would rush over and tear the lid off. That was one of the extras Anubis Air had plugged in its ad. Per Bill's instructions, I'd also specified that he be first off the plane.

So far, so good.

I cast a look at the dusky sky. The lights around the field had come on minutes ago. The black jackal's head on the airplane's tail looked savage in the harsh light, which created deep shadows where none had been. I checked my watch again.

'Yes. I'm very sorry.'

I glanced sideways at my unwanted companion. Had he gotten on the plane in Baton Rouge? I couldn't remember his face, but then, I'd been pretty nervous the whole flight. 'Sorry,' I said. 'For what? Is there some kind of problem?'

He looked elaborately astonished. 'Well,' he said, nodding his head toward the coffin, which was now descending on the ramp on a roller system. 'Your bereavement. Was this a loved one?' He edged a little closer to me.

'Well, sure,' I said, poised between puzzlement and aggravation. Why was he out here? Surely the airline didn't pay a priest to meet every person traveling with a coffin? Especially one being unloaded from Anubis Air. 'Why else would I be standing here?'

I began to worry.

Slowly, carefully, I slid down my mental shields and began to examine the man beside me. I know, I know: an invasion of his privacy. But I was responsible for not only my own safety, but Bill's.

The priest, who happened to be a strong broadcaster, was thinking about approaching nightfall as intently as I was, and with a lot more fear. He was hoping his friends were where they were supposed to be.

Trying not to show my increasing anxiety, I looked upward again. Deep into dusk, there was only the faintest trace of light remaining in the Texas sky.

'Your husband, maybe?' He curved his fingers around my arm.

Was this guy creepy, or what? I glanced over at him. His eyes were fixed on the baggage handlers who were clearly visible in the hold of the plane. They were wearing black and silver jumpsuits with the Anubis logo on the left chest. Then his gaze flickered down to the airline employee on the ground, who was preparing to guide the coffin onto the padded, flat-bedded baggage cart. The priest wanted . . . what did he want? He was trying to catch the men all looking away, preoccupied. He didn't want them to see. While he . . . what?

'Nah, it's my boyfriend,' I said, just to keep our pretence up. My grandmother had raised me to be polite, but she hadn't raised me to be stupid. Surreptitiously, I opened my shoulder bag with one hand and extracted the pepper spray Bill had given me for emergencies. I held the little cylinder down by my thigh. I was edging away from the false priest and his unclear intentions, and his hand was tightening on my arm, when the lid of the coffin swung open.

The two baggage handlers in the plane had swung down to the ground. Now they bowed deeply. The one who'd guided the coffin onto the cart said, 'Shit!' before he bowed, too (new guy, I guess). This little piece of obsequious behavior was also an airline extra, but I considered it way over the top.

The priest said, 'Help me, Jesus!' But instead of falling to his knees, he jumped to my right, seized me by the arm holding the spray, and began to yank at me.

At first, I thought he felt he was trying to remove me from the danger represented by the opening coffin, by pulling me to safety. And I guess that was what it looked like to the baggage handlers, who were wrapped up in their role-playing as Anubis Air attendants. The upshot was, they didn't help me, even though I yelled, 'Let go!' at the top of my well-developed lungs. The 'priest' kept yanking at my arm and trying to run, and I kept digging in my two-inch heels and pulling back. I flailed at him with my free hand. I'm not letting anyone haul me off somewhere I don't want to go, not without a good fight.

'Bill!' I was really frightened. The priest was not a big man, but he was taller and heavier than me, and almost as determined. Though I was making his struggle as hard as possible, inch by inch he was moving me toward a staff door into the terminal. A wind had sprung up from nowhere, a hot dry wind, and if I sprayed the chemicals they would blow right back in my face.

The man inside the coffin sat up slowly, his large dark eyes taking in the scene around him. I caught a glimpse of him running a hand over his smooth brown hair.

The staff door opened and I could tell there was someone right inside, reinforcements for the priest.

'Bill!'

There was a whoosh through the air around me, and all of a sudden the priest let go and zipped through the door like a rabbit at a greyhound track. I staggered and would have landed on my butt if Bill hadn't slowed to catch me.

'Hey, baby,' I said, incredibly relieved. I yanked at the jacket of my new gray suit, and felt glad I'd put on some more lipstick when the plane landed. I looked in the direction the priest had taken. '*That* was pretty weird.' I tucked the pepper spray back in my purse.

'Sookie,' Bill said, 'are you all right?' He leaned down to give me a kiss, ignoring the awed whispers of the baggage handlers at work on a charter plane next to the Anubis gate. Even though the world at large had learned two years ago that vampires were not only the stuff of legends and horror movies, but truly led a centuries-long existence among us, lots of people had never seen a vampire in the flesh.

Bill ignored them. Bill is good at ignoring things that he doesn't feel are worth his attention.

'Yes, I'm fine,' I said, a little dazed. 'I don't know why he was trying to grab me.'

'He misunderstood our relationship?'

'I don't think so. I think he knew I was waiting for you and he was trying to get me away before you woke up.'

'We'll have to think about this,' said Bill, master of the understatement. 'Other than this bizarre incident, how did the evening go?'

'The flight was all right,' I said, trying not to stick my bottom lip out.

'Did anything else untoward happen?' Bill sounded just a wee bit dry. He was quite aware that I considered myself put-upon.

'I don't know what normal is for airplane trips, never having done it before,' I said tartly, 'but up until the time the priest appeared, I'd say things pretty much ran smooth.' Bill raised one eyebrow in that superior way he has, so I'd elaborate. 'I don't think that man was really a priest at all. What did he meet the plane for? Why'd he come over to talk to me? He was just waiting till everyone working on the plane was looking in another direction.'

'We'll talk about it in a more private place,' my vampire said, glancing at the men and women who'd begun to gather around the plane to check out the commotion. He stepped over to the uniformed Anubis employees, and in a quiet voice he chastised them for not coming to my help. At least, I assumed that was the burden of his conversation, from the way they turned white and began to babble. Bill slid an arm around my waist and we began to stroll to the terminal.

'Send the coffin to the address on the lid,' Bill called back over his shoulder. 'The Silent Shore Hotel.' The Silent Shore was the only hotel in the Dallas area that had undergone the extensive renovation necessary to accommodate vampire patrons. It was one of the grand old downtown hotels, the brochure had said, not that I'd ever seen downtown Dallas or any of its grand old hotels before.

We stopped in the stairwell of a grubby little flight leading up to the main passenger concourse. 'Now, tell me,' he demanded. I glanced up at him while I related the odd little incident from start to finish. He was very white. I knew he must be hungry. His eyebrows looked black against the pallor of his skin, and his eyes looked an even darker brown than they really were.

He held open a door and I passed through into the bustle and confusion of one of the biggest airports in the world.

'You didn't listen to him?' I could tell Bill didn't mean with my ears.

'I was still pretty heavily shielded from the plane,' I said. 'And by the time I got concerned, began to try to read him, you came out of your coffin and he took off. I had the funniest feeling, before he ran . . .' I hesitated, knowing this was far-fetched.

Bill just waited. He's not one to waste words. He lets me finish what I'm saying. We stopped walking for a second, edged over to the wall.

'I felt like he was there to kidnap me,' I said. 'I know that sounds nuts. Who would know who I am, here in Dallas? Who would know to be meeting the plane? But that's definitely the impression I got.' Bill took my warm hands in his cool ones.

I looked up into Bill's eyes. I'm not that short, and he's not that tall, but I still have to look up at him. And it's a little pride issue with me, that I can meet his eyes and not get glamoured. Sometimes I wish Bill *could* give me a different set of memories – for example, I wouldn't mind forgetting about the maenad – but he can't.

Bill was thinking over what I'd said, filing it away for future reference. 'So the flight itself was boring?' he asked.

'Actually, it was pretty exciting,' I admitted. 'After I made sure the Anubis people had stowed you on their plane, and I was boarded on mine, the woman showed us what to do when we crashed. I was sitting on the row with the emergency exit. She said to switch if we didn't think we could handle that. But I think I could, don't you? Handle an emergency? She brought me a drink and a magazine.' I seldom got waited on myself, being a barmaid by profession, you might say, so I really enjoyed being served.

'I'm sure you can handle just about anything, Sookie. Were you frightened when the plane took off?'

'No. I was just a little worried about this evening. Aside from that, it went fine.'

'Sorry I couldn't be with you,' he murmured, his cool and liquid voice flowing around me. He pressed me against his chest.

'That's okay,' I said into his shirt, mostly meaning it. 'First time flying, you know, it's kind of nerve-wracking. But it went all right. Until we landed.'

I might grouse and I might moan, but I was truly glad Bill had risen in time to steer me through the airport. I was feeling more and more like the poor country cousin.

We didn't talk any more about the priest, but I knew Bill hadn't forgotten. He walked me through collecting our luggage and finding transportation. He would've parked me somewhere and arranged it all, except, as he reminded me frequently, I'd have to do this on my own sometime, if our business demanded we land somewhere in full daylight.

Despite the fact that the airport seemed incredibly crowded, full of people who all appeared heavily burdened and unhappy, I managed to follow the signs with a little nudge from Bill; after reinforcing my mental shields. It was bad enough, getting washed with the weary misery of the travelers, without listening to their specific laments. I directed the porter with our luggage (which Bill could easily have carried under one arm) to the taxi stand, and Bill and I were on our way to the hotel within forty minutes of Bill's emergence. The Anubis people had sworn up and down that his coffin would be delivered within three hours.

We'd see. If they didn't make it, we got a free flight.

I'd forgotten the sprawl of Dallas, in the seven years since I'd graduated from high school. The lights of the city were amazing, and the busyness. I stared out of the windows at everything we passed, and Bill smiled at me with an irritating indulgence.

'You look very pretty, Sookie. Your clothes are just right.'

'Thanks,' I said, relieved and pleased. Bill had insisted that I needed to look 'professional,' and after I'd said, 'Professional what?' he'd given me one of those looks. So I was wearing a gray suit over a white shell, with pearl earrings and a black purse and heels. I'd even smoothed my hair back into a twisted shape at the back of my head with one of those Hairagamis I'd ordered from TV. My friend Arlene had helped me. To my mind, I looked like a professional, all right – a professional funeral home attendant – but Bill seemed to approve. And I'd charged the whole outfit to him at Tara's Togs, since it was a legitimate business expense. So I couldn't complain about the cost.

I'd have been more comfortable in my barmaid's outfit. Give me shorts and a T-shirt over a dress and hose any day. And I could've been wearing my Adidas with my barmaid uniform, not these damn heels. I sighed.

The taxi pulled up to the hotel, and the driver got out to extract our luggage. There was enough of it for three days. If the vampires of Dallas had followed my directions, I could wind this up and we could go back to Bon Temps tomorrow night, to live there unmolested and uninvolved in vampire politics – at least until the next time Bill got a phone call. But it was better to bring extra clothes than to count on that.

I scooted across the seat to emerge after Bill, who was paying the driver. A uniformed bellboy from the hotel was loading the luggage onto a rolling cart. He turned his thin face to Bill and said, 'Welcome to Silent Shore Hotel, sir! My name is Barry, and I'll . . .' Then Bill stepped forward, the light from the lobby door spilling onto his face. 'I'll be your porter,' Barry finished weakly.

'Thank you,' I said, to give the boy, who couldn't be more than eighteen, a second to compose himself. His hands were a little trembly. I cast a mental net out to check the source of his distress.

To my startled delight, I realized (after a quick rummage in Barry's head) that he was a telepath, like me! But he was at the level of organization and development I'd been when I was, maybe, twelve years old. He was a mess, that boy. He couldn't control himself at all, and his shields were a shambles. He was heavy into denial. I didn't know whether to grab him and hug him, or smack him upside the head. Then I realized his secret was not mine to give away. I glanced off in another direction, and shifted from one foot to another, as if I were bored.

'I'll just follow you with your luggage,' Barry mumbled, and Bill smiled at him gently. Barry smiled tentatively back, and then got busy bringing in the cart. It had to be Bill's appearance that unnerved Barry, since he couldn't read Bill's mind, the great attraction of the undead for people like me. Barry was going to have to learn how to relax around vampires, since he'd agreed to work at a hotel that catered to them.

Some people think all vampires look terrifying. To me, it depends on the vampire. I remember thinking, when I first met Bill, that he looked incredibly different; but I hadn't been frightened.

The one that was waiting for us in the lobby of Silent Shores, now, *she* was scary. I bet she made ole Barry wet his pants. She approached after we'd checked in, as Bill was putting his credit card back in his wallet (you just try applying for a credit card when you're a hundred sixty years old; that process had been a *bear*) and I sidled a little closer to him as he tipped Barry, hoping she wouldn't notice me.

'Bill Compton? The detective from Louisiana?' Her voice was as calm and cool as Bill's, with considerably less inflection. She had been dead a long time. She was as white as paper and as flat as a board, and her thin ankle-length blue-and-gold dress didn't do a thing for her except accentuate both whiteness and flatness. Light brown hair (braided and long enough to tap her butt) and glittery green eyes emphasized her otherness.

'Yes.' Vampires don't shake hands, but the two made eye contact and gave each other a curt nod.

'This is the woman?' She had probably gestured toward me with one of those lightning quick movements, because I caught a blur from the corner of my eyes.

'This is my companion and coworker, Sookie Stackhouse,' Bill said.

After a moment, she nodded to show she was picking up the hint. 'I am Isabel Beaumont,' she said, 'and after you take your luggage to your room and take care of your needs, you are to come with me.'

Bill said, 'I have to feed.'

Isabel swiveled an eye toward me thoughtfully, no doubt wondering why I wasn't supplying blood for my escort, but it was none of her business. She said, 'Just punch the telephone button for room service.'

Measly old mortal me would just have to order from the menu. But as I considered the time frame, I realized I'd feel much better if I waited to eat after this evening's business was finished.

After our bags had been put in the bedroom (big enough for the coffin and a bed), the silence in the little living room became uncomfortable. There was a little refrigerator well stocked with PureBlood, but this evening Bill would want the real thing.

'I have to call, Sookie,' Bill said. We'd gone over this before the trip.

'Of course.' Without looking at him, I retreated into the bedroom and shut the door. He might have to feed off someone else so I could keep my strength up for coming events, but I didn't have to watch it or like it. After a few minutes, I heard a knock on the corridor door and I heard Bill admit someone – his Meal on Wheels. There was a little murmur of voices and then a low moan.

Unfortunately for my tension level, I had too much common sense to do something like throw my hairbrush or one of the damn high heels across the room. Maybe retaining some dignity figured in there, too; and a healthy sense of how much temperament Bill would put up with. So I unpacked my suitcase and laid my makeup out in the bathroom, using the facility even though I didn't feel especially needy. Toilets were optional in the vampire world, I'd learned, and even if a functional facility was available in a house occupied by vampires, occasionally they forgot to stock toilet paper.

Soon I heard the outer door open and close again, and Bill knocked lightly before coming into the bedroom. He looked rosy and his face was fuller.

'Are you ready?' he asked. Suddenly, the fact that I was going out on my first real job for the vampires hit me, and I felt scared all over again. If I wasn't a success, my life would become out-and-out perilous, and Bill might become even deader than he was now. I nodded, my throat dry with fear.

'Don't bring your purse.'

'Why not?' I stared down at it, astonished. Who could object?

'Things can be hidden in purses.' Things like stakes, I assumed. 'Just slip a room key into . . . does that skirt have a pocket?'

'No.'

'Well, slip the key into your underthings.'

I raised my hem so Bill could see exactly what underthings I had to tuck something into. I enjoyed the expression on his face more than I can say.

'Those are . . . would that be a . . . thong?' Bill seemed a little preoccupied all of a sudden.

'It would. I didn't see the need to be professional down to the skin.'

'And what skin it is,' Bill murmured. 'So tan, so . . . smooth.'

'Yep, I figured I didn't need to wear any hose.' I tucked the plastic rectangle – the 'key' – under one of the side straps.

'Oh, I don't think it'll stay there,' he said, his eyes large and luminous. 'We might get separated, so you definitely need to take it with you. Try another spot.'

I moved it somewhere else.

'Oh, Sookie. You'll never get at it in a hurry there. We have . . . ah, we have to go.' Bill seemed to shake himself out of his trance.

'All right, if you insist,' I said, smoothing the skirt of the suit over my 'underthings.'

He gave me a dark look, patted his pockets like men do, just to make sure they got everything. It was an oddly human gesture, and it touched me in a way I couldn't even describe to myself. We gave each other a sharp nod and walked down the corridor to the elevator. Isabel Beaumont would be waiting, and I had a distinct feeling she wasn't used to that.

The ancient vampire, who looked no more than thirty-five, was standing exactly where we'd left her. Here at the Silent Shore Hotel, Isabel felt free to be her vampire self, which included immobile downtime. People fidget. They are compelled to look engaged in an activity, or purposeful. Vampires can just occupy space without feeling obliged to justify it. As we came out of the elevator, Isabel looked exactly like a statue. You could have hung your hat on her, though you'd have been sorry.

Some early warning system kicked in when we were within six feet of the vamp. Isabel's eyes flicked in our direction and her right hand moved, as though someone had thrown her 'on' switch. 'Come with me,' she said, and glided out the main door. Barry could hardly open it for her fast enough. I noticed he had enough training to cast his eyes down as she passed. Everything you've heard about meeting vampires' eyes is true.

Predictably, Isabel's car was a black Lexus loaded with options. Vampires won't go around in any Geo. Isabel waited until I'd buckled my seat belt (she and Bill didn't bother to use them) before pulling away from the curb, which surprised me. Then we were driving through Dallas, down a main thoroughfare. Isabel seemed to be the strong silent type, but after we'd been in the car for maybe five minutes, she seemed to shake herself, as if she had been reminded she had orders.

We began a curve to the left. I could see some sort of grassy area, and a vague shape that would be some kind of historical marker, maybe. Isabel pointed to her right with a long bony finger. 'The Texas School Book Depository,' she said, and I understood she felt obliged to inform me. That meant she had been ordered to do so, which was very interesting. I followed her finger eagerly, taking in as much of the brick building as I could see. I was surprised it didn't look more notable.

'That's the grassy knoll?' I breathed, excited and impressed. It was like I'd happened upon the *Hindenburg* or some other fabled artifact.

Isabel nodded, a barely perceptible movement that I only caught because her braid jerked. 'There is a museum in the old depository,' she said.

Now, that was something I'd like to see in the daytime. If we were here long enough, I'd walk or maybe find out how to catch a cab while Bill was in his coffin.

Bill smiled over his shoulder at me. He could pick up on my slightest mood, which was wonderful about eighty percent of the time.

We drove for at least twenty more minutes, leaving business areas and entering residential. At first the structures were modest and boxy; but gradually, though the lots didn't seem that much larger, the houses began to grow as if they'd taken steroids. Our final destination was a huge house shoehorned onto a small lot. With its little ruffle of land around the cube of the house, it looked ridiculous, even in the dark.

I sure could have stood a longer ride and more delay.

We parked on the street in front of the mansion, for so it seemed to me. Bill opened my door for me. I stood for a moment, reluctant to start the – project. I knew there were vampires inside, lots of them. I knew it the same way I would be able to discern that humans were waiting. But instead of positive surges of thought, the kind I'd get to indicate people, I got mental pictures of . . . how can I put it? There were holes in the air inside the house. Each hole represented a vampire. I went a few feet down the short sidewalk to the front door, and there, finally, I caught a mental whiff of human.

The light over the door was on, so I could tell the house was of beige brick with white trim. The light, too, was for my benefit; any vampire could see far better than the sharpest-eyed human. Isabel led the way to the front door, which was framed in graduating arches of brick. There was a tasteful wreath of grapevines and dried flowers on the door, which almost disguised the peephole. This was clever mainstreaming. I realized there was nothing apparent in this house's appearance to indicate that it was any different from any of the other oversized houses we'd passed, no outward indication that within lived vampires.

But they were there, in force. As I followed Isabel inside, I counted four in the main room onto which the front door opened, and there were two in the hall and at least six in the vast kitchen, which looked designed to produce meals for twenty people at a time. I knew immediately that the house had been purchased, not built, by a vampire, because vampires always plan tiny kitchens, or leave the kitchen out entirely. All they need is a refrigerator, for the synthetic blood, and a microwave, to heat it up. What are they going to cook?

At the sink, a tall, lanky human was washing a few dishes, so perhaps some humans did live here. He half-turned as we passed through, and nodded to me. He was wearing glasses and his shirtsleeves were rolled up. I didn't have a chance to speak, because Isabel was ushering us into what appeared to be the dining room.

Bill was tense. I might not be able to read his mind, but I knew him well enough to interpret the set of his shoulders. No vampire is ever comfortable entering another vamp's territory. Vampires have as many rules and regulations as any other society; they just try to keep them secret. But I was figuring things out.

Among all the vampires in the house, I quickly spotted the leader. He was one of those sitting at the long table in the large dining room. He was a total geek. That was my first impression. Then I realized that he was carefully disguised as a geek: he was quite . . . other. His sandy hair was slicked back, his physique was narrow and unimpressive, his black-rimmed glasses were sheer camouflage, and his pinstriped oxford cloth shirt was tucked into cotton-polyester blend pants. He was pale – well, duh – and freckled, with invisible eyelashes and minimal eyebrows.

'Bill Compton,' the geek said.

'Stan Davis,' Bill said.

'Yeah, welcome to the city.' There was a faint trace of foreign accent in the geek's voice. *He used to be Stanislaus Davidowitz*, I thought, and then wiped my mind clean like a slate. If any of them found out that every now and then I picked a stray thought out of the silence of their minds, I'd be bloodless before I hit the floor.

Even Bill didn't know that.

I packed the fear down in the cellar of my mind as the pale eyes fixed on me and scrutinized me feature by feature.

'She comes in an agreeable package,' he said to Bill, and I supposed that was meant to be a compliment, a pat on the back, for Bill.

Bill inclined his head.

Vampires didn't waste time saying a lot of things humans would under similar circumstances. A human executive would ask Bill how Eric, his boss, was doing; would threaten Bill a little in case I didn't perform; would maybe introduce Bill and me to at least the more important people in the room. Not Stan Davis, head vampire. He lifted his hand, and a young Hispanic vampire with bristly black hair left the room and returned with a human girl in tow. When she saw me, she gave a screech and lunged, trying to break free of the grip the vampire had on her upper arm.

'Help me,' she shrieked. 'You have to help me!'

I knew right away that she was stupid. After all, what could I do against a roomful of vampires? Her appeal was ridiculous. I told myself that several times, very fast, so I could go through with what I had to do.

I caught her eyes, and held up my finger to tell her to be silent. Once she'd looked at me, locked on to me, she obeyed. I don't have the hypnotic eyes of a vamp, but I don't look the least bit threatening. I look exactly like the girl you'd see in a low-paying job any place in any town in the South: blond and bosomy and tan and young. Possibly, I don't look very bright. But I think it's more that people (and vampires) assume that if you're pretty and blond and have a low-paying job, you are ipso facto dumb.

I turned to Stan Davis, very grateful that Bill was right behind me. 'Mr. Davis, you understand that I need more privacy when I question this girl. And I have to know what you need from her.'

The girl began to sob. It was slow and heartrending, and almost unbelievably irritating under the circumstances.

Davis's pale eyes fastened on mine. He was not trying to glamour me, or subdue me; he was just examining me. 'I understood your escort knew the terms of my agreement with his leader,' Stan Davis said. All right, I got the point. I was beneath contempt since I was a human. My talking to Stan was like a chicken talking to the buyer from KFC. But still, I had to know our goal. 'I'm aware you met Area 5's conditions,' I said, keeping my voice as steady as I could, 'and I'm going to do my best. But without a goal, I can't get started.'

'We need to know where our brother is,' he said, after a pause.

I tried not to look as astonished as I felt.

As I've said, some vampires, like Bill, live by themselves. Others feel more secure in a cluster, called a nest. They call each other brother and sister when they've been in the same nest for a while, and some nests lasted decades. (One in New Orleans has lasted two centuries.) I knew from Bill's briefing before we left Louisiana that the Dallas vampires lived in an especially large nest.

I'm no brain surgeon, but even I realized that for a vampire as powerful as Stan to be missing one of his nest brothers was not only very unusual, it was humiliating.

Vampires like to be humiliated about as much as people do.

'Explain the circumstances, please,' I said in my most neutral voice.

'My brother Farrell has not returned to his nest for five nights,' Stan Davis said.

I knew they would have checked Farrell's favorite hunting grounds, have asked every other vampire in the Dallas nest to find out if Farrell had been seen. Nevertheless, I opened my mouth to ask, as humans are compelled to do. But Bill touched my shoulder, and I glanced behind me to see a tiny headshake. My questions would be taken as a serious insult.

'This girl?' I asked instead. She was still quiet, but she was shivering and shaking. The Hispanic vampire seemed to be the only thing holding her up.

'Works in the club where he was last seen. It's one we own, The Bat's Wing.' Bars were favorite enterprises for vampires, naturally, because their heaviest traffic came at night. Somehow, fanged all-night dry cleaners didn't have the same allure that a vampire-studded bar did.

In the past two years, vampire bars had become the hottest form of nightlife a city could boast. The pathetic humans who became obsessed with vampires – fangbangers – hung out in vampire bars, often in costumes, in the hopes of attracting the attention of the real thing. Tourists came in to gape at the undead and the fangbangers. These bars weren't the safest place to work.

I caught the eyes of the Hispanic vampire, and indicated a chair on my side of the long table. He eased the girl into it. I looked down at her, preparing to slide into her thoughts. Her mind had no protection whatsoever. I closed my eyes.

Her name was Bethany. She was twenty-one, and she had thought of herself as a wild child, a real bad girl. She had had no idea what trouble that could get her into, until now. Getting a job at the Bat's Wing had been the rebellious gesture of her life, and it might just turn out to be fatal.

I turned my eyes back to Stan Davis. 'You understand,' I said, taking a great risk, 'that if she yields the information you want, she goes free, unharmed.' He'd said he understood the terms, but I had to be sure.

Bill heaved a sigh behind me. Not a happy camper. Stan Davis's eyes actually glowed for a second, so angry was he. 'Yes,' he said, biting out the words, his fangs half out, 'I agreed.' We met each other's eyes for a second. We both knew that even two years ago, the vampires of Dallas would have kidnapped Bethany and tortured her until they had every scrap of information she had stored in her brain, and some she'd made up.

Mainstreaming, going public with the fact of their existence, had many benefits – but it also had its price. In this instance, the price was my service.

'What does Farrell look like?'

'Like a cowboy.' Stan said this without a trace of humor. 'He wears one of those string ties, jeans, and shirts with fake pearl snaps.'

The Dallas vampires didn't seem to be into haute couture. Maybe I could have worn my barmaid outfit after all. 'What color hair and eyes?'

'Brown hair going gray. Brown eyes. A big jaw. About . . . five feet, eleven inches.' Stan was translating from some other method of measurement. 'He would look about thirty-eight, to you,' Stan said. 'He's clean-shaven, and thin.'

'Would you like me to take Bethany somewhere else? You got a smaller room, less crowded?' I tried to look agreeable, because it seemed like such a good idea.

Stan made a movement with his hand, almost too fast for me to detect, and in a second – literally – every vampire, except Stan himself and Bill, had left the kitchen. Without looking, I knew that Bill was standing against the wall, ready for anything. I took a deep breath. Time to start this venture.

'Bethany, how are you?' I said, making my voice gentle.

'How'd you know my name?' she asked, slumping down in her seat. It was a breakfast nook chair on wheels, and I rolled it out from the table and turned it to face the one I now settled in. Stan was still sitting at the head of the table, behind me, slightly to my left.

'I can tell lots of things about you,' I said, trying to look warm and omniscient. I began picking thoughts out of the air, like apples from a laden tree. 'You had a dog named Woof when you were little, and your mother makes the best coconut cake in the world. Your dad lost too much money at a card game one time, and you had to hock your VCR to help him pay up, so your mom wouldn't find out.'

Her mouth was hanging open. As much as it was possible, she had forgotten the fact that she was in terrible danger. 'That's amazing, you're as good as the psychic on TV, the one in the ads!'

'Well, Bethany, I'm not a psychic,' I said, a little too sharply. 'I'm a telepath, and what I do is read your thoughts, even some you maybe didn't know you had. I'm going to relax you, first, and then we're going to remember the evening you worked at the bar – not tonight, but five nights ago.' I glanced back at Stan, who nodded.

'But I wasn't thinking about my mother's cake!' Bethany said, stuck on what had struck her.

I tried to suppress my sigh.

'You weren't aware of it, but you did. It slid across your mind when you looked at the palest vampire – Isabel – because her face was as white as the icing for the cake. And you thought of how much you missed your dog when you were thinking of how your parents would miss you.'

I knew that was a mistake as soon as the words went out of my mouth, and sure enough, she began crying again, recalled to her present circumstances.

'So what are you here for?' she asked between sobs.

'I'm here to help you remember.'

'But you said you're not psychic.'

'And I'm not.' Or was I? Sometimes I thought I had a streak mixed in with my other 'gift,' which was what the vampires thought it was. I had always thought of it as more of a curse, myself, until I'd met Bill. 'Psychics can touch objects and get information about the wearers. Some psychics see visions of past or future events. Some psychics can communicate with the dead. I'm a telepath. I can read some peoples' thoughts. Supposedly, I can send thoughts, too, but I've never tried that.' Now that I'd met another telepath, the attempt was an exciting possibility, but I stowed that idea away to explore at my leisure. I had to concentrate on the business at hand.

As I sat knee to knee with Bethany, I was making a series of decisions. I was new to the idea of using my 'listening in' to some purpose. Most of my life had been spent struggling not to hear. Now, hearing was my job, and Bethany's life probably depended on it. Mine almost certainly did.

'Listen, Bethany, here's what we're going to do. You're going to remember that evening, and I'm going to go through it with you. In your mind.'

'Will it hurt?'

'No, not a bit.'

'And after that?'

'Why, you'll go.'

'Go home?'

'Sure.' With an amended memory that wouldn't include me, or this evening, courtesy of a vampire.

'They won't kill me?'

'No way.'

'You promise?'

'I do.' I managed to smile at her.

'Okay,' she said, hesitantly. I moved her a little, so she couldn't see Stan over my shoulder. I had no idea what he was doing. But she didn't need to see that white face while I was trying to get her to relax.

'You're pretty,' she said suddenly.

'Thanks, and back at you.' At least, she might be pretty under better circumstances. Bethany had a mouth that was too small for her face, but that was a feature some men found attractive, since it looked like she was always puckered up. She had a great quantity of brown hair, thick and bushy, and a thin body with small breasts. Now that another woman was looking at her, Bethany was worried about her wrinkled clothes and stale makeup.

'You look fine,' I said quietly, taking her hands into mine. 'Now, we're just gonna hold hands here for a minute – I swear I'm not making a pass.' She giggled, and her fingers relaxed a little more. Then I began my spiel.

This was a new wrinkle for me. Instead of trying to avoid using my telepathy, I'd been trying to develop it, with Bill's encouragement. The human staff at Fangtasia had acted as guinea pigs. I'd found out, almost by accident, that I could hypnotize people in a jiffy. It didn't put them under my spell or anything, but it let me into their minds with a frightening ease. When you can tell what really relaxes someone, by reading his or her mind, it's relatively easy to relax that person right into a trancelike state.

'What do you enjoy the most, Bethany?' I asked. 'Do you get a massage every now and then? Or maybe you like getting your nails done?' I looked in Bethany's mind delicately. I selected the best channel for my purpose.

'You're getting your hair fixed,' I said, keeping my voice soft and even, 'by your favorite hairdresser . . . Jerry. He's combed it and combed it, there's not a tangle left. He's sectioned it off, so carefully, because your hair is so thick. It's gonna take him a long time to cut it, but he's looking forward to it, because your hair is healthy and shiny. Jerry's lifting a lock, and trimming it . . . the scissors give a little snick. A little bit of hair falls on the plastic cape and slides off to the floor. You feel his fingers in your hair again. Over and over, his fingers move in your hair, lift a lock, snip it. Sometimes he combs it again, to see if he got it even. It feels so good, just sitting and having someone work on your hair. There's no one else . . .' No, wait. I'd raised a hint of unease. 'There's only a few people in the shop, and they're just as busy as Jerry. Someone's got a blow dryer going. You can barely hear voices murmuring in the next booth. His fingers run through, lift, snip, comb, over and over . . .'

I didn't know what a trained hypnotist would say about my technique, but it worked for me this time, at least. Bethany's brain was in a restful, fallow state, just waiting to be given a task. In the same even voice I said, 'While he's working on your hair, we're going to walk through that night at work. He won't stop cutting, okay? Start with getting ready to go to the bar. Don't mind me, I'm just a puff of air right behind your shoulder. You might hear my voice, but it's coming from another booth in that beauty salon. You won't even be able to hear what I'm saying unless I use your name.' I was informing Stan as well as reassuring Bethany. Then I submerged deeper into the girl's memory.

Bethany was looking at her apartment. It was very small, fairly neat, and she shared it with another Bat's Wing employee, who went by the name Desiree Dumas. Desiree Dumas, as seen by Bethany, looked exactly like her made-up name: a self-designated siren, a little too plump, a little too blond, and convinced of her own eroticism.

Taking the waitress through this experience was like watching a film, a really dull one. Bethany's memory was almost too good. Skipping over the boring parts, like Bethany and Desiree's argument over the relative merits of two brands of mascara, what Bethany remembered was this: she had prepared for work as she always did, and she and Desiree had ridden together to their job. Desiree worked in the gift shop section of the Bat's Wing. Dressed in a red bustier and black boots, she hawked vampire souvenirs for big bucks. Wearing artificial fangs, she posed for pictures with tourists for a good tip. Bony and shy Bethany was a humble waitress; for a year she'd been waiting for an opening in the more congenial gift shop, where she wouldn't make the big tips but her base salary would be higher, and she could sit down when she wasn't busy. Bethany hadn't gotten there yet. Big grudge against Desiree, there, on Bethany's part; irrelevant, but I heard myself telling Stan about it as if it were crucial information.

I had never been this deep into someone else's mind. I was trying to weed as I went, but it wasn't working. Finally, I just let it all come. Bethany was completely relaxed, still getting that haircut. She had excellent visual recall, and she was as deeply engaged as I was in the evening she'd spent at work.

In her mind, Bethany served synthetic blood to only four vampires: a red-haired female; a short, stocky Hispanic female with eyes as black as pitch; a blond teenager with ancient tattoos; and a brown-haired man with a jutting jaw and a bolo tie. There! Farrell was embedded in Bethany's memory. I had to suppress my surprise and recognition, and try to steer Bethany with more authority.

'That's the one, Bethany,' I whispered. 'What do you remember about him?'

'Oh, him,' Bethany said out loud, startling me so much I almost jumped out of my chair. In her mind, she turned to look at Farrell, thinking of him. He'd had two synthetic bloods, O positive, and he'd left her a tip.

There was a crease between Bethany's eyebrows as she became focused on my request. She was trying hard now, searching her memory. Bits of the evening began to compact, so she could reach the parts containing the memory of the brown-haired vampire. 'He went back to the bathroom with the blond,' she said, and I saw in her mind the image of the blond tattooed vampire, the very young-looking one. If I'd been an artist, I could have drawn him.

'Young vampire, maybe sixteen. Blond, tattoo,' I murmured to Stan, and he looked surprised. I barely caught that, having so much to concentrate on – this was like trying to juggle – but I did think surprise was the flash of feeling on Stan's face. That was puzzling.

'Sure he was a vampire?' I asked Bethany.

'He drank the blood,' she said flatly. 'He had that pale skin. He gave me the creeps. Yes, I'm sure.'

And he'd gone into the bathroom with Farrell. I was disturbed. The only reason a vampire would enter a bathroom was if there were a human inside he wanted to have sex with, or drink from, or (any vamp's favorite) do both simultaneously. Submerging myself again in Bethany's recollections, I watched her serve a few more customers, no one I recognized, though I got as good a look as I could at the other patrons. Most of them seemed like harmless tourist types. One of them, a dark-complexioned man with a bushy mustache, seemed familiar, so I tried to note his companions: a tall, thin man with shoulder-length blond hair and a squatty woman with one of the worst haircuts I'd ever seen.

I had some questions to ask Stan, but I wanted to finish up with Bethany first. 'Did the cowboy-looking vampire come out again, Bethany?'

'No,' she said after a perceptible pause. 'I didn't see him again.' I checked her carefully for blank spots in her mind; I could never replace what had been erased, but I might know if her memory had been tampered with. I found nothing. And she was trying to remember, I could tell. I could sense her straining to recall another glimpse of Farrell. I realized, from the sense of her straining, that I was losing control of Bethany's thoughts and memories.

'What about the young blond one? The one with the tattoos?'

Bethany pondered that. She was about half out of her trance now. 'I didn't see him neither,' she said. A name slid through her head.

'What's that?' I asked, keeping my voice very quiet and calm.

'Nothing! Nothing!' Bethany's eyes were wide open now. Her haircut was over: I'd lost her. My control was far from perfect.

She wanted to protect someone; she wanted him not to go through the same thing she was going through. But she couldn't stop herself from thinking the name, and I caught it. I couldn't quite understand why she thought this man would know something else, but she did. I knew no purpose would be served by letting her know I'd picked up on her secret, so I smiled at her and told Stan, without turning to look at him, 'She can go. I've gotten everything.'

I absorbed the look of relief on Bethany's face before I turned to look at Stan. I was sure he realized I had something up my sleeve, and I didn't want him to say anything. Who can tell what a vampire is thinking when the vamp is being guarded? But I had the distinct feeling Stan understood me.

He didn't speak out loud, but another vampire came in, a girl who'd been about Bethany's age when she went over. Stan had made a good choice. The girl leaned over Bethany, took her hand, smiled with fangs fully retracted, and said, 'We'll take you home now, okay?'

'Oh, great!' Bethany's relief was written in neon on her forehead. 'Oh, great,' she said again, less certainly. 'Ah, you really are going to my house? You . . .'

But the vampire had looked directly into Bethany's eyes and now she said, 'You won't remember anything about today or this evening except the party.'

'Party?' Bethany's voice sounded sluggish. Only mildly curious.

'You went to a party,' the vampire said as she led Bethany from the room. 'You went to a great party, and you met a cute guy there. You've been with him.' She was still murmuring to Bethany as they went out. I hoped she was giving her a good memory.

'What?' Stan asked, when the door shut behind the two.

'Bethany thought the club bouncer would know more. She watched him go into the men's room right on the heels of your friend Farrell and the vampire you didn't know.' What *I* didn't know, and hardly liked to ask Stan, was whether vampires ever had sex with each other. Sex and food were so tied together in the vampire life system that I couldn't imagine a vampire having sex with someone nonhuman, that is, someone he couldn't get blood from. Did vampires ever take blood from each other in noncrisis situations? I knew if a vampire's life was at stake (har de har) another vampire would donate blood to revive the damaged one, but I had never heard of another situation involving blood exchange. I hardly liked to ask Stan. Maybe I'd broach the subject with Bill, when we got out of this house.

'What you uncovered in her mind was that Farrell was at the bar, and that he went into the toilet room with another vampire, a young male with long blond hair and many tattoos,' Stan summarized. 'The bouncer went into the toilet while the two were in there.'

'Correct.'

There was a sizeable pause while Stan made up his mind about what to do next. I waited, delighted not to hear one word of his inner debate. No flashes, no glimpses.

At least such momentary glimpses into a vampire mind were extremely rare. And I'd never had one from Bill; I hadn't known it was possible for some time after I'd been introduced to the vampiric world. So his company remained pure pleasure to me. It was possible, for the first time in my life, to have a normal relationship with a male. Of course, he wasn't a *live* male, but you couldn't have everything.

As if he knew I'd been thinking of him, I felt Bill's hand on my shoulder. I put my own over it, wishing I could get up and give him a full-length hug. Not a good idea in front of Stan. Might make him hungry.

'We don't know the vampire who went in with Farrell,' Stan said, which seemed a little bit of an answer after all that thinking. Maybe he'd imagined giving me a longer explanation, but decided I wasn't smart enough to understand the answer. I would rather be underestimated than overrated any day. Besides, what real difference did it make? But I filed my question away under facts I needed to know.

'So, who's the bouncer at the Bat's Wing?'

'A man called Re-Bar,' Stan said. There was a trace of distaste in the way he said it. 'He is a fangbanger.'

So Re-Bar had his dream job. Working with vampires, working for vampires, and being around them every night. For someone who had gotten fascinated by the undead, Re-Bar had hit a lucky streak. 'What could he do if a vampire got rowdy?' I asked, out of sheer curiosity.

'He was only there for the human drunks. We found that a vampire bouncer tended to overuse his strength.'

I didn't want to think about that too much. 'Is Re-Bar here?'

'It will take a short time,' Stan said, without consulting anyone in his entourage. He almost certainly had some kind of mind contact with them. I'd never seen that before, and I was sure Eric couldn't approach Bill mentally. It must be Stan's special gift.

While we waited, Bill sat down in the chair next to me. He reached over and took my hand. I found it very comforting, and loved Bill for it. I kept my mind relaxed, trying to maintain energy for the questioning ahead. But I was beginning to frame some worries, very serious worries, about the situation of the vampires of Dallas. And I was concerned about the glimpse I'd had of the bar patrons, especially the man I'd thought I recognized.

'Oh, no,' I said sharply, suddenly recalling where I'd seen him.

The vampires shot to full alert. 'What, Sookie?' Bill asked.

Stan looked like he'd been carved from ice. His eyes actually glowed green, I wasn't just imagining it.

I stumbled all over my words in my haste to explain what I was thinking. 'The priest,' I told Bill. 'The man that ran away at the airport, the one who tried to grab me. He was at the bar.' The different clothes and setting had fooled me when I was deep into Bethany's memory, but now I was sure.

'I see,' Bill said slowly. Bill seems to have almost total recall, and I could rely on him to have the man's face imprinted in his memory.

'I didn't think he was really a priest then, and now I know he was at the bar the night Farrell vanished,' I said.

'Dressed in regular clothes. Not, ah, the white collar and black shirt.'

There was a pregnant pause.

Stan said, delicately, 'But this man, this pretend priest, at the bar, even with two human companions, he could not have taken Farrell if Farrell didn't want to go.'

I looked directly down at my hands and didn't say one word. I didn't want to be the one to say this out loud. Bill, wisely, didn't speak either. At last, Stan Davis, head vampire of Dallas, said, 'Someone went in the bathroom with Farrell, Bethany recalled. A vampire I didn't know.'

I nodded, keeping my gaze directed elsewhere.

'Then this vampire must have helped to abduct Farrell.'

'Is Farrell gay?' I asked, trying to sound as if my question had just oozed out of the walls.

'He prefers men, yes. You think –'

'I don't think a thing.' I shook my head emphatically, to let him know how much I wasn't thinking. Bill squeezed my fingers. Ouch.

The silence was tense until the teenage-looking vamp returned with a burly human, one I'd seen in Bethany's memories. He didn't look like Bethany saw him, though; through her eyes, he was more robust, less fat; more glamorous, less unkempt. But he was recognizable as Re-Bar.

It was apparent to me immediately that something was wrong with the man. He followed after the girl vamp readily enough, and he smiled at everyone in the room; but that was off, wasn't it? Any human who sensed vampire trouble would be worried, no matter how clear his conscience. I got up and went over to him. He watched me approach with cheerful anticipation.

'Hi, buddy,' I said gently, and shook his hand. I dropped it as soon as I decently could. I took a couple of steps back. I wanted to take some Advil and lie down.

'Well,' I said to Stan, 'he sure enough has a hole in his head.'

Stan examined Re-Bar's skull with a skeptical eye. 'Explain,' he said.

'How ya doin', Mr. Stan?' Re-Bar asked. I was willing to bet no one had ever spoken to Stan Davis that way, at least not in the past five hundred years or so.

'I'm fine, Re-Bar. How are you?' I gave Stan credit for keeping it calm and level.

'You know, I just feel great,' Re-Bar said, shaking his head in wonderment. 'I'm the luckiest sumbitch on earth – 'scuse me, lady.'

'You're excused.' I had to force the words out.

Bill said, 'What has been done to him, Sookie?'

'He's had a hole burned in his head,' I said. 'I don't know how else to explain it, exactly. I can't tell how it was done, because I've never seen it before, but when I look in his thoughts, his memories, there's just a big old ragged hole. It's like Re-Bar needed a tiny tumor removed, but the surgeon took his spleen and maybe his appendix, too, just to be sure. You know when y'all take away someone's memory, you replace it with another one?' I waved a hand to show I meant all vampires. 'Well, someone took a chunk out of Re-Bar's mind, and didn't replace it with anything. Like a lobotomy,' I added, inspired. I read a lot. School was tough for me with my little problem, but reading by myself gave me a means of escape from my situation. I guess I'm self-educated.

'So whatever Re-Bar knew about Farrell's disappearance is lost,' Stan said.

'Yep, along with a few components of Re-Bar's personality and a lot of other memories.'

'Is he still functional?'

'Why, yeah, I guess so.' I'd never encountered anything like this, never even realized it was possible. 'But I don't know how effective a bouncer he'll be,' I said, trying to be honest.

'He was hurt while he was working for us. We'll take care of him. Maybe he can clean the club after it closes,' Stan said. I could tell from Stan's voice that he wanted to be sure I was marking this down mentally; that vampires could be compassionate, or at least fair.

'Gosh, that would be great!' Re-Bar beamed at his boss. 'Thanks, Mr. Stan.'

'Take him back home,' Mr. Stan told his minion. She departed directly, with the lobotomized man in tow.

'Who could've done such a crude job on him?' Stan wondered. Bill did not reply, since he wasn't there to stick his neck out, but to guard me and do his own detecting when it was required. A tall red-haired female vampire came in, the one who'd been at the bar the night Farrell was taken.

'What did you notice the evening Farrell vanished?' I asked her, without thinking about protocol. She snarled at me, her white teeth standing out against her dark tongue and brilliant lipstick.

Stan said, 'Cooperate.' At once her face smoothed out, all expression vanishing like wrinkles in a bedspread when you run your hand over it.

'I don't remember,' she said finally. So Bill's ability to recall what he'd seen in minute detail was a personal gift. 'I don't remember seeing Farrell more than a minute or two.'

'Can you do the same thing to Rachel that you did to the barmaid?' Stan asked.

'No,' I said immediately, my voice maybe a little too emphatic. 'I can't read vampire minds at all. Closed books.'

Bill said, 'Can you remember a blond – one of us – who looks about sixteen years old? One with ancient blue tattooing on his arms and torso?'

'Oh, yes,' red-haired Rachel said instantly. 'The tattoos were from the time of the Romans, I think. They were crude but interesting. I wondered about him, because I hadn't seen him coming here to the house to ask Stan for hunting privileges.'

So vamps passing through someone else's territory were required to sign in at the visitors' center, so to speak. I filed that away for future reference.

'He was with a human, or at least had some conversation with him,' the red-haired vampire continued. She was wearing blue jeans and a green sweater that looked incredibly hot to me. But vamps don't worry about the actual temperature. She looked at Stan, then Bill, who made a beckoning gesture to indicate he wanted whatever memories she had. 'The human was dark-haired, and had a mustache, if I am recalling him correctly.' She made a gesture with her hands, an open-fingered sweep that seemed to say, 'They're all so much alike!'

After Rachel left, Bill asked if there was a computer in the house. Stan said there was, and looked at Bill with actual curiosity when Bill asked if he could use it for a moment, apologizing for not having his laptop. Stan nodded. Bill was about to leave the room when he hesitated and looked back at me. 'Will you be all right, Sookie?' he asked.

'Sure.' I tried to sound confident.

Stan said, 'She will be fine. There are more people for her to see.'

I nodded, and Bill left. I smiled at Stan, which is what I do when I'm strained. It's not a happy smile, but it's better than screaming.

'You and Bill have been together for how long?' Stan asked.

'For a few months.' The less Stan knew about us, the happier I'd be.

'You are content with him?'

'Yes.'

'You love him?' Stan sounded amused.

'None of your business,' I said, grinning. 'Did you mention there were more people I needed to check?'

Following the same procedure I had with Bethany, I held a variety of hands and checked a boring bunch of brains. Bethany had definitely been the most observant person in the bar. These people – another barmaid, the human bartender, and a frequent patron (a fangbanger) who'd actually volunteered for this – had dull boring thoughts and limited powers of recollection. I did find out the bartender fenced stolen household goods on the side, and after the guy had left, I recommended to Stan that he get another employee behind the bar, or he'd be sucked into any police investigation. Stan seemed more impressed by this than I hoped he'd be. I didn't want him to get too enamored of my services.

Bill returned as I finished up the last bar employee, and he looked just a little pleased, so I concluded he'd been successful. Bill had been spending most of his waking hours on the computer lately, which had not been too popular an idea with me.

'The tattooed vampire,' Bill said when Stan and I were the only two left in the room, 'is named Godric, though for the past century he's gone by Godfrey. He's a renouncer.' I don't know about Stan, but I was impressed. A few minutes on the computer, and Bill had done a neat piece of detective work.

Stan looked appalled, and I suppose I looked puzzled.

'He's allied himself with radical humans. He plans to commit suicide,' Bill told me in a soft voice, since Stan was wrapped in thought. 'This Godfrey plans to meet the sun. His existence has turned sour on him.'

'So he's gonna take someone with him?' Godfrey would expose Farrell along with himself?

'He has betrayed us to the Fellowship,' Stan said.

Betrayed is a word that packs a lot of melodrama, but I didn't dream of smirking when Stan said it. I'd heard of the Fellowship, though I'd never met anyone who claimed to actually belong to it. What the Klan was to African Americans, the Fellowship of the Sun was to vampires. It was the fastest-growing cult in America.

Once again, I was in deeper waters than I could swim in.

Chapter 5

There were lots of humans who hadn't liked discovering they shared the planet with vampires. Despite the fact that they had always done so – without knowing it – once they believed that vampires were real, these people were bent on the vampires' destruction. They weren't any choosier about their methods of murder than a rogue vampire was about his.

Rogue vampires were the backward-looking undead; they hadn't wanted to be made known to humans any more than the humans wanted to know about them. Rogues refused to drink the synthetic blood that was the mainstay of most vampires' diets these days. Rogues believed the only future for vampires lay in a return to secrecy and invisibility. Rogue vampires would slaughter humans for the fun of it, now, because they actually welcomed a return of persecution of their own kind. Rogues saw it as a means of persuading mainstream vampires that secrecy was best for the future of their kind; and then, too, persecution was a form of population control.

Now I learned from Bill that there were vampires who became afflicted with terrible remorse, or perhaps ennui after a long life. These renouncers planned to 'meet the sun,' the vampire term for committing suicide by staying out past daybreak.

Once again, my choice of boyfriend had led me down paths I never would have trod otherwise. I wouldn't have needed to know any of this, would never have even dreamed of dating someone definitely deceased, if I hadn't been born with the disability of telepathy. I was kind of a pariah to human guys. You can imagine how impossible it is to date someone whose mind you can read. When I met Bill, I began the happiest time of my life. But I'd undoubtedly encountered more trouble in the months I'd known him than I had in my entire twenty-five years previously. 'So, you're thinking Farrell is already dead?' I asked, forcing myself to focus on the current crisis. I hated to ask, but I needed to know.

'Maybe,' Stan said after a long pause.

'Possibly they're keeping him somewhere,' said Bill. 'You know how they invite the press to these . . . ceremonies.'

Stan stared into space for a long moment. Then he stood. 'The same man was in the bar and at the airport,' he said, almost to himself. Stan, the geeky head vampire of Dallas, was pacing now, up and down the room. It was making me nuts, though saying so was out of the question. This was Stan's house, and his 'brother' was missing. But I'm not one for long, brooding silences. I was tired, and I wanted to go to bed.

'So,' I said, doing my best to sound brisk, 'how'd they know I was going to be there?'

If there's anything worse than having a vampire stare at you, it's having two vampires stare at you.

'To know you were coming ahead of time . . . there is a traitor,' Stan said. The air in the room began to tremble and crackle with the tension he was producing.

But I had a less dramatic idea. I picked up a notepad lying on the table and wrote, 'MAYBE YOU'RE BUGGED.' They both glared at me as if I'd offered them a Big Mac. Vampires, who individually have incredible and various powers, are sometimes oblivious to the fact that humans have developed some powers of their own. The two men gave each other a look of speculation, but neither of them offered any practical suggestion.

Well, to heck with them. I'd only seen this done in movies, but I figured if someone had planted a bug in this room, they'd done it in a hurry and they'd been scared to death. So the bug would be close and not well hidden. I shrugged off the gray jacket and kicked off my shoes. Since I was a human and had no dignity to lose in Stan's eyes, I dropped below the table and began crawling down its length, pushing the rolling chairs away as I went. For about the millionth time, I wished I'd worn slacks.

I'd gotten about two yards from Stan's legs when I saw something odd. There was a dark bump adhering to the underside of the blond wood of the table. I looked at it as closely as I could without a flashlight. It was not old gum.

Having found the little mechanical device, I didn't know what to do. I crawled out, somewhat dustier for the experience, and found myself right at Stan's feet. He held out his hand and I took it reluctantly. Stan pulled gently, or it seemed gently, but suddenly I was on my feet facing him. He wasn't very tall, and I looked more into his eyes than I really wanted. I held up my finger in front of my face to be sure he was paying attention. I pointed under the table.

Bill left the room in a flash. Stan's face grew even whiter, and his eyes blazed. I looked anywhere but directly at him. I didn't want to be the sight filling his eyes while he digested the fact that someone had planted a bug in his audience chamber. He had indeed been betrayed, just not in the fashion he'd expected.

I cast around in my mind for something to do that would help. I beamed at Stan. Reaching up automatically to straighten my ponytail, I realized my hair was still in its roll on the back of my head, though considerably less neat. Fiddling with it gave me a good excuse to look down.

I was considerably relieved when Bill reappeared with Isabel and the dishwashing man, who was carrying a bowl of water. 'I'm sorry, Stan,' Bill said. 'I'm afraid Farrell is already dead, if you go by what we have discovered this evening. Sookie and I will return to Louisiana tomorrow, unless you need us further.' Isabel pointed to the table, and the man set the bowl down.

'You might as well,' Stan replied, in a voice as cold as ice. 'Send me your bill. Your master, Eric, was quite adamant about that. I will have to meet him someday.' His tone indicated the meeting would not be pleasant for Eric.

Isabel said abruptly, 'You stupid human! You've spilled my drink!' Bill reached past me to snatch the bug from under the table and drop it in the water, and Isabel, walking even more smoothly to keep the water from slopping over the sides of the bowl, left the room. Her companion remained behind.

That had been disposed of simply enough. And it was at least possible that whoever had been listening in had been fooled by that little bit of dialogue. We all relaxed, now that the bug was gone. Even Stan looked a little less frightening.

'Isabel says you have reason to think Farrell might have been abducted by the Fellowship,' the man said. 'Maybe this young lady and I could go to the Fellowship Center tomorrow, and try to find out if there're plans for any kind of ceremony soon.'

Bill and Stan regarded him thoughtfully.

'That's a good idea,' Stan said. 'A couple would seem less noticeable.'

'Sookie?' Bill asked.

'Certainly none of you can go,' I said. 'I think maybe we could at least get the layout of the place. If you think there's really a chance Farrell's being held there.' If I could find out more about the situation at the Fellowship Center, maybe I could keep the vampires from attacking. They sure weren't going to go down to the police station to file a missing persons report to prod the police into searching the Center. No matter how much the Dallas vampires wanted to remain within the boundaries of human law so they could successfully reap the benefits of mainstreaming, I knew that if a Dallas vampire was being held captive in the Center, humans would die right, left, and sideways. I could maybe prevent that from happening, and locate the missing Farrell, too.

'If this tattooed vampire is a renouncer and plans to meet the sun, taking Farrell with him, and if this is being arranged through the Fellowship, then this pretend priest who tried to grab you at the airport must work for them. They know you now,' Bill pointed out. 'You would have to wear your wig.' He smiled with gratification. The wig had been his idea.

A wig in this heat. Oh, hell. I tried not to look petulant. After all, it would be better to have an itchy head than to be identified as a woman who associated with vampires, while I was visiting a Fellowship of the Sun Center. 'It would be better if there were another human with me,' I admitted, sorry as I was to involve anyone else in danger.

'This is Isabel's current man,' Stan said. He was silent for a minute, and I guessed he was 'beaming' at her, or however he contacted his underlings.

Sure enough, Isabel glided in. It must be handy, being able to summon people like that. You wouldn't need an intercom, or a telephone. I wondered how far away other vamps could be and still receive his message. I was kind of glad Bill couldn't signal me without words, because I'd feel too much like his slave girl. Could Stan summon humans the way he called his vamps? Maybe I didn't really want to know.

The man reacted to Isabel's presence the way a bird dog does when he senses quail. Or maybe it was more like a hungry man who gets served a big steak, and then has to wait for grace. You could almost see his mouth water. I hoped I didn't look like that when I was around Bill.

'Isabel, your man has volunteered to go with Sookie to the Fellowship of the Sun Center. Can he be convincing as a potential convert?'

'Yes, I think he can,' Isabel said, staring into the man's eyes.

'Before you go – are there visitors this evening?'

'Yes, one, from California.'

'Where is he?'

'In the house.'

'Has he been in this room?' Naturally, Stan would love the bug-planter to be a vamp or human he didn't know..

'Yes.'

'Bring him.'

A good five minutes later, Isabel returned with a tall blond vampire in tow. He must have been six foot four, or maybe even more. He was brawny, clean-shaven, and he had a mane of wheat-colored hair. I looked down at my feet immediately, just as I sensed Bill going immobile.

Isabel said, 'This is Leif.'

'Leif,' Stan said smoothly, 'welcome to my nest. This evening we have a problem here.'

I stared at my toes, wishing more than I'd ever wished anything that I could be completely alone with Bill for two minutes and find out what the hell was going on, because this vampire wasn't any 'Leif,' and he wasn't from California.

It was Eric.

Bill's hand came into my line of vision and closed around mine. He gave my fingers a very careful little squeeze, and I returned it. Bill slid his arm around me, and I leaned against him. I needed to relax, by golly.

'How may I help you?' Eric – no, Leif, for the moment – asked courteously.

'It seems that someone has entered this room and performed an act of spying.'

That seemed a nice way to put it. Stan wanted to keep the bugging a secret for right now, and in view of the fact that there surely was a traitor here, that was probably a great idea.

'I am a visitor to your nest, and I have no problem with you or any of yours.'

Leif's calm and sincere denial was quite impressive, given that I knew for a fact that his whole presence was an imposture to further some unfathomable vampire purpose.

'Excuse me,' I said, sounding as frail and human as I possibly could.

Stan looked quite irritated at the interruption, but screw him.

'The, uh, item, would have had to be put in here earlier than today,' I said, trying to sound like I was sure Stan had already thought of this fact. 'To get the details of our arrival in Dallas.'

Stan was staring at me with no expression whatsoever.

In for a penny, in for a pound. 'And excuse me, but I am really worn out. Could Bill take me back to the hotel now?'

'We will have Isabel take you back by yourself,' Stan said dismissively.

'No, sir.'

Behind the fake glasses, Stan's pale eyebrows flew up. 'No?' He sounded as though he'd never heard the word.

'By the terms of my contract, I don't go anywhere without a vampire from my area. Bill is that vampire. I go nowhere without him, at night.'

Stan gave me another good long stare. I was glad I had found the bug and proved myself useful otherwise, or I wouldn't last long in Stan's bailiwick. 'Go,' he said and Bill and I didn't waste any time. We couldn't help Eric if Stan came to suspect him, and we might quite possibly give him away. I would be by far the more likely to do that by some word or gesture, with Stan watching me. Vampires have studied humans for centuries, in the way predators learn as much as they can about their prey.

Isabel came out with us, and we got back into her Lexus for the ride back to the Silent Shore Hotel. The streets of Dallas, though not empty, were at least much quieter than when we'd arrived at the nest hours earlier. I estimated it was less than two hours until dawn.

'Thank you,' I said politely when we pulled under the porte cochere of the hotel.

'My human will come to get you at three o'clock in the afternoon,' Isabel told me.

Repressing the urge to say, 'Yes, ma'am!' and click my heels together, I just told her that would be fine. 'What's his name?' I asked.

'His name is Hugo Ayres,' she said.

'Okay.' I already knew that he was a quick man with an idea. I went into the lobby and waited for Bill. He was only seconds behind me, and we went up in the elevator in silence.

'Do you have your key?' he asked me at the room door.

I had been half-asleep. 'Where's yours?' I asked, none too graciously.

'I'd just like to see you recover yours,' he said.

Suddenly I was in a better mood. 'Maybe you'd like to find it,' I suggested.

A male vampire with a waist-length black mane strolled down the hall, his arm around a plump girl with a head of curly red hair. When they'd entered a room farther down the hall, Bill began searching for the key.

He found it pretty fast.

Once we'd gotten inside, Bill picked me up and kissed me at length. We needed to talk, since a lot had happened during this long night, but I wasn't in the mood and he wasn't, either.

The nice thing about skirts, I discovered, was that they just slide up, and if you were only wearing a thong underneath, it could vanish in a jiffy. The gray jacket was on the floor, the white shell was discarded, and my arms were locked around Bill's neck before you could say, 'Screw a vampire.'

Bill was leaning against the sitting room wall trying to open his slacks with me still wrapped around him when there was a knock at the door.

'Damn,' he whispered in my ear. 'Go away,' he said, somewhat louder. I wriggled against him and his breath caught in his throat. He pulled the bobby pins and the Hairagami out of my hair to let it roll down my back.

'I need to talk to you,' said a familiar voice, somewhat muffled by the thick door.

'No,' I moaned. 'Say it isn't Eric.' The only creature in the world we *had* to admit.

'It's Eric,' said the voice.

I unlocked my legs from around Bill's waist, and he gently lowered me to the floor. In a real snit, I stomped into the bedroom to put on my bathrobe. To hell with rebuttoning all those clothes.

I came back out as Eric was telling Bill that Bill had done well this evening.

'And, of course, you were marvelous, Sookie,' Eric said, taking in the pink, short bathrobe with a comprehensive glance. I looked up at him – and up, and up – and wished him at the bottom of the Red River, spectacular smile, golden hair, and all.

'Oh,' I said malignantly, 'thanks so much for coming up to tell us this. We couldn't have gone to bed without a pat on the back from you.'

Eric looked as blandly delighted as he possibly could. 'Oh, dear,' he said. 'Did I interrupt something? Would these – well, this – be yours, Sookie?' He held up the black string that had formerly been one side of my thong.

Bill said, 'In a word, yes. Is there anything else you would like to discuss with us, Eric?' Ice would've been surprised by how cold Bill could sound.

'We haven't got time tonight,' Eric said regretfully, 'since daylight is so soon, and there are things I need to see to before I sleep. But tomorrow night we must meet. When you find out what Stan wants you to do, leave me a note at the desk, and we'll make an arrangement.'

Bill nodded. 'Good-bye, then,' he said.

'You don't want a nightcap?' Was he hoping to be offered a bottle of blood? Eric's eyes went to the refrigerator, then to me. I was sorry I was wearing a thin nylon robe instead of something bulky and chenille. 'Warm from the vessel?' Bill maintained a stony silence.

His gaze lingering on me until the last minute, Eric stepped through the door and Bill locked it behind him.

'You think he's listening outside?' I asked Bill, as he untied the sash of my robe.

'I don't care,' Bill said, and bent his head to other things.

When I got up, about one o'clock in the afternoon, the hotel had a silent feel to it. Of course, most of the guests were sleeping. Maids would not come into a room during the day. I had noted the security last night – vampire guards. The daytime would be different, since daytime guarding was what the guests were paying so heavily for. I called room service for the first time in my life and ordered breakfast. I was as hungry as a horse, since I hadn't eaten last night at all. I was showered and wrapped up in my robe when the waiter knocked on the door, and after I'd made sure he was who he said he was, I let him in.

After my attempted abduction at the airport the day before, I wasn't taking anything for granted. I held the pepper spray down by my side as the young man laid out the food and the coffeepot. If he took one step toward the door behind which Bill slept in his coffin, I would zap him. But this fellow, Arturo, had been well trained, and his eyes never even strayed toward the bedroom. He never looked directly at me, either. He was thinking about me, though, and I wished I'd put on a bra before I let him in.

When he'd gone – and as Bill had instructed me, I added a tip to the room ticket I signed – I ate everything he'd brought: sausage and pancakes and a bowl of melon balls. Oh gosh, it tasted good. The syrup was real maple syrup, and the fruit was just ripe enough. The sausage was wonderful. I was glad Bill wasn't around to watch and make me feel uncomfortable. He didn't really like to see me eat, and he hated it if I ate garlic.

I brushed my teeth and hair and got my makeup situated. It was time to prepare for my visit to the Fellowship Center. I sectioned my hair and pinned it up, and got the wig out of its box. It was short and brown and really undistinguished. I had thought Bill was nuts when he'd suggested I get a wig, and I still wondered why it had occurred to him I might need one, but I was glad to have it. I had a pair of glasses like Stan's, serving the same camouflaging purpose, and I put them on. There was a little magnification in the bottom part, so I could legitimately claim they were reading glasses.

What did fanatics wear to go to a fanatic gathering place? In my limited experience, fanatics were usually conservative in dress, either because they were too preoccupied with other concerns to think about it or because they saw something evil in dressing stylishly. If I'd been at home I'd have run to Wal-Mart and been right on the money, but I was here in the expensive, windowless Silent Shores. However, Bill had told me to call the front desk for anything I needed. So I did.

'Front desk,' said a human who was trying to copy the smooth cool voice of an older vampire. 'How may I help you?' I felt like telling him to give it up. Who wants an imitation when the real thing is under the roof?

'This is Sookie Stackhouse in three-fourteen. I need a long denim skirt, size eight, and a pastel flowered blouse or knit top, same size.'

'Yes, ma'am,' he said, after a longish pause. 'When shall I have those for you?'

'Soon.' Gee, this was a lot of fun. 'As a matter of fact, the sooner the better.' I was getting into this. I loved being on someone else's expense account.

I watched the news while I waited. It was the typical news of any American city: traffic problems, zoning problems, homicide problems.

'A woman found dead last night in a hotel Dumpster has been identified,' said a newscaster, his voice appropriately grave. He bent down the corners of his mouth to show serious concern. 'The body of twenty-one-year-old Bethany Rogers was found behind the Silent Shore Hotel, famous for being Dallas's first hotel catering to the undead. Rogers had been killed by a single gunshot wound to the head. Police described the murder as 'execution-style.' Detective

Tawny Kelner told our reporter that police are following up several leads.' The screen image shifted from the artificially grim face to a genuinely grim one. The detective was in her forties, I thought, a very short woman with a long braid down her back. The camera shot swiveled to include the reporter, a small dark man with a sharply tailored suit. 'Detective Kelner, is it true that Bethany Rogers worked at a vampire bar?'

The detective's frown grew even more formidable. 'Yes, that's true,' she said. 'However, she was employed as a waitress, not an entertainer.' An entertainer? What did entertainers do at the Bat's Wing? 'She had only been working there a couple of months.'

'Doesn't the site used to dump her body indicate that there's some kind of vampire involvement?' The reporter was more persistent than I would've been.

'On the contrary, I believe the site was chosen to send a message to the vampires,' Kelner snapped, and then looked as if she regretted speaking. 'Now, if you'll excuse me . . .'

'Of course, detective,' the reporter said, a little dazed. 'So, Tom,' and he turned to face the camera, as if he could see through it back to the anchor in the station, 'that's a provocative issue.'

Huh?

The anchor realized the reporter wasn't making any sense, too, and quickly moved to another topic.

Poor Bethany was dead, and there wasn't anyone I could discuss that with. I pushed back tears; I hardly felt I had a right to cry for the girl. I couldn't help but wonder what had happened to Bethany Rogers last night after she'd been led from the room at the vampire nest. If there'd been no fang marks, surely a vampire hadn't killed her. It would be a rare vampire who could pass up the blood.

Sniffling from repressed tears and miserable with dismay, I sat on the couch and hunted through my purse to find a pencil. At last, I unearthed a pen. I used it to scratch up under the wig. Even in the air-conditioned dark of the hotel, it itched. In thirty minutes, there was a knock at the door. Once again, I looked through the peephole. There was Arturo again, with garments draped across his arm.

'We'll return the ones you don't want,' he said, handing me the bundle. He tried not to stare at my hair.

'Thanks,' I said, and tipped him. I could get used to this in a hurry.

It wasn't long until I was supposed to be meeting the Ayres guy, Isabel's honey bun. Dropping the robe where I stood, I looked at what Arturo'd brought me. The pale peachy blouse with the off-white flowers, that would do, and the skirt . . . hmmm. He hadn't been able to find denim, apparently, and the two he'd brought were khaki. That would be all right, I figured, and I pulled one on. It looked too tight for the effect I needed, and I was glad he'd brought another style. It was just right for the image. I slid my feet into flat sandals, put some tiny earrings in my pierced ears, and I was good to go. I even had a battered straw purse to carry with the ensemble. Unfortunately, it was my regular purse. But it fit right in. I dumped out my identifying items, and wished I had thought of that earlier instead of at the last minute. I wondered what other crucial safety measures I might have forgotten.

I stepped out into the silent corridor. It was exactly as it had been the night before. There were no mirrors and no windows, and the feeling of enclosure was complete. The dark red of the carpet and the federal blue, red, and cream of the wallpaper didn't help. The elevator snicked open when I touched the call button, and I rode down by myself. No elevator music, even. The Silent Shore was living up to its name.

There were armed guards on either side of the elevator, when I reached the lobby. They were looking at the main doors to the hotel. Those doors were obviously locked. There was a television set mounted by the doors, and it showed the sidewalk outside of the doors. Another television set showed a wider view.

I thought a terrible attack must be imminent and I froze, my heart racing, but after a few seconds of calm I figured out they must be there all the time. This was why vampires stayed here, and at other similar specialty hotels. No one would get past these guards to the elevators. No one would make it into the hotel rooms where sleeping and helpless vampires lay. This was why the fee for the hotel was exorbitant. The two guards on duty at the moment were both huge, and wearing the black livery of the hotel. (Ho, hum. Everyone seemed to think vampires were obsessed with black.) The guards' sidearms seemed gigantic to me, but then, I'm not too familiar with guns. The men glanced at me and then went back to their bored forward stare.

Even the desk clerks were armed. There were shotguns on racks behind the counter. I wondered how far they would go to protect their guests. Would they really shoot other humans, intruders? How would the law handle it?

A man wearing glasses sat in one of the padded chairs that punctuated the marble floor of the lobby. He was about thirty, tall and lanky, with sandy hair. He was wearing a suit, a lightweight summer khaki suit, with a conservative tie and penny loafers. The dishwasher, sure enough.

'Hugo Ayres?' I asked.

He sprang up to shake my hand. 'You must be Sookie? But your hair . . . last night, you were blond?'

'I am. I'm wearing a wig.'

'It looks very natural.'

'Good. Are you ready?'

'My car's outside.' He touched my back briefly to point me in the right direction, as if I wouldn't see the doors otherwise. I appreciated the courtesy, if not the implication. I was trying to get a feel for Hugo Ayres. He wasn't a broadcaster.

'How long have you been dating Isabel?' I asked as we buckled up in his Caprice.

'Ah, um, I guess about eleven months,' Hugo Ayres said. He had big hands, with freckles on the back. I was surprised he wasn't living in the suburbs with a wife with streaked hair and two sandy children.

'Are you divorced?' I asked impulsively. I was sorry when I saw the grief cross his face.

'Yes,' he said. 'Pretty recently.'

'Too bad.' I started to ask about the children, decided it was none of my business. I could read him well enough to know he had a little girl, but I couldn't discover her name and age.

'Is it true you can read minds?' he asked.

'Yes, it's true.'

'No wonder you're so attractive to them.'

Well, *ouch*, Hugo. 'That's probably a good part of the reason,' I said, keeping my voice flat and even. 'What's your day job?'

'I'm a lawyer,' Hugo said.

'No wonder you're so attractive to them,' I said, in the most neutral voice I could manage.

After a longish silence, Hugo said, 'I guess I deserved that.'

'Let's move on past it. Let's get a cover story.'

'Could we be brother and sister?'

'That's not out of the question. I've seen brother and sister teams that looked less like each other than we do. But I think boyfriend-girlfriend would account for the gaps in our knowledge of each other more, if we get separated and questioned. I'm not predicting that'll happen, and I'd be amazed if it did, but as brother and sister we'd have to know all about each other.'

'You're right. Why don't we say that we met at church? You just moved to Dallas, and I met you in Sunday school at Glen Craigie Methodist. That's actually my church.'

'Okay. How about I'm manager of a . . . restaurant?' From working at Merlotte's, I thought I could be convincing in the role if I wasn't questioned too intensively.

He looked a little surprised. 'That's just different enough to sound good. I'm not much of an actor, so if I just stick to being me, I'll be okay.'

'How did you meet Isabel?' Of course I was curious.

'I represented Stan in court. His neighbors sued to have the vampires barred from the neighborhood. They lost.' Hugo had mixed feelings about his involvement with a vampire woman, and wasn't entirely sure he should've won the court case, either. In fact, Hugo was deeply ambivalent about Isabel.

Oh, good, that made this errand much more frightening. 'Did that get in the papers? The fact that you represented Stan Davis?'

He looked chagrined. 'Yes, it did. Dammit, someone at the Center might recognize my name. Or me, from my picture being in the papers.'

'But that might be even better. You can tell them you saw the error of your ways, after you'd gotten to know vampires.'

Hugo thought that over, his big freckled hands moving restlessly on the steering wheel. 'Okay,' he said finally. 'Like I said, I'm not much of an actor, but I think I can bring that off.'

I acted all the time, so I wasn't too worried about myself. Taking a drink order from a guy while pretending you don't know whether he's speculating on whether you're blond all the way down can be excellent acting training. You can't blame people – mostly – for what they're thinking on the inside. You have to learn to rise above it.

I started to suggest to the lawyer that he hold my hand if things got tense today, to send me thoughts that I could act on. But his ambivalence, the ambivalence that wafted from him like a cheap cologne, gave me pause. He might be in sexual thrall to Isabel, he might even love her and the danger she represented, but I didn't think his heart and mind were wholly committed to her.

In an unpleasant moment of self-examination, I wondered if the same could be said of Bill and me. But now was not the time and place to ponder this. I was getting enough from Hugo's mind to wonder if he were completely trustworthy in terms of this little mission of ours. It was just a short step from there to wondering how safe I was in his company. I also wondered how much Hugo Ayres actually knew about me. He hadn't been in the room when I'd been working the night before. Isabel hadn't struck me as a chatterer. It was possible he didn't know much about me.

The four-lane road, running through a huge suburb, was lined with all the usual fast-food places and chain stores of all kinds. But gradually, the shopping gave way to residences, and the concrete to greenery. The traffic seemed unrelenting. I could never live in a place this size, cope with this on a daily basis.

Hugo slowed and put on his turn signal when we came to a major intersection. We were about to turn into the parking lot of a large church; at least, it had formerly been a church. The sanctuary was huge, by Bon Temps standards. Only Baptists could count that kind of attendance, in my neck of the woods, and that's if all their congregations joined together. The two-story sanctuary was flanked by two long one-story wings. The whole building was white-painted brick, and all the windows were tinted. There was a chemically green lawn surrounding the whole, and a huge parking lot.

The sign on the well-tended lawn read THE FELLOWSHIP OF THE SUN CENTER – Only Jesus Rose from the Dead.

I snorted as I opened my door and emerged from Hugo's car. 'That right there is false,' I pointed out to my companion. 'Lazarus rose from the dead, too. Jerks can't even get their scripture right.'

'You better banish that attitude from your head,' Hugo warned me, as he got out and hit the lock button. 'It'll make you careless. These people are dangerous. They've accepted responsibility, publicly, for handing over two vampires to the Drainers, saying at least humanity can benefit from the death of a vampire in some way.'

'They deal with Drainers?' I felt sick. Drainers followed

an extremely hazardous profession. They trapped vampires, wound them around with silver chains, and drained the blood from them for sale on the black market. 'These people in here have handed over vampires to the Drainers?'

'That's what one of their members said in a newspaper interview. Of course, the leader was on the news the next day, denying the report vehemently, but I think that was just smokescreen. The Fellowship kills vampires any way they can, thinks they're unholy and an abomination, and they're capable of anything. If you're a vampire's best friend, they can bring tremendous pressure to bear. Just remember that, every time you open your mouth in here.'

'You, too, Mr. Ominous Warning.'

We walked to the building slowly, looking it over as we went. There were about ten other cars in the parking lot, ranging from aging and dented to brand new and upscale. My favorite was a pearly white Lexus, so nice it might almost have belonged to a vampire.

'Someone's doing well out of the hate business,' Hugo observed.

'Who's the head of this place?'

'Guy named Steve Newlin.'

'Bet this is his car.'

'That would account for the bumper sticker.'

I nodded. It read TAKE THE *UN* OUT OF *UNDEAD*. Dangling from the mirror inside was a replica – well, maybe a replica – of a stake.

This was a busy place, for a Saturday afternoon. There were children using the swing set and jungle gym in a fenced yard to the side of the building. The kids were being watched by a bored teenager, who looked up every now and then from picking at his nails. Today was not as hot as the day before – summer was losing its doomed last stand, and thank God for that – and the door of the building was propped open to take advantage of the beautiful day and moderate temperature.

Hugo took my hand, which made me jump until I realized he was trying to make us look loverlike. He had zero interest in me personally, which was fine with me. After a second's adjustment we managed to look fairly natural. The contact made Hugo's mind just that more open to me, and I could tell that he was anxious but resolute. He found touching me distasteful, which was a little bit too strong a feeling for me to feel comfortable about; lack of attraction was peachy, but this actual distaste made me uneasy. There was something behind that feeling, some basic attitude . . . but there were people ahead of us, and I pulled my mind back to my job. I could feel my lips pull into their smile.

Bill had been careful to leave my neck alone last night, so I didn't have to worry about concealing any fang marks, and in my new outfit and on this lovely day it was easier to look carefree as we nodded at a middle-aged couple who were on their way out.

We passed into the dimness of the building, into what must have been the Sunday school wing of the church. There were fresh signs outside the rooms up and down the corridor, signs that read BUDGETING AND FINANCE, ADVERTISING, and most ominously, MEDIA RELATIONS.

A woman in her forties came out of a door farther down the hall, and turned to face us. She looked pleasant, even sweet, with lovely skin and short brown hair. Her definitely pink lipstick matched her definitely pink fingernails, and her lower lip was slightly pouty, which gave her an unexpectedly sensuous air; it sat with odd provocation on her pleasantly round body. A denim skirt and a knit shirt, neatly tucked in, were the echo of my own outfit, and I patted myself on the back mentally.

'Can I help you?' she asked, looking hopeful.

'We want to find out more about the Fellowship,' Hugo said, and he seemed every bit as nice and sincere as our new friend. She had on a nametag, I noticed, which read S. NEWLIN.

'We're glad you're here,' she said. 'I'm the wife of the director, Steve Newlin? I'm Sarah?' She shook hands with Hugo, but not with me. Some women don't believe in shaking hands with another woman, so I didn't worry about it.

We exchanged pleasedtomeetyou's, and she waved a manicured hand toward the double doors at the end of the hall. 'If you'll just come with me, I'll show you where we get things done.' She laughed a little, as if the idea of meeting goals was a touch ludicrous.

All of the doors in the hall were open, and within the rooms there was evidence of perfectly open activity. If the Newlins' organization was keeping prisoners or conducting covert ops, it was accomplishing its goals in some other part of the building. I looked at everything as hard as I could, determined to fill myself with information. But so far the interior of the Fellowship of the Sun was as blindingly clean as the outside, and the people hardly seemed sinister or devious.

Sarah covered ground ahead of us with an easy walk. She clutched a bundle of file folders to her chest and chattered over her shoulder as she moved at a pace that seemed relaxed, but actually was a bit challenging. Hugo and I, abandoning the handholding, had to step out to keep up.

This building was proving to be far larger than I'd estimated. We'd entered at the far end of one wing. Now we crossed the large sanctuary of the former church, set up for meetings like any big hall, and we passed into the other wing. This wing was divided into fewer and larger rooms; the one closest to the sanctuary was clearly the office of the former pastor. Now it had a sign on the door that read G. STEVEN NEWLIN, DIRECTOR.

This was the only closed door I'd seen in the building.

Sarah knocked and, having waited for a moment, entered. The tall, lanky man behind the desk stood to beam at us with an air of pleased expectancy. His head didn't seem quite big enough for his body. His eyes were a hazy blue, his nose was on the beaky side, and his hair was almost the same dark brown as his wife's, with a threading of gray. I don't know what I'd been expecting in a fanatic, but this man was not it. He seemed a little amused by his own life.

He'd been talking to a tall woman with iron gray hair. She was wearing a pair of slacks and a blouse, but she looked as if she'd have been more comfortable in a business suit. She was formidably made up, and she was less than pleased about something – maybe our interruption.

'What can I do for you today?' Steve Newlin asked, indicating that Hugo and I should be seated. We took green leather armchairs pulled up opposite his desk, and Sarah, unasked, plopped down in a smaller chair that was against the wall on one side. 'Excuse me, Steve,' she said to her husband. 'Listen, can I get you two some coffee? Soda?'

Hugo and I looked at each other and shook our heads.

'Honey, this is – oh, I didn't even ask your names?' She looked at us with charming ruefulness.

'I'm Hugo Ayres, and this is my girlfriend, Marigold.'

Marigold? Was he *nuts*? I kept my smile pasted on my face with an effort. Then I saw the pot of marigolds on the table beside Sarah, and at least I could understand his selection. We'd certainly made a large mistake already; we should have talked about this on the drive over. It stood to reason that if the Fellowship was responsible for the bug, the Fellowship knew the name of Sookie Stackhouse. Thank God Hugo had figured that out.

'Don't we know Hugo Ayres, Sarah?' Steve Newlin's face had the perfect quizzical expression – brow slightly wrinkled, eyebrows raised inquiringly, head tilted to one side.

'Ayres?' said the gray-haired woman. 'By the way, I'm Polly Blythe, the Fellowship ceremonies officer.'

'Oh, Polly, I'm sorry, I got sidetracked.' Sarah tilted her head right back. Her forehead wrinkled, too. Then it smoothed out and she beamed at her husband. 'Wasn't an Ayres the lawyer representing the vampires in University Park?'

'So he was,' Steve said, leaning back in his chair and crossing his long legs. He waved to someone passing by in the corridor and wrapped his laced fingers around his knee. 'Well, it's very interesting that you're paying us a call, Hugo. Can we hope that you've seen the other side of the vampire question?' Satisfaction rolled off Steve Newlin like scent off a skunk.

'It's appropriate that you should put it that way –' Hugo began, but Steve's voice just kept rolling on:

'The bloodsucking side, the dark side of vampire existence? Have you found that they want to kill us all, dominate us with their foul ways and empty promises?'

I knew my eyes were as round as plates. Sarah was nodding thoughtfully, still looking as sweet and bland as a vanilla pudding. Polly looked as if she were having some really grim kind of orgasm. Steve said – and he was still smiling – 'You know, eternal life on this earth may sound good, but you'll lose your soul and eventually, when we catch up with you – maybe not me, of course, maybe my son, or eventually my granddaughter – we'll stake you and burn you and then you'll be in true hell. And it won't be any the better for having been put off. God has a special corner for vampires who've used up humans like toilet tissue and then flushed . . .'

Well, ick. This was going downhill in a hurry. And what I was getting off of Steve was just this endless, gloating satisfaction, along with a heavy dash of cleverness. Nothing concrete or informative.

'Excuse me, Steve,' said a deep voice. I swiveled in my chair to see a handsome black-haired man with a crewcut and a bodybuilder's muscles. He smiled at all of us in the room with the same goodwill they were all showing. It had impressed me earlier. Now, I thought it was just creepy. 'Our guest is asking for you.'

'Really? I'll be there in a minute.'

'I wish you would come now. I'm sure your guests wouldn't mind waiting?' Black Crewcut glanced at us appealingly. Hugo was thinking of some deep place, a flash of thought which seemed very peculiar to me.

'Gabe, I'll be there when I've finished with our visitors,' Steve said very firmly.

'Well, Steve . . .' Gabe wasn't willing to give up that easily, but he got a flash from Steve's eyes and Steve sat up and uncrossed his legs, and Gabe got the message. He shot Steve a look that was anything but worshipful, but he left.

That exchange was promising. I wondered if Farrell was behind some locked door, and I could picture myself returning to the Dallas nest, telling Stan exactly where his nest brother was trapped. And then . . .

Uh-oh. And then Stan would come and attack the Fellowship of the Sun and kill all the members and free Farrell, and then . . .

Oh dear.

'We just wanted to know if you have some upcoming events we can attend, something that'll give us an idea of the scope of the programs here.' Hugo's voice sounded mildly inquiring, nothing more. 'Since Miss Blythe is here, maybe she can answer that.'

I noticed Polly Blythe glanced at Steve before she spoke, and I noticed that his face remained shuttered. Polly Blythe was very pleased to be asked to give information, and she was very pleased about Hugo and me being there at the Fellowship.

'We do have some upcoming events,' the gray-haired woman said. 'Tonight, we're having a special lock-in, and following that, we have a Sunday dawn ritual.'

'That sounds interesting,' I said. 'Literally, at dawn?'

'Oh, yes, exactly. We call the weather service and everything,' Sarah said, laughing.

Steve said, 'You'll never forget one of our dawn services. It's inspiring beyond belief.'

'What kind of – well, what happens?' Hugo asked.

'You'll see the evidence of God's power right before you,' Steve said, smiling.

That sounded really, really ominous. 'Oh, Hugo,' I said. 'Doesn't that sound exciting?'

'It sure does. What time does the lock-in start?'

'At six-thirty. We want our members to get here before *they* rise.'

For a second I envisioned a tray of rolls set in some warm place. Then I realized Steve meant he wanted members to get here before the vampires rose for the night.

'But what about when your congregation goes home?' I could not refrain from asking.

'Oh, you must not have gone to a lock-in as a teenager!' Sarah said. 'It's loads of fun. Everyone comes and brings their sleeping bags, and we eat and have games and Bible readings and a sermon, and we all spend the night actually in the church.' I noticed that the Fellowship was a church, in Sarah's eyes, and I was pretty sure that reflected the view of the rest of the management. If it looked like a church, and functioned like a church, then it was a church, no matter what its tax status was.

I'd been to a couple of lock-ins as a teenager, and I'd scarcely been able to endure the experience. A bunch of kids locked in a building all night, closely chaperoned, provided with an endless stream of movies and junk food, activities and sodas. I had suffered through the mental bombardment of teenage hormone-fueled ideas and impulses, the shrieking and the tantrums.

This would be different, I told myself. These would be adults, and purposeful adults, at that. There weren't likely to be a million bags of chips around, and there might be decent sleeping arrangements. If Hugo and I came, maybe we'd get a chance to search around the building and rescue Farrell, because I was sure that he was the one who was going to get to meet the dawn on Sunday, whether or not he got to choose.

Polly said, 'You'd be very welcome. We have plenty of food and cots.'

Hugo and I looked at each other uncertainly.

'Why don't we just go tour the building now, and you can see all there is to see? Then you can make up your minds,' Sarah suggested. I took Hugo's hand, got a wallop of ambivalence. I was filled with dismay at Hugo's torn emotions. He thought, Let's get out of here.

I jettisoned my previous plans. If Hugo was in such turmoil, we didn't need to be here. Questions could wait until later. 'We should go back to my place and pack our sleeping bags and pillows,' I said brightly. 'Right, baby?'

'And I've got to feed the cat,' Hugo said. 'But we'll be back here at . . . six-thirty, you said?'

'Gosh, Steve, don't we have some bedrolls left in the supply room? From when that other couple came to stay here for a while?'

'We'd love to have you stay until everyone gets here,' Steve urged us, his smile as radiant as ever. I knew we were being threatened, and I knew we needed to get out, but all I was receiving from the Newlins psychically was a wall of determination. Polly Blythe seemed to actually be almost – gloating. I hated to push and probe, now that I was aware they had some suspicion of us. If we could just get out of here right now, I promised myself I'd never come back. I'd give up this detecting for the vampires, I'd just tend bar and sleep with Bill.

'We really do need to go,' I said with firm courtesy. 'We are so impressed with you all here, and we want to come to the lock-in tonight, but there is still enough time before then for us to get some of our errands done. You know how it is when you work all week. All those little things pile up.'

'Hey, they'll still be there when the lock-in ends tomorrow!' Steve said. 'You need to stay, both of you.'

There wasn't any way to get out of here without dragging everything out into the open. And I wasn't going to be the first one to do that, not while there was any hope left we could get out. There were lots of people around. We turned left when we came out of Steve Newlin's office, and with Steve ambling behind us, and Polly to our right, and Sarah ahead of us, we went down the hall. Every time we passed an open door, someone inside would call, 'Steve, can I see you for a minute?' or 'Steve, Ed says we have to change the wording on this!' But aside from a blink or a minor tremor in his smile, I could not see much reaction from Steve Newlin to these constant demands.

I wondered how long this movement would last if Steve were removed. Then I was ashamed of myself for thinking this, because what I meant was, if Steve were killed. I was beginning to think either Sarah or Polly would be able to step into his shoes, if they were allowed, because both seemed made of steel.

All the offices were perfectly open and innocent, if you considered the premise on which the organization was founded to be innocent. These all looked like average, rather cleaner-cut-than-normal, Americans, and there were even a few people who were non-Caucasian.

And one nonhuman.

We passed a tiny, thin Hispanic woman in the hall, and as her eyes flicked over to us, I caught a mental signature I'd only felt once before. Then, it came from Sam Merlotte.

This woman, like Sam, was a shapeshifter, and her big eyes widened as she caught the waft of 'difference' from me. I tried to catch her gaze, and for a minute we stared at each other, me trying to send her a message, and her trying not to receive it.

'Did I tell you the first church to occupy this site was built in the early sixties?' Sarah was saying, as the tiny woman went on down the hall at a fast clip. She glanced back over her shoulder, and I met her eyes again. Hers were frightened. Mine said, 'Help.'

'No,' I said, startled at the sudden turn in the conversation.

'Just a little bit more,' Sarah coaxed. 'We'll have seen the whole church.' We'd come to the last door at the end of the corridor. The corresponding door on the other wing had led to the outside. The wings had seemed to be exactly balanced from the outside of the church. My observations had obviously been faulty, but still . . .

'It's certainly a large place,' said Hugo agreeably. Whatever ambivalent emotions had been plaguing him seemed to have subsided. In fact, he no longer seemed at all concerned. Only someone with no psychic sense at all could fail to be worried about this situation.

That would be Hugo. No psychic sense at all. He looked only interested when Polly opened the last door, the door flat at the end of the corridor. It should have led outside.

Instead, it led down.

Chapter 6

'You know, I have a touch of claustrophobia,' I said instantly. 'I didn't know many Dallas buildings had a basement, but I have to say, I just don't believe I want to see it.' I clung to Hugo's arm and tried to smile in a charming but self-deprecating way.

Hugo's heart was beating like a drum because he was scared shitless – I'll swear he was. Faced with those stairs, somehow his calm was eroding again. What was with Hugo? Despite his fear, he gamely patted my shoulder and smiled apologetically at our companions. 'Maybe we should go,' he murmured.

'But I really think you should see what we've got underground. We actually have a bomb shelter,' Sarah said, almost laughing in her amusement. 'And it's fully equipped, isn't it, Steve?'

'Got all kinds of things down there,' Steve agreed. He still looked relaxed, genial, and in charge, but I no longer saw those as benign characteristics. He stepped forward, and since he was behind us, I had to step forward or risk him touching me, which I found I very much did not want.

'Come on,' Sarah said enthusiastically. 'I'll bet Gabe's down here, and Steve can go on and see what Gabe wanted while we look at the rest of the facility.' She trotted down the stairs as quickly as she'd moved down the hall, her round butt swaying in a way I probably would have considered cute if I hadn't been just on the edge of terrified.

Polly waved us down ahead of her, and down we went. I was going along with this because Hugo seemed absolutely confident that no harm would come to him. I was picking that up very clearly. His earlier fear had completely abated. It was as though he'd resigned himself to some program, and his ambivalence had vanished. Vainly, I wished he were easier to read. I turned my focus on Steve Newlin, but what I got from him was a thick wall of self-satisfaction.

We moved farther down the stairs, despite the fact that my steps had slowed, and then become slower again. I could tell Hugo was convinced that he would get to walk back up these stairs: after all, he was a civilized person. These were all civilized people.

Hugo really couldn't imagine that anything irreparable could happen to him, because he was a middle-class white American with a college education, as were all the people on the stairs with us.

I had no such conviction. I was not a wholly civilized person.

That was a new and interesting thought, but like many of my ideas that afternoon, it had to be stowed away, to be explored at leisure. If I ever had leisure again.

At the base of the stairs there was another door, and Sarah knocked on it in a pattern. Three fast, skip, two fast, my brain recorded. I heard locks shooting back.

Black Crewcut – Gabe – opened the door. 'Hey, you brought me some visitors,' he said enthusiastically. 'Good show!' His golf shirt was tucked neatly into his pleated Dockers, his Nikes were new and spotless, and he was shaved as clean as a razor could get. I was willing to bet he did fifty push-ups every morning. There was an undercurrent of excitement in his every move and gesture; Gabe was really pumped about something.

I tried to 'read' the area for life, but I was too agitated to concentrate.

'I'm glad you're here, Steve,' Gabe said. 'While Sarah is showing our visitors the shelter, maybe you can give our guest room a look-see.' He nodded his head to the door in the right side of the narrow concrete hall. There was another door at the end of it, and a door to the left.

I hated it down here. I had pleaded claustrophobia to get out of this. Now that I had been coerced into coming down the stairs, I was finding that it was a true failing of mine. The musty smell, the glare of the artificial light, and the sense of enclosure . . . I hated it all. I didn't want to stay here. My palms broke out in a sweat. My feet felt anchored to the ground. 'Hugo,' I whispered. 'I don't want to do this.' There was very little act in the desperation in my voice. I didn't like to hear it, but it was there.

'She really needs to get back upstairs,' Hugo said apologetically. 'If you all don't mind, we'll just go back up and wait for you there.'

I turned around, hoping this would work, but I found myself looking up into Steve's face. He wasn't smiling anymore. 'I think you two need to wait in the other room over there, until I'm through with my business. Then, we'll talk.' His voice brooked no discussion, and Sarah opened the door to disclose a bare little room with two chairs and two cots.

'No,' I said, 'I can't do that,' and I shoved Steve as hard as I could. I am very strong, very strong indeed, since I've had vampire blood, and despite his size, he staggered. I nipped up the stairs as fast as I could move, but a hand closed around my ankle, and I fell most painfully. The edges of the stairs hit me everywhere, across my left cheekbone, my breasts, my hipbones, my left knee. It hurt so much I almost gagged.

'Here, little lady,' said Gabe, hauling me to my feet.

'What have you – how could you hurt her like that?' Hugo was sputtering, genuinely upset. 'We come here thinking of joining your group, and this is the way you treat us?'

'Drop the act,' Gabe advised, and he twisted my arm behind my back before I had gotten my wits back from the fall. I gasped with the new pain, and he propelled me into the room, at the last minute grabbing my wig and yanking it off my head. Hugo stepped in behind me, though I gasped, '*No!*' and then they shut the door behind him.

And we heard it lock.

And that was that.

'Sookie,' Hugo said, 'there's a dent across your cheekbone.'

'No shit,' I muttered weakly.

'Are you badly hurt?'

'What do you think?'

He took me literally. 'I think you have bruises and maybe a concussion. You didn't break any bones, did you?'

'Not but one or two,' I said.

'And you're obviously not hurt badly enough to cut out the sarcasm,' Hugo said. If he could be angry with me, it would make him feel better, I could tell, and I wondered why. But I didn't wonder too hard. I was pretty sure I knew.

I was lying on one of the cots, an arm across my face, trying to keep private and do some thinking. We hadn't been able to hear much happening in the hall outside. Once I thought I'd heard a door opening, and we'd heard muted voices, but that was all. These walls were built to withstand a nuclear blast, so I guess the quiet was to be expected.

'Do you have a watch?' I asked Hugo.

'Yes. It's five-thirty.'

A good two hours until the vampires rose.

I let the quiet go on. When I knew hard-to-read Hugo must have relapsed into his own thoughts, I opened my mind and I listened with complete concentration.

Not supposed to happen like this, don't like this, surely everything'll be okay, what about when we need to go to the bathroom, I can't haul it out in front of her, maybe Isabel won't ever know, I should have known after that girl last night, how can I get out of this still practicing law, if I begin to distance myself after tomorrow maybe I can kind of ease out of it . . .

I pressed my arm against my eyes hard enough to hurt, to stop myself from jumping up and grabbing a chair and beating Hugo Ayres senseless. At present, he didn't fully understand my telepathy, and neither did the Fellowship, or they wouldn't have left me in here with him.

Or maybe Hugo was as expendable to them as he was to me. And he certainly would be to the vampires; I could hardly wait to tell Isabel that her boy toy was a traitor.

That sobered up my bloodlust. When I realized what Isabel would do to Hugo, I realized that I would take no real satisfaction in it if I witnessed it. In fact, it would terrify me and sicken me.

But part of me thought he richly deserved it.

To whom did this conflicted lawyer owe fealty?

One way to find out.

I sat up painfully, pressed my back against the wall. I would heal pretty fast – the vampire blood, again – but I was still a human, and I still felt awful. I knew my face was badly bruised, and I was willing to believe my cheekbone was fractured. The left side of my face was swelling something fierce. But my legs weren't broken, and I could still run, given the chance; that was the main thing.

Once I was braced and as comfortable as I was going to get, I said, 'Hugo, how long have you been a traitor?'

He flushed an incredible red. 'To whom? To Isabel, or to the human race?'

'Take your pick.'

'I betrayed the human race when I took the side of the vampires in court. If I'd had any idea of what they were . . . I took the case sight unseen, because I thought it would be an interesting legal challenge. I have always been a civil rights lawyer, and I was convinced vampires had the same civil rights as other people.'

Mr. Floodgates. 'Sure,' I said.

'To deny them the right to live anywhere they wanted to, that was un-American, I thought,' Hugo continued. He sounded bitter and world-weary.

He hadn't *seen* bitter, yet.

'But you know what, Sookie? Vampires aren't American. They aren't even black or Asian or Indian. They aren't Rotarians or Baptists. They're all just plain vampires. That's their color and their religion and their nationality.'

Well, that was what happened when a minority went underground for thousands of years. Duh.

'At the time, I thought if Stan Davis wanted to live on Green Valley Road, or in the Hundred-Acre Wood, that was his right as an American. So I defended him against the neighborhood association, and I won. I was real proud of myself. Then I got to know Isabel, and I took her to bed one night, feeling real daring, really the big man, the emancipated thinker.'

I stared at him, not blinking or saying a word.

'As you know, the sex is great, the best. I was in thrall to her, couldn't get enough. My practice suffered. I started seeing clients only in the afternoon, because I couldn't get up in the morning. I couldn't make my court dates in the morning. I couldn't leave Isabel after dark.'

This sounded like an alcoholic's tale, to me. Hugo had become addicted to vampiric sex. I found the concept fascinating and repellent.

'I started doing little jobs she found for me. This past month, I've been going over there and doing the housekeeping chores, just so I can hang around Isabel. When she wanted me to bring the bowl of water into the dining room, I was excited. Not at doing such a menial task – I'm a *lawyer*, for God's sake! But because the Fellowship had called me, asked me if I could give them any insight into what the vampires of Dallas intended to do. At the time they called, I was mad at Isabel. We'd had a fight about the way she treated me. So I was open to listening to them. I'd heard your name pass between Stan and Isabel, so I passed it on to the Fellowship. They have a guy who works for Anubis Air. He found out when Bill's plane was coming in, and they tried to grab you at the airport so they could find out what the vamps wanted with you. What they'd do to get you back. When I came in with the bowl of water, I heard Stan or Bill call you by name, so I knew they'd missed you at the airport. I felt like I had something to tell them, to make up for losing the bug I'd put in the conference room.'

'You betrayed Isabel,' I said. 'And you betrayed me, though I'm human, like you.'

'Yes,' he said. He didn't look me in the eyes.

'What about Bethany Rogers?'

'The waitress?'

He was stalling. 'The dead waitress,' I said.

'They took her,' he said, shaking his head from side to side, as if he were actually saying, No, they couldn't have done what they did. 'They took her, and I didn't know what they were going to do. I knew she was the only one who'd seen Farrell with Godfrey, and I'd told them that. When I got up today and I heard she'd been found dead, I just couldn't believe it.'

'They abducted her after you told them she'd been at Stan's. After you told them she was the only true witness.'

'Yes, they must have.'

'You called them last night.'

'Yes, I have a cell phone. I went out in the backyard and I called. I was really taking a chance, because you know how well the vamps can hear, but I called.' He was trying to convince himself that had been a brave, bold thing to do. Place a phone call from vamp headquarters to lay the finger on poor, pathetic Bethany, who'd ended up shot in an alley.

'She was shot after you betrayed her.'

'Yes, I . . . I heard that on the news.'

'Guess who did that, Hugo.'

'I . . . just don't know.'

'Sure you do, Hugo. She'd been an eyewitness. And she was a lesson, a lesson to the vampires. "This is what we'll do to people who work for you or make their living from you, if they go against the Fellowship." What do you think they're going to do with you, Hugo?'

'I've been helping them,' he said, surprised.

'Who else knows that?'

'No one.'

'So who would die? The lawyer that helped Stan Davis live where he wanted.'

Hugo was speechless.

'If you're so all-fired important to them, how come you're in this room with me?'

'Because up until now, you didn't know what I'd done,' he pointed out. 'Up until now, it was possible you would give me other information we could use against them.'

'So now, now that I know what you are, they'll let you out. Right? Why don't you try it and see? I'd much rather be alone.'

Just then a small aperture in the door opened. I hadn't even known it was there, having been preoccupied while I was out in the hall. A face appeared at the opening, which measured perhaps ten inches by ten inches.

It was a familiar face. Gabe, grinning. 'How you doing in there, you two?'

'Sookie needs a doctor,' Hugo said. 'She's not complaining, but I think her cheekbone is broken.' He sounded reproachful. 'And she knows about my alliance with the Fellowship, so you might as well let me out.'

I didn't know what Hugo thought he was doing, but I tried to look as beaten as possible. That was pretty easy.

'I have me an idea,' Gabe said. 'I've gotten kind of bored down here, and I don't expect Steve or Sarah – or even old Polly – will be coming back down here any time soon. We got another prisoner over here, Hugo, might be glad to see you. Farrell? You meet him over at the headquarters of the Evil Ones?'

'Yes,' said Hugo. He looked very unhappy about this turn of the conversation.

'You know how fond Farrell's gonna be of you? And he's gay, too, a queer bloodsucker. We're so deep underground that he's been waking up early. So I thought I might just put you in there with him, while I have me a little fun with the female traitor, here.' And Gabe smiled at me in a way that made my stomach lurch.

Hugo's face was a picture. A real picture. Several things crossed my mind, pertinent things to say. I forewent the doubtful pleasure. I needed to save my energy.

One of my Gran's favorite adages popped into my mind irresistibly as I looked at Gabe's handsome face. 'Pretty is as pretty does,' I muttered, and began the painful process of getting to my feet to defend myself. My legs might not be broken, but my left knee was surely in bad shape. It was already badly discolored and swollen.

I wondered if Hugo and I together could take Gabe down when he opened the door, but as soon as it swung outward, I saw he'd armed himself with a gun and a black, menacing-looking object I decided might be a stun gun.

'Farrell!' I called. If he were awake, he'd hear me; he was a vampire.

Gabe jumped, looked at me suspiciously.

'Yes?' came a deep voice from the room farther down the hall. I heard chains clink as the vampire moved. Of course, they'd have to chain him with silver. Otherwise he could rip the door off its hinges.

'Stan sent us!' I yelled, and then Gabe backhanded me with the hand that held the gun. Since I was against the wall, my head bounced off it. I made an awful noise, not quite a scream but too loud for a moan.

'Shut up, bitch!' Gabe screamed. He was pointing the gun at Hugo and had the stun gun held at the ready a few inches from me. 'Now, Lawyer, you get out here in the hall. Keep away from me, you hear?'

Hugo, sweat pouring down his face, edged past Gabe and into the hall. I was having a hard time tracking what was happening, but I noticed that in the narrow width Gabe had to maneuver, he came very close to Hugo on his way to open Farrell's cell. Just when I thought he was far enough down the hall for me to make it, he told Hugo to close my cell door, and though I frantically shook my head at Hugo, he did so.

I don't think Hugo even saw me. He was turned completely inward. Everything inside him was collapsing, his thoughts were in chaos. I'd done my best for him by telling Farrell we were from Stan, which in Hugo's case was stretching it considerably, but Hugo was too frightened or disillusioned or ashamed to show any backbone. Considering his deep betrayal, I was very surprised I'd bothered. If I hadn't held his hand and seen the images of his children, I wouldn't have.

'There's nothing to you, Hugo,' I said. His face reappeared at the still-open window momentarily, his face white with distress of all kinds, but then he vanished. I heard a door open, I heard the clink of chains, and I heard a door close.

Gabe had forced Hugo into Farrell's cell. I took deep breaths, one right after another, until I felt I might hyperventilate. I picked up one of the chairs, a plastic one with four metal legs, the kind you've sat on a million times in churches and meetings and classrooms. I held it lion-tamer style, with the legs facing outward. It was all I could think of to do. I thought of Bill, but that was too painful. I thought of my brother, Jason, and I wished he were there with me. It had been a long time since I'd wished that about Jason.

The door opened. Gabe was already smiling as he came in. It was a nasty smile, letting all the ugliness leak out of his soul through his mouth and eyes. This really was his idea of a good time.

'You think that little chair is going to keep you safe?' he asked.

I wasn't in the mood for talking, and I didn't want to listen to the snakes in his mind. I closed myself off, contained myself tightly, bracing myself.

He'd holstered the gun, but kept the stun gun in his hand. Now, such was his confidence, he put it in a little leather pouch on his belt, on the left side. He seized the legs of the chair and began to yank the chair from side to side.

I charged.

I almost had him out the door, so unexpected was my strong counterattack, but at the last minute he managed to twist the legs sideways, so that they couldn't pass through the narrow doorway. He stood against the wall on the other side of the hall, panting, his face red.

'Bitch,' he hissed, and came at me again, and this time he tried to pull the chair out of my hands altogether. But as

I've said before, I've had vampire blood, and I didn't let him have it. And I didn't let him have me.

Without my seeing it, he'd drawn the stun gun and, quick as a snake, he reached over the chair and touched it to my shoulder.

I didn't collapse, which he expected, but I went down on my knees, still holding the chair. While I was still trying to figure out what had happened to me, he yanked the chair from my hands, and knocked me backwards.

I could hardly move, but I could scream and lock my legs together, and I did.

'Shut up!' he yelled, and since he was touching me, I could tell that he really wanted me unconscious, he would enjoy raping me while I was unconscious; in fact, that was his ideal.

'Don't like your women awake,' I panted, 'do you?' He stuck a hand between us and yanked open my blouse.

I heard Hugo's voice, yelling, as if that would do any good. I bit at Gabe's shoulder.

He called me a bitch again, which was getting old. He'd opened his own pants, now he was trying to pull up my skirt. I was fleetingly glad I'd bought a long one.

'You afraid they'll complain, if they're awake?' I yelled. 'Let me go, get off me! Get off, get off, *get off!*' Finally, I'd unpinned my arms. In a moment, they'd recovered enough from the electric jolt to function. I formed two cups with my hands. As I screamed at him, I clapped my hands over his ears.

He roared, and reared back, his own hands going to his head. He was so full of rage it escaped him and washed over me; it felt like bathing in fury. I knew then that he would kill me if he could, no matter what reprisals he faced. I tried to roll to one side, but he had me pinned with his legs. I watched as his right hand formed a fist, which seemed as big as a boulder to me. And with a sense of doom, I watched the arc of that fist as it descended to my face, knowing this one would knock me out and it would be all over . . .

And it didn't happen.

Up in the air Gabe went, pants open and dick hanging out, his fist landing on air, his shoes kicking at my legs.

A short man was holding Gabe up in the air; not a man, I realized at second glance, a teenager. An ancient teenager.

He was blond and shirtless, and his arms and chest were covered with blue tattoos. Gabe was yelling and flailing, but the boy stood calmly, his face expressionless, until Gabe ran down. By the time Gabe was silent, the boy had transferred his grip to a kind of bear hug encircling Gabe's waist, and Gabe was hanging forward.

The boy looked down at me dispassionately. My blouse had been torn open, and my bra was ripped down the middle.

'Are you badly hurt?' the boy asked, almost reluctantly.

I had a savior, but not an enthusiastic one.

I stood up, which was more of a feat than it sounds. It took me quite a while. I was trembling violently from the emotional shock. When I was upright, I was on an eye level with the boy. In human years, he would've been about sixteen when he'd been made vampire. There was no telling how many years ago that had been. He must be older than Stan, older than Isabel. His English was clear, but heavily accented. I had no idea what kind of accent it was. Maybe his original language was not even spoken anymore. What a lonely feeling that would be.

'I'll mend,' I said. 'Thank you.' I tried to rebutton my blouse – there were a few remaining buttons – but my hands were shaking too badly. He wasn't interested in seeing my skin, anyway. It didn't do a thing for him. His eyes were quite dispassionate.

'Godfrey,' Gabe said. His voice was thready. 'Godfrey, she was trying to escape.'

Godfrey shook him, and Gabe shut up.

So, Godfrey was the vampire I'd seen through Bethany's eyes – the only eyes that could remember seeing him at the Bat's Wing that evening. The eyes that were no longer seeing anything.

'What do you intend to do?' I asked him, keeping my voice quiet and even.

Godfrey's pale blue eyes flickered. He didn't know.

He'd gotten the tattoos while he was alive, and they were very strange, symbols whose meaning had been lost centuries ago, I was willing to bet. Probably some scholar would give his eyeteeth to have a look at those tattoos. Lucky me, I was getting to see them for nothing.

'Please let me out,' I said with as much dignity as I could muster. 'They'll kill me.'

'But you consort with vampires,' he said.

My eyes darted from one side to another, as I tried to figure this one out.

'Ah,' I said hesitantly. 'You're a vampire, aren't you?'

'Tomorrow I atone for my sin publicly,' Godfrey said. 'Tomorrow I greet the dawn. For the first time in a thousand years, I will see the sun. Then I will see the face of God.'

Okay. 'You chose,' I said.

'Yes.'

'But I didn't. I don't want to die.' I spared a glance for Gabe's face, which was quite blue. In his agitation, Godfrey was squeezing Gabe much tighter than he ought to. I wondered if I should say something.

'You do consort with vampires,' Godfrey accused, and I switched my gaze back to his face. I knew I'd better not let my concentration wander again.

'I'm in love,' I said.

'With a vampire.'

'Yes. Bill Compton.'

'All vampires are damned, and should all meet the sun. We're a taint, a blot on the face of the earth.'

'And these people' – I pointed upward to indicate I meant the Fellowship – 'these people are better, Godfrey?'

The vampire looked uneasy and unhappy. He was starving, I noticed; his cheeks were almost concave, and they were as white as paper. His blond hair almost floated around his head, it was so electric, and his eyes looked like blue marbles against his pallor. 'They, at least, are human, part of God's plan,' he said quietly. 'Vampires are an abomination.'

'Yet you've been nicer to me than this human.' Who was dead, I realized, as I glanced down at his face. I tried not to flinch, and refocused on Godfrey, who was much more important to my future.

'But we take the blood of the innocents.' Godfrey's pale blue eyes fixed on mine.

'Who is innocent?' I asked rhetorically, hoping I didn't sound too much like Pontius Pilate asking, What is truth? when he knew damn well.

'Well, children,' Godfrey said.

'Oh, you . . . fed on children?' I put my hand over my mouth.

'I killed children.'

I couldn't think of a thing to say for a long time. Godfrey stood there, looking at me sadly, holding Gabe's body in his arms, forgotten.

'What stopped you?' I asked.

'Nothing will stop me. Nothing but my death.'

'I'm so sorry,' I said inadequately. He was suffering, and I was truly sorry for that. But if he'd been human, I'd have said he deserved the electric chair without thinking twice.

'How soon is it until dark?' I asked, not knowing what else to say.

Godfrey had no watch, of course. I assumed he was up only because he was underground and he was very old. Godfrey said, 'An hour.'

'Please let me go. If you help me, I can get out of here.'

'But you will tell the vampires. They will attack. I will be prevented from meeting the dawn.'

'Why wait till the morning?' I asked, suddenly irritated. 'Walk outside. Do it now.'

He was astounded. He dropped Gabe, who landed with a thud. Godfrey didn't even spare him a glance. 'The ceremony is planned for dawn, with many believers there to witness it,' he explained. 'Farrell will also be brought up to face the sun.'

'What part would I have played in this?'

He shrugged. 'Sarah wanted to see if the vampires would exchange one of their own for you. Steve had other plans. His idea was to lash you to Farrell, so that when he burned, so would you.'

I was stunned. Not that Steve Newlin had had the idea, but that he thought it would appeal to his congregation, for that was what they were. Newlin was further over the top than even I had guessed. 'And you think lots of people would enjoy seeing that, a young woman executed without any kind of trial? That they would think it was a valid religious ceremony? You think the people who planned this terrible death for me are truly religious?'

For the first time, he seemed a shade doubtful. 'Even for humans, that seems a little extreme,' he agreed. 'But Steve thought it would be a powerful statement.'

'Well, sure it would be a powerful statement. It would say, "I'm nuts." I know this world has plenty of bad people and bad vampires, but I don't believe the majority of the people in this country, or for that matter just here in Texas, would be edified by the sight of a screaming woman burning to death.'

Godfrey looked doubtful. I could see I was voicing thoughts that had occurred to him, thoughts he had denied to himself he was entertaining. 'They have called the media,' he said. It was like the protest of a bride slated to marry a groom she suddenly doubted. But the invitations have been sent out, Mother.

'I'm sure they have. But it'll be the end of their organization, I can tell you that flat out. I repeat, if you really want to make a statement that way, a big "I'm sorry," then you walk out of this church right now and stand on the lawn. God'll be watching, I promise you. That's who you should care about.'

He struggled with it; I'll give him that.

'They have a special white robe for me to wear,' he said. (But I've already bought the dress and reserved the church.)

'Big damn deal. If we're arguing clothes, you don't really want to do it. I bet you'll chicken out.'

I had definitely lost sight of my goal. When the words came out of my mouth, I regretted them.

'You will see,' he said firmly.

'I don't want to see, if I'm tied to Farrell at the time. I am not evil, and I don't want to die.'

'When was the last time you were in church?' He was issuing me a challenge.

'About a week ago. And I took Communion, too.' I was never happier to be a churchgoer, because I couldn't have lied about that.

'Oh.' Godfrey looked dumbfounded.

'See?' I felt I was robbing him of all his wounded majesty by this argument, but dammit, I didn't want to die by burning. I wanted Bill, wanted him with a longing so intense I hoped it would pop his coffin open. If only I could tell him what was going on . . . 'Come on,' said Godfrey, holding out his hand.

I didn't want to give him a chance to rethink his position, not after this long do-si-do, so I took his hand and stepped over Gabe's prone form out into the hall. There was an ominous lack of conversation from Farrell and Hugo, and to tell the truth, I was too scared to call out to find out what was going on with them. I figured if I could get out, I could rescue them both, anyway.

Godfrey sniffed the blood on me, and his face was swept with longing. I knew that look. But it was devoid of lust. He didn't care a thing for my body. The link between blood and sex is very strong for all vampires, so I considered myself lucky that I was definitely adult in form. I inclined my face to him out of courtesy. After a long hesitation, he licked the trickle of blood from the cut on my cheekbone. He closed his eyes for a second, savoring the taste, and then we started for the stairs.

With a great deal of help from Godfrey, I made it up the steep flight. He used his free arm to punch in a combination on the door, and swung it open. 'I've been staying down here, in the room at the end,' he explained, in a voice that was hardly more than a disturbance of the air.

The corridor was clear, but any second someone might come out of one of the offices. Godfrey didn't seem to fear that at all, but I did, and I was the one whose freedom was at stake. I didn't hear any voices; apparently the staff had gone home to get ready for the lock-in, and the lock-in guests had not yet started arriving. Some of the office doors were closed, and the windows in the offices were the only means of sunlight getting to the hall. It was dark enough for Godfrey to be comfortable, I assumed, since he didn't even wince. There was bright artificial light coming from under the main office door.

We hurried, or at least tried to, but my left leg was not very cooperative. I wasn't sure what door Godfrey was heading toward, perhaps double doors I'd seen earlier at the back of the sanctuary. If I could get safely out of those, I wouldn't have to traverse the other wing. I didn't know what I'd do when I got outside. But being outside would definitely be better than being inside. Just as we reached the open doorway to the next-to-last office on the left, the one from which the tiny Hispanic woman had come, the door to Steve's office opened. We froze. Godfrey's arm around me felt like an iron band. Polly stepped out, still facing into the room. We were only a couple of yards away.

'. . . bonfire,' she was saying.

'Oh, I think we've got enough,' Sarah's sweet voice said. 'If everyone returned their attendance cards, we'd know for sure. I can't believe how bad people are about not replying. It's so inconsiderate, after we made it as easy as possible for them to tell us whether or not they'd be here!'

An argument about etiquette. Gosh, I wished Miss Manners were here to give me advice on this situation. *I was an uninvited guest of a small church, and I left without saying good-bye. Am I obliged to write a thank-you note, or may I simply send flowers?*

Polly's head began turning, and I knew any moment she would see us. Even as the thought formed, Godfrey pushed me into the dark empty office.

'Godfrey! What are you doing up here?' Polly didn't sound frightened, but she didn't sound happy, either. It was more like she'd found the yardman in the living room, making himself at home.

'I came to see if there is anything more I need to do.'

'Isn't it awfully early for you to be awake?'

'I am very old,' he said politely. 'The old don't need as much sleep as the young.'

Polly laughed. 'Sarah,' she said brightly, 'Godfrey's up!'

Sarah's voice sounded closer, when she spoke. 'Well, hey, Godfrey!' she said, in an identical bright tone. 'Are you excited? I bet you are!'

They were talking to a thousand-year-old vampire like he was a child on his birthday eve.

'Your robe's all ready,' Sarah said. 'All systems go!'

'What if I changed my mind?' Godfrey asked.

There was a long silence. I tried to breathe very slowly and quietly. The closer it got to dark the more I could imagine I had a chance of getting out of this.

If I could telephone . . . I glanced over at the desk in the office. There was a telephone on it. But wouldn't the buttons in the offices light up, the buttons for that line, if I used the phone? At the moment, it would make too much noise.

'You changed your mind? Can this be possible?' Polly asked. She was clearly exasperated. 'You came to us, remember? You told us about your life of sin, and the shame you felt when you killed children and . . . did other things. Has any of this changed?'

'No,' Godfrey said, sounding more thoughtful than anything else. 'None of this has changed. But I see no need to include any humans in this sacrifice of mine. In fact, I believe that Farrell should be left to make his own peace with God. We shouldn't force him into immolation.'

'We need to get Steve back here,' Polly said to Sarah in an undertone.

After that, I just heard Polly, so I assumed Sarah had gone back into the office to call Steve.

One of the lights on the phone lit up. Yep, that was what she was doing. She'd know if I tried to use one of the other lines. Maybe in a minute.

Polly was trying sweet reason with Godfrey. Godfrey was not talking much, himself, and I had no idea what was going through his head. I stood helplessly, pressed against the wall, hoping no one would come into the office, hoping no one would go downstairs and raise the alarm, hoping Godfrey wouldn't have yet another change of heart.

Help, I said in my mind. If only I could call for help that way, through my other sense!

A flicker of an idea crossed my mind. I made myself stand calmly, though my legs were still trembling with shock, and my knee and face hurt like the six shades of hell. Maybe I *could* call someone: Barry, the bellboy. He was a telepath, like me. He could be able to hear me. Not that I'd ever made such an attempt before – well, I'd never met another telepath, had I? I tried desperately to locate myself in relation to Barry, assuming he was at work. This was about the same time we'd arrived from Shreveport, so he might be. I pictured my location on the map, which luckily I'd looked up with Hugo – though I knew now that he had been pretending not to know where the Fellowship Center was – and I figured we were southwest of the Silent Shore Hotel.

I was in new mental territory. I gathered up what energy I had and tried to roll it into a ball, in my mind. For a second, I felt absolutely ridiculous, but when I thought of getting free of this place and these people, there was very little to gain in not being ridiculous. I thought to Barry. It's hard to peg down exactly how I did it, but I projected. Knowing his name helped, and knowing his location helped.

I decided to start easy. *Barry Barry Barry Barry . . .*

What do you want? He was absolutely panicked. This had never happened to him before.

I've never done this either. I hoped I sounded reassuring. *I need help. I'm in big trouble.*

Who are you?

Well, that would help. Stupid me. *I'm Sookie, the blond who came in last night with the brown-haired vampire. Third-floor suite.*

The one with the boobs? Oh, sorry.

At least he'd apologized. *Yes. The one with the boobs. And the boyfriend.*

So, what's the matter?

Now, all this sounds very clear and organized, but it wasn't words. It was like we were sending each other emotional telegrams and pictures.

I tried to think how to explain my predicament. *Get my vampire as soon as he wakes.*

And then?

Tell him I'm in danger. Dangerdangerdanger . . .

Okay, I get the idea. Where?

Church. I figured that would be shorthand for the Fellowship Center. I couldn't think how to convey that to Barry.

He knows where?

He knows where. Tell him, Go down the stairs.

Are you for real? I didn't know there was anyone else . . .

I'm for real. Please, help me.

I could feel a complicated bundle of emotions racing through Barry's mind. He was scared of talking to a vampire, he was frightened that his employers would discover he had a 'weird brain thing,' he was just excited that there was someone like him. But mostly he was scared of this part of him that had puzzled and frightened him for so long.

I knew all those feelings. *It's okay, I understand*, I told him. *I wouldn't ask if I wasn't going to be killed.*

Fear struck him again, fear of his own responsibility in this. I should never have added that.

And then, somehow, he erected a flimsy barrier between us, and I wasn't sure what Barry was going to do.

While I'd been concentrating on Barry, things had been moving right along in the hall. When I began listening again, Steve had returned. He, too, was trying to be reasonable and positive with Godfrey.

'Now, Godfrey,' he was saying, 'if you didn't want to do this, all you had to do was say so. You committed to it, we all did, and we've moved forward with every expectation that you would keep to your word. A lot of people are going to be very disappointed if you lose your commitment to the ceremony.'

'What will you do with Farrell? With the man Hugo, and the blond woman?'

'Farrell's a vampire,' said Steve, still the voice of sweet reason. 'Hugo and the woman are vampires' creatures. They should go to the sun, too, tied to a vampire. That is the lot they chose in their lives, and it should be their lot in death.'

'I am a sinner, and I know it, so when I die my soul will go to God,' Godfrey said. 'But Farrell does not know this. When he dies, he won't have a chance. The man and woman, too, have not had a chance to repent their ways. Is it fair to kill them and condemn them to hell?'

'We need to go into my office,' Steve said decisively. And I realized, finally, that that was what Godfrey had been aiming for all along. There was a certain amount of foot shuffling, and I heard Godfrey murmur, 'After you,' with great courtesy.

He wanted to be last so he could shut the door behind him.

My hair finally felt dry, freed from the wig that had drenched it in sweat. It was hanging around my shoulders in separate locks, because I'd been silently unpinning it during the conversation. It had seemed a casual thing to be doing, while listening to my fate being settled, but I had to keep occupied. Now I cautiously pocketed the bobby pins, ran my fingers through the tangled mess, and prepared to sneak out of the church.

I peered cautiously from the doorway. Yes, Steve's door was closed. I tiptoed out of the dark office, took a left, and continued to the door leading into the sanctuary. I turned its knob very quietly and eased it open. I stepped into the sanctuary, which was very dusky. There was just enough light from the huge stained-glass windows to help me get down the aisle without falling over the pews.

Then I heard voices, getting louder, coming from the far wing. The lights in the sanctuary came on. I dove into a row and rolled under the pew. A family group came in, all talking loudly, the little girl whining about missing some favorite show on television because she had to go to the stinky old lock-in.

That got her a slap on the bottom, sounded like, and her father told her she was lucky she was going to get to see such an amazing evidence of the power of God. She was going to see salvation in action.

Even under the circumstances, I took issue with that. I wondered if this father really understood that his leader planned for the congregation to watch two vampires burn to death, at least one of them clutching a human who would also burn. I wondered how the little girl's mental health would fare after that 'amazing evidence of the power of God.'

To my dismay, they proceeded to put their sleeping bags up against a wall on the far side of the sanctuary, still talking. At least this was a family that communicated. In addition to the whiny little girl, there were two older kids, a boy and a girl, and like true siblings they fought like cats and dogs.

A pair of small flat red shoes trotted by the end of my pew and disappeared through the door into Steve's wing. I wondered if the group in his office was still debating.

The feet went by again after a few seconds, this time going very fast. I wondered about that, too.

I waited about five more minutes, but nothing else happened.

From now on, there would be more people coming in. It was now or never. I rolled out from under the pew and got up. By my good fortune, they were all looking down at their task when I stood up, and I began walking briskly to the double doors at the back of the church. By their sudden silence, I knew they'd spotted me.

'Hi!' called the mother. She rose to her feet beside her bright blue sleeping bag. Her plain face was full of curiosity. 'You must be new at the Fellowship. I'm Francie Polk.'

'Yes,' I called, trying to sound cheerful. 'Gotta rush! Talk to you later!'

She drew closer. 'Have you hurt yourself?' she asked. 'You – excuse me – you look awful. Is that blood?'

I glanced down at my blouse. There were some small stains on my chest.

'I had a fall,' I said, trying to sound rueful. 'I need to go home and do a little first aid, change my clothes, like that. I'll be back!'

I could see the doubt on Francie Polk's face. 'There's a first aid kit in the office, why don't I just run and get that?' she asked.

Because I don't want you to. 'You know, I need to get a fresh blouse, too,' I said. I wrinkled my nose to show my low opinion of going around in a spotted blouse all evening.

Another woman had come in the very doors I was hoping to go out of, and she stood listening to the conversation, her dark eyes darting back and forth from me to the determined Francie.

'Hey, girl!' she said in a lightly accented voice, and the little Hispanic woman, the shapeshifter, gave me a hug. I come from a hugging culture, and it was automatic to hug her right back. She gave me a meaningful pinch while we were clenched.

'How are you?' I asked brightly. 'It's been too long.'

'Oh, you know, same old same old,' she said. She beamed up at me, but there was caution in her eyes. Her hair was a very dark brown, rather than black, and it was coarse and abundant. Her skin was the color of a milky caramel, and she had dark freckles. Generous lips were painted an outstanding fuchsia. She had big white teeth, flashing at me in her wide smile. I glanced down at her feet. Flat red shoes.

'Hey, come outside with me while I have a cigarette,' she said.

Francie Polk was looking more satisfied.

'Luna, can't you see your friend needs to go to the doctor?' she said righteously.

'You do have a few bumps and bruises,' Luna said, examining me. 'Have you fallen down again, girl?'

'You know Mama always tells me, "Marigold, you're as clumsy as an elephant."'

'That mama of yours,' Luna said, shaking her head in disgust. 'Like that would make you less clumsy!'

'What can you do?' I said, shrugging. 'If you'll excuse us, Francie?'

'Well, sure,' she said. 'I'll see you later, I guess.'

'Sure will,' said Luna. 'I wouldn't miss it for anything.'

And with Luna, I strolled out of the Fellowship of the Sun meeting hall. I concentrated ferociously on keeping my gait even, so Francie wouldn't see me limp and become even more suspicious.

'Thank God,' I said, when we were outside.

'You knew me for what I was,' she said rapidly. 'How did you know?'

'I have a friend who's a shapeshifter.'

'Who is he?'

'He's not local. And I won't tell you without his consent.'

She stared at me, all pretence of friendship dropped in that instant.

'Okay, I respect that,' she said. 'Why are you here?'

'What's it to you?'

'I just saved your ass.'

She had a point, a good point. 'Okay. I am a telepath, and I was hired by your vampire area leader to find out what had become of a missing vampire.'

'That's better. But it ain't *my* area leader. I'm a supe, but I ain't no freaking vampire. What vamp did you deal with?'

'I don't need to tell you that.'

She raised her eyebrows.

'I don't.'

She opened her mouth as if to yell.

'Yell away. There're some things I just won't tell. What's a supe?'

'A supernatural being. Now, you listen to me,' Luna said. We were walking through the parking lot now, and cars were beginning to pull in regularly from the road. She did a lot of smiling and waving, and I tried to at least look happy. But the limp was no longer concealable, and my face was swelling like a bitch, as Arlene would say.

Gosh, I was homesick all of a sudden. But I thrust that feeling away to pay attention to Luna, who clearly had things to tell me.

'You tell the vampires *we* have this place under surveillance –'

'"We" being who?'

'"We" being the shapeshifters of the greater Dallas area.'

'You guys are organized? Hey, that's great! I'll have to tell . . . my friend.'

She rolled her eyes, clearly not impressed with my intellect. 'Listen here, missy, you tell the vampires that as soon as the Fellowship figures out about us, they will be on us, too. And we aren't going to mainstream. We're underground for good. Stupid freakin' vampires. So we're keeping an eye on the Fellowship.'

'If you're keeping such a good eye, how come you didn't call the vampires and tell them about Farrell being in the basement? And about Godfrey?'

'Hey, Godfrey wants to kill himself, no skin off our teeth. He came to the Fellowship; they didn't go to him. They about peed their pants, they were so glad to have him, after they got over the shock of sitting in the same room with one of the damned.'

'What about Farrell?'

'I didn't know who was down there,' Luna admitted. 'I knew they'd captured someone, but I'm not exactly in the inner circle yet, and I couldn't find out who. I even tried buttering up that asshole Gabe, but that didn't help.'

'You'll be pleased to know that Gabe is dead.'

'Hey!' She smiled genuinely for the first time. 'That *is* good news.'

'Here's the rest. As soon as I get in touch with the vampires, they're going to be here to get Farrell. So if I were you, I wouldn't go back to the Fellowship tonight.'

She chewed on her lower lip for a minute. We were at the far end of the parking lot.

'In fact,' I said, 'it would be perfect if you would give me a lift to the hotel.'

'Well, I'm not in the business of making your life perfect,' she snarled, recalled to her tough cookie persona. 'I got to get back in that church before the shit hits the fan, and get some papers out. Think about this, girl. What are the vampires gonna do with Godfrey? Can they let him live? He's a child molester and a serial killer; so many times over you couldn't even count. He can't stop, and he knows it.'

So there was a good side to the church . . . it gave vampires like Godfrey a venue to commit suicide while being watched?

'Maybe they should just put it on pay-per-view,' I said.

'They would if they could.' Luna was serious. 'Those vampires trying to mainstream, they're pretty harsh to anyone who might upset their plan. Godfrey's no poster boy.'

'I can't solve every problem, Luna. By the way, my real name is Sookie. Sookie Stackhouse. Anyway, I've done what I could. I did the job I was hired to do, and now I have to get back and report. Godfrey lives or Godfrey dies. I think Godfrey will die.'

'You better be right,' she said ominously.

I couldn't figure out why it was my fault if Godfrey changed his mind. I had just questioned his chosen venue. But maybe she was right. I might have some responsibility, here.

It was all just too much for me.

'Good-bye,' I said, and began limping along the back of the parking lot to the road. I hadn't gotten far when I heard a hue and cry arise from the church, and all the outside lights popped on. The sudden glare was blinding.

'Maybe I won't go back in the Fellowship Center after all. Not a good idea,' Luna said from the window of a Subaru Outback. I scrambled into the passenger's seat, and we sped toward the nearest exit onto the four-lane road. I fastened my seat belt automatically.

But as swiftly as we had moved, others had moved even more swiftly. Various family vehicles were being positioned to block the exits from the parking lot.

'Crap,' said Luna.

We sat idling for a minute while she thought.

'They'll never let me out, even if we hide you somehow. I can't get you back into the church. They can search the parking lot too easily.' Luna chewed on her lip some more.

'Oh, freak this job, anyway,' she said, and threw the Outback into gear. She drove conservatively at first, trying to attract as little attention as possible. 'These people wouldn't know what religion was if it bit them in the ass,' she said. Up by the church, Luna drove over the curb separating the parking lot from the lawn. Then we were flooring it over the lawn, circling the fenced play area, and I discovered I was grinning from ear to ear, though it hurt to do so.

'Yee-hah!' I yelled, as we hit a sprinkler head on the lawn watering system. We flew across the front yard of the church, and, out of sheer shock, no one was pursuing us. They'd organize themselves in a minute, though, the diehards. Those people who didn't espouse the more extreme measures of this Fellowship were going to get a real wake-up call tonight.

Sure enough, Luna looked in her rearview mirror and said, 'They've unblocked the exits, and someone's coming after us.' We pulled out into traffic on the road running in front of the church, another major four-lane road, and horns honked all around at our sudden entry into the traffic flow.

'Holy shit,' Luna said. She slowed down to a reasonable speed and kept looking in her rearview mirror. 'It's too dark now, I can't tell which headlights are them.'

I wondered if Barry had alerted Bill.

'You got a cell phone?' I asked her.

'It's in my pursc, along with my driver's license, which is still sitting in my office in the church. That's how I knew you were loose. I went in my office, smelled your scent. Knew you'd been hurt. So I went outside and scouted around, and when I couldn't find you, I came back in. We're damn lucky I had my keys in my pocket.'

God bless shapeshifters. I felt wistful about the phone, but it couldn't be helped. I suddenly wondered where my purse was. Probably back in the Fellowship of the Sun office. At least I'd taken all my i.d. out of it.

'Should we stop at a pay phone, or the police station?'

'If you call the police, what are they going to do?' asked Luna, in the encouraging voice of someone leading a small child to wisdom.

'Go to the church?'

'And what will happen then, girl?'

'Ah, they'll ask Steve why he was holding a human prisoner?'

'Yep. And what will he say?'

'I don't know.'

'He'll say, "We never held her prisoner. She got into some kind of argument with our employee Gabe, and he ended up dead. Arrest her!"'

'Oh. You think?'

'Yeah, I think.'

'What about Farrell?'

'If the police start coming in, you can better believe they've got someone detailed to hustle down to the basement and stake him. By the time the cops get there, no more Farrell. They could do the same to Godfrey, if he wouldn't back them up. He would probably stand still for it. He wants to die, that Godfrey.'

'Well, what about Hugo?'

'You think Hugo is going to explain how come he got locked in a basement there? I don't know what that jerk would say, but he won't tell the truth. He's led a double life for months now, and he can't say whether his head is on straight or not.'

'So we can't call the police. Who can we call?'

'I got to get you with your people. You don't need to meet mine. They don't want to be known, you understand?'

'Sure.'

'You have to be something weird yourself, huh? To recognize us.'

'Yes.'

'So what are you? Not a vamp, for sure. Not one of us, either.'

'I'm a telepath.'

'You are! No shit! Well, woooo woooo,' Luna said, imitating the traditional ghost sound.

'No more woo woo than you are,' I said, feeling I could be pardoned for sounding a bit testy.

'Sorry,' she said, not meaning it. 'Okay, here's the plan—'

But I didn't get to hear what the plan was, because at that moment we were hit from the rear.

*

The next thing I knew, I was hanging upside down in my seat belt. A hand was reaching in to pull me out. I recognized the fingernails; it was Sarah. I bit her.

With a shriek, the hand withdrew. 'She's obviously out of it,' I heard Sarah's sweet voice gabbling to someone else, someone unconnected with the church, I realized, and knew I had to act.

'Don't you listen to her. It was her car that hit us,' I called. 'Don't you let her touch me.'

I looked over at Luna, whose hair now touched the ceiling. She was awake but not talking. She was wriggling around, and I figured she was trying to undo her seat belt.

There was lots of conversation outside the window, most of it contentious.

'I tell you, I am her sister, and she is just drunk,' Polly was telling someone.

'I am not. I demand to have a sobriety test right now,' I said, in as dignified a voice as I could manage, considering that I was shocked silly and hanging upside down. 'Call the police immediately, please, and an ambulance.'

Though Sarah began spluttering, a heavy male voice said, 'Lady, doesn't sound like she wants you around. Sounds like she's got some good points.'

A man's face appeared in the window. He was kneeling and bent sideways to see in. 'I've called nine-one-one,' the heavy voice said. He was disheveled and stubbly and I thought he was beautiful.

'Please stay here till they come,' I begged.

'I will,' he promised, and his face vanished.

There were more voices now. Sarah and Polly were getting shrill. They'd hit our car. Several people had witnessed it. Them claiming to be sisters or whatever didn't go over well with this crowd. Also, I gathered, they had two Fellowship males with them who were being less than endearing.

'Then we'll just go,' Polly said, fury in her voice.

'No, you won't,' said my wonderful belligerent male. 'You gotta trade insurance with them, anyway.'

'That's right,' said a much younger male voice. 'You just don't want to pay for getting their car fixed. And what if they're hurt? Don't you have to pay their hospital?'

Luna had managed to unbuckle herself, and she twisted when she fell to the roof that was now the floor of the car. With a suppleness I could only envy, she worked her head out of the open window, and then began to brace her feet against whatever purchase she could find. Gradually, she began to wriggle her way out of the window. One of the purchases happened to be my shoulder, but I didn't even peep. One of us needed to be free.

There were exclamations outside as Luna made her appearance, and then I heard her say, 'Okay, which one of you was driving?'

Various voices chimed in, some saying one, some saying another, but they all knew Sarah and Polly and their henchmen were the perpetrators and Luna was a victim. There were so many people around that when yet another car of men from the Fellowship pulled up, there wasn't any way they could just haul us off. God bless the American spectator, I thought. I was in a sentimental mood.

The paramedic that ended up extricating me from the car was the cutest guy I'd ever seen. His name was Salazar, according to his bar pin, and I said, 'Salazar,' just to be sure I could say it. I had to sound it out carefully.

'Yep, that's me,' he said while lifting my eyelid to look at my eye. 'You're kinda banged up, lady.'

I started to tell him that I'd had some of these injuries before the car accident, but then I heard Luna say, 'My calendar flew off the dashboard and hit her in the face.'

'Be a lot safer if you'd keep your dash clear, ma'am,' said a new voice with a flat twang to it.

'I hear you, Officer.'

Officer? I tried to turn my head and got admonished by Salazar. 'You just keep still till I finish looking you over,' he said sternly.

'Okay.' After a second I said, 'The police are here?'

'Yes, ma'am. Now, what hurts?'

We went through a whole list of questions, most of which I was able to answer.

'I think you're going to be fine, ma'am, but we need to take you and your friend to the hospital just to check you out.' Salazar and his partner, a heavy Anglo woman, were matter-of-fact about this necessity.

'Oh,' I said anxiously, 'we don't need to go to the hospital, do we, Luna?'

'Sure,' she said, as surprised as she could be. 'We have to get you X-rayed, honey bunch. I mean, that cheek of yours looks bad.'

'Oh.' I was a little stunned by this turn of events. 'Well, if you think so.'

'Oh, yeah.'

So Luna walked to the ambulance, and I was loaded in on a gurney, and with siren blaring, we started off. My last view before Salazar shut the doors was of Polly and Sarah talking to a very tall policeman. Both of them looked very upset. That was good.

The hospital was like all hospitals. Luna stuck to me like white to rice, and when we were in the same cubicle and a nurse entered to take down still more details, Luna said, 'Tell Dr. Josephus that Luna Garza and her sister are here.'

The nurse, a young African American woman, gave Luna a doubtful look, but said, 'Okay,' and left immediately.

'How'd you do that?' I asked.

'Get a nurse to stop filling out charts? I asked for this hospital on purpose. We've got someone at every hospital in the city, but I know our man here best.'

'Our?'

'Us. The Two-Natured.'

'Oh.' The shapeshifters. I could hardly wait to tell Sam about this.

'I'm Dr. Josephus,' said a calm voice. I raised my head to see that a spare, silver-haired man had stepped into our curtained area. His hair was receding and he had a sharp nose on which a pair of wire-rimmed glasses perched. He had intent blue eyes, magnified by his glasses.

'I'm Luna Garza, and this is my friend, ah, Marigold.' Luna said this as if she were a different person. In fact, I glanced over to see if it was the same Luna. 'We met with misfortune tonight in the line of duty.'

The doctor looked at me with some mistrust.

'She is worthy,' Luna said with great solemnity. I didn't want to ruin the moment by giggling, but I had to bite the inside of my mouth.

'You need X-rays,' the doctor said after looking at my face and examining my grotesquely swollen knee. I had various abrasions and bruises, but those were my only really significant injuries.

'Then we need them very quickly, and then we need out of here in a secure way,' Luna said in a voice that would brook no denial.

No hospital had ever moved so quickly. I could only suppose that Dr. Josephus was on the board of directors. Or maybe he was the chief of staff. The portable X-ray machine was wheeled in, the X-rays were taken, and in a few minutes Dr. Josephus told me that I had a hairline fracture of the cheekbone which would mend on its own. Or I could see a plastic surgeon when the swelling had gone down. He gave me a prescription for pain pills, a lot of advice, and an ice pack for my face and another for my knee, which he called 'wrenched.'

Within ten minutes after that, we were on our way out of the hospital. Luna was pushing me in a wheelchair, and Dr. Josephus was leading us through a kind of service tunnel. We passed a couple of employees on their way in. They appeared to be poor people, the kind who take low-paying jobs like hospital janitor and cook. I couldn't believe the massively self-assured Dr. Josephus had ever come down this tunnel before, but he seemed to know his way, and the staff didn't act startled at the sight of him. At the end of the tunnel, he pushed open a heavy metal door.

Luna Garza nodded to him regally, said, 'Many thanks,' and wheeled me out into the night. There was a big old car parked out there. It was dark red or dark brown. As I looked around a little more, I realized that we were in an alley. There were big trash bins lining the wall, and I saw a cat pouncing on something – I didn't want to know what – between two of the bins. After the door whooshed pneumatically shut behind us, the alley was quiet. I began to feel afraid again.

I was incredibly tired of being afraid.

Luna went over to the car, opened the rear door, and said something to whoever was inside. Whatever answer she got, it made her angry. She expostulated in another language.

There was further argument.

Luna stomped back to me. 'You have to be blindfolded,' she said, obviously certain I would take great offense.

'No problem,' I said, with a sweep of one hand to indicate how trifling a matter this was.

'You don't mind?'

'No. I understand, Luna. Everyone likes his privacy.'

'Okay, then.' She hurried back to the car and returned with a scarf in her hands, of green and peacock blue silk. She folded it as if we were going to play pin-the-tail, and tied it securely behind my head. 'Listen to me,' she said in my ear, 'these two are tough. You watch it.' Good. I wanted to be more frightened.

She rolled me over to the car and helped me in. I guess she wheeled the chair back to the door to await pickup; anyway, after a minute she got in the other side of the car.

There were two presences in the front seat. I felt them mentally, very delicately, and discovered both were shapeshifters; at least, they had the shapeshifter feel to their brains, the semiopaque snarly tangle I got from Sam and Luna. My boss, Sam, usually changes into a collie. I wondered what Luna preferred. There was a difference about these two, a pulsing sort of heaviness. The outline of their heads seemed subtly different, not exactly human.

There was only silence for a few minutes, while the car bumped out of the alley and drove through the night.

'Silent Shore Hotel, right?' said the driver. She sounded

kind of growly. Then I realized it was almost the full moon. Oh, hell. They had to change at the full moon. Maybe that was why Luna had kicked over the traces so readily at the Fellowship tonight, once it got dark. She had been made giddy by the emergence of the moon.

'Yes, please,' I said politely.

'Food that talks,' said the passenger. His voice was even closer to a growl.

I sure didn't like that, but had no idea how to respond. There was just as much for me to learn about shapeshifters as there was about vampires, apparently.

'You two can it,' Luna said. 'This is my guest.'

'Luna hangs with puppy chow,' said the passenger. I was beginning to really not like this guy.

'Smells more like hamburger to me,' said the driver. 'She's got a scrape or two, doesn't she, Luna?'

'Y'all are giving her a great impression of how civilized we are,' Luna snapped. 'Show some control. She's already had a bad night. She's got a broken bone, too.'

And the night wasn't even halfway over yet. I shifted the ice pack I was holding to my face. You can only stand so much freezing cold on your sinus cavity.

'Why'd Josephus have to send for freakin' werewolves?' Luna muttered into my ear. But I knew they'd heard; Sam heard everything, and he was by no means as powerful as a true werewolf. Or at least, that was my evaluation. To tell you the truth, until this moment, I hadn't been sure werewolves actually existed.

'I guess,' I said tactfully and audibly, 'he thought they could defend us best if we're attacked again.'

I could feel the creatures in the front seat prick up their ears. Maybe literally.

'We were doing okay,' Luna said indignantly. She twitched and fidgeted on the seat beside me like she'd drunk sixteen cups of coffee.

'Luna, we got rammed and your car got totaled. We were in the emergency room. "Okay" in what sense?'

Then I had to answer my own question. 'Hey, I'm sorry, Luna. You got me out of there when they would've killed me. It's not your fault they rammed us.'

'You two have a little roughhouse tonight?' asked the passenger, more civilly. He was spoiling for a fight. I didn't know if all werewolves were as feisty as this guy, or if it was just his nature.

'Yeah, with the fucking Fellowship,' Luna said, more than a trace of pride in her voice. 'They had this chick stuck in a cell. In a dungeon.'

'No shit?' asked the driver. She had the same hyper pulsing to her – well, I just had to call it her aura, for lack of a better word.

'No shit,' I said firmly. 'I work for a shifter, at home,' I added, to make conversation.

'No kidding? What's the business?'

'A bar. He owns a bar.'

'So, are you far from home?'

'Too far,' I said.

'This little bat saved your life tonight, for real?'

'Yes.' I was absolutely sincere about that. 'Luna saved my life.' Could they mean that literally? Did Luna shapeshift into a . . . oh golly.

'Way to go, Luna.' There was a fraction more respect in the deeper growly voice.

Luna found the praise pleasant, as she ought to, and she patted my hand. In a more agreeable silence, we drove maybe five more minutes, and then the driver said, 'The Silent Shore, coming up.'

I breathed out a long sigh of relief.

'There's a vampire out front, waiting.'

I almost ripped off the blindfold, before I realized that would be a really tacky thing to do. 'What does he look like?'

'Very tall, blond. Big head of hair. Friend or foe?'

I had to think about that. 'Friend,' I said, trying not to sound doubtful.

'Yum, yum,' said the driver. 'Does he cross-date?'

'I don't know. Want me to ask?'

Luna and the passenger both made gagging sounds. 'You can't date a deader!' Luna protested. 'Come on, Deb – uh, girl!'

'Oh, okay,' said the driver. 'Some of them aren't so bad. I'm pulling into the curb, little Milkbone.'

'That would be you,' Luna said in my ear.

We came to a stop, and Luna leaned over me to open my door. As I stepped out, guided and shoved by her hands, I heard an exclamation from the sidewalk. Quick as a wink Luna slammed the door shut behind me. The car full of shapeshifters pulled away from the curb with a screech of tires. A howl trailed behind it in the thick night air.

'Sookie?' said a familiar voice.

'Eric?'

I was fumbling with the blindfold, but Eric just grabbed the back of it and pulled. I had acquired a beautiful, if somewhat stained, scarf. The front of the hotel, with its heavy blank doors, was brilliantly lit in the dark light, and Eric looked remarkably pale. He was wearing an absolutely conventional navy blue pinstripe suit, of all things.

I was actually glad to see him. He grabbed my arm to keep me from wobbling and looked down at me with an unreadable face. Vampires were good at that. 'What has happened to you?' he said.

'I got . . . well, it's hard to explain in a second. Where is Bill?'

'First he went to the Fellowship of the Sun to get you out. But we heard along the way, from one of us who is a policeman, that you had been involved in an accident and gone to a hospital. So then he went to the hospital. At the hospital, he found out you had left outside the proper channels. No one would tell him anything, and he couldn't threaten them properly.' Eric looked extremely frustrated. The fact that he had to live within human laws was a constant irritant to Eric, though he greatly enjoyed the benefits. 'And then there was no trace of you. The doorman had only heard the once from you, mentally.'

'Poor Barry. Is he all right?'

'The richer for several hundred dollars, and quite happy about it,' Eric said in a dry voice. 'Now we just need Bill. What a lot of trouble you are, Sookie.' He pulled a cell phone out of his pocket and punched in a number. After what seemed a long time, it was answered.

'Bill, she is here. Some shapeshifters brought her in.' He looked me over. 'Battered, but walking.' He listened some more. 'Sookie, do you have your key?' he asked. I felt in the pocket of my skirt where I'd stuffed the plastic rectangle about a million years ago.

'Yes,' I said, and simply could not believe that something had gone right. 'Oh, wait! Did they get Farrell?'

Eric held up his hand to indicate he'd get to me in a minute. 'Bill, I'll take her up and start doctoring.' Eric's back stiffened. 'Bill,' he said and there was a world of threat in his voice. 'All right then. Good-bye.' He turned back to me as if there'd been no interruption.

'Yes, Farrell is safe. They raided the Fellowship.'

'Did . . . did many people get hurt?'

'Most of them were too frightened to approach. They scattered and went home. Farrell was in an underground cell with Hugo.'

'Oh, yes, Hugo. What happened to Hugo?'

My voice must have been very curious, because Eric looked at me sideways while we were progressing toward the elevator. He was matching my pace, and I was limping very badly.

'May I carry you?' he asked.

'Oh, I don't think so. I've made it this far.' I would've taken Bill up on the offer instantly. Barry, at the bell captain's desk, gave me a little wave. He would've run up to me if I hadn't been with Eric. I gave him what I hoped was a significant look, to say I'd talk to him again later, and then the elevator door dinged open and we got on. Eric punched the floor button and leaned against the mirrored wall of the car opposite me. In looking at him, I got a look at my own reflection.

'Oh, no,' I said, absolutely horrified. 'Oh, no.' My hair had been flattened by the wig, and then combed out with my fingers, so it was a disaster. My hands went up to it, helplessly and painfully, and my mouth shook with suppressed tears. And my hair was the least of it. I had visible bruises ranging from mild to severe on most of my body, and that was just the part you could see. My face was swollen and discolored on one side. There was a cut in the middle of the bruise over my cheekbone. My blouse was missing half its buttons, and my skirt was ripped and filthy. My right arm was ridged with bloody lumps.

I began crying. I looked so awful; it just broke what was left of my spirit.

To his credit, Eric didn't laugh, though he may have wanted to. 'Sookie, a bath and clean clothes and you will be put to rights,' he said as if he were talking to a child. To tell you the truth, I didn't feel much older at the moment.

'The werewolf thought you were cute,' I said, and sobbed some more. We stepped out of the elevator.

'The werewolf? Sookie, you have had adventures tonight.' He gathered me up like an armful of clothes and held me to him. I got his lovely suit jacket wet and snotty, and his pristine white shirt was spotless no more.

'Oh, I'm so sorry!' I held back and looked at his ensemble. I swabbed it with the scarf.

'Don't cry again,' he said hastily. 'Just don't start crying again, and I won't mind taking this to the cleaners. I won't even mind getting a whole new suit.'

I thought it was pretty amusing that Eric, the dread master vampire, was afraid of weeping women. I sniggered through the residual sobs.

'Something funny?' he asked.

I shook my head.

I slid my key in the door and we went in. 'I'll help you into the tub if you like, Sookie,' Eric offered.

'Oh, I don't think so.' A bath was what I wanted more than anything else in the world, that and to never put on these clothes again, but I sure wasn't taking a bath with Eric anywhere around.

'I'll bet you are a treat, naked,' Eric said, just to boost my spirits.

'You know it. I'm just as tasty as a big éclair,' I said, and carefully settled into a chair. 'Though at the moment I feel more like boudain.' Boudain is Cajun sausage, made of all kinds of things, none of them elegant. Eric pushed over a straight chair and lifted my leg to elevate the knee. I resettled the ice pack on it and closed my eyes. Eric called down to the desk for some tweezers, a bowl, and some antiseptic ointment, plus a rolling chair. The items arrived within ten minutes. This staff was good.

There was a small desk by one wall. Eric moved it over to the right side of my chair, lifted my arm, and laid it over the top of the desk. He switched on the lamp. After swabbing off my arm with a wet washcloth, Eric began removing the lumps. They were tiny pieces of glass from Luna's Outback's window. 'If you were an ordinary girl, I could glamour you and you wouldn't feel this,' he commented. 'Be brave.' It hurt like a bitch, and tears streamed down my face the whole time he worked. I worked hard keeping silent.

At last, I heard another key in the door, and I opened my eyes. Bill glanced at my face, winced, and then examined what Eric was doing. He nodded approvingly to Eric.

'How did this happen?' he asked, laying the lightest of touches on my face. He pulled the remaining chair closer and sat in it. Eric continued with his work.

I began to explain. I was so tired my voice faltered from time to time. When I got to the part about Gabe, I didn't have enough wits to tone the episode down, and I could see Bill was holding on to his temper with iron control. He gently lifted my blouse to peer at the ripped bra and the bruises on my chest, even with Eric there. (He looked, of course.)

'What happened to this Gabe?' Bill asked, very quietly.

'Well, he's dead,' I said. 'Godfrey killed him.'

'You saw Godfrey?' Eric leaned forward. He hadn't said a thing up till this point. He'd finished doctoring my arm. He'd put antibiotic ointment all over it as if he were protecting a baby from diaper rash.

'You were right, Bill. He was the one who kidnapped Farrell, though I didn't get any details. And Godfrey stopped Gabe from raping me. Though I got to say, I had gotten in a few good licks myself.'

'Don't brag,' said Bill with a small smile. 'So, the man is dead.' But he didn't seem satisfied.

'Godfrey was very good in stopping Gabe and helping me get out. Specially since he just wanted to think about meeting the dawn. Where is he?'

'He ran into the night during our attack on the Fellowship,' Bill explained. 'None of us could catch him.'

'What happened at the Fellowship?'

'I'll tell you, Sookie. But let's say good night to Eric, and I will tell you while I bathe you.'

'Okay,' I agreed. 'Good night, Eric. Thanks for the first aid.'

'I think those are the main points,' Bill said to Eric. 'If there is more, I'll come to your room later.'

'Good.' Eric looked at me, his eyes half open. He'd had a lick or two at my bloody arm while he doctored it and the taste seemed to have intoxicated him. 'Rest well, Sookie.'

'Oh,' I said, my eyes opening all the way suddenly. 'You know, we owe the shapeshifters.'

Both the vampires stared at me. 'Well, maybe not you guys, but I sure do.'

'Oh, they'll put in a claim,' Eric predicted. 'Those shapeshifters never perform any service for free. Good night, Sookie. I am glad you weren't raped and killed.' He gave his sudden flashing grin, and looked a lot more like himself.

'Gee, thanks a lot,' I said, my eyes closing again. 'Night.'

When the door had closed behind Eric, Bill gathered me up out of the chair and took me in the bathroom. It was about as big as most hotel bathrooms, but the tub was adequate. Bill ran it full of hot water and very carefully took off my clothes.

'Just toss 'em, Bill,' I said.

'Maybe I will, at that.' He was eyeing the bruises again, his lips pressed together in a straight line.

'Some of these are from the fall on the stairs, and some are from the car accident,' I explained.

'If Gabe wasn't dead I would find him and kill him,' Bill said, mostly to himself. 'I would take my time.' He lifted me as easily as if I were a baby and put me in the bath, and began washing me with a cloth and a bar of soap.

'My hair is so nasty.'

'Yes, it is, but we may have to take care of your hair in the morning. You need sleep.'

Beginning with my face, Bill gently scrubbed me all the way down. The water became discolored with dirt and old blood. He checked my arm thoroughly, to make sure Eric had gotten all the glass. Then he emptied the tub and refilled it, while I shivered. This time, I got clean. After I moaned about my hair a second time, he gave in. He wet my head and shampooed my hair, rinsing it laboriously. There is nothing more wonderful than feeling head-to-toe clean after you've been filthy, having a comfortable bed with clean sheets, being able to sleep in it in safety.

'Tell me about what happened at the Fellowship,' I said as he carried me to the bed. 'Keep me company.'

Bill inserted me under the sheet and crawled in the other side. He slid his arm under my head and scooted close. I carefully touched my forehead to his chest and rubbed it.

'By the time we got there, it was like a disrupted anthill,' he said. 'The parking lot was full of cars and people, and more kept arriving for the – all-night sleep-over?'

'Lock-in,' I murmured, carefully turning on my right side to burrow against him.

'There was a certain amount of turmoil when we arrived. Almost all of them piled into their cars and left as fast as traffic would allow. Their leader, Newlin, tried to deny us entrance to the Fellowship hall – surely that was a church at one time? – and he told us we would burst into flames if we entered, because we were the damned.' Bill snorted. 'Stan picked him up and set him aside. And into the church we went, Newlin and his woman trailing right behind us. Not a one of us burst into flames, which seemed to shake up the people a great deal.'

'I'll bet,' I mumbled into his chest.

'Barry told us that when he communicated with you, he had the sense you were "down" – below ground level. He thought he picked up the word "stairs" from you. There were six of us – Stan, Joseph Velasquez, Isabel, and others – and it took us perhaps six minutes to eliminate all the possibilities and find the stairs.'

'What did you do about the door?' It had had stout locks, I remembered.

'We ripped it from its hinges.'

'Oh.' Well, that would provide quick access, sure enough.

'I thought you were still down there, of course. When I found the room with the dead man, who had his pants open . . .' He paused a long moment. 'I was sure you had been there. I could smell you in the air still. There was a smear of blood on him, your blood, and I found other traces of it around. I was very worried.'

I patted him. I felt too tired and weak to pat very vigorously, but it was the only consolation I had to offer at the moment.

'Sookie,' he said very carefully, 'is there anything more you want to tell me?'

I was too sleepy to figure this one through. 'No,' I said and yawned. 'I think I pretty much covered my adventures earlier.'

'I thought maybe since Eric was in the room earlier, you wouldn't want to say everything?'

I finally heard the other shoe drop. I kissed his chest, over his heart. 'Godfrey really was in time.'

There was a long silence. I looked up to see Bill's face set so rigidly that he looked like a statue. His dark eyelashes stood out against his pallor with amazing clarity. His dark eyes seemed bottomless. 'Tell me the rest,' I said.

'Then we went farther into the bomb shelter and found the larger room, along with an extended area full of supplies – food and guns – where it was obvious another vampire had been staying.'

I hadn't seen that part of the bomb shelter, and I certainly had no plans to revisit it to view what I'd missed.

'In the second cell we found Farrell and Hugo.'

'Was Hugo alive?'

'Just barely.' Bill kissed my forehead. 'Luckily for Hugo, Farrell likes his sex with younger men.'

'Maybe that was why Godfrey chose Farrell to abduct, when he decided to make an example of another sinner.'

Bill nodded. 'That is what Farrell said. But he had been without sex and blood for a long time, and he was hungry in every sense. Without the silver manacles, Hugo would have . . . had a bad time. Even with silver on his wrists and ankles, Farrell was able to feed from Hugo.'

'Did you know that Hugo was the traitor?'

'Farrell heard your conversation with him.'

'How – oh, right, vampire hearing. Stupid me.'

'Farrell would also like to know what you did to Gabe to make him scream.'

'Clapped him over the ears.' I cupped one hand to show him.

'Farrell was delighted. This Gabe was one of those men who enjoys power over others. He subjected Farrell to many indignities.'

'Farrell's just lucky he's not a woman,' I said. 'Where is Hugo now?'

'He is somewhere safe.'

'Safe for who?'

'Safe for vampires. Away from the media. They would enjoy Hugo's story all too much.'

'What are they gonna do with him?'

'That's for Stan to decide.'

'Remember the deal we had with Stan? If humans are found guilty by evidence of mine, they don't get killed.'

Bill obviously didn't want to debate me on this now. His face shut down. 'Sookie, you have to go to sleep now. We'll talk about it when you get up.'

'But by then he may be dead.'

'Why should you care?'

'Because that was the deal! I know Hugo is a shit, and I hate him, too, but I feel sorry for him, and I don't think I can be implicated in his death and live with a clear conscience.'

'Sookie, he will still be alive when you get up. We'll talk about it then.'

I felt sleep pulling me under like the undertow of the surf. It was hard to believe it was only two o'clock in the morning.

'Thanks for coming after me.'

Bill said, after a pause, 'First you weren't at the Fellowship, just traces of your blood and dead rapist. When I found you weren't at the hospital, that you had been spirited out of there somehow . . .'

'Mmmmh?'

'I was very, very scared. No one had any idea where you were. In fact, while I stood there talking to the nurse who admitted you, your name went off the computer screen.'

I was impressed. Those shapeshifters were organized to an amazing degree. 'Maybe I should send Luna some flowers,' I said, hardly able to get the words out of my mouth.

Bill kissed me, a very satisfying kiss, and that was the last thing I remembered.

Chapter 7

I turned over laboriously and peered at the illuminated clock on the bedside table. It was not yet dawn, but dawn would come soon. Bill was in his coffin already: the lid was closed. Why was I awake? I thought it over.

There was something I had to do. Part of me stood back in amazement at my own stupidity as I pulled on some shorts and a T-shirt and slid my feet into sandals. I looked even worse in the mirror, to which I gave only a sideways glance. I stood with my back to it to brush my hair. To my astonishment and pleasure, my purse was sitting on the table in the sitting room. Someone had retrieved it from the Fellowship headquarters the night before. I stuck my plastic key in it and made my way painfully down the silent halls.

Barry was not on duty anymore, and his replacement was too well trained to ask me what the hell I was doing going around looking like something a train had dragged in. He got me a cab and I told the driver where I needed to go. The driver looked at me in the rearview mirror. 'Wouldn't you rather go to a hospital?' he suggested uneasily.

'No. I've already been.' That hardly seemed to reassure him.

'Those vampires treat you so bad, why do you hang around them?'

'People did this to me,' I said. 'Not vampires.'

We drove off. Traffic was light, it being nearly dawn on a Sunday morning. It only took fifteen minutes to get to the same place I'd been the night before, the Fellowship parking lot.

'Can you wait for me?' I asked the driver. He was a man in his sixties, grizzled and missing a front tooth. He wore a plaid shirt with snaps instead of buttons.

'I reckon I can do that,' he said. He pulled a Louis L'Amour western out from under his seat and switched on a dome light to read.

Under the glare of the sodium lights, the parking lot showed no visible traces of the events of the night before. There were only a couple of vehicles remaining, and I figured they'd been abandoned the night before. One of these cars was probably Gabe's. I wondered if Gabe had had a family; I hoped not. For one thing, he was such a sadist he must have made their lives miserable, and for another, for the rest of their lives they'd have to wonder how and why he'd died. What would Steve and Sarah Newlin do now? Would there be enough members left of their Fellowship to carry on? Presumably the guns and provisions were still in the church. Maybe they'd been stockpiling against the apocalypse.

Out of the dark shadows next to the church a figure emerged. Godfrey. He was still bare-chested, and he still looked like a fresh-faced sixteen. Only the alien character of the tattoos and his eyes gave the lie to his body.

'I came to watch,' I said, when he was close to me, though maybe 'bear witness' would have been more accurate.

'Why?'

'I owe it to you.'

'I am an evil creature.'

'Yes, you are.' There just wasn't any getting around that. 'But you did a good thing, saving me from Gabe.'

'By killing one more man? My conscience hardly knew the difference. There have been so many. At least I spared you some humiliation.'

His voice grabbed at my heart. The growing light in the sky was still so faint that the parking lot security lights remained on, and by their glow I examined the young, young face.

All of a sudden, absurdly, I began to cry.

'That's nice,' Godfrey said. His voice was already remote. 'Someone to cry for me at the end. I had hardly expected that.' He stepped back to a safe distance.

And then the sun rose.

When I got back in the cab, the driver stowed away his book.

'They have a fire going over there?' he asked. 'I thought I saw some smoke. I almost came to see what was happening.'

'It's out now,' I said.

I mopped at my face for a mile or so, and then I stared out the window as the stretches of city emerged from the night.

Back at the hotel, I let myself into our room again. I pulled off my shorts, lay down on the bed, and just as I was preparing myself for a long period of wakefulness, I fell deep asleep.

Bill woke me up at sundown, in his favorite way. My T-shirt was pushed up, and his dark hair brushed my chest. It was like waking up halfway down the road, so to speak; his mouth was sucking so tenderly on half of what he told me was the most beautiful pair of breasts in the world. He was very careful of his fangs, which were fully down. That was only one of the evidences of his arousal. 'Do you feel up to doing this, enjoying it, if I am very, very careful?' he whispered against my ear.

'If you treat me like I was made of glass,' I murmured, knowing that he could.

'But that doesn't feel like glass,' he said, his hand moving gently. 'That feels warm. And wet.'

I gasped.

'That much? Am I hurting you?' His hand moved more forcefully.

'Bill' was all I could say. I put my lips on his, and his tongue began a familiar rhythm.

'Lie on your side,' he whispered. 'I will take care of everything.'

And he did.

'Why were you partly dressed?' he asked, later. He'd gotten up to get a bottle of blood from the refrigerator in the room, and he'd warmed it in the microwave. He hadn't taken any of my blood, in consideration of my weakened state.

'I went to see Godfrey die.'

His eyes glowed down at me. 'What?'

'Godfrey met the dawn.' The phrase I had once considered embarrassingly melodramatic flowed quite naturally from my mouth.

There was a long silence.

'How did you know he would? How did you know where?'

I shrugged as much as you can while you're lying in a bed. 'I just figured he'd stick with his original plan. He seemed pretty set on it. And he'd saved my life. It was the least I could do.'

'Did he show courage?'

I met Bill's eyes. 'He died very bravely. He was eager to go.'

I had no idea what Bill was thinking. 'We have to go see Stan,' he said. 'We'll tell him.'

'Why do we have to go see Stan again?' If I hadn't been such a mature woman, I would've pouted. As it was, Bill gave me one of those looks.

'You have to tell him your part, so he can be convinced we've performed our service. Also, there's the matter of Hugo.'

That was enough to make me gloomy. I was so sore the idea of any more clothes than necessary touching my skin made me feel ill, so I pulled on a long sleeveless taupe dress made out of a soft knit and slid my feet carefully into sandals, and that was my outfit. Bill brushed my hair and put in my earrings for me, since raising my arms was uncomfortable, and he decided I needed a gold chain. I looked like I was going to a party at the outpatient ward for battered women. Bill called down for a rental car to be brought around. When the car had arrived in the underground garage, I had no idea. I didn't even know who had arranged for it. Bill drove. I didn't look out the window anymore. I was sick of Dallas.

When we got to the house on Green Valley Road it looked as quiet as it had two nights ago. But after we'd been admitted, I found it was abuzz with vampires. We'd arrived in the midst of a welcome-home party for Farrell, who was standing in the living room with his arm around a handsome young man who might be all of eighteen. Farrell had a bottle of TrueBlood O negative in one hand, and his date had a Coke. The vampire looked almost as rosy as the boy.

Farrell had never actually seen me, so he was delighted to make my acquaintance. He was clad from head to toe in western regalia, and as he bowed over my hand, I expected to hear spurs clink.

'You are so lovely,' he said extravagantly, waving the bottle of synthetic blood, 'that if I slept with women, you would receive my undivided attention for a week. I know you are self-conscious about your bruises, but they only set off your beauty.'

I couldn't help laughing. Not only was I walking like I was about eighty, my face was black-and-blue on the left side.

'Bill Compton, you are one lucky vampire,' Farrell told Bill.

'I am well aware of that,' Bill said, smiling, though somewhat coolly.

'She is brave and beautiful!'

'Thanks, Farrell. Where's Stan?' I decided to break this stream of praise. Not only did it make Bill antsy, but Farrell's young companion was getting entirely too curious. My intention was to relate this story once again, and only once.

'He's in the dining room,' the young vampire said, the one who'd brought poor Bethany into the dining room when we'd been here before. This must be Joseph

Velasquez. He was maybe five foot eight, and his Hispanic ancestry gave him the toast-colored complexion and dark eyes of a don, while his vampire state gave him an unblinking stare and the instant willingness to do damage. He was scanning the room, waiting for trouble. I decided he was sort of the sergeant at arms of the nest. 'He will be glad to see both of you.'

I glanced around at all the vampires and the sprinkling of humans in the large rooms of the house. I didn't see Eric. I wondered if he'd gone back to Shreveport. 'Where's Isabel?' I asked Bill, keeping my voice quiet.

'Isabel is being punished,' he said, almost too softly to hear. He didn't want to talk about this any louder, and when Bill thought that was a wise idea, I knew I better shut up. 'She brought a traitor into the nest, and she has to pay a price for that.'

'But –'

'Shhh.'

We came into the dining room to find it as crowded as the living room. Stan was in the same chair, wearing virtually the same outfit he had been wearing last time I saw him. He stood up when we entered, and from the way he did this, I understood this was supposed to mark our status as important.

'Miss Stackhouse,' he said formally, shaking my hand with great care. 'Bill.' Stan examined me with his eyes, their washed-out blue not missing a detail of my injuries. His glasses had been mended with Scotch tape. Stan was nothing if not thorough with his disguise. I thought I'd send him a pocket-protector for Christmas.

'Please tell me what happened to you yesterday, omitting nothing,' Stan said.

This reminded me irresistibly of Archie Goodwin reporting to Nero Wolfe. 'I'll bore Bill,' I said, hoping to get out of this recitation.

'Bill will not mind being bored for a little.'

There was no getting around this. I sighed, and began with Hugo picking me up from the Silent Shore Hotel. I tried to leave Barry's name out of my narrative, since I didn't know how he'd feel about being known by the vampires of Dallas. I just called him 'a bellboy at the hotel.' Of course, they could learn who he was if they tried.

When I got to the part where Gabe sent Hugo into Farrell's cell and then tried to rape me, my lips yanked up in a tight grin. My face felt so taut that I thought it might crack.

'Why does she do that?' Stan asked Bill, as though I weren't there.

'When she is tense . . .' Bill said.

'Oh.' Stan looked at me even more thoughtfully. I reached up and began to pull my hair into a ponytail. Bill handed me an elastic band from his pocket, and with considerable discomfort, I held the hair in a tight hank so I could twist the band around it three times.

When I told Stan about the help the shapeshifters had given me, he leaned forward. He wanted to know more than I told, but I would not give any names away. He was intensely thoughtful after I told him about being dropped off at the hotel. I didn't know whether to include Eric or not; I left him out, completely. He was supposed to be from California. I amended my narrative to say I'd gone up to our room to wait for Bill.

And then I told him about Godfrey.

To my amazement, Stan could not seem to absorb Godfrey's death. He made me repeat the story. He swiveled in his chair to face the other way while I spoke. Behind his back, Bill gave me a reassuring caress. When Stan turned back to us, he was wiping his eyes with a red-stained handkerchief. So it was true that vampires could cry. And it was true that vampire tears were bloody.

I cried right along with him. For his centuries of molesting and killing children, Godfrey had deserved to die. I wondered how many humans were in jail for crimes Godfrey had committed. But Godfrey had helped me, and Godfrey had carried with him the most tremendous load of guilt and grief I'd ever encountered.

'What resolution and courage,' Stan said admiringly. He hadn't been grieved at all, but lost in admiration. 'It makes me weep.' He said this in such a way that I knew it was meant to be a great tribute. 'After Bill identified Godfrey the other night, I made some inquiries and found he had belonged to a nest in San Francisco. His nest mates will be grieved to hear of this. And of his betrayal of Farrell. But his courage in keeping his word, in fulfilling his plan!' It seemed to overwhelm Stan.

I just ached all over. I rummaged in my purse for a small bottle of Tylenol, and poured two out in my palm. At Stan's gesture, the young vampire brought me a glass of water, and I said, 'Thank you,' to his surprise.

'Thank you for your efforts,' Stan said quite abruptly, as if he'd suddenly recalled his manners. 'You have done the job we hired you to do, and more. Thanks to you we discovered and freed Farrell in time, and I'm sorry you sustained so much damage in the process.'

That sounded mighty like dismissal.

'Excuse me,' I said, sliding forward in the chair. Bill made a sudden movement behind me, but I disregarded him.

Stan raised his light eyebrows at my temerity. 'Yes? Your check will be mailed to your representative in Shreveport, as per our agreement. Please stay with us this evening as we celebrate Farrell's return.'

'Our agreement was that if what I discovered resulted in a human being found at fault, that human would not be punished by the vampires but would be turned over to the police. For the court system to deal with. Where is Hugo?'

Stan's eyes slid from my face to focus on Bill's behind me. He seemed to be silently asking Bill why he couldn't control his human better.

'Hugo and Isabel are together,' said Stan cryptically.

I *so* didn't want to know what that meant. But I was honor-bound to see this through. 'So you are not going to honor your agreement?' I said, knowing that was a real challenge to Stan.

There should be an adage, proud as a vampire. They all are, and I'd pinked Stan in his pride. The implication that he was dishonorable enraged the vampire. I almost backed down, his face grew so scary. He really had nothing human left about him after a few seconds. His lips drew away from his teeth, his fangs extended, and his body hunched and seemed to elongate.

After a moment he stood, and with a curt little jerk of his hand, indicated I should follow him. Bill helped me up, and we trailed after Stan as he walked deeper into the house. There must have been six bedrooms in the place, and all the doors to them were closed. From behind one door came the unmistakable sounds of sex. To my relief, we passed that door by. We went up the stairs, which was quite uncomfortable for me. Stan never looked back and never slowed down. He went up the stairs at exactly the same pace at which he walked. He stopped at a door that looked like all the others. He unlocked it. He stood aside and gestured to me to go in.

That was something I didn't want to do – oh, so much. But I had to. I stepped forward and looked in.

Except for the dark blue wall-to-wall, the room was bare. Isabel was chained to the wall on one side of the room – with silver, of course. Hugo was on the other. He was chained, too. They were both awake, and they both looked at the doorway, naturally.

Isabel nodded as if we'd met in the mall, though she was naked. I saw that her wrists and ankles were padded to prevent the silver from burning her, though the chains would still keep her weak.

Hugo was naked, too. He could not take his eyes off Isabel. He barely glanced at me to see who I was before his gaze returned to her. I tried not to be embarrassed, because that seemed such a petty consideration; but I think it was the first time I'd seen another naked adult in my life, besides Bill.

Stan said, 'She cannot feed off him, though she is hungry. He cannot have sex with her, though he is addicted. This is their punishment, for months. What would happen to Hugo in human courts?'

I considered. What had Hugo actually done that was indictable?

He'd deceived the vampires in that he'd been in the Dallas nest under false pretenses. That is, he actually loved Isabel, but he'd betrayed her compadres. Hmmm. No law about that.

'He bugged the dining room,' I said. That was illegal. At least, I thought it was.

'How long in jail would he get for that?' Stan asked.

Good question. Not much, was my guess. A human jury might feel bugging a vampire hangout was even justified. I sighed, sufficient answer for Stan.

'What other time would Hugo serve?' he asked.

'He got me to the Fellowship under false pretenses . . . not illegal. He . . . well, he . . .'

'Exactly.'

Hugo's infatuated gaze never shifted from Isabel.

Hugo had caused and abetted evil, just as surely as Godfrey had committed evil.

'How long will you keep them there?' I asked.

Stan shrugged. 'Three or four months. We will feed Hugo, of course. Not Isabel.'

'And then?'

'We'll unchain him first. He will get a day's head start.'

Bill's hand clamped down on my wrist. He didn't want me to ask any more questions.

Isabel looked at me and nodded. This seemed fair to her, she was saying. 'All right,' I said, holding my palms forward in the 'Stop' position. 'All right.' And I turned and made my way slowly and carefully down the stairs.

I had lost some integrity, but for the life of me, I couldn't figure out what I could do differently. The more I tried to think about it, the more confused I got. I am not used to thinking through moral issues. Things are bad to do, or they aren't.

Well, there was a gray area. That's where a few things fell, like sleeping with Bill though we weren't married or telling Arlene her dress looked good, when in fact it made her look like hell. Actually, I couldn't marry Bill. It wasn't legal. But then, he hadn't asked me.

My thoughts wandered in a dithery circle around the miserable couple in the upstairs bedroom. To my amazement, I felt much sorrier for Isabel than for Hugo. Hugo, after all, was guilty of active evil. Isabel was only guilty of negligence.

I had a lot of time to maunder on and on through similar dead-end thought patterns, since Bill was having a rip-roaring good time at the party. I'd only been to a mixed vampire and human party once or twice before and it was a mixture that was still uneasy after two years of legally recognized vampirism. Open drinking – that is, bloodsucking – from humans was absolutely illegal and I am here to tell you that in Dallas's vampire headquarters, that law was strictly observed. From time to time, I saw a couple vanish for a while upstairs, but all the humans seemed to come back in good health. I know, because I counted and watched.

Bill had mainstreamed for so many months that apparently it was a real treat for him to get together with other vampires. So he was deep in conversation with this vamp or that, reminiscing about Chicago in the twenties or investment opportunities in various vampire holdings around the world. I was so shaky physically that I was content to sit on a soft couch and watch, sipping from time to time at my Screwdriver. The bartender was a pleasant young man, and we talked bars for a little while. I should have been enjoying my break from waiting tables at Merlotte's, but I would gladly have dressed in my uniform and taken orders. I wasn't used to big changes in my routine.

Then a woman maybe a little younger than me plopped

down on the couch beside me. Turned out she was dating the vampire who acted as sergeant at arms, Joseph Velasquez, who'd gone to the Fellowship Center with Bill the night before. Her name was Trudi Pfeiffer. Trudi had hair done in deep red spikes, a pierced nose and tongue, and macabre makeup, including black lipstick. She told me proudly its color was called Grave Rot. Her jeans were so low I wondered how she got up and down in them. Maybe she wore them so low-cut to show off her navel ring. Her knit top was cropped very short. The outfit I'd worn the night the maenad had gotten me paled in comparison. So, there was lots of Trudi to see.

When you talked to her, she wasn't as bizarre as her appearance led you to believe. Trudi was a college student. I discovered, through absolutely legitimate listening, that she believed herself to be waving the red flag at the bull, by dating Joseph. The bull was her parents, I gathered.

'They would even rather I dated someone *black*,' she told me proudly.

I tried to look appropriately impressed. 'They really hate the dead scene, huh?'

'Oh, do they ever.' She nodded several times and waved her black fingernails extravagantly. She was drinking Dos Equis. 'My mom always says, "Can't you date someone *alive*?"' We both laughed.

'So, how are you and Bill?' She waggled her eyebrows up and down to indicate how significant the question was.

'You mean . . .?'

'How's he in bed? Joseph is un-fucking-believable.'

I can't say I was surprised, but I was dismayed. I cast around in my mind for a minute. 'I'm glad for you,' I finally said. If she'd been my good friend Arlene, I might have winked and smiled, but I wasn't about to discuss my sex life with a total stranger, and I really didn't want to know about her and Joseph.

Trudi lurched up to get another beer, and remained in conversation with the bartender. I shut my eyes in relief and weariness, and felt the couch depress beside me. I cut my gaze to the right to see what new companion I had. Eric. Oh, great.

'How are you?' he asked.

'Better than I look.' That wasn't true.

'You've seen Hugo and Isabel?'

'Yes.' I looked at my hands folded in my lap.

'Appropriate, don't you think?'

I thought that Eric was trying to provoke me.

'In a way, yes,' I said. 'Assuming Stan sticks to his word.'

'You didn't say that to him, I hope.' But Eric looked only amused.

'No, I didn't. Not in so many words. You're all so damn proud.'

He looked surprised. 'Yes, I guess that's true.'

'Did you just come to check up on me?'

'To Dallas?'

I nodded.

'Yes.' He shrugged. He was wearing a knit shirt in a pretty tan-and-blue pattern, and the shrug made his shoulders look massive. 'We are loaning you out for the first time. I wanted to see that things went smoothly without being here in my official capacity.'

'Do you think Stan knows who you are?'

He looked interested in the idea. 'It's not far-fetched,' he said at last. 'He would probably have done the same thing in my place.'

'Do you think from now on, you could just let me stay at home, and leave me and Bill alone?' I asked.

'No. You are too useful,' he said. 'Besides, I'm hoping that the more you see me, the more I'll grow on you.'

'Like a fungus?'

He laughed, but his eyes were fixed on me in a way that meant business. Oh, hell.

'You look especially luscious in that knit dress with nothing underneath,' Eric said. 'If you left Bill and came to me of your own free will, he would accept that.'

'But I'm not going to do any such thing,' I said, and then something caught at the edges of my consciousness.

Eric started to say something else to me, but I put my hand across his mouth. I moved my head from side to side, trying to get the best reception; that's the best way I can explain it.

'Help me up,' I said.

Without a word, Eric stood and gently pulled me to my feet. I could feel my eyebrows draw together.

They were all around us. They circled the house.

Their brains were wound up to fever pitch. If Trudi hadn't been babbling earlier, I might have heard them as they crept up to circle the house.

'Eric,' I said, trying to catch as many thoughts as I could, hearing a countdown, oh, God!

'Hit the floor!' I yelled at the top of my lungs.

Every vampire obeyed.

So when the Fellowship opened fire, it was the humans that died.

Chapter 8

A yard away, Trudi was cut down by a shotgun blast. The dyed dark red of her hair turned another shade of red and her open eyes stared at me forever. Chuck, the bartender, was only wounded, since the structure of the bar itself offered him some protection.

Eric was lying on top of me. Given my sore condition, that was very painful, and I started to shove at him. Then I realized that if he were hit with bullets, he would most likely survive. But I wouldn't. So I accepted his shelter gratefully for the horrible minutes of the first wave of the attack, when rifles and shotguns and handguns were fired into the suburban mansion over and over.

Instinctively, I shut my eyes while the blasting lasted. Glass shattered, vampires roared, humans screamed. The noise battered at me, just as the tidal wave of scores of brains at high gear washed over me. When it began to taper off, I looked up into Eric's eyes. Incredibly, he was excited. He smiled at me. 'I knew I'd get on top of you somehow,' he said.

'Are you trying to make me mad so I'll forget how scared I am?'

'No, I'm just opportunistic.'

I wiggled, trying to get out from under him, and he said, 'Oh, do that again. It felt great.'

'Eric, that girl I was just talking to is about three feet away from us with part of her head missing.'

'Sookie,' he said, suddenly serious, 'I've been dead for a few hundred years. I am used to it. But she is not quite gone. There is a spark. Do you want me to bring her over?'

I was shocked speechless. How could I make that decision?

And while I thought about it, he said, 'She is gone.'

While I stared up at him, the silence became complete. The only noise in the house was the sobbing of Farrell's wounded date, who was pressing both hands to his reddened thigh. From outside came the remote sounds of vehicles pulling out in a hurry up and down the quiet suburban street. The attack was over. I seemed to be having trouble breathing, and figuring out what I should do next. Surely there was something, some action, I should be taking?

This was as close to war as I would ever come.

The room was full of the survivors' screams and the vampires' howls of rage. Bits of stuffing from the couch and chairs floated in the air like snow. There was broken glass on everything and the heat of the night poured into the room. Several of the vampires were already up and giving chase, Joseph Velasquez among them, I noticed.

'No excuse to linger,' Eric said with a mock sigh, and lifted off of me. He looked down at himself. 'My shirts always get ruined when I am around you.'

'Oh shit, Eric.' I got to my knees with clumsy haste. 'You're bleeding. You got hit. Bill! Bill!' My hair was slithering around my shoulders as I turned from side to side searching the room. The last time I'd noticed him he'd been talking to a black-haired vampire with a pronounced widow's peak. She'd looked something like Snow White, to me. Now I half-stood to search the floor and I saw her sprawled close to a window. Something was protruding from her chest. The window had been hit by a shotgun blast, and some splinters had flown into the room. One of them had pierced her chest and killed her. Bill was not in sight, among the living or the dead.

Eric pulled off his sodden shirt and looked down at his shoulder. 'The bullet is right inside the wound, Sookie,' Eric said, through clenched teeth. 'Suck it out.'

'What?' I gaped at him.

'If you don't suck it out, it will heal inside my flesh. If you are so squeamish, go get a knife and cut.'

'But I can't do that.' My tiny party purse had a pocketknife inside, but I had no idea where I'd put it down, and I couldn't gather my thoughts to search.

He bared his teeth at me. 'I took this bullet for you. You can get it out for me. You are no coward.'

I forced myself to steady. I used his discarded shirt as a swab. The bleeding was slowing, and by peering into the torn flesh, I could just see the bullet. If I'd had long fingernails like Trudi, I'd have been able to get it out, but my fingers are short and blunt, and my nails are clipped close. I sighed in resignation.

The phrase 'biting the bullet' took on a whole new meaning as I bent to Eric's shoulder.

Eric gave a long moan as I sucked, and I felt the bullet pop into my mouth. He'd been right. The rug could hardly be stained any worse than it already was, so though it made me feel like a real heathen, I spat the bullet onto the floor along with most of the blood in my mouth. But some of it, inevitably, I swallowed. His shoulder was already healing. 'This room reeks of blood,' he whispered.

'Well, there,' I said, and looked up. 'That was the grossest –'

'Your lips are bloody.' He seized my face in both hands and kissed me.

It's hard not to respond when a master of the art of kissing is laying one on you. And I might have let myself enjoy it – well, enjoy it more – if I hadn't been so worried about Bill; because let's face it, brushes with death have that effect. You want to reaffirm the fact that you're alive. Though vampires actually aren't, it seems they are no more immune to that syndrome than humans, and Eric's libido was up because of the blood in the room.

But I was worried about Bill, and I was shocked by the violence, so after a long hot moment of forgetting the horror around me, I pulled away. Eric's lips were bloody now. He licked them slowly. 'Go look for Bill,' he said in a thick voice.

I glanced at his shoulder again, to see the hole had begun to close. I picked up the bullet off the carpet, tacky as it was with blood, and wrapped it in a scrap from Eric's shirt. It seemed like a good memento, at the time. I really don't know what I was thinking. There were still the injured and dead on the floor in the room, but most of those who were still alive had help from other humans or from two vampires who hadn't joined in the chase.

Sirens were sounding in the distance.

The beautiful front door was splintered and pitted. I stood to one side to open it, just in case there was a lone vigilante in the yard, but nothing happened. I peered around the doorframe.

'Bill?' I called. 'Are you okay?'

Just then he sauntered back in the yard looking positively rosy.

'Bill,' I said, feeling old and grim and gray. A dull horror, that really was just a deep disappointment, filled the pit of my stomach.

He stopped in his tracks.

'They fired at us and killed some of us,' he said. His fangs gleamed, and he was shiny with excitement.

'You just killed somebody.'

'To defend us.'

'To get vengeance.'

There was a clear difference between the two, in my mind, at that moment. He seemed nonplussed.

'You didn't even wait to see if I was okay,' I said. Once a vampire, always a vampire. Tigers can't change their stripes. You can't teach an old dog new tricks. I heard every warning anyone had ever fed me, in the warm drawl of home.

I turned and went back into the house, walking obliviously through the bloodstains and chaos and mess as if I saw such things every day. Some of the things I saw I didn't even register I'd seen, until the next week when my brain would suddenly throw out a picture for my viewing: maybe a closeup of a shattered skull, or a spouting artery. What was important to me at the moment was that I find my purse. I found that purse in the second place I looked. While Bill fussed with the wounded so he wouldn't have to talk to me, I walked out of that house and got in that rental car and, despite my anxiety, I drove. Being at this house was worse than the fear of big city traffic. I pulled away from the house right before the police got there.

After I'd driven a few blocks, I parked in front of a library and extricated the map from the glove compartment. Though it took twice as long as it should have, since my brain was so shell-shocked it was almost not functioning, I figured out how to get to the airport.

And that's where I went. I followed the signs that said RENTAL CARS and I parked the car and left the keys in it and walked away. I got a seat on the next flight to Shreveport, which was leaving within the hour. I thanked God I had my own credit card.

Since I'd never done it before, it took me a few minutes to figure out the pay phone. I was lucky enough to get hold of Jason, who said he'd meet me at the airport.

I was home in bed by early morning.

I didn't start crying until the next day.

Chapter 9

We'd fought before, Bill and I. I'd gotten fed up before, tired of the vampirey stuff I had to learn to accommodate, frightened of getting in deeper. Sometimes, I just wanted to see humans for a while.

So for over three weeks, that was what I did. I didn't call Bill; he didn't call me. I knew he was back from Dallas because he left my suitcase on my front porch. When I unpacked it, I found a black velvet jeweler's box tucked in the side pocket. I wish I'd had the strength to keep from opening it, but I didn't. Inside was a pair of topaz earrings, and a note that said, 'To go with your brown dress.' Which meant the taupe knit thing I'd worn to the vampires' headquarters. I stuck my tongue out at the box, and drove over to his house that afternoon to leave it in his mailbox. He'd finally gone out and bought me a present, and here I had to return it.

I didn't even try to 'think things through.' I figured my brain would clear up in a while, and then I would know what to do.

I did read the papers. The vampires of Dallas and their

human friends were now martyrs, which probably suited Stan down to the ground. The Dallas Midnight Massacre was being touted in all the newsmagazines as the perfect example of a hate crime. Legislatures were being pressured to pass all kinds of laws that would never make it onto the books, but it made people feel better to think they might; laws that would provide vampire-owned buildings with federal protection, laws that would permit vampires to hold certain elected positions (though no one yet suggested a vampire could run for the U.S. Senate or serve as a representative). There was even a motion in the Texas legislature to appoint a vampire as legal executioner of the state. After all, a Senator Garza was quoted as saying, 'Death by vampire bite is at least supposed to be painless, and the vampire receives nutrition from it.'

I had news for Senator Garza. Vampire bites were only pleasant by the will of the vampire. If the vampire didn't glamour you first, a serious vampire bite (as opposed to a love nip) hurt like hell.

I wondered if Senator Garza was related to Luna, but Sam told me that 'Garza' was as common among Americans of Mexican descent as 'Smith' was among Americans of English stock.

Sam didn't ask why I wanted to know. That made me feel a little forlorn, because I was used to feeling important to Sam. But he was preoccupied these days, on the job and off. Arlene said she thought he was dating someone, which was a first, as far as any of us could remember. Whoever she was, none of us got to see her, which was strange in and of itself. I tried to tell him about the shapeshifters of Dallas, but he just smiled and found an excuse to go do something else.

My brother, Jason, dropped by the house for lunch one day. It wasn't like it had been when my grandmother was alive. Gran would have a huge meal on the table at lunchtime, and then we'd just eat sandwiches at night. Jason had come by pretty frequently then; Gran had been an excellent cook. I managed to serve him meatloaf sandwiches and potato salad (though I didn't tell him it was from the store), and I had some peach tea fixed, which was lucky.

'What's with you and Bill?' he asked bluntly, when he was through. He'd been real good about not asking on the drive back from the airport.

'I got mad at him,' I said.

'Why?'

'He broke a promise to me,' I said. Jason was trying hard to act like a big brother, and I should try to accept his concern instead of getting mad. It occurred to me, not for the first time, that possibly I had a pretty hot temper. Under some circumstances. I locked my sixth sense down firmly, so I would only hear what Jason was actually saying.

'He's been seen over in Monroe.'

I took a deep breath. 'With someone else?'

'Yes.'

'Who?'

'You're not going to believe this. Portia Bellefleur.'

I couldn't have been more surprised if Jason had told me Bill had been dating Hillary Clinton (though Bill *was* a Democrat). I stared at my brother as if he'd suddenly announced he was Satan. The only things Portia Bellefleur and I had in common were a birthplace, female organs, and long hair. 'Well,' I said blankly. 'I don't know whether to pitch a fit or laugh. What do you make of that?'

Because if anyone knew about man-woman stuff, it was Jason. At least, he knew about it from the man's point of view.

'She's your opposite,' he said, with undue thoughtfulness. 'In every way that I can think of. She's real educated, she comes from an, I guess you'd call it, aristocratic background, and she's a lawyer. Plus, her brother's a cop. And they go to symphonies and shit.'

Tears prickled at my eyes. I would have gone to a symphony with Bill, if he'd ever asked me.

'On the other hand, you're smart, you're pretty, and you're willing to put up with his little ways.' I wasn't exactly sure what Jason meant by that, and thought it better not to ask. 'But we sure ain't aristocracy. You work in a bar, and your brother works on a road crew.' Jason smiled at me lopsidedly.

'We've been here as long as the Bellefleurs,' I said, trying not to sound sullen.

'I know that, and you know that. And Bill sure knows that, because he was alive then.' True enough.

'What's happening about the case against Andy?' I asked.

'No charges brought against him yet, but the rumors are flying around town thick and fast about this sex club thing. Lafayette was so pleased to have been asked; evidently he mentioned it to quite a few people. They say that since the first rule of the club is Keep Silent, Lafayette got whacked for his enthusiasm.'

'What do you think?'

'I think if anyone was forming a sex club around Bon Temps, they woulda called me,' he said, dead serious.

'You're right,' I said, struck again by how sensible Jason could be. 'You'd be number one on the list.' Why hadn't I thought of that before? Not only did Jason have a reputation as a guy who'd heated up many a bed, he was both very attractive and unmarried.

'The only thing I can think of,' I said slowly, 'Lafayette was gay, as you well know.'

'And?'

'And maybe this club, if it exists, only accepts people who are all right with that.'

'You might have a point there,' Jason said.

'Yes, Mr. Homophobe.'

Jason smiled and shrugged. 'Everybody's got a weak point,' he said. 'Plus, as you know, I've been going out with Liz pretty steady. I think anyone with a brain would see Liz ain't about to share a napkin, much less a boyfriend.'

He was right. Liz's family notoriously took 'Neither a borrower nor a lender be' to a complete extreme.

'You are a piece of work, brother,' I said, focusing on his shortcomings, rather than those of Liz's folks. 'There are so many worse things to be than gay.'

'Such as?'

'Thief, traitor, murderer, rapist . . .'

'Okay, okay, I get the idea.'

'I hope you do,' I said. Our differences grieved me. But I loved Jason anyway; he was all I had left.

I saw Bill out with Portia that same night. I caught a glimpse of them together in Bill's car, driving down Claiborne Street. Portia had her head turned to Bill, talking; he was looking straight ahead, expressionless, as far as I could tell. They didn't see me. I was coming from the automated teller at the bank, on my way to work.

Hearing of and seeing directly are two very different things. I felt an overwhelming surge of rage; and I understood how Bill had felt, when he'd seen his friends dying. I wanted to kill someone. I just wasn't sure who I wanted to kill.

Andy was in the bar that evening, sitting in Arlene's section. I was glad, because Andy looked bad. He was not clean-shaven, and his clothes were rumpled. He came up to me as he was leaving, and I could smell the booze. 'Take him back,' he said. His voice was thick with anger. 'Take the damn vampire back so he'll leave my sister alone.'

I didn't know what to say to Andy Bellefleur. I just stared at him until he stumbled out of the bar. It crossed my mind that people wouldn't be as surprised to hear of a dead body in his car now as they had been a few weeks ago.

The next night I had off, and the temperature dropped. It was a Friday, and suddenly I was tired of being alone. I decided to go to the high school football game. This is a townwide pastime in Bon Temps, and the games are discussed thoroughly on Monday morning in every store in town. The film of the game is shown twice on a local-access channel, and boys who show promise with pig-skin are minor royalty, more's the pity.

You don't show up at the game all disheveled.

I pulled my hair back from my forehead in an elastic band and used my curling iron on the rest, so I had thick curls hanging around my shoulders. My bruises were gone. I put on complete makeup, down to the lip liner. I put on black knit slacks and a black-and-red sweater. I wore my black leather boots, and my gold hoop earrings, and I pinned a red-and-black bow to hide the elastic band in my hair. (Guess what our school colors are.)

'Pretty good,' I said, viewing the result in my mirror. 'Pretty *damn* good.' I gathered up my black jacket and my purse and drove into town.

The stands were full of people I knew. A dozen voices called to me, a dozen people told me how cute I looked, and the problem was . . . I was miserable. As soon as I realized this, I pasted a smile on my face and searched for someone to sit with.

'Sookie! Sookie!' Tara Thornton, one of my few good high school friends, was calling me from high up in the stands. She made a frantic beckoning gesture, and I smiled back and began to hike up, speaking to more people along the way. Mike Spencer, the funeral home director, was there, in his favorite western regalia, and my grandmother's good friend Maxine Fortenberry, and her grandson Hoyt, who was a buddy of Jason's. I saw Sid Matt Lancaster, the ancient lawyer, bundled up beside his wife.

Tara was sitting with her fiancé, Benedict Tallie, who was inevitably and regrettably called 'Eggs.' With them was Benedict's best friend, JB du Rone. When I saw JB, my spirits began to rise, and so did my repressed libido. JB could have been on the cover of a romance novel, he was so lovely. Unfortunately, he didn't have a brain in his head, as I'd discovered on our handful of dates. I'd often thought I'd hardly have to put up any mental shield to be with JB, because he had no thoughts to read.

'Hey, how ya'll doing?'

'We're great!' Tara said, with her party-girl face on. 'How about you? I haven't seen you in a coon's age!' Her dark hair was cut in a short pageboy, and her lipstick could have lit a fire, it was so hot. She was wearing off-white and black with a red scarf to show her team spirit, and she and Eggs were sharing a drink in one of the paper cups sold in the stadium. It was spiked; I could smell the bourbon from where I stood. 'Move over, JB, and let me sit with you,' I said with an answering smile.

'Sure, Sookie,' he said, looking very happy to see me. That was one of JB's charms. The others included white perfect teeth, an absolutely straight nose, a face so masculine yet so handsome that it made you want to reach out and stroke his cheeks, and a broad chest and trim waist. Maybe not quite as trim as it used to be, but then, JB was human, and that was a Good Thing. I settled in between Eggs and JB, and Eggs turned to me with a sloppy smile.

'Want a drink, Sookie?'

I am kind of spare on drinking, since I see its results every day. 'No, thank you,' I said. 'How you been doing, Eggs?'

'Good,' he said, after considering. He'd had more to drink than Tara. He'd had too much to drink.

We talked about mutual friends and acquaintances until the kickoff, after which the game was the sole topic of conversation. The Game, broadly, because every game for the past fifty years lay in the collective memory of Bon Temps, and this game was compared to all other games, these players to all others. I could actually enjoy this occasion a little, since I had developed my mental shielding to such an extent. I could pretend people were exactly what they said, since I was absolutely not listening in.

JB snuggled closer and closer, after a shower of compliments on my hair and my figure. JB's mother had taught him early on that appreciated women are happy women, and it was a simple philosophy that had kept JB's head above water for some time.

'You remember that doctor at that hospital, Sookie?' he asked me suddenly, during the second quarter.

'Yes. Dr. Sonntag. Widow.' She'd been young to be a widow, and younger to be a doctor. I'd introduced her to JB.

'We dated for a while. Me and a doctor,' he said wonderingly.

'Hey, that's great.' I'd hoped as much. It had seemed to me that Dr. Sonntag could sure use what JB had to offer, and JB needed . . . well, he needed someone to take care of him.

'But then she got rotated back to Baton Rouge,' he told me. He looked a little stricken. 'I guess I miss her.' A health care system had bought our little hospital, and the emergency room doctors were brought in for four months at a stretch. His arm tightened around my shoulders. 'But it's awful good to see you,' he reassured me.

Bless his heart. 'JB, you could go to Baton Rouge to see her,' I suggested. 'Why don't you?'

'She's a doctor. She doesn't have much time off.'

'She'd make time off for you.'

'Do you think so?'

'Unless she's an absolute idiot,' I told him.

'I might do that. I did talk to her on the phone the other night. She did say she wished I was there.'

'That was a pretty big hint, JB.'

'You think?'

'I sure do.'

He looked perkier. 'Then I'm fixing to drive to Baton Rouge tomorrow,' he said again. He kissed my cheek. 'You make me feel good, Sookie.'

'Well, JB, right back at you.' I gave him a peck on the lips, just a quick one.

Then I saw Bill staring a hole in me.

He and Portia were in the next section of seats, close to the bottom. He had twisted around and was looking up at me.

If I'd planned it, it couldn't have worked out better. This was a magnificent Screw-him moment.

And it was ruined.

I just wanted him.

I turned my eyes away and smiled at JB, and all the time what I wanted was to meet with Bill under the stands and have sex with him right then and there. I wanted him to pull down my pants and get behind me. I wanted him to make me moan.

I was so shocked at myself I didn't know what to do. I could feel my face turning a dull red. I could not even pretend to smile.

After a minute, I could appreciate that this was almost funny. I had been brought up as conventionally as possible, given my unusual disability. Naturally, I'd learned the facts of life pretty early since I could read minds (and, as a child, had no control over what I absorbed). And I'd always thought the idea of sex was pretty interesting, though the same disability that had led to me learning so much about it theoretically had kept me from putting that theory into practice. After all, it's hard to get really involved in sex when you know your partner is wishing you were Tara Thornton instead (for example), or when he's hoping you remembered to bring a condom, or when he's criticizing your body parts. For successful sex, you have to keep your concentration fixed on what your partner's *doing*, so you can't get distracted by what he's *thinking*.

With Bill, I couldn't hear a single thing. And he was so experienced, so smooth, so absolutely dedicated to getting it right. It appeared I was as much a junkie as Hugo.

I sat through the rest of the game, smiling and nodding when it seemed indicated, trying not to look down and to my left, and finding after the halftime show was over that I hadn't heard a single song the band had played. Nor had I noticed Tara's cousin's twirling solo. As the crowd moved slowly to the parking lot after the Bon Temps Hawks had won, 28–18, I agreed to drive JB home. Eggs had sobered some by then, so I was pretty sure he and Tara would be okay; but I was relieved to see Tara take the wheel.

JB lived close to downtown in half a duplex. He asked me very sweetly to come in, but I told him I had to get home. I gave him a big hug, and I advised him to call Dr. Sonntag. I still didn't know her first name.

He said he would, but then, with JB, you couldn't really tell.

Then I had to stop and get gas at the only late-night gas station, where I had a long conversation with Arlene's cousin Derrick (who was brave enough to take the night shift), so I was a little later getting home than I had planned.

As I unlocked the front door, Bill came out of the darkness. Without a word, he grabbed my arm and turned me to him, and then he kissed me. In a minute we were pressed against the door with his body moving rhythmically against mine. I reached one hand behind myself to fumble with the lock, and the key finally turned. We stumbled into the house, and he turned me to face the couch. I gripped it with my hands and, just as I'd imagined, he pulled down my pants, and then he was in me.

I made a hoarse noise I'd never heard come from my throat before. Bill was making noises equally as primitive. I didn't think I could form a word. His hands were under my sweater, and my bra was in two pieces. He was relentless. I almost collapsed after the first time I came. 'No,' he growled when I was flagging, and he kept pounding. Then he increased the pace until I was almost sobbing, and then my sweater tore, and his teeth found my shoulder. He made a deep, awful sound, and then, after long seconds, it was over.

I was panting as if I'd run a mile, and he was shivering, too. Without bothering to refasten his clothing, he turned me around to face him, and he bent his head to my shoulder again to lick the little wound. When it had stopped bleeding and begun healing, he took off everything I had on, very slowly. He cleaned me below; he kissed me above.

'You smell like him' was the only thing he said. He proceeded to erase that smell and replace it with his own.

Then we were in the bedroom, and I had a moment to be glad I'd changed the sheets that morning before he bent his mouth to mine again.

If I'd had doubts up until then, I had them no longer. He was not sleeping with Portia Bellefleur. I didn't know what he was up to, but he did not have a true relationship with her. He slid his arms underneath me and held me to him as tightly as possible; he nuzzled my neck, kneaded my hips, ran his fingers down my thighs, and kissed the backs of my knees. He bathed in me. 'Spread your legs for me, Sookie,' he whispered, in his cold dark voice, and I did. He was ready again, and he was rough with it, as if he were trying to prove something.

'Be sweet,' I said, the first time I had spoken.

'I can't. It's been too long, next time I'll be sweet, I swear,' he said, running his tongue down the line of my jaw.

His fangs grazed my neck. Fangs, tongue, mouth, fingers, manhood; it was like being made love to by the Tasmanian Devil. He was everywhere, and everywhere in a hurry.

When he collapsed on top of me, I was exhausted. He shifted to lie by my side, one leg draped over mine, one arm across my chest. He might as well have gotten out a branding iron and had done with it, but it wouldn't have been as much fun for me.

'Are you okay?' he mumbled.

'Except for having run into a brick wall a few times,' I said indistinctly.

We both drifted off to sleep for a little, though Bill woke first, as he always did at night. 'Sookie,' he said quietly. 'Darling. Wake up.'

'Oo,' I said, slowly coming to consciousness. For the first time in weeks, I woke with the hazy conviction that all was right with the world. With slow dismay, I realized that things were far from right. I opened my eyes. Bill's were right above me.

'We have to talk,' he said, stroking the hair back from my face.

'So talk.' I was awake now. What I was regretting was not the sex, but having to discuss the issues between us.

'I got carried away in Dallas,' he said immediately. 'Vampires do, when the chance to hunt presents itself so obviously. We were attacked. We have the right to hunt down those who want to kill us.'

'That's returning to days of lawlessness,' I said.

'But vampires hunt, Sookie. It is our nature,' he said very seriously. 'Like leopards; like wolves. We are not human. We can pretend to be, when we're trying to live with people . . . in your society. We can sometimes remember what it was like to be among you, one of you. But we are not the same race. We are no longer of the same clay.'

I thought this over. He'd told me this, over and over, in different words, since we'd begun seeing each other.

Or maybe, he'd been seeing me, but I hadn't been seeing him: clearly, truly. No matter how often I thought I'd made my peace with his otherness, I realized that I still expected him to react as he would if he were JB du Rone, or Jason, or my church pastor.

'I think I'm finally getting this,' I said. 'But you got to realize, sometimes I'm not going to like that difference. Sometimes I have to get away and cool down. I'm really going to try. I really love you.' Having done my best to promise to meet him halfway, I was reminded of my own grievance. I grabbed his hair and rolled him over so I was looking down at him. I looked right in his eyes.

'Now, you tell me what you're doing with Portia.'

Bill's big hands rested on my hips as he explained.

'She came to me after I got back from Dallas, the first night. She had read about what happened there, wondered if I knew anyone who'd been there that day. When I said that I had been there myself – I didn't mention you – Portia said she had information that some of the arms used in the attack had come from a place in Bon Temps, Sheridan's Sport Shop. I asked her how she had heard this; she said as a lawyer, she couldn't say. I asked her why she was so concerned, if there wasn't anything further she'd tell me about it; she said she was a good citizen and hated to see other citizens persecuted. I asked her why she came to me; she said I was the only vampire she knew.'

I believed that like I believed Portia was a secret belly dancer.

I narrowed my eyes as I worked this through. 'Portia doesn't care one damn thing about vampire rights,' I said. 'She might want to get in your pants, but she doesn't care about vampire legal issues.'

'"Get in my pants?" What a turn of phrase you have.'

'Oh, you've heard that before,' I said, a little abashed.

He shook his head, amusement sparkling in his face. 'Get in my pants,' he repeated, sounding it out slowly. 'I would be in your pants, if you had any on.' He rubbed his hands up and down to demonstrate.

'Cut that out,' I said. 'I'm trying to think.'

His hands were pressing my hips, then releasing, moving me back and forth on him. I began to have difficulty forming thoughts.

'Stop, Bill,' I said. 'Listen, I think Portia wants to be seen with you so she might be asked to join that supposed sex club here in Bon Temps.'

'Sex club?' Bill said with interest, not stopping in the least.

'Yes, didn't I tell you . . . oh, Bill, no . . . Bill, I'm still worn out from last . . . Oh. Oh, God.' His hands had gripped me with their great strength, and moved me purposefully, right onto his stiffness. He began rocking me again, back and forth. 'Oh,' I said, lost in the moment. I began to see colors floating in front of my eyes, and then I was being rocked so fast I couldn't keep track of my motion. The end came at the same time for both of us, and we clung together panting for several minutes.

'We should never separate again,' Bill said.

'I don't know, this makes it almost worth it.'

A little aftershock rippled his body. 'No,' he said. 'This is wonderful, but I would rather just leave town for a few days, than fight with you again.' He opened his eyes wide. 'Did you really suck a bullet from Eric's shoulder?'

'Yeah, he said I had to get it out before his flesh closed over it.'

'Did he tell you he had a pocketknife in his pocket?'

I was taken aback. 'No. Did he? Why would he do that?'

Bill raised his eyebrows, as if I had said something quite ridiculous.

'Guess,' he said.

'So I would suck on his shoulder? You can't mean that.'

Bill just maintained the skeptical look.

'Oh, Bill. I fell for it. Wait a minute – he got shot! That bullet could have hit me, but instead it hit him. He was guarding me.'

'How?'

'Well, by lying on top of me . . .'

'I rest my case.' There was nothing old-fashioned about Bill at the moment. On the other hand, there was a pretty old-fashioned look on his face.

'But, Bill . . . you mean he's that devious?'

Again with the raised eyebrows.

'Lying on top of me is not such a big treat,' I protested, 'that someone should take a bullet for it. Geez. That's nuts!'

'It got some of his blood in you.'

'Only a drop or two. I spit the rest out,' I said.

'A drop or two is enough when you are as old as Eric is.'

'Enough for what?'

'He will know some things about you, now.'

'What, like my dress size?'

Bill smiled, not always a relaxing sight. 'No, like how you are feeling. Angry, horny, loving.'

I shrugged. 'Won't do him any good.'

'Probably it is not too important, but be careful from now on,' Bill warned me. He seemed quite serious.

'I still can't believe someone would put themselves in a position to take a bullet for me just in the hopes I'd ingest a drop of blood getting the bullet out. That's ridiculous. You know, it seems like to me you introduced this subject so I'd quit bugging you about Portia, but I'm not going to. I think Portia believes if she's dating you, someone will ask her to go to this sex club, since if she's willing to ball a vampire, she's willing to do anything. They *think*,' said hastily after looking at Bill's face. 'So Portia figures she'll go, she'll learn stuff, she'll find out who actually killed Lafayette, Andy'll be off the hook.'

'That's a complicated plot.'

'Can you refute it?' I was proud to use *refute*, which had been on my Word of the Day calendar.

'As a matter of fact, I can't.' He became immobile. His eyes were fixed and unblinking, and his hands relaxed. Since Bill doesn't breathe, he was absolutely still.

Finally he blinked. 'It would have been better if she had told me the truth to begin with.'

'You better not have had sex with her,' I said, finally admitting to myself that the bare possibility had made me nearly blind with jealousy.

'I wondered when you were going to ask me,' he said calmly. 'As if I would ever bed a Bellefleur. No, she has not the slightest desire to have sex with me. She even has a hard time pretending she wants to at some later date. Portia is not much of an actress. Most of the time we are together, she takes me on wild goose chases to find this cache of arms the Fellowship has stowed here, saying all the Fellowship sympathizers are hiding them.'

'So why'd you go along with any of this?'

'There's something about her that's honorable. And I wanted to see if you would be jealous.'

'Oh, I see. Well, what do you think?'

'I think,' he said, 'I had better never see you within a yard of that handsome moron again.'

'JB? I'm like his sister,' I said.

'You forget, you've had my blood, and I can tell what you are feeling,' Bill said. 'I don't think you feel exactly like a sister to him.'

'That would explain why I'm here in bed with you, right?'

'You love me.'

I laughed, up against his throat.

'It's close to dawn,' he said. 'I have to go.'

'Okay, baby.' I smiled up at him as he gathered up his clothes. 'Hey, you owe me a sweater and a bra. Two bras. Gabe tore one, so that was a work-related clothes injury. And you tore one last night, plus my sweater.'

'That's why I bought a women's clothing store,' he said smoothly. 'So I could rip if the spirit moves me.'

I laughed and lay back down. I could sleep for a couple more hours. I was still smiling when he let himself out of my house, and I woke up in the middle of the morning with a lightness in my heart that hadn't been there for a long time. (Well, it felt like a long time.) I walked, somewhat gingerly, into the bathroom to soak in a tubful of hot water. When I began to wash, I felt something in my earlobes. I stood up in the tub and looked over at the mirror above the sink. He'd put the topaz earrings in while I was asleep.

Mr. Last Word.

*

Since our reunion had been secret, it was I who got invited to the club first. It had never occurred to me that that might happen; but after it did, I realized that if Portia had figured she might be invited after going with a vampire, I was even primer meat.

To my surprise and disgust, the one to broach the subject was Mike Spencer. Mike was the funeral home director and the coroner in Bon Temps, and we had not always had a completely cordial relationship. However, I'd known him all my life and was used to offering him respect, a hard habit to break. Mike was wearing his funeral home duds when he came in to Merlotte's that evening, because he'd come from Mrs. Cassidy's visitation. A dark suit, white shirt, subdued striped tie, and polished wing tips changed Mike Spencer from the guy who really preferred bolo ties and pointy-toed cowboy boots.

Since Mike was at least twenty years older than me, I'd always related to him as an elder, and it shocked me silly when he approached me. He was sitting by himself, which was unusual enough to be noteworthy. I brought him a hamburger and a beer. As he paid me, he said casually, 'Sookie, some of us are getting together at Jan Fowler's lake house tomorrow night and we wondered if we could get you to come.'

I am fortunate I have a well-schooled face. I felt as if a pit had opened beneath my feet, and I was actually a little nauseated. I understood immediately, but I couldn't quite believe it. I opened my mind to him, while my mouth was saying, 'You said "some of us"? Who would that be, Mr. Spencer?'

'Why don't you call me Mike, Sookie?' I nodded, looking inside his head all the while. Oh, geez Louise. Ick.

'Well, some of your friends will be there. Eggs, and Portia, and Tara. The Hardaways.'

Tara and Eggs . . . that really shocked me.

'So, what goes on at these parties? Is this just a drinking and dancing type thing?' This was not an unreasonable question. No matter how many people knew I was supposed to be able to read minds, they almost never believed it, no matter how much evidence to the contrary they'd witnessed. Mike simply could not believe that I could receive the images and concepts floating in his mind.

'Well, we get a little wild. We thought since you'd broken up with your boyfriend, that you might want to come let your hair down a little.'

'Maybe I'll come,' I said, without enthusiasm. It wouldn't do to look eager. 'When?'

'Oh, ten o'clock tomorrow night.'

'Thanks for the invite,' I said, as if remembering my manners, and then sauntered off with my tip. I thought furiously, in the odd moments I had to myself during the rest of my shift.

What good could my going serve? Could I really learn anything that would solve the mystery of Lafayette's death? I didn't like Andy Bellefleur much, and now I liked Portia even less, but it wasn't fair that Andy might be prosecuted, his reputation ruined, for something that wasn't his fault. On the other hand, it stood to reason that no one present at a party at the lake house would trust me with any deep dark secrets until I'd become a regular, and I just couldn't stomach that. I wasn't even sure I could get through one gathering. The last thing in the world I wanted to see was my friends and my neighbors 'letting their hair down.' I didn't want to see them let down their hair, or anything else.

'What's the matter, Sookie?' Sam asked, so close to me that I jumped.

I looked at him, wishing that I could ask what he thought. Sam was strong and wiry, and he was clever too. The bookkeeping, the ordering, the maintenance and planning, he never seemed to be taxed with any of it. Sam was a self-sufficient man, and I liked and trusted him.

'I'm just in a little quandary,' I said. 'What's up with you, Sam?'

'I got an interesting phone call last night, Sookie.'

'Who from?'

'A squeaky woman in Dallas.'

'Really?' I found myself smiling, really, not the grin I used to cover my nerves. 'Would that be a lady of Mexican descent?'

'I believe so. She spoke of you.'

'She's feisty,' I said.

'She's got a lot of friends.'

'Kind of friends you'd want to have?'

'I already have some good friends,' Sam said, squeezing my hand briefly. 'But it's always nice to know people who share your interests.'

'So, are you driving over to Dallas?'

'I just might. In the meantime, she's put me in touch with some people in Ruston who also . . .'

Change their appearance when the moon is full, I finished mentally.

'How did she trace you? I didn't give her your name, on purpose, because I didn't know if you'd want me to.'

'She traced you,' Sam said. 'And she found out who your boss was through local . . . people.'

'How come you had never hooked up with them on your own?'

'Until you told me about the maenad,' Sam said, 'I never realized that there were so many more things I had to learn.'

'Sam, you haven't been hanging around with her?'

'I've spent a few evenings in the woods with her, yes. As Sam, and in my other skin.'

'But she's so evil,' I blurted.

Sam's back stiffened. 'She's a supernatural creature like me,' he said evenly. 'She's neither evil nor good, she just is.'

'Oh, bullshit.' I couldn't believe I was hearing this from Sam. 'If she's feeding you this line, then she wants something from you.' I remembered how beautiful the maenad had been, if you didn't mind bloodstains. And Sam, as a shapeshifter, wouldn't. 'Oh,' I said, comprehension sweeping me. Not that I could read Sam's mind clearly, since he was a supernatural creature, but I could get a lock on his emotional state, which was – embarrassed, horny, resentful, and horny.

'Oh,' I said again, somewhat stiffly. 'Excuse me, Sam. I didn't mean to speak ill of someone you . . . you, ah . . .' I could hardly say, 'are screwing,' however apropos it might be. 'You're spending time with,' I finished lamely. 'I'm sure she's lovely once you get to know her. Of course, the fact that she cut my back to bloody ribbons may have something to do with my prejudice against her. I'll try to be more open-minded.' And I stalked off to take an order, leaving Sam openmouthed behind me.

I left a message on Bill's answering machine. I didn't know what Bill intended to do about Portia, and I guessed there was a possibility someone else would be there when he played his messages, so I said, 'Bill, I got invited to that party tomorrow night. Let me know if you think I should go.' I didn't identify myself, since he'd know my voice. Possibly, Portia had left an identical message, an idea that just made me furious.

When I drove home that night, I half-hoped Bill would be waiting to ambush me again in an erotic way, but the house and yard were silent. I perked up when I noticed the light on my answering machine was blinking.

'Sookie,' said Bill's smooth voice, 'stay out of the woods. The maenad was dissatisfied with our tribute. Eric will be in Bon Temps tomorrow night to negotiate with her, and he may call you. The – other people – of Dallas, the ones who helped you, are asking for outrageous recompense from the vampires of Dallas, so I am going over there on Anubis to meet with them, with Stan. You know where I'll be staying.'

Yikes. Bill wouldn't be in Bon Temps to help me, and he was out of my reach. Or was he? It was one in the morning. I called the number I'd put in my address book, for the Silent Shore. Bill had not yet checked in, though his coffin (which the concierge referred to as his 'baggage') had been put in his room. I left a message, which I had to phrase so guardedly that it might be incomprehensible.

I was really tired, since I hadn't gotten much sleep the night before, but I had no intention of going to the next night's party alone. I sighed deeply, and called Fangtasia, the vampire bar in Shreveport.

'You've reached Fantasia, where the undead live again every night,' said a recording of Pam's voice. Pam was a co-owner. 'For bar hours, press one. To make a party reservation, press two. To talk to a live person or a dead vampire, press three. Or, if you were intending to leave a humorous prank message on our answering machine, know this: we will find you.'

I pressed three.

'Fangtasia,' Pam said, as if she were bored more completely than anyone had ever been bored.

'Hi,' I said, weighing in on the perky side to counteract the ennui. 'This is Sookie, Pam. Is Eric around?'

'He is enthralling the vermin,' Pam said. I took that to mean Eric was sprawling in a chair on the main floor of the bar, looking gorgeous and dangerous. Bill had told me that some vampires were under contract to Fangtasia, to put in one or two appearances a week of a stated duration, so the tourists would keep coming. Eric, as an owner, was there almost every night. There was another bar where vampires went of their own accord, a bar a tourist would never enter. I'd never been in it, because frankly, I see enough of bars while I'm at work.

'Could you take him the phone, please, ma'am?'

'Oh, all right,' she said grudgingly. 'I hear you had quite a time in Dallas,' she said as she walked. Not that I could hear her steps, but the noise in the background ebbed and flowed.

'Unforgettable.'

'What did you think of Stan Davis?'

Hmmm. 'He's one of a kind.'

'I like that nerdy, geeky look myself.'

I was glad she wasn't there to see the astonished look I gave the telephone. I'd never realized Pam liked guys, too. 'He certainly didn't seem to be dating anyone,' I said, I hoped casually.

'Ah. Maybe I'll take a vacation to Dallas soon.'

It was also news to me that vampires were interested in each other. I'd never actually seen two vampires together.

'I am here,' Eric said.

'And I am here.' I was a little amused at Eric's phone answering technique.

'Sookie, my little bullet-sucker,' he said, sounding fond and warm.

'Eric, my big bullshitter.'

'You want something, my darling?'

'I'm not your darling, and you know it, for one thing. For another – Bill said you were coming over here tomorrow night?'

'Yes, to tromp up in the woods looking for the maenad. She finds our offerings of vintage wine and a young bull inadequate.'

'You took her live bull?' I was momentarily sidetracked by the vision of Eric herding a cow into a trailer and driving it to the shoulder of the interstate and shooing it into the trees.

'Yes, indeed we did. Pam and Indira and I.'

'Was it fun?'

'Yes,' he said, sounding faintly surprised. 'It had been several centuries since I dealt with livestock. Pam is a city girl. Indira had too much awe of the bull to be a lot of help. But if you like, the next time I have to transport animals I will give you a call, and you can go along.'

'Thanks, that would be lovely,' I said, feeling pretty confident that was a call I'd never get. 'The reason I called you is that I need you to go to a party with me tomorrow night.'

A long silence.

'Bill is no longer your bedmate? The differences you developed in Dallas are permanent?'

'What I should have said is, "I need a bodyguard for tomorrow night." Bill's in Dallas.' I was smacking myself on the forehead with the heel of my hand. 'See, there's a long explanation, but the situation is that I need to go to a party tomorrow night that's really just a . . . well, it's a . . . kind of orgy thing? And I need someone with me in case . . . just in case.'

'That's fascinating,' Eric said, sounding fascinated. 'And since I'm going to be in the neighborhood, you thought I might do as an escort? To an orgy?'

'You can look almost human,' I said.

'This is a human orgy? One that excludes vampires?'

'It's a human orgy that doesn't know a vampire is coming.'

'So, the more human I look the less frightening I'll be?'

'Yes, I need to read their thoughts. Pick their brains. And if I get them thinking about a certain thing, and pick their brains, then we can get out of there.' I'd just had a great idea about how to get them to think about Lafayette. Telling Eric was going to be the problem.

'So you want me to go to a human orgy, where I will not be welcome, and you want us to leave before I get to enjoy myself?'

'Yes,' I said, almost squeaking in my anxiety. In for a penny, in for a pound. 'And . . . do you think you could pretend to be gay?'

There was a long silence. 'What time do I need to be there?' Eric asked softly.

'Um. Nine-thirty? So I can brief you?'

'Nine-thirty at your house.'

'I am carrying the phone back,' Pam informed me. 'What did you say to Eric? He is shaking his head back and forth with his eyes shut.'

'Is he laughing, even a little bit?'

'Not that I can tell,' Pam said.

Chapter 10

Bill didn't call back that night, and I left for work before sunset the next day. He'd left a message on the answering machine when I came home to dress for the 'party.'

'Sookie, I had a hard time making out what the situation was, from your very guarded message,' he said. His usually calm voice was definitely on the unhappy side. Miffed. 'If you are going to this party, don't go alone, whatever you do. It isn't worth it. Get your brother or Sam to go with you.'

Well, I'd gotten someone even stronger to go with me, so I should be feeling pretty virtuous. Somehow, I didn't think that my having Eric with me would reassure Bill.

'Stan Davis and Joseph Velasquez send their regards, and Barry the bellhop.'

I smiled. I was sitting cross-legged on my bed wearing only an old chenille bathrobe, giving my hair a brushing while I listened to my messages.

'I haven't forgotten Friday night,' Bill said, in the voice that always made me shiver. 'I will never forget.'

'So what happened Friday night?' Eric asked.

I shrieked. Once I could feel my heart was going to stay in my chest cavity, I scrambled off the bed and strode over to him with my fists balled.

'You are old enough to know you don't come in someone's house without knocking on the door and having it answered. Besides, when did I ever invite you inside?' I had to have extended the invitation, or else Eric couldn't have crossed the threshold.

'When I stopped by last month to see Bill. I did knock,' Eric said, trying his best to look wounded. 'You didn't answer, and I thought I heard voices, so I came in. I even called your name.'

'You may have whispered my name.' I was still furious. 'But you acted bad, and you know it!'

'What are you wearing to the party?' Eric asked, effectively changing the subject. 'If this is to be an orgy, what does a good girl like you wear?'

'I just don't know,' I said, deflated by the reminder. 'I'm sure I'm supposed to look like the kind of girl who goes to orgies, but I've never been to one and I have no idea how to start out, though I have a pretty clear idea of how I'm supposed to end up.'

'I have been to orgies,' he offered.

'Why does that not surprise me? What do you wear?'

'The last time I wore an animal hide; but this time I settled for this.' Eric had been wearing a long trench coat. Now he threw it off dramatically, and I could only stand and stare. Normally, Eric was a blue-jeans-and-T-shirt kind of guy. Tonight, he wore a pink tank top and Lycra leggings. I don't know where he got them; I didn't know any company made Lycra leggings in Men's Xtra Large Tall.

They were pink and aqua, like the swirls down the sides of Jason's truck.

'Wow,' I said, since it was all I could think of to say. 'Wow. That's some outfit.' When you've got a big guy wearing Lycra it doesn't leave a whole lot to the imagination. I resisted the temptation to ask Eric to turn around.

'I don't believe I could be convincing as a queen,' Eric said, 'but I decided this sent such a mixed signal, almost anything was possible.' He fluttered his eyelashes at me. Eric was definitely enjoying this.

'Oh, yes,' I said, trying to find somewhere else to look.

'Shall I go through your drawers and find something for you to wear?' Eric suggested. He had actually opened the top drawer of my bureau before I said, 'No, no! I'll find something!' But I couldn't find anything more informally sexy than shorts and a tee shirt. However, the shorts were some I had left over from my junior high days, and they encased me 'like a caterpillar embraces a butterfly,' Eric said poetically.

'More like Daisy Dukes,' I muttered, wondering if the lace pattern of my bikini underwear would be imprinted on my butt for the rest of my life. I wore a matching steel blue bra with a dipping white tank top that exposed a lot of the decoration on the bra. This was one of my replacement bras, and Bill hadn't even gotten to see it yet, so I sure hoped nothing happened to it. My tan was still holding up, and I wore my hair loose.

'Hey, our hair's the same color,' I said, eyeing us side by side in the mirror.

'Sure is, girlfriend.' Eric grinned at me. 'But are you blond all the way down?'

'Don't you wish you knew?'

'Yes,' he said simply.

'Well, you'll just have to wonder.'

'I am,' he said. 'Blond everywhere.'

'I could tell as much from your chest hair.'

He raised my arm to check my armpit. 'You silly women, shaving your body hair,' he said, dropping my arm.

I opened my mouth to say something else on the topic, suddenly realized that would lead to disaster, and said instead, 'We need to go.'

'Aren't you going to wear perfume?' He was sniffing all the bottles on top of my dressing table. 'Oh, wear this!' He tossed me a bottle and I caught it without thinking. His eyebrows flew up. 'You have had more vampire blood than I thought, Miss Sookie.'

'Obsession,' I said, looking at the bottle. 'Oh, okay.' Carefully not responding to his observation, I dabbed a little bit of Obsession between my breasts and behind my knees. I figured that way I was covered from head to toe.

'What is our agenda, Sookie?' Eric asked, eyeing this procedure with interest.

'What we're going to do is go to this stupid so-called sex party and do as little as possible in that line while I gather information from the minds of the people there.'

'Pertaining to?'

'Pertaining to the murder of Lafayette Reynold, the cook at Merlotte's Bar.'

'And why are we doing this?'

'Because I liked Lafayette. And to clear Andy Bellefleur of the suspicion that he murdered Lafayette.'

'Bill knows you are trying to save a Bellefleur?'

'Why do you ask that?'

'You know Bill hates the Bellefleurs,' Eric said, as if that were the best-known fact in Louisiana.

'No,' I said. 'No, I didn't know that at all.' I sat down on the chair by my bed, my eyes fixed on Eric's face. 'Why?'

'You'll have to ask Bill that, Sookie. And this is the only reason we're going? You're not cleverly using this as an excuse to make out with me?'

'I'm not that clever, Eric.'

'I think you deceive yourself, Sookie,' Eric said with a brilliant smile.

I remembered he could now sense my moods, according to Bill. I wondered what Eric knew about me that I didn't know.

'Listen, Eric,' I began, as we went out the door and across the porch. Then I had to stop and cast around in my mind for how to say what I wanted to say.

He waited. The evening had been cloudy, and the woods felt closer around the house. I knew the night just seemed oppressive because I was going to go to an event personally distasteful to me. I was going to learn things about people that I didn't know and didn't want to know. It seemed stupid to be seeking the kind of information that I'd spent my life learning how to block out. But I felt a sort of public service obligation to Andy Bellefleur to discover the truth; and I respected Portia, in an odd way, for her willingness to subject herself to something unpleasant in order to save her brother. How Portia could feel a genuine distaste for Bill was simply incomprehensible to me, but if Bill said she was frightened of him, it was true. This coming evening, the idea of seeing the true secret face of people I'd known forever was just as frightening to me.

'Don't let anything happen to me, okay?' I said to Eric

directly. 'I have no intention of getting intimate with any of those people. I guess I'm scared that something will happen, someone will go too far. Even for the sake of Lafayette's murder being avenged, I won't willingly have sex with any of those people.' That was my real fear, one I hadn't admitted to myself until this moment: that some cog would slip, some safeguard fail, and I would be a victim. When I'd been a child, something had happened to me, something that I could neither prevent nor control, something incredibly vile. I would almost rather die than be subjected to abuse like that again. That was why I'd fought so hard against Gabe and been so relieved when Godfrey had killed him.

'You trust me?' Eric sounded surprised.

'Yes.'

'That's . . . crazy, Sookie.'

'I don't think so.' Where that surety had come from, I didn't know, but it was there. I pulled on a thigh-length heavy sweater I had brought out with me.

Shaking his blond head, his trench coat drawn close around him, Eric opened the door to his red Corvette. I would be arriving at the orgy in style.

I gave Eric directions to Mimosa Lake, and I filled him in as much as I could on the background of this series of events as we drove (flew) down the narrow two-lane. Eric drove with great zest and élan – and the recklessness of someone extremely hard to kill.

'Remember, I'm mortal,' I said, after going around a curve at a speed that made me wish my fingernails were long enough to bite.

'I think about that often,' Eric said, his eyes fixed on the road ahead of him.

I didn't know what to make of that, so I let my mind drift to relaxing things. Bill's hot tub. The nice check I would get from Eric when the check from the Dallas vampires cleared. The fact that Jason had dated the same woman several months in a row, which might mean he was serious about her, or might mean he'd run through all the available women (and a few who shouldn't have been) in Renard Parish. That it was a beautiful, cool night and I was riding in a wonderful car.

'You are happy,' Eric said.

'Yes. I am.'

'You will be safe.'

'Thanks. I know I will.'

I pointed to the little sign marked FOWLER that indicated a driveway almost hidden by a stand of myrtle and hawthorn. We turned down a short, rutted gravel driveway lined with trees. It canted sharply downhill. Eric frowned as the Corvette lurched along the deep ruts. By the time the drive leveled out into the clearing where the cabin stood, the slope was enough to render the roof a little below the height of the road around the lake. There were four cars parked on the beaten dirt in front of the cabin. The windows were open to admit the sharp cool of the evening, but the shades were drawn. I could hear voices drifting out, though I couldn't make out words. I was suddenly, deeply reluctant to enter Jan Fowler's cabin.

'I could be bisexual?' Eric asked. It didn't seem to bother him; he seemed, if anything, amused. We stood by Eric's car, facing each other, my hands stuffed in the sweater pockets.

'Okay.' I shrugged. Who cared? This was make believe. I caught a movement out of the corner of my eye. Someone was watching us through a partially raised shade. 'We're being watched.'

'Then I'll act friendly.'

We were out of the car by that time. Eric bent, and without yanking me to him, set his mouth on mine. He didn't grab me, so I felt fairly relaxed. I'd known that at the very minimum I'd have to kiss other people. So I set my mind to it.

Maybe I had natural talent, which had been nurtured by a great teacher. Bill had pronounced me an excellent kisser, and I wanted to do him proud.

Judging from the state of Eric's Lycra, I succeeded.

'Ready to go in?' I asked, doing my best to keep my eyes above his chest.

'Not really,' Eric said. 'But I suppose we have to. At least I look in the mood.'

Though it was dismaying to think that this was the second time I had kissed Eric and that I had enjoyed it more than I should, I could feel a smile twitch the corners of my mouth as we crossed the bumpy ground of the clearing. We went up the steps to a large wooden deck, strewn with the usual aluminum folding chairs and a large gas grill. The screen door screeched as Eric pulled it open, and I knocked lightly on the inner door. 'Who is it?' Jan's voice said.

'It's Sookie and a friend,' I answered.

'Oh, goodie! Come on in!' she called.

When I pushed open the door, all the faces in the room were turned toward us. The welcoming smiles turned to startled looks as Eric came in behind me.

Eric stepped to my side, his coat over his arm, and I almost hooted at the variety of expressions. After the shock of realizing Eric was vampire, which everyone in the room did after a minute or so, eyes flickered up and down the length of Eric's body, taking in the panorama.

'Hey, Sookie, who's your friend?' Jan Fowler, a multiple divorcée in her thirties, was wearing what looked like a lace slip. Jan's hair was streaked and professionally tousled, and her makeup would have seemed in place on stage, though for a cabin by Mimosa Lake the effect was a bit much. But as hostess, I guess she felt she could wear what she wanted to her own orgy. I slid out of my sweater and endured the embarrassment of receiving the same scrutiny Eric had been given.

'This is Eric,' I said. 'I hope you don't mind me bringing a friend?'

'Oh, the more the merrier,' she said with undoubted sincerity. Her eyes never rose to Eric's face. 'Eric, what can I get you to drink?'

'Blood?' Eric asked hopefully.

'Yeah, I think I've got some O here,' she said, unable to tear her gaze away from the Lycra. 'Sometimes we . . . pretend.' She raised her eyebrows significantly, and kind of leered at Eric.

'No need to pretend anymore,' he said, giving her back look for look. On his way to join her at the refrigerator, he managed to stroke Eggs's shoulder, and Eggs's face lit up.

Oh. Well, I'd known I'd learn some things. Tara, beside him, was sulking, her dark brows drawn down over dark eyes. Tara was wearing a bra and panties of shrieking red, and she looked pretty good. Her toenails and fingernails were painted so they matched, and so did her lipstick. She'd come prepared. I met her eyes, and she looked away. It didn't take a mind reader to recognize shame.

Mike Spencer and Cleo Hardaway were on a dilapidated couch against the left-hand wall. The whole cottage, basically one large room with a sink and stove against the right-hand wall and a walled-in bathroom in the far corner, was furnished in cast-offs, because in Bon Temps that was what you did with your old furniture. However, most lake cabins would not have featured such a thick soft rug and such a lot of pillows tossed around at random, and there would not have been such thick shades drawn at all the windows. Plus, the knickknacks strewn around on that soft rug were simply nasty. I didn't even know what some of them were.

But I pasted a cheerful smile on my face, and hugged Cleo Hardaway, as I usually did when I saw her. Granted, she had always been wearing more clothes when she ran the high school cafeteria. But panties were more than Mike was wearing, which was not a stitch.

Well, I'd known it would be bad, but I guess you just can't prepare yourself for some sights. Cleo's huge milk-chocolate brown boobs were glistening with some kind of oil, and Mike's private parts were equally shiny. I didn't even want to think about that.

Mike tried to grab my hand, probably to assist with the oil, but I slithered away and edged over to Eggs and Tara.

'I sure never thought you'd come,' Tara said. She was smiling, too, but not real happily. In fact, she looked pretty damn miserable. Maybe the fact that Tom Hardaway was kneeling in front of her smooching up the inside of her leg had something to do with that. Maybe it was Eggs's obvious interest in Eric. I tried to meet Tara's eyes, but I felt sick.

I'd only been here five minutes, but I was willing to bet this was the longest five minutes of my life.

'Do you do this real often?' I asked Tara, absurdly. Eggs, his eyes on Eric's bottom while Eric stood talking at the refrigerator with Jan, began fumbling with the button on my shorts. Eggs had been drinking again. I could smell it. His eyes were glassy and his jaw was slack. 'Your friend is really big,' he said, as if his mouth were watering, and maybe it was.

'Lots bigger than Lafayette,' I whispered, and his gaze jerked up to meet mine. 'I figured he'd be welcome.'

'Oh, yes,' Eggs said, deciding not to confront my statement. 'Yes, Eric's . . . very large. It's good to have some diversity.'

'This is as rainbow as Bon Temps gets,' I said, trying hard not to sound perky. I endured Eggs's continued struggle with the button. This had been a big mistake. Eggs was just thinking about Eric's butt. And other things about Eric.

Speaking of the devil, he snugged up behind me and ran his arms around me, pulling me to him and removing me from Eggs's clumsy fingers. I leaned back into Eric, really glad he was there. I realized that was because I *expected* Eric to misbehave. But seeing people you'd known all your life act like this, well, it was deeply disgusting. I wasn't too sure I could keep my face from showing this, so I wiggled against Eric, and when he made a happy sound, I turned in his arms to face him. I put my arms up around his neck and raised my face. He happily complied with my silent suggestion. With my face concealed, my mind was free to roam. I opened myself up mentally, just as Eric parted my lips with his tongue, so I felt completely unguarded. There were some strong 'senders' in that room, and I no longer felt like myself, but like a pipeline for other people's overwhelming needs.

I could taste the flavor of Eggs's thoughts. He was remembering Lafayette, thin brown body, talented fingers, and heavily made up eyes. He was remembering Lafayette's whispered suggestions. Then he was choking those happy memories off with more unpleasant ones, Lafayette protesting violently, shrilly . . .

'Sookie,' Eric said in my ear, so low that I don't think another person in the room could've heard him. 'Sookie, relax. I have you.'

I made my hand stroke his neck. I found that someone else was behind Eric, sort of making out with him from behind.

Jan's hand reached around Eric and began rubbing my rear. Since she was touching me, her thoughts were absolutely clear; she was an exceptional 'sender.' I flicked through her mind like the pages of a book, and read nothing of interest. She was only thinking of Eric's anatomy, and worrying about her own fascination with Cleo's chest. Nothing there for me.

I reached in another direction, wormed into the head of Mike Spencer, found the nasty tangle I'd expected, found that as he rolled Cleo's breasts in his hands he was seeing other brown flesh, limp and lifeless. His own flesh rose as he remembered this. Through his memories I saw Jan asleep on the lumpy couch, Lafayette's protest that if they didn't stop hurting him he would tell everyone what he'd done and with whom, and then Mike's fists descending, Tom Hardaway kneeling on the thin dark chest . . .

I had to get out of here. I couldn't bear it, even if I hadn't just learned what I needed to know. I didn't see how

Portia could have endured it, either, especially since she would have had to stay to learn anything, not having the 'gift' I had.

I felt Jan's hand massaging my ass. This was the most joyless excuse for sex I had ever seen: sex separated from mind and spirit, from love or affection. Even simple liking.

According to my four-times-married friend Arlene, men had no problem with this. Evidently, some women didn't either.

'I have to get out,' I breathed into Eric's mouth. I knew he could hear me.

'Go along with me,' he replied, and it was almost as if I was hearing him in my head.

He lifted me and slung me over his shoulder. My hair trailed down almost to the middle of his thigh.

'We're going outside for a minute,' he told Jan, and I heard a big smacking noise. He'd given her a kiss.

'Can I come, too?' she asked, in a breathless Marlene Dietrich voice. It was lucky my face wasn't showing.

'Give us a minute. Sookie is still a little shy,' Eric said in a voice as full of promise as a tub of a new flavor of ice cream.

'Warm her up good,' Mike Spencer said in a muffled voice. 'We all want to see our Sookie fired up.'

'She will be hot,' Eric promised.

'Hot damn,' said Tom Hardaway, from between Tara's legs.

Then, bless Eric, we were out the door and he laid me out on the hood of the Corvette. He lay on top of me, but most of his weight was supported by his hands resting on the hood on either side of my shoulders.

He was looking down at me, his face clamped down like a ship's deck during a storm. His fangs were out. His eyes were wide. Since the whites were so purely white, I could see them. It was too dark to see the blue of his eyes, even if I'd wanted to.

I didn't want. 'That was . . .' I began, and had to stop. I took a deep breath. 'You can call me a goody two-shoes if you want to, and I wouldn't blame you, after all this was my idea. But you know what I think? I think that's awful. Do men really like that? Do women, for that matter? Is it fun to have sex with someone you don't even like?'

'Do you like me, Sookie?' Eric asked. He rested more heavily on me and moved a little.

Uh-oh. 'Eric, remember why we're here?'

'They're watching.'

'Even if they are, remember?'

'Yes, I remember.'

'So we need to go.'

'Do you have any evidence? Do you know what you wanted to find out?'

'I don't have any more evidence than I had before tonight, not evidence you can hand out in court.' I made myself put my arms around his ribs. 'But I know who did it. It was Mike, Tom, and maybe Cleo.'

'This is interesting,' Eric said, with a complete lack of sincerity. His tongue flicked into my ear. I happen to particularly like that, and I could feel my breathing speed up. Maybe I wasn't as immune to uninvolved sex as I'd thought. But then, I liked Eric, when I wasn't afraid of him.

'No, I just hate this,' I said, reaching some inner conclusion. 'I don't like any part of this.' I shoved Eric hard, though it didn't make a bit of difference. 'Eric, you listen to me. I've done everything for Lafayette and Andy Bellefleur I can, though it's precious little. He'll just have to go from here on the little snatches I caught. He's a cop. He can find court evidence. I'm not selfless enough to go any further with this.'

'Sookie,' Eric said. I didn't think he'd heard a word. 'Yield to me.'

Well, that was pretty direct.

'No,' I said, in the most definite voice I could summon. 'No.'

'I will protect you from Bill.'

'You're the one that's gonna need protection!' When I reflected on that sentence, I was not proud of it.

'You think Bill is stronger than me?'

'I am not having this conversation.' Then I proceeded to have it. 'Eric, I appreciate your offering to help me, and I appreciate your willingness to come to an awful place like this.'

'Believe me, Sookie, this little gathering of trash is nothing, nothing, compared to some of the places I have been.'

And I believed him utterly. 'Okay, but it's awful to me. Now, I realize that I should've known this would, ah, rouse your expectations, but you know I did not come out here tonight to have sex with anyone. Bill is my boyfriend.' Though the words *boyfriend* and *Bill* sounded ludicrous in the same sentence, 'boyfriend' was Bill's function in my world, anyway.

'I am glad to hear it,' said a cool, familiar voice. 'This scene would make me wonder, otherwise.'

Oh, great.

Eric rose up off of me, and I scrambled off the hood of the car and stumbled in the direction of Bill's voice.

'Sookie,' he said, when I drew near, 'it's getting to where I just can't let you go anywhere alone.'

As far as I could tell in the poor lighting, he didn't look very glad to see me. But I couldn't blame him for that. 'I sure made a big mistake,' I said, from the bottom of my heart. I hugged him.

'You smell like Eric,' he said into my hair. Well, hell, I was forever smelling like other men to Bill. I felt a flood of misery and shame, and I realized things were about to happen.

But what happened was not what I expected.

Andy Bellefleur stepped out of the bushes with a gun in his hand. His clothes looked torn and stained, and the gun looked huge.

'Sookie, step away from the vampire,' he said.

'No.' I wrapped myself around Bill. I didn't know if I was protecting him or he was protecting me. But if Andy wanted us separated, I wanted us joined.

There was a sudden surge of voices on the porch of the cabin. Someone clearly had been looking out of the window – I had kind of wondered if Eric had made that up – because, though no voices had been raised, the showdown in the clearing had attracted the attention of the revelers inside. While Eric and I had been in the yard, the orgy had progressed. Tom Hardaway was naked, and Jan, too. Eggs Tallie looked drunker.

'You smell like Eric,' Bill repeated, in a hissing voice.

I reared back from him, completely forgetting about Andy and his gun. And I lost my temper.

This is a rare thing, but not as rare as it used to be. It was kind of exhilarating. 'Yeah, uh-huh, and I can't even tell what you smell like! For all I know you've been with six women! Hardly fair, is it?'

Bill gaped at me, stunned. Behind me, Eric started laughing. The crowd on the sundeck was silently enthralled. Andy didn't think we should all be ignoring the man with the gun.

'Stand together in a group,' he bellowed. Andy had had a lot to drink.

Eric shrugged. 'Have you ever dealt with vampires, Bellefleur?' he asked.

'No,' Andy said. 'But I can shoot you dead. I have silver bullets.'

'That's –' I started to say, but Bill's hand covered my mouth. Silver bullets were only definitely fatal to werewolves, but vampires also had a terrible reaction to silver, and a vampire hit in a vital place would certainly suffer.

Eric raised an eyebrow and sauntered over to the orgiasts on the deck. Bill took my hand, and we joined them. For once, I would have loved to know what Bill was thinking.

'Which one of you was it, or was it all of you?' Andy bellowed.

We all kept silent. I was standing by Tara, who was shivering in her red underwear. Tara was scared, no big surprise. I wondered if knowing Andy's thoughts would help any, and I began to focus on him. Drunks don't make for good reading, I can tell you, because they only think about stupid stuff, and their ideas are quite unreliable. Their memories are shaky, too. Andy didn't have too many thoughts at the moment. He didn't like anyone in the clearing, not even himself, and he was determined to get the truth out of someone.

'Sookie, come here,' he yelled.

'No,' Bill said very definitely.

'I have to have her right here beside me in thirty seconds, or I shoot – her!' Andy said, pointing his gun right at me.

'You will not live thirty seconds after, if you do,' Bill said.

I believed him. Evidently Andy did, too.

'I don't care,' Andy said. 'She's not much loss to the world.'

Well, that made me mad all over again. My temper had begun to die down, but that made it flare up in a big way.

I yanked free from Bill's hand and stomped down the steps to the yard. I wasn't so blind with anger that I ignored the gun, though I was sorely tempted to grab Andy by his balls and squeeze. He'd still shoot me, but he'd hurt, too. However, that was as self-defeating as drinking was. Would the moment of satisfaction be worth it?

'Now, Sookie, you read the minds of those people and you tell me which one did it,' Andy ordered. He gripped the back of my neck with his big hands, like I was an untrained puppy, and swiveled me around to face the deck.

'What the hell do you think I was doing here, you stupid shit? Do you think this is the way I like to spend my time, with assholes like these?'

Andy shook me by my neck. I am very strong, and there was a good chance that I could break free from him and grab the gun, but it was not close enough to a sure thing to make me comfortable. I decided to wait for a minute. Bill was trying to tell me something with his face, but I wasn't sure what it was. Eric was trying to cop a feel from Tara. Or Eggs. It was hard to tell.

A dog whined at the edge of the woods. I rolled my eyes in that direction, unable to turn my head. Well, great. Just great.

'That's my collie,' I told Andy. 'Dean, remember?' I could have used some human-shaped help, but since Sam had arrived on the scene in his collie persona, he'd have to stay that way or risk exposure.

'Yeah. What's your dog doing out here?'

'I don't know. Don't shoot him, okay?'

'I'd never shoot a dog,' he said, sounding genuinely shocked.

'Oh, but me, it's okay,' I said bitterly.

The collie padded over to where we were standing. I wondered what was on Sam's mind. I wondered if he retained much human thinking while he was in his favorite form. I rolled my eyes toward the gun, and Sam/Dean's eyes followed mine, but how much comprehension was in there, I just couldn't estimate.

The collie began to growl. His teeth were bared and he was glaring at the gun.

'Back up, dog,' Andy said, annoyed.

If I could just hold Andy still for a minute, the vampires could get him. I tried to work out all the moves in my mind. I'd have to grab his gun hand with both of my hands and force it up. But with Andy holding me out from him like this, that wasn't going to be easy.

'No, sweetheart,' Bill said.

My eyes flashed over to him. I was considerably startled. Bill's eyes moved from my face to behind Andy. I could take a hint.

'Oh, who is being held like a little cub?' inquired a voice behind Andy.

Oh, this was just *peachy*.

'It is my messenger!' The maenad sauntered around Andy in a wide circle and came to stand to his right, a few feet before him. She was not between Andy and the group on the deck. She was clean tonight, and wearing nothing at all. I guessed she and Sam had been out in the woods making whoopee, before they heard the crowd. Her black hair fell in a tangled mass all the way to her hips. She didn't seem cold. The rest of us (except the vampires) were definitely feeling the nip in the air. We'd come dressed for an orgy, not an outdoors party.

'Hello, messenger,' the maenad said to me. 'I forgot to introduce myself last time, my canine friend reminds me. I am Callisto.'

'Miss Callisto,' I said, since I had no idea what to call her. I would have nodded, but Andy had hold of my neck. It was sure beginning to hurt.

'Who is this stalwart brave gripping you?' Callisto moved a little closer.

I had no idea what Andy looked like, but everyone on the deck was enthralled and terrified, Eric and Bill excepted. They were easing back, away from the humans. This wasn't good.

'This is Andy Bellefleur,' I croaked. 'He has a problem.'

I could tell from the way my skin crawled that the maenad had eased forward a little.

'You have never seen anything like me, have you?' she said to Andy.

'No,' Andy admitted. He sounded dazed.

'Am I beautiful?'

'Yes,' he said, without hesitation.

'Do I deserve tribute?'

'Yes,' he said.

'I love drunkenness, and you are very drunk,' Callisto said happily. 'I love pleasures of the flesh, and these people are full of lust. This is my kind of place.'

'Oh, good,' Andy said uncertainly. 'But one of these people is a murderer, and I need to know which.'

'Not just one,' I muttered. Reminded I was on the end of his arm, Andy shook me again. I was getting really tired of this.

The maenad had gotten close enough now to touch me. She gently stroked my face, and I smelled earth and wine on her fingers.

'You are not drunk,' she observed.

'No, ma'am.'

'And you have not had the pleasures of the flesh this evening.'

'Oh, just give me time,' I said.

She laughed. It was a high, whooping laugh. It went on and on.

Andy's grip loosened, as he grew more and more disconcerted by the maenad's nearness. I don't know what the people on the deck thought they saw. But Andy knew he was seeing a creature of the night. He let go of me, quite suddenly.

'Come on up here, new girl,' called Mike Spencer. 'Let's have a look at you.'

I was on a heap on the ground by Dean, who was licking my face enthusiastically. From that point of view, I could see the maenad's arm snake around Andy's waist. Andy transferred his gun to his left hand so he could return the compliment.

'Now, what did you want to know?' she asked Andy.

Her voice was calm and reasonable. She idly waved the long wand with the tuft on the end. It was called a thyrsis; I'd looked *maenad* up in the encyclopedia. Now I could die educated.

'One of those people killed a man named Lafayette, and I want to know which one,' Andy said with the belligerence of the drunk.

'Of course you do, my darling,' the maenad crooned. 'Shall I find out for you?'

'Please,' he begged.

'All right.' She scanned the people, and crooked her finger at Eggs. Tara held on to his arm to try to keep him with her, but he lurched down the steps and over to the maenad, grinning foolishly all the while.

'Are you a girl?' Eggs asked.

'Not by any stretch of the imagination,' Callisto said. 'You have had a lot of wine.' She touched him with the thyrsis.

'Oh, yeah,' he agreed. He wasn't smiling anymore. He looked into Callisto's eyes, and he shivered and shook. Her eyes were glowing. I looked at Bill, and saw he had his own eyes focused on the ground. Eric was looking at the hood of his car. Ignored by everyone, I began to crawl toward Bill.

This was a fine kettle of fish.

The dog paced beside me, nosing me anxiously. I felt he wanted me to move faster. I reached Bill's legs and gripped them. I felt his hand on my hair. I was scared to make the large movement of rising to my feet.

Callisto wrapped her thin arms around Eggs and began to whisper to him. He nodded and whispered back. She kissed him, and he went rigid. When she left him to glide over to the deck, he stood absolutely still, staring into the woods.

She stopped by Eric, who was closer to the deck than we were. She looked him up and down, and smiled that terrifying smile again. Eric looked at her chest fixedly, careful not to meet her eyes. 'Lovely,' she said, 'just lovely. But not for me, you beautiful piece of dead meat.'

Then she was up amongst the people on the deck. She took a deep breath, inhaling the scents of drinking and sex. She sniffed as if she were following a trail, and then she swung to face Mike Spencer. His middle-aged body did not fare well in the chilly air, but Callisto seemed delighted with him.

'Oh,' she said as happily as though she'd just gotten a present, 'you're so proud! Are you a king? Are you a great soldier?'

'No,' Mike said. 'I own a funeral home.' He didn't sound too sure. 'What are you, lady?'

'Have you ever seen anything like me before?'

'No,' he said, and all the others shook their heads.

'You don't remember my first visit?'

'No, ma'am.'

'But you've made me an offering before.'

'I have? An offering?'

'Oh, yes, when you killed the little black man. The pretty one. He was a lesser child of mine, and a fitting tribute for me. I thank you for leaving him outside the drinking place; bars are my particular delight. Could you not find me in the woods?'

'Lady, we didn't make no offering,' Tom Hardaway said, his dark skin all over goose pimples and his penis gone south.

'I saw you,' she said.

Everything fell silent then. The woods around the lake, always full of little noises and tiny movements, became still. I very carefully rose to my feet beside Bill.

'I love the violence of sex, I love the reek of drink,' she said dreamily. 'I can run from miles away to be there for the end.'

The fear pouring out of their heads began to fill mine up, and run out. I covered my face with my hands. I threw up the strongest shields I could fashion, but I could still barely contain the terror. My back arched, and I bit my tongue to keep from making a sound. I could feel the movement as Bill turned to me, and then Eric was by his side and they were both mashing me between them. There is not a thing erotic about being pressed between two vampires under those circumstances. Their own urgent desire for my silence fed the fear, because what would frighten vampires? The dog pressed against our legs as if he offered us protection.

'You hit him during sex,' the maenad said to Tom. 'You hit him, because you are proud, and his subservience disgusted and excited you.' She stretched her bony hand to caress Tom's dark face. I could see the whites of his eyes. 'And you' – she patted Mike with her other hand – 'you beat him, too, because you were seized with the madness. Then he threatened to tell.' Her hand left Tom and rubbed his wife, Cleo. Cleo had thrown on a sweater before she went out, but it wasn't buttoned.

Since she had avoided notice, Tara began backing up. She was the only one who wasn't paralyzed by fear. I could feel the tiny spark of hope in her, the desire to survive. Tara crouched under a wrought-iron table on the deck, made herself into a little ball, and squeezed her eyes shut. She was making a lot of promises to God about her future behavior, if he'd get her out of this. That poured into my mind, too. The reek of fear from the others built to a peak, and I could feel my body go into tremors as they broadcast so heavily that it broke through all my barriers. I had nothing left of myself. I was only fear. Eric and Bill locked arms with each other, to hold me upright and immobile between them.

Jan, in her nudity, was completely ignored by the maenad. I can only suppose that there was nothing in Jan that appealed to the creature; Jan was not proud, she was pathetic, and she hadn't had a drink that night. She embraced sex out of other needs than the need for its loss of self – needs that had nothing to do with leaving one's mind and body for a moment of wonderful madness. Trying, as always, to be the center of the group, Jan reached out with a would-be flirty smile and took the maenad's hand. Suddenly she began to convulse, and the noises coming from her throat were horrible. Foam came from her mouth, and her eyes rolled up. She collapsed to the deck, and I could hear her heels drumming the wood.

Then the silence resumed. But something was brewing a few yards away in the little group on the deck: something terrible and fine, something pure and horrible. Their fear was subsiding, and my body began to calm again. The awful pressure eased in my head. But as it ebbed, a new force began to build, and it was indescribably beautiful and absolutely evil.

It was pure madness, it was mindless madness. From the maenad poured the berserker rage, the lust of pillage, the hubris of pride. I was overwhelmed when the people on the deck were overwhelmed, I jerked and thrashed as the insanity rolled off Callisto and into their brains, and only

Eric's hand across my mouth kept me from screaming as they did. I bit him and tasted his blood, and heard him grunt at the pain.

It went on and on and on, the screaming, and then there were awful wet sounds. The dog, pressed against our legs, whimpered.

Suddenly, it was over.

I felt like a dancing puppet whose strings have suddenly been severed. I went limp. Bill laid me down on Eric's car hood again. I opened my eyes. The maenad looked down at me. She was smiling again, and she was drenched in blood. It was like someone had poured a bucket of red paint over her head; her hair was drenched, as was every bit of her bare body, and she reeked of the copper smell, enough to set your teeth on edge.

'You were close,' she said to me, her voice as sweet and high as a flute. She moved a little more deliberately, as if she'd eaten a heavy meal. 'You were very close. Maybe as close as you'll ever come, maybe not. I've never seen anyone maddened by the insanity of others. An entertaining thought.'

'Entertaining for you, maybe,' I gasped. The dog bit my leg to bring me to myself. She looked down at him.

'My dear Sam,' she murmured. 'Darling, I must leave you.'

The dog looked up at her with intelligent eyes.

'We've had some good nights running through the woods,' she said, and stroked his head. 'Catching little rabbits, little coons.'

The dog wagged his tail.

'Doing other things.'

The dog grinned and panted.

'But it's time for me to go, darling. The world is full of woods and people that need to learn their lesson. I must be paid tribute. They mustn't forget me. I'm owed,' she said, in her sated voice, 'owed the madness and death.' She began to drift to the edge of the woods.

'After all,' she said over her shoulder, 'it can't always be hunting season.'

Chapter 11

Even if I'd wanted to, I couldn't have walked over to see what was on the deck. Bill and Eric seemed subdued, and when vampires seem subdued, it means you don't really want to go investigate.

'We'll have to burn the cabin,' Eric said from a few yards away. 'I wish Callisto had taken care of her own mess.'

'She never has,' Bill said. 'that I have heard. It is the madness. What does true madness care about discovery?'

'Oh, I don't know,' Eric said carelessly. He sounded as if he was lifting something. There was a heavy thud. 'I have seen a few people who were definitely mad and quite crafty with it.'

'That's true,' Bill said. 'Shouldn't we leave a couple of them on the porch?'

'How can you tell?'

'That's true, too. It's a rare night I can agree with you this much.'

'She called me and asked me to help.' Eric was responding to the subtext rather than the statement.

'Then, all right. But you remember our agreement.'

'How can I forget?'

'You know Sookie can hear us.'

'Quite all right with me,' Eric said, and laughed. I stared up at the night and wondered, not too curiously, what the hell they were talking about. It's not like I was Russia, to be parceled out to the strongest dictator. Sam was resting beside me, back in his human form, and stark naked. At the moment, I could not have cared less. The cold didn't bother Sam, since he was a shapeshifter.

'Whoops, here's a live one,' Eric called.

'Tara,' Sam called.

Tara scrambled down the steps of the deck and over to us. She flung her arms around me and began sobbing. With tremendous weariness, I held her and let her boo-hoo. I was still in my Daisy Duke outfit, and she was in her fire-engine lingerie. We were like big white water lilies in a cold pond, we two. I made myself straighten up and hold Tara.

'Would there be a blanket in that cabin, you think?' I asked Sam. He trotted over to the steps, and I noticed the effect was interesting from behind. After a minute, he trotted back – wow, this view was even more arresting – and wrapped a blanket around the two of us.

'I must be gonna live,' I muttered.

'Why do you say that?' Sam was curious. He didn't seem unduly surprised by the events of the night.

I could hardly tell him it was because I'd watched him bounce around, so I said, 'How are Eggs and Andy?'

'Sounds like a radio show,' Tara said suddenly, and giggled. I didn't like the sound of it.

'They're still standing where she left them,' Sam reported. 'Still staring.'

'I'm – still – staring,' Tara sang, to the tune of Elton's 'I'm Still Standing.'

Eric laughed.

He and Bill were just about to start the fire. They strolled over to us for a last-minute check.

'What car did you come in?' Bill asked Tara.

'Ooo, a vampire,' she said. 'You're Sookie's honey, aren't you? Why were you at the game the other night with a dog like Portia Bellefleur?'

'She's kind, too,' Eric said. He looked down at Tara with a sort of beneficent but disappointed smile, like a dog breeder regarding a cute, but inferior, puppy.

'What car did you come in?' Bill asked again. 'If there is a sensible side to you, I want to see it now.'

'I came in the white Camaro,' she said, quite soberly. 'I'll drive it home. Or maybe I better not. Sam?'

'Sure, I'll drive you home. Bill, you need my help here?'

'I think Eric and I can cope. Can you take the skinny one?'

'Eggs? I'll see.'

Tara gave me a kiss on the cheek and began picking her way across the yard to her car. 'I left the keys in it,' she called.

'What about your purse?' The police would surely wonder if they found Tara's purse in a cabin with a lot of bodies.

'Oh . . . it's in there.'

I looked at Bill silently, and he went in to fetch the purse. He returned with a big shoulder bag, large enough to contain not only makeup and everyday items, but also a change of clothing.

'This is yours?'

'Yes, thanks,' Tara said, taking the bag from him as if she were afraid his fingers might touch hers. She hadn't been so picky earlier in the evening, I thought.

Eric was carrying Eggs to her car. 'He will not remember any of this,' Eric told Tara as Sam opened the back door of the Camaro so Eric could lay Eggs inside.

'I wish I could say the same.' Her face seemed to sag on its bones under the weight of the knowledge of what had happened this night. 'I wish I'd never seen that thing, whatever she is. I wish I'd never come here, to start with. I hated doing this. I just thought Eggs was worth it.' She gave a look to the inert form in the backseat of her car. 'He's not. No one is.'

'I can remove your memory, too.' Eric made the offer offhandedly.

'No,' she said. 'I need to remember some of this, and it's worth carrying the burden of the rest.' Tara sounded twenty years older. Sometimes we can grow up all in a minute; I'd done that when I was about seven and my parents died. Tara had done that this night.

'But they're all dead, all but me and Eggs and Andy. Aren't you afraid we'll talk? Are you gonna come after us?'

Eric and Bill exchanged glances. Eric moved a little closer to Tara. 'Look, Tara,' he began, in a very reasonable voice, and she made the mistake of glancing up. Then, once her gaze was fixed, Eric began to erase the memory of the night. I was just too tired to protest, as if that would do any good. If Tara could even raise the question, she shouldn't be burdened with the knowledge. I hoped she wouldn't repeat her mistakes, having been separated from the knowledge of what they had cost her; but she couldn't be allowed to tell tales.

Tara and Eggs, driven by Sam (who had borrowed Eggs's pants), were on their way back to town when Bill began arranging a natural-looking fire to consume the cabin. Eric was apparently counting bones up on the deck, to make sure the bodies there were complete enough to reassure the investigators. He went across the yard to check on Andy.

'Why does Bill hate the Bellefleurs so much?' I asked him again.

'Oh, that's an old story,' Eric said. 'Back from before Bill had even changed over.' He seemed satisfied by Andy's condition and went back to work.

I heard a car approaching, and Bill and Eric both appeared in the yard instantly. I could hear a faint crackle from the far side of the cabin. 'We can't start the fire from more than one place, or they may be able to tell it wasn't natural,' Bill said to Eric. 'I hate these strides in police science.'

'If we hadn't decided to go public, they'd have to blame it on one of them,' Eric said. 'But as it is, we are such attractive scapegoats . . . it's galling, when you think of how much stronger we are.'

'Hey, guys, I'm not a Martian, I'm a human, and I can hear you just fine,' I said. I was glaring at them, and they were looking perhaps one-fiftieth embarrassed, when Portia Bellefleur got out of her car and ran to her brother. 'What have you done to Andy?' she said, her voice harsh and cracking. 'You damn vampires.' She pulled the collar of Andy's shirt this way and that, looking for puncture marks.

'They saved his life,' I told her.

Eric looked at Portia for a long moment, evaluating her, and then he began to search the cars of the dead revelers. He'd gotten their car keys, which I didn't want to picture.

Bill went over to Andy and said, 'Wake up,' in the quietest voice, so quiet it could hardly be heard a few feet away.

Andy blinked. He looked over at me, confused that I wasn't still in his grasp, I guess. He saw Bill, so close to him, and he flinched, expecting retaliation. He registered that Portia was at his side. Then he looked past Bill at the cabin.

'It's on fire,' he observed, slowly.

'Yes,' Bill said. 'They are all dead, except the two who've gone back into town. They knew nothing.'

'Then . . . these people did kill Lafayette?'

'Yes,' I said. 'Mike, and the Hardaways, and I guess maybe Jan knew about it.'

'But I haven't got any proof.'

'Oh, I think so,' Eric called. He was looking down into the trunk of Mike Spencer's Lincoln.

We all moved to the car to see. Bill's and Eric's superior vision made it easy for them to tell there was blood in the trunk, blood and some stained clothes and a wallet. Eric reached down and carefully flipped the wallet open.

'Can you read whose it is?' Andy asked.

'Lafayette Reynold,' Eric said.

'So if we just leave the cars like this, and we leave, the police will find what's in the trunk and it'll all be over. I'll be clear.'

'Oh, thank God!' Portia said, and gave a kind of sobbing gasp. Her plain face and thick chestnut hair caught a gleam of moonlight filtering through the trees. 'Oh, Andy, let's go home.'

'Portia,' Bill said, 'look at me.'

She glanced up at him, then away. 'I'm sorry I led you on like that,' she said rapidly. She was ashamed to apologize to a vampire, you could tell. 'I was just trying to get one of the people who came here to invite me, so I could find out for myself what was going on.'

'Sookie did that for you,' Bill said mildly.

Portia's gaze darted over to me. 'I hope it wasn't too awful, Sookie,' she said, surprising me.

'It was really horrible,' I said. Portia cringed. 'But it's over.'

'Thank you for helping Andy,' Portia said bravely.

'I wasn't helping Andy. I was helping Lafayette,' I snapped.

She took a deep breath. 'Of course,' she said, with some dignity. 'He was your coworker.'

'He was my *friend*,' I corrected.

Her back straightened. 'Your friend,' she said.

The fire was catching in the cabin now, and soon there would be police and firefighters. It was definitely time to leave.

I noticed neither Eric nor Bill offered to remove any memories from Andy.

'You better get out of here,' I said to him. 'You better go back to your house, with Portia, and tell your grandmama to swear you were there all night.'

Without a word, brother and sister piled into Portia's Audi and left. Eric folded himself into the Corvette for the drive back to Shreveport, and Bill and I went through the woods to Bill's car, concealed in the trees across the road. He carried me, as he enjoyed doing. I have to say, I enjoyed it, too, on occasion. This was definitely one of the occasions.

It wasn't far from dawn. One of the longest nights of my life was about to come to a close. I lay back against the seat of the car, tired beyond reckoning.

'Where did Callisto go?' I asked Bill.

'I have no idea. She moves from place to place. Not too many maenads survived the loss of the god, and the ones that did find woods, and roam them. They move before their presence is discovered. They're crafty like that. They love war and its madness. You'll never find them far from a battlefield. I think they'd all move to the Middle East if there were more woods.'

'Callisto was here because . . .?'

'Just passing through. She stayed maybe two months, now she'll work her way . . . who knows? To the Everglades, or up the river to the Ozarks.'

'I can't understand Sam, ah, palling around with her.'

'That's what you call it? Is that what we do, pal around?'

I reached over and poked him in the arm, which was like pressing on wood. 'You,' I said.

'Maybe he just wanted to walk on the wild side,' Bill said. 'After all, it's hard for Sam to find someone who can accept his true nature.' Bill paused significantly.

'Well, that can be hard to do,' I said. I recalled Bill coming back in the mansion in Dallas, all rosy, and I gulped. 'But people in love are hard to pry apart.' I thought of how I'd felt when I'd heard he'd been seeing Portia, and I thought of how I'd reacted when I'd seen him at the football game. I stretched my hand over to rest on his thigh and I gave it a gentle squeeze.

With his eyes on the road, he smiled. His fangs ran out a little.

'Did you get everything settled with the shapeshifters in Dallas?' I asked after a moment.

'I settled it in an hour, or rather Stan did. He offered them his ranch for the nights of the full moon, for the next four months.'

'Oh, that was nice of him.'

'Well, it doesn't cost him anything exactly. And he doesn't hunt, so the deer need culling anyway, as he pointed out.'

'Oh,' I said in acknowledgment, and then after a second, 'ooooh.'

'They hunt.'

'Right. Gotcha.'

When we got back to my house, it didn't lack much till dawn. Eric would just make it to Shreveport, I figured. While Bill showered, I ate some peanut butter and jelly, since I hadn't had anything for more hours than I could add up. Then I went and brushed my teeth.

At least he didn't have to rush off. Bill had spent several nights the month before creating a place for himself at my house. He'd cut out the bottom of the closet in my old bedroom, the one I'd used for years before my grandmother died and I'd started using hers. He'd made the whole closet floor into a trapdoor, so he could open it, climb in, and pull it shut after him, and no one would be the wiser but me. If I was still up when he went to earth, I put an old suitcase in the closet and a couple of pairs of shoes to make it look more natural. Bill kept a box in the crawl space to sleep in, because it was mighty nasty down there. He didn't often stay there, but it had come in handy from time to time.

'Sookie,' Bill called from my bathroom. 'Come, I have time to scrub you.'

'But if you scrub me, I'll have a hard time getting to sleep.'

'Why?'

'Because I'll be frustrated.'

'Frustrated?'

'Because I'll be clean but . . . unloved.'

'It is close to dawn,' Bill admitted, his head poking around the shower curtain. 'But we'll have our time tomorrow night.'

'If Eric doesn't make us go somewhere else,' I muttered, when his head was safely under the cascade of water. As usual, he was using up most of my hot. I wriggled out of the damn shorts and resolved to throw them away tomorrow. I pulled the tee shirt over my head and stretched out on my bed to wait for Bill. At least my new bra was intact. I turned on one side, and closed my eyes against the light coming from the half-closed bathroom door.

'Darling?'

'You out of the shower?' I asked drowsily.

'Yes, twelve hours ago.'

'What?' My eyes flew open. I looked at the windows. They were not pitch black, but very dark.

'You fell asleep.'

I had a blanket over me, and I was still wearing the steel blue bra and panty set. I felt like moldy bread. I looked at Bill. He was wearing nothing at all.

'Hold that thought,' I said and paid a visit to the bathroom. When I came back, Bill was waiting for me on the bed, propped on one elbow.

'Did you notice the outfit you got me?' I rotated to give him the full benefit of his generosity.

'It's lovely, but you may be slightly overdressed for the occasion.'

'What occasion would that be?'

'The best sex of your life.'

I felt a lurch of sheer lust down low. But I kept my face still. 'And can you be sure it will be the best?'

'Oh, yes,' he said, his voice becoming so smooth and cold it was like running water over stones. 'I can be sure, and so can you.'

'Prove it,' I said, smiling very slightly.

His eyes were in the shadows, but I could see the curve of his lips as he smiled back. 'Gladly,' he said.

Some time later, I was trying to recover my strength, and he was draped over me, an arm across my stomach, a leg across mine. My mouth was so tired it could barely pucker to kiss his shoulder. Bill's tongue was gently licking the tiny puncture marks on my shoulder.

'You know what we need to do?' I said, feeling too lazy to move ever again.

'Um?'

'We need to get the newspaper.'

After a long pause, Bill slowly unwrapped himself from me and strolled to the front door. My paperwoman pulls up my driveway and tosses it in the general direction of the porch because I pay her a great big tip on that understanding.

'Look,' said Bill, and I opened my eyes. He was holding a foil-wrapped plate. The paper was tucked under his arm.

I rolled off the bed and we went automatically to the kitchen. I pulled on my pink robe as I padded after Bill. He was still natural, and I admired the effect.

'There's a message on the answering machine,' I said, as I put on some coffee. The most important thing done, I rolled back the aluminum foil and saw a two-layer cake with chocolate icing, studded with pecans in a star pattern on the top.

'That's old Mrs. Bellefleur's chocolate cake,' I said, awe in my voice.

'You can tell whose it is by looking?'

'Oh, this is a famous cake. It's a legend. Nothing is as good as Mrs. Bellefleur's cake. If she enters it in the county fair, the ribbon's as good as won. And she brings it when someone dies. Jason said it was worth someone dying, just to get a piece of Mrs. Bellefleur's cake.'

'What a wonderful smell,' Bill said, to my amazement. He bent down and sniffed. Bill doesn't breathe, so I haven't exactly figured out how he smells, but he does. 'If you could wear that as a perfume, I would eat you up.'

'You already did.'

'I would do it a second time.'

'I don't think I could stand it.' I poured myself a cup of coffee. I stared at the cake, full of wonderment. 'I didn't even know she knew where I live.'

Bill pressed the message button on my answering machine. 'Miss Stackhouse,' said the voice of a very old, very Southern, aristocrat. 'I knocked on your door, but you must have been busy. I left a chocolate cake for you, since I didn't know what else to do to thank you for what Portia tells me you've done for my grandson Andrew. Some people have been kind enough to tell me that the cake is good. I hope you enjoy it. If I can ever be of service to you, just give me a call.'

'Didn't say her name.'

'Caroline Holliday Bellefleur expects everyone to know who she is.'

'Who?'

I looked up at Bill, who was standing by the window. I was sitting at the kitchen table, drinking coffee from one of my grandmother's flowered cups.

'Caroline Holliday Bellefleur.'

Bill could not get any paler, but he was undoubtedly stunned. He sat down very abruptly into the chair across from me. 'Sookie, do me a favor.'

'Sure, baby. What is it?'

'Go over to my house and get the Bible that is in the glass-fronted bookshelf in the hallway.'

He seemed so upset, I grabbed my keys and drove over in my bathrobe, hoping I wouldn't meet anyone along the way. Not too many people live out on our parish road, and none of them were out at four in the morning.

I let myself into Bill's house and found the Bible exactly where he'd said. I eased it out of the bookcase very carefully. It was obviously quite old. I was so nervous carrying it up the steps to my house that I almost tripped. Bill was sitting where I'd left him. When I'd set the Bible in front of him, he stared at it for a long minute. I began to wonder if he could touch it. But he didn't ask for help, so I waited. His hand reached out and the white fingers caressed the worn leather cover. The book was massive, and the gold lettering on the cover was ornate.

Bill opened the book with gentle fingers and turned a page. He was looking at a family page, with entries in faded ink, made in several different handwritings.

'I made these,' he said in a whisper. 'These here.' He pointed at a few lines of writing.

My heart was in my throat as I came around the table to look over his shoulder. I put my own hand on his shoulder, to link him to the here and now.

I could barely make out the writing.

William Thomas Compton, his mother had written, or perhaps his father. *Born April 9, 1840.* Another hand had written *Died November 25, 1868.*

'You have a birthday,' I said, of all the stupid things to say. I'd never thought of Bill having a birthday.

'I was the second son,' Bill said. 'The only son who grew up.'

I remembered that Robert, Bill's older brother, had died when he was twelve or so, and two other babies had died in infancy. There all these births and deaths were recorded, on the page under Bill's fingers.

'Sarah, my sister, died childless.' I remembered that. 'Her young man died in the war. All the young men died in the war. But I survived, only to die later. This is the date of my death, as far as my family is concerned. It's in Sarah's handwriting.'

I held my lips pressed tight, so I wouldn't make a sound. There was something about Bill's voice, the way he touched the Bible that was almost unbearable. I could feel my eyes fill with tears.

'Here is the name of my wife,' he said, his voice quieter and quieter.

I bent over again to read, *Caroline Isabelle Holliday*. For one second, the room swung sideways, until I realized it just could not be.

'And we had children,' he said. 'We had three children.'

Their names were there, too. *Thomas Charles Compton, b. 1859.* She'd gotten pregnant right after they'd married, then.

I would never have Bill's baby.

Sarah Isabelle Compton, b. 1861. Named after her aunt (Bill's sister) and her mother. She'd been born around the time Bill had left for the war. *Lee Davis Compton, b. 1866.* A homecoming baby. *Died 1867*, a different hand had added.

'Babies died like flies then,' Bill whispered. 'We were so poor after the war, and there wasn't any medicine.'

I was about to take my sad weepy self out of the kitchen, but then I realized that if Bill could stand this, I pretty much had to.

'The other two children?' I asked.

'They lived,' he said, the tension in his face easing a little. 'I had left then, of course. Tom was only nine when I died, and Sarah was seven. She was towheaded, like her mother.' Bill smiled a little, a smile that I'd never seen on his face before. He looked quite human. It was like seeing a different being sitting here in my kitchen, not the same person I'd made love with so thoroughly not an hour earlier. I pulled a Kleenex out of the box on the baker's rack and dabbed at my face. Bill was crying, too, and I handed him one. He looked at it in surprise, as if he'd expected to see something different – maybe a monogrammed cotton handkerchief. He patted his own cheeks. The Kleenex turned pink.

'I hadn't ever looked to see what became of them,' he said wonderingly. 'I cut myself off so thoroughly. I never came back, of course, while there was any chance any one of them would be alive. That would be too cruel.' He read down the page.

'My descendant Jessie Compton, from whom I received my house, was the last of my direct line,' Bill told me. 'My mother's line, too, has thinned down, until the remaining Loudermilks are only distantly related to me. But Jessie did descend from my son Tom, and apparently, my daughter Sarah married in 1881. She had a baby in – Sarah had a baby! She had four babies! But one of them was born dead.'

I could not even look at Bill. Instead, I looked at the window. It had begun raining. My grandmother had loved her tin roof, so when it had had to be replaced, we'd gotten tin again, and the drumming of the rain was normally the most relaxing sound I knew. But not tonight.

'Look, Sookie,' Bill said, pointing. 'Look! My Sarah's daughter, named Caroline for her grandmother, married a cousin of hers, Matthew Phillips Holliday. And her second child was Caroline Holliday.' His face was glowing.

'So old Mrs. Bellefleur is your great-granddaughter.'

'Yes,' he said unbelievingly.

'So Andy,' I continued, before I could think twice about it, 'is your, ah, great-great-great-grandson. And Portia . . .'

'Yes,' he said, less happily.

I had no idea what to say, so for once, I said nothing. After a minute, I got the feeling it might be better if I made myself scarce, so I tried to slip by him to get out of the small kitchen.

'What do they need?' he asked me, seizing my wrist.

Okay. 'They need money,' I said instantly. 'You can't help them with their personality problems, but they are cash-poor in the worst possible way. Old Mrs. Bellefleur won't give up that house, and it's eating every dime.'

'Is she proud?'

'I think you could tell from her phone message. If I hadn't known her middle name was Holliday, I would have thought it was "Proud."' I eyed Bill. 'I guess she comes by it natural.'

Somehow, now that Bill knew he could do something for his descendants, he seemed to feel much better. I knew he would be reminiscing for a few days, and I would not grudge him that. But if he decided to take up Portia and Andy as permanent causes, that might be a problem.

'You didn't like the name Bellefleur before this,' I said, surprising myself. 'Why?'

'When I spoke to your grandmother's club, you remember, the Descendants of the Glorious Dead?'

'Yes, sure.'

'And I told the story, the story of the wounded soldier out in the field, the one who kept calling for help? And how my friend Tolliver Humphries tried to rescue him?'

I nodded.

'Tolliver died in the attempt,' Bill said bleakly. 'And the wounded soldier resumed calling for help after his death. We managed to retrieve him during the night. His name was Jebediah Bellefleur. He was seventeen years old.'

'Oh my gosh. So that was all you knew of the Bellefleurs until today.'

Bill nodded.

I tried to think of something of significance to say. Something about cosmic plans. Something about throwing your bread upon the waters. What goes around, comes around?

I tried to leave again. But Bill caught my arm, pulled me to him. 'Thank you, Sookie.'

That was the last thing I had expected him to say. 'Why?'

'You made me do the right thing with no idea of the eventual reward.'

'Bill, I can't make you do anything.'

'You made me think like a human, like I was still alive.'

'The good you do is in you, not in me.'

'I am a vampire, Sookie. I have been a vampire far longer than I was human. I have upset you many times. To tell the truth, sometimes I can't understand why you do what you do sometimes, because it's been so long since I was a person. It's not always comfortable to remember what it was like to be a man. Sometimes I don't want to be reminded.'

These were deep waters for me. 'I don't know if I'm right or wrong, but I don't know how to be different,' I said. 'I'd be miserable if it wasn't for you.'

'If anything happens to me,' Bill said, 'you should go to Eric.'

'You've said that before,' I told him. 'If anything happens to you, I don't have to go to anyone. I'm my own person. I get to make up my mind what I want to do. You've got to make sure nothing happens to you.'

'We'll be having more trouble from the Fellowship in the years to come,' Bill said. 'Actions will have to be taken that may be repugnant to you as a human. And there are the dangers attached to your job.' He didn't mean waiting tables.

'We'll cross that bridge when we get to it.' Sitting on Bill's lap was a real treat, especially since he was still naked. My life had not exactly been full of treats until I met Bill. Now every day held a treat, or two.

In the low-lit kitchen, with the coffee smelling as beautiful (in its own way) as the chocolate cake did, and the rain drumming on the roof, I was having a beautiful moment with my vampire, what you might call a warm human moment.

But maybe I shouldn't call it that, I reflected, rubbing my cheek against Bill's. This evening, Bill had looked quite human. And I – well, I had noticed while we made love on our clean sheets, that in the darkness Bill's skin had been glowing in its beautiful otherworldly way.

And mine had, too.

CLUB DEAD

Also by Charlaine Harris

SOOKIE STACKHOUSE

Dead Until Dark
Living Dead in Dallas
Club Dead
Dead to the World
Dead as a Doornail
Definitely Dead
All Together Dead
From Dead to Worse
Dead and Gone

HARPER CONNELLY

Grave Sight
Grave Surprise
An Ice Cold Grave
Grave Secret

CLUB DEAD

CHARLAINE HARRIS

First published in Great Britain in 2004 by
Little, Brown

This edition published in Great Britain in 2009 by
Gollancz
An imprint of the Orion Publishing Group
Orion House, 5 Upper St Martin's Lane, London WC2H 9EA
An Hachette UK Company

A CIP catalogue record for this book
is available from the British Library

ISBN 978 0 575 08940 2

7 9 10 8

Printed and bound in the UK by
CPI Mackays, Chatham ME5 8TD

www.orionbooks.co.uk

*This book is dedicated to my middle child,
Timothy Schulz, who told me flatly
he wanted a book all to himself.*

Acknowledgments

My thanks go to Lisa Weissenbuehler, Kerie L. Nickel, Marie La Salle, and the incomparable Doris Ann Norris for their input on car trunks, great and small. My further thanks to Janet Davis, Irene, and Sonya Stocklin, also cybercitizens of DorothyL, for their information on bars, bourree (a card game), and the parish governments of Louisiana. Joan Coffey was most gracious with supplying information about Jackson. The wonderful and obliging Jane Lee drove me patiently around Jackson for many hours, entering thoroughly into the spirit of finding the perfect location for a vampire bar.

Chapter 1

Bill was hunched over the computer when I let myself in his house. This was an all-too-familiar scenario in the past month or two. He'd torn himself away from his work when I came home, until the past couple of weeks. Now it was the keyboard that attracted him.

'Hello, sweetheart,' he said absently, his gaze riveted to the screen. An empty bottle of type O TrueBlood was on the desk beside the keyboard. At least he'd remembered to eat.

Bill, not a jeans-and-tee kind of guy, was wearing khakis and a plaid shirt in muted blue and green. His skin was glowing, and his thick dark hair smelled like Herbal Essence. He was enough to give any woman a hormonal surge. I kissed his neck, and he didn't react. I licked his ear. Nothing.

I'd been on my feet for six hours straight at Merlotte's Bar, and every time some customer had under-tipped, or some fool had patted my fanny, I'd reminded myself that in a short while I'd be with my boyfriend, having incredible sex and basking in his attention.

That didn't appear to be happening.

I inhaled slowly and steadily and glared at Bill's back. It was a wonderful back, with broad shoulders, and I had planned on seeing it bare with my nails dug into it. I had counted on that very strongly. I exhaled, slowly and steadily.

'Be with you in a minute,' Bill said. On the screen, there was a snapshot of a distinguished man with silver hair and a dark tan. He looked sort of Anthony Quinn-type sexy, and he looked powerful. Under the picture was a name, and under that was some text. 'Born 1756 in Sicily,' it began. Just as I opened my mouth to comment that vampires *did* appear in photographs despite the legend, Bill twisted around and realized I was reading.

He hit a button and the screen went blank.

I stared at him, not quite believing what had just happened.

'Sookie,' he said, attempting a smile. His fangs were retracted, so he was totally not in the mood in which I'd hoped to find him; he wasn't thinking of me carnally. Like all vampires, his fangs are only fully extended when he's in the mood for the sexy kind of lust, or the feeding-and-killing kind of lust. (Sometimes, those lusts all get kind of snarled up, and you get your dead fang-bangers. But that element of danger is what attracts most fang-bangers, if you ask me.) Though I've been accused of being one of those pathetic creatures that hang around vampires in the hope of attracting their attention, there's only one vampire I'm involved with (at least voluntarily) and it was the one sitting right in front of me. The one who was keeping secrets from me. The one who wasn't nearly glad enough to see me.

'Bill,' I said coldly. Something was Up, with a capital *U*. And it wasn't Bill's libido. (Libido had just been on my Word-A-Day calendar.)

'You didn't see what you just saw,' he said steadily. His dark brown eyes regarded me without blinking.

'Uh-huh,' I said, maybe sounding just a little sarcastic. 'What are you up to?'

'I have a secret assignment.'

I didn't know whether to laugh or stalk away in a snit. So I just raised my eyebrows and waited for more. Bill was the investigator for Area 5, a vampire division of Louisiana. Eric, the head of Area 5, had never given Bill an 'assignment' that was secret from me before. In fact, I was usually an integral part of the investigation team, however unwilling I might be.

'Eric must not know. None of the Area 5 vampires can know.'

My heart sank. 'So – if you're not doing a job for Eric, who are you working for?' I knelt because my feet were so tired, and I leaned against Bill's knees.

'The queen of Louisiana,' he said, almost in a whisper.

Because he looked so solemn, I tried to keep a straight face, but it was no use. I began to laugh, little giggles that I couldn't suppress.

'You're serious?' I asked, knowing he must be. Bill was almost always a serious kind of fellow. I buried my face on his thigh so he couldn't see my amusement. I rolled my eyes up for a quick look at his face. He was looking pretty pissed.

'I am as serious as the grave,' Bill said, and he sounded so steely, I made a major effort to change my attitude.

'Okay, let me get this straight,' I said in a reasonably

level tone. I sat back on the floor, cross-legged, and rested my hands on my knees. 'You work for Eric, who is the boss of Area 5, but there is also a queen? Of Louisiana?'

Bill nodded.

'So the state is divided up into Areas? And she's Eric's superior, since he runs a business in Shreveport, which is in Area 5.'

Again with the nod. I put my hand over my face and shook my head. 'So, where does she live, Baton Rouge?' The state capital seemed the obvious place.

'No, no. New Orleans, of course.'

Of *course*. Vampire central. You could hardly throw a rock in the Big Easy without hitting one of the undead, according to the papers (though only a real fool would do so). The tourist trade in New Orleans was booming, but it was not exactly the same crowd as before, the hard-drinking, rollicking crowd who'd filled the city to party hearty. The newer tourists were the ones who wanted to rub elbows with the undead; patronize a vampire bar, visit a vampire prostitute, watch a vampire sex show.

This was what I'd heard; I hadn't been to New Orleans since I was little. My mother and father had taken my brother, Jason, and me. That would have been before I was seven, because that's when they died.

Mama and Daddy died nearly twenty years before vampires had appeared on network television to announce the fact that they were actually present among us, an announcement that had followed on the Japanese development of synthetic blood that actually maintained a vampire's life without the necessity of drinking from humans.

The United States vampire community had let the

Japanese vampire clans come forth first. Then, simultaneously, in most of the nations of the world that had television – and who doesn't these days? – the announcement had been made in hundreds of different languages, by hundreds of carefully picked personable vampires.

That night, two and half years ago, we regular old live people learned that we had always lived with monsters among us.

'But' – the burden of this announcement had been – 'now we can come forward and join with you in harmony. You are in no danger from us anymore. We don't need to drink from you to live.'

As you can imagine, this was a night of high ratings and tremendous uproar. Reaction varied sharply, depending on the nation.

The vampires in the predominantly Islamic nations had fared the worst. You don't even want to know what happened to the undead spokesman in Syria, though perhaps the female vamp in Afghanistan died an even more horrible – and final – death. (What were they thinking, selecting a female for that particular job? Vampires could be so smart, but they sometimes didn't seem quite in touch with the present world.)

Some nations – France, Italy, and Germany were the most notable – refused to accept vampires as equal citizens. Many – like Bosnia, Argentina, and most of the African nations – denied any status to the vampires, and declared them fair game for any bounty hunter. But America, England, Mexico, Canada, Japan, Switzerland, and the Scandinavian countries adopted a more tolerant attitude.

It was hard to determine if this reaction was what the

vampires had expected or not. Since they were still struggling to maintain a foothold in the stream of the living, the vampires remained very secretive about their organization and government, and what Bill was telling me now was the most I'd ever heard on the subject.

'So, the Louisiana queen of the vampires has you working on a secret project,' I said, trying to sound neutral. 'And this is why you have lived at your computer every waking hour for the past few weeks.'

'Yes,' Bill said. He picked up the bottle of TrueBlood and tipped it up, but there were only a couple of drops left. He went down the hall into the small kitchen area (when he'd remodeled his old family home, he'd pretty much left out the kitchen, since he didn't need one) and extracted another bottle from the refrigerator. I was tracking him by sound as he opened the bottle and popped it into the microwave. The microwave went off, and he reentered, shaking the bottle with his thumb over the top so there wouldn't be any hot spots.

'So, how much more time do you have to spend on this project?' I asked – reasonably, I thought.

'As long as it takes,' he said, less reasonably. Actually, Bill sounded downright irritable.

Hmmm. Could our honeymoon be over? Of course I mean figurative honeymoon, since Bill's a vampire and we can't be legally married, practically anywhere in the world.

Not that he's asked me.

'Well, if you're so absorbed in your project, I'll just stay away until it's over,' I said slowly.

'That might be best,' Bill said, after a perceptible pause, and I felt like he'd socked me in the stomach. In a flash, I was on my feet and pulling my coat back over my cold-weather waitress outfit – black slacks, white boat-neck long-sleeved tee with 'Merlotte's' embroidered over the left breast. I turned my back to Bill to hide my face.

I was trying not to cry, so I didn't look at him even after I felt Bill's hand touch my shoulder.

'I have to tell you something,' Bill said in his cold, smooth voice. I stopped in the middle of pulling on my gloves, but I didn't think I could stand to see him. He could tell my backside.

'If anything happens to me,' he continued (and here's where I should have begun worrying), 'you must look in the hiding place I built at your house. My computer should be in it, and some disks. Don't tell anyone. If the computer isn't in the hiding place, come over to my house and see if it's here. Come in the daytime, and come armed. Get the computer and any disks you can find, and hide them in my hidey-hole, as you call it.'

I nodded. He could see that from the back. I didn't trust my voice.

'If I'm not back, or if you don't get word from me, in say . . . eight weeks – yes, eight weeks, then tell Eric everything I said to you today. And place yourself under his protection.'

I didn't speak. I was too miserable to be furious, but it wouldn't be long before I reached meltdown. I acknowledged his words with a jerk of my head. I could feel my ponytail switch against my neck.

'I am going to . . . Seattle soon,' Bill said. I could feel his cool lips touch the place my ponytail had brushed.

He was lying.

'When I come back, we'll talk.'

Somehow, that didn't sound like an entrancing prospect. Somehow, that sounded ominous.

Again I inclined my head, not risking speech because I was actually crying now. I would rather have died than let him see the tears.

And that was how I left him, that cold December night.

The next day on my way to work, I took an unwise detour. I was in that kind of mood where I was rolling in how awful everything was. Despite a nearly sleepless night, something inside me told me I could probably make my mood a little worse if I drove along Magnolia Creek Road: so sure enough, that's what I did.

The old Bellefleur mansion, Belle Rive, was a beehive of activity, even on a cold and ugly day. There were vans from the pest control company, a kitchen design firm, and a siding contractor parked at the kitchen entrance to the antebellum home. Life was just humming for Caroline Holliday Bellefleur, the ancient lady who had ruled Belle Rive and (at least in part) Bon Temps for the past eighty years. I wondered how Portia, a lawyer, and Andy, a detective, were enjoying all the changes at Belle Rive. They had lived with their grandmother (as I had lived with mine) for all their adult lives. At the very least, they had to be enjoying her pleasure in the mansion's renovation.

My own grandmother had been murdered a few months ago.

The Bellefleurs hadn't had anything to do with it, of course. And there was no reason Portia and Andy would share the pleasure of this new affluence with me. In fact, they both avoided me like the plague. They owed me, and they couldn't stand it. They just didn't know how *much* they owed me.

The Bellefleurs had received a mysterious legacy from a relative who had 'died mysteriously over in Europe somewhere,' I'd heard Andy tell a fellow cop while they were drinking at Merlotte's. When she dropped off some raffle tickets for Gethsemane Baptist Church's Ladies' Quilt, Maxine Fortenberry told me Miss Caroline had combed every family record she could unearth to identify their benefactor, and she was still mystified at the family's good fortune.

She didn't seem to have any qualms about spending the money, though.

Even Terry Bellefleur, Portia and Andy's cousin, had a new pickup sitting in the packed dirt yard of his doublewide. I liked Terry, a scarred Viet Nam vet who didn't have a lot of friends, and I didn't grudge him a new set of wheels.

But I thought about the carburetor I'd just been forced to replace in my old car. I'd paid for the work in full, though I'd considered asking Jim Downey if I could just pay half and get the rest together over the next two months. But Jim had a wife and three kids. Just this morning I'd been thinking of asking my boss, Sam Merlotte, if he could add to my hours at the bar. Especially with Bill gone to 'Seattle,' I could just about live at Merlotte's, if Sam could use me. I sure needed the money.

I tried real hard not to be bitter as I drove away from Belle Rive. I went south out of town and then turned left onto Hummingbird Road on my way to Merlotte's. I tried to pretend that all was well; that on his return from Seattle – or wherever – Bill would be a passionate lover again, and Bill would treasure me and make me feel valuable once more. I would again have that feeling of belonging with someone, instead of being alone.

Of course, I had my brother, Jason. Though as far as intimacy and companionship goes, I had to admit that he hardly counted.

But the pain in my middle was the unmistakable pain of rejection. I knew the feeling so well, it was like a second skin.

I sure hated to crawl back inside it.

Chapter 2

I tested the doorknob to make sure I'd locked it, turned around, and out of the corner of my eye glimpsed a figure sitting in the swing on my front porch. I stifled a shriek as he rose. Then I recognized him.

I was wearing a heavy coat, but he was in a tank top; that didn't surprise me, really.

'El –' Uh-oh, close call. 'Bubba, how are you?' I was trying to sound casual, carefree. I failed, but Bubba wasn't the sharpest tool in the shed. The vampires admitted that bringing him over, when he'd been so very close to death and so saturated with drugs, had been a big mistake. The night he'd been brought in, one of the morgue attendants happened to be one of the undead, and also happened to be a huge fan. With a hastily constructed and elaborate plot involving a murder or two, the attendant had 'brought him over' – made Bubba a vampire. But the process doesn't always go right, you know. Since then, he's been passed around like idiot royalty. Louisiana had been hosting him for the past year.

'Miss Sookie, how you doin'?' His accent was still thick

and his face still handsome, in a jowly kind of way. The dark hair tumbled over his forehead in a carefully careless style. The heavy sideburns were brushed. Some undead fan had groomed him for the evening.

'I'm just fine, thank you,' I said politely, grinning from ear to ear. I do that when I'm nervous. 'I was just fixing to go to work,' I added, wondering if it was possible I would be able to simply get in my car and drive away. I thought not.

'Well, Miss Sookie, I been sent to guard you tonight.'

'You have? By who?'

'By Eric,' he said proudly. 'I was the only one in the office when he got a phone call. He tole me to get my ass over here.'

'What's the danger?' I peered around the clearing in the woods in which my old house stood. Bubba's news made me very nervous.

'I don't know, Miss Sookie. Eric, he tole me to watch you tonight till one of them from Fangtasia gets here – Eric, or Chow, or Miss Pam, or even Clancy. So if you go to work, I go with you. And I take care of anyone who bothers you.'

There was no point in questioning Bubba further, putting strain on that fragile brain. He'd just get upset, and you didn't want to see that happen. That was why you had to remember not to call him by his former name . . . though every now and then he would sing, and that was a moment to remember.

'You can't come in the bar,' I said bluntly. That would be a disaster. The clientele of Merlotte's is used to the occasional vampire, sure, but I couldn't warn *everyone* not to say his name. Eric must have been desperate; the vampire community kept mistakes like Bubba out of sight, though from time to time he'd take it in his head to wander off on his own. Then you got a 'sighting,' and the tabloids went crazy.

'Maybe you could sit in my car while I work?' The cold wouldn't affect Bubba.

'I got to be closer than that,' he said, and he sounded immovable.

'Okay, then, how about my boss's office? It's right off the bar, and you can hear me if I yell.'

Bubba still didn't look satisfied, but finally, he nodded. I let out a breath I didn't realize I'd been holding. It would be easiest for me to stay home, call in sick. However, not only did Sam expect me to show up, but also, I needed the paycheck.

The car felt a little small with Bubba in the front seat beside me. As we bumped off my property, through the woods and out to the parish road, I made a mental note to get the gravel company to come dump some more gravel on my long, meandering driveway. Then I canceled that order, also mentally. I couldn't afford that right now. It'd have to wait until spring. Or summer.

We turned right to drive the few miles to Merlotte's, the bar where I work as a waitress when I'm not doing Heap Big Secret Stuff for the vampires. It occurred to me when we were about halfway there that I hadn't seen a car Bubba could've used to drive to my house. Maybe he'd flown? Some vamps could. Though Bubba was the least talented vampire I'd met, maybe he had a flair for it.

A year ago I would've asked him, but not now. I'm used to hanging around with the undead now. Not that I'm a vampire. I'm a telepath. My life was hell on wheels until I met a man whose mind I couldn't read. Unfortunately, I couldn't read his mind because he was dead. But Bill and I had been together for several months now, and until recently, our relationship had been real good. And the other vampires need me, so I'm safe – to a certain extent. Mostly. Sometimes.

Merlotte's didn't look too busy, judging from the half-empty parking lot. Sam had bought the bar about five years ago. It had been failing – maybe because it had been cut out of the forest, which loomed all around the parking lot. Or maybe the former owner just hadn't found the right combination of drinks, food, and service.

Somehow, after he renamed the place and renovated it, Sam had turned balance sheets around. He made a nice living off it now. But tonight was a Monday night, not a big drinking night in our neck of the woods, which happened to be in northern Louisiana. I pulled around to the employee parking lot, which was right in front of Sam Merlotte's trailer, which itself is behind and at right angles to the employee entrance to the bar. I hopped out of the driver's seat, trotted through the storeroom, and peeked through the glass pane in the door to check the short hall with its doors to the rest rooms and Sam's office. Empty. Good. And when I knocked on Sam's door, he was behind his desk, which was even better.

Sam is not a big man, but he's very strong. He's a strawberry blond with blue eyes, and he's maybe three years older than my twenty-six. I've worked for him for about that many years. I'm fond of Sam, and he's starred in some of my favorite fantasies; but since he dated a beautiful but homicidal creature a couple of months before, my enthusiasm has somewhat faded. He's for sure my friend, though.

''Scuse me, Sam,' I said, smiling like an idiot.

'What's up?' He closed the catalog of bar supplies he'd been studying.

'I need to stash someone in here for a little while.'

Sam didn't look altogether happy. 'Who? Has Bill gotten back?'

'No, he's still traveling.' My smile got even brighter. 'But, um, they sent another vampire to sort of guard me? And I need to stow him in here while I work, if that's okay with you.'

'Why do you need to be guarded? And why can't he just sit out in the bar? We have plenty of TrueBlood.' TrueBlood was definitely proving to be the front-runner among competing blood replacements. 'Next best to the drink of life,' its first ad had read, and vampires had responded to the ad campaign.

I heard the tiniest of sounds behind me, and I sighed. Bubba had gotten impatient.

'Now, I asked you –' I began, starting to turn, but never got further. A hand grasped my shoulder and whirled me around. I was facing a man I'd never seen before. He was cocking his fist to punch me in the head.

Though the vampire blood I had ingested a few months ago (to save my life, let me point out) has mostly worn off – I barely glow in the dark at all now – I'm still quicker than most people. I dropped and rolled into the man's legs, which made him stagger, which made it easier for Bubba to grab him and crush his throat.

I scrambled to my feet and Sam rushed out of his office. We stared at each other, Bubba, and the dead man.

Well, now we were really in a pickle.

'I've kilt him,' Bubba said proudly. 'I saved you, Miss Sookie.'

Having the Man from Memphis appear in your bar, realizing he's become a vampire, and watching him kill a would-be assailant – well, that was a lot to absorb in a couple of minutes, even for Sam, though he himself was more than he appeared.

'Well, so you have,' Sam said to Bubba in a soothing voice. 'Do you know who he was?'

I had never seen a dead man – outside of visitation at the local funeral home – until I'd started dating Bill (who of course was technically dead, but I mean human dead people).

It seems I run across them now quite often. Lucky I'm not too squeamish.

This particular dead man had been in his forties, and every year of that had been hard. He had tattoos all over his arms, mostly of the poor quality you get in jail, and he was missing some crucial teeth. He was dressed in what I thought of as biker clothes: greasy blue jeans and a leather vest, with an obscene T-shirt underneath.

'What's on the back of the vest?' Sam asked, as if that would have significance for him.

Bubba obligingly squatted and rolled the man to his side. The way the man's hand flopped at the end of his arm made me feel pretty queasy. But I forced myself to look at the vest. The back was decorated with a wolf's head insignia. The wolf was in profile, and seemed to be howling. The head was silhouetted against a white circle, which I decided was supposed to be the moon. Sam looked even more worried when he saw the insignia. 'Werewolf,' he said tersely. That explained a lot.

The weather was too chilly for a man wearing only a vest, if he wasn't a vampire. Weres ran a little hotter than regular people, but mostly they were careful to wear coats in cold weather, since Were society was still secret from the human race (except for lucky, lucky me, and probably a few hundred others). I wondered if the dead man had left a coat out in the bar hanging on the hooks by the main entrance; in which case, he'd been back here hiding in the men's room, waiting for me to appear. Or maybe he'd come through the back door right after me. Maybe his coat was in his vehicle.

'You see him come in?' I asked Bubba. I was maybe just a little light-headed.

'Yes, ma'am. He must have been waiting in the big parking lot for you. He drove around the corner, got out of his car, and went in the back just a minute after you did. You hightailed it through the door, and then he went in. And I followed him. You mighty lucky you had me with you.'

'Thank you, Bubba. You're right; I'm lucky to have you. I wonder what he planned to do with me.' I felt cold all over as I thought about it. Had he just been looking for a lone woman to grab, or did he plan on grabbing me specifically? Then I realized that was dumb thinking. If Eric had been alarmed enough to send a bodyguard, he must have known there was a threat, which pretty much ruled out me being targeted at random. Without comment, Bubba strode out the back door. He returned in just a minute.

'He's got him some duct tape and gags on the front seat of his car,' Bubba said. 'That's where his coat is. I brought it to put under his head.' He bent to arrange the heavily padded camouflage jacket around the dead man's face and neck. Wrapping the head was a real good idea, since the man was leaking a little bit. When he had finished his task, Bubba licked his fingers.

Sam put an arm around me because I had started shaking.

'This is strange, though,' I was saying, when the door to the hall from the bar began to open. I glimpsed Kevin Pryor's face. Kevin is a sweet guy, but he's a cop, and that's the last thing we needed.

'Sorry, toilet's back-flowing,' I said, and pushed the door shut on his narrow, astonished, face. 'Listen, fellas, why don't I hold this door shut while you two take this guy and put him in his car? Then we can figure out what to do with him.' The floor of the hall would need swabbing. I discovered the hall door actually locked. I'd never realized that.

Sam was doubtful. 'Sookie, don't you think that we should call the police?' he asked.

A year ago I would have been on the phone dialing 911 before the corpse even hit the floor. But that year had been one long learning curve. I caught Sam's eye and inclined my head toward Bubba. 'How do you think he'd handle jail?' I murmured. Bubba was humming the opening line to 'Blue Christmas.' 'Our hands are hardly strong enough to have done this,' I pointed out.

After a moment of indecision, Sam nodded, resigned to the inevitable. 'Okay, Bubba, let's you and me tote this guy out to his car.'

I ran to get a mop while the men – well, the vampire and the shape-shifter – carried Biker Boy out the back door. By the time Sam and Bubba returned, bringing a gust of cold air in their wake, I had mopped the hall and the men's bathroom (as I would if there really had been an overflow). I sprayed some air freshener in the hall to improve the environment.

It was a good thing we'd acted quickly, because Kevin was pushing open the door as soon as I'd unlocked it.

'Everything okay back here?' he asked. Kevin is a runner, so he has almost no body fat, and he's not a big guy. He looks kind of like a sheep, and he still lives with his mom. But for all that, he's nobody's fool. In the past, whenever I'd listened to his thoughts, they were either on police work, or his black amazon of a partner, Kenya Jones. Right now, his thoughts ran more to the suspicious.

'I think we got it fixed,' Sam said. 'Watch your feet, we just mopped. Don't slip and sue me!' He smiled at Kevin.

'Someone in your office?' Kevin asked, nodding his head toward the closed door.

'One of Sookie's friends,' Sam said.

'I better get out there and hustle some drinks,' I said cheerfully, beaming at them both. I reached up to check that my ponytail was smooth, and then I made my Reeboks move. The bar was almost empty, and the woman I was replacing (Charlsie Tooten) looked relieved. 'This is one slow night,' she muttered to me. 'The guys at table six have been nursing that pitcher for an hour, and Jane Bodehouse has tried to pick up every man who's come in. Kevin's been writing something in a notebook all night.'

I glanced at the only female customer in the bar, trying to keep the distaste off my face. Every drinking establishment has its share of alcoholic customers, people who open and close the place. Jane Bodehouse was one of ours. Normally, Jane drank by herself at home, but every two weeks or so she'd take it into her head to come in and pick up a man. The pickup process was getting more and more iffy, since not only was Jane in her fifties, but lack of regular sleep and proper nutrition had been taking a toll for the past ten years.

This particular night, I noticed that when Jane had applied her makeup, she had missed the actual perimeters of her eyebrows and lips. The result was pretty unsettling. We'd have to call her son to come get her. I could tell at a glance she couldn't drive.

I nodded to Charlsie, and waved at Arlene, the other waitress, who was sitting at a table with her latest flame, Buck Foley. Things were really dead if Arlene was off her feet. Arlene waved back, her red curls bouncing.

'How're the kids?' I called, beginning to put away some of the glasses Charlsie had gotten out of the dishwasher. I felt like I was acting real normal until I noticed that my hands were shaking violently.

'Doing great. Coby made the All-A honor roll and Lisa won the spelling bee,' she said with a broad smile. To anyone who believed that a four-times married woman couldn't be good mother, I would point at Arlene. I gave Buck a quick smile, too, in Arlene's honor. Buck is about the average kind of guy Arlene dates, which is not good enough for her.

'That's great! They're smart kids, like their mama,' I said.

'Hey, did that guy find you?'

'What guy?' Though I had a feeling I already knew.

'That guy in the motorcycle gear. He asked me was I the waitress dating Bill Compton, since he'd got a delivery for that waitress.'

'He didn't know my name?'

'No, and that's pretty weird, isn't it? Oh my God, Sookie, if he didn't know your name, how could he have come from Bill?'

Possibly Coby's smarts had come through his daddy, since it had taken Arlene this long to figure that out. I loved Arlene for her nature, not her brain.

'So, what did you tell him?' I asked, beaming at her. It was my nervous smile, not my real one. I don't always know when I'm wearing it.

'I told him I liked my men warm and breathing,' she said, and laughed. Arlene was occasionally completely tactless, too. I reminded myself to reevaluate why she was my good friend. 'No, I didn't really say that. I just told him you would be the blond who came in at nine.'

Thanks, Arlene. So my attacker had known who I was because my best friend had identified me; he hadn't known my name or where I lived, just that I worked at Merlotte's and dated Bill Compton. That was a little reassuring, but not a lot.

Three hours dragged by. Sam came out, told me in a whisper that he'd given Bubba a magazine to look at and a bottle of Life Support to sip on, and began to poke around behind the bar. 'How come that guy was driving a car instead of a motorcycle?' Sam muttered in a low voice. 'How come his car's got a Mississippi license plate?' He hushed when Kevin came up to check that we were going to call Jane's son, Marvin. Sam phoned while Kevin stood there so he could relay the son's promise to be at Merlotte's in twenty minutes. Kevin pushed off after that, his notebook tucked under his arm. I wondered if Kevin was turning into a poet, or writing his resume.

The four men who'd been trying to ignore Jane while sipping their pitcher at the speed of a turtle finished their beer and left, each dropping a dollar on the table by way of tip. Big spenders. I'd never get my driveway regraveled with customers like these.

With only half an hour to wait, Arlene did her closing chores and asked if she could go on and leave with Buck. Her kids were still with her mom, so she and Buck might have the trailer to themselves for a little while.

'Bill coming home soon?' she asked me as she pulled on her coat. Buck was talking football with Sam.

I shrugged. He'd called me three nights before, telling me he'd gotten to 'Seattle' safely and was meeting with – whomever he was supposed to meet with. The Caller ID had read 'Unavailable.' I felt like that said quite a lot about the whole situation. I felt like that was a bad sign.

'You . . . missing him?' Her voice was sly.

'What do you think?' I asked, with a little smile at the corners of my mouth. 'You go on home, have a good time.'

'Buck is very good at good times,' she said, almost leering.

'Lucky you.'

So Jane Bodehouse was the only customer in Merlotte's when Pam arrived. Jane hardly counted; she was so out of it.

Pam is a vampire, and she is co-owner of Fangtasia, a tourist bar in Shreveport. She's Eric's second in command. Pam is blond, probably two hundred-plus years old, and actually has a sense of humor – not a vampire trademark. If a vampire can be your friend, she was as close as I'd gotten.

She sat on a bar stool and faced me over the shining expanse of wood.

This was ominous. I had *never* seen Pam anywhere but Fangtasia. 'What's up?' I said by way of greeting. I smiled at her, but I was tense all over.

'Where's Bubba?' she asked, in her precise voice. She

looked over my shoulder. 'Eric's going to be angry if Bubba didn't make it here.' For the first time, I noticed that Pam had a faint accent, but I couldn't pin it down. Maybe just the inflections of antique English.

'Bubba's in the back, in Sam's office,' I said, focusing on her face. I wished the ax would go on and fall. Sam came to stand beside me, and I introduced them. Pam gave him a more significant greeting than she would have given a plain human (whom she might not have acknowledged at all), since Sam was a shapeshifter. And I expected to see a flicker of interest, since Pam is omnivorous in matters of sex, and Sam is an attractive supernatural being. Though vampires aren't well-known for facial expressions, I decided that Pam's was definitely unhappy.

'What's the deal?' I asked, after a moment of silence.

Pam met my gaze. We're both blue-eyed blonds, but that's like saying two animals are both dogs. That's as far as any resemblance went. Pam's hair was straight and pale, and her eyes were very dark. Now they were full of trouble. She looked at Sam, her stare significant. Without a word, he went over to help Jane's son, a worn-looking man in his thirties, shift Jane to the car.

'Bill's missing,' Pam said, shooting from the conversational hip.

'No, he's not. He's in Seattle,' I said. Willfully obtuse. I had learned that word from my Word-A-Day calendar only that morning, and here I was getting to use it.

'He lied to you.'

I absorbed that, made a 'come on' gesture with my hand.

'He's been in Mississippi all this time. He drove to Jackson.'

I stared down at the heavily polyurethane-coated wood of

the bar. I'd pretty much figured Bill had lied to me, but hearing it said out loud, baldly, hurt like hell. He'd lied to me, and he was missing.

'So . . . what are you going to do to find him?' I asked, and hated how unsteady my voice was.

'We're looking. We're doing everything we can,' Pam said. 'Whoever got him may be after you, too. That's why Eric sent Bubba.'

I couldn't answer. I was struggling to control myself.

Sam had returned, I suppose when he saw how upset I was. From about an inch behind my back, he said, 'Someone tried to grab Sookie on her way into work tonight. Bubba saved her. The body's out behind the bar. We were going to move him after we'd closed.'

'So quickly,' Pam said. She sounded even unhappier. She gave Sam a once-over, nodded. He was a fellow supernatural being, though that was definitely second best to him being another vampire. 'I'd better go over the car and see what I can find.' Pam took it quite for granted that we'd dispose of the body ourselves rather than doing something more official. Vampires are having trouble accepting the authority of law enforcement and the obligation of citizens to notify the police when trouble arises. Though vamps can't join the armed services, they can become cops, and actually enjoy the hell out of the job. But vamp cops are often pariahs to the other undead.

I would a lot rather think about vampire cops than what Pam had just told me.

'When did Bill go missing?' Sam asked. His voice managed to stay level, but there was anger just under the surface.

'He was due in last night,' Pam said. My head snapped

up. I hadn't known that. Why hadn't Bill told me he was coming home? 'He was going to drive into Bon Temps, phone us at Fangtasia to let us know he'd made it home, and meet with us tonight.' This was practically babbling, for a vampire.

Pam punched in numbers on a cell phone; I could hear the little beeps. I listened to her resultant conversation with Eric. After relaying the facts, Pam told him, 'She's sitting here. She's not speaking.'

She pressed the phone into my hand. I automatically put it to my ear.

'Sookie, are you listening?' I knew Eric could hear the sounds of my hair moving over the receiver, the whisper of my breath.

'I can tell you are,' he said. 'Listen and obey me. For now, tell no one what's happened. Act just as normal. Live your life as you always do. One of us will be watching you all the time, whether you think so or not. Even in the day, we'll find some way to guard you. We will avenge Bill, and we will protect you.'

Avenge Bill? So Eric was sure Bill was dead. Well, non-existent.

'I didn't know he was supposed to be coming in last night,' I said, as if that was the most important fact I'd learned.

'He had – bad news he was going to tell you,' Pam said suddenly.

Eric overheard her and made a disgusted sound. 'Tell Pam to shut up,' he said, sounding overtly furious for the first time since I'd known him. I didn't see any need to relay the message, because I figured Pam had been able to hear him, too. Most vampires have very acute hearing.

'So you knew this bad news and you knew he was coming back,' I said. Not only was Bill missing and possibly dead – permanently dead – but he had lied to me about where he was going and why, and he'd kept some important secret from me, something concerning me. The pain went so deep, I could not even feel the wound. But I knew I would later.

I handed the phone back to Pam, and I turned and left the bar.

I faltered as I was getting into my car. I should stay at Merlotte's to help dispose of the body. Sam wasn't a vampire, and he was only involved in this for my sake. This wasn't fair to him.

But after only a second's hesitation, I drove away. Bubba could help him, and Pam – Pam, who knew all, while I knew nothing.

Sure enough, I caught a glimpse of a white face in the woods when I got home. I almost called out to the watcher, invited the vampire in to at least sit on the couch during the night. But then I thought, No. I had to be by myself. None of this was any of my doing. I had no action to take. I had to remain passive, and I was ignorant through no will of my own.

I was as wounded and as angry as it was possible for me to be. Or at least I thought I was. Subsequent revelations would prove me wrong.

I stomped inside my house and locked the door behind me. A lock wouldn't keep the vampire out, of course, but lack of an invitation to enter would. The vampire could definitely keep any humans out, at least until dawn.

I put on my old long-sleeved blue nylon gown, and I sat at my kitchen table staring blankly at my hands. I wondered where Bill was now. Was he even walking the earth; or was he a pile of ashes in some barbecue pit? I thought of his dark brown hair, the thick feel of it beneath my fingers. I considered the secrecy of his planned return. After what seemed like a minute or two, I glanced at the clock on the stove. I'd been sitting at the table, staring into space, for over an hour.

I should go to bed. It was late, and cold, and sleeping would be the normal thing to do. But nothing in my future would be normal again. Oh, wait! If Bill were gone, my future *would* be normal.

No Bill. So, no vampires: no Eric, Pam, or Bubba.

No supernatural creatures: no Weres, shape-shifters, or maenads. I wouldn't have encountered them, either, if it hadn't been for my involvement with Bill. If he'd never come into Merlotte's, I'd just be waiting tables, listening to the unwanted thoughts of those around me: the petty greed, the lust, the disillusionment, the hopes, and the fantasies. Crazy Sookie, the village telepath of Bon Temps, Louisiana.

I'd been a virgin until Bill. Now the only sex I might possibly have would be with JB du Rone, who was so lovely that you could almost overlook the fact that he was dumb as a stump. He had so few thoughts that his companionship was nearly comfortable for me. I could even touch JB without receiving unpleasant pictures. But *Bill* . . . I found that my right hand was clenched in a fist, and I pounded it on the table so hard, it hurt like hell.

Bill had told me that if anything happened to him, I was to 'go to' Eric. I'd never been sure if he was telling me that Eric would see to it that I received some financial legacy of Bill's, or that Eric would protect me from other vampires, or that I'd be Eric's . . . well, that I'd have to have the same relationship with Eric that I had with Bill. I'd told Bill I wasn't going to be passed around like a Christmas fruitcake.

But Eric had already come to me, so I didn't even have the chance to decide whether or not to follow Bill's last piece of advice.

I lost the trail of my thought. It had never been a clear one anyway.

Oh, Bill, where are you? I buried my face in my hands.

My head was throbbing with exhaustion, and even my cozy kitchen was chilly in this small hour. I rose to go to bed, though I knew I wouldn't sleep. I needed Bill with such gut-clenching intensity that I wondered if it was somehow abnormal, if I'd been enchanted by some supernatural power.

Though my telepathic ability provided immunity from the vampires' glamour, maybe I was vulnerable to another power? Or maybe I was just missing the only man I'd ever loved. I felt eviscerated, empty, and betrayed. I felt worse than I had when my grandmother had died, worse than when my parents had drowned. When my parents had died, I'd been very young, and maybe I hadn't fully comprehended, all at once, that they were permanently gone. It was hard to remember now. When my grandmother had died a few months ago, I had taken comfort in the ritual surrounding death in the South.

And I'd known they hadn't willingly left me.

I found myself standing in the kitchen doorway. I switched off the overhead light.

Once I was wrapped up in bed in the dark, I began crying, and I didn't stop for a long, long time. It was not a night to count my blessings. It was a night when every loss I'd ever had pressed hard on me. It did seem I'd had more bad luck than most people. Though I made a token attempt to fend off a deluge of self-pity, I wasn't too successful. It was pretty much twined in there with the misery of not knowing Bill's fate.

I wanted Bill to curl up against my back; I wanted his cool lips on my neck. I wanted his white hands running down my stomach. I wanted to talk to him. I wanted him to laugh off my terrible suspicions. I wanted to tell him about my day; about the stupid problem I was having with the gas company, and the new channels our cable company had added. I wanted to remind him that he needed a new washer on the sink in his bathroom, let him know that my brother, Jason, had found out he wasn't going to be a father after all (which was good, since he wasn't a husband, either).

The sweetest part of being a couple was sharing your life with someone else.

But my life, evidently, had not been good enough to share.

Chapter 3

When the sun came up, I'd managed a half hour of sleep. I started to rise and make some coffee, but there didn't seem to be much point. I just stayed in bed. The phone rang during the morning, but I didn't pick it up. The doorbell rang, but I didn't answer it.

At some point toward the middle of the afternoon, I realized that there was one thing I had to do, the task Bill had insisted on my accomplishing if he was delayed. This situation exactly fit what he'd told me.

Now I sleep in the largest bedroom, formerly my grandmother's. I wobbled across the hall to my former room. A couple of months before, Bill had taken out the floor of my old closet and made it into a trapdoor. He'd established a light-tight hidey-hole for himself in the crawl space under the house. He'd done a great job.

I made sure I couldn't be seen from the window before I opened the closet door. The floor of the closet was bare of everything but the carpet, which was an extension of the one cut to fit the room. After I'd retracted the flap that covered the closet floor, I ran a pocketknife around the flooring and eventually pried it up. I looked down into the black box below. It was full: Bill's computer, a box of disks, even his monitor and printer.

So Bill had foreseen this might happen, and he'd hidden his work before he'd left. He'd had some faith in me, no matter how faithless he might have been himself. I nodded, and rolled the carpet back into place, fitting it carefully into the corners. On the floor of the closet I put out-of-season things – shoe boxes containing summer shoes, a beach bag filled with big sunbathing towels and one of my many tubes of suntan lotion, and my folding chaise that I used for tanning. I stuck a huge umbrella back in the corner, and decided that the closet looked realistic enough. My sundresses hung from the bar, along with some very lightweight bathrobes and nightgowns. My flare of energy faded as I realized I'd finished the last service Bill had asked of me, and I had no way to let him know I had followed his wishes.

Half of me (pathetically) wanted to let him know I'd kept the faith; half of me wanted to get in the toolshed and sharpen me some stakes.

Too conflicted to form any course of action, I crawled back to my bed and hoisted myself in. Abandoning a lifetime of making the best of things, and being strong and cheerful and practical, I returned to wallowing in my grief and my overwhelming sense of betrayal.

When I woke, it was dark again, and Bill was in bed with me. Oh, thank God! Relief swept over me. Now all would be well. I felt his cool body behind me, and I rolled over, half asleep, and put my arms around him. He eased up my long nylon gown, and his hand stroked my leg. I put my head against his silent chest and nuzzled him. His arms tightened around me, he pressed firmly against me, and I sighed with joy, inserting a hand between us to unfasten his pants. Everything was back to normal.

Except he smelled different.

My eyes flew open, and I pushed back against rock-hard shoulders. I let out a little squeak of horror.

'It's me,' said a familiar voice.

'Eric, what are you doing here?'

'Snuggling.'

'You son of a bitch! I thought you were Bill! I thought he was back!'

'Sookie, you need a shower.'

'What?'

'Your hair is dirty, and your breath could knock down a horse.'

'Not that I care what you think,' I said flatly.

'Go get cleaned up.'

'Why?'

'Because we have to talk, and I'm pretty sure you don't want to have a long conversation in bed. Not that I have any objection to being in bed with you' – he pressed himself against me to prove how little he objected – 'but I'd enjoy it more if I were with the hygienic Sookie I've come to know.'

Possibly nothing he could have said would have gotten me out of the bed faster than that. The hot shower felt wonderful to my cold body, and my temper took care of warming up my insides. It wasn't the first time Eric had surprised me in my own home. I was going to have to rescind his invitation to enter. What had stopped me from that drastic step before – what stopped me now – was the idea that if I ever needed help, and he couldn't enter, I might be dead before I could yell, 'Come in!'

I'd entered the bathroom carrying my jeans and underwear and a red-and-green Christmas sweater with reindeer on it, because that's what had been at the top of my drawer. You only get a month to wear the darn things, so I make the most of it. I used a blow-dryer on my hair, wishing Bill were there to comb it out for me. He really enjoyed doing that, and I enjoyed letting him. At that mental image, I almost broke down again, but I stood with my head resting against the wall for a long moment while I gathered my resolve. I took a deep breath, turned to the mirror, and slapped on some makeup. My tan wasn't great this far into the cold season; but I still had a nice glow, thanks to the tanning bed at Bon Temps Video Rental.

I'm a summer person. I like the sun, and the short dresses, and the feeling you had many hours of light to do whatever you chose. Even Bill loved the smells of summer; he loved it when he could smell suntan oil and (he told me) the sun itself on my skin.

But the sweet part of winter was that the nights were much longer – at least, I'd thought so when Bill was around to share those nights with me. I threw my hairbrush across the bathroom. It made a satisfying clatter as it ricocheted into the tub. 'You *bastard*!' I screamed at the top of my lungs. Hearing my voice saying such a thing out loud calmed me down as nothing else could have.

When I emerged from the bathroom, Eric was completely dressed. He had on a freebie T-shirt from one of the breweries that supplied Fangtasia ('This Blood's For You,' it read) and blue jeans, and he had thoughtfully made the bed.

'Can Pam and Chow come in?' he asked.

I walked through the living room to the front door and opened it. The two vampires were sitting silently on the porch swing. They were in what I thought of as downtime. When vampires don't have anything in particular to do, they sort of go blank; retreat inside themselves, sitting or standing utterly immobile, eyes open but vacant. It seems to refresh them.

'Please come in,' I said.

Pam and Chow entered slowly, looking around them with interest, as if they were on a field trip. Louisiana farmhouse, circa early twenty-first century. The house had belonged to our family since it was built over a hundred and sixty years ago. When my brother, Jason, had struck out on his own, he'd moved into the place my parents had built when they'd married. I'd stayed here, with Gran, in this much-altered, much-renovated house; and she'd left it to me in her will.

The living room had been the total original house. Other additions, like the modern kitchen and the bathrooms, were relatively new. The next floor, which was much smaller than the ground level, had been added in the early 1900s to accommodate a generation of children who all survived. I rarely went up there these days. It was awfully hot upstairs in the summer, even with the window air conditioners.

All my furniture was aged, styleless, and comfortable – absolutely conventional. The living room had couches and chairs and a television and a VCR, and then you passed through a hall that had my large bedroom with its own bath on one side, and a hall bathroom and my former bedroom and some closets – linen, coat – on the other. Through that passage, you were into the kitchen/dining area, which had been added on soon after my grandparents' wedding. After the kitchen, there was a big roofed back porch, which I'd just had screened in. The porch housed a useful old bench, the washer and dryer, and a bunch of shelves.

There was a ceiling fan in every room and a fly swatter, too, hung in a discreet spot on a tiny nail. Gran wouldn't turn on the air conditioner unless she absolutely had to.

Though they didn't venture upstairs, no detail escaped Pam and Chow on the ground floor.

By the time they settled at the old pine table where Stackhouses had eaten for a few generations, I felt like I lived in a museum that had just been cataloged. I opened the refrigerator and got out three bottles of TrueBlood, heated them up in the microwave, gave them a good shake, and plonked them down on the table in front of my guests.

Chow was still practically a stranger to me. He'd been working at Fangtasia only a few months. I assume he'd bought into the bar, as the previous bartender had. Chow had amazing tattoos, the dark blue Asian kind that are so intricate, they are like a set of fancy clothes. These were so different from my attacker's jailhouse decorations that it was hard to believe they were the same art form. I'd been told Chow's were Yakuza tattoos but I had never had the nerve to ask him, especially since it wasn't exactly my business. However, if these were true Yakuza tats, Chow was not that old for a vampire. I'd looked up the Yakuza, and the tattooing was a (relatively) recent development in that criminal organization's long history. Chow had long black hair (no surprise there), and I'd heard from many sources that he was a tremendous draw at Fangtasia. Most evenings, he worked shirtless. Tonight, as a concession to the cold, he was wearing a zipped red vest.

I couldn't help but wonder if he ever really felt naked; his body was so thoroughly decorated. I wished I could ask him, but of course that was out of the question. He was the only person of Asian descent I had ever met, and no matter how you know individuals don't represent their whole race, you do kind of expect at least some of the generalizations to be valid. Chow did seem to have a strong sense of privacy. But far from being silent and inscrutable, he was chattering away with Pam, though in a language I couldn't understand. And he smiled at me in a disconcerting way. Okay, maybe he was too far from inscrutable. He was probably insulting the hell out of me, and I was too dumb to know it.

Pam was dressed, as always, in sort of middle-class anonymous clothes. This evening it was a pair of winter white knit pants and a blue sweater. Her blond hair was shining, straight and loose, down her back. She looked like Alice in Wonderland with fangs.

'Have you found out anything else about Bill?' I asked, when they'd all had a swallow of their drinks.

Eric said, 'A little.'

I folded my hands in my lap and waited.

'I know Bill's been kidnapped,' he said, and the room swam around my head for a second. I took a deep breath to make it stop.

'Who by?' Grammar was the least of my worries.

'We aren't sure,' Chow told me. 'The witnesses are not agreeing.' His English was accented, but very clear.

'Let me at them,' I said. 'If they're human, I'll find out.'

'If they were under our dominion, that would be the logical thing to do,' Eric said agreeably. 'But, unfortunately, they're not.'

Dominion, my foot. 'Please explain.' I was sure I was showing extraordinary patience under the circumstances.

'These humans owe allegiance to the king of Mississippi.'

I knew my mouth was falling open, but I couldn't seem to stop it. 'Excuse me,' I said, after a long moment, 'but I could have sworn you said . . . the king? Of Mississippi?'

Eric nodded without a trace of a smile.

I looked down, trying to keep a straight face. Even under the circumstances, it was impossible. I could feel my mouth twitch. 'For real?' I asked helplessly. I don't know why it seemed even funnier that Mississippi had a king – after all, Louisiana had a queen – but it did. I reminded myself I wasn't supposed to know about the queen. Check.

The vampires looked at one another. They nodded in unison.

'Are you the king of Louisiana?' I asked Eric, giddy with all my mental effort to keep varying stories straight. I was laughing so hard that it was all I could do to keep upright in the chair. Possibly there was a note of hysteria.

'Oh, no,' he said. 'I am the sheriff of Area 5.'

That really set me off. I had tears running down my face, and Chow was looking uneasy. I got up, made myself some Swiss Miss microwave hot chocolate, and stirred it with a spoon so it would cool off. I was calming down as I performed the little task, and by the time I returned to the table, I was almost sober.

'You never told me all this before,' I said, by way of explanation. 'You all have divided up America into kingdoms, is that right?'

Pam and Chow looked at Eric with some surprise, but he didn't regard them. 'Yes,' he said simply. 'It has been so since vampires came to America. Of course, over the years the system's changed with the population. There were far fewer vampires in America for the first two hundred years, because the trip over was so perilous. It was hard to work out the length of the voyage with the available blood supply.' Which would have been the crew, of course. 'And the Louisiana Purchase made a great difference.'

Well, of course it *would*. I stifled another bout of giggles. 'And the kingdoms are divided into . . .?'

'Areas. Used to be called fiefdoms, until we decided that was too behind the times. A sheriff controls each area. As you know, we live in Area 5 of the kingdom of Louisiana. Stan, whom you visited in Dallas, is sheriff of Area 6 in the kingdom of . . . in Texas.'

I pictured Eric as the sheriff of Nottingham, and when that had lost amusement value, as Wyatt Earp. I was definitely on the light-headed side. I really felt pretty bad physically. I told myself to pack away my reaction to this information, to focus on the immediate problem. 'So, Bill was kidnapped in daylight, I take it?'

Multiple nods all around.

'This kidnapping was witnessed by some humans who live in the kingdom of Mississippi.' I just loved to say that. 'And they're under the control of a vampire king?'

'Russell Edgington. Yes, they live in his kingdom, but a few of them will give me information. For a price.'

'This king won't let you question them?'

'We haven't asked him yet. It could be Bill was taken on his orders.'

That raised a whole new crop of questions, but I told myself to stay focused. 'How can I get to them? Assuming I decide I want to.'

'We've thought of a way you may be able to gather information from humans in the area where Bill disappeared,' said Eric. 'Not just people I have bribed to let me know what's happening there, but all the people that associated with Russell. It's risky. I had to tell you what I have, to make it work. And you may be unwilling. Someone's already tried to get you once. Apparently, whoever has Bill must not have much information about you yet. But soon, Bill will talk. If you're anywhere around when he breaks, they'll have you.'

'They won't really need me then,' I pointed out. 'If he's already broken.'

'That's not necessarily true,' Pam said. They did some more of the enigmatic-gaze-swapping thing.

'Give me the whole story,' I said. I noticed that Chow had finished his blood, so I got up to get him some more.

'As Russell Edgington's people tell it, Betty Jo Pickard, Edgington's second in command, was supposed to begin a flight to St. Louis yesterday. The humans responsible for taking her coffin to the airport took Bill's identical coffin by mistake. When they delivered the coffin to the hangar Anubis Airlines leases, they left it unguarded for perhaps ten minutes while they were filling out paperwork. During that time – they claim – someone wheeled the coffin, which was on a kind of gurney, out of the back of the hangar, loaded it onto a truck, and drove away.'

'Someone who could penetrate Anubis security,' I said, doubt heavy in my voice. Anubis Airlines had been established to transport vampires safely both day and night, and their guarantee of heavy security to guard the coffins of sleeping vampires was their big calling card. Of course, vampires don't have to sleep in coffins, but it sure is easy to ship them that way. There had been unfortunate 'accidents' when vampires had tried to fly Delta. Some fanatic had gotten in the baggage hold and hacked open a couple of coffins with an ax. Northwest had suffered the same problem. Saving money suddenly didn't seem so attractive to the undead, who now flew Anubis almost exclusively.

'I'm thinking that someone could have mingled with Edgington's people, someone the Anubis employees thought was Edgington's, and Edgington's people thought belonged to Anubis. He could have wheeled Bill out as Edgington's people left, and the guards would be none the wiser.'

'The Anubis people wouldn't ask to see papers? On a departing coffin?'

'They say they did see papers, Betty Jo Pickard's. She was on her way to Missouri to negotiate a trade agreement with the vampires of St. Louis.' I had a blank moment of wondering what on earth the vampires of Mississippi could be trading with the vampires of Missouri, and then I decided I just didn't want to know.

'There was also extra confusion at the time,' Pam was saying. 'A fire started under the tail of another Anubis plane, and the guards were distracted.'

'Oh, accidentally-on-purpose.'

'I think so,' Chow said.

'So, why would anyone want to snatch Bill?' I asked. I was afraid I knew. I was hoping they'd provide me with something else. Thank God Bill had prepared for this moment.

'Bill's been working on a little special project,' Eric said, his eyes on my face. 'Do you know anything about that?'

More than I wanted to. Less than I ought to.

'What project?' I said. I've spent my whole life concealing my thoughts, and I called on all my skill now. That life depended on my sincerity.

Eric's gaze flickered over to Pam, to Chow. They both gave some infinitesimal signal. He focused on me again, and said, 'That is a little hard to believe, Sookie.'

'How come?' I asked, anger in my voice. When in doubt, attack. 'When do any of you exactly spill your emotional guts to a human? And Bill is definitely one of you.' I infused that with as much rage as I could muster.

They did that eye-flicker thing at one another again.

'You think we'll believe that Bill didn't tell you what he was working on?'

'Yes, I think so. Because he didn't.' I had more or less figured it out all by myself anyway.

'Here's what I'm going to do,' Eric said finally. He looked at me from across the table, his blue eyes as hard as marbles and just as warm. No more Mr. Nice Vampire. 'I can't tell if you're lying or not, which is remarkable. For your sake, I hope you are telling the truth. I could torture you until you told me the truth, or until I was sure you had been telling me the truth from the beginning.'

Oh, brother. I took a deep breath, blew it out, and tried to think of an appropriate prayer. *God, don't let me scream too loud* seemed kind of weak and negative. Besides, there was no one to hear me besides the vampires, no matter how loudly I shrieked. When the time came, I might as well let it rip.

'But,' Eric continued thoughtfully, 'that might damage you too badly for the other part of my plan. And really, it doesn't make that much difference if you know what Bill has been doing behind our backs or not.'

Behind their backs? Oh, *shit.* And now I knew whom to blame for my very deep predicament. My own dear love, Bill Compton.

'That got a reaction,' Pam observed.

'But not the one I expected,' Eric said slowly.

'I'm not too happy about the torture option.' I was in so much trouble, I couldn't even begin to add it up, and I was so overloaded with stress that I felt like my head was floating somewhere above my body. 'And I miss Bill.' Even though at the moment I would gladly kick his ass, I did miss him. And if I could just have ten minutes' conversation with him, how much better prepared I would be to face the coming days. Tears rolled down my face. But there was more they had to tell me; more I had to hear, whether I wanted to or not. 'I do expect you to tell me why he lied about this trip, if you know. Pam mentioned bad news.'

Eric looked at Pam with no love in his eyes at all.

'She's leaking again,' Pam observed, sounding a little uncomfortable. 'I think before she goes to Mississippi, she should know the truth. Besides, if she has been keeping secrets for Bill, this will . . .'

Make her spill the beans? Change her loyalty to Bill? Force her to realize she has to tell us?

It was obvious that Chow and Eric had been all for keeping me in ignorance and that they were acutely unhappy with Pam for hinting to me that, though I supposedly didn't know it, all was not well with Bill and me. But they both eyed Pam intently for a long minute, and then Eric nodded curtly.

'You and Chow wait outside,' Eric said to Pam. She gave him a very pointed look, and then they walked out, leaving their drained bottles sitting on the table. Not even a thank-you for the blood. Didn't even rinse the bottles out. My head felt lighter and lighter as I contemplated poor vampire manners. I felt my eyelids flicker, and it occurred to me that I was on the edge of fainting. I am not one of these frail gals who keels over at every little thing, but I felt I was justified right now. Plus, I vaguely realized I hadn't eaten in over twenty-four hours.

'Don't you do it,' Eric said. He sounded definite. I tried to concentrate on his voice, and I looked at him.

I nodded to indicate I was doing my best.

He moved over to my side of the table, turned the chair Pam had occupied until it faced me and was very close. He sat and leaned over to me, his big white hand covering both of mine, still folded neatly in my lap. If he closed his hand, he could crush all my fingers. I'd never work as a waitress again.

'I don't enjoy seeing you scared of me,' he said, his face too close to mine. I could smell his cologne – Ulysse, I thought. 'I have always been very fond of you.'

He'd always wanted to have sex with me.

'Plus, I want to fuck you.' He grinned, but at this moment it didn't do a thing to me. 'When we kiss . . . it's very exciting.' We had kissed in the line of duty, so to speak, and not as recreation. But it had been exciting. How not? He was gorgeous, and he'd had several hundred years to work on his smooching technique.

Eric got closer and closer. I wasn't sure if he was going to bite me or kiss me. His fangs had run out. He was angry, or horny, or hungry, or all three. New vampires tended to lisp while they talked until they got used to their fangs; you couldn't even tell, with Eric. He'd had centuries of perfecting that technique, too.

'Somehow, that torture plan didn't make me feel very sexy,' I told him.

'It did something for Chow, though,' Eric whispered in my ear.

I wasn't shaking, but I should have been. 'Could you cut to the chase here?' I asked. 'Are you gonna torture me, or not? Are you my friend, or my enemy? Are you gonna find Bill, or let him rot?'

Eric laughed. It was short and unfunny, but it was better than him getting closer, at least at the moment. 'Sookie, you are too much,' he said, but not as though he found that particularly endearing. 'I'm not going to torture you. For one thing, I would hate to ruin that beautiful skin; one day, I will see all of it.'

I just hoped it was still on my body when that happened.

'You won't always be so afraid of me,' he said, as if he were absolutely certain of the future. 'And you won't always be as devoted to Bill as you are now. There is something I must tell you.'

Here came the Big Bad. His cool fingers twined with mine, and without wanting to, I held his hand hard. I couldn't think of a word to say, at least a word that was safe. My eyes fixed on his.

'Bill was summoned to Mississippi,' Eric told me, 'by a vampire – a female – he'd known many years ago. I don't know if you've realized that vampires almost never mate with other vampires, for any longer than a rare one-night affair. We don't do this because it gives us power over each other forever, the mating and sharing of blood. This vampire . . .'

'Her name,' I said.

'Lorena,' he said reluctantly. Or maybe he wanted to tell me all along, and the reluctance was just for show. Who the heck knows, with a vampire.

He waited to see if I would speak, but I did not.

'She was in Mississippi. I am not sure if she regularly lives there, or if she went there to ensnare Bill. She had been living in Seattle for years, I know, because she and Bill lived there together for many years.'

I had wondered why he'd picked Seattle as his fictitious destination. He hadn't just plucked it out of the air.

'But whatever her intention in asking him to meet her there . . . what excuse she gave him for not coming here . . . maybe he was just being careful of you . . .'

I wanted to die at that moment. I took a deep breath and looked down at our joined hands. I was too humiliated to look in Eric's eyes.

'He was – he became – instantly enthralled with her, all over again. After a few nights, he called Pam to say that he was coming home early without telling you, so he could arrange your future care before he saw you again.'

'Future care?' I sounded like a crow.

'Bill wanted to make a financial arrangement for you.'

The shock of it made me blanch. 'Pension me off,' I said numbly. No matter how well he had meant, Bill could not have offered me any greater offense. When he'd been in my life, it had never occurred to him to ask me how my finances were faring – though he could hardly wait to help his newly discovered descendants, the Bellefleurs.

But when he was going to be out of my life, and felt guilty for leaving pitiful, pitiable me – then he started worrying.

'He wanted . . .' Eric began, then stopped and looked

closely at my face. 'Well, leave that for now. I would not have told you any of this, if Pam hadn't interfered. I would have sent you off in ignorance, because then it wouldn't have been words from my mouth that hurt you so badly. And I would not have had to plead with you, as I'm going to plead.'

I made myself listen. I gripped Eric's hand as if it were a lifeline.

'What I'm going to do – and you have to understand, Sookie, my hide depends on this, too . . .'

I looked him straight in the face, and he saw the rush of my surprise.

'Yes, my job, and maybe my life, too, Sookie – not just yours, and Bill's. I'm sending you a contact tomorrow. He lives in Shreveport, but he has a second apartment in Jackson. He has friends among the supernatural community there, the vampires, shifters, and Weres. Through him you can meet some of them, and their human employees.'

I was not completely in my head right now, but I felt like I'd understand all this when I played it back. So I nodded. His fingers stroked mine, over and over.

'This man is a Were,' Eric said carelessly, 'so he is scum. But he is more reliable than some others, and he owes me a big personal favor.'

I absorbed that, nodded again. Eric's long fingers seemed almost warm.

'He'll take you out and about in the vampire community in Jackson, and you can pick brains there among human employees. I know it's a long shot, but if there's something to discover, if Russell Edgington did abduct Bill, you may pick up a hint. The man who tried to abduct you was from Jackson, going by the bills in his car, and he was a Were, as the wolf's head on his vest indicates. I don't know why they came after you. But I suspect it means Bill is alive, and they wanted to grab you to use as leverage over him.'

'Then I guess they should have abducted Lorena,' I said. Eric's eyes widened in appreciation.

'Maybe they already have her,' he said. 'But maybe Bill has realized it is Lorena who betrayed him. He wouldn't have been taken if she hadn't revealed the secret he had told her.'

I mulled that over, nodded yet again.

'Another puzzle is why she happened to be there at all,' Eric said. 'I think I would have known if she'd been a regular member of the Mississippi group. But I'll be thinking about that in my spare time.' From his grim face, Eric had already put in considerable brain time on that question. 'If this plan doesn't work within about three days, Sookie, we may have to kidnap one of the Mississippi vampires in return. This would almost certainly lead to a war, and a war – even with Mississippi – would be costly in lives and money. And in the end, they would kill Bill anyway.'

Okay, the weight of the world was resting on my shoulders. Thanks, Eric. I needed more responsibility and pressure.

'But know this: If they have Bill – if he is still alive – we will get him back. And you will be together again, if that's what you want.'

Big if.

'To answer your question: I am your friend, and that will last as long as I can be your friend without jeopardizing my own life. Or the future of my area.'

Well, that laid it on the line. I appreciated his honesty. 'As long as it's convenient for you, you mean,' I said calmly, which was both unfair and inaccurate. However, I thought it was odd that my characterization of his attitude actually seemed to bother him. 'Let me ask you something, Eric.'

He raised his eyebrows to tell me he was waiting. His hands traveled up and down my arms, absently, as if he wasn't thinking of what he was doing. The movement reminded me of a man warming his hands at a fire.

'If I'm understanding you, Bill was working on a project for the . . .' I felt a wild bubble of laughter rising, and I ruthlessly suppressed it. 'For the queen of Louisiana,' I finished. 'But you didn't know about it. Is this right?'

Eric stared at me for a long moment, while he thought about what to tell me. 'She told me she had work for Bill to do,' he said. 'But not what it was, or why he had to be the one to do it, or when it would be complete.'

That would miff almost any leader, having his underling co-opted like that. Especially if the leader was kept in ignorance. 'So, why isn't this queen looking for Bill?' I asked, keeping my voice carefully neutral.

'She doesn't know he's gone.'

'Why is that?'

'We haven't told her.'

Sooner or later he'd quit answering. 'Why not?'

'She would punish us.'

'Why?' I was beginning to sound like a two-year-old.

'For letting something happen to Bill, when he was doing a special project for her.'

'What would that punishment be?'

'Oh, with her it's difficult to tell.' He gave a choked laugh. 'Something very unpleasant.'

Eric was even closer to me, his face almost touching my

hair. He was inhaling, very delicately. Vampires rely on smell, and hearing, much more than sight, though their eyesight is extremely accurate. Eric had had my blood, so he could tell more about my emotions than a vampire who hadn't. All bloodsuckers are students of the human emotional system, since the most successful predators know the habits of their prey.

Eric actually rubbed his cheek against mine. He was like a cat in his enjoyment of contact.

'Eric.' He'd given me more information than he knew.

'Mmm?'

'Really, what will the queen do to you if you can't produce Bill on the date her project is due?'

My question got the desired result. Eric pulled away from me and looked down at me with eyes bluer than mine and harder than mine and colder than the Arctic waste.

'Sookie, you really don't want to know,' he said. 'Producing his work would be good enough. Bill's actual presence would be a bonus.'

I returned his look with eyes almost as cold as his. 'And what will I get in return for doing this for you?' I asked.

Eric managed to look both surprised and pleased. 'If Pam hadn't hinted to you about Bill, his safe return would have been enough and you would have jumped at the chance to help,' Eric reminded me.

'But now I know about Lorena.'

'And knowing, do you agree to do this for us?'

'Yes, on one condition.'

Eric looked wary. 'What would that be?' he asked.

'If something happens to me, I want you to take her out.'

He gaped at me for at least a whole second before he

roared with laughter. 'I would have to pay a huge fine,' he said when he'd quit chortling. 'And I'd have to accomplish it first. That's easier said than done. She's three hundred years old.'

'You've told me that what will happen to you if all this comes unraveled would be pretty horrible,' I reminded him.

'True.'

'You've told me you desperately need me to do this for you.'

'True.'

'That's what I ask in return.'

'You might make a decent vampire, Sookie,' Eric said finally. 'All right. Done. If anything happens to you, she'll never fuck Bill again.'

'Oh, it's not just that.'

'No?' Eric looked very skeptical, as well he might.

'It's because she betrayed him.'

Eric's hard blue eyes met mine. 'Tell me this, Sookie: Would you ask this of me if she were a human?' His wide, thin-lipped mouth, most often amused, was in a serious straight line.

'If she were a human, I'd take care of it myself,' I said, and stood to show him to the door.

After Eric had driven away, I leaned against the door and laid my cheek against the wood. Did I mean what I'd told him? I'd long wondered if I were really a civilized person, though I kept striving to be one. I knew that at the moment I'd said I would take care of Lorena myself, I had meant it. There was something pretty savage inside me, and I'd always controlled it. My grandmother had not raised me to be a murderess.

As I plodded down the hall to my bedroom, I realized

that my temper had been showing more and more lately. Ever since I'd gotten to know the vampires.

I couldn't figure out why that should be. They exerted tremendous control over themselves. Why should mine be slipping?

But that was enough introspection for one night.

I had to think about tomorrow.

Chapter 4

Since it seemed I was going out of town, there was laundry to be done, and stuff in the refrigerator that needed throwing away. I wasn't particularly sleepy after spending so long in bed the preceding day and night, so I got out my suitcase, opened it, and tossed some clothes into the washer out on the freezing back porch. I didn't want to think about my own character any longer. I had plenty of other items to mull over.

Eric had certainly adopted a shotgun approach to bending me to his will. He'd bombarded me with many reasons to do what he wanted: intimidation, threat, seduction, an appeal for Bill's return, an appeal for his (and Pam's, and Chow's) life and/or well-being – to say nothing of my own health. 'I might have to torture you, but I want to have sex with you; I need Bill, but I'm furious with him because he deceived me; I have to keep peace with Russell Edgington, but I have to get Bill back from him; Bill is my serf, but he's secretly working more for my boss.'

Darn vampires. You can see why I'm glad their glamour doesn't affect me. It's one of the few positives my mind-reading ability has yielded me. Unfortunately, humans with psychic glitches are very attractive to the undead.

I certainly could not have foreseen any of this when I'd become attached to Bill. Bill had become almost as necessary to me as water; and not entirely because of my deep feelings for him, or my physical pleasure in his lovemaking. Bill was the only insurance I had against being annexed by another vampire, against my will.

After I'd run a couple of loads through the washer and dryer and folded the clothes, I felt much more relaxed. I was almost packed, and I'd put in a couple of romances and a mystery in case I got a little time to read. I am self-educated from genre books.

I stretched and yawned. There was a certain peace of mind to be found in having a plan, and my uneasy sleep of the past day and night had not refreshed me as much as I thought. I might be able to fall asleep easily.

Even without help from the vampires, I could maybe find Bill, I thought, as I brushed my teeth and climbed into bed. But breaking him out of whatever prison he was in and making a successful escape, that was another question. And then I'd have to decide what to do about our relationship.

I woke up at about four in the morning with an odd feeling there was an idea just waiting to be acknowledged. I'd had a thought at some point during the night; it was the kind of idea that you just know has been bubbling in your brain, waiting to boil over.

Sure enough, after a minute the idea resurfaced. What if Bill had not been abducted, but had defected? What if he'd become so enamored or addicted to Lorena that he'd decided to leave the Louisiana vampires and join with the

Mississippi group? Immediately, I had doubts that that had been Bill's plan; it would be a very elaborate one, with the leakage of informants to Eric concerning Bill's abduction, the confirmed presence of Lorena in Mississippi. Surely there'd be a less dramatic, and simpler, way to arrange his disappearance.

I wondered if Eric, Chow, and Pam were even now searching Bill's house, which lay across the cemetery from mine. They weren't going to find what they were looking for. Maybe they'd come back here. They wouldn't have to get Bill back at all, if they could find the computer files the queen wanted so badly. I fell to sleep out of sheer exhaustion, thinking I heard Chow laugh outside.

Even the knowledge of Bill's betrayal did not stop me from searching for him in my dreams. I must have rolled over three times, reaching out to see if he'd slid into bed with me, as he often did. And every time, the other side of the bed was empty and cold.

However, that was better than finding Eric there instead.

I was up and showering at first light, and I'd made a pot of coffee before the knock at the front door came.

'Who is it?' I stood to one side of the door as I asked.

'Eric sent me,' a gruff voice said.

I opened the door and looked up. And looked up some more.

He was huge. His eyes were green. His tousled hair was curly and thick and black as pitch. His brain buzzed and pulsed with energy; kind of a red effect. Werewolf.

'Come on in. You want some coffee?'

Whatever he'd expected, it wasn't what he was seeing. 'You bet, chere. You got some eggs? Some sausage?'

'Sure.' I led him to the kitchen. 'I'm Sookie Stackhouse,'

I said, over my shoulder. I bent over to get the eggs out of the refrigerator. 'You?'

'Alcide,' he said, pronouncing it *Al-see*, with the *d* barely sounded. 'Alcide Herveaux.'

He watched me steadily while I lifted out the skillet – my grandmother's old, blackened iron skillet. She'd gotten it when she got married, and fired it, like any woman worth her salt would do. Now it was perfectly seasoned. I turned the gas eye on at the stove. I cooked the sausage first (for the grease), plopped it on a paper towel on a plate and stuck it in the oven to keep warm. After asking Alcide how he wanted the eggs, I scrambled them and cooked them quickly, sliding them onto the warm plate. He opened the right drawer for the silverware on the first try, and poured himself some juice and coffee after I silently pointed out which cabinet contained the cups. He refilled my mug while he was at it.

He ate neatly. And he ate everything.

I plunged my hands into the hot, soapy water to clean the few dishes. I washed the skillet last, dried it, and rubbed some Crisco into the blackness, taking occasional glances at my guest. The kitchen smelled comfortably of breakfast and soapy water. It was a peculiarly peaceful moment.

This was anything but what I had expected when Eric had told me someone who owed him a favor would be my entrée into the Mississippi vampire milieu. As I looked out the kitchen window at the cold landscape, I realized that this was how I had envisioned my future; on the few occasions I'd let myself imagine a man sharing my house.

This was the way life was supposed to be, for normal people. It was morning, time to get up and work, time for a woman to cook breakfast for a man, if he had to go out and earn. This big rough man was eating real food. He almost certainly had a pickup truck sitting out in front of my house.

Of course, he was a werewolf. But a Were could live a more close-to-human life than a vampire.

On the other hand, what I didn't know about Weres could fill a book.

He finished, put his plate in the water in the sink, and washed and dried it himself while I wiped the table. It was as smooth as if we'd choreographed it. He disappeared into the bathroom for a minute while I ran over my mental list of things that had to be done before I left. I needed to talk to Sam, that was the main thing. I'd called my brother the night before to tell him I'd be gone for a few days. Liz had been at Jason's, so he hadn't really thought a lot about my departure. He'd agreed to pick up my mail and my papers for me.

Alcide came to sit opposite me at the table. I was trying to think about how we should talk about our joint task; I was trying to anticipate any sore paws I might tread on. Maybe he was worrying about the same things. I can't read the minds of shape-shifters or werewolves with any consistency; they're supernatural creatures. I can reliably interpret moods, and pick up on the occasional clear idea. So the humans-with-a-difference are much less opaque to me than the vampires. Though I understand there's a contingent of shape-shifters and Weres who wants to change things, the fact of their existence still remains a secret. Until they see how publicity works out for the vampires, the supernaturals of the two-natured variety are ferocious about their privacy.

Werewolves are the tough guys of the shape-shifting world. They're shape-shifters by definition, but they're the only ones who have their own separate society, and they will not allow anyone else to be called 'Were' in their hearing. Alcide Herveaux looked plenty tough. He was big as a boulder, with biceps that I could do pullups on. He would have to shave a second time if he planned on going out in the evening. He would fit right in on a construction site or a wharf.

He was a proper man.

'How are they forcing you to do this?' I asked.

'They have a marker of my dad's,' he said. He put his massive hands on the table and leaned into them. 'They own a casino in Shreveport, you know?'

'Sure.' It was a popular weekend excursion for people in this area, to go over to Shreveport or up to Tunica (in Mississippi, right below Memphis) and rent a room for a couple of nights, play the slots, see a show or two, eat lots of buffet food.

'My dad got in too deep. He owns a surveying company – I work for him – but he likes to gamble.' The green eyes smoldered with rage. 'He got in too deep in the casino in Louisiana, so your vamps own his marker, his debt. If they call it in, our company will go under.' Werewolves seemed to respect vampires about as much as vampires respect them. 'So, to get the marker back, I have to help you hang around with the vamps in Jackson.' He leaned back in the chair, looking me in the eyes. 'That's not a hard thing, taking a pretty woman to Jackson and out barhopping. Now that I've met you, I'm glad to do it, to get my father out from under the debt. But why the hell you want to do that? You look like a real woman, not one of those sick bitches who get off on hanging around the vamps.'

This was a refreshingly direct conversation, after my

conference with the vampires. 'I only hang around with one vampire, by choice,' I said bitterly. 'Bill, my – well, I don't know if he's even my boyfriend anymore. It seems the vampires of Jackson may have kidnapped him. Someone tried to grab me last night.' I thought it only fair to let him know. 'Since the kidnapper didn't seem to know my name, just that I worked at Merlotte's, I'll probably be safe in Jackson if no one figures out I'm the woman who goes with Bill. I have to tell you, the man who tried to grab me was a werewolf. And he had a Hinds County car plate.' Jackson was in Hinds County.

'Wearing a gang vest?' Alcide asked. I nodded. Alcide looked thoughtful, which was a good thing. This was not a situation I took lightly, and it was a good sign that he didn't, either. 'There's a small gang in Jackson made up of Weres. Some of the bigger shifters hang around the edges of this gang – the panther, the bear. They hire themselves out to the vamps on a pretty regular basis.'

'There's one less of them now,' I said.

After a moment's digestion of that information, my new companion gave me a long, challenging stare. 'So, what good is a little human gal going to do against the vampires of Jackson? You a martial artist? You a great shot? You been in the Army?'

I had to smile. 'No. You never heard my name?'

'You're famous?'

'Guess not.' I was pleased that he didn't have any preconceptions about me. 'I think I'll just let you find out about me.'

'Long as you're not gonna turn into a snake.' He stood up. 'You're not a guy, are you?' That late-breaking thought made his eyes widen.

'No, Alcide. I'm a woman.' I tried to say that matter-of-factly, but it was pretty hard.

'I was willing to put money on that.' He grinned at me. 'If you're not some kind of superwoman, what are you going to do when you know where your man is?'

'I'm going to call Eric, the . . .' Suddenly I realized that telling vampire secrets is a bad idea. 'Eric is Bill's boss. He'll decide what to do after that.'

Alcide looked skeptical. 'I don't trust Eric. I don't trust any of 'em. He'll probably double-cross you.'

'How?'

'He might use your man as leverage. He might demand restitution, since they have one of his men. He might use your man's abduction as an excuse to go to war, in which case your man will be executed tout de suite.'

I had not thought that far. 'Bill knows stuff,' I said. 'Important stuff.'

'Good. That may keep him alive.' Then he saw my face, and chagrin ran across his own. 'Hey, Sookie, I'm sorry. I don't think before I talk sometimes. We'll get him back, though it makes me sick to think of a woman like you with one of those bloodsuckers.'

This was painful, but oddly refreshing.

'Thanks, I guess,' I said, attempting a smile. 'What about you? Do you have a plan about how to introduce me to the vampires?'

'Yeah. There's a nightclub in Jackson, close to the capitol. It's for Supes and their dates only. No tourists. The vamps can't make it pay on their own, and it's a convenient meeting place for them, so they let us low-lifes share the fun.' He grinned. His teeth were perfect – white and sharp. 'It won't be suspicious if I go there. I always drop in when I'm in

Jackson. You'll have to go as my date.' He looked embarrassed. 'Uh, I better tell you, you seem like you're a jeans kind of person like me – but this club, they like you to dress kind of party style.' He feared I had no fancy dresses in my closet; I could read that clearly. And he didn't want me to be humiliated by appearing in the wrong clothes. What a man.

'Your girlfriend won't be crazy about this,' I said, angling for information out of sheer curiosity.

'She lives in Jackson, as a matter of fact. But we broke up a couple of months ago,' he said. 'She took up with another shape-shifter. Guy turns into a damn owl.'

Was she *nuts*? Of course, there'd be more to the story. And of course, it fell into the category of 'none of your business.'

So without comment, I went to my room to pack my two party dresses and their accessories in a hanging bag. Both were purchases from Tara's Togs, managed (and now owned) by my friend Tara Thornton. Tara was real good about calling me when things went on clearance. Bill actually owned the building that housed Tara's Togs, and had told all the businesses housed in there to run a tab for me that he would pay, but I had resisted the temptation. Well, except for replacing clothes that Bill himself had ripped in our more thrilling moments.

I was very proud of both these dresses, since I'd never had anything like them before, and I zipped the bag shut with a smile.

Alcide stuck his head in the bedroom to ask if I was ready. He looked at the cream-and-yellow bed and curtains, and nodded approvingly. 'I got to call my boss,' I said. 'Then we'll be good to go.' I perched on the side of the bed and picked up the receiver.

Alcide propped himself against the wall by my closet door while I dialed Sam's personal number. His voice was sleepy when he answered, and I apologized for calling so early. 'What's happening, Sookie?' he asked groggily.

'I have to go away for a few days,' I said. 'I'm sorry for not giving you more notice, but I called Sue Jennings last night to see if she'd work for me. She said yes, so I gave her my hours.'

'Where are you going?' he asked.

'I have to go to Mississippi,' I said. 'Jackson.'

'You got someone lined up to pick up your mail?'

'My brother. Thanks for asking.'

'Plants to water?'

'None that won't live till I get back.'

'Okay. Are you going by yourself?'

'No,' I said hesitantly.

'With Bill?'

'No, he, uh, he hasn't shown up.'

'Are you in trouble?'

'I'm just fine,' I lied.

'Tell him a man's going with you,' Alcide rumbled, and I gave him an exasperated look. He was leaning against the wall, and he took up an awful lot of it.

'Someone's there?' Sam's nothing if not quick on the uptake.

'Yes, Alcide Herveaux,' I said, figuring it was a smart thing to tell someone who cared about me that I was leaving the area with this guy. First impressions can be absolutely false, and Alcide needed to be aware there was someone who would hold him accountable.

'Aha,' Sam said. The name did not seem to be unfamiliar to him. 'Let me talk to him.'

'Why?' I can take a lot of paternalism, but I was about up to my ears.

'Hand over the damn phone.' Sam almost never curses, so I made a face to show what I thought of his demand and gave the phone to Alcide. I stomped out to the living room and looked through the window. Yep. A Dodge Ram, extended cab. I was willing to bet it had everything on it that could be put on.

I'd rolled my suitcase out by its handle, and I'd slung my carrying bag over a chair by the door, so I just had to pull on my heavy jacket. I was glad Alcide had warned me about the dress-up rule for the bar, since it never would have occurred to me to pack anything fancy. Stupid vampires. Stupid dress code.

I was Sullen, with a capital *S*.

I wandered back down the hall, mentally reviewing the contents of my suitcase, while the two shape-shifters had (presumably) a 'man talk.' I glanced through the doorway of my bedroom to see that Alcide, with the phone to his ear, was perched on the side of my bed where I'd been sitting. He looked oddly at home there.

I paced restlessly back into the living room and stared out the window some more. Maybe the two were having shape-shifting talk. Though to Alcide, Sam (who generally shifted into a collie, though he was not limited to that form) would rank as a lightweight, at least they were from the same branch of the tree. Sam, on the other hand, would be a little leery of Alcide; werewolves had a bad rep.

Alcide strode down the hall, safety shoes clomping on the hardwood floor. 'I promised him I'd take care of you,' he said. 'Now, we'll just hope that works out.' He wasn't smiling.

I had been tuning up to be aggravated, but his last sentence was so realistic that the hot air went out of me as if I'd been punctured. In the complex relationship between vampire, Were, and human, there was a lot of leeway for something to go wrong somewhere. After all, my plan was thin, and the vampires' hold over Alcide was tenuous. Bill might not have been taken unwillingly; he might be happy being held captive by a king, as long as the vampire Lorena was on site. He might be enraged that I had come to find him.

He might be dead.

I locked the door behind me and followed Alcide as he stowed my things in the extended cab of the Ram.

The outside of the big truck gleamed, but inside, it was the littered vehicle of a man who spent his working life on the road; a hard hat, invoices, estimates, business cards, boots, a first-aid kit. At least there wasn't any food trash. As we bumped down my eroded driveway, I picked up a rubber-banded sheaf of brochures whose cover read, 'Herveaux and Son, AAA Accurate Surveys.' I eased out the top one and studied it carefully as Alcide drove the short distance to interstate 20 to go east to Monroe, Vicksburg, and then to Jackson.

I discovered that the Herveauxes, father and son, owned a bi-state surveying company, with offices in Jackson, Monroe, Shreveport, and Baton Rouge. The home office, as Alcide had told me, was in Shreveport. There was a photo inside of the two men, and the older Herveaux was just as impressive (in a senior way) as his son.

'Is your dad a werewolf, too?' I asked, after I'd digested the information and realized that the Herveaux family was at least prosperous, and possibly rich. They'd worked hard for it, though; and they'd keep working hard, unless the older Mr. Herveaux could control his gambling.

'Both my parents,' Alcide said, after a pause.

'Oh, sorry.' I wasn't sure what I was apologizing for, but it was safer than not.

'That's the only way to produce a Were child,' he said, after a moment. I couldn't tell if he was explaining to be polite, or because he really thought I should know.

'So how come America's not full of werewolves and shapeshifters?' I asked, after I'd considered his statement.

'Like must marry like to produce another, which is not always doable. And each union only produces one child with the trait. Infant mortality is high.'

'So, if you marry another werewolf, one of your kids will be a werebaby?'

'The condition will manifest itself at the onset of, ah, puberty.'

'Oh, that's awful. Being a teenager is tough enough.'

He smiled, not at me, but at the road. 'Yeah, it does complicate things.'

'So, your ex-girlfriend . . . she a shifter?'

'Yeah. I don't normally date shifters, but I guess I thought with her it would be different. Weres and shifters are strongly attracted to each other. Animal magnetism, I guess,' Alcide said, as an attempt at humor.

My boss, also a shifter, had been glad to make friends with other shifters in the area. He had been hanging out with a maenad ('dating' would be too sweet a word for their relationship), but she'd moved on. Now, Sam was hoping to find another compatible shifter. He felt more comfortable with a strange human, like me, or another shifter, than he did with regular women. When he'd told me that, he'd meant it as a compliment, or maybe just as a simple statement; but it had hurt me a little, though my abnormality had been borne in on me since I was very young.

Telepathy doesn't wait for puberty.

'How come?' I asked baldly. 'How come you thought it would be different?'

'She told me she was sterile. I found out she was on birth control pills. Big difference. I'm not passing this along. Even a shifter and a werewolf may have a child who has to change at the full moon, though only kids of a pure couple – both Weres or both shifters – can change at will.'

Food for thought, there. 'So you normally date regular old girls. But doesn't it make it hard to date? Keeping secret such a big, ah, factor, in your life?'

'Yeah,' he admitted. 'Dating regular girls can be a pain. But I have to date someone.' There was an edge of desperation to his rumbly voice.

I gave that a long moment's contemplation, and then I closed my eyes and counted to ten. I was missing Bill in a most elemental and unexpected way. My first clue had been the tug-below-the-waist I'd felt when I'd watched my tape of *The Last of the Mohicans* the week before and I'd fixated on Daniel Day-Lewis bounding through the forest. If I could appear from behind a tree before he saw Madeleine Stowe . . .

I was going to have to watch my step.

'So, if you bite someone, they won't turn into a werewolf?' I decided to change the direction of my thoughts. Then I remembered the last time Bill had bitten me, and felt a rush of heat through . . . oh, *hell*.

'That's when you get your wolf-man. Like the ones in the movies. They die pretty quick, poor people. And that's not passed along, if they, ah, engender children in their human form. If it's when they're in their altered form, the baby is miscarried.'

'How interesting.' I could not think of one other thing to say.

'But there's that element of the supernatural, too, just like with vampires,' Alcide said, still not looking in my direction. 'The tie-in of genetics and the supernatural element, that's what no one seems to understand. We just can't tell the world we exist, like the vampires did. We'd be locked up in zoos, sterilized, ghettoized – because we're sometimes animals. Going public just seems to make the vampires glamorous and rich.' He sounded more than a little bitter.

'So how come you're telling me all this, right off the bat? If it's such a big secret?' He had given me more information in ten minutes than I'd had from Bill in months.

'If I'm going to be spending a few days with you, it will make my life a lot easier if you know. I figure you have your own problems, and it seems the vampires have some power over you, too. I don't think you'll tell. And if the worst happens, and I've been utterly wrong about you, I'll ask Eric to pay you a visit and wipe out your memory.' He shook his head in baffled irritation. 'I don't know why, really. I just feel like I know you.'

I couldn't think of a response to that, but I had to speak. Silence would lend too much importance to his last sentence. 'I'm sorry the vampires have a hold on your dad. But I have to find Bill. If this is the only way I can do it, this is what I have to do. I at least owe him that much, even if . . .' My voice trailed off. I didn't want to finish the sentence. All the possible endings were too sad, too final.

He shrugged, a large movement on Alcide Herveaux. 'Taking a pretty girl to a bar isn't that big a deal,' he reassured me again, trying to bolster my spirits.

In his position, I might not have been so generous. 'Is your dad a constant gambler?'

'Only since my mother died,' Alcide said, after a long pause.

'I'm sorry.' I kept my eyes off his face in case he needed some privacy. 'I don't have either of my parents,' I offered.

'They been gone long?'

'Since I was seven.'

'Who raised you?'

'My grandmother raised me and my brother.'

'She still living?'

'No. She died this year. She was murdered.'

'Tough.' He was matter-of-fact.

'Yeah.' I had one more question. 'Did both your parents tell you about yourself?'

'No. My grandfather told me when I was about thirteen. He'd noticed the signs. I just don't know how orphaned Weres get through it without guidance.'

'That would be really rough.'

'We try to keep aware of all the Weres breeding in the area, so no one will go unwarned.'

Even a secondhand warning would be better than no warning at all. But still, such a session would be a major trauma in anyone's life.

We stopped in Vicksburg to get gas. I offered to pay for filling the tank, but Alcide told me firmly this could go on his books as a business expense, since he did in fact need to see some customers. He waved off my offer to pump the gas, too. He did accept the cup of coffee I bought him, with as many thanks as if it had been a new suit. It was a cold, bright day, and I took a brisk walk around the travel center to stretch my legs before climbing back into the cab of the truck.

Seeing the signs for the battlefield reminded me of one of the most taxing days I'd had as an adult. I found myself telling Alcide about my grandmother's favorite club, the Descendants of the Glorious Dead, and about their field trip to the battlefield two years before. I'd driven one car, Maxine Fortenberry (grandmother of one of my brother Jason's good buddies) another, and we'd toured at length. Each of the Descendants had brought a favorite text covering the siege, and an early stop at the visitors' center had gotten the Descendants all tanked up with maps and memorabilia. Despite the failure of Velda Cannon's Depends, we'd had a great time. We'd read every monument, we'd had a picnic lunch by the restored USS *Cairo*, and we'd gone home laden with souvenir booty and exhausted. We'd even gone into the Isle of Capri Casino for an hour of amazed staring, and some tentative slot machine feeding. It had been a very happy day for my grandmother, almost as happy a time as the evening she'd inveigled Bill into speaking at the Descendants meeting.

'Why did she want him to do that?' Alcide asked. He was smiling at my description of our supper stop at a Cracker Barrel.

'Bill's a vet,' I said. 'An Army vet, not an animal-doctor vet.'

'So?' After a beat, he said, 'You mean your boyfriend is a veteran of the *Civil War*?'

'Yeah. He was human then. He wasn't brought over until after the war. He had a wife and children.' I could hardly keep calling him my boyfriend, since he'd been on the verge of leaving me for someone else.

'Who made him a vampire?' Alcide asked. We were in Jackson now, and he was making his way downtown to the apartment his company maintained.

'I don't know,' I said. 'He doesn't talk about it.'

'That seems a little strange to me.'

Actually, it seemed a little strange to me, too; but I figured it was something really personal, and when Bill wanted to tell me about it, he would. The relationship was very strong, I knew, between the older vampire and the one he'd 'brought over.'

'I guess he really isn't my boyfriend anymore,' I admitted. Though 'boyfriend' seemed a pretty pale term for what Bill had been to me.

'Oh, yeah?'

I flushed. I shouldn't have said anything. 'But I still have to find him.'

We were silent for a while after that. The last city I'd visited had been Dallas, and it was easy to see that Jackson was nowhere close to that size. (That was a big plus, as far as I was concerned.) Alcide pointed out the golden figure on the dome of the new capitol, and I admired it appropriately. I thought it was an eagle, but I wasn't sure, and I was a little embarrassed to ask. Did I need glasses? The building we were going to was close to the corner of High and State streets. It was not a new building; the brick had started out a golden tan, and now it was a grimy light brown.

'The apartments here are larger than they are in new buildings,' Alcide said. 'There's a small guest bedroom. Everything should be all ready for us. We use the apartment cleaning service.'

I nodded silently. I could not remember if I'd ever been in an apartment building before. Then I realized I had, of course. There was a two-story U-shaped apartment building in Bon Temps. I had surely visited someone there; in the past seven years, almost every single person in Bon Temps had rented a place in Kingfisher Apartments at some point in his or her dating career.

Alcide's apartment, he told me, was on the top floor, the fifth. You drove in from the street down a ramp to park. There was a guard at the garage entrance, standing in a little booth. Alcide showed him a plastic pass. The heavy-set guard, who had a cigarette hanging out of his mouth, barely glanced at the card Alcide held out before he pressed a button to raise the barrier. I wasn't too impressed with the security. I felt like I could whip that guy, myself. My brother, Jason, could pound him into the pavement.

We scrambled out of the truck and retrieved our bags from the rudimentary backseat. My hanging bag had fared pretty well. Without asking me, Alcide took my small suitcase. He led the way to a central block in the parking area, and I saw a gleaming elevator door. He punched the button, and it opened immediately. The elevator creaked its way up after Alcide punched the button marked with a 5. At least the elevator was very clean, and when the door swished open, so were the carpet and the hall beyond.

'They went condo, so we bought the place,' Alcide said, as if it was no big deal. Yes, he and his dad had made some money. There were four apartments per floor, Alcide told me.

'Who are your neighbors?'

'Two state senators own 501, and I'm sure they've gone home for the holiday season,' he said. 'Mrs. Charles

Osburgh the Third lives in 502, with her nurse. Mrs. Osburgh was a grand old lady until the past year. I don't think she can walk anymore. Five-oh-three is empty right now, unless the realtor sold it this past two weeks.' He unlocked the door to number 504, pushed it open, and gestured for me to enter ahead of him. I entered the silent warmth of the hall, which opened on my left into a kitchen enclosed by counters, not walls, so the eye was unobstructed in sweeping the living room/dining area. There was a door immediately on my right, which probably opened onto a coat closet, and another a little farther down, which led into a small bedroom with a neatly made-up double bed. A door past that revealed a small bathroom with white-and-blue tiles and towels hung just so on the racks.

Across the living room, to my left, was a door that led into a larger bedroom. I peered inside briefly, not wanting to seem overly interested in Alcide's personal space. The bed in that room was a king. I wondered if Alcide and his dad did a lot of entertaining when they visited Jackson.

'The master bedroom has its own bath,' Alcide explained. 'I'd be glad to let you have the bigger room, but the phone's in there, and I'm expecting some business calls.'

'The smaller bedroom is just fine,' I said. I peeked around a little more after my bags were stowed in my room.

The apartment was a symphony in beige. Beige carpet, beige furniture. Sort of oriental bamboo-y patterned wallpaper with a beige background. It was very quiet and very clean.

As I hung my dresses in the closet, I wondered how many nights I'd have to go to the club. More than two, and I'd have to do some shopping. But that was impossible, at the least imprudent, on my budget. A familiar worry settled hard on my shoulders.

My grandmother hadn't had much to leave me, God bless her, especially after her funeral expenses. The house had been a wonderful and unexpected gift.

The money she'd used to raise Jason and me, money that had come from an oil well that had petered out, was long gone. The fee I'd gotten paid for moonlighting for the Dallas vampires had mostly gone to buy the two dresses, pay my property taxes, and have a tree cut down because the previous winter's ice storm had loosened its roots and it had begun to lean too close to the house. A big branch had already fallen, damaging the tin roof a bit. Luckily, Jason and Hoyt Fortenberry had known enough about roofing to repair that for me.

I recalled the roofing truck outside of Belle Rive.

I sat on the bed abruptly. Where had that come from? Was I petty enough to be angry that my boyfriend had been thinking of a dozen different ways to be sure his descendants (the unfriendly and sometimes snooty Bellefleurs) prospered, while I, the love of his afterlife, worried herself to tears about her finances?

You bet, I was petty enough.

I should be ashamed of myself.

But later. My mind was not through toting up grievances.

As long as I was considering money (lack of), I wondered if it had even occurred to Eric when he dispatched me on this mission that since I'd be missing work, I wouldn't get paid. Since I wouldn't get paid, I couldn't pay the electric company, or the cable, or the phone, or my car insurance . . . though I had a moral obligation to find Bill, no matter what had happened to our relationship, right?

I flopped back on the bed and told myself that this would all work out. I knew, in the back of my mind, that all I had to do was sit down with Bill – assuming I ever got him back – and explain my situation to him, and he'd . . . he'd do something.

But I couldn't just take money from Bill. Of course, if we were married, it would be okay; husband and wife held all in common. But we couldn't get married. It was illegal.

And he hadn't asked me.

'Sookie?' a voice said from the doorway.

I blinked and sat up. Alcide was lounging against the jamb, his arms crossed over his chest.

'You okay?'

I nodded uncertainly.

'You missing him?'

I was too ashamed to mention my money troubles, and they weren't more important than Bill, of course. To simplify things, I nodded.

He sat beside me and put his arm around me. He was so warm. He smelled like Tide detergent, and Irish Spring soap, and man. I closed my eyes and counted to ten again.

'You miss him,' he said, confirming. He reached across his body to take my left hand, and his right arm tightened around me.

You don't know *how I miss him*, I thought.

Apparently, once you got used to regular and spectacular sex, your body had a mind of its own (so to speak) when it was deprived of that recreation; to say nothing of missing the hugging and cuddling part. My body was begging me to knock Alcide Herveaux back onto the bed so it could have its way with him. *Right now*.

'I do miss him, no matter what problems we have,' I said, and my voice came out tiny and shaky. I wouldn't open my eyes, because if I did, I might see on his face a tiny impulse, some little inclination, and that would be all it would take.

'What time do you think we should go to the club?' I asked, firmly steering in another direction.

He was so *warm*.

Other direction! 'Would you like me to cook supper before we go?' Least I could do. I shot up off the bed like a bottle rocket; turned to face him with the most natural smile I could muster. Get out of close proximity, or jump his bones.

'Oh, let's go to the Mayflower Cafe. It looks like an old diner – it is an old diner – but you'll enjoy it. Everyone goes there – senators and carpenters, all kinds of people. They just serve beer, that okay?'

I shrugged and nodded. That was fine with me. 'I don't drink much,' I told him.

'Me neither,' he said. 'Maybe because, every so often, my dad tends to drink too much. Then he makes bad decisions.' Alcide seemed to regret having told me this. 'After the Mayflower, we'll go to the club,' Alcide said, much more briskly. 'It gets dark real early these days, but the vamps don't show up till they've had some blood, picked up their dates, done some business. We should get there about ten. So we'll go out to eat about eight, if that suits you?'

'Sure, that'll be great.' I was at a loss. It was only two in the afternoon. His apartment didn't need cleaning. There was no reason to cook. If I wanted to read, I had romance novels in my suitcase. But in my present condition, it was hardly likely to help my state of . . . mind.

'Listen, would it be okay if I ran out to visit some clients?' he asked.

'Oh, that would be fine.' I thought it would be all to the good if he wasn't in my immediate vicinity. 'You go do whatever you need to do. I have books to read, and there's the television.' Maybe I could begin the mystery novel.

'If you want to . . . I don't know . . . my sister, Janice, owns a beauty shop about four blocks away, in one of the older neighborhoods. She married a local guy. You want to, you could walk over and get the works.'

'Oh, I . . . well, that . . .' I didn't have the sophistication to think of a smooth and plausible refusal, when the glaring roadblock to such a treat was my lack of money.

Suddenly, comprehension crossed his face. 'If you stopped by, it would give Janice the opportunity to look you over. After all, you're supposed to be my girlfriend, and she hated Debbie. She'd really enjoy a visit.'

'You're being awful nice,' I said, trying not to sound as confused and touched as I felt. 'That's not what I expected.'

'You're not what I expected, either,' he said, and left his sister's shop number by the phone before heading out on his business.

Chapter 5

Janice Herveaux Phillips (married two years, mother of one, I learned quickly) was exactly what I might have expected of a sister of Alcide's. She was tall, attractive, plain-spoken, and confident; and she ran her business efficiently.

I seldom went into beauty parlors. My gran had always done her own home perms, and I had never colored my hair or done anything else to it, besides a trim now and then. When I confessed this to Janice, who'd noticed I was looking around me with the curiosity of the ignorant, her broad face split in a grin. 'Then you'll need everything,' she said with satisfaction.

'No, no, no,' I protested anxiously. 'Alcide –'

'Called me on his cell phone and made it clear I was to give you the works,' Janice said. 'And frankly, honey, anyone who helps him recover from that Debbie is my best friend.'

I had to smile. 'But I'll pay,' I told her.

'No, your money's no good here,' she said. 'Even if you break up with Alcide tomorrow, just getting him through tonight will be worth it.'

'Tonight?' I began to have a sinking feeling that once again, I didn't know everything there was to know.

'I happen to know that tonight that bitch is going to announce her engagement at that club they go to,' Janice said.

Okay, this time what I didn't know was something pretty major. 'She's marrying the – man she took up with after she dumped Alcide?' (I barely stopped myself from saying, 'The shape-shifter?')

'Quick work, huh? What could he have that my brother doesn't have?'

'I can't imagine,' I said with absolutely sincerity, earning a quick smile from Janice. There was sure to be a flaw in her brother somewhere – maybe Alcide came to the supper table in his underwear, or picked his nose in public.

'Well, if you find out, you let me know. Now, let's get you going.' Janice glanced around her in a businesslike way. 'Corinne is going to give you your pedicure and manicure, and Jarvis is going to do your hair. You sure have a great head of it,' Janice said in a more personal way.

'All mine, all natural,' I admitted.

'No color?'

'Nope.'

'You're the lucky one,' Janice said, shaking her head.

That was a minority opinion.

Janice herself was working on a client whose silver hair and gold jewelry proclaimed she was a woman of privilege, and while this cold-faced lady examined me with indifferent eyes, Janice fired off some instructions to her employees and went back to Ms. Big Bucks.

I had never been so pampered in my life. And everything was new to me. Corinne (manicures and pedicures), who was as plump and juicy as one of the sausages I'd cooked that morning, painted my toenails and fingernails screaming red to match the dress I was going to wear. The only male in the shop, Jarvis, had fingers as light and quick as butterflies. He was thin as a reed and artificially platinum blond. Entertaining me with a stream of chatter, he washed and set my hair and established me under the dryer. I was one chair down from the rich lady, but I got just as much attention. I had a *People* magazine to read, and Corinne brought me a Coke. It was so nice to have people urging me to relax.

I was feeling kind of roasted under the dryer when the timer binged. Jarvis got me out from under it and set me back in his chair. After consulting with Janice, he whipped his preheated curling iron from a sort of holster mounted on the wall, and painstakingly arranged my hair in loose curls trailing down my back. I looked spectacular. Looking spectacular makes you happy. This was the best I'd felt since Bill had left.

Janice came over to talk every moment she was able. I caught myself forgetting that I wasn't Alcide's real girlfriend, with a real chance of becoming Janice's sister-in-law. This kind of acceptance didn't come my way too often.

I was wishing I could repay her kindness in some way, when a chance presented itself. Jarvis's station mirrored Janice's, so my back was to Janice's customer's back. Left on my own while Jarvis went to get a bottle of the conditioner he thought I should try, I watched (in the mirror) Janice take off her earrings and put them in a little china dish. I might never have observed what happened next if I hadn't picked up a clear covetous thought from the rich lady's head, which was, simply, 'Aha!' Janice walked away to get another towel, and in the clear reflection, I watched the silver-haired customer deftly sweep up the earrings and stuff them into her jacket pocket, while Janice's back was turned.

By the time I was finished, I'd figured out what to do. I was just waiting to say good-bye to Jarvis, who'd had to go to the telephone; I knew he was talking to his mother, from the pictures I got from his head. So I slid out of my vinyl chair and walked over to the rich woman. who was writing a check for Janice.

''Scuse me,' I said, smiling brilliantly. Janice looked a little startled, and the elegant woman looked snooty. This was a client who spent a lot of money here, and Janice wouldn't want to lose her. 'You got a smear of hair gel on your jacket. If you'll please just slide out of it for a second, I'll get it right off.'

She could hardly refuse. I grasped the jacket shoulders and gently tugged, and she automatically helped me slide the green-and-red plaid jacket down her arms. I carried it behind the screen that concealed the hairwashing area, and wiped at a perfectly clean area just for verisimilitude (a great word from my Word of the Day calendar). Of course, I also extracted the earrings and put them in my own pocket.

'There you are, good as new!' I beamed at her and helped her into the jacket.

'Thanks, Sookie,' Janice said, too brightly. She suspected something was amiss.

'You're welcome!' I smiled steadily.

'Yes, of course,' said the elegant woman, somewhat confusedly. 'Well, I'll see you next week, Janice.'

She clicked on her high heels all the way out the door,

not looking back. When she was out of sight, I reached in my pocket and held out my hand to Janice. She opened her hand under mine, and I dropped the earrings into her palm.

'Good God almighty,' Janice said, suddenly looking about five years older. 'I forgot and left something where she could reach it.'

'She does this all the time?'

'Yeah. That's why we're about the fifth beauty salon she's patronized in the past ten years. The others put up with it for a while, but eventually she did that one thing too many. She's so rich, and so educated, and she was brought up right. I don't know why she does stuff like this.'

We shrugged at each other, the vagaries of the white-collar well-to-do beyond our comprehension. It was a moment of perfect understanding. 'I hope you don't lose her as a customer. I tried to be tactful,' I said.

'And I really appreciate that. But I would have hated losing those earrings more than losing her as a client. My husband gave them to me. They tend to pinch after a while, and I didn't even think when I pulled them off.'

I'd been thanked more than enough. I pulled on my own coat. 'I better be off,' I said. 'I've really enjoyed the wonderful treat.'

'Thank my brother,' Janice said, her broad smile restored. 'And, after all, you just paid for it.' She held up the earrings.

I was smiling, too, as I left the warmth and camaraderie of the salon, but that didn't last too long. The thermometer had dropped and the sky was getting darker by the minute. I walked the distance back to the apartment building very briskly. After a chilly ride on a creaky elevator, I was glad to use the key Alcide had given me and step into the warmth. I switched on a lamp and turned on the television for a little company, and I huddled on the couch and thought about the pleasures of the afternoon. Once I'd thawed out, I realized Alcide must have turned down the thermostat. Though pleasant compared to the out-of-doors, the apartment was definitely on the cool side.

The sound of the key in the door roused me out of my reverie, and Alcide came in with a clipboard full of paperwork. He looked tired and preoccupied, but his face relaxed when he saw me waiting.

'Janice called me to tell me you'd come by,' he said. His voice warmed up as he spoke. 'She wanted me to say thank you again.'

I shrugged. 'I appreciate my hair and my new nails,' I said. 'I've never done that before.'

'You've never been to a beauty shop before?'

'My grandmother went every now and then. I had my ends trimmed, once.'

He looked as stunned as if I'd confessed I'd never seen a flush toilet.

To cover my embarrassment, I fanned my nails out for his admiration. I hadn't wanted very long ones, and these were the shortest ones Corinne could in all conscience manage, she had told me. 'My toenails match,' I told my host.

'Let's see,' he said.

I untied my sneakers and pulled off my socks. I held out my feet. 'Aren't they pretty?' I asked.

He was looking at me kind of funny. 'They look great,' he said quietly.

I glanced at the clock on top of the television. 'I guess I better go get ready,' I said, trying to figure out how to take a bath without affecting my hair and nails. I thought of Janice's news about Debbie. 'You're really ready to dress up tonight, right?'

'Sure,' he said gamely.

''Cause I'm going all out.'

That interested him. 'That would mean . . .?'

'Wait and see.' This was a nice guy, with a nice family, doing me a heavy-duty favor. Okay, he'd been coerced into it. But he was being extremely gracious to me, under any circumstances.

I rolled out of my room an hour later. Alcide was standing in the kitchen, pouring himself a Coke. It ran over the edge of the glass while he took me in.

That was a real compliment.

While Alcide mopped up the counter with a paper towel, he kept darting glances at me. I turned around slowly.

I was wearing red – screaming red, fire engine red. I was going to freeze most of the evening, because my dress didn't have any shoulders, though it did have long sleeves that you slid on separately. It zipped up the back. It flared below the hips, what there *was* below the hips. My grandmother would have flung herself across the doorsill to keep me from going out the door in this dress. I loved it. I had got it on extreme sale at Tara's Togs; I suspected Tara had kind of put it aside for me. Acting on a huge and unwise impulse, I'd bought the shoes and lipstick to go with it. And now the nails, thanks to Janice! I had a gray-and-black fringed silk shawl to wrap around myself, and a little bitty bag that matched my shoes. The bag was beaded.

'Turn around again,' Alcide suggested a little hoarsely.

He himself was wearing a conventional black suit with a white shirt and a green patterned tie that matched his eyes. Nothing, apparently, could tame his hair. Maybe he should have gone to Janice's beauty shop instead of me. He looked handsome and rough, though 'attractive' might be a more accurate word than 'handsome.'

I rotated slowly. I wasn't confident enough to keep my eyebrows from arching in a silent question as I completed my turn.

'You look *mouthwatering*,' he said sincerely. I released a breath I hadn't realized I'd been holding.

'Thanks,' I said, trying not to beam like an idiot.

I had a trying time getting into Alcide's truck, what with the shortness of the dress and the highness of the heels, but with Alcide giving me a tactical boost, I managed.

Our destination was a small place on the corner of Capitol and Roach. It wasn't impressive from the outside, but the Mayflower Cafe was as interesting as Alcide had predicted. Some of the people at the tables scattered on the black-and-white tile floor were dressed to the nines, like Alcide and me. Some of them were wearing flannel and denim. Some had brought their own wine or liquor. I was glad we weren't drinking; Alcide had one beer, and that was it. I had iced tea. The food was really good, but not fancy. Dinner was long, drawn-out, and interesting. Lots of people knew Alcide, and they came by the table to say hello to him and to find out who I was. Some of these visitors were involved in the state government, some were in the building trade like Alcide, and some appeared to be friends of Alcide's dad's.

A few of them were not law-abiding men at all; even

though I've always lived in Bon Temps, I know hoods when I see the product of their brains. I'm not saying they were thinking about bumping off anyone, or bribing senators, or anything specific like that. Their thoughts were greedy – greedy of money, greedy of me, and in one case, greedy of Alcide (to which he was completely oblivious, I could tell).

But most of all, these men – all of them – were greedy for power. I guess in a state capital, that lust for power was inevitable, even in as poverty-plagued a state as Mississippi.

The women with the greediest men were almost all extremely well groomed and very expensively dressed. For this one evening, I could match them, and I held my head up. One of them thought I looked like a high-priced whore, but I decided that was a compliment, at least for tonight. At least she thought I was expensive. One woman, a banker, knew Debbie the-former-girlfriend, and she examined me from head to toe, thinking Debbie would want a detailed description.

None of these people, of course, knew one thing about me. It was wonderful to be among people who had no idea of my background and upbringing, my occupation or my abilities. Determined to enjoy the feeling, I concentrated on not speaking unless I was spoken to, not spilling any food on my beautiful dress, and minding my manners, both table and social. While I was enjoying myself, I figured it would be a pity if I caused Alcide any embarrassment, since I was entering his life so briefly.

Alcide snatched the bill before I could reach it, and scowled at me when I opened my mouth to protest. I finally gave a little bob of my head. After that silent struggle, I was glad to observe that Alcide was a generous tipper. That raised him in my estimation. To tell the truth, he was entirely too high in my estimation already. I was on the alert to pick out something negative about the man. When we got back in Alcide's pickup – this time he gave me even more help when he boosted me up to the seat, and I was pretty confident he enjoyed the procedure – we were both quiet and thoughtful.

'You didn't talk much at supper,' he said. 'You didn't have a good time?'

'Oh, sure, I did. I just didn't think it was a real good time to start broadcasting any opinions.'

'What did you think of Jake O'Malley?' O'Malley, a man in his early sixties with thick steel-colored eyebrows, had stood talking to Alcide for at least five minutes, all the while stealing little sideways glances at my boobs.

'I think he's planning on screwing you six ways from Sunday.'

It was lucky we hadn't pulled away from the curb yet. Alcide switched on the overhead light and looked at me. His face was grim. 'What are you talking about?' he asked.

'He's going to underbid you on the next job, because he's bribed one of the women in your office – Thomasina something? – to let him know what you all's bid is. And then –'

'What?'

I was glad the heater was running full blast. When werewolves got mad, you could feel it in the air around you. I had so hoped I wouldn't have to explain myself to Alcide. It had been so neat, being unknown.

'You are . . . what?' he asked, to make sure I understood him.

'Telepath,' I said, kind of mumbling.

A long silence fell, while Alcide digested this.

'Did you hear *anything* good?' he asked, finally.

'Sure. Mrs. O'Malley wants to jump your bones,' I told him, smiling brightly. I had to remind myself not to pull at my hair.

'That's good?'

'Comparatively,' I said. 'Better to be screwed physically than financially.' Mrs. O'Malley was at least twenty years younger than Mr. O'Malley, and she was the most groomed person I'd ever seen. I was betting she brushed her eyebrows a hundred strokes a night.

He shook his head. I had no clear picture of what he was thinking. 'What about me, you read me?'

Aha. 'Shape-shifters are not so easy,' I said. 'I can't pick out a clear line of thought, more a general mood, intentions, sort of. I guess if you thought directly at me, I'd get it. You want to try? Think something at me.'

The dishes I use at the apartment have a border of yellow roses.

'I wouldn't call them roses,' I said doubtfully. 'More like zinnias, if you ask me.'

I could feel his withdrawal, his wariness. I sighed. Same old, same old. It sort of hurt, since I liked him. 'But just to pick your own thoughts out of your head, that's a murky area,' I said. 'I can't consistently do that, with Weres and shifters.' (A few Supes were fairly easy to read, but I saw no need to bring that up at this point in time.)

'Thank God.'

'Oh?' I said archly, in an attempt to lighten the mood. 'What are you afraid I'll read?'

Alcide actually grinned at me before he turned off the dome light and we pulled out of our parking space. 'Never mind,' he said, almost absently. 'Never mind. So what you're going to be doing tonight is reading minds, to try to pick up clues about your vampire's whereabouts?'

'That's right. I can't read vampires; they don't seem to put out any brainwaves. That's just how I put it. I don't know how I do this, or if there's a scientific way to phrase it.' I wasn't exactly lying: Undead minds really were unreadable – except for a little split second's glimpse every now and then (which hardly counted, and no one could know about). If vampires thought I could read their minds, not even Bill could save me. If he would.

Every time I forgot for a second that our relationship had radically changed, it hurt all over again to be reminded.

'So what's your plan?'

'I'm aiming for humans dating or serving local vampires. Humans were the actual abductors. He was snatched in daytime. At least, that's what they told Eric.'

'I should have asked you about this earlier,' he said, mostly to himself. 'Just in case I hear something the regular way – through my ears – maybe you should tell me the circumstances.'

As we drove by what Alcide said was the old train station, I gave him a quick summary. I caught a glimpse of a street sign reading 'Amite' as we pulled up to an awning that stretched over a deserted length of sidewalk in the outskirts of downtown Jackson. The area directly under the awning was lit with a brilliant and cold light. Somehow that length of sidewalk seemed creepily ominous, especially since the rest of the street was dark. Uneasiness crawled down my back. I felt a deep reluctance to stop at that bit of sidewalk.

It was a stupid feeling, I told myself. It was just a stretch of cement. No beasts were in sight. After the businesses closed at five, downtown Jackson was not exactly teeming, even under ordinary circumstances. I was willing to bet that most of the sidewalks in the whole state of Mississippi were bare on this cold December night.

But there was something ominous in the air, a watchfulness laced with a charge of malice. The eyes observing us were invisible; but they were observing us, nonetheless. When Alcide climbed out of the truck and came around to help me down, I noticed that he left the keys in the ignition. I swung my legs outward and put my hands on his shoulders, my long silk stole wound firmly around me and trailing behind, fringe trembling in a gust of chilled air. I pushed off as he lifted, and then I was on the sidewalk.

The truck drove away.

I looked at Alcide sideways, to see if this was startling to him, but he looked quite matter-of-fact. 'Vehicles parked in front would attract attention from the general public,' he told me, his voice hushed in the vast silence of that coldly lit bit of pavement.

'They can come in? Regular people?' I asked, nodding toward the single metal door. It looked as uninviting as a door can look. There was no name anywhere on it, or on the building, for that matter. No Christmas decorations, either. (Of course, vampires don't observe holidays, except for Halloween. It's the ancient festival of Samhain dressed up in trappings that the vamps find delightful. So Halloween's a great favorite, and it's celebrated worldwide in the vamp community.)

'Sure, if they want to pay a twenty-dollar cover charge to drink the worst drinks in five states. Served by the rudest waiters. Very slowly.'

I tried to smother my smile. This was not a smiley kind of place. 'And if they stick that out?'

'There's no floor show, no one speaks to them, and if

they last much longer, they find themselves out on the sidewalk getting into their car with no memory of how they got there.'

He grasped the handle of the door and pulled it open. The dread that soaked the air did not seem to affect Alcide.

We stepped into a tiny hall that was blocked by another door after about four feet. There, again, I knew we were being watched, though I couldn't see a camera or a peephole anywhere.

'What's the name of this place?' I whispered.

'The vamp that owns it calls it Josephine's,' he said, just as quietly. 'But Weres call it Club Dead.'

I thought about laughing, but the inner door opened just then.

The doorman was a goblin.

I had never seen one before, but the word 'goblin' popped into my mind as if I had a supernatural dictionary printed on the inside of my eyeballs. He was very short and very cranky-looking, with a knobby face and broad hands. His eyes were full of fire and malignance. He glared up at us as if customers were the last things he needed.

Why any ordinary person would walk into Josephine's after the cumulative effect of the haunted sidewalk, the vanishing vehicle, and the goblin at the door . . . well, some people are just born asking to be killed, I guess.

'Mr. Herveaux,' the goblin said slowly, in a deep, growly voice. 'Good to have you back. Your companion is . . .?'

'Miss Stackhouse,' Alcide said. 'Sookie, this is Mr. Hob.' The goblin examined me with glowing eyes. He looked faintly troubled, as if he couldn't quite fit me into a slot; but after a second, he stood aside to let us pass.

Josephine's was not very crowded. Of course, it was

somewhat early for its patrons. After the eerie build-up, the large room looked almost disappointingly like any other bar. The serving area itself was in the middle of the room, a large square bar with a lift-up panel for the staff to go to and fro. I wondered if the owner had been watching reruns of *Cheers*. The glasses hung down, suspended on racks, and there were artificial plants and low music and dim lighting. There were polished bar stools set evenly all around the square. To the left of the bar was a small dance floor, and even farther left was a tiny stage for a band or a disc jockey. On the other three sides of the square were the usual small tables, about half of which were in use.

Then I spotted the list of ambiguous rules on the wall, rules designed to be understood by the regular habitues, but not by the occasional tourist. 'No Changing on the Premises,' one said sternly. (Weres and shifters could not switch from animal to human when they were at the bar; well, I could understand that.) 'No Biting of Any Kind,' said another. 'No Live Snacks,' read a third. Ick.

The vampires were scattered throughout the bar, some with others of their own kind, some with humans. There was a raucous party of shifters in the southeast corner, where several tables had been drawn together to accommodate the size of the party. The center of this group appeared to be a tall young woman with gleaming short black hair, an athletic build, and a long, narrow face. She was draped over a square man of her own age, which I guessed to be about twenty-eight. He had round eyes and a flat nose and the softest looking hair I'd ever seen – it was almost baby fine, and so light a blond, it was nearly white. I wondered if this were the engagement party, and I wondered if Alcide had known it was to take place. His attention was definitely focused on that group.

Naturally, I immediately checked out what the other women in the bar were wearing. The female vampires and the women with male vampires were dressed about at my level. The shifter females tended to dress down a bit more. The black-haired woman I'd pegged for Debbie was wearing a gold silk blouse and skintight brown leather pants, with boots. She laughed at some comment of the blond man's, and I felt Alcide's arm grow rigid under my fingers. Yep, this must be the ex-girlfriend, Debbie. Her good time had certainly escalated since she'd glimpsed Alcide's entrance.

Phony bitch, I decided in the time it takes to snap your fingers, and I made up my mind to behave accordingly. The goblin Hob led the way to an empty table within view of the happy party, and held out a chair for me. I nodded to him politely, and unwound my wrap, folding it and tossing it onto an empty chair. Alcide sat in the chair to my right, so he could put his back to the corner where the shifters were having such a raucous good time.

A bone-thin vampire came to take our order. Alcide asked my pleasure with an inclination of his head. 'A champagne cocktail,' I said, having no idea what one tasted like. I'd never gone to the trouble to mix myself one at Merlotte's, but now that I was in someone else's bar, I thought I'd give it a shot. Alcide ordered a Heineken. Debbie was casting many glances our way, so I leaned forward and smoothed back a lock of Alcide's curly black hair. He looked surprised, though of course Debbie couldn't see that.

'Sookie?' he said, rather doubtfully.

I smiled at him, not my nervous smile – because I

wasn't, for once. Thanks to Bill, I now had a little confidence about my own physical attractiveness. 'Hey, I'm your date, remember? I'm acting date-like,' I told him.

The thin vampire brought our drinks just then, and I clinked my glass against his bottle. 'To our joint venture,' I said, and his eyes lit up. We sipped.

I loved champagne cocktails.

'Tell me more about your family,' I said, because I enjoyed listening to his rumbly voice. I would have to wait until there were more humans in the bar before I began listening in to others' thoughts.

Alcide obligingly began telling me about how poor his dad had been when he started his surveying business, and how long it had taken for him to prosper. He was just beginning to tell me about his mother when Debbie sashayed up:

It had only been a matter of time.

'Hello, Alcide,' she purred. Since he hadn't been able to see her coming, his strong face quivered. 'Who's your new friend? Did you borrow her for the evening?'

'Oh, longer than that,' I said clearly, and smiled at Debbie, a smile that matched her own for sincerity.

'Really?' If her eyebrows had crawled any higher, they'd have been in heaven.

'Sookie is a good friend,' Alcide said impassively.

'Oh?' Debbie doubted his word. 'It wasn't too long ago you told me you'd never have another "friend" if you couldn't have . . . Well.' She smirked.

I covered Alcide's huge hand with my own and gave her a look that implied much.

'Tell me,' Debbie said, her lips curling in a skeptical way, 'how do you like that birthmark of Alcide's?'

Who could have predicted she was willing to be a bitch so openly? Most women try to hide it, at least from strangers.

It's on my right butt cheek. It's shaped like a rabbit. Well, how nice. Alcide had remembered what I'd said, and he'd thought directly at me.

'I love bunnies,' I said, still smiling, my hand drifting down Alcide's back to caress, very lightly, the top of his right buttock.

For a second, I saw sheer rage on Debbie's face. She was so focused, so controlled, that her mind was a lot less opaque than most shifters'. She was thinking about her owl fiancé, about how he wasn't as good in the sack as Alcide, but he had a lot of ready cash and he was willing to have children, which Alcide wasn't. And she was stronger than the owl, able to dominate him.

She was no demon (of course, her fiancé would have a really short shelf life if she *were*) but she was no sweetie, either.

Debbie still could have recovered the situation, but her discovery that I knew Alcide's little secret made her nuts. She made a big mistake.

She raked me over with a glare that would have paralyzed a lion. 'Looks like you went to Janice's salon today,' she said, taking in the casually tumbled curls, the fingernails. Her own straight black hair had been cut in asymmetrical clumps, tiny locks of different lengths, making her look a little like a dog in a very good show, maybe an Afghan. Her narrow face increased the resemblance. 'Janice never sends anyone out looking like they live in this century.'

Alcide opened his mouth, rage tensing all his muscles. I laid my hand on his arm.

'What do you think of my hair?' I asked softly, moving my head so it slithered over my bare shoulders. I took his hand and held it gently to the curls falling over my chest. Hey, I was pretty good at this! Sookie the sex kitten.

Alcide caught his breath. His fingers trailed through the length of my hair, and his knuckles brushed my collarbone. 'I think it's beautiful,' he said, and his voice was both sincere and husky.

I smiled at him.

'I guess instead of borrowing you, he rented you,' Debbie said, goaded into irreparable error.

It was a terrible insult, to both of us. It took every bit of resolution I had to hang on to a ladylike self-control. I felt the primitive self, the truer me, swim nearly to the surface. We sat staring at the shifter, and she blanched at our silence. 'Okay, I shouldn't have said that,' she said nervously. 'Just forget it.'

Because she was a shifter, she'd beat me in a fair fight. Of course, I had no intention of fighting fair, if it came to that.

I leaned over and touched one red fingertip to her leather pants. 'Wearing Cousin Elsie?' I asked.

Unexpectedly, Alcide burst into laughter. I smiled at him as he doubled over, and when I looked up, Debbie was stalking back to her party, who had fallen silent during our exchange.

I reminded myself to skip going to the ladies' room alone this evening.

By the time we ordered our second drinks, the place was full. Some Were friends of Alcide's came in, a large group – Weres like to travel in packs, I understand. Shifters, it depended on the animal they most often shifted to. Despite their theoretical versatility, Sam had told me that shapeshifters most often changed to the same animal every time, some creature they had a special affinity for. And they might call themselves by that animal: weredog, or werebat, or weretiger. But never just 'Weres' – that term was reserved for the wolves. The true werewolves scorned such variance in form, and they didn't think much of shifters in general. They, the werewolves, considered themselves the cream of the shapeshifting world.

Shifters, on the other hand, Alcide explained, thought of werewolves as the thugs of the supernatural scene. 'And you do find a lot of us in the building trades,' he said, as if he were trying hard to be fair. 'Lots of Weres are mechanics, or brick masons, or plumbers, or cooks.'

'Useful occupations,' I said.

'Yes,' he agreed. 'But not exactly white-collar. So though we all cooperate with each other, to some extent, there's a lot of class discrimination.'

A small group of Weres in motorcycle gear strode in. They wore the same sort of leather vest with wolf's heads on the back that had been worn by the man who'd attacked me at Merlotte's. I wondered if they'd started searching for their comrade yet. I wondered if they had a clearer idea of who they were looking for, what they'd do if they realized who I was. The four men ordered several pitchers of beer and began talking very secretively, heads close together and chairs pulled right up to the table.

A deejay – he appeared to be a vampire – began to play records at the perfect level; you could be sure what the song was, but you could still talk.

'Let's dance,' Alcide suggested.

I hadn't expected that; but it would put me closer to the vampires and their humans, so I accepted. Alcide held my chair for me, and took my hand as we went over to the minuscule dance floor. The vampire changed the music from some heavy metal thing to Sarah Mc-Lachlan's 'Good Enough,' which is slow, but with a beat.

I can't sing, but I can dance; as it happened, Alcide could, too.

The good thing about dancing is that you don't have to talk for a while, if you feel chatted out. The bad thing is it makes you hyperconscious of your partner's body. I had already been uncomfortably aware of Alcide's – excuse me – animal magnetism. Now, so close to him, swaying in rhythm with him, following his every move, I found myself in a kind of trance. When the song was over, we stayed on the little dance floor, and I kept my eyes on the floor. When the next song started up, a faster piece of music – though for the life of me I couldn't have told you what – we began dancing again, and I spun and dipped and moved with the werewolf.

Then the muscular squat man sitting at a bar stool behind us said to his vampire companion, 'He hasn't talked yet. And Harvey called today. He said they searched the house and didn't find anything.'

'Public place,' said his companion, in a sharp voice. The vampire was a very small man – perhaps he'd become a vampire when men were shorter.

I knew they were talking about Bill, because the human was thinking of Bill when he said, 'He hasn't talked.' And the human was an exceptional broadcaster, both sound and visuals coming through clearly.

When Alcide tried to lead me away from their orbit, I

resisted his lead. Looking up into his surprised face, I cut my eyes toward the couple. Comprehension filtered into his eyes, but he didn't look happy.

Dancing and trying to read another person's mind at the same time is not something I'd recommend. I was straining mentally, and my heart was pounding with shock at the glimpse of Bill's image. Luckily, Alcide excused himself to go to the men's room just then, parking me on a stool at the bar right by the vampire. I tried to keep looking around at different dancers, at the deejay, at anything but the man to the vampire's left, the man whose mind I was trying to pick through.

He was thinking about what he'd done during the day; he'd been trying to keep someone awake, someone who really needed to sleep – a vampire. Bill.

Keeping a vampire awake during the day was the worst kind of torture. It was difficult to do, too. The compulsion to sleep when the sun came up was imperative, and the sleep itself was like death.

Somehow, it had never crossed my mind – I guess since I'm an American – that the vampires who had snatched Bill might be resorting to evil means to get him to talk. If they wanted the information, naturally they weren't just going to wait around until Bill felt like telling them. Stupid me – dumb, dumb, dumb. Even knowing Bill had betrayed me, even knowing he had thought of leaving me for his vampire lover, I was struck deep with pain for him.

Engrossed in my unhappy thoughts, I didn't recognize trouble when it was standing right beside me. Until it grabbed me by the arm.

One of the Were gang members, a big dark-haired man, very heavy and very smelly, had grabbed hold of my arm.

He was getting his greasy fingerprints all over my beautiful red sleeves, and I tried to pull away from him.

'Come to our table and let us get to know you, sweet thing,' he said, grinning at me. He had a couple of earrings in one ear. I wondered what happened to them during the full moon. But almost immediately, I realized I had more serious problems to solve. The expression on his face was too frank; men just didn't look at women that way unless those women were standing on a street corner in hot pants and a bra: in other words, he thought I was a sure thing.

'No, thank you,' I said politely. I had a weary, wary feeling that this wasn't going to be the end of it, but I might as well try. I'd had plenty of experience at Merlotte's with pushy guys, but I always had backup at Merlotte's. Sam wouldn't tolerate the servers being pawed or insulted.

'Sure, darlin'. You want to come see us,' he said insistently.

For the first time in my life, I wished Bubba were with me.

I was getting far too used to people who bothered me meeting a bad end. And maybe I was getting too accustomed to having some of my problems solved by others.

I thought of scaring the Were by reading his mind. It would have been an easy read – he was wide open, for a Were. But not only were his thoughts boring and unsurprising (lust, aggression), if his gang was charged with searching for the girlfriend of Bill the vampire, and they knew she was a barmaid and a telepath, and they found a telepath, well . . .

'No, I don't want to come sit with you,' I said definitely. 'Leave me alone.' I slid off the stool so I wouldn't be trapped in one position.

'You don't have no man here. We're real men, honey.' With his free hand, he cupped himself. Oh, charming. That really made me horny. 'We'll keep you happy.'

'You couldn't make me happy if you were Santa Claus,' I said, stomping on his instep with all my strength. If he hadn't been wearing motorcycle boots, it might have been effective. As it was, I came close to breaking the heel of my shoe. I was mentally cursing my false nails because they made it hard to form a fist. I was going to hit him in the nose with my free hand; a blow to the nose really hurts badly. He'd have to let go.

He snarled at me, really snarled, when my heel hit his instep, but he didn't loosen his grip. His free hand seized my bare shoulder, and his fingers dug in.

I'd been trying to be quiet, hoping to resolve this without hubbub, but I was past that point right now. 'Let *go*!' I yelled, as I made a heroic attempt to knee him in the balls. His thighs were heavy and his stance narrow, so I couldn't get a good shot. But I did make him flinch, and though his nails gouged my shoulder, he let go.

Part of this was due to the fact that Alcide had a hold on the scruff of his neck. And Mr. Hob stepped in, just as the other gang members surged around the bar to come to the aid of their buddy. The goblin who'd ushered us into the club doubled as the bouncer, it happened. Though he looked like a very small man on the outside, he wrapped his arms around the biker's waist and lifted him with ease. The biker began shrieking, and the smell of burned flesh began to circulate in the bar. The rail-thin bartender switched on a heavy-duty exhaust fan, which helped a lot, but we could hear the screams of the biker all the way down a narrow dark hall I hadn't noticed before. It must lead to the rear exit of the building. Then there was a big clang, a yell, and the same clang sounding again. Clearly, the back door of the bar had been opened and the offender tossed outside.

Alcide swung around to face the biker's friends, while I stood shaking with reaction behind him. I was bleeding from the imprints of the biker's fingernails in the flesh of my shoulder. I needed some Neosporin, which was what my grandmother had put on every injury when I'd objected to Campho-Phenique. But any little first-aid concerns were going to have to wait: It looked as though we faced another fight. I glanced around for a weapon, and saw the bartender had gotten a baseball bat out and laid it on the bar. She was keeping a wary eye on the situation. I seized the bat and went to stand beside Alcide. I swung the bat into position and waited for the next move. As my brother, Jason, had taught me – based on his many fights in bars, I'm afraid – I picked out one man in particular, pictured myself swinging the bat and bringing it to strike on his knee, which was more accessible to me than his head. That would bring him down, sure enough.

Then someone stepped into the no-man's-land between Alcide and me and the Weres. It was the small vampire, the one who'd been talking with the human whose mind had been such a source of unpleasant information.

Maybe five feet five with his shoes on, he was also slight of build. When he'd died, he'd been in his early twenties, I guessed. Clean-shaven and very pale, he had eyes the color of bitter chocolate, a jarring contrast with his red hair.

'Miss, I apologize for this unpleasantness,' he said, his voice soft and his accent heavily Southern. I hadn't heard an accent that thick since my great-grandmother had died twenty years ago.

'I'm sorry the peace of the bar has been disturbed,' I said, summoning up as much dignity as I could while gripping a baseball bat. I'd instinctively kicked off my heels so I could fight. I straightened up from my fighting stance, and inclined my head to him, acknowledging his authority.

'You men should leave now,' the little man said, turning to the group of Weres, 'after apologizing to this lady and her escort.'

They milled around uneasily, but none wanted to be the first to back down. One of them, who was apparently younger and dumber than the others, was a blond with a heavy beard and a bandanna around his head in a particularly stupid-looking style. He had the fire of battle in his eyes; his pride couldn't handle the whole situation. The biker telegraphed his move before he'd even begun it, and quick as lightning I held out the bat to the vampire, who snatched it in a move so fast, I couldn't even glimpse it. He used it to break the werewolf's leg.

The bar was absolutely silent as the screaming biker was carried out by his friends. The Weres chorused, 'Sorry, sorry,' as they lifted the blond and removed him from of the bar.

Then the music started again, the small vampire returned the bat to the bartender, Alcide began checking me over for damage, and I began shaking.

'I'm fine,' I said, pretty much just wanting everyone to look somewhere else.

'But you're bleeding, my dear,' said the vampire.

It was true; my shoulder was trailing blood from the biker's fingernails. I knew etiquette. I leaned toward the vampire, offering him the blood.

'Thank you,' he said instantly, and his tongue flicked

out. I knew I would heal better and quicker with his saliva anyway, so I held quite still, though to tell the truth, it was like letting someone feel me up in public. Despite my discomfort, I smiled, though I know it can't have been a comfortable smile. Alcide held my hand, which was reassuring.

'Sorry I didn't come out quicker,' he said.

'Not something you can predict.' Lick, lick, lick. Oh, come on, I had to have stopped bleeding by now.

The vampire straightened, ran his tongue over his lips, and smiled at me. 'That was quite an experience. May I introduce myself? I'm Russell Edgington.'

Russell Edgington, the king of Mississippi; from the reaction of the bikers, I had suspected as much. 'Pleased to meet you,' I said politely, wondering if I should curtsey. But he hadn't introduced himself by his title. 'I'm Sookie Stackhouse, and this is my friend Alcide Herveaux.'

'I've known the Herveaux family for years,' the king of Mississippi said. 'Good to see you, Alcide. How's that father of yours?' We might have been standing in the Sunday sunlight outside the First Presbyterian Church, rather than in a vampire bar at midnight.

'Fine, thank you,' Alcide said, somewhat stiffly. 'We're sorry there was trouble.'

'Not your fault,' the vampire said graciously. 'Men sometimes have to leave their ladies alone, and ladies are not responsible for the bad manners of fools.' Edgington actually bowed to me. I had no idea what to do in response, but an even deeper head-inclination seemed safe. 'You're like a rose blooming in an untended garden, my dear.'

And you're full of bull hockey. 'Thank you, Mr. Edgington,' I said, casting my eyes down lest he read the skepticism in them. Maybe I should have called him 'Your Highness'? 'Alcide, I'm afraid I need to call it a night,' I said, trying to sound soft and gentle and shaken. It was a little too easy.

'Of course, darlin',' he said instantly. 'Let me get your wrap and purse.' He began making his way to our table immediately, God bless him.

'Now, Miss Stackhouse, we want you to come back tomorrow night,' Russell Edgington said. His human friend stood behind Edgington, his hands resting on Edgington's shoulders. The small vampire reached up and patted one of those hands. 'We don't want you scared off by the bad manners of one individual.'

'Thanks, I'll mention that to Alcide,' I said, not letting any enthusiasm leak into my voice. I hoped I appeared subservient to Alcide without being spineless. Spineless people didn't last long around vampires. Russell Edgington believed he was projecting the appearance of an old-style Southern gentleman, and if that was his thing, I might as well feed it.

Alcide returned, and his face was grim. 'I'm afraid your wrap had an accident,' he said, and I realized he was furious. 'Debbie, I guess.'

My beautiful silk shawl had a big hole burned in it. I tried to keep my face impassive, but I didn't manage very well. Tears actually welled up in my eyes, I suppose because the incident with the biker had shaken me already.

Edgington, of course, was soaking this all in.

'Better the shawl than me,' I said, attempting a shrug. I made the corners of my mouth turn up. At least my little purse appeared intact, though I hadn't had any more in it than a compact and a lipstick, and enough cash to pay for supper. To my intense embarrassment, Alcide shrugged out of his suit coat and held it for me to slide into. I began to protest, but the look on his face said he wasn't going to take no for an answer.

'Good night, Miss Stackhouse,' the vampire said. 'Herveaux, see you tomorrow night? Does your business keep you in Jackson?'

'Yes, it does,' Alcide said pleasantly. 'It was good to talk to you, Russell.'

The truck was outside the club when we emerged. The sidewalk seemed no less full of menace than it had when we arrived. I wondered how all these effects were achieved, but I was too depressed to question my escort.

'You shouldn't have given me your coat, you must be freezing,' I said, after we'd driven a couple of blocks.

'I have on more clothes than you,' Alcide said.

He wasn't shivering like I was, even without his coat. I huddled in it, enjoying the silk lining, and the warmth, and his smell.

'I should never have left you by yourself with those jerks in the club.'

'Everyone has to go to the bathroom,' I said mildly.

'I should have asked someone else to sit with you.'

'I'm a big girl. I don't need a perpetual guard. I handle little incidents like that all the time at the bar.' If I sounded weary of it, I was. You just don't get to see the best side of men when you're a barmaid; even at a place like Merlotte's, where the owner watches out for his servers and almost all the clientele is local.

'Then you shouldn't be working there.' Alcide sounded very definite.

'Okay, marry me and take me away from all this,' I said,

deadpan, and got a frightened look in return. I grinned at him. 'I have to make my living, Alcide. And mostly, I like my job.'

He looked unconvinced and thoughtful. It was time to change the subject.

'They've got Bill,' I said.

'You know for sure.'

'Yeah.'

'Why? What does he know that Edgington would want to know so badly, badly enough to risk a war?'

'I can't tell you.'

'But you do know?'

To tell him would be to say I trusted him. I was in the same kind of danger as Bill if it was known that I knew what he knew. And I'd break a lot faster.

'Yes,' I said. 'I know.'

Chapter 6

We were silent in the elevator. As Alcide unlocked his apartment, I leaned against the wall. I was a mess: tired, conflicted, and agitated by the fracas with the biker and Debbie's vandalism.

I felt like apologizing, but I didn't know what for.

'Good night,' I said, at the door to my room. 'Oh, here. Thanks.' I shrugged out of his coat and held it out to him. He hung it over the back of one of the bar stools at the eat-in counter.

'Need help with your zipper?' he asked.

'It would be great if you could get it started.' I turned my back to him. He'd zipped it up the last couple of inches when I was getting dressed, and I appreciated his thinking of this before he vanished into his room.

I felt his big fingers against my back, and the little hiss of the zipper. Then something unexpected happened; I felt him touch me again.

I shivered all over as his fingers trailed down my skin.

I didn't know what to do.

I didn't know what I wanted to do.

I made myself turn to face him. His face was as uncertain as mine.

'Worst possible time,' I said. 'You're on the rebound. I'm looking for my boyfriend; granted, he's my unfaithful boyfriend, but still . . .'

'Bad timing,' he agreed, and his hands settled on my shoulders. Then he bent down and kissed me. It took about a half a second for my arms to go around his waist and his tongue to slide into my mouth. He kissed soft. I wanted to run my fingers through his hair and find out how broad his chest was and if his butt was really as high and round as it looked in his pants . . . oh, hell. I gently pushed back.

'Bad timing,' I said. I flushed, realizing that with my dress half unzipped, Alcide could see my bra and the tops of my bosom easily. Well, it was good I had a pretty bra on.

'Oh, God,' he said, having gotten an eyeful. He made a supreme effort and squeezed those green eyes shut. 'Bad timing,' he agreed again. 'Though I can hope that, real soon, it might seem like better timing.'

I smiled. 'Who knows?' I said, and stepped back into my room while I could still make myself move in that direction. After shutting the door gently, I hung up the red dress, pleased it still looked good and unstained. The sleeves were a disaster, with greasy fingerprints and a little blood on them. I sighed regretfully.

I'd have to flit from door to door to use the bathroom. I didn't want to be a tease, and my robe was definitely short, nylon, and pink. So I scooted, because I could hear Alcide rummaging around in the kitchen. What with one thing and another, I was in the little bathroom for a while. When I came out, all the lights in the apartment were off except the one in my bedroom. I closed the shades, feeling a little silly doing so since no other building on the block was five stories high. I put on my pink nightgown, and crawled in the bed to read a chapter of my romance by way of calming down. It was the one where the heroine finally beds the hero, so it didn't work too well, but I did stop thinking about the biker's skin burning from contact with the goblin, and about Debbie's malicious narrow face. And about the idea of Bill being tortured.

The love scene (actually, the sex scene) steered my mind more toward Alcide's warm mouth.

I switched off the bedside lamp after I'd put my bookmark in my book. I snuggled down in the bed and piled the covers high on top of me, and felt – finally – warm and safe.

Someone knocked at my window.

I let out a little shriek. Then, figuring who it must be, I yanked on my robe, belted it, and opened the shades.

Sure enough, Eric was floating just outside. I switched on the lamp again, and struggled with the unfamiliar window.

'What the hell do you want?' I was saying, as Alcide dashed into the room.

I barely spared him a glance over my shoulder. 'You better leave me alone and let me get some sleep,' I told Eric, not caring if I sounded like an old scold, 'and you better stop showing up outside places in the middle of the night and expecting me to let you in!'

'Sookie, let me in,' Eric said.

'No! Well, actually, this is Alcide's place. Alcide, what you want to do?'

I turned to look at him for the first time, and tried not to let my mouth fall open. Alcide slept in those long drawstring pants, period. Whoa. If he'd been shirtless thirty minutes before, the timing might have seemed just perfect.

'What do you want, Eric?' Alcide asked, much more calmly than I had done.

'We need to talk,' Eric said, sounding impatient.

'If I let him in now, can I rescind it?' Alcide asked me.

'Sure.' I grinned at Eric. 'Any moment, you can rescind it.'

'Okay. You can come in, Eric.' Alcide took the screen off the window, and Eric slid in feetfirst. I eased the window shut behind him. Now I was cold again. There was gooseflesh all over Alcide's chest, too, and his nipples . . . I forced myself to keep an eye on Eric.

Eric gave both of us a sharp look, his blue eyes as brilliant as sapphires in the lamplight. 'What have you found out, Sookie?'

'The vampires here do have him.'

Eric's eyes may have widened a little, but that was his only reaction. He appeared to be thinking intently.

'Isn't it a little dangerous for you to be on Edgington's turf, unannounced?' Alcide asked. He was doing his leaning-against-the-wall thing again. He and Eric were both big men and the room really seemed crowded all of a sudden. Maybe their egos were using up all the oxygen.

'Oh, yes,' Eric said. 'Very dangerous.' He smiled radiantly.

I wondered if they'd notice if I went back to bed. I yawned. Two pairs of eyes swung to focus on me. 'Anything else you need, Eric?' I asked.

'Do you have anything else to report?'

'Yes, they've tortured him.'

'Then they won't let him go.'

Of course not. You wouldn't let loose a vampire you'd tortured. You'd be looking over your shoulder for the rest of your life. I hadn't thought that through, but I could see its truth.

'You're going to attack?' I wanted to be nowhere around Jackson when that happened.

'Let me think on it,' Eric said. 'You are going back to the bar tomorrow night?'

'Yes, Russell invited us specifically.'

'Sookie attracted his attention tonight,' Alcide said.

'But that's perfect!' Eric said. 'Tomorrow night, sit with the Edgington crew and pick their brains, Sookie.'

'Well, that would never have occurred to me, Eric,' I said, wonderingly. 'Gosh, I'm glad you woke me up tonight to explain that to me.'

'No problem,' Eric said. 'Anytime you want me to wake you up, Sookie, you have only to say.'

I sighed. 'Go away, Eric. Good night again, Alcide.'

Alcide straightened, waiting for Eric to go back out the window. Eric waited for Alcide to leave.

'I rescind your invitation into my apartment,' Alcide said, and abruptly Eric walked to the window, reopened it, and launched himself out. He was scowling. Once outside, he regained his composure and smiled at us, waving as he vanished downward.

Alcide slammed the window shut and let the blinds back down.

'No, there are lots of men who don't like me at all,' I told him. He'd been easy to read that time, all right.

He gave me an odd look. 'Is that so?'

'Yes, it is.'

'If you say so.'

'Most people, regular people, that is . . . they think I'm nuts.'

'Is that right?'

'Yes, that's right! And it makes them very nervous to have me serve them.'

He began laughing, a reaction that was so far from what I had intended that I had no idea what to say next.

He left the room, still more or less chuckling to himself.

Well, that had been weird. I turned out the lamp and took off the robe, tossing it across the foot of the bed. I snuggled between the sheets again, the blanket and spread pulled up to my chin. It was cold and bleak outside, but here I was, finally, warm and safe and alone. Really, really alone.

The next morning Alcide was already gone when I got up. Construction and surveying people get going early, naturally, and I was used to sleeping late because of my job at the bar and because I hung around with a vampire. If I wanted to spend time with Bill, it had to be at night, obviously.

There was a note propped up on the coffeepot. I had a slight headache since I am not used to alcohol and I'd had two drinks the night before – the headache was not quite a hangover, but I wasn't my normal cheerful self, either. I squinted at the tiny printing.

'Running errands. Make yourself at home. I'll be back in the afternoon.'

For a minute I felt disappointed and deflated. Then I got a hold of myself. It wasn't like he'd called me up and scheduled this as a romantic weekend, or like we really knew each other. Alcide had had my company foisted on him. I shrugged, and poured myself a cup of coffee. I made some toast and turned on the news. After I'd watched one cycle of CNN headlines, I decided to shower. I took my time. What else was there to do?

I was in danger of experiencing an almost unknown state – boredom.

At home, there was always something to do, though it might not be something I particularly enjoyed. If you have a house, there's always some little job waiting for your attention. And when I was in Bon Temps, there was the library to go to, or the dollar store, or the grocery. Since I'd taken up with Bill, I'd also been running errands for him that could only be done in the daytime when offices were open.

As Bill crossed my mind, I was plucking a stray hair from my eyebrow line, leaning over the sink to peer in the bathroom mirror. I had to lay down the tweezers and sit on the edge of the tub. My feelings for Bill were so confused and conflicting, I had no hope of sorting them out anytime soon. But knowing he was in pain, in trouble, and I didn't know how to find him – that was a lot to bear. I had never supposed that our romance would go smoothly. It was an interspecies relationship, after all. And Bill was a lot older than me. But this aching chasm I felt now that he was gone – that, I hadn't ever imagined.

I pulled on some jeans and a sweater and made my bed. I lined up all my makeup in the bathroom I was using, and hung the towel just so. I would have straightened up Alcide's room if I hadn't felt it would be sort of impertinent to handle his things. So I read a few chapters of my book, and then decided I simply could not sit in the apartment any longer.

I left a note for Alcide telling him I was taking a walk, and then I rode down in the elevator with a man in casual clothes, lugging a golf bag. I refrained from saying, 'Going to play golf?' and confined myself to mentioning that it was a good day to be outside. It was bright and sunny, clear as a bell, and probably in the fifties. It was a happy day, with all the Christmas decorations looking bright in the sun, and lots of shopping traffic.

I wondered if Bill would be home for Christmas. I wondered if Bill could go to church with me on Christmas Eve, or if he would. I thought of the new Skil saw I'd gotten Jason; I'd had it on layaway at Sears in Monroe for months, and just picked it up a week ago. I had gotten a toy for each of Arlene's kids, and a sweater for Arlene. I really didn't have anyone else to buy a gift for, and that was pathetic. I decided I'd get Sam a CD this year. The idea cheered me. I love to give presents. This would have been my first Christmas with a boyfriend . . .

Oh, hell, I'd come full cycle, just like *Headline News*.

'Sookie!' called a voice.

Startled out of my dreary round of thoughts, I looked around to see that Janice was waving at me out of the door of her shop, on the other side of the street. I'd unconsciously walked the direction I knew. I waved back at her.

'Come on over!' she said.

I went down to the corner and crossed with the light. The shop was busy, and Jarvis and Corinne had their hands full with customers.

'Christmas parties tonight,' Janice explained, while her hands were busy rolling up a young matron's black shoulder-length hair. 'We're not usually open after noon on Saturdays.' The young woman, whose hands were decorated with an impressive set of diamond rings, kept riffling through a copy of *Southern Living* while Janice worked on her head.

'Does this sound good?' she asked Janice. 'Ginger meatballs?' One glowing fingernail pointed to the recipe.

'Kind of oriental?' Janice asked.

'Um, sort of.' She read the recipe intently. 'No one else would be serving them,' she muttered. 'You could stick toothpicks in 'em.'

'Sookie, what are you doing today?' Janice asked, when she was sure her customer was thinking about ground beef.

'Just hanging out,' I said. I shrugged. 'Your brother's out running errands, his note said.'

'He left you a note to tell you what he was doing? Girl, you should be proud. That man hasn't set pen to paper since high school.' She gave me a sideways look and grinned. 'You all have a good time last night?'

I thought it over. 'Ah, it was okay,' I said hesitantly. The dancing had been fun, anyway.

Janice burst out laughing. 'If you have to think about it that hard, it must not have been a perfect evening.'

'Well, no,' I admitted. 'There was like a little fight in the bar, and a man had to be evicted. And then, Debbie was there.'

'How did her engagement party go?'

'There was quite a crowd at her table,' I said. 'But she came over after a while and asked a lot of questions.' I smiled reminiscently. 'She sure didn't like seeing Alcide with someone else!'

Janice laughed again.

'Who got engaged?' asked her customer, having decided against the recipe.

'Oh, Debbie Pelt? Used to go with my brother?' Janice said.

'I know her,' said the black-haired woman, pleasure in her voice. 'She used to date your brother, Alcide? And now she's marrying someone else?'

'Marrying Charles Clausen,' Janice said, nodding gravely. 'You know him?'

'Sure I do! We went to high school together. He's marrying Debbie Pelt? Well, better him than your brother,' Black Hair said confidentially.

'I'd already figured that out,' Janice said. 'You know something I don't know, though?'

'That Debbie, she's into some weird stuff,' Black Hair said, raising her eyebrows to mark deep significance.

'Like what?' I asked, hardly breathing as I waited to hear what would come out. Could it be that this woman actually knew about shape-shifting, about werewolves? My eyes met Janice's and I saw the same apprehension in them.

Janice knew about her brother. She knew about his world.

And she knew I did, too.

'Devil worship, they say,' Black Hair said. 'Witchcraft.'

We both gaped at her reflection in the mirror. She had gotten the reaction she'd been looking for. She gave a satisfied nod. Devil worship and witchcraft weren't synonymous, but I wasn't going to argue with this woman; this was the wrong time and place.

'Yes, ma'am, that's what I hear. At every full moon, she and some friends of hers go out in the woods and do stuff. No one seems to know exactly what,' she admitted.

Janice and I exhaled simultaneously.

'Oh, my goodness,' I said weakly.

'Then my brother's well out of a relationship with her. We don't hold with such doings,' Janice said righteously.

'Of course not,' I agreed.

We didn't meet each other's eyes.

After that little passage, I made motions about leaving, but Janice asked me what I was wearing that night.

'Oh, it's kind of a champagne color,' I said. 'Kind of a shiny beige.'

'Then the red nails won't do,' Janice said. 'Corinne!'

Despite all my protests, I left the shop with bronze finger- and toenails, and Jarvis worked on my hair again. I tried to pay Janice, but the most she would let me do was tip her employees.

'I've never been pampered so much in my life,' I told her.

'What do you do, Sookie?' Somehow that hadn't come up the day before.

'I'm a barmaid,' I said.

'That *is* a change from Debbie,' Janice said. She looked thoughtful.

'Oh, yeah? What does Debbie do?'

'She's a legal assistant.'

Debbie definitely had an educational edge. I'd never been able to manage college; financially, it would have been rough, though I could've found a way, I guess. But my disability had made it hard enough to get out of high school. A telepathic teenager has an extremely hard time of it, let me tell you. And I had so little control then. Every day had been full of dramas – the dramas of other kids. Trying to concentrate on listening in class, taking tests in a roomful of buzzing brains . . . the only thing I'd ever excelled in was homework.

Janice didn't seem to be too concerned that I was a

barmaid, which was an occupation not guaranteed to impress the families of those you dated.

I had to remind myself all over again that this setup with Alcide was a temporary arrangement he'd never asked for, and that after I'd discovered Bill's whereabouts – right, Sookie, remember Bill, your *boyfriend*? – I'd never see Alcide again. Oh, he might drop into Merlotte's, if he felt like getting off the interstate on his way from Shreveport to Jackson, but that would be all.

Janice was genuinely hoping I would be a permanent member of her family. That was so nice of her. I liked her a lot. I almost found myself wishing that Alcide really liked me, that there was a real chance of Janice being my sister-in-law.

They say there's no harm in daydreaming, but there is.

Chapter 7

Alcide was waiting for me when I got back. A pile of wrapped presents on the kitchen counter showed me how he'd spent at least part of his morning. Alcide had been completing his Christmas shopping.

Judging from his self-conscious look (Mr. Subtle, he wasn't), he'd done something he wasn't sure I'd like. Whatever it was, he wasn't ready to reveal it to me, so I tried to be polite and stay out of his head. As I was passing through the short hall formed by the bedroom wall and the kitchen counter, I sniffed something less than pleasant. Maybe the garbage needed to be tossed? What garbage could we have generated in our short stay that would produce that faint, unpleasant odor? But the past pleasure of my chat with Janice and the present pleasure of seeing Alcide made it easy to forget.

'You look nice,' he said.

'I stopped in to see Janice.' I was worried for fear he would think I was imposing on his sister's generosity. 'She has a way of getting you to accept things you had no intention of accepting.'

'She's good,' he said simply. 'She's known about me since we were in high school, and she's never told a soul.'

'I could tell.'

'How –? Oh, yeah.' He shook his head. 'You seem like the most regular person I ever met, and it's hard to remember you've got all this extra stuff.'

No one had ever put it quite like that.

'When you were coming in, did you smell something strange by –' he began, but then the doorbell rang.

Alcide went to answer it while I took off my coat.

He sounded pleased, and I turned to face the door with a smile. The young man coming in didn't seem surprised to see me, and Alcide introduced him as Janice's husband, Dell Phillips. I shook his hand, expecting to be as pleased with him as I was with Janice.

He touched me as briefly as possible, and then he ignored me. 'I wondered if you could come by this afternoon and help me set up our outside Christmas lights,' Dell said – to Alcide, and Alcide only.

'Where's Tommy?' Alcide asked. He looked disappointed. 'You didn't bring him by to see me?' Tommy was Janice's baby.

Dell looked at me, and shook his head. 'You've got a woman here, it didn't seem right. He's with my mom.'

The comment was so unexpected, all I could do was stand in silence. Dell's attitude had caught Alcide flat-footed, too. 'Dell,' he said, 'don't be rude to my friend.'

'She's staying in your apartment, that says more than friend,' Dell said matter-of-factly. 'Sorry, miss, this just isn't right.'

'Judge not, that ye be not judged,' I told him, hoping I didn't sound as furious as my clenched stomach told me I was. It felt wrong to quote the Bible when you were in a towering rage. I went into the guest bedroom and shut the door.

After I heard Dell Phillips leave, Alcide knocked on the door.

'You want to play Scrabble?' he asked.

I blinked. 'Sure.'

'When I was shopping for Tommy, I picked up a game.'

He'd already put it on the coffee table in front of the couch, but he hadn't been confident enough to unwrap it and set it up.

'I'll pour us a Coke,' I said. Not for the first time, I noticed that the apartment was quite cool, though of course it was much warmer than outside. I wished I had brought a light sweater to put on, and I wondered if it would offend Alcide if I asked him to turn the heat up. Then I remembered how warm his skin was, and I figured he was one of those people who runs kind of hot. Or maybe all Weres were like that? I pulled on the sweatshirt I'd worn yesterday, being very careful when I eased it over my hair.

Alcide had folded himself onto the floor on one side of the table, and I settled on the other. It had been a long time since either of us played Scrabble, so we studied the rules for a while before we began the game.

Alcide had graduated from Louisiana Tech. I'd never been to college, but I read a lot, so we were about even on the extent of our vocabulary. Alcide was the better strategist. I seemed to think a little faster.

I scored big with 'quirt,' and he stuck his tongue out at me. I laughed, and he said, 'Don't read my mind, that would be cheating.'

'Of course I wouldn't do any such thing,' I said demurely, and he scowled at me.

I lost – but only by twelve points. After a pleasantly quarrelsome rehash of the game, Alcide got up and took our glasses over to the kitchen. He put them down and began to search through the cabinets, while I stored the game pieces and replaced the lid.

'Where you want me to put this?' I asked.

'Oh, in the closet by the door. There are a couple of shelves in there.'

I tucked the box under one arm and went to the closet. The smell I'd noticed earlier seemed to be stronger.

'You know, Alcide,' I said, hoping I wasn't being tacky, 'there's something that smells almost rotten, right around here.'

'I'd noticed it, too. That's why I'm over here looking through the cabinets. Maybe there's a dead mouse?'

As I spoke, I was turning the doorknob.

I discovered the source of the smell.

'Oh, no,' I said. 'Oh, *nononono.*'

'Don't tell me a rat got in there and died,' Alcide said.

'Not a rat,' I said. 'A werewolf.'

The closet had a shelf above a hanging bar, and it was a small closet, intended only for visitors' coats. Now it was filled by the swarthy man from Club Dead, the man who'd grabbed me by the shoulder. He was really dead. He'd been dead for several hours.

I didn't seem to be able to look away.

Alcide's presence at my back was an unexpected comfort. He stared over my head, his hands gripping my shoulders.

'No blood,' I said in a jittery voice.

'His neck.' Alcide was at least as shaken as I was.

His head really was resting on his shoulder, while still attached to his body. Ick, ick, ick. I gulped hard. 'We should call the police,' I said, not sounding very positive about the process. I noted the way the body had been stuffed into the closet. The dead man was almost standing up. I figured he'd been shoved in, and then whoever had done the shoving had forced the door closed. He'd sort of hardened in position.

'But if we call the police . . .' Alcide's voice trailed off. He took a deep breath. 'They'll never believe we didn't do it. They'll interview his friends, and his friends will tell them he was at Club Dead last night, and they'll check it out. They'll find out he got into trouble for bothering you. No one will believe we didn't have a hand in killing him.'

'On the other hand,' I said slowly, thinking out loud, 'do you think they'd mention a word about Club Dead?'

Alcide pondered that. He ran his thumb over his mouth while he thought. 'You may be right. And if they couldn't bring up Club Dead, how could they describe the, uh, confrontation? You know what they'd do? They'd want to take care of the problem themselves.'

That was an *excellent* point. I was sold: no police. 'Then we need to dispose of him,' I said, getting down to brass tacks. 'How are we gonna do that?'

Alcide was a practical man. He was used to solving problems, starting with the biggest.

'We need to take him out to the country somewhere. To do that, we have to get him down to the garage,' he said after a few moments' thought. 'To do that, we have to wrap him up.'

'The shower curtain,' I suggested, nodding my head in

the direction of the bathroom I'd used. 'Um, can we close the closet and go somewhere else while we work this out?'

'Sure,' Alcide said, suddenly as anxious as I was to stop looking at the gruesome sight before us.

So we stood in the middle of the living room and had a planning session. The first thing I did was turn off the heat in the apartment altogether, and open all the windows. The body had not made its presence known earlier only because Alcide liked the temperature kept cool, and because the closet door fit well. Now we had to disperse the faint but pervasive smell.

'It's five flights down, and I don't think I can carry him that far,' Alcide said. 'He needs to go at least some of the distance in the elevator. That's the most dangerous part.'

We kept discussing and refining, until we felt we had a workable procedure. Alcide asked me twice if I was okay, and I reassured him both times; it finally dawned on me that he was thinking I might break into hysterics, or faint.

'I've never been able to afford to be too finicky,' I said. 'That's not my nature.' If Alcide expected or wanted me to ask for smelling salts, or to beg him to save little me from the big bad wolf, he had the wrong woman.

I might be determined to keep my head, but that's not to say I felt exactly calm. I was so jittery when I went to get the shower curtain that I had to restrain myself from ripping it from the clear plastic rings. Slow and steady, I told myself fiercely. Breathe in, breathe out, get the shower curtain, spread it on the hall floor.

It was blue and green with yellow fish swimming serenely in even rows.

Alcide had gone downstairs to the parking garage to move his truck as close to the stair door as possible. He'd thoughtfully brought a pair of work gloves back up with him. While he pulled them on, he took a deep breath – maybe a mistake, considering the body's proximity. His face a frozen mask of determination, Alcide gripped the corpse's shoulders and gave a yank.

The results were dramatic beyond our imagining. In one stiff piece, the biker toppled out of the closet. Alcide had to leap to his right to avoid the falling body, which banged against the kitchen counter and then fell sideways onto the shower curtain.

'Wow,' I said in a shaky voice, looking down at the result. 'That turned out well.'

The body was lying almost exactly as we wanted it. Alcide and I gave each other a sharp nod and knelt at each end. Acting in concert, we took one side of the plastic curtain and flipped it over the body, then the other. We both relaxed when the man's face was covered. Alcide had also brought up a roll of duct tape – real men always have duct tape in their trucks – and we used it to seal the wrapped body in the curtain. Then we folded the ends over, and taped them. Luckily, though a hefty guy, the Were hadn't been very tall.

We stood up and let ourselves have a little moment of recovery. Alcide spoke first. 'It looks like a big green burrito,' he observed.

I slapped a hand over my mouth to stifle a fit of the giggles.

Alcide's eyes were startled as he stared at me over the wrapped corpse. Suddenly, he laughed, too.

After we'd settled down, I asked, 'You ready for phase two?'

He nodded, and I pulled on my coat and scooted past the

body and Alcide. I went out to the elevator, closing the apartment door behind me very quickly, just in case someone passed by.

The minute I punched the button, a man appeared around the corner and came to stand by the elevator door. Perhaps he was a relative of old Mrs. Osburgh, or maybe one of the senators was making a flying trip back to Jackson. Whoever he was, he was well dressed and in his sixties, and he was polite enough to feel the obligation of making conversation.

'It's really cold today, isn't it?'

'Yes, but not as cold as yesterday.' I stared at the closed doors, willing them to open so he would be gone.

'Did you just move in?'

I had never been so irritated with a courteous person before. 'I'm visiting,' I said, in the kind of flat voice that should indicate the conversation is closed.

'Oh,' he said cheerfully. 'Who?'

Luckily the elevator chose that moment to arrive and its doors snicked open just in time to save this too-genial man from getting his head snapped off. He gestured with a sweep of his hand, wanting me to precede him, but I took a step back, said, 'Oh my gosh, I forgot my keys!' and walked briskly off without a backward glance. I went to the door of the apartment next to Alcide's, the one he'd told me was empty, and I knocked on the door. I heard the elevator doors close behind me, and I breathed a sigh of relief.

When I figured Mr. Chatty had had time to get to his car and drive out of the garage – unless he was talking the ears off the security guard – I recalled the elevator. It was Saturday, and there was no telling what people's schedules would be like. According to Alcide, many of the condos had been bought as an investment and were subleased to legislators, most of who would be gone for the pre-holidays. The year-round tenants, however, would be moving around in atypical ways, since it was not only the weekend, but also only two weekends before Christmas. When the creaky contraption came back to the fifth floor, it was empty.

I dashed back to 504, knocked twice on the door, and dashed back to the elevator to hold the doors open. Preceded by the legs of the corpse, Alcide emerged from the apartment. He moved as quickly as a man can while he's carrying a stiff body over his shoulder.

This was our most vulnerable moment. Alcide's bundle looked like nothing on this earth but a corpse wrapped in a shower curtain. The plastic kept the smell down, but it was still noticeable in the small enclosure. We made it down one floor safely, then the next. At the third floor, our nerve ran out. We stopped the elevator, and to our great relief it opened onto an empty corridor. I darted out and over to the stair door, holding it open for Alcide. Then I scampered down the stairs ahead of him, and looked through the pane of glass in the door to the garage.

'Whoa,' I said, holding my hand up. A middle-aged woman and a teenage girl were unloading packages from the trunk of their Toyota, simultaneously having a vigorous disagreement. The girl had been invited to an all-night party. No, her mother said.

She had to go, all her friends would be there. No, her mother said.

But Mom, everyone else's mom was letting them go. No, her mother said.

'Please don't decide to take the stairs,' I whispered.

But the argument raged on as they got in the elevator. I

clearly heard the girl break her train of complaint long enough to say, 'Ew, something smells in here!' before the doors closed.

'What's happening?' Alcide whispered.

'Nothing. Let's see if that lasts a minute longer.'

It did, and I stepped out of the door and over to Alcide's truck, darting glances from side to side to make sure I was really alone. We weren't quite in sight of the security guard, who was in his little glass hut up the slope of the ramp.

I unlocked the back of Alcide's pickup; fortunately, his pickup bed had a cover. With one more comprehensive look around the garage, I hurried back to the stair door and rapped on it. After a second, I pulled it open.

Alcide shot out and over to his truck faster than I would have believed he could move, burdened as he was. We pushed as hard as we could, and the body slowly retreated into the truck bed. With tremendous relief, we slammed the tailgate shut and locked it.

'Phase two complete,' Alcide said with an air that I would have called giddy if he hadn't been such a big man.

Driving through the streets of a city with a body in your vehicle is a terrifying exercise in paranoia.

'Obey every single traffic rule,' I reminded Alcide, unhappy with how tense my voice sounded.

'Okay, okay,' he growled, his voice equally tense.

'Do you think those people in that Jimmy are looking at us?'

'No.'

It would obviously be a good thing for me to keep quiet, so I did. We got back on I-20, the same way we'd entered Jackson, and drove until there was no city, only farmland.

When we got to the Bolton exit, Alcide said, 'This looks good.'

'Sure,' I said. I didn't think I could stand driving around with the body any longer. The land between Jackson and Vicksburg is pretty low and flat, mostly open fields broken up by a few bayous, and this area was typical. We exited the interstate and headed north toward the woods. After a few miles Alcide took a right onto a road that had needed repaving for years. The trees grew up on either side of the much-patched strip of gray. The bleak winter sky didn't stand a chance of giving much light with this kind of competition, and I shivered in the cab of the truck.

'Not too much longer,' Alcide said. I nodded jerkily.

A tiny thread of a road led off to the left, and I pointed. Alcide braked, and we examined the prospect. We gave each other a sharp nod of approval. Alcide backed in, which surprised me; but I decided that it was a good idea. The farther we went into the woods, the more I liked our choice of venue. The road had been graveled not too long ago, so we wouldn't leave tire tracks, for one thing. And I thought the chances were good that this rudimentary road led to a hunting camp, which wouldn't be in much use now that deer season was over.

Sure enough, after we'd crunched a few yards down the track, I spotted a sign nailed to a tree. It proclaimed, 'Kiley-Odum Hunt Club private property – KEEP OUT.'

We proceeded down the track, Alcide backing slowly and carefully.

'Here,' he said, when we'd gone far enough into the woods that it was almost certain we couldn't be seen from the road. He put the truck into Park. 'Listen, Sookie, you don't have to get out.'

'It'll be quicker if we work together.'

He tried to give me a menacing glare, but I gave him a stone face right back, and finally, he sighed. 'Okay, let's get this over with,' he said.

The air was cold and wet, and if you stood still for a moment the chilling damp would creep into your bones. I could tell the temperature was taking a dive, and the bright sky of the morning was a fond memory. It was an appropriate day to dump a body. Alcide opened the back of the truck, we both pulled on gloves, and we grasped the bright blue-and-green bundle. The cheerful yellow fish looked almost obscene out here in the freezing woods.

'Give it everything you got,' Alcide advised me, and on a count of three, we yanked with all our might. That got the bundle half out, and the end of it protruded over the tailgate in a nasty way. 'Ready? Let's go again. One, two, three!' Again I yanked, and the body's own gravity shot it out of the truck and onto the road.

If we could have driven off then and there, I would have been much happier; but we had decided we had to take the shower curtain with us. Who was to say what fingerprints might be found somewhere on the duct tape or the curtain itself? There was sure to be other, microscopic evidence that I couldn't even imagine.

I don't watch the Discovery Channel for nothing.

Alcide had a utility knife, and I did let him have the honor of this particular task. I held open a garbage bag while he cut the plastic away and stuffed it into the opening. I tried not to look, but of course I did.

The body's appearance had not improved.

That job, too, was finished sooner than I expected. I half turned to get back in the truck, but Alcide stood, his face raised to the sky. He looked as if he was smelling the forest.

'Tonight's the full moon,' he said. His whole body seemed to quiver. When he looked at me, his eyes looked alien. I couldn't say that they had changed in color or contour, but it was as if a different person was looking out of them.

I was very alone in the woods with a comrade who had suddenly taken on a whole new dimension. I fought conflicting impulses to scream, burst into tears, or run. I smiled brightly at him and waited. After a long, fraught pause, Alcide said, 'Let's get back in the truck.'

I was only too glad to scramble up into the seat.

'What do you think killed him?' I asked, when it seemed to me Alcide had had time to return to normal.

'I think someone gave his neck a big twist,' Alcide said. 'I can't figure out how he got into the apartment. I know I locked the door last night. I'm sure of it. And this morning it was locked again.'

I tried to figure that out for a while, but I couldn't. Then I wondered what actually killed you if your neck was broken. But I decided that wasn't really a great thing to think about.

En route to the apartment, we made a stop at WalMart. On a weekend this close to Christmas, it was swarming with shoppers. Once again, I thought, *I haven't gotten anything for Bill.*

And I felt a sharp pain in my heart as I realized that I might never buy Bill a Christmas present, not now, not ever.

We needed air fresheners, Resolve (to clean the carpet), and a new shower curtain. I packed my misery away and walked a little more briskly. Alcide let me pick out the shower curtain, which I actually enjoyed. He paid cash, so there wouldn't be any record of our visit.

I checked out my nails after we had climbed back in the truck. They were fine. Then I thought of how callous I must be, worrying about my fingernails. I'd just finished disposing of a dead man. For several minutes, I sat there feeling mighty unhappy about myself.

I relayed this to Alcide, who seemed more approachable now that we were back in civilization minus our silent passenger.

'Well, you didn't kill him,' he pointed out. 'Ah – did you?'

I met his green eyes, feeling only a little surprise. 'No, I certainly did not. Did you?'

'No,' he said, and from his expression I could tell he'd been waiting for me to ask him. It had never occurred to me to do so.

While I'd never suspected Alcide, of course someone had made the Were into a body. For the first time I tried to figure who could have stuffed the body in the closet. Up until this point, I'd just been busy trying to make the body go away.

'Who has keys?' I asked.

'Just Dad and me, and the cleaning woman who does most of the apartments in the building. She doesn't keep a key of her own. The building manager gives her one.' We pulled around behind the row of stores, and Alcide tossed in the garbage bag containing the old shower curtain.

'That's a pretty short list.'

'Yes,' Alcide said slowly. 'Yes, it is. But I know my dad's in Jackson. I talked to him on the phone this morning, right after I got up. The cleaning woman only comes in when we leave a message with the building manager. He keeps a copy of our key, hands it to her when she needs it, and she returns it to him.'

'What about the security guard in the garage? Is he on duty all night?'

'Yes, because he's the only line of defense between people sneaking into the garage and taking the elevator. You've always come in that way, but there are actually front doors to the building that face onto the major street. Those front doors are locked all the time. There's no guard there, but you do have to have a key to get in.'

'So if someone could sneak past the guard, they could ride up in the elevator to your floor, without being stopped.'

'Oh, sure.'

'And that someone would have to pick the lock to the door.'

'Yes, and carry in a body, and stuff it in the closet. That sounds pretty unlikely,' said Alcide.

'But that's apparently what happened. Oh, um . . . did you ever give Debbie a key? Maybe someone borrowed hers?' I tried hard to sound totally neutral. That probably didn't work too well.

Long pause.

'Yes, she had a key,' Alcide said stiffly.

I bit down on my lips so I wouldn't ask the next question.

'No, I didn't get it back from her.'

I hadn't even needed to ask.

Breaking a somewhat charged silence, Alcide suggested we eat a late lunch. Oddly enough, I found I was really hungry.

We ate at Hal and Mal's, a restaurant close to downtown. It was in an old warehouse, and the tables were just far enough apart to make our conversation possible without anyone calling the police.

'I don't think,' I murmured, 'that anyone could walk around your building with a body over his shoulder, no matter what the hour.'

'We just did,' he said, unanswerably. 'I figure it had to have happened between, say, two a.m. and seven. We were asleep by two, right?'

'More like three, considering Eric's little visit.'

Our eyes met. Eric. Eureka!

'But why would he have done that? Is he nuts about you?' Alcide asked bluntly.

'Not so much nuts,' I muttered, embarrassed.

'Oh, wants to get in your pants.'

I nodded, not meeting his eyes.

'Lot of that going around,' Alcide said, under his breath.

'Huh,' I said dismissively. 'You're still hung up on that Debbie, and you know it.'

We looked right at each other. Better to haul this out of the shadows now, and put it to rest.

'You can read my mind better than I thought,' Alcide said. His broad face looked unhappy. 'But she's not . . . Why do I care about her? I'm not sure I even like her. I like the hell out of you.'

'Thanks,' I said, smiling from my heart. 'I like the hell out of you, too.'

'We're obviously better for each other than either of the people we're dating are for us,' he said.

Undeniably true. 'Yes, and I would be happy with you.'

'And I'd enjoy sharing my day with you.'

'But it looks like we're not going to get there.'

'No.' He sighed heavily. 'I guess not.'

The young waitress beamed at us as we left, making sure Alcide noticed how well packed into her jeans she was.

'What I think I'll do,' Alcide said, 'is I'll do my best to yank Debbie out of me by the roots. And then I'll turn up on your doorstep, one day when you least expect it, and I'll hope by then you will have given up on your vampire.'

'And then we'll be happy ever after?' I smiled.

He nodded.

'Well, that'll be something to look forward to,' I told him.

Chapter 8

I was so tired by the time we entered Alcide's apartment that I was sure all I was good for was a nap. It had been one of the longest days of my life, and it was only the middle of the afternoon.

But we had some housekeeping chores to do first. While Alcide hung the new shower curtain, I cleaned the carpet in the closet with Resolve, and opened one of the air fresheners and placed it on the shelf. We closed all the windows, turned on the heat, and breathed experimentally, our eyes locked on each other's.

The apartment smelled okay. We simultaneously breathed out a sigh of relief.

'We just did something really illegal,' I said, still uneasy about my own immorality. 'But all I really feel is happy we got away with it.'

'Don't worry about not feeling guilty,' Alcide said. 'Something'll come along pretty soon that you'll feel guilty about. Save it up.'

This was such good advice that I decided to try it. 'I'm going to take a nap,' I said, 'so I'll be at least a little alert tonight.' You didn't want to be slow on the uptake around vampires.

'Good idea,' Alcide said. He cocked an eyebrow at me, and I laughed, shaking my head. I went in the smaller bedroom and shut the door, taking off my shoes and falling onto the bed with a feeling of quiet delight. I reached over the side of the bed after a moment, grabbed the fringe of the chenille bedspread, and wrapped it around me. In the quiet apartment, with the heating system blowing a steady stream of warm air into the bedroom, it took only a few minutes to fall asleep.

I woke all of a sudden, and I was completely awake. I knew there was someone else in the apartment. Maybe on some level I'd heard a knock on the front door; or maybe I'd registered the rumble of voices in the living room. I swung silently off the bed and padded to the door, my socks making no noise at all on the beige carpet. I had pushed my door to, but not latched it, and now I turned my head to position my ear at the crack.

A deep, gravelly voice said, 'Jerry Falcon came to my apartment last night.'

'I don't know him,' Alcide replied. He sounded calm, but wary.

'He says you got him into trouble at Josephine's last night.'

'I got him into trouble? If he's the guy who grabbed my date, he got himself into trouble!'

'Tell me what happened.'

'He made a pass at my date while I was in the men's room. When she protested, he started manhandling her, and she drew attention to the situation.'

'He hurt her?'

'Shook her up. And he drew some blood on her shoulder.'

'A blood offense.' The voice had become deadly serious.

'Yes.'

So the fingernail gouges on my shoulder constituted a blood offense, whatever that was.

'And then?'

'I came out of the men's room, hauled him off of her. Then Mr. Hob stepped in.'

'That explains the burns.'

'Yes. Hob threw him out the back door. And that was the last I saw of him. You say his name is Jerry Falcon?'

'Yeah. He came right to my house then, after the rest of the boys left the bar.'

'Edgington intervened. They were about to jump us.'

'Edgington was there?' The deep voice sounded very unhappy.

'Oh, yes, with his boyfriend.'

'How did Edgington get involved?'

'He told them to leave. Since he's the king, and they work for him from time to time, he expected obedience. But a pup gave him some trouble, so Edgington broke his knee, made the others carry the guy out. I'm sorry there was trouble in your city, Terence. But it was none of our doing.'

'You've got guest privileges with our pack, Alcide. We respect you. And those of us who work for the vampires, well, what can I say? Not the best element. But Jerry is their leader, and he was shamed in front of his people last night. How much longer you going to be in our city?'

'Just one more night.'

'And it's a full moon.'

'Yeah, I know, I'll try to keep a low profile.'

'What are you going to do tonight? Try to avoid the change, or come out to my hunting land with me?'

'I'll try to stay out of the moon, try to avoid stress.'

'Then you'll keep out of Josephine's.'

'Unfortunately, Russell pretty much demanded that we come back tonight. He felt apologetic that my date went through so much aggravation. He made a point of insisting she come back.'

'Club Dead on a full-moon night, Alcide. This isn't wise.'

'What am I gonna do? Russell calls the shots in Mississippi.'

'I can understand. But watch out, and if you see Jerry Falcon there, you turn the other way. This is my city.' The deep voice was heavy with authority.

'I understand, Packmaster.'

'Good. Now that you and Debbie Pelt have broken up, I hope it's a while before we see you back here, Alcide. Give things a chance to settle down. Jerry's a vindictive son of a bitch. He'll do you an injury if he can, without starting a feud.'

'He was the one who caused a blood offense.'

'I know, but because of his long association with the vampires, Jerry has too good an opinion of himself. He doesn't always follow the pack traditions. He only came to me, as he should, because Edgington backed the other side.'

Jerry wasn't going to be following any tradition anymore. Jerry was lying in the woods to the west.

While I'd napped, it had gotten dark outside. I heard a tap on the glass of the window. I jumped, of course, but then I padded across as quietly as I could. I opened the curtain and held a finger across my lips. It was Eric. I hoped no one on the street outside looked up. He smiled at me and motioned me to open the window. I shook my head vehemently and held my finger across my lips again. If I let Eric in now, Terence would hear, and my presence would be discovered. Terence, I knew instinctively, would not like to find he had been overheard. I tiptoed back to the door and listened. Goodbyes were being said. I glanced back at the window, to see that Eric was watching me with great interest. I held up one finger to indicate it would just be a minute.

I heard the apartment door close. Moments later, there was a knock at my door. As I let Alcide in, I hoped I didn't have those funny creases on my face.

'Alcide, I heard most of that,' I said. 'I'm sorry I eavesdropped, but it did seem like it concerned me. Um, Eric is here.'

'So I see,' Alcide said unenthusiastically. 'I guess I'd better let him in. Enter, Eric,' he said, as he slid open the window.

Eric entered as smoothly as a tall man can enter a small window. He was wearing a suit, complete with vest and tie. His hair was slicked back into a ponytail. He was also wearing glasses.

'Are you in disguise?' I asked. I could hardly believe it.

'Yes, I am.' He looked down at himself proudly. 'Don't I look different?'

'Yes,' I admitted. 'You look just like Eric, dressed up for once.'

'Do you like the suit?'

'Sure,' I said. I have limited knowledge of men's clothes, but I was willing to bet this sort of olive-brown three-piece ensemble had cost more than I made in two weeks. Or four.

I might not have picked this out for a guy with blue eyes, but I had to admit he looked spectacular. If they put out a vampire issue of *GQ*, he'd definitely be in the running for a photo shoot. 'Who did your hair?' I asked, noticing for the first time that it had been braided in an intricate pattern.

'Oooh, jealous?'

'No, I thought maybe they could teach me how to do that to mine.'

Alcide had had enough of fashion commentary. He said belligerently, 'What do you mean by leaving the dead man in my closet?'

I have seldom seen Eric at a loss for words, but he was definitely speechless – for all of thirty seconds.

'It wasn't Bubba in the closet, was it?' he asked.

It was our turn to stand with mouths open, Alcide because he didn't know who the hell Bubba was, and me because I couldn't imagine what could have happened to the dazed vampire.

I hastily filled Alcide in on Bubba.

'So that explains all the sightings,' he said, shaking his head from side to side. 'Damn – they were all for real!'

'The Memphis group wanted to keep him, but it was just impossible,' Eric explained. 'He kept wanting to go home, and then there'd be incidents. So we started passing him around.'

'And now you've lost him,' Alcide observed, not too chagrined by Eric's problem.

'It's possible that the people who were trying to get to Sookie in Bon Temps got Bubba instead,' Eric said. He tugged on his vest and looked down with some satisfaction. 'So, who was in the closet?'

'The biker who marked Sookie last night,' Alcide said.

'He made a pretty rough pass at her while I was in the men's room.'

'Marked her?'

'Yes, blood offense,' Alcide said significantly.

'You didn't say anything about this last night.' Eric raised an eyebrow at me.

'I didn't want to talk about it,' I said. I didn't like the way that came out, kind of forlorn. 'Besides, it wasn't much blood.'

'Let me see.'

I rolled my eyes, but I knew darn good and well that Eric wouldn't give up. I pulled my sweatshirt off my shoulder, along with my bra strap. Luckily, the sweatshirt was so old, the neck had lost its elasticity, and it afforded enough room. The fingernail gouges on my shoulder were crusted half-moons, puffy and red, though I'd scrubbed the area carefully the night before. I know how many germs are under fingernails. 'See,' I said. 'No big deal. I was more mad than scared or hurt.'

Eric kept his eyes on the little nasty wounds until I shrugged my clothes back into order. Then he switched his eyes to Alcide. 'And he was dead in the closet?'

'Yes,' Alcide said. 'Had been dead for hours.'

'What killed him?'

'He hadn't been bitten,' I said. 'He looked as though his neck might have been broken. We didn't feel like looking that closely. You're saying you aren't the guilty party?'

'No, though it would have been a pleasure to have done it.'

I shrugged, not willing to explore that dark thought. 'So, who put him there?' I asked, to get the discussion going again.

'And why?' Alcide asked.

'Would it be too much to ask where he is now?' Eric managed to look as if he were indulging two rowdy children.

Alcide and I shot each other glances. 'Um, well, he's . . .' My voice trailed away.

Eric inhaled, sampling the apartment's atmosphere. 'The body's not here. You called the police?'

'Well, no,' I muttered. 'Actually, we, ah . . .'

'We dumped him out in the country,' Alcide said. There just wasn't a nice way to say it.

We had surprised Eric a second time. 'Well,' he said blankly. 'Aren't you two enterprising?'

'We worked it all out,' I said, maybe sounding a tad defensive.

Eric smiled. It was not a happy sight. 'Yes, I'll bet you did.'

'The packmaster came to see me today,' Alcide said. 'Just now, in fact. And he didn't know that Jerry was missing. In fact, Jerry went complaining to Terence after he left the bar last night, telling Terence he had a grievance against me. So he was seen and heard after the incident at Josephine's.'

'So you may have gotten away with it.'

'I think we did.'

'You should have burned him,' Eric said. 'It would have killed any trace of your smell on him.'

'I don't think anyone could pick out our smell,' I told him. 'Really and truly. I don't think we ever touched him with our bare skin.'

Eric looked at Alcide, and Alcide nodded. 'I agree,' he said. 'And I'm one of the two-natured.'

Eric shrugged. 'I have no idea who would have killed

him and put him in the apartment. Obviously, someone wanted his death blamed on you.'

'Then why not call the police from a pay phone and tell them there's a dead body in 504?'

'A good question, Sookie, and one I can't answer right now.' Eric seemed to lose interest all of a sudden. 'I will be at the club tonight. If I need to talk to you, Alcide, tell Russell that I am your friend from out of town, and I've been invited to meet Sookie, your new girlfriend.'

'Okay,' said Alcide. 'But I don't understand why you want to be there. It's asking for trouble. What if one of the vamps recognizes you?'

'I don't know any of them.'

'Why are you taking this chance?' I asked. 'Why go there at all?'

'There may be something I can pick up on that you won't hear of, or that Alcide won't know because he is not a vampire,' Eric said reasonably. 'Excuse us for a minute, Alcide. Sookie and I have some business to discuss.'

Alcide looked at me to make sure I was okay with this, before he nodded grudgingly and went out to the living room.

Eric said abruptly, 'Do you want me to heal the marks on your shoulder?'

I thought of the ugly, crusty crescents, and I thought about the thin shoulder straps on the dress I'd brought to wear. I almost said yes, but then I had a second thought. 'How would I explain that, Eric? The whole bar saw him grab me.'

'You're right.' Eric shook his head, his eyes closed, as if he were angry with himself. 'Of course. You're not Were, you're not undead. How would you have healed so quickly?'

Then he did something else unexpected. Eric took my right hand with both of his and gripped it. He looked directly into my face. 'I have searched Jackson. I have looked in warehouses, cemeteries, farmhouses, and anyplace that had a trace of vampire scent about it: every property Edgington owns, and some his followers own. I haven't found a trace of Bill. I am very afraid, Sookie, that it is becoming most likely that Bill is dead. Finally dead.'

I felt like he'd smacked me in the middle of the forehead with a sledgehammer. My knees just folded, and if he hadn't moved quick as lightning, I'd have been on the floor. Eric sat on a chair that was in the corner of the room, and he gathered me up into a bundle in his lap. He said, 'I've upset you too much. I was trying to be practical, and instead I was . . .'

'Brutal.' I felt a tear trickle out of each eye.

Eric's tongue darted out, and I felt a tiny trace of moisture as he licked up my tears. Vampires just seem to like any body fluid, if they can't get blood, and that didn't particularly bother me. I felt glad someone was holding me in a comforting way, even if it was Eric. I sunk deeper into misery while Eric spent a few moments thinking.

'The only place I haven't checked is Russell Edgington's compound – his mansion, with its outbuildings. It would be amazing if Russell were rash enough to keep another vampire prisoner in his own home. But he's been king for a hundred years. It could be that he is that confident. Maybe I could sneak in over the wall, but I wouldn't come out again. The grounds are patrolled by Weres. It's very unlikely we'll get access to such a secure place, and he won't invite us in except in very unusual circumstances.' Eric let all this sink in. 'I think you must tell me what you know about Bill's project.'

'Is that what all this holding and niceness is about?' I was furious. 'You want to get some information out of me?' I leaped up, revitalized with wrath.

Eric jumped up himself and did his best to loom over me. 'I think Bill is dead,' he said. 'And I'm trying to save my own life, and yours, you stupid woman.' Eric sounded just as angry as I was.

'I will find Bill,' I said, enunciating each word carefully. I wasn't sure how I was going to accomplish this, but I'd just do some very good spying tonight, and something would turn up. I am no Pollyanna, but I have always been optimistic.

'You can't make eyes at Edgington, Sookie. He's not interested in women. And if I flirted with him, he would be suspicious. A vampire mating with another – that's unusual. Edgington hasn't gotten where he is by being gullible. Maybe his second, Betty Joe, would be interested in me, but she is a vampire, too, and the same rule applies. I can't tell you how unusual Bill's fascination with Lorena is. In fact, we disapprove of vampires loving others of our kind.'

I ignored his last two sentences. 'How'd you find all this out?'

'I met up with a young female vampire last night, and her boyfriend also went to parties at Edgington's place.'

'Oh, he's bi?'

Eric shrugged. 'He's a werewolf, so I guess he's two-natured in more ways than one.'

'I thought vamps didn't date werewolves, either.'

'She is being perverse. The young ones like to experiment.'

I rolled my eyes. 'So, what you're saying is that I need to

concentrate on getting an invitation into Edgington's compound, since there's nowhere else in Jackson that Bill can be hidden?'

'He could be somewhere else in the city,' Eric said cautiously. 'But I don't think so. The possibility is faint. Remember, Sookie, they've had him for days now.' When Eric looked at me, what I saw in his face was pity.

That frightened me more than anything.

Chapter 9

I had the shivery, shaky feeling that precedes walking into danger. This was the last night that Alcide could go to Club Dead: Terence had warned him away, very definitely. After this, I would be on my own, if I were even allowed into the club when Alcide did not escort me.

As I dressed, I found myself wishing I were going to an ordinary vampire bar, the kind where regular humans came to gape at the undead. Fangtasia, Eric's bar in Shreveport, was such a place. People would actually come through on tours, make an evening of wearing all black, maybe pouring on a little fake blood or inserting some cheesy fake fangs. They'd stare at the vampires carefully planted throughout the bar, and they'd thrill at their own daring. Every now and then, one of these tourists would step across the line that kept them safe. Maybe he'd make a pass at one of the vamps, or maybe he'd disrespect Chow, the bartender. Then, perhaps, that tourist would find out what he'd been messing with.

At a bar like Club Dead, all the cards were out on the table. Humans were the adornments, the frills. The supernaturals were the necessity.

I'd been excited this time the night before. Now I just felt a detached sort of determination, like I was on a powerful drug that divorced me from all my more ordinary emotions. I pulled on my hose and some pretty black garters that Arlene had given me for my birthday. I smiled as I thought of my red-haired friend and her incredible optimism about men, even after four marriages. Arlene would tell me to enjoy the minute, the second, with every bit of zest I could summon up. She would tell me I never knew what man I might meet, maybe tonight would be the magic night. Maybe wearing garters would change the course of my life, Arlene would tell me.

I can't say I exactly summoned up a smile, but I felt a little less grim as I pulled my dress over my head. It was the color of champagne. There wasn't much of it. I had on black heels and jet earrings, and I was trying to decide if my old coat would look too horrible, or if I should just freeze my butt off out of vanity. Looking at the very worn blue cloth coat, I sighed. I carried it into the living room over my arm. Alcide was ready, and he was standing in the middle of the room waiting for me. Just as I registered the fact that he was looking distinctly nervous, Alcide pulled one of the wrapped boxes out of the pile he'd collected during his morning shopping. He got that self-conscious look on his face, the one he'd been wearing when I'd returned to the apartment.

'I think I owe you this,' he said. And handed me the large box.

'Oh, Alcide! You got me a present?' I know, I know, I was standing there holding the box. But you have to understand, this is not something that happens to me very often.

'Open it,' he said gruffly.

I tossed the coat onto the nearest chair and I unwrapped the gift awkwardly – I wasn't used to my fake nails. After a little maneuvering, I opened the white cardboard box to find that Alcide had replaced my evening wrap. I pulled out the long rectangle slowly, savoring every moment. It was beautiful; a black velvet wrap with beading on the ends. I couldn't help but realize that it cost five times what I'd spent on the one that had been damaged.

I was speechless. That hardly ever happens to me. But I don't get too many presents, and I don't take them lightly. I wrapped the velvet around me, luxuriating in the feel of it. I rubbed my cheek against it.

'Thank you,' I said, my voice wobbling.

'You're welcome,' he said. 'God, don't cry, Sookie. I meant you to be happy.'

'I'm real happy,' I said. 'I'm not going to cry.' I choked back the tears, and went to look at myself in the mirror in my bathroom. 'Oh, it's beautiful,' I said, my heart in my voice.

'Good, glad you like it,' Alcide said brusquely. 'I thought it was the least I could do.' He arranged the wrap so that the material covered the red, scabbed marks on my left shoulder.

'You didn't owe me a thing,' I said. 'It's me that owes you.' I could tell that my being serious worried Alcide just as much as my crying. 'Come on,' I said. 'Let's go to Club Dead. We'll learn everything, tonight, and no one will get hurt.'

Which just goes to prove I don't have second sight.

Alcide was wearing a different suit and I a different dress, but Josephine's seemed just the same. Deserted sidewalk, atmosphere of doom. It was even colder tonight, cold enough for me to see my breath on the air, cold enough to make me pathetically grateful for the warmth of the velvet wrap. Tonight, Alcide practically leaped from the truck to the cover of the awning, not even helping me down, and then stood under it waiting for me.

'Full moon;' he explained tersely. 'It'll be a tense night.'

'I'm sorry,' I said, feeling helpless. 'This must be awfully hard on you.' If he hadn't been obliged to accompany me, he could have been off bounding through the woods after deer and bunnies. He shrugged my apology off. 'There'll always be tomorrow night,' he said. 'That's almost as good.' But he was humming with tension.

Tonight I didn't jump quite so much when the truck rolled away, apparently on its own, and I didn't even quiver when Mr. Hob opened the door. I can't say the goblin looked pleased to see us, but I couldn't tell you what his ordinary facial expression really meant. So he could have been doing emotional cartwheels of joy, and I wouldn't have known it.

Somehow, I doubted he was that excited about my second appearance in his club. Or was he the owner? It was hard to imagine Mr. Hob naming a club 'Josephine's.' 'Dead Rotten Dog,' maybe, or 'Flaming Maggots,' but not 'Josephine's.'

'We won't have trouble tonight,' Mr. Hob told us grimly. His voice was bumpy and rusty, as if he didn't talk much, and didn't enjoy it when he did.

'It wasn't her fault,' Alcide said.

'Nonetheless,' Hob said, and left it at that. He probably felt he didn't need to say anything else, and he was right. The short, lumpy goblin jerked his head at a group of tables that had been pushed together. 'The king is waiting for you.'

The men stood as I reached the table. Russell Edgington and his special friend Talbot were facing the dance floor; and across from them were an older (well, he'd become undead when he was older) vampire, and a woman, who of course stayed seated. My gaze trailed over her, came back, and I shrieked with delight.

'Tara!'

My high school friend shrieked right back and jumped up. We gave each other a full frontal hug, rather than the slightly less enthusiastic half-hug that was our norm. We were both strangers in a strange land, here at Club Dead.

Tara, who is several inches taller than I am, has dark hair and eyes and olive skin. She was wearing a long-sleeved gold-and-bronze dress that shimmered as she moved, and she had on high, high heels. She had attained the height of her date.

Just as I was disengaging from the embrace and giving her a happy pat on the back, I realized that seeing Tara was the worst thing that could have happened. I went into her mind, and I saw that, sure enough, she was about to ask me why I was with someone who wasn't Bill.

'Come on, girlfriend, come to the ladies' with me for a second!' I said cheerfully, and she grabbed her purse, while giving her date a perfect smile, both promising and rueful. I gave Alcide a little wave, asked the other gentlemen to excuse us, and we walked briskly to the rest rooms, which were off the passage leading to the back door. The ladies' room was empty. I pressed my back against the door to keep other females out. Tara was facing me, her face lit up with questions.

'Tara, please, don't say anything about Bill or anything about Bon Temps.'

'You want to tell me why?'

'Just . . .' I tried to think of something reasonable, couldn't. 'Tara, it'll cost me my life if you do.'

She twitched, and gave me a steady stare. Who wouldn't? But Tara had been through a lot in her life, and she was a tough, if wounded, bird. 'I'm so happy to see you here,' she said. 'It was lonely being in this crowd by myself. Who's your friend? What is he?'

I always forgot that other people couldn't tell. And sometimes I nearly forgot that other people didn't know about Weres and shifters. 'He's a surveyor,' I said. 'Come on, I'll introduce you.'

'Sorry we left so quickly,' I said, smiling brightly at all the men. 'I forgot my manners.' I introduced Tara to Alcide, who looked appropriately appreciative. Then it was Tara's turn. 'Sook, this is Franklin Mott.'

'A pleasure to meet you,' I said, and extended my hand before I realized my faux pas. Vampires don't shake hands. 'I beg your pardon,' I said hastily, and gave him a little wave instead. 'Do you live here in Jackson, Mr. Mott?' I was determined not to embarrass Tara.

'Please call me Franklin,' he said. He had a wonderful mellow voice with a light Italian accent. When he had died, he had probably been in his late fifties or early sixties; his hair and mustache were iron gray, and his face was lined. He looked vigorous and very masculine. 'Yes, I do, but I own a business that has a franchise in Jackson, one in Ruston, and one in Vicksburg. I met Tara at a gathering in Ruston.'

Gradually we progressed through the social do-si-do of

getting seated, explaining to the men how Tara and I had attended high school together, and ordering drinks. All the vampires, of course, ordered synthetic blood, and Talbot, Tara, Alcide, and I got mixed drinks. I decided another champagne cocktail would be good. The waitress, a shifter, was moving in an odd, almost slinking manner, and she didn't seem inclined to talk much. The night of the full moon was making itself felt in all kinds of ways.

There were far fewer of the two-natured in the bar this night of the moon cycle. I was glad to see Debbie and her fiancé were missing, and there were only a couple of the Were bikers. There were more vampires, and more humans. I wondered how the vampires of Jackson kept this bar a secret. Among the humans who came in with Supe dates, surely one or two were inclined to talk to a reporter or just tell a group of friends about the bar's existence?

I asked Alcide, and he said quietly, 'The bar's spellbound. You wouldn't be able to tell anyone how to get here if you tried.'

I'd have to experiment with that later, see if it worked. I wonder who did the spell casting, or whatever it was called. If I could believe in vampires and werewolves and shapeshifters, it was not too far a stretch to believe in witches.

I was sandwiched between Talbot and Alcide, so by way of making conversation I asked Talbot about secrecy. Talbot didn't seem averse to chatting with me, and Alcide and Franklin Mott had found they had acquaintances in common. Talbot had on too much cologne, but I didn't hold that against him. Talbot was a man in love, and furthermore, he was a man addicted to vampiric sex . . . the two states are not always combined. He was a ruthless, intelligent man who could not understand how his life had taken such an exotic turn. (He was a big broadcaster, too, which was why I could pick up so much of his life.)

He repeated Alcide's story about the spell on the bar. 'But the way what happens here is kept a secret, that's different,' Talbot said, as if he was considering a long answer and a short answer. I looked at his pleasant, handsome face and reminded myself that he knew Bill was being tortured, and he didn't care. I wished he would think about Bill again, so I could learn more; at least I would know if Bill was dead or alive. 'Well, Miss Sookie, what goes on here is kept secret by terror and punishment.'

Talbot said that with relish. He liked that. He liked that he had won the heart of Russell Edgington, a being who could kill easily, who deserved to be feared. 'Any vampire or Were – in fact, any sort of supernatural creature, and you haven't seen quite a few of them, believe me – who brings in a human is responsible for that human's behavior. For example, if you were to leave here tonight and call a tabloid, it would be Alcide's bounden duty to track and kill you.'

'I see.' And indeed, I did. 'What if Alcide couldn't bring himself to do that?'

'Then his life would be forfeit, and one of the bounty hunters would be commissioned to do the job.'

Jesus Christ, Shepherd of Judea. 'There are bounty hunters?' Alcide could have told me a lot more than he had; that was an unpleasant discovery. My voice may have been a little on the croaky side.

'Sure. The Weres who wear the motorcycle gear, in this area. In fact, they're asking questions around the bar tonight because . . .' His expression sharpened, became suspicious. 'The man who was bothering you . . . did you see him again last night? After you left the bar?'

'No,' I said, speaking the technical truth. I hadn't seen him again – last night. I knew what God thought about technical truths, but I also figured he expected me to save my own life. 'Alcide and I, we went right back to the apartment. I was pretty upset.' I cast my eyes down like a modest girl unused to approaches in bars, which was also a few steps away from the truth. (Though Sam keeps such incidents down to a minimum, and it was widely known I was crazy and therefore undesirable, I certainly had to put up with the occasional aggressive advance, as well as a certain amount of half-hearted passes from guys who got too drunk to care that I was supposed to be crazy.)

'You were sure plucky when it looked like there was going to be a fight,' Talbot observed. Talbot was thinking that my courage last night didn't jibe with my demure demeanor this evening. Darn it, I'd overplayed my role.

'Plucky is the word for Sookie,' Tara said. It was a welcome interruption. 'When we danced together on stage, about a million years ago, she was the one who was brave, not me! I was shaking in my shoes.'

Thank you, Tara.

'You danced?' asked Franklin Mott, his attention caught by the conversation.

'Oh, yes, and we won the talent contest,' Tara told him. 'What we didn't realize, until we graduated and had some experience in the world, was that our little routine was really, ah –'

'Suggestive,' I said, calling a spade a spade. 'We were the most innocent girls in our little high school, and there we were, with this dance routine we lifted straight off MTV.'

'It took us years to understand why the principal was sweating so hard,' Tara said, her smile just rascally enough to be charming. 'As a matter of fact, let me go talk to the deejay right now.' She sprang up and worked her way over to the vampire who'd set up his gear on the small stage. He bent over and listened intently, and then he nodded.

'Oh, no.' I was going to be horribly embarrassed.

'What?' Alcide was amused.

'She's going to make us do it all over again.'

Sure enough, Tara wiggled her way through the crowd to get back to me, and she was beaming. I had thought of twenty-five good reasons not to do what she wanted by the time she seized my hands and pulled me to my feet. But it was evident that the only way I could get out of this was to go forward. Tara had her heart set on this exhibition, and Tara was my friend. The crowd made a space as Pat Benatar's 'Love Is a Battlefield' began to play.

Unfortunately, I remembered every bump and grind, every hip thrust.

In our innocence, Tara and I had planned our routine almost like pairs figure skating, so we were touching (or very near) during the whole thing. Could it have looked more like some lesbian tease act performed in a stripper bar? Not much. Not that I'd ever been to a stripper bar, or a porno movie house; but I assume the rise of communal lust I felt in Josephine's that night was similar. I didn't like being the object of it – but yet, I discovered I felt a certain flood of power.

Bill had informed my body about good sex, and I was sure that now I danced like I knew about enjoying sex – and so did Tara. In a perverse way, we were having an 'I am woman, hear me roar' moment. And, by golly, love sure *was* a battlefield. Benatar was right about that.

We had our sides to the audience, Tara gripping my

waist, for the last few bars, and we pumped our hips in unison, and brought our hands sweeping to the floor. The music stopped. There was a tiny second of silence, and then a lot of applause and whistling.

The vampires thought of the blood flowing in our veins, I was sure from the hungry looks on their faces – especially those lower main lines on our inner thighs. And I could hear that the werewolves were imagining how good we would taste. So I was feeling quite edible as I made my way back to our table. Tara and I were patted and complimented along the way, and we received many invitations. I was halfway tempted to accept the dance offer of a curly-haired brunette vamp who was just about my size and cute as a bunny. But I just smiled and kept on going.

Franklin Mott was delighted. 'Oh, you were so right,' he said as he held Tara's chair for her. Alcide, I observed, remained seated and glowered at me, forcing Talbot to lean over and pull my chair out for me, an awkward and makeshift courtesy. (He did get a caress on the shoulder from Russell for his gesture.) 'I can't believe you girls didn't get expelled,' Talbot said, covering the awkward moment. I never would have pegged Alcide for a possessive jerk.

'We had no clue,' Tara protested, laughing. 'None. We couldn't understand what all the fuss was about.'

'What bit your ass?' I asked Alcide, very quietly. But when I listened carefully, I could pick out the source of his dissatisfaction. He was resenting the fact that he had acknowledged to me that he still had Debbie in his heart, because otherwise he'd make a determined effort to share my bed tonight. He felt both guilty and angry about that, since it was the full moon – come to think of it, his time of the month. In a way.

'Not looking for your boyfriend too hard, are you?' he said coldly, in a nasty undertone.

It was like he'd thrown a bucket of cold water in my face. It was a shock, and it hurt terribly. Tears welled up in my eyes. It was also completely obvious to everyone at the table that he had said something to upset me.

Talbot, Russell, and Franklin all gave Alcide level looks practically laden with threat. Talbot's look was a weak echo of his lover's, so it could be disregarded, but Russell was the king, after all, and Franklin was apparently an influential vampire. Alcide recalled where he was, and with whom.

'Excuse me, Sookie, I was just feeling jealous,' he said, loud enough for all at the table to hear. 'That was really interesting.'

'Interesting?' I said, as lightly as I could. I was pretty damn mad, myself. I ran my fingers through his hair as I leaned over to his chair. 'Just interesting?' We smiled at each other quite falsely, but the others bought it. I felt like taking a handful of that black hair and giving it a good hard yank. He might not be a mind reader like me, but he could read that impulse loud and clear. Alcide had to force himself not to flinch.

Tara stepped in once again to ask Alcide what his occupation was – God bless her – and yet another awkward moment passed harmlessly by. I pushed my chair a little farther back from the circle around the table and let my mind roam. Alcide had been right about the fact that I needed to be at work, rather than amusing myself; but I didn't see how I could have refused Tara something she enjoyed so much.

A parting of the bodies crowding the little dance floor gave me a glimpse of Eric, leaning against the wall behind the small stage. His eyes were on me, and they were full of heat. *There* was someone who wasn't pissed off at me, someone who had taken our little routine in the spirit in which it was offered.

Eriç looked quite nice in the suit and glasses. The glasses made him seem somehow less threatening, I decided, and turned my mind to business. Fewer Weres and humans made it easier to listen in to each one, easier to track the thread of thought back to its owner. I closed my eyes to help me concentrate, and almost immediately I caught a snatch of inner monologue that shook me up.

'Martyrdom,' the man was thinking. I knew the thinker was a man, and that his thoughts were coming from the area behind me, the area right around the bar. My head began to turn, and I stopped myself. Looking wouldn't help, but it was an almost irresistible impulse. I looked down instead, so the movements of the other patrons wouldn't distract me.

People don't really think in complete sentences, of course. What I'm doing, when I spell out their thoughts, is translating.

'When I die, my name will be famous,' he thought. 'It's almost here. God, please let it not hurt. At least he's here with me . . . I hope the stake's sharp enough.'

Oh, dammit. The next thing I knew I was on my feet, walking away from the table.

I was inching along, blocking the noise of the music and the voices so I could listen sharply to what was being said silently. It was like walking underwater. At the bar, slugging back a glass of synthetic blood, was a woman with a poof of teased hair. She was dressed in a tight-bodiced dress with a full skirt fluffing out around it. Her muscular arms and broad shoulders looked pretty strange with the outfit; but I'd never tell her so, nor would any sane person. This had to be Betty Joe Pickard, Russell Edgington's second in command. She had on white gloves and pumps, too. All she needed was a little hat with a half-veil, I decided. I was willing to bet Betty Joe had been a big fan of Mamie Eisenhower's.

And standing behind this formidable vampire, also facing the bar, were two male humans. One was tall, and oddly familiar. His gray-threaded brown hair was long, but neatly combed. It looked like a regular men's haircut, allowed to grow however it wanted to grow. The hairstyle looked odd with his suit. His shorter companion had rough black hair, tousled and flecked with gray. This second man wore a sports coat that maybe came off the rack from JCPenney on a sale day.

And inside that cheap coat, in a specially sewn pocket, he carried a stake.

Horribly enough, I hesitated. If I stopped him, I would be revealing my hidden talent, and to reveal that would be to unmask my identity. The consequences of this revelation would depend on what Edgington knew about me; he apparently knew Bill's girlfriend was a barmaid at Merlotte's in Bon Temps, but not her name. That's why I'd been free to introduce myself as Sookie Stackhouse. If Russell knew Bill's girlfriend was a telepath, and he discovered I was a telepath, who knew what would happen then?

Actually, I could make a good guess.

As I dithered, ashamed and frightened, the decision was made for me. The man with the black hair reached inside his coat and the fanaticism roiling in his head reached fever pitch. He pulled out the long sharpened piece of ash, and then a lot happened.

I yelled, '*STAKE!*' and lunged for the fanatic's arm, gripping it desperately with both my hands. The vampires and their humans whirled around looking for the threat, and the shifters and Weres wisely scattered to the walls to leave the floor free for the vampires. The tall man beat at me, his big hands pounding at my head and shoulders, and his dark-haired companion kept twisting his arm, trying to free it from my grasp. He heaved from side to side to throw me off.

Somehow, in the melee, my eyes met those of the taller man, and we recognized each other. He was G. Steve Newlin, former leader of the Brotherhood of the Sun, a militant anti-vampire organization whose Dallas branch had more or less bit the dust after I'd paid it a visit. He was going to tell them who I was, I just knew it, but I had to pay attention to what the man with the stake was doing. I was staggering around on my heels, trying to keep my feet, when the assassin finally had a stroke of brilliance and transferred the stake from his pinned right hand to his free left.

With a final punch to my back, Steve Newlin dashed for the exit, and I caught a flash of creatures bounding in pursuit. I heard lots of yowling and tweeting, and then the black-haired man threw back his left arm and plunged the stake into my waist on my right side.

I let go of his arm then, and stared down at what he'd done to me. I looked back up into his eyes for a long moment, reading nothing there but a horror to mirror my own. Then Betty Joe Pickard swung back her gloved fist and hit him twice – boom-boom. The first blow snapped his neck. The second shattered his skull. I could hear the bones break.

And then he went down to the floor, and since my legs were tangled with his, I went down, too. I landed flat on my back.

I lay looking up at the ceiling of the bar, at the fan that was rotating solemnly above my head. I wondered why the fan was on in the middle of winter. I saw a hawk fly across the ceiling, narrowly avoiding the fan blades. A wolf came to my side and licked my face and whined, but turned and dashed away. Tara was screaming. I was not. I was so cold.

With my right hand, I covered the spot where the stake entered my body. I didn't want to see it, and I was scared I'd look down. I could feel the growing wetness around the wound.

'Call nine-one-one!' Tara yelled as she landed on her knees beside me. The bartender and Betty Joe exchanged a look over her head. I understood.

'Tara,' I said, and it came out like a croak. 'Honey, all the shifters are changing. It's full moon. The police can't come in here, and they'll come if anyone calls nine-one-one.'

The shifter part just didn't seem to register with Tara, who didn't know such things were possible. 'The vampires are not gonna let you die,' Tara said confidently. 'You just saved one of them!'

I wasn't so sure about that. I saw Franklin Mott's face above Tara. He was looking at me, and I could read his expression.

'Tara,' I whispered, 'you have to get out of here. This is getting crazy, and if there's any chance the police are coming, you can't be here.'

Franklin Mott nodded in approval.

'I'm not going to leave you until you have help,' Tara said, her voice full of determination. Bless her heart.

The crowd around me consisted of vampires. One of them was Eric. I could not decipher his face.

'The tall blond will help me,' I told Tara, my voice barely a rasp. I pointed a finger at Eric. I didn't look at him for fear I'd read rejection in his eyes. If Eric wouldn't help me, I suspected I would lie here and die on this polished wood floor in a vampire bar in Jackson, Mississippi.

My brother, Jason, would be so pissed off.

Tara had met Eric in Bon Temps, but their introduction had been on a very stressful night. She didn't seem to identify the tall blond she'd met that night with the tall blond she saw tonight, wearing glasses and a suit and with his hair pulled back strictly into a braid.

'Please help Sookie,' she said to him directly, as Franklin Mott almost yanked her to her feet.

'This young man will be glad to help your friend,' Mott said. He gave Eric a sharp look that told Eric he damn well better agree.

'Of course. I'm a good friend of Alcide's,' Eric said, lying without a blink.

He took Tara's place by my side, and I could tell after he was on his knees that he caught the smell of my blood. His face went even whiter, and his bones stood out starkly under his skin. His eyes blazed.

'You don't know how hard it is,' he whispered to me, 'not to bend over and lick.'

'If you do, everyone else will,' I said. 'And they won't just lick, they'll bite.' There was a German shepherd staring at me with luminous yellow eyes, just past my feet.

'That's the only thing stopping me.'

'Who are you?' asked Russell Edgington. He was giving Eric a careful once-over. Russell was standing to my other side, and he bent over both of us. I had been loomed over enough, I can tell you that, but I was in no position to do a damn thing about it.

'I'm a friend of Alcide's,' Eric repeated. 'He invited me here tonight to meet his new girlfriend. My name is Leif.'

Russell could look down at Eric, since Eric was kneeling, and his golden brown eyes bored into Eric's blue ones. 'Alcide doesn't hang with many vampires,' Russell said.

'I'm one of the few.'

'We have to get this young lady out of here,' Russell said.

The snarling a few feet away increased in intensity. There appeared to be a knot of animals gathered around something on the floor.

'Take that out of here!' roared Mr. Hob. 'Out the back door! You know the rules!'

Two of the vampires lifted the corpse, for that was what the Weres and shifters were squabbling over, and carried it out the back door, followed by all the animals. So much for the black-haired fanatic.

Just this afternoon Alcide and I had disposed of a corpse. We'd never thought of just bringing it down to the club, laying it in the alley. Of course, this one was fresh.

'. . . maybe has nicked a kidney,' Eric was saying. I had been unconscious, or at least somewhere else, for a few moments.

I was sweating heavily, and the pain was excruciating. I felt a flash of chagrin when I realized I was sweating all over my dress. But possibly the big bloody hole had already ruined the dress anyway, huh?

'We'll take her to my place,' Russell said, and if I hadn't been sure I was very badly hurt, I might have laughed. 'The limo's on its way. I'm sure a familiar face would make her more comfortable, don't you agree?'

What I thought was, Russell didn't want to get his suit nasty picking me up. And Talbot probably couldn't lug me. Though the small vampire with curly black hair was still there, and still smiling, I would be awful bulky for him . . .

And I lost some more time.

'Alcide turned into a wolf and chased after the assassin's companion,' Eric was telling me, though I didn't remember asking. I started to tell Eric who the companion was, and then I realized that I'd better not. 'Leif,' I muttered, trying to commit the name to memory. 'Leif. I guess my garters are showing. Does that mean . . .?'

'Yes, Sookie?'

. . . and I was out again. Then I was aware I was moving, and I realized that Eric was carrying me. Nothing had ever hurt so badly in my life, and I reflected, not for the first time, that I'd never even been in a hospital until I'd met Bill, and now I seemed to spend half my time battered or recovering from being battered. This was very significant and important.

A lynx padded out of the bar beside us. I looked down into the golden eyes. What a night this was turning out to be for Jackson. I hoped all the good people had decided to stay home tonight.

And then we were in the limo. My head was resting on Eric's thigh, and in the seat across from us sat Talbot, Russell, and the small curly-haired vampire. As we stopped at a light, a bison lumbered by.

'Lucky no one's out in downtown Jackson on a weekend night in December,' Talbot was remarking, and Eric laughed.

We drove for what seemed like some time. Eric smoothed my skirt over my legs, and brushed my hair out of my face. I looked up at him, and . . .

'. . . did she know what he was going to do?' Talbot was asking.

'She saw him pull the stake out, she said,' Eric said mendaciously. 'She was going to the bar to get another drink.'

'Lucky for Betty Joe,' Russell said in his smooth Southern drawl. 'I guess she's still hunting the one that got away.'

Then we pulled up into a driveway and stopped at a gate. A bearded vampire came up and peered in the window, looking at all the occupants carefully. He was far more alert than the indifferent guard at Alcide's apartment building. I heard an electronic hum, and the gate opened. We went up a driveway (I could hear the gravel crunching) and then we swung around in front of a mansion. It was lit up like a birthday cake, and as Eric carefully extracted me from the limo, I could see we were under a porte cochere that was as fancy as all get-out. Even the carport had columns. I expected to see Vivian Leigh come down the steps.

I had a blank moment again, and then we were in the foyer. The pain seemed to be fading away, and its absence left me giddy.

As the master of this mansion, Russell's return was a big event, and when the inhabitants smelled fresh blood, they were doubly quick to come thronging. I felt like I'd landed in the middle of a romance cover model contest. I had never seen so many cute men in one place in my life. But I could tell they were not for me. Russell was like the gay vampire Hugh Hefner, and this was the Playboy Mansion, with an emphasis on the 'boy.'

'Water, water, everywhere, nor any drop to drink,' I said, and Eric laughed out loud. That was why I liked him, I thought rosily; he 'got' me.

'Good, the shot's taking effect,' said a white-haired man in a sports shirt and pleated trousers. He was human, and he might as well have had a stethoscope tattooed around his neck, he was so clearly a doctor. 'Will you be needing me?'

'Why don't you stay for a while?' Russell suggested. 'Josh will keep you company, I'm sure.'

I didn't get to see what Josh looked like, because Eric was carrying me upstairs then.

'Rhett and Scarlet,' I said.

'I don't understand,' Eric told me.

'You haven't seen *Gone with the Wind*?' I was horrified. But then, why should a vampire Viking have seen that staple of the Southern mystique? But he'd read *The Rhyme of the Ancient Mariner*, which I had worked my way through in high school. 'You'll have to watch it on video. Why am I acting so stupid? Why am I not scared?'

'That human doctor gave you a big dose of drugs,' Eric said, smiling down at me. 'Now I am carrying you to a bedroom so you can be healed.'

'He's here,' I told Eric.

His eyes flashed caution at me. 'Russell, yes. But I'm afraid that Alcide made less than a stellar choice, Sookie. He raced off into the night after the other attacker. He should have stayed with you.'

'Screw him,' I said expansively.

'He wishes, especially after seeing you dance.'

I wasn't feeling quite good enough to laugh, but it did cross my mind. 'Giving me drugs maybe wasn't such a great idea,' I told Eric. I had too many secrets to keep.

'I agree, but I am glad you're out of pain.'

Then we were in a bedroom, and Eric was laying me on a gosh-to-goodness canopied four-poster. He took the opportunity to whisper, 'Be careful,' in my ear. And I tried to bore that thought into my drug-addled brain. I might blurt out the fact that I knew, beyond a doubt, that Bill was somewhere close to me.

Chapter 10

There was quite a crowd in the bedroom, I noticed. Eric had gotten me situated on the bed, which was so high, I might need a stepstool to get down. But it would be convenient for the healing, I had heard Russell comment, and I was beginning to worry about what constituted 'the healing.' The last time I'd been involved in a vampire 'healing,' the treatment had been what you might call nontraditional.

'What's gonna happen?' I asked Eric, who was standing at the side of the bed on my left, non-wounded, side.

But it was the vampire who had taken his place to my right who answered. He had a long, horsy face, and his blond eyebrows and eyelashes were almost invisible against his pallor. His bare chest was hairless, too. He was wearing a pair of pants, which I suspected were vinyl. Even in the winter, they must be, um, unbreathing. I wouldn't like to peel those suckers off. This vamp's saving grace was his lovely straight pale hair, the color of white corn.

'Miss Stackhouse, this is Ray Don,' Russell said.

'How de do.' Good manners would make you welcome anywhere, my gran had always told me.

'Pleased to meet you,' he responded correctly. He had been raised right, too, though no telling when that had been. 'I'm not going to ask you how you're doing, cause I can see you got a great big hole in your side.'

'Kind of ironic, isn't it, that it was the human that got staked,' I said socially. I hoped I would see that doctor again, because I sure wanted to ask him what he'd given me. It was worth its weight in gold.

Ray Don gave me a dubious look, and I realized I'd just shot out of his comfort zone, conversationally. Maybe I could give Ray Don a Word of the Day calendar, like Arlene gave me every Christmas.

'I'll tell you what's going to happen, Sookie,' Eric said. 'You know, when we start to feed and our fangs come out, they release a little anticoagulant?'

'Um-hum.'

'And when we are ready to finish feeding, the fangs release a little coagulant and a little trace of the, the –'

'Stuff that helps you all heal so fast?'

'Yes, exactly.'

'So, Ray Don is going to what?'

'Ray Don, his nest mates say, has an extra supply of all these chemicals in his body. This is his talent.'

Ray Don beamed at me. He was proud of that.

'So he will start the process on a volunteer, and when he has fed, he will begin cleaning your wound and healing it.'

What Eric had left out of this narrative was that at some point during this process, the stake was going to have to come out, and that no drug in the world could keep that from hurting like a son of a bitch. I realized that in one of my few moments of clarity.

'Okay,' I said. 'Let's get the show on the road.'

The volunteer turned out to be a thin blond human teenager, who was no taller than me and probably no wider in the shoulders. He seemed to be quite willing. Ray Don gave him a big kiss before he bit him, which I could have done without, since I'm not into public displays of carnal affection. (When I say 'big,' I don't mean a loud smack, but the intense, moaning, tonsil-sucking kind.) When that was done, to both their satisfactions, Blondie inclined his head to one side, and the taller Ray Don sank his fangs in. There was much cleaving, and much panting – and even to drug-addled me, Ray Don's vinyl pants didn't leave enough to the imagination.

Eric watched without apparent reaction. Vampires seem, as a whole, to be extremely tolerant of any sexual preference; I guess there aren't that many taboos when you've been alive a few hundred years.

When Ray Don drew back from Blondie and turned to face the bed, he had a bloody mouth. My euphoria evaporated as Eric instantly sat on the bed and pinned my shoulders. The Big Bad Thing was coming.

'Look at me,' he demanded. 'Look at me, Sookie.'

I felt the bed indent, and I assumed Ray Don was kneeling beside it and leaning over to my wound.

There was a jar in the torn flesh of my side that jolted me down to the marrow of my bones. I felt the blood leave my face and felt hysteria bubbling up my throat like my blood was leaving the wound.

'Don't, Sookie! Look at me!' Eric said urgently.

I looked down to see that Ray Don had grabbed the stake.

Next he would . . .

I screamed over and over, until I didn't have the energy.

I met Eric's eyes as I felt Ray Don's mouth sucking at the wound. Eric was holding my hands, and I was digging my nails into him like we were doing something else. He won't mind, I thought, as I realized I'd drawn blood.

And sure enough, he didn't. 'Let go,' he advised me, and I loosened my grip on his hands. 'No, not of me,' he said, smiling. 'You can hold on to me as long as you want. Let go of the pain, Sookie. Let go. You need to drift away.'

It was the first time I had relinquished my will to someone else. As I looked at him, it became easy, and I retreated from the suffering and uncertainty of this strange place.

The next thing I knew, I was awake. I was tucked in the bed, lying on my back, my formerly beautiful dress removed. I was still wearing my beige lace underwear, which was good. Eric was in the bed with me, which was not. He was really making a habit of this. He was lying on his side, his arm draped over me, one leg thrown over mine. His hair was tangled with my hair, and the strands were almost indistinguishable, the color was so similar. I contemplated that for a while, in a sort of misty, drifting state.

Eric was having downtime. He was in that absolutely immobile state into which vampires retreat when they have nothing else to do. It refreshes them, I think, reduces the wear and tear of the world that ceaselessly passes them by, year after year, full of war and famine and inventions that they must learn how to master, changing mores and conventions and styles that they must adopt in order to fit in. I pulled down the covers to check out my side. I was still in pain, but it was greatly reduced. There was a large circle of scar tissue on the site of the wound. It was hot and shiny and red and somehow glossy.

'It's much better,' Eric said, and I gasped. I hadn't felt him rouse from his suspended animation.

Eric was wearing silk boxers. I would have figured him for a Jockey man.

'Thank you, Eric.' I didn't care for how shaky I sounded, but an obligation is an obligation.

'For what?' His hand gently stroked my stomach.

'For standing by me in the club. For coming here with me. For not leaving me alone with all these people.'

'How grateful are you?' he whispered, his mouth hovering over mine. His eyes were very alert now, and his gaze was boring into mine.

'That kind of ruins it, when you say something like that,' I said, trying to keep my voice gentle. 'You shouldn't want me to have sex with you just because I owe you.'

'I don't really care why you have sex with me, as long as you do it,' he said, equally gently. His mouth was on mine then. Try as I might to stay detached, I wasn't too successful. For one thing, Eric had had hundreds of years to practice his kissing technique, and he'd used them to good advantage. I snuck my hands up to his shoulders, and I am ashamed to say I responded. As sore and tired as my body was, it wanted what it wanted, and my mind and will were running far behind. Eric seemed to have six hands, and they were everywhere, encouraging my body to have its way. A finger slid under the elastic of my (minimal) panties, and glided right into me.

I made a noise, and it was not a noise of rejection. The finger began moving in a wonderful rhythm. Eric's mouth seemed bent on sucking my tongue down his throat. My hands were enjoying the smooth skin and the muscles that worked underneath it.

Then the window flew open, and Bubba crawled in.

'Miss Sookie! Mr. Eric! I tracked you down!' Bubba was proud.

'Oh, good for you, Bubba,' Eric said, ending the kiss. I clamped my hand on his wrist, and pulled his hand away. He allowed me to do it. I am nowhere near as strong as the weakest vampire.

'Bubba, have you been here the whole time? Here in Jackson?' I asked, once I had some wits in my head. It was a good thing Bubba had come in, though Eric didn't think so.

'Mr. Eric told me to stick with you,' Bubba said simply. He settled into a low chair tastefully upholstered in flowered material. He had a dark lock of hair falling over his forehead, and he was wearing a gold ring on every finger. 'You get hurt bad at that club, Miss Sookie?'

'It's a lot better now,' I said.

'I'm sorry I didn't do my job, but that little critter guarding the door wouldn't let me in. He didn't seem to know who I was, if you can believe that.'

Since Bubba himself hardly remembered who he was, and had a real fit when he did, maybe it wasn't too surprising that a goblin wouldn't be current on American popular music.

'But I saw Mr. Eric carrying you out, so I followed you.'

'Thank you, Bubba. That was real smart.'

He smiled, in a slack and dim sort of way. 'Miss Sookie, what you doing in bed with Mr. Eric if Bill is your boyfriend?'

'That's a real good question, Bubba,' I said. I tried to sit up, but I couldn't do it. I made a little pain sound, and Eric cursed in another language.

'I am going to give her blood, Bubba,' Eric said. 'Let me tell you what I need you to do.'

'Sure,' Bubba said agreeably.

'Since you got over the wall and into the house without being caught, I need you to search this estate. We think Bill is here somewhere. They are keeping him prisoner. Don't try to free him. This is an order. Come back here and tell us when you have found him. If they see you, don't run. Just don't say anything. Nothing. Not about me, or Sookie, or Bill. Nothing more than, 'Hi, my name is Bubba.'

'Hi, my name is Bubba.'

'Right.'

'Hi, my name is Bubba.'

'Yes. That's fine. Now, you sneak, and you be quiet and invisible.'

Bubba smiled at us. 'Yes, Mr. Eric. But after that, I gotta go find me some food. I'm mighty hungry.'

'Okay, Bubba. Go search now.'

Bubba scrambled back out the window, which was on the second story. I wondered how he was going to get to the ground, but if he'd gotten into the window, I was sure he could get out of it.

'Sookie,' Eric said, right in my ear. 'We could have a long argument about you taking my blood, and I know everything you would say. But the fact is, dawn is coming. I don't know if you will be allowed to stay the day here or not. I will have to find shelter, here or elsewhere. I want you strong and able to defend yourself; at least able to move quickly.'

'I know Bill is here,' I said, after I'd thought this over for a moment. 'And no matter what we almost just did – thank God for Bubba – I need to find Bill. The best time to get him out of here would be while all you vampires are asleep. Can he move at all during the daytime?'

'If he knows he is in great danger, he may be able to stagger,' Eric said, slowly and thoughtfully. 'Now I am even more sure you will need my blood, because you need strength. He will need to be covered thoroughly. You will need to take the blanket off this bed; it's thick. How will you get him out of here?'

'That's where you come in.' I said. 'After we do this blood thing, you need to go get me a car – a car with a great big trunk, like a Lincoln or a Caddy. And you need to get the keys to me. And you'll need to sleep somewhere else. You don't want to be here when they wake up and find their prisoner is gone.' Eric's hand was resting quietly on my stomach, and we were still wrapped up together in the bedding. But the situation felt completely different.

'Sookie, where will you take him?'

'An underground place,' I said uncertainly. 'Hey, maybe Alcide's parking garage! That's better than being out in the open.'

Eric sat up against the headboard. The silk boxers were royal blue. He spread his legs and I could see up the leg hole. Oh, Lord. I had to close my eyes. He laughed.

'Sit up with your back against my chest, Sookie. That will make you more comfortable."

He carefully eased me up against him, my back to his chest, and wrapped his arms around me. It was like leaning against a firm, cool, pillow. His right arm vanished, and I heard a little crunch sound. Then his wrist appeared in front of my face, blood running from the two wounds in his skin.

'This will cure you of everything,' Eric said.

I hesitated, then derided myself for my foolish hesitation. I knew that the more of Eric's blood I had in me, the more he would know me. I knew that it would give him some kind of power over me. I knew that I would be stronger for a long time, and given how old Eric was, I would be very strong. I would heal, and I would feel wonderful. I would be more attractive. This was why vampires were preyed upon by Drainers, humans who worked in teams to capture vamps, chain them with silver, and drain their blood into vials, which sold for varying sums on the black market. Two hundred dollars had been the going price for one vial last year; God knows what Eric's blood would bring, since he was so old. Proving that provenance would definitely be a problem for the Drainer. Draining was an extremely hazardous occupation, and it was also extremely illegal.

Eric was giving me a great gift.

I have never been what you would call squeamish, thank goodness. I closed my mouth over the little wounds, and I sucked.

Eric moaned, and I could tell quickly that he was once again pleased to be in such close contact. He began to move a little, and there wasn't a lot I could do about it. His left arm was keeping me firmly clamped against him, and his right arm was, after all, feeding me. It was still hard not to be icked out by the process. But Eric was definitely having a good time, and since with every pull I felt better, it was hard to argue with myself that this was a bad thing to be doing. I tried not to think, and I tried not to move myself in response. I remembered the time I'd taken Bill's blood because I needed extra strength, and I remembered Bill's reaction.

Eric pressed against me even harder, and suddenly he said, 'Ohhhhh,' and relaxed all over. I felt wetness against my back, and I took one deep, last draw. Eric groaned again, a deep and guttural sound, and his mouth trailed down the side of my neck.

'Don't bite me,' I said. I was holding on to the remnants of my sanity with difficulty. What had excited me, I told myself, was my memory of Bill; his reaction when I'd bitten him, his intense arousal. Eric just happened to be here. I couldn't have sex with a vampire, especially Eric, just because I found him attractive – not when there would be such dire consequences. I was just too strung out to enumerate those consequences to myself. I was an adult, I told myself sternly; true adults don't have sex just because the other person is skilled and pretty.

Eric's fangs scraped my shoulder.

I launched myself out of that bed like a rocket. Intending to locate a bathroom, I flung open the door to find the short brunette vampire, the one with the curly hair, standing just outside, his left arm draped with clothes, his right raised to knock.

'Well, look at you,' he said, smiling. And he certainly was looking. He burned his candle at both ends, apparently.

'You needed to talk to me?' I leaned against the door frame, doing my best to look wan and frail.

'Yes, after we cut your beautiful dress off, Russell figured you'd need some clothes. I happened to have these in my closet, and since we're the same height . . .'

'Oh,' I said faintly. I'd never shared clothes with a guy. 'Well, thank you so much. This is very kind of you.' And it was. He'd brought some sweats (powder blue) and socks, and a silk bathrobe, and even some fresh panties. I didn't want to think about that too closely.

'You seem better,' the small man said. His eyes were admiring, but not in any real personal way. Maybe I'd overestimated my charms.

'I am very shaky,' I said quietly. 'I was up because I was on my way to the bathroom.'

Curly's brown eyes flared, and I could tell he was looking at Eric over my shoulder. This view definitely was more to his taste, and his smile became frankly inviting. 'Leif, would you like to share my coffin today?' he asked, practically batting his eyelashes.

I didn't dare turn to look at Eric. There was a patch on my back that was still wet. I was suddenly disgusted with myself. I'd had thoughts about Alcide, and more than had thoughts about Eric. I was not pleased with my moral fiber. It was no excuse that I knew Bill had been unfaithful to me, or at least it wasn't much of an excuse. It was probably also not an excuse that being with Bill had accustomed me to regular, spectacular sex. Or not much of an excuse.

It was time to pull my moral socks up and behave myself. Just deciding that made me feel better.

'I have to run an errand for Sookie,' Eric was telling the curly-haired vamp. 'I am not sure I'll return before daybreak, but if I do, you can be sure I'll seek you out.' Eric was flirting back. While all this repartee was flying around me, I pulled on the silk robe, which was black and pink and white, all flowers. It was really outstanding. Curly spared me a glance, and seemed more interested than he had when I'd just appeared in my undies.

'Yum,' he said simply.

'Again, thanks,' I said. 'Could you tell me where the nearest bathroom is?'

He pointed down the hall to a half-open door.

'Excuse me,' I said to both of them, and reminded myself to walk slowly and carefully, as if I was still in pain, as I made my way down the hall. Past the bathroom, by maybe two doors, I could see the head of the staircase. Okay, I knew the way out now. That was actually a comfort.

The bathroom was just a regular old bathroom. It was full of the stuff that usually clutters bathrooms: hair dryers, hot curlers, deodorant, shampoo, styling gel. Some makeup. Brushes and combs and razors.

Though the counter was clean and orderly, it was apparent several people shared the room. I was willing to bet Russell Edgington's personal bathroom looked nothing like this one. I found some bobby pins and secured my hair on top of my head, and I took the quickest shower on record. Since my hair had just been washed that morning, which now seemed years ago and took forever to dry besides, I was glad to skip it in favor of scrubbing my skin vigorously with the scented soap in the built-in dish. There were clean towels in the closet, which was a relief.

I was back in the bedroom within fifteen minutes. Curly was gone, Eric was dressed, and Bubba was back.

Eric did not say one word about the embarrassing incident that had taken place between us. He eyed the robe appreciatively but silently.

'Bubba has scoped out the territory, Sookie,' Eric said, clearly quoting.

Bubba was smiling his slightly lopsided smile. He was pleased with himself. 'Miss Sookie, I found Bill,' he said triumphantly. 'He ain't in such good shape, but he's alive.'

I sank into a chair with no forewarning. I was just lucky it was behind me. My back was still straight – but all of a sudden, I was sitting instead of standing. It was one more strange sensation in a night full of them.

When I was able to think of anything else, I noticed vaguely that Eric's expression was a bewildering blend of things: pleasure, regret, anger, satisfaction. Bubba just looked happy.

'Where is he?' My voice didn't even sound like my own.

'There's a big building in back of here, like a four-car garage, but it's got apartments on top of it and a room to the side.'

Russell liked to keep his help handy.

'Are there other buildings? Could I get confused?'

'There's a swimming pool, Miss Sookie, and it's got a little building right by it for people to change into their bathing suits. And there's a great big toolshed, I think that's what it's for, but it's separate from the garage.'

Eric said, 'What part of the garage is he being kept in?'

Bubba said, 'The room to the right side. I think maybe the garage used to be stables, and the room is where they kept the saddles and stuff. It isn't too big.'

'How many are in there with him?' Eric was asking some good questions. I could not get over Bubba's assurance that Bill was still alive and that I was very close to him.

'They got three in there right now, Mr. Eric, two men and one woman. All three are vamps. She's the one with the knife.'

I shrank inside myself. 'Knife,' I said.

'Yes'm, she's cut him up pretty bad.'

This was no time to falter. I'd been priding myself on my

lack of squeamishness earlier. This was the moment to prove I'd been telling the truth to myself.

'He's held out this long,' I said.

'He has,' Eric agreed. 'Sookie, I will go to get a car. I'll try to park it back there by the stables.'

'Do you think they'll let you back in?'

'If I take Bernard with me.'

'Bernard?'

'The little one.' Eric smiled at me, and his own smile was a little lopsided.

'You mean . . . Oh, if you take Curly with you, they'll let you back in because he lives here?'

'Yes. But I may have to stay here. With him.'

'You couldn't, ah, get out of it?'

'Maybe, maybe not. I don't want to be caught here, rising, when they discover Bill is gone, and you with him.'

'Miss Sookie, they'll put werewolves to guarding him during the day.'

We both looked at Bubba simultaneously.

'Those werewolves that have been on your trail? They'll be guarding Bill when the vamps go to sleep.'

'But tonight is the full moon,' I said. 'They'll be worn out when it's their turn to take over. If they show up at all.'

Eric looked at me with some surprise. 'You're right, Sookie. This is the best opportunity we're going to get.'

We talked it over some more; perhaps I could act very weak and hole up in the house, waiting for a human ally of Eric's to arrive from Shreveport. Eric said he would call the minute he got out of the immediate area, on his cell phone.

Eric said, 'Maybe Alcide could lend a hand tomorrow morning.'

I have to admit, I was tempted by the idea of calling him

in again. Alcide was big and tough and competent, and something hidden and weak in me suggested that surely Alcide would be able to manage everything better than I would. But my conscience gave an enormous twinge. Alcide, I argued, could not be involved further. He'd done his job. He had to deal with these people in a business way, and it would ruin him if Russell figured out his part in the escape of Bill Compton.

We couldn't spend any more time in discussion, because it lacked only two hours until dawn. With a lot of details still loose, Eric went to find Curly – Bernard – and coyly request his company on an errand to obtain a car I assumed he intended to rent, and what car rental place would be open at this hour was a mystery to me, but Eric didn't seem to anticipate any trouble. I tried to dismiss my doubts from my mind. Bubba agreed to go over Russell's wall again, as he'd entered, and find a place to go to ground for the day. Only the fact that this was the night of the full moon had saved Bubba's life, Eric said, and I was willing to believe it. The vampire guarding the gate might be good, but he couldn't be everywhere.

My job was to play weak until day, when the vampires would retire, and then somehow get Bill out of the stable and into the trunk of the car Eric would provide. They'd have no reason to stop me from leaving.

'This is maybe the worst plan I have ever heard,' Eric said.

'You got that right, but it's all we have.'

'You'll do great, Miss Sookie,' Bubba told me encouragingly.

That's what I needed, a positive attitude. 'Thank you, Bubba,' I said, trying to sound as grateful as I felt. I was energized by Eric's blood. I felt like my eyes were shooting sparks and my hair was floating around my head in a electric halo.

'Don't get too carried away,' Eric advised. He reminded me that this was a common problem with people who ingested black-market vampire blood. They attempted crazy things since they felt so strong, so invincible, and sometimes they just weren't up to the attempted feat – like the guy who tried to fight a whole gang at once, or the woman who took on an oncoming train. I took a deep breath, trying to impress his warning on my brain. What I wanted to do was lean out the window and see if I could crawl up the wall to the roof. Wow, Eric's blood was *awesome*. That was a word I'd never used before, but it was accurate. I'd never realized what a difference there would be between taking Bill's blood and taking Eric's.

There was a knock at the door, and we all looked at it as if we could see through it.

In an amazingly short time, Bubba was out the window, Eric was sitting in the chair by the bed, and I was in the bed trying to look weak and shaky.

'Come in,' Eric called in a hushed voice, as befitted the companion of someone recuperating from a terrible wound.

It was Curly – that is, Bernard. Bernard was wearing jeans and a dark red sweater, and he looked good enough to eat. I closed my eyes and gave myself a stern lecture. The blood infusion had made me very lively.

'How is she doing?' Bernard asked, almost whispering. 'Her color is better.'

'Still in pain, but healing, thanks to the generosity of your king.'

'He was glad to do it,' Bernard said courteously. 'But he

will be, ah, best pleased if she can leave on her own tomorrow morning. He is sure by then her boyfriend will be back at his apartment after he has enjoyed the moon tonight. I hope this doesn't seem too brusque?'

'No, I can understand his concern,' Eric said, being polite right back.

Apparently, Russell was afraid that I would stay for several days, cashing in on my act of heroism. Russell, unused to having human female houseguests, wanted me to go back to Alcide, when he was sure Alcide would be able to see after me. Russell was a little uneasy about an unknown woman wandering around his compound during the day, when he and all his retinue would be in their deep sleep.

Russell was quite right to worry about this.

'Then I'll go get her a car and park it in the area to the rear of the house, and she can drive herself out tomorrow. If you can arrange that she'll have safe passage through the front gates – I assume they are guarded during the day? – I will have fulfilled my obligation to my friend Alcide.'

'That sounds very reasonable,' Bernard said, giving me a fraction of the smile he was aiming at Eric. I didn't return it. I closed my eyes wearily. 'I'll leave word at the gate when we go. My car okay? It's just a little old egg-beater, but it'll get us to . . . where did you want to go?'

'I'll tell you when we're on the road. It's close to the home of a friend of mine. He knows a man who'll loan me the car for a day or two.'

Well, he'd found a way to obtain a car without a paper trail. Good.

I felt movement to my left. Eric bent over me. I knew it was Eric, because his blood inside me informed me so. This was really scary, and this was why Bill had warned me against taking blood from any vampire other than him. Too late. Rock and a hard place.

He kissed my cheek in a chaste, friend-of-the-boyfriend way. 'Sookie,' he said very quietly. 'Can you hear me?'

I nodded just a trifle.

'Good. Listen, I am going to get you a car. I'll leave the keys up here by the bed when I get back. In the morning, you need to drive out of here and back to Alcide's. Do you understand?'

I nodded again. 'Bye,' I said, trying to make my voice drowsy. 'Thank you.'

'My pleasure,' he said, and I heard the edge in his voice. With an effort, I kept my face straight.

It's hard to credit, but I actually fell asleep after they left. Bubba had evidently obeyed, and gone over the fence to arrange shelter for the day. The mansion became very quiet as the night's revelries drew to a close. I supposed the werewolves were off having their last howl somewhere. As I was drifting off, I wondered how the other shape-shifters had fared. What did they do with their clothes? Tonight's drama at Club Dead had been a fluke; I was sure they had a normal procedure. I wondered where Alcide was. Maybe he had caught that son of a bitch Newlin.

I woke up when I heard the chink of keys.

'I'm back,' Eric said. His voice was very quiet, and I had to open my eyes a little to make sure he was actually there. 'It's a white Lincoln. I parked out by the garage; there wasn't room inside, which is a real pity. They wouldn't let me get any closer to confirm what Bubba said. Are you hearing me?'

I nodded.

'Good luck.' Eric hesitated. 'If I can disentangle myself,

I'll meet you in the parking garage at first dark tonight. If you aren't there, I'll go back to Shreveport.'

I opened my eyes. The room was dark, still; I could see Eric's skin glowing. Mine was, too. That scared the tar out of me. I had just stopped glowing from taking Bill's blood (in an emergency situation), when here came another crisis, and now I was shining like a disco ball. Life around vampires was just one continuous emergency, I decided.

'We'll talk later,' Eric said ominously.

'Thanks for the car,' I said.

Eric looked down at me. He seemed to have a hickey on his neck. I opened my mouth, and then shut it again. Better not to comment.

'I don't like having feelings,' Eric said coldly, and he left.

That was a tough exit line to top.

Chapter 11

There was a line of light in the sky when I crept out of the mansion of the king of Mississippi. It was a little warmer this morning, and the sky was dark with not just night, but rain. I had a little roll of my belongings under my arm. Somehow my purse and my black velvet shawl had made it here to the mansion from the nightclub, and I had rolled my high heels in the shawl. The purse did have the key to Alcide's apartment in it, the one he'd loaned me, so I felt reassured that I could find shelter there if need be. I had the blanket from the bed folded neatly under my other arm. I'd made the bed up, so its loss would not be obvious for a little while.

What Bernard had not loaned me was a jacket. When I'd snuck out, I'd snagged a dark blue quilted jacket that had been hanging on the banister. I felt very guilty. I'd never stolen anything before. Now I had taken the blanket and the jacket. My conscience was protesting vigorously.

When I considered what I might have to do to get out of this compound, taking a jacket and a blanket seemed pretty mild. I told my conscience to shut up.

As I crept through the cavernous kitchen and opened the back door, my feet were sliding around in the elastic-sided slippers Bernard had included in the bundle of clothes he'd brought to my room. The socks and slippers were better than teetering in the heels, by a long shot.

I hadn't seen anyone so far. I seemed to have hit the magic time. Almost all the vampires were securely in their coffins, or beds, or in the ground, or whatever the heck they did during the day. Almost all the Were creatures, of whatever persuasion, were not back from their last night's binge or were already sleeping it off. But I was vibrating with tension, because at any moment this luck might run out.

Behind the mansion, there was indeed a smallish swimming pool, covered for the winter by a huge black tarp. It had weighted edges that extended far beyond the actual perimeter of the pool. The tiny pool house was completely dark. I moved silently down a pathway created with uneven flagstones, and after I passed through a gap in a dense hedge, I found myself in a paved area. With my enhanced vision, I was able to see instantly that I had found the courtyard in front of the former stables. It was a large edifice sided with white clapboards, and the second story (where Bubba had spotted apartments) had gable-style windows. Though this was the fanciest garage I had ever seen, the bays for cars did not have doors, but open archways. I could count four vehicles parked inside, from the limo to a Jeep. And there, on the right, instead of a fifth archway, there was a solid wall, and in it, a door.

Bill, I thought. *Bill. My* heart was pounding now. With an overwhelming sense of relief, I spotted the Lincoln parked close to the door. I turned the key in the driver's door, and it clicked open. When I opened the door, the dome light came on, but there didn't seem to be anyone here to see it. I tucked my little bundle of belongings on the passenger seat, and I eased the driver's door almost shut. I found a little switch and turned off the dome light. I took a precious minute to look at the dashboard, though I was so excited and terrified, it was hard to focus. Then I went to the rear of the vehicle and unlocked the trunk. It was just huge – but not clean, like the interior. I had the idea that Eric had gathered up all the large contents and tossed them in the trash, leaving the bottom littered with cigarette rolling papers, plastic bags, and spots of white powder on the floor. Hmmm. Well, okay. That couldn't be too important. Eric had stuck in two bottles of blood, and I moved them over to one side. The trunk was dirty, yes, but clear of anything that would cause Bill discomfort.

I took a deep breath, and clutched the blanket to my chest. Wrapped in its folds was the stake that had hurt me so badly. It was the only weapon I had, and despite its grisly appearance (it was still stained with my blood and a little tissue), I had retrieved it from the wastebasket and brought it with me. After all, I knew for sure it could cause damage.

The sky was a shade lighter, but when I felt raindrops on my face, I felt confident the darkness would last a little longer. I skulked my way to the garage. Creeping around surely looked suspicious, but I simply could not make myself stride purposefully over to the door. The gravel made silence almost impossible, but still I tried to step lightly.

I put my ear to the door, listened with all my enhanced ability. I was picking up nothing. At least I knew there was no human inside. Turning the knob slowly, easing it back into position after I pushed, I stepped into the room.

The floor was wooden, and covered with stains. The smell was awful. I knew immediately that Russell had used this room for torture before. Bill was in the center of the room, lashed to a straight-back chair by silver chains.

After the confused emotions and unfamiliar surroundings of the past few days, I felt like the world suddenly came into focus.

Everything was clear. Here was Bill. I would save him.

And after I'd had a good look at him in the light of the naked bulb hanging from the ceiling, I knew I would do *anything* to save him.

I had never imagined anything so bad.

There were burn marks under the silver chains, which were draped all around him. I knew that silver caused unremitting agony to a vampire, and my Bill was suffering that now. He had been burned with other things, and cut, cut more than he could heal. He had been starved, and he had been denied sleep. He was slumped over now, and I knew he was taking what respite he could while his tormenters were gone. His dark hair was matted with blood.

There were two doors leading out of the windowless room. One, to my right, led to a dormitory of sorts. I could see some beds through the open doorway. There was a man passed out on one, just sprawled across the cot fully clothed. One of the werewolves, back after his monthly toot. He was snoring, and there were dark smears around his mouth that I didn't want to look at more closely. I couldn't see the rest of the room, so I couldn't be sure if there were others; it would be smart to assume there were.

The door at the rear of the room led farther back into the

garage, perhaps to the stairs going up to the apartments. I couldn't spare the time to investigate. I had a feeling of urgency, impelling me to get Bill out as fast as I could. I was trembly with the need to hurry. So far, I had encountered enormous luck. I couldn't count on its holding.

I took two steps closer to Bill.

I knew when he smelled me, realized it was me.

His head snapped up and his eyes blazed at me. A terrible hope shone on his filthy face. I held up a finger; I stepped quietly over to the open door to the dormitory, and gently, gently, slid it almost shut. Then I glided behind him, looking down at the chains. There were two small padlocks, like the ones you put on your locker at school, holding the chains together. 'Key?' I breathed in Bill's ear. He had an unbroken finger, and that was the one he used to point at the door I'd come in by. Two keys hung on a nail by the door, quite high from the floor, and always in Bill's sight. Of course they'd think of that. I put the blanket and stake on the floor by Bill's feet. I crept across the stained floor, and reached up as far as I could strain. I couldn't reach the keys. A vampire who could float would be able to get them. I reminded myself I was strong, strong from Eric's blood.

There was a shelf on the wall that held interesting things like pokers and pincers. Pincers! I stood on my tiptoes and lifted them off the shelf, trying hard to keep my gorge from rising when I saw they were crusted with – oh, horrible stuff. I held them up, and they were very heavy, but I managed to clamp them on the keys, work them forward off the nail, and lower the pincers until I could take the keys from their pointed ends. I exhaled a giant sigh of relief, as silently as you can exhale. That hadn't been so hard.

In fact, that was the last easy thing I encountered. I began the horrible task of unwrapping Bill, while trying to keep the movement of the chains as silent as I could. It was oddly difficult to unwind the shiny rope of links. In fact, they seemed to be sticking to Bill, whose whole body was rigid with tension.

Then I understood. He was trying not to scream out loud as the chains were pulled out of his charred flesh. My stomach lurched. I had to stop my task for a few precious seconds, and I had to inhale very carefully. If it was this hard for me to witness his agony, how much harder must it be for Bill to endure it?

I braced up my mental fortitude, and I began working again. My grandmother always told me women could do whatever they had to do, and once again, she was right.

There were literally yards of silver chain, and the careful unwinding took more time than I liked. Any time was more time than I liked. The danger lurked right over my shoulder. I was breathing disaster, in and out, with every breath. Bill was very weak, and struggling to stay awake now that the sun had risen. It helped that the day was so dark, but he would not be able to move much when the sun was high, no matter how dreary the day.

The last bit of chain slid to the floor.

'You have to stand up,' I said in Bill's ear. 'You just have to. I know it hurts. But I can't carry you.' At least, I didn't think I could. 'There's a big Lincoln outside, and the trunk is open. I'm putting you in the trunk, wrapped in this blanket, and we're driving out of here. Understand, babe?'

Bill's dark head moved a fraction of an inch.

Right then our luck ran out.

'Who the hell are you?' asked a heavily accented voice. Someone had come through the door at my back.

Bill flinched under my hands. I whirled to face her, dipping to pick up the stake as I did so, and then she was on me.

I had talked myself into believing they were all in their coffins for the day, but this one was doing her best to kill me.

I would have been dead in a minute if she hadn't been as shocked as I was. I twisted my arm from her grasp and pivoted around Bill in his chair. Her fangs were all out, and she was snarling at me over Bill's head. She was a blond, like me, but her eyes were brown and her build was smaller; she was a tiny woman. She had dried blood on her hands, and I knew it was Bill's. A flame started up inside me. I could feel it flicker through my eyes.

'You must be his little human bitch whore,' she said. 'He was fucking me, all this time, you understand. The minute he saw me, he forgot about you, except for pity.'

Well, Lorena wasn't elegant, but she knew where to sink the verbal knife. I batted the words aside, because she wanted to distract me. I shifted my grip on the stake to be ready, and she leaped across Bill to land on top of me.

As she moved, without a conscious decision I whipped up the stake and pointed it at an angle. As she came down on me, the sharp point went in her chest and out the other side. Then we were on the floor. I was still gripping the end of the stake, and she was holding herself off of me with her arms. She looked down at the wood in her chest, astonished. Then she looked in my eyes, her mouth agape, her fangs retracting. 'No,' she said. Her eyes went dull.

I used the stake to push her to my left side, and I

scrambled up off the floor. I was panting, and my hands shook violently. She didn't move. The whole incident had been so swift and so quiet that it hardly felt real.

Bill's eyes went from the thing on the floor to me. His expression was unreadable. 'Well,' I told him, 'I killed *her* ass.'

Then I was on my knees beside her, trying not to vomit.

It took me more precious seconds to regain control of myself. I had a goal I had to meet. Her death would not do me a bit of good if I couldn't get Bill out of here before someone else came in. Since I had done something so horrible, I had to get something, some advantage out of it.

It would be a smart thing to conceal the body – which was beginning to shrivel – but that had to take second place to removing Bill. I wrapped the blanket around his shoulders as he sat slumped in the stained chair. I'd been afraid to look at his face since I'd done this thing.

'That was Lorena?' I whispered in Bill's ear, plagued by a sudden doubt. 'She did this to you?'

He gave that tiny nod again.

Ding dong, the witch was dead.

After a pause, while I waited to feel something, the only thing I could think of was asking Bill why someone named Lorena would have a foreign accent. That was dumb, so I forgot about it.

'You got to wake up. You got to stay awake till I get you in the car, Bill.' I was trying to keep a mental eye open for the Weres in the next room. One of them began snoring behind the closed door, and I felt the mental stir of another, one I hadn't been able to spot. I froze for several seconds, before I could feel that mind settle into a sleep pattern again. I took a deep, deep breath and pulled a flap of blanket over Bill's head. Then I got his left arm draped around my neck, and I heaved. He came up out of the chair, and though he gave a ragged hiss of pain, he managed to shuffle to the door. I was more than half carrying him, so I was glad to stop there and grab the knob and twist it. Then I almost lost hold of him, since he was literally sleeping on his feet.

Only the danger that we would be caught was stimulating him enough to afford movement.

The door opened, and I checked to make sure the blanket, which happened to be fuzzy and yellow, completely covered his head. Bill moaned and went almost completely limp when he felt the sunlight, weak and watery as it was. I began talking to him under my breath, cursing him and challenging him to move, telling him I could keep him awake if that bitch Lorena could, telling him I would beat him up if he didn't make it to the car.

Finally, with a tremendous effort that left me trembling, I got Bill to the trunk of the car. I pushed it open. 'Bill, just sit on the lip here,' I told him, tugging at him until he was facing me and sitting on the edge of the trunk. But the life left him completely at that point, and he simply collapsed backward. As he folded into the space, he made a deep pain noise that tore at my heart, and then he was absolutely silent and limp. It was always terrifying to see Bill die like that. I wanted to shake him, scream at him, pound on his chest.

There was no point in any of that.

I made myself shove all the sticking-out bits – a leg, an arm – into the trunk with him, and then I closed it. I allowed myself the luxury of a moment of intense relief.

Standing in the dim daylight in the deserted courtyard,

I conducted a brief inner debate. Should I attempt to hide Lorena's body? Would such an effort be worth the time and energy?

I changed my mind about six times in the course of thirty seconds. I finally decided that yeah, it might be worth it. If there was no body to see, the Weres might suppose that Lorena had taken Bill somewhere for a little extra torture session. And Russell and Betty Joe would be dead to the world and unavailable to give instructions. I had no illusions that Betty Joe would be grateful enough to me to spare me, if I should get caught right now. A somewhat quicker death would be the most I could hope for.

My decision reached, back into that awful blood-stained room I went. Misery had soaked into the walls, along with the stains. I wondered how many humans, Weres, and vampires had been held prisoner in this room. Gathering up the chains as silently as I could, I stuffed them in Lorena's blouse, so anyone checking out the room might assume they were still around Bill. I looked around to see if there was any more cleanup I needed to do. There was so much blood in the room already, Lorena's made no difference.

Time to get her out of there.

To keep her heels from dragging and making noise, I had to lift her onto my shoulder. I had never done such a thing, and the procedure was awkward. Lucky for me she was so small, and lucky I'd practiced blocking things out of my mind all these years. Otherwise, the way Lorena dangled, completely limp, and the way she was beginning to flake away, would have freaked me out. I gritted my teeth, to hold back the bubble of hysteria starting up my throat.

It was raining heavily as I carried the body to the pool. Without Eric's blood, I could never have lifted the weighted edge of the pool cover, but I managed it with one hand and pushed what was left of Lorena into the pool with one foot. I was aware at any second that someone could look out the windows at the back of the mansion and see me, realize what I was doing – but if any of the humans living in the house did so, they decided to keep silent.

I was beginning to feel overwhelmingly weary. I trudged back down the flagstone path through the hedge to the car. I leaned on it for a minute, just breathing, gathering myself. Then I got in the driver's seat, and turned the key in the ignition. The Lincoln was the biggest car I'd ever driven, and one of the most luxurious cars I'd ever been in, but just at the moment I could take no interest or pleasure in it. I buckled my seat belt, adjusted the mirror and the seat, and looked at the dashboard carefully. I was going to need the windshield wipers, of course. This car was a new one, and the lights came on automatically, so that was one less worry.

I took a deep breath. This was at least phase three of the rescue of Bill. It was scary how much of this had happened by sheer chance, but the best-laid plans never take every happenstance into account anyway. Not possible. Generally, my plans tended to be what I called roomy.

I swung the car around and drove out of the courtyard. The drive swept in a graceful curve and went across the front of the main building. For the first time, I saw the facade of the mansion. It was as beautiful – white painted siding, huge columns – as I had imagined. Russell had spent a pretty penny renovating the place.

The driveway wound through grounds that still looked manicured even in their winter brown state, but that long driveway was all too short. I could see the wall ahead of me.

There was the checkpoint at the gate, and it was manned. I was sweating despite the cold.

I stopped just before the gate. There was a little white cubicle to one side, and it was glass from waist level up. It extended inside and outside the wall, so guards could check both incoming and outgoing vehicles. I hoped it was heated, for the sake of the two Weres on duty. Both of them were wearing their leathers and looking mighty grumpy. They'd had a hard night, no doubt about it. As I pulled to a stop, I resisted an almost overwhelming temptation to plow right through those gates. One of the Weres came out. He was carrying a rifle, so it was a good thing I hadn't acted on that impulse.

'I guess Bernard told you all I'd be leaving this morning?' I said, after I'd rolled down my window. I attempted a smile.

'You the one who got staked last night?' My questioner was surly and stubbly, and he smelled like a wet dog.

'Yeah.'

'How you feeling?'

'Better, thank you.'

'You coming back for the crucifixion?'

Surely I hadn't heard him right. 'Excuse me?' I asked faintly.

His companion, who'd come to stand in the hut's door, said, 'Doug, shut up.'

Doug glowered at his fellow Were, but he shrugged after the glower didn't have any effect. 'Okay, you're cleared to go.'

The gates opened, way too slowly to suit me. When they were wide, and the Weres had stepped back, I drove sedately through. I suddenly realized I had no idea which way to go, but it seemed correct to turn left, since I wanted to head back to Jackson. My subconscious was telling me we had turned right to enter the driveway the night before.

My subconscious was a big fat liar.

After five minutes, I was fairly positive I was lost, and the sun continued to rise, naturally, even through the mass of clouds. I couldn't remember how well the blanket covered Bill, and I wasn't sure how light-tight the trunk would be. After all, safe transportation of vampires was not something the car makers would cover in their list of specs.

On the other hand, I told myself, the trunk would have to be waterproof – that was sure important – so lightproof couldn't be far behind. Nonetheless, it seemed vitally important to find a dark place to park the Lincoln for the remaining hours of the day. Though every impulse told me to drive hard and get as far away from the mansion as I could, just in case someone went checking for Bill and put two and two together, I pulled over to the side of the road and opened the glove compartment. God bless America! There was a map of Mississippi with an inset for Jackson.

Which would have helped if I'd had any idea where I was at the moment.

People making desperate escapes aren't supposed to get lost.

I took a few deep breaths. I pulled back out into the road and drove on until I saw a busy gas station. Though the Lincoln's tank was full (thank you, Eric) I pulled in and parked at one of the pumps. The car on the other side was a black Mercedes, and the woman pumping the gas was an intelligent-looking middle-aged woman dressed in casual, comfortable, nice clothes. As I got the windshield squeegee out of its vat of water, I said, 'You wouldn't happen to know how to get back to I-20 from here, would you?'

'Oh, sure,' she said. She smiled. She was the kind of person who just loves to help other people, and I was thanking my lucky stars I'd spotted her. 'This is Madison, and Jackson is south of here. I-55 is maybe a mile over that way.' She pointed west. 'You take I-55 south, and you'll run right into I-20. Or, you could take . . .'

I was about to be overloaded with information. 'Oh, that sounds perfect. Let me just do that, or I'll lose track.'

'Sure, glad I could help.'

'Oh, you surely did.'

We beamed at each other, just two nice women. I had to fight an impulse to say, 'There's a tortured vampire in my trunk,' out of sheer giddiness. I had rescued Bill, and I was alive, and tonight we would be on our way back to Bon Temps. Life would be wonderfully trouble-free. Except, of course, for dealing with my unfaithful boyfriend, finding out if the werewolf's body we'd disposed of in Bon Temps had been found, waiting to hear the same about the werewolf who'd been stuffed in Alcide's closet, and waiting for the reaction of the queen of Louisiana to Bill's indiscretion with Lorena. His verbal indiscretion: I didn't think for one minute that she would care about his sexual activities.

Other than that, we were hunky-dory.

'Sufficient unto the day is the evil thereof,' I told myself. That had been Gran's favorite Bible quotation. When I was about nine, I'd asked her to explain that to me, and she'd said, 'Don't go looking for trouble; it's already looking for you.'

Bearing that in mind, I cleared my mental decks. My next goal was simply to get back to Jackson and the shelter of the garage. I followed the instructions the kind woman had given me, and I had the relief of entering Jackson within a half hour.

I knew if I could find the state capitol, I could find Alcide's apartment building. I hadn't allowed for one-way streets, and I hadn't been paying awful close attention to directions when Alcide gave me my little tour of downtown Jackson. But there aren't that many five-story buildings in the whole state of Mississippi, even in the capital. After a tense period of cruising, I spotted it.

Now, I thought, *all my troubles will be over*. Isn't it dumb to think that? Ever?

I pulled into the area by the little guard cubicle, where you had to wait to be recognized while the guy flipped the switch, or punched the button, or whatever made the barrier lift up. I was terrified he might deny me entrance because I didn't have a special sticker, like Alcide did on his truck.

The man wasn't there. The cubicle was empty. Surely that was wrong? I frowned, wondering what to do. But here the guard came, in his heavy brown uniform, trudging up the ramp. When he saw I was waiting, he looked stricken, and hurried up to the car. I sighed. I would have to talk to him after all. I pushed the button that would lower my window.

'I'm sorry I was away from my post,' he said instantly. 'I had to, ah . . . personal needs.'

I had a little leverage here.

'I had to go borrow me a car,' I said. 'Can I get a temporary sticker?' I looked at him in a way that clued him in to my mindset. That look said, 'Don't hassle me about getting the sticker, and I won't say a word about you leaving your post.'

'Yes, ma'am. That's apartment 504?'

'You have a wonderful memory,' I said, and his seamed face flushed.

'Part of the job,' he said nonchalantly, and handed me a laminated number that I stuck on the dashboard. 'If you'll just hand that in when you leave for good, please? Or if you plan on staying, you'll have to fill out a form we can have on file, and we'll give you a sticker. Actually,' he said, stumbling a little, embarrassed, 'Mr. Herveaux will have to fill it out, as the property owner.'

'Sure,' I said. 'No problem.' I gave him a cheery wave, and he retreated to the cubicle to raise the barrier.

I drove into the dark parking garage, feeling that rush of relief that follows clearing a major hurdle.

Reaction set in. I was shaking all over when I took the keys out of the ignition. I thought I saw Alcide's pickup over a couple of rows, but I had parked as deeply in the garage as I could – in the darkest corner, away from all the other cars, as it happened. This was as far as I had planned. I had no idea what to do next. I hadn't really believed I would get this far. I leaned back in the comfortable seat just for a minute, to relax and stop shaking before I got out. I'd had the heater on full blast during my drive from the mansion, so it was toasty warm inside the car.

When I woke up, I'd been asleep for hours.

The car was cold, and I was colder, despite the stolen quilted jacket. I got out of the driver's seat stiffly, stretching and bending to relieve cramped joints.

Maybe I should check on Bill. He had gotten rolled around in the trunk, I was sure, and I needed to make sure he was covered.

Actually, I just wanted to see him again. My heart actually beat faster at the thought. I was a real idiot.

I checked my distance from the weak sunlight at the entrance; I was well away. And I had parked so the trunk opening was pointed away from that bit of sunlight.

Yielding to temptation, I stepped around to the back of the car. I turned the key in the lock, pulled it out and popped it in my jacket pocket, and watched as the lid rose.

In the dim garage, I couldn't see too well, and it was hard to make out even the fuzzy yellow blanket. Bill appeared to be pretty well concealed. I bent over a little more, so I could arrange a fold further over his head. I had only a second's warning, a scuff of a shoe against the concrete, and then I felt a forceful shove from behind.

I fell into the trunk on top of Bill.

An instant and extra shove brought my legs in, and the trunk slammed shut.

Now Bill and I were locked in the trunk of the Lincoln.

Chapter 12

Debbie. I figured it had been Debbie. After I got over my initial flood of panic, which lasted longer than I wanted to admit, I tried to relive the few seconds carefully. I'd caught a trace of brain pattern, enough to inform me that my attacker was a shifter. I figured it must have been Alcide's former girlfriend – his not-so-former girlfriend, apparently, since she was hanging around his garage.

Had she been waiting for me to return to Alcide since the night before? Or had she met up with him at some point during the craziness of the full moon? Debbie had been even more angered by my escorting Alcide than I could have imagined. Either she loved him, or she was extremely possessive.

Not that her motivation was any big concern right now. My big concern was air. For the first time, I felt lucky that Bill didn't breathe.

I made my own breath slow and even. No deep, panicky gasps, no thrashing. I made myself figure things out. Okay, I'd entered the trunk probably about, hmm, one p.m. Bill would wake around five, when it was getting dark. Maybe he'd sleep a little longer, because he'd been so exhausted – but no later than six-thirty, for sure. When he was awake, he'd be able to get us out of here. Or would he? He was very weak. He'd been terribly injured, and his injuries would take a while in healing, even for a vampire. He would need rest and blood before he'd be up to par. And he hadn't had any blood in a week. As that thought passed through my mind, I suddenly felt cold.

Cold all over.

Bill would be hungry. Really, really hungry. Crazy hungry.

And here I was – fast food.

Would he know who I was? Would he realize it was me, in time to stop?

It hurt even worse to think that he might not care enough anymore – care enough about me – to stop. He might just keep sucking and sucking, until I was drained dry. After all, he'd had an affair with Lorena. He'd seen me kill her, right in front of his eyes. Granted, she'd betrayed and tortured him, and that should have doused his ardor, right there. But aren't relationships crazy anyway?

Even my grandmother would have said, 'Oh, *shit*.'

Okay. I had stay calm. I had to breathe shallow and slow to save air. And I had to rearrange our bodies, so I could be more comfortable. I was relieved this was the biggest trunk I'd ever seen, because that made such a maneuver possible. Bill was limp – well, he was dead, of course. So I could sort of shove him without worrying too much about the consequences. The trunk was cold, too, and I tried to unwrap Bill a little bit so I could share the blanket.

The trunk was also quite dark. I could write the car

designer a letter, and let him know I could vouch for its light-tightness, if that was how you'd put it. If I got out of here alive, that is. I felt the shape of the two bottles of blood. Maybe Bill would be content with that?

Suddenly, I remembered an article I'd read in a news magazine while I was waiting in the dentist's office. It was about a woman who'd been taken hostage and forced into the trunk of her own car, and she'd been campaigning ever since to have inside latches installed in trunks so any captive could release herself. I wondered if she'd influenced the people who made Lincolns. I felt all around the trunk, at least the parts I could reach, and I did feel a latch release, maybe; there was a place where wires were sticking into the trunk. But whatever handle they'd been attached to had been clipped off.

I tried pulling, I tried yanking to the left or right. Damn it, this just wasn't right. I almost went nuts, there in that trunk. The means of escape was in there with me, and I couldn't make it work. My fingertips went over and over the wires, but to no purpose.

The mechanism had been disabled.

I tried real hard to figure out how that could have happened. I am ashamed to confess, I wondered if somehow Eric knew I'd be shut in the trunk, and this was his way of saying, 'That's what you get for preferring Bill.' But I just couldn't believe that. Eric sure had some big blank moral blind spots, but I didn't think he'd do that to me. After all, he hadn't reached his stated goal of having me, which was the nicest way I could put it to myself.

Since I had nothing else to do but think, which didn't take up extra oxygen, as far as I knew, I considered the car's previous owner. It occurred to me that Eric's friend had pointed out a car that would be easy to steal; a car belonging to someone who was sure to be out late at night, someone who could afford a fine car, someone whose trunk would hold the litter of cigarette papers, powder, and Baggies.

Eric had liberated the Lincoln from a drug dealer, I was willing to bet. And that drug dealer had disabled the inner trunk release for reasons I didn't even want to think about too closely.

Oh, give me a break, I thought indignantly. (It was easy just then to forget the many breaks I'd had during the day.) Unless I got a final break, and got out of this trunk before Bill awoke, none of the others would exactly count.

It was a Sunday, and very close to Christmas, so the garage was silent. Maybe some people had gone home for the holidays, and the legislators had gone home to their constituency, and the other people were busy doing . . . Christmas, Sunday stuff. I heard one car leave while I lay there, and then I heard voices after a time; two people getting off the elevator. I screamed, and banged on the trunk lid, but the sound was swallowed up in the starting of a big engine. I quieted immediately, frightened of using more air than I could afford.

I'll tell you, time spent in the nearly pitch-black dark, in a confined space, waiting for something to happen – that's pretty awful time. I didn't have a watch on; I would have had to have one with those hands that light up, anyway. I never fell asleep, but I drifted into an odd state of suspension. This was mostly due to the cold, I expect. Even with the quilted jacket and the blanket, it was very cold in the trunk. Still, cold, unmoving, dark, silent. My mind drifted.

Then I was terrified.

Bill was moving. He stirred, made a pain noise. Then his body seemed to go tense. I knew he had smelled me.

'Bill,' I said hoarsely, my lips almost too stiff with cold to move. 'Bill, it's me, Sookie. Bill, are you okay? There's some bottled blood in here. Drink it now.'

He struck.

In his hunger, he made no attempt to spare me anything, and it hurt like the six shades of hell.

'Bill, it's me,' I said, starting to cry. 'Bill, it's me. Don't do this, honey. Bill, it's Sookie. There's TrueBlood in here.'

But he didn't stop. I kept talking, and he kept sucking, and I was becoming even colder, and very weak. His arms were clamping me to him, and struggling was no use, it would only excite him more. His leg was slung over my legs.

'Bill,' I whispered, thinking it was already maybe too late. With the little strength I had left, I pinched his ear with the fingers of my right hand. 'Please listen, Bill.'

'Ow,' he said. His voice sounded rough; his throat was sore. He had stopped taking blood. Now another need was on him, one closely related to feeding. His hands pulled down my sweatpants, and after a lot of fumbling and rearranging and contorting, he entered me with no preparation at all. I screamed, and he clapped a hand over my mouth. I was crying, sobbing, and my nose was all stopped up, and I needed to breathe through my mouth. All restraint left me and I began fighting like a wildcat. I bit and scratched and kicked, not caring about the air supply, not caring that I would enrage him. I just had to have air.

After a few seconds, his hand fell away. And he stopped moving. I drew air in with a deep, shuddering gasp. I was crying in earnest, one sob after another.

'Sookie?' Bill said uncertainly. 'Sookie?'

I couldn't answer.

'It's you,' he said, his voice hoarse and wondering. 'It's you. You were really there in that room?'

I tried to gather myself, but I felt very fuzzy and I was afraid I was going to faint. Finally, I was able to say, 'Bill,' in a whisper.

'It is you. Are you all right?'

'No,' I said almost apologetically. After all, it was Bill who'd been held prisoner and tortured.

'Did I . . .' He paused, and seemed to brace himself. 'Have I taken more blood than I should?'

I couldn't answer. I laid my head on his arm. It seemed too much trouble to speak.

'I seem to be having sex with you in a closet,' Bill said in a subdued voice. 'Did you, ah, volunteer?'

I turned my head from side to side, then let it loll on his arm again.

'Oh, no,' he whispered. 'Oh, no.' He pulled out of me and fumbled around a lot for the second time. He was putting me back to rights; himself, too, I guess. His hands patted our surroundings. 'Car trunk,' he muttered.

'I need air,' I said, in a voice almost too soft to hear.

'Why didn't you say so?' Bill punched a hole in the trunk. He *was* stronger. Good for him.

Cold air rushed in and I sucked it deep. Beautiful beautiful oxygen.

'Where are we?' he asked, after a moment.

'Parking garage,' I gasped. 'Apartment building. Jackson.' I was so weak, I just wanted to let go and float away.

'Why?'

I tried to gather enough energy to answer him. 'Alcide lives here,' I managed to mutter, eventually.

'Alcide who? What are we supposed to do now?'

'Eric's . . . coming. Drink the bottled blood.'

'Sookie? Are you all right?'

I couldn't answer. If I could have, I might have said 'Why do you care? You were going to leave me anyway.' I might have said, 'I forgive you,' though that doesn't seem real likely. Maybe I would have just told him that I'd missed him, and that his secret was still safe with me; faithful unto death, that was Sookie Stackhouse.

I heard him open a bottle.

As I was drifting off in a boat down a current that seemed to be moving ever faster, I realized that Bill had never revealed my name. I knew they had tried to find it out, to kidnap me and bring me to be tortured in front of him for extra leverage. And he hadn't told.

The trunk opened with a noise of tearing metal.

Eric stood outlined by the fluorescent lights of the garage. They'd come on when it got dark. 'What are you two doing in here?' he asked.

But the current carried me away before I could answer.

'She's coming around, Eric observed. 'Maybe that was enough blood.' My head buzzed for a minute, went silent again.

'She really is,' he was saying next, and my eyes flickered open to register three anxious male faces hovering above me: Eric's, Alcide's, and Bill's. Somehow, the sight made me want to laugh. So many men at home were scared of me, or didn't want to think about me, and here were the three men in the world who wanted to have sex with me, or who at least had thought about it seriously; all crowding around the bed. I giggled, actually giggled, for the first time in maybe ten years. 'The Three Musketeers,' I said.

'Is she hallucinating?' Eric asked.

'I think she's laughing at us,' Alcide said. He didn't sound unhappy about that. He put an empty TrueBlood bottle on the vanity table behind him. There was a large pitcher beside it, and a glass.

Bill's cool fingers laced with mine. 'Sookie,' he said, in that quiet voice that always sent shivers down my spine. I tried to focus on his face. He was sitting on the bed to my right.

He looked better. The deepest cuts were scars on his face, and the bruises were fading.

'They said, was I coming back for the crucifixion?' I told him.

'Who said that to you?' He bent over me, his face intent, dark eyes wide.

'Guards at the gate.'

'The guards at the gates of the mansion asked you if you were coming back for a crucifixion tonight? This night?'

'Yes.'

'Whose?'

'Don't know.'

'I would have expected you to say, 'Where am I? What happened to me?' Eric said. 'Not ask whose crucifixion would be taking place – perhaps is taking place,' he corrected himself, glancing at the clock by the bed.

'Maybe they meant mine?' Bill looked a little stunned by the idea. 'Maybe they decided to kill me tonight?'

'Or perhaps they caught the fanatic who tried to stake Betty Joe?' Eric suggested. 'He would be a prime candidate for crucifixion.'

I thought it over, as much as I was able to reason through the weariness that kept threatening to overwhelm me. 'Not the picture I got,' I whispered. My neck was very, very sore.

'You were able to read something from the Weres?' Eric asked.

I nodded. 'I think they meant Bubba,' I whispered, and everyone in the room froze.

'That cretin,' Eric said savagely, after he'd had time to process that. 'They caught him?'

'Think so.' That was the impression I'd gotten.

'We'll have to retrieve him,' Bill said. 'If he's still alive.'

It was very brave for Bill to say he would go back in that compound. I would never have said that, if I'd been him.

The silence that had fallen was distinctly uneasy.

'Eric?' Bill's dark eyebrows arched; he was waiting for a comment.

Eric looked royally angry. 'I guess you are right. We have the responsibility of him. I can't believe his home state is willing to execute him! Where is their loyalty?'

'And you?' Bill's voice was considerably cooler as he asked Alcide.

Alcide's warmth filled the room. So did the confused tangle of his thoughts. He'd spent part of last night with Debbie, all right.

'I don't see how I can,' Alcide said desperately. 'My business, my father's, depends on my being able to come here often. And if I'm on the outs with Russell and his crew, that would be almost impossible. It's going to be difficult enough when they realize Sookie must be the one who stole their prisoner.'

'And killed Lorena,' I added.

Another pregnant silence.

Eric began to grin. 'You offed Lorena?' He had a good grasp of the vernacular, for a very old vampire.

It was hard to interpret Bill's expression. 'Sookie staked her,' he said. 'It was a fair kill.'

'She killed Lorena in a fight?' Eric's grin grew even broader. He was as proud as if he'd heard his firstborn reciting Shakespeare.

'Very *short* fight,' I said, not wanting to take any credit that was not due me. If you could term it credit.

'Sookie killed a vampire,' Alcide said, as if that raised me in his evaluation, too. The two vampires in the room scowled.

Alcide poured and handed me a big glass of water. I drank it, slowly and painfully. I felt appreciably better after a minute or two.

'Back to the original subject,' Eric said, giving me another meaningful look to show me he had more to say about the killing of Lorena. 'If Sookie has not been pegged as having helped Bill escape, she is the best choice to get us back on the grounds without setting off alarms. They might not be expecting her, but they won't turn her away, either, I'm sure. Especially if she says she has a message for Russell from the queen of Louisiana, or if she says she has something she wants to return to Russell . . .' He shrugged, as if to say surely we could make up a good story.

I didn't want to go back in there. I thought of poor Bubba, and tried to worry about his fate – which he might have already met – but I was just too weak to worry about it.

'Flag of truce?' I suggested. I cleared my throat. 'Do the vampires have such a thing?'

Eric looked thoughtful. 'Of course, then I'd have to explain who I am,' he said.

Happiness had made Alcide a lot easier to read. He was thinking about how soon he could call Debbie.

I opened my mouth, reconsidered, shut it, opened it again. What the hell. 'Know who pushed me in the trunk and slammed it shut?' I asked Alcide. His green eyes locked onto me. His face became still, contained, as if he was afraid emotion would leak out. He turned and left the room, pulling the door shut behind him. For the first time, I registered that I was back in the guest bedroom in his apartment.

'So, who did the deed, Sookie?' Eric asked.

'His ex-girlfriend. Not so ex, after last night.'

'Why would she do that?' Bill asked.

There was another significant silence. 'Sookie was represented as Alcide's new girlfriend to gain entrée to the club,' Eric said delicately.

'Oh,' Bill said. 'Why did you need to go to the club?'

'You must have gotten hit on the head a few times, Bill,' Eric said coldly. 'She was trying to "hear" where they had taken you.'

This was getting too close to things Bill and I had to talk about alone.

'It's dumb to go back in there,' I said. 'What about a phone call?'

They both stared at me like I was turning into a frog.

'Well, what a good idea,' Eric said.

The phone, as it turned out, was just listed under Russell Edgington's name; not 'Mansion of Doom,' or 'Vampires R Us.' I worked on getting my story straight as I downed the contents of a big opaque plastic mug. I hated the taste of the synthetic blood Bill insisted I drink, so he'd mixed it with apple juice, and I was trying not to look as I gulped it down.

They'd made me drink it straight when they'd gotten up to Alcide's apartment that evening; and I didn't ask them how. At least I knew why the clothes I'd borrowed from Bernard were really horrible now. I looked like I'd had my throat cut, instead of mangled by Bill's painful bite. It was still very sore, but it was better.

Of course I had been picked to make the call. I never met a man yet, above the age of sixteen, who liked to talk on the phone.

'Betty Joe Pickard, please,' I said to the male voice that answered the phone.

'She's busy,' he said promptly.

'I need to talk to her right now.'

'She's otherwise engaged. May I take your number?'

'This is the woman who saved her life last night.' No point beating around the bush. 'I need to talk to her, right now. Tout de suite.'

'I'll see.'

There was a long pause. I could hear people walking by the phone from time to time, and I heard a lot of cheering that sounded as if it was coming from a distance. I didn't want to think about that too much. Eric, Bill, and Alcide – who had finally stomped back into the room when Bill had asked him if we could borrow his phone – were standing there making all kinds of faces at me, and I just shrugged back.

Finally, there was the click, click, click of heels on tile.

'I'm grateful, but you can't bank on this forever,' Betty Jo Pickard said briskly. 'We arranged for your healing, you had a place to stay to recuperate. We didn't erase your memory,' she added, as if that was a little detail that had escaped her until just this moment. 'What have you called to ask?'

'You have a vampire there, an Elvis impersonator?'

'So?' Suddenly she sounded very wary. 'We caught an intruder within our walls last night, yes.'

'This morning, after I left your place, I was stopped again,' I said. We had figured this would sound convincing because I sounded so hoarse and weak.

There was a long silence while she thought through the implications. 'You have a habit of being in the wrong place,' she said, as if she were remotely sorry for me.

'They are getting me to call you now,' I said carefully. 'I am supposed to tell you that the vampire you have there, he's the real thing.'

She laughed a little. 'Oh, but . . .' she began. Then she fell silent. 'You're shitting me, right?' Mamie Eisenhower would never have said *that*, I was willing to swear.

'Absolutely not. There was a vamp working in the morgue that night,' I croaked. Betty Jo made a sound that came out between a gasp and a choke. 'Don't call him by his real name. Call him "Bubba." And for goodness' sake, don't hurt him.'

'But we've already . . . hold on!'

She ran. I could hear the urgent sound die away.

I sighed, and waited. After a few seconds, I was completely nuts with the two guys standing around looking down at me. I was strong enough to sit up, I figured.

Bill gently held me up, while Eric propped pillows behind my back. I was glad to see one of them had had the presence of mind to spread the yellow blanket over the bed so I wouldn't stain the bedspread. All this while, I'd held the phone clamped to my ear, and when it squawked, I was actually startled.

'We got him down in time,' Betty Joe said brightly.

'The call came in time,' I told Eric. He closed his eyes and seemed to be offering up a prayer. I wondered to whom Eric prayed. I waited for further instructions.

'Tell them,' he said, 'to just let him go, and he will take himself home. Tell them that we apologize for letting him stray.'

I relayed that message from my 'abductors.'

Betty Jo was quick to dismiss the directions. 'Would you ask if he could stay and sing to us a little? He's in pretty good shape,' she said.

So I relayed *that*. Eric rolled his eyes. 'She can ask him, but if he says no, she must take it to heart and not ask him anymore,' he said. 'It just upsets him, if he's not in the mood. And sometimes when he does sing, it brings back memories, and he gets, ah, obstreperous.'

'All right,' she said, after I'd explained. 'We'll do our best. If he doesn't want to sing, we'll let him go right away.' From the sound of it, she turned to someone by her. 'He can sing, if he'll consent,' she said, and the someone said, 'Yippee!' Two big nights in a row for the crowd at the king of Mississippi's mansion, I guess.

Betty Joe said into the telephone, 'I hope you get out of your difficulties. I don't know how whoever's got you got lucky enough to have the care of the greatest star in the world. Would he consider negotiating?'

She didn't know yet about the troubles that entailed. 'Bubba' had an unfortunate predilection for cat blood, and he was addlepated, and he could only follow the simplest directions; though every now and then, he exhibited a streak of shrewdness. He followed directions quite literally.

'She wants permission to keep him,' I told Eric. I was tired of being the go-between. But Betty Joe couldn't meet with Eric, or she'd know he was the supposed friend of Alcide's who'd helped me get to the mansion the night before.

This was all too complicated for me.

'Yes?' Eric said into the telephone. Suddenly he had an English accent. Mr. Master of Disguise. Soon he was saying things like, 'He's a sacred trust,' and, 'You don't know what you're biting off,' into the phone. (If I'd had any sense of humor that night, I would have thought the last statement was pretty funny.) After a little more conversation, he hung up, with a pleased air.

I was thinking how strange it was that Betty Joe hadn't indicated that anything else was amiss at the compound. She hadn't accused Bubba of taking their prisoner, and she hadn't commented on finding the body of Lorena. Not that she'd necessarily mention these things in a phone conversation with a human stranger; and, for that matter, not that there'd be much to find; vampires disintegrate pretty quickly. But the silver chains would still be in the pool, and maybe enough sludge to identify as the corpse of a vampire. Of course, why would anyone look under the pool cover? But surely someone had noticed their star prisoner was gone?

Maybe they were assuming Bubba had freed Bill while he was roaming the compound. We'd told him not to say anything, and he would follow that directive to the letter.

Maybe I was off the hook. Maybe Lorena would be completely dissolved by the time they started to clean the pool in the spring.

The topic of corpses reminded me of the body we'd found stuffed in the closet of this apartment. Someone sure knew where we were, and someone sure didn't like us. Leaving the body there was an attempt to tie us to the crime of murder, which, actually, I had committed. I just hadn't done that particular murder. I wondered if the body of Jerry Falcon had been discovered yet. The chance seemed remote. I opened my mouth to ask Alcide if it had been on the news, and then I closed it again. I lacked the energy to frame the sentence.

My life was spinning out of control. In the space of two days I'd hidden one corpse and created another one. And all because I'd fallen in love with a vampire. I gave Bill an unloving glance. I was so absorbed in my thoughts, I hardly heard the telephone. Alcide, who had gone into the kitchen, must have answered it on the first ring.

Alcide appeared in the door of the bedroom. 'Move,' he said, 'you all have to move next door into the empty apartment. Quick, quick!'

Bill scooped me up, blanket and all. We were out the door and Eric was breaking the lock on the apartment next to Alcide's before you could say 'Jack Daniels.' I heard the slow grumble of the elevator arriving on the fifth floor as Bill closed the door behind us.

We stood stock-still in the empty cold living room of the barren apartment. The vampires were listening intently to what was going on next door. I began to shiver in Bill's arms.

To tell the truth, it felt great to be held by him, no matter how angry I had been at him, no matter how many issues we had to settle. To tell the truth, I had a dismayingly wonderful sense of homecoming. To tell the truth, no matter how battered my body was – and battered at his hands, or rather, his fangs – that body could hardly wait to meet up with his body again, buck naked, despite the terrible incident in the trunk. I sighed. I was disappointed in myself. I would have to stand up for my psyche, because my body was ready to betray me, big time. It seemed to be blacking out Bill's mindless attack.

Bill laid me on the floor in the smaller guest bedroom of this apartment as carefully as if I'd cost him a million dollars, and he swaddled me securely in the blanket. He and Eric listened at the wall, which was shared with Alcide's bedroom.

'What a bitch,' Eric murmured. Oh. Debbie was back.

I closed my eyes. Eric made a little noise of surprise and I opened them again. He was looking at me, and there was that disconcerting amusement in his face again.

'Debbie stopped by his sister's house last night to grill her about you. Alcide's sister likes you very much,' Eric said in a tiny whisper. 'This angers the shapeshifter Debbie. She is insulting his sister in front of him.'

Bill's face showed he was not so thrilled.

Suddenly every line in Bill's body became tense, as if someone had jammed Bill's finger in an electric socket. Eric's jaw dropped and he looked at me with an unreadable expression.

There was the unmistakable sound of a slap – even I could hear it – from the next room.

'Leave us for a moment,' Bill said to Eric. I didn't like the sound of his voice.

I closed my eyes. I didn't think I was up to whatever would come next. I didn't want to argue with Bill, or upbraid him for his unfaithfulness. I didn't want to listen to explanations and excuses.

I heard the whisper of movement as Bill knelt beside me on the carpet. Bill stretched out beside me, turned on his side, and laid his arm across me.

'He just told this woman how good you are in bed,' Bill murmured gently.

I came up from my prone position so fast that it tore my healing neck and gave me a twinge in my nearly healed side.

I clapped my hand to my neck and gritted my teeth so I wouldn't moan. When I could talk, I could only say, 'He what? He what?' I was almost incoherent with anger. Bill gave me a piercing look, put his finger over his lips to remind me to be quiet.

'I *never* did,' I whispered furiously. 'But even if I had, you know what? It would serve you right, you betraying son of a bitch.' I caught his eyes with mine and stared right into them. Okay, we were going to do this now.

'You're right,' he murmured. 'Lie down, Sookie. You are hurting.'

'Of course I'm hurting,' I whispered, and burst into tears. 'And to have the others tell me, to hear that you were just going to pension me off and go live with her without even having the courage to talk to me about it yourself! Bill, how could you be capable of such a thing! I was idiot enough to think you really loved me!' With a savagery I could scarcely believe was coming from inside me, I tossed off the blanket and threw myself on him, my fingers scrabbling for his throat.

And to hell with the pain.

My hands could not circle his neck, but I dug in as hard as I could and I felt a red rage carry me away. I wanted to kill him.

If Bill had fought back, I could have kept it up, but the longer I squeezed, the more the fine rage ebbed away, leaving me cold and empty. I was straddling Bill, and he was prone on the floor, lying passively with his hands at his sides. My hands eased off of his neck and I used them to cover my face.

'I hope that hurt like hell,' I said, my voice choking but clear enough.

'Yes,' he said. 'It hurt like hell.'

Bill pulled me down to the floor by him, covered us both with the blanket. He gently pushed my head into the notch of his neck and shoulder.

We lay there in silence for what seemed like a long time, though maybe it was only minutes. My body nestled into his out of habit and out of a deep need; though I didn't know if the need was for Bill specifically, or the intimacy I'd only shared with him. I hated him. I loved him.

'Sookie,' he said, against my hair, 'I'm –'

'Hush,' I said. 'Hush.' I huddled closer against him. I relaxed. It was like taking off an Ace bandage, one that had been wrapped too tight.

'You're wearing someone else's clothes,' he whispered, after a minute or two.

'Yes, a vampire named Bernard. He gave me clothes to wear after my dress got ruined at the bar.'

'At Josephine's?'

'Yes.'

'How did your dress get ruined?'

'I got staked.'

Everything about him went still. 'Where? Did it hurt?' He folded down the blanket. 'Show me.'

'Of course it hurt,' I said deliberately. 'It hurt like hell.' I lifted the hem of the sweatshirt carefully.

His fingers stroked the shiny skin. I would not heal like Bill. It might take a night or two more for him to become as smooth and perfect as he had been, but he would look just as before, despite a week of torture. I would have a scar the rest of my life, vampire blood or no vampire blood. The scar might not be as severe, and it was certainly forming at a phenomenal rate, but it was undeniably red and ugly, the flesh underneath it still tender, the whole area sore.

'Who did this to you?'

'A man. A fanatic. It's a long story.'

'Is he dead?'

'Yeah. Betty Joe Pickard killed him with two big blows of her fist. It kind of reminded me of a story I read in elementary school, about Paul Bunyan.'

'I don't know that story.' His dark eyes caught mine.

I shrugged.

'As long as he's dead now.' Bill had a good grip on that idea.

'Lots of people are dead now. All because of your program.'

There was a long moment of silence.

Bill cast a glance at the door Eric had tactfully closed behind him. Of course, he was probably listening right outside, and like all vampires, Eric had excellent hearing. 'It's safe?'

'Yes.'

Bill's mouth was right by my ear. It tickled when he whispered, 'Did they search my house?'

'I don't know. Maybe the vamps from Mississippi went

in. I never had a chance to get over there after Eric and Pam and Chow came to tell me you'd been snatched.'

'And they told you . . .?'

'That you were planning on leaving me. Yes. They told me.'

'I already got paid back for that piece of madness,' Bill said.

'You might have been paid back enough to suit *you*,' I said, 'but I don't know if you've been paid back enough to suit *me*.'

There was a long silence in the cold, empty room. It was quiet out in the living room, too. I hoped Eric had worked out what we were going to do next, and I hoped it involved going home. No matter what happened between Bill and me, I needed to be home in Bon Temps. I needed to go back to my job and my friends and I needed to see my brother. He might not be much, but he was what I had.

I wondered what was happening in the next apartment.

'When the queen came to me and said she'd heard I was working on a program that had never been attempted before, I was flattered,' Bill told me. 'The money she offered was very good, and she would have been within her rights not to offer any, since I am her subject.'

I could feel my mouth twisting at hearing yet another reminder of how different Bill's world was from mine. 'Who do you think told her?' I asked.

'I don't know. I don't really want to,' Bill said. His voice sounded offhand, even gentle, but I knew better.

'You know I had been working on it for some time,' Bill said, when he figured I wasn't going to say anything.

'Why?'

'Why?' He sounded oddly disconcerted. 'Well, because

it seemed like a good idea to me. Having a list of all America's vampires, and at least some of the rest of the world's? That was a valuable project, and actually, it was kind of fun to compile. And once I started doing research, I thought of including pictures. And aliases. And histories. It just grew.'

'So you've been, um, compiling a – like a directory? Of vampires?'

'Exactly.' Bill's glowing face lit up even brighter. 'I just started one night, thinking how many other vampires I'd come across in my travels over the past century, and I started making a list, and then I started adding a drawing I'd done or a photograph I'd taken.'

'So vampires do photograph? I mean, they show up in pictures?'

'Sure. We never liked to have our picture made, when photography became a common thing in America, because a picture was proof we'd been in a particular place at a particular time, and if we showed up looking exactly the same twenty years later, well, it was obvious what we were. But since we have admitted our existence, there is no point clinging to the old ways.'

'I'll bet some vampires still do.'

'Of course. There are some who still hide in the shadows and sleep in crypts every night.'

(This from a guy who slept in the soil of the cemetery from time to time.)

'And other vampires helped you with this?'

'Yes,' he said, sounding surprised. 'Yes, a few did. Some enjoyed the exercise of memory . . . some used it as a reason to search for old acquaintances, travel to old haunts. I am sure that I don't have all the vampires in America, especially the recent immigrants, but I think I have probably eighty percent of them.'

'Okay, so why is the queen so anxious to have this program? Why would the other vampires want it, once they learned about it? They could assemble all the same information, right?'

'Yes,' he said. 'But it would be far easier to take it from me. And as for why it's so desirable to have this program . . . wouldn't you like to have a booklet that listed all the other telepaths in the United States?'

'Oh, sure,' I said. 'I could get lots of tips on how to handle my problem, or maybe how to use it better.'

'So, wouldn't it be good to have a directory of vampires in the United States, what they're good at, where their gifts lie?'

'But surely some vampires really wouldn't want to be in such a book,' I said. 'You've told me that some vamps don't want to come out, that they want to stay in the darkness and hunt secretly.'

'Exactly.'

'Those vamps are in there, too?'

Bill nodded.

'Do you want to get yourself staked?'

'I never realized how tempting this project would be to anyone else. I never thought of how much power it would give to the one who owned it, until others began trying to steal it.'

Bill looked glum.

The sound of shouting in the apartment next door drew our attention.

Alcide and Debbie were at it again. They were really bad for each other. But some mutual attraction kept them ricocheting back to each other. Maybe, away from Alcide, Debbie was a nice person.

Nah, I couldn't bring myself to believe that. But maybe she was at least tolerable when Alcide's affections weren't an issue.

Of course they should separate. They should never be in the same room again.

And I had to take this to heart.

Look at me. Mangled, drained, staked, battered. Lying in a cold apartment in a strange city with a vampire who had betrayed me.

A big decision was standing right in front of my face, waiting, to be recognized and enacted.

I shoved Bill away, and wobbled to my feet. I pulled on my stolen jacket. With his silence heavy at my back, I opened the door to the living room. Eric was listening with some amusement to the battle going on in the next apartment.

'Take me home,' I said.

'Of course,' he said. 'Now?'

'Yes. Alcide can drop my things by when he goes back to Baton Rouge.'

'Is the Lincoln drivable?'

'Oh, yes.' I pulled the keys out of my pocket. 'Here.'

We walked out of the empty apartment and took the elevator down to the garage.

Bill didn't follow.

Chapter 13

Eric caught up with me as I was climbing into the Lincoln.

'I had to give Bill a few instructions about cleaning up the mess he caused,' he said, though I didn't ask.

Eric was used to driving sports cars, and he had a few issues with the Lincoln.

'Had it occurred to you,' he said, after we'd rolled out of the city's center, 'that you tend to walk away when things between you and Bill become rocky? Not that I mind, necessarily, since I would be glad for you two to sever your association. But if this is the pattern you follow in your romantic attachments, I want to know now.'

I thought of several things to say, discarded the first few, which would have blistered my grandmother's ears, and drew a deep breath.

'Firstly, Eric, what happens between Bill and me is just none of your damn business.' I let that sink in for a few seconds. 'Second, my relationship with Bill is the only one I've ever had, so I've never had any idea what I'm going to do even from day to day, much less establishing a policy.' I paused to work on phrasing my next idea. 'Third, I'm through with you all. I'm tired of seeing all this sick stuff. I'm tired of having to be brave, and having to do things that scare me, and having to hang out with the bizarre and the supernatural. I am just a regular person, and I just want to date regular people. Or at least people who are *breathing*.'

Eric waited to see if I'd finished. I cast a quick glance over at him, and the streetlights illuminated his strong profile with its knife-edge nose. At least he wasn't laughing at me. He wasn't even smiling.

He glanced at me briefly before turning his attention back to the road. 'I'm listening to what you say. I can tell you mean it. I've had your blood: I know your feelings.'

A mile of darkness went by. I was pleased Eric was taking me seriously. Sometimes he didn't; and sometimes he didn't seem to care what he said to me.

'You are spoiled for humans,' Eric said. His slight foreign accent was more apparent.

'Maybe I am. Though I don't see that as much of a loss, since I didn't have any luck with guys before.' Hard to date, when you know exactly what your date is thinking. So much of the time, knowing a man's exact thoughts can erase desire and even liking. 'But I'd be happier with no one than I am now.'

I'd been considering the old Ann Landers rule of thumb: Would I be better off with him, or without him? My grandmother and Jason and I had read Ann Landers every day when Jason and I had been growing up. We'd discussed all Ann's responses to reader questions. A lot of the advice she'd ladled out had been intended to help women deal with guys like Jason, so he certainly brought perspective to the conversations.

Right at this moment, I was pretty darn sure I was better off without Bill. He'd used me and abused me, betrayed me and drained me.

He'd also defended me, avenged me, worshiped me with his body, and provided hours of uncritical companionship, a very major blessing.

Well, I just didn't have my scales handy. What I had was a heart full of hurt and a way to go home. We flew through the black night, wrapped in our own thoughts. Traffic was light, but this was an interstate, so of course there were cars around us from time to time.

I had no idea what Eric was thinking about, a wonderful feeling. He might be debating pulling over to the shoulder and breaking my neck, or he might be wondering what tonight's take at Fangtasia would add up to. I wanted him to talk to me. I wished he would tell me about his life before he became a vampire, but that's a real touchy subject with lots of vamps, and I wasn't about to bring it up tonight of all nights.

About an hour out of Bon Temps, we took an exit ramp. We were a little low on gas, and I needed to use the ladies' room. Eric had already begun to fill the tank as I eased my sore body carefully out of the car. He had dismissed my offer to pump the gas with a courteous, 'No, thank you.' One other car was filling up, and the woman, a peroxide blond about my age, hung up the nozzle as I got out of the Lincoln.

At one in the morning, the gas station/convenience store was almost empty besides the young woman, who was heavily made up and wrapped in a quilted coat. I spied a battered Toyota pickup parked by the side of the filling station, in the only shadow on the lot. Inside the pickup, two men were sitting, involved in a heated conversation.

'It's too cold to be sitting outside in a pickup,' the dark-rooted blond said, as we went through the glass doors together. She gave an elaborate shiver.

'You'd think so,' I commented. I was halfway down the aisle by the back of the store, when the clerk, behind a high counter on a raised platform, turned away from his little television to take the blond's money.

The door to the bathroom was hard to shut behind me, since the wooden sill had swollen during some past leakage. In fact, it probably didn't shut all the way behind me, since I was in something of a hurry. But the stall door shut and locked, and it was clean enough. In no hurry to get back in the car with the silent Eric, I took my time after using the facilities. I peered in the mirror over the sink, expecting I'd look like holy hell and not being contradicted by what I saw reflected there.

The mangled bite mark on my neck looked really disgusting, as though a dog had had hold of me. As I cleaned the wound with soap and wet paper towels, I wondered if having ingested vampire blood would give me a specific quantity of extra strength and healing, and then be exhausted, or if it was good for a certain amount of time like a time-release capsule, or what the deal was. After I'd had Bill's blood, I'd felt great for a couple of months.

I didn't have a comb or brush or anything, and I looked like something the cat dragged in. Trying to tame my hair with my fingers just made a bad thing worse. I washed my face and neck, and stepped back into the glare of the store. I hardly registered that once again the door didn't shut behind me, instead lodged quietly on the swollen sill. I emerged behind the last long aisle of groceries, crowded with CornNuts and Lays Chips and Moon Pies and Scotch Snuf and Prince Albert in a can . . .

And two armed robbers up by the clerk's platform inside the door.

Holy Moses, why don't they just give these poor clerks shirts with big targets printed on them? That was my first thought, detached, as if I were watching a movie with a convenience store robbery. Then I snapped into the here and now, tuned in by the very real strain on the clerk's face. He was awfully young – a reedy, blotched teenager. And he was facing the two big guys with guns. His hands were in the air, and he was mad as hell. I would have expected blubbering for his life, or incoherence, but this boy was furious.

It was the fourth time he'd been robbed, I read fresh from his brain. And the third time at gunpoint. He was wishing he could grab the shotgun under the seat in his truck behind the store and blast these sumbitches to hell.

And no one acknowledged that I was there. They didn't seem to know.

Not that I was complaining, okay?

I glanced behind me, to verify that the door to the bathroom had stuck open again, so its sound would not betray me. The best thing for me to do would be to creep out the back door to this place, if I could find it, and run around the building to get Eric to call the police.

Wait a minute. Now that I was thinking of Eric, where was he? Why hadn't he come in to pay for the gas?

If it was possible to have a foreboding any more ominous than the one I already had, that fit the bill. If Eric hadn't come in yet, Eric wasn't coming. Maybe he'd decided to leave. Leave me.

Here.

Alone.

Just like Bill left you, my mind supplied helpfully. Well, thanks a hell of a lot, Mind.

Or maybe they'd shot him. If he'd taken a head wound . . . and there was no healing a heart that had taken a direct hit with a big-caliber bullet.

There was no point whatsoever in standing there worrying.

This was a typical convenience store. You came in the front door, and the clerk was behind a long counter to your right, up on a platform. The cold drinks were in the refrigerator case that took up the left wall. You were facing three long aisles running the width of the store, plus various special displays and stacks of insulated mugs and charcoal briquettes and birdseed. I was all the way at the back of the store and I could see the clerk (easily) and the crooks (just barely) over the top of the groceries. I had to get out of the store, preferably unseen. I spotted a splintered wooden door, marked 'Employees Only' farther along the back wall. It was actually beyond the counter behind which the clerk stood. There was a gap between the end of the counter and the wall, and from the end of my aisle to the beginning of that counter, I'd be exposed.

Nothing would be gained by waiting.

I dropped to my hands and knees and began crawling. I moved slowly, so I could listen, too.

'You seen a blond come in here, about this tall?' the burlier of the two robbers was saying, and all of a sudden I felt faint.

Which blond? Me, or Eric? Or the peroxide blond? Of course, I couldn't see the height indication. Were they looking for a male vampire or a female telepath? Or . . . after all, I wasn't the only woman in the world who could get into trouble, I reminded myself.

'Blond woman come in here five minutes ago, bought some cigarettes,' the boy said sullenly. Good for you, fella!

'Naw, that one done drove off. We want the one who was with the vampire.'

Yep, that would be me.

'I didn't see no other woman,' the boy said. I glanced up a little and saw the reflection off a mirror mounted up in the corner of the store. It was a security mirror so the clerk could detect shoplifters. I thought, *He can see me crouching here. He knows I'm here.*

God bless him. He was doing his best for me. I had to do my best for him. At the same time, if we could avoid getting shot, that would be a very good thing. And where the hell was Eric?

Blessing my borrowed sweatpants and slippers for being soft and silent, I crept deliberately toward the stained wooden 'Employees Only' door. I wondered if it creaked. The two robbers were still talking to the clerk, but I blocked out their voices so I could concentrate on reaching the door.

I'd been scared before, plenty of times, but this was right up there with the scariest events of my life. My dad had hunted, and Jason and his buddies hunted, and I'd watched a massacre in Dallas. I knew what bullets could do. Now that I'd reached the end of the aisle, I'd come to the end of my cover.

I peered around the display counter's end. I had to cross about four feet of open floor to reach the partial shelter of the long counter that ran in front of the cash register. I would be lower and well hidden from the robbers' perspective, once I crossed that empty space.

'Car pulling in,' the clerk said, and the two robbers automatically looked out the plate glass window to see. If I hadn't known what he was doing telepathically, I might have hesitated too long. I scuttled across the exposed linoleum faster than I would have believed possible.

'I don't see no car,' said the less bulky man.

The clerk said, 'I thought I heard the bell ring, the one that goes when a car drives across it.'

I reached up and turned the knob on the door. It opened quietly.

'It rings sometimes when there ain't nobody there,' the boy continued, and I realized he was trying to make noise and hold their attention so I could get out the door. God bless him, all over again.

I pushed the door a little wider, and duck-walked through. I was in a narrow passage. There was another door at the end of it, a door that presumably led to the area behind the convenience store. In the door was a set of keys. They wisely kept the back door locked. From one of a row of nails by the back door hung a heavy camo jacket. I poked my hand down in the pocket on the right and came up with the boy's keys. That was just a lucky guess. It happens. Clutching them to prevent their jingling, I opened the back door and stepped outside.

There was nothing out here but a battered pickup and a reeking Dumpster. The lighting was poor, but at least there was some light. The blacktop was cracked. Since it was winter, the weeds that had sprouted up from those cracks were dry and bleached. I heard a little sound to my left and drew in a shaky breath after I'd jumped about a foot. The sound was caused by a huge old raccoon, and he ambled off into the small patch of woods behind the store.

I exhaled just as shakily as I'd drawn the air in. I made myself focus on the bunch of keys. Unfortunately, there were about twenty. This boy had more keys than squirrels had acorns. No one on God's green earth could possibly use this many keys. I flicked through them desperately, and finally selected one that had GM stamped on a black rubber cover. I unlocked the door and reached into the musty interior, which smelled strongly of cigarettes and dogs. Yes, the shotgun was under the seat. I broke it open. It was loaded. Thank God Jason believed in self-defense. He'd showed me how to load and fire his new Benelli.

Despite my new protection, I was so scared, I wasn't sure I could get around to the front of the store. But I had to scout out the situation, and find out what had happened to Eric. I eased down the side of the building where the old Toyota truck was parked. Nothing was in the back, except a little spot that picked up a stray fraction of light. The shotgun cradled in one arm, I reached down to run a finger over it.

Fresh blood. I felt old and cold. I stood with my head bowed for a long moment, and then I braced myself.

I looked in the driver's window to find the cab was unlocked. Well, happy days. I opened the door quietly, glanced in. There was a sizeable open box on the front seat, and when I checked its contents, my heart sank so low, I thought it'd come out the bottom of my shoes. On the outside, the box was stamped 'Contents: Two.' Now it contained one silver mesh net, the kind sold in 'mercenary' magazines, the kind always advertised as 'vampire proof.'

That was like calling a shark cage a sure deterrent from shark bites.

Where was Eric? I glanced over the immediate vicinity, but I saw no other trace. I could hear traffic whooshing by on the interstate, but the silence hung over this bleak parking lot.

My eyes lit on a pocketknife on the dash. Yahoo! Carefully placing the shotgun on the front seat, I scooped up the knife, opened it and held it ready to sink into the tire. Then I thought twice. A wholehearted tire-slashing was proof someone had been out here while the robbers were inside. That might not be a good thing. I contented myself with poking a single hole in the tire. It was just a smallish hole that might have come from anything, I told myself. If they did drive off, they'd have to stop somewhere down the road. Then I pocketed the knife – I was certainly quite the thief lately – and returned to the shadows around the building. This hadn't taken as long as you might think, but still it had been several minutes since I'd assessed the situation in the convenience store.

The Lincoln was still parked by the pumps. The gas port was closed, so I knew Eric had finished refueling before something had happened to him. I sidled around the corner of the building, hugging its lines. I found good cover at the front, in the angle formed by the ice machine and the front wall of the store. I risked standing up enough to peek over the top of the machine.

The robbers had come up into the higher area where the clerk stood, and they were beating on him.

Hey, now. That had to stop. They were beating him because they wanted to know where I was hiding, was my guess; and I couldn't let someone else get beaten up on my behalf.

'Sookie,' said a voice right behind me.

The next instant a hand clapped across my mouth just as I was about to scream.

'Sorry,' Eric whispered. 'I should have thought of a better way to let you know I was here.'

'Eric,' I said, when I could speak. He could tell I was calmer, and he moved his hand. 'We gotta save him.'

'Why?'

Sometimes vampires just astound me. Well, people, too, but tonight it was a vampire.

'Because he's getting beaten for our sakes, and they're probably gonna kill him, and it'll be our fault!'

'They're robbing the store,' Eric said, as if I were particularly dim. 'They had a new vampire net, and they thought they'd try it out on me. They don't know it yet, but it didn't work. But they're just opportunistic scum.'

'They're looking for us,' I said furiously.

'Tell me,' he whispered, and I did.

'Give me the shotgun,' he said.

I kept a good grip on it. 'You know how to use one of these things?'

'Probably as well as you.' But he looked at it dubiously.

'That's where you're wrong,' I told him. Rather than have a prolonged argument while my new hero was getting internal injuries, I ran in a crouch around the ice machine, the propane gas rack, and through the front door into the store. The little bell over the door rang like crazy, and though with all the shouting they didn't seem to hear it, they sure paid attention when I fired a blast through the ceiling over their heads. Tiles, dust, and insulation rained down.

It almost knocked me flat – but not quite. I leveled the gun right on them. They were frozen. It was like playing Swing the Statue when I was little. But not quite. The poor pimply clerk had a bloody face, and I was sure his nose was broken, and some of his teeth knocked loose.

I felt a fine rage break out behind my eyes. 'Let the young man go,' I said clearly.

'You gonna shoot us, little lady?'

'You bet your ass I am,' I said.

'And if she misses, I will get you,' said Eric's voice, above and behind me. A big vampire makes great backup.

'The vampire got loose, Sonny.' The speaker was a thinnish man with filthy hands and greasy boots.

'I see that,' said Sonny, the heavier one. He was darker, too. The smaller man's head was covered with that no-color hair, the kind people call 'brown' because they have to call it something.

The young clerk pulled himself up out of his pain and fear and came around the counter as fast as he could move. Mixed with the blood on his face was a lot of white powder from me shooting into the ceiling. He looked a sight.

'I see you found my shotgun,' he said as he passed by me, carefully not getting between the bad guys and me. He pulled a cell phone out of his pocket, and I heard the tiny beeps as he pressed numbers. His growly voice was soon in staccato conversation with the police.

'Before the police get here, Sookie, we need to find out who sent these two imbeciles,' Eric said. If I'd been them, I'd have been mighty scared at the tone of his voice, and they seemed to be aware of what an angry vampire could do. For the first time Eric stepped abreast of me and then a little bit ahead, and I could see his face. Burns crisscrossed it like angry strings of poison ivy welts. He was lucky only his face had been bare, but I doubt he was feeling very lucky.

'Come down here,' Eric said, and he caught the eyes of Sonny.

Sonny immediately walked down from the clerk's platform and around the counter while his companion was gaping.

'Stay,' said Eric. The no-color man squeezed his eyes shut so he couldn't glimpse Eric, but he opened them just a crack when he heard Eric take a step closer, and that was enough. If you don't have any extra abilities yourself, you just can't look a vampire in the eyes. If they want to, they'll get you.

'Who sent you here?' Eric asked softly.

'One of the Hounds of Hell,' Sonny said, with no inflection in his voice.

Eric looked startled. 'A member of the motorcycle gang,' I explained carefully, mindful that we had a civilian audience who was listening with great curiosity. I was getting a great amplification of the answers through their brains.

'What did they tell you to do?'

'They told us to wait along the interstate. There are more fellas waiting at other gas stations.'

They'd called about forty thugs altogether. They'd outlaid a lot of cash.

'What were you supposed to watch for?'

'A big dark guy and a tall blond guy. With a blond woman, real young, with nice tits.'

Eric's hand moved too fast for me to track. I was only sure he'd moved when I saw the blood running down Sonny's face.

'You are speaking of my future lover. Be more respectful. Why were you looking for us?'

'We were supposed to catch you. Take you back to Jackson.'

'Why?'

'The gang suspected you mighta had something to do with Jerry Falcon's disappearance. They wanted to ask you some questions about it. They had someone watching some apartment building, seen you two coming out in a Lincoln, had you followed part of the way. The dark guy wasn't with you, but the woman was the right one, so we started tracking you.'

'Do the vampires of Jackson know anything about this plan?'

'No, the gang figured it was their problem. But they also got a lot of other problems, a prisoner escape and so on, and lots of people out sick. So what with one thing and another, they recruited a bunch of us to help.'

'What are these men?' Eric asked me.

I closed my eyes and thought carefully. 'Nothing,' I said. 'They're nothing.' They weren't shifters, or Weres, or anything. They were hardly human beings, in my opinion, but nobody died and made me God.

'We need to get out of here,' Eric said. I agreed heartily. The last thing I wanted to do was spend the night at the police station, and for Eric, that was an impossibility. There wasn't an approved vampire jail cell any closer than Shreveport. Heck, the police station in Bon Temps had just gotten wheelchair accessible.

Eric looked into Sonny's eyes. 'We weren't here,' he said. 'This lady and myself.'

'Just the boy,' Sonny agreed.

Again, the other robber tried to keep his eyes tight shut,

but Eric blew in his face, and just as a dog would, the man opened his eyes and tried to wiggle back. Eric had him in a second, and repeated his procedure.

Then he turned to the clerk and handed him the shotgun. 'Yours, I believe,' Eric said.

'Thanks,' the boy said, his eyes firmly on the barrel of the gun. He aimed at the robbers. 'I know you weren't here,' he growled, keeping his gaze ahead of him. 'And I ain't saying nothing to the police.'

Eric put forty dollars on the counter. 'For the gas,' he explained. 'Sookie, let's make tracks.'

'A Lincoln with a big hole in the trunk does stand out,' the boy called after us.

'He's right.' I was buckling up and Eric was accelerating as we heard sirens, pretty close.

'I should have taken the truck,' Eric said. He seemed pleased with our adventure, now that it was over.

'How's your face?'

'It's getting better.'

The welts were not nearly as noticeable.

'What happened?' I asked, hoping this was not a very touchy subject.

He cast me a sideways glance. Now that we were back on the interstate, we had slowed down to the speed limit, so it wouldn't seem to any of the many police cars converging on the convenience store that we were fleeing.

'While you were tending to your human needs in the bathroom,' he said, 'I finished putting gas in the tank. I had hung up the pump and was almost at the door when those two got out of the truck and just tossed a net over me. It is very humiliating, that they were able to do that, two fools with a silver net.'

'Your mind must have been somewhere else.'

'Yes,' he said shortly. 'It was.'

'So then what happened?' I asked, when it seemed he was going to stop there.

'The heavier one hit me with the butt of his gun, and it took me a small time to recover,' Eric said.

'I saw the blood.'

He touched a place on the back of his head. 'Yes, I bled. After getting used to the pain, I snagged a corner of the net on the bumper of their truck and managed to roll out of it. They were inept in that, as well as robbery. If they had tied the net shut with silver chains, the result might have been different.'

'So you got free?'

'The head blow was more of a problem than I thought at first,' Eric said stiffly. 'I ran along the back of the store to the water spigot on the other side. Then I heard someone coming out of the back. When I was recovered, I followed the sounds and found you.' After a long moment's silence, Eric asked me what had happened in the store.

'They got me confused with the other woman who went in the store at the same time I went to the ladies' room,' I explained. 'They didn't seem to be sure I was in the store, and the clerk was telling them that there had been only one woman, and she'd gone. I could tell he had a shotgun in his truck – you know, I heard it in his head – and I went and got it, and I disabled their truck, and I was looking for you because I figured something had happened to you.'

'So you planned to save me and the clerk, together?'

'Well . . . yeah.' I couldn't understand the odd tone of his voice. 'I didn't feel like I had a whole lot of choices there.'

The welts were just pink lines now.

The silence still didn't seem relaxed. We were about forty minutes from home now. I started to let it drop. I didn't.

'You don't seem too happy about something,' I said, a definite edge to my voice. My own temper was fraying around the edges. I *knew* I was heading in the wrong direction conversationally; I *knew* I should just be content with silence, however brooding and pregnant.

Eric took the exit for Bon Temps and turned south.

Sometimes, instead of going down the road less taken, you just charge right down the beaten path.

'Would there be something wrong with me rescuing the two of you?' We were driving through Bon Temps now. Eric turned east after the buildings along Main gradually thinned and vanished. We passed Merlotte's, still open. We turned south again, on a small parish road. Then we were bumping down my driveway.

Eric pulled over and killed the engine. 'Yes,' he said. 'There is something wrong with that. And why the hell don't you get your driveway fixed?'

The string of tension that had stretched between us popped. I was out of the car in a New York minute, and he was, too. We faced each other across the roof of the Lincoln, though not much of me showed. I charged around it until I was right in front of him.

'Because I can't afford it, that's why! I don't have any money! And you all keep asking me to take time off from my job to do stuff for you! I can't! I can't do it anymore!' I shrieked. 'I quit!'

There was a long moment of silence while Eric regarded me. My chest was heaving underneath my stolen jacket. Something felt funny, something was bothering me about the appearance of my house, but I was too het up to examine my worry.

'Bill . . .' Eric began cautiously, and it set me off like a rocket.

'He's spending all his money on the freaking Bellefleurs,' I said, my tone this time low and venomous, but no less sincere. 'He never thinks about giving me money. And how could I take it? It would make me a kept woman, and I'm not his whore, I'm his . . . I used to be his girlfriend.'

I took a deep, shuddering breath, dismally aware that I was going to cry. It would be better to get mad again. I tried. 'Where do you get off, telling them that I'm your . . . your lover? Where'd that come from?'

'What happened to the money you earned in Dallas?' Eric asked, taking me completely by surprise.

'I paid my property taxes with it.'

'Did you ever think that if you told me where Bill's hiding his computer program, I would give you anything you asked for? Did you not realize that Russell would have paid you handsomely?'

I sucked in my breath, so offended, I hardly knew where to begin.

'I see you didn't think of those things.'

'Oh, yeah, I'm just an angel.' Actually, none of those things had occurred to me, and I was almost defensive they hadn't. I was shaking with fury, and all my good sense went out the window. I would feel the presence of other brains at work, and the fact that someone was in my place enraged me farther. The rational part of my mind crumpled under the weight of my anger.

'Someone's waiting in my house, Eric.' I swung around and stomped over to my porch, finding the key I'd hidden under the rocker my grandmother had loved. Ignoring everything my brain was trying to tell me, ignoring the beginning of a bellow from Eric, I opened the front door and got hit with a ton of bricks.

Chapter 14

'We got her,' said a voice I didn't recognize. I had been yanked to my feet, and I was swaying between two men who were holding me up.

'What about the vamp?'

'I shot him twice, but he's in the woods. He got away.'

'That's bad news. Work fast.'

I could sense that there were many men in the room with me, and I opened my eyes. They'd turned on the lights. They were in my house. They were in my home. As much as the blow to my jaw, that made me sick. Somehow, I'd assumed my visitors would be Sam or Arlene or Jason.

There were five strangers in my living room, if I was thinking clearly enough to count. But before I could form another idea, one of the men – and now I realized he was wearing a familiar leather vest – punched me in the stomach.

I didn't have enough breath to scream.

The two men holding me pulled me back upright.

'Where is he?'

'Who?' I really couldn't remember, at this point, what

particular missing person he wanted me to locate. But, of course, he hit me again. I had a dreadful minute when I needed to gag but hadn't the air to do it. I was strangling and suffocating.

Finally, I drew in a long breath. It was noisy and painful and just heaven.

My Were interrogator, who had light hair shaved close to his scalp and a nasty little goatee, slapped me, hard, open-handed. My head rocked on my neck like a car on faulty shock absorbers. 'Where's the vampire, bitch?' the Were said. He drew his fist back.

I couldn't take any more of this. I decided to speed things up. I pulled my legs up, and while the two at my sides kept desperate grips on my arms, I kicked the Were in front of me with both feet. If I hadn't had on bedroom slippers, it probably would have been more effective. I'm never wearing safety boots when I need them. But Nasty Goatee did stagger back, and then he came for me with my death in his eyes.

By then my legs had swung back to the floor, but I made them keep going backward, and threw my two captors completely off balance. They staggered, tried to recover, but their frantic footing was in vain. Down we all went, the Were along with us.

This might not be better, but it was an improvement over waiting to get hit.

I'd landed on my face, since my arms and hands weren't under my control. One guy did let go as we fell, and when I got that hand underneath me for leverage, I yanked away from the other man.

I'd gotten halfway to my feet when the Were, quicker than the humans, managed to grab my hair. He dealt a slap to my face while he wound my hair around his hand for a better grip. The other hired hands closed in, either to help the two on the floor to rise, or just to see me get battered.

A real fight is over in a few minutes because people wear out quick. It had been a very long day, and the fact was, I was ready to give up against these overwhelming odds. But I had a little pride and I went for the guy closest to me, a potbellied pig of a man with greasy dark hair. I dug my fingers into his face, trying to cause any damage I could, while I could.

The Were kneed me in the belly and I screamed, and the pig-man began to yell for the others to get me off of him, and the front door crashed open as Eric came in, blood covering his chest and right leg. Bill was right behind him.

They lost all control.

I saw firsthand what a vampire could do.

After a second, I realized my help would not be needed, and I decided the Goddess of Really Tough Gals would have to excuse me while I closed my eyes.

In two minutes, all the men in my living room were dead.

'Sookie? Sookie?' Eric's voice was hoarse. 'Do we need to take her to the hospital?' he asked Bill.

I felt cool fingers on my wrist, touching my neck. I almost explained that for once I was conscious, but it was just too hard. The floor seemed like a good place to be.

'Her pulse is strong,' Bill reported. 'I'm going to turn her over.'

'She's alive?'

'Yes.'

Eric's voice, suddenly closer, said, 'Is the blood hers?'

'Yes, some of it.'

He drew a deep, shuddering breath. 'Hers is different.'

'Yes,' Bill said coldly. 'But surely you are full by now.'

'It's been a long time since I had real blood in quantity,' Eric said, just exactly like my brother, Jason, would have remarked it had been a long time since he'd had blackberry cobbler.

Bill slid his hands underneath me. 'For me, too. We'll need to put them all out in the yard,' he said casually, 'and clean up Sookie's house.'

'Of course.'

Bill began rolling me over, and I began crying. I couldn't help it. As strong as I wanted to be, all I could think of was my body. If you've ever been really beaten, you'll know what I mean. When you've been really beaten, you realize that you are just an envelope of skin, an easily penetrated envelope that holds together a lot of fluids and some rigid structures, which in their turn can simply be broken and invaded. I thought I'd been badly hurt in Dallas a few weeks before, but this felt worse. I knew that didn't mean it was worse; there was a lot of soft tissue damage. In Dallas, my cheekbone had been fractured and my knee twisted. I thought maybe the knee had been compromised all over again, and I thought maybe one of the slaps had rebroken the cheekbone. I opened my eyes, blinked, and opened them again. My vision cleared after a few seconds.

'Can you speak?' Eric said, after a long, long moment.

I tried, but my mouth was so dry, nothing came out.

'She needs a drink.' Bill went to the kitchen, having to take a less than direct route, since there were a lot of obstructions in the way.

Eric's hands stroked back my hair. He'd been shot, I

remembered, and I wanted to ask him how he felt, but I couldn't. He was sitting on his butt beside me, leaning on the cushions of my couch. There was blood on his face, and he looked pinker than I'd ever seen him, ruddy with health. When Bill returned with my water – he'd even added a straw – I looked at his face. Bill looked almost sunburned.

Bill held me up carefully and put the straw to my lips. I drank, and it was the best thing I'd ever tasted.

'You killed them all,' I said in a creaky voice.

Eric nodded.

I thought of the circle of brutish faces that had surrounded me. I thought of the Were slapping me in the face.

'Good,' I said. Eric looked a little amused, just for a second. Bill didn't look anything in particular.

'How many?'

Eric looked around vaguely, and Bill pointed a finger silently as he toted them up.

'Seven?' Bill said doubtfully. 'Two in the yard and five in the house?'

'I was thinking eight,' Eric murmured.

'Why did they come after you like that?'

'Jerry Falcon.'

'Oh,' said Bill, a different note in his voice. 'Oh, yes. I've encountered him. In the torture room. He is first on my list.'

'Well, you can cross him off,' Eric said. 'Alcide and Sookie disposed of his body in the woods yesterday.'

'Did this Alcide kill him?' Bill looked down at me, reconsidered. 'Or Sookie?'

'He says no. They found the corpse in the closet of

Alcide's apartment, and they hatched a plan to hide his remains.' Eric sounded like that had been kind of cute of us.

'My Sookie hid a corpse?'

'I don't think you can be too sure about that possessive pronoun.'

'Where did you learn that term, Northman?'

'I took "English as a Second Language" at a community college in the seventies.'

Bill said, 'She is mine.'

I wondered if my hands would move. They would. I raised both of them, making an unmistakable one-fingered gesture.

Eric laughed, and Bill said, 'Sookie!' in shocked admonishment.

'I think that Sookie is telling us she belongs to herself,' Eric said softly. 'In the meantime, to finish our conversation, whoever stuffed the corpse in the closet meant to saddle Alcide with the blame, since Jerry Falcon had made a blatant pass at Sookie in the bar the night before, and Alcide had taken umbrage.'

'So all this plot might be directed at Alcide instead of us?'

'Hard to say. Evidently, from what the armed robbers at the gas station told us, what's remaining of the gang called in all the thugs they knew and stationed them along the interstate to intercept us on the way back. If they'd just called ahead, they wouldn't now be in jail for armed robbery. And I'm certainly sure that's where they are.'

'So how'd these guys get here? How'd they know where Sookie lived, who she really was?'

'She used her own name at Club Dead. They didn't know the name of Bill's human girlfriend. You were faithful.'

'I hadn't been faithful in other ways,' Bill said bleakly. 'I thought it was the least I could do for her.'

And this was the guy whom I'd shot the bird. On the other hand, this was the guy who was talking like I wasn't in the room. And most importantly, this was the guy who'd had another 'darling,' for whom he'd planned to leave me flat.

'So the Weres may not know she was your girlfriend; they only know she was staying in the apartment with Alcide when Jerry disappeared. They know Jerry may have come by the apartment. This Alcide says that the pack-master in Jackson told Alcide to leave and not return for a while, but that he believed Alcide had not killed Jerry.'

'This Alcide . . . he seemed to have a troubled relationship with his girlfriend.'

'She is engaged to someone else. She believes he is attached to Sookie.'

'And is he? He has the gall to tell this virago Debbie that Sookie is good in bed.'

'He wanted to make her jealous. He has not slept with Sookie.'

'But he likes her.' Bill made it sound like a capital crime.

'Doesn't everyone?'

I said, with great effort, 'You just killed a bunch of guys who didn't seem to like me at all.' I was tired of them talking about me right above my head, as illuminating as it was. I was hurting real bad, and my living room was full of dead men. I was ready for both those situations to be remedied.

'Bill, how'd you get here?' I asked in a raspy whisper.

'My car. I negotiated a deal with Russell, since I didn't want to be looking over my shoulder for the rest of my existence. Russell was in a tantrum when I called him. Not only had I disappeared and Lorena vanished, but his hired Weres had disobeyed him and thus jeopardized business dealings Russell has with this Alcide and his father.'

'Who was Russell angriest with?' Eric asked.

'Lorena, for letting me escape.'

They had a good laugh over that one before Bill continued his story. Those vamps. A laugh a minute.

'Russell agreed to return my car and leave me alone if I would tell him how I'd escaped, so he could plug the hole I'd wiggled out of. And he asked me to put in a bid for him to share in the vampire directory.'

If Russell had just done that in the first place, it would have saved everyone a lot of grief. On the other hand, Lorena would still be alive. So would the thugs who'd beaten me, and perhaps so would Jerry Falcon, whose death was still a mystery.

'So,' Bill continued, 'I sped down the highway, on the way to tell you two that the Weres and their hired hands were pursuing you, and that they had gone ahead to lie in wait. They had discovered, via the computer, that Alcide's girlfriend Sookie Stackhouse lived in Bon Temps.'

'These computers are dangerous things,' Eric said. His voice sounded weary, and I remembered the blood on his clothes. Eric had been shot twice, because he'd been with me.

'Her face is swelling,' Bill said. His voice was both gentle and angry.

'Eric okay?' I asked wearily, figuring I could skip a few words if I got the idea across.

'I will heal,' he said, from a great distance. 'Especially since having all that good . . .'

And then I fell asleep, or passed out, or some blend of the two.

Sunshine. It had been so long since I'd seen sunshine; I'd almost forgotten how good it looked.

I was in my own bed, and I was in my soft blue brushed-nylon nightgown, and I was wrapped up like a mummy. I really, really had to get up and get to the bathroom. Once I moved enough to establish how awful walking was going to be, only my bladder compelled me to get out of that bed.

I took tiny steps across the floor, which suddenly seemed as wide and empty as the desert. I covered it inch by painful inch. My toenails were still painted bronze, to match my nails. I had a lot of time to look at my toes as I made my journey.

Thank God I had indoor plumbing. If I'd had to make it into the yard to an outhouse, as my grandmother had as a child, I would've given up.

When I had completed my journey and pulled on a fleecy blue robe, I inched my way down the hall to the living room to examine the floor. I noticed along the way that the sun outside was brilliant and the sky was the deep rich blue of heaven. It was forty-two, said the thermometer Jason had given me on my birthday. He'd mounted it for me on the window frame, so I could just peek out to read it.

The living room looked real good. I wasn't sure how long the vampire cleaning crew had been at work the night before, but there were no body parts visible. The wood of the floor was gleaming, and the furniture looked spanky clean. The old throw rug was missing, but I didn't care. It had been no wonderful heirloom anyway, just a sort of pretty rug Gran had picked up at a flea market for thirty-five dollars. Why did I remember that? It didn't matter at all. And my grandmother was dead.

I felt the sudden danger of weeping, and I pushed it away. I wasn't going to fall back into a trough of self-pity. My reaction to Bill's unfaithfulness seemed faint and far away now; I was a colder woman, or maybe my protective hide had just grown thicker. I no longer felt angry with him, to my surprise. He'd been tortured by the woman – well, the vampire he'd thought loved him. And she'd tortured him for financial gain – that was the worst.

To my startled horror, suddenly I relived the moment when the stake had gone in under her ribs, and I was feeling the movement of the wood as it plowed through her body.

I made it back to the hall bathroom just in time.

Okay, I'd killed someone.

I'd once hurt someone who was trying to kill me, but that had never bothered me: oh, the odd dream or two. But the horror of staking the vampire Lorena felt worse. She would've killed me a lot quicker, and I was sure it would have been no problem whatsoever for Lorena. She probably would've laughed her ass off.

Maybe that was what had gotten to me so much. After I'd sunk the stake in, I was sure I'd had a moment, a second, a flash of time in which I'd thought, *So there, bitch.* And it had been pure pleasure.

A couple of hours later, I'd discovered it was the early afternoon, and it was Monday. I called my brother on his cell phone, and he came by with my mail. When I opened my door, he stood for a long minute, looking me up and down.

'If he did that to you, I'm heading over there with a torch and a sharpened broom handle,' he said.

'No, he didn't.'

'What happened to the ones who did?'

'You better not think about it too much.'

'At least he does some things right.'

'I'm not gonna see him anymore.'

'Uh-huh. I've heard that before.'

He had a point. 'For a while,' I said firmly.

'Sam said you'd gone off with Alcide Herveaux.'

'Sam shouldn't have told you.'

'Hell, I'm your brother. I need to know who you're going around with.'

'It was business,' I said, trying a little smile on for size.

'You going into surveying?'

'You know Alcide?'

'Who doesn't, at least by name? Those Herveauxes, they're well known. Tough guys. Good to work for. Rich.'

'He's a nice guy.'

'He coming around anymore? I'd like to meet him. I don't want to be on a road crew working for the parish my whole life.'

That was news to me. 'Next time I see him, I'll call you. I don't know if he'll be stopping by anytime soon, but if he does, you'll know about it.'

'Good.' Jason glanced around. 'What happened to the rug?'

I noticed a spot of blood on the couch, about where Eric had leaned. I sat down so my legs were covering it. 'The rug? I spilled some tomato sauce on it. I was eating spaghetti out here while I watched TV.'

'So you took it to get it cleaned?'

I didn't know how to answer. I didn't know if that was what the vampires had done with the rug, or if it'd had to be torched. 'Yes,' I said, with some hesitation. 'But they may not be able to get the stain out, they said.'

'New gravel looks good.'

I stared at him in gape-mouthed surprise. 'What?'

He looked at me as if I were a fool. 'The new gravel. On the driveway. They did a good job, getting it level. Not a single pothole.'

Completely forgetting the bloodstain, I heaved myself up from the couch with some difficulty and peered out the front window, this time really looking.

Not only was the driveway done, but also there was a new parking area in front of the house. It was outlined with landscaping timbers. The gravel was the very expensive kind, the kind that's supposed to interlock so it doesn't roll out of the desired area I put my hand over my mouth as I calculated how much it had cost. 'It's done like that all the way to the road?' I asked Jason, my voice hardly audible.

'Yeah, I saw the Burgess and Sons crew out here when I drove by earlier,' he said slowly. 'Didn't you fix it up to have it done?'

I shook my head.

'Damn, they did it by mistake?.' Quick to rage, Jason flushed. 'I'll call that Randy Burgess and ream his ass. Don't you pay the bill! Here's the note that was stuck to the front door.' Jason pulled a rolled receipt from his front pocket. 'Sorry, I was going to hand that to you before I noticed your face.'

I unrolled the yellow sheet and read the note scribbled across it. 'Sookie – Mr. Northman said not to knock on your door, so I'm sticking this to it. You may need this in case something is wrong. Just call us. Randy.'

'It's paid for,' I said, and Jason calmed a little.

'The boyfriend? The ex?'

I remembered screaming at Eric about my driveway. 'No,' I said. 'Someone else.' I caught myself wishing the man who'd been so thoughtful had been Bill.

'You sure are getting around these days,' Jason said. He didn't sound as judgmental as I expected, but then Jason was shrewd enough to know he could hardly throw many stones.

I said flatly, 'No, I'm not.'

He eyed me for a long moment. I met his gaze. 'Okay,' he said slowly. 'Then someone owes you, big time.'

'That would be closer to the truth,' I said, and wondered in turn if I myself was being truthful. 'Thanks for getting my mail for me, Big Bro. I need to crawl back in bed.'

'No problem. You want to go to the doctor?'

I shook my head. I couldn't face the waiting room.

'Then you let me know if you need me to get you some groceries.'

'Thanks,' I said again, with more pleasure. 'You're a good brother.' To our mutual surprise, I stood on tiptoe and gave him a kiss on the cheek. He awkwardly put his arm around me, and I made myself keep the smile on my face, rather than wincing from the pain.

'Get back in bed, Sis,' he said, shutting the door behind him carefully. I noticed he stood on the porch for a full minute, surveying all that premium gravel. Then he shook his head and got back into his pickup, always clean and gleaming, the pink and aqua flames startling against the black paint that covered the rest of the truck.

I watched a little television. I tried to eat, but my face hurt too much. I felt lucky when I discovered some yogurt in the refrigerator.

A big pickup pulled up to the front of the house about three o'clock. Alcide got out with my suitcase. He knocked softly.

He might be happier if I didn't answer, but I figured I wasn't in the business of making Alcide Herveaux happy, and I opened the door.

'Oh, Jesus Christ,' he said, not irreverently, as he took me in.

'Come in,' I said, through jaws that were getting so sore I could barely part them. I knew I'd said I'll call Jason if Alcide came by; but Alcide and I needed to talk.

He came in and stood looking at me. Finally, he put the suitcase back in my room, fixed me a big glass of iced tea with a straw in it, and put it on the table by the couch. My eyes filled with tears. Not everyone would have realized that a hot drink made my swollen face hurt.

'Tell me what happened, chere,' he said, sitting on the couch beside me. 'Here, put your feet up while you do.' He helped me swivel sideways and lay my legs over his lap. I had plenty of pillows propped behind me, and I did feel comfortable, or as comfortable as I was going to feel for a couple of days.

I told him everything.

'So, you think they'll come after me in Shreveport?' he asked. He didn't seem to be blaming me for bringing all this on his head, which frankly I'd half expected.

I shook my head helplessly. 'I just don't know. I wish we knew what had really happened. That might get them off our backs.'

'Weres are nothing if not loyal,' Alcide said.

I took his hand. 'I know that.'

Alcide's green eyes regarded me steadily.

'Debbie asked me to kill you,' he said.

For a moment I felt cold down to my bones. 'What did you tell her back?' I asked, through stiff lips.

'I told her she could go fuck herself, excuse my language.'

'And how do you feel now?'

'Numb. Isn't that stupid? I'm pulling her out of me by the roots, though. I told you I would. I had to do it. It's like being addicted to crack. She's awful.'

I thought of Lorena. 'Sometimes,' I said, and even to my own ears I sounded sad, 'the bitch wins.' Lorena was far from dead between Bill and me. Speaking of Debbie raised yet another unpleasant memory. 'Hey, you told her we had been to bed together, when you two were fighting!'

He looked profoundly embarrassed, his olive skin flushing. 'I'm ashamed of that. I knew she'd been having a good time with her fiancé; she bragged about it. I sort of used your name in vain when I was really mad. I apologize.'

I could understand that, even though I didn't like it. I raised my eyebrows to indicate that wasn't quite enough.

'Okay, that was really low. A double apology and a promise to never do it again.'

I nodded. I would accept that.

'I hated to hustle you all out of the apartment like that, but I didn't want her to see the three of you, in view of conclusions she might have drawn. Debbie can get really mad, and I thought if she saw you in conjunction with the vampires, she might hear a rumor that Russell was missing a prisoner and put two and two together. She might even be mad enough to call Russell.'

'So much for loyalty among Weres.'

'She's a shifter, not a Were,' Alcide said instantly, and a suspicion of mine was confirmed. I was beginning to believe that Alcide, despite his stated conviction that he was determined to kept the Were gene to himself, would never be happy with anyone but another Were. I sighed: I tried to keep it a nice, quiet sigh. I might be wrong, after all.

'Debbie aside,' I said, waving my hand to show how completely Debbie was out of our conversational picture, '*someone* killed Jerry Falcon and put him in your closet. That's caused me – and you – a lot more trouble that the original mission, which was searching for Bill. Who would do something like that? It would have to be someone really malicious.'

'Or someone really stupid,' Alcide said fairly.

'I know Bill didn't do it, because he was a prisoner. And I'd swear Eric was telling the truth when he said he didn't do it.' I hesitated, hating to bring a name back up. 'But what about Debbie? She's . . .' I stopped myself from saying 'a real bitch,' because only Alcide should call her that. 'She was angry with you for having a date,' I said mildly. 'Maybe she would put Jerry Falcon in your closet to cause you trouble?'

'Debbie's mean and she can cause trouble, but she's never killed anyone,' Alcide said. 'She doesn't have the, the . . . grit for it, the sand. The will to kill.'

Okay. Just call me Sandy.

Alcide must have read my dismay on my face. 'Hey, I'm a Were,' he said, shrugging. 'I'd do it if I had to. Especially at the right time of the moon.'

'So maybe a fellow pack member did him in, for reasons we don't know, and decided to lay the blame on you?' Another possible scenario.

'That doesn't feel right. Another Were would have – well, the body would've looked different.' Alcide said, trying to spare my finer feelings. He meant the body would have been ripped to shreds. 'And I think I would've smelled another Were on him. Not that I got that close.'

We just didn't have any other ideas, though if I'd tape-recorded that conversation and played it back, I would have thought of another possible culprit easily enough.

Alcide said he had to get back to Shreveport, and I lifted my legs for him to rise. He got up, but went down on one knee by the head of the couch to tell me goodbye. I said the polite things, how nice it had been of him to give me a place to stay, how much I'd enjoyed meeting his sister, how much fun it had been to hide a body with him. No, I didn't really say that, but it crossed my mind, as I was being Gran's courteous product.

'I'm glad I met you,' he said. He was closer to me than I'd thought, and he gave me a peck on the lips in farewell. But after the peck, which was okay, he returned for a longer good-bye. His lips felt so warm; and after a second, his tongue felt even warmer. His head turned slightly to get a better angle, and then he went at it again. His right hand hovered above me, trying to find a place to settle that wouldn't hurt me. Finally he covered my left hand with his. Oh boy, this was good. But only my mouth and my lower pelvis were happy. The rest of me hurt. His hand slid, in a questioning sort of way, up to my breast, and I gave a sharp gasp.

'Oh, God, I hurt you!' he said. His lips looked very full

and red after the long kiss, and his eyes were brilliant.

I felt obliged to apologize. 'I'm just so sore,' I said.

'What did they do to you?' he asked. 'Not just a few slaps across the face?'

He had imagined my swollen face was my most serious problem.

'I wish that had been it,' I said, trying to smile.

He truly looked stricken. 'And here I am, making a pass at you.'

'Well, I didn't push you away,' I said mildly. (I was too sore to push.) 'And I didn't say, "No, sir, how dare you force your attentions on me!"'

Alcide looked somewhat startled. 'I'll come back by soon,' he promised. 'If you need anything, you call me.' He fished a card out of his pocket and laid it on the table by the couch. 'This has got my work number on it, and I'm writing my cell number on the back, and my home number. Give me yours.' Obediently, I recited the numbers to him, and he wrote them down in, no kidding, a little black book. I didn't have the energy to make a joke.

When he was gone, the house felt extra empty. He was so big and so energetic – so alive – he filled large spaces with his personality and presence.

It was a day for me to sigh.

Having talked to Jason at Merlotte's, Arlene came by at half past five. She surveyed me, looked as if she were suppressing a lot of comments she really wanted to make, and heated me up some Campbell's. I let it cool before I ate it very carefully and slowly, and felt the better for it. She put the dishes in the dishwasher, and asked me if I needed any other help. I thought of her children waiting for her at home, and I said I was just fine. It did me good to see

Arlene, and to know she was struggling with herself about speaking out of turn made me feel even better.

Physically, I was feeling more and more stiff. I made myself get up and walk a little (though it looked more like a hobble), but as my bruises became fully developed and the house grew colder, I began to feel much worse. This was when living alone really got to you, when you felt bad or sick and there was no one there.

You might feel a little sorry for yourself, too, if you weren't careful.

To my surprise, the first vampire to arrive after dark was Pam. Tonight she was wearing a trailing black gown, so she was scheduled to work at Fangtasia. Ordinarily, Pam shunned black; she was a pastels kind of female. She yanked at the chiffon sleeves impatiently.

'Eric says you may need a female to help you,' she said impatiently. 'Though why I am supposed to be your lady's maid, I don't know. Do you really need help, or is he just trying to curry favor with you? I like you well enough, but after all, I am vampire, and you are human.'

That Pam, what a sweetie.

'You could sit and visit with me for a minute,' I suggested, at a loss as to how to proceed. Actually, it would be nice to have help getting into and out of the bathtub, but I knew Pam would be offended to be asked to perform such a personal task. After all, she was vampire, I was human. . . .

Pam settled into the armchair facing the couch. 'Eric says you can fire a shotgun,' she said, more conversationally. 'Would you teach me?'

'I'd be real glad to, when I'm better.'

'Did you really stake Lorena?'

The shotgun lessons were more important than the death of Lorena, it seemed.

'Yes. She would've killed me.'

'How'd you do it?'

'I had the stake that had been used on me.'

Then Pam had to hear about that, and ask me how it felt, since I was the only person she knew who'd survived being staked, and then she asked me exactly how I'd killed Lorena, and there we were, back at my least favorite topic.

'I don't want to talk about it,' I admitted.

'Why not?' Pam was curious. 'You say she was trying to kill you.'

'She was.'

'And after she had done that, she would have tortured Bill more, until he broke, and you would have been dead, and it all would have been for nothing.'

Pam had a point, a good one, and I tried to think about it as a practical step to have taken, rather than a desperate reflex.

'Bill and Eric will be here soon,' Pam said, looking at her watch.

'I wish you had told me that earlier,' I said, struggling to my feet.

'Got to brush your teeth and hair?' Pam was cheerfully sarcastic. 'That's why Eric thought you might need my help.'

'I think I can manage my own grooming, if you wouldn't mind heating up some blood in the microwave – of course, for yourself as well. I'm sorry, I wasn't being polite.'

Pam gave me a skeptical look, but trotted off to the kitchen without further comment. I listened for a minute to make sure she knew how to operate a microwave, and I heard reassuringly unhesitating beeps as she punched in the numbers and hit Start.

Slowly and painfully, I washed off in the sink, brushed my hair and teeth, and put on some silky pink pajamas and a matching robe and slippers. I wished I had the energy to dress, but I just couldn't face underwear and socks and shoes.

There was no point putting on makeup over the bruises. There was no way I could cover them. In fact, I wondered why I'd gotten up from the couch to put myself through this much pain. I looked in the mirror and told myself I was an idiot to make any preparation for their arrival. I was just plain primping. Given my overall misery (mental and physical), my behavior was ridiculous. I was sorry I had felt the impulse, and even sorrier Pam had witnessed it.

But the first male caller I had was Bubba.

He was all decked out. The vampires of Jackson had enjoyed Bubba's company, it was apparent. Bubba was wearing a red jumpsuit with rhinestones on it (I wasn't too surprised one of the boy toys at the mansion had had one) complete with wide belt and half boots. Bubba looked good.

He didn't seem pleased, though. He seemed apologetic. 'Miss Sookie, I'm sorry I lost you last night,' he said right away. He brushed past Pam, who looked surprised. 'I see something awful happened to you last night, and I wasn't there to stop it like Eric told me to be. I was having a good time in Jackson, those guys there really know how to throw themselves a party.'

I had an idea, a blindingly simple idea. If I'd been in a comic strip, it would have shown itself as a lightning bolt over my head. 'You've been watching me every night,' I said, as gently as I could, trying hard to keep all excitement out of my voice. 'Right?'

'Yes'm, ever since Mr. Eric told me to.' He was standing straighter, his head full of carefully combed hair gelled into the familiar style. The guys at Russell's mansion had really worked hard on him.

'So you were out there the night we came back from the club? The first night?'

'You bet, Miss Sookie.'

'Did you see anyone else outside the apartment?'

'I sure did.' He looked proud.

Oh, boy. 'Was this a guy in gang leathers?'

He looked surprised. 'Yes'm, it was that guy hurt you in the bar. I seen him when the doorman threw him out back. Some of his buddies came around back there, and they were talking about what had happened. So I knew he'd offended you. Mr. Eric said not to come up to you or him in public, so I didn't. But I followed you back to the apartment, in that truck. Bet you didn't even know I was in the back.'

'No, I sure didn't know you were in the back of the pickup. That was real smart. Now tell me, when you saw the Were later, what was he doing?'

'He had picked the lock on the apartment door by the time I snuck up behind him. I just barely caught that sucker in time.'

'What did you do with him?' I smiled at Bubba.

'I broke his neck and stuffed him in the closet,' Bubba said proudly. 'I didn't have time to take the body anywhere, and I figured you and Mr. Eric could figure out what to do about it.'

I had to look away. So simple. So direct. Solving that

mystery had just taken asking the right person the right question.

Why hadn't we thought of it? You couldn't give Bubba orders and expect him to adapt them to circumstances. Quite possibly, he had saved my life by killing Jerry Falcon, since my bedroom was the first one the Were would have come to. I had been so tired when I finally got to bed, I might not have woken until it was too late.

Pam had been looking back and forth between us with a question on her face. I held up a hand to indicate I'd explain later, and I made myself smile at Bubba and tell him he'd done the right thing. 'Eric will be so pleased,' I said. And telling Alcide would be an interesting experience.

Bubba's whole face relaxed. He smiled, that upper lip curling just a little. 'I'm glad to hear you say so,' he said. 'You got any blood? I'm mighty thirsty.'

'Sure,' I said. Pam was thoughtful enough to fetch the blood, and Bubba took a big swig.

'Not as good as a cat's,' he observed. 'But mighty fine just the same. Thank you, thank you very much.'

Chapter 15

What a cozy evening it was turning out to be – yours truly and four vampires, after Bill and Eric arrived separately but almost simultaneously. Just me and my buds, hanging at the house.

Bill insisted on braiding my hair for me, just so he could show his familiarity with my house and habits by going in the bathroom and getting my box of hair doo-dads. Then he put me on the ottoman in front of him as he sat behind me to brush and fix my hair. I have always found this a very soothing process, and it aroused memories of another evening Bill and I had begun just about the same way, with a fabulous finale. Of course, Bill was well aware he was pushing those memories to the fore.

Eric observed this with the air of one taking notes, and Pam sneered openly. I could not for the life of me understand why they all had to be here at the same time, and why they all didn't get sick of one another – and me – and go away. After a few minutes of having a comparative crowd in my house, I longed to be alone once more. Why had I thought I was lonely?

Bubba left fairly quickly, anxious to do some hunting. I didn't want to think too closely about that. When he'd left, I was able to tell the other vampires about what had really happened to Jerry Falcon.

Eric didn't seem too upset that his directions to Bubba had caused the death of Jerry Falcon, and I'd already admitted to myself that I couldn't be too wrought up about it, either. If it came down to him, or me, well, I liked me better. Bill was indifferent to Jerry's fate, and Pam thought the whole thing was funny.

'That he followed you to Jackson, when his instructions were just for here, for one night . . . that he kept following his instructions, no matter what! It's not very vampiric, but he's certainly a good soldier.'

'It would have been much better if he'd told Sookie what he'd done and why he'd done it,' Eric observed.

'Yes, a note would have been nice,' I said sarcastically. 'Anything would have been better than opening that closet and finding the body stuffed in there.'

Pam hooted with laughter. I'd really found the way to tickle her funny bone. Wonderful.

'I can just see your face,' she said. 'You and the Were had to hide the body? That's priceless.'

'I wish I'd known all this when Alcide was here today,' I said. I'd closed my eyes when the full effect of the hair brushing had soothed me. But the sudden silence was delightful. At last, I was getting to amuse my own self a little bit.

Eric said, 'Alcide Herveaux came here?'

'Yeah, he brought my bag. He stayed to help me out, seeing as how I'm banged up.'

When I opened my eyes, because Bill had quit brushing,

I caught Pam's eyes. She winked at me. I gave her a tiny smile.

'I unpacked your bag for you, Sookie,' Pam said smoothly. 'Where did you get that beautiful velvet shawl-thing?'

I pressed my lips together firmly. 'Well, my first evening wrap got ruined at Club – I mean, at Josephine's. Alcide very kindly went shopping and bought it to surprise me . . . he said he felt responsible for the first one getting burned.' I was delighted I'd carried it up to the apartment from its place on the front seat of the Lincoln. I didn't remember doing that.

'He has excellent taste, for a Were,' Pam conceded. 'If I borrow your red dress, can I borrow the shawl, too?'

I hadn't known Pam and I were on clothes-swapping terms. She was definitely up to mischief. 'Sure,' I said.

Shortly after that, Pam said she was leaving. 'I think I'll run home through the woods,' she said. 'I feel like experiencing the night.'

'You'll run all the way back to Shreveport?' I said, astonished.

'It won't be the first time,' she said. 'Oh, by the way, Bill, the queen called Fangtasia this evening to find out why you are late with her little job. She had been unable to reach you at your home for several nights, she said.'

Bill resumed brushing my hair. 'I will call her back later,' he said. 'From my place. She'll be glad to hear that I've completed it.'

'You nearly lost everything,' Eric said, his sudden outburst startling everyone in the room.

Pam slipped out the front door after she'd looked from Eric to Bill. That kind of scared me.

'Yes, I'm well aware of that,' Bill said. His voice, always cool and sweet, was absolutely frigid. Eric, on the other hand, tended toward the fiery.

'You were a fool to take up with that she-demon again,' Eric said.

'Hey, guys, I'm sitting right here,' I said.

They both glared at me. They seemed determined to finish this quarrel, and I figured I would leave them to go at it. Once they were outside. I hadn't thanked Eric for the driveway yet, and I wanted to, but tonight was maybe not the time.

'Okay,' I said. 'I'd hoped to avoid this, but . . . Bill, I rescind your invitation into my house.' Bill began walking backward to the door, a helpless look on his face, and my brush still in his hand. Eric grinned at him triumphantly. 'Eric,' I said, and his smile faded. 'I rescind your invitation into my house.' And backward he went, out my door and off my porch. The door slammed shut behind (or maybe in front of?) them.

I sat on the ottoman, feeling relief beyond words at the sudden silence. And all of a sudden, I realized that the computer program so desired by the queen of Louisiana, the computer program that had cost lives and the ruin of my relationship with Bill, was in my house . . . which not Eric, or Bill, or even the queen, could enter without my say-so.

I hadn't laughed so hard in weeks.

DEAD AS A DOORNAIL

Also by Charlaine Harris

SOOKIE STACKHOUSE

Dead Until Dark
Living Dead in Dallas
Club Dead
Dead to the World
Dead as a Doornail
Definitely Dead
All Together Dead
From Dead to Worse
Dead and Gone

HARPER CONNELLY

Grave Sight
Grave Surprise
An Ice Cold Grave
Grave Secret

DEAD AS A DOORNAIL

CHARLAINE HARRIS

First published in Great Britain in 2007 by
Gollancz
An imprint of the Orion Publishing Group
Orion House, 5 Upper St Martin's Lane, London WC2H 9EA
An Hachette UK Company

This edition published in Great Britain in 2009 by
Gollancz

7 9 10 8 6

A CIP catalogue record for this book
is available from the British Library

ISBN 978 0 575 09105 4

Printed and bound in the UK by
CPI Mackays, Chatham ME5 8TD

The Orion Publishing Group's policy is to use papers that are natural, renewable and recyclable products and made from wood grown in sustainable forests. The logging and manufacturing processes are expected to conform to the environmental regulations of the country of origin.

www.orionbooks.co.uk

This book is dedicated to a wonderful woman I don't get to see often enough. Janet Hutchings (then an editor at Walker, now editor of *Ellery Queen Mystery Magazine*) was brave enough to take me on many years ago after I'd taken a long sabbatical from writing. God bless her.

ACKNOWLEDGMENTS

I didn't thank Patrick Schulz for loaning me his Benelli for the last book—sorry, Son. My friend Toni L. P. Kelner, who pointed out some problems in the first half of the book, is due a big hats-off. My friend Paula Woldan gave me moral support and some information on pirates, and was willing to endure me on Talk Like a Pirate Day. Her daughter Jennifer saved my life by helping me prepare the manuscript. Shay, a Faithful Reader, had the great idea for the calendar. And in thanking the Woldan family, I have to include Jay, a volunteer firefighter for many years, who shared his knowledge and expertise with me.

1

I KNEW MY BROTHER WOULD TURN INTO A PANTHER before he did. As I drove to the remote crossroads community of Hotshot, my brother watched the sunset in silence. Jason was dressed in old clothes, and he had a plastic Wal-Mart bag containing a few things he might need—toothbrush, clean underwear. He hunched inside his bulky camo jacket, looking straight ahead. His face was tense with the need to control his fear and his excitement.

"You got your cell phone in your pocket?" I asked, knowing I'd already asked him as soon as the words left my mouth. But Jason just nodded instead of snapping at me. It was still afternoon, but at the end of January the dark comes early.

Tonight would be the first full moon of the New Year.

When I stopped the car, Jason turned to look at me, and even in the dim light I saw the change in his eyes. They weren't blue like mine anymore. They were yellowish. The shape of them had changed.

"My face feels funny," he said. But he still hadn't put two and two together.

Tiny Hotshot was silent and still in the waning light. A cold wind was blowing across the bare fields, and the pines and oaks were shivering in the gusts of frigid air. Only one man was visible. He was standing outside one of the little houses, the one that was freshly painted. This man's eyes were closed, and his bearded face was raised to the darkening sky. Calvin Norris waited until Jason was climbing out the passenger's door of my old Nova before he walked over and bent to my window. I rolled it down.

His golden-green eyes were as startling as I'd remembered, and the rest of him was just as unremarkable. Stocky, graying, sturdy, he looked like a hundred other men I'd seen in Merlotte's Bar, except for those eyes.

"I'll take good care of him," Calvin Norris said. Behind him, Jason stood with his back to me. The air around my brother had a peculiar quality; it seemed to be vibrating.

None of this was Calvin Norris's fault. He hadn't been the one who'd bitten my brother and changed him forever. Calvin, a werepanther, had been born what he was; it was his nature. I made myself say, "Thank you."

"I'll bring him home in the morning."

"To my house, please. His truck is at my place."

"All right, then. Have a good night." He raised his face to the wind again, and I felt the whole community was waiting, behind their windows and doors, for me to leave.

So I did.

Jason knocked on my door at seven the next morning. He still had his little Wal-Mart bag, but he hadn't used anything in it. His face was bruised, and his hands were covered with scratches. He didn't say a word. He just stared at me when I asked him how he was, and walked past me through the living room and down the hall. He closed the door to the hall bathroom with a decisive click. I heard the water running after a second, and I heaved a weary sigh all to myself. Though I'd gone to work and come home tired at about two a.m., I hadn't gotten much sleep.

By the time Jason emerged, I'd fixed him some bacon and eggs. He sat down at the old kitchen table with an air of pleasure: a man doing a familiar and pleasant thing. But after a second of staring down at the plate, he leaped to his feet and ran back into the bathroom, kicking the door shut behind him. I listened to him throw up, over and over.

I stood outside the door helplessly, knowing he wouldn't want me to come in. After a moment, I went back to the kitchen to dump the food into the trash can, ashamed of the waste but utterly unable to force myself to eat.

When Jason returned, he said only, "Coffee?" He looked green around the gills, and he walked like he was sore.

"Are you okay?" I asked, not sure if he would be able to answer or not. I poured the coffee into a mug.

"Yes," he said after a moment, as though he'd had to think about it. "That was the most incredible experience of my life."

For a second, I thought he meant throwing up in my bathroom, but that was sure no new experience for Jason. He'd been quite a drinker in his teens, until he'd figured out that there was nothing glamorous or attractive about hanging over a toilet bowl, heaving your guts out.

"Shifting," I said tentatively.

He nodded, cradling his coffee mug in his hands. He held his face over the steam rising from the hot, strong blackness. He met my eyes. His own were once again their ordinary blue. "It's the most incredible rush," he said. "Since I was bitten, not born, I don't get to be a true panther like the others."

I could hear envy in his voice.

"But even what I become is amazing. You feel the magic inside you, and you feel your bones moving around and adapting, and your vision changes. Then you're lower to the ground and you walk in a whole different way, and as for running, damn, you can *run*. You can chase. . . ." And his voice died away.

I would just as soon not know that part, anyway.

"So it's not so bad?" I asked, my hands clasped together. Jason was all the family I had, except for a cousin who'd drifted away into the underworld of drugs years before.

"It's not so bad," Jason agreed, scraping up a smile to give me. "It's great while you're actually the animal. Everything's so simple. It's when you're back to being human that you start to worry about stuff."

He wasn't suicidal. He wasn't even despondent. I wasn't aware I'd been holding my breath until I let it out. Jason was going to be able to live with the hand he'd been dealt. He was going to be okay.

The relief was incredible, like I'd removed something jammed painfully between my teeth or shaken a sharp rock out of my shoe. For days, weeks even, I'd been worried, and now that anxiety was gone. That didn't mean Jason's life as a shape-shifter would be worry-free, at least from my point of view. If he married a regular human woman, their kids would be normal. But if he married into the shifter community at Hotshot, I'd have nieces or nephews who turned into animals once a month. At least, they would after puberty; that would give them, and their auntie Sook, some preparation time.

Luckily for Jason, he had plenty of vacation days, so he wasn't due at the parish road department. But I had to work tonight. As soon as Jason left in his flashy pickup truck, I crawled back into bed, jeans and all, and in about five minutes I was fast asleep. The relief acted as a kind of sedative.

When I woke up, it was nearly three o'clock and time for me to get ready for my shift at Merlotte's. The sun outside was bright and clear, and the temperature was fifty-two, said my indoor-outdoor thermometer. This isn't too unusual in north Louisiana in January. The temperature would drop after the sun went down, and Jason would shift. But he'd have some fur—not a full coat, since he turned into half-man, half-cat—and he'd be with other panthers. They'd go hunting. The woods around Hotshot, which lay in a remote corner of Renard Parish, would be dangerous again tonight.

As I went about eating, showering, folding laundry, I thought of a dozen things I'd like to know. I wondered if the shifters would kill a human being if they came upon one in the woods. I wondered how much of their human consciousness they retained in their animal form. If they mated in panther form, would they have a kitten or a baby? What happened when a pregnant werepanther saw the full moon? I wondered if Jason knew the answer to all these questions yet, if Calvin had given him some kind of briefing.

But I was glad I hadn't questioned Jason this morning while everything was still so new to him. I'd have plenty of chances to ask him later.

For the first time since New Year's Day, I was thinking about the future. The full moon symbol on my calendar no longer seemed to be a period marking the end of something, but just another way of counting time. As I pulled on my waitress outfit (black pants and a white boat-neck T-shirt and black Reeboks), I felt almost giddy with cheer. For once, I left my hair down instead of pulling it back and up into a ponytail. I put in some bright red dot earrings and matched my lipstick to the color. A little eye makeup and some blush, and I was good to go.

I'd parked at the rear of the house last night, and I checked the back porch carefully to make sure there weren't any lurking vampires before I shut and locked the back door behind me. I'd been surprised before, and it wasn't a pleasant feeling. Though it was barely dark, there might be some early risers around. Probably the last thing the Japanese had expected when they'd developed synthetic blood was that its availability would bring vampires out of the realm of legend and into the light of fact. The Japanese had just been trying to make a few bucks hawking the blood substitute to ambulance companies and hospital emergency rooms. Instead, the way we looked at the world had changed forever.

Speaking of vampires (if only to myself), I wondered if Bill Compton was home. Vampire Bill had been my first love, and he lived right across the cemetery from me. Our houses lay on a parish road outside the little town of Bon Temps and south of the bar where I worked. Lately, Bill had been traveling a lot. I only found out he was home if he happened to come into Merlotte's, which he did every now and then to mix with the natives and have some warm O-positive. He preferred TrueBlood, the most expensive Japanese synthetic. He'd told me it almost completely satisfied his cravings for blood fresh from the source. Since I'd witnessed Bill going into a bloodlust fit, I could only thank God for TrueBlood. Sometimes I missed Bill an awful lot.

I gave myself a mental shake. Snapping out of a slump, that was what today was all about. No more worry! No more fear! Free and twenty-six! Working! House paid for! Money in the bank! These were all good, positive things.

The parking lot was full when I got to the bar. I could see I'd be busy tonight. I drove around back to the employees' entrance. Sam Merlotte, the owner and my boss, lived back there in a very nice double-wide that even had a little yard surrounded by a hedge, Sam's equivalent of a white picket fence. I locked my car and went in the employees' back door, which opened into the hallway off of which lay the men's and the ladies', a large stock room, and Sam's office. I stowed my purse and coat in an empty desk drawer, pulled up my red socks, shook my head to make my hair hang right, and went through the doorway (this door was almost always propped open) that led to the big room of the bar/restaurant. Not that the kitchen produced anything but the most basic stuff: hamburgers, chicken strips, fries and onion rings, salads in the summer and chili in the winter.

Sam was the bartender, the bouncer, and on occasion the cook, but lately we'd been lucky in getting our positions filled: Sam's seasonal allergies had hit hard, making him less than ideal as a food handler. The new cook had shown up in answer to Sam's ad just the week before. Cooks didn't seem to stay long at Merlotte's, but I was hoping that Sweetie Des Arts would stick around a while. She showed up on time, did her job well, and never gave the rest of the staff any trouble. Really, that was all you could ask for. Our last cook, a guy, had given my friend Arlene a big rush of hope that he was The One—in this case, he'd have been her fourth or fifth One—before he'd decamped overnight with her plates and forks and a CD player. Her kids had been devastated; not because they'd loved the guy, but because they missed their CD player.

I walked into a wall of noise and cigarette smoke that made it seem like I was passing into another universe. Smokers all sit on the west side of the room, but the smoke doesn't seem to know it should stay there. I put a smile on my face and stepped behind the bar to give Sam a pat on the arm. After he expertly filled a glass with beer and slid it to a patron, he put another glass under the tap and began the process all over again.

"How are things?" Sam asked carefully. He knew all about Jason's problems, since he'd been with me the night I'd found Jason being held prisoner in a toolshed in Hotshot. But we had to be roundabout in our speech; vampires had gone public, but shape-shifters and Weres were still cloaked in secrecy. The underground world of supernatural beings was waiting to see how vampires fared before they followed the vampire example by going public.

"Better than I expected." I smiled up at him, though not too far up, since Sam's not a big man. He's built lean, but he's much stronger than he looks. Sam is in his thirties—at least, I think he is—and he has reddish gold hair that halos his head. He's a good man, and a great boss. He's also a shape-shifter, so he can change into any animal. Most often, Sam turns into a very cute collie with a gorgeous coat. Sometimes he comes over to my place and I let him sleep on the rug in the living room. "He's gonna be fine."

"I'm glad," he said. I can't read shifter minds as easily as I read human minds, but I can tell if a mood is true or not. Sam was happy because I was happy.

"When are you taking off?" I asked. He had that faraway look in his eyes, the look that said he was mentally running through the woods, tracking possums.

"As soon as Terry gets here." He smiled at me again, but this time the smile was a bit strained. Sam was getting antsy.

The door to the kitchen was just outside the bar area at the west end, and I stuck my head in the door to say hi to Sweetie. Sweetie was bony and brunette and fortyish, and she wore a lot of makeup for someone who was going to be out of sight in the kitchen all evening. She also seemed a little sharper, perhaps better educated, than any of Merlotte's previous short-order cooks.

"You doing okay, Sookie?" she called, flipping a hamburger as she spoke. Sweetie was in constant motion in the kitchen, and she didn't like anyone getting in her way. The teenager who assisted her and bussed tables was terrified of Sweetie, and he took care to dodge her as she moved from griddle to fryer. This teenage boy got the plates ready, made the salads, and went to the window to tell the barmaids which order was up. Out on the floor, Holly Cleary and her best friend, Danielle, were working hard. They'd both looked relieved when they'd seen me come in. Danielle worked the smoking section to the west, Holly usually worked the middle area in front of the bar, and I worked the east when three of us were on duty.

"It looks like I better get moving," I told Sweetie.

She gave me a quick smile and turned back to the griddle. The cowed teenager, whose name I had yet to catch, gave me a ducked-head nod and went back to loading the dishwasher.

I wished Sam had called me before things had gotten so busy; I wouldn't have minded coming in a little earlier. Of course, he wasn't exactly himself tonight. I began checking the tables in my section, getting fresh drinks and clearing off food baskets, collecting money and bringing change.

"Barmaid! Bring me a Red Stuff!" The voice was unfamiliar, and the order was unusual. Red Stuff was the cheapest artificial blood, and only the newest vampires would be caught dead asking for it. I got a bottle from the clear-fronted refrigerator and stuck it in the microwave. While it warmed, I scanned the crowd for the vamp. He was sitting with my friend Tara Thornton. I'd never seen him before, which was worrisome. Tara'd been dating an older vampire (much older: Franklin Mott had been older than Tara in human years before he died, and he'd been a vampire for over three hundred years), and he'd been giving her lavish gifts—like a Camaro. What was she doing with this new guy? At least Franklin had nice manners.

I put the warm bottle on a tray and carried it over to the couple. The lighting in Merlotte's at night isn't particularly bright, which is how patrons like it, and it wasn't until I'd gotten quite near that I could appreciate Tara's companion. He was slim and narrow shouldered with slicked-back hair. He had long fingernails and a sharp face. I supposed that, in a way, he was attractive—if you like a liberal dose of danger with your sex.

I put the bottle down in front of him and glanced uncertainly at Tara. She looked great, as usual. Tara is tall, slim, and dark haired, and she has a wardrobe of wonderful clothes. She'd overcome a truly horrible childhood to own her own business and actually join the chamber of commerce. Then she started dating the wealthy vampire, Franklin Mott, and she quit sharing her life with me.

"Sookie," she said, "I want you to meet Franklin's friend Mickey." She didn't sound like she wanted us to meet. She sounded like she wished I'd never come over with Mickey's drink. Her own glass was almost empty, but she said, "No," when I asked her if she was ready for another.

I exchanged a nod with the vampire; they don't shake hands, not normally. He was watching me as he took a gulp from the bottled blood, his eyes as cold and hostile as a snake's. If he was a friend of the ultra-urbane Franklin, I was a silk purse. Hired hand, more like. Maybe a bodyguard? Why would Franklin give Tara a bodyguard?

She obviously wasn't going to talk openly in front of this slimeball, so I said, "Catch you later," and took Mickey's money to the till.

I was busy all night, but in the spare moments I had, I thought about my brother. For a second night, he was out frolicking under the moon with the other beasties. Sam had taken off like a shot the moment Terry Bellefleur arrived, though his office wastebasket was full of crumpled tissues. His face had been tense with anticipation.

It was one of those nights that made me wonder how the humans around me could be so oblivious to the other world operating right beside ours. Only willful ignorance could ignore the charge of magic in the air. Only a group lack of imagination could account for people not wondering what went on in the dark around them.

But not too long ago, I reminded myself, I'd been as willfully blind as any of the crowd in Merlotte's. Even when the vampires had made their carefully coordinated worldwide announcement that their existence was fact, few authorities or citizens seemed to take the next mental step: *If vampires exist, what else could be lurking just outside the edge of the light?*

Out of curiosity, I began to dip into the brains around me, testing to see their fears. Most of the people in the bar were thinking about Mickey. The women, and some of the men, were wondering what it would be like to be with him. Even stick-in-the-mud lawyer Portia Bellefleur was peeking around her conservative beau to study Mickey. I could only wonder at these speculations. Mickey was terrifying. That negated any physical attraction I might have felt toward him. But I had lots of evidence that the other humans in the bar didn't feel the same way.

I've been able to read minds all my life. The ability is no great gift. Most peoples' minds don't bear reading. Their thoughts are boring, disgusting, disillusioning, but very seldom amusing. At least Bill had helped me learn how to cut out some of the buzz. Before he'd given me some clues, it had been like tuning in to a hundred radio stations simultaneously. Some of them had come in crystal clear, some had been remote, and some, like the thoughts of shape-shifters, had been full of static and obscurity. But they'd all added up to cacophony. No wonder lots of people had treated me as a half-wit.

Vampires were silent. That was the great thing about vamps, at least from my point of view: They were dead. Their minds were dead, too. Only once in a coon's age did I get any kind of flash from a vampire mind.

Shirley Hunter, my brother's boss at his parish roadwork job, asked me where Jason was when I brought a pitcher of beer to his table. Shirley was universally known as "Catfish."

"Your guess is as good as mine," I said mendaciously, and he winked at me. The first guess as to where Jason was always involved a woman, and the second guess usually included another woman. The tableful of men, still in their working clothes, laughed more than the answer warranted, but then they'd had a lot of beer.

I raced back to the bar to get three bourbon-and-Cokes from Terry Bellefleur, Portia's cousin, who was working under pressure. Terry, a Vietnam vet with a lot of physical and emotional scars, appeared to be holding up well on this busy night. He liked simple jobs that required concentration. His graying auburn hair was pulled back in a ponytail and his face was intent as he plied the bottles. The drinks were ready in no time, and Terry smiled at me as I put them on my tray. A smile from Terry was a rare thing, and it warmed me.

Just as I was turning with my tray resting on my right hand, trouble erupted. A Louisiana Tech student from Ruston got into a one-on-one class war with Jeff LaBeff, a redneck who had many children and made a kind of living driving a garbage truck. Maybe it was just a case of two stubborn guys colliding and really didn't have much to do with town vs. gown (not that we were that close to Ruston). Whatever the reason for the original quarrel, it took me a few seconds to realize the fight was going to be more than a shouting match.

In those few seconds, Terry tried to intervene. Moving quickly, he got between Jeff and the student and caught firm hold of both their wrists. I thought for a minute it would work, but Terry wasn't as young or as active as he had been, and all hell broke loose.

"You could stop this," I said furiously to Mickey as I hurried past his and Tara's table on my way to try to make peace.

He sat back in his chair and sipped his drink. "Not my job," he said calmly.

I got that, but it didn't endear the vampire to me, especially when the student whirled and took a swing at me as I approached him from behind. He missed, and I hit him over the head with my tray. He staggered to one side, maybe bleeding a little, and Terry was able to subdue Jeff LaBeff, who was looking for an excuse to quit.

Incidents like this had been happening with more frequency, especially when Sam was gone. It was evident to me that we needed a bouncer, at least on weekend nights . . . and full-moon nights.

The student threatened to sue.

"What's your name?" I asked.

"Mark Duffy," the young man said, clutching his head.

"Mark, where you from?"

"Minden."

I did a quick evaluation of his clothes, his demeanor, and the contents of his head. "I'm gonna enjoy calling your mama and telling her you took a swing at a woman," I said. He blanched and said no more about suing, and he and his buds left soon after. It always helps to know the most effective threat.

We made Jeff leave, too.

Terry resumed his place behind the bar and began dispensing drinks, but he was limping slightly and had a strained look in his face, which worried me. Terry's war experiences hadn't left him real stable. I'd had enough trouble for one night.

But of course the night wasn't over yet.

About an hour after the fight, a woman came into Merlotte's. She was plain and plainly dressed in old jeans and a camo coat. She had on boots that had been wonderful when they'd been new, but that had been a long time ago. She didn't carry a purse, and she had her hands thrust into her pockets.

There were several indicators that made my mental antennae twitch. First of all, this gal didn't look right. A local woman might dress like that if she were going hunting or doing farm work, but not to come to Merlotte's. For an evening out at the bar, most women fixed themselves up. So this woman was in a working mode; but she wasn't a whore by the same reasoning.

That meant drugs.

To protect the bar in Sam's absence, I tuned in to her thoughts. People don't think in complete sentences, of course, and I'm smoothing it out, but what was running through her head was along the order of: *Three vials left getting old losing power gotta sell it tonight so I can get back to Baton Rouge and buy some more. Vampire in the bar if he catches me with vamp blood I'm dead. This town is a dump. Back to the city first chance I get.*

She was a Drainer, or maybe she was just a distributor. Vampire blood was the most intoxicating drug on the market, but of course vamps didn't give it up willingly. Draining a vampire was a hazardous occupation, boosting prices of the tiny vials of blood to amazing sums.

What did the drug user get for parting with a lot of money? Depending on the age of the blood—that is, the time since it'd been removed from its owner—and the age of the vampire from whom the blood had been removed, and the individual chemistry of the drug user, it could be quite a lot. There was the feeling of omnipotence, the increased strength, acute vision, and hearing. And most important of all for Americans, an enhanced physical appearance.

Still, only an idiot would drink black-market vampire blood. For one thing, the results were notoriously unpredictable. Not only did the effects vary, but those effects could last anywhere from two weeks to two months. For another thing, some people simply went mad when the blood hit their system—sometimes homicidally mad. I'd heard of dealers who sold gullible users pig's blood or contaminated human blood. But the most important reason to avoid the black market in vamp blood was this: Vampires hated Drainers, and they hated the users of the drained blood (commonly known as bloodheads). You just don't want a vampire pissed off at you.

There weren't any off-duty police officers in Merlotte's that night. Sam was out wagging his tail somewhere. I hated to tip off Terry, because I didn't know how he'd react. I had to do something about this woman.

Truly, I try not to intervene in events when my only connection comes through my telepathy. If I stuck my oar in every time I learned something that would affect the lives around me (like knowing the parish clerk was embezzling, or that one of the local detectives took bribes), I wouldn't be able to live in Bon Temps, and it was my home. But I couldn't permit this scraggy woman to sell her poison in Sam's bar.

She perched on an empty barstool and ordered a beer

from Terry. His gaze lingered on her. Terry, too, realized something was wrong about the stranger.

I came to pick up my next order and stood by her. She needed a bath, and she'd been in a house heated by a wood fireplace. I made myself touch her, which always improved my reception. Where was the blood? It was in her coat pocket. Good.

Without further ado, I dumped a glass of wine down her front.

"Dammit!" she said, jumping off the stool and patting ineffectually at her chest. "You are the clumsiest-ass woman I ever saw!"

" 'Scuse me," I said abjectly, putting my tray on the bar and meeting Terry's eyes briefly. "Let me put some soda on that." Without waiting for her permission, I pulled her coat down her arms. By the time she understood what I was doing and began to struggle, I had taken charge of the coat. I tossed it over the bar to Terry. "Put some soda on that, please," I said. "Make sure the stuff in her pockets didn't get wet, too." I'd used this ploy before. I was lucky it was cold weather and she'd had the stuff in her coat, not in her jeans pocket. That would have taxed my inventiveness.

Under the coat, the woman was wearing a very old Dallas Cowboys T-shirt. She began shivering, and I wondered if she'd been sampling more conventional drugs. Terry made a show of patting soda on the wine stain. Following my hint, he delved into the pockets. He looked down at his hand with disgust, and I heard a clink as he threw the vials in the trash can behind the bar. He returned everything else to her pockets.

She'd opened her mouth to shriek at Terry when she realized she really couldn't. Terry stared directly at her, daring her to mention the blood. The people around us watched with interest. They knew something was up, but not what, because the whole thing had gone down very quickly. When Terry was sure she wasn't going to start yelling, he handed me the coat. As I held it so she could slide her arms in, Terry told her, "Don't you come back here no more."

If we kept throwing people out at this rate, we wouldn't have many customers.

"You redneck son of a bitch," she said. The crowd around us drew in a collective breath. (Terry was almost as unpredictable as a bloodhead.)

"Doesn't matter to me what you call me," he said. "I guess an insult from you is no insult at all. You just stay away." I expelled a long breath of relief.

She shoved her way through the crowd. Everyone in the room marked her progress toward the door, even Mickey the vampire. In fact, he was doing something with a device in his hands. It looked like one of those cell phones that can take a picture. I wondered to whom he was sending it. I wondered if she'd make it home.

Terry pointedly didn't ask how I'd known the scruffy woman had something illegal in her pockets. That was another weird thing about the people of Bon Temps. The rumors about me had been floating around as long as I could remember, from when I was little and my folks put me through the mental health battery. And yet, despite the evidence at their disposal, almost everyone I knew would much rather regard me as a dim and peculiar young woman than acknowledge my strange ability. Of course, I was careful not to stick it in their faces. And I kept my mouth shut.

Anyway, Terry had his own demons to fight. Terry subsisted on some kind of government pension, and he cleaned Merlotte's early in the morning, along with a couple of other businesses. He stood in for Sam three or four times a month. The rest of his time was his own, and no one seemed to know what he did with it. Dealing with people exhausted Terry, and nights like tonight were simply not good for him.

It was lucky he wasn't in Merlotte's the next night, when all hell broke loose.

2

At first, I thought everything had returned to normal. The bar seemed a little calmer the next night. Sam was back in place, relaxed and cheerful. Nothing seemed to rile him, and when I told him what had happened with the dealer the night before, he complimented me on my finesse.

Tara didn't come in, so I couldn't ask her about Mickey. But was it really any of my business? Probably not my business—but my concern, definitely.

Jeff LaBeff was back and sheepish about getting riled by the college kid the night before. Sam had learned about the incident through a phone call from Terry, and he gave Jeff a word of warning.

Andy Bellefleur, a detective on the Renard parish force and Portia's brother, came in with the young woman he was dating, Halleigh Robinson. Andy was older than me, and I'm twenty-six. Halleigh was twenty-one—just old enough to be in Merlotte's. Halleigh taught at the elementary school, she was right out of college, and she was real attractive, with short earlobe-length brown hair and huge brown eyes and a nicely rounded figure. Andy had been dating Halleigh for about two months, and from the little I saw of the couple, they seemed to be progressing in their relationship at a predictable rate.

Andy's true thoughts were that he liked Halleigh very much (though she was a tad boring), and he was really ready for her to give it up. Halleigh thought Andy was sexy and a real man of the world, and she really loved the newly restored Bellefleur family mansion, but she didn't believe he'd hang around long after she slept with him. I hate knowing more about relationships than the people in them know—but no matter how battened down I am, I pick up a trickle of stuff.

Claudine came in the bar that night, toward closing time. Claudine is six feet tall, with black hair that ripples down her back and bruised-looking white skin that looks thin and glossy like a plum's. Claudine dresses for attention. Tonight she was wearing a terra-cotta pants suit, cut very snug on her Amazonian body. She works in the complaint department of a big store at the mall in Ruston during the day. I wished she'd brought her brother, Claude, with her. He doesn't swing in my direction, but he's a treat for the eyes.

He's a fairy. I mean, literally. So's Claudine, of course.

She waved at me across the heads of the crowd. I waved back smiling. Everyone's happy around Claudine, who is always cheerful when there are no vampires in her vicinity. Claudine is unpredictable and a lot of fun, though like all fairies, she's as dangerous as a tiger when she's angry. Fortunately, that doesn't happen often.

Fairies occupy a special place in the hierarchy of magical

creatures. I haven't figured out exactly what it is yet, but sooner or later I'll piece it together.

Every man in the bar was drooling over Claudine, and she was eating it up. She gave Andy Bellefleur a long, big-eyed look, and Halleigh Robinson glared, mad enough to spit, until she remembered she was a sweet southern girl. But Claudine abandoned all interest in Andy when she saw he was drinking ice tea with lemon. Fairies are even more violently allergic to lemon than vampires are to garlic.

Claudine worked her way over to me, and she gave me a big hug, to the envy of every male in the bar. She took my hand to pull me into Sam's office. I went with her out of sheer curiosity.

"Dear friend," Claudine said, "I have bad news for you."

"What?" I'd gone from bemused to scared in a heartbeat.

"There was a shooting early this morning. One of the werepanthers was hit."

"Oh, no! Jason!" But surely one of his friends would've called if he hadn't gone into work today?

"No, your brother is fine, Sookie. But Calvin Norris was shot."

I was stunned. Jason hadn't called to tell me this? I had to find out from someone else?

"Shot dead?" I asked, hearing my voice shake. Not that Calvin and I were close—far from it—but I was shocked. Heather Kinman, a teenager, had been fatally shot the week before. What was happening in Bon Temps?

"Shot in the chest. He's alive, but he's bad hurt."

"Is he in the hospital?"

"Yes, his nieces took him to Grainger Memorial."

Grainger was a town farther southeast than Hotshot, and a shorter drive from there than the parish hospital in Clarice.

"Who did it?"

"No one knows. Someone shot him early this morning, when Calvin was on his way to work. He'd come home from his, um, time of the month, changed, and started into town for his shift." Calvin worked at Norcross.

"How'd you come to know all this?"

"One of his cousins came into the store to buy some pajamas, since Calvin didn't have any. Guess he sleeps in the buff," Claudette said. "I don't know how they think they're going to get a pajama top on over the bandages. Maybe they just needed the pants? Calvin wouldn't like to be shuffling around the hospital with only one of those nasty gowns between him and the world."

Claudine often took long side trails in her conversation.

"Thanks for telling me," I said. I wondered how the cousin had known Claudine, but I wasn't going to ask.

"That's okay. I knew you'd want to know. Heather Kinman was a shape-shifter, too. Bet you didn't know that. Think about it."

Claudine gave me a kiss on the forehead—fairies are very touchy-feely—and we went back into the bar area. She'd stunned me into silence. Claudine herself was back to business as usual. The fairy ordered a 7-and-7 and was surrounded by suitors in about two minutes flat. She never left with anyone, but the men seemed to enjoy trying. I'd decided that Claudine fed off this admiration and attention.

Even Sam was beaming at her, and she didn't tip.

By the time we were closing the bar, Claudine had left to go back to Monroe, and I'd passed along her news to Sam. He was as appalled by the story as I was. Though Calvin Norris was the leader of the small shifter community of Hotshot, the rest of the world knew him as a steady, quiet bachelor who owned his own home and had a good job as crew foreman at the local lumber mill. It was hard to imagine either of his personas leading to an assassination attempt. Sam decided to send some flowers from the bar's staff.

I pulled on my coat and went out the bar's back door just ahead of Sam. I heard him locking the door behind me. Suddenly I remembered that we were getting low on bottled blood, and I turned to tell Sam this. He caught my movement and stopped, waiting for me to speak, his face expectant. In the length of time it takes to blink, his expression changed from expectant to shocked, dark red began to spread on his left leg, and I heard the sound of a shot.

Then blood was everywhere, Sam crumpled to the ground, and I began to scream.

I'd never had to pay the cover charge at Fangtasia before. The few times I'd come through the public entrance, I'd been with a vampire. But now I was by myself and feeling mighty conspicuous. I was exhausted from an especially long night. I'd been at the hospital until six in the morning, and I'd had only a few hours' fitful sleep after I'd gotten home.

Pam was taking the cover charge and showing the customers to tables. She was wearing the long filmy black outfit she usually wore when she was on door duty. Pam never looked happy when she was dressed like a fictional vampire. She was the real thing and proud of it. Her personal taste leaned more toward slack sets in pastel colors and penny loafers. She looked as surprised as a vampire can look when she saw me.

"Sookie," she said, "do you have an appointment with Eric?" She took my money without a blink.

I was actually happy to see her: pathetic, huh? I don't have a lot of friends, and I value the ones I have, even if I suspect they dream about catching me in a dark alley and having their bloody way with me. "No, but I do need to talk to him. Business," I added hastily. I didn't want anyone thinking I was courting the romantic attention of the undead head honcho of Shreveport, a position called "sheriff" by the vamps. I shrugged off my new cranberry-colored coat and folded it carefully over my arm. WDED, the Baton Rouge–based all-vampire radio station, was being piped over the sound system. The smooth voice of the early night deejay, Connie the Corpse, said, "And here's a song for all you lowlifes who were outside howling earlier this week . . . 'Bad Moon Rising,' an old hit from Creedence Clearwater Revival." Connie the Corpse was giving a private tip of the hat to the shapeshifters.

"Wait at the bar while I tell him you're here," Pam said. "You'll enjoy the new bartender."

Bartenders at Fangtasia didn't tend to last long. Eric and Pam always tried to hire someone colorful—an exotic bartender drew in the human tourists who came by the busloads to take a walk on the wild side—and in this they were successful. But somehow the job had acquired a high attrition rate.

The new man gave me a white-toothed smile when I perched on one of the high stools. He was quite an eyeful. He had a head full of long, intensely curly hair, chestnut brown in color. It clustered thickly on his shoulders. He also sported a mustache and a Vandyke. Covering his left eye was a black eye patch. Since his face was narrow and the features on it sizable, his face was crowded. He was about my height, five foot six, and he was wearing a black poet shirt and black pants and high black boots. All he needed was a bandanna tied around his head and a pistol.

"Maybe a parrot on your shoulder?" I said.

"Aaargh, dear lady, you are not the first to suggest such a thing." He had a wonderful rich baritone voice. "But I understand there are health department regulations against having an uncaged bird in an establishment serving drinks." He bowed to me as deeply as the narrow area behind the bar permitted. "May I get you a drink and have the honor of your name?"

I had to smile. "Certainly, sir. I'm Sookie Stackhouse." He'd caught the whiff of otherness about me. Vampires almost always pick up on it. The undead usually note me; humans don't. It's kind of ironic that my mind reading doesn't work on the very creatures who believe it distinguishes me from the rest of the human race, while humans would rather believe I was mentally ill than credit me with an unusual ability.

The woman on the barstool next to me (credit cards maxed out, son with ADD) half turned to listen in. She was jealous, having been trying to entice the bartender into showing her some attention for the past thirty minutes. She eyed me, trying to figure out what had caused the vamp to choose to open a conversation with me. She wasn't impressed at all with what she saw.

"I am delighted to meet you, fair maiden," the new vampire said smoothly, and I grinned. Well, at least I was fair—in the blond-and-blue-eyed sense. His eyes took me in; of course, if you're a woman who works in a bar, you're used to that. At least he didn't look at me offensively; and believe me, if you're a woman who works in a bar, you can tell the difference between an evaluation and an eye fuck.

"I bet good money she's no maiden," said the woman next to me.

She was right, but that was beside the point.

"You must be polite to other guests," the vampire told her, with an altered version of his smile. Not only were his fangs slightly extended, but I also noticed he had crooked (though beautifully white) teeth. American standards of tooth straightness are very modern.

"No one tells me how to act," the woman said combatively. She was sullen because the evening wasn't going as she'd planned. She'd thought it would be easy to attract a vampire, that any vamp would think he was lucky to have her. She'd planned to let one bite her neck, if he'd just settle her credit card bills.

She was overestimating herself and underestimating vampires.

"I beg your pardon, madam, but while you are in Fangtasia, most definitely I shall tell you how to act," the bartender said.

She subsided after he fixed her with his quelling gaze, and I wondered if he hadn't given her a dose of glamour.

"My name," he said, returning his attention to me, "is Charles Twining."

"Pleased to meet you," I said.

"And the drink?"

"Yes, please. A ginger ale." I had to drive back to Bon Temps after I'd seen Eric.

He raised his arched brows but poured me the drink and placed it on a napkin in front of me. I paid him and deposited a good tip in the jar. The little white napkin had some fangs outlined in black, with a single drop of red falling from the right fang—custom-made napkins for the vampire bar. "Fangtasia" was printed in jazzy red script on the opposite corner of the napkin, duplicating the sign outside. Cute. There were T-shirts for sale in a case over in a corner, too, along with glasses decorated with the same logo. The legend underneath read, "Fangtasia—The Bar with a Bite." Eric's merchandising expertise had made great strides in the past few months.

As I waited my turn for Eric's attention, I watched Charles Twining work. He was polite to everyone, served the drinks swiftly, and never got rattled. I liked his technique much better than that of Chow, the previous bartender, who'd always made patrons feel like he was doing them a favor by bringing them drinks at all. Long Shadow, the bartender before Chow, had had too much of an eye for the female customers. That'll cause a lot of strife in a bar.

Lost in my own thoughts, I didn't realize Charles Twining was right across the bar from me until he said, "Miss Stackhouse, may I tell you how lovely you look tonight?"

"Thank you, Mr. Twining," I said, entering into the spirit of the encounter. The look in Charles Twining's one visible brown eye let me know that he was a first-class rogue, and I didn't trust him any farther than I could throw him, which was maybe two feet. (The effects of my last infusion of vampire blood had worn off, and I was my regular human self. Hey, I'm no junkie; it had been an emergency situation calling for extra strength.)

Not only was I back at average stamina for a fit woman in her twenties, my looks were back to normal; no vampire-blood enhancement. I hadn't dressed up, since I didn't want Eric to think I was dressing up for him, but I hadn't wanted to look like a slob, either. So I was wearing low-riding blue jeans and a fuzzy white long-sleeved sweater with a boatneck. It stopped just at my waist, so some tummy showed when I walked. That tummy wasn't fish-belly white, either, thanks to the tanning bed at the video rental place.

"Please, dear lady, call me Charles," the bartender said, pressing his hand to his heart.

I laughed out loud, despite my weariness. The gesture's theatricality wasn't diminished by the fact that Charles's heart wasn't beating.

"Of course," I said agreeably. "If you'll call me Sookie."

He rolled his eyes up as if the excitement was too much for him, and I laughed again. Pam tapped me on the shoulder.

"If you can tear yourself away from your new buddy, Eric's free."

I nodded to Charles and eased off the stool to follow Pam. To my surprise, she didn't lead me back to Eric's office, but to one of the booths. Evidently, tonight Eric was on bar duty. All the Shreveport-area vampires had to agree to show themselves at Fangtasia for a certain number of hours each week so the tourists would keep coming; a vampire bar without any actual vampires is a money-losing establishment. Eric set a good example for his underlings by sitting out in the bar at regular intervals.

Usually the sheriff of Area Five sat in the center of the room, but tonight he was in the corner booth. He watched me approach. I knew he was taking in my jeans, which were on the tight side, and my tummy, which was on the flat side, and my soft fuzzy white sweater, which was filled with natural bounty. I should have worn my frumpiest clothes. (Believe me, I have plenty in my closet.) I shouldn't have carried the cranberry coat, which Eric had given me. I should have done *anything* but look good for Eric—and I had to admit to myself that that had been my goal. I'd blindsided myself.

Eric slid out of the booth and rose to his considerable height—around six foot four. His mane of blond hair rippled down his back, and his blue eyes sparkled from his white, white face. Eric has bold features, high cheekbones, and a square jaw. He looks like a lawless Viking, the kind that could pillage a village in no time at all; and that's exactly what he had been.

Vampires don't shake hands except under extraordinary circumstances, so I didn't expect any salutation from Eric. But he bent to give me a kiss on the cheek, and he gave it lingeringly, as if he wanted me to know he'd like to seduce me.

He didn't realize he'd already kissed just about every inch of Sookie Stackhouse. We'd been as up close and personal as a man and a woman could be.

Eric just couldn't remember anything about it. I wanted it to stay that way. Well, not exactly *wanted*; but I knew it was better all the way around if Eric didn't recall our little fling.

"What pretty nail polish," Eric said, smiling. He had a slight accent. English was not his second language, of course; it was maybe his twenty-fifth.

I tried not to smile back, but I was pleased at his compliment. Trust Eric to pick out the one thing that was new and different about me. I'd never had long nails until recently, and they were painted a wonderful deep red—cranberry, in fact, to match the coat.

"Thank you," I murmured. "How you been doing?"

"Just fine." He raised a blond eyebrow. Vampires didn't have variable health. He waved a hand at the empty side of the booth, and I slid into it.

"Had any trouble picking up the reins?" I asked, to clarify.

A few weeks previously, a witch had given Eric amnesia, and it had taken several days to restore his sense of identity. During that time, Pam had parked him with me to keep him concealed from the witch who'd cursed him. Lust had taken its course. Many times.

"Like riding a bicycle," Eric said, and I told myself to focus. (Though I wondered when bicycles had been invented, and if Eric had had anything to do with it.) "I did receive a call from Long Shadow's sire, an American Indian whose name seems to be Hot Rain. I'm sure you remember Long Shadow."

"I was just thinking of him," I said.

Long Shadow had been the first bartender of Fangtasia. He'd been embezzling from Eric, who had coerced me into interrogating the barmaids and other human employees until I discovered the culprit. About two seconds before Long Shadow would have ripped out my throat, Eric had executed the bartender with the traditional wooden stake. Killing another vampire is a very serious thing, I gathered, and Eric had had to pay a stiff fine—to whom, I hadn't known, though now I was sure the money had gone to Hot Rain. If Eric had killed Long Shadow without any justification, other penalties would have come into play. I was content to let those remain a mystery.

"What did Hot Rain want?" I said.

"To let me know that though I had paid him the price set by the arbitrator, he didn't consider himself satisfied."

"Did he want more money?"

"I don't think so. He seemed to think financial recompense was not all he required." Eric shrugged. "As far as I'm concerned, the matter is settled." Eric took a swallow of synthetic blood, leaned back in his chair, and looked at me with unreadable blue eyes. "And so is my little amnesia episode. The crisis is over, the witches are dead, and order is restored in my little piece of Louisiana. How have things been for you?"

"Well, I'm here on business," I said, and I put my business face on.

"What can I do for you, my Sookie?" he asked.

"Sam wants to ask you for something," I said.

"And he sends you to ask for it. Is he very clever or very stupid?" Eric asked himself out loud.

"Neither," I said, trying not to sound snippy. "He's very leg-broken. That is to say, he got his leg broken last night. He got shot."

"How did this come about?" Eric's attention sharpened.

I explained. I shivered a little when I told him Sam and I had been alone, how silent the night had been.

"Arlene was just out of the parking lot. She went on home without knowing a thing. The new cook, Sweetie—she'd just left, too. Someone shot him from the trees north of the parking lot." I shivered again, this time with fear.

"How close were you?"

"Oh," I said, and my voice shook. "I was real close. I'd just turned to . . . then he was . . . There was blood all over."

Eric's face looked hard as marble. "What did you do?"

"Sam had his cell phone in his pocket, thank God, and I held one hand over the hole in his leg and I dialed nine-one-one with the other."

"How is he?"

"Well." I took a deep breath and tried to make myself still. "He's pretty good, all things considered." I'd put that quite calmly. I was proud. "But of course, he's down for a while, and so much . . . so many odd things have been happening at the bar lately. . . . Our substitute bartender, he just can't handle it for more than a couple of nights. Terry's kind of damaged."

"So what's Sam's request?"

"Sam wants to borrow a bartender from you until his leg heals."

"Why's he making this request of me, instead of the packmaster of Shreveport?" Shifters seldom got organized, but the city werewolves had. Eric was right: It would have been far more logical for Sam to make the request of Colonel Flood.

I looked down at my hands wrapped around the ginger ale glass. "Someone's gunning for the shifters and Weres in

Bon Temps," I said. I kept my voice very low. I knew he would hear me through the music and the talk of the bar.

Just then a man lurched up to the booth, a young serviceman from Barksdale Air Force Base, which is a part of the Shreveport area. (I pigeonholed him instantly from his haircut, fitness, and his running buddies, who were more or less clones.) He rocked on his heels for a long moment, looking from me to Eric.

"Hey, you," the young man said to me, poking my shoulder. I looked up at him, resigned to the inevitable. Some people court their own disaster, especially when they drink. This young man, with his buzz haircut and sturdy build, was far from home and determined to prove himself.

There's not much I dislike more than being addressed as "Hey, you" and being poked with a finger. But I tried to present a pleasant face to the young man. He had a round face and round dark eyes, a small mouth and thick brown brows. He was wearing a clean knit shirt and pressed khakis. He was also primed for a confrontation.

"I don't believe I know you," I said gently, trying to defuse the situation.

"You shouldn't be sitting with a vamp," he said. "Human girls shouldn't go with dead guys."

How often had I heard that? I'd gotten an earful of this kind of crap when I'd been dating Bill Compton.

"You should go back over there to your friends, Dave. You don't want your mama to get a phone call about you being killed in a bar fight in Louisiana. Especially not in a vampire bar, right?"

"How'd you know my name?" he asked slowly.

"Doesn't make any difference, does it?"

From the corner of my eye, I could see that Eric was shaking his head. Mild deflection was not his way of dealing with intrusion.

Abruptly, Dave began to simmer down.

"How'd you know about me?" he asked in a calmer voice.

"I have x-ray vision," I said solemnly. "I can read your driver's license in your pants."

He began to smile. "Hey, can you see other stuff through my pants?"

I smiled back at him. "You're a lucky man, Dave," I said ambiguously. "Now, I'm actually here to talk business with this guy, so if you'd excuse us . . ."

"Okay. Sorry, I . . ."

"No problem at all," I assured him. He went back to his friends, walking cocky. I was sure he'd give them a highly embellished account of the conversation.

Though everyone in the bar had tried to pretend they weren't watching the incident, which had so much potential for some juicy violence, they had to scramble to look busy when Eric's eyes swept the surrounding tables.

"You were starting to tell me something when we were so rudely interrupted," he said. Without my asking, a barmaid came up and deposited a fresh drink in front of me, whisking my old glass away. Anyone sitting with Eric got the deluxe treatment.

"Yes. Sam isn't the only shape-shifter who's been shot in Bon Temps lately. Calvin Norris was shot in the chest a few days ago. He's a werepanther. And Heather Kinman was shot before that. Heather was just nineteen, a werefox."

Eric said, "I still don't see why this is interesting."

"Eric, she was killed."

He still looked inquiring.

I clenched my teeth together so I wouldn't try to tell him what a nice girl Heather Kinman had been: She'd just graduated from high school and she was working at her first job as a clerk at Bon Temps Office Supplies. She'd been drinking a milkshake at the Sonic when she'd been shot. Today, the crime lab would be comparing the bullet that had shot Sam with the bullet that had killed Heather, and both of those with the bullet from Calvin's chest. I assumed the bullets would match.

"I'm trying to explain to you why Sam doesn't want to ask another shape-shifter or Were to step in to help," I said through clenched teeth. "He thinks that might be putting him or her in danger. And there's just not a local human who's got the qualifications for the job. So he asked me to come to you."

"When I stayed at your house, Sookie . . ."

I groaned. "Oh, Eric, give it a *rest*."

It griped Eric's butt that he couldn't remember what had happened while he was cursed. "Someday I'll remember," he said almost sullenly.

When he remembered everything, he wouldn't just recall the sex.

He'd also recall the woman who'd been waiting in my kitchen with a gun. He'd remember that he'd saved my life by taking the bullet meant for me. He'd remember that I'd shot her. He'd remember disposing of the body.

He'd realize that he had power over me forever.

He might also recall that he'd humbled himself enough to offer to abandon all his businesses and come to live with me.

The sex, he'd enjoy remembering. The power, he'd enjoy remembering. But somehow I didn't think Eric would enjoy remembering that last bit.

"Yes," I said quietly, looking down at my hands. "Someday, I expect you will remember." WDED was playing an old Bob Seger song, "Night Moves." I noticed Pam was twirling unself-consciously in her own dance, her unnaturally strong and limber body bending and twisting in ways human bodies couldn't.

I'd like to see her dance to live vampire music. You ought

to hear a vampire band. You'll never forget that. They mostly play New Orleans and San Francisco, sometimes Savannah or Miami. But when I'd been dating Bill, he'd taken me to hear a group playing in Fangtasia for one night while making their way south to New Orleans. The lead singer of the vampire band—Renfield's Masters, they'd called themselves—had wept tears of blood as he sang a ballad.

"Sam was clever to send you to ask me," Eric said after a long pause. I had nothing to say to that. "I'll spare someone." I could feel my shoulders relax with relief. I focused on my hands and took a deep breath. When I glanced over at him, Eric was looking around the bar, considering the vampires present.

I'd met most of them in passing. Thalia had long black ringlets down her back and a profile that could best be described as classical. She had a heavy accent—Greek, I thought—and she also had a hasty temper. Indira was a tiny Indian vamp, complete with doe eyes and tikal; no one would take her seriously until things got out of hand. Maxwell Lee was an African-American investment banker. Though strong as any vampire, Maxwell tended to enjoy more cerebral pastimes than acting as a bouncer.

"What if I send Charles?" Eric sounded casual, but I knew him well enough to suspect he wasn't.

"Or Pam," I said. "Or anyone else who can keep their temper." I watched Thalia crush a metal mug with her fingers to impress a human male who was trying to put the moves on her. He blanched and scurried back to his table. Some vampires enjoy human company, but Thalia was not one of them.

"Charles is the least temperamental vampire I've ever met, though I confess I don't know him well. He's been working here only two weeks."

"You seem to be keeping him busy here."

"I can spare him." Eric gave me a haughty look that said quite clearly it was up to him to decide how busy he wanted to keep his employee.

"Um . . . okeydokey." The patrons of Merlotte's would like the pirate just fine, and Sam's revenue would jump in consequence.

"Here are the terms," Eric said, fixing me with his gaze. "Sam supplies unlimited blood for Charles and a secure place to stay. You might want to keep him in your house, as you did me."

"And I might not," I said indignantly. "I'm not running any hostel for traveling vampires." Frank Sinatra began to croon "Strangers in the Night" in the background.

"Oh, of course, I forgot. But you were generously paid for my board."

He'd touched on a sore spot. In fact, he'd poked it with a sharp stick. I flinched. "That was my brother's idea," I said. I saw Eric's eyes flash, and I flushed all over. I'd just confirmed a suspicion he'd had. "But he was absolutely right," I said with conviction. "Why should I have put a vampire up in my house without getting paid? After all, I needed the money."

"Is the fifty thousand already gone?" Eric said very quietly. "Did Jason ask for a share of it?"

"None of your business," I said, my voice exactly as sharp and indignant as I'd intended it to be. I'd given Jason only a fifth of it. He hadn't exactly asked, either, though I had to admit to myself he'd clearly expected me to give him some. Since I needed it a lot worse, I'd kept more of it than I'd initially planned.

I had no health insurance. Jason, of course, was covered through the parish plan. I'd begun thinking, *What if I was disabled? What if I broke my arm or had to have my appendix out?* Not only would I not put in my hours at work, but I'd have hospital bills. And any stay in a hospital, in this day and age, is an expensive one. I'd incurred a few medical bills during the past year, and it had taken me a long, painful time to pay them off.

Now I was profoundly glad I'd had that twinge of caution. In the normal course of things, I don't look real far ahead, because I'm used to living day to day. But Sam's injury had opened my eyes. I'd been thinking of how badly I needed a new car—well, a newer secondhand one. I'd been thinking of how dingy the living room drapes were, how pleasant it would be to order new ones from JCPenney. It had even crossed my mind that it would be a lot of fun to buy a dress that wasn't on sale. But I'd been shocked out of such frivolity when Sam had his leg broken.

As Connie the Corpse introduced the next song ("One of These Nights"), Eric examined my face. "I wish that I could read your mind as you can read the minds of others," he said. "I wish very much that I could know what was going on in your head. I wish I knew why I cared what's going on in that head."

I gave him a lopsided smile. "I agree to the terms: free blood and lodging, though the lodging won't necessarily be with me. What about the money?"

Eric smiled. "I'll take my payment in kind. I like Sam owing me a favor."

I called Sam with the cell phone he'd lent me. I explained.

Sam sounded resigned. "There's a place in the bar the vamp can sleep. All right. Room and board, and a favor. When can he come?"

I relayed the question to Eric.

"Right now." Eric beckoned to a human waitress, who was wearing the low-cut long black dress all the female human employees wore. (I'll tell you something about vampires: They don't like to wait tables. And they're pretty poor at it, too. You won't catch a vamp bussing tables, either. The vamps almost always hire humans to do the grubbier work at their establishments.) Eric told her to fetch Charles from behind the bar. She bowed, fist to her opposite shoulder, and said, "Yes, Master."

Honestly, it just about made you sick.

Anyway, Charles leapt over the bar theatrically, and while patrons applauded, he made his way to Eric's booth.

Bowing to me, he turned to Eric with an air of attentiveness that should have seemed subservient but instead seemed simply matter-of-fact.

"This woman will tell you what to do. As long as she needs you, she is your master." I just couldn't decipher Charles Twining's expression as he heard Eric's directive. Lots of vampires simply wouldn't agree to being at a human's beck and call, no matter what their head honcho said.

"No, Eric!" I was shocked. "If you make him answerable to anyone, it should be Sam."

"Sam sent you. I'm entrusting Charles's direction to you." Eric's face closed down. I knew from experience that once Eric got that expression, there was no arguing with him.

I couldn't see where this was going, but I knew it wasn't good.

"Let me get my coat, and I'll be ready anytime it pleases you to leave," Charles Twining said, bowing in a courtly and gracious way that made me feel like an idiot. I made a strangled noise in acknowledgment, and though he was still in the down position, his patch-free eye rolled up to give me a wink. I smiled involuntarily and felt much better.

Over the music system, Connie the Corpse said, "Hey, you night listeners. Continuing ten in a row for us genuine deadheads, here's a favorite." Connie began playing "Here Comes the Night," and Eric said, "Will you dance?"

I looked over at the little dance floor. It was empty.

However, Eric had arranged for a bartender and bouncer for Sam as Sam had asked. I should be gracious. "Thank you," I said politely, and slid out of the booth. Eric offered me his hand, I took it, and he put his other hand on my waist.

Despite the difference in our heights, we managed quite well. I pretended I didn't know everyone in the bar was looking at us, and we glided along as if we knew what we were doing. I focused on Eric's throat so I wouldn't be looking up into his eyes.

When the dance was over, he said, "Holding you seems very familiar, Sookie."

With a tremendous effort, I kept my eyes fixed on his Adam's apple. I had a dreadful impulse to say, "You told me you loved me and would stay with me forever."

"You wish," I said briskly instead. I let go of his hand as quickly as I could and stepped away from his embrace. "By the way, have you ever run across a kind of mean-looking vampire named Mickey?"

Eric grabbed my hand again and squeezed it. I said, "Ow!" and he eased up.

"He was in here last week. Where have you seen Mickey?" he demanded.

"In Merlotte's." I was astonished at the effect my last-minute question had had on Eric. "What's the deal?"

"What was he doing?"

"Drinking Red Stuff and sitting at a table with my friend Tara. You know, you saw her? At Club Dead, in Jackson?"

"When I saw her she was under the protection of Franklin Mott."

"Well, they were dating. I can't understand why he'd let her go out with Mickey. I hoped maybe Mickey was just there as her bodyguard or something." I retrieved my coat from the booth. "So, what's the bottom line on this guy?" I asked.

"Stay away from him. Don't talk to him, don't cross him, and don't try to help your friend Tara. When he was here, Mickey talked mostly to Charles. Charles tells me he is a rogue. He's capable of . . . things that are barbarous. Don't go around Tara."

I opened my hands, asking Eric to explain.

"He'll do things the rest of us won't," Eric said.

I stared up at Eric, shocked and deeply worried. "I can't just ignore her situation. I don't have so many friends that I can afford to let one go down the drain."

"If she's involved with Mickey, she's just meat on the hoof," Eric said with a brutal simplicity. He took my coat from me and held it while I slid into it. His hands massaged my shoulders after I'd buttoned it.

"It fits well," he said. It didn't take a mind reader to guess that he didn't want to say any more about Mickey.

"You got my thank-you note?"

"Of course. Very, ah, seemly."

I nodded, hoping to indicate this was the end of the subject. But, of course, it wasn't.

"I still wonder why your old coat had bloodstains on it," Eric murmured, and my eyes flashed up to his. I cursed my carelessness once again. When he'd come back to thank me for keeping him, he'd roamed the house while I was busy until he'd come across the coat. "What did we do, Sookie? And to whom?"

"It was chicken blood. I killed a chicken and cooked it," I lied. I'd seen my grandmother do that when I was little, many a time, but I'd never done it myself.

"Sookie, Sookie. My bullshit meter is reading that as a 'false,' " Eric said, shaking his head in a chiding way.

I was so startled I laughed. It was a good note on which to leave. I could see Charles Twining standing by the front door, thoroughly modern padded jacket at the ready. "Good-bye,

Eric, and thanks for the bartender," I said, as if Eric had loaned me some AA batteries or a cup of rice. He bent and brushed my cheek with his cool lips.

"Drive safely," he said. "And stay away from Mickey. I need to find out why he's in my territory. Call me if you have any problems with Charles." (If the batteries are defective, or if the rice is full of worms.) Beyond him I could see the same woman was still sitting at the bar, the one who'd remarked that I was no maiden. She was obviously wondering what I had done to secure the attention of a vampire as ancient and attractive as Eric.

I often wondered the same thing.

4

THE DRIVE BACK TO BON TEMPS WAS PLEASANT. Vampires don't smell like humans or act like humans, but they're sure relaxing to my brain. Being with a vampire is almost as tension-free as being alone, except, of course, for the blood-sucking possibilities.

Charles Twining asked a few questions about the work for which he'd been hired and about the bar. My driving seemed to make him a little uneasy—though possibly his unease was due to simply being in a car. Some of the pre–Industrial Revolution vamps loathe modern transportation. His eye patch was on his left eye, on my side, which gave me the curious feeling I was invisible.

I'd run him by the vampire hostel where he'd been living so he could gather a few things. He had a sports bag with him, one large enough to hold maybe three days' worth of clothes. He'd just moved into Shreveport, he told me, and hadn't had time to decide where he would settle.

After we'd been on our way for about forty minutes, the vampire said, "And you, Miss Sookie? Do you live with your father and mother?"

"No, they've been gone since I was seven," I said. Out of the corner of my eye, I caught a hand gesture inviting me to continue. "There was a whole lot of rain in a real short time one night that spring, and my dad tried to cross a little bridge that had water already over it. They got swept away."

I glanced to my right to see that he was nodding. People died, sometimes suddenly and unexpectedly, and sometimes for very little reason. A vampire knew that better than anyone. "My brother and I grew up with my grandmother," I said. "She died last year. My brother has my parents' old house, and I have my grandmother's."

"Lucky to have a place to live," he commented.

In profile, his hooked nose was an elegant miniature. I wondered if he cared that the human race had gotten larger, while he had stayed the same.

"Oh, yes," I agreed. "I'm major lucky. I've got a job, I've got my brother, I've got a house, I've got friends. And I'm healthy."

He turned to look at me full-face, I think, but I was passing a battered Ford pickup, so I couldn't return his gaze. "That's interesting. Forgive me, but I was under the impression from Pam that you have some kind of disability."

"Oh, well, yeah."

"And that would be . . . ? You look very, ah, robust."

"I'm a telepath."

He mulled that over. "And that would mean?"

"I can read other humans' minds."

"But not vampires."

"No, not vampires."

"Very good."

"Yes, I think so." If I could read vampire minds, I'd have been dead long ago. Vampires value their privacy.

"Did you know Chow?" he asked.

"Yes." It was my turn to be terse.

"And Long Shadow?"

"Yes."

"As the newest bartender at Fangtasia, I have a definite interest in their deaths."

Understandable, but I had no idea how to respond. "Okay," I said cautiously.

"Were you there when Chow died again?" This was the way some vamps referred to the final death.

"Um . . . yes."

"And Long Shadow?"

"Well . . . yes."

"I would be interested in hearing what you had to say."

"Chow died in what they're calling the Witch War. Long Shadow was trying to kill me when Eric staked him because he'd been embezzling."

"You're sure that's why Eric staked him? For embezzling?"

"I was there. I oughta know. End of subject."

"I suppose your life has been complicated," Charles said after a pause.

"Yes."

"Where will I be spending the sunlight hours?"

"My boss has a place for you."

"There is a lot of trouble at this bar?"

"Not until recently." I hesitated.

"Your regular bouncer can't handle shifters?"

"Our regular bouncer is the owner, Sam Merlotte. He is a shifter. Right now, he's a shifter with a broken leg. He got shot. And he's not the only one."

This didn't seem to astonish the vampire. "How many?"

"Three that I know of. A werepanther named Calvin

Norris, who wasn't mortally wounded, and then a shifter girl named Heather Kinman, who's dead. She was shot at the Sonic. Do you know what Sonic is?" Vampires didn't always pay attention to fast-food restaurants, because they didn't eat. (Hey, how many blood banks can you locate off the top of your head?)

Charles nodded, his curly chestnut hair bouncing on his shoulders. "That's the one where you eat in your car?"

"Yes, right," I said. "Heather had been in a friend's car, talking, and she got out to walk back to her car a few slots down. The shot came from across the street. She had a milkshake in her hand." The melting chocolate ice cream had blended with blood on the pavement. I'd seen it in Andy Bellefleur's mind. "It was late at night, and all the businesses on the other side of the street had been closed for hours. So the shooter got away."

"All three shootings were at night?"

"Yes."

"I wonder if that's significant."

"Could be; but maybe it's just that there's better concealment at night."

Charles nodded.

"Since Sam got hurt, there's been a lot of anxiety among the shifters because it's hard to believe three shootings could be a coincidence. And regular humans are worried because in their view three people have been shot at random, people with nothing in common and few enemies. Since everyone's tense, there are more fights in the bar."

"I've never been a bouncer before," Charles said conversationally. "I was the youngest son of a minor baronet, so I've had to make my own way, and I've done many things. I've worked as a bartender before, and many years ago I was shill for a whorehouse. Stood outside, trumpeted the wares of the strumpets—that's a neat phrase, isn't it?—threw out men who got too rough with the whores. I suppose that's the same as being a bouncer."

I was speechless at this unexpected confidence.

"Of course, that was after I lost my eye, but before I became a vampire," the vampire said.

"Of course," I echoed weakly.

"Which was while I was a pirate," he continued. He was smiling. I checked with a sideways glance.

"What did you, um, pirate?" I didn't know if that was a verb or not, but he got my meaning clearly.

"Oh, we'd try to catch almost anyone unawares," he said blithely. "Off and on I lived on the coast of America, down close to New Orleans, where we'd take small cargo ships and the like. I sailed aboard a small hoy, so we couldn't take on too large or well defended a ship. But when we caught up with some bark, then there was fighting!" He sighed—recalling the happiness of whacking at people with a sword, I guess.

"And what happened to you?" I asked politely, meaning how did he come to depart his wonderful warm-blooded life of rapine and slaughter for the vampire edition of the same thing.

"One evening, we boarded a galleon that had no living crew," he said. I noticed that his hands had curled into fists. His voice chilled. "We had sailed to the Tortugas. It was dusk. I was first man to go down into the hold. What was in the hold got me first."

After that little tale, we fell silent by mutual consent.

Sam was on the couch in the living room of his trailer. Sam had had the double-wide anchored so it was at a right angle to the back of the bar. That way, at least he opened his front door to a view of the parking lot, which was better than looking at the back of the bar, with its large garbage bin between the kitchen door and the employees' entrance.

"Well, there you are," Sam said, and his tone was grumpy. Sam was never one for sitting still. Now that his leg was in a cast, he was fretting from the inactivity. What would he do during the next full moon? Would the leg be healed enough by then for him to change? If he changed, what would happen to the cast? I'd known other injured shape-shifters before, but I hadn't been around for their recuperation, so this was new territory for me. "I was beginning to think you'd gotten lost on the way back." Sam's voice returned me to the here and now. It had a distinct edge.

" 'Gee, thanks, Sookie, I see you returned with a bouncer,' " I said. " 'I'm so sorry you had to go through the humiliating experience of asking Eric for a favor on my behalf.' " At that moment, I didn't care if he was my boss or not.

Sam looked embarrassed.

"Eric agreed, then," he said. He nodded at the pirate.

"Charles Twining, at your service," said the vampire.

Sam's eyes widened. "Okay. I'm Sam Merlotte, owner of the bar. I appreciate your coming to help us out here."

"I was ordered to do so," the vampire said coolly.

"So the deal you struck was room, board, and favor," Sam said to me. "I owe Eric a favor." This was said in a tone that a kind person would describe as grudging.

"Yes." I was mad now. "You sent me to make a deal. I checked the terms with you! That's the deal I made. You asked Eric for a favor; now he gets a favor in return. No matter what you told yourself, that's what it boils down to."

Sam nodded, though he didn't look happy. "Also, I changed my mind. I think Mr. Twining, here, should stay with you."

"And why would you think that?"

"The closet looked a little cramped. You have a light-tight place for vampires, right?"

"You didn't ask me if that was okay."

"You're refusing to do it?"

"Yes! I'm not the vampire hotel keeper!"

"But you work for me, and he works for me . . ."

"Uh-huh. And would you ask Arlene or Holly to put him up?"

Sam looked even more amazed. "Well, no, but that's because—" He stopped then.

"Can't think of how to finish the sentence, can you?" I snarled. "Okay, buddy, I'm out of here. I spent a whole evening putting myself in an embarrassing situation for you. And what do I get? *No effing thanks!*"

I stomped out of the double-wide. I didn't slam the door because I didn't want to be childish. Door slamming just isn't adult. Neither is whining. Okay, maybe stomping out isn't, either. But it was a choice between making an emphatic verbal exit or slapping Sam. Normally Sam was one of my favorite people in the world, but tonight . . . not.

I was working the early shift for the next three days—not that I was sure I had a job anymore. When I got into Merlotte's at eleven the next morning, dashing to the employees' door through the pouring rain in my ugly but useful rain slicker, I was nearly sure that Sam would tell me to collect my last paycheck and hit the door. But he wasn't there. I had a moment of what I recognized as disappointment. Maybe I'd been spoiling for another fight, which was odd.

Terry Bellefleur was standing in for Sam again, and Terry was having a bad day. It wasn't a good idea to ask him questions or even to talk to him beyond the necessary relay of orders.

Terry particularly hated rainy weather, I'd noticed, and he also didn't like Sheriff Bud Dearborn. I didn't know the reason for either prejudice. Today, gray sheets of rain battered at the walls and roof, and Bud Dearborn was pontificating to five of his cronies over on the smoking side. Arlene caught my eye and widened her eyes to give me a warning.

Though Terry was pale, and perspiring, he'd zipped up the light jacket he often wore over his Merlotte's T-shirt. I noticed his hands shaking as he pulled a draft beer. I wondered if he could last until dark.

At least there weren't many customers, if something did go wrong. Arlene drifted over to catch up with a married couple who'd come in, friends of hers. My section was almost empty, with the exception of my brother, Jason, and his friend Hoyt.

Hoyt was Jason's sidekick. If they weren't both definitely heterosexual, I would have recommended they marry, they complemented each other so well. Hoyt enjoyed jokes, and Jason enjoyed telling them. Hoyt was at a loss to fill his free time, and Jason was always up to something. Hoyt's mother was a little overwhelming, and Jason was parent-free. Hoyt was firmly anchored in the here and now, and had an iron sense of what the community would tolerate and what it would not. Jason didn't.

I thought of what a huge secret Jason now had, and I wondered if he was tempted to share it with Hoyt.

"How you doing, Sis?" Jason asked. He held up his glass, indicating he'd like a refill on his Dr Pepper. Jason didn't drink until after his workday was over, a large point in his favor.

"Fine, Brother. You want some more, Hoyt?" I asked.

"Please, Sookie. Ice tea," Hoyt said.

In a second I was back with their drinks. Terry glared at me when I went behind the bar, but he didn't speak. I can ignore a glare.

"Sook, you want to go with me to the hospital in Grainger this afternoon after you get off?" Jason asked.

"Oh," I said. "Yeah, sure." Calvin had always been good to me.

Hoyt said, "Sure is crazy, Sam and Calvin and Heather getting shot. What do you make of it, Sookie?" Hoyt has decided I am an oracle.

"Hoyt, you know as much about it as I do," I told him. "I think we all should be careful." I hoped the significance of this wasn't lost on my brother. He shrugged.

When I looked up, I saw a stranger waiting to be seated and hurried over to him. His dark hair, turned black by the rain, was pulled back in a ponytail. His face was scarred with one long thin white line that ran along one cheek. When he pulled off his jacket, I could see that he was a bodybuilder.

"Smoking or non?" I asked, with a menu already in my hand.

"Non," he said, and followed me to a table. He carefully hung his wet jacket on the back of a chair and took the menu after he was seated. "My wife will be along in a few minutes," he said. "She's meeting me here."

I put another menu at the adjacent place. "Do you want to order now or wait for her?"

"I'd like some hot tea," he asked. "I'll wait until she comes to order food. Kind of a limited menu here, huh?" He glanced over at Arlene and then back at me. I began to feel uneasy. I knew he wasn't here because this place was convenient for lunch.

"That's all we can handle," I said, taking care to sound relaxed. "What we've got, it's good."

When I assembled the hot water and a tea bag, I put a saucer with a couple of lemon slices on the tray, too. No fairies around to offend.

"Are you Sookie Stackhouse?" he asked when I returned with his tea.

"Yes, I am." I put the saucer gently on the table, right beside the cup. "Why do you want to know?" I already knew why, but with regular people, you had to ask.

"I'm Jack Leeds, a private investigator," he said. He laid a business card on the table, turned so I could read it. He waited for a beat, as if he usually got a dramatic reaction to that statement. "I've been hired by a family in Jackson, Mississippi—the Pelt family," he continued, when he saw I wasn't going to speak.

My heart sank to my shoes before it began pounding at an accelerated rate. This man believed that Debbie was dead. And he thought there was a good chance I might know something about it.

He was absolutely right.

I'd shot Debbie Pelt dead a few weeks before, in self-defense. Hers was the body Eric had hidden. Hers was the bullet Eric had taken for me.

Debbie's disappearance after leaving a "party" in Shreveport, Louisiana (in fact a life-and-death brawl between witches, vamps, and Weres), had been a nine days' wonder. I'd hoped I'd heard the end of it.

"So the Pelts aren't satisfied with the police investigation?" I asked. It was a stupid question, one I picked out of the air at random. I had to say something to break up the gathering silence.

"There really wasn't an investigation," Jack Leeds said. "The police in Jackson decided she probably vanished voluntarily." He didn't believe that, though.

His face changed then; it was like someone had switched on a light behind his eyes. I turned to look where he was looking, and I saw a blond woman of medium height shaking her umbrella out at the door. She had short hair and pale skin, and when she turned, I saw that she was very pretty; at least, she would have been if she had been more animated.

But that wasn't a factor to Jack Leeds. He was looking at the woman he loved, and when she saw him, the same light switched on behind her eyes, too. She came across the floor to his table as smoothly as if she were dancing, and when she shed her own wet jacket, I saw her arms were as muscular as his. They didn't kiss, but his hand slid over hers and squeezed just briefly. After she'd taken her chair and asked for some diet Coke, her eyes went to the menu. She was thinking that all the food Merlotte's offered was unhealthy. She was right.

"Salad?" Jack Leeds asked.

"I have to have something hot," she said. "Chili?"

"Okay. Two chilis," he told me. "Lily, this is Sookie Stackhouse. Ms. Stackhouse, this is Lily Bard Leeds."

"Hello," she said. "I've just been out to your house."

Her eyes were light blue, and she had a stare like a laser. "You saw Debbie Pelt the night she disappeared." Her mind added, *You're the one she hated so much.*

They didn't know Debbie Pelt's true nature, and I was relieved that the Pelts hadn't been able to find a Were investigator. They wouldn't out their daughter to regular detectives. The longer the two-natured could keep the fact of their existence a secret, the better, as far as they were concerned.

"Yes," I said. "I saw her that night."

"Can we come talk to you about that? After you get off work?"

"I have to go see a friend in the hospital after work," I said.

"Sick?" Jack Leeds asked.

"Shot," I said.

Their interest quickened. "By someone local?" the blond woman asked.

Then I saw how it might all work. "By a sniper," I said. "Someone's been shooting people at random in this area."

"Have any of them vanished?" Jack Leeds asked.

"No," I admitted. "They've all been left lying. Of course, there were witnesses to all of the shootings. Maybe that's why." I hadn't heard of anyone actually seeing Calvin get shot, but someone had come along right afterward and called 911.

Lily Leeds asked me if they could talk to me the next day before I went to work. I gave them directions to my house and told them to come at ten. I didn't think talking to them was a very good idea, but I didn't think I had much of a choice, either. I would become more of an object of suspicion if I refused to talk about Debbie.

I found myself wishing I could call Eric tonight and tell him about Jack and Lily Leeds; worries shared are worries halved. But Eric didn't remember any of it. I wished that I could forget Debbie's death, too. It was awful to know something so heavy and terrible, to be unable to share it with a soul.

I knew so many secrets, but almost none of them were my own. This secret of mine was a dark and bloody burden.

Charles Twining was due to relieve Terry at full dark. Arlene was working late, since Danielle was attending her daughter's dance recital, and I was able to lighten my mood a little by briefing Arlene on the new bartender/bouncer. She was intrigued. We'd never had an Englishman visit the bar, much less an Englishman with an eye patch.

"Tell Charles I said hi," I called as I began to put on my rain gear. After a couple of hours of sprinkling, the drops were beginning to come faster again.

I splashed out to my car, the hood pulled well forward over my face. Just as I unlocked the driver's door and pulled it open, I heard a voice call my name. Sam was standing on crutches in the door of his trailer. He'd added a roofed porch a couple of years before, so he wasn't getting wet, but he didn't need to be standing there, either. Slamming the car door shut, I leaped over puddles and across the stepping-stones. In a second or two, I was standing on his porch and dripping all over it.

"I'm sorry," he said.

I stared at him. "You should be," I said gruffly.

"Well, I am."

"Okay. Good." I resolutely didn't ask him what he'd done with the vampire.

"Anything happen over at the bar today?"

I hesitated. "Well, the crowd was thin, to put it mildly. But . . ." I started to tell him about the private detectives, but then I knew he'd ask questions. And I might end up telling him the whole sorry story just for the relief of confessing to someone. "I have to go, Sam. Jason's taking me to visit Calvin Norris in the hospital in Grainger."

He looked at me. His eyes narrowed. The lashes were the same red-gold as his hair, so they showed up only when you were close to him. And I had no business at all thinking about Sam's eyelashes, or any other part of him, for that matter.

"I was a shit yesterday," he said. "I don't have to tell you why."

"Well, I guess you do," I said, bewildered. "Because I sure don't understand."

"The point is, you know you can count on me."

To get mad at me for no reason? To apologize afterward? "You've really confused me a lot lately," I said. "But you've been my friend for years, and I have a very high opinion of you." That sounded way too stilted, so I tried smiling. He smiled back, and a drop of rain fell off my hood and splashed on my nose, and the moment was over. I said, "When do you think you'll get back to the bar?"

"I'll try to come in tomorrow for a while," he said. "At least I can sit in the office and work on the books, get some filing done."

"See you."

"Sure."

And I dashed back to my car, feeling that my heart was much lighter than it had been before. Being at odds with Sam had felt wrong. I didn't realize how that wrongness had colored my thoughts until I was right with him again.

5

THE RAIN PELTED DOWN AS WE PULLED IN TO THE parking lot of the Grainger hospital. It was as small as the one in Clarice, the one most Renard Parish people were carried to. But the Grainger hospital was newer and had more of the diagnostic machines modern hospitals seemed to require.

I'd changed into jeans and a sweater, but I'd resumed wearing my lined slicker. As Jason and I hurried to the sliding glass doors, I was patting myself on the back for wearing boots. Weather-wise, the evening was proving as nasty as the morning had been.

The hospital was roiling with shifters. I could feel their anger as soon as I was inside. Two of the werepanthers from Hotshot were in the lobby; I figured they were acting as guards. Jason went to them and took their hands firmly. Maybe he exchanged some kind of secret shake or something;

I don't know. At least they didn't rub against one another's legs. They didn't seem quite as happy to see Jason as he was to see them, and I noticed that Jason stepped back from them with a little frown between his eyes. The two looked at me intently. The man was of medium height and stocky, and he had thick brownish-blond hair. His eyes were full of curiosity.

"Sook, this is Dixon Mayhew," Jason said. "And this is Dixie Mayhew, his twin sister." Dixie wore her hair, the same color as her brother's, almost as short as Dixon's, but she had dark, almost black, eyes. The twins were certainly not identical.

"Has it been quiet here?" I asked carefully.

"No problems so far," Dixie said, keeping her voice low. Dixon's gaze was fixed on Jason. "How's your boss?"

"He's in a cast, but he'll heal."

"Calvin was shot bad." Dixie eyed me for a minute. "He's up in 214."

Having been given the seal of approval, Jason and I went to the stairs. The twins watched us all the way. We passed the hospital auxiliary "pink lady" on duty at the visitors' desk. I felt kind of worried about her: white-haired, heavy glasses, sweet face with a full complement of wrinkles. I hoped nothing would happen during her watch to upset her worldview.

It was easy to pick which room was Calvin's. A slab of muscle was leaning against the wall outside, a barrel-shaped man I'd never seen. He was a werewolf. Werewolves make good bodyguards, according to the common wisdom of the two-natured, because they are ruthless and tenacious. From what I've seen, that's just the bad-boy image Weres have. But it's true that as a rule, they're the roughest element of the two-natured community. You won't find too many Were doctors, for example, but you will find a lot of Weres in construction work. Jobs relating to motorcycles are heavily dominated by Weres, too. Some of those gangs do more than drink beer on the full-moon nights.

Seeing a Were disturbed me. I was surprised the panthers of Hotshot had brought in an outsider. Jason murmured, "That's Dawson. He owns the small engine repair shop between Hotshot and Grainger."

Dawson was on the alert as we came down the hall.

"Jason Stackhouse," he said, identifying my brother after a minute. Dawson was wearing a denim shirt and jeans, but his biceps were about to burst through the material. His black leather boots were battle scarred.

"We've come to see how Calvin is doing," Jason said. "This here's my sister, Sookie."

"Ma'am," Dawson rumbled. He eyeballed me slowly, and there wasn't anything lascivious about it. I was glad I'd left my purse in the locked truck. He would've gone through it, I was sure. "You want to take off that coat and turn around for me?"

I didn't take offense; Dawson was doing his job. I didn't want Calvin to get hurt again, either. I took off my slicker, handed it to Jason, and rotated. A nurse who'd been entering something in a chart watched this procedure with open curiosity. I held Jason's jacket as he took his turn. Satisfied, Dawson knocked on the door. Though I didn't hear a response, he must have, because he opened the door and said, "The Stackhouses."

Just a whisper of a voice came from the room. Dawson nodded.

"Miss Stackhouse, you can go in," he said. Jason started to follow me, but Dawson put a massive arm in front of him. "Only your sister," he said.

Jason and I began to protest at the same moment, but then Jason shrugged. "Go ahead, Sook," he said. There was obviously no budging Dawson, and there was no point to upsetting a wounded man, for that matter. I pushed the heavy door wide open.

Calvin was by himself, though there was another bed in the room. The panther leader looked awful. He was pale and drawn. His hair was dirty, though his cheeks above his trim beard had been shaved. He was wearing a hospital gown, and he was hooked up to lots of things.

"I'm so sorry," I blurted. I was horrified. Though many brains had indicated as much, I could see that if Calvin hadn't been two-natured, the wound would have killed him instantly. Whoever had shot him had wanted his death.

Calvin turned his head to me, slowly and with effort. "It's not as bad as it looks," he said dryly, his voice a thread. "They're going to take me off some of this stuff tomorrow."

"Where were you hit?" I asked.

Calvin moved one hand to touch his upper left chest. His golden brown eyes captured mine. I went closer to him and covered his hand with mine. "I'm so sorry," I said again. His fingers curled under mine until he was holding my hand.

"There've been others," he said in a whisper of a voice.

"Yes."

"Your boss."

I nodded.

"That poor girl."

I nodded again.

"Whoever's doing this, they've got to be stopped."

"Yes."

"It's got to be someone who hates shifters. The police will never find out who's doing this. We can't tell them what to look for."

Well, that was part of the problem of keeping your condition a secret. "It'll be harder for them to find the person," I conceded. "But maybe they will."

"Some of my people wonder if the shooter is someone

who's a shifter," Calvin said. His fingers tightened around mine. "Someone who didn't want to become a shifter in the first place. Someone who was bitten."

It took a second for the light to click on in my head. I am such an idiot.

"Oh, no, Calvin, no, no," I said, my words stumbling over each other in my haste. "Oh, Calvin, please don't let them go after Jason. Please, he's all I've got." Tears began to run down my cheeks as if someone had turned on a faucet in my head. "He was telling me how much he enjoyed being one of you, even if he couldn't be exactly like a born panther. He's so new, he hasn't had time to figure out who all else is two-natured. I don't think he even realized Sam and Heather were. . . ."

"No one's gonna take him out until we know the truth," Calvin said. "Though I might be in this bed, I'm still the leader." But I could tell he'd had to argue against it, and I also knew (from hearing it right out of Calvin's brain) that some of the panthers were still in favor of executing Jason. Calvin couldn't prevent that. He might be angry afterward, but if Jason were dead, that wouldn't make one little bit of difference. Calvin's fingers released mine, and his hand rose with an effort to wipe the tears off my cheek.

"You're a sweet woman," he said. "I wish you could love me."

"I wish I could, too," I said. So many of my problems would be solved if I loved Calvin Norris. I'd move out to Hotshot, become a member of the secretive little community. Two or three nights a month, I'd have to be sure to stay inside, but other than that, I'd be safe. Not only would Calvin defend me to the death, but so would the other members of the Hotshot clan.

But the thought of it just made me shudder. The windswept open fields, the powerful and ancient crossroads around which the little houses clustered . . . I didn't think I could handle the perpetual isolation from the rest of the world. My Gran would have urged me to accept Calvin's offer. He was a steady man, was a shift leader at Norcross, a job that came with good benefits. You might think that's laughable, but wait until you have to pay for your insurance all by yourself; then laugh.

It occurred to me (as it should have right away) that Calvin was in a perfect position to force my compliance—Jason's life for my companionship—and he hadn't taken advantage of it.

I leaned over and gave Calvin a kiss on the cheek. "I'll pray for your recovery," I said. "Thank you for giving Jason a chance." Maybe Calvin's nobility was partly due to the fact that he was in no shape to take advantage of me, but it was nobility, and I noted and appreciated it. "You're a good man," I said, and touched his face. The hair of his neat beard felt soft.

His eyes were steady as he said good-bye. "Watch out for that brother of yours, Sookie," he said. "Oh, and tell Dawson I don't want no more company tonight."

"He won't take my word for it," I said.

Calvin managed to smile. "Wouldn't be much of a bodyguard if he did, I guess."

I relayed the message to the Were. But sure enough, as Jason and I walked back to the stairs, Dawson was going into the room to check with Calvin.

I debated for a couple of minutes before I decided it would be better if Jason knew what he was up against. In the truck, as he drove home, I relayed my conversation with Calvin to my brother.

He was horrified that his new buddies in the werepanther world could believe such a thing of him. "If I'd thought of that before I changed for the first time, I can't say it wouldn't have been tempting," Jason said as we drove back to Bon Temps through the rain. "I was mad. Not just mad, furious. But now that I've changed, I see it different." He went on and on while my thoughts ran around inside my head in a circle, trying to think of a way out of this mess.

The sniping case had to be solved by the next full moon. If it wasn't, the others might tear Jason up when they changed. Maybe he could just roam the woods around his house when he turned into his panther-man form, or maybe he could hunt the woods around my place—but he wouldn't be safe out at Hotshot. And they might come looking for him. I couldn't defend him against them all.

By the next full moon, the shooter had to be in custody.

Until I was washing my few dishes that night, it didn't strike me as odd that though Jason was being accused by the werepanther community of being an assassin, I was the one who'd actually shot a shifter. I'd been thinking of the private detectives' appointment to meet me here the next morning. And, as I found myself doing out of habit, I'd been scanning the kitchen for signs of the death of Debbie Pelt. From watching the Discovery Channel and the Learning Channel, I knew that there was no way I could completely eradicate the traces of blood and tissue that had spattered my kitchen, but I'd scrubbed and cleaned over and over. I was certain that no casual glance—in fact, no careful inspection by the naked eye—could reveal anything amiss in this room.

I had done the only thing I could, short of standing there to be murdered. Was that what Jesus had meant by turning the other cheek? I hoped not, because every instinct in me had urged me to defend myself, and the means at hand had been a shotgun.

Of course, I should immediately have reported it. But by

then, Eric's wound had healed, the one made when Debbie'd hit him while trying to shoot me. Aside from the testimony of a vampire and myself, there was no proof that she'd fired first, and Debbie's body would have been a powerful statement of our guilt. My first instinct had been to cover up her visit to my house. Eric hadn't given me any other advice, which also might have changed things.

No, I wasn't blaming my predicament on Eric. He hadn't even been in his right mind at the time. It was my own fault that I hadn't sat down to think things through. There would have been gunshot residue on Debbie's hand. Her gun had been fired. Some of Eric's dried blood would have been on the floor. She'd broken in through my front door, and the door had shown clear signs of her trespass. Her car was hidden across the road, and only her fingerprints would've been in it.

I'd panicked, and blown it.

I just had to live with that.

But I was very sorry about the uncertainty her family was suffering. I owed them certainty—which I couldn't deliver.

I wrung out the washcloth and hung it neatly over the sink divider. I dried off my hands and folded the dish towel. Okay, now I'd gotten my guilt straight. That was so much better! *Not.* Angry with myself, I stomped out to the living room and turned on the television: another mistake. There was a story about Heather's funeral; a news crew from Shreveport had come to cover the modest service this afternoon. Just think of the sensation it would cause if the media realized how the sniper was selecting his victims. The news anchor, a solemn African-American man, was saying that police in Renard Parish had discovered other clusters of apparently random shootings in small towns in Tennessee and Mississippi. I was startled. A serial shooter, here?

The phone rang. "Hello," I said, not expecting anything good.

"Sookie, hi, it's Alcide."

I found myself smiling. Alcide Herveaux, who worked in his father's surveying business in Shreveport, was one of my favorite people. He was a Were, he was both sexy and hardworking, and I liked him very much. He'd also been Debbie Pelt's fiancé. But Alcide had abjured her before she vanished, in a rite that made her invisible and inaudible to him—not literally, but in effect.

"Sookie, I'm at Merlotte's. I'd thought you might be working tonight, so I drove over. Can I come to the house? I need to talk to you."

"You know you're in danger, coming to Bon Temps."

"No, why?"

"Because of the sniper." I could hear the bar sounds in the background. There was no mistaking Arlene's laugh. I was betting the new bartender was charming one and all.

"Why would I worry about that?" Alcide hadn't been thinking about the news too hard, I decided.

"All the people who got shot? They were two-natured," I said. "Now they're saying on the news there've been a lot more across the south. Random shootings in small towns. Bullets that match the one recovered from Heather Kinman here. And I'm betting all the other victims were shapeshifters, too."

There was a thoughtful silence on the end of the line, if silence can be characterized.

"I hadn't realized," Alcide said. His deep, rumbly voice was even more deliberate than normal.

"Oh, and have you talked to the private detectives?"

"What? What are you talking about?"

"If they see us talking together, it'll look very suspicious to Debbie's family."

"Debbie's family has hired private eyes to look for her?"

"That's what I'm saying."

"Listen, I'm coming to your house." He hung up the phone.

I didn't know why on earth the detectives would be watching my house, or where they'd watch it from, but if they saw Debbie's former fiancé tootling down my driveway, it would be easy to connect the dots and come up with a totally erroneous picture. They'd think Alcide killed Debbie to clear the way for me, and nothing could be more wrong. I hoped like hell that Jack Leeds and Lily Bard Leeds were sound asleep rather than staked out in the woods somewhere with a pair of binoculars.

Alcide hugged me. He always did. And once again I was overwhelmed by the size of him, the masculinity, the familiar smell. Despite the warning bell ringing in my head, I hugged him back.

We sat on the couch and half turned to face each other. Alcide was wearing work clothes, which in this weather consisted of a flannel shirt worn open over a T-shirt, heavy jeans, and thick socks under his work boots. His tangle of black hair had a crease in it from his hard hat, and he was beginning to look a little bristly.

"Tell me about the detectives," he said, and I described the couple and told him what they'd said.

"Debbie's family didn't say anything to me about it," Alcide said. He turned it over in his head for a minute. I could follow his thinking. "I think that means they're sure I made her vanish."

"Maybe not. Maybe they just think you're so grieved they don't want to bring it up."

"Grieved." Alcide mulled that over for a minute. "No. I spent all the . . ." He paused, grappling for words. "I used up all the energy I had to spare for her," he said finally. "I was so blind, I almost think she used some kind of magic on me. Her mother's a spellcaster and half shifter. Her dad's a full-blooded shifter."

"You think that's possible? Magic?" I wasn't questioning that magic existed, but that Debbie had used it.

"Why else would I stick with her for so long? Ever since she's gone missing, it's been like someone took a pair of dark glasses off my eyes. I was willing to forgive her so much, like when she pushed you into the trunk."

Debbie had taken an opportunity to push me in a car trunk with my vampire boyfriend, Bill, who'd been starved for blood for days. And she'd walked off and left me in the trunk with Bill, who was about to awake.

I looked down at my feet, pushing away the recollection of the desperation, the pain.

"She let you get raped," Alcide said harshly.

Him saying it like that, flat out, shocked me. "Hey, Bill didn't know it was me," I said. "He hadn't had anything to eat for days and days, and the impulses are so closely related. I mean, he stopped, you know? He stopped, when he knew it was me." I couldn't put it like that to myself; I couldn't say that word. I knew beyond a doubt that Bill would rather have chewed off his own hand than done that to me if he'd been in his right mind. At that time, he'd been the only sex partner I'd ever had. My feelings about the incident were so confused that I couldn't even bear to try to pick through them. When I'd thought of rape before, when other girls had told me what had happened to them or I'd read it in their brains, I hadn't had the ambiguity I felt over my own short, awful time in the trunk.

"He did something you didn't want him to do," Alcide said simply.

"He wasn't himself," I said.

"But he did it."

"Yes, he did, and I was awful scared." My voice began to shake. "But he came to his senses, and he *stopped,* and I was okay, and he was really, really sorry. He's never laid a finger on me since then, never asked me if we could have sex, never . . ." My voice trailed off. I stared down at my hands. "Yes, Debbie was responsible for that." Somehow, saying that out loud made me feel better. "She knew what would happen, or at least she didn't care what would happen."

"And even then," Alcide said, returning to his main point, "she kept coming back and I kept trying to rationalize her behavior. I can't believe I would do that if I wasn't under some kind of magical influence."

I wasn't about to try to make Alcide feel guiltier. I had my own load of guilt to carry. "Hey, it's over."

"You sound sure."

I looked Alcide directly in the eyes. His were narrow and green. "Do you think there's the slightest chance that Debbie's alive?" I asked.

"Her family . . ." Alcide stopped. "No, I don't."

I couldn't get rid of Debbie Pelt, dead or alive.

"Why'd you need to talk to me in the first place?" I asked. "You said over the phone you needed to tell me something."

"Colonel Flood died yesterday."

"Oh, I'm so sorry! What happened?"

"He was driving to the store when another driver hit him broadside."

"That's awful. Was anyone in the car with him?"

"No, he was by himself. His kids are coming back to Shreveport for the funeral, of course. I wondered if you'd come to the funeral with me."

"Of course. It's not private?"

"No. He knew so many people still stationed at the Air Force base, and he was head of his Neighborhood Watch group and the treasurer of his church, and of course he was the packmaster."

"He had a big life," I said. "Lots of responsibility."

"It's tomorrow at one. What's your work schedule?"

"If I can swap shifts with someone, I'd need to be back here at four thirty to change and go to work."

"That shouldn't be a problem."

"Who'll be packmaster now?"

"I don't know," Alcide said, but his voice wasn't as neutral as I'd expected.

"Do you want the job?"

"No." He seemed a little hesitant, I thought, and I felt the conflict in his head. "But my father does." He wasn't finished. I waited.

"Were funerals are pretty ceremonial," he said, and I realized he was trying to tell me something. I just wasn't sure what it was.

"Spit it out." Straightforward is always good, as far as I'm concerned.

"If you think you can overdress for this, you can't," he said. "I know the rest of the shifter world thinks Weres only go for leather and chains, but that's not true. For funerals, we go all out." He wanted to give me even more fashion tips, but he stopped there. I could see the thoughts crowding right behind his eyes, wanting to be let out.

"Every woman wants to know what's appropriate to wear," I said. "Thanks. I won't wear pants."

He shook his head. "I know you can do that, but I'm always taken by surprise." I could hear that he was disconcerted. "I'll pick you up at eleven thirty," he said.

"Let me see about swapping shifts."

I called Holly and found it suited her to switch shifts with me. "I can just drive over there and meet you," I offered.

"No," he said. "I'll come get you and bring you back."

Okay, if he wanted to go to the trouble of fetching me, I could live with it. I'd save mileage on my car, I figured. My old Nova was none too reliable.

"All right. I'll be ready."

"I better go," he said. The silence drew out. I knew Alcide was thinking of kissing me. He leaned over and kissed me lightly on the lips. We regarded each other from a few inches apart.

"Well, I have some things I need to be doing, and you should be going back to Shreveport. I'll be ready at eleven thirty tomorrow."

After Alcide left, I got my library book, Carolyn Haines's latest, and tried to forget my worries. But for once, a book just couldn't do the trick. I tried a hot soak in the bathtub, and I shaved my legs until they were perfectly smooth. I painted my toenails and fingernails a deep pink and then I plucked my eyebrows. Finally, I felt relaxed, and when I crawled into my bed I had achieved peace through pampering. Sleep came upon me in such a rush that I didn't finish my prayers.

6

YOU HAVE TO FIGURE OUT WHAT TO WEAR TO A FUneral, just like any other social occasion, even if it seems your clothes should be the last thing on your mind. I had liked and admired Colonel Flood during our brief acquaintance, so I wanted to look appropriate at his burial service, especially after Alcide's comments.

I just couldn't find anything in my closet that seemed right. About eight the next morning, I phoned Tara, who told me where her emergency key was. "Get whatever you need out of my closet," Tara said. "Just be sure you don't go into any other rooms, okay? Go straight from the back door to my room and back out again."

"That's what I'd be doing anyway," I said, trying not to sound offended. Did Tara think I'd rummage around her house just to pry?

"Of course you would, but I just feel responsible."

Suddenly, I understood that Tara was telling me that there was a vampire sleeping in her house. Maybe it was the bodyguard Mickey, maybe Franklin Mott. After Eric's warning, I wanted to stay far away from Mickey. Only the very oldest vampires could rise before dark, but coming across a sleeping vampire would give me a nasty start in and of itself.

"Okay, I get you," I said hastily. The idea of being alone with Mickey made me shiver, and not with happy anticipation. "Straight in, straight out." Since I didn't have any time to waste, I jumped in my car and drove into town to Tara's little house. It was a modest place in a modest part of town, but Tara's owning her own home was a miracle, when I recalled the place where she'd grown up.

Some people should never breed; if their children have the misfortune to be born, those children should be taken away immediately. That's not allowed in our country, or any country that I know of, and I'm sure in my brainier moments that's a good thing. But the Thorntons, both alcoholics, had been vicious people who should have died years earlier than they did. (I forget my religion when I think of them.) I remember Myrna Thornton tearing my grandmother's house up looking for Tara, ignoring my grandmother's protests, until Gran had to call the sheriff's department to come drag Myrna out. Tara had run out our back door to hide in the woods behind our house when she had seen the set of her mother's shoulders as Mrs. Thornton staggered to our door, thank God. Tara and I had been thirteen at the time.

I can still see the look on my grandmother's face while she talked to the deputy who'd just put Myrna Thornton in the back of the patrol car, handcuffed and screaming.

"Too bad I can't drop her off in the bayou on the way back to town," the deputy had said. I couldn't recall his name, but his words had impressed me. It had taken me a minute to be sure what he meant, but once I was, I realized that other people knew what Tara and her siblings were going through. These other people were all-powerful adults. If they knew, why didn't they solve the problem?

I sort of understood now that it hadn't been so simple; but I still thought the Thornton kids could have been spared a few years of their misery.

At least Tara had this neat little house with all-new appliances, and a closet full of clothes, and a rich boyfriend. I had an uneasy feeling that I didn't know everything that was happening in Tara's life, but on the surface of it, she was still way ahead of the predictions.

As she'd directed, I went through the spanky-clean kitchen, turned right, and crossed a corner of the living room to pass through the doorway to Tara's bedroom. Tara hadn't had a chance to make her bed that morning. I pulled the sheets straight in a flash and made it look nice. (I couldn't help it.) I couldn't decide if that was a favor to her or not, since now she'd know I minded it not being made, but for the life of me I couldn't mess it up again.

I opened her walk-in closet. I spotted exactly what I needed right away. Hanging in the middle of the rear rack was a knit suit. The jacket was black with creamy pink facings on the lapels, meant to be worn over the matching pink shell on the hanger beneath it. The black skirt was pleated. Tara had had it hemmed up; the alteration tag was still on the plastic bag covering the garment. I held the skirt up to me and looked in Tara's full-length mirror. Tara was two or three inches taller than I, so the skirt fell just an inch above my knees, a fine length for a funeral. The sleeves of the jacket were a little long, but that wasn't so obvious. I had some black pumps and a purse, and even some black gloves that I'd tried to save for nice.

Mission accomplished, in record time.

I slid the jacket and shell into the plastic bag with the skirt and walked straight out of the house. I'd been in Tara's place less than ten minutes. In a hurry, because of my ten o'clock appointment, I began getting ready. I French braided my hair and rolled the remaining tail under, securing everything with some antique hairpins my grandmother had stashed away; they'd been her grandmother's. I had some black hose, fortunately, and a black slip, and the pink of my fingernails at least coordinated with the pink of the jacket and shell. When I heard a knock on the front door at ten, I was ready except for my shoes. I stepped into my pumps on the way to the door.

Jack Leeds looked openly astonished at my transformation, while Lily's eyebrows twitched.

"Please come in," I said. "I'm dressed for a funeral."

"I hope you're not burying a friend," Jack Leeds said. His companion's face might have been sculpted from marble. Had the woman never heard of a tanning bed?

"Not a close one. Won't you sit down? Can I get you anything? Coffee?"

"No, thank you," he said, his smile transforming his face.

The detectives sat on the couch while I perched on the edge of the La-Z-Boy. Somehow, my unaccustomed finery made me feel braver.

"About the evening Ms. Pelt vanished," Leeds began. "You saw her in Shreveport?"

"Yes, I was invited to the same party she was. At Pam's place." All of us who'd lived through the Witch War—Pam, Eric, Clancy, the three Wiccans, and the Weres who had survived—had agreed on our story: Instead of telling the police that Debbie had left from the dilapidated and abandoned store where the witches had established their hideout, we'd said that we'd stayed the whole evening at Pam's house, and Debbie had left in her car from that address. The neighbors might have testified that everyone had left earlier en masse if the Wiccans hadn't done a little magic to haze their memories of the evening.

"Colonel Flood was there," I said. "Actually, it's his funeral I'm going to."

Lily looked inquiring, which was probably the equivalent of someone else exclaiming, "Oh, you've got to be kidding!"

"Colonel Flood died in a car accident two days ago," I told them.

They glanced at each other. "So, were there quite a few people at this party?" Jack Leeds said. I was sure he had a complete list of the people who'd been sitting in Pam's living room for what had been essentially a war council.

"Oh, yes. Quite a few. I didn't know them all. Shreveport people." I'd met the three Wiccans that evening for the first time. I'd known the werewolves slightly. The vampires, I'd known.

"But you'd met Debbie Pelt before?"

"Yes."

"When you were dating Alcide Herveaux?"

Well. They'd certainly done their homework.

"Yes," I said. "When I was dating Alcide." My face was as smooth and impassive as Lily's. I'd had lots of practice in keeping secrets.

"You stayed with him once at the Herveaux apartment in Jackson?"

I started to blurt out that we'd stayed in separate bedrooms, but it really wasn't their business. "Yes," I said with a certain edge to my voice.

"You two ran into Ms. Pelt one night in Jackson at a club called Josephine's?"

"Yes, she was celebrating her engagement to some guy named Clausen," I said.

"Did something happen between you that night?"

"Yes." I wondered whom they'd been talking to; someone had given the detectives a lot of information that they shouldn't have. "She came over to the table, made a few remarks to us."

"And you also went to see Alcide at the Herveaux office a few weeks ago? You two were at a crime scene that afternoon?"

They'd done *way* too much homework. "Yes," I said.

"And you told the officers at that crime scene that you and Alcide Herveaux were engaged?"

Lies will come back to bite you in the butt. "I think it was Alcide who said that," I said, trying to look thoughtful.

"And was his statement true?"

Jack Leeds was thinking that I was the most erratic woman he'd ever met, and he couldn't understand how someone who could get engaged and unengaged so adeptly could be the sensible hardworking waitress he'd seen the day before.

She was thinking my house was very clean. (Strange, huh?) She also thought I was quite capable of killing Debbie Pelt, because she'd found people were capable of the most horrible things. She and I shared more than she'd ever know. I had the same sad knowledge, since I'd heard it directly from their brains.

"Yes," I said. "At the time, it was true. We were engaged for, like, ten minutes. Just call me Britney." I hated lying. I almost always knew when someone else was lying, so I felt I had LIAR printed in big letters on my forehead.

Jack Leeds's mouth quirked, but my reference to the pop singer's fifty-five-hour marriage didn't make a dent in Lily Bard Leeds.

"Ms. Pelt object to your seeing Alcide?"

"Oh, yes." I was glad I'd had years of practice of hiding my feelings. "But Alcide didn't want to marry her."

"Was she angry with you?"

"Yes," I said, since undoubtedly they knew the truth of that. "Yes, you could say that. She called me some names. You've probably heard that Debbie didn't believe in hiding her emotions."

"So when did you last see her?"

"I last saw her . . ." *(with half her head gone, sprawled on my kitchen floor, her legs tangled up in the legs of a chair)* "Let me think. . . . As she left the party that night. She walked off into the dark by herself." Not from Pam's, but from another location altogether; one full of dead bodies, with blood splashed on the walls. "I just assumed she was starting back to Jackson." I shrugged.

"She didn't come by Bon Temps? It's right off the interstate on her return route."

"I can't imagine why she would. She didn't knock on my door." She'd broken in.

"You didn't see her after the party?"

"I have not seen her since that night." Now, *that* was the absolute truth.

"You've seen Mr. Herveaux?"

"Yes, I have."

"Are you engaged now?"

I smiled. "Not that I know of," I said.

I wasn't surprised when the woman asked if she could use my bathroom. I'd let down my guard to find out how suspicious the detectives were, so I knew she wanted to have a more extensive look at my house. I showed her to the bathroom in the hall, not the one in my bedroom; not that she'd find anything suspicious in either of them.

"What about her car?" Jack Leeds asked me suddenly. I'd been trying to steal a glimpse of the clock on the mantel over the fireplace, because I wanted to be sure the duo were gone before Alcide picked me up for the funeral.

"Hmm?" I'd lost track of the conversation.

"Debbie Pelt's car."

"What about it?"

"Do you have any idea where it is?"

"Not an idea in the world," I said with complete honesty.

As Lily came back into the living room, he asked, "Ms. Stackhouse, just out of curiosity, what do you think happened to Debbie Pelt?"

I thought, *I think she got what was coming to her*. I was a little shocked at myself. Sometimes I'm not a very nice person, and I don't seem to be getting any nicer. "I don't know, Mr. Leeds," I said. "I guess I have to tell you that except for her family's worry, I don't really care. We didn't like each other. She burned a hole in my shawl, she called me a whore, and she was awful to Alcide; though since he's a grown-up, that's his problem. She liked to jerk people around. She liked to make them dance to her tune." Jack Leeds was looking a little dazed at this flow of information. "So," I concluded, "that's the way I feel."

"Thanks for your honesty," he said, while his wife fixed me with her pale blue eyes. If I'd had any doubt, I understood clearly now that she was the more formidable of the two. Considering the depth of the investigation Jack Leeds had performed, that was saying something.

"Your collar is crooked," she said quietly. "Let me fix it." I held still while her deft fingers reached behind me and twitched the jacket until the collar lay down correctly.

They left after that. After I watched their car go down the driveway, I took my jacket off and examined it very carefully. Though I hadn't picked up any such intention from her brain, maybe she'd put a bug on me? The Leeds might be more suspicious than they'd sounded. No, I discovered: she really was the neat freak she'd seemed, and she really had been unable to withstand my turned-up collar. As long as I was being suspicious, I inspected the hall bathroom. I hadn't been in it since the last time I'd cleaned it a week ago, so it looked quite straight and as fresh and as sparkly as a very old bathroom in a very old house can look. The sink was damp, and the towel had been used and refolded, but that was all. Nothing extra was there, and nothing was missing, and if the detective had opened the bathroom cabinet to check its contents, I just didn't care.

My heel caught on a hole where the flooring had worn through. For about the hundredth time, I wondered if I could teach myself how to lay linoleum, because the floor could sure use a new layer. I also wondered how I could conceal the fact that I'd killed a woman in one minute, and worry about the cracked linoleum in the bathroom the next.

"She was bad," I said out loud. "She was mean and bad, and she wanted me to die for no very good reason at all."

That was how I could do it. I'd been living in a shell of guilt, but it had just cracked and fallen apart. I was tired of being all angst-y over someone who would have killed me in a New York minute, someone who'd tried her best to cause my death. I would never have lain in wait to ambush Debbie, but I hadn't been prepared to let her kill me just because it suited her to have me dead.

To hell with the whole subject. They'd find her, or they wouldn't. No point in worrying about it either way.

Suddenly, I felt a lot better.

I heard a vehicle coming through the woods. Alcide was right on time. I expected to see his Dodge Ram, but to my surprise he was in a dark blue Lincoln. His hair was as smooth as it could be, which wasn't very, and he was wearing a sober charcoal gray suit and a burgundy tie. I gaped at him through the window as he came up the stepping-stones to the front porch. He looked good enough to eat, and I tried not to giggle like an idiot at the mental image.

When I opened the door, he seemed equally stunned. "You look wonderful," he said after a long stare.

"You, too," I said, feeling almost shy.

"I guess we need to get going."

"Sure, if we want to be there on time."

"We need to be there ten minutes early," he said.

"Why that, exactly?" I picked up my black clutch purse, glanced in the mirror to make sure my lipstick was still fresh, and locked the front door behind me. Fortunately, the day was just warm enough for me to leave my coat at home. I didn't want to cover up my outfit.

"This is a Were funeral," he said in a tone of significance.

"That's different from a regular funeral how?"

"It's a packmaster's funeral, and that makes it more . . . formal."

Okay, he'd told me that the day before. "How do you keep regular people from realizing?"

"You'll see."

I felt misgivings about the whole thing. "Are you sure I should be going to this?"

"He made you a friend of the pack."

I remembered that, though at the time I hadn't realized it was a title, the way Alcide made it sound now: Friend of the Pack.

I had an uneasy feeling that there was a lot more to know

about Colonel Flood's funeral ceremony. Usually I had more information than I could handle about any given subject, since I could read minds; but there weren't any Weres in Bon Temps, and the other shifters weren't organized like the wolves were. Though Alcide's mind was hard to read, I could tell he was preoccupied with what was going to happen in the church, and I could tell he was worried about a Were named Patrick.

The service was being held at Grace Episcopal, a church in an older, affluent suburb of Shreveport. The church edifice was very traditional, built of gray stone, and topped with a steeple. There wasn't an Episcopal church in Bon Temps, but I knew that the services were similar to those of the Catholic church. Alcide had told me that his father was attending the funeral, too, and that we'd come over from Bon Temps in his father's car. "My truck didn't look dignified enough for the day, my father thought," Alcide said. I could tell that his father was foremost in Alcide's thoughts.

"Then how's your dad getting here?" I asked.

"His other car," Alcide said absently, as if he weren't really listening to what I was saying. I was a little shocked at the idea of one man owning two cars: In my experience, men might have a family car and a pickup, or a pickup and a four-wheeler. My little shocks for the day were just beginning. By the time we had reached I-20 and turned west, Alcide's mood had filled up the car. I wasn't sure what it was, but it involved silence.

"Sookie," Alcide said abruptly, his hands tightening on the wheel until his knuckles were white.

"Yes?" The fact that bad stuff was coming into the conversation might as well have been written in blinking letters above Alcide's head. Mr. Inner Conflict.

"I need to talk to you about something."

"What? Is there something suspicious about Colonel

Flood's death?" *I should have wondered!* I chided myself. But the other shifters had been shot. A traffic accident was such a contrast.

"No," Alcide said, looking surprised. "As far as I know, the accident was just an accident. The other guy ran a red light."

I settled back into the leather seat. "So what's the deal?"

"Is there anything you want to tell me?"

I froze. "Tell you? About what?"

"About that night. The night of the Witch War."

Years of controlling my face came to my rescue. "Not a thing," I said calmly enough, though I may have been clenching my hands as I said it.

Alcide said nothing more. He parked the car and came around to help me out, which was unnecessary but nice. I'd decided I wouldn't need to take my purse inside, so I stuck it under the seat and Alcide locked the car. We started toward the front of the church. Alcide took my hand, somewhat to my surprise. I might be a friend of the pack, but I was apparently supposed to be friendlier with one member of the pack than the others.

"There's Dad," Alcide said as we approached a knot of mourners. Alcide's father was a little shorter than Alcide, but he was a husky man like his son. Jackson Herveaux had iron-gray hair instead of black, and a bolder nose. He had the same olive skin as Alcide. Jackson looked all the darker because he was standing by a pale, delicate woman with gleaming white hair.

"Father," Alcide said formally, "this is Sookie Stackhouse."

"A pleasure to meet you, Sookie," Jackson Herveaux said. "This is Christine Larrabee." Christine, who might have been anything from fifty-seven to sixty-seven, looked like a painting done in pastels. Her eyes were a washed-out blue, her smooth skin was magnolia pale with the faintest tinge of pink, her white hair was immaculately groomed. She was wearing a light blue suit, which I personally wouldn't have worn until the winter was completely over, but she looked great in it, for sure.

"Nice to meet you," I said, wondering if I should curtsy. I'd shaken hands with Alcide's father, but Christine didn't extend hers. She gave me a nod and a sweet smile. Probably didn't want to bruise me with her diamond rings, I decided after a squint at her fingers. Of course, they matched her earrings. I was outclassed, no doubt about it. *Eff it,* I thought. It seemed to be my day for shrugging off unpleasant things.

"Such a sad occasion," Christine said.

If she wanted to do polite chitchat, I was up to it. "Yes, Colonel Flood was a wonderful man," I said.

"Oh, you knew him, dear?"

"Yes," I said. As a matter of fact, I'd seen him naked, but in decidedly unerotic circumstances.

My brief answer didn't leave her much of anywhere to go. I saw genuine amusement lurking in her pale eyes. Alcide and his dad were exchanging low-voiced comments, which we were obviously supposed to be ignoring. "You and I are strictly decorations today," Christine said.

"Then you know more than I do."

"I expect so. You're not one of the two-natured?"

"No." Christine was, of course. She was a full-blooded Were, like Jackson and Alcide. I couldn't picture this elegant woman changing into a wolf, especially with the down-and-dirty reputation the Weres had in the shifter community, but the impressions I got from her mind were unmistakable.

"The funeral of the packmaster marks the opening of the campaign to replace him," Christine said. Since that was more solid information than I'd gotten in two hours from Alcide, immediately I felt kindly disposed toward the older woman.

"You must be something extraordinary, for Alcide to choose you as his companion today," Christine continued.

"I don't know about *extra*ordinary. In the literal sense, I guess I am. I have extras that aren't ordinary."

"Witch?" Christine guessed. "Fairy? Part goblin?"

Gosh. I shook my head. "None of the above. So what's going to happen in there?"

"There are more roped-off pews than usual. The whole pack will sit at the front of the church, the mated ones with their mates, of course, and their children. The candidates for packmaster will come in last."

"How are they chosen?"

"They announce themselves," she said. "But they'll be put to the test, and then the membership votes."

"Why is Alcide's dad bringing you, or is that a real personal question?"

"I'm the widow of the packmaster prior to Colonel Flood," Christine Larrabee said quietly. "That gives me a certain influence."

I nodded. "Is the packmaster always a man?"

"No. But since strength is part of the test, males usually win."

"How many candidates are there?"

"Two. Jackson, of course, and Patrick Furnan." She inclined her patrician head slightly to her right, and I gave a closer look at the couple that had been on the periphery of my attention.

Patrick Furnan was in his mid-forties, somewhere between Alcide and his father. He was a thick-bodied man with a light brown crew cut and a very short beard shaved into a fancy shape. His suit was brown, too, and he'd had trouble buttoning the jacket. His companion was a pretty woman who believed in a lot of lipstick and jewelry. She had short brown hair, too, but it was highlighted with blond streaks and elaborately styled. Her heels were at least three inches high. I eyed the shoes with awe. I would break my neck if I tried to walk in them. But this woman maintained a smile and offered a good word to everyone who approached. Patrick Furnan was colder. His narrow eyes measured and assessed every Were in the gathering crowd.

"Tammy Faye, there, is his wife?" I asked Christine in a discreetly low tone.

Christine made a sound that I would have called snigger if it had issued from someone less patrician. "She does wear a lot of makeup," Christine said. "Her name is Libby, actually. Yes, she's his wife and a full-blooded Were, and they have two children. So he's added to the pack."

Only the oldest child would become a Were at puberty.

"What does he do for a living?" I asked.

"He owns a Harley-Davidson dealership," Christine said.

"That's a natural." Weres tended to like motorcycles a lot.

Christine smiled, probably as close as she came to laughing out loud.

"Who's the front-runner?" I'd been dumped into the middle of a game, and I needed to learn the rules. Later, I was going to let Alcide have it right between the eyes; but right now, I was going to get through the funeral, since that's what I'd come for.

"Hard to say," Christine murmured. "I wouldn't have thrown in with either one, given a choice, but Jackson called on our old friendship, and I had to come down on his side."

"That's not nice."

"No, but it's practical," she said, amused. "He needs all the support he can get. Did Alcide ask you to endorse his father?"

"No. I'd be completely ignorant of the situation if you hadn't been kind enough to fill me in." I gave her a nod of thanks.

"Since you're not a Were—excuse me, honey, but I'm just trying to figure this out—what can you do for Alcide, I wonder? Why'd he drag you into this?"

"He'll have to tell me that real soon," I said, and if my voice was cold and ominous, I just didn't care.

"His last girlfriend disappeared," Christine said thoughtfully. "They were pretty on-again, off-again, Jackson tells me. If his enemies had something to do with it, you might watch your step."

"I don't think I'm in danger," I said.

"Oh?"

But I'd said enough.

"Hmmmm," Christine said after a long, thoughtful look at my face. "Well, she was too much of a diva for someone who isn't even a Were." Christine's voice expressed the contempt the Weres feel for the other shifters. ("Why bother to change, if you can't change into a wolf?" I'd heard a Were say once.)

My attention was caught by the dull gleam of a shaved head, and I stepped a bit to my left to have a better view. I'd never seen this man before. I would certainly have remembered him; he was very tall, taller than Alcide or even Eric, I thought. He had big shoulders and arms roped with muscle. His head and arms were the brown of a Caucasian with a real tan. I could tell, because he was wearing a sleeveless black silk tee tucked into black pants and shiny dress shoes. It was a nippy day at the end of January, but the cold didn't seem to affect him at all. There was a definite space between him and the people around him.

As I looked at him, wondering, he turned and looked at me, as if he could feel my attention. He had a proud nose, and his face was as smooth as his shaved head. At this distance, his eyes looked black.

"Who is that?" I asked Christine, my voice a thread in the wind that had sprung up, tossing the leaves of the holly bushes planted around the church.

Christine darted a look at the man, and she must have known whom I meant, but she didn't answer.

Regular people had gradually been filtering through the Weres, going up the steps and into the church. Now two men in black suits appeared at the doors. They crossed their hands in front of them, and the one on the right nodded at Jackson Herveaux and Patrick Furnan.

The two men, with their female companions, came to stand facing each other at the bottom of the steps. The assembled Weres passed between them to enter the church. Some nodded at one, some at the other, some at both. Fence-sitters. Even after their ranks had been reduced by the recent war with the witches, I counted twenty-five full-blooded adult Weres in Shreveport, a very large pack for such a small city. Its size was attributable to the Air Force base, I figured.

Everyone who walked between the two candidates was a full Were. I saw only two children. Of course, some parents might have left their kids in school rather than bring them to the funeral. But I was pretty sure I was seeing the truth of what Alcide had told me: Infertility and a high infant mortality rate plagued the Weres.

Alcide's younger sister, Janice, had married a human. She herself would never change shape, since she was not the firstborn child. Her son's recessive Were traits, Alcide had told me, might show as increased vigor and a great healing ability. Many professional athletes came from couples whose genetic pool contained a percentage of Were blood.

"We go in a second," Alcide murmured. He was standing beside me, scanning the faces as they went by.

"I'm going to kill you later," I told him, keeping my face calm for the Weres passing by. "Why didn't you explain this?"

The tall man walked up the steps, his arms swinging as he walked, his large body moving with purpose and grace. His head swung toward me as he went by, and I met his eyes. They were very dark, but still I couldn't distinguish the color. He smiled at me.

Alcide touched my hand, as if he knew my attention had wandered. He leaned over to whisper in my ear, "I need your help. I need you to find a chance after the funeral to read Patrick's mind. He's going to do something to sabotage my father."

"Why didn't you just ask me?" I was confused, and mostly I was hurt.

"I thought you might feel like you owed me anyway!"

"How do you figure that?"

"I know you killed Debbie."

If he'd slapped me, it couldn't have shocked me more. I have no idea what my face looked like. After the impact of the shock and the reflexive guilt wore off, I said, "You'd abjured her. What's it to you?"

"Nothing," he said. "Nothing. She was already dead to me." I didn't believe that for a minute. "But you thought it would be a big deal to me, and you concealed it. I figure you'd guess you owed me."

If I'd had a gun in my purse, I would've been tempted to pull it out then. "I don't owe you squat," I said. "I think you came to get me in your dad's car because you knew I'd drive away once you said that."

"No," he said. We were still keeping our voices down, but I could see from the sideways glances we were getting that our intense colloquy was attracting attention. "Well, maybe. Please, forget what I said about you owing me. The fact is, my dad's in trouble and I'd do just about anything to help him out. And you can help."

"Next time you need help, just *ask*. Don't trying blackmailing me into it or maneuvering me into it. I like to help people. But I hate to be pushed and tricked." He'd lowered his eyes, so I grabbed his chin and made him look into mine. *"I hate it."*

I glanced up at the top of the steps to gauge how much interest our quarrel was attracting. The tall man had reappeared. He was looking down at us without perceptible expression. But I knew we had his attention.

Alcide glanced up, too. His face reddened. "We need to go in now. Will you go with me?"

"What is the meaning of me going in with you?"

"It means you're on my father's side in his bid for the pack."

"What does that oblige me to do?"

"Nothing."

"Then why is it important for me to do it?"

"Though choosing a packmaster is pack business, it may influence those who know how much you helped us during the Witch War."

Witch Skirmish would have been more accurate, because though it had certainly been them vs. us, the total number of people involved had been fairly small—say, forty or fifty. But in the history of the Shreveport pack, it was an epic episode, I gathered.

I glared down at my black pumps. I struggled with my

warring instincts. They seemed about equally strong. One said, "You're at a funeral. Don't make a scene. Alcide has been good to you, and it wouldn't hurt you to do this for him." The other said, "Alcide helped you in Jackson because he was trying to get his dad out of trouble with the vampires. Now, again, he's willing to involve you in something dangerous to help his dad out." The first voice chipped in, "He knew Debbie was bad. He tried to pull away from her, and then he abjured her." The second said, "Why'd he love a bitch like Debbie in the first place? Why'd he even consider sticking with her when he had clear evidence she was evil? No one else has suggested she had spellcasting power. This 'spellcasting' thing is a cheap excuse." I felt like Linda Blair in the *The Exorcist,* with her head whirling around on her neck.

Voice number one won out. I put my hand on Alcide's crooked elbow and we went up the stairs and into the church.

The pews were full of regular people. The front three rows on both sides had been saved for the pack. But the tall man, who would stand out anywhere, sat in the back row. I caught a glimpse of his big shoulders before I had to pay strict attention to the pack ceremony. The two Furnan children, cute as the dickens, went solemnly down to the front pew on the right of the church. Then Alcide and I entered, preceding the two candidates for packmaster. This seating ceremony was oddly like a wedding, with Alcide and me being the best man and maid of honor. Jackson and Christine and Patrick and Libby Furnan would enter like the parents of the bride and groom.

What the civilians made of this I don't know.

I knew they were all staring, but I'm used to that. If being a barmaid will get you used to anything, it's being looked over. I was dressed appropriately and I looked as good as I could make myself look, and Alcide had done the same, so let them stare. Alcide and I sat on the front row on the left side of the church, and moved in. I saw Patrick Furnan and his wife, Libby, enter the pew across the aisle. Then I looked back to see Jackson and Christine coming in slowly, looking fittingly grave. There was a slight flutter of heads and hands, a tiny buzz of whispers, and then Christine sidled into the pew, Jackson beside her.

The coffin, draped with an elaborately embroidered cloth, was wheeled up the aisle as we all stood, and then the somber service began.

After going through the litany, which Alcide showed me in the Prayer Book, the priest asked if anyone would like to say a few words about Colonel Flood. One of his Air Force friends went first and spoke of the colonel's devotion to duty and his sense of pride in his command. One of his fellow church members took the next turn, praising the colonel's generosity and applauding the time he'd spent balancing the church's books.

Patrick Furnan left his pew and strode to the lectern. He didn't do a good stride; he was too stout for that. But his speech was certainly a change from the elegies the two previous men had given. "John Flood was a remarkable man and a great leader," Furnan began. He was a much better speaker than I'd expected. Though I didn't know who'd written his remarks, it was someone educated. "In the fraternal order we shared, he was always the one who told us the direction we should take, the goal we should achieve. As he grew older, he remarked often that this was a job for the young."

A right turn from eulogy to campaign speech. I wasn't the only one who'd noticed this; all around me there were little movements, whispered comments.

Though taken aback by the reaction he'd aroused, Patrick Furnan plowed ahead. "I told John that he was the finest man for the job we'd ever had, and I still believe that. No matter who follows in his footsteps, John Flood will never be forgotten or replaced. The next leader can only hope to work as hard as John. I'll always be proud that John put his trust in me more than once, that he even called me his right hand." With those sentences, the Harley dealer underscored his bid to take Colonel's Flood's job as packmaster (or, as I referred to it internally, Leader of the Pack).

Alcide, to my right, was rigid with anger. If he hadn't been sitting in the front row of a funeral, he would have loved to address a few remarks to me on the subject of Patrick Furnan. On the other side of Alcide, I could just barely see Christine, whose face looked carved out of ivory. She was suppressing quite a few things herself.

Alcide's dad waited a moment to begin his trip to the lectern. Clearly, he wanted us to cleanse our mental palate before he gave his address.

Jackson Herveaux, wealthy surveyor and werewolf, gave us the chance to examine his maturely handsome face. He began, "We will not soon see the likes of John Flood. A man whose wisdom had been tempered and tested by the years . . ." Oh, ouch. This wasn't going to be pointed or anything, no sirree.

I tuned out for the rest of the service to think my own thoughts. I had plenty of food for thought. We stood as John Flood, Air Force colonel and packmaster, exited this church for the last time. I remained silent during the ride to the cemetery, stood by Alcide's side during the graveside service, and got back in the car when it was over and all the post-funeral handshaking was done.

I looked for the tall man, but he wasn't at the cemetery.

On the drive back to Bon Temps, Alcide obviously wanted to keep our silence nice and clean, but it was time to answer some questions.

"How did you know?" I asked.

He didn't even try to pretend to misunderstand what I was talking about. "When I came to your house yesterday, I could smell a very, very faint trace of her at your front door," he said. "It took me a while to think it through."

I'd never considered the possibility.

"I don't think I would've picked up on it if I hadn't known her so well," he offered. "I certainly didn't pick up a whiff anywhere else in the house."

So all my scrubbing had been to some avail. I was just lucky Jack and Lily Leeds weren't two-natured. "Do you want to know what happened?"

"I don't think so," he said after an appreciable pause. "Knowing Debbie, I'm guessing you only did what you had to do. After all, it was her scent at your house. She had no business there."

This was far from a ringing endorsement.

"And Eric was still at your house then, wasn't he? Maybe it was Eric?" Alcide sounded almost hopeful.

"No," I said.

"Maybe I do want the whole story."

"Maybe I've changed my mind about telling it to you. You either believe in me, or you don't. Either you think I'm the kind of person who'd kill a woman for no good reason, or you know I'm not." Truly, I was hurt more than I thought I'd be. I was very careful not to slip into Alcide's head, because I was afraid I might pick up on something that would have been even more painful.

Alcide tried several times to open another conversation, but the drive couldn't end soon enough for me. When he pulled into the clearing and I knew I was yards away from being in my own house, the relief was overwhelming. I couldn't scramble out of that fancy car fast enough.

But Alcide was right behind me.

"I don't care," he said in a voice that was almost a growl.

"What?" I'd gotten to my front door, and the key was in the lock.

"I don't care."

"I don't believe that for one minute."

"What?"

"You're harder to read than a plain human, Alcide, but I can see the pockets of reservation in your mind. Since you wanted me to help you out with your dad, I'll tell you: Patrick Whatsisname plans to bring up your dad's gambling problems to show he's unsuitable as packleader." Nothing more underhanded and supernatural than the truth. "I'd read his mind before you asked me to. I don't want to see you for a long, long, long time."

"What?" Alcide said again. He looked like I'd hit him in the head with an iron.

"Seeing you . . . listening to your head . . . makes me feel bad." Of course, there were several different reasons they did, but I didn't want to enumerate them. "So, thanks for the ride to the funeral." (I may have sounded a bit sarcastic.) "I appreciate your thinking of me." (Even a higher probability of sarcasm here.) I entered the house, shut the door on his startled face, and locked it just to be on the safe side. I marched across the living room so he could hear my steps, but then I stopped in the hall and waited to listen while he got back in the Lincoln. I listened to the big car rocket down the driveway, probably putting ruts in my beautiful gravel.

As I shed Tara's suit and bundled it up to drop at the dry

cleaner's, I confess I was mopey. They say when one door shuts, another one opens. But they haven't been living at my house.

Most of the doors I open seem to have something scary crouched behind them, anyway.

7 ~

SAM WAS IN THE BAR THAT NIGHT, SEATED AT A CORner table like a visiting king, his leg propped up on another chair cushioned with pillows. He was keeping one eye on Charles, one eye on the clientele's reaction to a vampire bartender.

People would stop by, drop down in the chair across from him, visit for a few minutes, and then vacate the chair. I knew Sam was in pain. I can always read the preoccupation of people who are hurting. But he was glad to be seeing other people, glad to be back in the bar, pleased with Charles's work.

All this I could tell, and yet when it came to the question of who had shot him, I didn't have a clue. Someone was gunning for the two-natured, someone who'd killed quite a few and wounded even more. Discovering the identity of the shooter was imperative. The police didn't suspect Jason, but his own people did. If Calvin Norris's people decided to take matters into their own hands, they could easily find a chance to take out Jason. They didn't know there were more victims than those in Bon Temps.

I probed into minds, I tried to catch people in unguarded moments, I even tried to think of the most promising candidates for the role of assassin so I wouldn't waste time listening to (for example) Liz Baldwin's worries about her oldest granddaughter.

I assumed the shooter was almost certainly a guy. I knew plenty of women who went hunting and plenty more with access to rifles. But weren't snipers always men? The police were baffled by this sniper's selection of targets, because they didn't know the true nature of all the victims. The two-natured were hampered in their search because they were looking only at local suspects.

"Sookie," Sam said as I passed close to him. "Kneel down here a minute."

I sank to one knee right by his chair so he could speak in a low voice.

"Sookie, I hate to ask you again, but the closet in the storeroom isn't working out for Charles." The cleaning supplies closet in the storeroom was not exactly built to be light tight, but it was inaccessible to daylight, which was good enough. After all, the closet had no windows, and it was inside a room with no windows.

It took me a minute to switch my train of thought to another track. "You can't tell me he's not able to sleep," I said incredulously. Vampires could sleep in the daytime under any circumstances. "And I'm sure you put a lock on the inside of the door, too."

"Yes, but he has to kind of huddle on the floor, and he says it smells like old mops."

"Well, we did keep the cleaning stuff in there."

"What I'm saying is, would it be so bad for him to stay at your place?"

"Why do you really want me to have him at the house?" I asked. "There's got to be a reason more than a strange vampire's comfort during the day, when he's dead, anyway."

"Haven't we been friends a long time, Sookie?"

I smelled something big and rotten.

"Yes," I admitted, standing so that he would have to look up at me. "And?"

"I hear through the grapevine that the Hotshot community has hired a Were bodyguard for Calvin's hospital room."

"Yeah, I think that's kind of strange, too." I acknowledged his unspoken concern. "So I guess you heard what they suspect."

Sam nodded. His bright blue eyes caught mine. "You have to take this seriously, Sookie."

"What makes you think I don't?"

"You refused Charles."

"I don't see what telling him he couldn't sleep in my house has to do with worrying about Jason."

"I think he'd help you protect Jason, if it came to that. I'm down with this leg, or I'd . . . I don't believe it was Jason who shot me."

A knot of tension within me relaxed when Sam said that. I hadn't realized I'd been worried about what he thought, but I had.

My heart softened a little. "Oh, all right," I said with poor grace. "He can come stay with me." I stomped off grumpily, still not certain why I'd agreed.

Sam beckoned Charles over, conferred with him briefly. Later in the evening Charles borrowed my keys to stow his bag in the car. After a few minutes, he was back at the bar and signaled he'd returned my keys to my purse. I nodded, maybe a little curtly. I wasn't happy, but if I had to be saddled with a houseguest, at least he was a polite houseguest.

Mickey and Tara came into Merlotte's that night. As before, the dark intensity of the vampire made everyone in the bar a little excited, a little louder. Tara's eyes followed me with a kind of sad passivity. I was hoping to catch her alone, but I didn't see her leave the table for any reason. I found that was another cause for alarm. When she'd come into the bar with Franklin Mott, she'd always taken a minute to give me a hug, chat with me about family and work.

I caught a glimpse of Claudine the fairy across the room, and though I planned to work my way over to have a word with her, I was too preoccupied with Tara's situation. As usual, Claudine was surrounded by admirers.

Finally, I got so anxious that I took the vampire by the fangs and went over to Tara's table. The snakelike Mickey was staring at our flamboyant bartender, and he scarcely flicked a gaze at me as I approached. Tara looked both hopeful and frightened, and I stood by her and laid my hand on her shoulder to get a clearer picture of her head. Tara has done so well for herself I seldom worry over her one weakness: She picks the wrong men. I was remembering when she dated "Eggs" Benedict, who'd apparently died in a fire the previous fall. Eggs had been a heavy drinker and a weak personality. Franklin Mott had at least treated Tara with respect and had showered her with presents, though the nature of the presents had said, "I'm a mistress," rather than "I'm an honored girlfriend." But how had it come to pass that she was in Mickey's company—Mickey, whose name made even Eric hesitate?

I felt like I'd been reading a book only to discover that someone had ripped a few pages from the middle.

"Tara," I said quietly. She looked up at me, her big brown eyes dull and dead: past fear, past shame.

To the outer eye she looked almost normal. She was well groomed and made up, and her clothing was fashionable and attractive. But inside, Tara was in torment. What was wrong with my friend? Why hadn't I noticed before that something was eating her up from the inside out?

I wondered what to do next. Tara and I were just staring at each other, and though she knew what I was seeing inside her, she wasn't responding. "Wake up," I said, not even knowing where the words were coming from. "Wake up, Tara!"

A white hand grabbed my arm and removed my hand from Tara's shoulder forcibly. "I'm not paying you to touch my date," Mickey said. He had the coldest eyes I'd ever seen—mud colored, reptilian. "I'm paying you to bring our drinks."

"Tara is my friend," I said. He was still squeezing my arm, and if a vampire squeezes you, you know about it. "You're doing something to her. Or you're letting someone else hurt her."

"It's none of your concern."

"It is my concern," I said. I knew my eyes were tearing up from the pain, and I had a moment of sheer cowardice. Looking into his face, I knew he could kill me and be out of the bar before anyone there could stop him. He could take Tara with him, like a pet dog or his livestock. Before the fear could get a grip, I said, "Let go of me." I made each word clear and distinct, even though I knew he could hear a pin drop in a storm.

"You're shaking like a sick dog," he said scornfully.

"Let go of me," I repeated.

"Or you'll do—what?"

"You can't stay awake forever. If it's not me, it'll be someone else."

Mickey seemed to be reconsidering. I don't think it was my threat, though I meant it from the tips of my toes to the roots of my hair.

He looked down at Tara, and she spoke, as though he'd pulled a string. "Sookie, don't make such a big deal out of nothing. Mickey is my man now. Don't embarrass me in front of him."

My hand dropped back to her shoulder and I risked taking my eyes off Mickey to look down at her. She definitely wanted me to back off; she was completely sincere about that. But her thinking about her motivation was curiously murky.

"Okay, Tara. Do you need another drink?" I asked slowly. I was feeling my way through her head, and I was meeting a wall of ice, slippery and nearly opaque.

"No, thank you," Tara said politely. "Mickey and I need to be going now."

That surprised Mickey, I could tell. I felt a little better; Tara was in charge of herself, at least to some extent.

"I'll return your suit. I took it by the cleaner's, already," I said.

"No hurry."

"All right. I'll see you later." Mickey had a firm grip on my friend's arm as the two made their way through the crowd.

I got the empty glasses off the table, swabbed it down, and turned back to the bar. Charles Twining and Sam were on alert. They'd been observing the whole small incident. I shrugged, and they relaxed.

When we closed the bar that night, the new bouncer was waiting at the back door for me when I pulled on my coat and got my keys out of my purse.

I unlocked my car doors and he climbed in.

"Thanks for agreeing to have me in your home," he said.

I made myself say the polite thing back. No point in being rude.

"Do you think Eric will mind my being here?" Charles asked as we drove down the narrow parish road.

"It's not his say-so," I said curtly. It irked me that he automatically wondered about Eric.

"He doesn't come to see you often?" enquired Charles with unusual persistence.

I didn't answer until we'd parked behind my house. "Listen," I said, "I don't know what you heard, but he's not . . . we're not . . . like that." Charles looked at my face and wisely said nothing as I unlocked my back door.

"Feel free to explore," I said after I'd invited him over the threshold. Vampires like to know entrances and exits. "Then I'll show you your sleeping place." While the bouncer looked curiously around the humble house where my family had lived for so many years, I hung up my coat and put my purse in my room. I made myself a sandwich after asking Charles if he wanted some blood. I keep some type O in the refrigerator, and he seemed glad to sit down and drink after he'd studied the house. Charles Twining was a peaceful sort of guy to be around, especially for a vampire. He didn't letch after me, and he didn't seem to want anything from me.

I showed him the lift-up floor panel in the guest bedroom closet. I told him how the television remote worked, showed him my little collection of movies, and pointed out the books on the shelves in the guest bedroom and living room.

"Is there anything else you can think of you might need?" I asked. My grandmother brought me up right, though I don't think she ever imagined I'd have to be hostess to a bunch of vampires.

"No, thank you, Miss Sookie," Charles said politely. His

long white fingers tapped his eye patch, an odd habit of his that gave me the cold gruesomes.

"Then, if you'll excuse me, I'll say good night." I was tired, and it was exhausting work making conversation with a near stranger.

"Of course. Rest easy, Sookie. If I want to roam in the woods . . . ?"

"Feel free," I said immediately. I had an extra key to the back door, and I got it out of the drawer in the kitchen where I kept all the keys. This had been the odds and ends drawer for perhaps eighty years, since the kitchen had been added onto the house. There were at least a hundred keys in it. Some, those that were old when the kitchen was added, were mighty strange looking. I'd labeled the ones from my generation, and I'd put the back door key on a bright pink plastic key ring from my State Farm insurance agent. "Once you're in for the night—well, for good—shoot the dead bolt, please."

He nodded and took the key.

It was usually a mistake to feel sympathy for a vampire, but I couldn't help but think there was something sad about Charles. He struck me as lonely, and there's always something pathetic about loneliness. I'd experienced it myself. I would ferociously deny I was pathetic, but when I viewed loneliness in someone else, I could feel the tug of pity.

I scrubbed my face and pulled on some pink nylon pajamas. I was already half-asleep as I brushed my teeth and crawled into the high old bed my grandmother had slept in until she died. My great-grandmother had made the quilt I pulled over me, and my great-aunt Julia had embroidered the pattern on the edges of the bedspread. Though I might actually be alone in the world—with the exception of my brother, Jason—I went to sleep surrounded by my family.

My deepest sleep is around three a.m., and sometime

during that period I was awakened by the grip of a hand on my shoulder.

I was shocked into total awareness, like a person being thrown into a cold pool. To fight off the shock that was close to paralyzing me, I swung my fist. It was caught in a chilly grip.

"No, no, no, ssshhh" came a piercing whisper out of the darkness. English accent. Charles. "Someone's creeping around outside your house, Sookie."

My breath was as wheezy as an accordion. I wondered if I was going to have a heart attack. I put a hand over my heart, as if I could hold it in when it seemed determined to pound its way out of my chest.

"Lie down!" he said right into my ear, and then I felt him crouch beside my bed in the shadows. I lay down and closed my eyes almost all the way. The headboard of the bed was situated between the two windows in the room, so whoever was creeping around my house couldn't really get a good look at my face. I made sure I was lying still and as relaxed as I could get. I tried to think, but I was just too scared. If the creeper was a vampire, he or she couldn't come in—unless it was Eric. Had I rescinded Eric's invitation to enter? I couldn't remember. *That's the kind of thing I need to keep track of,* I babbled to myself.

"He's passed on," Charles said in a voice so faint it was almost the ghost of a voice.

"What is it?" I asked in a voice I hoped was nearly as soundless.

"It's too dark outside to tell." If a vampire couldn't see what was out there, it must be really dark. "I'll slip outside and find out."

"No," I said urgently, but it was too late.

Jesus Christ, shepherd of Judea! What if the prowler was Mickey? He'd kill Charles—I just knew it.

"Sookie!" The last thing I expected—though frankly, I was way beyond consciously expecting anything—was for Charles to call to me. "Come out here, if you please!"

I slid my feet into my pink fuzzy slippers and hurried down the hall to the back door; that was where the voice had been coming from, I thought.

"I'm turning on the outside light," I yelled. Didn't want anyone to be blinded by the sudden electricity. "You sure it's safe out there?"

"Yes," said two voices almost simultaneously.

I flipped the switch with my eyes shut. After a second, I opened them and stepped to the door of the screened-in back porch, in my pink jammies and slippers. I crossed my arms over my chest. Though it wasn't cold tonight, it was cool.

I absorbed the scene in front of me. "Okay," I said slowly. Charles was in the graveled area where I parked, and he had an elbow around the neck of Bill Compton, my neighbor. Bill is a vampire, has been since right after the Civil War. We have a history. It's probably just a pebble of a history in Bill's long life, but in mine, it's a boulder.

"Sookie," Bill said between clenched teeth. "I don't want to cause this foreigner harm. Tell him to get his hands off me."

I mulled that over at an accelerated rate. "Charles, I think you can let him go," I said, and as fast as I could snap my fingers, Charles was standing beside me.

"You know this man?" Charles's voice was steely.

Just as coldly, Bill said, "She does know me, intimately."

Oh, *gack*.

"Now, is that polite?" I may have had a little cold steel in my own voice. "I don't go around telling everyone the details of our former relationship. I would expect the same of any gentleman."

To my gratification, Charles glared at Bill, raising one eyebrow in a very superior and irritating way.

"So this one is sharing your bed now?" Bill jerked his head toward the smaller vampire.

If he'd said anything else, I could've held on to my temper. I don't lose it a lot, but when I do, it's well and truly lost. "Is that any of your business?" I asked, biting off each word. "If I sleep with a hundred men, or a hundred sheep, it's not any of your business! Why are you creeping around my house in the middle of the night? You scared me halfway to death."

Bill didn't look remotely repentant. "I'm sorry you wakened and were frightened," he said insincerely. "I was checking on your safety."

"You were roaming around the woods and smelled another vampire," I said. He'd always had an extremely acute sense of smell. "So you came over here to see who it was."

"I wanted to be sure you weren't being attacked," Bill said. "I thought I caught a sniff of human, too. Did you have a human visitor today?"

I didn't believe for a minute Bill was only concerned with my safety, but I didn't want to believe jealousy brought him to my window, or some kind of prurient curiosity. I just breathed in and out for a minute, calming down and considering.

"Charles is not attacking me," I said, proud I was speaking so levelly.

Bill sneered. "Charles," he repeated in tones of great scorn.

"Charles Twining," said my companion, bowing—if you could call a slight inclination of his curly brown head a bow.

"Where did you come up with this one?" Bill's voice had regained its calm.

"Actually, he works for Eric, like you do."

"Eric's provided you with a bodyguard? You need a bodyguard?"

"Listen, bozo," I said through clenched jaws, "my life goes on while you're gone. So does the town. People are getting shot around here, among them Sam. We needed a substitute bartender, and Charles was volunteered to help us out." That may not have been entirely accurate, but I was not in the accuracy business at the moment. I was in the Make My Point business.

At least Bill was appropriately taken aback by the information.

"Sam. Who else?"

I was shivering, since it wasn't nylon pajama weather. But I didn't want Bill in the house. "Calvin Norris and Heather Kinman."

"Shot dead?"

"Heather was. Calvin was pretty badly wounded."

"Have the police arrested anyone?"

"No."

"Do you know who did it?"

"No."

"You're worried about your brother."

"Yes."

"He turned at the full moon."

"Yes."

Bill looked at me with what might have been pity. "I'm sorry, Sookie," he said, and he meant it.

"No point telling me about it," I snapped. "Tell Jason—it's him who turns fuzzy."

Bill's face went cold and stiff. "Excuse my intrusion," he said. "I'll go." He melted into the woods.

I don't know how Charles reacted to the episode, because I turned and stalked back into the house, turning off the outside light as I went. I threw myself back in bed and lay there, fuming and fussing silently. I pulled the covers up over my head so the vampire would take the hint that I didn't want to discuss the incident. He moved so quietly, I couldn't be sure where he was in the house; I think he paused in the doorway for a second, and then moved on.

I lay awake for at least forty-five minutes, and then I found myself settling back into sleep.

Then someone shook me by the shoulder. I smelled sweet perfume, and I smelled something else, something awful. I was terribly groggy.

"Sookie, your house is on fire," a voice said.

"Couldn't be," I said. "I didn't leave anything on."

"You have to get out now," the voice insisted. A persistent shriek reminded me of fire drills at the elementary school.

"Okay," I said, my head thick with sleep and (I saw when I opened my eyes) smoke. The shriek in the background, I slowly realized, was my smoke detector. Thick gray plumes were drifting through my yellow and white bedroom like evil genies. I wasn't moving fast enough for Claudine, who yanked me out of bed and carried me out the front door. A woman had never lifted me, but, of course, Claudine was no ordinary woman. She set me on my feet in the chilly grass of the front yard. The cold feel of it suddenly woke me up. This was not a nightmare.

"My house caught on fire?" I was still struggling to be alert.

"The vampire says it was that human, there," she said, pointing to the left of the house. But for a long minute my eyes were fixed on the terrible sight of flames, and the red glow of fire lighting the night. The back porch and part of the kitchen were blazing.

I made myself look at a huddled form on the ground, close to a forsythia in bud. Charles was kneeling by it.

"Have you called the fire department?" I asked them both as I picked my way around the house in my bare feet to have a look at the recumbent figure. I peered at the dead man's slack face in the poor light. He was white, clean-shaven, and probably in his thirties. Though conditions were hardly ideal, I didn't recognize him.

"Oh, no, I didn't think of it." Charles looked up from the body. He came from a time before fire departments.

"And I forgot my cell phone," said Claudine, who was thoroughly modern.

"Then I have to go back in and do it, if the phones still work," I said, turning on my heel. Charles rose to his inconsiderable height and stared at me.

"You will not go back in there." This was definitely an order from Claudine. "New man, you run fast enough to do that."

"Fire," Charles said, "is very quickly fatal to vampires."

It was true; they went up like a torch once they caught. Selfishly, for a second I almost insisted; I wanted my coat and my slippers and my purse.

"Go call from Bill's phone," I said, pointing in the right direction, and off he took like a jackrabbit. The minute he was out of sight and before Claudine could stop me, I dashed back in the front door and made my way to my room. The smoke was much thicker, and I could see the flames a few feet down the hall in the kitchen. As soon as I saw the flames I knew I'd made a huge mistake by reentering the house, and it was hard not to panic. My purse was right where I'd left it, and my coat was tossed over the slipper chair in a corner of my room. I couldn't find my slippers, and I knew I couldn't stay. I fumbled in a drawer for a pair of socks, since I knew for sure they were there, and then I ran out of my room, coughing and choking. Acting through sheer instinct, I turned briefly to my left to shut the door to the kitchen, and then whirled to hurry out the front door. I fell over a chair in the living room.

"That was stupid," said Claudine the fairy, and I shrieked. She grabbed me around the waist and ran out of the house again, with me under her arm like a rolled-up carpet.

The combination of shrieking and coughing tied my respiratory system in knots for a minute or two, during which time Claudine moved me farther away from my house. She sat me down on the grass and put the socks on my feet. Then she helped me stand up and get my arms into the coat. I buttoned it around me gratefully.

This was the second time Claudine had appeared out of nowhere when I was about to get into serious trouble. The first time, I'd fallen asleep at the wheel after a very long day.

"You're making it awfully hard on me," she said. She still sounded cheerful, but maybe not quite as sweet.

Something changed about the house, and I realized the night-light in the hall had gone out. Either the electricity was out, or the line had been shut down in town by the fire department.

"I'm sorry," I said, feeling that was appropriate, though I had no idea why Claudine felt put upon when it was my house that was burning. I wanted to hurry to the backyard to get a better view, but Claudine caught hold of my arm.

"No closer," she said simply, and I could not break her hold. "Listen, the trucks are coming."

Now I could hear the fire engines, and I blessed every person who was coming to help. I knew the pagers had gone off all over the area, and the volunteers had rushed to the firehouse straight from their beds.

Catfish Hunter, my brother's boss, pulled up in his car. He leaped out and ran right to me. "Anyone left inside?" he asked urgently. The town's fire truck pulled in after him, scattering my new gravel all to hell.

"No," I said.

"Is there a propane tank?"

"Yes."

"Where?"

"Backyard."

"Where's your car, Sookie?"

"In the back," I said, and my voice was starting to shake.

"Propane tank in the back!" Catfish bellowed over his shoulder.

There was an answering yell, followed by a lot of purposeful activity. I recognized Hoyt Fortenberry and Ralph Tooten, plus four or five other men and a couple of women.

Catfish, after a quick conversation with Hoyt and Ralph, called over a smallish woman who seemed swamped by her gear. He pointed to the still figure in the grass, and she threw off her helmet and knelt beside him. After some peering and touching, she shook her head. I barely recognized her as Dr. Robert Meredith's nurse, Jan something.

"Who's the dead man?" asked Catfish. He didn't seem too upset by the corpse.

"I have no idea," I said. I only discovered how shocked I was by the way my voice came out—quavery, small. Claudine put her arm around me.

A police car pulled in to the side of the fire truck, and Sheriff Bud Dearborn got out of the driver's seat. Andy Bellefleur was his passenger.

Claudine said, "Ah-oh."

"Yeah," I said.

Then Charles was with me again, and Bill was right on his heels. The vampires took in the frantic but purposeful activity. They noticed Claudine.

The small woman, who'd stood to resume her gear, called, "Sheriff, do me a favor and call an ambulance to take this body away."

Bud Dearborn glanced at Andy, who turned away to speak into the car radio.

"Having one dead beau ain't enough, Sookie?" Bud Dearborn asked me.

Bill snarled, the firefighters broke out the window by my great-great-grandmother's dining table, and a visible rush of heat and sparks gushed into the night. The pumper truck made a lot of noise, and the tin roof that covered the kitchen and porch separated from the house.

My home was going up in flames and smoke.

8

CLAUDINE WAS ON MY LEFT. BILL CAME TO STAND TO my right and took my hand. Together, we watched the firefighters aim the hose through the broken window. A sound of shattering glass from the other side of the house indicated they were breaking the window over the sink, too. While the firefighters concentrated on the fire, the police concentrated on the body. Charles stepped up to bat right away.

"I killed him," he said calmly. "I caught him setting fire to the house. He was armed, and he attacked me."

Sheriff Bud Dearborn looked more like a Pekinese than any human should look. His face was practically concave. His eyes were round and bright, and at the moment extremely curious. His brown hair, liberally streaked with gray, was combed back from his face all around, and I expected him to snuffle when he spoke. "And you would be?" he asked the vampire.

"Charles Twining," Charles answered gracefully. "At your service."

I wasn't imagining the snort the sheriff gave or Andy Bellefleur's eye roll.

"And you'd be on the spot because . . . ?"

"He's staying with me," Bill said smoothly, "while he works at Merlotte's."

Presumably the sheriff had already heard about the new bartender, because he just nodded. I was relieved at not having to confess that Charles was supposed to be sleeping in my closet, and I blessed Bill for having lied about that. Our eyes met for a moment.

"So you admit you killed this man?" Andy asked Charles. Charles nodded curtly.

Andy beckoned to the woman in hospital scrubs who'd been waiting by her car—which made maybe five cars in my front yard, plus the fire truck. This new arrival glanced at me curiously as she walked past to the huddled form in the bushes. Pulling a stethoscope from a pocket, she knelt by the man and listened to various parts of his body. "Yep, dead as a doornail," she called.

Andy had gotten a Polaroid out of the police car to take pictures of the body. Since the only light was the flash of the camera and the flicker of flame from my burning house, I didn't think the pictures would turn out too well. I was numb with shock, and I watched Andy as if this were an important activity.

"What a pity. It would have been a good thing to find out why he torched Sookie's house," Bill said as he watched Andy work. His voice rivaled a refrigerator for coldness.

"In my fear for Sookie's safety, I suppose I struck too hard." Charles tried to look regretful.

"Since his neck seems to be broken, I suppose you did," said the doctor, studying Charles's white face with the same careful attention she'd given mine. The doctor was in her thirties, I thought; a woman slim to the point of skinny, with very short red hair. She was about five foot three, and she had elfin features, or at least the kind I'd always thought of as elfin: a short, turned-up nose, wide eyes, large mouth. Her words were both dry and bold, and she didn't seem at all disconcerted by or excited at being called out in the middle of the night for something like this. She must be the parish coroner, so I must have voted for her, but I couldn't recall her name.

"Who are you?" Claudine asked in her sweetest voice.

The doctor blinked at the vision of Claudine. Claudine, at this ungodly hour of the morning, was in full makeup and a fuchsia knit top with black knit leggings. Her shoes were fuchsia and black striped, and her jacket was, too. Claudine's black rippling hair was held off her face with fuchsia combs.

"I'm Dr. Tonnesen. Linda. Who are you?"

"Claudine Crane," the fairy said. I'd never known the last name Claudine used.

"And why were you here on the spot, Ms. Crane?" Andy Bellefleur asked.

"I'm Sookie's fairy godmother," Claudine said, laughing. Though the scene was grim, everyone else laughed, too. It was like we just couldn't stop being cheerful around Claudine. But I wondered very much about Claudine's explanation.

"No, really," Bud Dearborn said. "Why are you here, Ms. Crane?"

Claudine smiled impishly. "I was spending the night with Sookie," she said, winking.

In a second, we were the objects of fascinated scrutiny from every male within hearing, and I had to lock down my head as if it were a maximum-security prison to block the mental images the guys were broadcasting.

Andy shook himself, closed his mouth, and squatted by

the dead man. "Bud, I'm going to roll him," he said a little hoarsely, and turned the corpse so he could feel inside the dead man's pockets. The man's wallet proved to be in his jacket, which seemed a little unusual to me. Andy straightened and stepped away from the body to examine the billfold's contents.

"You want to have a look, see if you recognize him?" Sheriff Dearborn asked me. Of course I didn't, but I also saw that I really didn't have a choice. Nervously, I inched a little closer and looked again at the face of the dead man. He still looked ordinary. He still looked dead. He might be in his thirties. "I don't know him," I said, my voice small in the din of the firefighters and the water pouring onto the house.

"What?" Bud Dearborn was having trouble hearing me. His round brown eyes were locked onto my face.

"Don't know him!" I said, almost yelling. "I've never seen him, that I remember. Claudine?"

I don't know why I asked Claudine.

"Oh, yes, I've seen him," she said cheerfully.

That attracted the undivided attention of the two vampires, the two lawmen, the doctor, and me.

"Where?"

Claudine threw her arm around my shoulders. "Why, he was in Merlotte's tonight. You were too worried about your friend to notice, I guess. He was over in the side of the room where I was sitting." Arlene had been working that side.

It wasn't too amazing that I'd missed one male face in a crowded bar. But it did bother me that I'd been listening in to people's thoughts and I'd missed out on thoughts that must have been relevant to me. After all, he was in the bar with me, and a few hours later he'd set fire to my house. He must have been mulling me over, right?

"This driver's license says he's from Little Rock, Arkansas," Andy said.

"That wasn't what he told me," Claudine said. "He said he was from Georgia." She looked just as radiant when she realized he'd lied to her, but she wasn't smiling. "He said his name was Marlon."

"Did he tell you why he was in town, Ms. Crane?"

"He said he was just passing through, had a motel room up on the interstate."

"Did he explain any further?"

"Nope."

"Did you go to his motel, Ms. Crane?" Bud Dearborn asked in his best nonjudgmental voice.

Dr. Tonnesen was looking from speaker to speaker as if she was at a verbal tennis match.

"Gosh, no, I don't do things like that." Claudine smiled all around.

Bill looked as if someone had just waved a bottle of blood in front of his face. His fangs extended, and his eyes fixed on Claudine. Vampires can only hold out so long when fairies are around. Charles had stepped closer to Claudine, too.

She had to leave before the lawmen observed how the vampires were reacting. Linda Tonnesen had already noticed; she herself was pretty interested in Claudine. I hoped she'd just attribute the vamps' fascination to Claudine's excellent looks, rather than the overwhelming allure fairies held for vamps.

"Fellowship of the Sun," Andy said. "He has an honest-to-God membership card in here. There's no name written on the card; that's strange. His license is issued to Jeff Marriot." He looked at me questioningly.

I shook my head. The name meant nothing to me.

It was just like a Fellowship member to think that he could do something as nasty as torching my house—with me in it—and no one would question him. It wasn't the first time the Fellowship of the Sun, an anti-vampire hate group, had tried to burn me alive.

"He must have known you've had, ah, an association with vampires," Andy said into the silence.

"I'm losing my home, and I could have died, because I know vampires?"

Even Bud Dearborn looked a little embarrassed.

"Someone must have heard you used to date Mr. Compton, here," Bud muttered. "I'm sorry, Sookie."

I said, "Claudine needs to leave."

The abrupt change of subject startled both Andy and Bud, as well as Claudine. She looked at the two vampires, who were perceptibly closer to her, and hastily said, "Yes, I'm sorry, I have to get back home. I have to work tomorrow."

"Where's your car, Ms. Crane?" Bud Dearborn looked around elaborately. "I didn't see any car but Sookie's, and it's parked in the back."

"I'm parked over at Bill's," Claudine lied smoothly, having had years of practice. Without waiting for further discussion, she disappeared into the woods, and only my hands gripping their arms prevented Charles and Bill from gliding into the darkness after her. They were staring into the blackness of the trees when I pinched them, hard.

"What?" asked Bill, almost dreamily.

"Snap out of it," I muttered, hoping Bud and Andy and the new doctor wouldn't overhear. They didn't need to know that Claudine was supernatural.

"That's quite a woman," Dr. Tonnesen said, almost as dazed as the vampires. She shook herself. "The ambulance will come get, uh, Jeff Marriot. I'm just here because I had my scanner turned on as I was driving back from my shift at the Clarice hospital. I need to get home and get some sleep. Sorry about your fire, Ms. Stackhouse, but at least you didn't end up like this guy here." She nodded down at the corpse.

As she got into her Ranger, the fire chief trudged up to us. I'd known Catfish Hunter for years—he'd been a friend of my dad's—but I'd never seen him in his capacity as volunteer fire chief. Catfish was sweating despite the cold, and his face was smudged with smoke.

"Sookie, we done got it out," he said wearily. "It's not as bad as you might think."

"It's not?" I asked in a small voice.

"No, honey. You lost your back porch and your kitchen and your car, I'm afraid. He splashed some gas in that, too. But most of the house should be okay."

The kitchen . . . where the only traces of the death I'd caused could have been found. Now not even the technicians featured on the Discovery Channel could find any blood traces in the scorched room. Without meaning to, I began to laugh. "The kitchen," I said between giggles. "The kitchen's all gone?"

"Yes," said Catfish uneasily. "I hope you got you some homeowners insurance."

"Oh," I said, trying hard not to giggle any more. "I do. It was hard for me to keep up the payments, but I kept the policy Grandmother had on the house." Thank God my grandmother had been a great believer in insurance. She'd seen too many people drop policy payments to cut their monthly expenses and then suffer losses they were unable to recoup.

"Who's it with? I'll call right now." Catfish was so anxious to stop me laughing, he was ready to make clown faces and bark if I asked him to.

"Greg Aubert," I said.

The whole night suddenly rose up and whalloped me one. My house had burned, at least partially. I'd had more than one prowler. I had a vampire in residence for whom daytime cover had to be provided. My car was gone. There was a dead man named Jeff Marriot in my yard, and he'd set fire to my house and car out of sheer prejudice. I was overwhelmed.

"Jason isn't at home," Catfish said from a distance. "I tried him. He'd want her to come over to his house."

"She and Charles—that is, Charles and I will take her over to my house," Bill said. He seemed to be equally far away.

"I don't know about that," Bud Dearborn said doubtfully. "Sookie, is that okay with you?"

I could barely make my mind shuffle through a few options. I couldn't call Tara because Mickey was there. Arlene's trailer was as crowded as it needed to be already.

"Yes, that would be all right," I said, and my voice sounded remote and empty, even to my own ears.

"All right, long's we know where to reach you."

"I called Greg, Sookie, and left a message on his office answering machine. You better call him yourself in the morning," Catfish said.

"Fine," I said.

And all the firefighters shuffled by, and they all told me how sorry they were. I knew every one of them: friends of my father's, friends of Jason's, regulars at the bar, high school acquaintances.

"You all did the best you could," I said over and over. "Thanks for saving most of it."

And the ambulance came to cart away the arsonist.

By then, Andy had found a gasoline can in the bushes, and the corpse's hands reeked of gasoline, Dr. Tonnesen said.

I could hardly believe that a stranger had decided I should lose my home and my life because of my dating preference. Thinking at that moment of how close I'd come to death, I didn't feel it was unjust that he'd lost his own life in the process. I admitted to myself that I thought Charles had done a good thing. I might owe my life to Sam's insistence that the vampire be billeted at my house. If Sam had been there at the moment, I would have given him a very enthusiastic thank-you.

Finally Bill and Charles and I started over to Bill's house. Catfish had advised me not to go back into my house until the morning, and then only after the insurance agent and the arson investigator had checked it over. Dr. Tonnesen had told me that if I felt wheezy, to come in to her office in the morning. She'd said some other stuff, but I hadn't quite absorbed it.

It was dark in the woods, of course, and by then it was maybe five in the morning. After a few paces into the trees, Bill picked me up and carried me. I didn't protest, because I was so tired I'd been wondering how I was going to manage stumbling through the cemetery.

He put me down when we reached his house. "Can you make it up the stairs?" he asked.

"I'll take you," offered Charles.

"No, I can do it," I said, and started up before they could say anything more. To tell the truth, I was not so sure I could, but slowly I made my way up to the bedroom I'd used when Bill had been my boyfriend. He had a snug light-tight place somewhere on the ground floor of the house, but I'd never asked him exactly where. (I had a pretty good idea it was in the space the builders had lopped off the kitchen to create the hot tub/plant room.) Though the water table is too high in Louisiana for houses to have basements, I was almost as sure there was another dark hole concealed somewhere. He had room for Charles without them bunking together, anyway—not that that was too high on my list of concerns. One of my nightgowns still lay in the drawer in the old-fashioned bedroom, and there was still a toothbrush of mine in the hall bathroom. Bill hadn't put my things in the trash; he'd left them, like he'd expected me to return.

Or maybe he just hadn't had much reason to go upstairs since we'd broken up.

Promising myself a long shower in the morning, I took off my smelly, stained pajamas and ruined socks. I washed my face and pulled on the clean nightgown before I crawled in the high bed, using the antique stool still positioned where I'd left it. As the incidents of the day and night buzzed in my head like bees, I thanked God for the fact that my life had been spared, and that was all I had time to say to Him before sleep swallowed me up.

I slept only three hours. Then worry woke me up. I was up in plenty of time to meet Greg Aubert, the insurance agent. I dressed in a pair of Bill's jeans and a shirt of his. They'd been left outside my door, along with heavy socks. His shoes were out of the question, but to my delight I found an old pair of rubber-soled slippers I'd left at the very back of the closet. Bill still had some coffee and a coffeemaker in his kitchen from our courtship, and I was grateful to have a mug to carry with me as I made my way carefully across the cemetery and through the belt of woods surrounding what was left of my house.

Greg was pulling into the front yard as I stepped from the trees. He got out of his truck, scanned my oddly fitting ensemble, and politely ignored it. He and I stood side by side, regarding the old house. Greg had sandy hair and rimless glasses, and he was an elder in the Presbyterian Church. I'd always liked him, at least in part because whenever I'd taken my grandmother by to pay her premiums, he'd come out of his office to shake her hand and make her feel like a valued client. His business acumen was matched only by his luck. People had said for years that his personal good fortune extended to his policyholders, though of course they said this in a joking kind of way.

"If only I could have foreseen this," Greg said. "Sookie, I am so sorry this happened."

"What do you mean, Greg?"

"Oh, I'm just . . . I wish I'd thought of you needing more coverage," he said absently. He began walking around to the back of the house, and I trailed behind him. Curious, I began to listen in to his head, and I was startled out of my gloom by what I heard there.

"So casting spells to back up your insurance really works?" I asked.

He yelped. There's no other word for it. "It's true about you," he gasped. "I—I don't—it's just . . ." He stood outside my blackened kitchen and gaped at me.

"It's okay," I said reassuringly. "You can pretend I don't know if it'll help you feel better."

"My wife would just die if she knew," he said soberly. "And the kids, too. I just want them kept separate from this part of my life. My mother was . . . she was . . ."

"A witch?" I supplied helpfully.

"Well, yes." Greg's glasses glinted in the early morning sun as he looked at what was left of my kitchen. "But my dad always pretended he didn't know, and though she kept training me to take her place, I wanted to be a normal man more than anything in the world." Greg nodded, as if to say he'd achieved his goal.

I looked down into my mug of coffee, glad I had something to hold in my hands. Greg was lying to himself in a major way, but it wasn't up to me to point that out to him. It was something he'd have to square with his God and his conscience. I wasn't saying Greg's method was a bad one, but it sure wasn't a normal man's choice. Insuring your livelihood (literally) by the use of magic had to be against some kind of rule.

"I mean, I'm a good agent," he said, defending himself, though I hadn't said a word. "I'm careful about what I insure. I'm careful about checking things out. It's not all the magic."

"Oh, no," I said, because he would just explode with anxiety if I didn't. "People have accidents anyway, right?"

"Regardless of what spells I use," he agreed gloomily. "They drive drunk. And sometimes metal parts give way, no matter what."

The idea of conventional Greg Aubert going around Bon Temps putting spells on cars was almost enough to distract me from the ruin of my house . . . but not quite.

In the clear chilly daylight, I could see the damage in full. Though I kept telling myself it could have been much worse—and that I was very lucky that the kitchen had extended off the back of the house, since it had been built at a later date—it had also been the room that had held big-ticket items. I'd have to replace the stove, the refrigerator, the hot water heater, and the microwave, and the back porch had been home to my washer and drier.

After the loss of those major appliances, there came the dishes and the pots and the pans and the silverware, some of it very old indeed. One of my greats had come from a family with a little money, and she'd brought a set of fine china and a silver tea service that had been a pain to polish. I'd never have to polish it again, I realized, but there was no joy in the thought. My Nova was old, and I'd needed to replace it for a long time, but I hadn't planned on that being now.

Well, I had insurance, and I had money in the bank, thanks to the vampires who'd paid me for keeping Eric when he'd lost his memory.

"And you had smoke detectors?" Greg was asking.

"Yes, I did," I said, remembering the high-pitched pulsing that had started up right after Claudine had woken me.

"If the ceiling in the hall is still there, you'll be able to see one."

There were no more back steps to get us up onto the porch, and the porch floorboards looked very unsteady. In fact, the washer had half fallen through and was tilted at an odd angle. It made me sick, seeing my everyday things, things I'd touched and used hundreds of times, exposed to the world and ruined.

"We'll go through from the front door," Greg suggested, and I was glad to agree.

It was still unlocked, and I felt a flutter of alarm before I realized how ludicrous that was. I stepped in. The first thing I noticed was the smell. Everything reeked of smoke. I opened the windows, and the cool breeze that blew through began to clear the smell out until it was just tolerable.

This end of the house was better than I'd expected. The furniture would need cleaning, of course. But the floor was solid and undamaged. I didn't even go up the stairs; I seldom used the rooms up there, so whatever had happened up there could wait.

My arms were crossed under my breasts. I looked from side to side, moving slowly across the room toward the hall. I felt the floor vibrate as someone else came in. I knew without looking around that Jason was behind me. He and Greg said something to each other, but after a second Jason fell silent, as shocked as I was.

We passed into the hall. The door to my bedroom and the door to the bedroom across the hall were both open. My bedding was still thrown back. My slippers were beside the night table. All the windows were smudged with smoke and moisture, and the dreadful odor grew even stronger. There was the smoke detector on the hall ceiling. I pointed to it silently. I opened the door to the linen closet and found that everything in it felt damp. Well, these things could be washed. I went into my room and opened my closet door. My closet shared a wall with the kitchen. At first glance my clothes looked intact, until I noticed that each garment hanging on a wire hanger had a line across the shoulders where the heated hanger had singed the cloth. My shoes had baked. Maybe three pairs were usable.

I gulped.

Though I felt shakier by the second, I joined my brother and the insurance agent as they carefully continued down the hall to the kitchen.

The floor closest to the old part of the house seemed okay. The kitchen had been a large room, since it had also served as the family dining room. The table was partially burned, as were two of the chairs. The linoleum on the floor was all broken up, and some of it was charred. The hot water heater had gone through the floor, and the curtains that had covered the window over the sink were hanging in strips. I remembered Gran making those curtains; she hadn't enjoyed sewing, but the ones from JCPenney that she'd liked were just too much. So she'd gotten out her mother's old sewing machine and bought some cheap but pretty flowered material at Hancock's, and she'd measured, and cursed under her breath, and worked and worked until finally she'd gotten them done. Jason and I had admired them extravagantly to make her feel it had been worth the effort, and she'd been so pleased.

I opened one drawer, the one that had held all the keys. They were melted together. I pressed my lips together, hard. Jason stood beside me, looked down.

"Shit," he said, his voice low and vicious. That helped me push the tears back.

I held on to his arm for just a minute. He patted me awkwardly. Seeing items so familiar, items made dear by use, irrevocably altered by fire was a terrible shock, no matter how many times I reminded myself that the whole house could have been consumed by the flames; that I could have died, too. Even if the smoke detector had wakened me in time, there was every likelihood I would have run outside to be confronted by the arsonist, Jeff Marriot.

Almost everything on the east side of the kitchen was ruined. The floor was unstable. The kitchen roof was gone.

"It's lucky the rooms upstairs don't extend over the kitchen," Greg said when he came down from examining the two bedrooms and the attic. "You'll have to get a builder to let you know, but I think the second story is essentially sound."

I talked to Greg about money after that. When would it come? How much would it be? What deductible would I have to pay?

Jason wandered around the yard while Greg and I stood by his car. I could interpret my brother's posture and movements. Jason was very angry: at my near-death escape, at what had happened to the house. After Greg drove off, leaving me with an exhausting list of things to do and phone calls to make (from where?) and work to get ready for (wearing what?), Jason meandered over to me and said, "If I'd been here, I coulda killed him."

"In your new body?" I asked.

"Yeah. It would've given that sumbitch the scare of his life before he left it."

"I think Charles probably was pretty scary, but I appreciate the thought."

"They put the vamp in jail?"

"No, Bud Dearborn just told him not to leave town. After all, the Bon Temps jail doesn't have a vampire cell. And regular cells don't hold 'em, plus they have windows."

"That's where the guy was from—Fellowship of the Sun? Just a stranger who came to town to do you in?"

"That's what it looks like."

"What they got against you? Other than you dating Bill and associating with some of the other vamps?"

Actually, the Fellowship had quite a bit against me. I'd been responsible for their huge Dallas church being raided and one of their main leaders going underground. The papers had been full of what the police had found in the Fellowship building in Texas. Arriving to find the members dashing in turmoil around their building, claiming vampires had attacked them, the police entered the building to search it and found a basement torture chamber, illegal arms adapted to shoot wooden stakes into vampires, and a corpse. The police failed to see a single vampire. Steve and Sarah Newlin, the leaders of the Fellowship church in Dallas, had been missing since that night.

I'd seen Steve Newlin since then. He'd been at Club Dead in Jackson. He and one of his cronies had been preparing to stake a vampire in the club when I'd prevented them. Newlin had escaped; his buddy hadn't.

It appeared that the Newlins' followers had tracked me down. I hadn't foreseen such a thing, but then, I'd never foreseen anything that had happened to me in the past year. When Bill had been learning how to use his computer, he'd told me that with a little knowledge and money, anyone could be found through a computer.

Maybe the Fellowship had hired private detectives, like the couple who had been in my house yesterday. Maybe Jack and Lily Leeds had just been pretending to be hired by the Pelt family? Maybe the Newlins were their real employers? They hadn't struck me as politicized people, but the power of the color green is universal.

"I guess dating a vampire was enough for them to hate me," I told Jason. We were sitting on the tailgate of his truck, staring dismally at the house. "Who do you think I should call about rebuilding the kitchen?"

I didn't think I needed an architect: I just wanted to replace what was missing. The house was raised up off the ground, so slab size wasn't a factor. Since the floor was burned through in the kitchen and would have to be completely replaced, it wouldn't cost much more to make the kitchen a little bigger and enclose the back porch completely. The washer and dryer wouldn't be so awful to use in bad weather, I thought longingly. I had more than enough money to satisfy the deductible, and I was sure the insurance would pay for most of the rest.

After a while, we heard another truck coming. Maxine Fortenberry, Hoyt's mother, got out with a couple of laundry baskets. "Where's your clothes, girl?" she called. "I'm gonna take them home and wash them, so you'll have something to wear that don't smell like smoke."

After I protested and she insisted, we went into the chokingly unpleasant air of the house to get some clothes. Maxine also insisted on getting an armful of linens out of the linen closet to see if some of them could be resurrected.

Right after Maxine left, Tara drove her new car into the clearing, followed by her part-time help, a tall young woman called McKenna, who was driving Tara's old car.

After a hug and a few words of sympathy, Tara said, "You drive this old Malibu while you're getting your insurance stuff straightened out. It's just sitting in my carport doing nothing, and I was just about to put it in the paper in the For Sale column. You can be using it."

"Thank you," I said in a daze. "Tara, that's so nice of you." She didn't look good, I noticed vaguely, but I was too sunk in my own troubles to really evaluate Tara's demeanor. When she and McKenna left, I gave them a limp wave good-bye.

After that, Terry Bellefleur arrived. He offered to demolish the burned part for a very nominal sum, and for a little bit more he'd haul all the resultant trash to the parish dump. He'd start as soon as the police gave him the go-ahead, he said, and to my astonishment he gave me a little hug.

Sam came after that, driven by Arlene. He stood and looked at the back of the house for a few minutes. His lips were tightly compressed. Almost any man would have said, "Pretty lucky I sent the vampire home with you, huh?" But Sam didn't. "What can I do?" he said instead.

"Keep me working," I said, smiling. "Forgive me coming to work in something besides my actual work clothes." Arlene walked all around the house, and then hugged me wordlessly.

"That's easily done," he said. He still wasn't smiling. "I hear that the guy who started the fire was a Fellowship member, that this is some kind of payback for you dating Bill."

"He had the card in his wallet, and he had a gas can." I shrugged.

"But how'd he find you? I mean, no one around here . . ." Sam's voice trailed off as he considered the possibility more closely.

He was thinking, as I had, that though the arson could be just because I'd dated Bill, it seemed a drastic overreaction. A more typical retaliation was a Fellowship member throwing pig's blood on humans who dated, or had a work partnership with, a vampire. That had happened more than once, most notably to a designer from Dior who'd employed all vampire models for one spring show. Such incidents usually occurred in big cities, cities that hosted large Fellowship "churches" and a bigger vampire population.

What if the man had been hired to set fire to my house by someone else? What if the Fellowship card in his wallet was planted there for misdirection?

Any of these things could be true; or all of them, or none of them. I couldn't decide what I believed. So, was I the target of an assassin, like the shape-shifters? Should I, too, fear the shot from the dark, now that the fire had failed?

That was such a frightening prospect that I flinched from pursuing it. Those were waters too deep for me.

The state police arson investigator appeared while Sam and Arlene were there. I was eating a lunch plate Arlene had brought me. That Arlene was not much of a food person is the nicest way to put it, so my sandwich was made of cheap bologna and plastic cheese, and my canned drink was off-brand sugared tea. But she'd thought of me and she'd brought them to me, and her kids had drawn a picture for me. I would have been happy if she'd brought me just a slice of bread under those conditions.

Automatically, Arlene made eyes at the arson investigator. He was a lean man in his late forties named Dennis Pettibone. Dennis had a camera, a notebook, and a grim outlook. It took Arlene maybe two minutes of conversation to coax a little smile from Mr. Pettibone's lips, and his brown eyes were admiring her curves after two more minutes had passed. Before Arlene drove Sam home, she had a promise from the investigator that he'd drop by the bar that evening.

Also before she left, Arlene offered me the foldout couch in her trailer, which was sweet of her, but I knew it would crowd her and throw off her get-the-kids-to-school morning routine, so I told her I had a place to stay. I didn't think Bill would evict me. Jason had mentioned his house was open to me, and to my amazement, before he left, Sam said, "You can stay with me, Sookie. No strings. I have two empty bedrooms in the double-wide. There's actually a bed in one of them."

"That's so nice of you," I said, putting all my sincerity into my voice. "Every soul in Bon Temps would have us on the way to being married if I did that, but I sure do appreciate it."

"You don't think they won't make assumptions if you stay with Bill?"

"I can't marry Bill. Not legal," I replied, cutting off that argument. "Besides, Charles is there, too."

"Fuel to the fire," Sam pointed out. "That's even spicier."

"That's kind of flattering, crediting me with enough pizzazz to take care of two vampires at a go."

Sam grinned, which knocked about ten years off his age. He looked over my shoulder as we heard the sound of gravel crunching under yet another vehicle. "Look who's coming," he said.

A huge and ancient pickup lumbered to a stop. Out of it stepped Dawson, the huge Were who'd been acting as Calvin Norris's bodyguard.

"Sookie," he rumbled, his voice so deep I expected the ground to vibrate.

"Hey, Dawson." I wanted to ask, "What are you doing here?" but I figured that would sound plain rude.

"Calvin heard about your fire," Dawson said, not wasting time with preliminaries. "He told me to come by here and see was you hurt, and to tell you that he is thinking about you and that if he were well, he would be here pounding nails already."

I saw from the corner of my eye that Dennis Pettibone was eyeing Dawson with interest. Dawson might as well have been wearing a sign that said DANGEROUS DUDE on it.

"You tell him I'm real grateful for the thought. I wish he were well, too. How's he doing, Dawson?"

"He got a couple of things unhooked this morning, and he's been walking a little. It was a bad wound," Dawson said. "It'll take a bit." He glanced over to see how far away the arson investigator was. "Even for one of us," he added.

"Of course," I said. "I appreciate your coming by."

"Also, Calvin says his house is empty while he's in the hospital, if you need a place to stay. He'd be glad to give you the use of it."

That, too, was kind, and I said so. But I would feel very awkward, being obliged to Calvin in such a significant way.

Dennis Pettibone called me over. "See, Ms. Stackhouse," he said. "You can see where he used the gasoline on your porch. See the way the fire ran out from the splash he made on the door?"

I gulped. "Yes, I see."

"You're lucky there wasn't any wind last night. And most of all, you're lucky that you had that door shut, the one between the kitchen and the rest of the house. The fire would have gone right down that hall if you hadn't shut the door. When the firefighters smashed that window on the north side, the fire ran that way looking for oxygen, instead of trying to make it into the rest of the house."

I remembered the impulse that had pushed me back into the house against all common sense, the last-minute slam of that door.

"After a couple of days, I don't think the bulk of the house will even smell as bad," the investigator told me. "Open the windows now, pray it don't rain, and fairly soon I don't think you'll have much problem. Course, you got to call the power company and talk to them about the electricity. And the propane company needs to take a look at the tank. So the house ain't livable, from that point of view."

The gist of what he was saying was, I could just sleep there to have a roof over my head. No electricity, no heat, no hot water, no cooking. I thanked Dennis Pettibone and excused myself to have a last word with Dawson, who'd been listening in.

"I'll try to come see Calvin in a day or two, once I get this straightened out," I said, nodding toward the blackened back of my house.

"Oh, yeah," the bodyguard said, one foot already in his pickup. "Calvin said let him know who done this, if it was ordered by someone besides the sumbitch dead at the scene."

I looked at what remained of my kitchen and could almost count the feet from the flames to my bedroom. "I appreciate that most of all," I said, before my Christian self could smother the thought. Dawson's brown eyes met mine in a moment of perfect accord.

9

THANKS TO MAXINE, I HAD CLEAN-SMELLING clothes to wear to work, but I had to go buy some footwear at Payless. Normally, I put a little money into my shoes since I have to stand up so much, but there was no time to go to Clarice to the one good shoe shop there or to drive over to Monroe to the mall. When I got to work, Sweetie Des Arts came out of the kitchen to hug me, her thin body wrapped in a white cook's apron. Even the boy who bussed the tables told me he was sorry. Holly and Danielle, who were switching off shifts, each gave me a pat on the shoulder and told me they hoped things got better for me.

Arlene asked me if I thought that handsome Dennis Pettibone would be coming by, and I told her I was sure he would.

"I guess he has to travel a lot," she said thoughtfully. "I wonder where he's based."

"I got his business card. He's based in Shreveport. He told me he bought himself a small farm right outside of Shreveport, now that I think about it."

Arlene's eyes narrowed. "Sounds like you and Dennis had a nice talk."

I started to protest that the arson investigator was a little long in the tooth for me, but since Arlene had stuck to saying she was thirty-six for the past three years, I figured that would be less than tactful. "He was just passing the time of day," I told her. "He asked me how long I'd worked with you, and did you have any kids."

"Oh. He did?" Arlene beamed. "Well, well." She went to check on her tables with a cheerful strut to her walk.

I set about my work, having to take longer than usual to do everything because of the constant interruptions. I knew some other town sensation would soon eclipse my house fire. Though I couldn't hope anyone else would experience a similar disaster, I would be glad when I wasn't the object of discussion of every single bar patron.

Terry hadn't been able to handle the light daytime bar duties today, so Arlene and I pitched in to cover it. Being busy helped me feel less self-conscious.

Though I was coasting on three hours of sleep, I managed okay until Sam called me from the hallway that led to his office and the public bathrooms.

Two people had come in earlier and gone up to his corner table to talk to him; I'd noted them only in passing. The woman was in her sixties, very round and short. She used a cane. The young man with her was brown haired, with a sharp nose and heavy brows to give his face some character. He reminded me of someone, but I couldn't make the reference pop to the top of my head. Sam had ushered them back into his office.

"Sookie," Sam said unhappily, "the people in my office want to talk to you."

"Who are they?"

"She's Jeff Marriot's mother. The man is his twin."

"Oh my God," I said, realizing the man reminded me of the corpse. "Why do they want to talk to me?"

"They don't think he ever had anything to do with the Fellowship. They don't understand anything about his death."

To say I dreaded this encounter was putting it mildly. "Why talk to me?" I said in a kind of subdued wail. I was nearly at the end of my emotional endurance.

"They just . . . want answers. They're grieving."

"So am I," I said. "My home."

"Their loved one."

I stared at Sam. "Why should I talk to them?" I asked. "What is it you want from me?"

"You need to hear what they have to say," Sam said with a note of finality in his voice. He wouldn't push any more, and he wouldn't explain any more. Now the decision was up to me.

Because I trusted Sam, I nodded. "I'll talk to them when I get off work," I said. I secretly hoped they'd leave by then. But when my shift was over, the two were still sitting in Sam's office. I took off my apron, tossed it in the big trash can labeled DIRTY LINEN (reflecting for the hundredth time that the trash can would probably implode if anyone put some actual linen in it), and plodded into the office.

I looked the Marriots over more carefully now that we were face-to-face. Mrs. Marriot (I assumed) was in bad shape. Her skin was grayish, and her whole body seemed to sag. Her glasses were smeared because she'd been weeping so much, and she was clutching damp tissues in her hands. Her son was shocked expressionless. He'd lost his twin, and he was sending me so much misery I could hardly absorb it.

"Thanks for talking to us," he said. He rose from his seat automatically and extended his hand. "I'm Jay Marriot, and this is my mother, Justine."

This was a family that found a letter of the alphabet it liked and stuck to it.

I didn't know what to say. Could I tell them I was sorry their loved one was dead, when he'd tried to kill me? There was no rule of etiquette for this; even my grandmother would have been stymied.

"Miss—Ms.—Stackhouse, had you ever met my brother before?"

"No," I said. Sam took my hand. Since the Marriots were seated in the only two chairs Sam's office could boast, he and I leaned against the front of his desk. I hoped his leg wasn't hurting.

"Why would he set fire to your house? He'd never been arrested before, for anything," Justine spoke for the first time. Her voice was rough and choked with tears; it had an undertone of pleading. She was asking me to let this not be true, this allegation about her son Jeff.

"I sure don't know."

"Could you tell us how this happened? His—death, I mean?"

I felt a flare of anger at being obliged to pity them—at the necessity for being delicate, for treating them specially. After all, who had almost died here? Who had lost part of her home? Who was facing a financial crunch that only chance had reduced from a disaster? Rage surged through me, and Sam let go of my hand and put his arm around me. He could feel the tension in my body. He was hoping I would control the impulse to lash out.

I held on to my better nature by my fingernails, but I held on.

"A friend woke me up," I said. "When we got outside, we found a vampire who is staying with my neighbor—also a vampire—standing by Mr. Marriot's body. There was a gasoline can near to the . . . nearby. The doctor who came said there was gas on his hands."

"What killed him?" The mother again.

"The vampire."

"Bit him?"

"No, he . . . no. No biting."

"How, then?" Jay was showing some of his own anger.

"Broke his neck, I think."

"That was what we heard at the sheriff's office," Jay said. "But we just didn't know if they were telling the truth."

Oh, for goodness's sake.

Sweetie Des Arts stuck her head in to ask Sam if she could borrow the storeroom keys because she needed a case of pickles. She apologized for interrupting. Arlene waved a hand at me as she went down the hall to the employees' door, and I wondered if Dennis Pettibone had come in the bar. I'd been so sunk in my own problems, I hadn't noticed. When the outside door clunked shut behind her, the silence seemed to gather in the little room.

"So why was the vampire in your yard?" Jay asked impatiently. "In the middle of the night?"

I did not tell him it was none of his business. Sam's hand stroked my arm. "That's when they're up. And he was staying at the only other house out by mine." That's what we'd told the police. "I guess he heard someone in my yard while he was close and came to investigate."

"We don't know how Jeff got there," Justine said. "Where is his car?"

"I don't know."

"And there was a card in his wallet?"

"Yes, a Fellowship of the Sun membership card," I told her.

"But he had nothing particular against vampires," Jay protested. "We're twins. I would have known if he'd had some big grudge. This just doesn't make any sense."

"He did give a woman in the bar a fake name and hometown," I said, as gently as I could.

"Well, he was just passing through," Jay said. "I'm a married man, but Jeff 's divorced. I don't like to say this in front of my mother, but it's not unknown for men to give a false name and history when they meet a woman in a bar."

This was true. Though Merlotte's was primarily a neighborhood bar, I'd listened to many a tale from out-of-towners who'd dropped in; and I'd known for sure they were lying.

"Where was the wallet?" Justine asked. She looked up at me like an old beaten dog, and it made my heart sick.

"In his jacket pocket," I said.

Jay stood up abruptly. He began to move, pacing in the small space he had at his disposal. "There again," he said, his voice more animated, "that's just not like Jeff. He kept his billfold in his jeans, same as me. We never put our wallets in our jacket."

"What are you saying?" Sam asked.

"I'm saying that I don't think Jeff did this," his twin said. "Even those people at the Fina station, they could be mistaken."

"Someone at the Fina says he bought a can of gas there?" Sam asked.

Justine flinched again, the soft skin of her chin shaking.

I'd been wondering if there might be something to the Marriots' suspicions, but that idea was extinguished now. The phone rang, and all of us jumped. Sam picked it up and said, "Merlotte's," in a calm voice. He listened, said,

"Um-hum," and "That right?" and finally, "I'll tell her." He hung up.

"Your brother's car's been found," he told Jay Marriot. "It's on a little road almost directly across from Sookie's driveway."

The light went out completely on the little family's ray of hope, and I could only feel sorry for them. Justine seemed ten years older than she had when she'd come into the bar, and Jay looked like he'd gone days without sleep or food. They left without another word to me, which was a mercy. From the few sentences they exchanged with each other, I gathered they were going to see Jeff's car and ask if they could remove any of his belongings from it. I thought they would meet another blank wall there.

Eric had told me that that little road, a dirt track leading back to a deer camp, was where Debbie Pelt had hidden her car when she'd come to kill me. Might as well put up a sign: PARKING FOR SOOKIE STACKHOUSE NIGHTTIME ATTACKS.

Sam came swinging back into the room. He'd been seeing the Marriots out. He stood by me propped against his desk and set his crutches aside. He put his arm around me. I turned to him and slid my arms around his waist. He held me to him, and I felt peaceful for a wonderful minute. The heat of his body warmed me, and the knowledge of his affection comforted me.

"Does your leg hurt?" I asked when he moved restlessly.

"Not my leg," he said.

I looked up, puzzled, to meet his eyes. He looked rueful. Suddenly, I became aware of exactly what was hurting Sam, and I flushed red. But I didn't let go of him. I was reluctant to end the comfort of being close to someone—no, of being close to Sam. When I didn't move away, he slowly put his lips to mine, giving me every chance to step out of reach. His mouth brushed mine once, twice. Then he settled in to kissing me, and the heat of his tongue filled my mouth, stroking.

That felt incredibly good. With the visit of the Marriot family, I'd been browsing the Mystery section. Now I'd definitely wandered over to the Romances.

His height was close enough to mine that I didn't have to strain upward to meet his mouth. His kiss became more urgent. His lips strayed down my neck, to the vulnerable and sensitive place just at the base, and his teeth nipped very gently.

I gasped. I just couldn't help it. If I'd had the gift of teleportation, I would've had us somewhere more private in an instant. Remotely, I felt there was something kind of tacky at feeling this lustful in a messy office in a bar. But the heat surged as he kissed me again. We'd always had something between us, and the smoldering ember had just burst into flame.

I struggled to hold on to some sense. Was this survivor lust? What about his leg? Did he really need the buttons on his shirt?

"Not good enough for you here," he said, doing a little gasping of his own. He pulled away and reached for his crutches, but then he hauled me back and kissed me again. "Sookie, I'm going to—"

"What are you going to do?" asked a cold voice from the doorway.

If I was shocked senseless, Sam was enraged. In a split second I was pushed to one side, and he launched himself at the intruder, broken leg and all.

My heart was thumping like a scared rabbit's, and I put one hand over it to make sure it stayed in my chest. Sam's sudden attack had knocked Bill to the floor. Sam pulled back his fist to get in a punch, but Bill used his greater weight and strength to roll Sam until he was on the bottom. Bill's fangs were out and his eyes were glowing.

"Stop!" I yelled at a reduced volume, scared the patrons would come running. In a little fast action of my own, I gripped Bill's smooth dark hair with both hands and used it to yank his head back. In the excitement of the moment, Bill reached behind him to catch my wrists in his hands, and he began twisting. I choked with pain. Both my arms were about to break when Sam took the opportunity to sock Bill in the jaw with all his power. Shifters are not as powerful as Weres and vampires, but they can pack quite a punch, and Bill was rocked sideways. He also came to his senses. Releasing my arms, he rose and turned to me in one graceful movement.

My eyes welled full of tears from the pain, and I opened them wide, determined not to let the drops roll down my cheeks. But I'm sure I looked exactly like someone who was trying hard not to cry. I was holding my arms out in front of me, wondering when they'd stop hurting.

"Since your car was burned, I came to get you because it was time for you to get off work," Bill said, his fingers gently evaluating the marks on my forearms. "I swear I just intended to do you a favor. I swear I wasn't spying on you. I swear I never intended you any harm."

That was a pretty good apology, and I was glad he'd spoken first. Not only was I in pain, I was totally embarrassed. Naturally, Bill had no way of knowing that Tara had loaned me a car. I should have left him a note or left a message on his answering machine, but I'd driven straight to work from the burned house, and it simply hadn't crossed my mind. Something else did occur to me, as it should have right away.

"Oh, Sam, did your leg get hurt worse?" I brushed past Bill to help Sam to his feet. I took as much of his weight as I could, knowing he'd rather lie on the floor forever than accept any assistance from Bill. Finally, with some difficulty, I maneuvered Sam upright, and I saw he was careful to keep his weight on his good leg. I couldn't even imagine how Sam must be feeling.

He was feeling pretty pissed off, I discovered directly. He glared past me at Bill. "You come in without calling out, without knocking? I'm sure you don't expect me to say I'm sorry for jumping you." I'd never seen Sam so angry. I could tell that he was embarrassed that he hadn't "protected" me more effectively, that he was humiliated that Bill had gained the upper hand and furthermore had hurt me. Last but not least, Sam was coping with the backwash from all those hormones that had been exploding when we'd been interrupted.

"Oh, no. I don't expect that." Bill's voice dropped in temperature when he spoke to Sam. I expected to see icicles form on the walls.

I wished I were a thousand miles away. I longed for the ability to walk out, get into my own car, and drive to my own home. Of course, I couldn't. At least I had the use of a car, and I explained that to Bill.

"Then I needn't have gone to the trouble of coming to get you, and you two could have continued uninterrupted," he said in an absolutely lethal tone. "Where are you going to spend the night, if I may ask? I was going to go to the store to buy food for you."

Since Bill hated grocery shopping, that would have been a major effort, and he wanted to be sure I knew about it. (Of course, it was also possible that he was making this up on the spot to be sure I felt as guilty as possible.)

I reviewed my options. Though I never knew what I'd walk into over at my brother's, that seemed my safest choice. "I'm going to run by my house to get some makeup out of the bathroom, and then I'm going to Jason's," I said.

"Thank you for putting me up last night, Bill. I guess you brought Charles to work? Tell him if he wants to spend the night at my house, I guess the, ah, hole is okay."

"Tell him yourself. He's right outside," Bill said in a voice I can only characterize as grumpy. Bill's imagination had evidently spun a whole different scenario for the evening. The way events were unfolding was making him mighty unhappy.

Sam was in so much pain (I could see it hovering like a red glow around him) that the most merciful thing I could do was clear out of there before he gave into it. "I'll see you tomorrow, Sam," I said, and kissed him on the cheek.

He tried to smile at me. I didn't dare offer to help him over to his trailer while the vampires were there, because I knew Sam's pride would suffer. At the moment, that was more important to him than the state of his injured leg.

Charles was behind the bar and already busy. When Bill offered accommodations again for a second day, Charles accepted rather than opting for my untested hidey hole. "We have to check your hiding place, Sookie, for cracks that may have occurred during the fire," Charles said seriously.

I could understand the necessity, and without saying a word to Bill, I got into the loaner car and drove to my house. We'd left the windows open all day, and the smell had largely dissipated. That was a welcome development. Thanks to the strategy of the firefighters and the inexpert way the fire had been set, the bulk of my house would be livable in short order. I'd called a contractor, Randall Shurtliff, that evening from the bar, and he'd agreed to stop by the next day at noon. Terry Bellefleur had promised to start removing the remains of the kitchen early the next day. I would have to be there to set aside anything I could salvage. I felt like I had two jobs now.

I was suddenly and completely exhausted, and my arms

ached. I would have huge bruises the next day. It was almost too warm to justify long sleeves, but I'd have to wear them. Armed with a flashlight from the glove compartment of Tara's car, I got my makeup and some more clothes from my bedroom, throwing them all into a sport duffle I'd won at the Relay for Life. I tossed in a couple of paperbacks I hadn't read yet—books I'd traded for at the library swap rack. That prompted another line of thought. Did I have any movies that needed to go back to the rental place? No. Library books? Yes, had to return some, and I needed to air them out first. Anything else that belonged to another person? Thank goodness I'd dropped Tara's suit at the cleaner's.

There was no point in closing and locking the windows, which I'd left open to dissipate the odor, as the house was easily accessible through the burned kitchen. But when I went out my front door, I locked it behind me. I'd gotten to Hummingbird Road before I realized how silly that had been, and as I drove to Jason's, I found myself smiling for the first time in many, many hours.

10

MY MELANCHOLY BROTHER WAS GLAD TO SEE ME. The fact that his new "family" didn't trust him had been eating away at Jason all day. Even his panther girlfriend, Crystal, was nervous about seeing him while the cloud of suspicion hung around him. She'd sent him packing when he'd shown up on her front doorstep this evening. When I found out he'd actually driven out to Hotshot, I exploded. I told my brother in no uncertain terms that he apparently had a death wish and I was not responsible for whatever happened to him. He responded that I'd never been responsible for anything that he did, anyway, so why would I start now?

It went on like that for a while.

After he'd grudgingly agreed to stay away from his fellow shifters, I carried my bag down the short hall to the guest bedroom. This was where he kept his computer, his old high school trophies from the baseball team and the football team, and an ancient foldout couch on hand primarily for visitors who drank too much and couldn't drive home. I didn't even bother to unfold it but spread out an ancient quilt over the glossy Naugahyde. I pulled another one over me.

After I said my prayers, I reviewed my day. It had been so full of incident that I got tired trying to remember everything. In about three minutes, I was out like a light. I dreamed about growling animals that night: they were all around me in the fog, and I was scared. I could hear Jason screaming somewhere in the mist, though I couldn't find him to defend him.

Sometimes you don't need a psychiatrist to interpret a dream, right?

I woke up just a bit when Jason left for work in the morning, mostly because he slammed the door behind him. I dozed off again for another hour, but then I woke up decisively. Terry would be coming to my house to begin tearing down the ruined part, and I needed to see if any of my kitchen things could be saved.

Since this was liable to be a dirty job, I borrowed Jason's blue jumpsuit, the one he put on when he worked on his car. I looked in his closet and pulled out an old leather jacket Jason wore for rough work. I also appropriated a box of garbage bags. As I started Tara's car, I wondered how on earth I could repay her for its use. I reminded myself to pick up her suit. Since it was on my mind, I made a slight detour to retrieve it from the dry cleaner's.

Terry was in a stable mood today, to my relief. He was smiling as he smacked away at the charred boards of the back porch with a sledgehammer. Though the day was very cool, Terry wore only a sleeveless T-shirt tucked in his jeans. It covered most of the dreadful scars. After greeting him and registering that he didn't want to talk, I went in through the front door. I was drawn down the hall to the kitchen to look again at the damage.

The firefighters had said the floor was safe. It made me nervous to step out onto the scorched linoleum, but after a moment or two, I felt easier. I pulled on gloves and began to work, going through cabinets and cupboards and drawers. Some things had melted or twisted with the heat. A few things, like my plastic colander, were so warped it took me a second or two to identify what I was holding.

I tossed the ruined things directly out the south kitchen window, away from Terry.

I didn't trust any of the food that had been in the cabinets that were on the outer wall. The flour, the rice, the sugar—they'd all been in Tupperware containers, and though the seals had held, I just didn't want to use the contents. The same held true of the canned goods; for some reason, I felt uneasy about using food from cans that had gotten so hot.

Fortunately, my everyday stoneware and the good china that had belonged to my great-great-grandmother had survived, since they were in the cabinet farthest from the flames. Her sterling silver was in fine shape, too. My far more useful stainless tableware, much closer to the fire, was warped and twisted. Some of the pots and pans were usable.

I worked for two or three hours, consigning things to the growing pile outside the window or bagging them in Jason's garbage bags for future use in a new kitchen. Terry worked hard, too, taking a break every now and then to drink bottled water while he perched on the tailgate of his pickup. The temperature rose to the upper sixties. We might have a few more hard frosts, and there was always the chance of an ice storm, but it was possible to count on spring coming soon.

It wasn't a bad morning. I felt like I was taking a step toward regaining my home. Terry was an undemanding companion, since he didn't like to talk, and he was exorcising his demons with hard work. Terry was in his late fifties now. Some of the chest hair I could see above his T-shirt neck was gray. The hair on his head, once auburn, was fading as he aged. But he was a strong man, and he swung his sledgehammer with vigor and loaded boards onto the flatbed of his truck with no sign of strain.

Terry left to take a load to the parish dump. While he was gone, I went into my bedroom and made my bed—a strange and foolish thing to do, I know. I would have to take the sheets off and wash them; in fact, I'd have to wash almost every piece of fabric in the house to completely rid it of the smell of burning. I'd even have to wash the walls and repaint the hall, though the paint in the rest of the house seemed clean enough.

I was taking a break out in the yard when I heard a truck approaching a moment before it appeared, coming out of the trees that surrounded the driveway. To my astonishment, I recognized it as Alcide's truck, and I felt a pang of dismay. I'd told him to stay away.

He seemed miffed about something when he leaped out of the cab. I'd been sitting in the sunshine on one of my aluminum lawn chairs, wondering what time it was and wondering when the contractor would get here. After the all-round discomfort of my night at Jason's, I was also planning on finding somewhere else to stay while the kitchen was being rebuilt. I couldn't imagine the rest of my house being habitable until the work was complete, and that might be months from now. Jason wouldn't want me around that long, I was sure. He'd have to put up with me if I wanted to stay—he was my brother, after all—but I didn't want to strain his fraternal spirit. There wasn't *anyone* I wanted to stay with for a couple of months, when I came to consider the matter.

"Why didn't you tell me?" Alcide bellowed as his feet touched the ground.

I sighed. Another angry man.

"We aren't big buddies right now," I reminded him. "But I would have gotten around to it. It's only been a couple of days."

"You should have called me first thing," he told me, striding around the house to survey the damage. He stopped right in front of me. "You could have died," he said, as if it was big news.

"Yes," I said. "I know that."

"A vampire had to save you." There was disgust in his voice. Vamps and Weres just didn't get along.

"Yes," I agreed, though actually my savior had been Claudine. But Charles had killed the arsonist. "Oh, would you rather I'd burned?"

"No, of course not!" He turned away, looked at the mostly dismantled porch. "Someone's working on tearing down the damaged part already?"

"Yes."

"I could have gotten a whole crew out here."

"Terry volunteered."

"I can get you a good rate on the reconstruction."

"I've lined up a contractor."

"I can loan you the money to do it."

"I have the money, thank you very much."

That startled him. "You do? Where'd—" He stopped before saying something inexcusable. "I didn't think your grandmother had had much to leave you," he said, which was almost as bad.

"I earned the money," I said.

"You earned the money from Eric?" he guessed accurately.

Alcide's green eyes were hot with anger. I thought he was going to shake me.

"You just calm down, Alcide Herveaux," I said sharply. "How I earned it is none of your damn business. I'm glad to have it. If you'll get down off your high horse, I'll tell you that I'm glad you're concerned about me, and I'm grateful you're offering help. But don't treat me like I'm a slow fifth grader in the special class."

Alcide stared down at me while my speech soaked in. "I'm sorry. I thought you—I thought we were close enough for you to've called me that night. I thought . . . maybe you needed help."

He was playing the "you hurt my feelings" card.

"I don't mind asking for help when I need it. I'm not that proud," I said. "And I'm glad to see you." (Not totally true.) "But don't act like I can't do things for myself, because I can, and I am."

"The vampires paid you for keeping Eric while the witches were in Shreveport?"

"Yes," I said. "My brother's idea. It embarrassed me. But now I'm grateful I've got the money. I won't have to borrow any to get the house put into shape."

Terry Bellefleur returned with his pickup just then, and I introduced the two men. Terry didn't seem at all impressed by meeting Alcide. In fact, he went right back to work after he gave Alcide's hand a perfunctory shake. Alcide eyed Terry doubtfully.

"Where are you staying?" Alcide had decided not to ask questions about Terry's scars, thank goodness.

"I'm staying with Jason," I said promptly, leaving out the fact that I hoped that would be temporary.

"How long is it gonna take to rebuild?"

"Here's the guy who can tell me," I said gratefully. Randall Shurtliff was in a pickup, too, and he had his wife and partner with him. Delia Shurtliff was younger than Randall, pretty as a picture, and tough as nails. She was Randall's second wife. When he'd gotten divorced from his "starter" wife, the one who'd had three children and cleaned his house for twelve years, Delia had already been working for Randall and had gradually begun to run his business for him far more efficiently than he'd ever done. He was able to give his first wife and sons more advantages with the money his second wife had helped him earn than he otherwise might have, had he married someone else. It was common knowledge (by which I mean I wasn't the only one who knew this) that Delia was very ready for Mary Helen to remarry and for the three Shurtliff boys to graduate from high school.

I shut out Delia's thoughts with a firm resolve to work on keeping my shields up. Randall was pleased to meet Alcide, whom he'd known by sight, and Randall was even more eager to take on rebuilding my kitchen when he knew I was a friend of Alcide's. The Herveaux family carried a lot of weight personally and financially in the building trade. To my irritation, Randall began addressing all his remarks to Alcide instead of to me. Alcide accepted this quite naturally.

I looked at Delia. Delia looked at me. We were very unlike, but we were of one mind at that moment.

"What do you think, Delia?" I asked her. "How long?"

"He'll huff and he'll puff," she said. Her hair was paler than mine, courtesy of the beauty salon, and she wore emphatic eye makeup, but she was dressed sensibly in khakis and a polo shirt with "Shurtliff Construction" in script above her left breast. "But he's got that house over on Robin Egg to finish. He can work on your kitchen before he begins a house in Clarice. So, say, three to four months from now, you'll have you a usable kitchen."

"Thanks, Delia. Do I need to sign something?"

"We'll get an estimate ready for you. I'll bring it to the bar for you to check. We'll include the new appliances, because we can get a dealer discount. But I'll tell you right now, you're looking at this ballpark."

She showed me the estimate on a kitchen renovation they had done a month before.

"I have it," I said, though I gave one long shriek deep inside. Even with the insurance money, I'd be using up a big chunk of what I had in the bank.

I should be thankful, I reminded myself sternly, that Eric had paid me all that money, that I had it to spend. I wouldn't have to borrow from the bank or sell the land or take any other drastic step. I should think of that money as just passing through my account rather than living there. I hadn't actually owned it. I'd just had custody of it for a while.

"You and Alcide good friends?" Delia asked, our business concluded.

I gave it some thought. "Some days," I answered honestly.

She laughed, a harsh cackle that was somehow sexy. Both men looked around, Randall smiling, Alcide quizzical. They were too far away to hear what we were saying.

"I'll tell you something," Delia Shurtliff said to me quietly. "Just between you and me and the fencepost. Jackson Herveaux's secretary, Connie Babcock—you met her?"

I nodded. I'd at least seen her and talked to her when I'd dropped by Alcide's office in Shreveport.

"She got arrested this morning for stealing from Herveaux and Son."

"What did she take?" I was all ears.

"This is what I don't understand. She was caught sneaking some papers out of Jackson Herveaux's office. Not business papers, but personal, the way I heard it. She said she'd been paid to do it."

"By?"

"Some guy who owns a motorcycle dealership. Now, does that make sense?"

It did if you knew that Connie Babcock had been sleeping with Jackson Herveaux, as well as working in his office. It did if you suddenly realized that Jackson had taken Christine Larrabee, a pure Were and influential, to the funeral of Colonel Flood, instead of taking the powerless human Connie Babcock.

While Delia elaborated on the story, I stood, lost in thought. Jackson Herveaux was without a doubt a clever businessman, but he was proving to be a stupid politician. Having Connie arrested was dumb. It drew attention to the Weres, had the potential to expose them. A people so secretive would not appreciate a leader who couldn't manage a problem with more finesse than that.

As a matter of fact, since Alcide and Randall were still discussing the rebuilding of my house with each other instead of with me, a lack of finesse appeared to run in the Herveaux family.

Then I frowned. It occurred to me that Patrick Furnan might be devious and clever enough to have engineered the whole thing—bribing the spurned Connie to steal Jackson's private papers, then ensuring she was caught—knowing that Jackson would react with a hot head. Patrick Furnan might be much smarter than he looked, and Jackson Herveaux much stupider, at least in the way that mattered if you wanted to be packmaster. I tried to shake off these disturbing speculations. Alcide hadn't said a word about Connie's arrest, so I had to conclude that he considered it none of my business. Okay, maybe he thought I had enough to worry about, and he was right. I turned my mind back to the moment.

"You think they'd notice if we left?" I asked Delia.

"Oh, yeah," Delia said confidently. "It might take Randall a minute, but he'd look around for me. He'd get lost if he couldn't find me."

Here was a woman who knew her own worth. I sighed and thought about getting in my borrowed car and driving away. Alcide, catching sight of my face, broke off his discussion with my contractor and looked guilty. "Sorry," he called. "Habit."

Randall came back to where I was standing quite a bit faster than he'd wandered away. "Sorry," he apologized. "We were talking shop. What did you have in mind, Sookie?"

"I want the same dimensions for the kitchen as before," I said, having dropped visions of a larger room after seeing the estimate. "But I want the new back porch to be just as wide as the kitchen, and I want to enclose it."

Randall produced a tablet, and I sketched what I wanted.

"You want the sinks where they were? You want all the appliances where they were?"

After some discussion, I drew everything I wanted, and Randall said he'd call me when it was time to pick out the cabinets and the sinks and all the other incidentals.

"One thing I wish you'd do for me today or tomorrow is fix the door from the hall into the kitchen," I said. "I want to be able to lock the house."

Randall rummaged around in the back of his pickup for a minute or two and came up with a brand-new doorknob with a lock, still in its package. "This won't keep out anyone really determined," he said, still in the apologetic vein, "but it's better'n nothing." He had it installed within fifteen minutes, and I was able to lock the sound part of the house away from the burned part. I felt much better, though I knew this lock wasn't worth much. I needed to put a dead bolt on the inside of the door; that would be even better. I wondered if I could do it myself, but I recalled that would entail cutting away some of the door frame, and I wasn't anything of a carpenter. Surely I could find someone who'd help me with that task.

Randall and Delia left with many assurances that I would be next on the list, and Terry resumed work. Alcide said, "You're never alone," in mildly exasperated tones.

"What did you want to talk about? Terry can't hear us over here." I led the way over to where my aluminum chair was sitting under a tree. Its companion was leaning up against the rough bark of the oak, and Alcide unfolded it. It creaked a little under his weight as he settled into it. I assumed he was going to tell me about the arrest of Connie Babcock.

"I upset you the last time I talked to you," he said directly.

I had to change mental gears at the unexpected opening. Okay, I liked a man who could apologize. "Yes, you did."

"You didn't want me to tell you I knew about Debbie?"

"I just hate that the whole thing happened. I hate that her family is taking it so hard. I hate that they don't know, that they're suffering. But I'm glad to be alive, and I'm not going to jail for defending myself."

"If it'll make you feel any better, Debbie wasn't that close to her family. Her parents always preferred Debbie's little sister, though she didn't inherit any shifter characteristics. Sandra is the apple of their eye, and the only reason they're pursuing this with such vigor is that Sandra expected it."

"You think they'll give up?"

"They think I did it," Alcide said. "The Pelts think that because Debbie got engaged to another man, I killed her. I got an e-mail from Sandra in response to mine about the private eyes."

I could only gape at him. I had a horrible vista of the future in which I saw myself going down to the police station and confessing to save Alcide from a jail term. Even to be suspected of a murder he hadn't committed was an awful thing, and I couldn't permit it. It just hadn't occurred to me that someone else would be blamed for what I'd done.

"But," Alcide continued, "I can prove I didn't. Four pack members have sworn I was at Pam's house after Debbie left, and one female will swear I spent the night with her."

He had been with the pack members, just somewhere else. I slumped with relief. I was not going to have a jealous spasm about the female. He wouldn't have called her that if he'd actually had sex with her.

"So the Pelts will just have to suspect someone else. That's not what I wanted to talk to you about, anyway."

Alcide took my hand. His were big, and hard, and enclosed mine like he was holding something wild that would fly away if he relaxed his grip. "I want you to think about seeing me on a steady basis," Alcide said. "As in, every day."

Once again, the world seemed to rearrange itself around me. "Huh?" I said.

"I like you very much," he said. "I think you like me, too. We want each other." He leaned over to kiss me once on the cheek and then, when I didn't move, on the mouth. I was too surprised to get into it and unsure whether I wanted to anyway. It's not often a mind reader gets taken by surprise, but Alcide had achieved it.

He took a deep breath and continued. "We enjoy each other's company. I want to see you in my bed so much it makes me ache. I wouldn't have spoken this soon, without us being together more, but you need a place to live right now. I have a condo in Shreveport. I want you to think about staying with me."

If he'd whomped me upside the head with a two-by-four, I couldn't have been more stunned. Instead of trying so hard to stay out of people's heads, I should consider getting back into them. I started several sentences in my head, discarded them all. The warmth of him, the attraction of his big body, was something I had to fight as I struggled to sort my thoughts.

"Alcide," I began at last, speaking over the background noise of Terry's sledgehammer knocking down the boards of my burned kitchen, "you're right that I like you. In fact, I more than like you." I couldn't even look at his face. I looked instead at his big hands, with their dusting of dark hair across the backs. If I looked down past his hands, I could see his muscular thighs and his . . . Well, back to the hands. "But the timing seems all wrong. I think you need more time to get over your relationship with Debbie, since you seemed so enslaved to her. You may feel that just saying the words 'I abjure you' got rid of all your feelings for Debbie, but I'm not convinced that's so."

"It's a powerful ritual of my people," Alcide said stiffly, and I risked a quick glance at his face.

"I could tell it was a powerful ritual," I assured him, "and it had a big effect on everyone there. But I can't believe that, quick as a flash, every single feeling you had for Debbie was uprooted when you said the words. That's just not how people work."

"That's how werewolves work." He looked stubborn. And determined.

I thought very hard about what I wanted to say.

"I'd love for someone to step in and solve all my problems," I told him. "But I don't want to accept your offer because I need a place to live and we're hot for each other. When my house is rebuilt, then we'll talk, if you still feel the same."

"This is when you need me the most," he protested, the words spilling out of his mouth in his haste to persuade me. "You need me *now.* I need you *now.* We're right for each other. You know it."

"No, I don't. I know that you're worried about a lot of

things right now. You lost your lover, however it happened. I don't think it's sunk into you yet that you'll never see her again."

He flinched.

"I shot her, Alcide. With a shotgun."

His whole face clenched.

"See? Alcide, I've seen you rip into a person's flesh when you were being a wolf. And it didn't make me scared of you. Because *I'm on your side.* But you loved Debbie, at least for a time. We get into a relationship now, at some point you're going to look up and say, 'Here's the one who ended her life.'"

Alcide opened his mouth to protest, but I held up a hand. I wanted to finish.

"Plus, Alcide, your dad's in this succession struggle. He wants to win the election. Maybe you being in a settled relationship would help his ambitions. I don't know. But I don't want any part of Were politics. I didn't appreciate you dragging me into it cold last week at the funeral. You should have let me decide."

"I wanted them to get used to the sight of you by my side," Alcide said, his face stiffening with offense. "I meant it as an honor to you."

"I might have appreciated that honor more if I'd known about it," I snapped. It was a relief to hear another vehicle approaching, to see Andy Bellefleur get out of his Ford and watch his cousin knocking down my kitchen. For the first time in months, I was glad to see Andy.

I introduced Andy to Alcide, of course, and watched them size each other up. I like men in general, and some men in specific, but when I saw them practically circle each other as they sniffed each other's butts—excuse me, exchanged greetings—I just had to shake my head. Alcide was the taller by a good four inches, but Andy Bellefleur had been on his college wrestling team, and he was still a block of muscle. They were about the same age. I would put even money on them in a fight, providing that Alcide kept his human form.

"Sookie, you asked me to keep you posted on the man who died here," Andy said.

Sure, but it had never occurred to me he'd actually do it. Andy did not have any very high opinion of me, though he'd always been a big fan of my rear end. It's wonderful being telepathic, huh?

"He has no prior record," Andy said, looking down at the little notebook he'd produced. "He has no known association with the Fellowship of the Sun."

"But that doesn't make sense," I said into the little silence that followed. "Why would he set the fire otherwise?"

"I was hoping you could tell me that," Andy said, his clear gray eyes meeting mine.

I'd had it with Andy, abruptly and finally. In our dealings over the years, he'd insulted me and wounded me, and now I'd encountered that last straw.

"Listen to me, Andy," I said, and I looked right back into his eyes. "I never did anything to you that I know of. I've never been arrested. I've never even jaywalked, or been late paying my taxes, or sold a drink to an underage teen. I've never even had a speeding ticket. Now someone tried to barbecue me inside my own home. Where do you get off, making me feel like I've done something wrong?" *Other than shoot Debbie Pelt,* a voice whispered in my head. It was the voice of my conscience.

"I don't think there's anything in this guy's past that would indicate he'd do this to you."

"Fine! Then find out who did! Because someone burned my house, and it sure wasn't me!" I was yelling when I got to the last part, partly to drown the voice. My only recourse was to turn and walk away, striding around the house until I was out of Andy's sight. Terry gave me a sidelong look, but he didn't stop swinging his sledgehammer.

After a minute, I heard someone picking his way through the debris behind me. "He's gone," Alcide said, his deep voice just a tiny bit amused. "I guess you're not interested in going any further with our conversation."

"You're right," I said briefly.

"Then I'll go back to Shreveport. Call me if you need me."

"Sure." I made myself be more polite. "Thanks for your offer of help."

" 'Help'? I asked you to live with me!"

"Then thank you for asking me to live with you." I couldn't help it if I didn't sound completely sincere. I said the right words. Then my grandmother's voice sounded in my head, telling me that I was acting like I was seven years old. I made myself turn around.

"I do appreciate your . . . affection," I said, looking up into Alcide's face. Even this early in the spring, he had a tan line from wearing a hard hat. His olive complexion would be shades darker in a few weeks. "I do appreciate . . ." I trailed off, not sure how to put it. I appreciated his willingness to consider me as an eligible woman to mate with, which so many men didn't, as well as his assumption that I would make a good mate and a good ally. This was as close as I could get to phrasing what I meant.

"But you're not having any." The green eyes regarded me steadily.

"I'm not saying that." I drew a breath. "I'm saying now is not the time to work on a relationship with you." *Though I wouldn't mind jumping your bones,* I added to myself wistfully.

But I wasn't going to do that on a whim, and certainly not with a man like Alcide. The new Sookie, the rebound

Sookie, wasn't going to make the same mistake twice in a row. I was double rebounding. (If you rebound from the two men you've had so far, do you end up a virgin again? To what state are you rebounding?) Alcide gave me a hard hug and dropped a kiss on my cheek. He left while I was still mulling that over. Soon after Alcide left, Terry knocked off for the day. I changed from the jumpsuit into my work clothes. The afternoon had chilled, so I pulled on the jacket I'd borrowed from Jason's closet. It smelled faintly of Jason.

I detoured on the way to work to drop off the pink and black suit at Tara's house. Her car wasn't there, so I figured she was still at the shop. I let myself in and went back to her bedroom to put the plastic bag in her closet. The house was dusky and deep shadowed. It was almost dark outside. Suddenly my nerves thrummed with alarm. I shouldn't be here. I turned away from the closet and stared around the room. When my eyes got to the doorway, it was filled with a slim figure. I gasped before I could stop myself. Showing them you're scared is like waving a red flag in front of a bull.

I couldn't see Mickey's face to read his expression, if he had any.

"Where did that new bartender at Merlotte's come from?" he asked.

If I'd expected anything, it wasn't that.

"When Sam got shot, we needed another bartender in a hurry. We borrowed him from Shreveport," I said. "From the vampire bar."

"Had he been there long?"

"No," I said, managing to feel surprised even through my creeping fear. "He hadn't been there long at all."

Mickey nodded, as if that confirmed some conclusion he'd reached. "Get out of here," he said, his deep voice quite calm. "You're a bad influence on Tara. She doesn't need anything but me, until I'm tired of her. Don't come back."

The only way out of the room was through the door he was filling. I didn't trust myself to speak. I walked toward him as confidently as I could, and I wondered if he would move when I reached him. It felt like three hours later by the time I rounded Tara's bed and eased my way around her dressing table. When I showed no sign of slowing down, the vampire stepped aside. I couldn't stop myself from looking up at his face as I passed him, and he was showing fang. I shuddered. I felt so sick for Tara that I couldn't stop myself. How had this happened to her?

When he saw my revulsion, he smiled.

I tucked the problem of Tara away in my heart to pull out later. Maybe I could think of something to do for her, but as long as she seemed willing to stay with this monstrous creature, I didn't see what I could do to help.

Sweetie Des Arts was outside smoking a cigarette when I parked my car at the back of Merlotte's. She looked pretty good, despite being wrapped in a stained white apron. The outside floodlights lit up every little crease in her skin, revealing that Sweetie was a little older than I'd thought, but she still looked very fit for someone who cooked most of the day. In fact, if it hadn't been for the white apron swathing her and the lingering perfume of cooking oil, Sweetie might have been a sexy woman. She certainly carried herself like a person who was used to being noticed.

We'd had such a succession of cooks that I hadn't made much effort to know her. I was sure she'd drift away sooner or later—probably sooner. But she raised a hand in greeting and seemed to want to talk to me, so I paused.

"I'm sorry about your house," she said. Her eyes were shining in the artificial light. It didn't smell so great here by the Dumpster, but Sweetie was as relaxed as if she were on an Acapulco beach.

"Thanks," I said. I just didn't want to talk about it. "How are you today?"

"Fine, thanks." She waved the hand with the cigarette around, indicating the parking lot. "Enjoying the view. Hey, you got something on your jacket." Holding her hand carefully to one side so she wouldn't get ash on me, she leaned forward, closer than my comfort zone permitted, and flicked something off my shoulder. She sniffed. Maybe the smokey smell of the burned wood clung to me, despite all my efforts.

"I need to go in. Time for my shift," I said.

"Yeah, I gotta get back in myself. It's a busy night." But Sweetie stayed where she was. "You know, Sam's just nuts about you."

"I've worked for him for a long time."

"No, I think it goes a little beyond that."

"Ah, I don't think so, Sweetie." I couldn't think of any polite way to conclude a conversation that had gotten way too personal.

"You were with him when he got shot, right?"

"Yeah, he was heading for his trailer and I was heading for my car." I wanted to make it clear we were going in different directions.

"You didn't notice anything?" Sweetie leaned against the wall and tilted her head back, her eyes closed as if she were sunbathing.

"No. I wish I had. I'd like the police to catch whoever's doing this."

"Did you ever think there might be a reason those people were targeted?"

"No," I lied stoutly. "Heather and Sam and Calvin have nothing in common."

Sweetie opened one brown eye and squinted up at me. "If we were in a mystery, they'd all know the same secret, or they'd have witnessed the same accident, or something. Or the police would find out they all had the same dry cleaner." Sweetie flicked the ashes off her cigarette.

I relaxed a little. "I see what you're getting at," I said. "But I think real life doesn't have as many patterns as a serial killer book. I think they were all chosen at random."

Sweetie shrugged. "You're probably right." I saw she'd been reading a Tami Hoag suspense novel, now tucked into an apron pocket. She tapped her book with one blunt fingernail. "Fiction just makes it all more interesting. Truth is so boring."

"Not in my world," I said.

11

BILL BROUGHT A DATE INTO MERLOTTE'S THAT night. I assumed this was payback for my kissing Sam, or maybe I was just being proud. This possible payback was in the form of a woman from Clarice. I'd seen her in the bar before every once in a while. She was a slim brunette with shoulder-length hair, and Danielle could hardly wait to tell me she was Selah Pumphrey, a real estate saleswoman who'd gotten the million-dollar sales award the year before.

I hated her instantly, utterly, and passionately.

So I smiled as brightly as a thousand-watt bulb and brought them Bill's warm TrueBlood and her cold screwdriver quick as a wink. I didn't spit in the screwdriver, either. That was beneath me, I told myself. Also, I didn't have enough privacy.

Not only was the bar crowded, but Charles was eyeing me watchfully. The pirate was in fine form tonight, wearing a white shirt with billowing sleeves and navy blue Dockers, a bright scarf pulled through the belt loops for a dash of color. His eye patch matched the Dockers, and it was embroidered with a gold star. This was as exotic as Bon Temps could get.

Sam beckoned me over to his tiny table, which we'd wedged into a corner. He had his bad leg propped up on another chair. "Are you all right, Sookie?" Sam murmured, turning away from the crowd at the bar so no one could even read his lips.

"Sure, Sam!" I gave him an amazed expression. "Why not?" At that moment, I hated him for kissing me, and I hated me for responding.

He rolled his eyes and smiled for a fleeting second. "I think I've solved your housing problem," he said to distract me. "I'll tell you later." I hurried off to take an order. We were swamped that night. The warming weather and the attraction of a new bartender had combined to fill Merlotte's with the optimistic and the curious.

I'd left *Bill,* I reminded myself proudly. Though he'd cheated on me, he hadn't wanted us to break up. I had to keep telling myself that, so I wouldn't hate everyone present who was witnessing my humiliation. Of course, none of the people knew any of the circumstances, so they were free to imagine that Bill had dropped me for this brunette bitch. Which was *so* not the case.

I stiffened my back, broadened my smile, and hustled drinks. After the first ten minutes, I began to relax and see that I was behaving like a fool. Like millions of couples, Bill and I had broken up. Naturally, he'd begun dating someone else. If I'd had the normal run of boyfriends, starting when I was thirteen or fourteen, my relationship with Bill would just be another in a long line of relationships that hadn't panned out. I'd be able to take this in stride, or at least in perspective.

I had no perspective. Bill was my first love, in every sense.

The second time I brought drinks to their table, Selah Pumphrey looked at me uneasily when I beamed at her. "Thanks," she said uncertainly.

"Don't mention it," I advised her through clenched teeth, and she blanched.

Bill turned away. I hoped he wasn't hiding a smile. I went back to the bar.

Charles said, "Shall I give her a good scare, if she spends the night with him?"

I'd been standing behind the bar with him, staring into the glass-fronted refrigerator we kept back there. It held soft drinks, bottled blood, and sliced lemons and limes. I'd come to get a slice of lemon and a cherry to put on a Tom Collins, and I'd just stayed. He was entirely too perceptive.

"Yes, please," I said gratefully. The vampire pirate was turning into an ally. He'd saved me from burning, he'd killed the man who'd set fire to my house, and now he was offering to scare Bill's date. You had to like that.

"Consider her terrified," he said in a courtly way, bowing with a florid sweep of his arm, his other hand on his heart.

"Oh, you," I said with a more natural smile, and got out the bowl of sliced lemons.

It took every ounce of self-control I had to stay out of Selah Pumphrey's head. I was proud of myself for making the effort.

To my horror, the next time the door opened, Eric came in. My heart rate picked up immediately, and I felt almost faint. I was going to have to stop reacting like this. I wished I could forget our "time together" (as one of my favorite romance novels might term it) as thoroughly as Eric had. Maybe I should track down a witch, or a hypnotherapist, and give myself a dose of amnesia. I bit down on the inside of my cheek, hard, and carried two pitchers of beer over to a table of young couples who were celebrating the promotion of one of the men to supervisor—of someone, somewhere.

Eric was talking to Charles when I turned around, and though vampires can be pretty stone-faced when they're dealing with each other, it seemed apparent to me that Eric wasn't happy with his loaned-out bartender. Charles was nearly a foot shorter than his boss, and his head was tilted up as they talked. But his back was stiff, his fangs protruded a bit, and his eyes were glowing. Eric was pretty scary when he was mad, too. He was now definitely looking toothy. The humans around the bar were tending to find something to do somewhere else in the room, and any minute they'd start finding something to do at some other bar.

I saw Sam grabbing at a cane—an improvement over the crutches—so he could get up and go over to the pair, and I sped over to his table in the corner. "You stay put," I told him in a very firm low voice. "Don't you think about intervening."

I heel and toed it over to the bar. "Hi, Eric! How you doing? Is there anything I can help you with?" I smiled up at him.

"Yes. I need to talk to you, too," he growled.

"Then why don't you come with me? I was just going to step out back to take a break," I offered.

I took hold of his arm and towed him through the door and down the hall to the employees' entrance. We were outside in the night-cold air before you could say Jack Robinson.

"You better not be about to tell me what to do," I said instantly. "I've had enough of that for one day, and Bill's in here with a woman, and I lost my kitchen. I'm in a bad mood." I underlined this by squeezing Eric's arm, which was like gripping a small tree trunk.

"I care nothing about your mood," he said instantly, and

he was showing fang. "I pay Charles Twining to watch you and keep you safe, and who hauls you out of the fire? A fairy. While Charles is out in the yard, killing the fire setter rather than saving his hostess's life. Stupid Englishman!"

"He's supposed to be here as a favor to Sam. He's supposed to be here helping Sam out." I peered at Eric doubtfully.

"Like I give a damn about a shifter," the vampire said impatiently.

I stared up at him.

"There's something about you," Eric said. His voice was cold, but his eyes were not. "There is something I am almost on the verge of knowing about you, and it's under my skin, this feeling that something happened while I was cursed, something I should know about. Did we have sex, Sookie? But I can't think that was it, or it alone. Something happened. Your coat was ruined with brain tissue. Did I kill someone, Sookie? Is that it? You're protecting me from what I did while I was cursed?" His eyes were glowing like lamps in the darkness.

I'd never thought he might be wondering whom he'd killed. But frankly, if it had occurred to me, I wouldn't have thought Eric would care; what difference would one human life make to a vampire as old as this one? But he seemed mighty upset. Now that I understood what he was worried about, I said, "Eric, you did not kill anyone at my house that night." I stopped short.

"You have to tell me what happened." He bent a little to look into my face. "I hate not knowing what I did. I've had a life longer than you can even imagine, and I remember every second of it, except for those days I spent with you."

"I can't make you remember," I said as calmly as I could. "I can only tell you that you stayed with me for several days, and then Pam came to get you."

Eric stared into my eyes a little longer. "I wish I could

get in your head and get the truth out of you," he said, which alarmed me more than I wanted to show. "You've had my blood. I can tell you're concealing things from me." After a moment's silence, he said, "I wish I knew who's trying to kill you. And I hear you had a visit from some private detectives. What did they want of you?"

"Who told you that?" Now I had something else to worry about. Someone was informing on me. I could feel my blood pressure rise. I wondered if Charles was reporting to Eric every night.

"Is this something to do with the woman who's missing, that bitch the Were loved so much? Are you protecting him? If I didn't kill her, did he? Did she die in front of us?"

Eric had gripped my shoulders, and the pressure was excruciating.

"Listen, you're hurting me! Let go."

Eric's grip loosened, but he didn't remove his hands.

My breath began to come faster and shallower, and the air was full of the crackling of danger. I was sick to death of being threatened.

"Tell me now," he demanded.

He would have power over me for the rest of my life if I told him he'd seen me kill someone. Eric already knew more about me than I wanted him to, because I'd had his blood, and he'd had mine. Now I rued our blood exchange more than ever. Eric was sure I was concealing something important.

"You were so sweet when you didn't know who you were," I said, and whatever he'd been expecting me to say, it wasn't that. Astonishment played tag with outrage across his handsome face. Finally, he was amused.

"Sweet?" he said, one corner of his mouth turning up in a smile.

"Very," I said, trying to smile back. "We gossiped like old buddies." My shoulders ached. Probably everyone in the bar needed a new drink. But I couldn't go back in just yet. "You were scared and alone, and you liked to talk to me. It was fun having you around."

"Fun," he said thoughtfully. "I'm not fun now?"

"No, Eric. You're too busy being . . . yourself." Head boss vampire, political animal, budding tycoon.

He shrugged. "Is myself so bad? Many women seem to think not."

"I'm sure they do." I was tired to the bone.

The back door opened. "Sookie, are you all right?" Sam had hobbled to my rescue. His face was stiff with pain.

"Shifter, she doesn't need your assistance," Eric said.

Sam didn't say anything. He just kept Eric's attention.

"I was rude," Eric said, not exactly apologetically, but civilly enough. "I'm on your premises. I'll be gone. Sookie," he said to me, "we haven't finished this conversation, but I see this isn't the time or place."

"I'll see you," I said, since I knew I had no choice.

Eric melted into the darkness, a neat trick that I'd love to master someday.

"What is he so upset about?" Sam asked. He hobbled out of the doorway and leaned against the wall.

"He doesn't remember what happened while he was cursed," I said, speaking slowly out of sheer weariness. "That makes him feel like he's lost control. Vampires are big on having control. I guess you noticed."

Sam smiled—a small smile, but genuine. "Yes, that had come to my attention," he admitted. "I'd also noticed they're pretty possessive."

"You're referring to Bill's reaction when he walked in on us?" Sam nodded. "Well, he seems to have gotten over it."

"I think he's just repaying you in kind."

I felt awkward. Last night, I'd been on the verge of going to bed with Sam. But I was far from feeling passionate at this moment, and Sam's leg had been hurt badly in his fall. He didn't look as if he could romance a rag doll, much less a robust woman like me. I knew it was wrong to think of indulging in some sex play with my boss, though Sam and I had been teetering on a fine edge for months. Coming down on the "no" side was the safest, sanest thing to do. Tonight, particularly after the emotionally jangling events of the past hour, I wanted to be safe.

"He stopped us in time," I said.

Sam raised a fine red-gold eyebrow. "Did you want to be stopped?"

"Not at that moment," I admitted. "But I guess it was for the best."

Sam just looked at me for a moment. "What I was going to tell you, though I was going to wait until after the bar closed, is that one of my rental houses is empty right now. It's the one next to—well, you remember, the one where Dawn . . ."

"Died," I finished.

"Right. I had that one redone, and it's rented out now. So you'd have a neighbor, and you're not used to that. But the empty side is furnished. You'd only have to bring a few linens, your clothes, and some pots and pans." Sam smiled. "You could get that in a car. By the way, where'd you get this?" He nodded at the Malibu.

I told him how generous Tara had been, and I also told him I was worried about her. I repeated the warning Eric had given me about Mickey.

When I saw how anxious Sam looked, I felt like a selfish creep for burdening him with all this. Sam had enough to worry about. I said, "I'm sorry. You don't need to hear more troubles. Come on, let's go back inside."

Sam stared at me. "I do need to sit down," he said after a moment.

"Thanks for the rental. Of course I'll pay you. I'm so glad to have a place to live where I can come and go without bothering anyone! How much is it? I think my insurance will pay for me renting a place to live while my house is being fixed."

Sam gave me a hard look, and then named a price that I was sure was well below his usual rate. I slid my arm around him because his limp was so bad. He accepted the help without a struggle, which made me think even better of him. He hobbled down the hall with my help and settled in the rolling chair behind his desk with a sigh. I pushed over one of the visitor chairs so he could put his leg up on it if he wanted, and he used it immediately. Under the strong fluorescent light in his office, my boss looked haggard.

"Get back to work," he said mock-threateningly. "I'll bet they're mobbing Charles."

The bar was just as chaotic as I'd feared, and I began tending to my tables immediately. Danielle shot me a dirty look, and even Charles looked less than happy. But gradually, moving as fast as I could, I served fresh drinks, took away empty glasses, dumped the occasional ashtray, wiped the sticky tables, and smiled at and spoke to as many people as I could. I could kiss my tips good-bye, but at least peace was restored.

Bit by bit, the pulse of the bar slowed and returned to normal. Bill and his date were deep in conversation, I noticed . . . though I made a great effort not to keep glancing their way. To my dismay, every single time I saw them as a couple, I felt a wave of rage that did not speak well for my character. For another thing, though my feelings were a matter of indifference to almost ninety percent of the bar's patrons, the other ten percent were watching like hawks to see if Bill's date was making me suffer. Some of them would be glad to see it, and some wouldn't—but it was no one's business, either way.

As I was cleaning off a table that had just been vacated, I felt a tap on my shoulder. I picked up a foreshadowing just as I turned, and that enabled me to keep my smile in place. Selah Pumphrey was waiting for my attention, her own smile bright and armor plated.

She was taller than I, and perhaps ten pounds lighter. Her makeup was expensive and expert, and she smelled like a million bucks. I reached out and touched her brain without even thinking twice.

Selah was thinking she had it all over me, unless I was fantastic in bed. Selah thought that lower-class women must always be better in bed, because they were less inhibited. She knew she was slimmer, was smarter, made more money, and was far more educated and better read than the waitress she was looking at. But Selah Pumphrey doubted her own sexual skill and had a terror of making herself vulnerable. I blinked. This was more than I wanted to know.

It was interesting to discover that (in Selah's mind) since I was poor and uneducated, I was more in touch with my nature as a sexual being. I'd have to tell all the other poor people in Bon Temps. Here we'd been having a wonderful time screwing one another, having much better sex than smart upper-class people, and we hadn't even appreciated it.

"Yes?" I asked.

"Where is the ladies' room?" she asked.

"Through that door there. The one with 'Restrooms' on the sign above it." I should be grateful I was clever enough to read signs.

"Oh! Sorry, I didn't notice."

I just waited.

"So, um, you got any tips for me? About dating a vampire?" She waited, looking nervous and defiant all at once.

"Sure," I said. "Don't eat any garlic." And I turned away from her to wipe down the table.

Once I was certain she was out of the room, I swung around to carry two empty beer mugs to the bar, and when I turned back, Bill was standing there. I gave a gasp of surprise. Bill has dark brown hair and of course the whitest skin you can imagine. His eyes are as dark as his hair. Right at the moment, those eyes were fixed on mine.

"Why did she talk to you?" he asked.

"Wanted to know the way to the bathroom."

He cocked an eyebrow, glancing up at the sign.

"She just wanted to take my measure," I said. "At least, that's my guess." I felt oddly comfortable with Bill at that moment, no matter what had passed between us.

"Did you scare her?"

"I didn't try to."

"Did you scare her?" he asked again in a sterner voice. But he smiled at me.

"No," I said. "Did you want me to?"

He shook his head in mock disgust. "Are you jealous?"

"Yes." Honesty was always safest. "I hate her skinny thighs and her elitist attitude. I hope she's a dreadful bitch who makes you so miserable that you howl when you remember me."

"Good," said Bill. "That's good to hear." He gave me a brush of lips on my cheek. At the touch of his cool flesh, I shivered, remembering. He did, too. I saw the heat flare in his eyes, the fangs begin to run out. Then Catfish Hunter yelled to me to stir my stumps and bring him another bourbon and Coke, and I walked away from my first lover.

It had been a long, long day, not only from a physical-energy-expended measurement, but also from an emotional-depths-plumbed point of view. When I let myself into my brother's house, there were giggles and squeakings coming from his bedroom, and I deduced Jason was consoling himself in the usual way. Jason might be upset that his new community suspected him of a foul crime, but he was not so upset that it affected his libido.

I spent as brief a time in the bathroom as I could and went into the guest room, shutting the door firmly behind me. Tonight the couch looked a lot more inviting than it had the evening before. As I curled up on my side and pulled the quilt over me, I realized that the woman spending the night with my brother was a shifter; I could feel it in the faint pulsing redness of her brain.

I hoped she was Crystal Norris. I hoped Jason had somehow persuaded the girl that he had nothing to do with the shootings. If Jason wanted to compound his troubles, the best way possible would be to cheat on Crystal, the woman he'd chosen from the werepanther community. And surely even Jason wasn't that stupid. Surely.

He wasn't. I met Crystal in the kitchen the next morning after ten o'clock. Jason was long gone, since he had to be at work by seven forty-five. I was drinking my first mug of coffee when Crystal stumbled in, wearing one of Jason's shirts, her face blurry with sleep.

Crystal was not my favorite person, and I was not hers, but she said, "Morning" civilly enough. I agreed that it was morning, and I got out a mug for her. She grimaced and got out a glass, filling it with ice and then Coca-Cola. I shuddered.

"How's your uncle?" I asked, when she seemed conscious.

"He's doing better," she said. "You ought to go see him. He liked having you visit."

"I guess you're sure Jason didn't shoot him."

"I am," she said briefly. "I didn't want to talk to him at first, but once he got me on the phone, he just talked his way out of me suspecting him."

I wanted to ask her if the other inhabitants of Hotshot were willing to give Jason the benefit of the doubt, but I hated to bring up a touchy subject.

I thought of what I had to do today: I had to go get enough clothes, some sheets and blankets, and some kitchen gear from the house, and get those things installed in Sam's duplex.

Moving into a small, furnished place was a perfect solution to my housing problem. I had forgotten Sam owned several small houses on Berry Street, three of them duplexes. He worked on them himself, though sometimes he hired JB du Rone, a high school friend of mine, to do simple repairs and maintenance chores. Simple was the best way to keep it, with JB.

After I retrieved my things, I might have time to go see Calvin. I showered and dressed, and Crystal was sitting in the living room watching TV when I left. I assumed that was okay with Jason.

Terry was hard at work when I pulled into the clearing. I walked around back to check his progress, and I was delighted to see he'd done more than I'd have thought possible. He smiled when I said so, and paused in loading broken boards into his truck. "Tearing down is always easier than building up," he said. This was no big philosophical statement, but a builder's summary. "I should be done in two more days, if nothing happens to slow me down. There's no rain in the forecast."

"Great. How much will I owe you?"

"Oh," he muttered, shrugging and looking embarrassed. "A hundred? Fifty?"

"No, not enough." I ran a quick estimate of his hours in my head, multiplied. "More like three."

"Sookie, I'm not charging you that much." Terry got his stubborn face on. "I wouldn't charge you anything, but I got to get a new dog."

Terry bought a very expensive Catahoula hunting dog about every four years. He wasn't turning in the old models for new ones. Something always seemed to happen to Terry's dogs, though he took great care of them. After he'd had the first hound about three years, a truck had hit him. Someone had fed poisoned meat to the second. The third one, the one he'd named Molly, had gotten snake-bit, and the bite had turned septic. For months now, Terry had been on the list for one in the next litter born at the kennel in Clarice that bred Catahoulas.

"You bring that puppy around for me to hug," I suggested, and he smiled. Terry was at his best in the outdoors, I realized for the first time. He always seemed more comfortable mentally and physically when he was not under a roof, and when he was outside with a dog, he seemed quite normal.

I unlocked the house and went in to gather what I might need. It was a sunny day, so the absence of electric light wasn't a problem. I filled a big plastic laundry basket with two sets of sheets and an old chenille bedspread, some more clothes, and a few pots and pans. I would have to get a new coffeepot. My old one had melted.

And then, standing there looking out the window at the coffeemaker, which I'd pitched to the top of the trash heap, I understood how close I'd come to dying. The realization hit me broadside.

One minute I was standing at my bedroom window, looking out at the misshaped bit of plastic; the next I was sitting on the floor, staring at the painted boards and trying to breathe.

Why did it hit me now, after three days? I don't know. Maybe there was something about the way the Mr. Coffee looked: cord charred, plastic warped with the heat. The plastic had literally bubbled. I looked at the skin of my hands and shuddered. I stayed on the floor, shivering and shaking, for an unmeasured bit of time. For the first minute or two after that, I had no thoughts at all. The closeness of my brush with death simply overwhelmed me.

Claudine had not only most probably saved my life; she had certainly saved me from pain so excruciating that I would have wanted to be dead. I owed her a debt I would never be able to repay.

Maybe she really was my fairy godmother.

I got up, shook myself. Grabbing up the plastic basket, I left to go move into my new home.

12 ~

I LET MYSELF IN WITH THE KEY I'D GOTTEN FROM SAM. I was on the right side of a duplex, the mirror of the one next door presently occupied by Halleigh Robinson, the young schoolteacher dating Andy Bellefleur. I figured I was likely to have police protection at least part of the time, and Halleigh would be gone during most of the day, which was nice considering my late hours.

The living room was small and contained a flowered couch, a low coffee table, and an armchair. The next room was the kitchen, which was tiny, of course. But it had a stove, a refrigerator, and a microwave. No dishwasher, but I'd never had one. Two plastic chairs were tucked under a tiny table.

After I'd glanced at the kitchen I went through into the small hall that separated the larger (but still small) bedroom on the right from the smaller (tiny) bedroom and the bathroom on the left. At the end of the hall there was a door to the little back porch.

This was a very basic accommodation, but it was quite clean. There was central heating and cooling, and the floors were level. I ran a hand around the windows. They fit well. Nice. I reminded myself I'd have to keep the venetian blinds drawn down, since I had neighbors.

I made up the double bed in the larger bedroom. I put my clothes away in the freshly painted chest of drawers. I started a list of other things I needed: a mop, a broom, a bucket, some cleaning products . . . those had been on the back porch. I'd have to get my vacuum cleaner out of the house. It had been in the closet in the living room, so it should be fine. I'd brought one of my phones to plug in over here, so I would have to arrange with the phone company for them to route calls to this address. I'd loaded my television into my car, but I had to arrange for my cable to be hooked up here. I'd have to call from Merlotte's. Since the fire, all my time was being absorbed with the mechanics of living.

I sat on the hard couch, staring into space. I tried to think of something fun, something I could look forward to. Well, in two months, it'd be sunbathing time. That made me smile. I enjoyed lying in the sun in a little bikini, timing myself carefully so I didn't burn. I loved the smell of coconut oil. I took pleasure in shaving my legs and removing most of my other body hair so I'd look smooth as a baby's bottom. And I don't want to hear any lectures about how bad tanning is for you. That's my vice. Everybody gets one.

More immediately, it was time to go to the library and get another batch of books; I'd retrieved my last bagful while I was at the house, and I'd spread them out on my tiny porch here so they'd air out. So going to the library—that would be fun.

Before I went to work, I decided I'd cook myself something in my new kitchen. That necessitated a trip to the grocery store, which took longer than I'd planned because I kept seeing staples I was sure I'd need. Putting the groceries away in the duplex cabinets made me feel that I really lived there. I browned a couple of pork chops and put them in the oven, microwaved a potato, and heated some peas. When I had to work nights, I usually went to Merlotte's at about five, so my home meal on those days was a combination lunch and dinner.

After I'd eaten and cleaned up, I thought I just had time to drive down to visit Calvin in the Grainger hospital.

The twins had not arrived to take up their post in the lobby again, if they were still keeping vigil. Dawson was still stationed outside Calvin's room. He nodded to me, gestured to me to stop while I was several feet away, and stuck his head in Calvin's room. To my relief, Dawson swung the door wide open for me to enter and even patted my shoulder as I went in.

Calvin was sitting up in the padded chair. He clicked off the television as I came in. His color was better, his beard and hair were clean and trimmed, and he looked altogether more like himself. He was wearing pajamas of blue broadcloth. He still had a tube or two in, I saw. He actually tried to push himself up out of the chair.

"No, don't you dare get up!" I pulled over a straight chair and sat in front of him. "Tell me how you are."

"Glad to see you," he said. Even his voice was stronger. "Dawson said you wouldn't take any help. Tell me who set that fire."

"That's the strange thing, Calvin. I don't know why this man set the fire. His family came to see me . . ." I hesitated, because Calvin was recuperating from his own brush with death, and he shouldn't have to worry about other stuff.

But he said, "Tell me what you're thinking," and he sounded so interested that I ended up relating everything to the wounded shifter: my doubts about the arsonist's motives, my relief that the damage could be repaired, my concern about the trouble between Eric and Charles Twining. And I told Calvin that the police here had learned of more clusters of sniper activity.

"That would clear Jason," I pointed out, and he nodded. I didn't push it.

"At least no one else has been shot," I said, trying to think of something positive to throw in with the dismal mix.

"That we know of," Calvin said.

"What?"

"That we know of. Maybe someone else has been shot, and no one's found 'em yet."

I was astonished at the thought, and yet it made sense. "How'd you think of that?"

"I don't have nothing else to do," he said with a small smile. "I don't read, like you do. I'm not much one for television, except for sports." Sure enough, the station he'd had on when I'd entered had been ESPN.

"What do you do in your spare time?" I asked out of sheer curiosity.

Calvin was pleased I'd asked him a personal question. "I work pretty long hours at Norcross," he said. "I like to hunt, though I'd rather hunt at the full moon." In his panther body. Well, I could understand that. "I like to fish. I love mornings when I can just sit in my boat on the water and not worry about a thing."

"Uh-huh," I said encouragingly. "What else?"

"I like to cook. We have shrimp boils sometimes, or we cook up a whole mess of catfish and we eat outside—catfish and hush puppies and slaw and watermelon. In the summer, of course."

It made my mouth water just to think about it.

"In the winter, I work on the inside of my house. I go out and cut wood for the people in our community who can't cut their own. I've always got something to do, seems like."

Now I knew twice as much about Calvin Norris as I had.

"Tell me how you're recovering," I asked.

"I've still got the damn IV in," he said, gesturing with his arm. "Other than that, I'm a lot better. We heal pretty good, you know."

"How are you explaining Dawson to the people from your work who come to visit?" There were flower arrangements and bowls of fruit and even a stuffed cat crowding the level surfaces in the room.

"Just tell 'em he's my cousin here to make sure I won't get too wore out with visitors."

I was pretty sure no one would question Dawson directly.

"I have to get to work," I said, catching a glimpse of the clock on the wall. I was oddly reluctant to leave. I'd enjoyed having a regular conversation with someone. Little moments like these were rare in my life.

"Are you still worried about your brother?" he asked.

"Yes." But I'd made my mind up I wouldn't beg again. Calvin had heard me out the first time. There wasn't any need for a repeat.

"We're keeping an eye on him."

I wondered if the watcher had reported to Calvin that Crystal was spending the night with Jason. Or maybe Crystal herself was the watcher? If so, she was certainly taking her job seriously. She was watching Jason about as close as he could be watched.

"That's good," I said. "That's the best way to find out he didn't do it." I was relieved to hear Calvin's news, and the longer I pondered it, the more I realized I should have figured it out myself.

"Calvin, you take care." I rose to leave, and he held up his cheek. Rather reluctantly, I touched my lips to it.

He was thinking that my lips were soft and that I smelled good. I couldn't help but smile as I left. Knowing someone simply finds you attractive is always a boost to the spirits.

I drove back to Bon Temps and stopped by the library before I went to work. The Renard Parish library is an old ugly brown-brick building erected in the thirties. It looks every minute of its age. The librarians had made many justified complaints about the heating and cooling, and the electrical wiring left a lot to be desired. The library's parking lot was in bad shape, and the old clinic next door, which had opened its doors in 1918, now had boarded-up windows—always a depressing sight. The long-closed clinic's overgrown lot looked more like a jungle than a part of downtown.

I had allotted myself ten minutes to exchange my books. I was in and out in eight. The library parking lot was almost empty, since it was just before five o'clock. People were shopping at Wal-Mart or already home cooking supper.

The winter light was fading. I was not thinking about anything in particular, and that saved my life. In the nick of time, I identified intense excitement pulsing from another brain, and reflexively I ducked, feeling a sharp shove in my shoulder as I did so, and then a hot lance of blinding pain, and then wetness and a big noise. This all happened so fast I could not definitely sequence it when I later tried to reconstruct the moment.

A scream came from behind me, and then another. Though I didn't know how it had happened, I found myself on my knees beside my car, and blood was spattered over the front of my white T-shirt.

Oddly, my first thought was *Thank God I didn't have my new coat on.*

The person who'd screamed was Portia Bellefleur. Portia was not her usual collected self as she skidded across the parking lot to crouch beside me. Her eyes went one way, then another, as she tried to spot danger coming from any direction.

"Hold still," she said sharply, as though I'd proposed running a marathon. I was still on my knees, but keeling over appeared to be a pleasant option. Blood was trickling down my arm. "Someone shot you, Sookie. Oh my God, oh my God."

"Take the books," I said. "I don't want to get blood on the books. I'll have to pay for them."

Portia ignored me. She was talking into her cell phone. People talked on their phones at the damnedest times! In the library, for goodness's sake, or at the optometrist. Or in the bar. Jabber, jabber, jabber. As if everything was so important it couldn't wait. So I put the books on the ground beside me all by myself.

Instead of kneeling, I found myself sitting, my back against my car. And then, as if someone had taken a slice out of my life, I discovered I was lying on the pavement of the library parking lot, staring at someone's big old oil stain. People should take better care of their cars. . . .

Out.

"Wake up," a voice was saying. I wasn't in the parking lot, but in a bed. I thought my house was on fire again, and Claudine was trying to get me out. People were always trying to get me out of bed. Though this didn't sound like Claudine; this sounded more like . . .

"Jason?" I tried to open my eyes. I managed to peer through my barely parted lids to identify my brother. I was in a dimly lit blue room, and I hurt so bad I wanted to cry.

"You got shot," he said. "You got shot, and I was at Merlotte's, waiting for you to get there."

"You sound . . . happy," I said through lips that felt oddly thick and stiff. Hospital.

"I couldn't have done it! I was with people the whole time! I had Hoyt in the truck with me from work to Merlotte's, because his truck's in the shop. I am *covered*."

"Oh, good. I'm glad I got shot, then. As long as you're okay." It was such an effort to say it, I was glad when Jason picked up on the sarcasm.

"Yeah, hey, I'm sorry about that. At least it wasn't serious."

"It isn't?"

"I forgot to tell you. Your shoulder got creased, and it's going to hurt for a while. Press this button if it hurts. You can give yourself pain medication. Cool, huh? Listen, Andy's outside."

I pondered that, finally deduced Andy Bellefleur was there in his official capacity. "Okay," I said. "He can come in." I stretched out a finger and carefully pushed the button.

I blinked then, and it must have been a long blink, because when I pried my eyes open again, Jason was gone and Andy was in his place, a little notebook and a pen in his hands. There was something I had to tell him, and after a moment's reflection, I knew what it was.

"Tell Portia I said thank you," I told him.

"I will," he said seriously. "She's pretty shook up. She's never been that close to violence before. She thought you were gonna die."

I could think of nothing to say to that. I waited for him to ask me what he wanted to know. His mouth moved, and I guess I answered him.

". . . said you ducked at the last second?"

"I heard something, I guess," I whispered. That was the truth, too. I just hadn't heard something with my ears. . . . But Andy knew what I meant, and he was a believer. His eyes met mine and widened.

And out again. The ER doctor had certainly given me some excellent painkiller. I wondered which hospital I was in. The one in Clarice was a little closer to the library; the one in Grainger had a higher-rated ER. If I was in Grainger, I might as well have saved myself the time driving back to Bon Temps and going to the library. I could have been shot right in the hospital parking lot when I left from visiting Calvin, and that would have saved me the trip.

"Sookie," said a quiet, familiar voice. It was cool and dark, like water running in a stream on a moonless night.

"Bill," I said, feeling happy and safe. "Don't go."

"I'll be right here."

And he was there, reading, in a chair by my bed when I woke up at three in the morning. I could feel the minds in the rooms around me all shut down in sleep. But the brain in the head of the man next to me was a blank. At that moment, I realized that the person who'd shot me had not been a vampire, though all the shootings had taken place at dusk or full dark. I'd heard the shooter's brain in the second before the shot, and that had saved my life.

Bill looked up the instant I moved. "How are you feeling?" he asked.

I pushed the button to raise the head of the bed. "Like hell warmed over," I said frankly after evaluating my shoulder. "My pain stuff has lapsed, and my shoulder aches like it's going to fall off. My mouth feels like an army has marched through it, and I need to go to the bathroom in the worst way."

"I can help you take care of that," he said, and before I could get embarrassed, he'd moved the IV pole around the bed and helped me up. I stood cautiously, gauging how steady my legs were. He said, "I won't let you fall."

"I know," I said, and we started across the floor to the bathroom. When he got me settled on the toilet, he tactfully stepped out, but left the door cracked while he waited just outside. I managed everything awkwardly, but I became profoundly aware I was lucky I'd been shot in my left shoulder instead of my right. Of course, the shooter must have been aiming for my heart.

Bill got me back into the bed as deftly as if he'd been nursing people all his life. He'd already smoothed the bed and shaken the pillows, and I felt much more comfortable. But the shoulder continued to nag me, and I pressed the pain button. My mouth was dry, and I asked Bill if there was water in the plastic pitcher. Bill pressed the Nurse button. When her tinny voice came over the intercom, Bill said, "Some water for Miss Stackhouse," and the voice squawked back that she'd be right down. She was, too. Bill's presence might have had something to do with her speed. People might have accepted the reality of vampires, but that didn't meant they liked undead Americans. Lots of middle-class Americans just couldn't relax around vamps. Which was smart of them, I thought.

"Where are we?" I asked.

"Grainger," he said. "I get to sit with you in a different hospital this time." Last time, I'd been in Renard Parish Hospital in Clarice.

"You can go down the hall and visit Calvin."

"If I had any interest in doing so."

He sat on the bed. Something about the deadness of the hour, the strangeness of the night, made me feel like being frank. Maybe it was just the drugs.

"I never was in a hospital till I knew you," I said.

"Do you blame me?"

"Sometimes." I watched his face glow. Other people didn't always know a vamp when they saw one; that was hard for me to understand.

"When I met you, that first night I came into Merlotte's,

I didn't know what to think of you," he said. "You were so pretty, so full of vitality. And I could tell there was something different about you. You were interesting."

"My curse," I said.

"Or your blessing." He put one of his cool hands on my cheek. "No fever," he said to himself. "You'll heal." Then he sat up straighter. "You slept with Eric while he was staying with you."

"Why are you asking, if you already know?" There was such a thing as too much honesty.

"I'm not asking. I knew when I saw you together. I smelled him all over you; I could tell how you felt about him. We've had each other's blood. It's hard to resist Eric," Bill went on in a detached way. "He's as vital as you are, and you share a zest for life. But I'm sure you know that . . ." He paused, seemed to be trying to think how to frame what he wanted to say.

"I know that you'd be happy if I never slept with anyone else in my life," I said, putting his thoughts into words for him.

"And how do you feel about me?"

"The same. Oh, but wait, you already *did* sleep with someone else. Before we even broke up." Bill looked away, the line of his jaw like granite. "Okay, that's water under the bridge. No, I don't want to think about you with Selah, or with anyone. But my head knows that's unreasonable."

"Is it unreasonable to hope that we'll be together again?"

I considered the circumstances that had turned me against Bill. I thought of his infidelity with Lorena; but she had been his maker, and he had had to obey her. Everything I'd heard from other vamps had confirmed what he'd told me about that relationship. I thought of his near-rape of me in the trunk of a car; but he'd been starved and tortured, and hadn't known what he was doing. The minute he'd come to his senses, he'd stopped.

I remembered how happy I'd been when I'd had what I thought was his love. I'd never felt more secure in my life. How false a feeling that had been: He'd become so absorbed in his work for the Queen of Louisiana that I'd begun to come in a distant second. Out of all the vampires who could have walked into Merlotte's Bar, I'd gotten the workaholic.

"I don't know if we can ever have the same relationship again," I said. "It might be possible, when I'm a little less raw from the pain of it. But I'm glad you're here tonight, and I wish you would lie down with me for a little while . . . if you want to." I moved over on the narrow bed and turned on my right side, so the wounded shoulder was up. Bill lay down behind me and put his arm over me. No one could approach me without him knowing. I felt perfectly secure, absolutely safe, and cherished. "I'm so glad you're here," I mumbled as the medicine kicked in. As I was drifting off to sleep again, I remembered my New Year's Eve resolution: I wanted not to get beaten up. Note to self: I should have included "shot."

I was released the next morning. When I went to the business office, the clerk, whose name tag read MS. BEESON, said, "It's already been taken care of."

"By who?" I asked.

"The person wishes to remain anonymous," the clerk said, her round brown face set in a way that implied I shouldn't look gift horses in the mouth.

This made me uneasy, very uneasy. I actually had the money in the bank to pay the whole bill, instead of sending a check each month. And nothing comes without a price. There were some people to whom I just didn't want to be beholden. When I absorbed the total at the bottom of the bill, I was shocked to find how very beholden I'd be.

Maybe I should have stayed in the office longer and argued with Ms. Beeson more forcefully, but I just didn't feel up to it. I wanted to shower, or at least bathe—something more thorough than the high-spots scrub I'd given myself (very slowly and carefully) that morning. I wanted to eat my own food. I wanted some solitude and peace. So I got back in the wheelchair and let the aide wheel me out of the main entrance. I felt like the biggest idiot when it occurred to me that I didn't have a way home. My car was still in the library parking lot in Bon Temps—not that I was supposed to drive it for a couple of days.

Just as I was about to ask the aide to wheel me back inside so I could ride up to Calvin's room (maybe Dawson could give me a lift), a sleek red Impala came to a halt in front of me. Claudine's brother, Claude, leaned over to push open the passenger door. I sat gaping at him. He said irritably, "Well, are you going to get in?"

"Wow," muttered the aide. "Wow." I thought her blouse buttons were going to pop open, she was breathing so hard.

I'd met Claudine's brother Claude only once before. I'd forgotten what an impact he made. Claude was absolutely breathtaking, so lovely that his proximity made me tense as a high wire. Relaxing around Claude was like trying to be nonchalant with Brad Pitt.

Claude had been a stripper on ladies' night at Hooligans, a club in Monroe, but lately he'd not only moved into managing the club, he'd also branched into print and runway modeling. The opportunities for such work were few and far between in northern Louisiana, so Claude (according to Claudine) had decided to compete for Mr. Romance at a romance readers' convention. He'd even had his ears surgically altered so they weren't pointed anymore. The big payoff was the chance to appear on a romance cover. I didn't know too much about the contest, but I knew what I saw when I looked at Claude. I felt pretty confident Claude would win by acclamation.

Claudine had mentioned that Claude had just broken up with his boyfriend, too, so he was unattached: all six feet of him, accessorized with rippling black hair and rippling muscles and a six-pack that could have been featured in *Abs Weekly*. Mentally add to that a pair of brown velour-soft eyes, a chiseled jaw, and a sensuous mouth with a pouty bottom lip, and you've got Claude. Not that I was noticing.

Without the help of the aide, who was still saying, "Wow, wow, wow," very quietly, I got out of the wheelchair and eased myself into the car. "Thanks," I said to Claude, trying not to sound as astonished as I felt.

"Claudine couldn't get off work, so she called me and woke me up so I'd be here to chauffeur you," Claude said, sounding totally put out.

"I'm grateful for the ride," I said, after considering several possible responses.

I noticed that Claude didn't have to ask me for directions to Bon Temps, though I'd never seen him in the area—and I think I've made the point that he was hard to miss.

"How is your shoulder?" he said abruptly, as if he'd remembered that was the polite question to ask.

"On the mend," I said. "And I have a prescription for some painkillers to fill."

"So I guess you need to do that, too?"

"Um, well, that would be nice, since I'm not supposed to drive for another day or two."

When we reached Bon Temps, I directed Claude to the pharmacy, where he found a parking slot right in front. I managed to get out of the car and take in the prescription, since Claude didn't offer. The pharmacist, of course, had heard what had happened already and wanted to know what this world was coming to. I couldn't tell him.

I passed the time while he was filling my prescription by speculating on the possibility that Claude was bisexual—even a little bit? Every woman who came into the pharmacy had a glazed look on her face. Of course, they hadn't had the privilege of having an actual conversation with Claude, so they hadn't had the benefit of his sparkling personality.

"Took you long enough," Claude said as I got back in the car.

"Yes, Mr. Social Skills," I snapped. "I'll try to hurry from now on. Why should getting shot slow me down? I apologize."

Out of the corner of my eye, I noticed Claude's cheeks reddening.

"I'm sorry," he said stiffly. "I was abrupt. People tell me I'm rude."

"No! Really?"

"Yes," he admitted, and then realized I'd been a tad sarcastic. He gave me a look I would have called a glower from a less beautiful creature. "Listen, I have a favor to ask you."

"You're certainly off to a good start. You've softened me up now."

"Would you stop that? I know I'm not . . . not . . ."

"Polite? Minimally courteous? Gallant? Going about this the right way?"

"Sookie!" he bellowed. "Be quiet!"

I wanted one of my pain pills. "Yes, Claude?" I said in a quiet, reasonable voice.

"The people running the pageant want a portfolio. I'll go to the studio in Ruston for some glamour shots, but I think it might be a good idea to do some posed pictures, too. Like the covers of the books Claudine is always reading. Claudine says I should have a blonde pose with me, since I'm dark. I thought of you."

I guess if Claude had told me he wanted me to have his baby I could have been more surprised, but only just. Though Claude was the surliest man I'd ever encountered, Claudine had a habit of saving my life. For her sake, I wanted to oblige.

"Would I need, like, a costume?"

"Yes. But the photographer also does amateur dramatics and he rents out Halloween costumes, so he thought he might have some things that would do. What size do you wear?"

"An eight." Sometimes more like a ten. But then again, once in a blue moon, a six, okay?

"So when can you do this?"

"My shoulder has to heal," I said gently. "The bandage wouldn't look good in the pictures."

"Oh, right. So you'll call me?"

"Yes."

"You won't forget?"

"No. I'm so looking forward to it." Actually, at the moment what I wanted was my own space, free and clear of any other person, and a Diet Coke, and one of the pills I was clutching in my hand. Maybe I'd have a little nap before I took the shower that also featured on my list.

"I've met the cook at Merlotte's before," Claude said, the floodgates evidently now wide open.

"Uh-huh. Sweetie."

"That's what she's calling herself? She used to work at the Foxy Femmes."

"She was a stripper?"

"Yeah, until the accident."

"Sweetie was in an accident?" I was getting more worn out by the second.

"Yeah, so she got scarred and didn't want to strip anymore. It would've required too much makeup, she said. Besides, by then she was getting a little on the, ah, old side to be stripping."

"Poor thing," I said. I tried to picture Sweetie parading down a runway in high heels and feathers. Disturbing.

"I'd never let her hear you say that," he advised.

We parked in front of the duplex. Someone had brought my car back from the library parking lot. The door to the other side of the duplex opened, and Halleigh Robinson stepped out, my keys in her hand. I was wearing the black pants I'd had on since I had been on my way to work, but my Merlotte's T-shirt had been ruined so the hospital had given me a white sweatshirt that someone had left there once upon a time. It was huge on me, but that wasn't why Halleigh was standing stock-still, catching flies with her mouth. Claude had actually gotten out to help me into the house, and the sight of him had paralyzed the young schoolteacher.

Claude eased his arm tenderly around my shoulders, bent his head to look adoringly into my face, and winked.

This was the first hint I'd had that Claude had a sense of humor. It pleased me to find he wasn't universally disagreeable.

"Thanks for bringing me my keys," I called, and Halleigh suddenly remembered she could walk.

"Um," she said. "Um, sure." She put the keys somewhere in the vicinity of my hand, and I snagged them.

"Halleigh, this is my friend Claude," I said with what I hoped was a meaningful smile.

Claude moved his arm down to circle my waist and gave her a distracted smile of his own, hardly moving his eyes from mine. Oh, brother. "Hello, Halleigh," he said in his richest baritone.

"You're lucky to have someone to bring you home from

the hospital," Halleigh said. "That's very nice of you, uh, Claude."

"I would do anything for Sookie," Claude said softly.

"Really?" Halleigh shook herself. "Well, how nice. Andy drove your car back over here, Sookie, and he asked if I'd give you your keys. It's lucky you caught me. I just ran home to eat lunch. I, um, I have to go back to . . ." She gave Claude a final comprehensive stare before getting into her own little Mazda to drive back to the elementary school.

I unlocked my door clumsily and stepped into my little living room. "This is where I'm staying while my house is being rebuilt," I told Claude. I felt vaguely embarrassed at the small sterile room. "I just moved in the day I got shot. Yesterday," I said with some wonder.

Claude, his faux admiration having been dropped when Halleigh pulled away, eyed me with some disparagement. "You have mighty bad luck," he observed.

"In some ways," I said. But I thought of all the help I'd already gotten, and of my friends. I remembered the simple pleasure of sleeping close to Bill the night before. "My luck could definitely be worse," I added, more or less to myself.

Claude was massively uninterested in my philosophy.

After I thanked him again and asked him to give Claudine a hug from me, I repeated my promise to call him when my wound had healed enough for the posing session.

My shoulder was beginning to ache now. When I locked the door behind him, I swallowed a pill. I'd called the phone company from the library the afternoon before, and to my surprise and pleasure I got a dial tone when I picked up my phone. I called Jason's cell to tell him I was out of the hospital, but he didn't answer so I left a message on his voice mail. Then I called the bar to tell Sam I'd be back at work the next day. I'd missed two days' worth of pay and tips, and I couldn't afford any more.

I stretched out on the bed and took a long nap.

When I woke up, the sky was darkening in a way that meant rain. In the front yard of the house across the street, a small maple was whipping around in an alarming way. I thought of the tin roof my Gran had loved and of the clatter the rain made when it hit the hard surface. Rain here in town was sure to be quieter.

I was looking out my bedroom window at the identical duplex next door, wondering who my neighbor was, when I heard a sharp knock. Arlene was breathless from running through the first drops of rain. She had a bag from Wendy's in her hand, and the smell of the food made my stomach wake up with a growl.

"I didn't have time to cook you anything," she said apologetically as I stood aside to let her in. "But I remembered you liked to get the double hamburger with bacon when you were feeling low, and I figured you'd be feeling pretty low."

"You figured right," I said, though I was discovering I was much better than I'd been that morning. I went to the kitchen to get a plate, and Arlene followed, her eyes going to every corner.

"Hey, this is nice!" she said. Though it looked barren to me, my temporary home must have looked wonderfully uncluttered to her.

"What was it like?" Arlene asked. I tried not to hear that she was thinking that I got into more trouble than anyone she knew. "You must have been so scared!"

"Yes." I was serious, and my voice showed it. "I was very scared."

"The whole town is talking about it," Arlene said artlessly. That was just what I wanted to hear: that I was the subject of many conversations. "Hey, you remember that Dennis Pettibone?"

"The arson expert?" I said. "Sure."

"We've got a date tomorrow night."

"Way to go, Arlene. What are you all gonna do?"

"We're taking the kids to the roller rink in Grainger. He's got a girl, Katy. She's thirteen."

"Well, that sounds like fun."

"He's on stakeout tonight," Arlene said importantly.

I blinked. "What's he staking out?"

"They needed all the officers they could call in. They're staking out different parking lots around town to see if they can catch this sniper in the act."

I could see a flaw in their plan. "What if the sniper sees them first?"

"These are professionally trained men, Sookie. I think they know how to handle this." Arlene looked, and sounded, quite huffy. All of a sudden, she was Ms. Law Enforcement.

"Chill," I said. "I'm just concerned." Besides, unless the lawmen were Weres, they weren't in danger. Of course, the big flaw in that theory was that I had been shot. And I was no Were, no shifter. I still hadn't figured out how to work that into my scenario.

"Where's the mirror?" Arlene asked, and I looked around.

"I guess the only big one's in the bathroom," I said, and it felt strange to have to think about the location of an item in my own place. While Arlene fussed with her hair, I put my food on a plate, hoping I'd get to eat while it was still warm. I caught myself standing like a fool with the empty food bag in my hand, wondering where the garbage can was. Of course there wasn't a garbage can until I went out to buy one. I'd never lived anywhere but my Gran's house for the past nineteen years. I'd never had to start housekeeping from the ground up.

"Sam's still not driving, so he can't come to see you, but

he's thinking about you," Arlene called. "You gonna be able to work tomorrow night?"

"I'm planning on it."

"Good. I'm scheduled to be off, Charlsie's granddaughter's in the hospital with pneumonia, so she's gone, and Holly doesn't always show up when she's scheduled. Danielle's going to be out of town. That new girl, Jada—she's better than Danielle, anyway."

"You think?"

"Yeah." Arlene snorted. "I don't know if you've noticed, but Danielle just doesn't seem to care anymore. People can be wanting drinks and calling to her, and it doesn't make a smidge of difference to her. She'll just stand there talking to her boyfriend while people holler at her."

It was true that Danielle had been less than scrupulous about her work habits since she'd started steady-dating a guy from Arcadia. "You think she's gonna quit?" I asked, and that opened up another conversational pit we mined for about five minutes, though Arlene had said she was in a hurry. She'd ordered me to eat while the food was good, so I chewed and swallowed while she talked. We didn't say anything startlingly new or original, but we had a good time. I could tell that Arlene (for once) was just enjoying sitting with me, being idle.

One of the many downsides to telepathy is the fact that you can tell the difference between when someone's really listening to you, and when you're talking to just a face instead of a mind.

Andy Bellefleur arrived as Arlene was getting into her car. I was glad I'd stuffed the bag from Wendy's in a cabinet just to get it out of the way.

"You're right next to Halleigh," Andy said—an obvious opening gambit.

"Thanks for leaving my keys with her and getting my car over here," I said. Andy had his moments.

"She says the guy that brought you home from the hospital was really, ah, interesting." Andy was obviously fishing. I smiled at Andy. Whatever Halleigh had said had made him curious and maybe a little jealous.

"You could say that," I agreed.

He waited to see if I'd expound. When I didn't, he became all business.

"The reason I'm here, I wanted to find out if you remembered any more about yesterday."

"Andy, I didn't know anything then, much less now."

"But you ducked."

"Oh, Andy," I said, exasperated, since he knew good and well about my condition, "you don't have to ask why I ducked."

He turned red, slowly and unbecomingly. Andy was a fireplug of a man and an intelligent police detective, but he had such ambiguity toward things he knew to be true, even if those things weren't completely conventional items of common knowledge.

"We're here all by ourselves," I pointed out. "And the walls are thick enough that I don't hear Halleigh moving around."

"Is there more?" he asked suddenly, his eyes alight with curiosity. "Sookie, is there more?"

I knew exactly what he meant. He would never spell it out, but he wanted to know if there was even more in this world than humans, and vampires, and telepaths. "So much more," I said, keeping my voice quiet and even. "Another world."

Andy's eyes met mine. His suspicions had been confirmed, and he was intrigued. He was right on the edge of asking me about the people who'd been shot—right on the verge of making the leap—but at the last instant, he drew back. "You didn't see anything or hear anything that would help us? Was there anything different about the night Sam was shot?"

"No," I said. "Nothing. Why?"

He didn't answer, but I could read his mind like a book. The bullet from Sam's leg didn't match the other recovered bullets.

After he left, I tried to dissect that quick impression I'd gotten, the one that had prompted me to duck. If the parking lot hadn't been empty, I might not have caught it at all, since the brain that had made it had been at some distance. And what I'd felt had been a tangle of determination, anger, and above all, disgust. The person who'd been shooting had been sure I was loathsome and inhuman. Stupidly enough, my first reaction was hurt—after all, no one likes to be despised. Then I considered the strange fact that Sam's bullet didn't match any of the previous Were shootings. I couldn't understand that at all. I could think of many explanations, but all of them seemed far-fetched.

The rain began to pour down outside, hitting the north-facing windows with a hiss. I didn't have a reason to call anyone, but I felt like making one up. It wasn't a good night to be out of touch. As the pounding of the rain increased, I became more and more anxious. The sky was a leaden gray; soon it would be full dark.

I wondered why I was so twitchy. I was used to being by myself, and it seldom bothered me. Now I was physically closer to people than I'd ever been in my house on Hummingbird Road, but I felt more alone.

Though I wasn't supposed to drive, I needed things for the duplex. I would have made the errand a necessity and gone to Wal-Mart despite the rain—or because of the rain—if the nurse hadn't made such a big deal out of resting my shoulder. I went restlessly from room to room until the crunch of gravel told me that I was having yet more company. This was town living, for sure.

When I opened the door, Tara was standing there in a leopard-print raincoat with a hood. Of course I asked her in, and she tried her best to shake out the coat on the little front porch. I carried it into the kitchen to drip on the linoleum.

She hugged me very gently and said, "Tell me how you are."

After I went over the story once again, she said, "I've been worried about you. I couldn't get away from the shop until now, but I just had to come see you. I saw the suit in my closet. Did you come to my house?"

"Yes," I said. "The day before yesterday. Didn't Mickey tell you?"

"He was in the house when you were there? I warned you," she said, almost panic-stricken. "He didn't hurt you, did he? He didn't have anything to do with you getting shot?"

"Not that I know of. But I did go into your house kind of late, and I know you told me not to. It was just dumb. He did, ah, try to scare me. I wouldn't let him know you've been to see me, if I were you. How were you able to come here tonight?"

A shutter dropped over Tara's face. Her big dark eyes hardened, and she pulled away from me. "He's out somewhere," she said.

"Tara, can you tell me how you came to be involved with him? What happened to Franklin?" I tried to ask these questions as gently as I could, because I knew I was treading on delicate ground.

Tara's eyes filled with tears. She was struggling to answer me, but she was ashamed. "Sookie," she began at last, almost whispering, "I thought Franklin really cared about me, you know? I mean, I thought he respected me. As a person."

I nodded, intent on her face. I was scared of disrupting the flow of her story now that she'd finally begun to talk to me.

"But he . . . he just passed me along when he was through with me."

"Oh, no, Tara! He . . . surely he explained to you why you two were breaking up. Or did you have a big fight?" I didn't want to believe Tara had been passed from vamp to vamp like some fang-banger at a bloodsucker's party.

"He said, 'Tara, you're a pretty girl and you've been good company, but I owe a debt to Mickey's master, and Mickey wants you now.' "

I knew my mouth was hanging open, and I didn't care. I could scarcely believe what Tara was telling me. I could hear the humiliation rolling off of her in waves of self-loathing. "You couldn't do anything about it?" I asked. I was trying to keep the incredulity out of my voice.

"Believe me, I tried," Tara said bitterly. She wasn't blaming me for my question, which was a relief. "I told him I wouldn't. I told him I wasn't a whore, that I'd been dating him because I liked him." Her shoulders collapsed. "But you know, Sookie, I wasn't telling the whole truth, and he knew it. I took all the presents he gave me. They were expensive things. But they were freely given, and he didn't tell me there were strings attached! I never asked for anything!"

"So he was saying that because you'd accepted his gifts, you were bound to do as he said?"

"He said—" Tara began weeping, and her sobs made everything come out in little jerks. "He said that I was acting like a mistress, and he'd paid for everything I had, and that I might as well be of more use to him. I said I wouldn't, that I'd give him back everything, and he said he didn't want it. He told me this vamp named Mickey had seen me out with him, that Franklin owed Mickey a big favor."

"But this is America," I protested. "How can they do that?"

"Vampires are awful," Tara said dismally. "I don't know how you can stand hanging out with them. I thought I was so cool, having a vamp boyfriend. Okay, he was more like a sugar daddy, I guess." Tara sighed at the admission. "It was just so nice being, you know, treated so well. I'm not used to that. I really thought he liked me, too. I wasn't just being greedy."

"Did he take blood from you?" I asked.

"Don't they always?" she asked, surprised. "During sex?"

"As far as I know," I said. "Yeah. But you know, after he had your blood, he could tell how you felt about him."

"He could?"

"After they've had your blood, they're tuned in to your feelings." I was quite sure that Tara hadn't been as fond of Franklin Mott as she'd been saying, that she was much more interested in his lavish gifts and courteous treatment than in him. Of course, he'd known that. He might not have much cared if Tara liked him for himself or not, but that had surely made him more inclined to trade her off. "So how'd it happen?"

"Well, it wasn't so abrupt as I've made it sound," she said. She stared down at her hands. "First Franklin said he couldn't go somewhere with me, so would it be okay if this other guy took me instead? I thought he was thinking of me, of how disappointed I'd be if I didn't get to go—it was a concert—so I really didn't brood over it. Mickey was on his best behavior, and it wasn't a bad evening. He left me at the door, like a gentleman."

I tried not to raise my eyebrows in disbelief. The snake-like Mickey, whose every pore breathed "bad to the bone," had persuaded Tara he was a gentleman? "Okay, so then what?"

"Then Franklin had to go out of town, so Mickey came by to see if I had everything I needed, and he brought me a present, which I thought was from Franklin."

Tara was lying to me, and halfway lying to herself. She had surely known the present, a bracelet, was from Mickey. She had persuaded herself it was kind of a vassal's tribute to his lord's lady, but she had known it wasn't from Franklin.

"So I took it, and we went out, and then when we came back that night, he started making advances. And I broke that off." She gave me a calm and regal face.

She may have repulsed his advances that night, but she hadn't done it instantly and decisively.

Even Tara forgot I could read her mind.

"So that time he left," she said. She took a deep breath. "The next time, he didn't."

He'd given plenty of advance warning of his intentions.

I looked at her. She flinched. "I know," she wailed. "I know, I did wrong!"

"So, is he living at your place?"

"He's got a day place somewhere close," she said, limp with misery. "He shows up at dark, and we're together the whole night. He takes me to meetings, he takes me out, and he . . ."

"Okay, okay." I patted her hand. That didn't seem like enough, and I hugged her closer. Tara was taller than I, so it wasn't a very maternal hug, but I just wanted my friend to know I was on her side.

"He's real rough," Tara said very quietly. "He's going to kill me some day."

"Not if we kill him first."

"Oh, we can't."

"You think he's too strong?"

"I think I can't kill someone, even him."

"Oh." I had thought Tara had more grit to her, after what her parents had put her through. "Then we have to think of a way to pry him off you."

"What about your friend?"

"Which one?"

"Eric. Everyone says that Eric has a thing for you."

"Everyone?"

"The vampires around here. Did Bill pass you to Eric?"

He'd told me once I should go to Eric if anything happened to him, but I hadn't taken that as meaning Eric should assume the same role that Bill had in my life. As it turned out, I had had a fling with Eric, but under entirely different circumstances.

"No, he didn't," I said with absolute clarity. "Let me think." I mulled it over, feeling the terrible pressure of Tara's eyes. "Who's Mickey's boss?" I asked. "Or his sire?"

"I think it's a woman," Tara said. "At least, Mickey's taken me to a place in Baton Rouge a couple of times, a casino, where he's met with a female vamp. Her name is Salome."

"Like in the Bible?"

"Yeah. Imagine naming your kid that."

"So, is this Salome a sheriff?"

"What?"

"Is she a regional boss?"

"I don't know. Mickey and Franklin never talked about that stuff."

I tried not to look as exasperated as I felt. "What's the name of the casino?"

"Seven Veils."

Hmmm. "Okay, did he treat her with deference?" That was a good Word of the Day entry from my calendar, which I hadn't seen since the fire.

"Well, he kind of bowed to her."

"Just his head, or from the waist?"

"From the waist. Well, more than the head. I mean, he bent over."

"Okay. What did he call her?"

"Mistress."

"Okay." I hesitated, and then asked again, "You're sure we can't kill him?"

"Maybe you can," she said morosely. "I stood over him with an ice pick for fifteen minutes one night when he went to sleep after, you know, sex. But I was too scared. If he finds out I've been here to see you, he'll get mad. He doesn't like you at all. He thinks you're a bad influence."

"He got that right," I said with a confidence I was far from feeling. "Let me see what I can think of."

Tara left after another hug. She even managed a little smile, but I didn't know how justified her flash of optimism might be.

There was only one thing I could do.

The next night I'd be working. It was full dark by now, and he'd be up.

I had to call Eric.

13

"FANGTASIA," SAID A BORED FEMININE VOICE. "Where all your bloody dreams come true."

"Pam, it's Sookie."

"Oh, hello," she said more cheerfully. "I hear you're in even more trouble. Got your house burned. You won't live much longer if you keep that up."

"No, maybe not," I agreed. "Listen, is Eric there?"

"Yes, he's in his office."

"Can you transfer me to him?"

"I don't know how," she said disdainfully.

"Could you take the phone to him, please, ma'am?"

"Of course. Something always happens around here after you call. It's quite the break in routine." Pam was carrying the phone through the bar; I could tell by the change in the ambient noise. There was music in the background. KDED again: "The Night Has a Thousand Eyes" this time. "What's happening in Bon Temps, Sookie?" Pam asked, saying in a clear aside to some bar patron, "Step aside, you son of a misbegotten whore!

"They like that kind of talk," she said to me conversationally. "Now, what's up?"

"I got shot."

"Oh, too bad," she said. "Eric, do you know what Sookie is telling me? Someone shot her."

"Don't get so emotional, Pam," I said. "Someone might think you care."

She laughed. "Here is the man," she said.

Sounding just as matter-of-fact as Pam had, Eric said, "It can't be critical or you wouldn't be talking to me."

This was true, though I would have enjoyed a more horrified reaction. But this was no time to think of little issues. I took a deep breath. I knew, sure as shooting, what was coming, but I had to help Tara. "Eric," I said with a feeling of doom, "I need a favor."

"Really?" he said. Then, after a notable pause, "Really?"

He began to laugh.

"Gotcha," he said.

He arrived at the duplex an hour later and paused on the doorsill after I'd responded to his knock. "New building," he reminded me.

"You are welcome to come in," I said insincerely, and he stepped in, his white face practically blazing with—triumph? Excitement? Eric's hair was wet with rain and straggled over his shoulders in rattails. He was wearing a golden brown silk T-shirt and brown pleated trousers with a magnificent belt that was just barbaric: lots of leather, and gold, and dangling tassels. You can take the man out of the Viking era, but you can't take the Viking out of the man.

"Can I get you a drink?" I said. "I'm sorry, I don't have any

TrueBlood, and I'm not supposed to drive, so I couldn't go get any." I knew that was a big breach of hospitality, but there was nothing I could do about it. I hadn't been about to ask anyone to bring me blood for Eric.

"Not important," he said smoothly, looking around the small room.

"Please sit down."

Eric said onto the couch, his right ankle on the knee of his left leg. His big hands were restless. "What's the favor you need, Sookie?" He was openly gleeful.

I sighed. At least I was pretty sure he'd help, since he could practically taste the leverage he'd have over me.

I perched on the edge of the lumpy armchair. I explained about Tara, about Franklin, about Mickey. Eric got serious in a hurry. "She could leave during the day and she doesn't," he pointed out.

"Why should she leave her business and her home? He's the one should leave," I argued. (Though I have to confess, I'd wondered to myself why Tara didn't just take a vacation. Surely Mickey wouldn't stick around too long if his free ride was gone?) "Tara would be looking over her shoulder for the rest of her life if she tried to shake him loose by running," I said firmly.

"I've learned more about Franklin since I met him in Mississippi," Eric said. I wondered if Eric had learned this from Bill's database. "Franklin has an outdated mind-set."

This was rich, coming from a Viking warrior whose happiest days had been spent pillaging and raping and laying waste.

"Vampires used to pass willing humans around," Eric explained. "When our existence was secret, it was convenient to have a human lover, to maintain that person . . . that is, not to take too much blood . . . and then, when there was no one left who wanted her—or him," Eric added hastily, so my feminist side would not be offended, "that person would be, ah, completely used."

I was disgusted and showed it. "You mean drained," I said.

"Sookie, you have to understand that for hundreds, thousands, of years we have considered ourselves better than humans, separate from humans." He thought for a second. "Very much in the same relationship to humans as humans have to, say, cows. Edible like cows, but cute, too."

I was knocked speechless. I had sensed this, of course, but to have it spelled out was just . . . nauseating. Food that walked and talked, that was us. McPeople.

"I'll just go to Bill. He knows Tara, and she rents her business premises from him, so I bet he'll feel obliged to help her," I said furiously.

"Yes. He'd be obliged to try to kill Salome's underling. Bill doesn't rank any higher than Mickey, so he can't order him to leave. Who do you think would survive the fight?"

The idea paralyzed me for a minute. I shuddered. What if Mickey won?

"No, I'm afraid I'm your best hope here, Sookie." Eric gave me a brilliant smile. "I'll talk to Salome and ask her to call her dog off. Franklin is not her child, but Mickey is. Since he's been poaching in my area, she'll be obliged to recall him."

He raised a blond eyebrow. "And since you're asking me to do this for you, of course, you owe me."

"Gosh, I wonder what you want in return?" I asked, maybe a little on the dry and sarcastic side.

He grinned at me broadly, giving me a flash of fang. "Tell me what happened while I was staying with you. Tell me completely, leaving out nothing. After that, I'll do what you want." He put both feet on the floor and leaned forward, focused on me.

"All right." Talk about being caught between a rock and a hard place. I looked down at my hands clasped in my lap.

"Did we have sex?" he asked directly.

For about two minutes, this might actually be fun. "Eric," I said, "we had sex in every position I could imagine, and some I couldn't. We had sex in every room in my house, and we had sex outdoors. You told me it was the best you'd ever had." (At the time he couldn't recall all the sex he'd ever had. But he'd paid me a compliment.) "Too bad you can't remember it," I concluded with a modest smile.

Eric looked like I'd hit him in the forehead with a mallet. For all of thirty seconds his reaction was completely gratifying. Then I began to be uneasy.

"Is there anything else I should know?" he said in a voice so level and even that it was simply scary.

"Um, yes."

"Then perhaps you'll enlighten me."

"You offered to give up your position as sheriff and come to live with me. And get a job."

Okay, maybe this *wasn't* going so well. Eric couldn't get any whiter or stiller. "Ah," he said. "Anything else?"

"Yes." I ducked my head because I'd gotten to the absolutely un-fun part. "When we came home that last night, the night we'd had the battle with the witches in Shreveport, we came in the back door, right, like I always do. And Debbie Pelt—you remember her. Alcide's—oh, whatever she was to him . . . Debbie was sitting at my kitchen table. And she had a gun and was gonna shoot me." I risked a glance and found Eric's brows had drawn in together in an ominous frown. "But you threw yourself in front of me." I leaned forward very quickly and patted him on the knee. Then I retreated into my own space. "And you took the bullet, which was really, really sweet of you. But she was going to shoot again, and I pulled out my brother's shotgun, and I killed her." I hadn't cried at all that night, but I felt a tear run down my cheek now. "I killed her," I said, and gasped for breath.

Eric's mouth opened as though he was going to ask a question, but I held up a hand in a *wait* gesture. I had to finish. "We gathered up the body and bagged it, and you took it and buried her somewhere while I cleaned the kitchen. And you found her car and you hid it. I don't know where. It took me hours to get the blood out of the kitchen. It was on everything." I grabbed desperately at my self-possession. I rubbed my eyes with the back of my wrist. My shoulder ached, and I shifted in the chair, trying to ease it.

"And now someone else has shot at you and I wasn't there to take the bullet," Eric said. "You must be living wrong. Do you think the Pelt family is trying to get revenge?"

"No," I said. I was pleased that Eric was taking all this so calmly. I don't know what I'd expected, but it wasn't this. He seemed, if anything, subdued. "They hired private detectives, and as far as I know, the private detectives didn't find any reason to suspect me any more than anyone else. The only reason I was a suspect anyway was because when Alcide and I found that body in Shreveport at Verena Rose's, we told the police we were engaged. We had to explain why we went together to a bridal shop. Since he had such an on-and-off relationship with Debbie, him saying we were getting married naturally raised a red flag when the detectives checked it out. He had a good alibi for the time she died, as it turned out. But if they ever seriously suspect me, I'll be in trouble. I can't give you as an alibi, because of course you weren't even here, as far as anyone knows. You can't give me an alibi because you don't remember that night; and of course, I'm just plain old guilty. I killed her. I had to do it." I'm sure Cain had said that when he'd killed Abel.

"You're talking too much," Eric said.

I pressed my lips together. One minute he wanted me to tell him everything; the next minute he wanted me to stop talking.

For maybe five minutes, Eric just looked at me. I wasn't always sure he was seeing me. He was lost in some deep thoughts.

"I told you I would leave everything for you?" he said at the end of all this rumination.

I snorted. Trust Eric to select that as the pertinent idea.

"And how did you respond?"

Okay, that astonished me. "You couldn't just stay with me, not remembering. That wouldn't be right."

He narrowed his eyes. I got tired of being regarded through slits of blue. "So," I said, curiously deflated. Maybe I'd expected a more emotional scene than this. Maybe I'd expected Eric to grab me and kiss me silly and tell me he still felt the same. Maybe I was too fond of daydreams. "I did your favor. Now you do mine."

Not taking his eyes off me, Eric whipped a cell phone from his pocket and dialed a number from memory. "Rose-Anne," he said. "Are you well? Yes, please, if she's free. Tell her I have information that will interest her." I couldn't hear the response on the other end, but Eric nodded, as he would if the speaker had been present. "Of course I'll hold. Briefly." In a minute, he said, "And hello to you, too, most beautiful princess. Yes, it keeps me busy. How's business at the casino? Right, right. There's one born every minute. I called to tell you something about your minion, that one named Mickey. He has some business connection with Franklin Mott?"

Then Eric's eyebrows rose, and he smiled slightly. "Is that right? I don't blame you. Mott is trying to stick to the old ways, and this is America." He listened again. "Yes, I'm giving you this information for free. If you choose not to grant me a small favor in return, of course that's of no consequence. You know in what esteem I hold you." Eric smiled charmingly at the telephone. "I did think you should know about Mott's passing on a human woman to Mickey. Mickey's keeping her under his thumb by threatening her life and property. She's quite unwilling."

After another silence, during which his smile widened, Eric said, "The small favor is removing Mickey. Yes, that's all. Just make sure he knows he should never again approach this woman, Tara Thornton. He should have nothing more to do with her, or her belongings and friends. The connection should be completely severed. Or I'll have to see about severing some part of Mickey. He's done this in my area, without the courtesy of coming to visit me. I really expected better manners of any child of yours. Have I covered all the bases?"

That Americanism sounded strange, coming from Eric Northman. I wondered if he'd ever played baseball.

"No, you don't need to thank me, Salome. I'm glad to be of service. And if you could let me know when the thing is accomplished? Thanks. Well, back to the grindstone." Eric flipped the phone shut and began tossing it in the air and catching it, over and over.

"You knew Mickey and Franklin were doing something wrong to start with," I said, shocked but oddly unsurprised. "You know their boss would be glad to find out they were breaking the rules, since her vamp was violating your territory. So this won't affect you at all."

"I only realized that when you told me what you wanted," Eric pointed out, the very essence of reason. He grinned at me. "How could I know that your heart's desire would be for me to help someone else?"

"What did you think I wanted?"

"I thought maybe you wanted me to pay for rebuilding

your house, or you would ask me to help find out who's shooting the Weres. Someone who could have mistaken you for a Were," Eric told me, as if I should have known that. "Who had you been with before you were shot?"

"I'd been to visit Calvin Norris," I said, and Eric looked displeased.

"So you had his smell on you."

"Well, I gave him a hug good-bye, so yeah."

Eric eyed me skeptically. "Had Alcide Herveaux been there?

"He came by the house site," I said.

"Did he hug you, too?"

"I don't remember," I said. "It's no big deal."

"It is for someone looking for shifters and Weres to shoot. And you are hugging too many people."

"Maybe it was Claude's smell," I said thoughtfully. "Gosh, I didn't think of that. No, wait, Claude hugged me after the shooting. So I guess the fairy smell didn't matter."

"A fairy," Eric said, the pupils of his eyes actually dilating. "Come here, Sookie."

Ah-oh. I might have overplayed my hand out of sheer irritation.

"No," I said. "I told you what you wanted, you did what I asked, and now you can go back to Shreveport and let me get some sleep. Remember?" I pointed to my bandaged shoulder.

"Then I'll come to you," Eric said, and knelt in front of me. He pressed against my legs and leaned over so his head was against my neck. He inhaled, held it, exhaled. I had to choke back a nervous laugh at the similarity the process held to smoking dope. "You reek," Eric said, and I stiffened. "You smell of shifter and Were and fairy. A cocktail of other races."

I stayed completely immobile. His lips were about two millimeters from my ear. "Should I just bite you, and end it all?" he whispered. "I would never have to think about you again. Thinking about you is an annoying habit, and one I want to be rid of. Or should I start arousing you, and discover if sex with you was really the best I've ever had?"

I didn't think I was going to get a vote on this. I cleared my throat. "Eric," I said, a little hoarsely, "we need to talk about something."

"No. No. No," he said. With each "no" his lips brushed my skin.

I was looking past his shoulder at the window. "Eric," I breathed, "someone's watching us."

"Where?" His posture didn't change, but Eric had shifted from a mood that was definitely dangerous to me to one that was dangerous for someone else.

Since the eyes-at-the-window scenario was an eerie echo of the situation the night my house had burned, and that night the skulker had proved to be Bill, I hoped the watcher might be Bill again. Maybe he was jealous, or curious, or just checking up on me. If the trespasser was a human, I could have read his brain and found out who he was, or at least what he intended; but this was a vampire, as the blank hole where the brain pattern should be had informed me.

"It's a vampire," I told Eric in the tiniest whisper I could manage, and he put his arms around me and pulled me into him.

"You're so much trouble," Eric said, and yet he didn't sound exasperated. He sounded excited. Eric loved the action moments.

By then, I was sure that the lurker wasn't Bill, who would have made himself known. And Charles was presumably busy at Merlotte's, mixing daiquiris. That left one vampire in the area unaccounted for. "Mickey," I breathed, my fingers gripping Eric's shirt.

"Salome moved more quickly than I thought," Eric said

in a regular voice. "He's too angry to obey her, I suppose. He's never been in here, correct?"

"Correct." Thank God.

"Then he can't come inside."

"But he can break the window," I said as glass shattered to our left. Mickey had thrown a large rock as big as my fist, and to my dismay the rock hit Eric squarely in the head. He went down like a—well, like a rock. He lay without moving. Dark blood welled from a deep cut in his temple. I leaped to my feet, completely stunned at seeing the powerful Eric apparently out cold.

"Invite me in," said Mickey, just outside the window. His face, white and angry, shone in the pelting rain. His black hair was plastered to his head.

"Of course not," I said, kneeling beside Eric, who blinked, to my relief. Not that he could be dead, of course, but still, when you see someone take a blow like that, vampire or not, it's just plain terrifying. Eric had fallen in front of the armchair, which had its back to the window, so Mickey couldn't see him.

But now I could see what Mickey was holding by one hand: Tara. She was almost as pale as he was, and she'd been beaten to a pulp. Blood was running out of the corner of her mouth. The lean vampire had a merciless grip on her arm. "I'll kill her if you don't let me in," he said, and to prove his point, he put both hands around her neck and began to squeeze. A clap of thunder and a bolt of lightning lit up Tara's desperate face as she clawed weakly at his arms. He smiled, fangs completely exposed.

If I let him in, he'd kill all of us. If I left him out there, I would have to watch him kill Tara. I felt Eric's hands take hold of my arm. "Do it," I said, not moving my gaze from Mickey. Eric bit, and it hurt like hell. He wasn't finessing this at all. He was desperate to heal in a hurry.

I'd just have to swallow the pain. I tried hard to keep my face still, but then I realized I had a great reason to look upset. "Let her go!" I yelled at Mickey, trying to buy a few seconds. I wondered if any of the neighbors were up, if they could hear the ruckus, and I prayed they wouldn't come searching to find out what was going on. I was even afraid for the police, if they came. We didn't have any vampire cops to handle vampire lawbreakers, like the cities did.

"I'll let her go when you let me in," Mickey yelled. He looked like a demon out there in the rain. "How's your tame vamp doing?"

"He's still out," I lied. "You hurt him bad." It didn't take any effort at all to make my voice crack as if I were on the verge of tears. "I can see his skull," I wailed, looking down at Eric to see that he was still feeding as greedily as a hungry baby. His head was mending as I watched. I'd seen vamps heal before, but it was still amazing. "He can't even open his eyes," I added in a heartbroken way, and just then Eric's blue eyes blazed up at me. I didn't know if he was in fighting trim yet, but I could not watch Tara being choked. "Not yet," Eric said urgently, but I had already told Mickey to come in.

"Oops," I said, and then Mickey slithered through the window in an oddly boneless movement. He knocked the broken glass out of the way carelessly, like it didn't hurt him to get cut. He dragged Tara through after him, though at least he'd switched his grip from her neck to her arm. Then he dropped her on the floor, and the rain coming in the window pelted down on her, though she couldn't be any wetter than she already was. I wasn't even sure she was conscious. Her eyes were closed in her bloody face, and her bruises were turning dark. I stood, swaying with the blood loss, but keeping my wrist concealed by resting it on the back of the armchair. I'd felt Eric lick it, but it would take a few minutes to heal.

"What do you want?" I asked Mickey. As if I didn't know.

"Your head, bitch," he said, his narrow features twisted with hatred, his fangs completely out. They were white and glistening and sharp in the bright overhead light. "Get down on your knees to your betters!" Before I could react in any way—in fact before I could blink—the vampire backhanded me, and I stumbled across the small room, landing half on the couch before I slid to the floor. The air went out of me in a big whoosh, and I simply couldn't move, couldn't even gasp for air, for an agonizingly long minute. In the meantime, Mickey was on top of me, his intentions completely clear when he reached down to unzip his pants. "This is all you're good for!" he said, contempt making him even uglier. He tried to push his way into my head, too, forcing the fear of him into my brain to cow me.

And my lungs inflated. The relief of breathing was exquisite, even under the circumstances. With air came rage, as if I'd inhaled it along with oxygen. This was the trump card male bullies played, always. I was sick of it—sick of being scared of the bogeyman's dick.

"No!" I screamed up at him. *"No!"* And finally I could think again; finally the fear let loose of me. "Your invitation is *rescinded*!" I yelled, and it was his turn to panic. He reared up off of me, looking ridiculous with his pants open, and he went backward out of the window, stepping on poor Tara as he went. He tried to bend, to grip her so he could yank her with him, but I lunged across the little room to grab her ankles, and her arms were too slick with rain to give him purchase, and the magic that had hold of him was too strong. In a second, he was outside looking in, screaming with rage. Then he looked east, as if he heard someone calling, and he vanished into the darkness.

Eric pushed himself to his feat, looking almost as startled

as Mickey. "That was clearer thinking than most humans can manage," he said mildly into the sudden silence. "How are you, Sookie?" He reached down a hand and pulled me to my feet. "I myself am feeling much better. I've had your blood without having to talk you into it, and I didn't have to fight Mickey. You did all the work."

"You got hit in the head with a rock," I pointed out, content just to stand for a minute, though I knew I had to call an ambulance for Tara. I was feeling a little on the weak side myself.

"A small price to pay," Eric told me. He brought out his cell phone, flipped it open, and pressed the REDIAL button. "Salome," Eric said, "glad you answered the phone. He's trying to run. . . ."

I heard the gleeful laughter coming from the other end of the phone. It was chilling. I couldn't feel the least bit sorry for Mickey, but I was glad I wouldn't have to witness his punishment.

"Salome'll catch him?" I asked.

Eric nodded happily as he returned his phone to his pocket. "And she can do things to him more painful than anything I could imagine," he said. "Though I can imagine plenty right now."

"She's that, ah, creative?"

"He's hers. She's his sire. She can do with him what she wishes. He can't disobey her and go unpunished. He has to go to her when she calls him, and she's calling."

"Not on the phone, I take it," I ventured.

His eyes glinted down at me. "No, she won't need a phone. He's trying to run away, but he'll go to her eventually. The longer he holds out, the more severe his torture will be. Of course," he added, in case I missed the point, "that's as it should be."

"Pam is yours, right?" I asked, falling to my knees and putting my fingers to Tara's cold neck. I didn't want to look at her.

"Yes," Eric said. "She's free to leave when she wants, but she comes back when I let her know I need her help."

I didn't know how I felt about that, but it didn't really make a hell of a lot of difference. Tara gasped and moaned. "Wake up, girl," I said. "Tara! I'm gonna call an ambulance for you.

"No," she said sharply. "No." There was a lot of that word going around tonight.

"But you're bad hurt."

"I can't go to the hospital. Everyone will know."

"Everyone will know someone beat the shit out of you when you can't go to work for a couple of weeks, you idiot."

"You can have some of my blood," Eric offered. He was looking down at Tara without any obvious emotion.

"No," she said. "I'd rather die."

"You might," I said, looking her over. "Oh, but you've had blood from Franklin or Mickey." I was assuming some tit-for-tat in their lovemaking.

"Of course not," she said, shocked. The horror in her voice took me aback. I'd had vampire blood when I'd needed it. The first time, I'd have died without it.

"Then you have to go to the hospital." I was really concerned that Tara might have internal injuries. "I'm scared for you to move," I protested, when she tried to push herself to a seated position. Mr. Super Strength didn't help, which irritated me, since he could have shifted her easily.

But at last Tara managed to sit with her back against the wall, the empty window allowing the chilly wind to gust in and blow the curtains to and fro. The rain had abated until only a drop or two was coming in. The linoleum in front of the window was wet with water and blood, and the glass lay in glittering sharp fragments, some stuck to Tara's damp clothes and skin.

"Tara, listen to me," Eric said. She looked up at him. Since he was close to the fluorescent light, she had to squint. I thought she looked pitiful, but Eric didn't seem to see the same person I was seeing. "Your greed and selfishness put my—my friend Sookie in danger. You say you're her friend, too, but you don't act like it."

Hadn't Tara loaned me a suit when I needed one? Hadn't she loaned me her car when mine burned? Hadn't she helped me on other occasions when I needed it? "Eric, this isn't any of your business," I said.

"You called me and asked me for my help. That makes it my business. I called Salome and told her what her child was doing, and she's taken him away and to punish him for it. Isn't that what you wanted?"

"Yes," I said, and I'm ashamed to say I sounded sullen.

"Then I'm going to make my point with Tara." He looked back down at her. "Do you understand me?"

Tara nodded painfully. The bruises on her face and throat seemed to be darkening more every minute.

"I'm getting some ice for your throat," I told her, and ran into the kitchen to dump ice from the plastic trays into a Ziploc bag. I didn't want to listen to Eric scold her; she seemed so pitiful.

When I came back less than a minute later, Eric had finished whatever he was going to say to Tara. She was touching her neck gingerly, and she took the bag from me and held it to her throat. While I was leaning over her, anxious and scared, Eric was back on his cell phone.

I twitched with worry. "You need a doctor," I urged her.

"No," she said.

I looked up at Eric, who was just finishing his phone call. He was the injury expert.

"She'll heal without going to the hospital," he said briefly. His indifference made a chill run down my spine. Just when I thought I was used to them, vampires would show me their true face, and I would have to remind myself all over again that they were a different race. Or maybe it was centuries of conditioning that made the difference; decades of disposing of people as they chose, taking what they wanted, enduring the dichotomy of being the most powerful beings on earth in the darkness, and yet completely helpless and vulnerable during the hours of light.

"But will she have some permanent damage? Something doctors could fix if she got to them quick?"

"I'm fairly certain that her throat is only badly bruised. She has some broken ribs from the beating, possibly some loose teeth. Mickey could have broken her jaw and her neck very easily, you know. He probably wanted her to be able to talk to you when he brought her here, so he held back a little. He counted on you panicking and letting him in. He didn't think you could gather your thoughts so quickly. If I'd been him, my first move would have been to damage your mouth or neck so you couldn't rescind my entrance."

That possibility hadn't occurred to me, and I blanched.

"When he backhanded you, I think that was what he was aiming for," Eric continued dispassionately.

I'd heard enough. I thrust a broom and dustpan into his hands. He looked at them as if they were ancient artifacts and he could not fathom their use.

"Sweep up," I said, using a wet washcloth to clean the blood and dirt off my friend. I didn't know how much of this conversation Tara was absorbing, but her eyes were open and her mouth was shut, so maybe she was listening. Maybe she was just working through the pain.

Eric moved the broom experimentally and made an attempt to sweep the glass into the pan while it lay in the middle of the floor. Of course, the pan slid away. Eric scowled.

I'd finally found something Eric did poorly.

"Can you stand?" I asked Tara. She focused on my face and nodded very slightly. I squatted and took her hands. Slowly and painfully, she drew her knees up, and then she pushed as I pulled. Though the window had broken mostly in big pieces, a few bits of glass fell from her as she rose, and I flicked an eye at Eric to make sure he understood he should clean them up. He had a truculent set to his mouth.

I tried to put my arm around Tara to help her into my bedroom, but my wounded shoulder gave a throb of pain so unexpected that I flinched. Eric tossed down the dustpan. He picked up Tara in one smooth gesture and put her on the couch instead of my bed. I opened my mouth to protest and he looked at me. I shut my mouth. I went into the kitchen and fetched one of my pain pills, and I got Tara to swallow one, which took some coaxing. The medicine seemed to knock her out, or maybe she just didn't want to acknowledge Eric anymore. Anyway, she kept her eyes closed and her body slack, and gradually her breathing grew even and deep.

Eric handed me the broom with a triumphant smile. Since he'd lifted Tara, clearly I was stuck with his task. I was awkward because of my bad shoulder, but I finished sweeping up the glass and disposing of it in a garbage bag. Eric turned toward the door. I hadn't heard anyone arrive, but Eric opened the door to Bill before Bill even knocked. Eric's earlier phone conversation must have been with Bill. In a way, that made sense; Bill lived in Eric's fiefdom, or whatever they called it. Eric needed help, so Bill was obliged to supply it. My ex was burdened with a large piece of plywood, a hammer, and a box of nails.

"Come in," I said when Bill halted in the doorway, and without speaking a word to each other, the two vampires nailed the wood across the window. To say I felt awkward would be an understatement, though thanks to the events of the evening I wasn't as sensitive as I would've been at another time. I was mostly preoccupied with the pain in my shoulder, and Tara's recovery, and the current whereabouts of Mickey. In the extra space I had left over after worrying about those items, I crammed in some anxiety about replacing Sam's window, and whether the neighbors had heard enough of this fracas to call the police. On the whole, I thought they hadn't; someone would be here by now.

After Bill and Eric finished their temporary repair, they both watched me mopping up the water and blood on the linoleum. The silence began to weigh heavily on all three of us: at least, on my third of the three of us. Bill's tenderness in caring for me the night before had touched me. But Eric's just acquired knowledge of our intimacy raised my self-consciousness to a whole new level. I was in the same room with two guys who both knew I'd slept with the other.

I wanted to dig a hole and lie down in it and pull the opening inside with me, like a character in a cartoon. I couldn't look either of them in the face.

If I rescinded both their invitations, they'd have to walk outside without a word; but in view of the fact that they'd both just helped me, such a procedure would be rude. I'd solved my problems with them before in exactly that way. Though I was tempted to repeat it to ease my personal embarrassment, I simply couldn't. So what did we do next?

Should I pick a fight? Yelling at one another might clear the air. Or maybe a frank acknowledgment of the situation . . . no.

I had a sudden mental picture of us all three climbing in the double bed in the little bedroom. Instead of *duking* out our conflicts, or *talking* out our problems, we could . . . no. I could feel my face flame red, as I was torn between semi-hysterical amusement and a big dash of shame at even thinking the thought. Jason and his buddy Hoyt had often discussed (in my hearing) that every male's fantasy was to be in bed with two women. And men who came into the bar echoed that idea, as I knew from checking Jason's theory by reading a random sample of male minds. Surely I was allowed to entertain the same kind of fantasy? I gave a hysterical kind of giggle, which definitely startled both vampires.

"This is amusing?" Bill asked. He gestured from the plywood, to the recumbent Tara, to the bandage on my shoulder. He omitted pointing from Eric to himself. I laughed out loud.

Eric cocked a blond eyebrow. "*We* are amusing?"

I nodded wordlessly. I thought, *Instead of a cook-off, we could have a cock-off. Instead of a fishing derby, we could have a . . .*

At least in part because I was tired, and strained, and blood depleted, I went way into the silly zone. I laughed even harder when I looked at Eric's and Bill's faces. They wore almost identical expressions of exasperation.

Eric said, "Sookie, we haven't finished our discussion."

"Oh yes, we have," I said, though I was still smiling. "I asked you for a favor: releasing Tara from her bondage to Mickey. You asked me for payment for that favor: telling you what happened when you lost your memory. You performed your side of the bargain, and so did I. Bought and paid for. The end."

Bill looked from Eric to me. Now he knew that Eric knew what I knew. . . . I giggled again. Then the giddiness just poofed out of me. I was a deflated balloon, for sure. "Good night, both of you," I said. "Thanks, Eric, for taking that rock in the head, and for sticking to your phone throughout the evening. Thanks, Bill, for turning out so late with window-repair supplies. I appreciate it, even if you got volunteered by Eric." Under ordinary circumstances—if there were such things as ordinary circumstances with vampires around—I would've given them each a hug, but that just seemed too weird. "Shoo," I said. "I have to go to bed. I'm all worn out."

"Shouldn't one of us stay here with you tonight?" Bill asked.

If I'd had to say yes to that, had to pick one of them to stay with me that night, it would have been Bill—if I could have counted on him to be as undemanding and gentle as he'd been the night before. When you're down and hurting, the most wonderful thing in the world is to feel cherished. But that was too big a bunch of if's for tonight.

"I think I'll be fine," I said. "Eric assures me that Salome will scoop up Mickey in no time, and I need sleep more than anything. I appreciate both of you coming out tonight."

For a long moment I thought they might just say "No" and try to outwait each other. But Eric kissed me on the forehead and left, and Bill, not to be outdone, brushed my lips with his and took his leave. When the two vampires had departed, I was delighted to be by myself.

Of course, I wasn't exactly alone. Tara was passed out on the couch. I made sure she was comfortable—took off her shoes, got the blanket off my bed to cover her—and then I fell into my own bed.

14 ~

I SLEPT FOR HOURS.

When I woke up, Tara was gone.

I felt a stab of panic, until I realized she'd folded the blanket, washed her face in the bathroom (wet washcloth), and put her shoes on. She had left me a little note, too, on an old envelope that already held the beginnings of my shopping list. It said, "I'll call you later. T"—a terse note, and not exactly redolent of sisterly love.

I felt a little sad. I figured I wouldn't be Tara's favorite person for a while. She'd had to look more closely at herself than she wanted to look.

There are times to think, and times to lie fallow. Today was a fallow day. My shoulder felt much better, and I decided I would drive to the Wal-Mart Supercenter in Clarice and get all my shopping over with in one trip. Also, there I wouldn't see as many people I knew, and I wouldn't have to discuss getting shot.

It was very peaceful, being anonymous in the big store. I moved slowly and read labels, and I even selected a shower curtain for the duplex bathroom. I took my time completing my list. When I transferred the bags from the buggy into the car, I tried to do all the lifting with my right arm. I was practically reeking with virtue when I got back to the house on Berry Street.

The Bon Temps Florist van was in the driveway. Every woman has a little lift in her heart when the florist's van pulls up, and I was no exception.

"I have a multiple delivery here," said Bud Dearborn's wife, Greta. Greta was flat-faced like the sheriff and squatty like the sheriff, but her nature was happy and unsuspicious. "You're one lucky girl, Sookie."

"Yes, ma'am, I am," I agreed, with only a tincture of irony. After Greta had helped me carry in my bags, she began carrying in flowers.

Tara had sent me a little vase of daisies and carnations. I am very fond of daisies, and the yellow and white looked pretty in my little kitchen. The card just read "From Tara."

Calvin had sent a very small gardenia bush wrapped up in tissue and a big bow. It was ready to pop out of the plastic tub and be planted as soon as the danger of a frost was over. I was impressed with the thoughtfulness of the gift, since the gardenia bush would perfume my yard for years. Because he'd had to call in the order, the card bore the conventional sentiment "Thinking of you—Calvin."

Pam had sent a mixed bouquet, and the card read, "Don't get shot anymore. From the gang at Fangtasia." That made me laugh a little. I automatically thought of writing thank-you notes, but of course I didn't have my stationery with me. I'd stop by the pharmacy and get some. The downtown pharmacy had a corner that was a card shop, and also it accepted packages for UPS pickup. You had to be diverse in Bon Temps.

I put away my purchases, awkwardly hung the shower curtain, and got cleaned up for work.

Sweetie Des Arts was the first person I saw when I came through the employees' entrance. She had an armful of kitchen towels, and she'd tied on her apron. "You're a hard woman to kill," she remarked. "How you feeling?"

"I'm okay," I said. I felt like Sweetie had been waiting for me, and I appreciated the gesture.

"I hear you ducked just in time," she said. "How come? Did you hear something?"

"Not exactly," I said. Sam limped out of his office then, using his cane. He was scowling. I sure didn't want to explain my little quirk to Sweetie on Sam's time. I said, "I just had a feeling," and shrugged, which was unexpetedly painful.

Sweetie shook her head at my close call and turned to go through the bar and back to the kitchen.

Sam jerked his head toward his office, and with a sinking heart I followed him in. He shut the door behind us. "What were you doing when you got shot?" he asked. His eyes were bright with anger.

I wasn't going to get blamed for what had happened to me. I stood right up to Sam, got in his face. "I was just checking out library books," I said through my teeth.

"So why would he think you're a shifter?"

"I have no idea."

"Who had you been around?"

"I'd been to see Calvin, and I'd . . ." My voice trailed off as I caught at the tail end of a thought.

"So, who can tell you smell like a shifter?" I asked slowly.

"No one but another shifter, right? Or someone with shifter blood. Or a vampire. Some supernatural thing."

"But we haven't had any strange shifters around here lately."

"Have you gone to where the shooter must have been, to smell?"

"No, the only time I was on the spot at a shooting, I was too busy screaming on the ground with blood running out of my leg."

"But maybe now you could pick up something."

Sam looked down at his leg doubtfully. "It's rained, but I guess it's worth a try," he conceded. "I should have thought of it myself. Okay, tonight, after work."

"It's a date," I said flippantly as Sam sank down in his squeaky chair. I put my purse in the drawer Sam kept empty and went out to check my tables.

Charles was hard at work, and he gave me a nod and a smile before he concentrated on the level of beer in the pitcher he was holding to the tap. One of our consistent drunks, Jane Bodehouse, was seated at the bar with Charles fixed in her sights. It didn't seem to make the vampire uncomfortable. I saw that the rhythm of the bar was back to normal; the new bartender had been absorbed into the background.

After I'd worked about an hour, Jason came in. He had Crystal cuddled up in the curve of his arm. He was as happy as I'd ever seen him. He was excited by his new life and very pleased with Crystal's company. I wondered how long that would last. But Crystal herself seemed of much the same mind.

She told me that Calvin would be getting out of the hospital the next day and going home to Hotshot. I made sure to mention the flowers he'd sent and told her I'd be fixing Calvin some dish to mark his homecoming.

Crystal was pretty sure she was pregnant. Even through

the tangle of shifter brain, I could read that thought as clear as a bell. It wasn't the first time I'd learned that some girl "dating" Jason was sure he was going to be a dad, and I hoped that this time was as false as the last time. It wasn't that I had anything against Crystal . . . Well, that was a lie I was telling myself. I did have something against Crystal. Crystal was part of Hotshot, and she'd never leave it. I didn't want any niece or nephew of mine to be brought up in that strange little community, within the pulsing magic influence of the crossroads that formed its center.

Crystal was keeping her late period a secret from Jason right now, determined to stay quiet until she was sure what it meant. I approved. She nursed one beer while Jason downed two, and then they were off to the movies in Clarice. Jason gave me a hug on the way out while I was distributing drinks to a cluster of law enforcement people. Alcee Beck, Bud Dearborn, Andy Bellefleur, Kevin Pryor, and Kenya Jones, plus Arlene's new crush, arson investigator Dennis Pettibone, were all huddled around two tables pushed together in a corner. There were two strangers with them, but I picked up easily enough that the two men were cops, too, part of some task force.

Arlene might have liked to wait on them, but they were clearly in my territory, and they clearly were talking about something heap big. When I was taking drink orders, they all hushed up, and when I was walking away, they'd start their conversation back up. Of course, what they said with their mouths didn't make any difference to me, since I knew what each and every one of them was thinking.

And they all knew this good and well; and they all forgot it. Alcee Beck, in particular, was scared to death of me, but even he was quite oblivious to my ability, though I'd demonstrated it for him before. The same could be said of Andy Bellefleur.

"What's the law enforcement convention in the corner cooking up?" asked Charles. Jane had tottered off to the ladies', and he was temporarily by himself at the bar.

"Let me see," I said, closing my eyes so I could concentrate better. "Well, they're thinking of moving the stakeout for the shooter to another parking lot tonight, and they're convinced that the arson is connected to the shootings and that Jeff Marriot's death is tied in with everything, somehow. They're even wondering if the disappearance of Debbie Pelt is included in this clutch of crimes, since she was last seen getting gas on the interstate at the filling station closest to Bon Temps. And my brother, Jason, disappeared for a while a couple of weeks ago; maybe that's part of the picture, too." I shook my head and opened my eyes to find that Charles was disconcertingly close. His one good eye, his right, stared hard into my left.

"You have very unusual gifts, young woman," he said after a moment. "My last employer collected the unusual."

"Who'd you work for before you came into Eric's territory?" I asked. He turned away to get the Jack Daniel's.

"The King of Mississippi," he said.

I felt as if someone had pulled the rug out from under my feet. "Why'd you leave Mississippi and come here?" I asked, ignoring the hoots from the table five feet away.

The King of Mississippi, Russell Edgington, knew me as Alcide's girlfriend, but he didn't know me as a telepath occasionally employed by vampires. It was quite possible Edgington might have a grudge against me. Bill had been held in the former stables behind Edgington's mansion and tortured by Lorena, the creature who'd turned Bill into a vampire over a hundred and forty years before. Bill had escaped. Lorena had died. Russell Edgington didn't necessarily know I was the agent of these events. But then again, he might.

"I got tired of Russell's ways," Sir Charles said. "I'm not

of his sexual persuasion, and being surrounded by perversity became tiresome."

Edgington enjoyed the company of men, it was true. He had a house full of them, as well as a steady human companion, Talbot.

It was possible Charles had been there while I was visiting, though I hadn't noticed him. I'd been severely injured the night I was brought to the mansion. I hadn't seen all its inhabitants, and I didn't necessarily remember the ones I'd seen.

I became aware that the pirate and I were maintaining our eye contact. If they've survived for any length of time, vampires read human emotions very well, and I wondered what Charles Twining was gleaning from my face and demeanor. This was one of the few times I wished I could read a vampire's mind. I wondered, very much, if Eric was aware of Charles's background. Surely Eric wouldn't have taken him on without a background check? Eric was a cautious vampire. He'd seen history I couldn't imagine, and he'd lived through it because he was careful.

Finally I turned to answer the summons of the impatient roofers who'd been trying to get me to refill their beer pitchers for several minutes.

I avoided speaking to our new bartender for the rest of the evening. I wondered why he'd told me as much as he had. Either Charles wanted me to know he was watching me, or he really had no idea I'd been in Mississippi recently.

I had a lot to think about.

The working part of the night finally came to an end. We had to call Jane's son to come get his soused relative, but that was nothing new. The pirate bartender had been working at a good clip, never making mistakes, being sure to give every patron a good word as he filled the orders. His tip jar looked healthy.

Bill arrived to pick up his boarder as we were closing up for the night. I wanted to have a quiet word with him, but Charles was by Bill's side in a flash, so I didn't have an opportunity. Bill gave me an odd look, but they were gone without my making an opportunity to talk to him. I wasn't sure what I would say, anyway. I was reassured when I realized that of course Bill had seen the worst employees of Russell Edgington, because those employees had tortured him. If Charles Twining was unknown to Bill, he might be okay.

Sam was ready to go on our sniffing mission. It was cold and brilliant outside, the stars glittering in the night sky. Sam was bundled up, and I pulled on my pretty red coat. I had a matching set of gloves and a hat, and I would need them now. Though spring was coming closer every day, winter hadn't finished with us yet.

No one was at the bar but us. The entire parking lot was empty, except for Jane's car. The glare of the security lights made the shadows deeper. I heard a dog bark way off in the distance. Sam was moving carefully on his crutches, trying to negotiate the uneven parking lot.

Sam said, "I'm going to change." He didn't mean his clothes.

"What'll happen to your leg if you do?"

"Let's find out."

Sam was full-blood shifter on both sides. He could change when it wasn't the full moon, though the experiences were very different, he'd said. Sam could change into more than one animal, though dogs were his preference, and a collie was his choice among dogs.

Sam retired behind the hedge in front of his trailer to doff his clothes. Even in the night, I saw the air disturbance that signaled magic was working all around him. He fell to his knees and gasped, and then I couldn't see him anymore through the dense bushes. After a minute, a bloodhound trotted out, a red one, his ears swinging from side to side. I wasn't used to seeing Sam this way, and it took me a second to be sure it was him. When the dog looked up at me, I knew my boss was inside.

"Come on, Dean," I said. I'd named Sam that in his animal guise before I'd realized the man and the dog were the same being. The bloodhound trotted ahead of me across the parking lot and into the woods where the shooter had waited for Sam to come out of the club. I watched the way the dog was moving. It was favoring its right rear leg, but not drastically.

In the cold night woods, the sky was partially blocked. I had a flashlight, and I turned it on, but somehow that just made the trees creepier. The bloodhound—Sam—had already reached the place the police had decided marked the shooter's vantage point. The dog, jowls jouncing, bent its head to the ground and moved around, sorting through all the scent information he was receiving. I stayed out of the way, feeling useless. Then Dean looked up at me and said, "Rowf." He began making his way back to the parking lot. I guessed he'd gathered all he could.

As we'd arranged, I loaded Dean in the Malibu to take him to another shooting site, the place behind some old buildings opposite the Sonic where the shooter had hidden on the night poor Heather Kinman had been killed. I turned into the service alley behind the old stores and parked behind Patsy's Cleaners, which had moved to a new and more convenient location fifteen years ago. Between the cleaners and the dilapidated and long-empty Louisiana Feed and Seed, a narrow gap afforded a great view of the Sonic. The drive-in restaurant was closed for the night but still bright with light. Since the Sonic was on the town's main drag, there were lights up and down the street, and I could actually see pretty well in the areas where the structures allowed light to go; unfortunately, that made the shadows impenetrable.

Again, the bloodhound worked the area, paying particular interest to the weedy strip of ground between the two old stores, a strip so narrow it was no more than a gap wide enough for one person. He seemed pretty excited at some particular scent he found. I was excited, too, hoping that he'd found something we could translate into evidence for the police.

Suddenly Dean let out a "Whoof!" and raised his head to look past me. He was certainly focusing on something, or someone. Almost unwillingly, I turned to see. Andy Bellefleur stood at the point where the service alley crossed the gap between the buildings. Only his face and upper torso were in the light.

"Jesus Christ, Shepherd of Judea! Andy, you scared the hell out of me!" If I hadn't been watching the dog so intently, I would've sensed him coming. The stakeout, dammit. I should have remembered.

"What are you doing here, Sookie? Where'd you get the dog?"

I couldn't think of a single answer that would sound plausible. "It seemed worth a try to see if a trained dog could pick up a single scent from the places where the shooter stood," I said. Dean leaned against my legs, panting and slobbering.

"So when did you get on the parish payroll?" Andy asked conversationally. "I didn't realize you'd been hired as an investigator."

Okay, this wasn't going well.

"Andy, if you'll move out of the way, me and the dog'll just get back into my car, and we'll drive away, and you won't have to be mad at me anymore." He was plenty mad, and he was determined to have it out with me, whatever that entailed. Andy wanted to get the world realigned, with facts he knew forming the tracks it should run on. I didn't fit in that world. I wouldn't run on those tracks. I could read his mind, and I didn't like what I was hearing.

I realized, too late, that Andy'd had one drink too many during the conference at the bar. He'd had enough to remove his usual constraints.

"You shouldn't be in our town, Sookie," he said.

"I have as much right to be here as you, Andy Bellefleur."

"You're a genetic fluke or something. Your grandmother was a real nice woman, and people tell me your dad and mom were good people. What happened to you and Jason?"

"I don't think there's much wrong with me and Jason, Andy," I said calmly, but his words stung like fire ants. "I think we're regular people, no better and no worse than you and Portia."

Andy actually snorted.

Suddenly the bloodhound's side, pressed against my legs, began to vibrate. Dean was growling almost inaudibly. But he wasn't looking at Andy. The hound's heavy head was turned in another direction, toward the dark shadows of the other end of the alley. Another live mind: a human. Not a regular human, though.

"Andy," I said. My whisper pierced his self-absorption. "You armed?"

I didn't know whether I felt that much better when he drew his pistol.

"Drop it, Bellefleur," said a no-nonsense voice, one that sounded familiar.

"Bullshit," Andy sneered. "Why should I?"

"Because I got a bigger gun," said the voice, cool and sarcastic. Sweetie Des Arts stepped from the shadows, carrying a rifle. It was pointed at Andy, and I had no doubt she was ready to fire. I felt like my insides had turned to Jell-O.

"Why don't you just leave, Andy Bellefleur?" Sweetie asked. She was wearing a mechanic's coverall and a jacket, and her hands were gloved. She didn't look anything like a short-order cook. "I've got no quarrel with you. You're just a person."

Andy was shaking his head, trying to clear it. I noticed he hadn't dropped his gun yet. "You're the cook at the bar, right? Why are you doing this?"

"You should know, Bellefleur. I heard your little conversation with the shifter here. Maybe this dog is a human, someone you know." She didn't wait for Andy to answer. "And Heather Kinman was just as bad. She turned into a fox. And the guy that works at Norcross, Calvin Norris? He's a damn panther."

"And you shot them all? You shot me, too?" I wanted to be sure Andy was registering this. "There's just one thing wrong with your little vendetta, Sweetie. I'm not a shifter."

"You smell like one," Sweetie said, clearly sure she was right.

"Some of my friends are shifters, and that day I'd hugged a few of 'em. But me myself—not a shifter of any kind."

"Guilty by association," Sweetie said. "I'll bet you got a dab of shifter from somewhere."

"What about you?" I asked. I didn't want to get shot again. The evidence suggested that Sweetie was not a sharpshooter: Sam, Calvin, and I had lived. I knew aiming at night had to be difficult, but still, you would've thought she could have done better. "Why are you on this vendetta?"

"I'm just a fraction of a shifter," she said, snarling just as much as Dean. "I got bit when I had a car wreck. This half-man half-wolf . . . thing . . . ran out of the woods near where I lay bleeding, and the damn thing bit me . . . and then another car came around the curve and it ran away. But the first full moon after that, my hands changed! My parents threw up."

"What about your boyfriend? You had one?" I kept speaking, trying to distract her. Andy was moving as far away from me as he could get, so she couldn't shoot both of us quickly. She planned on shooting me first, I knew. I wanted the bloodhound to move away from me, but he stayed loyally pressed against my legs. She wasn't sure the dog was a shifter. And, oddly, she hadn't mentioned shooting Sam.

"I was a stripper then, living with a great guy," she said, rage bubbling through her voice. "He saw my hands and the extra hair and he loathed me. He left when the moon was full. He'd take business trips. He'd go golfing with his buddies. He'd be stuck at a late meeting."

"So how long have you been shooting shifters?"

"Three years," she said proudly. "I've killed twenty-two and wounded forty-one."

"That's awful," I said.

"I'm proud of it," she said. "Cleaning the vermin off the face of the earth."

"You always find work in bars?"

"Gives me a chance to see who's one of the brethren," she said, smiling. "I check out the churches and restaurants, too. The day care centers."

"Oh, no." I thought I was going to throw up.

My senses were hyperalert, as you can imagine, so I knew there was someone coming up the alley behind Sweetie. I could feel the anger roiling in a two-natured head. I didn't look, trying to keep Sweetie's attention for as long as I could. But there was a little noise, maybe the sound of a piece of paper trash rustling against the ground, and that was enough for Sweetie. She whirled around with the rifle up to her shoulder, and she fired. There was a shriek from the darkness at the south end of the alley, and then a high whining.

Andy took his moment and shot Sweetie Des Arts while her back was turned. I pressed myself against the uneven bricks of the old Feed and Seed, and as the rifle dropped from her hand, I saw the blood come out of her mouth, black in the starlight. Then she folded to the earth.

While Andy was standing over her, his gun dangling from his hand, I made my way past them to find out who had come to our aid. I switched on my flashlight to discover a werewolf, terribly wounded. Sweetie's bullet had hit him in the middle of the chest, as best I could tell through the thick fur, and I yelled at Andy, "Use your cell phone! Call for help!" I was pressing down on the bubbling wound as hard as I could, hoping I was doing the right thing. The wound kept moving in a very disconcerting way, since the Were was in the process of changing back into a human. I glanced back to see that Andy was still lost in his own little vale of horror at what he'd done. "Bite him," I told Dean, and Dean padded over to the policeman and nipped his hand.

Andy cried out, of course, and raised his gun as if he were going to shoot the bloodhound. "No!" I yelled, jumping up from the dying Were. "Use your phone, you idiot. Call an ambulance."

Then the gun swung around to point at me.

For a long, tense moment I thought for sure the end of my life had come. We'd all like to kill what we don't understand, what scares us, and I powerfully scared Andy Bellefleur.

But then the gun faltered and dropped back to Andy's side. His broad face stared at me with dawning comprehension. He fumbled in his pocket, withdrew a cell phone. To my profound relief, he holstered the gun after he punched in a number.

I turned back to the Were, now wholly human and naked, while Andy said, "There's been a multiple shooting in the alley behind the old Feed and Seed and Patsy's Cleaners, across Magnolia Street from Sonic. Right. Two ambulances, two gunshot wounds. No, I'm fine."

The wounded Were was Dawson. His eyes flickered open, and he tried to gasp. I couldn't even imagine the pain he must be suffering. "Calvin," he tried to say.

"Don't worry now. Help's on the way," I told the big man. My flashlight was lying on the ground beside me, and by its oddly skewed light I could see his huge muscles and bare hairy chest. He looked cold, of course, and I wondered where his clothes were. I would have been glad to have his shirt to wad up over the wound, which was steadily leaking blood. My hands were covered in it.

"Told me to finish out my last day by watching over you," Dawson said. He was shuddering all over. He tried to smile. "I said, 'Piece of cake.' " And then he didn't say anything else, but lost consciousness.

Andy's heavy black shoes came to stand in my field of vision. I thought Dawson was going to die. I didn't even know his first name. I had no idea how we were going to explain a naked guy to the police. Wait . . . was that up to me? Surely Andy was the one who'd have the hard explaining to do?

As if he'd been reading my mind—for a change—Andy said, "You know this guy, right?"

"Slightly."

"Well, you're going to have to say you know him better than that, to explain his lack of clothes."

I gulped. "Okay," I said, after a brief, grim pause.

"You two were back here looking for his dog. You," Andy said to Dean. "I don't know who you are, but you stay a dog, you hear me?" Andy stepped away nervously. "And I came back here because I'd followed the woman—she was acting suspiciously."

I nodded, listening to the air rattle in Dawson's throat. If I could only give him blood to heal him, like a vampire. If I only knew a medical procedure . . . But I could already hear the police cars and the ambulances coming closer. Nothing in Bon Temps was very far from anything else, and on this side of town, the south side, the Grainger hospital would be closest.

"I heard her confess," I said. "I heard her say she shot the others."

"Tell me something, Sookie," Andy said in a rush. "Before they get here. There's nothing weird about Halleigh, right?"

I stared up at him, amazed he could think of such a thing at this moment. "Nothing aside from the stupid way she spells her name." Then I reminded myself who'd shot the bitch lying on the ground five feet away. "No, not a thing," I said. "Halleigh is just plain old normal."

"Thank God," he said. "Thank God."

And then Alcee Beck dashed down the alley and stopped in his tracks, trying to make sense of the scene before him. Right behind him was Kevin Pryor, and Kevin's partner Kenya crept along hugging the wall with her gun out. The ambulance teams were hanging back until they were sure the scene was secure. I was up against the wall getting searched before I knew what was happening. Kenya kept saying, "Sorry, Sookie" and "I have to do this," until I told her, "Just get it done. Where's my dog?"

"He run off," she said. "I guess the lights spooked him. He's a bloodhound, huh? He'll come home." When she'd done her usual thorough job, Kenya said, "Sookie? How come this guy is naked?"

This was just the beginning. My story was extremely

thin. I read disbelief written large on almost every face. It wasn't the temperature for outdoor loving, and I was completely dressed. But Andy backed me up every step of the way, and there was no one to say it hadn't happened the way I told it.

About two hours later, they let me get back in my car to return to the duplex. The first thing I did when I got inside was phone the hospital to find out how Dawson was. Somehow, Calvin got ahold of the phone. "He's alive," he said tersely.

"God bless you for sending him after me," I said. My voice was as limp as a curtain on a still summer day. "I'd be dead if it wasn't for him."

"I hear the cop shot her."

"Yes, he did."

"I hear a lot of other stuff."

"It was complicated."

"I'll see you this week."

"Yes, of course."

"Go get some sleep."

"Thanks again, Calvin."

My debt to the werepanther was piling up at a rate that scared me. I knew I'd have to work it off later. I was tired and aching. I was filthy inside from Sweetie's sad story, and filthy outside from being on my knees in the alley, helping the bloody Were. I dropped my clothes on the floor of the bedroom, went into the bathroom, and stood under the shower, trying hard to keep my bandage dry with a shower cap, the way one of the nurses had shown me.

When the doorbell rang the next morning, I cursed town living. But as it turned out, this was no neighbor who wanted to borrow a cup of flour. Alcide Herveaux was standing outside, holding an envelope.

I glared at him through eyes that felt crusty with sleep. Without saying a word, I plodded back to my bedroom and crawled into the bed. This wasn't enough to deter Alcide, who strode in after me.

"You're now doubly a friend of the pack," he said, as if he was sure that was the concern uppermost in my mind. I turned my back to him and snuggled under the covers. "Dawson says you saved his life."

"I'm glad Dawson's well enough to speak," I muttered, closing my eyes tightly and wishing Alcide would go away. "Since he got shot on my account, your pack doesn't owe me a damn thing."

From the movement of the air, I could tell that Alcide was kneeling at the side of the bed. "That's not for you to decide, but us," he said chidingly. "You're summoned to the contest for the packleader."

"What? What do I have to do?"

"You just watch the proceedings and congratulate the winner, no matter who it is."

Of course, to Alcide, this struggle for succession was the most important thing going. It was hard for him to get that I didn't have the same priorities. I was getting swamped by a wave of supernatural obligations.

The werewolf pack of Shreveport said they owed me. I owed Calvin. Andy Bellefleur owed me and Dawson and Sam for solving his case. I owed Andy for saving my life. Though I'd cleared Andy's mind about Halleigh's complete normality, so maybe that canceled my debt to him for shooting Sweetie.

Sweetie had owed payback to her assailant.

Eric and I were even, I figured.

I owed Bill slightly.

Sam and I were more or less caught up.

Alcide personally owed me, as far as I was concerned. I had showed up for this pack shit and tried to follow the rules to help him out.

In the world I lived in, the world of human people, there were ties and debts and consequences and good deeds. That was what bound people to society; maybe that was what constituted society. And I tried to live in my little niche in it the best way I could.

Joining in the secret clans of the two-natured and the undead made my life in human society much more difficult and complicated.

And interesting.

And sometimes . . . fun.

Alcide had been talking at least some of the time I'd been thinking, and I'd missed a lot of it. He was picking up on that. He said, "I'm sorry if I'm boring you, Sookie," in a stiff voice.

I rolled over to face him. His green eyes were full of hurt. "Not bored. I just have a lot to think about. Leave the invitation, okay? I'll get back with you on that." I wondered what you wore to a fighting-for-packmaster event. I wondered if the senior Mr. Herveaux and the somewhat pudgy motorcycle dealership owner would actually roll on the ground and grapple.

Alcide's green eyes were full of puzzlement. "You're acting so strange, Sookie. I felt so comfortable with you before. Now I feel like I don't know you."

Valid had been one of my Words of the Day last week. "That's a valid observation," I said, trying to sound matter-of-fact. "I felt just as comfortable with you when I first met you. Then I started to find out stuff. Like about Debbie, and shifter politics, and the servitude of some shifters to the vamps."

"No society is perfect," Alcide said defensively. "As for Debbie, I don't ever want to hear her name again."

"So be it," I said. God knew I couldn't get any sicker of hearing her name.

Leaving the cream envelope on the bedside table, Alcide took my hand, bent over it, and laid a kiss on the back of it. It was a ceremonial gesture, and I wished I knew its significance. But the moment I would have asked, Alcide was gone.

"Lock the door behind you," I called. "Just turn the little button on the doorknob." I guess he did, because I went right back to sleep, and no one woke me up until it was almost time for me to go to work. Except there was a note on my front door that said, "Got Linda T. to stand in for you. Take the night off. Sam." I went back inside and took off my waitress clothes and pulled on some jeans. I'd been ready to go to work, and now I felt oddly at a loss.

I was almost cheered to realize I had another obligation, and I went into the kitchen to start fulfilling it.

After an hour and a half of struggling to cook in an unfamiliar kitchen with about half the usual paraphernalia, I was on my way to Calvin's house in Hotshot with a dish of chicken breasts baked with rice in a sour-cream sauce, and some biscuits. I didn't call ahead. I planned to drop off the food and go. But when I reached the little community, I saw there were several cars parked on the road in front of Calvin's trim little house. "Dang," I said. I didn't want to get involved any further with Hotshot than I already was. My brother's new nature and Calvin's courting had already dragged me in too far.

Heart sinking, I parked and ran my arm through the handle of the basket full of biscuits. I took the hot dish of chicken and rice in oven-mitted hands, gritted my teeth against the ache in my shoulder, and marched my butt up to Calvin's front door. Stackhouses did the right thing.

Crystal answered the door. The surprise and pleasure on her face shamed me. "I'm so glad you're here," she said, doing her best to be offhand. "Please come in." She stood back, and now I could see that the small living room was full of people, including my brother. Most of them were werepanthers, of course. The werewolves of Shreveport had sent a representative; to my astonishment, it was Patrick Furnan, contender for the throne and Harley-Davidson salesman.

Crystal introduced me to the woman who appeared to be acting as hostess, Maryelizabeth Norris. Maryelizabeth moved as if she hadn't any bones. I was willing to bet Maryelizabeth didn't often leave Hotshot. The shifter introduced me around the room very carefully, making sure I understood the relationship Calvin bore to each individual. They all began to blur after a bit. But I could see that (with a few exceptions) the natives of Hotshot ran to two types: the small, dark-haired, quick ones like Crystal, and the fairer, stockier ones with beautiful green or golden-brown eyes, like Calvin. The surnames were mostly Norris or Hart.

Patrick Furnan was the last person Crystal reached. "Why, of course I know you," he said heartily, beaming at me as if we'd danced at a wedding together. "This here's Alcide's girlfriend," he said, making sure he was heard by everyone in the room. "Alcide's the son of the other candidate for packmaster."

There was long silence, which I would definitely characterize as "charged."

"You're mistaken," I said in a normal conversational tone. "Alcide and I are friends." I smiled at him in such a way as to let him know he better not be alone with me in an alley anytime soon.

"My mistake," he said, smooth as silk.

Calvin was receiving a hero's welcome home. There were balloons and banners and flowers and plants, and his house was meticulously clean. The kitchen had been full of food. Now Maryelizabeth stepped forward, turned her back to cut

Patrick Furnan dead, and said, "Come this way, honey. Calvin's ready to see you." If she'd had a trumpet handy, she'd have blown a flourish on it. Maryelizabeth was not a subtle woman, though she had a deceptive air of mystery due to her wide-spaced golden eyes.

I guess I could have been more uncomfortable, if there'd been a bed of red-hot coals to walk on.

Maryelizabeth ushered me into Calvin's bedroom. His furniture was very nice, with spare, clean lines. It looked Scandinavian, though I know little about furniture—or style, for that matter. He had a high bed, a queen-size, and he was propped up in it against sheets with an African motif of hunting leopards. (Someone had a sense of humor, anyway.) Against the deep colors in the sheets and the deep orange of the bedspread, Calvin looked pale. He was wearing brown pajamas, and he looked exactly like a man who'd just been released from the hospital. But he was glad to see me. I found myself thinking there was something a bit sad about Calvin Norris, something that touched me despite myself.

"Come sit," he said, indicating the bed. He moved over a little so I'd have room to perch. I guess he'd made some signal, because the man and the woman who'd been in the room—Dixie and Dixon—silently eased out through the door, shutting it behind them.

I perched, a little uneasily, on the bed beside him. He had one of those tables you most often see in hospitals, the kind that can be rolled across the bed. There was a glass of ice tea and a plate on it, steam rising from the food. I gestured that he should begin. He bowed his head and said a silent prayer while I sat quietly. I wondered to whom the prayer was addressed.

"Tell me about it," Calvin said as he unfolded his napkin, and that made me a lot more comfortable. He ate while I told him what had happened in the alley. I noticed that the food on the tray was the chicken-and-rice casserole I'd brought, with a dab of mixed vegetable casserole and two of my biscuits. He wanted me to see that he was eating the food I'd prepared for him. I was touched, which sounded a warning bell at the back of my brain.

"So, without Dawson, there's no telling what would've happened," I concluded. "I thank you for sending him. How is he?"

Calvin said, "Hanging on. They airlifted him from Grainger to Baton Rouge. He would be dead, if he wasn't a Were. He's lasted this long; I think he'll make it."

I felt terrible.

"Don't go blaming yourself for this," Calvin said, his voice suddenly sounding deeper. "This is Dawson's choice."

"Huh?" would've sounded ignorant, so I said, "How so?"

"His choice of professions. His choice of actions. Maybe he should have leaped for her a few seconds earlier. Why'd he wait? I don't know. How'd she know to aim low, given the poor light? I don't know. Choices lead to consequences." Calvin was struggling to express something. He was not naturally an articulate man, and he was trying to convey a thought both important and abstract. "There's no blame," he said finally.

"It would be nice to believe that, and I hope some day I do," I said. "Maybe I'm on my way to believing it." It was true that I was sick of self-blame and second-guessing.

"I suspect the Weres are going to invite you to their little packleader shindig," Calvin said. He took my hand. His was warm and dry.

I nodded.

"I bet you'll go," he said.

"I think I have to," I said uneasily, wondering what his goal was.

"I'm not going to tell you what to do," Calvin said. "I have no authority over you." He didn't sound too happy about that. "But if you go, please watch your back. Not for my sake; that don't mean nothing to you, yet. But for yourself."

"I can promise that," I said after a careful pause. Calvin was not a guy to whom you blurted the first idea in your head. He was a serious man.

Calvin gave me one of his rare smiles. "You're a damn fine cook," he said. I smiled back.

"Thank you, sir," I said, and got up. His hand tightened on mine and pulled. You don't fight a man who's just gotten out of the hospital, so I bent toward him and laid my cheek to his lips.

"No," he said, and when I turned a little to find out what was wrong, he kissed me on the lips.

Frankly, I expected to feel nothing. But his lips were as warm and dry as his hands, and he smelled like my cooking, familiar and homey. It was surprising, and surprisingly comfortable, to be so close to Calvin Norris. I backed off a little, and I am sure my face showed the mild shock I felt. The werepanther smiled and released my hand.

"The good thing about being in the hospital was you coming to see me," he said. "Don't be a stranger now that I'm home."

"Of course not," I said, ready to be out of the room so I could regain my composure.

The outer room had emptied of most of its crowd while I talked to Calvin. Crystal and Jason had vanished, and Maryelizabeth was gathering up plates with the help of an adolescent werepanther. "Terry," Maryelizabeth said with a sideways inclination of her head. "My daughter. We live next door."

I nodded to the girl, who gave me a darting look before turning back to her task. She was not a fan of mine. She was from the fairer bloodstock, like Maryelizabeth and Calvin, and she was a thinker. "Are you going to marry my dad?" she asked me.

"I'm not planning on marrying anyone," I said cautiously. "Who's your dad?"

Maryelizabeth gave Terry a sidelong look that promised Terry she'd be sorry later. "Terry is Calvin's," she said.

I was still puzzled for a second or two, but suddenly, the stance of both the younger and the older woman, their tasks, their air of comfort in this house, clicked into place.

I didn't say a word. My face must have shown something, for Maryelizabeth looked alarmed, and then angry.

"Don't presume to judge how we live our life," she said. "We are not like you."

"That's true," I said, swallowing my revulsion. I forced a smile to my lips. "Thank you for introducing me around. I appreciate it. Is there anything I can help you with?"

"We can take care of it," said Terry, giving me another look that was a strange combination of respect and hostility.

"We should never have sent you to school," Maryelizabeth said to the girl. Her wide-spaced golden eyes were both loving and regretful.

"Good-bye," I said, and after I recovered my coat, I left the house, trying not to hurry. To my dismay, Patrick Furnan was waiting for me beside my car. He was holding a motorcycle helmet under his arm, and I spotted the Harley a little farther down the road.

"You interested in hearing what I've got to say?" the bearded Were asked.

"No, actually not," I told him.

"He's not going to keep on helping you out for nothing," Furnan said, and my whole head snapped around so I could look at this man.

"What are you talking about?"

"A thank-you and a kiss ain't going to hold him. He's going to demand payment sooner or later. Won't be able to help it."

"I don't recall asking you for advice," I said. He stepped closer. "And you keep your distance." I let my gaze roam to the houses surrounding us. The watchful gaze of the community was full upon us; I could feel its weight.

"Sooner or later," Furnan repeated. He grinned at me suddenly. "I hope it's sooner. You can't two-time a Were, you know. Or a panther. You'll get ripped to shreds between 'em."

"I'm not two-timing *anyone,*" I said, frustrated almost beyond bearing at his insistence that he knew my love life better than I did. "I'm not dating either of them."

"Then you have no protection," he said triumphantly.

I just couldn't win.

"Go to hell," I said, completely exasperated. I got in my car and drove away, letting my eyes glide over the Were as if he weren't there. (This "abjure" concept could come in handy.) The last thing I saw in my rearview mirror was Patrick Furnan sliding his helmet on, still watching my retreating car.

If I hadn't really cared who won the King of the Mountain contest between Jackson Herveaux and Patrick Furnan, I did now.

15 ~

I WAS WASHING THE DISHES I'D USED AS I COOKED FOR Calvin. My little duplex was peaceful. If Halleigh was home, she was being quiet as a mouse. I didn't mind washing dishes, to tell you the truth. It was a good time to let my mind drift around, and often I made good decisions while I was doing something completely mundane. Not too surprisingly, I was thinking of the night before. I was trying to remember exactly what Sweetie had said. Something about it had struck me wrong, but at the moment I hadn't exactly been in a position to raise my hand to ask a question. It had something to do with Sam.

I finally recalled that though she'd told Andy Bellefleur that the dog in the alley was a shapeshifter, she hadn't known it was Sam. There wasn't anything strange about that, since Sam had been in a bloodhound shape, not his usual collie form.

After I'd realized what had been bothering me, I thought my mind would be at peace. That didn't happen. There was something else—something else Sweetie had said. I thought and thought, but it just wouldn't pop to the top of my brain.

To my surprise, I found myself calling Andy Bellefleur at home. His sister Portia was just as surprised as I was when she answered, and she said rather coldly that she'd find Andy.

"Yes, Sookie?" Andy sounded neutral.

"Let me ask a question, Andy."

"I'll listen."

"When Sam was shot," I said, and paused, trying to figure out what to say.

"Okay," Andy said. "What about it?"

"Is it true that the bullet didn't match the others?"

"We didn't retrieve a bullet in every case." Not a direct answer, but probably as good as I was going to get.

"Hmmm. Okay," I said, then thanked him and hung up, uncertain if I'd learned what I wanted or not. I had to push it out of my mind and do something else. If there was a question there, it would eventually work its way to the top of the heap of the issues that burdened my thoughts.

What remained of the evening was quiet, which was getting to be a rare pleasure. With so little house to clean, and so little yard to care for, there would be lots of free hours to come. I read for an hour, worked a crossword puzzle, and went to bed at about eleven.

Amazingly, no one woke me all night. No one died, there weren't any fires, and no one had to alert me to any emergency.

The next morning I rose feeling better than I had in a week. A glance at the clock told me I'd slept all the way through to ten o'clock. Well, that wasn't so surprising. My shoulder felt nearly healed; my conscience had settled itself. I didn't think I had many secrets to keep, and that was a tremendous relief. I was used to keeping other people's secrets, but not my own.

The phone rang as I swallowed the last of my morning coffee. I put my paperback facedown on the kitchen table to mark my place and got up to answer it. "Hello," I said cheerfully.

"It's today," Alcide said, voice vibrating with excitement. "You need to come."

Thirty minutes my peace had lasted. Thirty minutes.

"I'm guessing you mean the contest for the position of packmaster."

"Of course."

"And I need to be there why?"

"You need to be there because the entire pack and all friends of the pack have to be there," Alcide said, his voice brooking no dissent. "Christine especially thought you should be a witness."

I might have argued if he hadn't added the bit about Christine. The wife of the former packmaster had struck me as a very intelligent woman with a cool head.

"All right," I said, trying not to sound grumpy. "Where and when?"

"At noon, be at the empty building at 2005 Clairemont. It used to be David & Van Such, the printing company."

I got a few directions and hung up. While I showered, I reasoned that this was a sporting event, so I dressed in my old denim skirt with a long-sleeved red tee. I pulled on some red tights (the skirt was quite short) and some black Mary Janes. They were a little scuffed, so I hoped that Christine would not look down at my shoes. I tucked my silver cross into my shirt; the religious significance wouldn't bother the Weres at all, but the silver might.

The defunct printing company of David & Van Such had been in a very modern building, in an equally modern industrial park, largely deserted this Saturday. All the businesses had been constructed to match: low gray stone and dark glass edifices, with crepe myrtle bushes all around, grass medians, and nice curbing. David & Van Such featured an ornamental bridge over an ornamental pond, and a red front door. In the spring, and after some restorative maintenance, it would be as pretty as a modern business building could get. Today, in the fading phase of winter, the dead weeds that had grown high during the previous summer waved in a chilly breeze. The skeletal crepe myrtles needed pruning back, and the water in the pond looked stagnant, with trash floating dismally here and there. The David & Van Such parking lot contained about thirty cars, including—ominously—an ambulance.

Though I wore a jacket, the day suddenly seemed colder as I went from the parking lot and across the bridge to the front door. I was sorry I'd left my heavier coat at home, but it hadn't seemed worth bringing for a brief run between enclosed spaces. The glass front of David & Van Such, broken only by the red door, reflected the clear pale blue sky and the dead grass.

It didn't seem right to knock at a business door, so I slipped inside. Two people were ahead of me, having crossed the now-empty reception area. They passed through plain gray double doors. I followed them, wondering what I was getting into.

We entered what had been the manufacturing area, I suppose; the huge presses were long gone. Or maybe this cavern of a room had been full of desks manned by clerks taking orders or doing accounting work. Skylights in the roof let in some illumination. There was a cluster of people close to the middle of the space.

Well, I hadn't gotten the clothes thing right. The women were mostly wearing nicer pants outfits, and I glimpsed a dress here and there. I shrugged. Who could have known?

There were a few people in the crowd I hadn't seen at the funeral. I nodded at a red-haired Were named Amanda (I knew her from the Witch War), and she nodded back. I was surprised to spot Claudine and Claude. The twins looked marvelous, as always. Claudine was wearing a deep green sweater and black pants, and Claude was wearing a black sweater and deep green pants. The effect was striking. Since the two fairies were the only obvious non-Weres in attendance, I went to stand with them.

Claudine bent and kissed me on the cheek, and so did Claude. Their kisses felt exactly the same.

"What's going to happen?" I whispered the question because the group was abnormally quiet. I could see things hanging from the ceiling, but in the poor light I couldn't imagine what they were.

"There will be several tests," Claudine murmured. "You're not much of a screamer, right?"

I never had been, but I wondered if I'd break new ground today.

A door opened on the far side of the room, and Jackson Herveaux and Patrick Furnan came in. They were naked. Having seen very few men naked, I didn't have much basis for comparison, but I have to say that these two Weres weren't my ideal. Jackson, though certainly fit, was an older man with skinny legs, and Patrick (though he, too, looked strong and muscular) was barrel-like in form.

After I'd adjusted to the nakedness of the men, I noticed that each was accompanied by another Were. Alcide followed his father, and a young blond man trailed Patrick. Alcide and the blond Were remained fully clothed. "It would've been nice if *they'd* been naked, huh?" Claudine whispered, nodding at the younger men. "They're the seconds."

Like in a duel. I looked to see if they carried pistols or swords, but their hands were empty.

I noticed Christine only when she went to the front of the crowd. She reached above her head and clapped her hands one time. There hadn't been much chatter before this, but now the huge space fell completely silent. The delicate woman with her silver hair commanded all attention.

She consulted a booklet before she began. "We meet to discern the next leader of the Shreveport pack, also called the Long Tooth pack. To be the leader of the pack, these Weres must compete in three tests." Christine paused to look down at the book.

Three was a good mystical number. I would have expected three.

I hoped none of these tests involved blood. Fat chance.

"The first test is the test of agility." Christine gestured behind her at a roped-off area. It looked like a giant playground in the dim light. "Then the test of endurance." She pointed at a carpeted area to her left. "Then the test of might in battle." She waved a hand at a structure behind her.

So much for no blood.

"Then the winner must mate with another Were, to ensure the survival of the pack."

I sure hoped part four would be symbolic. After all, Patrick Furnan had a wife, who was standing apart with a group that was definitely pro-Patrick.

That seemed like four tests to me, not three, unless the mating part was kind of like the winner's trophy.

Claude and Claudine took my hands and gave them a simultaneous squeeze. "This is gonna be bad," I whispered, and they nodded in unison.

I saw two uniformed paramedics standing toward the back of the crowd. They were both shifters of some kind, their brain patterns told me. With them was a person—well, maybe a creature—I hadn't seen for months: Dr. Ludwig. She caught my eye and bowed to me. Since she was around three feet tall, she didn't have far to lean. I bowed back. Dr. Ludwig had a large nose, olive skin, and thick wavy brown hair. I was glad she was there. I had no idea what Dr. Ludwig actually was, other than nonhuman, but she was a good doctor. My back would have been permanently scarred—assuming I'd lived—if Dr. Ludwig hadn't treated me after a maenad attack. I'd escaped with a couple of bad days and a fine white tracery across my shoulder blades, thanks to the tiny doctor.

The contestants entered the "ring"—actually a large square marked off by those velvet ropes and metal-topped posts that they use in hotels. I'd thought the enclosed area looked like a playground, but now, as the lights came up, I realized I was seeing something more like a jumping arena for horses crossed with a gymnastics arena—or a course for a dog agility competition for giant dogs.

Christine said, "You will change." Christine moved away to melt back into the crowd. Both candidates dropped to the ground, and the air around them began to shimmer and distort. Changing quickly at one's desire was a great source of pride among shifters. The two Weres achieved their change at nearly the same instant. Jackson Herveaux became a huge black wolf, like his son. Patrick Furnan was pale gray, broad in the chest, a bit shorter in length.

As the small crowd drew closer, hugging the velvet ropes, one of the biggest men I'd ever seen emerged from the darkest shadows to step into the arena. I recognized him as the man whom I'd last seen at Colonel Flood's funeral. At least six and half feet tall, today he was bare-chested and barefoot. He was impressively muscular, and his chest was as hairless as his head. He looked like a genie; he would have appeared quite natural with a sash and pantaloons. Instead, he was wearing aged blue jeans. His eyes were pits of pitch. Of course, he was a shape-shifter of some kind, but I could not imagine what he turned into.

"Whoa," breathed Claude.

"Hooboy," whispered Claudia.

"Wowzers," I muttered.

Standing between the contenders, the tall man led them to the start of the course.

"Once the test begins, no pack member can interrupt," he said, looking from one Were to the other.

"First contestant is Patrick, wolf of this pack," the tall man said. His bass voice was as dramatic as the distant rumble of drums.

I understood, then; he was the referee. "Patrick goes first, by coin flip," the tall man said.

Before I could think it was pretty funny that all this ceremony included a coin toss, the pale wolf was off, moving so fast that I could hardly keep track of him. He flew up a ramp, leaped three barrels, hit the ground on the far side at a dash, went up another ramp and through a ring hanging from the ceiling (which rocked violently after he was through it), and dropped down on the ground, crawling on all fours through a clear tunnel that was very narrow and twisted at intervals. It was like the one sold in pet stores for ferrets or gerbils, just bigger. Once out of the tunnel, the wolf, mouth open in a pant, came to a level area covered with Astroturf. Here, he paused and considered before putting out a foot. Every step was like that, as the wolf worked its way across the twenty yards or so of this particular area. Suddenly a section of Astroturf leaped up as a trap snapped shut, narrowly missing the wolf's hind leg. The wolf yipped in consternation, frozen in place. It must have been agonizing, trying to restrain himself from dashing for the safety of the platform that was now only a few feet away.

I was shivering, though this contest had little to do with me. The tension was clearly showing among the Weres. They didn't seem to be moving quite as humans did anymore. Even the overly made-up Mrs. Furnan had wide round eyes now, eyes that didn't look like a woman's even under all that makeup.

As the gray wolf took his final test, a leap from a dead stop that had to cover the length of perhaps two cars, a howl of triumph erupted from Patrick's mate's throat. The gray wolf stood safely on the platform. The referee checked a stopwatch in his hand.

"Second candidate," said the big man, "Jackson Herveaux, wolf of this pack." A brain close to me supplied me with the big man's name.

"Quinn," I whispered to Claudine. Her eyes opened wide. The name was significant to her in a way I could not guess.

Jackson Herveaux began the same test of skills that Patrick had already completed. He was more graceful going through the suspended hoop; it scarcely moved as he sailed through. He took a little longer, I thought, getting through the tunnel. He seemed to realize it, too, because he stepped into the trap field more hastily than I thought wise. He stopped dead, maybe coming to the same conclusion. He bent to use his nose more carefully. The information he got from this made him quiver all over. With exquisite care, the werewolf raised one black forepaw and moved it a fraction of an inch. We were holding our breath as he worked forward in a completely different style from his predecessor. Patrick Furnan had moved in big steps, with longish pauses in between for careful sniffing, a sort of hurry-up-and-wait style. Jackson Herveaux moved very steadily in small increments, his nose always busy, his movements cannily plotted.

To my relief, Alcide's father made it across unharmed, without springing any of the traps.

The black wolf gathered himself for the final long leap and launched himself into the air with all his power. His landing was less than graceful, as his hind paws had to scrabble to cling to the edge of the landing site. But he made it, and a few congratulatory yips echoed through the empty space.

"Both candidates pass the agility test," Quinn said. His eyes roamed the crowd. When they passed over our odd trio—two tall black-haired twin fairies and a much shorter blond human—his gaze may have lingered a moment, but it was hard to say.

Christine was trying to get my attention. When she saw I was looking at her, she gave a tiny, sharp nod of her head to a spot by the test-of-endurance pen. Puzzled but obedient, I eased through the crowd. I didn't know the twins had followed me until they resumed standing to either side of me. There was something about this that Christine wanted me to see, to . . . Of course. She wanted me to use my talent here. She suspected . . . skulduggery. As Alcide and his blond counterpart took their places in the pen, I noticed they were both gloved. Their attention was totally absorbed by this contest; leaving nothing for me to sieve from that focus. That left the two wolves. I'd never tried to look inside the mind of a shifted person.

With considerable anxiety, I concentrated on opening myself to their thoughts. As you might expect, the blend of human and dog thought patterns was quite challenging. At first scan I could only pick up the same kind of focus, but then I detected a difference.

As Alcide lifted an eighteen-inch-long silver rod, my stomach felt cold and shivery. Watching the blond Were next to him repeat the gesture, I felt my lips draw back in distaste. The gloves were not totally necessary, because in human form, a Were's skin would not be damaged by the silver. In wolf form, silver was terribly painful.

Furnan's blond second ran his covered hands over the silver, as if testing the bar for hidden faults.

I had no idea why silver weakened vampires and burned them, and why it could be fatal to Weres, while it had no effect on fairies—who, however, could not bear prolonged exposure to iron. But I knew these things were true, and I knew the upcoming test would be awful to watch.

However, I was there to witness it. Something was going to happen that needed my attention. I turned my mind back to the little difference I'd read in Patrick's thoughts. In his Were form, these were so primitive they hardly qualified as "thoughts."

Quinn stood between the two seconds, his smooth scalp picking up a gleam of light. He had a timing watch in his hands.

"The candidates will take the silver now," he said, and with his gloved hands Alcide put the bar in his father's mouth. The black wolf clamped down and sat, just as the light gray wolf did with his silver bar. The two seconds drew back. A high whine of pain came from Jackson Herveaux, while Patrick Furnan showed no signs of stress other than heavy panting. As the delicate skin of his gums and lips began to smoke and smell a little, Jackson's whining became louder. Patrick's skin showed the same painful symptoms, but Patrick was silent.

"They're so brave," whispered Claude, watching with fascinated horror at the torment the two wolves were enduring. It was becoming apparent that the older wolf would not win this contest. The visible signs of pain were increasing every second, and though Alcide stood there focusing solely on his father to add his support, at any moment it would be over. Except . . .

"He's cheating," I said clearly, pointing at the gray wolf.

"No member of the pack may speak." Quinn's deep voice was not angry, merely matter-of-fact.

"I'm not a pack member."

"You challenge the contest?" Quinn was looking at me now. All the pack members who'd been standing close around me dropped back until I stood alone with the two fairies, who were looking down at me with some surprise and dismay.

"You bet your ass I do. Smell the gloves Patrick's second was wearing."

The blond second looked completely blindsided. And guilty.

"Drop the bars," Quinn commanded, and the two wolves complied, Jackson Herveaux with a whimper. Alcide dropped to his knees by his father, putting his arms around the older wolf.

Quinn, moving as smoothly as if his joints were oiled, knelt to retrieve the gloves that Patrick's second had tossed to the floor. Libby Furnan's hand darted over the velvet rope to snatch them up, but a deep snarl from Quinn told her to stop. It made my own spine tingle, and I was much farther away than Libby.

Quinn picked up the gloves and smelled them.

He looked down at Patrick Furnan with a contempt so heavy that I was surprised the wolf didn't crumple under its weight.

He turned to face the rest of the crowd. "The woman is right." Quinn's deep voice gave the words the gravity of stone. "There's a drug on the gloves. It made Furnan's skin numb when the silver was placed in his mouth, so he could last longer. I declare him loser of this part of the contest.

The pack will have to decide whether he should forfeit any right to continue, and whether his second should still be a pack member." The fair-haired Were was cringing as if he expected someone to hit him. I didn't know why his punishment should be worse than Patrick's; maybe the lower your rank, the worse your punishment? Not exactly fair; but then, I wasn't a Were.

"The pack will vote," Christine called. She met my eyes and I knew this was why she wanted me here. "If the rest of you would step into the outer room?"

Quinn, Claude, Claudine, and three shape-shifters moved with me to the doors leading into the other room. There was more natural light there, which was a pleasure. Less of a pleasure was the curiosity that pooled around me. My shields were still down, and I felt the suspicion and conjecture flowing from the brains of my companions, except, of course, from the two fairies. To Claude and Claudine, my peculiarity was a rare gift, and I was a lucky woman.

"Come here," Quinn rumbled, and I thought about telling him to take his commands and shove them where the sun don't shine. But that would be childish, and I had nothing to fear. (At least that's what I told myself about seven times in rapid succession.) I made my spine stiffen, and I strode up to him and looked up into his face.

"You don't have to stick your jaw out like that," he said calmly. "I'm not going to hit you."

"I never thought you were," I said with a snap in my voice that I was proud of. I found that his round eyes were the very dark, rich, purple-brown of pansies. Wow, they were pretty! I smiled out of sheer pleasure . . . and a dollop of relief.

Unexpectedly, he smiled back. He had full lips, very even white teeth, and a sturdy column of a neck.

"How often do you have to shave?" I asked, fascinated with his smoothness.

He laughed from the belly.

"Are you scared of anything?" he asked.

"So many things," I said regretfully.

He considered that for a moment. "Do you have an extrasensitive sense of smell?"

"Nope."

"Do you know the blond one?"

"Never saw him before."

"Then how did you know?"

"Sookie is a telepath," Claude said. When he got the full weight of the big man's stare, he looked like he was sorry he'd interrupted. "My sister is her, ah, guardian," Claude concluded in a rush.

"Then you're doing a terrible job," Quinn told Claudine.

"Don't you get onto Claudine," I said indignantly. "Claudine's saved my life a bunch."

Quinn looked exasperated. "Fairies," he muttered. "The Weres aren't going to be happy about your piece of information," he told me. "At least half of them are going to wish you were dead. If your safety is Claudine's top priority, she should have held your mouth shut."

Claudine looked crushed.

"Hey," I said, "cut it out. I know you've got friends in there you're worried about, but don't take that out on Claudine. Or me," I added hastily, as his eyes fixed on mine.

"I have no friends in there. And I shave every morning," he said.

"Okay, then." I nodded, nonplussed.

"Or if I'm going out in the evening."

"Gotcha."

"To do something special."

What would Quinn consider special?

The doors opened, interrupting one of the strangest conversations I'd ever had.

"You can come back in," said a young Were in three-inch-high fuck-me shoes. She was wearing a burgundy sheath, and when we followed her back into the big room, she gave her walk some extra sway. I wondered whom she was trying to entrance, Quinn or Claude. Or maybe Claudine?

"This is our judgment," said Christine to Quinn. "We'll resume the contest where it ended. According to the vote, since Patrick cheated on the second test, he is declared the loser of that test. Of the agility test, too. However, he's allowed to stay in the running. But, to win, he has to win the last test decisively." I wasn't sure what "decisively" meant in this context. From Christine's face, I was certain it didn't bode well. For the first time, I realized that justice might not prevail.

Alcide looked very grim, when I found his face in the crowd. This judgment seemed clearly biased in favor of his father's opponent. I hadn't realized that there were more Weres in the Furnan camp than the Herveaux camp, and I wondered when that shift had occurred. The balance had seemed more even at the funeral.

Since I had already interfered, I felt free to interfere some more. I began wandering among the pack members, listening to their brains. Though the twisted and turned brains of all Weres and shifters are difficult to decipher, I began to pick up a clue here and there. The Furnans, I learned, had followed their plan of leaking stories about Jackson Herveaux's gambling habits, talking up how unreliable that made Jackson as a leader.

I knew from Alcide that the stories about his father's gambling were true. Though I didn't admire the Furnans for playing this card, I didn't consider it stacking the deck, either.

The two competitors were still in wolf form. If I had understood correctly, they had been scheduled to fight anyway. I was standing by Amanda. "What's changed about the last test?" I asked. The redhead whispered that now the fight was no longer a regular match, with the contestant left standing after five minutes declared the winner. Now, to win the fight "decisively," the loser had to be dead or disabled.

This was more than I'd bargained for, but I knew without asking that I couldn't leave.

The group gathered around a wire dome that reminded me irresistibly of *Mad Max Beyond Thunderdome*. You remember—"Two men enter, one man leaves." I guess this was the wolf equivalent. Quinn opened the door, and the two large wolves slunk in, casting their gazes from side to side as they counted their supporters. Or at least, that's what I guessed they were doing.

Quinn turned and beckoned to me.

Ah-oh. I frowned. The dark, purple-brown eyes were intent. The man meant business. I approached him reluctantly.

"Go read their minds again," he told me. He laid a huge hand on my shoulder. He turned me to face him, which brought me face-to-face—well, so to speak—with his dark brown nipples. Disconcerted, I looked up. "Listen, blondie, all you have to do is go in there and do your thing," he said reassuringly.

He couldn't have had this idea while the wolves were outside the cage? What if he shut the door on me? I looked over my shoulder at Claudine, who was frantically shaking her head.

"Why do I need to? What purpose will it serve?" I asked, not being a total idiot.

"Is he gonna cheat again?" Quinn asked so softly that I knew no one else could hear him. "Does Furnan have some means of cheating that I can't see?"

"Do you guarantee my safety?"

He met my eyes. "Yes," he said without hesitation. He opened the door to the cage. Though he had to stoop, he came in behind me.

The two wolves approached me cautiously. Their smell was strong; like dog, but muskier and wilder. Nervously, I laid my hand on Patrick Furnan's head. I looked in his head as hard as I could, and I could discern nothing but rage at me for costing him his win in the endurance contest. There was a glowing coal of purpose about the coming battle, which he intended to win by sheer ruthlessness.

I sighed, shook my head, moved my hand away. To be fair, I put my hand on Jackson's shoulders, which were so high I was startled all over. The wolf was literally vibrating, a faint shiver that made his fur quiver under my touch. His whole resolve was bent toward rending his rival limb from limb. But Jackson was afraid of the younger wolf.

"All clear," I said, and Quinn turned away to open the door. He crouched to step through, and I was about to follow him when the burgundy-sheathed girl shrieked. Moving faster than I thought such a large man could move, Quinn spun on his foot, grabbed my arm with one hand, and yanked with all his might. With his other hand he slammed shut the door, and I heard something crash against it.

The noises behind me told me the battle had already started, but I was pinned against a huge expanse of smooth tan skin.

With my ear to Quinn's chest, I could hear the rumble inside as well as outside as he asked, "Did he get you?"

I had my own shaking and quivering going on. My leg was wet, and I saw that my tights were ripped, and blood was running from an abrasion on the side of my right calf. Had my leg scraped the door when Quinn had shut it so quickly, or had I been bitten? Oh my God, if I'd been bitten . . .

Everyone else was pressed against the wire cage, watching the snarling, whirling wolves. Their spittle and blood flew in fine sprays, dotting the spectators. I glanced back to see Jackson's grip on Patrick's hind leg broken when Patrick bent himself backward to bite Jackson's muzzle. I caught a glimpse of Alcide's face, intent and anguished.

I didn't want to watch this. I would rather look at this stranger's hide than watch the two men killing each other.

"I'm bleeding," I told Quinn. "It's not bad."

A high yip from the cage suggested that one of the wolves had scored a hit. I cringed.

The big man half carried me over to the wall. That was a good distance from the fight. He helped me turn and sink down into a sitting position.

Quinn lowered himself to the floor, too. He was so graceful for someone so large that I was absorbed in just watching him move. He knelt by me to pull off my shoes, and then my tights, which were ripped to shreds and dabbled with blood. I was silent and shaking as he sank down to lie on his stomach. He gripped my knee and my ankle in his huge hands as if my leg were a large drumstick. Without saying a word, Quinn began to lick the blood from my calf. I was afraid this was preparatory to taking a bite, but Dr. Ludwig trotted over, looked down, and nodded. "You'll be fine," she said dismissively. After patting me on the head as if I were an injured dog, the tiny doctor trotted back to her attendants.

Meanwhile, though I would not have thought it was possible for me to be anything but on the knife-edge of suspense, the leg-licking thing was providing an entirely unexpected diversion. I shifted restlessly, stifling a gasp. Maybe I should remove my leg from Quinn's possession? Watching the gleaming bald head bob up and down as he licked was making me think of something worlds away from the life-and-death battle taking place across the room. Quinn was working more and more slowly, his tongue warm and a little rough as he cleaned my leg. Though his brain was the most opaque shifter brain I'd ever encountered, I got the idea he was having the same reaction that I was.

When he finished, he laid his head on my thigh. He was breathing heavily, and I was trying not to. His hands released their grip but stroked my leg deliberately. He looked up at me. His eyes had changed. They were golden, solid gold. The color filled his eyes. Whoa.

I guess he could tell from my face that I was, to put it mildly, conflicted about our little interlude.

"Not our time and place, babe," he said. "God, that was . . . great." He stretched, and it wasn't an outward extension of arms and chest, the way humans stretch. He rippled from the base of his spine to his shoulders. It was one of the oddest things I'd ever seen, and I'd seen a lot of odd things. "Do you know who I am?" he asked.

I nodded. "Quinn?" I said, feeling my cheeks color.

"I've heard your name is Sookie," he said, rising to his knees.

"Sookie Stackhouse," I said.

He put his hand under my chin so I'd look up at him. I stared into his eyes as hard as I could. He didn't blink.

"I wonder what you're seeing," he said finally, and removed his hand.

I glanced down at my leg. The mark on it, now clear of blood, was almost certainly a scrape from the metal of the door. "Not a bite," I said, my voice faltering on the last word. The tension left me in a rush.

"Nope. No she-wolf in your future," he agreed, and flowed to his feet. He held out his hand. I took it, and he had me on my feet in a second. A piercing yelp from the cage yanked me back into the here and now.

"Tell me something. Why the hell can't they just vote?" I asked him.

Quinn's round eyes, back to their purple-brown color and properly surrounded with white, crinkled at the corners with amusement.

"Not the way of the shifter, babe. You're going to see me later," Quinn promised. Without another word he strode back to the cage, and my little field trip was over. I had to turn my attention back to the truly important thing happening in this building.

Claudine and Claude were looking anxiously over their shoulders when I found them. They made a little space for me to ease in between them, and wrapped their arms around me when I was in place. They seemed very upset, and Claudine had two tears trailing down her cheeks. When I saw the situation in the cage, I understood why.

The lighter wolf was winning. The black wolf's coat was matted with blood. He was still on his feet, still snarling, but one of his hind legs was giving way under his weight from time to time. He managed to pull himself back up twice, but the third time the leg collapsed, the younger wolf was on him, the two spinning over and over in a terrifying blur of teeth, torn flesh, and fur.

Forgetting the silence rules, all the Weres were screaming their support of one contestant or the other, or just howling. The violence and the noise blended together to make a chaotic collage. I finally spotted Alcide pounding his hands against the metal in futile agitation. I had never felt so sorry for anyone in my life. I wondered if he'd try to break into the combat cage. But another look told me that even if Alcide's respect for pack rules broke down and he attempted to go to his father's aid, Quinn was blocking the door. That was why the pack had brought in an outsider, of course.

Abruptly, the fight was over. The lighter wolf had the

darker one by the throat. He was gripping, but not biting. Maybe Jackson would have gone on struggling if he hadn't been so severely wounded, but his strength was exhausted. He lay whining, quite unable to defend himself, disabled. The room fell completely silent.

"Patrick Furnan is declared the winner," said Quinn, his voice neutral.

And then Patrick Furnan bit down on Jackson Herveaux's throat and killed him.

16

QUINN TOOK OVER THE CLEANUP WITH THE SURE AUTHORITY of one who's supervised such things before. Though I was dull and stupid with shock, I noticed he gave clear, concise directions as to the dispersal of the testing materials. Pack members dismantled the cage into sections and took apart the agility arena with efficient dispatch. A cleanup crew took care of mopping up the blood and other fluids.

Soon the building was empty of all but the people. Patrick Furnan had reverted to his human form, and Dr. Ludwig was attending his many wounds. I was glad he had every one of them. I was only sorry they weren't worse. But the pack had accepted Furnan's choice. If they would not protest such unnecessary brutality, I couldn't.

Alcide was being comforted by Maria-Star Cooper, a young Were I knew slightly.

Maria-Star held him and stroked his back, providing

support by her sheer closeness. He didn't have to tell me that on this occasion, he preferred another Were's companionship to mine. I'd gone to hug him, but when I'd neared him and met his eyes, I'd known. That hurt, and it hurt bad; but today wasn't about me and my feelings.

Claudine was crying in her brother's arms. "She's so tenderhearted," I whispered to Claude, feeling a bit abashed that I wasn't crying myself. My concern was for Alcide; I'd hardly known Jackson Herveaux.

"She went through the second elf war in Iowa fighting with the best of them," Claude said, shaking his head. "I've seen a decapitated goblin stick its tongue out at her in its death throes, and she laughed. But as she gets closer to the light, she becomes more sensitive."

That effectively shut me up. I was not about to ask for any explanation of yet another arcane supernatural rule. I'd had a bellyful this day.

Now that all the mess was cleared away (that mess included Jackson's body, which Dr. Ludwig had taken somewhere to be altered, to make the story of how he'd met his death more plausible), all the pack members present gathered in front of Patrick Furnan, who hadn't resumed clothes. According to his body, victory had made him feel manly. Ick.

He was standing on a blanket; it was a red plaid stadium blanket, like you'd take to a football game. I felt my lips twitch, but I became completely sober when the new packmaster's wife led a young woman to him, a brown-haired girl who seemed to be in her late teens. The girl was as bare as the packmaster, though she looked considerably better in that state.

What the hell?

Suddenly I remembered the last part of the ceremony, and I realized Patrick Furman was going to fuck this girl in front of us. No. No way was I going to watch this. I tried to turn to walk out. But Claude hissed, "You can't leave." He covered my mouth and picked me up bodily to move me to the back of the crowd. Claudine moved with us and stood in front of me, but with her back to me, so I wouldn't have to see. I made a furious sound into Claude's hand.

"Shut up," the fairy said grimly, his voice as concentrated with sincerity as he could manage. "You'll land us all in trouble. If it makes you feel any better, this is traditional. The girl volunteered. After this, Patrick'll be a faithful husband once more. But he's already bred his whelp by his wife, and he has to make the ceremonial gesture of breeding another one. May take, may not, but it has to be done."

I kept my eyes shut and was grateful when Claudine turned to me and placed her tear-wet hands over my ears. A shout went up from the crowd when the thing was completed. The two fairies relaxed and gave me some room. I didn't see what happened to the girl. Furnan remained naked, but as long as he was in a calm state, I could handle that.

To seal his status, the new packmaster began to receive the pledges of his wolves. They went in turn, oldest to youngest, I figured, after a moment's observation. Each Were licked the back of Patrick Furnan's hand and exposed his or her neck for a ritual moment. When it was Alcide's turn, I suddenly realized there was potential for even more disaster.

I found I was holding my breath.

From the profound silence, I knew I wasn't the only one.

After a long hesitation, Furnan bent over and placed his teeth on Alcide's neck; I opened my mouth to protest, but Claudine clapped her hand over it. Furnan's teeth came away from Alcide's flesh, leaving it unscathed.

Packmaster Furnan had sent a clear signal.

By the time the last Were had performed the ritual, I was

exhausted from all the emotion. Surely this was an end to it? Yes, the pack was dispersing, some members giving the Furnans congratulatory hugs, and some striding out silently.

I dodged them myself and made a beeline for the door. The next time someone told me I had to watch a supernatural rite, I was going to tell him I had to wash my hair.

Once out in the open air, I walked slowly, my feet dragging. I had to think about things I'd put to one side, like what I'd seen in Alcide's head after the whole debacle was over. Alcide thought I'd failed him. He'd told me I had to come, and I had; I should have known he had some purpose in insisting I be present.

Now I knew that he'd suspected Furnan had some underhanded trick in mind. Alcide had primed Christine, his father's ally, ahead of time. She made sure I used my telepathy on Patrick Furnan. And, sure enough, I had found that Jackson's opponent was cheating. That disclosure should have ensured Jackson's win.

Instead, the will of the pack had gone against Jackson, and the contest had continued with the stakes even higher. I'd nothing to do with that decision. But right now Alcide, in his grief and rage, was blaming me.

I was trying to be angry, but I was too sad.

Claude and Claudine said good-bye, and they hopped into Claudine's Cadillac and peeled out of the parking lot as if they couldn't wait to get back to Monroe. I was of the same mind, but I was a lot less resilient than the fairies. I had to sit behind the wheel of the borrowed Malibu for five or ten minutes, steadying myself for the drive home.

I found myself thinking of Quinn. It was a welcome relief from thinking of torn flesh and blood and death. When I'd looked into his head, I'd seen a man who knew his way. And I still didn't have a clue as to what he was.

The drive home was grim.

I might as well have phoned in to Merlotte's that evening. Oh, sure, I went through all the motions of taking orders and carrying them to the right tables, refilling pitchers of beer, popping my tips in the tip jar, wiping up spills and making sure the temporary cook (a vampire named Anthony Bolivar; he'd subbed for us before) remembered the busboy was off limits. But I didn't have any sparkle, any joy, in my work.

I did notice that Sam seemed be getting around better. He was obviously restive, sitting in his corner watching Charles work. Possibly Sam was also a little piqued, since Charles just seemed to get more and more popular with the clientele. The vamp was charming, that was for sure. He was wearing a red sequined eye patch tonight and his usual poet shirt under a black sequined vest—flashy in the extreme, but entertaining, too.

"You seem depressed, beautiful lady," he said when I came to pick up a Tom Collins and a rum and Coke.

"Just been a long day," I said, making an effort to smile. I had so many other things to digest emotionally that I didn't even mind when Bill brought Selah Pumphrey in again. Even when they sat in my section, I didn't care. But when Bill took my hand as I was turning away to get their order, I snatched it away as if he'd tried to set me on fire.

"I only want to know what's wrong," he said, and for a second I remembered how good it had felt that night at the hospital when he'd lain down with me. My mouth actually began to open, but then I caught a glimpse of Selah's indignant face, and I shut my emotional water off at the meter.

"I'll be right back with that blood," I said cheerfully, smiling wide enough to show every tooth in my head.

To heck with him, I thought righteously. *Him and the horse he rode in on.*

After that it was strictly business. I smiled and worked,

and worked and smiled. I stayed away from Sam, because I didn't want to have a long conversation with yet another shifter that evening. I was afraid—since I didn't have any reason to be mad at Sam—that if he asked me what was wrong, I'd tell him; and I just didn't want to talk about it. You ever just feel like stomping around and being miserable for a while? That was the kind of mood I was in.

But I had to go over to Sam, after all, when Catfish asked if he could pay with a check for this evening's festivities. That was Sam's rule: he had to approve checks. And I had to stand close to Sam, because the bar was very noisy.

I thought nothing of it, aside from not wanting to get into my own mood with him, but when I bent over him to explain Catfish's cash-flow problem, Sam's eyes widened. "My God, Sookie," he said, "Who have you been around?"

I backed off, speechless. He was both shocked and appalled by a smell I hadn't even known I carried. I was tired of supes pulling this on me.

"Where'd you meet up with a tiger?" he asked.

"A tiger," I repeated numbly.

So now I knew what my new acquaintance Quinn turned into when the moon was full.

"Tell me," Sam demanded.

"No," I snapped, "I won't. What about Catfish?"

"He can write a check this once. If there's a problem, he'll never write another one here again."

I didn't relay this last sentence. I took Catfish's check and his alcohol-fueled gratitude, and deposited both where they belonged.

To make my bad mood worse, I snagged my silver chain on a corner of the bar when I bent over to pick up a napkin some slob had tossed to the floor. The chain broke, and I caught it up and dropped it in my pocket. Dammit. This had been a rotten day, followed by a rotten night.

I made sure to wave at Selah as she and Bill left. He'd left me a good tip, and I stuffed it in my other pocket with so much force I almost ripped the fabric. A couple of times during the evening, I had heard the bar phone ring, and when I was taking some dirty glasses to the kitchen hatch, Charles said, "Someone keeps calling and hanging up. Very irritating."

"They'll get tired and quit," I said soothingly.

About an hour later, as I put a Coke in front of Sam, the busboy came to tell me there was someone at the employees' entrance, asking for me.

"What were you doing outside?" Sam asked sharply.

The boy looked embarrassed. "I smoke, Mr. Merlotte," he said. "I was outside taking me a break, 'cause the vamp said he'd drain me if I lit up inside, when this man walked up outta nowhere."

"What's he look like?" I asked.

"Oh, he's old, got black hair," the boy said, shrugging. Not long on the gift of description.

"Okay," I said. I was glad to take a break. I suspected who the visitor might be, and if he'd come into the bar, he'd have caused a riot. Sam found an excuse to follow me out by saying that he needed a pit stop, and he picked up his cane and used it to hobble down the hall after me. He had his own tiny bathroom off his office, and he limped into it as I continued past the men's and women's to the back door. I opened it cautiously and peered outside. But then I began smiling. The man waiting for me had one of the most famous faces in the world—except, apparently, to adolescent busboys.

"Bubba," I said, pleased to see the vampire. You couldn't call him by his former name, or he got real confused and agitated. Bubba was formerly known as . . . Well, let me just put it this way. You wondered about all those sightings after his death? This was the explanation.

The conversion hadn't been a complete success because his system had been so fuddled with drugs; but aside from his predilection for cat blood, Bubba managed pretty well. The vampire community took good care of him. Eric kept Bubba on staff as an errand boy. Bubba's glossy black hair was always combed and styled, his long sideburns sharply trimmed. Tonight he was wearing a black leather jacket, new blue jeans, and a black-and-silver plaid shirt.

"Looking good, Bubba," I said admiringly.

"You too, Miss Sookie." He beamed at me.

"Did you want to tell me something?"

"Yessum. Mr. Eric sent me over here to tell you that he's not what he seems."

I blinked.

"Who, Bubba?" I asked, trying to keep my voice gentle.

"He's a hit man."

I stared at Bubba's face not because I thought staring would get me anywhere, but because I was trying to figure out the message. This was a mistake; Bubba's eyes began darting from side to side, and his face lost its smile. I should have turned to stare at the wall—it would've given me as much information, and Bubba wouldn't have become as anxious.

"Thanks, Bubba," I said, patting him on his beefy shoulder. "You did good."

"Can I go now? Back to Shreveport?"

"Sure," I said. I would just call Eric. Why hadn't he used the phone for a message as urgent and important as this one seemed to be?

"I found me a back way into the animal shelter," Bubba confided proudly.

I gulped. "Oh, well, great," I said, trying not to feel queasy.

"See ya later, alligator," he called from the edge of the parking lot. Just when you thought Bubba was the worst vampire in the world, he did something amazing like moving at a speed you simply could not track.

"After a while, crocodile," I said dutifully.

"Was that who I think it was?" The voice was right behind me.

I jumped. I spun around to find that Charles had deserted his post at the bar.

"You scared me," I said, as though he hadn't been able to tell.

"Sorry."

"Yes, that was him."

"Thought so. I've never heard him sing in person. It must be amazing." Charles stared out at the parking lot as though he were thinking hard about something else. I had the definite impression he wasn't listening to his own words.

I opened my mouth to ask a question, but before my words reached my lips I really thought about what the English pirate had just said, and the words froze in my throat. After a long hesitation, I knew I had to speak, or he would know something was wrong.

"Well, I guess I'd better get back to work," I said, smiling the bright smile that pops onto my face when I'm nervous. And, boy, was I nervous now. The one blinding revelation I'd had made everything begin to click into place in my head. Every little hair on my arms and neck stood straight up. My fight-or-flight reflex was fixed firmly on "flight." Charles was between the outside door and me. I began to back down the hall toward the bar.

The door from the bar into the hall was usually left open, because people had to pass into the hall all the time to use the bathrooms. But now it was closed. It had been open when I'd come down the hall to talk to Bubba.

This was bad.

"Sookie," Charles said, behind me. "I truly regret this."

"It was you who shot Sam, wasn't it?" I reached behind me, fumbled for the handle that would open that door. He wouldn't kill me in front of all those people, would he? Then I remembered the night Eric and Bill had polished off a roomful of men in my house. I remembered it had taken them only three or four minutes. I remembered what the men had looked like afterward.

"Yes. It was a stroke of luck when you caught the cook, and she confessed. But she didn't confess to shooting Sam, did she?"

"No, she didn't," I said numbly. "All the others, but not Sam, and the bullet didn't match."

My fingers found the knob. If I turned it, I might live. But I might not. How much did Charles value his own life?

"You wanted the job here," I said.

"I thought there was a good chance I'd come in handy when Sam was out of the picture."

"How'd you know I'd go to Eric for help?"

"I didn't. But I knew someone would tell him the bar was in trouble. Since that would mean helping you, he would do it. I was the logical one to send."

"Why are you doing all this?"

"Eric owes a debt."

He was moving closer, though not very quickly. Maybe he was reluctant to do the deed. Maybe he was hoping for a more advantageous moment, when he could carry me off in silence.

"It looks like Eric's found out I'm not from the Jackson nest, as I'd said."

"Yeah. You picked the wrong one."

"Why? It seemed ideal to me. Many men there; you wouldn't have seen them all. No one can remember all the men who've passed through that mansion."

"But they've heard Bubba sing," I said softly. "He sang for them one night. You'd never have forgotten that. I don't know how Eric found out, but I knew as soon as you said you'd never—"

He sprang.

I was on my back on the floor in a split second, but my hand was already in my pocket, and he opened his mouth to bite. He was supporting himself on his arms, courteously trying not to actually lie on top of me. His fangs were fully out, and they glistened in the light.

"I have to do this," he said. "I'm sworn. I'm sorry."

"I'm not," I said, and thrust the silver chain into his mouth, using the heel of my hand to snap his jaw shut.

He screamed and hit at me, and I felt a rib go, and smoke was coming out of his mouth. I scrambled away and did a little yelling of my own. The door flew open, and a flood of bar patrons thundered into the little hallway. Sam shot out of the door of his office like he'd been fired from a cannon, moving very well for a man with a broken leg, and to my amazement he had a stake in his hand. By that time, the screaming vampire was weighted down by so many beefy men in jeans you couldn't even see him. Charles was trying to bite whoever he could, but his burned mouth was so painful his efforts were weak.

Catfish Hunter seemed to be on the bottom of the pile, in direct contact. "You pass me that stake here, boy!" he called back to Sam. Sam passed it to Hoyt Fortenberry, who passed it to Dago Guglielmi, who transferred it to Catfish's hairy hand.

"We gonna wait for the vampire police, or we gonna take care of this ourselves?" Catfish asked. "Sookie?"

After a horrified second of temptation, I opened my mouth to say, "Call the police." The Shreveport police had a squad of vampire policemen, as well as the necessary special transportation vehicle and special jail cells.

"End it," said Charles, somewhere below the heaving pile of men. "I failed in my mission, and I can't abide jails."

"Okeydokey," Catfish said, and staked him.

After it was over and the body had disintegrated, the men went back into the bar and settled down at the tables where they'd been before they heard the fight going on in the hall. It was beyond strange. There wasn't much laughing, and there wasn't much smiling, and no one who'd stayed in the bar asked anyone who'd left what had happened.

Of course, it was tempting to think this was an echo of the terrible old days, when black men had been lynched if there was even a rumor they'd winked at a white woman.

But, you know, the simile just didn't hold. Charles was a different race, true. But he'd been guilty as hell of trying to kill me. I would have been a dead woman in thirty more seconds, despite my diversionary tactic, if the men of Bon Temps hadn't intervened.

We were lucky in a lot of ways. There was not one law enforcement person in the bar that night. Not five minutes after everyone resumed his table, Dennis Pettibone, the arson investigator, came in to have a visit with Arlene. (The busboy was still mopping the hall, in fact.) Sam had bound my ribs with some Ace bandages in his office, and I walked out, slowly and carefully, to ask Dennis what he wanted to drink.

We were lucky that there weren't any outsiders. No college guys from Ruston, no truckers from Shreveport, no relatives who'd dropped in for a beer with a cousin or an uncle.

We were lucky there weren't many women. I don't know why, but I imagined a woman would be more likely to get squeamish about Charles's execution. In fact, I felt pretty squeamish about it, when I wasn't counting my lucky stars I was still alive.

And Eric was lucky when he dashed into the bar about thirty minutes later, because Sam didn't have any more stakes handy. As jittery as everyone was, some foolhardy soul would have volunteered to take out Eric: but he wouldn't have come out of it relatively unscathed, as those who'd tackled Charles had.

And Eric was also lucky that the first words out of his mouth were "Sookie, are you all right?" In his anxiety, he grabbed me, one hand on either side of my waist, and I cried out.

"You're hurt," he said, and then realized five or six men had jumped to their feet.

"I'm just sore," I said, making a huge effort to look okay. "Everything's fine. This here's my friend Eric," I said a little loudly. "He's been trying to get in touch with me, and now I know why it was so urgent." I met the eyes of each man, and one by one, they dropped back into their seats.

"Let's us go sit and talk," I said very quietly.

"Where is he? I will stake the bastard myself, no matter what Hot Rain sends against me." Eric was furious.

"It's been taken care of," I hissed. "Will you *chill*?"

With Sam's permission, we went to his office, the only place in the building that offered both chairs and privacy. Sam was back behind the bar, perched on a high stool with his leg on a lower stool, managing the bartending himself.

"Bill searched his database," Eric said proudly. "The bastard told me he came from Mississippi, so I wrote him down as one of Russell's discarded pretty boys. I had even called Russell, to ask him if Twining had worked well for him. Russell said he had so many new vampires in the mansion, he had only the vaguest recollection of Twining. But Russell, as I observed at Josephine's Bar, is not the kind of manager I am."

I managed a smile. That was definitely true.

"So when I found myself wondering, I asked Bill to go to

work, and Bill traced Twining from his birth as a vampire to his pledge to Hot Rain."

"This Hot Rain was the one who made him a vampire?"

"No, no," Eric said impatiently. "Hot Rain made the pirate's sire a vampire. And when Charles's sire was killed during the French and Indian War, Charles pledged himself to Hot Rain. When Hot Rain was dissatisfied with Long Shadow's death, he sent Charles to exact payment for the debt he felt was owed."

"Why would killing me cancel the debt?"

"Because he decided after listening to gossip and much reconnoitering that you were important to me, and that your death would wound me the way Long Shadow's had him."

"Ah." I could not think of one thing to say. Not one thing.

At last I asked, "So Hot Rain and Long Shadow were doing the deed, once upon a time?"

Eric said, "Yes, but it wasn't the sexual connection, it was the . . . the affection. That was the valuable part of the bond."

"So because this Hot Rain decided the fine you paid him for Long Shadow's death just didn't give him closure, he sent Charles to do something equally painful to you."

"Yes."

"And Charles got to Shreveport, kept his ears open, found out about me, decided my death would fill the bill."

"Apparently."

"So he heard about the shootings, knew Sam is a shifter, and shot Sam so there'd be a good reason for him to come to Bon Temps."

"Yes."

"That's real, real complicated. Why didn't Charles just jump me some night?"

"Because he wanted it to look like an accident. He didn't want blame attached to a vampire at all, because not only did he not want to get caught, he didn't want Hot Rain to incur any penalty."

I closed my eyes. "He set fire to my house," I said. "Not that poor Marriot guy. I bet Charles killed him before the bar even closed that night and brought him back to my house so he'd take the blame. After all, the guy was a stranger to Bon Temps. No one would miss him. Oh my God! Charles borrowed my keys! I bet the man was in my trunk! Not dead, but hypnotized. Charles planted that card in the guy's pocket. The poor fella wasn't a member of the Fellowship of the Sun anymore than I am."

"It must have been frustrating for Charles, when he found you were surrounded by friends," Eric said a little coldly, since a couple of those "friends" had just clomped by noisily, using a trip to the john as a pretext to keep an eye on him.

"Yes, must have been." I smiled.

"You seem better than I expected," Eric said a little hesitantly. "Less traumatized, as they say now."

"Eric, I'm a lucky woman," I said. "Today I've seen more bad stuff than you can imagine. All I can think is, I escaped. By the way, Shreveport now has a new packmaster, and he's a lying, cheating bastard."

"Then I take it Jackson Herveaux lost his bid for the job."

"Lost more than that."

Eric's eyes widened. "So the contest was today. I'd heard Quinn was in town. Usually, he keeps transgressions to a minimum."

"It wasn't his choice," I said. "A vote went against Jackson; it should have helped him, but it . . . didn't."

"Why were you there? Was that blasted Alcide trying to use you for some purpose in the contest?"

"You should talk about using."

"Yes, but I'm straightforward about it," Eric said, his blue eyes wide and guileless.

I had to laugh. I hadn't expected to laugh for days, or weeks, and yet here I was, laughing. "True," I admitted.

"So, I'm to understand that Charles Twining is no more?" Eric asked quite soberly.

"That's correct."

"Well, well. The people here are unexpectedly enterprising. What damage have you suffered?"

"Broken rib."

"A broken rib is not much when a vampire is fighting for his life."

"Correct, again."

"When Bubba got back and I found he hadn't exactly delivered his message, I rushed here gallantly to rescue you. I had tried calling the bar tonight to tell you to beware, but Charles answered the phone every time."

"It was gallant of you, in the extreme," I admitted. "But, as it turns out, unnecessary."

"Well, then . . . I'll go back to my own bar and look at my own bar patrons from my own office. We're expanding our Fangtasia product line."

"Oh?"

"Yes. What would you think of a nude calendar? 'Fangtasia's Vampire Hunks' is what Pam thinks it should be called."

"Are you gonna be in it?"

"Oh, of course. Mr. January."

"Well, put me down for three. I'll give one to Arlene and one to Tara. And I'll put one up on my own wall."

"If you promise to keep it open to my picture, I'll give you one for free," Eric promised.

"You got a deal."

He stood up. "One more thing, before I go."

I stood, too, but much more slowly.

"I may need to hire you in early March."

"I'll check my calendar. What's up?"

"There's going to be a little summit. A meeting of the kings and queens of some of the southern states. The location hasn't been settled, but when it is, I wonder if you can get time off from your job here to accompany me and my people."

"I can't think that far ahead just at the moment, Eric," I said. I winced as I began to walk out of the office.

"Wait one moment," he said suddenly, and justlikethat he was in front of me.

I looked up, feeling massively tired.

He bent and kissed me on my mouth, as softly as a butterfly's fluttering.

"You said I told you you were the best I'd ever had," he said. "But did you respond in kind?"

"Don't you wish you knew?" I said, and went back to work.

Enjoyed this? Keep an eye out for more great Gollancz Romancz titles:

Grave Sight by Charlaine Harris
Warprize by Elizabth Vaughan
Rosa and the Veil of Gold by Kim Wilkins

DEAD TO THE WORLD

Also by Charlaine Harris

SOOKIE STACKHOUSE

Dead Until Dark
Living Dead in Dallas
Club Dead
Dead to the World
Dead as a Doornail
Definitely Dead
All Together Dead
From Dead to Worse
Dead and Gone

HARPER CONNELLY

Grave Sight
Grave Surprise
An Ice Cold Grave
Grave Secret

DEAD TO THE WORLD

CHARLAINE HARRIS

First published in Great Britain in 2005 by
Little, Brown

This edition published in Great Britain in 2009 by
Gollancz
An imprint of the Orion Publishing Group
Orion House, 5 Upper St Martin's Lane, London WC2H 9EA
An Hachette UK Company

A CIP catalogue record for this book
is available from the British Library

ISBN 978 0 575 08942 6

7 9 10 8

Printed and bound in the UK by
CPI Mackays, Chatham ME5 8TD

www.orionbooks.co.uk

Though they'll probably never read it, this book is dedicated to all the coaches – baseball, football, volleyball, soccer – who've worked through so many years, often for no monetary reward, to coax athletic performances out of my children and to instill in them an understanding of The Game. God bless you all, and thanks from one of the moms who crowds the stands through rain, cold, heat, and mosquitoes.

However, this mom always wonders who else might be watching the night games.

Acknowledgments

My thanks to Wiccans who answered my call for knowledge with more information than I could use – Maria Lima, Sandilee Lloyd, Holly Nelson, Jean Hontz, and M. R. 'Murv' Sellars. I owe further thanks to other experts in different fields: Kevin Ryer, who knows more about feral hogs than most people do about their own pets; Dr. D. P. Lyle, who is so gracious about answering medical questions; and, of course, Doris Ann Norris, reference librarian to the stars.

If I have made mistakes in the use of the knowledge these kind people imparted, I'll do my best to somehow blame it on them.

I found the note taped to my door when I got home from work. I'd had the lunch-to-early-evening shift at Merlotte's, but since we were at the tail end of December, the day darkened early. So Bill, my former boyfriend – that's Bill Compton, or Vampire Bill, as most of the regulars at Merlotte's call him – must have left his message within the previous hour. He can't get up until dark.

I hadn't seen Bill in over a week, and our parting hadn't been a happy one. But touching the envelope with my name written on it made me feel miserable. You'd think – though I'm twenty-six – I'd never had, and lost, a boyfriend before.

You'd be right.

Normal guys don't want to date someone as strange as I am. People have been saying I'm messed up in the head since I started school.

They're right.

That's not to say I don't get groped at the bar occasionally. Guys get drunk. I look good. They forget their misgivings about my reputation for strangeness and my ever-present smile.

But only Bill has ever gotten close to me in an intimate way. Parting from him had hurt me bad.

I waited to open the envelope until I was sitting at the old, scarred kitchen table. I still had my coat on, though I'd shucked my gloves.

Dearest Sookie – I wanted to come over to talk to you when you had somewhat recovered from the unfortunate events of earlier this month.

'Unfortunate events,' my round rear end. The bruises had finally faded, but I had a knee that still ached in the cold, and I suspected that it always would. Every injury I had incurred had been in the course of rescuing my cheating boyfriend from his imprisonment by a group of vampires that included his former flame, Lorena. I had yet to figure out why Bill had been so infatuated with Lorena that he'd answered her summons to Mississippi.

Probably, you have a lot of questions about what happened.

Damn straight.

If you'll talk to me face-to-face, come to the front door and let me in.

Yikes. I hadn't seen that one coming. I pondered for a minute. Deciding that while I didn't trust Bill anymore, I didn't believe that he would physically harm me, I went back through the house to the front door. I opened it and called, 'Okay, come on in.'

He emerged from the woods surrounding the clearing in which my old house stood. I ached at the sight of him. Bill was broad-shouldered and lean from his life of farming the land next to mine. He was hard and tough from his years as a Confederate soldier, before his death in 1867. Bill's nose was straight off a Greek vase. His hair was dark brown and clipped close to his head, and his eyes were just as dark. He looked exactly the same as he had while we were dating, and he always would.

He hesitated before he crossed the threshold, but I'd given him permission, and I moved aside so he could step past me into the living room filled with old, comfortable furniture and neat as a pin.

'Thank you,' he said in his cold, smooth voice, a voice that still gave me a twinge of sheer lust. Many things had gone wrong between us, but they hadn't started in bed. 'I wanted to talk to you before I left.'

'Where are you going?' I tried to sound as calm as he.

'To Peru. The queen's orders.'

'Still working on your, ah, database?' I knew almost nothing about computers, but Bill had studied hard to make himself computer literate.

'Yes. I've got a little more research to do. A very old vampire in Lima has a great fund of knowledge about those of our race on his continent, and I have an appointment to confer with him. I'll do some sight-seeing while I'm down there.'

I fought the urge to offer Bill a bottle of synthetic blood, which would have been the hospitable thing to do. 'Have a seat,' I said curtly, and nodded at the sofa. I sat on the edge of the old recliner catty-cornered to it. Then a silence fell, a silence that made me even more conscious of how unhappy I was.

'How's Bubba?' I asked finally.

'He's in New Orleans right now,' Bill said. 'The queen likes to keep him around from time to time, and he was so visible here over the last month that it seemed like a good idea to take him elsewhere. He'll be back soon.'

You'd recognize Bubba if you saw him; everyone knows

his face. But he hadn't been 'brought over' too successfully. Probably the morgue attendant, who happened to be a vampire, should have ignored the tiny spark of life. But since he was a great fan, he hadn't been able to resist the attempt, and now the entire southern vampire community shuffled Bubba around and tried to keep him from public view.

Another silence fell. I'd planned on taking off my shoes and uniform, putting on a cuddly robe, and watching television with a Freschetta pizza by my side. It was a humble plan, but it was my own. Instead, here I was, suffering.

'If you have something to say, you better go on and say it,' I told him.

He nodded, almost to himself. 'I have to explain,' he said. His white hands arranged themselves in his lap. 'Lorena and I—'

I flinched involuntarily. I never wanted to hear that name again. He'd dumped me for Lorena.

'I have to tell you,' he said, almost angrily. He'd seen me twitch. 'Give me this chance.' After a second, I waved a hand to tell him to continue.

'The reason I went to Jackson when she called me is that I couldn't help myself,' he said.

My eyebrows flew up. I'd heard *that* before. It means, 'I have no self-control,' or, 'It seemed worth it at the time, and I wasn't thinking north of my belt.'

'We were lovers long ago. As Eric says he told you, vampire liaisons don't tend to last long, though they're very intense while they are ongoing. However, what Eric did not tell you was that Lorena was the vampire who brought me over.'

'To the Dark Side?' I asked, and then I bit my lip. This was no subject for levity.

'Yes,' Bill agreed seriously. 'And we were together after that, as lovers, which is not always the case.'

'But you had broken up . . .'

'Yes, about eighty years ago, we came to the point where we couldn't tolerate each other any longer. I hadn't seen Lorena since, though I'd heard of her doings, of course.'

'Oh, sure,' I said expressionlessly.

'But I had to obey her summons. This is absolutely imperative. When your maker calls, you must respond.' His voice was urgent.

I nodded, trying to look understanding. I guess I didn't do too good a job.

'She *ordered* me to leave you,' he said. His dark eyes were peering into mine. 'She said she would kill you if I didn't.'

I was losing my temper. I bit the inside of my cheek, real hard, to make myself focus. 'So, without explanation or discussion with me, you decided what was best for me and for you.'

'I had to,' he said. 'I *had* to do her bidding. And I knew she was capable of harming you.'

'Well, you got that right.' In fact, Lorena had done her dead level best to harm me right into the grave. But I'd gotten her first – okay, by a fluke, but it had worked.

'And now you no longer love me,' Bill said, with the slightest of questions in his voice.

I didn't have any clear answer.

'I don't know,' I said. 'I wouldn't think you'd want to come back to me. After all, I killed your mom.' And there was the slightest of questions in my voice, too, but mostly I was bitter.

'Then we need more time apart. When I return, if you consent, we'll talk again. A kiss good-bye?'

To my shame, I would love to kiss Bill again. But it was such a bad idea, even wanting it seemed wrong. We stood, and I gave him a quick brush of lips to the cheek. His white skin shone with a little glow that distinguished vampires from humans. It had surprised me to learn that not everyone saw them like I did.

'Are you seeing the Were?' he asked, when he was nearly out the door. He sounded as though the words had been pulled out of him by their roots.

'Which one?' I asked, resisting the temptation to bat my eyelashes. He deserved no answer, and he knew it. 'How long will you be gone?' I asked more briskly, and he looked at me with some speculation.

'It's not a sure thing. Maybe two weeks,' he answered.

'We might talk then,' I said, turning my face away. 'Let me return your key.' I fished my keys out of my purse.

'No, please, keep it on your key ring,' he said. 'You might need it while I am gone. Go in the house as you will. My mail's getting held at the post office until I give them notice, and I think all my other loose ends are taken care of.'

So I was his last loose end. I damned up the trickle of anger that was all too ready to bubble out these days.

'I hope you have a safe trip,' I said coldly, and shut the door behind him. I headed back to my bedroom. I had a robe to put on and some television to watch. By golly, I was sticking to my plan.

But while I was putting my pizza in the oven, I had to blot my cheeks a few times.

Chapter 1

The New Year's Eve party at Merlotte's Bar and Grill was finally, finally, over. Though the bar owner, Sam Merlotte, had asked all his staff to work that night, Holly, Arlene, and I were the only ones who'd responded. Charlsie Tooten had said she was too old to put up with the mess we had to endure on New Year's Eve, Danielle had long-standing plans to attend a fancy party with her steady boyfriend, and a new woman couldn't start for two days. I guess Arlene and Holly and I needed the money more than we needed a good time.

And I hadn't had any invitations to do anything else. At least when I'm working at Merlotte's, I'm a part of the scenery. That's a kind of acceptance.

I was sweeping up the shredded paper, and I reminded myself again not to comment to Sam on what a poor idea the bags of confetti had been. We'd all made ourselves pretty clear about that, and even good-natured Sam was showing signs of wear and tear. It didn't seem fair to leave it all for Terry Bellefleur to clean, though sweeping and mopping the floors was his job.

Sam was counting the till money and bagging it up so he could go by the night deposit at the bank. He was looking tired but pleased.

He flicked open his cell phone. 'Kenya? You ready to take me to the bank? Okay, see you in a minute at the back door.' Kenya, a police officer, often escorted Sam to the night deposit, especially after a big take like tonight's.

I was pleased with my money take, too. I had earned a lot in tips. I thought I might have gotten three hundred dollars or more – and I needed every penny. I would have enjoyed the prospect of totting up the money when I got home, if I'd been sure I had enough brains left to do it. The noise and chaos of the party, the constant runs to and from the bar and the serving hatch, the tremendous mess we'd had to clean up, the steady cacophony of all those brains . . . it had combined to exhaust me. Toward the end I'd been too tired to keep my poor mind protected, and lots of thoughts had leaked through.

It's not easy being telepathic. Most often, it's not fun.

This evening had been worse than most. Not only had the bar patrons, almost all known to me for many years, been in uninhibited moods, but there'd been some news that lots of people were just dying to tell me.

'I hear yore boyfriend done gone to South America,' a car salesman, Chuck Beecham, had said, malice gleaming in his eyes. 'You gonna get mighty lonely out to your place without him.'

'You offering to take his place, Chuck?' the man beside him at the bar had asked, and they both had a we're-men-together guffaw.

'Naw, Terrell,' said the salesman. 'I don't care for vampire leavings.'

'You be polite, or you go out the door,' I said steadily. I felt warmth at my back, and I knew my boss, Sam Merlotte, was looking at them over my shoulder.

'Trouble?' he asked.

'They were just about to apologize,' I said, looking Chuck and Terrell in the eyes. They looked down at their beers.

'Sorry, Sookie,' Chuck mumbled, and Terrell bobbed his head in agreement. I nodded and turned to take care of another order. But they'd succeeded in hurting me.

Which was their goal.

I had an ache around my heart.

I was sure the general populace of Bon Temps, Louisiana, didn't know about our estrangement. Bill sure wasn't in the habit of blabbing his personal business around, and neither was I. Arlene and Tara knew a little about it, of course, since you have to tell your best friends when you've broken up with your guy, even if you have to leave out all the interesting details. (Like the fact that you'd killed the woman he left you for. Which I couldn't help. Really.) So anyone who told me Bill had gone out of the country, assuming I didn't know it yet, was just being malicious.

Until Bill's recent visit to my house, I'd last seen him when I'd given him the disks and computer he'd hidden with me. I'd driven up at dusk, so the machine wouldn't be sitting on his front porch for long. I'd put all his stuff up against the door in a big waterproofed box. He'd come out just as I was driving away, but I hadn't stopped.

An evil woman would have given the disks to Bill's boss, Eric. A lesser woman would have kept those disks and that computer, having rescinded Bill's (and Eric's) invitations to enter the house. I had told myself proudly that I was not an evil, or a lesser, woman.

Also, thinking practically, Bill could just have hired some human to break into my house and take them. I didn't think he would. But he needed them bad, or he'd be in trouble with his boss's boss. I've got a temper, maybe even a bad temper, once it gets provoked. But I'm not vindictive.

Arlene has often told me I am too nice for my own good, though I assure her I am not. (Tara never says that; maybe she knows me better?) I realized glumly that, sometime during this hectic evening, Arlene would hear about Bill's departure. Sure enough, within twenty minutes of Chuck and Terrell's gibing, she made her way through the crowd to pat me on the back. 'You didn't need that cold bastard anyway,' she said. 'What did he ever do for you?'

I nodded weakly at her to show how much I appreciated her support. But then a table called for two whiskey sours, two beers, and a gin and tonic, and I had to hustle, which was actually a welcome distraction. When I dropped off their drinks, I asked myself the same question. What had Bill done for me?

I delivered pitchers of beer to two tables before I could add it all up.

He'd introduced me to sex, which I really enjoyed. Introduced me to a lot of other vampires, which I didn't. Saved my life, though when you thought about it, it wouldn't have been in danger if I hadn't been dating him in the first place. But I'd saved his back once or twice, so that debt was canceled. He'd called me 'sweetheart,' and at the time he'd meant it.

'Nothing,' I muttered, as I mopped up a spilled piña colada and handed one of our last clean bar towels to the woman who'd knocked it over, since a lot of it was still in her skirt. 'He didn't do a thing for me.' She smiled and nodded, obviously thinking I was commiserating with her. The place was too noisy to hear anything anyway, which was lucky for me.

But I'd be glad when Bill got back. After all, he was my nearest neighbor. The community's older cemetery separated our properties, which lay along a parish road south of Bon Temps. I was out there all by myself, without Bill.

'Peru, I hear,' my brother Jason, said. He had his arm around his girl of the evening, a short, thin, dark twenty-one-year-old from somewhere way out in the sticks. (I'd carded her.) I gave her a close look. Jason didn't know it, but she was a shape-shifter of some kind. They're easy to spot. She was an attractive girl, but she changed into something with feathers or fur when the moon was full. I noticed Sam give her a hard glare when Jason's back was turned, to remind her to behave herself in his territory. She returned the glare, with interest. I had the feeling she didn't become a kitten, or a squirrel.

I thought of latching on to her brain and trying to read it, but shifter heads aren't easy. Shifter thoughts are kind of snarly and red, though every now and then you can get a good picture of emotions. Same with Weres.

Sam himself turns into a collie when the moon is bright and round. Sometimes he trots all the way over to my house, and I feed him a bowl of scraps and let him nap on my back porch, if the weather's good, or in my living room, if the weather's poor. I don't let him in the bedroom anymore, because he wakes up naked – in which state he looks *very* nice, but I just don't need to be tempted by my boss.

The moon wasn't full tonight, so Jason would be safe. I

decided not to say anything to him about his date. Everyone's got a secret or two. Her secret was just a little more colorful.

Besides my brother's date, and Sam of course, there were two other supernatural creatures in Merlotte's Bar that New Year's Eve. One was a magnificent woman at least six feet tall, with long rippling dark hair. Dressed to kill in a skintight long-sleeved orange dress, she'd come in by herself, and she was in the process of meeting every guy in the bar. I didn't know what she was, but I knew from her brain pattern that she was not human. The other creature was a vampire, who'd come in with a group of young people, most in their early twenties. I didn't know any of them. Only a sideways glance by a few other revelers marked the presence of a vampire. It just went to show the change in attitude in the few years since the Great Revelation.

Almost three years ago, on the night of the Great Revelation, the vampires had gone on TV in every nation to announce their existence. It had been a night in which many of the world's assumptions had been knocked sideways and rearranged for good.

This coming-out party had been prompted by the Japanese development of a synthetic blood that can keep vamps satisfied nutritionally. Since the Great Revelation, the United States has undergone numerous political and social upheavals in the bumpy process of accommodating our newest citizens, who just happen to be dead. The vampires have a public face and a public explanation for their condition – they claim an allergy to sunlight and garlic causes severe metabolic changes – but I've seen the other side of the vampire world. My eyes now see a lot of things most human beings don't ever see. Ask me if this knowledge has made me happy.

No.

But I have to admit, the world is a more interesting place to me now. I'm by myself a lot (since I'm not exactly Norma Normal), so the extra food for thought has been welcome. The fear and danger haven't. I've seen the private face of vampires, and I've learned about Weres and shifters and other stuff. Weres and shifters prefer to stay in the shadows – for now – while they watch how going public works out for the vamps.

See, I had all this to mull over while collecting tray after tray of glasses and mugs, and unloading and loading the dishwasher to help Tack, the new cook. (His real name is Alphonse Petacki. Can you be surprised he likes 'Tack' better?) When our part of the cleanup was just about finished, and this long evening was finally over, I hugged Arlene and wished her a happy New Year, and she hugged me back. Holly's boyfriend was waiting for her at the employees' entrance at the back of the building, and Holly waved to us as she pulled on her coat and hurried out.

'What're your hopes for the New Year, ladies?' Sam asked. By that time, Kenya was leaning against the bar, waiting for him, her face calm and alert. Kenya ate lunch here pretty regularly with her partner, Kevin, who was as pale and thin as she was dark and rounded. Sam was putting the chairs up on the tables so Terry Bellefleur, who came in very early in the morning, could mop the floor.

'Good health, and the right man,' Arlene said dramatically, her hands fluttering over her heart, and we laughed. Arlene has found many men – and she's been married four times – but she's still looking for Mr. Right. I could 'hear'

Arlene thinking that Tack might be the one. I was startled; I hadn't even known she'd looked at him.

The surprise showed on my face, and in an uncertain voice Arlene said, 'You think I should give up?'

'Hell, no,' I said promptly, chiding myself for not guarding my expression better. It was just that I was so tired. 'It'll be this year, for sure, Arlene.' I smiled at Bon Temp's only black female police officer. 'You have to have a wish for the New Year, Kenya. Or a resolution.'

'I always wish for peace between men and women,' Kenya said. 'Make my job a lot easier. And my resolution is to bench-press one-forty.'

'Wow,' said Arlene. Her dyed red hair contrasted violently with Sam's natural curly red-gold as she gave him a quick hug. He wasn't much taller than Arlene – though she's at least five foot eight, two inches taller than I. 'I'm going to lose ten pounds, that's my resolution.' We all laughed. That had been Arlene's resolution for the past four years. 'What about you, Sam? Wishes and resolutions?' she asked.

'I have everything I need,' he said, and I felt the blue wave of sincerity coming from him. 'I resolve to stay on this course. The bar is doing great, I like living in my double-wide, and the people here are as good as people anywhere.'

I turned to conceal my smile. That had been a pretty ambiguous statement. The people of Bon Temps were, indeed, as good as people anywhere.

'And you, Sookie?' he asked. Arlene, Kenya, and Sam were all looking at me. I hugged Arlene again, because I like to. I'm ten years younger – maybe more, since though Arlene says she's thirty-six, I have my doubts – but we've been friends ever since we started working at Merlotte's together after Sam bought the bar, maybe five years now.

'Come on,' Arlene said, coaxing me. Sam put his arm around me. Kenya smiled, but drifted away into the kitchen to have a few words with Tack.

Acting on impulse, I shared my wish. 'I just hope to not be beaten up,' I said, my weariness and the hour combining in an ill-timed burst of honesty. 'I don't want to go to the hospital. I don't want to see a doctor.' I didn't want to have to ingest any vampire blood, either, which would cure you in a hurry but had various side effects. 'So my resolution is to stay out of trouble,' I said firmly.

Arlene looked pretty startled, and Sam looked – well, I couldn't tell about Sam. But since I'd hugged Arlene, I gave him a big hug, too, and felt the strength and warmth in his body. You think Sam's slight until you see him shirtless unloading boxes of supplies. He is really strong and built really smooth, and he has a high natural body temperature. I felt him kiss my hair, and then we were all saying good night to each other and walking out the back door. Sam's truck was parked in front of his trailer, which is set up behind Merlotte's Bar but at a right angle to it, but he climbed in Kenya's patrol car to ride to the bank. She'd bring him home, and then Sam could collapse. He'd been on his feet for hours, as had we all.

As Arlene and I unlocked our cars, I noticed Tack was waiting in his old pickup; I was willing to bet he was going to follow Arlene home.

With a last 'Good night!' called through the chilly silence of the Louisiana night, we separated to begin our new years.

I turned off onto Hummingbird Road to go out to my place, which is about three miles southeast of the bar. The relief of finally being alone was immense, and I began to relax mentally. My headlights flashed past the close-packed trunks of the pines that formed the backbone of the lumber industry hereabouts.

The night was extremely dark and cold. There are no streetlights way out on the parish roads, of course. Creatures were not stirring, not by any means. Though I kept telling myself to be alert for deer crossing the road, I was driving on autopilot. My simple thoughts were filled with the plan of scrubbing my face and pulling on my warmest nightgown and climbing into my bed.

Something white appeared in the headlights of my old car.

I gasped, jolted out of my drowsy anticipation of warmth and silence.

A running man: At three in the morning on January first, he was running down the parish road, apparently running for his life.

I slowed down, trying to figure out a course of action. I was a lone unarmed woman. If something awful was pursuing him, it might get me, too. On the other hand, I couldn't let someone suffer if I could help. I had a moment to notice that the man was tall, blond, and clad only in blue jeans, before I pulled up by him. I put the car into park and leaned over to roll down the window on the passenger's side.

'Can I help you?' I called. He gave me a panicked glance and kept on running.

But in that moment I realized who he was. I leaped out of the car and took off after him.

'Eric!' I yelled. 'It's me!'

He wheeled around then, hissing, his fangs fully out. I stopped so abruptly I swayed where I stood, my hands out in front of me in a gesture of peace. Of course, if Eric decided to attack, I was a dead woman. So much for being a good Samaritan.

Why didn't Eric recognize me? I'd known him for many months. He was Bill's boss, in the complicated vampire hierarchy that I was beginning to learn. Eric was the sheriff of Area Five, and he was a vampire on the rise. He was also gorgeous and could kiss like a house afire, but that was not the most pertinent side of him right at the moment. Fangs and strong hands curved into claws were what I was seeing. Eric was in full alarm mode, but he seemed just as scared of me as I was of him. He didn't leap to attack.

'Stay back, woman,' he warned me. His voice sounded like his throat was sore, raspy and raw.

'What are you doing out here?'

'Who are you?'

'You known darn good and well who I am. What's up with you? Why are you out here without your car?' Eric drove a sleek Corvette, which was simply Eric.

'You know me? Who am I?'

Well, that knocked me for a loop. He sure didn't sound like he was joking. I said cautiously, 'Of course I know you, Eric. Unless you have an identical twin. You don't, right?'

'I don't know.' His arms dropped, his fangs seemed to be retracting, and he straightened from his crouch, so I felt there'd been a definite improvement in the atmosphere of our encounter.

'You don't know if you have a brother?' I was pretty much at sea.

'No. I don't know. Eric is my name?' In the glare of my headlights, he looked just plain pitiful.

'Wow.' I couldn't think of anything more helpful to say.

'Eric Northman is the name you go by these days. Why are you out here?'

'I don't know that, either.'

I was sensing a theme here. 'For real? You don't remember anything?' I tried to get past being sure that at any second he'd grin down at me and explain everything and laugh, embroiling me in some trouble that would end in me . . . getting beaten up.

'For real.' He took a step closer, and his bare white chest made me shiver with sympathetic goose bumps. I also realized (now that I wasn't terrified) how forlorn he looked. It was an expression I'd never seen on the confident Eric's face before, and it made me feel unaccountably sad.

'You know you're a vampire, right?'

'Yes.' He seemed surprised that I asked. 'And you are not.'

'No, I'm real human, and I have to know you won't hurt me. Though you could have by now. But believe me, even if you don't remember it, we're sort of friends.'

'I won't hurt you.'

I reminded myself that probably hundreds and thousands of people had heard those very words before Eric ripped their throats out. But the fact is, vampires don't have to kill once they're past their first year. A sip here, a sip there, that's the norm. When he looked so lost, it was hard to remember he could dismember me with his bare hands.

I'd told Bill one time that the smart thing for aliens to do (when they invaded Earth) would be to arrive in the guise of lop-eared bunnies.

'Come get in my car before you freeze,' I said. I was having that I'm-getting-sucked-in feeling again, but I didn't know what else to do.

'I do know you?' he said, as though he were hesitant about getting in a car with someone as formidable as a woman ten inches shorter, many pounds lighter, and a few centuries younger.

'Yes,' I said, not able to restrain an edge of impatience. I wasn't too happy with myself, because I still half suspected I was being tricked for some unfathomable reason. 'Now come on, Eric. I'm freezing, and so are you.' Not that vampires seemed to feel temperature extremes, as a rule; but even Eric's skin looked goosey. The dead can freeze, of course. They'll survive it – they survive almost everything – but I understand it's pretty painful. 'Oh my God, Eric, you're barefoot.' I'd just noticed.

I took his hand; he let me get close enough for that. He let me lead him back to the car and stow him in the passenger seat. I told him to roll up the window as I went around to my side, and after a long minute of studying the mechanism, he did.

I reached in the backseat for an old afghan I keep there in the winter (for football games, etc.) and wrapped it around him. He wasn't shivering, of course, because he was a vampire, but I just couldn't stand to look at all that bare flesh in this temperature. I turned the heater on full blast (which, in my old car, isn't saying much).

Eric's exposed skin had never made me feel cold before – when I'd seen this much of Eric before, I'd felt anything *but*. I was giddy enough by now to laugh out loud before I could censor my own thoughts.

He was startled, and looked at me sideways.

'You're the last person I expected to see,' I said. 'Were you coming out this way to see Bill? Because he's gone.'

'Bill?'

'The vampire who lives out here? My ex-boyfriend?'

He shook his head. He was back to being absolutely terrified.

'You don't know how you came to be here?'

He shook his head again.

I was making a big effort to think hard; but it was just that, an effort. I was worn out. Though I'd had a rush of adrenaline when I'd spotted the figure running down the dark road, that rush was wearing off fast. I reached the turnoff to my house and turned left, winding through the black and silent woods on my nice, level driveway – that, in fact, Eric had had re-graveled for me.

And that was why Eric was sitting in my car right now, instead of running through the night like a giant white rabbit. He'd had the intelligence to give me what I really wanted. (Of course, he'd also wanted me to go to bed with him for months. But he'd given me the driveway because I needed it.)

'Here we are,' I said, pulling around to the back of my old house. I switched off the car. I'd remembered to leave the outside lights on when I'd left for work that afternoon, thank goodness, so we weren't sitting there in total darkness.

'This is where you live?' He was glancing around the clearing where the old house stood, seemingly nervous about going from the car to the back door.

'Yes,' I said, exasperated.

He just gave me a look that showed white all around the blue of his eyes.

'Oh, come on,' I said, with no grace at all. I got out of the car and went up the steps to the back porch, which I don't keep locked because, hey, why lock a screened-in back porch? I do lock the inner door, and after a second's fumbling, I had it open so the light I leave on in the kitchen could spill out. 'You can come in,' I said, so he could cross the threshold. He scuttled in after me, the afghan still clutched around him.

Under the overhead light in the kitchen, Eric looked pretty pitiful. His bare feet were bleeding, which I hadn't noticed before. 'Oh, Eric,' I said sadly, and got a pan out from the cabinet, and started the hot water to running in the sink. He'd heal real quick, like vampires do, but I couldn't help but wash him clean. The blue jeans were filthy around the hem. 'Pull 'em off,' I said, knowing they'd just get wet if I soaked his feet while he was dressed.

With not a hint of a leer or any other indication that he was enjoying this development, Eric shimmied out of the jeans. I tossed them onto the back porch to wash in the morning, trying not to gape at my guest, who was now clad in underwear that was definitely over-the-top, a bright red bikini style whose stretchy quality was definitely being tested. Okay, another big surprise. I'd seen Eric's underwear only once before – which was once more than I ought to have – and he'd been a silk boxers guy. Did men change styles like that?

Without preening, and without comment, the vampire rewrapped his white body in the afghan. Hmmm. I was now convinced he wasn't himself, as no other evidence could have convinced me. Eric was way over six feet of pure magnificence (if a marble white magnificence), and he well knew it.

I pointed to one of the straight-back chairs at the kitchen table. Obediently, he pulled it out and sat. I crouched to put the pan on the floor, and I gently guided his big feet into the water. Eric groaned as the warmth touched his skin. I guess that even a vampire could feel the contrast. I got a clean rag from under the sink and some liquid soap, and I washed his feet. I took my time, because I was trying to think what to do next.

'You were out in the night,' he observed, in a tentative sort of way.

'I was coming home from work, as you can see from my clothes.' I was wearing our winter uniform, a long-sleeved white boat-neck T-shirt with 'Merlotte's Bar' embroidered over the left breast and worn tucked into black slacks.

'Women shouldn't be out alone this late at night,' he said disapprovingly.

'Tell me about it.'

'Well, women are more liable to be overwhelmed by an attack than men, so they should be more protected—'

'No, I didn't mean literally. I meant, I agree. You're preaching to the choir. I didn't want to be working this late at night.'

'Then why were you out?'

'I need the money,' I said, wiping my hand and pulling the roll of bills out of my pocket and dropping it on the table while I was thinking about it. 'I got this house to maintain, my car is old, and I have taxes and insurance to pay. Like everyone else,' I added, in case he thought I was complaining unduly. I hated to poor-mouth, but he'd asked.

'Is there no man in your family?'

Every now and then, their ages do show. 'I have a brother. I can't remember if you've ever met Jason.' A cut on his left foot looked especially bad. I put some more hot water into the basin to warm the remainder. Then I tried to get all the dirt out. He winced as I gently rubbed the washcloth over the margins of the wound. The smaller cuts and bruises seemed to be fading even as I watched. The hot water heater came on behind me, the familiar sound somehow reassuring.

'Your brother permits you to do this working?'

I tried to imagine Jason's face when I told him that I expected him to support me for the rest of my life because I was a woman and shouldn't work outside the home. 'Oh, for goodness sake, Eric.' I looked up at him, scowling. 'Jason's got his own problems.' Like being chronically selfish and a true tomcat.

I eased the pan of water to the side and patted Eric dry with a dishtowel. This vampire now had clean feet. Rather stiffly, I stood. My back hurt. My feet hurt. 'Listen, I think what I better do is call Pam. She'll probably know what's going on with you.'

'Pam?'

It was like being around a particularly irritating two-year-old.

'Your second-in-command.'

He was going to ask another question, I could just tell. I held up a hand. 'Just hold on. Let me call her and find out what's happening.'

'But what if she has turned against me?'

'Then we need to know that, too. The sooner the better.'

I put my hand on the old phone that hung on the kitchen wall right by the end of the counter. A high stool sat below it. My grandmother had always sat on the stool to conduct her lengthy phone conversations, with a pad and pencil handy. I missed her every day. But at the moment I had no room in my emotional palette for grief, or even nostalgia. I looked in my little address book for the number of Fangtasia, the vampire bar in Shreveport that provided Eric's principal income and served as the base of his operations, which I understood were far wider in scope. I didn't know how wide or what these other moneymaking projects were, and I didn't especially want to know.

I'd seen in the Shreveport paper that Fangtasia, too, had planned a big bash for the evening – 'Begin Your New Year with a Bite' – so I knew someone would be there. While the phone was ringing, I swung open the refrigerator and got out a bottle of blood for Eric. I popped it in the microwave and set the timer. He followed my every move with anxious eyes.

'Fangtasia,' said an accented male voice.

'Chow?'

'Yes, how may I serve you?' He'd remembered his phone persona of sexy vampire just in the nick of time.

'It's Sookie.'

'Oh,' he said in a much more natural voice. 'Listen, Happy New Year, Sook, but we're kind of busy here.'

'Looking for someone?'

There was a long, charged silence.

'Wait a minute,' he said, and then I heard nothing.

'Pam,' said Pam. She'd picked up the receiver so silently that I jumped when I heard her voice.

'Do you still have a master?' I didn't know how much I could say over the phone. I wanted to know if she'd been the one who'd put Eric in this state, or if she still owed him loyalty.

'I do,' she said steadily, understanding what I wanted to know. 'We are under . . . we have some problems.'

I mulled that over until I was sure I'd read between the lines. Pam was telling me that she still owed Eric her allegiance, and that Eric's group of followers was under some kind of attack or in some kind of crisis.

I said, 'He's here.' Pam appreciated brevity.

'Is he alive?'

'Yep.'

'Damaged?'

'Mentally.'

A long pause, this time.

'Will he be a danger to you?'

Not that Pam cared a whole hell of a lot if Eric decided to drain me dry, but I guess she wondered if I would shelter Eric. 'I don't think so at the moment,' I said. 'It seems to be a matter of memory.'

'I hate witches. Humans had the right idea, burning them at the stake.'

Since the very humans who had burned witches would have been delighted to sink that same stake into vampire hearts, I found that a little amusing – but not very, considering the hour. I immediately forgot what she'd been talking about. I yawned.

'Tomorrow night, we'll come,' she said finally. 'Can you keep him this day? Dawn's in less than four hours. Do you have a safe place?'

'Yes. But you get over here at nightfall, you hear me? I don't want to get tangled up in your vampire shit again.' Normally, I don't speak so bluntly; but like I say, it was the tail end of a long night.

'We'll be there.'

We hung up simultaneously. Eric was watching me with unblinking blue eyes. His hair was a snarly tangled mess of blond waves. His hair is the exact same color as mine, and I have blue eyes, too, but that's the end of the similarities.

I thought of taking a brush to his hair, but I was just too weary.

'Okay, here's the deal,' I told him. 'You stay here the rest of the night and tomorrow, and then Pam and them'll come get you tomorrow night and let you know what's happening.'

'You won't let anyone get in?' he asked. I noticed he'd finished the blood, and he wasn't quite as drawn as he'd been, which was a relief.

'Eric, I'll do my best to keep you safe,' I said, quite gently. I rubbed my face with my hands. I was going to fall asleep on my feet. 'Come on,' I said, taking his hand. Clutching the afghan with the other hand, he trailed down the hall after me, a snow white giant in tiny red underwear.

My old house has been added onto over the years, but it hasn't ever been more than a humble farmhouse. A second story was added around the turn of the century, and two more bedrooms and a walk-in attic are upstairs, but I seldom go up there anymore. I keep it shut off, to save money on electricity. There are two bedrooms downstairs, the smaller one I'd used until my grandmother died and her large one across the hall from it. I'd moved into the large one after her death. But the hidey-hole Bill had built was in the smaller bedroom. I led Eric in there, switched on the light, and made sure the blinds were closed and the curtains drawn across them. Then I opened the door of the closet, removed its few contents, and pulled back the flap of carpet that covered the closet floor, exposing the trapdoor. Underneath was a light-tight space that Bill had built a few months before, so that he could stay over during the day or use it as a hiding place if his own home was unsafe. Bill liked having a bolt-hole, and I was sure he had some that I didn't know about. If I'd been a vampire (God forbid), I would have, myself.

I had to wipe thoughts of Bill out of my head as I showed my reluctant guest how to close the trapdoor on top of him and that the flap of carpet would fall back into place. 'When I get up, I'll put the stuff back in the closet so it'll look natural,' I reassured him, and smiled encouragingly.

'Do I have to get in now?' he asked.

Eric, making a request of me: The world was really turned upside-down. 'No,' I said, trying to sound like I was concerned. All I could think of was my bed. 'You don't have to. Just get in before sunrise. There's no way you could miss that, right? I mean, you couldn't fall asleep and wake up in the sun?'

He thought for a moment and shook his head. 'No,' he said. 'I know that can't happen. Can I stay in the room with you?'

Oh, God, *puppy dog eyes.* From a six-foot-five ancient Viking vampire. It was just too much. I didn't have enough energy to laugh, so I just gave a sad little snigger. 'Come on,' I said, my voice as limp as my legs. I turned off the light in that room, crossed the hall, and flipped on the one in my own room, yellow and white and clean and warm, and folded down the bedspread and blanket and sheet. While Eric sat forlornly in a slipper chair on the other side of the bed, I pulled off my shoes and socks, got a nightgown out of a drawer, and retreated into the bathroom. I was out in ten minutes, with clean teeth and face and swathed in a very old, very soft flannel nightgown that was cream-colored with blue flowers scattered around. Its ribbons were raveled and the ruffle around the bottom was pretty sad, but it suited me just fine. After I'd switched off the lights, I remembered my hair was still up in its usual ponytail, so I pulled out the band that held it and I shook my head to make it fall loose. Even my scalp seemed to relax, and I sighed with bliss.

As I climbed up into the high old bed, the large fly in my personal ointment did the same. Had I actually told him he could get in bed with me? Well, I decided, as I wriggled down under the soft old sheets and the blanket and the comforter, if Eric had designs on me, I was just too tired to care.

'Woman?'

'Hmmm?'

'What's your name?'

'Sookie. Sookie Stackhouse.'

'Thank you, Sookie.'

'Welcome, Eric.'

Because he sounded so lost – the Eric I knew had never been one to do anything other than assume others should serve him – I patted around under the covers for his hand. When I found it, I slid my own over it. His palm was turned up to meet my palm, and his fingers clasped mine.

And though I would not have thought it was possible to go to sleep holding hands with a vampire, that's exactly what I did.

Chapter 2

I woke up slowly. As I lay snuggled under the covers, now and then stretching an arm or a leg, I gradually remembered the surrealistic happenings of the night before.

Well, Eric wasn't in bed with me now, so I had to assume he was safely ensconced in the hidey-hole. I went across the hall. As I'd promised, I put the contents back in the closet to make it look normal. The clock told me it was noon, and outside the sun was bright, though the air was cold. For Christmas, Jason had given me a thermometer that read the outside temperature and showed it to me on a digital readout inside. He'd installed it for me, too. Now I knew two things: it was noon, and it was thirty-four degrees outside.

In the kitchen, the pan of water I'd washed Eric's feet with was still sitting on the floor. As I dumped it into the sink, I saw that at some point he'd rinsed out the bottle that had held the synthetic blood. I'd have to get some more to have around when he rose, since you didn't want a hungry vampire in your house, and it would be only polite to have extra to offer Pam and whoever else drove over from

Shreveport. They'd explain things to me – or not. They'd take Eric away and work on whatever problems were facing the Shreveport vampire community, and I would be left in peace. Or not.

Merlotte's was closed on New Year's Day until four o'clock. On New Year's Day, and the day after, Charlsie and Danielle and the new girl were on the schedule, since the rest of us had worked New Year's Eve. So I had two whole days off . . . and at least one of them I got to spend alone in a house with a mentally ill vampire. Life just didn't get any better.

I had two cups of coffee, put Eric's jeans in the washer, read a romance for a while, and studied my brand-new Word of the Day calendar, a Christmas gift from Arlene. My first word for the New Year was 'exsanguinate.' This was probably not a good omen.

Jason came by a little after four, flying down my drive in his black pickup with pink and purple flames on the side. I'd showered and dressed by then, but my hair was still wet. I'd sprayed it with detangler and I was brushing through it slowly, sitting in front of the fireplace. I'd turned on the TV to a football game to have something to watch while I brushed, but I kept the sound way down. I was pondering Eric's predicament while I luxuriated in the feel of the fire's warmth on my back.

We hadn't used the fireplace much in the past couple of years because buying a load of wood was so expensive, but Jason had cut up a lot of trees that had fallen last year after an ice storm. I was well stocked, and I was enjoying the flames.

My brother stomped up the front steps and knocked perfunctorily before coming in. Like me, he had mostly grown up in this house. We'd come to live with Gran when my parents died, and she'd rented out their house until Jason said he was ready to live on his own, when he'd been twenty. Now Jason was twenty-eight and the boss of a parish road crew. This was a rapid rise for a local boy without a lot of education, and I'd thought it was enough for him until the past month or two, when he'd begun acting restless.

'Good,' he said, when he saw the fire. He stood squarely in front of it to warm his hands, incidentally blocking the warmth from me. 'What time did you get home last night?' he said over his shoulder.

'I guess I got to bed about three.'

'What did you think of that girl I was with?'

'I think you better not date her anymore.'

That wasn't what he'd expected to hear. His eyes slid sideways to meet mine. 'What did you get off her?' he asked in a subdued voice. My brother knows I am telepathic, but he would never discuss it with me, or anyone else. I've seen him get into fights with some man who accused me of being abnormal, but he knows I'm different. Everyone else does, too. They just choose not to believe it, or they believe I couldn't possibly read *their* thoughts – just someone else's. God knows, I try to act and talk like I'm not receiving an unwanted spate of ideas and emotions and regrets and accusations, but sometimes it just seeps through.

'She's not your kind,' I said, looking into the fire.

'She surely ain't a vamp,' he protested.

'No, not a vamp.'

'Well, then.' He glared at me belligerently.

'Jason, when the vampires came out – when we found

out they were real after all those decades of thinking they were just a scary legend – didn't you ever wonder if there were other tall tales that were real?'

My brother struggled with that concept for a minute. I knew (because I could 'hear' him) that Jason wanted to deny any such idea absolutely and call me a crazy woman – but he just couldn't. 'You know for a fact,' he said. It wasn't quite a question.

I made sure he was looking me in the eyes, and I nodded emphatically.

'Well, shit,' he said, disgusted. 'I really liked that girl, and she was a tiger in the sack.'

'Really?' I asked, absolutely stunned that she had changed in front of him when it wasn't the full moon. 'Are you okay?' The next second, I was chastising myself for my stupidity. Of course she hadn't.

He gaped at me for a second, before bursting out laughing. 'Sookie, you are one weird woman! You looked just like you thought she really could—' And his face froze. I could feel the idea bore a hole through the protective bubble most people inflate around their brain, the bubble that repels sights and ideas that don't jibe with their expectation of the everyday. Jason sat down heavily in Gran's recliner. 'I wish I didn't know that,' he said in a small voice.

'That may not be specifically what happens to her – the tiger thing – but believe me, something happens.'

It took a minute for his face to settle back into more familiar lines, but it did. Typical Jason behavior: There was nothing he could do about his new knowledge, so he pushed it to the back of his mind. 'Listen, did you see Hoyt's date last night? After they left the bar, Hoyt got stuck in a ditch over to Arcadia, and they had to walk two miles to get to a phone because he'd let his cell run down.'

'He did not!' I exclaimed, in a comforting and gossipy way. 'And her in those heels.' Jason's equilibrium was restored. He told me the town gossip for a few minutes, he accepted my offer of a Coke, and he asked me if I needed anything from town.

'Yes, I do.' I'd been thinking while he was talking. Most of his news I'd heard from other brains the nights before, in unguarded moments.

'Ah-oh,' he said, looking mock-frightened. 'What am I in for now?'

'I need ten bottles of synthetic blood and clothes for a big man,' I said, and I'd startled him again. Poor Jason, he deserved a silly vixen of a sister who bore nieces and nephews who called him Uncle Jase and held on to his legs. Instead, he got me.

'How big is the man, and where is he?'

'He's about six foot four or five, and he's asleep,' I said. 'I'd guess a thirty-four waist, and he's got long legs and broad shoulders.' I reminded myself to check the size label on Eric's jeans, which were still in the dryer out on the back porch.

'What kind of clothes?'

'Work clothes.'

'Anybody I know?'

'Me,' said a much deeper voice.

Jason whipped around as if he was expecting an attack, which shows his instincts aren't so bad, after all. But Eric looked as unthreatening as a vampire his size can look. And he'd obligingly put on the brown velour bathrobe that I'd left in the second bedroom. It was one I'd kept here for Bill, and it gave me a pang to see it on someone else. But I had to be practical; Eric couldn't wander around in red bikini underwear – at least, not with Jason in the house.

Jason goggled at Eric and cast a shocked glance at me. 'This is your newest man, Sookie? You didn't let any grass grow under your feet.' He didn't know whether to sound admiring or indignant. Jason still didn't realize Eric was dead. It's amazing to me that lots of people can't tell for a few minutes. 'And I need to get him clothes?'

'Yes. His shirt got torn last night, and his blue jeans are still dirty.'

'You going to introduce me?'

I took a deep breath. It would have been so much better if Jason hadn't seen Eric. 'Better not,' I said.

They both took that badly. Jason looked wounded, and the vampire looked offended.

'Eric,' he said, and stuck out a hand to Jason.

'Jason Stackhouse, this rude lady's brother,' Jason said.

They shook, and I felt like wringing both their necks.

'I'm assuming there's a reason why you two can't go out to buy him more clothes,' Jason said.

'There's a good reason,' I said. 'And there's about twenty good reasons you should forget you ever saw this guy.'

'Are you in danger?' Jason asked me directly.

'Not yet,' I said.

'If you do something that gets my sister hurt, you'll be in a world of trouble,' Jason told Eric the vampire.

'I would expect nothing less,' Eric said. 'But since you are being blunt with me, I'll be blunt with you. I think you should support her and take her into your household, so she would be better protected.'

Jason's mouth fell open again, and I had to cover my own

so I wouldn't laugh out loud. This was even better than I'd imagined.

'Ten bottles of blood and a change of clothes?' Jason asked me, and I knew by the change in his voice that he'd finally cottoned on to Eric's state.

'Right. Liquor store'll have the blood. You can get the clothes at Wal-Mart.' Eric had mostly been a jeans and T-shirt kind of guy, which was all I could afford, anyway. 'Oh, he needs some shoes, too.'

Jason went to stand by Eric and put his foot parallel to the vampire's. He whistled, which made Eric jump.

'Big feet,' Jason commented, and flashed me a look. 'Is the old saying true?'

I smiled at him. He was trying to lighten the atmosphere. 'You may not believe me, but I don't know.'

'Kind of hard to swallow . . . no joke intended. Well, I'm gone,' Jason said, nodding to Eric. In a few seconds, I heard his truck speeding around the curves in the driveway, through the dark woods. Night had fallen completely.

'I'm sorry I came out while he was here,' Eric said tentatively. 'You didn't want me to meet him, I think.' He came over to the fire and seemed to be enjoying the warmth as I had been doing.

'It's not that I'm embarrassed to have you here,' I said. 'It's that I have a feeling you're in a heap of trouble, and I don't want my brother drawn in.'

'He is your only brother?'

'Yes. And my parents are gone, my grandmother, too. He's all I have, except for a cousin who's been on drugs for years. She's lost, I guess.'

'Don't be so sad,' he said, as if he couldn't help himself.

'I'm fine.' I made my voice brisk and matter-of-fact.

'You've had my blood,' he said.

Ah-oh. I stood absolutely still.

'I wouldn't be able to tell how you feel if you hadn't had my blood,' he said. 'Are we – have we been – lovers?'

That was certainly a nice way to put it. Eric was usually pretty Anglo-Saxon about sex.

'No,' I said promptly, and I was telling the truth, though only by a narrow margin. We'd been interrupted in time, thank God. I'm not married. I have weak moments. He is gorgeous. What can I say?

But he was looking at me with intense eyes, and I felt color flooding my face.

'This is not your brother's bathrobe.'

Oh, boy. I stared into the fire as if it were going to spell out an answer for me.

'Whose, then?'

'Bill's,' I said. That was easy.

'He is your lover?'

I nodded. 'Was,' I said honestly.

'He is my friend?'

I thought that over. 'Well, not exactly. He lives in the area you're the sheriff of? Area Five?' I resumed brushing my hair and discovered it was dry. It crackled with electricity and followed the brush. I smiled at the effect in my reflection in the mirror over the mantel. I could see Eric in the reflection, too. I have no idea why the story went around that vampires can't be seen in mirrors. There was certainly plenty of Eric to see, because he was so tall and he hadn't wrapped the robe very tightly . . . I closed my eyes.

'Do you need something?' Eric asked anxiously.

More self-control.

'I'm just fine,' I said, trying not to grind my teeth. 'Your friends will be here soon. Your jeans are in the dryer, and I'm hoping Jason will be back any minute with some clothes.'

'My friends?'

'Well, the vampires who work for you. I guess Pam counts as a friend. I don't know about Chow.'

'Sookie, where do I work? Who is Pam?'

This was really an uphill conversation. I tried to explain to Eric about his position, his ownership of Fangtasia, his other business interests, but truthfully, I wasn't knowledgeable enough to brief him completely.

'You don't know much about what I do,' he observed accurately.

'Well, I only go to Fangtasia when Bill takes me, and he takes me when you make me do something.' I hit myself in the forehead with my brush. Stupid, stupid!

'How could I make you do anything? May I borrow the brush?' Eric asked. I stole a glance at him. He was looking all broody and thoughtful.

'Sure,' I said, deciding to ignore his first question. I handed over the brush. He began to use it on his own hair, making all the muscles in his chest dance around. *Oh, boy. Maybe I should get back in the shower and turn the water on cold?* I stomped into the bedroom and got an elastic band and pulled my hair back in the tightest ponytail I could manage, up at the crown of my head. I used my second-best brush to get it very smooth, and checked to make sure I'd gotten it centered by turning my head from side to side.

'You are tense,' Eric said from the doorway, and I yipped.

'Sorry, sorry!' he said hastily.

I glared at him, full of suspicion, but he seemed sincerely contrite. When he was himself, Eric would have laughed.

But darn if I didn't miss Real Eric. You knew where you were with him.

I heard a knock on the front door.

'You stay in here,' I said. He seemed pretty worried, and he sat on the chair in the corner of the room, like a good little fella. I was glad I'd picked up my discarded clothes the night before, so my room didn't seem so personal. I went through the living room to the front door, hoping for no more surprises.

'Who is it?' I asked, putting my ear to the door.

'We are here,' said Pam.

I began to turn the knob, stopped, then remembered they couldn't come in anyway, and opened the door.

Pam has pale straight hair and is as white as a magnolia petal. Other than that, she looks like a young suburban housewife who has a part-time job at a preschool.

Though I don't think you'd really ever want Pam to take care of your toddlers, I've never seen her do anything extraordinarily cruel or vicious. But she's definitely convinced that vampires are better than humans, and she's very direct and doesn't mince words. I'm sure if Pam saw that some dire action was necessary for her well-being, she'd do it without missing any sleep. She seems to be an excellent second-in-command, and not overly ambitious. If she wants to have her own bailiwick, she keeps that desire very well concealed.

Chow is a whole different kettle of fish. I don't want to know Chow any better than I already do. I don't trust him, and I've never felt comfortable around him. Chow is Asian, a small-built but powerful vampire with longish black hair. He is no more than five foot seven, but every inch of visible skin (except his face) is covered with those intricate tattoos that are true art dyed into human skin. Pam says they are yakuza tattoos. Chow acts as Fangtasia's bartender some evenings, and on other nights he just sits around to let patrons approach him. (That's the whole purpose of vampire bars, to let regular humans feel they're walking on the wild side by being in the same room with the in-the-flesh undead. It's very lucrative, Bill told me.)

Pam was wearing a fluffy cream sweater and golden-brown knit pants, and Chow was in his usual vest and slacks. He seldom wore a shirt, so the Fangtasia patrons could get the full benefit of his body art.

I called Eric, and he came into the room slowly. He was visibly wary.

'Eric,' Pam said, when she saw him. Her voice was full of relief. 'You're well?' Her eyes were fixed on Eric anxiously. She didn't bow, but she sort of gave a deep nod.

'Master,' Chow said, and bowed.

I tried not to overinterpret what I was seeing and hearing, but I assumed that the different greetings signified the relationships among the three.

Eric looked uncertain. 'I know you,' he said, trying to make it sound more statement than question.

The two other vampires exchanged a glance. 'We work for you,' Pam said. 'We owe you fealty.'

I began to ease out of the room, because they'd want to talk about secret vampire stuff, I was sure. And if there was anything I didn't want to know, it was more secrets.

'Please don't go,' Eric said to me. His voice was frightened. I froze and looked behind me. Pam and Chow were staring over Eric's shoulders at me, and they had quite different expressions. Pam looked almost amused. Chow looked openly disapproving.

I tried not to look in Eric's eyes, so I could leave him with a clear conscience, but it just didn't work. He didn't want to be left alone with his two sidekicks. I blew lots of air out, puffing up my cheeks. Well, *dammit*. I trudged back to Eric's side, glaring at Pam the whole way.

There was another knock at the door, and Pam and Chow reacted in a dramatic way. They were both ready to fight in an instant, and vampires in that readiness are very, very scary. Their fangs run out, their hands arch like claws, and their bodies are on full alert. The air seems to crackle around them.

'Yes?' I said from right inside the door. I *had* to get a peephole installed.

'It's your brother,' Jason said brusquely. He didn't know how lucky he was that he hadn't just walked in.

Something had put Jason into a foul mood, and I wondered if there was anyone with him. I almost opened the door. But I hesitated. Finally, feeling like a traitor, I turned to Pam. I silently pointed down the hall to the back door, making an opening-and-closing gesture so she could not mistake what I meant. I made a circle in the air with my finger – *Come around the house, Pam* – and pointed at the front door.

Pam nodded and ran down the hall to the back of the house. I couldn't hear her feet on the floor. Amazing.

Eric moved away from the door. Chow got in front of him. I approved. This was exactly what an underling was supposed to do.

In less than a minute, I heard Jason bellow from maybe six inches away. I jumped away from the door, startled.

Pam said, 'Open up!'

I swung the door wide to see Jason locked in Pam's arms.

She was holding him off the ground with no effort, though he was flailing wildly and making it as hard as he could, God bless him.

'You're by yourself,' I said, relief being my big emotion.

'Of course, dammit! Why'd you set her on me? Let me down!'

'It's my brother, Pam,' I said. 'Please put him down.'

Pam set Jason down, and he spun around to look at her. 'Listen, woman! You don't just sneak up on a man like that! You're lucky I didn't slap you upside the head!'

Pam looked amused all over again, and even Jason looked embarrassed. He had the grace to smile. 'I guess that might be pretty hard,' he admitted, picking up the bags he'd dropped. Pam helped him. 'It's lucky I got the blood in the big plastic bottles,' he said. 'Otherwise, this lovely lady would have to go hungry.'

He smiled at Pam engagingly. Jason loves women. With Pam, Jason was in way over his head, but didn't have the sense to know it.

'Thanks. You need to go now,' I said abruptly. I took the plastic bags from his hands. He and Pam were still in an eye-lock. She was putting the whammy on him. 'Pam,' I said sharply. 'Pam, this is my brother.'

'I know,' she said calmly. 'Jason, did you have something to tell us?'

I'd forgotten that Jason had sounded like he was barely containing himself when he'd come to the door.

'Yes,' he said, hardly able to tear his eyes away from the vampire. But when he glanced at me, he caught sight of Chow, and his eyes widened. He had enough sense to fear Chow, at least. 'Sookie?' he said. 'Are you all right?' He took a step into the room, and I could see the adrenaline left over from the fright Pam had given begin to pump through his system again.

'Yes. Everything's all right. These are just friends of Eric's who came to check on him.'

'Well, they better go take those wanted posters down.'

That got everyone's full attention. Jason enjoyed that.

'There's posters up at Wal-Mart, and Grabbit Kwik, and the Bottle Barn, and just about everywhere else in town,' he said. 'They all say, "Have you seen this man?" and they go on to tell about him being kidnapped and his friends being so anxious, and the reward for a confirmed sighting is fifty thousand dollars.'

I didn't process this too well. I was mostly thinking, *Huh?*, when Pam got the point.

'They're hoping to sight him and catch him,' she said to Chow. 'It will work.'

'We should take care of it,' he said, nodding toward Jason.

'Don't you lay one hand on my brother,' I said. I moved between Jason and Chow, and my hands itched for a stake or hammer or anything at all that would keep this vamp from touching Jason.

Pam and Chow focused on me with that unswerving attention. I didn't find it flattering, as Jason had. I found it deadly. Jason opened his mouth to speak – I could feel the anger building in him, and the impulse to confront – but my hand clamped down on his wrist, and he grunted, and I said, 'Don't say a word.' For a miracle, he didn't. He seemed to sense that events were moving forward too rapidly and in a grave direction.

'You'll have to kill me, too,' I said.

Chow shrugged. 'Big threat.'

Pam didn't say anything. If it came to a choice between upholding vamp interests and being my buddy . . . well, I guessed we were just going to have to cancel our sleepover, and here I'd been planning on French-braiding her hair.

'What is this about?' Eric asked. His voice was considerably stronger. 'Explain . . . Pam.'

A minute went by while things hung in the balance. Then Pam turned to Eric, and she may have been slightly relieved that she didn't have to kill me right at the moment. 'Sookie and this man, her brother, have seen you,' she explained. 'They're human. They need the money. They will turn you in to the witches.'

'What witches?' Jason and I said simultaneously.

'Thank you, Eric, for getting us into this shit,' Jason muttered unfairly. 'And could you let go of my wrist, Sook? You're stronger than you look.'

I was stronger than I should be because I'd had vampire blood – most recently, Eric's. The effects would last around three more weeks, maybe longer. I knew this from past experience.

Unfortunately, I'd needed that extra strength at a low point in my life. The very vampire who was now draped in my former boyfriend's bathrobe had donated that blood when I was grievously wounded but had to keep going.

'Jason,' I said in a level voice – as though the vampires couldn't hear me – 'please watch yourself.' That was as close as I could come to telling Jason to be smart for once in his life. He was way too fond of walking on the wild side.

Very slowly and cautiously, as if an uncaged lion were in the room, Jason and I went to sit on the old couch to one side of the fireplace. That notched the situation down a couple of degrees. After a brief hesitation, Eric sat on the floor and pressed himself into my legs. Pam settled on the edge of the recliner, closest to the fireplace, but Chow chose to remain standing (within what I calculated was lunging distance) near Jason. The atmosphere became less tense, though not by any means relaxed – but still, this was an improvement over the moments before.

'Your brother must stay and hear this,' Pam said. 'No matter how much you don't want him to know. He needs to learn why he mustn't try to earn that money.'

Jason and I gave quick nods. I was hardly in a position to throw them out. Wait, I could! I could tell them all that their invitation to come in was rescinded, and whoosh, out the door they'd go, walking backward. I found myself smiling. Rescinding an invitation was extremely satisfying. I'd done it once before; I'd sent both Bill and Eric zooming out of my living room, and it had felt so good I'd rescinded the entrance invite of every vampire I knew. I could feel my smile fading as I thought more carefully.

If I gave way to this impulse, I'd have to stay in my house every night for the rest of my life, because they'd return at dusk the next day and the day after that and so on, until they got me, because I had their boss. I glowered at Chow. I was willing to blame this whole thing on him.

'Several night ago, we heard – at Fangtasia,' Pam explained for Jason's benefit, 'that a group of witches had arrived in Shreveport. A human told us, one who wants Chow. She didn't know why we were so interested in that information.'

That didn't sound too threatening to me. Jason shrugged. 'So?' he said. 'Geez, you all are vampires. What can a bunch of girls in black do to you?'

'Real witches can do plenty to vampires,' Pam said, with

remarkable restraint. 'The "girls in black" you're thinking of are only poseurs. Real witches can be women or men of any age. They are very formidable, very powerful. They control magical forces, and our existence itself is rooted in magic. This group seems to have some extra . . .' She paused, casting around for a word.

'Juice?' Jason suggested helpfully.

'Juice,' she agreed. 'We haven't discovered what makes them so strong.'

'What was their purpose in coming to Shreveport?' I asked.

'A good question,' Chow said approvingly. 'A much better question.'

I frowned at him. I didn't need his damn approval.

'They wanted – they want – to take over Eric's businesses,' Pam said. 'Witches want money as much as anyone, and they figure they can either take over the businesses, or make Eric pay them to leave him alone.'

'Protection money.' This was a familiar concept to a television viewer. 'But how could they force you into anything? You guys are so powerful.'

'You have no idea how many problems a business can develop if witches want a piece of it. When we met with them for the first time, their leaders – a sister and brother team – spelled it out. Hallow made it clear she could curse our labor, turn our alcoholic drinks bad, and cause patrons to trip on the dance floor and sue us, to say nothing of plumbing problems.' Pam threw up her hands in disgust. 'It would make every night a bad dream, and our revenues would plummet, maybe to the point that the Fangtasia would become worthless.'

Jason and I gave each other cautious glances. Naturally,

vampires were heavily into the bar business, since it was most lucrative at night, and they were up then. They'd dabbled in all-night dry cleaners, all-night restaurants, all-night movie theaters . . . but the bar business paid best. If Fangtasia closed, Eric's financial base would suffer a blow.

'So they want protection money,' Jason said. He'd watched the *Godfather* trilogy maybe fifty times. I thought about asking him if he wanted to sleep with the fishes, but Chow was looking antsy, so I refrained. We were both of us just a snick and a snee away from an unpleasant death, and I knew it was no time for humor, especially humor that so nearly wasn't.

'So how did Eric end up running down the road at night without a shirt or shoes?' I asked, thinking it was time to get down to brass tacks.

Much exchanging of glances between the two subordinates. I looked down at Eric, pressed up against my legs. He seemed to be as interested in the answer as we were. His hand firmly circled my ankle. I felt like a large security blanket.

Chow decided to take a narrative turn. 'We told them we would discuss their threat. But last night, when we went to work, one of the lesser witches was waiting at Fangtasia with an alternative proposal.' He looked a little uncomfortable. 'During our initial meeting, the head of the coven, Hallow, decided she, uh, lusted after Eric. Such a coupling is very frowned upon among witches, you understand, since we are dead and witchcraft is supposed to be so . . . organic.' Chow spat the word out like it was something stuck to his shoe. 'Of course, most witches would never do what this coven was attempting. These are all people drawn to the power itself, rather than to the religion behind it.'

This was interesting, but I wanted to hear the rest of the story. So did Jason, who made a 'hurry along' gesture with his hand. With a little shake to himself, as if to rouse himself from his thoughts, Chow went on. 'This head witch, this Hallow, told Eric, through her subordinate, that if he would entertain her for seven nights, she would only demand a fifth of his business, rather than a half.'

'You must have some kind of reputation,' my brother said to Eric, his voice full of honest awe. Eric was not entirely successful at hiding his pleased expression. He was glad to hear he was such a Romeo. There was a slight difference in the way he looked up at me in the next moment, and I had a feeling of horrid inevitability – like when you see your car begin to roll downhill (though you're sure you left it in park), and you know there's no way you can catch up to it and put on the brakes, no matter how much you want to. That car is gonna crash.

'Though some of us thought he might be wise to agree, our master balked,' Chow said, shooting 'our master' a less than loving glance. 'And our master saw fit to refuse in such insulting terms that Hallow cursed him.'

Eric looked embarrassed.

'Why on earth would you turn down a deal like that?' Jason asked, honestly puzzled.

'I don't remember,' Eric said, moving fractionally closer to my legs. Fractionally was all the closer he could get. He looked relaxed, but I knew he wasn't. I could feel the tension in his body. 'I didn't know my name until this woman, Sookie, told me it.'

'And how did you come to be out in the country?'

'I don't know that either.'

'He just vanished from where he was,' Pam said. 'We

were sitting in the office with the young witch, and Chow and I were arguing with Eric about his refusal. And then we weren't.'

'Ring any bells, Eric?' I asked. I'd caught myself reaching out to stroke his hair, like I would a dog that was huddling close to me.

The vampire looked puzzled. Though Eric's English was excellent, every now and then an idiom would faze him.

'Do you recall anything about this?' I said, more plainly. 'Have any memories of it?'

'I was born the moment I was running down the road in the dark and the cold,' he said. 'Until you took me in, I was a void.'

Put that way, it sounded terrifying.

'This just doesn't track,' I said. 'This wouldn't just happen out of the blue, with no warning.'

Pam didn't look offended, but Chow tried to make the effort.

'You two did something, didn't you? You messed up. What did you do?' Both Eric's arms wrapped around my legs, so I was pinned in place. I suppressed a little ripple of panic. He was just insecure.

'Chow lost his temper with the witch,' Pam said, after a significant pause.

I closed my eyes. Even Jason seemed to grasp what Pam was saying, because his eyes got bigger. Eric turned his face to rub his cheek along my thigh. I wondered what he was making of this.

'And the minute she was attacked, Eric vanished?' I asked.

Pam nodded.

'So she was booby-trapped with a spell.'

'Apparently,' Chow said. 'Though I had never heard of such a thing, and I can't be held responsible.' His glare dared me to say anything.

I turned to Jason and rolled my eyes. Dealing with Chow's blunder was not my responsibility. I was pretty sure that if the whole story was told to the queen of Louisiana, Eric's overlord, she might have a few things to say to Chow about the incident.

There was a little silence, during which Jason got up to put another log on the fire. 'You've been in Merlotte's before, haven't you?' he asked the vampires. 'Where Sookie works?'

Eric shrugged; he didn't remember. Pam said, 'I have, but not Eric.' She looked at me to confirm, and after some thought, I nodded.

'So no one's going to instantly associate Eric with Sookie.' Jason dropped that observation casually, but he was looking very pleased and almost smug.

'No,' Pam said slowly. 'Maybe not.'

There was definitely something I ought to be worrying about right now, but I couldn't quite see the shape of it.

'So you're clear as far as Bon Temps goes,' Jason continued. 'I doubt if anyone saw him out last night, except Sookie, and I'm damned if I know why he ended up on that particular road.'

My brother had made a second excellent point. He was really operating on all his batteries tonight.

'But lots of people from here do drive to Shreveport to go to that bar, Fangtasia. I've been myself,' Jason said. This was news to me, and I gave him a narrow-eyed glare. He shrugged and looked just a tad embarrassed. 'So what's gonna happen when someone tries to claim the reward? When they call the number on the poster?'

Chow decided to contribute more to the conversation. 'Of course, the "close friend" who answers will come right away to talk to the informant firsthand. If the caller can convince the "close friend" that he saw Eric after the whore witch worked her spell on him, the witches will begin looking in a specific area. They're sure to find him. They'll try to contact the local witches, too, get them working on it.'

'No witches in Bon Temps,' Jason said, looking amazed that Chow would even suggest the idea. There my brother went again, making assumptions.

'Oh, I'll bet there are,' I said. 'Why not? Remember what I told you?' Though I'd been thinking of Weres and shifters when I'd warned him there were things in the world he wouldn't want to see.

My poor brother was getting overloaded with information this evening. 'Why not?' he repeated weakly. 'Who would they be?'

'Some women, some men,' Pam said, dusting her hands together as if she were talking about some infectious pest. 'They are like everyone else who has a secret life – most of them are quite pleasant, fairly harmless.' Though Pam didn't sound too positive when she said that. 'But the bad ones tend to contaminate the good.'

'However,' Chow said, staring thoughtfully at Pam, 'this is such a backwater that there may well be very few witches in the area. Not all of them are in covens, and getting an unattached witch to cooperate will be very difficult for Hallow and her followers.'

'Why can't the Shreveport witches just cast a spell to find Eric?' I asked.

'They can't find anything of his to use to cast such a spell,' Pam said, and she sounded as if she knew what she was talking about. 'They can't get into his daytime resting place to find a hair or clothes that bear his scent. And there's no one around who's got Eric's blood in her.'

Ah-oh. Eric and I looked at each other very briefly. There was me; and I was hoping devoutly that no one knew that but Eric.

'Besides,' Chow said, shifting from foot to foot, 'in my opinion, since we are dead, such things would not work to cast a spell.'

Pam's eyes latched on to Chow's. They were exchanging ideas again, and I didn't like it. Eric, the cause of all this message swapping, was looking back and forth between his two fellow vamps. Even to me he looked clueless.

Pam turned to me. 'Eric should stay here, where he is. Moving him will expose him to more danger. With him out of the way and in safety, we can take countermeasures against the witches.'

'Going to the mattresses,' Jason muttered in my ear, still stuck on the *Godfather* terminology.

Now that Pam had said it out loud, I could see clearly why I should have become concerned when Jason began emphasizing how impossible it was that anyone should associate Eric with me. No one would believe that a vampire of Eric's power and importance would be parked with a human barmaid.

My amnesiac guest looked bewildered. I leaned forward, gave in briefly to my impulse to stroke his hair, and then I held my hands over his ears. He permitted this, even putting his own hands on top of mine. I was going to pretend he couldn't hear what I was going to say.

'Listen, Chow, Pam. This is the worst idea of all time. I'll tell you why.' I could hardly get the words out fast enough, emphatically enough. 'How am I supposed to protect him? You know how this will end! I'll get beaten up. Or maybe even killed.'

Pam and Chow looked at me with twin blank expressions. They might as well have said, 'Your point being?'

'If my sister does this,' Jason said, disregarding me completely, 'she deserves to get paid for it.'

There was what you call a pregnant silence. I gaped at him.

Simultaneously, Pam and Chow nodded.

'At least as much as an informer would get if he called the phone number on the poster,' Jason said, his bright blue eyes going from one pale face to another. 'Fifty thousand.'

'Jason!' I finally found my voice, and I clamped my hands down even tighter over Eric's ears. I was embarrassed and humiliated, without being able to figure out exactly why. For one thing, my brother was arranging my business as though it were his.

'Ten,' Chow said.

'Forty-five,' Jason countered.

'Twenty.'

'Thirty-five.'

'Done.'

'Sookie, I'll bring you my shotgun,' Jason said.

Chapter 3

'How did this happen?' I asked the fire, when they were all gone.

All except for the big Viking vampire I was supposed to preserve and protect.

I was sitting on the rug in front of the fire. I'd just thrown in another piece of wood, and the flames were really lovely. I needed to think about something pleasant and comforting.

I saw a big bare foot out of the corner of my eye. Eric sank down to join me on the hearth rug. 'I think this happened because you have a greedy brother, and because you are the kind of woman who would stop for me even though she was afraid,' Eric said accurately.

'How are you feeling about all this?' I never would have asked the compos mentis Eric this question, but he still seemed so different, maybe not the completely terrified mess he'd been the night before, but still very un-Eric. 'I mean – it's like you're a package that they put in a storage locker, me being the locker.'

'I am glad they are afraid enough of me to take good care of me.'

'Huh,' I said intelligently. Not the answer I'd expected.

'I must be a frightening person, when I am myself. Or do I inspire so much loyalty through my good works and kind ways?'

I sniggered.

'I thought not.'

'You're okay,' I said reassuringly, though come to think of it, Eric didn't look like he needed much reassurance. However, now I was responsible for him. 'Aren't your feet cold?'

'No,' he said. But now I was in the business of taking care of Eric, who *so* didn't need taking care of. And I was being paid a staggering amount of money to do just that, I reminded myself sternly. I got the old quilt from the back of the couch and covered his legs and feet in green, blue, and yellow squares. I collapsed back onto the rug beside him.

'That's truly hideous,' Eric said.

'That's what Bill said.' I rolled over on my stomach and caught myself smiling.

'Where is this Bill?'

'He's in Peru.'

'Did he tell you he was going?'

'Yes.'

'Am I to assume that your relationship with him has waned?'

That was a pretty nice way to put it. 'We've been on the outs. It's beginning to look permanent,' I said, my voice even.

He was on his stomach beside me now, propped up on his elbows so we could talk. He was a little closer than I was comfortable with, but I didn't want to make a big issue out of scooting over. He half turned to toss the quilt over both of us.

'Tell me about him,' Eric said unexpectedly. He and Pam and Chow had all had a glass of TrueBlood before the other vampires left, and he was looking pinker.

'You know Bill,' I told him. 'He's worked for you for quite a while. I guess you can't remember, but Bill's – well, he's kind of cool and calm, and he's really protective, and he can't seem to get some things through his head.' I never thought I'd be rehashing my relationship with Bill with Eric, of all people.

'He loves you?'

I sighed, and my eyes watered, as they so often did when I thought of Bill – Weeping Willa, that was me. 'Well, he said he did,' I muttered dismally. 'But then when this vampire ho contacted him somehow, he went a-running.' For all I knew, she'd emailed him. 'He'd had an affair with her before, and she turned out to be his, I don't know what you call 'em, the one who turned him into a vampire. Brought him over, he said. So Bill took back up with her. He says he had to. And then he found out' – I looked sideways at Eric with a significant raise of the eyebrows, and Eric looked fascinated – 'that she was just trying to lure him over to the even-darker side.'

'Pardon?'

'She was trying to get him to come over to another vampire group in Mississippi and bring with him the really valuable computer data base he'd put together for your people, the Louisiana vamps,' I said, simplifying a little bit for the sake of brevity.

'What happened?'

This was as much fun as talking to Arlene. Maybe even

more, because I'd never been able to tell her the whole story. 'Well, Lorena, that's her name, she *tortured* him,' I said, and Eric's eyes widened. 'Can you believe that? She could torture someone she'd made love with? Someone she'd lived with for years?' Eric shook his head disbelievingly. 'Anyway, you told me to go to Jackson and find him, and I sort of picked up clues at this nightclub for Supes only.' Eric nodded. Evidently, I didn't have to explain that Supes meant supernatural beings. 'Its real name is Josephine's, but the Weres call it Club Dead. You told me to go there with this really nice Were who owed you a big favor, and I stayed at his place.' Alcide Herveaux still figured in my daydreams. 'But I ended up getting hurt pretty bad,' I concluded. Hurt pretty bad, as always.

'How?'

'I got staked, believe it or not.'

Eric looked properly impressed. 'Is there a scar?'

'Yeah, even though—' And here I stopped dead.

He gave every indication he was hanging on my words. 'What?'

'You got one of the Jackson vampires to work on the wound, so I'd survive for sure . . . and then you gave me blood to heal me quick, so I could look for Bill at daylight.' Remembering how Eric had given me blood made my cheeks turn red, and I could only hope Eric would attribute my flush to the heat of the fire.

'And you saved Bill?' he said, moving beyond that touchy part.

'Yes, I did,' I said proudly. 'I saved his ass.' I rolled onto my back and looked up at him. Gee, it was nice to have someone to talk to. I pulled up my T-shirt and inclined partially on my side to show Eric the scar, and he looked impressed. He touched the shiny area with a fingertip and shook his head. I rearranged myself.

'And what happened to the vampire ho?' he asked

I eyed him suspiciously, but he didn't seem to be making fun of me. 'Well,' I said, 'um, actually, I kind of . . . She came in while I was getting Bill untied, and she attacked me, and I kind of . . . killed her.'

Eric looked at me intently. I couldn't read his expression. 'Had you ever killed anyone before?' he asked.

'Of course not!' I said indignantly. 'Well, I did hurt a guy who was trying to kill me, but he didn't die. No, I'm a *human*. I don't have to kill anyone to live.'

'But humans kill other humans all the time. And they don't even need to eat them or drink their blood.'

'Not *all* humans.'

'True enough,' he said. 'We vampires are all murderers.'

'But in a way, you're like lions.'

Eric looked astonished. 'Lions?' he said weakly.

'Lions all kill stuff.' At the moment, this idea seemed like an inspiration. 'So you're predators, like lions and raptors. But you use what you kill. You have to kill to eat.'

'The catch in that comforting theory being that we look almost exactly like you. And we used to be you. And we can love you, as well as feed off you. You could hardly say the lion wanted to caress the antelope.'

Suddenly there was something in the air that hadn't been there the moment before. I felt a little like an antelope that was being stalked – by a lion that was a deviant.

I'd felt more comfortable when I was taking care of a terrified victim.

'Eric,' I said, very cautiously, 'you know you're my guest here. And you know if I tell you to leave, which I will if you're not straight with me, you'll be standing out in the middle of a field somewhere in a bathrobe that's too short for you.'

'Have I said something to make you uncomfortable?' He was (apparently) completely contrite, blue eyes blazing with sincerity. 'I'm sorry. I was just trying to continue your train of thought. Do you have some more TrueBlood? What clothes did Jason get for me? Your brother is a very clever man.' He didn't sound a hundred percent admiring when he told me this. I didn't blame him. Jason's cleverness might cost him thirty-five thousand dollars. I got up to fetch the Wal-Mart bag, hoping that Eric liked his new Louisiana Tech sweatshirt and cheap jeans.

I turned in about midnight, leaving Eric absorbed in my tapes of the first season of *Buffy the Vampire Slayer*. (Though welcome, these were actually a gag gift from Tara.) Eric thought the show was a hoot, especially the way the vampires' foreheads bulged out when they got blood-lusty. From time to time, I could hear Eric laughing all the way back in my room. But the sound didn't bother me. I found it reassuring to hear someone else in the house.

It took me a little longer than usual to fall asleep, because I was thinking over the things that had happened that day. Eric was in the witness protection program, in a way, and I was providing the safe house. No one in the world – well, except for Jason, Pam, and Chow – knew where the sheriff of Area Five actually was at this moment.

Which was, sliding into my bed.

I didn't want to open my eyes and quarrel with him. I was just at that cusp between waking and dreaming. When he'd climbed in the night before, Eric had been so afraid that I'd felt quite maternal, comfortable in holding his hand to reassure him. Tonight it didn't seem so, well, neutral, having him in the bed with me.

'Cold?' I murmured, as he huddled close.

'Um-hum,' he whispered. I was on my back, so comfortable I could not contemplate moving. He was on his side facing me, and he put an arm across my waist. But he didn't move another inch, and he relaxed completely. After a moment's tension, I did, too, and then I was dead to the world.

The next thing I knew, it was morning and the phone was ringing. Of course, I was by myself in bed, and through my open doorway I could see across the hall into the smaller bedroom. The closet door was open, as he'd had to leave it when dawn came and he'd lowered himself into the light-tight hole.

It was bright and warmer today, up in the forties and heading for the fifties. I felt much more cheerful than I'd felt upon waking the day before. I knew what was happening now; or at least I knew more or less what I was supposed to do, how the next few days would go. Or I thought I did. When I answered the phone, I discovered that I was way off.

'Where's your brother?' yelled Jason's boss, Shirley Hennessey. You thought a man named Shirley was funny only until you were face-to-face with the real deal, at which point you decided it would really be better to keep your amusement to yourself.

'How would I know?' I said reasonably. 'Probably slept over at some woman's place.' Shirley, who was universally known as Catfish, had never, ever called here before to track Jason down. In fact, I'd be surprised if he'd ever had to call anywhere. One thing Jason was good about was showing up at work on time and at least going through the motions until that time was up. In fact, Jason was pretty good at his job, which I'd never fully understood. It seemed to involve parking his fancy truck at the parish road department, getting into another truck with the Renard parish logo on the door, and driving around telling various road crews what to do. It also seemed to demand that he get out of the truck to stand with other men as they all stared into big holes in or near the road.

Catfish was knocked off balance by my frankness. 'Sookie, you shouldn't say that kind of thing,' he said, quite shocked at a single woman admitting she knew her brother wasn't a virgin.

'Are you telling me that Jason hasn't shown up at work? And you've called his house?'

'Yes and yes,' said Catfish, who in most respects was no fool. 'I even sent Dago out to his place.' Dago (road crew members had to have nicknames) was Antonio Guglielmi, who had never been farther from Louisiana than Mississippi. I was pretty sure the same could be said for his parents, and possibly his grandparents, though there was rumor they'd once been to Branson to take in the shows.

'Was his truck out there?' I was beginning to have that cold creeping feeling.

'Yes,' Catfish said. 'It was parked in front of his house, keys inside. Door hanging open.'

'The truck door or the house door?'

'What?'

'Hanging open. Which door?'

'Oh, the truck.'

'This is bad, Catfish,' I said. I was tingling all over with alarm.

'When you seen him last?'

'Just last night. He was over here visiting with me, and he left about . . . oh, let's see . . . it must have been nine-thirty or ten.'

'He have anybody with him?'

'No.' He hadn't brought anybody with him, so that was pretty much the truth.

'You think I oughta call the sheriff?' Catfish asked.

I ran a hand over my face. I wasn't ready for that yet, no matter how off the situation seemed. 'Let's give it another hour,' I suggested. 'If he hasn't dragged into work in an hour, you let me know. If he does come in, you make him call me. I guess it's me ought to tell the sheriff, if it comes to that.'

I hung up after Catfish had repeated everything he'd said several times, just because he hated to hang up and go back to worrying. No, I can't read minds over the telephone line, but I could read it in his voice. I've known Catfish Hennessey for many years. He was a buddy of my father's.

I carried the cordless phone into the bathroom with me while I took a shower to wake up. I didn't wash my hair, just in case I had to go outside right away. I got dressed, made some coffee, and braided my hair in one long braid. All the time while I performed these tasks, I was thinking, which is something that's hard for me to do when I'm sitting still.

I came up with these scenarios.

One. (This was my favorite.) Somewhere between my house and his house, my brother had met up with a woman and fallen in love so instantly and completely that he had abandoned his habit of years and forgotten all about work.

At this moment, they were in a bed somewhere, having great sex.

Two. The witches, or whatever the hell they were, had somehow found out that Jason knew where Eric was, and they'd abducted him to force the information from him. (I made a mental note to learn more about witches.) How long could Jason keep the secret of Eric's location? My brother had lots of attitude, but he actually is a brave man – or maybe stubborn is a little more accurate. He wouldn't talk easily. Maybe a witch could spell him into talking? If the witches had him, he might be dead already, since they'd had him for hours. And if he'd talked, I was in danger and Eric was doomed. They could be coming at any minute, since witches are not bound by darkness. Eric was dead for the day, defenseless. This was definitely the worst-case scenario.

Three. Jason had returned to Shreveport with Pam and Chow. Maybe they'd decided to pay him some up-front money, or maybe Jason just wanted to visit Fangtasia because it was a popular nightspot. Once there, he could have been seduced by some vamp girl and stayed up all night with her, since Jason was like Eric in that women really, really took a shine to him. If she'd taken a little too much blood, Jason could be sleeping it off. I guess number three was really a variation on number one.

If Pam and Chow knew where Jason was but hadn't phoned before they died for the day, I was real mad. My gut instinct was to go get the hatchet and start chopping some stakes.

Then I remembered what I was trying so hard to forget: how it had felt when the stake pushed into Lorena's body, the expression on her face when she'd realized her long,

long life was over. I shoved that thought away as hard as I could. You didn't kill someone (even an evil vampire) without it affecting you sooner or later: at least not unless you were a complete sociopath, which I wasn't.

Lorena would have killed me without blinking. In fact, she would have positively enjoyed it. But then, she was a vampire, and Bill never tired of telling me that vampires were different; that though they retained their human appearance (more or less), their internal functions and their personalities underwent a radical change. I believed him and took his warnings to heart, for the most part. It was just that they looked so human; it was so very easy to attribute normal human reactions and feelings to them.

The frustrating thing was, Chow and Pam wouldn't be up until dark, and I didn't know who – or what – I'd raise if I called Fangtasia during the day. I didn't think the two lived at the club. I'd gotten the impression that Pam and Chow shared a house . . . or a mausoleum . . . somewhere in Shreveport.

I was fairly sure that human employees came into the club during the day to clean, but of course a human wouldn't (couldn't) tell me anything about vampire affairs. Humans who worked for vampires learned pretty quick to keep their mouths shut, as I could attest.

On the other hand, if I went to the club I'd have a chance to talk to *someone* face-to-face. I'd have a chance to read a human mind. I couldn't read vampire minds, which had led to my initial attraction to Bill. Imagine the relief of silence after a lifetime of elevator music. (Now, why couldn't I hear vampire thoughts? Here's my big theory about that. I'm about as scientific as a Saltine, but I have read about neurons, which fire in your brain, right? When you're thinking? Since it's magic that animates vampires, not normal life force, their brains don't fire. So, nothing for me to pick up – except about once every three months, I'd get a flash from a vampire. And I took great care to conceal that, because that was a sure way to court instant death.)

Oddly enough, the only vampire I'd ever 'heard' twice was – you guessed it – Eric.

I'd been enjoying Eric's recent company so much for the same reason I'd enjoyed Bill's, quite apart from the romantic component I'd had with Bill. Even Arlene had a tendency to stop listening to me when I was talking, if she thought of something more interesting, like her children's grades or cute things they'd said. But with Eric, he could be thinking about his car needing new windshield wipers while I was pouring my heart out, and I was none the wiser.

The hour I'd asked Catfish to give me was almost up, and all my constructive thought had dwindled into the same murky maundering I'd gone through several times. Blah blah blah. This is what happens when you talk to yourself a lot.

Okay, action time.

The phone rang right at the hour, and Catfish admitted he had no news. No one had heard from Jason or seen him; but on the other hand, Dago hadn't seen anything suspicious at Jason's place except the truck's open door.

I was still reluctant to call the sheriff, but I didn't see that I had much choice. At this point, it would seem peculiar to skip calling him.

I expected a lot of hubbub and alarm, but what I got was even worse: I got benevolent indifference. Sheriff Bud Dearborn actually laughed.

'You callin' me because your tomcat of a brother is missing a day of work? Sookie Stackhouse, I'm surprised at you.' Bud Dearborn had a slow voice and the mashed-in face of a Pekinese, and it was all too easy to picture him snuffling into the phone.

'He never misses work, and his truck is at his house. The door was open,' I said.

He did grasp that significance, because Bud Dearborn is a man who knows how to appreciate a fine pickup.

'That does sound a little funny, but still, Jason is way over twenty-one and he has a reputation for . . .' *(Drilling anything that stands still*, I thought.) '. . . being real popular with the ladies,' Bud concluded carefully. 'I bet he's all shacked up with someone new, and he'll be real sorry to have caused you any worry. You call me back if you haven't heard from him by tomorrow afternoon, you hear?'

'Right,' I said in my most frozen voice.

'Now, Sookie, don't you go getting all mad at me, I'm just telling you what any lawman would tell you,' he said.

I thought, *Any lawman with lead in his butt.* But I didn't say it out loud. Bud was what I had to work with, and I had to stay on his good side, as much as possible.

I muttered something that was vaguely polite and got off the phone. After reporting back to Catfish, I decided my only course of action was to go to Shreveport. I started to call Arlene, but I remembered she'd have the kids at home since it was still the school holiday. I thought of calling Sam, but I figured he might feel like he ought to do something, and I couldn't figure out what that would be. I just wanted to share my worries with someone. I knew that wasn't right. No one could help me, but me. Having made up my mind to be brave and independent, I almost phoned

Alcide Herveaux, who is a well-to-do and hardworking guy based in Shreveport. Alcide's dad runs a surveying firm that contracts for jobs in three states, and Alcide travels a lot among the various offices. I'd mentioned him the night before to Eric; Eric had sent Alcide to Jackson with me. But Alcide and I had some man-woman issues that were still unresolved, and it would be cheating to call him when I only wanted help he couldn't give. At least, that was how I felt.

I was scared to leave the house in case there might be news of Jason, but since the sheriff wasn't looking for him, I hardly thought there would be any word soon.

Before I left, I made sure I'd arranged the closet in the smaller bedroom so that it looked natural. It would be a little harder for Eric to get out when the sun went down, but it wouldn't be extremely difficult. Leaving him a note would be a dead giveaway if someone broke in, and he was too smart to answer the phone if I called just after dark had fallen. But he was so discombobulated by his amnesia, he might be scared to wake all by himself with no explanation of my absence, I thought.

I had a brainwave. Grabbing a little square piece of paper from last year's Word of the Day calendar ('enthrallment'), *I wrote: Jason, if you should happen to drop by, call me! I am very worried about you. No one knows where you are. I'll be back this afternoon or evening. I'm going to drop by your house, and then I'll check to see if you went to Shreveport. Then, back here. Love, Sookie.* I got some tape and stuck the note to the refrigerator, just where a sister might expect her brother to head if he stopped by.

There. Eric was plenty smart enough to read between the lines. And yet every word of it was feasible, so if anyone did break in to search the house, they'd think I was taking a smart precaution.

But still, I was frightened of leaving the sleeping Eric so vulnerable. What if the witches came looking?

But why should they?

If they could have tracked Eric, they'd have been here by now, right? At least, that was the way I was reasoning. I thought of calling someone like Terry Bellefleur, who was plenty tough, to come sit in my house – I could use waiting on a call about Jason as my pretext – but it wasn't right to endanger anyone else in Eric's defense.

I called all the hospitals in the area, feeling all the while that the sheriff should be doing this little job for me. The hospitals knew the name of everyone admitted, and none of them was Jason. I called the highway patrol to ask about accidents the night before and found there had been none in the vicinity. I called a few women Jason had dated, and I received a lot of negative responses, some of them obscene.

I thought I'd covered all the bases. I was ready to go to Jason's house, and I remember I was feeling pretty proud of myself as I drove north on Hummingbird Road and then took a left onto the highway. As I headed west to the house where I'd spent my first seven years, I drove past Merlotte's to my right and then past the main turnoff into Bon Temps. I negotiated the left turn and I could see our old home, sure enough with Jason's pickup parked in front of it. There was another pickup, equally shiny, parked about twenty feet away from Jason's.

When I got out of my car, a very black man was examining the ground around the truck. I was surprised to discover that the second pickup belonged to Alcee Beck, the only African-American detective on the parish force. Alcee's presence was both reassuring and disturbing.

'Miss Stackhouse,' he said gravely. Alcee Beck was wearing a jacket and slacks and heavy scuffed boots. The boots didn't go with the rest of his clothes, and I was willing to bet he kept them in his truck for when he had to go tromping around out in the country where the ground was less than dry. Alcee (whose name was pronounced Al-SAY) was also a strong broadcaster, and I could receive his thoughts clearly when I let down my shields to listen.

I learned in short order that Alcee Beck wasn't happy to see me, didn't like me, and did think something hinky had happened to Jason. Detective Beck didn't care for Jason, but he was actually scared of me. He thought I was a deeply creepy person, and he avoided me as much as possible.

Which was okay by me, frankly.

I knew more about Alcee Beck than I was comfortable knowing, and what I knew about Alcee was really unpleasant. He was brutal to uncooperative prisoners, though he adored his wife and daughter. He was lining his own pockets whenever he got a chance, and he made sure the chances came along pretty frequently. Alcee Beck confined this practice to the African-American community, operating on the theory that they'd never report him to the other white law enforcement personnel, and so far he'd been right.

See what I mean about not wanting to know things I heard? This was a lot different from finding out that Arlene really didn't think Charlsie's husband was good enough for Charlsie, or that Hoyt Fortenberry had dented a car in the parking lot and hadn't told the owner.

And before you ask me what I do about stuff like that, I'll tell you. I don't do squat. I've found out the hard way that it almost never works out if I try to intervene. What happens is no one is happier, and my little freakishness is brought to everyone's attention, and no one is comfortable around me for a month. I've got more secrets than Fort Knox has money. And those secrets are staying locked up just as tight.

I'll admit that most of those little facts I accumulated didn't make much difference in the grand scheme of things, whereas Alcee's misbehavior actually led to human misery. But so far I hadn't seen a single way to stop Alcee. He was very clever about keeping his activities under control and hidden from anyone with the power to intervene. And I wasn't too awful sure that Bud Dearborn *didn't* know.

'Detective Beck,' I said. 'Are you looking for Jason?'

'The sheriff asked me to come by and see if I could find anything out of order.'

'And have you found anything?'

'No, ma'am, I haven't.'

'Jason's boss told you the door to his truck was open?'

'I closed it so the battery wouldn't run down. I was careful not to touch anything, of coursc. But I'm sure your brother will show back up any time now, and he'll be unhappy if we mess with his stuff for no reason.'

'I have a key to his house, and I'm going to ask you to go in there with me.'

'Do you suspect anything happened to your brother in his house?' Alcee Beck was being so careful to spell everything out that I wondered if he had a tape recorder rolling away in his pocket.

'Could be. He doesn't normally miss work. In fact, he never misses work. And I always know where he is. He's real good about letting me know.'

'He'd tell you if he was running off with a woman? Most brothers wouldn't do that, Miss Stackhouse.'

'He'd tell me, or he'd tell Catfish.'

Alcee Beck did his best to keep his skeptical look on his dark face, but it didn't sit there easily.

The house was still locked. I picked out the right key from the ones on my ring, and we went inside. I didn't have the feeling of homecoming when I entered, the feeling I used to have as a kid. I'd lived in Gran's house so much longer than this little place. The minute Jason had turned twenty, he'd moved over here full-time, and though I'd dropped in, I'd probably spent less than twenty-four hours total in this house in the last eight years.

Glancing around me, I realized that my brother really hadn't changed the house much in all that time. It was a small ranch-style house with small rooms, but of course it was a lot younger than Gran's house – my house – and a lot more heating- and cooling-efficient. My father had done most of the work on it, and he was a good builder.

The small living room was still filled with the maple furniture my mother had picked out at the discount furniture store, and its upholstery (cream with green and blue flowers that had never been seen in nature) was still bright, more's the pity. It had taken me a few years to realize that my mother, while a clever woman in some respects, had had no taste whatsoever. Jason had never come to that realization. He'd replaced the curtains when they frayed and faded, and he'd gotten a new rug to cover the most worn spots on the ancient blue carpet. The appliances were all new, and he'd worked hard on updating the bathroom. But my parents, if they could have entered their home, would have felt quite comfortable.

It was a shock to realize they'd been dead for nearly twenty years.

While I stood close to the doorway, praying I wouldn't see bloodstains, Alcee Beck prowled through the house, which certainly seemed orderly. After a second's indecision, I decided to follow him. There wasn't much to see; like I say, it's a small house. Three bedrooms (two of them quite cramped), the living room, a kitchen, one bathroom, a fair-sized family room, and a small dining room: a house that could be duplicated any number of times in any town in America.

The house was quite tidy. Jason had never lived like a pig, though sometimes he acted like one. Even the king-size bed that almost filled the biggest bedroom was more-or-less pulled straight, though I could see the sheets were black and shiny. They were supposed to look like silk, but I was sure they were some artificial blend. Too slithery for me; I liked percale.

'No evidence of any struggle,' the detective pointed out.

'While I'm here, I'm just going to get something,' I told him, going over to the gun cabinet that had been my dad's. It was locked, so I checked my key ring again. Yes, I had a key for that, too, and I remembered some long story Jason had told me about why I needed one – in case he was out hunting and he needed another rifle, or something. As if I'd drop everything and run to fetch another rifle for him!

Well, I might, if I wasn't due at work, or something.

All Jason's rifles, and my father's, were in the gun cabinet – all the requisite ammunition, too.

'All present?' The detective was shifting around impatiently in the doorway to the dining room.

'Yes. I'm just going to take one of them home with me.'

'You expecting trouble at your place?' Beck looked interested for the first time.

'If Jason is gone, who knows what it means?' I said, hoping that was ambiguous enough. Beck had a very low opinion of my intelligence, anyway, despite the fact that he feared me. Jason had said he would bring me the shotgun, and I knew I would feel the better for having it. So I got out the Benelli and found its shells. Jason had very carefully taught me how to load and fire the shotgun, which was his pride and joy. There were two different boxes of shells.

'Which?' I asked Detective Beck.

'Wow, a Benelli.' He took time out to be impressed with the gun. 'Twelve-gauge, huh? Me, I'd take the turkey loads,' he advised. 'Those target loads don't have as much stopping power.'

I popped the box he indicated into my pocket.

I carried the shotgun out to my car, Beck trailing on my heels.

'You have to lock the shotgun in your trunk and the shells in the car,' the detective informed me. I did exactly what he said, even putting the shells in the glove compartment, and then I turned to face him. He would be glad to be out of my sight, and I didn't think he would look for Jason with any enthusiasm.

'Did you check around back?' I asked.

'I had just gotten here when you pulled up.'

I jerked my head in the direction of the pond behind the house, and we circled around to the rear. My brother, aided by Hoyt Fortenberry, had put in a large deck outside the back door maybe two years ago. He'd arranged some nice outdoor furniture he'd gotten on end-of-season sale at

Wal-Mart. Jason had even put an ashtray on the wrought-iron table for his friends who went outside to smoke. Someone had used it. Hoyt smoked, I recalled. There was nothing else interesting on the deck.

The ground sloped down from the deck to the pond. While Alcee Beck checked the back door, I looked down to the pier my father had built, and I thought I could see a smear on the wood. Something in me crumpled at the sight, and I must have made a noise. Alcee came to stand by me, and I said, 'Look at the pier.'

He went on point, just like a setter. He said, 'Stay where you are,' in an unmistakably official voice. He moved carefully, looking down at the ground around his feet before he took each step. I felt like an hour passed before Alcee finally reached the pier. He squatted down on the sun-bleached boards to take a close look. He focused a little to the right of the smear, evaluating something I couldn't see, something I couldn't even make out in his mind. But then he wondered what kind of work boots my brother wore; that came in clear.

'Caterpillars,' I called. The fear built up in me till I felt I was vibrating with the intensity of it. Jason was all I had.

And I realized I'd made a mistake I hadn't done in years: I'd answered a question before it had been asked out loud. I clapped a hand over my mouth and saw the whites of Beck's eyes. He wanted away from me. And he was thinking maybe Jason was in the pond, dead. He was speculating that Jason had fallen and knocked his head against the pier, and then slid into the water. But there was a puzzling print . . .

'When can you search the pond?' I called.

He turned to look at me, terror on his face. I hadn't had

anyone look at me like that in years. I had him spooked, and I hadn't wanted to have that effect on him.

'The blood is on the dock,' I pointed out, trying to improve matters. Providing a reasonable explanation was second nature. 'I'm scared Jason went into the water.'

Beck seemed to settle down a little after that. He turned his eyes back to the water. My father had chosen the site for the house to include the pond. He'd told me when I was little that the pond was very deep and fed by a tiny stream. The area around two-thirds of the pond was mowed and maintained as yard; but the farthest edge of it was left thickly wooded, and Jason enjoyed sitting on the deck in the late evening with binoculars, watching critters come to drink.

There were fish in the pond. He kept it stocked. My stomach lurched.

Finally, the detective walked up the slope to the deck. 'I have to call around, see who can dive,' Alcee Beck said. 'It may take a while to find someone who can do it. And the chief has to okay it.'

Of course, such a thing would cost money, and that money might not be in the parish budget. I took a deep breath. 'Are you talking hours, or days?'

'Maybe a day or two,' he said at last. 'No way anyone can do it who isn't trained. It's too cold, and Jason himself told me it was deep.'

'All right,' I said, trying to suppress my impatience and anger. Anxiety gnawed at me like another kind of hunger.

'Carla Rodriguez was in town last night,' Alcee Beck told me, and after a long moment, the significance of that sank into my brain.

Carla Rodriguez, tiny and dark and electric, had been the

closest shave Jason had ever had with losing his heart. In fact, the little shifter Jason had had a date with on New Year's Eve had somewhat resembled Carla, who had moved to Houston three years ago, much to my relief. I'd been tired of the pyrotechnics surrounding her romance with my brother; their relationship had been punctuated by long and loud and public arguments, hung-up telephones, and slammed doors.

'Why? Who's she staying with?'

'Her cousin in Shreveport,' Beck said. 'You know, that Dovie.'

Dovie Rodriguez had visited Bon Temps a lot while Carla had lived here. Dovie had been the more sophisticated city cousin, down in the country to correct all our local yokel ways. Of course, we'd envied Dovie.

I thought that tackling Dovie was just what I wanted to do.

It looked like I'd be going to Shreveport after all.

Chapter 4

The detective hustled me off after that, telling me he was going to get the crime scene officer out to the house, and he'd be in touch. I got the idea, right out of his brain, that there was something he didn't want me to see, and that he'd thrown Carla Rodriguez at me to distract me.

And I thought he might take the shotgun away, since he seemed much more sure now he was dealing with a crime, and the shotgun might be part of some bit of evidence. But Alcee Beck didn't say anything, so I didn't remind him.

I was more shaken than I wanted to admit to myself. Inwardly, I'd been convinced that, though I needed to track my brother down, Jason was really okay – just misplaced. Or mislaid, more likely, ho ho ho. Possibly he was in some kind of not-too-serious trouble, I'd told myself. Now things were looking more serious.

I've never been able to squeeze my budget enough to afford a cell phone, so I began driving home. I was thinking of whom I should call, and I came up with the same answer as before. No one. There was no definite news to break. I felt as lonely as I ever have in my life. But I just didn't want to be Crisis Woman, showing up on friends' doorsteps with trouble on my shoulders.

Tears welled up in my eyes. I wanted my grandmother back. I pulled over to the side of the road and slapped myself on the cheek, hard. I called myself a few names.

Shreveport. I'd go to Shreveport and confront Dovie and Carla Rodriguez. While I was there, I'd find out if Chow and Pam knew anything about Jason's disappearance – though it was hours until they'd be up, and I'd just be kicking my heels in an empty club, assuming there'd be someone there to let me in. But I just couldn't sit at home, waiting. I could read the minds of the human employees and find out if they knew what was up.

On the one hand, if I went to Shreveport, I'd be out of touch with what was happening here. On the other hand, I'd be doing something.

While I was trying to decide if there were any more hands to consider, something else happened.

It was even odder than the preceding events of the day. There I was, parked in the middle of nowhere at the side of a parish road, when a sleek, black, brand-new Camaro pulled onto the shoulder behind me. Out of the passenger's side stepped a gorgeous woman, at least six feet tall. Of course, I remembered her; she'd been in Merlotte's on New Year's Eve. My friend Tara Thornton was in the driver's seat.

Okay, I thought blankly, staring into the rearview mirror, *this is weird*. I hadn't seen Tara in weeks, since we'd met by chance in a vampire club in Jackson, Mississippi. She'd been there with a vamp named Franklin Mott; he'd been very handsome in a senior-citizen sort of way, polished, dangerous, and sophisticated.

Tara always looks great. My high school friend has black hair, and dark eyes, and a smooth olive complexion, and she has a lot of intelligence that she uses running Tara's Togs, an upscale women's clothing store that rents space in a strip mall Bill owns. (Well, it's as upscale as Bon Temps has to offer.) Tara had become a friend of mine years before, because she came from an even sadder background than mine.

But the tall woman put even Tara in the shade. She was as dark-haired as Tara, though the new woman had reddish highlights that surprised the eye. She had dark eyes, too, but hers were huge and almond-shaped, almost abnormally large. Her skin was as pale as milk, and her legs were as long as a stepladder. She was quite gifted in the bosom department, and she was wearing fire engine red from head to toe. Her lipstick matched.

'Sookie,' Tara called. 'What's the matter?' She walked carefully up to my old car, watching her feet because she was wearing glossy, brown leather, high-heeled boots she didn't want to scuff. They'd have lasted five minutes on my feet. I spend too much of my time standing up to worry about footwear that only looks good.

Tara looked successful, attractive, and secure, in her sage green sweater and taupe pants. 'I was putting on my makeup when I heard over the police scanner that something was up at Jason's house,' she said. She slid in the passenger's seat and leaned over to hug me. 'When I got to Jason's, I saw you pulling out. What's up?' The woman in red was standing with her back to the car, tactfully looking out into the woods.

I'd adored my father, and I'd always known (and my mother herself definitely believed) that no matter what

Mother put me through, she was acting out of love. But Tara's parents had been evil, both alcoholics and abusers. Tara's older sisters and brothers had left home as fast as they could, leaving Tara, as the youngest, to foot the bill for their freedom.

Yet now that I was in trouble, here she was, ready to help.

'Well, Jason's gone missing,' I said, in a fairly level voice, but then I ruined the effect by giving one of those awful choking sobs. I turned my face so I'd be looking out my window. I was embarrassed to show such distress in front of the new woman.

Wisely ignoring my tears, Tara began asking me the logical questions: Had Jason called in to work? Had he called me the night before? Who had he been dating lately?

That reminded me of the shifter girl who'd been Jason's date New Year's Eve. I thought I could even talk about the girl's otherness, because Tara had been at Club Dead that night. Tara's tall companion was a Supe of some kind. Tara knew all about the secret world.

But she didn't, as it turned out.

Her memory had been erased. Or at least she pretended it had.

'What?' Tara asked, with almost exaggerated confusion. 'Werewolves? At that nightclub? I remember seeing you there. Honey, didn't you drink a little too much and pass out, or something?'

Since I drink very sparingly, Tara's question made me quite angry, but it was also the most unremarkable explanation Franklin Mott could have planted in Tara's head. I was so disappointed at not getting to confide in her that I closed my eyes so I wouldn't have to see the blank look on her face. I felt tears leaving little paths down my cheeks. I should have just let it go, but I said, in a low, harsh voice, 'No, I didn't.'

'Omigosh, did your date put something in your drink?' In genuine horror, Tara squeezed my hand. 'That Rohypnol? But Alcide looked like such a nice guy!'

'Forget it,' I said, trying to sound gentler. 'It doesn't really have anything to do with Jason, after all.'

Her face still troubled, Tara pressed my hand again.

All of a sudden, I was certain I didn't believe her. Tara knew vampires could remove memory, and she was pretending Franklin Mott had erased hers. I thought Tara remembered quite well what had happened at Club Dead, but she was pretending she didn't to protect herself. If she had to do that to survive, that was okay. I took a deep breath.

'Are you still dating Franklin?' I asked, to start a different conversation.

'He got me this car.'

I was a little shocked and more than a little dismayed, but I hoped I was not the kind to point fingers.

'It's a wonderful car. You don't know any witches, do you?' I asked, trying to change the subject before Tara could read my misgivings. I was sure she would laugh at me for asking her such a question, but it was a good diversion. I wouldn't hurt her for the world.

Finding a witch would be a great help. I was sure Jason's abduction – and I swore to myself it was an abduction, it was not a murder – was linked to the witches' curse on Eric. It was just too much coincidence otherwise. On the other hand, I had certainly experienced the twists and turns of a bunch of coincidences in the past few months. There, I knew I'd find a third hand.

'Sure I do,' Tara said, smiling proudly. 'Now there I can help you. That is, if a Wiccan will do?'

I had so many expressions I wasn't sure my face could fit them all in. Shock, fear, grief, and worry were tumbling around in my brain. When the spinning stopped, we would see which one was at the top.

'You're a witch?' I said weakly.

'Oh, gosh, no, not me. I'm a Catholic. But I have some friends who are Wiccan. Some of them are witches.'

'Oh, really?' I didn't think I'd ever heard the word Wiccan before, though maybe I'd read it in a mystery or romance novel. 'I'm sorry, I don't know what that means,' I said, my voice humble.

'Holly can explain it better than I can,' Tara said.

'Holly. The Holly who works with me?'

'Sure. Or you could go to Danielle, though she's not going to be as willing to talk. Holly and Danielle are in the same coven.'

I was so shocked by now I might as well get even more stunned. 'Coven,' I repeated.

'You know, a group of pagans who worship together.'

'I thought a coven had to be witches?'

'I guess not – but they have to, you know, be non-Christian. I mean, Wicca is a religion.'

'Okay,' I said. 'Okay. Do you think Holly would talk to me about this?'

'I don't know why not.' Tara went back to her car to get her cell phone, and paced back and forth between our vehicles while she talked to Holly. I appreciated a little respite to allow me to get back on my mental feet, so to speak. To be polite I got out of my car and spoke to the woman in red, who'd been very patient.

'I'm sorry to meet you on such a bad day,' I said. 'I'm Sookie Stackhouse.'

'I'm Claudine,' she said, with a beautiful smile. Her teeth were Hollywood white. Her skin had an odd quality; it looked glossy and thin, reminding me of the skin of a plum; like if you bit her, sweet juice would gush out. 'I'm here because of all the activity.'

'Oh?' I said, taken aback.

'Sure. You have vampires, and Weres, and lots of other stuff all tangled up here in Bon Temps – to say nothing of several important and powerful crossroads. I was drawn to all the possibilities.'

'Uh-huh,' I said uncertainly. 'So, do you plan on just observing all this, or what?'

'Oh, no. Just observing is not my way.' She laughed. 'You're quite the wild card, aren't you?'

'Holly's up,' Tara said, snapping her phone shut and smiling because it was hard not to with Claudine around. I realized I was smiling from ear to ear, not my usual tense grin but an expression of sunny happiness. 'She says come on over.'

'Are you coming with me?' I didn't know what to think of Tara's companion.

'Sorry, Claudine's helping me today at the shop,' Tara said. 'We're having a New Year's sale on our old inventory, and people are doing some heavy shopping. Want me to put something aside for you? I've got a few really pretty party dresses left. Didn't the one you wore in Jackson get ruined?'

Yeah, because a fanatic had driven a stake through my side. The dress had definitely suffered. 'It got stained,' I said with great restraint. 'It's real nice of you to offer, but I don't think I'll have time to try anything on. With Jason and everything, I've got so much to think about.' And precious little extra money, I told myself.

'Sure,' said Tara. She hugged me again. 'You call me if you need me, Sookie. It's funny that I don't remember that evening in Jackson any better. Maybe I had too much to drink, too. Did we dance?'

'Oh, yes, you talked me into doing that routine we did at the high school talent show.'

'I did not!' She was begging me to deny it, with a half smile on her face.

''Fraid so.' I knew damn well she remembered it.

'I wish I'd been there,' said Claudine. 'I love to dance.'

'Believe me, that night in Club Dead is one I wish I'd missed,' I said.

'Well, remind me never to go back to Jackson, if I did that dance in public,' Tara said.

'I don't think either of us better go back to Jackson.' I'd left some very irate vampires in Jackson, but the Weres were even angrier. Not that there were a lot of them left, actually. But still.

Tara hesitated a minute, obviously trying to frame something she wanted to tell me. 'Since Bill owns the building Tara's Togs is in,' she said carefully, 'I do have a number to call, a number he said he'd check in with while he was out of the country. So if you need to let him know anything . . . ?'

'Thanks,' I said, not sure if I felt thankful at all. 'He told me he left a number on a pad by the phone in his house.' There was a kind of finality to Bill's being out of the country, unreachable. I hadn't even thought of trying to get in touch with him about my predicament; out of all the people I'd considered calling, he hadn't even crossed my mind.

'It's just that he seemed pretty, you know, down.' Tara examined the toes of her boots. 'Melancholy,' she said, as if she enjoyed using a word that didn't pass her lips often. Claudine beamed with approval. What a strange gal. Her huge eyes were luminous with joy as she patted me on the shoulder.

I swallowed hard. 'Well, he's never exactly Mr. Smiley,' I said. 'I do miss him. But . . .' I shook my head emphatically. 'It was just too hard. He just . . . upset me too much. I thank you for letting me know I can call him if I need to, and I really, really appreciate your telling me about Holly.'

Tara, flushed with the deserved pleasure of having done her good deed for the day, got back in her spanky-new Camaro. After folding her long self into the passenger seat, Claudine waved at me as Tara pulled away. I sat in my car for a moment longer, trying to remember where Holly Cleary lived. I thought I remembered her complaining about the closet size in her apartment, and that meant the Kingfisher Arms.

When I got to the U-shaped building on the southern approach to Bon Temps, I checked the mailboxes to discover Holly's apartment number. She was on the ground floor, in number 4. Holly had a five-year-old son, Cody. Holly and her best friend, Danielle Gray, had both gotten married right out of high school, and both had been divorced within five years. Danielle's mom was a great help to Danielle, but Holly was not so lucky. Her long-divorced parents had both moved away, and her grandmother had died in the Alzheimer's wing of the Renard Parish nursing home. Holly had dated Detective Andy Bellefleur for a few months, but nothing had come of it. Rumor had it that old Caroline Bellefleur, Andy's grandmother, had thought Holly wasn't 'good' enough for Andy. I had no opinion on that. Neither Holly nor Andy was on my shortlist of favorite people, though I definitely felt cooler toward Andy.

When Holly answered her door, I realized all of a sudden how much she'd changed over the past few weeks. For years, her hair had been dyed a dandelion yellow. Now it was matte black and spiked. Her ears had four piercings apiece. And I noticed her hipbones pushing at the thin denim of her aged jeans.

'Hey, Sookie,' she said, pleasantly enough. 'Tara asked me if I would talk to you, but I wasn't sure if you'd show up. Sorry about Jason. Come on in.'

The apartment was small, of course, and though it had been repainted recently, it showed evidence of years of heavy use. There was a living room-dining room-kitchen combo, with a breakfast bar separating the galley kitchen from the rest of the area. There were a few toys in a basket in the corner of the room, and there was a can of Pledge and a rag on the scarred coffee table. Holly had been cleaning.

'I'm sorry to interrupt,' I said.

'That's okay. Coke? Juice?'

'No, thanks. Where's Cody?'

'He went to stay with his dad,' she said, looking down at her hands. 'I drove him over the day after Christmas.'

'Where's his dad living?'

'David's living in Springhill. He just married this girl, Allie. She already had two kids. The little girl is Cody's age, and he just loves to play with her. It's always, "Shelley this," and "Shelley that."' Holly looked kind of bleak.

David Cleary was one of a large clan. His cousin Pharr had been in my grade all through school. For Cody's genes' sake, I hoped that David was more intelligent than Pharr, which would be real easy.

'I need to talk to you about something pretty personal, Holly.'

Holly looked surprised all over again. 'Well, we haven't exactly been on those terms, have we?' she said. 'You ask, and I'll decide whether to answer.'

I tried to frame what I was going to say – to keep secret what I needed to keep secret and ask of her what I needed without offending.

'You're a witch?' I said, embarrassed at using such a dramatic word.

'I'm more of a Wiccan.'

'Would you mind explaining the difference?' I met her eyes briefly, and then decided to focus on the dried flowers in the basket on top of the television. Holly thought I could read her mind only if I was looking into her eyes. (Like physical touching, eye contact does make the reading easier, but it certainly isn't necessary.)

'I guess not.' Her voice was slow, as if she were thinking as she spoke. 'You're not one to spread gossip.'

'Whatever you tell me, I won't share with anyone.' I met her eyes again, briefly.

'Okay,' she said. 'Well, if you're a witch, of course, you practice magic rituals.'

She was using 'you' in the general sense, I thought, because saying 'I' would mean too bold a confession.

'You draw from a power that most people never tap into. Being a witch isn't being wicked, or at least it isn't supposed to be. If you're a Wiccan, you follow a religion, a pagan religion. We follow the ways of the Mother, and we have our own calendar of holy days. You can be both a

Wiccan and a witch; or more one, or more the other. It's very individualized. I practice a little witchcraft, but I'm more interested in the Wiccan life. We believe that your actions are okay if you don't hurt anyone else.'

Oddly, my first feeling was one of embarrassment, when I heard Holly tell me that she was a non-Christian. I'd never met anyone who didn't at least pretend to be a Christian or who didn't give lip service to the basic Christian precepts. I was pretty sure there was a synagogue in Shreveport, but I'd never even met a Jew, to the best of my knowledge. I was certainly on a learning curve.

'I understand. Do you know lots of witches?'

'I know a few.' Holly nodded repeatedly, still avoiding my eyes.

I spotted an old computer on the rickety table in the corner. 'Do you have, like, a chat room online, or a bulletin board, or something?'

'Oh, sure.'

'Have you heard of a group of witches that's come into Shreveport lately?'

Holly's face became very serious. Her straight dark brows drew together in a frown. 'Tell me you're not involved with them,' she said.

'Not directly. But I know someone they've hurt, and I'm afraid they might've taken Jason.'

'Then he's in bad trouble,' she said bluntly. 'The woman who leads this group is out-and-out ruthless. Her brother is just as bad. That group, they're not like the rest of us. They're not trying to find a better way to live, or a path to get in touch with the natural world, or spells to increase their inner peace. They're Wiccans. They're evil.'

'Can you give me any clues about where I might track

them down?' I was doing my best to keep my face in line. I could hear with my other sense that Holly was thinking that if the newly arrived coven had Jason, he'd be hurt badly, if not killed.

Holly, apparently in deep thought, looked out the front window of her apartment. She was afraid that they'd trace any information she gave me back to her, punish her – maybe through Cody. These weren't witches who believed in doing harm to no one else. These were witches whose lives were planned around the gathering of power of all kinds.

'They're all women?' I asked, because I could tell she was on the verge of resolving to tell me nothing.

'If you're thinking Jason would be able to charm them with his ways because he's such a looker, you can think again,' Holly told me, her face grim and somehow stripped down to basics. She wasn't trying for any effect; she wanted me to understand how dangerous these people were. 'There are some men, too. They're . . . these aren't normal witches. I mean, they weren't even normal *people*.'

I was willing to believe that. I'd had to believe stranger things since the night Bill Compton had walked into Merlotte's Bar.

Holly spoke like she knew far more about this group of witches than I'd ever suspected . . . more than the general background I'd hoped to glean from her. I prodded her a little. 'What makes them different?'

'They've had vampire blood.' Holly glanced to the side, as if she felt someone listening to her. The motion creeped me out. 'Witches – witches with a lot of power they're willing to use for evil – they're bad enough. Witches that strong who've also had vampire blood are . . . Sookie, you have no idea how dangerous they are. Some of them are Weres. Please, stay away from them.'

Werewolves? They were not only witches, but Weres? And they drank vampire blood? I was seriously scared. I didn't know how could you get any worse. 'Where are they?'

'Are you listening to me?'

'I am, but I have to know where they are!'

'They're in an old business not awful far from Pierre Bossier Mall,' she said, and I could see the picture of it in her head. She'd been there. She'd seen them. She had this all in her head, and I was getting a lot of it.

'Why were you there?' I asked, and she flinched.

'I was worried about talking to you,' Holly said, her voice angry. 'I shouldn't have even let you in. But I'd dated Jason . . . You're gonna get me killed, Sookie Stackhouse. Me and my boy.'

'No, I won't.'

'I was there because their leader sent out a call for all the witches in the area to have, like, a summit. It turned out that what she wanted to do was impose her will on all of us. Some of us were pretty impressed with her commitment and her power, but most of us smaller-town Wiccans, we didn't like her drug use – that's what drinking vampire blood amounts to – or her taste for the darker side of witchcraft. Now, that's all I want to say about it.'

'Thanks, Holly.' I tried to think of something I could tell her that would relieve her fear. But she wanted me to leave more than anything in the world, and I'd caused her enough upset. Holly's just letting me in the door had been a big concession, since she actually believed in my mind-reading ability. No matter what rumors they heard, people really wanted to believe that the contents of their heads were private, no matter what proof they had to the contrary.

I did myself.

I patted Holly on the shoulder as I left, but she didn't get up from the old couch. She stared at me with hopeless brown eyes, as if any moment someone was going to come in the door and cut off her head.

That look frightened me more than her words, more than her ideas, and I left the Kingfisher Arms as quickly as I could, trying to note the few people who saw me turn out of the parking lot. I didn't recognize any of them.

I wondered why the witches in Shreveport would want Jason, how they could have made a connection between the missing Eric and my brother. How could I approach them to find out? Would Pam and Chow help, or had they taken their own steps?

And whose blood had the witches been drinking?

Since vampires had made their presence known among us, nearly three years ago now, they'd become preyed upon in a new way. Instead of fearing getting staked through the heart by wanna-be Van Helsings, vampires dreaded modern entrepreneurs called Drainers. Drainers traveled in teams, singling out vampires by a variety of methods and binding them with silver chains (usually in a carefully planned ambush), then draining their blood into vials. Depending on the age of the vampire, a vial of blood could fetch from $200 to $400 on the black market. The effect of drinking this blood? Quite unpredictable, once the blood had left the vampire. I guess that was part of the attraction. Most commonly, for a few weeks, the drinker gained strength, visual acuity, a feeling of robust health, and enhanced attractiveness. It depended on the age of the drained vampire and the freshness of the blood.

Of course, those effects faded, unless you drank more blood.

A certain percentage of people who experienced drinking vampire blood could hardly wait to scratch up money for more. These blood junkies were extremely dangerous, of course. City police forces were glad to hire vampires to deal with them, since regular cops would simply get pulped.

Every now and then, a blood drinker simply went mad – sometimes in a quiet, gibbering kind of way, but sometimes spectacularly and murderously. There was no way to predict who would be stricken this way, and it could happen on the first drinking.

So there were men with glittering mad eyes in padded cells and there were electrifying movie stars who equally owed their condition to the Drainers. Draining was a hazardous job, of course. Sometimes the vampire got loose, with a very predictable result. A court in Florida had ruled this vampire retaliation justifiable homicide, in one celebrated case, because Drainers notoriously discarded their victims. They left a vampire, all but empty of blood, too weak to move, wherever the vamp happened to fall. The weakened vampire died when the sun came up, unless he had the good fortune to be discovered and helped to safety during the hours of darkness. It took years to recover from a draining, and that was years of help from other vamps. Bill had told me there were shelters for drained vamps, and that their location was kept very secret.

Witches with nearly the physical power of vampires – that seemed a very dangerous combination. I kept thinking of women when I thought of the coven that had moved into Shreveport, and I kept correcting myself. Men, Holly had said, were in the group.

I looked at the clock at the drive-through bank, and I saw it was just after noon. It would be full dark by a few minutes before six; Eric had gotten up a little earlier than that, at times. I could certainly go to Shreveport and come back by then. I couldn't think of another plan, and I just couldn't go home and sit and wait. Even wasting gas was better than going back to my house, though worry for Jason crawled up and down my spine. I could take the time to drop off the shotgun, but as long as it was unloaded and the shells were in a separate location, it should be legal enough to drive around with it.

For the first time in my life, I checked my rearview mirror to see if I was being followed. I am not up on spy techniques, but if someone was following me, I couldn't spot him. I stopped and got gas and an ICEE, just to see if anyone pulled into the gas station behind me, but no one did. That was real good, I decided, hoping that Holly was safe.

As I drove, I had time to review my conversation with Holly. I realized it was the first one I'd ever had with Holly in which Danielle's name had not come up once. Holly and Danielle had been joined at the hip since grade school. They probably had their periods at the same time. Danielle's parents, cradle members of the Free Will Church of God's Anointed, would have a fit if they knew, so it wasn't any wonder that Holly had been so discreet.

Our little town of Bon Temps had stretched its gates open wide enough to tolerate vampires, and gay people didn't have a very hard time of it anymore (kind of depending on how they expressed their sexual preference).

However, I thought the gates might snap shut for Wiccans.

The peculiar and beautiful Claudine had told me that she was attracted to Bon Temps for its very strangeness. I wondered what else was out there, waiting to reveal itself.

Chapter 5

Carla Rodriguez my most promising lead came first. I'd looked up the old address I had for Dovie, with whom I'd exchanged the odd Christmas card. I found the house with a little difficulty. It was well away from the shopping areas that were my only normal stops in Shreveport. The houses were small and close together where Dovie lived, and some of them were in bad repair.

I felt a distinct thrill of triumph when Carla herself answered the door. She had a black eye, and she was hung-over, both signs that she'd had a big night the night before.

'Hey, Sookie,' she said, identifying me after a moment. 'What're you doing here? I was at Merlotte's last night, but I didn't see you there. You still working there?'

'I am. It was my night off.' Now that I was actually looking at Carla, I wasn't sure how to explain to her what I needed. I decided to be blunt. 'Listen, Jason's not at work this morning, and I kind of wondered if he might be here with you.'

'Honey, I got nothing against you, but Jason's the last man on earth I'd sleep with,' Carla said flatly. I stared at her, hearing that she was telling me truth. 'I ain't gonna stick my hand in the fire twice, having gotten burnt the first time. I did look around the bar a little, thinking I might see him, but if I had, I'd have turned the other way.'

I nodded. That seemed all there was to say on the subject. We exchanged a few more polite sentences, and I chatted with Dovie, who had a toddler balanced on her hip, but then it was time for me to leave. My most promising lead had just evaporated in the length of two sentences.

Trying to suppress my desperation, I drove to a busy corner filling station and parked, to check my Shreveport map. It didn't take me long to figure out how to get from Dovie's suburb to the vampire bar.

Fangtasia was in a shopping center close to Toys 'R' Us. It opened at six P.M. year-round, but of course the vampires didn't show up until full dark, which depended on the season. The front of Fangtasia was painted flat gray, and the neon writing was all in red. 'Shreveport's Premier Vampire Bar,' read the newly added, smaller writing under the exotic script of thc bar's name. I winced and looked away.

Two summers before, a small group of vamps from Oklahoma had tried to set up a rival bar in adjacent Bossier City. After one particularly hot, short August night, they'd never been seen again, and the building they'd been renovating had burned to the ground.

Tourists thought stories like this were actually amusing and colorful. It added to the thrill of ordering overpriced drinks (from human waitresses dressed in trailing black 'vampire' outfits) while staring at real, honest-to-God, undead bloodsuckers. Eric made the Area Five vampires show up for this unappealing duty by giving them a set number of hours each week to present themselves at Fangtasia. Most of his underlings weren't enthusiastic about exhibiting themselves, but it did give them a chance to hook up with fang-bangers who actually yearned for the chance to be bitten. Such encounters didn't take place on the premises: Eric had rules about that. And so did the police department. The only legal biting that could take place between humans and vampires was between consenting adults, in private.

Automatically, I pulled around to the rear of the shopping center. Bill and I had almost always used the employee entrance. Back here, the door was just a gray door in a gray wall, with the name of the bar put on in stick-on letters from Wal-Mart. Right below that, a large, black, stenciled notice proclaimed STAFF ONLY. I lifted my hand to knock, and then I realized I could see that the inner dead bolt had not been employed.

The door was unlocked.

This was really, really bad.

Though it was broad daylight, the hair on the back of my neck stood up. Abruptly, I wished I had Bill at my back. I wasn't missing his tender love, either. It's probably a bad indicator of your lifestyle when you miss your ex-boyfriend because he's absolutely lethal.

Though the public face of the shopping center was fairly busy, the service side was deserted. The silence was crawling with possibilities, and none of them was pleasant. I leaned my forehead against the cold gray door. I decided to get back in my old car and get the hell out of there, which would have been amazingly smart.

And I would have gone, if I hadn't heard the moaning.

Even then, if I'd been able to spot a pay phone, I

would've just called 911 and stayed outside until someone official showed up. But there wasn't one in sight, and I couldn't stand the possibility that someone needed my help real bad, and I'd withheld it because I was chicken.

There was a heavy garbage can right by the back door, and after I'd yanked the door open – standing aside for a second to avoid anything that might dart out – I maneuvered the can to hold the door ajar. I had goose bumps all over my arms as I stepped inside.

Windowless Fangtasia requires electric light, twenty-four/seven. Since none of these lights were on, the interior was just a dark pit. Winter daylight extended weakly down the hall that led to the bar proper. On the right were the doors to Eric's office and the bookkeeper's room. On the left was the door to the large storeroom, which also contained the employee bathroom. This hall ended in a heavy door to discourage any fun lovers from penetrating to the back of the club. This door, too, was open, for the first time in my memory. Beyond it lay the black silent cavern of the bar. I wondered if anything was sitting at those tables or huddled in those booths.

I was holding my breath so I could detect the least little noise. After a few seconds, I heard a scraping movement and another sound of pain, coming from the storeroom. Its door was slightly ajar. I took four silent steps to that door. My heart was pounding all the way up in my throat as I reached into the darkness to flip the light switch.

The glare made me blink.

Belinda, the only half-intelligent fang-banger I'd ever met, was lying on the storeroom floor in a curiously contorted position. Her legs were bent double, her heels pressed against her hips. There was no blood – in fact, no visible mark – on her. Apparently, she was having a giant and perpetual leg cramp.

I knelt beside Belinda, my eyes darting glances in all directions. I saw no other movement in the room, though its corners were obscured with stacks of liquor cartons and a coffin that was used as a prop in a show the vampires sometimes put on for special parties. The employee bathroom door was shut.

'Belinda,' I whispered. 'Belinda, look at me.'

Belinda's eyes were red and swollen behind their glasses, and her cheeks were wet with tears. She blinked and focused on my face.

'Are they still here?' I asked, knowing she'd understand that I meant 'the people who did this to you.'

'Sookie,' she said hoarsely. Her voice was weak, and I wondered how long she'd lain there waiting for help. 'Oh, thank God. Tell Master Eric we tried to hold them off.' Still role-playing, you notice, even in her agony: 'Tell our chieftain we fought to the death' – you know the kind of thing.

'Who'd you try to hold off?' I asked sharply.

'The witches. They came in last night after we'd closed, after Pam and Chow had gone. Just Ginger and me . . .'

'What did they want?' I had time to notice that Belinda was still wearing her filmy black waitress outfit with the slit up the long skirt, and there were still puncture marks painted on her neck.

'They wanted to know where we'd put Master Eric. They seemed to think they'd done . . . something to him, and that we'd hidden him.' During her long pause, her face contorted, and I could tell she was in terrible pain, but I couldn't tell what was wrong with her. 'My legs,' she moaned. 'Oh . . .'

'But you didn't know, so you couldn't tell them.'

'I would never betray our master.'

And Belinda was the one with sense.

'Was anyone here besides Ginger, Belinda?' But she was so deep into a spasm of suffering that she couldn't answer. Her whole body was rigid with pain, that low moan tearing out of her throat again.

I called 911 from Eric's office, since I knew the location of the phone there. The room had been tossed, and some frisky witch had spray painted a big red pentagram on one of the walls. Eric was going to love that.

I returned to Belinda to tell her the ambulance was coming. 'What's wrong with your legs?' I asked, scared of the answer.

'They made the muscle in the back of my legs pull up, like it was half as long . . .' And she began moaning again. 'It's like one of those giant cramps you get when you're pregnant.'

It was news to me that Belinda had ever been pregnant.

'Where's Ginger?' I asked, when her pain seemed to have ebbed a little.

'She was in the bathroom.'

Ginger, a pretty strawberry blonde, as dumb as a rock, was still there. I don't think they'd meant to kill her. But they'd put a spell on her legs like they'd done to Belinda's, it looked like; her legs were drawn up double in the same peculiar and painful way, even in death. Ginger had been standing in front of the sink when she'd crumpled, and her head had hit the lip of the sink on her way down. Her eyes were sightless and her hair was matted with some clotted blood that had oozed from the depression in her temple.

There was nothing to be done. I didn't even touch

Ginger; she was so obviously dead. I didn't say anything about her to Belinda, who was in too much agony to understand, anyway. She had a couple more moments of lucidity before I took off. I asked her where to find Pam and Chow so I could warn them, and Belinda said they just showed up at the bar when it became dark.

She also said the woman who'd worked the spell was a witch named Hallow, and she was almost six feet tall, with short brown hair and a black design painted on her face.

That should make her easy to identify.

'She told me she was as strong as a vampire, too,' Belinda gasped. 'You see . . .' Belinda pointed beyond me. I whirled, expecting an attack. Nothing that alarming happened, but what I saw was almost as disturbing as what I'd imagined. It was the handle of the dolly the staff used to wheel cases of drinks around. The long metal handle had been twisted into a U.

'I know Master Eric will kill her when he returns,' Belinda said falteringly after a minute, the words coming out in jagged bursts because of the pain.

'Sure he will,' I said stoutly. I hesitated, feeling crummy beyond words. 'Belinda, I have to go because I don't want the police to keep me here for questioning. Please don't mention my name. Just say a passerby heard you, okay?'

'Where's Master Eric? Is he really missing?'

'I have no idea,' I said, forced to lie. 'I have to get out of here.'

'Go,' Belinda said, her voice ragged. 'We're lucky you came in at all.'

I had to get out of there. I knew nothing about what had happened at the bar, and being questioned for hours would cost me time I couldn't afford, with my brother missing.

Back in my car and on my way out of the shopping center, I passed the police cars and the ambulance as they headed in. I'd wiped the doorknob clean of my fingerprints. Other than that, I couldn't think of what I'd touched and what I hadn't, no matter how carefully I reviewed my actions. There'd be a million prints there, anyway; gosh, it was a bar.

After a minute, I realized I was just driving with no direction. I was overwhelmingly rattled. I pulled over into yet another filling station parking lot and looked at the pay phone longingly. I could call Alcide, ask him if he knew where Pam and Chow spent their daytime hours. Then I could go there and leave a message or something, warn them about what had happened.

I made myself take some deep breaths and think hard about what I was doing. It was extremely unlikely that the vamps would give a Were the address of their daytime resting place. This was not information that vampires passed out to anyone who asked. Alcide had no love for the vamps of Shreveport, who'd held his dad's gambling debt over Alcide's head until he complied with their wishes. I knew that if I called, he'd come, because he was just a nice guy. But his involvement could have serious consequences for his family and his business. However, if this Hallow really *was* a triple threat – a Were witch who drank vampire blood – she was very dangerous, and the Weres of Shreveport should know about her. Relieved I'd finally made up my mind, I found a pay phone that worked, and I got Alcide's card out of its slot in my billfold.

Alcide was in his office, which was a miracle. I described my location, and he gave me directions on how to reach his office. He offered to come get me, but I didn't want him to think I was an utter idiot.

I used a calling card to phone Bud Dearborn's office, to hear there was no news about Jason.

Following Alcide's directions very carefully, I arrived at Herveaux and Son in about twenty minutes. It was not too far off I-30, on the eastern edge of Shreveport, actually on my way back to Bon Temps.

The Herveauxes owned the building, and their surveying company was its sole occupant. I parked in front of the low brick building. At the rear, I spotted Alcide's Dodge Ram pickup in the large parking lot for employees. The one in front, for visitors, was much smaller. It was clear to see that the Herveauxes mostly went to their clients, rather than the clients coming to them.

Feeling shy and more than a little nervous, I pushed open the front door and glanced around. There was a desk just inside the door, with a waiting area opposite. Beyond a half wall, I could see five or six workstations, three of them occupied. The woman behind the desk was in charge of routing phone calls, too. She had short dark brown hair that was carefully cut and styled, she was wearing a beautiful sweater, and she had wonderful makeup. She was probably in her forties, but it hadn't lessened her impressiveness.

'I'm here to see Alcide,' I said, feeling embarrassed and self-conscious.

'Your name?' She was smiling at me, but she looked a little crisp around the edges, as if she didn't quite approve of a young and obviously unfashionable woman showing up at Alcide's workplace. I was wearing a bright blue-and-yellow knit top with long sleeves under my old thigh-length blue cloth coat, and aged blue jeans, and Reeboks. I'd been worried about finding my brother when

I dressed, not about standing inspection by the Fashion Police.

'Stackhouse,' I said.

'Ms. Stackhouse here to see you,' Crispy said into an intercom.

'Oh, good!' Alcide sounded very happy, which was a relief.

Crispy was saying into the intercom, 'Shall I send her back?' when Alcide burst through the door behind and to the left of her desk.

'Sookie!' he said, and he beamed at me. He stopped for a second, as if he couldn't quite decide what he should do, and then he hugged me.

I felt like I was smiling all over. I hugged him back. I was so happy to see him! I thought he looked wonderful. Alcide is a tall man, with black hair that apparently can't be tamed with a brush and comb, and he has a broad face and green eyes.

We'd dumped a body together, and that creates a bond.

He pulled gently on my braid. 'Come on back,' he said in my ear, since Ms. Crispy was looking on with an indulgent smile. I was sure the indulgent part was for Alcide's benefit. In fact, I knew it was, because she was thinking I didn't look chic enough or polished enough to date a Herveaux, and she didn't think Alcide's dad (with whom she'd been sleeping for two years) would appreciate Alcide taking up with a no-account girl like me. Oops, one of those things I didn't want to know. Obviously I wasn't shielding myself hard enough. Bill had made me practice, and now that I didn't see him anymore, I was getting sloppy. It wasn't entirely my fault; Ms. Crispy was a clear broadcaster.

Alcide was not, since he's a werewolf.

Alcide ushered me down a hall, which was nicely carpeted and hung with neutral pictures – insipid landscapes and garden scenes – which I figured some decorator (or maybe Ms. Crispy) had chosen. He showed me into his office, which had his name on the door. It was a big room, but not a grand or elegant one, because it was just chock-full of work stuff – plans and papers and hard hats and office equipment. Very utilitarian. A fax machine was humming, and set beside a stack of forms there was a calculator displaying figures.

'You're busy. I shouldn't have called,' I said, instantly cowed.

'Are you kidding? Your call is the best thing that's happened to me all day!' He sounded so sincere that I had to smile again. 'There's something I have to say to you, something I didn't tell you when I dropped your stuff off after you got hurt.' After I'd been beaten up by hired thugs. 'I felt so bad about it that I've put off coming to Bon Temps to talk to you face-to-face.'

Omigod, he'd gotten back with his nasty rotten fiancée, Debbie Pelt. I was getting Debbie's name from his brain.

'Yes?' I said, trying to look calm and open. He reached down and took my hand between his own large palms.

'I owe you a huge apology.'

Okay, that was unexpected. 'How would that be?' I asked, looking up at him with narrowed eyes. I'd come here to spill my guts, but it was Alcide who was spilling his instead.

'That last night, at Club Dead,' he began, 'when you needed my help and protection the most, I . . .'

I knew what was coming now. Alcide had changed into

a wolf rather than staying human and helping me out of the bar after I'd gotten staked. I put my free hand across his mouth. His skin was so warm. If you're used to touching vampires, you'll know just how roasty a regular human can feel, and a Were even more so, since they run a few degrees hotter.

I felt my pulse quicken, and I knew he could tell, too. Animals are good at sensing excitement. 'Alcide,' I said, 'never bring that up. You couldn't help it, and it all turned out okay, anyway.' Well, more or less – other than my heart breaking at Bill's perfidy.

'Thanks for being so understanding,' he said, after a pause during which he looked at me intently. 'I think I would have felt better if you'd been mad.' I believe he was wondering whether I was just putting a brave face on it or if I was truly sincere. I could tell he had an impulse to kiss me, but he wasn't sure if I'd welcome such a move or even allow it.

Well, I didn't know what I'd do, either, so I didn't give myself the chance to find out.

'Okay, I'm furious with you, but I'm concealing it real well,' I said. He relaxed all over when he saw me smile, though it might be the last smile we'd share all day. 'Listen, your office in the middle of day isn't a good time and place to tell you the things I need to tell you,' I said. I spoke very levelly, so he'd realize I wasn't coming on to him. Not only did I just plain old like Alcide, I thought he was one hell of a man – but until I was sure he was through with Debbie Pelt, he was off my list of guys I wanted to be around. The last I'd heard of Debbie, she'd been engaged to another shifter, though even that hadn't ended her emotional involvement with Alcide.

I was not going to get in the middle of that – not with the grief caused by Bill's infidelity still weighing heavily on my own heart.

'Let's go to the Applebee's down the road and have some coffee,' he suggested. Over the intercom, he told Crispy he was leaving. We went out through the back door.

It was about two o'clock by then, and the restaurant was almost empty. Alcide asked the young man who seated us to put us in a booth as far away from anyone else as we could get. I scooted down the bench on one side, expecting Alcide to take the other, but he slid in beside me. 'If you want to tell secrets, this is as close as we can get,' he said.

We both ordered coffee, and Alcide asked the server to bring a small pot. I inquired after his dad while the server was puttering around, and Alcide inquired after Jason. I didn't answer, because the mention of my brother's name was enough to make me feel close to crying. When our coffee had come and the young man had left, Alcide said, 'What's up?'

I took a deep breath, trying to decide where to begin. 'There's a bad witch coven in Shreveport,' I said flatly. 'They drink vampire blood, and at least a few of them are shifters.'

It was Alcide's turn to take a deep breath.

I help up a hand, indicating there was more to come. 'They're moving into Shreveport to take over the vampires' financial kingdom. They put a curse or a hex or something on Eric, and it took away his memory. They raided Fangtasia, trying to discover the day resting place of the vampires. They put some kind of spell on two of the waitresses, and one of them is in the hospital. The other one is dead.'

Alcide was already sliding his cell phone from his pocket.

'Pam and Chow have hidden Eric at my house, and I have to get back before dark to take care of him. And Jason is missing. I don't know who took him or where he is or if he's . . .' *Alive.* But I couldn't say the word.

Alcide's deep breath escaped in a whoosh, and he sat staring at me, the phone in his hand. He couldn't decide whom to call first. I didn't blame him.

'I don't like Eric being at your house,' he said. 'It puts you in danger.'

I was touched that his first thought was for my safety. 'Jason asked for a lot of money for doing it, and Pam and Chow agreed,' I said, embarrassed.

'But Jason isn't there to take the heat, and you are.'

Unanswerably true. But to give Jason credit, he certainly hadn't planned it that way. I told Alcide about the blood on the dock. 'Might be a red herring,' he said. 'If the type matches Jason's, then you can worry.' He took a sip of his coffee, his eyes focused inward. 'I've got to make some calls,' he said.

'Alcide, are you the packmaster for Shreveport?'

'No, no, I'm nowhere near important enough.'

That didn't seem possible to me, and I said as much. He took my hand.

'Packmasters are usually older than me,' he said. 'And you have to be really tough. Really, really tough.'

'Do you have to fight to get to be packmaster?'

'No, you get elected, but the candidates have to be very strong and clever. There's a sort of – well, you have a test you have to take.'

'Written? Oral?' Alcide looked relieved when he saw I was smiling. 'More like an endurance test?' I said.

He nodded. 'More like.'

'Don't you think your packmaster should know about this?'

'Yes. What else?'

'Why would they be doing this? Why pick on Shreveport? If they have that much going for them, the vampire blood and the will to do really bad things, why not set up shop in a more prosperous city?'

'That's a real good question.' Alcide was thinking hard. His green eyes squinted when he thought. 'I've never heard of a witch having this much power. I never heard of a witch being a shifter. I tend to think it's the first time this has ever happened.'

'The first time?'

'That a witch has ever tried to take control of a city, tried to take away the assets of the city's supernatural community,' he said.

'How do witches stand in the supernatural pecking order?'

'Well, they're humans who stay human.' He shrugged. 'Usually, the Supes feel like witches are just wanna-bes. The kind you have to keep an eye on, since they practice magic and we're magical creatures, but still . . .'

'Not a big threat?'

'Right. Looks like we might have to rethink that. Their leader takes vampire blood. Does she drain them herself?' He punched in a number and held the phone to his ear.

'I don't know.'

'And what does she shift into?' Shape-shifters had a choice, but there was one animal each shifter had an affinity for, her habitual animal. A shape-shifter could call herself a 'were-lynx' or a 'were-bat,' if she was out of hearing range of a werewolf. Werewolves objected very strenuously to any other two-natured creatures who termed themselves 'Were.'

'Well, she's . . . like you,' I said. The Weres considered themselves the kings of the two-natured community. They only changed into one animal, and it was the best. The rest of the two-natured community responded by calling the wolves thugs.

'Oh, no.' Alcide was appalled. At that moment, his packmaster answered the phone.

'Hello, this is Alcide.' A silence. 'I'm sorry to bother you when you were busy in the yard. Something important's come up. I need to see you as soon as possible.' Another silence. 'Yes, sir. With your permission, I'll bring someone with me.' After a second or two, Alcide pressed a button to end the conversation. 'Surely Bill knows where Pam and Chow live?' he asked me.

'I'm sure he does, but he's not here to tell me about it.' If he would.

'And where is he?' Alcide's voice was deceptively calm.

'He's in Peru.'

I'd been looking down at my napkin, which I'd pleated into a fan. I glanced up at the man next to me to see him staring down at me with an expression of incredulity.

'He's *gone*? He left you there alone?'

'Well, he didn't know anything was going to happen,' I said, trying not to sound defensive, and then I thought, *What am I saying?* 'Alcide, I haven't seen Bill since I came back from Jackson, except when he came over to tell me he was leaving the country.'

'But she told me you were back with Bill,' Alcide said in a very strange voice.

'Who told you that?'

'Debbie. Who else?'

I'm afraid my reaction was not very flattering. 'And you believed *Debbie*?'

'She said she'd stopped by Merlotte's on her way over to see me, and she'd seen you and Bill acting very, ah, friendly while she was there.'

'And you *believed* her?' Maybe if I kept shifting the emphasis, he'd tell me he was just joking.

Alcide was looking sheepish now, or as sheepish as a werewolf can look.

'Okay, that was dumb,' he admitted. 'I'll deal with her.'

'Right.' Pardon me if I didn't sound very convinced. I'd heard that before.

'Bill's really in Peru?'

'As far as I know.'

'And you're alone in the house with Eric?'

'Eric doesn't know he's Eric.'

'He doesn't remember his identity?'

'Nope. He doesn't remember his character, either, apparently.'

'That's a good thing,' Alcide said darkly. He had never viewed Eric with any sense of humor, as I did. I'd always been leery of Eric, but I'd appreciated his mischief, his single-mindedness, and his flair. If you could say a vampire had joie de vivre, Eric had it in spades.

'Let's go see the packmaster now,' Alcide said, obviously in a much grimmer mood. We slid out of the booth after he'd paid for the coffee, and without phoning in to work ('No point being the boss if I can't vanish from time to time'), he helped me up into his truck and we took off back into Shreveport. I was sure Ms. Crispy would assume we'd checked into a motel or gone to Alcide's apartment, but that was better than Ms. Crispy finding out her boss was a werewolf.

As we drove, Alcide told me that the packmaster was a retired Air Force colonel, formerly stationed at Barksdale Air Force Base in Bossier City, which flowed into Shreveport. Colonel Flood's only child, a daughter, had married a local, and Colonel Flood had settled in the city to be close to his grandchildren.

'His wife is a Were, too?' I asked. If Mrs. Flood was also a Were, their daughter would be, too. If Weres can get through the first few months, they live a good long while, barring accidents.

'She was; she passed away a few months ago.'

Alcide's packmaster lived in a modest neighborhood of ranch-style homes on smallish lots. Colonel Flood was picking up pinecones in his front yard. It seemed a very domestic and peaceable thing for a prominent werewolf to be doing. I'd pictured him in my head in an Air Force uniform, but of course he was wearing regular civilian outdoor clothes. His thick hair was white and cut very short, and he had a mustache that must have been trimmed with a ruler, it was so exact.

The colonel must have been curious after Alcide's phone call, but he asked us to come inside in a calm sort of way. He patted Alcide on the back a lot; he was very polite to me.

The house was as neat as his mustache. It could have passed inspection.

'Can I get you a drink? Coffee? Hot chocolate? Soda?' The colonel gestured toward his kitchen as if there were a servant standing there alert for our orders.

'No, thank you,' I said, since I was awash with

Applebee's coffee. Colonel Flood insisted we sit in the company living room, which was an awkwardly narrow rectangle with a formal dining area at one end. Mrs. Flood had liked porcelain birds. She had liked them a lot. I wondered how the grandchildren fared in this room, and I kept my hands tucked in my lap for fear I'd jostle something.

'So, what can I do for you?' Colonel Flood asked Alcide. 'Are you seeking permission to marry?'

'Not today,' Alcide said with a smile. I looked down at the floor to keep my expression to myself. 'My friend Sookie has some information that she shared with me. It's very important.' His smile died on the vine. 'She needs to relate what she knows to you.'

'And why do I need to listen?'

I understood that he was asking Alcide who I was – that if he was obliged to listen to me, he needed to know my bona fides. But Alcide was offended on my behalf.

'I wouldn't have brought her if it wasn't important. I wouldn't have introduced her to you if I wouldn't give my blood for her.'

I wasn't real certain what that meant, but I was interpreting it to assume Alcide was vouching for my truthfulness and offering to pay in some way if I proved false. Nothing was simple in the supernatural world.

'Let's hear your story, young woman,' said the colonel briskly.

I related all I'd told Alcide, trying to leave out the personal bits.

'Where is this coven staying?' he asked me, when I was through. I told him what I'd seen through Holly's mind.

'Not enough information,' Flood said crisply. 'Alcide, we need the trackers.'

'Yes, sir.' Alcide's eyes were gleaming at the thought of action.

'I'll call them. Everything I've heard is making me rethink something odd that happened last night. Adabelle didn't come to the planning committee meeting.'

Alcide looked startled. 'That's not good.'

They were trying to be cryptic in front of me, but I could read what was passing between the two shifters without too much difficulty. Flood and Alcide were wondering if their – hmmm, vice president? – Adabelle had missed the meeting for some innocent reason, or if the new coven had somehow inveigled her into joining them against her own pack.

'Adabelle has been chafing against the pack leadership for some time,' Colonel Flood told Alcide, with the ghost of a smile on his thin lips. 'I had hoped, when she got elected my second, that she'd consider that concession enough.'

From the bits of information I could glean from the packmaster's mind, the Shreveport pack seemed to be heavily on the patriarchal side. To Adabelle, a modern woman, Colonel Flood's leadership was stifling.

'A new regime might appeal to her,' Colonel Flood said, after a perceptible pause. 'If the invaders learned anything about our pack, it's Adabelle they'd approach.'

'I don't think Adabelle would ever betray the pack, no matter how unhappy she is with the status quo,' Alcide said. He sounded very sure. 'But if she didn't come to the meeting last night, and you can't raise her by phone this morning, I'm concerned.'

'I wish you'd go check on Adabelle while I alert the pack to action,' Colonel Flood suggested. 'If your friend wouldn't mind.'

Maybe his friend would like to get her butt back to Bon Temps and see to her paying guest. Maybe his friend would like to be searching for her brother. Though truly, I could not think of a single thing to do that would further the search for Jason, and it would be at least two hours before Eric rose.

Alcide said, 'Colonel, Sookie is not a pack member and she shouldn't have to shoulder pack responsibilities. She has her own troubles, and she's gone out of her way to let us know about a big problem we didn't even realize we had. We should have known. Someone in our pack hasn't been honest with us.'

Colonel Flood's face drew in on itself as if he'd swallowed a live eel. 'You're right about that,' he said. 'Thank you, Miss Stackhouse, for taking the time to come to Shreveport and to tell Alcide about our problem . . . which we should have known.'

I nodded to him in acknowledgment.

'And I think you're right, Alcide. One of us must have known about the presence of another pack in the city.'

'I'll call you about Adabelle,' Alcide said.

The colonel picked up the phone and consulted a red leather book before he dialed. He glanced sideways at Alcide. 'No answer at her shop.' He had as much warmth radiating from him as a little space heater. Since Colonel Flood kept his house about as cold as the great outdoors, the heat was quite welcome.

'Sookie should be named a friend of the pack.'

I could tell that was more than a recommendation. Alcide was saying something quite significant, but he sure wasn't going to explain. I was getting a little tired of the elliptical conversations going on around me.

'Excuse me, Alcide, Colonel,' I said as politely as I could. 'Maybe Alcide could run me back to my car? Since you all seem to have plans to carry out.'

'Of course,' the colonel said, and I could read that he was glad to be getting me out of the way. 'Alcide, I'll see you back here in, what? Forty minutes or so? We'll talk about it then.'

Alcide glanced at his watch and reluctantly agreed. 'I might stop by Adabelle's house while I'm taking Sookie to her car,' he said, and the colonel nodded, as if that were only pro forma.

'I don't know why Adabelle isn't answering the phone at work, and I don't believe she'd go over to the coven,' Alcide explained when we were back in his truck. 'Adabelle lives with her mother, and they don't get along too well. But we'll check there first. Adabelle's Flood's second in command, and she's also our best tracker.'

'What can the trackers do?'

'They'll go to Fangtasia and try to follow the scent trail the witches left there. That'll take them to the witches' lair. If they lose the scent, maybe we can call in help from the Shreveport covens. They have to be as worried as we are.'

'At Fangtasia, I'm afraid any scent might be obscured by all the emergency people,' I said regretfully. That would have been something to watch, a Were tracking through the city. 'And just so you know, Hallow has contacted all the witches hereabouts already. I talked to a Wiccan in Bon Temps who'd been called in to Shreveport to meet with Hallow's bunch.'

'This is bigger than I thought, but I'm sure the pack can handle it.' Alcide sounded quite confident.

Alcide backed the truck out of the colonel's driveway, and we began making our way through Shreveport once again. I was seeing more of the city this day than I'd seen in my whole life.

'Whose idea was it for Bill to go to Peru?' Alcide asked me suddenly.

'I don't know.' I was startled and puzzled. 'I think it was his queen's.'

'But he didn't tell you that directly.'

'No.'

'He might have been ordered to go.'

'I suppose.'

'Who had the power to do that?' Alcide asked, as if the answer would enlighten me.

'Eric, of course.' Since Eric was sheriff of Area Five. 'And then the queen.' That would be Eric's boss, the queen of Louisiana. Yeah, I know. It's dumb. But the vampires thought they were a marvel of modern organization.

'And now Bill's gone, and Eric's staying at your house.' Alcide's voice was coaxing me to reach an obvious conclusion.

'You think that Eric staged this whole thing? You think he ordered Bill out of the country, had witches invade Shreveport, had them curse him, began running half-naked out in the freezing cold when he supposed I might be near, and then just hoped I'd take him in and that Pam and Chow and my brother would talk to each other to arrange Eric's staying with me?'

Alcide looked properly flattened. 'You mean you'd thought of this?'

'Alcide, I'm not educated, but I'm not dumb.' Try getting educated when you can read the minds of all your classmates, not to mention your teacher. But I read a lot, and I've read lots of good stuff. Of course, now I read mostly mysteries and romances. So I've learned many curious odds and ends, and I have a great vocabulary. 'But the fact is, Eric would hardly go to this much trouble to get me to go to bed with him. Is that what you're thinking?' Of course, I knew it was. Were or not, I could see that much.

'Put that way . . .' But Alcide still didn't look satisfied. Of course, this was the man who had believed Debbie Pelt when she said that I was definitely back with Bill.

I wondered if I could get some witch to cast a truth spell on Debbie Pelt, whom I despised because she had been cruel to Alcide, insulted me grievously, burned a hole in my favorite wrap and – oh – tried to kill me by proxy. Also, she had stupid hair.

Alcide wouldn't know an honest Debbie if she came up and bit him in the ass, though backbiting was a specialty of the real Debbie.

If Alcide had known Bill and I had parted, would he have come by? Would one thing have led to another?

Well, *sure* it would have. And there I'd be, stuck with a guy who'd take the word of Debbie Pelt.

I glanced over at Alcide and sighed. This man was just about perfect in many respects. I liked the way he looked, I understood the way he thought, and he treated me with great consideration and respect. Sure, he was a werewolf, but I could give up a couple of nights of month. True, according to Alcide it would be difficult for me to carry his baby to term, but it was at least possible. Pregnancy wasn't part of the picture with a vampire.

Whoa. Alcide hadn't offered to father my babies, and he

was still seeing Debbie. What had happened to her engagement to the Clausen guy?

With the less noble side of my character – assuming my character had a noble side – I hoped that someday soon Alcide would see Debbie for the bitch she truly was, and that he'd finally take the knowledge to heart. Whether, consequently, Alcide turned to me or not, he deserved better than Debbie Pelt.

Adabelle Yancy and her mother lived in a cul-de-sac in an upper-middle-class neighborhood that wasn't too far from Fangtasia. The house was on a rolling lawn that raised it higher than the street, so the driveway mounted and went to the rear of the property. I thought Alcide might park on the street and we'd go up the brick walkway to the front door, but he seemed to want to get the truck out of sight. I scanned the cul-de-sac, but I didn't see anyone at all, much less anyone watching the house for visitors.

Attached to the rear of the house at a right angle, the three-car garage was neat as a pin. You would think cars were never parked there, that the gleaming Subaru had just strayed into the area. We climbed out of the truck.

'That's Adabelle's mother's car.' Alcide was frowning. 'She started a bridal shop. I bet you've heard of it – Verena Rose. Verena's retired from working there full-time. She drops in just often enough to make Adabelle crazy.'

I'd never been to the shop, but brides of any claim to prominence in the area made a point of shopping there. It must be a real profitable store. The brick home was in excellent shape, and no more than twenty years old. The yard was edged, raked, and landscaped.

When Alcide knocked at the back door, it flew open.

The woman who stood revealed in the opening was as put-together and neat as the house and yard. Her steel-colored hair was in a neat roll on the back of her head, and she was in a dull olive suit and low-heeled brown pumps. She looked from Alcide to me and didn't find what she was seeking. She pushed open the glass storm door.

'Alcide, how nice to see you,' she lied desperately. This was a woman in deep turmoil.

Alcide gave her a long look. 'We have trouble, Verena.'

If her daughter was a member of the pack, Verena herself was a werewolf. I looked at the woman curiously, and she seemed like one of the more fortunate friends of my grandmother's. Verena Rose Yancy was an attractive woman in her late sixties, blessed with a secure income and her own home. I could not imagine this woman down on all fours loping across a field.

And it was obvious that Verena didn't give a damn what trouble Alcide had. 'Have you seen my daughter?' she asked, and she waited for his answer with terror in her eyes. 'She can't have betrayed the pack.'

'No,' Alcide said. 'But the packmaster sent us to find her. She missed a pack officers' meeting last night.'

'She called me from the shop last night. She said she had an unexpected appointment with a stranger who'd called the shop right at closing time.' The woman literally wrung her hands. 'I thought maybe she was meeting that witch.'

'Have you heard from her since?' I said, in the gentlest voice I could manage.

'I went to bed last night mad at her,' Verena said, looking directly at me for the first time. 'I thought she'd decided to spend the night with one of her friends. One of her *girl* friends,' she explained, looking at me with eyebrows arched, so I'd get her drift. I nodded. 'She never would tell me ahead of time, she'd just say, "Expect me when you see me," or "I'll meet you at the shop tomorrow morning," or something.' A shudder rippled through Verena's slim body. 'But she hasn't come home and I can't get an answer at the shop.'

'Was she supposed to open the shop today?' Alcide asked.

'No, Wednesday's our closed day, but she always goes in to work on the books and get paperwork out of the way. She always does,' Verena repeated.

'Why don't Alcide and I drive over there and check the shop for you?' I said gently. 'Maybe she left a note.' This was not a woman you patted on the arm, so I didn't make that natural gesture, but I did push the glass door shut so she'd understand she had to stay there and she shouldn't come with us. She understood all too clearly.

Verena Rose's Bridal and Formal Shop was located in an old home on a block of similarly converted two-story houses. The building had been renovated and maintained as beautifully as the Yancys' residence, and I wasn't surprised it had such cachet. The white-painted brick, the dark green shutters, the glossy black ironwork of the railings on the steps, and the brass details on the door all spoke of elegance and attention to detail. I could see that if you had aspirations to class, this is where you'd come to get your wedding gear.

Set a little back from the street, with parking behind the store, the building featured one large bay window in front. In this window stood a faceless mannequin wearing a shining brown wig. Her arms were gracefully bent to hold a stunning bouquet. Even from the truck, I could see that the bridal dress, with its long embroidered train, was absolutely spectacular.

We parked in the driveway without pulling around back, and I jumped out of the pickup. Together we took the brick sidewalk that led from the drive to the front door, and as we got closer, Alcide cursed. For a moment, I imagined some kind of bug infestation had gotten into the store window and landed on the snowy dress. But after that moment, I knew the dark flecks were surely spatters of blood.

The blood had sprayed onto the white brocade and dried there. It was as if the mannequin had been wounded, and for a crazy second I wondered. I'd seen a lot of impossible things in the past few months.

'Adabelle,' Alcide said, as if he was praying.

We were standing at the bottom of the steps leading up to the front porch, staring into the bay window. The CLOSED sign was hanging in the middle of the glass oval inset in the door, and venetian blinds were closed behind it. There were no live brainwaves emanating from that house. I had taken the time to check. I'd discovered, the hard way, that checking was a good idea.

'Dead things,' Alcide said, his face raised to the cold breeze, his eyes shut to help him concentrate. 'Dead things inside and out.'

I took hold of the curved ironwork handrail with my left hand and went up one step. I glanced around. My eyes came to rest on something in the flowerbed under the bay window, something pale that stood out against the pine bark mulch. I nudged Alcide, and I pointed silently with my free right hand.

Lying by a pruned-back azalea, there was another hand – an unattached extra. I felt a shudder run through Alcide's body as he comprehended what he saw. There was that moment when you tried to recognize it as anything but what it was.

'Wait here,' Alcide said, his voice thick and hoarse.

That was just fine with me.

But when he opened the unlocked front door to enter the shop, I saw what lay on the floor just beyond. I had to swallow a scream.

It was lucky Alcide had his cell phone. He called Colonel Flood, told him what had happened, and asked him to go over to Mrs. Yancy's house. Then he called the police. There was just no way around it. This was a busy area, and there was a good chance someone had noticed us going to the front door.

It was surely a day for finding bodies – for me, and for the Shreveport police department. I knew there were some vampire cops on the force, but of course the vamps had to work the night shift, so we spoke to regular old human cops. There wasn't a Were or a shifter among 'em, not even a telepathic human. All these police officers were regular people who thought we were borderline suspicious.

'Why did you stop by here, buddy?' asked Detective Coughlin, who had brown hair, a weathered face, and a beer belly one of the Clydesdales would've been proud of.

Alcide looked surprised. He hadn't thought this far, which wasn't too amazing. I hadn't known Adabelle when she was alive, and I hadn't stepped inside the bridal shop as he had. I hadn't sustained the worst shock. It was up to me to pick up the reins.

'It was my idea, Detective,' I said instantly. 'My grandmother, who died last year? She always told me, "If you need a wedding dress, Sookie, you go to Verena Rose's for it." I didn't think to call ahead and check to see if they were open today.'

'So, you and Mr. Herveaux are going to be married?'

'Yes,' said Alcide, pulling me against him and wrapping his arms around me. 'We're headed for the altar.'

I smiled, but in an appropriately subdued way.

'Well, congratulations.' Detective Coughlin eyed us thoughtfully. 'So, Miss Stackhouse, you hadn't ever met Adabelle Yancy face-to-face?'

'I may have met the older Mrs. Yancy when I was a little girl,' I said cautiously. 'But I don't remember her. Alcide's family knows the Yancys, of course. He's lived here all his life.' Of course, they're also werewolves.

Coughlin was still focused on me. 'And you didn't go in the shop none? Just Mr. Herveaux here?'

'Alcide just stepped in while I waited out here.' I tried to look delicate, which is not easy for me. I am healthy and muscular, and while I am not Emme, I'm not Kate Moss either. 'I'd seen the – the hand, so I stayed out.'

'That was a good idea,' Detective Coughlin said. 'What's in there isn't fit for people to see.' He looked about twenty years older as he said that. I felt sorry that his job was so tough. He was thinking that the savaged bodies in the house were a waste of two good lives and the work of someone he'd love to arrest. 'Would either of you have any idea why anyone would want to rip up two ladies like this?'

'Two,' Alcide said slowly, stunned.

'Two?' I said, less guardedly.

'Why, yes,' the detective said heavily. He had aimed to get our reactions and now he had them; what he thought of them, I would find out.

'Poor things,' I said, and I wasn't faking the tears that filled my eyes. It was kind of nice to have Alcide's chest to lean against, and as if he were reading my mind he unzipped his leather jacket so I'd be closer to him, wrapping the open sides around me to keep me warmer. 'But if one of them is Adabelle Yancy, who is the other?'

'There's not much left of the other,' Coughlin said, before he told himself to shut his mouth.

'They were kind of jumbled up,' Alcide said quietly, close to my ear. He was sickened. 'I didn't know . . . I guess if I'd analyzed what I was seeing . . .'

Though I couldn't read Alcide's thoughts clearly, I could understand that he was thinking that Adabelle had managed to take down one of her attackers. And when the rest of the group was getting away, they hadn't taken all the appropriate bits with them.

'And you're from Bon Temps, Miss Stackhouse,' the detective said, almost idly.

'Yes, sir,' I said, with a gasp. I was trying not to picture Adabelle Yancy's last moments.

'Where you work there?'

'Merlotte's Bar and Grill,' I said. 'I wait tables.'

While he registered the difference in social status between me and Alcide, I closed my eyes and laid my head against Alcide's warm chest. Detective Coughlin was wondering if I was pregnant; if Alcide's dad, a well-known and well-to-do figure in Shreveport, would approve of such a marriage. He could see why I'd want an expensive wedding dress, if I were marrying a Herveaux.

'You don't have an engagement ring, Miss Stackhouse?'

'We don't plan on a long engagement,' Alcide said. I could hear his voice rumbling in his chest. 'She'll get her diamond the day we marry.'

'You're so bad,' I said fondly, punching him in the ribs as hard as I could without being obvious.

'Ouch,' he said in protest.

Somehow this bit of byplay convinced Detective Coughlin that we were really engaged. He took down our phone numbers and addresses, then told us we could leave. Alcide was as relieved as I was.

We drove to the nearest place where we could pull over in privacy – a little park that was largely deserted in the cold weather – and Alcide called Colonel Flood again. I waited in the truck while Alcide, pacing in the dead grass, gesticulated and raised his voice, venting some of his horror and anger. I'd been able to feel it building up in him. Alcide had trouble articulating emotions, like lots of guys. It made him seem more familiar and dear.

Dear? I'd better stop thinking like that. The engagement had been drummed up strictly for Detective Coughlin's benefit. If Alcide was anyone's 'dear,' it was the perfidious Debbie's.

When Alcide climbed back into the pickup, he was scowling.

'I guess I better go back to the office and take you to your car,' he said. 'I'm sorry about all this.'

'I guess I should be saying that.'

'This is a situation neither of us created,' he said firmly. 'Neither of us would be involved if we could help it.'

'That's the God's truth.' After a minute of thinking of

the complicated supernatural world, I asked Alcide what Colonel Flood's plan was.

'We'll take care of it,' Alcide said. 'I'm sorry, Sook, I can't tell you what we're going to do.'

'Are you going to be in danger?' I asked, because I just couldn't help it.

We'd gotten to the Herveaux building by then, and Alcide parked his truck by my old car. He turned a little to face me, and he reached over to take my hand. 'I'm gonna be fine. Don't worry,' he said gently. 'I'll call you.'

'Don't forget to do that,' I said. 'And I have to tell you what the witches did about trying to find Eric.' I hadn't told Alcide about the posted pictures, the reward. He frowned even harder when he thought about the cleverness of this ploy.

'Debbie was supposed to drive over this afternoon, get here about six,' he said. He looked at his watch. 'Too late to stop her coming.'

'If you're planning a big raid, she could help,' I said.

He gave me a sharp look. Like a pointed stick he wanted to poke in my eye. 'She's a shifter, not a Were,' he reminded me defensively.

Maybe she turned into a weasel or a rat.

'Of course,' I said seriously. I literally bit my tongue so I wouldn't make any of the remarks that waited just inside my mouth, dying to be spoken. 'Alcide, do you think the other body was Adabelle's girlfriend? Someone who just got caught at the shop with Adabelle when the witches came calling?'

'Since a lot of the second body was missing, I hope that the body was one of the witches. I hope Adabelle went down fighting.'

'I hope so, too.' I nodded, putting an end to that train of thought. 'I'd better get back to Bon Temps. Eric will be waking up soon. Don't forget to tell your dad that we're engaged.'

His expression provided the only fun I'd had all day.

Chapter 6

I thought all the way home about my day in Shreveport. I'd asked Alcide to call the cops in Bon Temps from his cell phone, and he'd gotten another negative message. No, they hadn't heard any more on Jason, and no one had called to say they'd seen him. So I didn't stop by the police station on my way home, but I did have to go to the grocery to buy some margarine and bread, and I did have to go in the liquor store to pick up some blood.

The first thing I saw when I pushed open the door of Super Save-A-Bunch was a little display of bottled blood, which saved me a stop at the liquor store. The second thing I saw was the poster with the headshot of Eric. I assumed it was the photo Eric had had made when he opened Fangtasia, because it was a very nonthreatening picture. He was projecting winsome worldliness; any person in this universe would know that he'd never, ever bite. It was headed, 'HAVE YOU SEEN THIS VAMPIRE?'

I read the text carefully. Everything Jason had said about it was true. Fifty thousand dollars is a lot of money. That Hallow must be really nuts about Eric to pay that much, if all she wanted was a hump. It was hard to believe gaining control of Fangtasia (and having the bed services of Eric) would afford her a profit after paying out a reward that large. I was increasingly doubtful that I knew the whole story, and I was increasingly sure I was sticking my neck out and might get it bitten off.

Hoyt Fortenberry, Jason's big buddy, was loading pizzas into his buggy in the frozen food aisle. 'Hey, Sookie, where you think ole Jason got to?' he called as soon as he saw me. Hoyt, big and beefy and no rocket scientist, looked genuinely concerned.

'I wish I knew,' I said, coming closer so we could talk without everyone in the store recording every word. 'I'm pretty worried.'

'You don't think he's just gone off with some girl he met? That girl he was with New Year's Eve was pretty cute.'

'What was her name?'

'Crystal. Crystal Norris.'

'Where's she from?'

'From round Hotshot, out thataway.' He nodded south.

Hotshot was even smaller than Bon Temps. It was about ten miles away and had a reputation for being a strange little community. The Hotshot kids who attended the Bon Temps school always stuck together, and they were all a smidge . . . different. It didn't surprise me at all that Crystal lived in Hotshot.

'So,' Hoyt said, persisting in making his point, 'Crystal might have asked him to come stay with her.' But his brain was saying he didn't believe it, he was only trying to comfort me and himself. We both knew that Jason would have phoned by now, no matter how good a time he was having with any woman.

But I decided I'd give Crystal a call when I had a clear ten minutes, which might not be any time tonight. I asked Hoyt to pass on Crystal's name to the sheriff's department, and he said he would. He didn't seem too happy about the idea. I could tell that if the missing man had been anyone but Jason, Hoyt would have refused. But Jason had always been Hoyt's source of recreation and general amusement, since Jason was far more clever and inventive than the slow-moving, slow-thinking Hoyt: If Jason never reappeared, Hoyt would have a dull life.

We parted in the Super Save-A-Bunch parking lot, and I felt relieved that Hoyt hadn't asked me about the TrueBlood I'd purchased. Neither had the cashier, though she'd handled the bottles with distaste. As I'd paid for it, I'd thought about how much I was in the hole from hosting Eric already. Clothes and blood mounted up.

It was just dark when I got to my house and pulled the plastic grocery bags out of the car. I unlocked my back door and went in, calling to Eric as I switched on the kitchen light. I didn't hear an answer, so I put the groceries away, leaving a bottle of TrueBlood out of the refrigerator so he could have it to hand when he got hungry. I got the shotgun out of my trunk and loaded it, sticking it in the shadow of the water heater. I took a minute to call the sheriff's department again. No news of Jason, said the dispatcher.

I slumped against the kitchen wall for a long moment, feeling dejected. It wasn't a good thing to just sit around, being depressed. Maybe I'd go out to the living room and pop a movie into the VCR, as entertainment for Eric. He'd gone through all my *Buffy* tapes, and I didn't have *Angel*. I wondered if he'd like *Gone with the Wind.* (For all

I knew, he'd been around when they were filming it. On the other hand, he had amnesia. Anything should be new to him.)

But as I went down the hall, I heard some small movement. I pushed open the door of my old room gently, not wanting to make a big noise if my guest wasn't yet up. Oh, but he was. Eric was pulling on his jeans, with his back to me. He hadn't bothered with underwear, not even the itty-bitty red ones. My breath stuck in my throat. I made a sound like 'Guck,' and made myself close my eyes tight. I clenched my fists.

If there were an international butt competition, Eric would win, hands down – or cheeks up. He would get a large, large trophy. I had never realized a woman could have to struggle to keep her hands off a man, but here I was, digging my nails into my palms, staring at the inside of my eyelids as though I could maybe see through them if I peered hard enough.

It was somehow degrading, craving someone so . . . so *voraciously* – another good calendar word – just because he was physically beautiful. I hadn't thought that was something women did, either.

'Sookie, are you all right?' Eric asked. I floundered my way back to sanity through a swamp of lust. He was standing right in front of me, his hands resting on my shoulders. I looked up into his blue eyes, now focused on me and apparently full of nothing but concern. I was right on a level with his hard nipples. They were the size of pencil erasers. I bit the inside of my lip. I would *not* lean over those few inches.

'Excuse me,' I said, speaking very softly. I was scared to speak loudly, or move at all. If I did, I might knock him down. 'I didn't mean to walk in on you. I should have knocked.'

'You have seen all of me before.'

Not the rear view, bare. 'Yes, but intruding wasn't polite.'

'I don't mind. You look upset.'

You think? 'Well, I have had a very bad day,' I said, through clenched teeth. 'My brother is missing, and the Were witches in Shreveport killed the – the vice president of the Were pack there, and her hand was in the flowerbed. Well, someone's was. Belinda's in the hospital. Ginger is dead. I think I'll take a shower.' I turned on my heel and marched into my room. I went in the bathroom and shucked my clothes, tossing them into the hamper. I bit my lip until I could smile at my own streak of wildness, and then I climbed into the spray of hot water.

I know cold showers are more traditional, but I was enjoying the warmth and relaxation the heat brought. I got my hair wet and groped for the soap.

'I'll do that for you,' Eric said, pulling back the curtain to step into the shower with me.

I gasped, just short of a shriek. He had discarded the jeans. He was also in the mood, the same mood I was in. You could really tell, with Eric. His fangs were out some, too. I was embarrassed, horrified, and absolutely ready to jump him. While I stood stock-still, paralyzed by conflicting waves of emotion, Eric took the soap out of my hands and lathered up his own, set the soap back in its little niche, and began to wash my arms, raising each in turn to stroke my armpit, down my side, never touching my breasts, which were practically quivering like puppies who wanted to be petted.

'Have we ever made love?' he asked.

I shook my head, still unable to speak.

'Then I was a fool,' he said, moving one hand in a circular motion over my stomach. 'Turn around, lover.'

I turned my back to him, and he began to work on that. His fingers were very strong and very clever, and I had the most relaxed and cleanest set of shoulder blades in Louisiana by the time Eric got through.

My shoulder blades were the only thing at ease. My libido was hopping up and down. Was I really going to do this? It seemed more and more likely that I was, I thought nervously. If the man in my shower had been the real Eric, I would have had the strength to back off. I would have ordered him out the minute he stepped in. The real Eric came with a whole package of power and politics, something of which I had limited understanding and interest. This was a different Eric – without the personality that I'd grown fond of, in a perverse way – but it was beautiful Eric, who desired me, who was hungry for me, in a world that often let me know it could do very well without me. My mind was about to switch off and my body was about to take over. I could feel part of Eric pressed against my back, and he wasn't standing that close. Yikes. Yahoo. Yum.

He shampooed my hair next.

'Are you trembling because you are frightened of me?' he asked.

I considered that. Yes, and no. But I wasn't about to have a long discussion over the pros and cons. The inner debate had been tough enough. Oh, yeah, I know, there wouldn't be a better time to have a long yada-yada with Eric about the moral aspects of mating with someone you didn't love. And maybe there would never be another time to lay ground rules about being careful to be gentle with me physically. Not that I thought Eric would beat me up, but his manhood (as my romance novels called it – in this case the popular adjectives 'burgeoning' or 'throbbing' might also be applied) was a daunting prospect to a relatively inexperienced woman like me. I felt like a car that had only been operated by one driver . . . a car its new prospective buyer was determined to take to the Daytona 500.

Oh, to hell with thinking.

I took the soap from the niche and lathered up my fingers. As I stepped very close to him, I kind of folded Mr. Happy up against Eric's stomach, so I could reach around him and get my fingers on that absolutely gorgeous butt. I couldn't look him in the face, but he let me know he was delighted that I was responding. He spread his legs obligingly and I washed him very thoroughly, very meticulously. He began to make little noises, to rock forward. I began to work on his chest. I closed my lips around his right nipple and sucked. He liked that a lot. His hands pressed against the back of my head. 'Bite, a little,' he whispered, and I used my teeth. His hands began to move restlessly over whatever bit of my skin they could find, stroking and teasing. When he pulled away, he had decided to reciprocate, and he bent down. While his mouth closed over my breast, his hand glided between my legs. I gave a deep sigh, and did a little moving of my own. He had long fingers.

The next thing I knew, the water was off and he was drying me with a fluffy white towel, and I was rubbing him with another one. Then we just kissed for while, over and over.

'The bed,' he said, a little raggedly, and I nodded. He

scooped me up and then we got into a kind of tangle with me trying to pull the bedspread down while he just wanted to dump me on the bed and proceed, but I had my way because it was just too cold for the top of the bed. Once we were arranged, I turned to him and we picked back up where we'd left off, but with an escalating tempo. His fingers and his mouth were busy learning my topography, and he pressed heavily against my thigh.

I was so on fire for him I was surprised that flames didn't flicker out of my fingertips. I curled my fingers around him and stroked.

Suddenly Eric was on top of me, about to enter. I was exhilarated and very ready. I reached between us to put him at just the right spot, rubbing the tip of him over my nub as I did so.

'My lover,' he said hoarsely, and pushed.

Though I'd been sure I was prepared, and I ached with wanting him, I cried out with the shock of it.

After a moment, he said, 'Don't close your eyes. Look at me, lover.' The way he said 'lover' was like a caress, like he was calling me by a name no other man had ever used before or ever would after. His fangs were completely extended and I stretched up to run my tongue over them. I expected he would bite my neck, as Bill nearly always did.

'Watch me,' he said in my ear, and pulled out. I tried to yank him back, but he began kissing his way down my body, making strategic stops, and I was hovering on the golden edge when he got all the way down. His mouth was talented, and his fingers took the place of his penis, and then all of a sudden he looked up the length of my body to make sure I was watching – I was – and he turned his face to my inner thigh, nuzzling it, his fingers moving steadily now, faster and faster, and then he bit.

I may have made a noise, I am sure I did, but in the next second I was floating on the most powerful wave of pleasure I'd ever felt. And the minute the shining wave subsided, Eric was kissing my mouth again, and I could taste my own fluids on him, and then he was back inside me, and it happened all over again. His moment came right after, as I was still experiencing aftershocks. He shouted something in a language I'd never heard, and he closed his own eyes, and then he collapsed on top of me. After a couple of minutes, he raised his head to look down. I wished he would pretend to breathe, as Bill always had during sex. (I'd never asked him, he'd just done it, and it had been reassuring.) I pushed the thought away. I'd never had sex with anyone but Bill, and I guess it was natural to think of that, but the truth was it hurt to remember my previous one-man status, now gone for good.

I yanked myself back into The Moment, which was fine enough. I stroked Eric's hair, tucking some behind his ear. His eyes on mine were intent, and I knew he was waiting for me to speak. 'I wish,' I said, 'I could save orgasms in a jar for when I need them, because I think I had a few extra.'

Eric's eyes widened, and all of a sudden he roared with laughter. That sounded good, that sounded like the real Eric. I felt comfortable with this gorgeous but unknown stranger, after I heard that laugh. He rolled onto his back and swung me over easily until I was straddling his waist.

'If I had known you would be this gorgeous with your clothes off, I would have tried to do this sooner,' he said.

'You did try to do this sooner, about twenty times,' I said, smiling down at him.

'Then I have good taste.' He hesitated for a long minute, some of the pleasure leaving his face. 'Tell me about us. How long have I known you?'

The light from the bathroom spilled onto the right side of his face. His hair spread over my pillow, shining and golden.

'I'm cold,' I said gently, and he let me lie beside him, pulling the covers up over us. I propped myself up on one elbow and he lay on his side, so we were facing each other. 'Let me think. I met you last year at Fangtasia, the vampire bar you own in Shreveport. And by the way, the bar got attacked today. Last night. I'm sorry, I should have told you that first, but I've been so worried about my brother.'

'I want to hear about today, but give me our background first. I find myself mightily interested.'

Another little shock: The real Eric cared about his own position first, relationships down about – oh, I don't know, tenth. This was definitely odd. I told him, 'You are the sheriff of Area Five, and my former boyfriend Bill is your subordinate. He's gone, out of the country. I think I told you about Bill.'

'Your unfaithful former boyfriend? Whose maker was the vampire Lorena?'

'That's the one,' I said briefly. 'Anyway, when I met you at Fangtasia . . .'

It all took longer than I thought, and by the time I had finished with the tale, Eric's hands were busy again. He latched onto one breast with his fangs extended, drawing a little blood and a sharp gasp from me, and he sucked powerfully. It was a strange sensation, because he was getting the blood and my nipple. Painful and very exciting – I felt like he was drawing the fluid from much lower. I gasped and jerked in arousal, and suddenly he raised my leg so he could enter me.

It wasn't such a shock this time, and it was slower. Eric wanted me to be looking into his eyes; that obviously flicked his Bic.

I was exhausted when it was over, though I'd enjoyed myself immensely. I'd heard a lot about men who didn't care if the woman had her pleasure, or perhaps such men assumed that if they were happy, their partner was, too. But neither of the men I'd been with had been like that. I didn't know if that was because they were vampires, or because I'd been lucky, or both.

Eric had paid me many compliments, and I realized I hadn't said anything to him that indicated my admiration. That hardly seemed fair. He was holding me, and my head was on his shoulder. I murmured into his neck, 'You are so beautiful.'

'What?' He was clearly startled.

'You've told me you thought my body was nice.' Of course that wasn't the adjective he'd used, but I was embarrassed to repeat his actual words. 'I just wanted you to know I think the same about you.'

I could feel his chest move as he laughed, just a little. 'What part do you like best?' he asked, his voice teasing.

'Oh, your butt,' I said instantly.

'My . . . bottom?'

'Yep.'

'I would have thought of another part.'

'Well, that's certainly . . . adequate,' I told him, burying my face in his chest. I knew immediately I'd picked the wrong word.

'*Adequate?*' He took my hand, placed it on the part in

question. It immediately began to stir. He moved my hand on it, and I obligingly circled it with my fingers. 'This is *adequate*?'

'Maybe I should have said it's a gracious plenty?'

'A gracious plenty. I like that,' he said.

He was ready again, and honestly, I didn't know if I could. I was worn out to the point of wondering if I'd be walking funny the next day.

I indicated I would be pleased with an alternative by sliding down in the bed, and he seemed delighted to reciprocate. After another sublime release, I thought every muscle in my body had turned to Jell-O. I didn't talk anymore about the worry I felt about my brother, about the terrible things that had happened in Shreveport, about anything unpleasant. We whispered some heartfelt (on my part) mutual compliments, and I was just out of it. I don't know what Eric did for the rest of the night, because I fell asleep.

I had many worries waiting for me the next day; but thanks to Eric, for a few precious hours I just didn't care.

Chapter 7

The next morning the sun was shining outside when I woke. I lay in bed in a mindless pool of contentment. I was sore, but pleasantly so. I had a little bruise or two nothing that would show. And the fang marks that were a dead giveaway (har-de-har) were not on my neck, where they'd been in the past. No casual observer was going to be able to tell I'd enjoyed a vampire's company, and I didn't have an appointment with a gynecologist – the only other person who'd have a reason to check that area.

Another shower was definitely called for, so I eased out of bed and wobbled across the floor to the bathroom. We'd left it in something of a mess, with towels tossed everywhere and the shower curtain half-ripped from its plastic hoops (when had *that* happened?), but I didn't mind picking it up. I rehung the curtain with a smile on my face and a song in my heart.

As the water pounded on my back, I reflected that I must be pretty simple. It didn't take much to make me happy. A long night with a dead guy had done the trick. It wasn't just the dynamic sex that had given me so much pleasure (though that had contained moments I'd remember till the day I died); it was the companionship. Actually, the intimacy.

Call me stereotypical. I'd spent the night with a man who'd told me I was beautiful, a man who'd enjoyed me and who'd given me intense pleasure. He had touched me and held me and laughed with me. We weren't in danger of making a baby with our pleasures, because vampires just can't do that. I wasn't being disloyal to anyone (though I'll admit I'd had a few pangs when I thought of Bill), and neither was Eric. I couldn't see the harm.

As I brushed my teeth and put on some makeup, I had to admit to myself that I was sure that the Reverend Fullenwilder wouldn't agree with my viewpoint.

Well, I hadn't been going to tell him about it, anyway. It would just be between God and me. I figured God had made me with the disability of telepathy, and he could cut me a little slack on the sex thing.

I had regrets, of course. I would love to get married and have babies. I'd be faithful as can be. I'd be a good mom, too. But I couldn't marry a regular guy, because I would always know when he lied to me, when he was angry with me, every little thought he had about me. Even dating a regular guy was more than I'd been able to manage. Vampires can't marry, not yet, not legally; not that a vampire had asked me, I reminded myself, tossing a washcloth into the hamper a little forcefully. Perhaps I could stand a long association with a Were or a shifter, since their thoughts weren't clear. But there again, where was the willing Were?

I had better enjoy what I had at this moment –

something I've become quite good at doing. What I had was a handsome vampire who'd temporarily lost his memory and, along with it, a lot of his personality: a vampire who needed reassurance just as much as I did.

In fact, as I put in my earrings, I figured out that Eric had been so delighted with me for more than one reason. I could see that after days of being completely without memories of his possessions or underlings, days lacking any sense of self, last night he had gained something of his own – me. His lover.

Though I was standing in front of a mirror, I wasn't really seeing my reflection. I was seeing, very clearly, that – at the moment – I was all in the world that Eric could think of as his own.

I had better not fail him.

I was rapidly bringing myself down from 'relaxed happiness' to 'guilty grim resolution,' so I was relieved when the phone rang. It had a built-in caller ID, and I noticed Sam was calling from the bar, instead of his trailer.

'Sookie?'

'Hey, Sam.'

'I'm sorry about Jason. Any news?'

'No. I called down to the sheriff's department when I woke up, and I talked to the dispatcher. She said Alcee Beck would let me know if anything new came up. That's what she's said the last twenty times I've called.'

'Want me to get someone to take your shift?'

'No. It would be better for me to be busy, than to sit here at home. They know where to reach me if they've got anything to tell me.'

'You sure?'

'Yes. Thanks for asking, though.'

'If I can do anything to help, you let me know.'

'There is something, come to think of it.'

'Name it.'

'You remember the little shifter Jason was in the bar with New Year's Eve?'

Sam gave it thought. 'Yes,' he said hesitantly. 'One of the Norris girls? They live out in Hotshot.'

'That's what Hoyt said.'

'You have to watch out for people from out there, Sookie. That's an old settlement. An inbred settlement.'

I wasn't sure what Sam was trying to tell me. 'Could you spell that out? I'm not up to unraveling subtle hints today.'

'I can't right now.'

'Oh, not alone?'

'No. The snack delivery guy is here. Just be careful. They're really, really different.'

'Okay,' I said slowly, still in the dark. 'I'll be careful. See you at four-thirty,' I told him, and hung up, vaguely unhappy and quite puzzled.

I had plenty of time to go out to Hotshot and get back before I had to go to work. I pulled on some jeans, sneakers, a bright red long-sleeved T-shirt, and my old blue coat. I looked up Crystal Norris's address in the phone book and had to get out my chamber of commerce map to track it down. I've lived in Renard Parish my whole life, and I thought I knew it pretty well, but the Hotshot area was a black hole in my otherwise thorough knowledge.

I drove north, and when I came to the T-junction, I turned right. I passed the lumber processing plant that was Bon Temps's main employer, and I passed a reupholstering place, and I flew past the water department. There was a liquor store or two, and then a country store at a crossroads that had a prominent COLD BEER AND BAIT sign left over from the summer and propped up facing the road. I turned right again, to go south.

The deeper I went into the countryside, the worse the road seemed to grow. The mowing and maintenance crews hadn't been out here since the end of summer. Either the residents of the Hotshot community had no pull whatsoever in the parish government, or they just didn't want visitors. From time to time, the road dipped in some low-lying areas as it ran between bayous. In heavy rains, the low spots would be flooded. I wouldn't be surprised at all to hear folks out here encountered the occasional gator.

Finally I came to another crossroads, compared to which the one with the bait shop seemed like a mall. There were a few houses scattered around, maybe eight or nine. These were small houses, none of them brick. Most of them had several cars in the front yard. Some of them sported a rusty swing set or a basketball hoop, and in a couple of yards I spotted a satellite dish. Oddly, all the houses seemed pulled away from the actual crossroads; the area directly around the road intersection was bare. It was like someone had tied a rope to a stake sunk in the middle of the crossing and drawn a circle. Within it, there was nothing. Outside it, the houses crouched.

In my experience, in a little settlement like this, you had the same kind of people you had anywhere. Some of them were poor and proud and good. Some of them were poor and mean and worthless. But all of them knew each other thoroughly, and no action went unobserved.

On this chilly day, I didn't see a soul outdoors to let me know if this was a black community or a white community.

It was unlikely to be both. I wondered if I was at the right crossroads, but my doubts were washed away when I saw an imitation green road sign, the kind you can order from a novelty company, mounted on a pole in front of one of the homes. It read, HOTSHOT.

I was in the right place. Now, to find Crystal Norris's house.

With some difficulty, I spotted a number on one rusty mailbox, and then I saw another. By process of elimination, I figured the next house must be the one where Crystal Norris lived. The Norris house was little different from any of the others; it had a small front porch with an old armchair and two lawn chairs on it, and two cars parked in front, one a Ford Fiesta and the other an ancient Buick.

When I parked and got out, I realized what was so unusual about Hotshot.

No dogs.

Any other hamlet that looked like this would have at least twelve dogs milling around, and I'd be wondering if I could safely get out of the car. Here, not a single yip broke the winter silence.

I crossed over the hard, packed dirt of the yard, feeling as though eyes were on every step I took. I opened the torn screen door to knock on the heavier wooden door. Inset in it was a pattern of three glass panes. Dark eyes surveyed me through the lowest one.

The door opened, just when the pause was beginning to make me anxious.

Jason's date from New Year's Eve was less festive today, in black jeans and a cream-colored T-shirt. Her boots had come from Payless, and her short curly hair was a sort of dusty black. She was thin, intense, and though I'd carded her, she just didn't look twenty-one.

'Crystal Norris?'

'Yeah?' She didn't sound particularly unfriendly, but she did sound preoccupied.

'I'm Jason Stackhouse's sister, Sookie.'

'Oh, yeah? Come in.' She stood back, and I stepped into the tiny living room. It was crowded with furniture intended for a much larger space: two recliners and a three-cushion couch of dark brown Naugahyde, the big buttons separating the vinyl into little hillocks. You'd stick to it in the summer and slide around on it in the winter. Crumbs would collect in the depression around the buttons.

There was a stained rug in dark red and yellows and browns, and there were toys strewn in an almost solid layer over it. A picture of the Last Supper hung above the television set, and the whole house smelled pleasantly of red beans and rice and cornbread.

A toddler was experimenting with Duplos in the doorway to the kitchen. I thought it was a boy, but it was hard to be sure. Overalls and a green turtleneck weren't exactly a clue, and the baby's wispy brown hair was neither cut short nor decorated with a bow.

'Your child?' I asked, trying to make my voice pleasant and conversational.

'No, my sister's,' Crystal said. She gestured toward one of the recliners.

'Crystal, the reason I'm here . . . Did you know that Jason is missing?'

She was perched on the edge of the couch, and she'd been staring down at her thin hands. When I spoke, she looked into my eyes intently. This was not fresh news to her.

'Since when?' she asked. Her voice had a pleasantly hoarse sound to it; you'd listen to what this girl had to say, especially if you were a man.

'Since the night of January first. He left my house, and then the next morning he didn't show up for work. There was some blood on that little pier out behind the house. His pickup was still in his front yard. The door to it was hanging open.'

'I don't know nothing about it,' she said instantly.

She was lying.

'Who told you I had anything to do with this?' she asked, working up to being bitchy. 'I got rights. I don't have to talk to you.'

Sure, that was Amendment 29 to the Constitution: Shifters don't have to talk to Sookie Stackhouse.

'Yes, you do.' Suddenly, I abandoned the nice approach. She'd hit the wrong button on me. 'I'm not like you. I don't have a sister or a nephew,' and I nodded at the toddler, figuring I had a fifty-fifty chance of being right. 'I don't have a mom or a dad or anything, *anything*, except my brother.' I took a deep breath. 'I want to know where Jason is. And if you know anything, you better tell me.'

'Or you'll do what?' Her thin face was twisted into a snarl. But she genuinely wanted to know what kind of pull I had; I could read that much.

'Yeah, what?' asked a calmer voice.

I looked at the doorway to see a man who was probably on the upside of forty. He had a trimmed beard salted with gray, and his hair was cut close to his head. He was a small man, perhaps five foot seven or so, with a lithe build and muscular arms.

'Anything I have to,' I said. I looked him straight in the

eyes. They were a strange golden green. He didn't seem inimical, exactly. He seemed curious.

'Why are you here?' he asked, again in that neutral voice.

'Who are you?' I had to know who this guy was. I wasn't going to waste my time repeating my story to someone who just had some time to fill. Given his air of authority, and the fact that he wasn't opting for mindless belligerence, I was willing to bet this man was worth talking to.

'I'm Calvin Norris. I'm Crystal's uncle.' From his brain pattern, he was also a shifter of some kind. Given the absence of dogs in this settlement, I assumed they were Weres.

'Mr. Norris, I'm Sookie Stackhouse.' I wasn't imagining the increased interest in his expression. 'Your niece here went to the New Year's Eve party at Merlotte's Bar with my brother, Jason. Sometime the next night, my brother went missing. I want to know if Crystal can tell me anything that might help me find him.'

Calvin Norris bent to pat the toddler on the head, and then walked over to the couch where Crystal glowered. He sat beside her, his elbows resting on his knees, his hands dangling, relaxed, between them. His head inclined as he looked into Crystal's sullen face.

'This is reasonable, Crystal. Girl wants to know where her brother is. Tell her, if you know anything about it.'

Crystal snapped at him, 'Why should I tell her anything? She comes out here, tries to threaten me.'

'Because it's just common courtesy to help someone in trouble. You didn't exactly go to her to volunteer help, did you?'

'I didn't think he was just missing. I thought he—' And

her voice cut short as she realized her tongue had led her into trouble.

Calvin's whole body tensed. He hadn't expected that Crystal actually knew anything about Jason's disappearance. He had just wanted her to be polite to me. I could read that, but not much else. I could not decipher their relationship. He had power over the girl, I could tell that easily enough, but what kind? It was more than the authority of an uncle; it felt more like he was her ruler. He might be wearing old work clothes and safety boots, he might look like any blue-collar man in the area, but Calvin Norris was a lot more.

Packmaster, I thought. But who would be in a pack, this far out in the boondocks? Just Crystal? Then I remembered Sam's veiled warning about the unusual nature of Hotshot, and I had a revelation. *Everyone* in Hotshot was two-natured.

Was that possible? I wasn't completely certain Calvin Norris was a Were – but I knew he didn't change into any bunny. I had to struggle with an almost irresistible impulse to lean over and put my hand on his forearm, touch skin to skin to read his mind as clearly as possible.

I was completely certain about one thing: I wouldn't want to be anywhere around Hotshot on the three nights of the full moon.

'You're the barmaid at Merlotte's,' he said, looking into my eyes as intently as he'd looked into Crystal's.

'I'm *a* barmaid at Merlotte's.'

'You're a friend of Sam's.'

'Yes,' I said carefully. 'I am. I'm a friend of Alcide Herveaux's, too. And I know Colonel Flood.'

These names meant something to Calvin Norris. I wasn't

surprised that Norris would know the names of some prominent Shreveport Weres – and he'd know Sam, of course. It had taken my boss time to connect with the local two-natured community, but he'd been working on it.

Crystal had been listening with wide dark eyes, in no better mood than she had been before. A girl wearing overalls appeared from the back of the house, and she lifted the toddler from his nest of Duplos. Though her face was rounder and less distinctive and her figure was fuller, she was clearly Crystal's younger sister. She was also just as apparently pregnant again.

'You need anything, Uncle Calvin?' she asked, staring at me over the toddler's shoulder.

'No, Dawn. Take care of Matthew.' She disappeared into the back of the house with her burden. I had guessed right on the sex of the kid.

'Crystal,' said Calvin Norris, in a quiet and terrifying voice, 'you tell us now what you done.'

Crystal had believed she'd gotten away with something, and she was shocked at being ordered to confess.

But she'd obey. After a little fidgeting, she did.

'I was out with Jason on New Year's Eve,' she said. 'I'd met him at Wal-Mart in Bon Temps, when I went in to get me a purse.'

I sighed. Jason could find potential bedmates anywhere. He was going to end up with some unpleasant disease (if he hadn't already) or slapped with a paternity suit, and there was nothing I could do about it except watch it happen.

'He asked me if I'd spend New Year's Eve with him. I had the feeling the woman he'd had a date with had changed her mind, 'cause he's not the kind of guy to go without lining up a date for something big like that.'

I shrugged. Jason could have made and broken dates with five women for New Year's Eve, for all I knew. And it wasn't infrequent for women to get so exasperated by his earnest pursuit of anything with a vagina that they broke off plans with him.

'He's a cute guy, and I like to get out of Hotshot, so I said yeah. He asked me if he could come pick me up, but I knew some of my neighbors wouldn't like that, so I said I'd just meet him at the Fina station, and then we'd go in his truck. So that's what we did. And I had a real good time with him, went home with him, had a good night.' Her eyes gleamed at me. 'You want to know how he is in bed?'

There was a blur of movement, and then there was blood at the corner of her mouth. Calvin's hand was back dangling between his legs before I even realized he'd moved. 'You be polite. Don't show your worst face to this woman,' he said, and his voice was so serious I made up my mind I'd be extra polite, too, just to be safe.

'Okay. That wasn't nice, I guess,' she admitted, in a softer and chastened voice. 'Well, I wanted to see him the night after, too, and he wanted to see me again. So I snuck out and went over to his place. He had to leave to see his sister – you? You're the only sister he's got?'

I nodded.

'And he said to stay there, he'd be back in a bit. I wanted to go with him, and he said if his sister didn't have company, that woulda been fine, but she had vamp company, and he didn't want me to mix with them.'

I think Jason knew what my opinion of Crystal Norris would be, and he wanted to dodge hearing it, so he left her at his house.

'Did he come back home?' Calvin said, nudging her out of her reverie.

'Yes,' she said, and I tensed.

'What happened then?' Calvin asked, when she stopped again.

'I'm not real sure,' she said. 'I was in the house, waiting for him, and I heard his truck pull up, and I'm thinking, "Oh, good, he's here, we can party," and then I didn't hear him come up the front steps, and I'm wondering what's happening, you know? Of course all the outside lights are on, but I didn't go to the window, 'cause I knew it was him.' Of course a Were would know his step, maybe catch his smell. 'I'm listening real good,' she went on, 'and I hear him going around the outside of the house, so I'm thinking he's going to come in the back door, for some reason – muddy boots, or something.'

I took a deep breath. She'd get to the point in just a minute. I just knew she would.

'And then, to the back of the house, and farther 'way, yards away from the porch, I hear a lot of noise, and some shouting and stuff, and then nothing.'

If she hadn't been a shifter, she wouldn't have heard so much. There, I knew I'd think of a bright side if I searched hard enough.

'Did you go out and look?' Calvin asked Crystal. His worn hand stroked her black curls, as if he were petting a favorite dog.

'No sir, I didn't look.'

'Smell?'

'I didn't get close enough,' she admitted, just on the good side of sullen. 'The wind was blowing the other way.

I caught a little of Jason, and blood. Maybe a couple of other things.'

'Like what?'

Crystal looked at her own hands. 'Shifter, maybe. Some of us can change when it's not the full moon, but I can't. Otherwise, I'd have had a better chance at the scent,' she said to me in near-apology.

'Vampire?' Calvin asked.

'I never smelled a vampire before,' she said simply. 'I don't know.'

'Witch?' I asked.

'Do they smell any different from regular people?' she asked doubtfully.

I shrugged. I didn't know.

Calvin said, 'What did you do after that?'

'I knew something had carried Jason off into the woods. I just . . . I lost it. I'm not brave.' She shrugged. 'I came home after that. Nothing more I could do.'

I was trying not to cry, but tears just rolled down my cheeks. For the first time, I admitted to myself that I wasn't sure I'd ever see my brother again. But if the attacker's intention was to kill Jason, why not just leave his body in the backyard? As Crystal had pointed out, the night of New Year's Day there hadn't been a full moon. There were things that didn't have to wait for the full moon . . .

The bad thing about learning about all the creatures that existed in the world besides us is that I could imagine that there were things that might swallow Jason in one gulp. Or a few bites.

But I just couldn't let myself think about that. Though I was still weeping, I made an effort to smile. 'Thank you so much,' I said politely. 'It was real nice of you to take the time to see me. I know you have things you need to do.'

Crystal looked suspicious, but her uncle Calvin reached over and patted my hand, which seemed to surprise everyone, himself included.

He walked me out to my car. The sky was clouding over, which made it feel colder, and the wind began to toss the bare branches of the large bushes planted around the yard. I recognized yellow bells (which the nursery calls forsythia), and spirea, and even a tulip tree. Around them would be planted jonquil bulbs, and iris – the same flowers that are in my grandmother's yard, the same bushes that have grown in southern yards for generations. Right now everything looked bleak and sordid. In the spring, it would seem almost charming, picturesque; the decay of poverty gilded by Mother Nature.

Two or three houses down the road, a man emerged from a shed behind his house, glanced our way, and did a double take. After a long moment, he loped back into his house. It was too far away to make out more of his features than thick pale hair, but his grace was phenomenal. The people out here more than disliked strangers; they seemed to be allergic to them.

'That's my house over there,' Calvin offered, pointing to a much more substantial home, small but foursquare, painted white quite recently. Everything was in good repair at Calvin Norris's house. The driveway and parking area were clearly defined; the matching white toolshed stood rust-free on a neat concrete slab.

I nodded. 'It looks real nice,' I said in a voice that wasn't too wobbly.

'I want to make you an offer,' Calvin Norris said.

I tried to look interested. I half turned to face him.

'You're a woman without protection now,' he said. 'Your brother's gone. I hope he comes back, but you don't have no one to stand up for you while he's missing.'

There were a lot of things wrong with this speech, but I wasn't in any mood to debate the shifter. He'd done me a large favor, getting Crystal to talk. I stood there in the cold wind and tried to look politely receptive.

'If you need some place to hide, if you need someone to watch your back or defend you, I'll be your man,' he said. His green and golden eyes met mine directly.

I'll tell you why I didn't dismiss this with a snort: He wasn't being superior about it. According to his mores, he was being as nice as he could be, extending a shield to me if I should need it. Of course he expected to 'be my man' in every way, along with protecting me; but he wasn't being lascivious in his manner, or offensively explicit. Calvin Norris was offering to incur injury for my sake. He meant it. That's not something to get all snitty about.

'Thanks,' I said. 'I'll remember you said that.'

'I heard about you,' he said. 'Shifters and Weres, they talk to each other. I hear you're different.'

'I am.' Regular men might have found my outer package attractive, but my inner package repelled them. If I ever began to get a swelled head, after the attention paid me by Eric, or Bill, or even Alcide, all I had to do was listen to the brains of some bar patrons to have my ego deflated. I clutched my old blue coat more closely around me. Like most of the two-natured, Calvin had a system that didn't feel cold as intensely as my completely human metabolism did. 'But my difference doesn't lie in being two-natured, though I appreciate your, ah, kindness.' This was as close as I could come to asking him why he was so interested.

'I know that.' He nodded in acknowledgment of my delicacy. 'Actually, that makes you more . . . The thing is, here in Hotshot, we've inbred too much. You heard Crystal. She can only change at the moon, and frankly, even then she's not full-powered.' He pointed at his own face. 'My eyes can hardly pass for human. We need an infusion of new blood, new genes. You're not two-natured, but you're not exactly an ordinary woman. Ordinary women don't last long here.'

Well, that was an ominous and ambiguous way to put it. But I was sympathetic, and I tried to look understanding. Actually, I did understand, and I could appreciate his concern. Calvin Norris was clearly the leader of this unusual settlement, and its future was his responsibility.

He was frowning as he looked down the road at the house where I'd seen the man. But he turned to me to finish telling me what he wanted me to know. 'I think you would like the people here, and you would be a good breeder. I can tell by looking.'

That was a real unusual compliment. I couldn't quite think how to acknowledge it in an appropriate manner.

'I'm flattered that you think so, and I appreciate your offer. I'll remember what you said.' I paused to gather my thoughts. 'You know, the police will find out that Crystal was with Jason, if they haven't already. They'll come out here, too.'

'They won't find nothing,' Calvin Norris said. His golden green eyes met mine with faint amusement. 'They've been out here at other times; they'll be out here again. They never learn a thing. I hope you find your brother. You need help, you let me know. I got a job at Norcross. I'm a steady man.'

'Thank you,' I said, and got into my car with a feeling of relief. I gave Calvin a serious nod as I backed out of Crystal's driveway. So he worked at Norcross, the lumber processing plant. Norcross had good benefits, and they promoted from within. I'd had worse offers; that was for sure.

As I drove to work, I wondered if Crystal had been trying to get pregnant during her nights with Jason. It hadn't seemed to bother Calvin at all to hear that his niece had had sex with a strange man. Alcide had told me that Were had to breed with Were to produce a baby that had the same trait, so the inhabitants of this little community were trying to diversify, apparently. Maybe these lesser Weres were trying to breed out; that is, have children by regular humans. That would be better than having a generation of Weres whose powers were so weak they couldn't function successfully in their second nature, but who also couldn't be content as regular people.

Getting to Merlotte's was like driving from one century into another. I wondered how long the people of Hotshot had been clustered around the crossroads, what significance it had originally held for them. Though I couldn't help but be a little curious, I found it was a real relief to discard these wonderings and return to the world as I knew it.

That afternoon, the little world of Merlotte's Bar was very quiet. I changed, tied on my black apron, smoothed my hair, and washed my hands. Sam was behind the bar with his arms crossed over his chest, staring into space. Holly was carrying a pitcher of beer to a table where a lone stranger sat.

'How was Hotshot?' Sam asked, since we were alone at the bar.

'Very strange.'

He patted me on the shoulder. 'Did you find out anything useful?'

'Actually, I did. I'm just not sure what it means.' Sam needed a haircut, I noticed; his curly red-gold hair formed an arc around his face in a kind of Renaissance-angel effect.

'Did you meet Calvin Norris?'

'I did. He got Crystal to talk to me, and he made me a most unusual offer.'

'What's that?'

'I'll tell you some other time.' For the life of me, I couldn't figure out how to phrase it. I looked down at my hands, which were busy rinsing out a beer mug, and I could feel my cheeks burning.

'Calvin's an okay guy, as far as I know,' Sam said slowly. 'He works at Norcross, and he's a crew leader. Good insurance, retirement package, everything. Some of the other guys from Hotshot own a welding shop. I hear they do good work. But I don't know what goes on in Hotshot after they go home at night, and I don't think anyone else does, either. Did you know Sheriff Dowdy, John Dowdy? He was sheriff before I moved here, I think.'

'Yeah, I remember him. He hauled Jason in one time for vandalism. Gran had to go get him out of jail. Sheriff Dowdy read Jason a lecture that had him scared straight, at least for a while.'

'Sid Matt told me a story one night. It seems that one spring, John Dowdy went out to Hotshot to arrest Calvin Norris's oldest brother, Carlton.'

'For what?' Sid Matt Lancaster was an old and well-known lawyer.

'Statutory rape. The girl was willing, and she was even experienced, but she was underage. She had a new stepdad, and he decided Carlton had disrespected him.'

No politically correct stance could cover all those circumstances. 'So what happened?'

'No one knows. Late that night, John Dowdy's patrol car was found halfway back into town from Hotshot. No one in it. No blood, no fingerprints. He hasn't ever been seen since. No one in Hotshot remembered seeing him that day, they said.'

'Like Jason,' I said bleakly. 'He just vanished.'

'But Jason was at his own house, and according to you, Crystal didn't seem to be involved.'

I threw off the grip of the strange little story. 'You're right. Did anyone ever find out what happened to Sheriff Dowdy?'

'No. But no one ever saw Carlton Norris again, either.'

Now, that was the interesting part. 'And the moral of this story is?'

'That the people of Hotshot take care of their own justice.'

'Then you want them on your side.' I extracted my own moral from the story.

'Yes,' Sam said. 'You definitely want them on your side. You don't remember this? It was around fifteen years ago.'

'I was coping with my own troubles then,' I explained. I'd been an orphaned nine-year-old, coping with my growing telepathic powers.

Shortly after that, people began to stop by the bar on their way home from work. Sam and I didn't get a chance to talk the rest of the evening, which was fine with me. I was very fond of Sam, who'd often had a starring role in some of my most private fantasies, but at this point, I had so much to worry about I just couldn't take on any more.

That night, I discovered that some people thought Jason's disappearance improved Bon Temps society. Among these were Andy Bellefleur and his sister, Portia, who stopped by Merlotte's for supper, since their grandmother Caroline was having a dinner party and they were staying out of the way. Andy was a police detective and Portia was a lawyer, and they were both not on my list of favorite people. For one thing (a kind of sour-grapey thing), when Bill had found out they were his descendants, he'd made an elaborate plan to give the Bellefleurs money anonymously, and they'd really enjoyed their mysterious legacy to the hilt. But they couldn't stand Bill himself, and it made me constantly irritated to see their new cars and expensive clothes and the new roof on the Bellefleur mansion, when they dissed Bill all the time – and me, too, for being Bill's girlfriend.

Andy had been pretty nice to me before I started dating Bill. At least he'd been civil and left a decent tip. I'd just been invisible to Portia, who had her own share of personal woes. She'd come up with a suitor, I'd heard, and I wondered maliciously if that might not be due to the sudden upsurge in the Bellefleur family fortunes. I also wondered, at times, if Andy and Portia got happy in direct proportion to my misery. They were in fine fettle this winter evening, both tucking into their hamburgers with great zest.

'Sorry about your brother, Sookie,' Andy said, as I refilled his tea glass.

I looked down at him, my face expressionless. *Liar*, I

thought. After a second, Andy's eyes darted uneasily away from mine to light on the saltshaker, which seemed to have become peculiarly fascinating.

'Have you seen Bill lately?' Portia asked, patting her mouth with a napkin. She was trying to break the uneasy silence with a pleasant query, but I just got angrier.

'No,' I said. 'Can I get you all anything else?'

'No, thanks, we're just fine,' she said quickly. I spun on my heel and walked away. Then my mouth puckered in a smile. Just as I was thinking, *Bitch*, Portia was thinking, *What a bitch.*

Her ass is hot, Andy chimed in. Gosh, telepathy. What a blast. I wouldn't wish it on my worst enemy. I envied people who only heard with their ears.

Kevin and Kenya came in, too, very carefully not drinking. Theirs was a partnership that had given the people of Bon Temps much hilarity. Lily white Kevin was thin and reedy, a long-distance runner; all the equipment he had to wear on his uniform belt seemed almost too much for him to carry. His partner, Kenya, was two inches taller, pounds heavier, and fifteen shades darker. The men at the bar had been putting bets down for two years on whether or not they'd become lovers – of course, the guys at the bar didn't put it as nicely as that.

I was unwillingly aware that Kenya (and her handcuffs and nightstick) featured in all too many patrons' daydreams, and I also knew that the men who teased and derided Kevin the most mercilessly were the ones who had the most lurid fantasies. As I carried hamburger baskets over to Kevin and Kenya's table, I could tell that Kenya was wondering whether she should suggest to Bud Dearborn that he call in the tracking dogs from a neighboring parish in the search for Jason, while Kevin was worried about his mother's heart, which had been acting up more than usual lately.

'Sookie,' Kevin said, after I'd brought them a bottle of ketchup, 'I meant to tell you, some people came by the police department today putting out posters about a vampire.'

'I saw one at the grocery,' I said.

'I realize that just because you were dating a vampire, you aren't an expert,' Kevin said carefully, because Kevin always did his best to be nice to me, 'but I wondered if you'd seen this vamp. Before he disappeared, I mean.'

Kenya was looking up at me, too, her dark eyes examining me with great interest. Kenya was thinking I always seemed to be on the fringes of bad things that happened in Bon Temps, without being bad myself (thanks, Kenya). She was hoping for my sake that Jason was alive. Kevin was thinking I'd always been nice to him and Kenya; and he was thinking he wouldn't touch me with a ten-foot pole. I sighed, I hoped imperceptibly. They were waiting for an answer. I hesitated, wondering what my best choice was. The truth is always easiest to remember.

'Sure, I've seen him before. Eric owns the vampire bar in Shreveport,' I said. 'I saw him when I went there with Bill.'

'You haven't seen him recently?'

'I sure didn't abduct him from Fangtasia,' I said, with quite a lot of sarcasm in my voice.

Kenya gave me a sour look, and I didn't blame her. 'No one said you did,' she told me, in a 'Don't give me any trouble' kind of voice. I shrugged and drifted away.

I had plenty to do, since some people were still eating supper (and some were drinking it), and some regulars were drifting in after eating at home. Holly was equally busy, and when one of the men who worked for the phone company spilled his beer on the floor, she had to go get the mop and bucket. She was running behind on her tables when the door opened. I saw her putting Sid Matt Lancaster's order in front of him, with her back to the door. So she missed the next entrance, but I didn't. The young man Sam had hired to bus the tables during our busy hour was occupied with clearing two tables pulled together that had held a large party of parish workers, and so I was clearing off the Bellefleurs' table. Andy was chatting with Sam while he waited for Portia, who'd visited the ladies' room. I'd just pocketed my tip, which was fifteen percent of the bill to the penny. The Bellefleur tipping habits had improved – slightly – with the Bellefleur fortunes. I glanced up when the door was held open long enough for a cold gust of air to chill me.

The woman coming in was tall and so slim and broad-shouldered that I checked her chest, just to be sure I'd registered her gender correctly. Her hair was short and thick and brown, and she was wearing absolutely no makeup. There was a man with her, but I didn't see him until she stepped to one side. He was no slouch in the size department himself, and his tight T-shirt revealed arms more developed than any I'd ever seen. Hours in the gym; no, years in the gym. His chestnut hair trailed down to his shoulders in tight curls, and his beard and mustache were perceptibly redder. Neither of the two wore coats, though it was definitely coat weather. The newcomers walked over to me.

'Where's the owner?' the woman asked.

'Sam. He's behind the bar,' I said, looking down as soon

as I could and wiping the table all over again. The man had looked at me curiously; that was normal. As they brushed past me, I saw that he carried some posters under his arm and a staple gun. He'd stuck his hand through a roll of masking tape, so it bounced on his left wrist.

I glanced over at Holly. She'd frozen, the cup of coffee in her hand halfway down on its way to Sid Matt Lancaster's placemat. The old lawyer looked up at her, followed her stare to the couple making their way between the tables to the bar. Merlotte's, which had been on the quiet and peaceful side, was suddenly awash in tension. Holly set down the cup without burning Mr. Lancaster and spun on her heel, going through the swinging door to the kitchen at warp speed.

I didn't need any more confirmation on the identity of the woman.

The two reached Sam and began a low-voiced conversation with him, with Andy listening in just because he was in the vicinity. I passed by on my way to take the dirty dishes to the hatch, and I heard the woman say (in a deep, alto voice) '. . . put up these posters in town, just in case anyone spots him.'

This was Hallow, the witch whose pursuit of Eric had caused such an upset. She, or a member of her coven, was probably the murderer of Adabelle Yancy. This was the woman who might have taken my brother, Jason. My head began pounding as if there were a little demon inside trying to break out with a hammer.

No wonder Holly was in such a state and didn't want Hallow to glimpse her. She'd been to Hallow's little meeting in Shreveport, and her coven had rejected Hallow's invitation.

'Of course,' Sam said. 'Put up one on this wall.' He indicated a blank spot by the door that led back to the bathrooms and his office.

Holly stuck her head out the kitchen door, glimpsed Hallow, ducked back in. Hallow's eyes flicked over to the door, but not in time to glimpse Holly, I hoped.

I thought of jumping Hallow, beating on her until she told me what I wanted to know about my brother. That was what the pounding in my head was urging me to do – initiate action, any action. But I had a streak of common sense, and luckily for me it came to the fore. Hallow was big, and she had a sidekick who could crush me – plus, Kevin and Kenya would make me stop before I could get her to talk.

It was horribly frustrating to have her right in front of me and at the same time be unable to discover what she knew. I dropped all my shields, and I listened in as hard as I could.

But she suspected something when I touched inside her head.

She looked vaguely puzzled and glanced around. That was enough warning for me. I scrambled back into my own head as quickly as I could. I continued back behind the bar, passing within a couple of feet of the witch as she tried to figure out who'd brushed at her brain.

This had never happened to me before. No one, *no one*, had ever suspected I was listening in. I squatted behind the bar to get the big container of Morton Salt, straightened, and carefully refilled the shaker I'd snatched from Kevin and Kenya's table. I concentrated on this as hard as anyone can focus on performing such a nothing little task, and when I was through, the poster had been mounted with the staple gun. Hallow was lingering, prolonging her talk with Sam so she could figure out who had touched the inside of her head, and Mr. Muscles was eyeing me – but only like a man looks at a woman – as I returned the shaker to its table. Holly hadn't reappeared.

'Sookie,' Sam called.

Oh, for goodness sake. I had to respond. He was my boss.

I went over to the three of them, dread in my heart and a smile on my face.

'Hey,' I said, by way of greeting, giving the tall witch and her stalwart sidekick a neutral smile. I raised my eyebrows at Sam to ask him what he'd wanted.

'Marnie Stonebrook, Mark Stonebrook,' he said.

I nodded to each of them. *Hallow, indeed*, I thought, half-amused. 'Hallow' was just a tad more spiritual than 'Marnie.'

'They're looking for this guy,' Sam said, indicating the poster. 'You know him?'

Of course Sam knew that I knew Eric. I was glad I'd had years of concealing my feelings and thoughts from the eyes of others. I looked the poster over deliberately.

'Sure, I've seen him,' I said. 'When I went to that bar in Shreveport? He's kind of unforgettable, isn't he?' I gave Hallow – Marnie – a smile. We were just gals together, Marnie and Sookie, sharing a gal moment.

'Handsome guy,' she agreed in her throaty voice. 'He's missing now, and we're offering a reward for anyone who can give us information.'

'I see that from the poster,' I said, letting a tiny hint of irritation show in my voice. 'Is there any particular reason you think he might be around here? I can't imagine what a Shreveport vampire would be doing in Bon Temps.' I looked at her questioningly. Surely I wasn't out of line in asking that?

'Good question, Sookie,' Sam said. 'Not that I mind having the poster up, but how come you two are searching this area for the guy? Why would he be here? Nothing happens in Bon Temps.'

'This town has a vampire in residence, doesn't it?' Mark Stonebrook said suddenly. His voice was almost a twin of his sister's. He was so buff you expected to hear a bass, and even an alto as deep as Marnie's sounded strange coming from his throat. Actually, from Mark Stonebrook's appearance, you'd think he'd just grunt and growl to communicate.

'Yeah, Bill Compton lives here,' Sam said. 'But he's out of town.'

'Gone to Peru, I heard,' I said.

'Oh, yes, I'd heard of Bill Compton. Where does he live?' Hallow asked, trying to keep the excitement out of her voice.

'Well, he lives out across the cemetery from my place,' I said, because I had no choice. If the two asked someone else and got a different answer than the one I gave them, they'd know I had something (or in this case, someone) to conceal. 'Out off Hummingbird Road.' I gave them directions, not very clear directions, and hoped they got lost out in somewhere like Hotshot.

'Well, we might drop by Compton's house, just in case Eric went to visit him,' Hallow said. Her eyes cut to her brother Mark, and they nodded at us and left the bar. They didn't care whether this made sense or not.

'They're sending witches to visit all the vamps,' Sam said softly. Of course. The Stonebrooks were going to the residences of all vampires who owed allegiance to Eric – the vamps of Area Five. They suspected that one of these vamps might be hiding Eric. Since Eric hadn't turned up, he was being hidden. Hallow had to be confident that her spell had worked, but she might not know exactly how it had worked.

I let the smile fade off my face, and I leaned against the bar on my elbows, trying to think real hard.

Sam said, 'This is big trouble, right?' His face was serious.

'Yes, this is big trouble.'

'Do you need to leave? There's not too much happening here. Holly can come out of the kitchen now that they're gone, and I can always see to the tables myself, if you need to get home . . .' Sam wasn't sure where Eric was, but he suspected, and he'd noticed Holly's abrupt bolt into the kitchen.

Sam had earned my loyalty and respect a hundred times over.

'I'll give them five minutes to get out of the parking lot.'

'Do you think they might have something to do with Jason's disappearance?'

'Sam, I just don't know.' I automatically dialed the sheriff's department and got the same answer I'd gotten all day – 'No news, we'll call you when we know something.' But after she said that, the dispatcher told me that the pond was going to be searched the next day; the police had managed to get hold of two search-and-rescue divers. I didn't know how to feel about this information. Mostly, I was relieved that Jason's disappearance was being taken seriously.

When I hung up the phone, I told Sam the news. After a second, I said, 'It seems too much to believe that two men could disappear in the Bon Temps area at the same time. At least, the Stonebrooks seem to think Eric's around here. I have to think that there's a connection.'

'Those Stonebrooks are Weres,' Sam muttered.

'*And* witches. You be careful, Sam. She's a killer. The Weres of Shreveport are out after her, and the vamps, too. Watch your step.'

'Why is she so scary? Why would the Shreveport pack have any trouble handling her?'

'She's drinking vampire blood,' I said, as close to his ear as I could get without kissing him. I glanced around the room, to see that Kevin was watching our exchange with a lot of interest.

'What does she want with Eric?'

'His business. All his businesses. And him.'

Sam's eyes widened. 'So it's business, and personal.'

'Yep.'

'Do you know where Eric is?' He'd avoided asking me directly until now.

I smiled at him. 'Why would I know that? But I confess, I'm worried about those two being right down the road from my house. I have a feeling they're going to break into Bill's place. They might figure Eric's hiding with Bill, or in Bill's house. I'm sure he's got a safe hole for Eric to sleep in and blood on hand.' That was pretty much all a vampire required, blood and a dark place.

'So you're going over to guard Bill's property? Not a good idea, Sookie. Let Bill's homeowners insurance take care of whatever damage they do searching. I think he told me he went with State Farm. Bill wouldn't want you hurt in defense of plants and bricks.'

'I don't plan on doing anything that dangerous,' I said,

and truly, I didn't plan it. 'But I do think I'll run home. Just in case. When I see their car lights leaving Bill's house, I'll go over and check it out.'

'You need me to come with you?'

'Nah, I'm just going to do damage assessment, that's all. Holly'll be enough help here?' She'd popped out of the kitchen the minute the Stonebrooks had left.

'Sure.'

'Okay, I'm gone. Thanks so much.' My conscience didn't twinge as much when I noticed that the place wasn't nearly as busy as it'd been an hour ago. You got nights like that, when people just cleared out all of a sudden.

I had an itchy feeling between my shoulder blades, and maybe all our patrons had, too. It was that feeling that something was prowling that shouldn't be: that Halloween feeling, I call it, when you kind of picture something bad is easing around the corner of your house, to peer into your windows.

By the time I grabbed my purse, unlocked my car, and drove back to my house, I was almost twitching from uneasiness. Everything was going to hell in a handbasket, seemed to me. Jason was missing, the witch was here instead of Shreveport, and now she was within a half mile of Eric.

As I turned from the parish road onto my long, meandering driveway and braked for the deer crossing it from the woods on the south side to the woods on the north – moving away from Bill's house, I noticed – I had worked myself into a state. Pulling around to the back door, I leaped from the car and bounded up the back steps.

I was caught in midbound by a pair of arms like steel bands. Lifted and whirled, I was wrapped around Eric's waist before I knew it.

'Eric,' I said, 'you shouldn't be out—'

My words were cut off by his mouth over mine.

For a minute, going along with this program seemed like a viable alternative. I'd just forget all the badness and screw his brains out on my back porch, cold as it was. But sanity seeped back in past my overloaded emotional state, and I pulled a little away. He was wearing the jeans and Louisiana Tech Bulldogs sweatshirt Jason had bought for him at Wal-Mart. Eric's big hands supported my bottom, and my legs circled him as if they were used to it.

'Listen, Eric,' I said, when his mouth moved down to my neck.

'Ssshh,' he whispered.

'No, you have to let me speak. We have to hide.'

That got his attention. 'From whom?' he said into my ear, and I shivered. The shiver was unrelated to the temperature.

'The bad witch, the one that's after you,' I scrambled to explain. 'She came into the bar with her brother and they put up that poster.'

'So?' His voice was careless.

'They asked what other vampires lived locally, and of course we had to say Bill did. So they asked for directions to Bill's house, and I guess they're over there looking for you.'

'And?'

'That's right across the cemetery from here! What if they come over here?'

'You advise me to hide? To get back in that black hole below your house?' He sounded uncertain, but it was clear to me his pride was piqued.

'Oh, yes. Just for a little while! You're my responsibility; I have to keep you safe.' But I had a sinking feeling I'd expressed my fears in the wrong way. This tentative stranger, however uninterested he seemed in vampire concerns, however little he seemed to remember of his power and possessions, still had the vein of pride and curiosity Eric had always shown at the oddest moments. I'd tapped right into it. I wondered if maybe I could talk him into at least getting into my house, rather than standing out on the porch, exposed.

But it was too late. You just never could tell Eric anything.

Chapter 8

'Come on, lover, let's have a look,' Eric said, giving me a quick kiss. He jumped off the back porch with me still attached to him – like a large barnacle – and he landed silently, which seemed amazing. I was the noisy one, with my breathing and little sounds of surprise. With a dexterity that argued long practice, Eric slung me around so that I was riding his back. I hadn't done this since I was a child and my father had carried me piggyback, so I was considerably startled.

Oh, I was doing one great job of hiding Eric. Here we were, bounding through the cemetery, going *toward* the Wicked Witch of the West, instead of hiding in a dark hole where she couldn't find us. This was *so* smart.

At the same time, I had to admit that I was kind of having fun, despite the difficulties of keeping a grip on Eric in this gently rolling country. The graveyard was somewhat downhill from my house. Bill's house, the Compton house, was quite a bit more uphill from Sweet Home Cemetery. The journey downhill, mild as the slope was, was exhilarating, though I glimpsed two or three parked cars on the narrow blacktop that wound through the graves. That startled me. Teenagers sometimes chose the cemetery for privacy, but not in groups. But before I could think it through, we had passed them, swiftly and silently. Eric managed the uphill portion more slowly, but with no evidence of exhaustion.

We were next to a tree when Eric stopped. It was a huge oak, and when I touched it I became more or less oriented. There was an oak this size maybe twenty yards to the north of Bill's house.

Eric loosened my hands so I'd slide down his back, and then he put me between him and the tree trunk. I didn't know if he was trying to trap me or protect me. I gripped both his wrists in a fairly futile attempt to keep him beside me. I froze when I heard a voice drifting over from Bill's house.

'This car hasn't moved in a while,' a woman said. Hallow. She was in Bill's carport, which was on this side of the house. She was close. I could feel Eric's body stiffen. Did the sound of her voice evoke an echo in his memory?

'The house is locked up tight,' called Mark Stonebrook, from farther away.

'Well, we can take care of that.' From the sound of her voice, she was on the move to the front door. She sounded amused.

They were going to break into Bill's house! Surely I should prevent that? I must have made some sudden move, because Eric's body flattened mine against the trunk of the tree. My coat was worked up around my waist, and the bark bit into my butt through the thin material of my black pants.

I could hear Hallow. She was chanting, her voice low and

somehow ominous. She was actually casting a spell. That should have been exciting and I should have been curious: a real magic spell, cast by a real witch. But I felt scared, anxious to get away. The darkness seemed to thicken.

'I smell someone,' Mark Stonebrook said.

Fee, fie, foe, fum.

'What? Here and now?' Hallow stopped her chant, sounding a little breathless.

I began to tremble.

'Yeah.' His voice came out deeper, almost a growl.

'Change,' she ordered, just like that. I heard a sound I knew I'd heard before, though I couldn't trace the memory. It was a sort of gloppy sound. Sticky. Like stirring a stiff spoon through some thick liquid that had hard things in it, maybe peanuts or toffee bits. Or bone chips.

Then I heard a real howl. It wasn't human at all. Mark had changed, and it wasn't the full moon. This was real power. The night suddenly seemed full of life. Snuffling. Yipping. Tiny movements all around us.

I was some great guardian for Eric, huh? I'd let him sweep me over here. We were about to be discovered by a vampire-blood drinking Were witch, and who knows what all else, and I didn't even have Jason's shotgun. I put my arms around Eric and hugged him in apology.

'Sorry,' I whispered, as tiny as a bee would whisper. But then I felt something brush against us, something large and furry, while I was hearing Mark's wolfy sounds from a few feet away on the other side of the tree. I bit my lip hard to keep from giving a yip myself.

Listening intently, I became sure there were more than two animals. I would have given almost anything for a floodlight. From maybe ten yards away came a short, sharp bark. Another wolf? A plain old dog, in the wrong place at the wrong time?

Suddenly, Eric left me. One minute, he was pressing me against the tree in the pitch-black dark, and the next minute, cold air hit me from top to bottom (so much for my holding on to his wrists). I flung my arms out, trying to discover where he was, and touched only air. Had he just stepped away so he could investigate what was happening? Had he decided to join in?

Though my hands didn't encounter any vampires, something big and warm pressed against my legs. I used my fingers to better purpose by reaching down to explore the animal. I touched lots of fur: a pair of upright ears, a long muzzle, a warm tongue. I tried to move, to step away from the oak, but the dog (wolf?) wouldn't let me. Though it was smaller than I and weighed less, it leaned against me with such pressure that there was no way I could move. When I listened to what was going on in the darkness – a lot of growling and snarling – I decided I was actually pretty glad about that. I sank to my knees and put one arm across the canine's back. It licked my face.

I heard a chorus of howls, which rose eerily into the cold night. The hair on my neck stood up, and I buried my face in the neck fur of my companion and prayed. Suddenly, over all the lesser noises, there was a howl of pain and a series of yips.

I heard a car start up, and headlights cut cones into the night. My side of the tree was away from the light, but I could see that I was huddled by a dog, not a wolf. Then the lights moved and gravel sprayed from Bill's driveway as the car reversed. There was a moment's pause, I presumed while the driver shifted into drive, and then the car screeched and I heard it going at high speed down the hill to the turnoff onto Hummingbird Road. There was a terrible thud and a high shrieking sound that made my heart hammer even harder. It was the sound of a pain a dog makes when it's been hit by a car.

'Oh, Jesus,' I said miserably, and clutched my furry friend. I thought of something I could do to help, now that it seemed the witches had left.

I got up and ran for the front door of Bill's house before the dog could stop me. I pulled my keys out of my pocket as I ran. They'd been in my hand when Eric had seized me at my back door, and I'd stuffed them into my coat, where a handkerchief had kept them from jingling. I felt around for the lock, counted my keys until I arrived at Bill's – the third on the ring – and opened his front door. I reached in and flipped the outside light switch, and abruptly the yard was illuminated.

It was full of wolves.

I didn't know how scared I should be. Pretty scared, I guessed. I was just assuming both of the Were witches had been in the car. What if one of them was among the wolves present? And where was my vampire?

That question got answered almost immediately. There was a sort of *whump* as Eric landed in the yard.

'I followed them to the road, but they went too fast for me there,' he said, grinning at me as if we'd been playing a game.

A dog – a collie – went up to Eric, looked up at his face and growled.

'Shoo,' Eric said, making an imperious gesture with his hand.

My boss trotted over to me and sat against my legs

again. Even in the darkness, I had suspected that my guardian was Sam. The first time I'd encountered him in this transformation, I'd thought he was a stray, and I'd named him Dean, after a man I knew with the same eye color. Now it was a habit to call him Dean when he went on four legs. I sat on Bill's front steps and the collie cuddled against me. I said, 'You are one great dog.' He wagged his tail. The wolves were sniffing Eric, who was standing stock-still.

A big wolf trotted over to me, the biggest wolf I'd ever seen. Weres turn into large wolves, I guess; I haven't seen that many. Living in Louisiana, I've never seen a standard wolf at all. This Were was almost pure black, which I thought was unusual. The rest of the wolves were more silvery, except for one that was smaller and reddish.

The wolf gripped my coat sleeve with its long white teeth and tugged. I rose immediately and went over to the spot where most of the other wolves were milling. We were at the outer edge of the light, so I hadn't noticed the cluster right away. There was blood on the ground, and in the middle of the spreading pool lay a young dark-haired woman. She was naked.

She was obviously and terribly injured.

Her legs were broken, and maybe one arm.

'Go get my car,' I told Eric, in the kind of voice that has to be obeyed.

I tossed him my keys, and he took to the air again. In one available corner of my brain, I hoped that he remembered how to drive. I'd noted that though he'd forgotten his personal history, his modern skills were apparently intact.

I was trying not to think about the poor injured girl right in front of me. The wolves circled and paced, whining. Then the big black one raised his head to the dark sky and howled again. This was a signal to all the others, who did the same thing. I glanced back to be sure that Dean was keeping away, since he was the outsider. I wasn't sure how much human personality was left after these two-natured people transformed, and I didn't want anything to happen to him. He was sitting on the small porch, out of the way, his eyes fixed on me.

I was the only creature with opposable thumbs on the scene, and I was suddenly aware that that gave me a lot of responsibility.

First thing to check? Breathing. Yes, she was! She had a pulse. I was no paramedic, but it didn't seem like a normal pulse to me – which would be no wonder. Her skin felt hot, maybe from the changeover back to human. I didn't see a terrifying amount of fresh blood, so I hoped that no major arteries had been ruptured.

I slid a hand beneath the girl's head, very carefully, and touched the dusty dark hair, trying to see if her scalp was lacerated. No.

Sometime during the process of this examination, I began shaking all over. Her injuries were really frightening. Everything I could see of her looked beaten, battered, broken. Her eyes opened. She shuddered. Blankets – she'd need to be kept warm. I glanced around. All the wolves were still wolves.

'It would be great if one or two of you could change back,' I told them. 'I have to get her to a hospital in my car, and she needs blankets from inside this house.'

One of the wolves, a silvery gray, rolled onto its side – okay, male wolf – and I heard the same gloppy noise again. A haze wrapped around the writhing figure, and when it dispersed, Colonel Flood was curled up in place of the wolf. Of course, he was naked, too, but I chose to rise above my natural embarrassment. He had to lie still for at least a minute or two, and it was obviously a great effort for him to sit up.

He crawled over to the injured girl. 'Maria-Star,' he said hoarsely. He bent to smell her, which looked very weird when he was in human form. He whined in distress.

He turned his head to look at me. He said, 'Where?' and I understood he meant the blankets.

'Go in the house, go up the stairs. There's a bedroom at the head of the stairs. There's a blanket chest at the foot of the bed. Get two blankets out of there.'

He staggered to his feet, apparently having to deal with some disorientation from his rapid change, before he began striding toward the house.

The girl – Maria-Star – followed him with her eyes.

'Can you talk?' I asked.

'Yes,' she said, barely audibly.

'Where does it hurt worst?'

'I think my hips and legs are broken,' she said. 'The car hit me.'

'Did it throw you up in the air?'

'Yes.'

'The wheels didn't pass over you?'

She shuddered. 'No, it was the impact that hurt me.'

'What's your full name? Maria-Star what?' I'd need to know for the hospital. She might not be conscious by then.

'Cooper,' she whispered.

By then, I could hear a car coming up Bill's drive.

The colonel, moving more smoothly now, sped out of the house with the blankets, and all the wolves and the one human instantly arrayed themselves around me and their wounded pack member. The car was obviously a threat until they learned likewise. I admired the colonel. It took quite a man to face an approaching enemy stark naked.

The new arrival was Eric, in my old car. He pulled up to Maria-Star and me with considerable panache and squealing brakes. The wolves circled restlessly, their glowing yellow eyes fixed on the driver's door. Calvin Norris's eyes had looked quite different; fleetingly, I wondered why.

'It's my car; it's okay,' I said, when one of the Weres began growling. Several pairs of eyes turned to fix on me consideringly. Did I look suspicious, or tasty?

As I finished wrapping Maria-Star in the blankets, I wondered which one of the wolves was Alcide. I suspected he was the largest, darkest one, the one that just that moment turned to look me in the eyes. Yes, Alcide. This was the wolf I'd seen at Club Dead a few weeks ago, when Alcide had been my date on a night that had ended catastrophically – for me and a few other people.

I tried to smile at him, but my face was stiff with cold and shock.

Eric leaped out of the driver's seat, leaving the car running. He opened the back door. 'I'll put her in,' he called, and the wolves began barking. They didn't want their pack sister handled by a vampire, and they didn't want Eric to be anywhere close to Maria-Star.

Colonel Flood said, 'I'll lift her.' Eric looked at the older man's slight physique and lifted a doubtful eyebrow, but had the sense to stand aside. I'd wrapped the girl as well as I could without jarring her, but the colonel knew this was going to hurt her even worse. At the last minute, he hesitated.

'Maybe we should call the ambulance,' he muttered.

'And explain this how?' I asked. 'A bunch of wolves and a naked guy, and her being up here next to a private home where the owner's absent? I don't think so!'

'Of course.' He nodded, accepting the inevitable. Without even a hitch in his breathing, he stood with the bundle that was the girl and went to the car. Eric did run to the other side, open that door, and reach in to help pull her farther onto the backseat. The colonel permitted that. The girl shrieked once, and I scrambled behind the wheel as fast as I could. Eric got in the passenger side, and I said, 'You can't go.'

'Why not?' He sounded amazed and affronted.

'I'll have twice the explaining to do if I have a vampire with me!' It took most people a few minutes to decide Eric was dead, but of course they would figure it out eventually. Eric stubbornly stayed put. 'And everyone's seeing your face on the damn posters,' I said, working to keep my voice reasonable but urgent. 'I live among pretty good people, but there's no one in this parish who couldn't use that much money.'

He got out, not happily, and I yelled, 'Turn off the lights and relock the house, okay?'

'Meet us at the bar when you have word about Maria-Star!' Colonel Flood yelled back. 'We've got to get our cars and clothes out of the cemetery.' Okay, that explained the glimpse I'd caught on the way over.

As I steered slowly down the driveway, the wolves watched me go, Alcide standing apart from the rest, his black furry face turning to follow my progress. I wondered what wolfy thoughts he was thinking.

The closest hospital was not in Bon Temps, which is way too small to have its own (we're lucky to have a Wal-Mart), but in nearby Clarice, the parish seat. Luckily, it's on the outskirts of the town, on the side nearest Bon Temps. The ride to the Renard Parish Hospital only seemed to take years; actually, I got there in about twenty minutes. My passenger moaned for the first ten minutes, and then fell ominously silent. I talked to her, begged her to talk to me, asked her to tell me how old she was, and turned on the radio in attempt to spark some response from Maria-Star.

I didn't want to take the time to pull over and check on her, and I wouldn't have known what to do if I had, so I drove like a bat out of hell. By the time I pulled up to the emergency entrance and called to the two nurses standing outside smoking, I was sure the poor Were was dead.

She wasn't, judging from the activity that surrounded her in the next couple of minutes. Our parish hospital is a little one, of course, and it doesn't have the facilities that a city hospital can boast. We counted ourselves lucky to have a hospital at all. That night, they saved the Were's life.

The doctor, a thin woman with graying spiked hair and huge black-rimmed glasses, asked me a few pointed questions that I couldn't answer, though I'd been working on my basic story all the way to the hospital. After finding me clueless, the doctor made it clear I was to get the hell out of the way and let her team work. So I sat in a chair in the hall and waited, and worked on my story some more.

There was no way I could be useful here, and the glaring fluorescent lights and the gleaming linoleum made a harsh, unfriendly environment. I tried to read a magazine, and tossed it on the table after a couple of minutes. For the seventh or eighth time, I thought of skipping out. But there was a woman stationed at the night reception desk, and she was keeping a close eye on me. After a few more minutes, I decided to visit the women's room to wash the blood off my hands. While I was in there, I took a few swipes at my coat with a wet paper towel, which was largely a wasted effort.

When I emerged from the women's room, there were two cops waiting for me. They were big men, both of them. They rustled with their synthetic padded jackets, and they creaked with the leather of their belts and equipment. I couldn't imagine them sneaking up on anyone.

The taller man was the older. His steel gray hair was clipped close to his scalp. His face was carved with a few deep wrinkles, like ravines. His gut overhung his belt. His partner was a younger man, maybe thirty, with light brown hair and light brown eyes and light brown skin – a curiously monochromatic guy. I gave them a quick but comprehensive scan with all my senses.

I could tell the two were both prepared to find out I'd had a hand in the injuries of the girl I'd brought in, or that I at least knew more than I was saying.

Of course, they were partially right.

'Miss Stackhouse? You brought in the young woman Dr. Skinner is treating?' the younger man said gently.

'Maria-Star,' I said. 'Cooper.'

'Tell us how you came to do that,' the older cop said.

It was definitely an order, though his tone was moderate. Neither man knew me or knew of me, I 'heard.' Good.

I took a deep breath and dove into the waters of mendacity. 'I was driving home from work,' I said. 'I work at Merlotte's Bar – you know where that is?'

They both nodded. Of course, police would know the location of every bar in the parish.

'I saw a body lying by the side of the road, on the gravel of the shoulder,' I said carefully, thinking ahead so I wouldn't say something I couldn't take back. 'So I stopped. There wasn't anyone else in sight. When I found out she was still alive, I knew I had to get to help. It took me a long time to get her into the car by myself.' I was trying to account for the passage of time since I'd left work and the gravel from Bill's driveway that I knew would be in her skin. I couldn't gauge how much care I needed to take in putting my story together, but more care was better than less.

'Did you notice any skid marks on the road?' The light brown policeman couldn't go long without asking a question.

'No, I didn't notice. They may have been there. I was just – after I saw her, all I thought about was her.'

'So?' the older man prompted.

'I could tell she was hurt real bad, so I got her here as fast as I could.' I shrugged. End of my story.

'You didn't think about calling an ambulance?'

'I don't have a cell phone.'

'Woman who comes home from work that late, by herself, really ought to have a cell phone, ma'am.'

I opened my mouth to tell him that if he felt like paying the bill, I'd be glad to have one, when I restrained myself. Yes, it *would* be handy to have a cell phone, but I could barely afford my regular phone. My only extravagance was cable TV, and I justified that by telling myself it was my only recreational spending. 'I hear you,' I said briefly.

'And your full name is?' This from the younger man. I looked up, met his eyes.

'Sookie Stackhouse,' I said. He'd been thinking I seemed kind of shy and sweet.

'You the sister of the man who's missing?' The gray-haired man bent down to look in my face.

'Yes, sir.' I looked down at my toes again.

'You're sure having a streak of bad luck, Miss Stackhouse.'

'Tell me about it,' I said, my voice shaking with sincerity.

'Have you ever seen this woman, the woman you brought in, before tonight?' The older officer was scribbling in a little notepad he'd produced from a pocket. His name was Curlew, the little pin on his pocket said.

I shook my head.

'You think your brother might have known her?'

I looked up, startled. I met the eyes of the brown man again. His name was Stans. 'How the heck would I know?' I asked. I knew in the next second that he'd just wanted me to look up again. He didn't know what to make of me. The monochromatic Stans thought I was pretty and seemed like a good little Samaritan. On the other hand, my job was one educated nice girls didn't often take, and my brother was well known as a brawler, though many of the patrol officers liked him.

'How is she doing?' I asked.

They both glanced at the door behind which the struggle to save the young woman went on.

'She's still alive,' Stans said.

'Poor thing,' I said. Tears rolled down my cheeks, and I began fumbling in my pockets for a tissue.

'Did she say anything to you, Miss Stackhouse?'

I had to think about that. 'Yes,' I said. 'She did.' The truth was safe, in this instance.

They both brightened at the news.

'She told me her name. She said her legs hurt worst, when I asked her,' I said. 'And she said that the car had hit her, but not run her over.'

The two men looked at each other.

'Did she describe the car?' Stans asked.

It was incredibly tempting to describe the witches' car. But I mistrusted the glee that bubbled up inside me at the idea. And I was glad I had, the next second, when I realized that the trace evidence they'd get off the car would be wolf fur. Good thinking, Sook.

'No, she didn't,' I said, trying to look as though I'd been groping through my memory. 'She didn't really talk much after that, just moaning. It was awful.' And the upholstery on my backseat was probably ruined, too. I immediately wished I hadn't thought of something so selfish.

'And you didn't see any other cars, trucks, any other vehicles on your way to your house from the bar, or even when you were coming back to town?'

That was a slightly different question. 'Not on my road,' I said hesitantly. 'I probably saw a few cars when I got closer to Bon Temps and went through town. And of course I saw more between Bon Temps and Clarice. But I don't recall any in particular.'

'Can you take us to the spot where you picked her up? The exact place?'

'I doubt it. There wasn't anything to mark it besides her,' I said. My coherence level was falling by the minute. 'No big tree, or road, or mile marker. Maybe tomorrow? In the daytime?'

Stans patted me on the shoulder. 'I know you're shook up, miss,' he said consolingly. 'You done the best you could for this girl. Now we gotta leave it up to the doctors and the Lord.'

I nodded emphatically, because I certainly agreed. The older Curlew still looked at me a little skeptically, but he thanked me as a matter of form, and they strode out of the hospital into the blackness. I stepped back a little, though I remained looking out into the parking lot. In a second or two, they reached my car and shone their big flashlights through the windows, checking out the interior. I keep the inside of my car spanky-clean, so they wouldn't see a thing but bloodstains in the backseat. I noticed that they checked out the front grille, too, and I didn't blame them one little bit.

They examined my car over and over, and finally they stood under one of the big lights, making notes on clipboards.

Not too long after that, the doctor came out to find me. She pulled her mask down and rubbed the back of her neck with a long, thin hand. 'Miss Cooper is doing better. She's stable,' she said.

I nodded, and then I closed my eyes for a moment with sheer relief. 'Thank you,' I croaked.

'We're going to airlift her to Schumpert in Shreveport. The helicopter'll be here any second.'

I blinked, trying to decide if that were a good thing or a bad thing. No matter what my opinion was, the Were had to go to the best and closest hospital. When she became able to talk, she'd have to tell them something. How could I ensure that her story jibed with mine?

'Is she conscious?' I asked.

'Just barely,' the doctor said, almost angrily, as if such injuries were an insult to her personally. 'You can speak to her briefly, but I can't guarantee she'll remember, or understand. I have to go talk to the cops.' The two officers were striding back into the hospital, I saw from my place at the window.

'Thank you,' I said, and followed her gesture to her left. I pushed open the door into the grim glaring room where they'd been working on the girl.

It was a mess. There were a couple of nurses in there even now, chatting about this or that and packing away some of the unused packages of bandages and tubes. A man with a bucket and mop stood waiting in a corner. He would clean the room when the Were – the girl – had been wheeled out to the helicopter. I went to the side of the narrow bed and took her hand.

I bent down close.

'Maria-Star, you know my voice?' I asked quietly. Her face was swollen from its impact with the ground, and it was covered with scratches and scrapes. These were the smallest of her injuries, but they looked very painful to me.

'Yes,' she breathed.

'I'm the one that found you by the *side of the road*,' I said. 'On the way to my house, south of Bon Temps. You were lying by the parish road.'

'Understand,' she murmured.

'I guess,' I continued carefully, 'that someone made you get out of his car, and that someone then hit you with the car. But you know how it is after a trauma, sometimes people don't remember *anything*.' One of the nurses turned to me, her face curious. She'd caught the last part of my sentence. 'So don't worry if you don't remember.'

'I'll try,' she said ambiguously, still in that hushed, far-away voice.

There was nothing more I could do here, and a lot more that could go wrong, so I whispered 'Good-bye,' told the nurses I appreciated them, and went out to my car. Thanks to the blankets (which I supposed I'd have to replace for Bill), my backseat wasn't messed up too bad.

I was glad to find something to be pleased about.

I wondered about the blankets. Did the police have them? Would the hospital call me about them? Or had they been pitched in the garbage? I shrugged. There was no point worrying about two rectangles of material anymore, when I had so much else crammed on my worry list. For one thing, I didn't like the Weres congregating at Merlotte's. That pulled Sam way too far into Were concerns. He was a shifter, after all, and shifters were much more loosely involved with the supernatural world. Shifters tended to be more 'every shifter for himself,' while the Weres were always organized. Now they were using Merlotte's for a meeting place, after hours.

And then there was Eric. Oh, Lord, Eric would be waiting for me at the house.

I found myself wondering what time it was in Peru. Bill had to be having more fun than I was. It seemed like I'd gotten worn out on New Year's Eve and never caught up; I'd never felt this exhausted.

I was just past the intersection where I'd turned left, the road that eventually passed Merlotte's. The headlights illuminated flashes of trees and bushes. At least there were no more vampires running down the side . . .

'Wake up,' said the woman sitting by me on the front seat.

'What?' My eyelids popped open. The car swerved violently.

'You were falling asleep.'

By this time, I wouldn't have been surprised if a beached whale had lain across the road.

'You're who?' I asked, when I felt my voice might be under my control.

'Claudine.'

It was hard to recognize her in the dashboard light, but sure enough, it seemed to be the tall and beautiful woman who'd been in Merlotte's New Year's Eve, who'd been with Tara the previous morning. 'How did you get in my car? Why are you here?'

'Because there's been an unusual amount of supernatural activity in this area in the past week or two. I'm the go-between.'

'Go between what?'

'Between the two worlds. Or, more accurately, between the three worlds.'

Sometimes life just hands you more than you take. Then you just accept.

'So, you're like an angel? That's how come you woke me up when I was falling asleep at the wheel?'

'No, I haven't gotten that far yet. You're too tired to take this in. You have to ignore the mythology and just accept me for what I am.'

I felt a funny jolt in my chest.

'Look,' Claudine pointed out. 'That man's waving to you.'

Sure enough, in Merlotte's parking lot there stood a semaphoring vampire. It was Chow.

'Oh, just great,' I said, in the grumpiest voice I could manage. 'Well, I hope you don't mind us stopping, Claudine. I need to go in.'

'Sure, I wouldn't miss it.'

Chow waved me to the rear of the bar, and I was astonished to find the employee parking area jam-packed with cars that had been invisible from the road.

'Oh, boy!' Claudine said. 'A party!' She got out of my car as if she could hardly restrain her glee, and I had the satisfaction of seeing that Chow was absolutely stupefied when he took in all six feet of her. It's hard to surprise a vampire.

'Let's go in,' Claudine said gaily, and took my hand.

Chapter 9

Every Supe I'd ever met was in Merlotte's. Or maybe it just seemed like that, since I was dead tired and wanted to be by myself. The Were pack was there, all in human form and all more or less dressed, to my relief.

Alcide was in khakis and an unbuttoned shirt in green and blue plaid. It was hard to believe he could run on four legs. The Weres were drinking coffee or soft drinks, and Eric (looking happy and healthy) was having some TrueBlood. Pam was sitting on a barstool, wearing an ash green tracksuit, which she managed to make prim-but-sexy. She had a bow in her hair and beaded sneakers on her feet. She'd brought Gerald with her, a vampire I'd met once or twice at Fangtasia. Gerald looked about thirty, but I'd heard him refer to Prohibition once as if he'd lived through it. What little I knew of Gerald didn't predispose me to getting closer to him.

Even in such a company, my entrance with Claudine was nothing short of sensational. In the improved lighting of the bar, I could see that Claudine's strategically rounded body was packed into an orange knit dress, and her long legs ended in the highest of high heels. She looked like a scrumptious slut, super-sized.

Nope, she couldn't be an angel – at least, as I understood angels.

Looking from Claudine to Pam, I decided it was massively unfair that they looked so clean and appealing. Like I needed to feel unattractive, in addition to being worn out and scared and confused! Doesn't every gal want to walk into a room side by side with a gorgeous woman who practically has 'I want to fuck' tattooed on her forehead? If I hadn't caught a glimpse of Sam, whom I'd dragged into this whole thing, I would've turned around and walked right out.

'Claudine,' said Colonel Flood. 'What brings you here?'

Pam and Gerald were both staring at the woman in orange intently, as if they expected her to take off her clothes any second.

'My girl, here' – and Claudine inclined her head toward me – 'fell asleep at the wheel. How come you aren't watching out for her better?'

The colonel, as dignified in his civvies as he had been in his skin, looked a little startled, as if it was news to him that he was supposed to provide protection for me. 'Ah,' he said. 'Uh . . .'

'Should have sent someone to the hospital with her,' Claudine said, shaking her waterfall of black hair.

'I offered to go with her,' Eric said indignantly. 'She said it would be too suspicious if she went to the hospital with a vampire.'

'Well, hel-lo, tall, blond, and *dead*,' Claudine said. She looked Eric up and down, admiring what she saw. 'You in the habit of doing what human women ask of you?'

Thanks a lot, Claudine, I told her silently. I was supposed to be guarding Eric, and now he wouldn't even shut the door if I told him to. Gerald was still ogling her in the same stunned way. I wondered if anyone would notice if I stretched out on one of the tables and went to sleep. Suddenly, just as Pam's and Gerald's had done, Eric's gaze sharpened and he seemed fixed on Claudine. I had time to think it was like watching cats that'd suddenly spotted something skittering along the baseboards before big hands spun me around and Alcide gathered me to him. He'd maneuvered through the crowd in the bar until he'd reached me. Since his shirt wasn't buttoned, I found my face pressed against his warm chest, and I was glad to be there. The curly black hair did smell faintly of dog, true, but otherwise I was comforted at being hugged and cherished. It felt delightful.

'Who are you?' Alcide asked Claudine. I had my ear against his chest and I could hear him from inside and outside, a strange sensation.

'I'm Claudine, the fairy,' the huge woman said. 'See?'

I had to turn to see what she was doing. She'd lifted her long hair to show her ears, which were delicately pointed.

'Fairy,' Alcide repeated. He sounded as astonished as I felt.

'Sweet,' said one of the younger Weres, a spiky-haired male who might be nineteen. He looked intrigued with the turn of events, and he glanced around at the other Weres seated at his table as if inviting them to share his pleasure. 'For real?'

'For a while,' Claudine said. 'Sooner or later, I'll go one way or another.' No one understood that, with the possible exception of the colonel.

'You are one mouthwatering woman,' said the young Were. To back up the fashion statement of the spiked hair, he wore jeans and a ragged Fallen Angel T-shirt; he was barefoot, though Merlotte's was cool, since the thermostat was turned down for the rest of the night. He was wearing toe rings.

'Thanks!' Claudine smiled down at him. She snapped her fingers, and there was the same kind of haze around her that enveloped the Weres when they shifted. It was the haze of thick magic. When the air cleared, Claudine was wearing a spangled white evening gown.

'Sweet,' the boy repeated in a dazed way, and Claudine basked in his admiration. I noticed she was keeping a certain distance from the vampires.

'Claudine, now that you've shown off, could we please talk about something besides you?' Colonel Flood sounded as tired as I felt.

'Of course,' Claudine said in an appropriately chastened voice. 'Just ask away.'

'First things first. Miss Stackhouse, how is Maria-Star?'

'She survived the ride to the hospital in Clarice. They're airlifting her to Shreveport, to Schumpert hospital. She may already be on her way. The doctor sounded pretty positive about her chances.'

The Weres all looked at one another, and most of them let out gusty noises of relief. One woman, about thirty years old, actually did a little happy dance. The vampires, by now almost totally fixated on the fairy, didn't react at all.

'What did you tell the emergency room doctor?' Colonel Flood asked. 'I have to let her parents know what the official line is.' Maria-Star would be their first-born, and their only Were child.

'I told the police that I found her by the side of the road, that I didn't see any signs of a car braking or anything. I told them she was lying on the gravel, so we won't have to worry about grass that isn't pressed down when it ought to be . . . I hope she got it. She was pretty doped up when I talked to her.'

'Very good thinking,' Colonel Flood said. 'Thanks, Miss Stackhouse. Our pack is indebted to you.'

I waved my hand to disclaim any debt. 'How did you come to show up at Bill's house at the right time?'

'Emilio and Sid tracked the witches to the right area.' Emilio must be the small, dark man with huge brown eyes. There was a growing immigrant Mexican population in our area, and Emilio was apparently a part of that community. The spike-haired boy gave me a little wave, and I assumed he must be Sid. 'Anyway, after dark, we started keeping an eye on the building where Hallow and her coven are holed up. It's hard to do; it's a residential neighborhood that's mostly black.' African-American twins, both girls, grinned at each other. They were young enough to find this exciting, like Sid. 'When Hallow and her brother left for Bon Temps, we followed them in our cars. We called Sam, too, to warn him.'

I looked at Sam reproachfully. He hadn't warned me, hadn't mentioned the Weres were heading our way, too.

Colonel Flood went on, 'Sam called me on my cell to tell me where he figured they were heading when they walked out of his bar. I decided an isolated place like the Compton house would be a good place to get them. We were able to park our cars in the cemetery and change, so we got there just in time. But they caught our scent early.' The colonel glared at Sid. Apparently, the younger Were had jumped the gun.

'So they got away,' I said, trying to sound neutral. 'And now they know you're on to them.'

'Yes, they got away. The murderers of Adabelle Yancy. The leaders of a group trying to take over not only the vamps' territory, but ours.' Colonel Flood had been sweeping the assembled Weres with a cold gaze, and they wilted under his stare, even Alcide. 'And now the witches'll be on their guard, since they know we're after them.'

Their attention momentarily pulled from the radiant fairy Claudine, Pam and Gerald seemed discreetly amused by the colonel's speech. Eric, as always these days, looked as confused as if the colonel were speaking in Sanskrit.

'The Stonebrooks went back to Shreveport when they left Bill's?' I asked.

'We assume so. We had to change back very quickly – no easy matter – and then get to our cars. A few of us went one way, a few another, but we caught no glimpse of them.'

'And now we're here. Why?' Alcide's voice was harsh.

'We're here for several reasons,' the packmaster said. 'First, we wanted to know about Maria-Star. Also, we wanted to recover for a bit before we drive back to Shreveport ourselves.'

The Weres, who seemed to have pulled their clothes on pretty hastily, did look a little ragged. The dark-moon transformation and the rapid change back to two-legged form had taken a toll on all of them.

'And why are you here?' I asked Pam.

'We have something to report, too,' she said. 'Evidently, we have the same goals as the Weres – on this matter, anyway.' She tore her gaze away from Claudine with an effort. She and Gerald exchanged glances, and as one, they turned to Eric, who looked back at them blankly. Pam sighed, and Gerald looked down at his booted feet.

'Our nest mate Clancy didn't return to us last night,' Pam said. Hard on this startling announcement, she focused once again on the fairy. Claudine seemed to have some overwhelming allure for the vampires.

Most of the Weres looked like they were thinking that one less vampire was a step in the right direction. But Alcide said, 'What do you think has happened?'

'We got a note,' Gerald said, one of the few times I'd ever heard him speak out loud. He had a faint English accent. 'The note said that the witches plan to drain one of our vampires for each day they have to search for Eric.'

All eyes went to Eric, who looked stunned. 'But why?' he asked. 'I can't understand what makes me such a prize.'

One of the Were girls, a tan blonde in her late twenties, took silent issue with that. She rolled her eyes toward me, and I could only grin back. But no matter how good Eric looked, and what ideas interested parties might have about the fun to be had with him in bed (and on top of that, the control he had over various vampire enterprises in Shreveport), this single-minded pursuit of Eric rang the 'Excessive' alarm. Even if Hallow had sex with Eric, and then drained him dry and consumed all his blood – Wait, there was an idea.

'How much blood can be got from one of you?' I asked Pam.

She stared at me, as close to surprised as I'd ever seen her. 'Let me see,' she said. She stared into space, and her fingers wiggled. It looked like Pam was translating from one unit of measurement to another. 'Six quarts,' she said at last.

'And how much blood do they sell in those little vials?'

'That's . . .' She did some more figuring. 'Well, that would be less than a fourth of a cup.' She anticipated where I was heading. 'So Eric contains over ninety-six saleable units of blood.'

'How much you reckon they could charge for that?'

'Well, on the street, the price has reached $225 for regular vampire blood,' Pam said, her eyes as cold as winter frost. 'For Eric's blood . . . He is so old . . .'

'Maybe $425 a vial?'

'Conservatively.'

'So, on the hoof, Eric's worth . . .'

'Over forty thousand dollars.'

The whole crowd stared at Eric with heightened interest – except for Pam and Gerald, who along with Eric had resumed their contemplation of Claudine. They appeared to have inched closer to the fairy.

'So, do you think that's enough motivation?' I asked. 'Eric spurned her. She wants him, she wants his stuff, and she wants to sell his blood.'

'That's a lot of motivation,' agreed a Were woman, a pretty brunette in her late forties.

'Plus, Hallow's nuts,' Claudine said cheerfully.

I didn't think the fairy had stopped smiling since she'd appeared in my car. 'How do you know that, Claudine?' I asked.

'I've been to her headquarters,' she said.

We all regarded her in silence for a long moment, but not as raptly as the three vampires did.

'Claudine, have you gone over?' Colonel Flood asked. He sounded more tired than anything else.

'James,' Claudine said. 'Shame on you! She thought I was an area witch.'

Maybe I wasn't the only one who was thinking that such overflowing cheer was a little weird. Most of the fifteen or so Weres in the bar didn't seem too comfortable around the fairy. 'It would have saved us a lot of trouble if you'd told us that earlier than tonight, Claudine,' the colonel said, his tone frosty.

'A real fairy,' Gerald said. 'I've only had one before.'

'They're hard to catch,' Pam said, her voice dreamy. She edged a little closer.

Even Eric had lost his blank and frustrated mien and took a step toward Claudine. The three vamps looked like chocaholics at the Hershey factory.

'Now, now,' Claudine said, a little anxiously. 'Anything with fangs, take a step back!'

Pam looked a bit embarrassed, and she tried to relax. Gerald subsided unwillingly. Eric kept creeping forward.

Neither of the vampires nor any of the Weres looked willing to take Eric on. I mentally girded my loins. After all, Claudine had awakened me before I could crash my car.

'Eric,' I said, taking three quick steps to stand between Eric and the fairy. 'Snap out of it!'

'What?' Eric paid no more attention to me than he would to a fly buzzing around his head.

'She's off limits, Eric,' I said, and Eric's eyes did flicker down to my face.

'Hi, remember me?' I put my hand on his chest to slow him down. 'I don't know why you're in such a lather, fella, but you need to hold your horses.'

'I want her,' Eric said, his blue eyes blazing down into mine.

'Well, she's gorgeous,' I said, striving for reasonable,

though actually I was a little hurt. 'But she's not available. Right, Claudine?' I aimed my voice back over my shoulder.

'Not available to a vampire,' the fairy said. 'My blood is intoxicating to a vampire. You don't want to know what they'd be like after they had me.' But she still sounded cheerful.

So I hadn't been too far wrong with the chocolate metaphor. Probably this was why I hadn't encountered any fairies before; I was too much in the company of the undead.

When you have thoughts like that, you know you're in trouble.

'Claudine, I guess we need you to step outside now,' I said a little desperately. Eric was pushing against me, not testing me seriously yet (or I'd be flat on my back), but I'd had to retreat a step already. I wanted to hear what Claudine had to tell the Weres, but I realized separating the vamps from the fairy was top priority.

'Just like a big petit four,' Pam sighed, watching Claudine twitch her white-spangled butt all the way out the front door with Colonel Flood close behind her. Eric seemed to snap to once Claudine was out of sight, and I breathed a sigh of relief.

'Vamps really like fairies, huh?' I said nervously.

'Oh, yeah,' they said simultaneously.

'You know, she saved my life, and she's apparently helping us out on this witch thing,' I reminded them.

They looked sulky.

'Claudine was actually quite helpful,' Colonel Flood said as he reentered, sounding surprised. The door swung shut behind him.

Eric's arm went around me, and I could feel one kind of hunger being morphed into another.

'Why was she in their coven headquarters?' Alcide asked, more angrily than was warranted.

'You know fairies. They love to flirt with disaster, they love to role-play.' The packmaster sighed heavily. 'Even Claudine, and she's one of the good ones. Definitely on her way up. What she tells me is this: This Hallow has a coven of about twenty witches. All of them are Weres or the larger shifters. They are all vampire blood users, maybe addicts.'

'Will the Wiccans help us fight them?' asked a middle-aged woman with dyed red hair and a couple of chins.

'They haven't committed to it yet.' A young man with a military haircut – I wondered if he was stationed at Barksdale Air Force Base – seemed to know the story on the Wiccans. 'Acting on our packmaster's orders, I called or otherwise contacted every Wiccan coven or individual Wiccan in the area, and they are all doing their best to hide from these creatures. But I saw signs that most of them were heading for a meeting tonight, though I don't know where. I think they are going to discuss the situation on their own. If they could mount an attack as well, it would help us.'

'Good work, Portugal,' said Colonel Flood, and the young man looked gratified.

Since we had our backs to the wall, Eric had felt free to let his hand roam over my bottom. I didn't object to the sensation, which was very pleasant, but I did object to the venue, which was too darn public.

'Claudine didn't say anything about prisoners who might have been there?' I asked, taking a step away from Eric.

'No, I'm sorry, Miss Stackhouse. She didn't see anyone

answering your brother's description, and she didn't see the vampire Clancy.'

I wasn't exactly surprised, but I was very disappointed. Sam said, 'I'm sorry, Sookie. If Hallow doesn't have him, where can he be?'

'Of course, just because she didn't see him, doesn't mean he's not there for sure,' the colonel said. 'We're sure she took Clancy, and Claudine didn't catch sight of him.'

'Back to the Wiccans,' suggested the red-haired Were. 'What should we do about them?'

'Tomorrow, Portugal, call all your Wiccan contacts again,' Colonel Flood said. 'Get Culpepper to help you.'

Culpepper was a young woman with a strong, handsome face and a no-nonsense haircut. She looked pleased to be included in something Portugal was doing. He looked pleased, too, but he tried to mask it under a brusque manner. 'Yes, sir,' he said snappily. Culpepper thought that was cute as hell; I was lifting that directly from her brain. Were she might be, but you couldn't disguise an admiration that intense. 'Uh, why am I calling them again?' Portugal asked after a long moment.

'We need to know what they plan to do, if they'll share that with us,' Colonel Flood said. 'If they're not with us, they can at least stay out of the way.'

'So, we're going to war?' This was from an older man, who seemed to be a pair with the red-haired woman.

'It was the vampires that started it,' the redheaded woman said.

'That is *so* untrue,' I said indignantly.

'Vamp humper,' she said.

I'd had worse things said about me, but not to my face, and not from people who intended me to hear them.

Eric had left the floor before I could decide if I was more hurt or more enraged. He had instantly opted for enraged, and it made him very effective. She was on the ground on her back and he was on top of her with fangs extended before anyone could even be alarmed. It was lucky for the red-haired woman that Pam and Gerald were equally swift, though it took both of them to lift Eric off the redheaded Were. She was bleeding only a little, but she was yelping nonstop.

For a long second, I thought the whole room was going to erupt into battle, but Colonel Flood roared, 'SILENCE!' and you didn't disobey that voice.

'Amanda,' he said to the red-haired woman, who was whimpering as though Eric had removed a limb, and whose companion was busy checking out her injuries in a wholly unnecessary panic, 'you will be polite to our allies, and you will keep your damn opinions to yourself. Your offense cancels out the blood he spilled. No retaliation, Parnell!' The male Were snarled at the colonel, but finally gave a grudging nod.

'Miss Stackhouse, I apologize for the poor manners of the pack,' Colonel Flood said to me. Though I was still upset, I made myself nod. I couldn't help but notice that Alcide was looking from me to Eric, and he looked – well, he looked appalled. Sam had the sense to be quite expressionless. My back stiffened, and I ran a quick hand over my eyes to dash away the tears.

Eric was calming down, but it was with an effort. Pam was murmuring in his ear, and Gerald was keeping a good grip on his arm.

To make my evening perfect, the back door to Merlotte's opened once again, and Debbie Pelt walked in.

'Y'all are having a party without me.' She looked at the odd assemblage and raised her eyebrows. 'Hey, baby,' she said directly to Alcide, and ran a possessive hand down his arm, twining her fingers with his. Alcide had an odd expression on his face. It was as though he was simultaneously happy and miserable.

Debbie was a striking woman, tall and lean, with a long face. She had black hair, but it wasn't curly and disheveled like Alcide's. It was cut in asymmetrical tiny clumps, and it was straight and swung with her movement. It was the dumbest haircut I'd ever seen, and it had undoubtedly cost an arm and a leg. Somehow, men didn't seem to be interested in her haircut.

It would have been hypocritical of me to greet her. Debbie and I were beyond that. She'd tried to kill me, a fact that Alcide knew; and yet she still seemed to exercise some fascination for him, though he'd thrown her out when he first learned of it. For a smart and practical and hardworking man, he had a great big blind spot, and here it was, in tight Cruel Girl jeans and a thin orange sweater that hugged every inch of skin. What was she doing here, so far from her own stomping grounds?

I felt a sudden impulse to turn to Eric and tell him that Debbie had made a serious attempt on my life, just to see what would happen. But I restrained myself yet again. All this restraint was plain painful. My fingers were curled under, transforming my hands into tight fists.

'We'll call you if anything more happens in this meeting,' Gerald said. It took me a minute to understand I was being dismissed, and that it was because I had to take Eric back to my house lest he erupt again. From the look on his face, it wouldn't take much. His eyes were glowing blue, and his fangs were at least half extended. I was more than ever tempted to . . . no, I was *not*. I would leave.

'Bye, bitch,' Debbie said, as I went out the door. I caught a glimpse of Alcide turning to her, his expression appalled, but Pam grabbed me by the arm and hustled me out into the parking lot. Gerald had a hold of Eric, which was a good thing, too.

As the two vampires handed us out to Chow, I was seething.

Chow thrust Eric into the passenger's seat, so it appeared I was the designated driver. The Asian vamp said, 'We'll call you later, go home,' and I was about to snap back at him. But I glanced over at my passenger and decided to be smart instead and get out of there quickly. Eric's belligerence was dissolving into a muddle. He looked confused and lost, as unlike the hair-trigger avenger he'd been only a few minutes before as you can imagine.

We were halfway home before Eric said anything. 'Why are vampires so hated by Weres?' he asked.

'I don't know,' I answered, slowing down because two deer bounded across the road. You see the first one, you always wait: There'll be another one, most often. 'Vamps feel the same about Weres and shifters. The supernatural community seems to band together against humans, but other than that, you guys squabble a lot, at least as far as I can tell.' I took a deep breath and considered phraseology. 'Um, Eric, I appreciate your taking my part, when that Amanda called me a name. But I'm pretty used to speaking up for myself when I think it's called for. If I were a vampire, you wouldn't feel you had to hit people on my behalf, right?'

'But you're not as strong as a vampire, not even as strong as a Were,' Eric objected.

'No argument there, honey. But I also wouldn't have even thought of hitting her, because that would give her a reason to hit me back.'

'You're saying I made it come to blows when I didn't need to.'

'That's exactly what I'm saying.'

'I embarrassed you.'

'No,' I said instantly. Then I wondered if that wasn't exactly the case. 'No,' I repeated with more conviction, 'you didn't embarrass me. Actually, it made me feel good, that you felt, ah, fond enough of me to be angry when Amanda acted like I was something stuck to her shoe. But I'm used to that treatment, and I can handle it. Though Debbie's taking it to a whole different level.'

The new, thoughtful Eric gave that a mental chewing over.

'Why are you used to that?' he asked.

It wasn't the reaction I'd expected. By that time we were at the house, and I checked out the surrounding clearing before I got out of the car to unlock the back door. When we were safely inside with the dead bolt shot, I said, 'Because I'm used to people not thinking much of barmaids. Uneducated barmaids. Uneducated telepathic barmaids. I'm used to people thinking I'm crazy, or at least off mentally. I'm not trying to sound like I think I'm Poor Pitiful Pearl, but I don't have a lot of fans, and I'm used to that.'

'That confirms my bad opinion of humans in general,' Eric said. He pulled my coat off my shoulders, looked at it with distaste, hung it on the back of one of the chairs pushed in under the kitchen table. 'You are beautiful.'

No one had ever looked me in the eyes and said that. I

found I had to lower my head. 'You are smart, and you are loyal,' he said relentlessly, though I waved a hand to ask him to quit. 'You have a sense of fun and adventure.'

'Cut it out,' I said.

'Make me,' he said. 'You have the most beautiful breasts I've ever seen. You're brave.' I put my fingers across his mouth, and his tongue darted out to give them a quick lick. I relaxed against him, feeling the tingle down to my toes. 'You're responsible and hardworking,' he continued. Before he could tell me that I was good about replacing the garbage can liner when I took the garbage out, I replaced my fingers with my lips.

'There,' he said softly, after a long moment. 'You're creative, too.'

For the next hour, he showed me that he, too, was creative.

It was the only hour in an extremely long day that I hadn't been consumed with fear: for the fate of my brother, about Hallow's malevolence, about the horrible death of Adabelle Yancy. There were probably a few more things that made me fearful, but in such a long day it was impossible to pick any one thing that was more awful than the other.

As I lay wrapped up in Eric's arms, humming a little wordless tune as I traced the line of his shoulder with an idle finger, I was bone-deep grateful for the pleasure he'd given me. A piece of happiness should never be taken as due.

'Thank you,' I said, my face pressed to his silent chest.

He put a finger under my chin so I would raise my eyes to his. 'No,' he said quietly. 'You took me in off the road and kept me safe. You're ready to fight for me. I can tell this about you. I can't believe my luck. When this witch is defeated, I would bring you to my side. I will share everything I have with you. Every vampire who owes me fealty will honor you.'

Was this medieval, or what? Bless Eric's heart, none of that was going to happen. At least I was smart enough, and realistic enough, not to deceive myself for a minute, though it was a wonderful fantasy. He was thinking like a chieftain with thralls at his disposal, not like a ruthless head vampire who owned a tourist bar in Shreveport.

'You've made me very happy,' I said, which was certainly the truth.

Chapter 10

The pond behind Jason's house had already been searched by the time I got up the next morning. Alcee Beck pounded on my door about ten o'clock, and since it sounded exactly like a lawman knocking, I pulled on my jeans and a sweatshirt before I went to the door.

'He's not in the pond,' Beck said, without preamble.

I sagged against the doorway. 'Oh, thank God.' I closed my eyes for a minute to do just that. 'Please come in.' Alcee Beck stepped over the threshold like a vampire, looking around him silently and with a certain wariness.

'Would you like some coffee?' I asked politely, when he was seated on the old couch.

'No, thank you,' he said stiffly, as uncomfortable with me as I was with him. I spotted Eric's shirt hanging on the doorknob of my bedroom, not quite visible from where Detective Beck was sitting. Lots of women wear men's shirts, and I told myself not to be paranoid about its presence. Though I tried not to listen to the detective's mind, I could tell that he was uneasy being alone in the house of a white woman, and he was wishing that Andy Bellefleur would get there.

'Excuse me for a minute,' I said, before I yielded to temptation and asked him why Andy was due to arrive. That would shake Alcee Beck to the core. I grabbed the shirt as I went into my room, folded it, and tucked it in a drawer before I brushed my teeth and washed my face. By the time I returned to the living room, Andy had made his appearance. Jason's boss, Catfish Hennessey, was with him. I could feel the blood leaving my head and I sat down very heavily on the ottoman sitting by the couch.

'What?' I said. I couldn't have uttered another word.

'The blood on the dock is probably feline blood, and there's a print in it, besides Jason's boot print,' said Andy. 'We've kept this quiet, because we didn't want those woods crawling with idiots.' I could feel myself swaying in an invisible wind. I would have laughed, if I hadn't had the 'gift' of telepathy. He wasn't thinking tabby or calico when he said feline; he was thinking panther.

Panthers were what we called mountain lions. Sure, there aren't mountains around here, but panthers – the oldest men hereabouts called them 'painters' – live in low bottomland, too. To the best of my knowledge, the only place panthers could be found in the wild was in Florida, and their numbers were dwindling to the brink of extinction. No solid evidence had been produced to prove that any live native panthers had been living in Louisiana in the past fifty years, give or take a decade.

But of course, there were stories. And our woods and streams could produce no end of alligators, nutria, possums, coons, and even the occasional black bear or wildcat. Coyotes, too. But there were no pictures, or scat, or print casts, to prove the presence of panthers . . . until now.

Andy Bellefleur's eyes were hot with longing, but not for

me. Any red-blooded male who'd ever gone hunting, or even any P.C. guy who photographed nature, would give almost anything to see a real wild panther. Despite the fact that these large predators were deeply anxious to avoid humans, humans would not return the favor.

'What are you thinking?' I asked, though I knew damn good and well what they were thinking. But to keep them on an even keel, I had to pretend not to; they'd feel better, and they might let something slip. Catfish was just thinking that Jason was most likely dead. The two lawmen kept fixing me in their gaze, but Catfish, who knew me better than they did, was sitting forward on the edge of Gran's old recliner, his big red hands clasped to each other so hard the knuckles were white.

'Maybe Jason spotted the panther when he came home that night,' Andy said carefully. 'You know he'd run and get his rifle and try to track it.'

'They're endangered,' I said. 'You think Jason doesn't know that panthers are endangered?' Of course, they thought Jason was so impulsive and brainless that he just wouldn't care.

'Are you sure that would be at the top of his list?' Alcee Beck asked, with an attempt at gentleness.

'So you think Jason shot the panther,' I said, having a little difficulty getting the words out of my mouth.

'It's a possibility.'

'And then what?' I crossed my arms over my chest.

All three men exchanged a glance. 'Maybe Jason followed the panther into the woods,' Andy said. 'Maybe the panther wasn't so badly wounded after all, and it got him.'

'You think my brother would trail a wounded and dangerous animal into the woods – at night, by himself.' Sure they did. I could read it loud and clear. They thought that would be absolutely typical Jason Stackhouse behavior. What they didn't get was that (reckless and wild as my brother was) Jason's favorite person in the entire universe was Jason Stackhouse, and he would not endanger that person in such an obvious way.

Andy Bellefleur had some misgivings about this theory, but Alcee Beck sure didn't. He thought I'd outlined Jason's procedure that night exactly. What the two lawmen didn't know, and what I couldn't tell them, was that if Jason had seen a panther at his house that night, the chances were good the panther was actually a shape-shifting human. Hadn't Claudine said that the witches had gathered some of the larger shifters into their fold? A panther would be a valuable animal to have at your side if you were contemplating a hostile takeover.

'Jay Stans, from Clarice, called me this morning,' Andy said. His round face turned toward me and his brown eyes locked on me. 'He was telling me about this gal you found by the side of the road last night.'

I nodded, not seeing the connection, and too preoccupied with speculation about the panther to guess what was coming.

'This girl have any connection to Jason?'

'What?' I was stunned. 'What are you talking about?'

'You find this girl, this Maria-Star Cooper, by the side of the road. They searched, but they didn't find any trace of an accident.'

I shrugged. 'I told them I wasn't sure I could pin the spot down, and they didn't ask me to go looking, after I offered. I'm not real surprised they couldn't find any evidence, not knowing the exact spot. I tried to pin it down, but it was at night, and I was pretty scared. Or she could have just been dumped where I found her.' I don't watch the Discovery Channel for nothing.

'See, what we were thinking,' Alcee Beck rumbled, 'is that this girl was one of Jason's discards, and maybe he was keeping her somewhere secret? But you let her go when Jason disappeared.'

'Huh?' It was like they were speaking Urdu or something. I couldn't make any sense out of it.

'With Jason getting arrested under suspicion of those murders last year and all, we wondered if there wasn't some fire under all that smoke.'

'You know who did those killings. He's in jail, unless something's happened that I don't know about. And he confessed.' Catfish met my eyes, and his were very uneasy. This line of questioning had my brother's boss all twitchy. Granted, my brother was a little kinky in the sex department (though none of the women he'd kinked with seemed to mind), but the idea of him keeping a sex slave that I had to deal with when he vanished? Oh, come on!

'He did confess, and he's still in jail,' Andy said. Since Andy had taken the confession, I should hope so. 'But what if Jason was his accomplice?'

'Wait a damn minute now,' I said. My pot was beginning to boil over. 'You can't have it both ways. If my brother is dead out in the woods after chasing a mythical wounded panther, how could he have been holding, what's her name, Maria-Star Cooper, hostage somewhere? You're thinking I've been in on my brother's supposed bondage activities, too? You think I hit her with my car? And then I loaded her in and drove her to the emergency room?'

We all glared at each other for a long moment. The men

were tossing out waves of tension and confusion like they were necklaces at Mardi Gras.

Then Catfish launched himself off the couch like a bottle rocket. 'No,' he bellowed. 'You guys asked me to come along to break this bad news about the panther to Sookie. No one said anything about this stuff about some girl that got hit by a car! This here is a nice girl.' Catfish pointed at me. 'No one's going to call her different! Not only did Jason Stackhouse never have to do more than crook his little finger at a girl for her to come running, much less take one hostage and do weird stuff to her, but if you're saying Sookie let this Cooper girl free when Jason didn't come home, and then tried to run over her, well, all I got to say is, you can go straight to hell!'

God bless Catfish Hennessey is all *I* had to say.

Alcee and Andy left soon after, and Catfish and I had a disjointed talk consisting mostly of him cursing the lawmen. When he ran down, he glanced at his watch.

'Come on, Sookie. You and me got to get to Jason's.'

'Why?' I was willing but bewildered.

'We got us a search party together, and I know you'll want to be there.'

I stared at him with my mouth open, while Catfish fumed about Alcee and Andy's allegations. I tried real hard to think of some way to cancel a search party. I hated to think of those men and women putting on all their winter gear to plow through the underbrush, now bare and brown, that made the woods so difficult to navigate. But there was no way to stop them, when they meant so well; and there was every reason to join them.

There was the remote chance that Jason *was* out there in the woods somewhere. Catfish told me he'd gotten together as many men as he could, and Kevin Pryor had agreed to be the coordinator, though off-duty. Maxine Fortenberry and her churchwomen were bringing out coffee and doughnuts from the Bon Temps Bakery. I began crying, because this was just overwhelming, and Catfish turned even redder. Weeping women were way high on Catfish's long list of things that made him uncomfortable.

I eased his situation by telling him I had to get ready. I threw the bed together, washed my face clean of tears, and yanked my hair back into a ponytail. I found a pair of earmuffs that I used maybe once a year, and pulled on my old coat and stuck my yard work gloves in my pocket, along with a wad of Kleenex in case I got weepy again.

The search party was the popular activity for the day in Bon Temps. Not only do people like to help in our small town – but also rumors had inevitably begun circulating about the mysterious wild animal footprint. As far as I could tell, the word 'panther' was not yet currency; if it had been, the crowd would have been even larger. Most of the men had come armed – well, actually, most of the men were always armed. Hunting is a way of life around here, the NRA provides most of the bumper stickers, and deer season is like a holy holiday. There are special times for hunting deer with a bow and arrow, with a muzzleloader, or with a rifle. (There may be a spear season, for all I know.) There must have been fifty people at Jason's house, quite a party on a workday for such a small community.

Sam was there, and I was so glad to see him I almost began crying again. Sam was the best boss I'd ever had, and a friend, and he always came when I was in trouble. His red-gold hair was covered with a bright orange knit cap, and he wore bright orange gloves, too. His heavy brown jacket looked somber in contrast, and like all of the men, he was wearing work boots. You didn't go out in the woods, even in winter, with ankles unprotected. Snakes were slow and sluggish, but they were there, and they'd retaliate if you stepped on them.

Somehow the presence of all these people made Jason's disappearance seem that much more terrifying. If all these people believed Jason might be out in the woods, dead or badly wounded, he might be. Despite every sensible thing I could tell myself, I grew more and more afraid. I had a few minutes of blanking out on the scene entirely while I imagined all the things that could have happened to Jason, for maybe the hundredth go-round.

Sam was standing beside me, when I could hear and see again. He'd pulled off a glove, and his hand found mine and clasped it. His felt warm and hard, and I was glad to be holding on to him. Sam, though a shifter, knew how to aim his thoughts at me, though he couldn't 'hear' mine in return. *Do you really believe he's out there?* he asked me.

I shook my head. Our eyes met and held.

Do you think he's still alive?

That was a lot harder. Finally, I just shrugged. He kept hold of my hand, and I was glad of it.

Arlene and Tack scrambled out of Arlene's car and came toward us. Arlene's hair was as bright red as ever, but quite a bit more snarled than she usually wore it, and the short-order cook needed to shave. So he hadn't started keeping a razor at Arlene's yet, was the way I read it.

'Did you see Tara?' Arlene asked.

'No.'

'Look.' She pointed, as surreptitiously as you can, and I saw Tara in jeans and rubber boots that came up to her knees. She looked as unlike the meticulously groomed clothing-store proprietor as I could imagine, though she was wearing an adorable fake-fur hat of white and brown that made you want to go up and stroke her head. Her coat matched the hat. So did her gloves. But from the waist down, Tara was ready for the woods. Jason's friend Dago was staring at Tara with the stunned look of the newly smitten. Holly and Danielle had come, too, and since Danielle's boyfriend wasn't around, the search party was turning out to have an unexpected social side.

Maxine Fortenberry and two other women from her church had let down the tailgate of Maxine's husband's old pickup, and there were several thermoses containing coffee set up there, along with disposable cups, plastic spoons, and packages of sugar. Six dozen doughnuts steamed up the long boxes they'd been packed in. A large plastic trash can, already lined with a black bag, stood ready. These ladies knew how to throw a search party.

I couldn't believe all this had been organized in the space of a few hours. I had to take my hand from Sam's to fish out a tissue and mop my face with it. I would have expected Arlene to come, but the presence of Holly and Danielle was just about stunning, and Tara's attendance was even more surprising. She wasn't a search-the-woods kind of woman. Kevin Pryor didn't have much use for Jason, but here he was, with a map and pad and pencil, organizing away.

I caught Holly's eye, and she gave me a sad sort of smile, the kind of little smile you gave someone at a funeral.

Just then Kevin banged the plastic trash can lid against the tailgate of the truck, and when everyone's attention was on him, he began to give directions for the search. I hadn't realized Kevin could be so authoritative; on most occasions, he was overshadowed by his clingy mother, Jeneen, or his oversized partner, Kenya. You wouldn't catch Kenya out in the woods looking for Jason, I reflected, and just then I spotted her and had to swallow my own thoughts. In sensible gear, she was leaning against the Fortenberrys' pickup, her brown face absolutely expressionless. Her stance suggested that she was Kevin's enforcer – that she'd move or speak only if he were challenged in some way. Kenya knew how to project silent menace; I'll give her that. She would throw a bucket of water on Jason if he were on fire, but her feelings for my brother were certainly not overwhelmingly positive. She'd come because Kevin was volunteering. As Kevin divided people up into teams, her dark eyes left him only to scan the faces of the searchers, including mine. She gave me a slight nod, and I gave her the same.

'Each group of five has to have a rifleman,' Kevin called. 'That can't be just anybody. It has to be someone who's spent time out in the woods hunting.' The excitement level rose to the boiling point with this directive. But after that, I didn't listen to the rest of Kevin's instructions. I was still tired from the day before, for one thing; what an exceptionally full day it had been. And the whole time, in the background, my fear for my brother had been nagging and eating at me. I'd been woken early this morning after a long night, and here I was standing in the cold outside my childhood home, waiting to participate in a touching wild goose chase – or at least I hoped it was a wild goose chase. I was too dazed to judge any more. A chill wind began to gust through the clearing around the house, making the tears on my cheeks unbearably cold.

Sam put his arms around me, though in our coats it was quite awkward. It seemed to me I could feel the warmth of him even through all the material.

'You know we won't find him out there,' he whispered to me.

'I'm pretty sure we won't,' I said, sounding anything but certain.

Sam said, 'I'll smell him if he's out there.'

That was so practical.

I looked up at him. I didn't have to look far, because Sam's not a real tall man. Right now, his face was very serious. Sam has more fun with his shifter self than most of the two-natured, but I could tell he was intent on easing my fear. When he was in his second nature, he had the dog's keen sense of smell; when he was in his human form, that sense was still superior to that of a one-natured man. Sam would be able to smell a fairly recent corpse.

'You're going out in the woods,' I said.

'Sure. I'll do my best. If he's there, I think I'll know.'

Kevin had told me the sheriff had tried to hire the tracking dogs trained by a Shreveport police officer, but the officer had said they were booked for the day. I wondered if that were true, or if the man just hadn't wanted to risk his dogs in the woods with a panther. Truthfully, I couldn't blame him. And here was a better offer, right in front of me.

'Sam,' I said, my eyes filling with tears. I tried to thank him, but the words wouldn't come. I was lucky to have a friend like Sam, and well I knew it.

'Hush, Sookie,' he said. 'Don't cry. We'll find out what happened to Jason, and we'll find a way to restore Eric to his mind.' He rubbed the tears off my cheeks with his thumb.

No one was close enough to hear, but I couldn't help glancing around to make sure.

'Then,' Sam said, a distinctly grim edge to his voice, 'we can get him out of your house and back to Shreveport where he belongs.'

I decided no reply was the best policy.

'What was your word for the day?' he asked, standing back.

I gave him a watery smile. Sam always asked about the daily offering of my Word a Day calendar. 'I didn't check this morning. Yesterday was "farrago,"' I said.

He raised his brows inquiringly.

'A confused mess,' I said.

'Sookie, we'll find a way out of this.'

When the searchers divided up into groups, I discovered that Sam was not the only two-natured creature out in Jason's yard that day. I was astonished to see a contingent from Hotshot. Calvin Norris, his niece Crystal, and a second man who seemed vaguely familiar were standing by themselves. After a moment of stirring the sludge of my memory, I realized that the second man was the one I'd seen emerging from the shed behind the house down from Crystal's. His thick pale hair triggered the memory, and I was sure of it when I saw the graceful way he moved. Kevin assigned the Reverend Jimmy Fullenwilder to the trio as their armed man. The combination of the three Weres with the reverend would have made me laugh under other circumstances.

Since they lacked a fifth, I joined them.

The three Weres from Hotshot gave me sober nods, Calvin's golden green eyes fixed on me thoughtfully. 'This here's Felton Norris,' he said, by way of introduction.

I nodded back to Felton, and Jimmy Fullenwilder, a gray-haired man of about sixty, shook hands. 'Of course I know Miss Sookie, but the rest of you I'm not sure of. I'm Jimmy Fullenwilder, pastor of Greater Love Baptist,' he said, smiling all around. Calvin absorbed this information with a polite smile, Crystal sneered, and Felton Norris (had they run out of last names in Hotshot?) grew colder. Felton was an odd one, even for an inbred werewolf. His eyes were remarkably dark, set under straight thick brown brows, which contrasted sharply with his pale hair. His face was broad at the eyes, narrowing a little too abruptly to a thin-lipped mouth. Though he was a bulky man, he moved lightly and quietly, and as we began to move out into the woods, I realized that all the Hotshot residents had that in common. In comparison with the Norrises, Jimmy Fullenwilder and I were blundering elephants.

At least the minister carried his 30-30 like he knew how to use it.

Following our instructions, we stood in a row, stretching out our arms at shoulder height so we were fingertip to fingertip. Crystal was on my right, and Calvin was on my left. The other groups did the same. We began the search in the fanlike shape determined by the curve of the pond.

'Remember who's in your group,' Kevin bellowed. 'We don't want to leave people out here! Now, start.'

We began scanning the ground ahead of us, moving at a steady pace. Jimmy Fullenwilder was a couple of steps ahead, since he was armed. It was apparent right away that there were woodcraft disparities between the Hotshot folks, the reverend, and me. Crystal seemed to flow through the undergrowth, without having to wade through it or push it aside, though I could hear her progress. Jimmy

Fullenwilder, an avid hunter, was at home in the woods and an experienced outdoorsman, and I could tell he was getting much more information from his surroundings than I was, but he wasn't able to move like Calvin and Felton. They glided through the woods like ghosts, making about as much noise.

Once, when I ran into a particularly dense thicket of thorny vines, I felt two hands clamp on either side of my waist, and I was just lifted over it before I had a chance to react. Calvin Norris put me down very gently and went right back to his position. I don't think anyone else noticed. Jimmy Fullenwilder, the only one who would have been startled, had gotten a little ahead.

Our team found nothing: not a shred of cloth or flesh, not a boot print or panther print, not a smell or a trace or a drop of blood. One of the other teams yelled over that they'd found a chewed-up possum corpse, but there was no immediate way to tell what had caused its death.

The going got tougher. My brother had hunted in these woods, allowed some friends of his to hunt there, but otherwise had not interfered with nature in the twenty acres around the house. That meant he hadn't cleared away fallen branches or pulled up seedlings, which compounded the difficulty of our movement.

My team happened to be the one that found his deer stand, which he and Hoyt had built together about five years ago.

Though the stand faced a natural clearing running roughly north-south, the woods were so thick around it that we were temporarily out of sight of the other searchers, which I would not have thought possible in winter, with the branches bare. Every now and then a human voice, raised in a distant call, would make its way through the pines and the bushes and the branches of the oaks and gum trees, but the sense of isolation was overwhelming.

Felton Norris swarmed up the deer stand ladder in such an unhuman way that I had to distract Reverend Fullenwilder by asking him if he'd mind praying in church for my brother's return. Of course, he told me he already had, and furthermore, he notified me he'd be glad to see me in his church on Sunday to add my voice to those lifted in prayer. Though I missed a lot of churchgoing because of my job, and when I did go I attended the Methodist church (which Jimmy Fullenwilder well knew), I pretty much had to say yes. Just then Felton called down that the stand was empty. 'Come down careful, this ladder's not too steady,' Calvin called back, and I realized Calvin was warning Felton to look human when he descended. As the shifter descended slowly and clumsily, I met Calvin's eyes, and he looked amused.

Bored by the wait at the foot of the deer stand, Crystal had flitted ahead of our point man, the Reverend Fullenwilder, something Kevin had warned us not to do. Just as I was thinking, *I can't see her*, I heard her scream.

In the space of a couple of seconds, Calvin and Felton had bounded over the clearing toward the sound of Crystal's voice, and the Reverend Jimmy and I were left to run behind. I hoped the agitation of the moment would obscure his perception of the way Calvin and Felton were moving. Up ahead of us, we heard an indescribable noise, a loud chorus of squeals and frenetic movement coming from the undergrowth. Then a hoarse shout and another shrill scream came to us muffled by the cold thickness of the woods.

We heard yelling from all directions as the other searchers responded, hurrying toward the alarming sounds.

My heel caught in a snarl of vines and I went down, ass over teacup. Though I rolled to my feet and began running again, Jimmy Fullenwilder had gotten ahead of me, and as I plunged through a stand of low pines, each no bigger around than a mailing tube, I heard the boom of the rifle.

Oh, my God, I thought. *Oh, my God.*

The little clearing was filled with blood and tumult. A huge animal was thrashing in the dead leaves, spraying scarlet drops on everything in its vicinity. But it was no panther. For the second time in my life, I was seeing a razorback hog, that ferocious feral pig that grows to a huge size.

In the time it took me to realize what was in front of me, the sow collapsed and died. She reeked of pig and blood. A crashing and squealing in the undergrowth around us indicated she hadn't been alone when Crystal stumbled upon her.

But not all the blood was the sow's.

Crystal Norris was swearing a blue streak as she sat with her back against an old oak, her hands clamped over her gored thigh. Her jeans were wet with her own blood, and her uncle and her – well, I didn't know what relationship Felton bore to Crystal, but I was sure there was one – kinsman were bending over her. Jimmy Fullenwilder was standing with his rifle still pointed at the beast, and he had an expression on his face that I can only describe as shell-shocked.

'How is she?' I asked the two men, and only Calvin looked up. His eyes had gone very peculiar, and I realized they'd gotten more yellow, rounder. He cast an unmistakable look at the huge carcass, a look of sheer desire. There was blood around his mouth. There was a patch of fur on the back of his hand, kind of buff-colored. He must make a strange-looking wolf. I pointed silently at this evidence of his nature, and he shivered with longing as he nodded acknowledgment. I yanked a handkerchief out of my coat pocket, spat on it, and wiped his face with it before Jimmy Fullenwilder could fall out of his fascination with his kill and observe his strange companions. When Calvin's mouth wasn't stained anymore, I knotted the handkerchief around his hand to conceal the fur.

Felton seemed to be normal, until I observed what was at the end of his arms. They weren't really hands anymore . . . but not really wolf paws, either. They were something very odd, something big and flat and clawed.

I couldn't read the men's thoughts, but I could feel their desires, and most of those desires had to do with raw red pig meat, and lots of it. Felton actually rocked back and forth once or twice with the force of his desire. Their silent struggle was painful to endure, even secondhand. I felt the change when the two men began to force their brains into human patterns. In a few seconds, Calvin managed to speak.

'She's losing blood fast, but if we get her to the hospital she'll be all right.' His voice was thick, and he spoke with an effort. Felton, his eyes still downcast, began tearing clumsily at his flannel shirt. With his hands misshapen, he couldn't manage the job, and I took it over. When Crystal's wound was bound as tightly as the makeshift bandage could compress it, the two men lifted the now white and silent Crystal and began to carry her rapidly out of the woods. The position of Felton's hands hid them from sight, thank God.

This all occurred so quickly that the other searchers converging on the clearing were just beginning to absorb what had happened, and react.

'I shot a hog,' Jimmy Fullenwilder was saying, shaking his head from side to side, as Kevin and Kenya burst into the clearing from the east. 'I can't believe it. It just threw her over and the other sows and little ones scattered and then the two men were on it, and then they got out of the way and I shot it in the throat.' He didn't know if he was a hero or if he was in big trouble with the Department of Wildlife. He'd had more to fear than he would ever realize. Felton and Calvin had almost gone into full Were mode at the threat to Crystal and the arousal of their own hunting instincts, and the fact that they'd thrown themselves away from the pig rather than change utterly proved they were very strong, indeed. But the fact that they'd begun to change, hadn't been able to stop it, seemed to argue the opposite. The line between the two natures of some of the denizens of Hotshot seemed be growing very blurred.

In fact, there were bite marks on the hog. I was so overwhelmed with anxiety that I couldn't keep up my guard, and all the excitement of all the searchers poured into my head – all the revulsion/fear/panic at the sight of the blood, the knowledge that a searcher had been seriously injured, the envy of other hunters at Jimmy Fullenwilder's coup. It was all too much, and I wanted to get away more than I've ever wanted anything.

'Let's go. This'll be the end of the search, at least for today,' Sam said at my elbow. We walked out of the woods together, very slowly. I told Maxine what had happened, and after I'd thanked her for her wonderful contribution and accepted a box of doughnuts, I drove home. Sam followed me. I was a little more myself by the time we got there.

As I unlocked the back door, it felt quite strange knowing that there was actually someone else already in the house. Was Eric conscious on some level of my footsteps on the floor above his head – or was he as dead as an ordinary dead person? But the wondering ran through my head and out the other side, because I was just too overloaded to consider it.

Sam began to make coffee. He was somewhat at home in the kitchen, as he'd dropped in a time or two when my Gran was alive, and he'd visited on other occasions.

As I hung up our coats, I said, 'That was a disaster.'

Sam didn't disagree.

'Not only did we not find Jason, which I truly never expected we would, but the guys from Hotshot almost got outed, and Crystal got hurt. I don't know why they thought they should be there anyway, frankly.' I know it wasn't nice of me to say that, but I was with Sam, who'd seen enough of my bad side to be under no illusions.

'I talked to them before you got there. Calvin wanted to show he was willing to court you, in a Hotshot kind of way,' Sam said, his voice quiet and even. 'Felton is their best tracker, so he made Felton come, and Crystal just wanted to find Jason.'

Instantly I felt ashamed of myself. 'I'm sorry,' I said, holding my head in my hands and dropping into a chair. 'I'm sorry.'

Sam knelt in front of me and put his hands on my knees. 'You're entitled to be cranky,' he said.

I bent over him and kissed the top of his head. 'I don't

know what I'd do without you,' I said, without any thought at all.

He looked up at me, and there was a long, odd moment, when the light in the room seemed to dance and shiver. 'You'd call Arlene,' he said with a smile. 'She'd come over with the kids, and she'd try to spike your coffee, and she'd tell you about Tack's angled dick, and she'd get you to laughing, and you'd feel better.'

I blessed him for letting the moment pass. 'You know, that kind of makes me curious, that bit about Tack, but it probably falls into the category of "too much information,"' I said.

'I thought so, too, but that didn't prevent me from hearing it when she was telling Charlsie Tooten.'

I poured us each a cup of coffee and put the half-empty sugar bowl within Sam's reach, along with a spoon. I glanced over at the kitchen counter to see how full the clear sugar canister was, and I noticed that the message light on the answering machine was blinking. I only had to get up and take a step to press the button. The message had been recorded at 5:01 A.M. Oh. I'd turned the phone ringer off when I'd gone to bed exhausted. Almost invariably my messages were real mundane – Arlene asking me if I'd heard a piece of gossip, Tara passing the time of day during a slow hour at the store – but this one was a real doozy.

Pam's clear voice said, 'Tonight we attack the witch and her coven. The Weres have persuaded the local Wiccans to join us. We need you to bring Eric. He can fight, even if he doesn't know who he is. He will be useless to us if we can't break the spell, anyway.' That Pam, ever practical. She was willing to use Eric for cannon fodder, since we might not be able to restore him to full Eric leadership mode. After a little pause, she continued, 'The Weres of Shreveport are allying with vampires in battle. You can watch history being made, my telepathic friend.'

The sound of the phone being put back in the cradle. The click that heralded the next message, which came in two minutes after the first.

'Thinking of that,' Pam said, as if she'd never hung up, 'there is the idea that your unusual ability can help us in our fight, and we want to explore that. Isn't that the right buzzword now? Explore? So get here as close to first dark as possible.' She hung up again.

Click. '"Here" is 714 Parchman Avenue,' Pam said. Hung up.

'How can I do that, with Jason still missing?' I asked, when it became clear Pam hadn't called again.

'You're going to sleep now,' Sam said. 'Come on.' He pulled me to my feet, led me to my room. 'You're going to take off your boots and jeans, crawl back in the bed, and take a long nap. When you get up, you'll feel better. You leave Pam's number so I can reach you. Tell the cops to call the bar if they learn anything, and I'll phone you if I hear from Bud Dearborn.'

'So you think I should do this?' I was bewildered.

'No, I'd give anything if you wouldn't. But I think you have to. It's not my fight; I wasn't invited.' Sam gave me a kiss on the forehead and left to go back to Merlotte's.

His attitude was kind of interesting, after all the vampire insistence (both Bill's and Eric's) that I was a possession to be guarded. I felt pretty empowered and gung-ho for about thirty seconds, until I remembered my New Year's resolution: *no getting beaten up.* If I went to Shreveport with Eric, then I was sure to see things I didn't want to see, learn things I didn't want to know, and get my ass whipped, too.

On the other hand, my brother Jason had made a deal with the vampires, and I had to uphold it. Sometimes I felt that my whole life had been spent stuck between a rock and a hard place. But then, lots of people had complicated lives.

I thought of Eric, a powerful vampire whose mind had been stripped clean of his identity. I thought of the carnage I'd seen in the bridal shop, the white lace and brocade speckled with dried blood and matter. I thought of poor Maria-Star, in the hospital in Shreveport. These witches were bad, and bad should be stopped; bad should be overcome. That's the American model.

It seemed kind of strange to think that I was on the side of vampires and werewolves, and that was the good side. That made me laugh a little, all to myself. Oh, yes, we good guys would save the day.

Chapter 11

Amazingly, I did sleep. I woke with Eric on the bed beside me. He was smelling me.

'Sookie, what is this?' he asked in a very quiet voice. He knew, of course, when I woke. 'You smell of the woods, and you smell of shifter. And something even wilder.'

I supposed the shifter he smelled was Sam. 'And Were,' I prompted, not wanting him to miss out on anything.

'No, not Were,' he said.

I was puzzled. Calvin had lifted me over the brambles, and his scent should still have been on me.

'More than one kind of shifter,' Eric said in the near-dark of my room. 'What have you been doing, my lover?'

He didn't exactly sound angry, but he didn't sound happy, either. Vampires. They wrote the book on possessive.

'I was in the search party for my brother, in the woods behind his home,' I said.

Eric was still for a minute. Then he wrapped his arms around me and hauled me up against him. 'I'm sorry,' he said. 'I know you are worried.'

'Let me ask you something,' I said, willing to test a theory of mine.

'Of course.'

'Look inside yourself, Eric. Are you really, really sorry? Worried about Jason?' Because the real Eric, in his right mind, would not have cared one little bit.

'Of course,' he protested. Then, after a long moment – I wished I could see his face – he said, 'Not really.' He sounded surprised. 'I know I should be. I should be concerned about your brother, because I love having sex with you, and I should want you to think well of me so you'll want sex, too.'

You just had to like the honesty. This was the closest to the real Eric I'd seen in days.

'But you'll listen, right? If I need to talk? For the same reason?'

'Of course, my lover.'

'Because you want to have sex with me.'

'That, of course. But also because I find I really do . . .' He paused, as if he were about to say something outrageous. 'I find I have feelings for you.'

'Oh,' I said into his chest, sounding as astonished as Eric had. His chest was bare, as I suspected the rest of him was. I felt the light sprinkling of curly blond hair against my cheek.

'Eric,' I said, after a long pause, 'I almost hate to say this, but I have feelings for you, too.' There was a lot I needed to tell Eric, and we should be in the car on our way to Shreveport already. But I was taking this moment to savor this little bit of happiness.

'Not love, exactly,' he said. His fingers were busy trying to find out how best to get my clothes off.

'No, but something close.' I helped him. 'We don't have much time, Eric,' I said, reaching down, touching him, making him gasp. 'Let's make it good.'

'Kiss me,' he said, and he wasn't talking about his mouth. 'Turn this way,' he whispered. 'I want to kiss you, too.'

It didn't take long, after all, for us to be holding each other, sated and happy.

'What's happened?' he asked. 'I can tell something is frightening you.'

'We have to go to Shreveport now,' I said. 'We're already past the time Pam said on the phone. Tonight's the night we face off against Hallow and her witches.'

'Then you must stay here,' he said immediately.

'No,' I said gently, putting my hand on his cheek. 'No, baby, I have to go with you.' I didn't tell him Pam thought using me in the battle would be a good idea. I didn't tell him he was going to be used as a fighting machine. I didn't tell him I was sure someone was going to die tonight; maybe quite a few someones, human and Were and vampire. It was probably the last time I would use an endearment when I addressed Eric. It was perhaps the last time Eric would wake up in my house. One of us might not survive this night, and if we did, there was no way to know how we'd be changed.

The drive to Shreveport was silent. We'd washed up and dressed without talking much, either. At least seven times, I thought of heading back to Bon Temps, with or without Eric.

But I didn't.

Eric's skills did not include map reading, so I had to pull over to check my Shreveport map to plot our course to

714 Parchman, something I hadn't foreseen before we got to the city. (I'd somehow expected Eric to remember the directions, but of course, he didn't.)

'Your word of the day was "annihilate,"' he told me cheerfully.

'Oh. Thanks for checking.' I probably didn't sound very thankful. 'You're sounding pretty excited about all this.'

'Sookie, there's nothing like a good fight,' he said defensively.

'That depends on who wins, I would think.'

That kept him quiet for a few minutes, which was fine. I was having trouble negotiating the strange streets in the darkness, with so much on my mind. But we finally got to the right street, and the right house on that street. I had always pictured Pam and Chow living in a mansion, but the vampires had a large ranch-style house in an upper-middle-class suburb. It was a trimmed-lawn, bike-riding, lawn-sprinkling street, from what I could tell.

The light by the driveway was on at 714, and the three-car garage around at the rear was full. I drove up the slope to the concrete apron that was placed for overflow parking. I recognized Alcide's truck and the compact car that had been parked in Colonel Flood's carport.

Before we got out of my old car, Eric leaned over to kiss me. We looked at each other, his eyes wide and blue, the whites so white you could hardly look away, his golden hair neatly brushed. He'd tied it back with one of my elastic bands, a bright blue one. He was wearing a pair of jeans and a new flannel shirt.

'We could go back,' he said. In the dome light of the car, his face looked hard as stone. 'We could go back to your house. I can stay with you always. We can know each other's bodies in every way, night after night. I could love you.' His nostrils flared, and he looked suddenly proud. 'I could work. You would not be poor. I would help you.'

'Sounds like a marriage,' I said, trying to lighten the atmosphere. But my voice was too shaky.

'Yes,' he said.

And he would never be himself again. He would be a false version of Eric, an Eric cheated out of his true life. Providing our relationship (such as it was) lasted, he would stay the same; but I wouldn't.

Enough with the negative thinking, Sookie, I told myself. I would be a total idiot to pass up living with this gorgeous creature for however long. We actually had a good time together, and I enjoyed Eric's sense of humor and his company, to say nothing of his lovemaking. Now that he'd lost his memory, he was lots of uncomplicated fun.

And that was the fly in the ointment. We would have a counterfeit relationship, because this was the counterfeit Eric. I'd come full loop.

I slid out of the car with a sigh. 'I'm a total idiot,' I said as he came around the back of the car to walk with me to the house.

Eric didn't say anything. I guess he agreed with me.

'Hello,' I called, pushing open the door after my knock brought no response. The garage door led into the laundry room and from there into the kitchen.

As you would expect in a vampire home, the kitchen was absolutely clean, because it wasn't used. This kitchen was small for a house the size of this one. I guess the real estate agent had thought it was her lucky day – her lucky night – when she'd shown it to vampires, since a real family who cooked at home would have trouble dealing with a kitchen the size of a king bed. The house had an open floor plan, so you could see over the breakfast bar into the 'family' room – in this case, the main room for a mighty odd family. There were three open doorways that probably led into the formal living room, the dining room, and the bedroom area.

Right at the moment, this family room was crammed with people. I got the impression, from the glimpses of feet and arms, that more people were standing in the open doorways into the other rooms.

The vampires were there: Pam, Chow, Gerald, and at least two more I recognized from Fangtasia. The two-natured were represented by Colonel Flood, red-haired Amanda (my big fan), the teenage boy with spiked brown hair (Sid), Alcide, Culpepper, and (to my disgust) Debbie Pelt. Debbie was dressed in the height of fashion – at least her version of fashion – which seemed a little out of place for a meeting of this kind. Maybe she wanted to remind me that she had a very good job working at an advertising agency.

Oh, good. Debbie's presence made the night just about perfect.

The group I didn't recognize had to be the local witches, by the process of elimination. I assumed that the dignified woman sitting on the couch was their leader. I didn't know what her correct title would be – coven master? Mistress? She was in her sixties, and she had iron gray hair. An African American with skin the color of coffee, she had brown eyes that looked infinitely wise and also skeptical. She'd brought a pale young man with glasses, who wore pressed khakis with a striped shirt and polished loafers. He might work in Office Depot or Super One Foods in some kind of managerial position, and his kids would think that he was out bowling or attending some church meeting on this cold January night. Instead, he and the young female witch beside him were about to embark on a fight to the death.

The remaining two empty chairs were clearly intended for Eric and me.

'We expected you earlier,' Pam said crisply.

'Hi, good to see you, too, thanks for coming on such short notice,' I muttered. For one long moment, everyone in the room looked at Eric, waiting for him to take charge of the action, as he had for years. And Eric looked back at them blankly. The long pause began to be awkward.

'Well, let's lay this out,' Pam said. All the assembled Supes turned their faces to her. Pam seemed to have taken the leadership bit between her teeth, and she was ready to run with it.

'Thanks to the Were trackers, we know the location of the building Hallow is using for her headquarters,' Pam told me. She seemed to be ignoring Eric, but I sensed it was because she didn't know what else to do. Sid grinned at me; I remembered he and Emilio had tracked the killers from the bridal shop to the house. Then I realized he was showing me he'd filed his teeth to points. Ick.

I could understand the presence of the vamps, the witches, and the Weres, but why was Debbie Pelt at this meeting? She was a shifter, not a Were. The Weres had always been so snobby about the shifters, and here was one; furthermore, one out of her own territory. I loathed and distrusted her. She must have insisted on being here, and that made me trust her even less, if that was possible.

If she was so determined to join in, put Debbie in the first line of fire, would be my advice. You wouldn't have to worry about what she was doing behind your back.

My grandmother would certainly have been ashamed of my vindictiveness; but then (like Alcide) she would have found it almost impossible to believe that Debbie had really tried to kill me.

'We'll infiltrate the neighborhood slowly,' Pam said. I wondered if she'd been reading a commando manual. 'The witches have already broadcast a lot of magic in the area, so there aren't too many people out on the streets. Some of the Weres are already in place. We won't be so obvious. Sookie will go in first.'

The assembled Supes turned their eyes to me at the same moment. That was pretty disconcerting: like being in a ring of pickup trucks at night, when they all turn on their headlights to illuminate the center.

'Why?' Alcide asked. His big hands gripped his knees. Debbie, who'd slumped down to sit on the floor beside the couch, smiled at me, knowing Alcide couldn't see her.

'Because Sookie is human,' Pam pointed out. 'And she's more of a natural phenomenon than a true Supe. They won't detect her.'

Eric had taken my hand. He was gripping it so hard that I thought I could hear my bones grinding together. Prior to his enchantment, he would have nipped Pam's plan in the bud, or maybe he would've enthusiastically endorsed it. Now he was too cowed to comment, which he clearly wanted to do.

'What am I supposed to do when I get there?' I was proud of myself for sounding so calm and practical. I'd rather be taking a complicated drink order from a table of drunken tree-trimmers than be first in the line of battle.

'Read the minds of the witches inside while we get into

position. If they detect us approaching, we lose the surprise of it, and we stand a greater chance of sustaining serious injury.' When she got excited, Pam had a slight accent, though I'd never been able to figure out what it was. I thought it might just be English as it had been spoken three hundred years ago. Or whatever. 'Can you count them? Is that possible?'

I thought for a second. 'Yes, I can do that.'

'That would be a big help, too.'

'What do we do when we get in the building?' asked Sid. Jittery with the thrill of it all, he was grinning, his pointed teeth showing.

Pam looked mildly astonished. 'We kill them all,' she said.

Sid's grin faded. I flinched. I wasn't the only one.

Pam seemed to realize she'd said something unpalatable. 'What else would we do?' she asked, genuinely amazed.

That was a stumper.

'They'll do their best to kill *us*,' Chow pointed out. 'They only made one attempt at negotiation, and it cost Eric his memory and Clancy his life. They delivered Clancy's clothes to Fangtasia this morning.' People glanced away from Eric, embarrassed. He looked stricken, and I patted his hand with my free one. His grip on my right hand relaxed a little. My circulation resumed in that hand, and it tingled. That was a relief.

'Someone needs to go with Sookie,' Alcide said. He glowered at Pam. 'She can't go close to that house by herself.'

'I'll go with her,' said a familiar voice from the corner of the room, and I leaned forward, searching the faces.

'Bubba!' I said, pleased to see the vampire. Eric stared in

wonder at the famous face. The glistening black hair was combed back in a pompadour, and the pouty lower lip was stretched in the trademark smile. His current keeper must have dressed him for the evening, because instead of a jumpsuit decked with rhinestones, or jeans and a T-shirt, Bubba was wearing camo.

'Pleased to see ya, Miss Sookie,' Bubba said. 'I'm wearing my Army duds.'

'I see that. Looking good, Bubba.'

'Thank you, ma'am.'

Pam considered. 'That might be a good idea,' she said. 'His, ah – the mental broadcast, the signature, you all get what I'm telling you? – is so, ah, atypical that they won't discover a vampire is near.' Pam was being very tactful.

Bubba made a terrible vampire. Though stealthy and obedient, he couldn't reason very clearly, and he liked cat blood better than human blood.

'Where's Bill, Miss Sookie?' he asked, as I could have predicted he would. Bubba had always been very fond of Bill.

'He's in Peru, Bubba. That's way down in South America.'

'No, I'm not,' said a cool voice, and my heart flip-flopped. 'I'm back.' Out of an open doorway stepped my former flame.

This was just an evening for surprises. I hoped some of them would be pleasant.

Seeing Bill so unexpectedly gave me a heavier jolt than I'd figured. I'd never had an ex-boyfriend before, my life having been pretty devoid of boyfriends altogether, so I didn't have much experience in handling my emotions about being in his presence, especially with

Eric gripping my hand like I was Mary Poppins and he was my charge.

Bill looked good in his khakis. He was wearing a Calvin Klein dress shirt I'd picked out for him, a muted plaid in shades of brown and gold. Not that I noticed.

'Good, we need you tonight,' Pam said. Ms. Businesslike. 'You'll have to tell me how the ruins were, the ones everyone talks about. You know the rest of the people here?'

Bill glanced around. 'Colonel Flood,' he said, nodding. 'Alcide.' His nod to Alcide had less cordiality. 'I haven't met these new allies,' he said, indicating the witches. Bill waited until the introductions were complete to ask, 'What is Debbie Pelt doing here?'

I tried not to gape at having my innermost thoughts spoken aloud. My question exactly! And how did Bill know Debbie? I tried to remember if their paths had crossed in Jackson, if they'd actually met face-to-face; and I couldn't recall such a meeting, though of course Bill knew what she'd done.

'She's Alcide's woman,' Pam said, in a cautious, puzzled sort of way.

I raised my eyebrows, looking at Alcide, and he turned a dusky red.

'She's here for a visit, and she decided to come along with him,' Pam went on. 'You object to her presence?'

'She joined in while I was being tortured in the king of Mississippi's compound,' Bill said. 'She enjoyed my pain.'

Alcide stood, looking as shocked as I'd ever seen him. 'Debbie, is this true?'

Debbie Pelt tried not to flinch, now that every eye was on her, and every eye was unfriendly. 'I just happened to be visiting a Were friend who lived there, one of the guards,' she said. Her voice didn't sound calm enough to match the words. 'Obviously, there was nothing I could do to free you. I would have been ripped to shreds. I can't believe you remember me being there very clearly. You were certainly out of it.' There was a hint of contempt in her words.

'You joined in the torture,' Bill said, his voice still impersonal and all the more convincing for it. 'You liked the pincers best.'

'You didn't tell anyone he was there?' Alcide asked Debbie. His voice was not impersonal at all. It held grief, and anger, and betrayal. 'You knew someone from another kingdom was being tortured at Russell's, and you didn't do anything?'

'He's a *vamp*, for God's sake,' Debbie said, sounding no more than irritated. 'When I found out later that you'd been taking Sookie around to hunt for him so you could get your dad out of hock with the vamps, I felt terrible. But at the time, it was just vamp business. Why should I interfere?'

'But why would any decent person join in torture?' Alcide's voice was strained.

There was a long silence.

'And of course, she tried to kill Sookie,' Bill said. He still managed to sound quite dispassionate.

'I didn't know you were in the trunk of the car when I pushed her in! I didn't know I was closing her in with a hungry vampire!' Debbie protested.

I don't know about anyone else, but I wasn't convinced for a second.

Alcide bent his rough black head to look down into his hands as if they held an oracle. He raised his face to look at Debbie. He was a man unable to dodge the bullet of truth any longer. I felt sorrier for him than I'd felt for anyone in a long, long time.

'I abjure you,' Alcide said. Colonel Flood winced, and young Sid, Amanda, and Culpepper looked both astonished and impressed, as if this were a ceremony they'd never thought to witness. 'I see you no longer. I hunt with you no longer. I share flesh with you no longer.'

This was obviously a ritual of great significance among the two-natured. Debbie stared at Alcide, aghast at his pronouncement. The witches murmured to one another, but otherwise the room remained silent. Even Bubba was wide-eyed, and most things went right over his shiny head.

'No,' Debbie said in a strangled voice, waving a hand in front of her, as if she could erase what had passed. 'No, Alcide!'

But he stared right through her. He saw her no longer.

Even though I loathed Debbie, her face was painful to see. Like most of the others present, as soon as I could, I looked anywhere else but at the shifter. Facing Hallow's coven seemed like a snap compared to witnessing this episode.

Pam seemed to agree. 'All right then,' she said briskly. 'Bubba will lead the way with Sookie. She will do her best to do whatever it is that she does – and she'll signal us.' Pam pondered for a moment. 'Sookie, a recap: We need to know the number of people in the house, whether or not they are all witches, and any other tidbit you can glean. Send Bubba back to us with whatever information you find and stand guard in case the situation changes while we move up. Once we're in position, you can retire to the cars, where you'll be safer.'

I had no problem with that whatsoever. In a crowd of witches, vampires, and Weres, I was no kind of combatant.

'This sounds okay, if I have to be involved at all,' I said. A tug on my hand drew my eyes to Eric's. He looked pleased at the prospect of fighting, but there was still uncertainty in his face and posture. 'But what will happen to Eric?'

'What do you mean?'

'If you go in and kill everyone, who'll un-curse him?' I turned slightly to face the experts, the Wiccan contingent. 'If Hallow's coven dies, do their spells die with them? Or will Eric still be without a memory?'

'The spell must be removed,' said the oldest witch, the calm African-American woman. 'If it is removed by the one who laid it in the first place, that's best. It can be lifted by someone else, but it will take more time, more effort, since we don't know what went into the making of the spell.'

I was trying to avoid looking at Alcide, because he was still shaking with the violence of the emotions that had led him to cast out Debbie. Though I hadn't known such an action was possible, my first reaction was to feel a little bitter about his *not* casting her out right after I'd told him a month ago she'd tried to kill me. However, he could have told himself I'd been mistaken, that it hadn't been Debbie I'd sensed near me before she'd pushed me into the Cadillac's trunk.

As far as I knew, this was the first time Debbie had admitted she had done it. And she'd protested she hadn't known Bill was in the trunk, unconscious. But shoving a person into a car trunk and shutting the lid was no kind of amusing prank, right?

Maybe Debbie had been lying to herself some, too.

I needed to listen to what was happening now. I'd have lots of time to think about the human ego's capacity to deceive itself, if I survived the night.

Pam was saying, 'So you're thinking we need to save Hallow? To take the spell off Eric?' She didn't sound happy at the prospect. I swallowed my painful feelings and made myself listen. This was no time to start brooding.

'No,' the witch said instantly. 'Her brother, Mark. There is too much danger in leaving Hallow alive. She must die as quickly as we can reach her.'

'What will you be doing?' Pam asked. 'How will you help us in this attack?'

'We will be outside, but within two blocks,' the man said. 'We'll be winding spells around the building to make the witches weak and indecisive. And we have a few tricks up our sleeves.' He and the young woman, who had on a huge amount of black eye makeup, looked pretty pleased at a chance to use those tricks.

Pam nodded as if winding spells was sufficient aid. I thought waiting outside with a flamethrower would have been better.

All this time, Debbie Pelt had been standing as if she'd been paralyzed. Now she began to pick her way through to the back door. Bubba leaped up to grab her arm. She hissed at him, but he didn't falter, though I would have.

None of the Weres reacted to this occurrence. It really was as though she were invisible to them.

'Let me leave. I'm not wanted,' she said to Bubba, fury and misery fighting for control of her face.

Bubba shrugged. He just held on to her, waiting for Pam's judgment.

'If we let you go, you might run to the witches and let them know we are coming,' Pam said. 'That would be of a piece with your character, apparently.'

Debbie had the gall to look outraged. Alcide looked as if he were watching the Weather Channel.

'Bill, you take charge of her,' Chow suggested. 'If she turns on us, kill her.'

'That sounds wonderful,' Bill said, smiling in a fangy way.

After a few more arrangements about transportation, and some more quiet consultation among the witches, who were facing a completely different kind of fight, Pam said, 'All right, let's go.' Pam, who looked more than ever like Alice in Wonderland in her pale pink sweater and darker pink slacks, stood up and checked her lipstick in the mirror on the wall close to where I'd been sitting. She gave her reflection an experimental smile, as I've seen women do a thousand times.

'Sookie, my friend,' she said, turning to aim the smile at me. 'Tonight is a great night.'

'It is?'

'Yes.' Pam put her arm around my shoulders. 'We defend what is ours! We fight for the restoration of our leader!' She grinned past me at Eric. 'Tomorrow, Sheriff, you will be back at your desk at Fangtasia. You'll be able to go to your own house, your own bedroom. We've kept it clean for you.'

I checked Eric's reaction. I'd never heard Pam address Eric by his title before. Though the head vampire for each section was called a sheriff, and I should have been used to that by now, I couldn't help but picture Eric in a cowboy outfit with a star pinned to his chest, or (my favorite) in black tights as the villainous sheriff of Nottingham. I found it interesting, too, that he didn't live here with Pam and Chow.

Eric gave Pam such a serious look that the grin faded right off her face. 'If I die tonight,' he said, 'pay this woman the money that was promised her.' He gripped my shoulder. I was just draped in vampires.

'I swear,' Pam said. 'Chow and Gerald will know, too.'

Eric said, 'Do you know where her brother is?'

Startled, I stepped away from Pam.

Pam looked equally taken aback. 'No, Sheriff.'

'It occurred to me that you might have taken him hostage to ensure she didn't betray me.'

The idea had never crossed my mind, but it should have. Obviously, I had a lot to learn about being devious.

'I wish I'd thought of that,' Pam said admiringly, echoing my thoughts with her own twist. 'I wouldn't have minded spending some time with Jason as my hostage.' I couldn't understand it: Jason's allure just seemed universal. 'But I didn't take him,' Pam said. 'If we get through this, Sookie, I'll look for him myself. Could it be Hallow's witches have him?'

'It's possible,' I said. 'Claudine said she didn't see any hostages, but she also said there were rooms she didn't look into. Though I don't know why they would have taken Jason, unless Hallow knows I have Eric? Then they might have used him to make me talk, just the way you would have used him to make me keep silent. But they haven't approached me. You can't use blackmail on someone who doesn't know anything about the hold you have on them.'

'Nonetheless, I'll remind all those who are going to enter the building to watch out for him,' Pam said.

'How is Belinda?' I asked. 'Have you made arrangements to pay her hospital bills?'

She looked at me blankly.

'The waitress who was hurt defending Fangtasia,' I reminded her, a little dryly. 'You remember? The friend of Ginger, who *died*?'

'Of course,' said Chow, from his place against the wall. 'She is recovering. We sent her flowers and candy,' he told Pam. Then he focused on me. 'Plus, we have a group insurance policy.' He was proud as a new father about that.

Pam looked pleased with Chow's report. 'Good,' she said. 'You have to keep them happy. Are we ready to go?'

I shrugged. 'I guess so. No point in waiting.'

Bill stepped in front of me as Chow and Pam consulted about which vehicle to take. Gerald had gone out to make sure everyone was on the same page as far as the plan of battle.

'How was Peru?' I asked Bill. I was very conscious of Eric, a huge blond shadow at my elbow.

'I made a lot of notes for my book,' Bill said. 'South America hasn't been good to vampires as a whole, but Peru is not as hostile as the other countries, and I was able to talk to a few vampires I hadn't heard of before.' For months, Bill had been compiling a vampire directory at the behest of the queen of Louisiana, who thought having such an item would be very handy. Her opinion was certainly not the universal opinion of the vampire community, some of whom had very strong objections to being outed, even among their own kind. I guess secrecy could be almost impossible to give up, if you'd clung to it for centuries.

There were vampires who still lived in graveyards, hunting every night, refusing to recognize the change in their status; it was like the stories about the Japanese soldiers who'd held out on Pacific islands long after World War II was over.

'Did you get to see those ruins you talked about?'

'Machu Picchu? Yes, I climbed up to them by myself. It was a great experience.'

I tried to picture Bill going up a mountain at night, seeing the ruins of an ancient civilization in the moonlight. I couldn't even imagine what that must have been like. I'd never been out of the country. I hadn't often been out of the state, for that matter.

'This is Bill, your former mate?' Eric's voice sounded a little . . . strained.

'Ah, this is – well, yes, sort of,' I said unhappily. The 'former' was correct; the 'mate' was a little off.

Eric placed both his hands on my shoulders and moved in close to me. I had no doubt he was staring over the top of my head at Bill, who was staring right back. Eric might as well have stuck a SHE'S MINE sign on top of my head. Arlene had told me that she loved moments like this, when her ex saw plainly that someone else valued her even if he didn't. All I can say is, my taste in satisfaction runs completely different. I hated it. I felt awkward and ridiculous.

'You really don't remember me,' Bill said to Eric, as if he'd doubted it up until this moment. My suspicion was confirmed when he told me, as if Eric wasn't standing there, 'Truly, I thought this was an elaborate scheme on Eric's part to stay in your house so he could talk his way into your bed.'

Since the same thought had occurred to me, though I'd discarded it pretty quickly, I couldn't protest; but I could feel myself turning red.

'We need to get in the car,' I told Eric, turning to catch a glimpse of his face. It was rock hard and expressionless, which usually signaled he was in a dangerous state of mind. But he came with me when I moved toward the door, and the whole house slowly emptied its inhabitants into the narrow suburban street. I wondered what the neighbors thought. Of course, they knew the house was inhabited by vampires – no one around during the day, all the yard work done by human hirelings, the people who came and went at night being so very pale. This sudden activity had to invite neighborhood attention.

I drove in silence, Eric beside me on the front seat. Every now and then he reached over to touch me. I don't know who Bill had caught a ride with, but I was glad it wasn't me. The testosterone level would have been too high in the car, and I might have been smothered.

Bubba was sitting in the backseat, humming to himself. It sounded like 'Love Me Tender.'

'This is a crappy car,' Eric said, out of the blue, as far as I was concerned.

'Yes,' I agreed.

'Are you afraid?'

'I am.'

'If this whole thing works, will you still see me?'

'Sure,' I said, to make him happy. I was convinced that after this confrontation, nothing would be the same. But without the true Eric's conviction of his own prowess and intelligence and ruthlessness, this Eric was pretty shaky. He'd be up for the actual battle, but right now he needed a boost.

Pam had plotted out where everyone should park, to prevent Hallow's coven from becoming alarmed by the sudden appearance of a lot of cars. We had a map with our spot marked on it. That turned out to be an E-Z Mart on the corner of a couple of larger roads in a down-sliding area that was changing over from residential to commercial. We parked in the most out-of-the-way corner the E-Z Mart afforded. Without further discussion, we set out to our appointed locations.

About half the houses on the quiet street had real-estate signs in the front lawn, and the ones that remained in private hands were not well maintained. Cars were as battered as mine, and big bare patches indicated that the grass wasn't fertilized or watered in the summer. Every lighted window seemed to show the flickering of a television screen.

I was glad it was winter so the people who lived here were all inside. Two white vampires and a blond woman would excite comment, if not aggression, in this neighborhood. Plus, one of the vampires was pretty recognizable, despite the rigors of his changeover – which was why Bubba was almost always kept out of sight.

Soon we were at the corner where Eric was supposed to part from us so he could rendezvous with the other vampires. I would have continued on to my appointed post without a word; by now I was keyed up to such a pitch of tension I felt I could vibrate if you tapped me with a finger. But Eric wasn't content with a silent separation. He gripped my arms and kissed me for all he was worth, and believe me, that was plenty.

Bubba made a sound of disapproval. 'You're not supposed to be kissing on anybody else, Miss Sookie,' he said. 'Bill said it was okay, but I don't like it.'

After one more second, Eric released me. 'I'm sorry if we

offended you,' he said coldly. He looked back down at me. 'I'll see you later, my lover,' he said very quietly.

I laid my hand against his cheek. 'Later,' I said, and I turned and walked away with Bubba at my heels.

'You ain't mad at me, are you, Miss Sookie?' he asked anxiously.

'No,' I said. I made myself smile at him, since I knew he could see me far more clearly than I could see him. It was a cold night, and though I was wearing my coat, it didn't seem to be as warm as it used to be. My bare hands were quivering with cold, and my nose felt numb. I could just detect a whiff of wood smoke from a fireplace, and automobile exhaust, and gasoline, and oil, and all the other car odors that combine to make City Smell.

But there was another smell permeating the neighborhood, an aroma that indicated this neighborhood was contaminated by more than urban blight. I sniffed, and the odor curled through the air in almost visible flourishes. After a moment's thought, I realized this must be the smell of magic, thick and stomach-clenching. Magic smells like I imagine a bazaar in some exotic foreign country might. It reeks of the strange, the different. The scent of a lot of magic can be quite overwhelming. Why weren't the residents complaining to the police about it? Couldn't everyone pick up on that odor?

'Bubba, do you smell something unusual?' I asked in a very low voice. A dog or two barked as we walked past in the black night, but they quickly quieted when they caught the scent of vampire. (To them, I guess, Bubba was the something unusual.) Dogs are almost always frightened of vampires, though their reaction to Weres and shifters is more unpredictable.

I found myself convinced I wanted nothing more than to go back to the car and leave. It was a conscious effort to make my feet move in the correct direction.

'Yeah, I sure do,' he whispered back. 'Someone's been laying some spells. Stay-away magic.' I didn't know if the Wiccans on our side, or the witches on Hallow's, had been responsible for this pervasive piece of craft, but it was effective.

The night seemed almost unnaturally silent. Maybe three cars passed us as we walked the maze of suburban streets. Bubba and I saw no other pedestrians, and the sense of ominous isolation grew. The stay-away intensified as we came closer to what we were supposed to stay away from.

The darkness between the pools of light below the street-lamps seemed darker, and the light didn't seem to reach as far. When Bubba took my hand, I didn't pull away. My feet seemed to drag at each step.

I'd caught a whiff of this smell before, at Fangtasia. Maybe the Were tracker had had an easier job than I'd thought.

'We're there, Miss Sookie,' Bubba said, his voice just a quiet thread in the night. We'd come around a corner. Since I knew there was a spell, and I knew I could keep walking, I did; but if I'd been a resident of the area, I would have found an alternative route, and I wouldn't have thought twice about it. The impulse to avoid this spot was so strong that I wondered if the people who lived on this block had been able to come home from their jobs. Maybe they were eating out, going to movies, drinking in bars – anything to avoid returning to their homes. Every house on the street looked suspiciously dark and untenanted.

Across the road, and at the opposite end of the block, was the center of the magic.

Hallow's coven had found a good place to hole up: a business up for lease, a large building that had held a combination florist shop-bakery. Minnie's Flowers and Cakes stood in a lonely position, the largest store in a strip of three that had, one by one, faded and gone out like flames on a candelabra. The building had apparently been empty for years. The big plate-glass windows were plastered with posters for events long past and political candidates long since defeated. Plywood nailed over the glass doors was proof that vandals had broken in more than once.

Even in the winter chill, weeds pushed up through cracks in the parking area. A big Dumpster stood to the right side of the parking lot. I viewed it from across the street, getting as much of a picture of the outside as I could before closing my eyes to concentrate on my other senses. I took a moment to be rueful.

If you'd asked me, I would've had a hard time tracing the steps that had led me to this dangerous place at this dangerous time. I was on the edges of a battle in which both sides were pretty dubious. If I'd fallen in with Hallow's witches first, I would probably have been convinced that the Weres and the vampires deserved to be eradicated.

At this time a year ago, no one in the world really understood what I was, or cared. I was just Crazy Sookie, the one with the wild brother, a woman others pitied and avoided, to varying degrees. Now here I was, on a freezing street in Shreveport, gripping the hand of a vampire whose face was legendary and whose brain was mush. Was this betterment?

And I was here not for amusement, or improvement, but to reconnoiter for a bunch of supernatural creatures, gathering information on a group of homicidal, blood-drinking, shape-changing witches.

I sighed, I hoped inaudibly. Oh, well. At least no one had hit me.

My eyes closed, and I dropped my shields and reached out with my mind to the building across the street.

Brains, busy busy busy. I was startled at the bundle of impressions I was receiving. Maybe the absence of other humans in the vicinity, or the overwhelming pervasion of magic, was responsible; but some factor had sharpened my other sense to the point of pain. Almost stunned by the flow of information, I realized I had to sort through it and organize it. First, I counted brains. Not literally ('One temporal lobe, two temporal lobes . . .'), but as a thought cluster. I came up with fifteen. Five were in the front room, which had been the showroom of the store, of course. One was in the smallest space, which was most likely the bathroom, and the rest were in the third and largest room, which lay to the rear. I figured it had been the work area.

Everyone in the building was awake. A sleeping brain still gives me a low mumble of a thought or two, in dreaming, but it's not the same as a waking brain. It's like the difference between a dog twitching in its sleep and an alert puppy.

To get as much information as possible, I had to get closer. I had never attempted to pick through a group to get details as specific as guilt or innocence, and I wasn't even sure that was possible. But if any of the people in the building were not evil witches, I didn't want them to be in the thick of what was to come.

'Closer,' I breathed to Bubba. 'But under cover.'

'Yes'm,' he whispered back. 'You gonna keep your eyes closed?'

I nodded, and he led me very carefully across the street and into the shadow of the Dumpster that stood about five yards south of the building. I was glad it was cold, because that kept the garbage smell at an acceptable level. The ghosts of the scents of doughnuts and blossoms lay on top of the funk of spoiled things and old diapers that passersby had tossed into the handy receptacle. It didn't blend happily with the magic smell.

I adjusted, blocked out the assault on my nose, and began listening. Though I'd gotten better at this, it was still like trying to hear twelve phone conversations at once. Some of them were Weres, too, which complicated matters. I could only get bits and pieces.

. . . hope that's not a vaginal infection I feel coming on . . .

She won't listen to me, she doesn't think men can do the job.

If I turned her into a toad, who could tell the difference?

. . . wish we'd gotten some diet Coke . . .

I'll find that damn vamp and kill him . . .

Mother of the Earth, listen to my pleas.

I'm in too deep . . .

I better get a new nail file.

This was not decisive, but no one had been thinking, 'Oh, these demonic witches have trapped me, won't somebody help?' or 'I hear the vampires approaching!' or anything dramatic like that. This sounded like a band of people who knew each other, were at least relaxed in each other's company, and therefore held the same goals. Even the one who was praying was not in any state of urgency or need. I hoped Hallow wouldn't sense the crush of my mind, but everyone I'd touched had seemed preoccupied.

'Bubba,' I said, just a little louder than a thought, 'you

go tell Pam there are fifteen people in there, and as far as I can tell, they're all witches.'

'Yes'm.'

'You remember how to get to Pam?'

'Yes'm.'

'So you can let go my hand, okay?'

'Oh. Okay.'

'Be silent and careful,' I whispered.

And he was gone. I crouched in the shadow that was darker than the night, beside the smells and cold metal, listening to the witches. Three brains were male, the rest female. Hallow was in there, because one of the women was looking at her and thinking of her . . . dreading her, which kind of made me uneasy. I wondered where they'd parked their cars – unless they flew around on broomsticks, ha ha. Then I wondered about something that should already have crossed my mind.

If they were so darn wary and dangerous, where were their sentries?

At that moment, I was seized from behind.

Chapter 12

'Who are you?' asked a thin voice.

Since she had one hand clapped over my mouth and the other was holding a knife to my neck, I couldn't answer. She seemed to grasp that after a second, because she told me, 'We're going in,' and began to push me toward the back of the building.

I couldn't have that. If she'd been one of the witches in the building, one of the blood-drinking witches, I couldn't have gotten away with this, but she was a plain old witch, and she hadn't watched Sam break up as many bar fights as I had. With both hands, I reached up and grabbed her knife wrist, and I twisted it as hard as I could while I hit her hard with my lower body. Over she went, onto the filthy cold pavement, and I landed right on top of her, pounding her hand against the ground until she released the knife. She was sobbing, the will seeping out of her.

'You're a lousy lookout,' I said to Holly, keeping my voice low.

'Sookie?' Holly's big eyes peered out from under a knit

watch cap. She'd dressed for utility tonight, but she still had on bright pink lipstick.

'What the hell are you doing here?'

'They told me they'd get my boy if I didn't help them.'

I felt sick. 'How long have you been helping them? Before I came to your apartment, asking for help? How long?' I shook her as hard as I could.

'When she came to the bar with her brother, she knew there was another witch there. And she knew it wasn't you or Sam, after she'd talked to you. Hallow can do anything. She knows everything. Late that night, she and Mark came to my apartment. They'd been in a fight; they were all messed up, and they were mad. Mark held me down while Hallow punched me. She liked that. She saw my picture of my son; she took it and said she could curse him long distance, all the way from Shreveport – make him run out in the traffic or load his daddy's gun . . .' Holly was crying by now. I didn't blame her. It made me sick to think of it, and he wasn't even my child. 'I had to say I'd help her,' Holly whimpered.

'Are there others like you in there?'

'Forced to do this? A few of them.'

That made some thoughts I'd heard more understandable.

'And Jason? He in there?' Though I'd looked at all three of the male brains in the building, I still had to ask.

'Jason is a Wiccan? For real?' She pulled off the watch cap and ran her fingers through her hair.

'No, no, no. Is she holding him hostage?'

'I haven't seen him. Why on earth would Hallow have Jason?'

I'd been fooling myself all along. A hunter would find

my brother's remains someday: it's always hunters, or people walking their dogs, isn't it? I felt a falling away beneath my feet, as if the ground had literally dropped out from under me, but I called myself back to the here and now, away from emotions I couldn't afford to feel until I was in a safer place.

'You have to get out of here,' I said in the lowest voice I could manage. 'You have to get out of this area now.'

'She'll get my son!'

'I guarantee she won't.'

Holly seemed to read something in the dim view she had of my face. 'I hope you kill them all,' she said as passionately as you can in a whisper. 'The only ones worth saving are Parton and Chelsea and Jane. They got blackmailed into this just like I did. Normally, they're just Wiccans who like to live real quiet, like me. We don't want to do no one no harm.'

'What do they look like?'

'Parton's a guy about twenty-five, brown hair, short, birthmark on his cheek. Chelsea is about seventeen, her hair's dyed that bright red. Jane, um, well – Jane's just an old woman, you know? White hair, pants, blouse with flowers on it. Glasses.' My grandmother would have reamed Holly for lumping all old women together, but God bless her, she wasn't around anymore, and I didn't have the time.

'Why didn't Hallow put one of her toughest people out here on guard duty?' I asked, out of sheer curiosity.

'They got a big ritual spell thing set up for tonight. I can't believe the stay-away spell didn't work on you. You must be resistant.' Then Holly whispered, with a little rill of laughter in her voice, 'Plus, none of 'em wanted to get cold.'

'Go on, get out of here,' I said almost inaudibly, and helped her up. 'It doesn't matter where you parked your car, go north out of here.' In case she didn't know which direction was north, I pointed.

Holly took off, her Nikes making almost no sound on the cracked sidewalk. Her dull dyed black hair seemed to soak up the light from the streetlamp as she passed beneath it. The smell around the house, the smell of magic, seemed to intensify. I wondered what to do now. Somehow I had to make sure that the three local Wiccans within the dilapidated building, the ones who'd been forced to serve Hallow, wouldn't be harmed. I couldn't think of a way in hell to do that. Could I even save one of them?

I had a whole collection of half thoughts and abortive impulses in the next sixty seconds. They all led to a dead end.

If I ran inside and yelled, 'Parton, Chelsea, Jane – out!' that would alert the coven to the impending attack. Some of my friends – or at least my allies – would die.

If I hung around and tried to tell the vampires that three of the people in the building were innocent, they would (most likely) ignore me. Or, if a bolt of mercy struck them, they'd have to save all the witches and then cull the innocent ones out, which would give the coven witches time to counterattack. Witches didn't need physical weapons.

Too late, I realized I should have kept a hold of Holly and used her as my entrée into the building. But endangering a frightened mother was not a good option, either.

Something large and warm pressed against my side. Eyes and teeth gleamed in the city's night light. I almost screamed until I recognized the wolf as Alcide. He was very large. The silver fur around his eyes made the rest of his coat seem even darker.

I put an arm across his back. 'There are three in there who mustn't die,' I said. 'I don't know what to do.'

Since he was a wolf, Alcide didn't know what to do, either. He looked into my face. He whined, just a little. I was supposed to be back at the cars by now; but here I was, smack in the danger zone. I could feel movement in the dark all around me. Alcide slunk away to his appointed position at the rear door of the building.

'What are you doing here?' Bill said furiously, though it sounded strange coming out in a tiny thread of a whisper. 'Pam told you to leave once you'd counted.'

'Three in there are innocent,' I whispered back. 'They're locals. They were forced.'

Bill said something under his breath, and it wasn't a happy something.

I passed along the sketchy descriptions Holly had given me.

I could feel the tension in Bill's body, and then Debbie joined us in our foxhole. What was she thinking, to pack herself in so closely with the vampire and the human who hated her most?

'I told you to stay back,' Bill said, and his voice was frightening.

'Alcide abjured me,' she told me, just as if I hadn't been there when it happened.

'What did you expect?' I was exasperated at her timing and her wounded attitude. Hadn't she ever heard of consequences?

'I have to do something to earn back his trust.'

She'd come to the wrong shop, if she wanted to buy some self-respect.

'Then help me save the three in there who are innocent.' I recounted my problem again. 'Why haven't you changed into your animal?'

'Oh, I can't,' she said bitterly. 'I've been abjured. I can't change with Alcide's pack anymore. They have license to kill me, if I do.'

'What did you shift into, anyway?'

'Lynx.'

That was appropriate.

'Come on,' I said. I began to wriggle toward the building. I loathed this woman, but if she could be of use to me, I had to ally with her.

'Wait, I'm supposed to go to the back door with the Were,' Bill hissed. 'Eric's already back there.'

'So go!'

I sensed that someone else was at my back and risked a quick glance to see that it was Pam. She smiled at me, and her fangs were out, so that was a little unnerving.

Maybe if the witches inside hadn't been involved in a ritual, and hadn't been relying on their less-than-dedicated sentry and their magic, we wouldn't have made it to the door undetected. But fortune favored us for those few minutes. We got to the front door of the building, Pam and Debbie and I, and there met up with the young Were, Sid. I could recognize him even in his wolf body. Bubba was with him.

I was struck with a sudden inspiration. I moved a few feet away with Bubba.

'Can you run back to the Wiccans, the ones on our side? You know where they are?' I whispered.

Bubba nodded his head vigorously.

'You tell them there are three local Wiccans inside

who're being forced into this. Ask if they can make up some spell to get the three innocent ones to stand out.'

'I'll tell them, Miss Sookie. They're real sweet to me.'

'Good fella. Be quick, be quiet.'

He nodded, and was gone into the darkness.

The smell around the building was intensifying to such a degree that I was having trouble breathing. The air was so permeated with scent, I was reminded of passing a candle shop in a mall.

Pam said, 'Where have you sent Bubba?'

'Back to our Wiccans. They need to make three innocent people stand out somehow so we won't kill 'em.'

'But he has to come back now. He has to break down the door for me!'

'But . . .' I was disconcerted at Pam's reaction. 'He can't go in without an invitation, like you.'

'Bubba is brain damaged, degraded. He's not altogether a true vampire. He can enter without an express invitation.'

I gaped at Pam. 'Why didn't you tell me?' She just raised her eyebrows. When I thought back, it was true that I could remember at least twice that Bubba had entered dwellings without an invitation. I'd never put two and two together.

'So I'll have to be the first through the door,' I said, more matter-of-factly than I was really feeling. 'Then I invite you all in?'

'Yes. Your invitation will be enough. The building doesn't belong to them.'

'Should we do this now?'

Pam gave an almost inaudible snort. She was smiling in the glow of the streetlight, suddenly exhilarated. 'You waiting for an engraved invite?'

Lord save me from sarcastic vampires. 'You think Bubba's had enough time to get to the Wiccans?'

'Sure. Let's nail some witch butt,' she said happily. I could tell the fate of the local Wiccans was very low on her list of priorities. Everyone seemed to be looking forward to this but me. Even the young Were was showing a lot of fang.

'I kick, you go in,' Pam said. She gave me a quick peck on the cheek, utterly surprising me.

I thought, *I* so *don't want to be here.*

Then I got up from my crouch, stood behind Pam, and watched in awe while she cocked a leg and kicked with the force of four or five mules. The lock shattered, the door sprang inward while the old wood nailed over it splintered and cracked, and I leaped inside and screamed 'Come in!' to the vampire behind me and the ones at the back door. For an odd moment, I was in the lair of the witches by myself, and they'd all turned to look at me in utter astonishment.

The room was full of candles and people sitting on cushions on the floor; during the time we'd waited outside, all the others in the building seemed to have come into this front room, and they were sitting cross-legged in a circle, each with a candle burning before her, and a bowl, and a knife.

Of the three I'd try to save, 'old woman' was easiest to recognize. There was only one white-haired woman in the circle. She was wearing bright pink lipstick, a little skewed and smeared, and there was dried blood on her cheek. I grabbed her arm and pushed her into a corner, while all about me was chaos. There were only three human men in the room. Hallow's brother, Mark, now being attacked by a pack of wolves, was one of them. The second male was a middle-aged man with concave cheeks and suspicious black hair, and he not only was muttering some kind of spell but pulling a switchblade from the jacket lying on the floor to his right. He was too far away for me to do anything about it; I had to rely on the others to protect themselves. Then I spotted the third man, birthmark on cheek – must be Parton. He was cowering with his hands over his head. I knew how he felt.

I grabbed his arm and pulled up, and he came up punching, of course. But I wasn't having any of that, no one was going to hit me, so I aimed my fist through his ineffectually flailing arms and got him right on the nose. He shrieked, adding another layer of noise to the already cacophonous room, and I yanked him over to the same corner where I'd stashed Jane. Then I saw that the older woman and the young man were both shining. Okay, the Wiccans had come through with a spell and it was working, though just a tad late. Now I had to find a shining young woman with dyed red hair, the third local.

But my luck ran out then; hers already had. She was shining, but she was dead. Her throat had been torn out by one of the wolves: one of ours, or one of theirs, it didn't really matter.

I scrambled though the melee back to the corner and seized both of the surviving Wiccans by the arm. Debbie Pelt came rushing up. 'Get out of here,' I said to them. 'Find the other Wiccans out there, or go home now. Walk, get a cab, whatever.'

'It's a bad neighborhood out there,' quavered Jane.

I stared at her. 'And this isn't?' The last I saw of the two, Debbie was pointing and giving them instructions. She had stepped out the doorway with them. I was about to take off after them, since I wasn't supposed to be here anyway, when one of the Were witches snapped at my leg. Its teeth missed flesh but snagged my pants leg, and that was enough to yank me back. I stumbled and nearly fell to the floor, but managed to grasp the doorjamb in time to regain my feet. At that moment, the second wave of Weres and vamps came through from the back room, and the wolf darted off to meet the new assault from the rear.

The room was full of flying bodies and spraying blood and screams.

The witches were fighting for all they were worth, and the ones who could shift had done so. Hallow had changed, and she was a snarling mass of snapping teeth. Her brother was trying to work some kind of magic, which required him to be in his human form, and he was trying to hold off the Weres and the vampires long enough to complete the spell.

He was chanting something, he and the concave-cheeked man, even as Mark Stonebrook drove a fist into Eric's stomach.

A heavy mist began to crawl through the room. The witches, who were fighting with knives or wolf teeth, got the idea, and those who could speak began to add to whatever Mark was saying. The cloud of mist in the room began to get thicker and thicker, until it was impossible to tell friend from foe.

I leaped for the door to escape from the suffocating cloud. This stuff made breathing a real effort. It was like trying to inhale and exhale cotton balls. I extended my hand, but the bit of wall I touched didn't include a door. It had been right there! I felt a curl of panic in my stomach as I patted frantically, trying to trace the outline of the exit.

Not only did I fail to find the doorjamb, I lost touch with the wall altogether on my next sideways step. I stumbled over a wolf's body. I couldn't see a wound, so I got hold of its shoulders and dragged, trying to rescue it from the thick smoke.

The wolf began to writhe and change under my hands, which was pretty disconcerting. Even worse, it changed into a naked Hallow. I didn't know anyone could change that fast. Terrified, I let go of her immediately and backed away into the cloud. I'd been trying to be a good Samaritan with the wrong victim. A nameless woman, one of the witches, grabbed me from behind with superhuman strength. She tried to grip my neck with one hand while holding my arm with the other, but her hand kept slipping, and I bit her as hard as I could. She might be a witch, and she might be a Were, and she might have drunk a gallon of vamp blood, but she was no warrior. She screamed and released me.

By now I was completely disoriented. Which way was out? I was coughing and my eyes were streaming. The only sense I was sure of was gravity. Sight, hearing, touch: all were affected by the thick white billows, which were getting ever denser. The vampires had an advantage in this situation; they didn't need to breathe. All the rest of us did. Compared to the thickening atmosphere in the old bakery, the polluted city air outside had been pure and delicious.

Gasping and weeping, I flung my arms out in front of me and tried to find a wall or a doorway, any sort of landmark. A room that had not seemed so large now seemed cavernous. I felt I'd stumbled through yards of nothingness, but that wasn't possible unless the witches had changed the dimensions of the room, and my prosaic mind just couldn't accept the possibility. From around me I heard screams and sounds that were muffled in the cloud, but no less frightening. A spray of blood suddenly appeared down the front of my coat. I felt the spatter hit my face. I made a noise of distress that I couldn't form into words. I knew it wasn't my blood, and I knew I hadn't been hurt, but somehow that was hard for me to believe.

Then something fell past me, and as it was on its way to the floor I glimpsed a face. It was the face of Mark Stonebrook, and he was in the process of dying. The smoke closed in around him, and he might as well have been in another city.

Maybe I should crouch, too? The air might be better close to the floor. But Mark's body was down there, and other things. So much for Mark removing the spell on Eric, I thought wildly. Now we'll need Hallow. 'The best-laid plans of mice and men . . .' Where'd my grandmother gotten that quote? Gerald knocked me sideways as he pushed past in pursuit of something I couldn't see.

I told myself I was brave and resourceful, but the words rang hollow. I blundered ahead, trying not trip over the debris on the floor. The witches' paraphernalia, bowls and knives and bits of bone and vegetation that I couldn't identify, had been scattered in the scuffle. A clear spot opened up unexpectedly, and I could see an overturned bowl and one of the knives on the floor at my feet. I scooped up the knife just before the cloud rolled back over it. I was sure the knife was supposed to be used for some ritual – but I wasn't a witch, and I needed it to defend myself. I felt better when I had the knife, which was real pretty and felt very sharp.

I wondered what our Wiccans were doing. Could they be responsible for the cloud? I wished I'd gotten to vote.

Our witches, as it turned out, were getting a live feed from the scene of the fight from one of their coven sisters, who was a scryer. (Though she was physically with them, she could see what was happening on the surface of a bowl of water, I learned later.) She could make out more using that method than we could, though why she didn't see just a bunch of white smoke billowing on the surface of that water, I don't know.

Anyway, our witches made it rain . . . in the building. Somehow the rain slowly cut back on the cloud cover, and though I felt damp and extremely cold, I also discovered I was close to the inner door, the one leading into the second, large room. Gradually, I became aware that I could see; the room had started to glow with light, and I could discern shapes. One bounded toward me on legs that seemed not-quite-human, and Debbie Pelt's face snarled at me. What was she doing here? She'd stepped out the door to show the Wiccans which way to find safety, and now she was back in the room.

I don't know if she could help it or not, or if she'd just gotten swept up in the madness of battle, but Debbie had partially changed. Her face was sprouting fur, and her teeth had begun to lengthen and sharpen. She snapped at my throat, but a convulsion caused by the change made her teeth fall short. I tried to step back, but I stumbled over something on the floor and took a precious second or two to regain my footing. She began to lunge again, her intent unmistakable, and I recalled that I had a knife in my hand. I slashed at her, and she hesitated, snarling.

She was going to use the confusion to settle our score. I

wasn't strong enough to fight a shape-shifter. I'd have to use the knife, though something inside me cringed at the thought.

Then from the tags and tatters of the mist came a big hand stained with blood, and that big hand grabbed Debbie Pelt's throat and squeezed. And squeezed. Before I could track the hand up the arm to the face of its owner, a wolf leaped from the floor to knock me down.

And sniff my face.

Okay, that was . . . then the wolf on top of me was knocked off and rolling on the floor, snarling and snapping at another wolf. I couldn't help, because the two were moving so quickly I couldn't be sure I'd help the right party.

The mist was dispersing at a good rate now, and I could see the room as a whole, though there were still patches of opaque fog. Though I'd been desperate for this moment, I was almost sorry now that it'd arrived. Bodies, both dead and wounded, littered the floor among the paraphernalia of the coven, and blood spattered the walls. Portugal, the handsome young Were from the air force base, lay sprawled in front of me. He was dead. Culpepper crouched beside him, keening. This was a small piece of war, and I hated it.

Hallow was still standing and completely in her human form, bare and smeared with blood. She picked up a wolf and slung it at the wall as I watched. She was magnificent and horrible. Pam was creeping up behind her, and Pam was disheveled and dirty. I'd never seen the vampire so much as ruffled, and I almost didn't recognize her. Pam launched herself, catching Hallow at the hips and knocking her to the floor. It was as good a tackle as I'd ever seen in years of Friday night football, and if Pam had caught

Hallow a little higher up and could have gotten a grip on her, it would have been all over. But Hallow was slippery with the misty rain and with blood, and her arms were free. She twisted in Pam's grasp and seized Pam's long straight hair in both hands and pulled, and clumps of the hair came off, attached to a good bit of scalp.

Pam shrieked like a giant teakettle. I'd never heard a noise that loud come out of a throat – in this case not a human throat, but a throat nonetheless. Since Pam was definitely of the 'get even' school, she pinned Hallow to the floor by gripping both her upper arms and pressing, pressing, until Hallow was flattened. Since the witch was so strong, it was a terrible struggle, and Pam was hampered by the blood streaming down her face. But Hallow was human, and Pam was not. Pam was winning until one of the witches, the hollow-cheeked man, crawled over to the two woman and bit into Pam's neck. Both her arms were occupied, and she couldn't stop him. He didn't just bite, he drank, and as he drank, his strength increased, as if his battery was getting charged. He was draining right from the source. No one seemed to be watching but me. I scrambled across the limp, furry body of a wolf and one of the vampires to pummel on the hollow-cheeked man, who simply ignored me.

I would have to use the knife. I'd never done something like this; when I'd struck back at someone, it had always been a life-or-death situation, and the life and the death had been mine. This was different. I hesitated, but I had to do something quick. Pam was weakening before my eyes, and she would not be able to restrain Hallow much longer. I took the black-bladed knife with its black handle, and I held it to his throat; I jabbed him, a little.

'Let go of her,' I said. He ignored me.

I jabbed harder, and a stream of scarlet ran down the skin of his neck. He let go of Pam then. His mouth was all covered in her blood. But before I could rejoice that he'd freed her, he spun over while he was still underneath me and came after me, his eyes absolutely insane and his mouth open to drink from me, too. I could feel the yearning in his brain, the *want, want, want.* I put the knife to his neck again, and just as I was steeling myself, he lunged forward and pushed the blade into his own neck.

His eyes went dull almost instantly.

He'd killed himself by way of me. I don't think he'd ever realized the knife was there.

This was a close killing, a right-in-my-face killing, and I'd been the instrument of death, however inadvertently.

When I could look up, Pam was sitting on Hallow's chest, her knees pinning Hallow's arms, and she was smiling. This was so bizarre that I looked around the room to find the reason, and I saw that the battle appeared to be over. I couldn't imagine how long it had lasted, that loud but invisible struggle in the thick mist, but now I could see the results all too clearly.

Vampires don't kill neat, they kill messy. Wolves, too, are not known for their table manners. Witches seemed to manage to splash a little less blood, but the end result was really horrible, like a very bad movie, the kind you were ashamed you'd paid to see.

We appeared to have won.

At the moment, I hardly cared. I was really tired, mentally and physically, and that meant all the thoughts of the humans, and some of the thoughts of the Weres, rolled around in my brain like clothes in a dryer. There was nothing I could do about it, so I let the tag ends drift around in my head while, using the last of my strength, I pushed off of the corpse. I lay on my back and stared up at the ceiling. Since I had no thoughts, I filled up with everyone else's. Almost everyone was thinking the same kind of thing I was: how tired they were, how bloody the room was, how hard it was to believe they'd gone through a fight like this and survived. The spiky-haired boy had reverted to his human form, and he was thinking how much more he'd enjoyed it than he thought he should. In fact, his unclothed body was showing visible evidence of how much he'd enjoyed it, and he was trying to feel embarrassed about that. Mostly, he wanted to track down that cute young Wiccan and find a quiet corner. Hallow was hating Pam, she was hating me, she was hating Eric, she was hating everyone. She began to try to mumble a spell to make us all sick, but Pam gave her an elbow in the neck, and that shut her right up.

Debbie Pelt got up from the floor in the door and surveyed the scene. She looked amazingly pristine and energetic, as if she'd never had a furry face and wouldn't even begin to know how to kill someone. She picked her way through the bodies strewn on the floor, some living and some not, until she found Alcide, still in his wolf form. She squatted down to check him over for wounds, and he growled at her in clear warning. Maybe she didn't believe he would attack, or maybe she just fooled herself into believing it, but she laid her hand on his shoulder, and he bit her savagely enough to draw blood. She shrieked and scrambled back. For a few seconds, she crouched there, cradling her bleeding hand and crying. Her eyes met mine and almost glowed with hatred. She would never forgive me. She would blame me the rest of her life for Alcide's discovery of her dark nature. She'd toyed with him for two years, pulling him to her, pushing him back, concealing from him the elements of her nature he would never accept, but wanting him with her nonetheless. Now it was all over.

And this was my fault?

But I wasn't thinking in Debbie terms, I was thinking like a rational human being, and of course Debbie Pelt was not. I wished the hand that had caught her neck during the struggle in the cloud had choked her to death. I watched her back as she pushed open the door and strode into the night, and at that moment I knew Debbie Pelt would be out to get me for the rest of her life. Maybe Alcide's bite would get infected and she'd get blood poisoning?

In reflex action, I chastised myself: That was an evil thought; God didn't want us to wish ill on anyone. I just hoped He was listening in to Debbie, too, the way you hope the highway patrolman who stopped you for a ticket is also going to stop the guy behind you who was trying to pass you on the double yellow line.

The redheaded Were, Amanda, came over to me. She was bitten here and there, and she had a swollen lump on her forehead, but she was quietly beaming. 'While I'm in a good mood, I want to apologize for insulting you,' she said directly. 'You came through in this fight. Even if you can tolerate vamps, I won't hold that against you anymore. Maybe you'll see the light.' I nodded, and she strolled away to check on her packmates.

Pam had tied up Hallow, and Pam, Eric, and Gerald had gone to kneel beside someone on the other side of the room. I wondered vaguely what was happening over there, but Alcide was shimmering back into human form, and when he'd oriented himself, he crawled over to me. I was too exhausted to care that he was naked, but I had a floating idea that I should try to remember the sight, since I'd want to recall it at my leisure later.

He had some grazes and bloody spots, and one deep laceration, but overall he looked pretty good.

'There's blood on your face,' he said, with an effort.

'Not mine.'

'Thank God,' he said, and he lay on the floor beside me. 'How bad are you hurt?'

'I'm not hurt, not really,' I said. 'I mean, I got shoved around a lot, and choked a little maybe, and snapped at, but no one hit me!' By golly, I was going to make my New Year's resolution come true, after all.

'I'm sorry we didn't find Jason here,' he said.

'Eric asked Pam and Gerald if the vampires were holding him, and they said no,' I remarked. 'He'd thought of a real good reason for the vamps to have him. But they didn't.'

'Chow is dead.'

'How?' I asked, sounding as calm as if it hardly mattered. Truthfully, I had never been very partial to the bartender, but I would have shown a decent concern if I hadn't been so tired.

'One of Hallow's group had a wooden knife.'

'I never saw one before,' I said after a moment, and that was all I could think to say about the death of Chow.

'Me, neither.'

After a long moment, I said, 'I'm sorry about Debbie.' What I meant was, I was sorry Debbie had hurt him so badly, had proved to be such a dreadful person that he'd had to take a drastic step to get her out of his life.

'Debbie who?' he asked, and rolled to his feet and padded away across the filthy floor strewn with blood, bodies, and supernatural debris.

Chapter 13

The aftermath of a battle is melancholy and nasty. I guess you could call what we'd had a battle . . . maybe more like a supernatural skirmish? The wounded have to be tended, the blood has to be cleaned up, the bodies have to be buried. Or, in this case, disposed of – Pam decided to burn the store down, leaving the bodies of Hallow's coven inside.

They hadn't all died. Hallow, of course, was still alive. One other witch survived, though she was badly hurt and very low on blood. Of the Weres, Colonel Flood was gravely wounded; Portugal had been killed by Mark Stonebrook. The others were more or less okay. Only Chow had died, out of the vampire contingent. The others had wounds, some very horrible, but vampires will heal.

It surprised me that the witches hadn't made a better showing.

'They were probably good witches, but they weren't good fighters,' Pam said. 'They were picked for their magical ability and their willingness to follow Hallow, not for their battle skills. She shouldn't have tried to take over Shreveport with such a following.'

'Why Shreveport?' I asked Pam.

'I'm going to find out,' Pam said, smiling.

I shuddered. I didn't want to consider Pam's methods. 'How are you going to keep her from doing a spell on you while you question her?'

Pam said, 'I'll think of something.' She was still smiling.

'Sorry about Chow,' I said, a little hesitantly.

'The job of bartender at Fangtasia doesn't seem to be a good-luck job,' she admitted. 'I don't know if I'll be able to find someone to replace Chow. After all, he and Long Shadow both perished within a year of starting work.'

'What are you going to do about un-hexing Eric?'

Pam seemed glad enough to talk to me, even if I was only a human, since she'd lost her sidekick. 'We'll make Hallow do it, sooner or later. And she'll tell us why she did it.'

'If Hallow just gives up the general outline of the spell, will that be enough? Or will she have to perform it herself?' I tried to rephrase that in my head so it was clearer, but Pam seemed to understand me.

'I don't know. We'll have to ask our friendly Wiccans. The ones you saved should be grateful enough to give us any help we need,' Pam said, while she tossed some more gasoline around the room. She'd already checked the building to remove the few things she might want from it, and the local coven had gathered up the magical paraphernalia, in case one of the cops who came to investigate this fire could recognize the remnants.

I glanced at my watch. I hoped that Holly had made it safely home by now. I would tell her that her son was safe.

I kept my eyes averted from the job the youngest witch was doing on Colonel Flood's left leg. He'd sustained an ugly gash in the quadriceps. It was a serious wound. He made light of it, and after Alcide fetched their clothes, the colonel limped around with a smile on his face. But when blood seeped through the bandage, the packmaster had to allow his Weres to take him to a doctor who happened to be two-natured and willing to help off the books, since no one could think of a good story that would explain such a wound. Before he left, Colonel Flood shook hands ceremoniously with the head witch and with Pam, though I could see the sweat beading on his forehead even in the frigid air of the old building.

I asked Eric if he felt any different, but he was still oblivious to his past. He looked upset and on the verge of terror. Mark Stonebrook's death hadn't made a bit of difference, so Hallow was in for a few dreadful hours, courtesy of Pam. I just accepted that. I didn't want to think about it closely. Or at all.

As for me, I was feeling completely at a loss. Should I go home to Bon Temps, taking Eric with me? (Was I in charge of him anymore?) Should I try to find a place to spend the remaining hours of the night here in the city? Shreveport was home for everyone but Bill and me, and Bill was planning on using Chow's empty bed (or whatever it was) for the coming day, at Pam's suggestion.

I dithered around indecisively for a few minutes, trying to make up my mind. But no one seemed to need me for anything specific, and no one sought me out for conversation. So when Pam got involved in giving the other vampires directions about Hallow's transportation, I just walked out. The night was quite as still as it had been, but a few dogs did bark as I walked down the street. The smell of magic had lessened. The night was just as dark, and even colder, and I was at low ebb. I didn't know what I'd say if a policeman stopped me; I was blood-spattered and tattered, and I had no explanation. At the moment, I found it hard to care.

I'd gotten maybe a block when Eric caught up with me. He was very anxious – almost fearful. 'You weren't there. I just looked around and you weren't there,' he said accusingly. 'Where are you going? Why didn't you tell me?'

'Please,' I said, and held up a hand to beg him to be silent. 'Please.' I was too tired to be strong for him, and I had to fight an overwhelming depression, though I couldn't have told you exactly why; after all, no one had hit me. I should be happy, right? The goals of the evening had been met. Hallow was conquered and in captivity; though Eric hadn't been restored to himself, he soon would be, because Pam was sure to bring Hallow around to the vampire way of thinking, in a painful and terminal way.

Undoubtedly, Pam would also discover why Hallow had begun this whole course of action. And Fangtasia would acquire a new bartender, some fangy hunk who would bring in the tourist bucks. She and Eric would open the strip club they'd been considering, or the all-night dry-cleaners, or the bodyguard service.

My brother would still be missing.

'Let me go home with you. I don't know them,' Eric said, his voice low and almost pleading. I hurt inside when Eric said something that was so contrary to his normal personality. Or was I seeing Eric's true nature? Was his flash and assurance something he'd assumed, like another skin, over the years?

'Sure, come on,' I said, as desperate as Eric was, but in my own way. I just wanted him to be quiet, and strong.

I'd settle for quiet.

He loaned me his physical strength, at least. He picked me up and carried me back to the car. I was surprised to find that my cheeks were wet with tears.

'You have blood all over you,' he said into my ear.

'Yes, but don't get excited about it,' I warned. 'It doesn't do a thing for me. I just want to shower.' I was at the hiccupping-sob stage of crying, almost done.

'You'll have to get rid of this coat now,' he said, with some satisfaction.

'I'll get it cleaned.' I was too tired to respond to disparaging comments about my coat.

Getting away from the weight and smell of the magic was almost as good as a big cup of coffee and a hit of oxygen. By the time I got close to Bon Temps, I wasn't feeling so ragged, and I was calm as I let us in the back door. Eric came in behind me and took a step to my right to go around the kitchen table, as I leaned left to flick on the light switch.

When I turned on the light, Debbie Pelt was smiling at me.

She had been sitting in the dark at my kitchen table, and she had a gun in her hand.

Without saying a word, she fired at me.

But she'd reckoned without Eric, who was so fast, faster than any human. He took the bullet meant for me, and he took it right in the chest. He went down in front of me.

She hadn't had time to search the house, which was lucky. From behind the water heater, I yanked the shotgun I'd taken from Jason's house. I pumped it – one of the scariest sounds in the world – and I shot Debbie Pelt while she was still staring, shocked, at Eric, who was on his knees and coughing up blood. I racked another shell, but I didn't need to shoot her again. Her fingers relaxed and her gun fell to the floor.

I sat on the floor myself, because I couldn't stay upright anymore.

Eric was now full length on the floor, gasping and twitching in a pool of blood.

There wasn't much left of Debbie's upper chest and neck.

My kitchen looked like I'd been dismembering pigs, pigs that'd put up a good fight.

I started to reach up to scrabble for the telephone at the end of the counter. My hand dropped back to the floor when I wondered whom I was going to call.

The law? Ha.

Sam? And mire him down further in my troubles? I didn't think so.

Pam? Let her see how close I'd come to letting my charge get killed? Uh-uh.

Alcide? Sure, he'd love seeing what I'd done with his fiancée, abjure or no abjure.

Arlene? She had her living to make, and two little kids. She didn't need to be around something illegal.

Tara? Too queasy.

This is when I would have called my brother, if I'd known where he was. When you have to clean the blood out of the kitchen, it's family you want.

I'd have to do this by myself.

Eric came first. I scrambled over to him, reclined by him with one elbow to prop me up.

'Eric,' I said loudly. His blue eyes opened. They were bright with pain.

The hole in his chest bubbled blood. I hated to think

what the exit wound looked like. Maybe it had been a twenty-two? Maybe the bullet was still inside? I looked at the wall behind where he'd been standing, and I couldn't see a spray of blood or a bullet hole. Actually, I realized, if the bullet had gone through him, it would have struck me. I looked down at myself, fumbled the coat off. No, no fresh blood.

As I watched Eric, he began to look a little better. 'Drink,' he said, and I almost put my wrist to his lips, when I reconsidered. I managed to get some TrueBlood out of the refrigerator and heat it up, though the front of the microwave was less than pristine.

I knelt to give it to him. 'Why not you?' he asked painfully.

'I'm sorry,' I apologized. 'I know you earned it, sweetie. But I have to have all my energy. I've got more work ahead.'

Eric downed the drink in a few big gulps. I'd unbuttoned his coat and his flannel shirt, and as I looked at his chest to mark the progression of his bleeding, I saw an amazing thing. The bullet that had hit him popped out of the wound. In another three minutes, or perhaps less, the hole had closed. The blood was still drying on his chest hair, and the bullet wound was gone.

'Another drink?' Eric asked.

'Sure. How do you feel?' I was numb myself.

His smile was crooked. 'Weak.'

I got him more blood and he drank this bottle more slowly. Wincing, he pulled himself to a full sitting position. He looked at the mess on the other side of the table.

Then he looked at me.

'I know, I know, I did terrible!' I said. 'I'm so sorry!' I could feel tears – again – trailing down my cheeks. I could hardly feel more miserable. I'd done a dreadful thing. I'd failed in my job. I had a massive cleanup ahead of me. And I looked awful.

Eric looked mildly surprised at my outburst. 'You might have died of the bullet, and I knew I wouldn't,' he pointed out. 'I kept the bullet from you in the most expedient way, and then you defended me effectively.'

That was certainly a skewed way to look at it, but oddly enough, I did feel less horrible.

'I killed another human,' I said. That made two in one night; but in my opinion, the hollow-cheeked witch had killed himself by pushing down on the knife.

I'd definitely fired the shotgun all by myself.

I shuddered and turned away from the ragged shell of bone and flesh that had once held Debbie Pelt.

'You didn't,' he said sharply. 'You killed a shifter who was a treacherous, murderous bitch, a shifter who had tried to kill you twice already.' So it had been Eric's hand that had squeezed her throat and made her let go of me. 'I should have finished the job when I had her earlier,' he said, by way of confirmation. 'It would have saved us both some heartache; in my case, literally.'

I had a feeling this was not what the Reverend Fullenwilder would be saying. I muttered something to that effect.

'I was never a Christian,' Eric said. Now, that didn't surprise me. 'But I can't imagine a belief system that would tell you to sit still and get slaughtered.'

I blinked, wondering if that wasn't exactly what Christianity taught. But I am no theologian or Bible scholar, and I would have to leave the judgment on my action to God, who was also no theologian.

Somehow I felt better, and I was in fact grateful to be alive.

'Thank you, Eric,' I said. I kissed him on the cheek. 'Now you go clean up in the bathroom while I start in here.'

But he was not having any of that. God bless him, he helped me with great zeal. Since he could handle the most disgusting things with no apparent qualms, I was delighted to let him.

You don't want to know how awful it was, or all the details. But we got Debbie together and bagged up, and Eric took her way out into the woods and buried her and concealed the grave, he swore, while I cleaned. I had to take down the curtains over the sink and soak them in the washing machine in cold water, and I stuck my coat in with them, though without much hope of its being wearable again. I pulled on rubber gloves and used bleach-soaked wipes to go over and over the chair and table and floor, and I sprayed the front of the cabinets with wood soap and wiped and wiped.

You just wouldn't believe where specks of blood had landed.

I realized that attention to these tiny details was helping me keep my mind off of the main event, and that the longer I avoided looking at it squarely – the longer I let Eric's practical words sink into my awareness – the better off I'd be. There was nothing I could undo. There was no way I could mend what I had done. I'd had a limited number of choices, and I had to live with the choice I'd made. My Gran had always told me that a woman – any woman worth her salt – could do whatever she had to. If you'd called Gran a liberated woman, she would have denied it vigorously, but she'd been the strongest woman I'd ever known, and if she believed I could complete this grisly task just because I had to, I would do it.

When I was through, the kitchen reeked of cleaning products, and to the naked eye it was literally spotless. I was sure a crime scene expert would be able to find trace evidence (a tip of the hat to the Learning Channel), but I didn't intend that a crime scene expert would ever have reason to come into my kitchen.

She'd broken in the front door. It had never occurred to me to check it before I came in the back. So much for my career as a bodyguard. I wedged a chair under the doorknob to keep it blocked for the remainder of the night.

Eric, returned from his burial detail, seemed to be high on excitement, so I asked him to go scouting for Debbie's car. She had a Mazda Miata, and she'd hidden it on a four-wheeler trail right across the parish road from the turnoff to my place. Eric had had the foresight to retain her keys, and he volunteered to drive her car somewhere else. I should have followed him, to bring him back to my house, but he insisted he could do the job by himself, and I was too exhausted to boss him around. I stood under a stream of water and scrubbed myself clean while he was gone. I was glad to be alone, and I washed myself over and over. When I was as clean as I could get on the outside, I pulled on a pink nylon nightgown and crawled in the bed. It was close to dawn, and I hoped Eric would be back soon. I had opened the closet and the hole for him, and put an extra pillow in it.

I heard him come in just as I was falling asleep, and he kissed me on the cheek. 'All done,' he said, and I mumbled, 'Thanks, baby.'

'Anything for you,' he said, his voice gentle. 'Good night, my lover.'

It occurred to me that I was lethal for exes. I'd dusted Bill's big love (and his mom); now I'd killed Alcide's off-and-on-again sweetie. I knew hundreds of men. I'd never gone homicidal on their exes. But creatures I cared about, well, that seemed to be different. I wondered if Eric had any old girlfriends around. Probably about a hundred or so. Well, they'd better beware of me.

After that, whether I willed it or not, I was sucked down into a black hole of exhaustion.

Chapter 14

I guess Pam worked on Hallow right up until dawn was peeking over the horizon. I myself was so heavily asleep, so in need of both physical and mental healing, I didn't wake until four in the afternoon. It was a gloomy winter day, the kind that makes you switch on the radio to see if an ice storm is coming. I checked to make sure I had three or four days' worth of firewood moved up onto the back porch.

Eric would be up early today.

I dressed and ate at the speed of a snail, trying to get a handle on my state of being.

Physically, I was fine. A bruise here or there, a little muscle soreness – that was nothing. It was the second week of January and I was sticking to my New Year's resolution just great.

On the other hand – and there's always another hand – mentally, or maybe emotionally, I was less than rock-steady. No matter how practical you are, no matter how strong-stomached you are, you can't do something like I'd done without suffering some consequences.

That's the way it should be.

When I thought of Eric getting up, I thought of maybe doing some snuggling before I had to go to work. And I thought of the pleasure of being with someone who thought I was so important.

I hadn't anticipated that the spell would have been broken.

Eric got up at five-thirty. When I heard movement in the guest bedroom, I tapped on the door and opened it. He whirled, his fangs running out and his hands clawing in front of him.

I'd almost said, 'Hi, honey,' but caution kept me mute.

'Sookie,' he said slowly. 'Am I in your house?'

I was glad I'd gotten dressed. 'Yes,' I said, regrouping like crazy. 'You've been here for safekeeping. Do you know what happened?'

'I went to a meeting with some new people,' he said, doubt in his voice. 'Didn't I?' He looked down at his Wal-Mart clothes with some surprise. 'When did I buy these?'

'I had to get those for you,' I said.

'Did you dress me, too?' he asked, running his hands down his chest and lower. He gave me a very Eric smile.

He didn't remember. Anything.

'No,' I said. I flashed on Eric in the shower with me. The kitchen table. The bed.

'Where is Pam?' he asked.

'You should call her,' I said. 'Do you recall anything about yesterday?'

'Yesterday I had the meeting with the witches,' he said, as if that was indisputable.

I shook my head. 'That was days ago,' I told him, unable to add the number of them up in my head. My heart sank even lower.

'You don't remember last night, after we came back from Shreveport,' I pressed him, suddenly seeing a gleam of light in all this.

'Did we make love?' he asked hopefully. 'Did you finally yield to me, Sookie? It's only a matter of time, of course.' He grinned at me.

No, last night we cleaned up a body, I thought.

I was the only one who knew. And even I didn't know where Debbie's remains were buried, or what had happened to her car.

I sat down on the edge of my old narrow bed. Eric looked at me closely. 'Something's wrong, Sookie? What happened while I was – Why don't I remember what happened?'

Least said, soonest mended.

All's well that ends well.

Out of sight, out of mind. (Oh, I wished that were true.)

'I bet Pam will be here any minute,' I said. 'I think I'll let her tell you all about it.'

'And Chow?'

'No, he won't be here. He died last night. Fangtasia seems to have a bad effect on bartenders.'

'Who killed him? I'll have vengeance.'

'You've already had.'

'Something more is wrong with you,' Eric said. He'd always been astute.

'Yes, lots of stuff is wrong with me.' I would've enjoyed hugging him right then, but it would just complicate everything. 'And I think it's going to snow.'

'Snow, here?' Eric was as delighted as a child. 'I love snow!'

Why was I not surprised?

'Maybe we will get snowed in together,' he said suggestively, waggling his blond eyebrows.

I laughed. I just couldn't help it. And it was a hell of a lot better than crying, which I'd done quite enough of lately. 'As if you'd ever let the weather stop you from doing what you wanted to do,' I said, and stood. 'Come on, I'll heat you up some blood.'

Even a few nights of intimacy had softened me enough that I had to watch my actions. Once I almost stroked his hair as I passed him; and once I bent to give him a kiss, and had to pretend I'd dropped something on the floor.

When Pam knocked on my front door thirty minutes later, I was ready for work, and Eric was antsy as hell.

Pam was no sooner seated opposite him than he began bombarding her with questions. I told them quietly that I was leaving, and I don't think they even noticed when I went out the kitchen door.

Merlotte's wasn't too busy that night, after we dealt with a rather large supper crowd. A few flakes of snow had convinced most of the regulars that going home sober might be a very good idea. There were enough customers left to keep Arlene and me moderately busy. Sam caught me as I was loading my tray with seven mugs of beer and wanted to be filled in on the night before.

'I'll tell you later,' I promised, thinking I'd have to edit my narrative pretty carefully.

'Any trace of Jason?' he asked.

'No,' I said, and felt sadder than ever. The dispatcher at the law enforcement complex had sounded almost snappish when I'd called to ask if there was any news.

Kevin and Kenya came in that night after they'd gotten off duty. When I took their drinks to the table (a bourbon and Coke and a gin and tonic), Kenya said, 'We've been looking for your brother, Sookie. I'm sorry.'

'I know you all have been trying,' I said. 'I appreciate you all organizing the search party so much! I just wish . . .' And then I couldn't think of anything else to say. Thanks to my disability, I knew something about each of them that the other didn't know. They loved each other. But Kevin knew his mother would stick her head in the oven before she'd see him married to a black woman, and Kenya knew her brothers would rather ram Kevin through a wall than see him walk down the aisle with her.

And I knew this, despite the fact that neither of them did; and I hated having this personal knowledge, this intimate knowledge, that I just couldn't help knowing.

Worse than knowing, even, was the temptation to interfere. I told myself very sternly that I had enough problems of my own without causing problems for other people. Luckily, I was busy enough the rest of the night to erase the temptation from my mind. Though I couldn't reveal those kinds of secrets, I reminded myself that I owed the two officers, big-time. If I heard of something I could let them know, I would.

When the bar closed, I helped Sam put the chairs up on the tables so Terry Bellefleur could come in and mop and clean the toilets early in the morning. Arlene and Tack had left, singing 'Let It Snow' while they went out the back door. Sure enough, the flakes were drifting down outside, though I didn't think they'd stick past morning. I thought of the creatures out in the woods tonight, trying to keep warm and dry. I knew that in some spot in the forest, Debbie Pelt lay in a hole, cold forever.

I wondered how long I'd think of her like that, and I

hoped very much I could remember just as clearly what an awful person she'd been, how vindictive and murderous.

In fact, I'd stood staring out the window for a couple of minutes when Sam came up behind me.

'What's on your mind?' he asked. He gripped my elbow, and I could feel the strength in his fingers.

I sighed, not for the first time. 'Just wondering about Jason,' I said. That was close enough to the truth.

He patted me in a consoling way. 'Tell me about last night,' he said, and for one second I thought he was asking me about Debbie. Then, of course, I knew he referred to the battle with the witches, and I was able to give him an account.

'So Pam showed up tonight at your place.' Sam sounded pleased about that. 'She must have cracked Hallow, made her undo the spell. Eric was himself again?'

'As far as I could tell.'

'What did he have to say about the experience?'

'He didn't remember anything about it,' I said slowly. 'He didn't seem to have a clue.'

Sam looked away from me when he said, 'How are you, with that?'

'I think it's for the best,' I told him. 'Definitely.' But I would be going home to an empty house again. The knowledge skittered at the edges of my awareness, but I wouldn't look at it directly.

'Too bad you weren't working the afternoon shift,' he said, somehow following a similar train of thought. 'Calvin Norris was in here.'

'And?'

'I think he came in hopes of seeing you.'

I looked at Sam skeptically. 'Right.'

'I think he's serious, Sookie.'

'Sam,' I said, feeling unaccountably wounded, 'I'm on my own, and sometimes that's no fun, but I don't have to take up with a werewolf just because he offers.'

Sam looked mildly puzzled. 'You wouldn't have to. The people in Hotshot aren't Weres.'

'He said they were.'

'No, not Weres with a capital W. They're too proud to call themselves shifters, but that's what they are. They're were-panthers.'

'What?' I swear I saw dots floating in the air around my eyes.

'Sookie? What's wrong?'

'Panthers? Didn't you know that the print on Jason's dock was the print of a panther?'

'No, no one told me about any print! Are you sure?'

I gave him an exasperated look. 'Of course, I'm sure. And he vanished the night Crystal Norris was waiting for him in his house. You're the only bartender in the world who doesn't know all the town gossip.'

'Crystal – *she's* the Hotshot girl he was with New Year's Eve? The skinny black-headed girl at the search?'

I nodded.

'The one Felton loves so much?'

'He what?'

'Felton, you know, the one who came along on the search. She's been his big love his whole life.'

'And you know this how?' Since I, the mind reader, didn't, I was distinctly piqued.

'He told me one night when he'd had too much to drink. These guys from Hotshot, they don't come in much, but when they do, they drink serious.'

'So why would he join in the search?'

'I think maybe we'd better go ask a few questions.'

'This late?'

'You got something better to do?'

He had a point, and I sure wanted to know if they had my brother or could tell me what had happened to him. But in a way, I was scared of finding out.

'That jacket's too light for this weather, Sookie,' Sam said, as we bundled up.

'My coat is at the cleaner's,' I said. Actually, I hadn't had a chance to put it in the dryer, or even to check to make sure all the blood had come out. And it had holes in it.

'Hmmm' was all Sam said, before he loaned me a green pullover sweater to wear under my jacket. We got in Sam's pickup because the snow was really coming down, and like all men, Sam was convinced he could drive in the snow, though he'd almost never done so.

The drive out to Hotshot seemed even longer in the dark night, with the snow swirling down in the headlights.

'I thank you for taking me out here, but I'm beginning to think we're crazy,' I said, when we were halfway there.

'Is your seat belt on?' Sam asked.

'Sure.'

'Good,' he said, and we kept on our way.

Finally we reached the little community. There weren't any streetlights out here, of course, but a couple of the residents had paid to have security lights put up on the electric poles. Windows were glowing in some of the houses.

'Where do you think we should go?'

'Calvin's. He's the one with the power,' Sam said, sounding certain.

I remembered how proud Calvin had been of his house, and I was a little curious to see the inside. His lights were on, and his pickup was parked in front of the house. Stepping out of the warm truck into the snowy night was like walking through a chilly wet curtain to reach the front door. I knocked, and after a long pause, the door came open. Calvin looked pleased until he saw Sam behind me.

'Come in,' he said, not too warmly, and stood aside. We stamped our feet politely before we entered.

The house was plain and clean, decorated with inexpensive but carefully arranged furniture and pictures. None of the pictures had people in them, which I thought interesting. Landscapes. Wildlife.

'This is a bad night to be out driving around,' Calvin observed.

I knew I'd have to tread carefully, as much as I wanted to grab the front of his flannel shirt and scream in his face. This man was a ruler. The size of the kingdom didn't really matter.

'Calvin,' I said, as calmly as I could, 'did you know that the police found a panther print on the dock, by Jason's bootprint?'

'No,' he said, after a long moment. I could see the anger building behind his eyes. 'We don't hear a lot of town gossip out here. I wondered why the search party had men with guns, but we make other people kind of nervous, and no one was talking to us much. Panther print. Huh.'

'I didn't know that was your, um, other identity, until tonight.'

He looked at me steadily. 'You think that one of us made off with your brother.'

I stood silent, not shifting my eyes from his. Sam was equally still beside me.

'You think Crystal got mad at your brother and did him harm?'

'No,' I said. His golden eyes were getting wider and rounder as I spoke to him.

'Are you afraid of me?' he asked suddenly.

'No,' I said. 'I'm not.'

'Felton,' he said.

I nodded.

'Let's go see,' he said.

Back out into the snow and darkness. I could feel the sting of the flakes on my cheeks, and I was glad my jacket had a hood. Sam's gloved hand took mine as I stumbled over some discarded tool or toy in the yard of the house next to Felton's. As we trailed up to the concrete slab that formed Felton's front porch, Calvin was already knocking at the door.

'Who is it?' Felton demanded.

'Open,' said Calvin.

Recognizing his voice, Felton opened the door immediately. He didn't have the same cleanliness bug as Calvin, and his furniture was not so much arranged as shoved up against whatever wall was handiest. The way he moved was not human, and tonight that seemed even more pronounced than it had at the search. Felton, I thought, was closer to reverting to his animal nature. Inbreeding had definitely left its mark on him.

'Where is the man?' Calvin asked without preamble.

Felton's eyes flared wide, and he twitched, as if he was thinking about running. He didn't speak.

'Where?' Calvin demanded again, and then his hand

changed into a paw and he swiped it across Felton's face. 'Does he live?'

I clapped my hands across my mouth so I wouldn't scream. Felton sank to his knees, his face crossed with parallel slashes filling with blood.

'In the shed in back,' he said indistinctly.

I went back out the front door so quickly that Sam barely caught up with me. Around the corner of the house I flew, and I fell full-length over a woodpile. Though I knew it would hurt later, I jumped up and found myself supported by Calvin Norris, who, as he had in the woods, lifted me over the pile before I knew what he intended. He vaulted it himself with easy grace, and then we were at the door of the shed, which was one of those you order from Sears or Penney's. You have your neighbors come help put it up, when the concrete truck comes to pour your slab.

The door was padlocked, but these sheds aren't meant to repel determined intruders, and Calvin was very strong. He broke the lock, and pushed back the door, and turned on the light. It was amazing to me that there was electricity out here, because that's certainly not the norm.

At first I wasn't sure I was looking at my brother, because this creature looked nothing like Jason. He was blond, sure, but he was so filthy and smelly that I flinched, even in the freezing air. And he was blue with the cold, since he had only pants on. He was lying on a single blanket on the concrete floor.

I was on my knees beside him, gathering him up as best I could in my arms, and his eyelids fluttered open. 'Sookie?' he said, and I could hear the disbelief in his voice. 'Sookie? Am I saved?'

'Yes,' I said, though I was by no means so sure. I remember what had happened to the sheriff who'd come out here and found something amiss. 'We're going to take you home.'

He'd been bitten.

He'd been bitten a lot.

'Oh, no,' I said softly, the significance of the bites sinking in.

'I didn't kill him,' Felton said defensively, from outside.

'You bit him,' I said, and my voice sounded like another person's. 'You wanted him to be like you.'

'So Crystal wouldn't like him better. She knows we need to breed outside, but she really likes me best,' Felton said.

'So you grabbed him, and you kept him, and you bit him.'

Jason was too weak to stand.

'Please carry him to the truck,' I said stiffly, unable to meet the eyes of anyone around me. I could feel the fury rising in me like a black wave, and I knew I had to restrain it until we were out of here. I had just enough control to do this. I knew I did.

Jason cried out when Calvin and Sam lifted him. They got the blanket, too, and sort of tucked it around him. I stumbled after them as they made their way back to Calvin's and the truck.

I had my brother back. There was a chance he was going to turn into a panther from time to time, but I had him back. I didn't know if the rules for all shifters were the same, but Alcide had told me that Weres who were bitten, not born – created Weres, rather than genetic Weres – changed into the half-man, half-beast creatures who populated horror movies. I forced myself to get off that track, to think of the joy of having my brother back, alive.

Calvin got Jason into the truck and slid him over, and Sam climbed into the driver's seat. Jason would be between us after I climbed into the truck. But Calvin had to tell me something first.

'Felton will be punished,' he said. 'Right now.'

Punishing Felton hadn't been at the top of my list of things to think about, but I nodded, because I wanted to get the hell out of there.

'If we're taking care of Felton, are you going to go to the police?' he asked. He was standing stiffly, as if he was trying to be casual about the question. But this was a dangerous moment. I knew what happened to people who drew attention to the Hotshot community.

'No,' I said. 'It was just Felton.' Though, of course, Crystal had to have known, at least on some level. She'd told me she'd smelled an animal that night at Jason's. How could she have mistaken the smell of panther, when she was one? And she had probably known all along that that panther had been Felton. His smell would be familiar to her. But it just wasn't the time to go into that; Calvin would know that as well as I, when he'd had a moment to think. 'And my brother may be one of you now. He'll need you,' I added, in the most even voice I could manage. It wasn't very even, at that.

'I'll come get Jason, next full moon.'

I nodded again. 'Thank you,' I told him, because I knew we would never have found Jason if he'd stonewalled us. 'I have to get my brother home now.' I knew Calvin wanted me to touch him, wanted me to connect with him somehow, but I just couldn't do it.

'Sure,' he said, after a long moment. The shape-shifter stepped back while I scrambled up into the cab. He seemed to know I wouldn't want any help from him right now.

I'd thought I'd gotten unusual brain patterns from the Hotshot people because they were inbred. It had never occurred to me they were something other than wolves. I'd assumed. I know what my high school volleyball coach always said about 'assume.' Of course, he'd also told us that we had to leave everything out on the court so it would be there when we came back, which I had yet to figure out.

But he'd been right about assumptions.

Sam had already gotten the heater in the truck going, but not at full blast. Too much heat too soon would be bad for Jason, I was sure. As it was, the second Jason began to warm up, his smell was pretty evident, and I nearly apologized to Sam, but sparing Jason any further humiliation was more important.

'Aside from the bites, and being so cold, are you okay?' I asked, when I thought Jason had stopped shivering and could speak.

'Yes,' he said. 'Yes. Every night, every damn night, he'd come in the shed, and he'd change in front of me, and I'd think, Tonight he's going to kill me and eat me. And every night, he'd bite me. And then he'd just change back and leave. I could tell it was hard for him, after he'd smelled the blood . . . but he never did more than bite.'

'They'll kill him tonight,' I said. 'In return for us not going to the police.'

'Good deal,' said Jason, and he meant it.

Chapter 15

Jason was able to stand on his own long enough to take a shower, which he said was the best one he'd taken in his life. When he was clean and smelled like every scented thing in my bathroom, and he was modestly draped with a big towel, I went all over him with Neosporin. I used up a whole tube on the bites. They seemed to be healing clean already, but I could not stop myself from trying to think of things to do for him. He'd had hot chocolate, and he'd eaten some hot oatmeal (which I thought was an odd choice, but he said all Felton had brought him to eat had been barely cooked meat), and he'd put on the sleeping pants I'd bought for Eric (too big, but the drawstring waist helped), and he'd put on a baggy old T-shirt I'd gotten when I'd done the Walk for Life two years before. He kept touching the material as if he was delighted to be dressed.

He seemed to want to be warm and to sleep, more than anything. I put him in my old room. With a sad glance at the closet, which Eric had left all askew, I told my brother good night. He asked me to turn the hall light on and leave the door cracked a little. It cost Jason to ask that, so I didn't say a word. I just did as he'd requested.

Sam was sitting in the kitchen, drinking a cup of hot tea. He looked up from watching the steam of it and smiled at me. 'How is he?'

I sank down into my usual spot. 'He's better than I thought he would be,' I said. 'Considering he spent the whole time in the shed with no heat and being bitten every day.'

'I wonder how long Felton would have kept him?'

'Until the full moon, I guess. Then Felton would've found out if he'd succeeded or not.' I felt a little sick.

'I checked your calendar. He's got a couple of weeks.'

'Good. Give Jason time to get his strength back before he has something else to face.' I rested my head in my hands for a minute. 'I have to call the police.'

'To let them know to stop searching?'

'Yep.'

'Have you made up your mind what to say? Did Jason mention any ideas?'

'Maybe that the male relatives of some girl had kidnapped him?' Actually, that was sort of true.

'The cops would want to know where he'd been held. If he'd gotten away on his own, they'd want to know how, and they'd be sure he'd have more information for them.'

I wondered if I had enough brainpower left to think. I stared blankly at the table: the familiar napkin holder that my grandmother had bought at a craft fair, and the sugar bowl, and the salt- and peppershakers shaped like a rooster and a hen. I noticed something had been tucked under the saltshaker.

It was a check for $50,000, signed by Eric Northman.

Eric had not only paid me, he had given me the biggest tip of my career.

'Oh,' I said, very gently. 'Oh, boy.' I looked at it for a minute more, to make sure I was reading it correctly. I passed it across the table to Sam.

'Wow. Payment for keeping Eric?' Sam looked up at me, and I nodded. 'What will you do with it?'

'Put it through the bank, first thing tomorrow morning.'

He smiled. 'I guess I was thinking longer term than that.'

'Just relax. It'll just relax me to have it. To know that . . .' To my embarrassment, here came tears. Again. *Damn*. 'So I won't have to *worry* all the time.'

'Things have been tight recently, I take it.' I nodded, and Sam's mouth compressed. 'You . . .' he began, and then couldn't finish his sentence.

'Thanks, but I can't do that to people,' I said firmly. 'Gran always said that was the surest way to end a friendship.'

'You could sell this land, buy a house in town, have neighbors,' Sam suggested, as if he'd been dying to say that for months.

'Move out of this house?' Some member of my family had lived in this house continuously for over a hundred and fifty years. Of course, that didn't make it sacred or anything, and the house had been added to and modernized many times. I thought of living in a small modern house with level floors and up-to-date bathrooms and a convenient kitchen with lots of plugs. No exposed water heater. Lots of blown-in insulation in the attic. A carport!

Dazzled at the vision, I swallowed. 'I'll consider it,' I said, feeling greatly daring to even entertain the idea. 'But

I can't think of anything much right now. Just getting through tomorrow will be hard enough.'

I thought of the police man-hours that had been put into searching for Jason. Suddenly I was so tired, I just couldn't make an attempt to fashion a story for the law.

'You need to go to bed,' Sam said astutely.

I could only nod. 'Thank you, Sam. Thank you so much.' We stood and I gave him a hug. It turned into a longer hug than I'd planned, because hugging him was unexpectedly restful and comfortable. 'Good night,' I said. 'Please drive careful going back.' I thought briefly of offering him one of the beds upstairs, but I kept that floor shut off and it would be awfully cold up there; and I'd have to go up and make the bed. He'd be more comfortable making the short drive home, even in the snow.

'I will,' he said, and released me. 'Call me in the morning.

'Thanks again.'

'Enough thank-yous,' he said. Eric had put a couple of nails in the front door to hold it shut, until I could get a dead bolt put on. I locked the back door behind Sam, and I barely managed to brush my teeth and change into a nightgown before I crawled in my bed.

The first thing I did the next morning was check on my brother. Jason was still deeply asleep, and in the light of day, I could clearly see the effects of his imprisonment. His face had a coating of stubble. Even in his sleep, he looked older. There were bruises here and there, and that was just on his face and arms. His eyes opened as I sat by the bed, looking at him. Without moving, he rolled his eyes around, taking in the room. They stopped when they came to my face.

'I didn't dream it,' he said. His voice was hoarse. 'You and Sam came and got me. They let me go. The panther let me go.'

'Yes.'

'So what's been happening while I was gone?' he asked next. 'Wait, can I go to the bathroom and get a cup of coffee before you tell me?'

I liked his asking instead of telling (a Jason trait, telling), and I was glad to tell him yes and even volunteer to get the coffee. Jason seemed happy enough to crawl back in bed with the mug of coffee and sugar, and prop himself up on the pillows while we talked.

I told him about Catfish's phone call, our to-and-fro with the police, the search of the yard and my conscription of his Benelli shotgun, which he immediately demanded to see.

'You fired it!' he said indignantly, after checking it over.

I just stared at him.

He flinched first. 'I guess it worked like a shotgun is 'spose to,' he said slowly. 'Since you're sitting here looking pretty much okay.'

'Thanks, and don't ask me again,' I said.

He nodded.

'Now we have to think of a story for the police.'

'I guess we can't just tell them the truth.'

'Sure, Jason, let's tell them that the village of Hotshot is full of were-panthers, and that since you slept with one, her boyfriend wanted to make you a were-panther, too, so she wouldn't prefer you over him. That's why he changed into a panther and bit you every day.'

There was a long pause.

'I can just see Andy Bellefleur's face,' Jason said in a

subdued kind of way. 'He still can't get over me being innocent of murdering those girls last year. He'd love to get me committed as being delusional. Catfish would have to fire me, and I don't think I'd like it at the mental hospital.'

'Well, your dating opportunities would sure be limited.'

'Crystal – God, that girl! You warned me. But I was so bowled over by her. And she turns out to be a . . . you know.'

'Oh, for goodness sake, Jason, she's a shape-shifter. Don't go on like she's the creature from the Black Lagoon, or Freddy Krueger, or something.'

'Sook, you know a lot of stuff we don't know, don't you? I'm getting that picture.'

'Yes, I guess so.'

'Besides vampires.'

'Right.'

'There's lots else.'

'I tried to tell you.'

'I believed what you said, but I just didn't get it. Some people I know – I mean besides Crystal – they're not always people, huh?'

'That's right.'

'Like how many?'

I counted up the two-natured I'd seen in the bar: Sam, Alcide, that little were-fox who'd been standing Jason and Hoyt drinks a couple of weeks ago . . . 'At least three,' I said.

'How do you know all this?'

I just stared at him.

'Right,' he said, after a long moment. 'I don't want to know.'

'And now, you,' I said gently.

'Are you sure?'

'No, and we won't be sure for a couple of weeks,' I said. 'But Calvin'll help you if you need it.'

'I won't take help from them!' Jason's eyes were blazing, and he looked positively feverish.

'You don't have a choice,' I said, trying not to snap. 'And Calvin didn't know you were there. He's an okay guy. But it's not even time to talk about it yet. We have to figure out what to tell the police right now.'

For at least an hour we went over and over our stories, trying to find threads of truth to help us stitch together a fabrication.

Finally, I called the police station. The day-shift dispatcher was tired of hearing my voice, but she was still trying to be nice. 'Sookie, like I told you yesterday, hon, we'll call you when we find out something about Jason,' she said, trying to suppress the note of exasperation beneath her soothing tone.

'I've got him,' I said.

'You – WHAT?' The shriek came over loud and clear. Even Jason winced.

'I've got him.'

'I'll send someone right over.'

'Good,' I said, though I didn't mean it.

I had the foresight to get the nails out of the front door before the police got there. I didn't want them asking what had happened to it. Jason had looked at me oddly when I got out the hammer, but he didn't say a word.

'Where's your car?' Andy Bellefleur asked first thing.

'It's at Merlotte's.'

'Why?'

'Can I just tell you and Alcee, together, one time?' Alcee

Beck was coming up the front steps. He and Andy came in the house together, and at the sight of Jason lying wrapped up on my couch, they both stopped dead in their tracks. I knew then that they'd never expected to see Jason alive again.

'Glad to see you safe and sound, man,' Andy said, and shook Jason's hand. Alcee Beck followed on his heels. They sat down, Andy in Gran's recliner and Alcee in the armchair I usually took, and I perched on the couch beside Jason's feet. 'We're glad you're in the land of the living, Jason, but we need to know where you've been and what happened to you.'

'I have no idea,' Jason said.

And he stuck to it for hours.

There had been no believable story Jason could tell that could account for everything: his absence, his poor physical condition, the bite marks, his sudden reappearance. The only possible line he could take was to say the last thing he remembered, he'd heard a funny noise outside while he was entertaining Crystal, and when he'd gone to investigate, he'd been hit on the head. He didn't remember anything until somehow he'd felt himself pushed from a vehicle to land in my yard the night before. I'd found him there when Sam brought me home from work. I'd ridden home with Sam because I was scared to drive in the snow.

Of course, we'd cleared this with Sam ahead of time, and he'd agreed, reluctantly, that it was the best we could come up with. I knew Sam didn't like to lie, and I didn't either, but we had to keep that particular can of worms closed.

The beauty of this story was its simplicity. As long as Jason could resist the temptation to embroider, he'd be safe. I'd known that would be hard for Jason; he loved to talk, and he loved to talk big. But as long as I was sitting there, reminding him of the consequences, my brother managed to restrain himself. I had to get up to get him another cup of coffee – the lawmen didn't want any more – and as I was coming back in the living room, Jason was saying he thought he remembered a cold dark room. I gave him a very plain look, and he said, 'But you know, my head is so confused, that may just be something I dreamed.'

Andy looked from Jason to me, clearly getting angrier and angrier. 'I just can't understand you two,' he said. His voice was almost a growl. 'Sookie, I know you worried about him. I'm not making that up, am I?'

'No, I am so glad to have him back.' I patted my brother's foot under the blanket.

'And you, you didn't want to be wherever you were, right? You missed work, you cost the parish thousands of dollars from our budget to search for you, and you disrupted the lives of hundreds of people. And you're sitting here lying to us!' Andy's voice was almost a shout as he finished. 'Now, the same night you show up, this missing vampire on all the posters called the police in Shreveport to say he's recovering from memory loss, too! And there's a strange fire in Shreveport with all kinds of bodies recovered! And you're trying to tell me there's no connection!'

Jason and I gaped at each other. Actually, there *was* no connection between Jason and Eric. It just hadn't occurred to me how strange that would look.

'What vampire?' Jason asked. It was so good, I almost believed him myself.

'Let's leave, Alcee,' Andy said. He slapped his notebook shut. He put his pen back in his shirt pocket with such an emphatic thrust that I was surprised he had a pocket left. 'This bastard won't even tell us the truth.'

'Don't you think I'd tell you if I could?' Jason said. 'Don't you think I'd like to lay hands on whoever did this to me?' He sounded absolutely, one hundred percent sincere, because he was. The two detectives were shaken in their disbelief, especially Alcee Beck. But they still left unhappy with the two of us. I felt sorry for it, but there was nothing I could do.

Later that day, Arlene picked me up so I could fetch my car from Merlotte's. She was happy to see Jason, and she gave him a big hug. 'You had your sister some kind of worried, you rascal,' she said, with mock ferocity. 'Don't you ever scare Sookie like that again.'

'I'll do my best,' Jason said, with a good approximation of his old roguish smile. 'She's been a good sister to me.'

'Now, that's God's truth,' I said, a little sourly. 'When I bring my car back, I think I might just run you home, big brother.'

Jason looked scared for a minute. Being alone had never been his favorite thing, and after hours by himself in the cold of the shed, it might be even harder.

'I bet girls all over Bon Temps are making food to bring to your place now that they heard you're back,' Arlene said, and Jason brightened perceptibly. ' 'Specially since I've been telling everyone what an invalid you are.'

'Thanks, Arlene,' Jason said, looking much more like himself.

I echoed that on the way into town. 'I really appreciate you cheering him up. I don't know what all he went through, but he's going to have a rough time getting over it, I think.'

'Honey, you don't need to worry about Jason. He's the original survivor. I don't know why he didn't try out for the show.'

We laughed all the way into town at the idea of staging a *Survivor* episode in Bon Temps.

'What with the razorbacks in the woods, and that panther print, they might have an exciting time of it if we had *Survivor: Bon Temps*,' Arlene said. 'Tack and me would just sit back and laugh at them.'

That gave me a nice opening to tease her about Tack, which she enjoyed, and altogether she cheered up me just as much as Jason. Arlene was good about stuff like that. I had a brief conversation with Sam in the storeroom of Merlotte's, and he told me Andy and Alcee had already been by to see if his story meshed with mine.

He hushed me before I could thank him again.

I took Jason home, though he hinted broadly he'd like to stay with me one more night. I took the Benelli with us, and I told him to clean it that evening. He promised he would, and when he looked at me, I could tell he wanted to ask me again why I'd had to use it. But he didn't. Jason had learned some things in the past few days, himself.

I was working the late shift again, so I would have a little time on my hands when I got home before I had to go in to work. The prospect felt good. I didn't see any running men on my way back to my house, and no one phoned or popped in with a crisis for a whole two hours. I was able to change the sheets on both beds, wash them, and sweep the kitchen and straighten up the closet concealing the hidey-hole, before the knock came at the front door.

I knew who it would be. It was full dark outside, and sure enough, Eric stood on my front porch.

He looked down at me with no very happy face. 'I find myself troubled,' he said without preamble.

'Then I've got to drop everything so I can help you out,' I said, going instantly on the offensive.

He cocked an eyebrow. 'I'll be polite and ask if I can come in.' I hadn't rescinded his invitation, but he didn't want to just stroll into my house. Tactful.

'Yes, you can.' I stepped back.

'Hallow is dead, having been forced to counter the curse on me, obviously.'

'Pam did a good job.'

He nodded. 'It was Hallow or me,' he said. 'I like me better.'

'Why'd she pick Shreveport?'

'Her parents were jailed in Shreveport. They were witches, too, but they also ran confidence games of some kind, using their craft to make their victims more convinced of their sincerity. In Shreveport, their luck ran out. The supernatural community refused to make any effort to get the older Stonebrooks out of jail. The woman ran afoul of a voodoo priestess while she was incarcerated, and the man ran afoul of a knife in some bathroom brawl.'

'Pretty good reason to have it in for the supernaturals of Shreveport.'

'They say I was here for several nights.' Eric had decided to change the subject.

'Yes,' I said. I tried to look agreeably interested in what he had to say.

'And in that time, we never . . . ?'

I didn't pretend to misunderstand him.

'Eric, does that seem likely?' I asked.

He hadn't sat down, and he moved closer to me, as if

looking at me hard would reveal the truth. It would have been easy to take a step, be even closer.

'I just don't know,' he said. 'And it's making me a little aggravated.'

I smiled. 'Are you enjoying being back at work?'

'Yes. But Pam ran everything well during my absence. I'm sending lots of flowers to the hospital. Belinda, and a wolf named Maria-Comet or something.'

'Maria-Star Cooper. You didn't send any to me,' I pointed out tartly.

'No, but I left you something more meaningful under the saltshaker,' he said, with much the same edge. 'You'll have to pay taxes on it. If I know you, you'll give your brother some of it. I hear you got him back.'

'I did,' I said briefly. I knew I was getting closer to bursting out with something, and I knew he should leave soon. I'd given Jason such good advice about being quiet, but it was hard to follow it myself. 'And your point is?'

'It won't last for long.'

I don't think Eric realized how much money fifty thousand dollars was, by my standards. 'What's your point? I can tell you have one, but I don't have an idea what it might be.'

'Was there a reason I found brain tissue on my coat sleeve?'

I felt all the blood drain from my face, the way it does when you're on the edge of passing out. The next thing I knew, I was on the couch and Eric was beside me.

'I think there are some things you're not telling me, Sookie, my dear,' he said. His voice was gentler, though.

The temptation was almost overwhelming.

But I thought of the power Eric would have over me, even more power than he had now; he would know I had slept with him, and he would know that I had killed a woman and he was the only one who'd witnessed it. He would know that not only did he owe me his life (most likely), I certainly owed him mine.

'I liked you a lot better when you didn't remember who you were,' I said, and with that truth forefront in my mind, I knew I had to keep quiet.

'Harsh words,' he said, and I almost believed he was really hurt.

Luckily for me, someone else came to my door. The knock was loud and peremptory, and I felt a jolt of alarm.

The caller was Amanda, the insulting redheaded female Were from Shreveport. 'I'm on official business today,' she said, 'so I'll be polite.'

That would be a nice change.

She nodded to Eric and said, 'Glad to have you back in your right mind, vampire,' in a completely unconcerned tone. I could see that the Weres and vampires of Shreveport had reverted to their old relationship.

'And good to see you, too, Amanda,' I said.

'Sure,' she said, but hardly as if she cared. 'Miss Stackhouse, we're making inquiries for the shifters of Jackson.'

Oh, no. 'Really? Won't you please sit down? Eric was just leaving.'

'No, I'd love to stay and hear Amanda's questions,' Eric said, beaming.

Amanda looked at me, eyebrows raised.

There wasn't a hell of a lot I could do about it.

'Oh, by all means, stay,' I said. 'Please sit down, both of you. I'm sorry, but I don't have a lot of time before I'm due at work.'

'Then I'll get right to the point,' Amanda said. 'Two nights ago, the woman that Alcide abjured – the shifter from Jackson, the one with the weird haircut?'

I nodded, to show I was on the same page. Eric looked pleasantly blank. He wouldn't in a minute.

'Debbie,' the Were recalled. 'Debbie Pelt.'

Eric's eyes widened. Now, that name he did know. He began to smile.

'Alcide abjured her?' he said.

'You were sitting right there,' snapped Amanda. 'Oh, wait, I forgot. That was while you were *under a curse.*'

She enjoyed the hell out of saying that.

'Anyway, Debbie didn't make it back to Jackson. Her family is worried about her, especially since they heard that Alcide abjured her, and they're afraid something might have happened to her.'

'Why do you think she would have said anything to me?'

Amanda made a face. 'Well, actually, I think she would rather have eaten glass than talked to you again. But we're obliged to check with everyone who was there.'

So this was just routine. I wasn't being singled out. I could feel myself relax. Unfortunately, so could Eric. I'd had his blood; he could tell things about me. He got up and wandered back to the kitchen. I wondered what he was doing.

'I haven't seen her since that night,' I said, which was true, since I didn't specify what time. 'I have no idea where she is now.' That was even truer.

Amanda told me, 'No one admits to having seen Debbie after she left the area of the battle. She drove off in her own car.'

Eric strolled back into the living room. I glanced at him, worried about what he was up to.

'Has her car been seen?' Eric asked.

He didn't know he'd been the one who'd hidden it.

'No, neither hide nor hair,' Amanda said, which was a strange image to use for a car. 'I'm sure she just ran off somewhere to get over her rage and humiliation. Being abjured; that's pretty awful. It's been years since I've heard the words said.'

'Her family doesn't think that's the case? That's she's gone somewhere to, ah, think things over?'

'They're afraid she's done something to herself.' Amanda snorted. We exchanged glances, showing we agreed perfectly about the likelihood of Debbie committing suicide. 'She wouldn't do anything that convenient,' Amanda said, since she had the nerve to say it out loud and I didn't.

'How's Alcide taking this?' I asked anxiously.

'He can hardly join in the search,' she pointed out, 'since he's the one who abjured her. He acts like he doesn't care, but I notice the colonel calls him to let him know what's happening. Which, so far, is nothing.' Amanda heaved herself to her feet, and I got up to walk her to the door. 'This sure has been a bad season for people going missing,' she said. 'But I hear through the grapevine that you got your brother back, and Eric's returned to his normal self, looks like.' She cast him a glance to make sure he knew how little she liked that normal self. 'Now Debbie has gone missing, but maybe she'll turn up, too. Sorry I had to bother you.'

'That's all right. Good luck,' I said, which was meaningless under the circumstances. The door closed behind her, and I wished desperately that I could just walk out and get in my car and drive to work.

I made myself turn around. Eric was standing.

'You're going?' I said, unable to keep from sounding startled and relieved.

'Yes, you said you had to get to work,' he said blandly.

'I do.'

'I suggest you wear that jacket, the one that's too light for the weather,' he said. 'Since your coat is still in bad shape.'

I'd run it through the washer on cold water wash, but I guess I hadn't checked it well enough to be sure everything had come off. That's where he'd been, searching for my coat. He'd found it on its hanger on the back porch, and examined it.

'In fact,' Eric said, as he went to the front door, 'I'd throw it away entirely. Maybe burn it.'

He left, closing the door behind him very quietly.

I knew, as sure as I knew my name, that tomorrow he would send me another coat, in a big fancy box, with a big bow on it. It would be the right size, it would be a top brand, and it would be warm.

It was cranberry red, with a removable liner, a detachable hood, and tortoiseshell buttons.

DEFINITELY DEAD

Also by Charlaine Harris

SOOKIE STACKHOUSE

Dead Until Dark

Living Dead in Dallas

Club Dead

Dead to the World

Dead as a Doornail

Definitely Dead

All Together Dead

From Dead to Worse

Dead and Gone

HARPER CONNELLY

Grave Sight

Grave Surprise

An Ice Cold Grave

Grave Secret

DEFINITELY DEAD

CHARLAINE HARRIS

First published in Great Britain in 2007 by
Gollancz
An imprint of the Orion Publishing Group
Orion House, 5 Upper St Martin's Lane, London WC2H 9EA
An Hachette UK Company

This edition published in Great Britain in 2009 by
Gollancz

7 9 10 8 6

A CIP catalogue record for this book
is available from the British Library

ISBN 978 0 575 09104 7

Printed and bound in the UK by
CPI Mackays, Chatham ME5 8TD

www.orionbooks.co.uk

Obviously, this book was finished months before Hurricane Katrina struck the Gulf Coast. Since much of the plot is set in New Orleans, I struggled with whether I would leave *Definitely Dead* as it was, or include the catastrophe of August and September. After much thought, since Sookie's visit takes place in the early spring of the year, I decided to let the book remain as it was originally written.

My heart goes out to the people of the beautiful city of New Orleans and to all the people of the coastal areas of Mississippi, my home state. My thoughts and prayers will be with you as you rebuild your homes and your lives.

ACKNOWLEDGMENTS

My thanks to so many people: Jerrilyn Farmer's son's Latin teacher; Toni L.P. Kelner and Steve Kelner, friends and sounding boards; Ivan Van Laningham, who has both knowledge and opinions about many, many subjects; Dr. Stacy Clanton, about whom I can say the same; Alexandre Dumas, author of the fabulous *The Three Musketeers*, which everyone ought to read; Anne Rice, for vampirizing New Orleans; and to the reader at Uncle Hugo's who guessed the plot of this book in advance . . . hats off to you all!

DEFINITELY DEAD

1

I WAS DRAPED OVER THE ARM OF ONE OF THE MOST beautiful men I'd ever seen, and he was staring into my eyes. "Think . . . Brad Pitt," I whispered. The dark brown eyes still regarded me with remote interest.

Okay, I was on the wrong track.

I pictured Claude's last lover, a bouncer at a strip joint.

"Think about Charles Bronson," I suggested. "Or, um, Edward James Olmos." I was rewarded by the beginnings of a hot glow in those long-lashed eyes.

In a jiffy, you would've thought Claude was going to hike up my long rustling skirt and yank down my low-cut push-up bodice and ravish me until I begged for mercy. Unfortunately for me—and all the other women of Louisiana—Claude batted for another team. Bosomy and blond was not

Claude's ideal; tough, rough, and brooding, with maybe a little whisker stubble, was what lit his fire.

"Maria-Star, reach in there and pull that lock of hair back," Alfred Cumberland directed from behind the camera. The photographer was a heavyset black man with graying hair and mustache. Maria-Star Cooper took a quick step in front of the camera to rearrange a stray strand of my long blond hair. I was bent backward over Claude's right arm, my invisible (to the camera, anyway) left hand desperately clutching the back of his black frock coat, my right arm raised to rest gently on his left shoulder. His left hand was at my waist. I think the pose was meant to suggest that he was lowering me to the ground to have his way with me.

Claude was wearing the black frock coat with black knee pants, white hose, and a white frothy shirt. I was wearing a long blue dress with a billowing skirt and a score of petticoats. As I've mentioned, the dress was scanty on the topside, with the little sleeves pushed down off my shoulders. I was glad the temperature in the studio was moderately warm. The big light (it looked to my eyes like a satellite dish) was not as hot as I'd expected.

Al Cumberland was snapping away as Claude smoldered down at me. I did my best to smolder right back. My personal life had been, shall we say, *barren* for the past few weeks, so I was all too ready to smolder. In fact, I was ready to burst into flames.

Maria-Star, who had beautiful light-toast skin and curly dark hair, was standing ready with a big makeup case and brushes and combs to perform last-minute repairs. When Claude and I had arrived at the studio, I'd been surprised to find that I recognized the photographer's young assistant. I hadn't seen Maria-Star since the Shreveport packleader had been chosen a few weeks before. I hadn't had much of a chance to observe her then, since the packmaster contest had been frightening and bloody. Today, I had the leisure to see that Maria-Star had completely recovered from being hit by a car this past January. Werewolves healed quickly.

Maria-Star had recognized me, too, and I'd been relieved when she smiled back at me. My standing with the Shreveport pack was, to say the least, uncertain. Without exactly volunteering to do so, I'd unwittingly thrown in my lot with the unsuccessful contestant for the packleader's job. That contestant's son, Alcide Herveaux, whom I'd counted as maybe more than a friend, felt I'd let him down during the contest; the new packleader, Patrick Furnan, knew I had ties to the Herveaux family. I'd been surprised when Maria-Star chatted away while she was zipping the costume and brushing my hair. She applied more makeup than I'd ever worn in my life, but when I stared into the mirror I had to thank her. I looked great, though I didn't look like Sookie Stackhouse.

If Claude hadn't been gay, he might have been impressed, too. He's the brother of my friend Claudine, and he makes his living stripping on ladies' night at Hooligans, a club he now owns. Claude is simply mouthwatering; six feet tall, with rippling black hair and large brown eyes, a perfect nose, and lips just full enough. He keeps his hair long to cover up his ears: they've been surgically altered to look rounded like human ears, not pointed as they originally were. If you're in the know supernaturally, you'll spot the ear surgery, and you'll know Claude is a fairy. I'm not using the pejorative term for his sexual orientation. I mean it literally; Claude's a fairy.

"Now the wind machine," Al instructed Maria-Star, and after a little repositioning, she switched on a large fan. Now we appeared to be standing in a gale. My hair billowed out in a blond sheet, though Claude's tied-back ponytail stayed in place. After a few shots to capture that look, Maria-Star unbound Claude's hair and directed it over one shoulder, so it would blow forward to form a backdrop for his perfect profile.

"Wonderful," Al said, and snapped some more. Maria-Star moved the machine a couple of times, causing the windstorm to strike from different directions. Eventually Al told me I could stand up. I straightened gratefully.

"I hope that wasn't too hard on your arm," I told Claude, who was looking cool and calm again.

"Nah, no problem. You have any fruit juice around?" he asked Maria-Star. Claude was not Mr. Social Skills.

The pretty Were pointed to a little refrigerator in the corner of the studio. "Cups are on the top," she told Claude. She followed him with her eyes and sighed. Women frequently did that after they'd actually talked to Claude. The sigh was a "what a pity" sigh.

After checking to make sure her boss was still fiddling intently with his gear, Maria-Star gave me a bright smile. Even though she was a Were, which made her thoughts hard to read, I was picking up on the fact that she had something she wanted to tell me . . . and she wasn't sure how I was going to take it.

Telepathy is no fun. Your opinion of yourself suffers when you know what others think of you. And telepathy makes it almost impossible to date regular guys. Just think about it. (And remember, I'll know—if you are, or if you aren't.)

"Alcide's had a hard time of it since his dad was defeated," Maria-Star said, keeping her voice low. Claude was occupied with studying himself in a mirror while he drank his juice. Al Cumberland had gotten a call on his cell phone and retreated to his office to hold his conversation.

"I'm sure he has," I said. Since Jackson Herveaux's opponent had killed him, it was only to be expected that Jackson's son was having his ups and his downs. "I sent a memorial to the ASPCA, and I know they'll notify Alcide and Janice," I said. (Janice was Alcide's younger sister, which made her a non-Were. I wondered how Alcide had explained their father's death to his sister.) In acknowledgment, I'd received a printed thank-you note, the kind the funeral home gives you, without one personal word written on it.

"Well . . ." She seemed to be unable to spit it out, whatever was stuck in her throat. I was getting a glimpse of the shape of it. Pain flickered through me like a knife, and then I locked it down and pulled my pride around me. I'd learned to do that all too early in life.

I picked an album of samples of Alfred's work and began to flip through them, hardly looking at the photographs of brides and grooms, bar mitzvahs, first communions, twenty-fifth wedding anniversaries. I closed that album and laid it down. I was trying to look casual, but I don't think it worked.

With a bright smile that echoed Maria-Star's own expression, I said, "Alcide and I weren't ever truly a couple, you know." I might have had longings and hopes, but they'd never had a chance to ripen. The timing had always been wrong.

Maria-Star's eyes, a much lighter brown than Claude's, widened in awe. Or was it fear? "I heard you could do that," she said. "But it's hard to believe."

"Yeah," I said wearily. "Well, I'm glad you and Alcide are dating, and I have no right to mind, even if I did. Which I don't." That came out kind of garbled (and it wasn't entirely true), but I think Maria-Star got my intention: to save my face.

When I hadn't heard from Alcide in the weeks following his father's death, I'd known that whatever feelings he'd had for me were quenched. That had been a blow, but not a fatal one. Realistically, I hadn't expected anything more from Alcide. But gosh darn it, I liked him, and it always smarts when you find out you've been replaced with apparent ease. After all, before his dad's death Alcide had suggested we live together. Now he was shacking up with this young Were, maybe planning to have puppies with her.

I stopped that line of thought in its tracks. Shame on me! No point in being a bitch. (Which, come to think of it, Maria-Star actually was, at least three nights a month.)

Double shame on me.

"I hope you're very happy," I said.

She wordlessly handed me another album, this one stamped EYES ONLY. When I opened it, I realized that the Eyes were supernatural. Here were pictures of ceremonies humans never got to see . . . a vampire couple dressed in elaborate costume, posed before a giant ankh; a young man in the middle of changing into a bear, presumably for the first time; a shot of a Were pack with all its members in wolf form. Al Cumberland, photographer of the weird. No wonder he had been Claude's first choice for his pictures, which Claude hoped would launch him on a cover-model career.

"Next shot," called Al, as he bustled out of his office, snapping his phone shut. "Maria-Star, we just got booked for a double wedding in Miss Stackhouse's neck of the woods." I wondered if he'd been engaged for regular human work or for a supernatural event, but it would be rude to ask.

Claude and I got up close and personal again. Following Al's instructions, I pulled up the skirt to display my legs. In the era my dress represented, I didn't think women tanned or shaved their legs, and I was brown and smooth as a baby's bottom. But what the hey. Probably guys hadn't walked around with their shirts unbuttoned, either.

"Raise your leg like you're going to wrap it around him," Alfred directed. "Now Claude, this is your chance to shine. Look like you're going to pull your pants off at any second. We want the readers to pant when they look at you!"

Claude's portfolio of shots would be used when he entered the Mr. Romance competition, orchestrated each year by *Romantic Times Bookclub* magazine.

When he'd shared his ambition with Al (I gathered they'd met at a party), Al had advised Claude to have some pictures made with the sort of woman that often appeared on the cover of romance novels; he'd told the fairy that Claude's dark looks would be set off by a blue-eyed blonde. I happened to be the only bosomy blonde of Claude's acquaintance who was willing to help him for free. Of course, Claude knew some strippers who would have done it, but they expected to be paid. With his usual tact, Claude had told me this on our way to the photographer's studio. Claude could have kept these details to himself, which would have left me feeling good about helping out my friend's brother—but in typical Claude fashion, he shared.

"Okay, Claude, now off with the shirt," Alfred called.

Claude was used to being asked to take off his clothes. He had a broad, hairless chest with impressive musculature, so he looked very nice indeed without his shirt. I was unmoved. Maybe I was becoming immune.

"Skirt, leg," Alfred reminded me, and I told myself that this was a job. Al and Maria-Star were certainly professional and impersonal, and you couldn't get cooler than Claude. But I wasn't used to pulling my skirt up in front of people, and it felt pretty personal to me. Though I showed this much leg when I wore shorts and never raised a blush, somehow the pulling up of the long skirt was a little more loaded with sexuality. I clenched my teeth and hiked up the material, tucking it at intervals so it would stay in position.

"Miss Stackhouse, you have to look like you're enjoying this," Al said. He peered at me from around his camera, his forehead creased in a definitely unhappy way.

I tried not to sulk. I'd told Claude I'd do him a favor, and favors should be done willingly. I raised my leg so my thigh was parallel with the floor, and pointed my bare toes to the floor in what I hoped was a graceful position. I put both hands on Claude's naked shoulders and looked up at him. His skin felt warm and smooth to the touch—not erotic or arousing.

"You look *bored*, Miss Stackhouse," Alfred said. "You're

supposed to look like you want to jump his bones. Maria-Star, make her look more . . . more." Maria darted over to push the little puff sleeves farther down my arms. She got a little too enthusiastic, and I was glad the bodice was tight.

The fact of the matter was, Claude could look beautiful and bare all day long, and I still wouldn't want him. He was grumpy and he had bad manners. Even if he'd been hetero, he wouldn't have been my cup of tea—after I'd had ten minutes' conversation with him.

Like Claude earlier, I'd have to resort to fantasy.

I thought of Bill the vampire, my first love in every way. But instead of lust, I felt anger. Bill was dating another woman, had been for a few weeks.

Okay, what about Eric, Bill's boss, the former Viking? Eric the vampire had shared my house and my bed for a few days in January. Nope, that way lay danger. Eric knew a secret I wanted to keep hidden for the rest of my days; though, since he'd had amnesia when he'd stayed at my place, he wasn't aware it was in his memory somewhere.

A few other faces popped into my mind—my boss, Sam Merlotte, the owner of Merlotte's Bar. No, don't go there, thinking about your boss naked is *bad.* Okay, Alcide Herveaux? Nope, that was a no-go, especially since I was in the company of his current girlfriend. . . . Okay, I was clean out of fantasy material and would have to fall back on one of my old fictional favorites.

But movie stars seemed bland after the supernatural world I'd inhabited since Bill came into Merlotte's. The last remotely erotic experience I'd had, oddly enough, had involved my bleeding leg getting licked. That had been . . . unsettling. But even under the circumstances, it had made things deep inside me twitch. I remembered how Quinn's bald head had moved while he cleaned my scrape in a very personal way, the firm grip his big warm fingers had had on my leg. . . .

"That'll do," Alfred said, and began snapping away. Claude put his hand on my bare thigh when he could feel my muscles begin to tremble from the effort of holding the position. Once again, a man had a hold of my leg. Claude gripped my thigh enough to give it some support. That helped considerably, but it wasn't a bit erotic.

"Now some bed shots," Al said, just when I'd decided I couldn't stand it any more.

"No," Claude and I said in chorus.

"But that's part of the package," Al said. "You don't need to undress, you know. I don't do that kind of picture. My wife would kill me. You just lie down on the bed like you are. Claude hikes up on one elbow and looks down at you, Miss Stackhouse."

"No," I said firmly. "Take some pictures of him standing by himself in the water. That would be better." There was a fake pond over in the corner, and shots of Claude, apparently naked, dripping water over his bare chest, would be extremely appealing (to any woman who hadn't actually met him).

"How does that grab you, Claude?" Al asked.

Claude's narcissism chimed in. "I think that would be great, Al," he said, trying not to sound too excited.

I started for the changing room, eager to shed the costume and get back into my regular jeans. I glanced around for a clock. I was due at work at five-thirty, and I had to drive back to Bon Temps and grab my work uniform before I went to Merlotte's.

Claude called, "Thanks, Sookie."

"Sure, Claude. Good luck with the modeling contracts." But he was already admiring himself in a mirror.

Maria-Star saw me out. "Goodbye, Sookie. It was good to see you again."

"You, too," I lied. Even through the reddish twisted passages of a Were mind, I could see that Maria-Star couldn't understand why I would pass up Alcide. After all, the Were was handsome in a rugged way, an entertaining companion, and a hot-blooded male of the heterosexual persuasion. Also, he now owned his own surveying company and was a wealthy man in his own right.

The answer popped into my head and I spoke before I thought. "Is anyone still looking for Debbie Pelt?" I asked, much the same way you poke a sore tooth. Debbie had been Alcide's longtime on-again, off-again lover. She'd been a piece of work.

"Not the same people," Maria-Star said. Her expression darkened. Maria-Star didn't like thinking about Debbie any more than I did, though doubtless for different reasons. "The detectives the Pelt family hired gave up, said they'd be fleecing the family if they'd kept on. That's what I heard. The police didn't exactly say it, but they'd reached a dead end, too. I've only met the Pelts once, when they came over to Shreveport right after Debbie disappeared. They're a pretty savage couple." I blinked. This was a fairly drastic statement, coming from a Were.

"Sandra, their daughter, is the worst. She was nuts about Debbie, and for her sake they're still consulting people, some way-out people. Myself, I think Debbie got abducted. Or maybe she killed herself. When Alcide abjured her, maybe she lost it big-time."

"Maybe," I murmured, but without conviction.

"He's better off. I hope she stays missing," Maria-Star said.

My opinion had been the same, but unlike Maria-Star, I knew exactly what had happened to Debbie; that was the wedge that had pushed Alcide and me apart.

"I hope he never sees her again," Maria-Star said, her pretty face dark and showing a little bit of her own savage side.

Alcide might be dating Maria-Star, but he hadn't confided in her fully. Alcide knew for a fact that he would never see Debbie again. And that was my fault, okay?

I'd shot her dead.

I'd more or less made my peace with my act, but the stark fact of it kept popping back up. There's no way you can kill someone and get to the other side of the experience unchanged. The consequences alter your life.

Two priests walked into the bar.

This sounds like the opening of a million jokes. But these priests didn't have a kangaroo with them, and there was not a rabbi sitting at the bar, or a blonde, either. I'd seen plenty of blondes, one kangaroo in a zoo, no rabbis. However, I'd seen these two priests plenty of times before. They had a standing appointment to have dinner together every other week.

Father Dan Riordan, clean shaven and ruddy, was the Catholic priest who came to the little Bon Temps church once a week on Saturday to celebrate mass, and Father Kempton Littrell, pale and bearded, was the Episcopal priest who held Holy Eucharist in the tiny Episcopal church in Clarice once every two weeks.

"Hello, Sookie," Father Riordan said. He was Irish; really Irish, not just of Irish extraction. I loved to hear him talk. He wore thick glasses with black frames, and he was in his forties.

"Evening, Father. And hi to you, Father Littrell. What can I get you all?"

"I'd like Scotch on the rocks, Miss Sookie. And you, Kempton?"

"Oh, I'll just have a beer. And a basket of chicken strips, please." The Episcopal priest wore gold-rimmed glasses, and he was younger than Father Riordan. He had a conscientious heart.

"Sure." I smiled at the two of them. Since I could read their thoughts, I knew them both to be genuinely good men, and that made me happy. It's always disconcerting to hear the contents of a minister's head and find out they're no better than you, and not only that, they're not trying to be.

Since it was full dark outside, I wasn't surprised when Bill Compton walked in. I couldn't say the same for the priests. The churches of America hadn't come to grips with the reality of vampires. To call their policies confused was putting it mildly. The Catholic Church was at this moment holding a convocation to decide whether the church would declare all vampires damned and anathema to Catholics, or accept them into the fold as potential converts. The Episcopal Church had voted against accepting vampires as priests, though they were allowed to take communion—but a substantial slice of the laity said that would be over their dead bodies. Unfortunately, most of them didn't comprehend how possible that was.

Both the priests watched unhappily as Bill gave me a quick kiss on the cheek and settled at his favorite table. Bill barely gave them a glance, but unfolded his newspaper and began to read. He always looked serious, as if he were studying the financial pages or the news from Iraq; but I knew he read the advice columns first, and then the comics, though he often didn't get the jokes.

Bill was by himself, which was a nice change. Usually, he brought the lovely Selah Pumphrey. I loathed her. Since Bill had been my first love and my first lover, maybe I would never be completely over him. Maybe he didn't want me to be. He did seem to drag Selah into Merlotte's every single date they had. I figured he was waving her in my face. Not exactly what you did if you didn't care any more, huh?

Without his having to ask, I took him his favorite beverage, TrueBlood type O. I set it neatly in front of him on a napkin, and I'd turned to go when a cool hand touched my arm. His touch always jolted me; maybe it always would. Bill had always made it clear I aroused him, and after a lifetime of no relationships and no sex, I began walking tall when Bill made it clear he found me attractive. Other men had looked at me as if I'd become more interesting, too. Now I knew why people thought about sex so much; Bill had given me a thorough education.

"Sookie, stay for a moment." I looked down into brown eyes, which looked all the darker in Bill's white face. His hair was brown, too, smooth and sleek. He was slim and broad-shouldered, his arms hard with muscles, like the farmer he had been. "How have you been?"

"I'm fine," I said, trying not to sound surprised. It wasn't often Bill passed the time of day; small talk wasn't his strong point. Even when we'd been a couple, he had not been what you'd call chatty. And even a vampire can be a workaholic; Bill had become a computer geek. "Have things been well with you?"

"Yes. When will you go to New Orleans to claim your inheritance?"

Now I was truly startled. (This is possible because I can't read vampire minds. That's why I like vampires so much. It's wonderful to be with someone who's a mystery to me.) My cousin had been murdered almost six weeks ago in New Orleans, and Bill had been with me when the Queen of Louisiana's emissary had come to tell me about it . . . and to deliver the murderer to me for my judgment. "I guess I'll go through Hadley's apartment sometime in the next month or so. I haven't talked to Sam about taking the time off."

"I'm sorry you lost your cousin. Have you been grieving?"

I hadn't seen Hadley in years, and it would have been stranger than I can say to see her after she'd become a vampire. But as a person with very few living relations, I hated to lose even one. "A bit," I said.

"You don't know when you might go?"

"I haven't decided. You remember her lawyer, Mr. Cataliades? He said he'd tell me when the will had gone through probate. He promised to keep the place intact for me, and when the queen's counselor tells you the place'll be intact, you have to believe it'll be untouched. I haven't really been too interested, to tell you the truth."

"I might go with you when you head to New Orleans, if you don't mind having a traveling companion."

"Gee," I said, with just a dash of sarcasm, "Won't Selah mind? Or were you going to bring her, too?" That would make for a merry trip.

"No." And he closed down. You just couldn't get anything out of Bill when he was holding his mouth like that, I knew from experience. Okay, color me confused.

"I'll let you know," I said, trying to figure him out. Though it was painful to be in Bill's company, I trusted him. Bill would never harm me. He wouldn't let anyone else harm me, either. But there's more than one kind of harm.

"Sookie," Father Littrell called, and I hurried away.

I glanced back to catch Bill smiling, a small smile with a lot of satisfaction packed into it. I wasn't sure what it meant, but I liked to see Bill smile. Maybe he was hoping to revive our relationship?

Father Littrell said, "We weren't sure if you wanted to be interrupted or not." I looked down at him, confused.

"We were a tad concerned to see you consorting with the vampire for so long, and so intently," Father Riordan said. "Was the imp of hell trying to bring you under his spell?"

Suddenly his Irish accent wasn't charming at all. I looked at Father Riordan quizzically. "You're joking, right? You know Bill and I dated for a good while. Obviously, you don't know much about imps from hell if you believe Bill's anything like one." I'd seen things *much* darker than Bill in and about our fair town of Bon Temps. Some of those things had been human. "Father Riordan, I understand my own life. I understand the nature of vampires better than you ever will. Father Littrell," I said, "you want honey mustard or ketchup with your chicken strips?"

Father Littrell chose honey mustard, in a kind of dazed way. I walked away, working to shrug the little incident off, wondering what the two priests would do if they knew what had happened in this bar a couple of months before when the bar's clientele had ganged up to rid me of someone who was trying to kill me.

Since that someone had been a vampire, they'd probably have approved.

Before he left, Father Riordan came over to "have a word" with me. "Sookie, I know you're not real happy with me at the moment, but I need to ask you something on behalf of someone else. If I've made you less inclined to listen by my behavior, please ignore that and give these people the same consideration you would have."

I sighed. At least Father Riordan tried to be a good man. I nodded reluctantly.

"Good girl. A family in Jackson has contacted me . . ."

All my alarms started going off. Debbie Pelt was from Jackson.

"The Pelt family, I know you've heard of them. They're still searching for news of their daughter, who vanished in January. Debbie, her name was. They called me because their priest knows me, knows I serve the Bon Temps congregation. The Pelts would like to come to see you, Sookie. They want to talk to everyone who saw their daughter the night she vanished, and they feared if they just showed up on your doorstep, you might not see them. They're afraid you're angry because their private detectives have interviewed you, and the police have talked to you, and maybe you might be indignant about all that."

"I don't want to see them," I said. "Father Riordan, I've told everything I know." That was true. I just hadn't told it to the police or the Pelts. "I don't want to talk about Debbie any more." That was also true, very true. "Tell them, with all due respect, there's nothing left to talk about."

"I'll tell them," he said. "But I've got to say, Sookie, I'm disappointed."

"Well, I guess it's been a bad night for me all around," I said. "Losing your good opinion, and all."

He left without another word, which was exactly what I'd wanted.

2

IT WAS CLOSE TO CLOSING TIME THE NEXT NIGHT WHEN another odd thing happened. Just as Sam gave us the signal to start telling our customers this would be their last drink, someone I thought I'd never see again came into Merlotte's.

He moved quietly for such a large man. He stood just inside the door, looking around for a free table, and I noticed him because of the quick gleam of the dim bar light on his shaven head. He was very tall, and very wide, with a proud nose and big white teeth. He had full lips and an olive complexion, and he was wearing a sort of bronze sports jacket over a black shirt and slacks. Though he would have looked more natural in motorcycle boots, he was wearing polished loafers.

"Quinn," Sam said quietly. His hands became still,

though he'd been in the middle of mixing a Tom Collins. "What is he doing here?"

"I didn't know you knew him," I said, feeling my face flush as I realized I'd been thinking about the bald man only the day before. He'd been the one who'd cleaned the blood from my leg with his tongue—an interesting experience.

"Everyone in my world knows Quinn," Sam said, his face neutral. "But I'm surprised you've met him, since you're not a shifter." Unlike Quinn, Sam's not a big man; but he's very strong, as shifters tend to be, and his curly red-gold hair haloes his head in an angelic way.

"I met Quinn at the contest for packmaster," I said. "He was the, ah, emcee." Naturally, Sam and I had talked about the change of leadership in the Shreveport pack. Shreveport isn't too far from Bon Temps, and what the Weres do is pretty important if you're any kind of a shifter.

A true shape-shifter, like Sam, can change into anything, though each shape-shifter has a favorite animal. And to confuse the issue, all those who can change from human form to animal form call themselves shape-shifters, though very few possess Sam's versatility. Shifters who can change to only one animal are were-animals: weretigers (like Quinn), werebears, werewolves. The wolves are the only ones who call themselves simply Weres, and they consider themselves superior in toughness and culture to any of the other shape-shifters.

Weres are also the most numerous subset of shifters, though compared to the total vampire population, there are mighty few of them. There are several reasons for this. The Were birthrate is low, infant mortality is higher than in the general population of humans, and only the first child born of a pure Were couple becomes a full Were. That happens during puberty—as if puberty weren't bad enough already.

Shape-shifters are very secretive. It's a hard habit to break, even around a sympathetic and strange human like me. The shifters have not come into the public view yet, and I'm learning about their world in little increments.

Even Sam has many secrets that I don't know, and I count him as a friend. Sam turns into a collie, and he often visits me in that form. (Sometimes he sleeps on the rug by my bed.)

I'd only seen Quinn in his human form.

I hadn't mentioned Quinn when I told Sam about the fight between Jackson Herveaux and Patrick Furnan for the Shreveport pack leadership. Sam was frowning at me now, displeased that I'd kept it from him, but I hadn't done it purposely. I glanced back at Quinn. He'd lifted his nose a little. He was sampling the air, following a scent. Who was he trailing?

When Quinn went unerringly to a table in my section, despite the many empty ones in the closer section that Arlene was working, I knew he was trailing me.

Okay, mixed feelings on that.

I glanced sideways at Sam to get his reaction. I had trusted him for five years now, and he had never failed me.

Now Sam nodded at me. He didn't look happy, though. "Go see what he wants," he said, his voice so low it was almost a growl.

I got more and more nervous the closer I came to the new customer. I could feel my cheeks redden. Why was I getting so flustered?

"Hello, Mr. Quinn," I said. It would be stupid to pretend I didn't recognize him. "What can I get you? I'm afraid we're about to close, but I have time to serve you a beer or a drink."

He closed his eyes and took a deep breath, as if he were inhaling me. "I'd recognize you in a pitch-black room," he said, and he smiled at me. It was a broad and beautiful smile.

I looked off in another direction, pinching back the involuntary grin that rose to my lips. I was acting sort of . . . shy.

I never acted shy. Or maybe *coy* would be a better term, and one I disliked. "I guess I should say thank you," I ventured cautiously. "That's a compliment?"

"Intended as one. Who's the dog behind the bar who's giving me the stay-away look?"

He meant *dog* as a statement of fact, not as a derogatory term.

"That's my boss, Sam Merlotte."

"He has an interest in you."

"I should hope so. I've worked for him for round about five years."

"Hmmm. How about a beer?"

"Sure. What kind?"

"Bud."

"Coming right up," I said, and turned to go. I knew he watched me all the way to the bar because I could feel his gaze. And I knew from his mind, though his was a closely guarded shifter mind, that he was watching me with admiration.

"What does he want?" Sam looked almost . . . bristly. If he'd been in dog form, the hair on his back would have been standing up.

"A Bud," I said.

Sam scowled at me. "That's not what I meant, and you know it."

I shrugged. I had no idea what Quinn wanted.

Sam slammed the full glass down on the bar right by my fingers, making me jump. I gave him a steady look to make sure he noted that I'd been displeased, and then I took the beer to Quinn.

Quinn gave me the cost of the beer and a good tip—not a ridiculously high one, which would have made me feel bought—which I slipped into my pocket. I began making the rounds of my other tables. "You visiting someone in this area?" I asked Quinn as I passed him on my way back from clearing another table. Most of the patrons were paying up and drifting out of Merlotte's. There was an afterhours place that Sam pretended he didn't know about, way out in the country, but most of the Merlotte's regulars would be going home to bed. If a bar could be family-oriented, Merlotte's was.

"Yes," he said. "You."

That left me with nowhere to go, conversationally.

I kept on going and unloaded the glasses from my tray so absently that I almost dropped one. I couldn't think of when I'd been so flustered.

"Business or personal?" I asked, the next time I was close.

"Both," he said.

A little of the pleasure drained away when I heard about the business part, but I was left with a sharpened attention . . . and that was a good thing. You needed all your wits honed when you dealt with the supes. Supernatural beings had goals and desires that regular people didn't fathom. I knew that, since for my entire life I have been the unwilling repository for human, "normal," goals and desires.

When Quinn was one of the few people left in the bar—besides the other barmaids and Sam—he stood and looked at me expectantly. I went over, smiling brightly, as I do when I'm tense. I was interested to find that Quinn was almost equally tense. I could feel the tightness in his brain pattern.

"I'll see you at your house, if that's agreeable to you." He looked down at me seriously. "If that makes you nervous, we can meet somewhere else. But I want to talk to you tonight, unless you're exhausted."

That had been put politely enough. Arlene and Danielle were trying hard not to stare—well, they were trying hard to stare when Quinn wouldn't catch them—but Sam had turned his back to fiddle around with something behind the bar, ignoring the other shifter. He was behaving very badly.

Quickly I processed Quinn's request. If he came out to my house, I'd be at his mercy. I live in a remote place. My nearest neighbor is my ex, Bill, and he lives clear across the cemetery. On the other hand, if Quinn had been a regular date of mine, I'd let him take me home without a second thought. From what I could catch from his thoughts, he meant me no harm.

"All right," I said, finally. He relaxed, and smiled his big smile at me again.

I whisked his empty glass away and became aware that three pairs of eyes were watching me disapprovingly. Sam was disgruntled, and Danielle and Arlene couldn't understand why anyone would prefer me to them, though Quinn gave even those two experienced barmaids pause. Quinn gave off a whiff of otherness that must be perceptible to even the most prosaic human. "I'll be through in just a minute," I said.

"Take your time."

I finished filling the little china rectangle on each table with packages of sugar and sweetener. I made sure the napkin holders were full and checked the salt and pepper shakers. I was soon through. I gathered my purse from Sam's office and called good-bye to him.

Quinn pulled out to follow me in a dark green pickup truck. Under the parking lot lights, the truck looked brand spanking new, with gleaming tires and hubcaps, an extended cab, and a covered bed. I'd bet good money it was loaded with options. Quinn's truck was the fanciest vehicle I'd seen in a long time. My brother, Jason, would have drooled, and he's got pink and aqua swirls painted on the side of *his* truck.

I drove south on Hummingbird Road and turned left into my driveway. After following the drive through two acres of woods, I reached the clearing where our old family home stood. I'd turned the outside lights on before I left, and there was a security light on the electric pole that was automatic, so the clearing was well lit. I pulled around back to park behind the house, and Quinn parked right beside me.

He got out of his truck and looked around him. The security light showed him a tidy yard. The driveway was in excellent repair, and I'd recently repainted the tool shed in the back. There was a propane tank, which no amount of landscaping could disguise, but my grandmother had planted plenty of flower beds to add to the ones my family had established over the hundred-and-fifty-odd years the family had lived here. I'd lived on this land, in this house, from age seven, and I loved it.

There's nothing grand about my home. It started out as a family farmhouse and it's been enlarged and remodeled over the years. I keep it clean, and I try to keep the yard in good trim. Big repairs are beyond my skills, but Jason sometimes helps me out. He hadn't been happy when Gran left me the house and land, but he'd moved to our parents' house when he'd turned twenty-one, and I'd never made him pay me for my half of that property. Gran's will had seemed fair to me. It had taken Jason a while to admit that had been the right thing for her to do.

We'd become closer in the past few months.

I unlocked the back door and led Quinn into the kitchen. He looked around him curiously as I hung my jacket on one of the chairs pushed under the table in the middle of the kitchen where I ate all my meals.

"This isn't finished," Quinn said.

The cabinets were resting on the floor, ready to be mounted. After that, the whole room would have to be painted and the countertops installed. Then I'd be able to rest easy.

"My old kitchen got burned down a few weeks ago,"

I said. "The builder had a cancellation and got this done in record time, but then when the cabinets didn't arrive on time, he put his crew on another job. By the time the cabinets got here, they were almost through there. I guess they'll come back eventually." In the meantime, at least I could enjoy being back in my own home. Sam had been tremendously kind in letting me live in one of his rent houses (and gosh, I'd enjoyed the level floors and the new plumbing and the neighbors), but there was nothing like being home.

The new stove was in, so I could cook, and I'd laid a sheet of plywood over the top of the cabinets so I could use it as a work station while I was cooking. The new refrigerator gleamed and hummed quietly, quite unlike the one Gran had had for thirty years. The newness of the kitchen struck me every time I crossed the back porch—now larger and enclosed—to unlock the new, heavier back door, with its peephole and deadbolt.

"This is where the old house begins," I said, going from the kitchen into the hall. Only a few boards had had to be replaced in the floor in the rest of the house, and everything was freshly cleaned and painted. Not only had the walls and ceilings been smoke-stained, but I'd had to eradicate the burned smell. I'd replaced some curtains, tossed out a throw rug or two, and cleaned, cleaned, cleaned. This project had occupied every extra waking moment I'd had for quite a while.

"A good job," Quinn commented, studying how the two parts had been united.

"Come into the living room," I said, pleased. I enjoyed showing someone the house now that I knew the upholstery was clean, there were no dust bunnies, and the glass over the pictures was simply gleaming. The living room curtains had been replaced, something I'd wanted to do for at least a year.

God bless insurance, and God bless the money I'd earned

hiding Eric from an enemy. I'd gouged a hole in my savings account, but I'd had it when I needed it, and that was something for which I could be grateful.

The fireplace was laid ready for a fire, but it was just too warm to justify lighting one. Quinn sat in an armchair, and I sat across from him. "Can I get you a drink—a beer, or some coffee or iced tea?" I asked, conscious of my role as hostess.

"No, thanks," he said. He smiled at me. "I've wanted to see you again since I met you in Shreveport."

I tried to keep my eyes on him. The impulse to look down at my feet or my hands was almost overwhelming. His eyes really were the deep, deep purple I remembered. "That was a tough day for the Herveauxes," I said.

"You dated Alcide for a while," he observed, in a neutral kind of voice.

I thought of a couple of possible answers. I settled for, "I haven't seen him since the packmaster contest."

He smiled widely. "So he's not your steady?"

I shook my head.

"Then you're unattached?"

"Yes."

"No toes I'd be stepping on?"

I tried to smile, but my effort was not a happy one. "I didn't say that." There were toes. Those toes wouldn't be happy piggies. But they didn't have any right to be in the way.

"I guess I can handle some disgruntled exes. So will you go out with me?"

I looked at him for a second or two, scouring my mind for considerations. From his brain I was getting nothing but hopefulness: I saw no deceit or self-serving. When I examined the reservations I had, they dissolved into nothing.

"Yes," I said. "I will." His beautiful white smile sparked me to smile in return, and this time my smile was genuine.

"There," he said. "We've negotiated the pleasure part. Now for the business part, which is unrelated."

"Okay," I said, and put my smile away. I hoped I'd have occasion to haul it out later, but any business he would have with me would be supe-related, and therefore cause for anxiety.

"You've heard about the regional summit?"

The vampire summit: the kings and queens from a group of states would gather to confer about . . . vampire stuff. "Eric said something about it."

"Has he hired you to work there yet?"

"He mentioned he might need me."

"Because the Queen of Louisiana found out I was in the area, and she asked me to request your services. I think her bid would have to cancel out Eric's."

"You'd have to ask Eric about that."

"I think you would have to *tell* him. The queen's wishes are Eric's orders."

I could feel my face fall. I didn't want to tell Eric, the sheriff of Louisiana's Area Five, anything. Eric's feelings for me were confused. I can assure you, vamps don't like feeling confused. The sheriff had lost his memory of the short time he'd spent hiding in my house. That memory gap had driven Eric nuts; he liked being in control, and that meant being cognizant of his own actions every second of the night. So he'd waited until he could perform an action on my behalf, and as payment for that action he'd demanded my account of what had passed while he stayed with me.

Maybe I'd carried the frankness thing a little too far. Eric wasn't exactly surprised that we'd had sex; but he was stunned when I told him he'd offered to give up his hard-won position in the vampire hierarchy and to come live with me.

If you knew Eric, you'd know that was pretty much intolerable to him.

He didn't talk to me any more. He stared at me when we met, as if he were trying to resurrect his own memories of that time, to prove me wrong. It made me sad to see that the relationship we'd had—not the secret happiness of the few days he'd spent with me, but the entertaining relationship between a man and a woman who had little in common but a sense of humor—didn't seem to exist any more.

I knew it was up to me to tell him that his queen had superseded him, but I sure didn't want to.

"Smile's all gone," Quinn observed. He looked serious himself.

"Well, Eric is a . . ." I didn't know how to finish the sentence. "He's a complicated guy," I said lamely.

"What shall we do on our first date?" Quinn asked. So he was a good subject changer.

"We could go to the movies," I said, to start the ball rolling.

"We could. Afterward, we could have dinner in Shreveport. Maybe Ralph and Kacoo's," he suggested.

"I hear their crawfish etouffee is good," I said, keeping the conversational ball rolling.

"And who doesn't like crawfish etouffee? Or we could go bowling."

My great-uncle had been an avid bowler. I could see his feet, in their bowling shoes, right in front of me. I shuddered. "Don't know how."

"We could go to a hockey game."

"That might be fun."

"We could cook together in your kitchen, and then watch a movie on your DVD."

"Better put that one on a back burner." That sounded a little too personal for a first date, not that I've had that much experience with first dates. But I know that proximity to a bedroom is never a good idea unless you're sure you wouldn't mind if the flow of the evening took you in that direction.

"We could go see *The Producers.* That's coming to the Strand."

"Really?" Okay, I was excited now. Shreveport's restored Strand Theater hosted traveling stage productions ranging from plays to ballet. I'd never seen a real play before. Wouldn't that be awfully expensive? Surely he wouldn't have suggested it if he couldn't afford it. "Could we?"

He nodded, pleased at my reaction. "I can make the reservations for this weekend. What about your work schedule?"

"I'm off Friday night," I said happily. "And, um, I'll be glad to chip in for my ticket."

"I invited you. My treat," Quinn said firmly. I could read from his thoughts that he thought it was surprising that I had offered. And touching. Hmmm. I didn't like that. "Okay then. It's settled. When I get back to my laptop, I'll order the tickets online. I know there are some good ones left, because I was checking out our options before I drove over."

Naturally, I began to wonder about appropriate clothes. But I stowed that away for later. "Quinn, where do you actually live?"

"I have a house outside Memphis."

"Oh," I said, thinking that seemed a long way away for a dating relationship.

"I'm partner in a company called Special Events. We're a sort of secret offshoot of Extreme(ly Elegant) Events. You've seen the logo, I know. E(E)E?" He made the parentheses with his fingers. I nodded. E(E)E did a lot of very fancy event designing nationally. "There are four partners who work full-time for Special Events, and we each employ a few people full- or part-time. Since we travel a lot, we have places we use all over the country; some of them are just rooms in houses of friends or associates, and some of them are real apartments. The place I stay in this area is in Shreveport, a guesthouse in back of the mansion of a shifter."

I'd learned a lot about him in two minutes flat. "So you put on events in the supernatural world, like the contest for packmaster." That had been a dangerous job and one requiring a lot of specialized paraphernalia. "But what else is there to do? A packmaster's contest can only come up every so now and then. How much do you have to travel? What other special events can you stage?"

"I generally handle the Southeast, Georgia across to Texas." He sat forward in his chair, his big hands resting on his knees. "Tennessee south through Florida. In those states, if you want to stage a fight for packmaster, or a rite of ascension for a shaman or witch, or a vampire hierarchal wedding—and you want to do it right, with all the trimmings—you come to me."

I remembered the extraordinary pictures in Alfred Cumberland's photo gallery. "So there's enough of that to keep you busy?"

"Oh, yes," he said. "Of course, some of it is seasonal. Vamps get married in the winter, since the nights are so much longer. I did a hierarchal wedding in New Orleans in January, this past year. And then, some of the occasions are tied to the Wiccan calendar. Or to puberty."

I couldn't begin to imagine the ceremonies he arranged, but a description would have to wait for another occasion. "And you have three partners who do this full-time, too? I'm sorry. I'm just grilling you, seems like. But this is such an interesting way to make a living."

"I'm glad you think so. You gotta have a lot of people skills, and you gotta have a mind for details and organization."

"You have to be really, really, tough," I murmured, adding my own thought.

He smiled, a slow smile. "No problem there."

Yep, didn't seem as though toughness was a problem for Quinn.

"And you have to be good at sizing up people, so you can steer clients in the right direction, leave them happy with the job you've done," he said.

"Can you tell me some stories? Or is there a client confidentiality clause with your jobs?"

"Customers sign a contract, but none of them have ever requested a confidentiality clause," he said. "Special Events, you don't get much chance to talk about what you do, obviously, since the clients are mostly still traveling beneath the surface of the regular world. It's actually kind of a relief to talk about it. I usually have to tell a girl I'm a consultant, or something bogus like that."

"It's a relief to me, too, to be able to talk without worrying I'm spilling secrets."

"Then it's lucky we found each other, huh?" Again, the white grin. "I'd better let you get some rest, since you just got off work." Quinn got up and stretched after he'd reached his full height. It was an impressive gesture on someone as muscular as he was. It was just possible Quinn knew how excellent he looked when he stretched. I glanced down to hide my smile. I didn't mind one bit that he wanted to impress me.

He reached for my hand and pulled me to my feet in one easy motion. I could feel his focus centered on me. His own hand was warm and hard. He could crack my bones with it.

The average woman would not be pondering how fast her date could kill her, but I'll never be an average woman. I'd realized that by the time I became old enough to understand that not every child could understand what her family members were thinking about her. Not every little girl knew when her teachers liked her, or felt contempt for her, or compared her to her brother (Jason had an easy charm even then). Not every little girl had a funny uncle who tried to get her alone at every family gathering.

So I let Quinn hold my hand, and I looked up into his pansy-purple eyes, and for a minute I indulged myself by letting his admiration wash over me like a bath of approval.

Yes, I knew he was a tiger. And I don't mean in bed, though I was willing to believe he was ferocious and powerful there, too.

When he kissed me good night, his lips brushed my cheek, and I smiled.

I like a man who knows when to rush things . . . and when not to.

I GOT A PHONE CALL THE NEXT NIGHT AT MERLOTTE'S. Of course, it's not a good thing to get phone calls at work; Sam doesn't like it, unless there's some kind of home emergency. Since I get the least of any of the barmaids—in fact, I could count the calls I'd gotten at work on one hand—I tried not to feel guilty when I gestured to Sam that I'd take the call back at the phone on his desk.

"Hello," I said cautiously.

"Sookie," said a familiar voice.

"Oh, Pam. Hi." I was relieved, but only for a second. Pam was Eric's second in command, and she was his child, in the vampire sense.

"The boss wants to see you," she said. "I'm calling from his office."

Eric's office, in the back of his club, Fangtasia, was well

soundproofed. I could barely hear KDED, the all-vampire radio station, playing in the background: Clapton's version of "After Midnight."

"Well, lah-de-dah. He's too lofty to make his own phone calls?"

"Yes," Pam said. That Pam—*literal-minded* was the phrase for her.

"What's this about?"

"I am following his instructions," she said. "He tells me to call the telepath, I call you. You are summoned."

"Pam, I need a little more explanation than that. I don't especially want to see Eric."

"You are being recalcitrant?"

Uh-oh. I hadn't had that on my Word of the Day calendar yet. "I'm not sure I understand." It's better to just go on and confess ignorance than try to fake my way through.

Pam sighed, a long-suffering gust of sound. "You're digging in your heels," she clarified, her English accent making itself known. "And you shouldn't be. Eric treats you very well." She sounded faintly incredulous.

"I'm not giving up work *or* free time to drive over to Shreveport because Mr. High and Mighty wants me to jump to do his bidding," I protested—reasonably, I thought. "He can haul his ass over here if he wants to tell me something. Or he can pick up the telephone his ownself." So there.

"If he had wanted to pick up the phone 'his ownself,' as you put it, he would have done so. Be here Friday night by eight, he bids me tell you."

"Sorry, no can do."

A significant silence.

"You won't come?"

"I can't. I have a date," I said, trying to keep any trace of smugness out of my voice.

There was another silence. Then Pam snickered. "Oh, that's

rich," she said, abruptly switching to American vernacular. "Oh, I'm going to love telling him that."

Her reaction made me begin to feel uneasy. "Um, Pam," I began, wondering if I should backpedal, "listen . . ."

"Oh, no," she said, almost laughing out loud, which was very un-Pam-like.

"You tell him I did say thanks for the calendar proofs," I said. Eric, always thinking of ways to make Fangtasia more lucrative, had come up with a vampire calendar to sell in the little gift shop. Eric himself was Mr. January. He'd posed with a bed and a long white fur robe. Eric and the bed were set against a pale gray background hung with giant glittering snowflakes. He wasn't wearing the robe: oh, no. He wasn't wearing anything. He had one bent knee on the rumpled bed, and the other foot was on the floor, and he was looking directly at the camera, smoldering. (He could have taught Claude a few lessons.) Eric's blond hair fell in a tousled mane around his shoulders, and his right hand gripped the robe tossed on the bed, so the white fur rose just high enough to cover his kit 'n' kaboodle. His body was turned just slightly to flaunt the curve of his world-class butt. A light trail of dark blond hair pointed south of his navel. It practically screamed, "Carrying concealed!"

I happened to know that Eric's pistol was more of a .357 Magnum than a snub-nose.

Somehow I'd never gotten past looking at January.

"Oh, I'll let him know," Pam said. "Eric said many people wouldn't like it if I were in the calendar made for women . . . so I'm in the one for men. Would you like me to send you a copy of my picture, as well?"

"That surprises me," I told her. "It really does. I mean, that you wouldn't mind posing." I had a hard time imagining her participation in a project that would pander to human tastes.

"Eric tells me to pose, I pose," she said matter-of-factly.

Though Eric had considerable power over Pam since he was her maker, I have to say that I'd never known Eric to ask Pam to do anything she wasn't ready to do. Either he knew her well (which, of course, he did) or Pam was willing to do just about anything.

"I have a whip in my picture," Pam said. "The photographer says it'll sell a million." Pam had wide-ranging tastes in the area of sex.

After a long moment while I contemplated the mental image that raised, I said, "I'm sure it will, Pam. But I'll give it a pass."

"We'll all get a percentage, all of us who agreed to pose."

"But Eric will get a bigger percentage than the rest."

"Well, he's the sheriff," Pam said reasonably.

"Right. Well, bye." I started to hang up.

"Wait, what am I to tell Eric?"

"Just tell him the truth."

"You know he'll be angry." Pam didn't sound at all scared. In fact, she sounded gleeful.

"Well, that's his problem," I said, maybe a bit childishly, and this time I did hang up. An angry Eric would surely be my problem, too.

I had a nasty feeling I'd taken a serious step in denying Eric. I had no idea what would happen now. When I'd first gotten to know the sheriff of Area Five, I'd been dating Bill. Eric had wanted to use my unusual talent. He'd simply held hurting Bill over my head to get me to comply. When I'd broken up with Bill, Eric had lacked any means of coercion until I'd needed a favor from him, and then I'd supplied Eric with the most potent ammunition of all—the knowledge that I'd shot Debbie Pelt. It didn't matter that he'd hidden her body and her car and he couldn't himself remember where; the accusation would be enough to ruin the rest of my life, even if it was never proved. Even if I could bring myself to deny it.

As I carried out my duties in the bar the rest of that night, I found myself wondering if Eric really would reveal my secret. If Eric told the police what I'd done, he'd have to admit he'd had a part in it, wouldn't he?

I was waylaid by Detective Andy Bellefleur when I was on my way to the bar. I've known Andy and his sister Portia all my life. They're a few years older than me, but we'd been through the same schools, grown up in the same town. Like me, they'd been largely raised by their grandmother. The detective and I have had our ups and downs. Andy had been dating a young schoolteacher, Halleigh Robinson, for a few months now.

Tonight, he had a secret to share with me and a favor to ask.

"Listen, she's going to order the chicken basket," he said, without preamble. I glanced over to their table, to make sure Halleigh was sitting with her back to me. She did. "When you bring the food to the table, make sure this is in it, covered up." He stuffed a little velvet-covered box into my hand. There was a ten-dollar bill under it.

"Sure, Andy, no problem," I said, smiling.

"Thanks, Sookie," he said, and for once he smiled back, a simple and uncomplicated and terrified smile.

Andy had been right on the money. Halleigh ordered the chicken basket when I went to their table.

"Make that extra fries," I said to our new cook when I turned in the order. I wanted plenty of camouflage. The cook turned from the grill to glare at me. We've had an assortment of cooks, of every age, color, gender, and sexual preference. We even had a vampire, once. Our current cook was a middle-aged black woman named Callie Collins. Callie was heavy, so heavy I didn't know how she could get through the hours she spent standing on her feet in the hot kitchen. "Extra fries?" Callie said, as if she'd never heard of such a thing. "Uh-huh. People get extra fries when they pay for them, not because they friends of yours."

It could be that Callie was so sharp-edged because she was old enough to remember the bad old days when blacks and whites had different schools, different waiting rooms, different water fountains. I didn't remember any of those things, and I was not willing to take into account Callie's bundle of baggage every time I talked to her.

"They paid extra," I lied, not wanting to call an explanation through the service pass-through that anyone close enough could overhear. I'd put a dollar of my tip into the till, instead, to make up the money. Despite our differences, I wished Andy and his schoolteacher well. Anyone who was going to be Caroline Bellefleur's granddaughter-in-law deserved a romantic moment.

When Callie called up the basket, I trotted over to get it. Slipping the little box under the fries was harder than I imagined, and it required a bit of surreptitious rearrangement. I wondered if Andy had realized that the velvet would get greasy and salty. Oh well, this wasn't my romantic gesture, but his.

I carried the tray to the table with happy anticipation. In fact, Andy had to warn me (with a severe glance) to pull my face into more neutral lines as I served their food. Andy already had a beer in front of him, and she had a glass of white wine. Halleigh wasn't a big drinker, as befitted an elementary school teacher. I turned away as soon as the food was on the table, even forgetting to ask them if they needed anything else, like a good waitress should.

It was beyond me to try to stay detached after that. Though I tried not to be obvious, I watched the couple as closely as I could. Andy was on pins and needles, and I could hear his brain, which was simply agitated. He really wasn't sure whether he'd be accepted, and his mind was running through the list of things she might object to: the fact that Andy was almost ten years older, his hazardous profession . . .

I knew the moment when she spied the box. Maybe it wasn't nice of me to eavesdrop mentally on a very special moment, but to tell you the truth, I didn't even think of that at the time. Though ordinarily I keep myself well guarded, I'm used to dropping into people's heads if I spy something interesting. I'm also used to believing that my ability is a minus, not a plus, so I guess I feel entitled to whatever fun I can have with it.

I had my back to them, clearing off a table, which I should have left for the busboy to do. So I was close enough to hear.

She was frozen for a long moment. "There's a box in my food," she said, finally, keeping her voice very low because she thought she'd upset Sam if she made a fuss.

"I know," he said. "It's from me."

She knew then; everything in her brain began to accelerate, and the thoughts practically tripped over themselves in their eagerness.

"Oh, Andy," she whispered. She must have opened the box. It was all I could do not to turn around and look right along with her.

"Do you like it?"

"Yes, it's beautiful."

"Will you wear it?"

There was a silence. Her head was so confused. Half of it was going "Yippee!" and half of it was troubled.

"Yes, with one stipulation," she said slowly.

I could feel his shock. Whatever Andy had expected, it wasn't this.

"And that would be?" he asked, suddenly sounding much more like a cop than a lover.

"We have to live in our own place."

"What?" Again, she'd surprised Andy.

"I've always gotten the idea that you assumed you'd stay in the family home, with your grandmother and your sister, even after you got married. It's a wonderful old house, and your grandmother and Portia are great women."

That was tactful. Good for Halleigh.

"But I'd like to have a home of my own," she said gently, earning my admiration.

And then I really had to haul ass; I had tables to tend to. But as I refilled beer mugs, cleared empty plates, and took more money to Sam at the cash register, I was filled with awe at Halleigh's stand, since the Bellefleur mansion was Bon Temps's premier residence. Most young women would give a finger or two to live there, especially since the big old house had been extensively remodeled and freshened with the influx of money from a mysterious stranger. That stranger was actually Bill, who'd discovered that the Bellefleurs were descendants of his. He'd known they wouldn't accept money from a vampire, so he'd arranged the whole "mysterious legacy" ruse, and Caroline Bellefleur had jumped into spending it on the mansion with as much relish as Andy ate a cheeseburger.

Andy caught up with me a few minutes later. He snagged me on the way to Sid Matt Lancaster's table, so the aged lawyer had to wait a bit extra for his hamburger and fries.

"Sookie, I have to know," he said urgently, but in a very low tone.

"What, Andy?" I was alarmed at his intensity.

"Does she love me?" There were edges of humiliation in his head, that he'd actually asked me. Andy was proud, and he wanted some kind of assurance that Halleigh didn't want his family name or his family home as he'd found other women had. Well, he'd found out about the home. Halleigh didn't want it, and he would move into some humble, small house with her, if she really loved him.

No one had ever demanded this of me before. After all the years of wanting people to believe in me, understand my freakish talent, I found I didn't enjoy being taken seriously, after all. But Andy was waiting for an answer, and I couldn't refuse. He was one of the most dogged men I'd ever met.

"She loves you as much as you love her," I said, and he let go of my arm. I continued on my way to Sid Matt's table. When I glanced back at him, he was staring at me.

Chew on that, Andy Bellefleur, I thought. Then I felt a little ashamed of myself. But he shouldn't have asked, if he didn't want to know the answer.

There was something in the woods around my house.

I'd gotten ready for bed as soon as I'd come home, because one of my favorite moments in every twenty-four hours is when I get to put on my nightgown. It was warm enough that I didn't need a bathrobe, so I was roaming around in my old blue knee-length sleep tee. I was just thinking of shutting the kitchen window, since the March night was getting a little chilly. I'd been listening to the sounds of the night while I washed dishes; the frogs and the bugs had been filling the air with their chorus.

Suddenly, the noises that had made the night seem as friendly and busy as the day had come to a stop, cut off in midcry.

I paused, my hands immersed in the hot soapy water. Peering out into the darkness didn't help a bit, and I realized how visible I must be, standing at an open window with its curtains flung wide apart. The yard was lit up with the security light, but beyond the trees that ringed the clearing, the woods lay dark and still.

Something was out there. I closed my eyes and tried to reach out with my brain, and I found some kind of activity. But it wasn't clear enough to define.

I thought about phoning Bill, but I'd called him before when I'd been worried about my safety. I couldn't let it become a habit. Hey, maybe the watcher in the woods was Bill himself? He sometimes roamed around at night, and he came to check on me from time to time. I looked longingly over at the telephone on the wall at the end of the counter. (Well, where the counter would be when it was all put together.) My new telephone was portable. I could grab it, retreat to my bedroom, and call Bill in a snap of the fingers, since he was on my speed dial. If he answered the phone, I'd know whatever was out in the woods was something I needed to worry about.

But if he was home, he'd come racing over here. He'd hear my call like this: "Oh, Bill, please come save me! I can't think of anything to do but call a big, strong vampire to come to my rescue!"

I made myself admit that I really knew that whatever was in the woods, it wasn't Bill. I'd gotten a brain signal of some kind. If the lurker had been a vampire, I would have sensed nothing. Only twice had I gotten a flicker of a signal from a vampire brain, and it had been like a flash of electricity in an outage.

And right by that telephone was the back door—which wasn't locked.

Nothing on earth could keep me at the sink after the fact of the open door had occurred to me. I simply ran for it. I stepped out onto the back porch, flipped the latch on the glass door there, and jumped back into the kitchen proper and locked the big wooden door, which I'd had outfitted with a thumb latch and a deadbolt.

I leaned against the door after it was safely locked. Better than anyone I could think of, I knew the futility of doors and locks. To a vampire, the physical barrier was nothing—but a vampire had to be invited in. To a Were, doors were of more consequence, but still not much of a problem; with their incredible strength, Weres could go wherever they damn well chose. The same held true of other shifters.

Why didn't I just hold an open house?

However, I felt wonderfully better with two locked doors between me and whatever was in the woods. I knew the front door was locked and bolted, since it hadn't been opened in days. I didn't get that many visitors, and I normally entered and departed through the back.

I crept back to the window, which I closed and locked. I drew the curtains, too. I'd done everything to increase my security I could do. I went back to the dishes. I got a wet circle on the front of my sleep tee because I had to lean against the edge of the sink to steady my shaking legs. But I made myself continue until all the dishes were safely in the drainer and the sink had been wiped clean.

I listened intently after that. The woods were still silent. No matter how I listened with every sense at my disposal, that faint signal did not impinge on my brain again. It was gone.

I sat in the kitchen for a while, brain still in high gear, but then I forced myself to follow my usual routine. My heart rate had returned to normal by the time I brushed my teeth, and as I climbed into bed I had almost persuaded myself that nothing had happened out there in the silent darkness. But I'm careful about being honest inside. I knew some creature had been out in my woods; and that creature had been something bigger and scarier than a raccoon.

Quite soon after I'd turned my bedside light off, I heard the bugs and the frogs resume their chorus. Finally, when it continued uninterrupted, I slept.

4

I PUNCHED IN THE NUMBER OF MY BROTHER'S CELL phone when I got up the next morning. I hadn't spent a very good night, but at least I'd gotten a bit of sleep. Jason answered on the second ring. He sounded a little preoccupied when he said, "Hello?"

"Hi, Brother. How's it going?"

"Listen, I need to talk to you. I can't right now. I'll be there, probably in a couple of hours." He hung up without saying good-bye, and he'd sounded pretty worried about something. Good. I needed another complication.

I glanced at the clock. A couple of hours would give me enough time to get cleaned up and run into town to go to the grocery store. Jason would be getting here about noon, and if I knew him he'd expect me to feed him lunch. I yanked my hair into a ponytail and then doubled the elastic band around it, making it into a kind of topknot. I had a little fan of the ends waving above my head. Though I tried not to admit it to myself, I thought this slapdash hairstyle was fun-looking and kind of cute.

It was one of those crisp, cool March mornings, the kind that promises a warm afternoon. The sky was so bright and sunny that my spirits rose, and I drove to Bon Temps with the window rolled down, singing along with the radio at the top of my voice. I would've sung along with Weird Al Yankovic that morning.

I drove past woods, the occasional house, and a field full of cows (and a couple of buffalo; you never know what people will raise).

The disc jockey played "Blue Hawaii" as a golden oldie, and I wondered where Bubba was—not my own brother, but the vampire now known only as Bubba. I hadn't seen him in three or four weeks. Maybe the vamps of Louisiana had moved him to another hiding place, or maybe he'd wandered off, as he does from time to time. That's when you get your long articles in the papers they keep by the grocery check-out stand.

Though I was having a blissful moment of being happy and content, I had one of those stray ideas you get at odd moments. I thought, *How nice it would be if Eric were here with me in the car. He'd look so good with the wind blowing his hair, and he'd enjoy the moment.* Well, yeah, before he burned to a crisp.

But I realized I'd thought of Eric because it was the kind of day you wanted to share with the person you cared about, the person whose company you enjoyed the most. And that would be Eric as he'd been while he was cursed by a witch: the Eric who hadn't been hardened by centuries of vampire politics, the Eric who had no contempt for humans and their affairs, the Eric who was not in charge of many financial enterprises and responsible for the lives and incomes of quite a few humans and vampires. In other words, Eric as he would never be again.

Ding-dong, the witch was dead, and Eric was restored to his character as it was now. The restored Eric was wary of me, was fond of me, and didn't trust me (or his feelings) an inch.

I sighed heavily, and the song vanished from my lips. It was nearly quenched in my heart until I told myself to stop being a melancholy idiot. I was young, I was healthy. The day was beautiful. And I had an actual date for Friday night. I promised myself a big treat. Instead of going directly to the grocery store, I went by Tara's Togs, owned and operated by my friend Tara Thornton.

I hadn't seen Tara in a while. She'd gone on a vacation to visit an aunt in south Texas, and since she'd returned she'd been working long hours at the store. At least, that's what she'd said when I'd called her to thank her for the car. When my kitchen had burned, my car had burned with it, and Tara had loaned me her old car, a two-year-old Malibu. She'd acquired a brand-new car (never mind how) and hadn't gotten around to selling the Malibu.

To my astonishment, about a month ago, Tara had mailed me the title and the bill of sale, with a letter telling me the car was now mine. I'd called to protest, but she had stonewalled me, and in the end, there didn't seem to be anything to do but accept the gift graciously.

She intended it as payment, since I'd extricated her from a terrible situation. But to help her, I'd had to indebt myself to Eric. I hadn't minded. Tara had been my friend all my life. Now she was safe, if she was smart enough to stay away from the supernatural world.

Though I was grateful and relieved to have the newest vehicle I'd ever owned, I would have been happier to have her uninterrupted friendship. I'd stayed away, since I assumed that I reminded her of too many bad things. But

I was in the mood to try to rip down that veil. Maybe Tara had had enough time.

Tara's Togs was in a strip mall on the south side of Bon Temps. There was one other car parked in front of the store. I decided it might be good that a third party would be there; it would depersonalize the meeting.

Tara was serving Andy Bellefleur's sister Portia when I went in, so I began flicking through the size tens, and then the eights. Portia was sitting at the Isabelle table, which was extremely interesting. Tara is the local representative for Isabelle's Bridal, a national company that produces a catalog that's become the bible of all things wedding-related. You can try on samples of the bridesmaid dresses at the local outlet, so you can order the right size, and each dress comes in about twenty colors. The wedding dresses are just as popular. Isabelle's has twenty-five models. The Company also offers wedding shower invitations, decorations, garters, bridesmaids' gifts, and any bit of wedding paraphernalia you can imagine. However, Isabelle's was pretty much a middle-class phenomenon, and Portia was definitely an upper-class woman.

Since she lived with her grandmother and her brother in the Bellefleur mansion on Magnolia Street, Portia had grown up in a sort of decayed gothic splendor. Now that the mansion was repaired and her grandmother entertained more, Portia had looked noticeably happier when I'd glimpsed her around town. She didn't come into Merlotte's that much, but when she was in the bar she had more time to spare for other people, and she smiled occasionally. A plain woman just past thirty, Portia's best feature was her thick, shining chestnut hair.

Portia was thinking *wedding*, and Tara was thinking *money.*

"I have to talk with Halleigh again, but I think we'll need four hundred invitations," Portia was saying, and I thought my jaw would drop.

"All right, Portia, if you don't mind paying the rush fee, we can have those in ten days."

"Oh, good!" Portia was definitely pleased. "Of course, Halleigh and I will be wearing different dresses, but we thought we might try to pick out the same bridesmaid's dress. Maybe in different colors. What do you think?"

I thought I was going to choke on my own curiosity. Portia was going to be married, too? To that stick of an accountant she'd been dating, the guy from Clarice? Tara caught a glimpse of my face over the top of the standing rack of dresses. Portia was looking at the catalog, so Tara winked at me. She was definitely pleased to have a rich customer, and we were definitely okay with each other. Relief flooded me.

"I think having the same style in different colors—coordinating colors, of course—would be really original," Tara said. "How many bridesmaids are there going to be?"

"Five apiece," Portia said, her attention on the page before her. "Can I take a copy of the catalog home? That way, Halleigh and I can look at it tonight."

"I only have one extra copy; you know, one of the ways Isabelle's makes money is charging an arm and a leg for the darn catalog," Tara said with a charming smile. Tara can lay it on when she needs to. "I'll let you take it home, if you cross your heart you'll bring it back tomorrow!"

Portia made the childish gesture, and tucked the thick catalog under her arm. She was wearing one of her "lawyer suits," a brownish tweedy-looking straight skirt and jacket with a silk blouse underneath. She had on beige hose and low-heeled pumps, and she carried a matching purse. Bo-ring.

Portia was excited, and her brain was cartwheeling with happy images. She knew she would look a little old as a bride, especially compared to Halleigh; but by God, she was finally going to be a bride. Portia would get her share of the fun, the presents, the attention, and the clothes, to say nothing of the validation of having a husband of her own. She looked up from the catalog and spied me lurking by the slacks rack. Her happiness was profound enough to encompass even me.

"Hello, Sookie!" she said, practically beaming. "Andy told me what a help you were to him, fixing up his little surprise for Halleigh. I really appreciate it."

"It was fun," I said, with my own version of a gracious smile. "Is it true that congratulations are in order for you, as well?" I know, you're not supposed to congratulate the bride, only the groom, but I didn't think Portia would mind.

Sure enough, she didn't. "Well, I am getting married," she confessed. "And we decided to have a double ceremony with Andy and Halleigh. The reception will be at the house."

Of course. Why have a mansion, if you couldn't have the reception there?

"That's going to be a lot of work, setting up a wedding by—when?" I said, trying to sound sympathetic and concerned.

"April. Tell me about it," Portia said, laughing. "Grandmother is already half-crazy. She's called every caterer she knows to try to book someone for the second weekend, and finally landed Extreme(ly Elegant) Events because they had a cancellation. Plus, the guy who runs Sculptured Forest in Shreveport is coming to see her this afternoon."

Sculptured Forest was the premier landscape planning center and nursery in the area, at least if you went by their omnipresent ads. Hiring both Sculptured Forest and Extreme(ly Elegant) Events meant that this double wedding would be the primo social occasion of the Bon Temps year.

"We're thinking an outdoor wedding at the house, with tents in the back yard," Portia said. "In case of rain, we'll have to move it to the church, and have the reception at the Renard Parish Community Building. But we'll keep our fingers crossed."

"Sounds wonderful." I really couldn't think of anything else to say. "How are you going to keep working, with all this wedding stuff to do?"

"Somehow I'll manage."

I wondered what the rush was. Why weren't the happy couples waiting until summer, when Halleigh wouldn't be working? Why not wait, so Portia could free her calendar for a proper wedding and honeymoon? And wasn't the man she'd been dating an accountant? Surely a wedding during tax season was the worst possible scheduling.

Oooo . . . maybe Portia was pregnant. But if she was in the family way, she wasn't thinking about it, and I hardly thought she would be doing otherwise. Gosh, if I ever found out I was pregnant, I'd be so happy! If the guy loved me and would marry me, that is—because I wasn't tough enough to raise a kid by myself, and my grandmother would roll over in her grave if I was an unmarried mother. Modern thinking on that subject had completely passed my grandmother by, without even ruffling her hair with its passage.

While all these thoughts were buzzing around in my head, it took me a minute to process Portia's words. "So try to keep the second Saturday in April free," she said with as close to a charming smile as Portia Bellefleur could manage.

I promised I would, trying not to trip over my own tongue with astonishment. She must be high on wedding fever. Why would my presence be desired at the wedding? I was no big buddy of any of the Bellefleurs.

"We're asking Sam to bartend at the reception," she continued, and my world realigned into a more familiar pattern. She wanted me there to assist Sam.

"An afternoon wedding?" I asked. Sam sometimes took outside bartending jobs, but Saturday was usually our heavy day at Merlotte's.

"No, night," she said, "but I already talked to Sam this morning, and he's agreed."

"Okay," I said.

She read more into my tone than I'd put there, and she flushed. "Glen has some clients that he wants to invite," she said, though I'd asked for no explanation. "They can only come after dark." Glen Vicks was the accountant. I was glad I'd retrieved his last name from my memory. Then everything clicked into place, and I understood Portia's embarrassment. Portia meant that Glen's clients were vampires. Well, well, well. I smiled at her.

"I'm sure it'll be a lovely wedding, and I look forward to being there," I said, "since you were kind enough to invite me." I'd deliberately misunderstood her, and as I'd foreseen, she flushed even redder. Then a related idea occurred to me, one so important I bent one of my personal rules.

"Portia," I said slowly, wanting to be sure she got my meaning, "you should invite Bill Compton."

Now Portia loathed Bill—disliked all vampires—but when she'd been forwarding one of her own plots, she'd dated Bill briefly. Which had been odd, because afterward Bill had discovered Portia was actually his great-great-great-great-great-granddaughter, or something like that.

Bill had gone along with her pretense of interest in him. At the time, he'd just wanted to find out what her goal was. He'd realized that it made Portia's skin crawl to be around him. But when he'd discovered the Bellefleurs were his only surviving kin, he'd anonymously given them a whacking great bunch of money.

I could "hear" that Portia thought I was purposely reminding her of the few times she'd dated Bill. She didn't want to be reminded of it, and it angered her that I'd done so.

"Why do you suggest that?" she asked coldly, and I gave her high points for not just stalking out of the shop. Tara was being studiously busy over by the Isabelle table, but I knew she could hear our conversation. Nothing wrong with Tara's hearing.

I had a ferocious internal debate. Finally, what Bill wanted prevailed over what I wanted for him. "Never mind," I said reluctantly. "Your wedding, your list."

Portia was looking at me as if she really saw me for the first time. "Are you still dating him?" she asked.

"No, he's dating Selah Pumphrey," I said, keeping my voice even and empty.

Portia gave me an unreadable look. Without another word, she went out to her car.

"What was all that about?" Tara asked.

I couldn't explain, so I changed the subject to one closer to Tara's retailing heart. "I'm delighted you're getting the business," I said.

"You and me both. If she didn't have to pull it together in such a short time, you can bet Portia Bellefleur wouldn't ever go Isabelle," Tara said frankly. "She'd drive to Shreveport and back a million times running errands, if she had the lead time. Halleigh is just trailing along in Portia's wake, poor thing. She'll come in this afternoon, and I'll show her the same things I've shown Portia, and she'll have to buckle under. But it's all good for me. They're getting the whole package, because the Isabelle system can deliver it all on time. Invitations, thank-you notes, dresses, garters, bridesmaids' gifts, even the mother-of-the-bride gowns—Miss Caroline will be buying one, and Halleigh's mother—they're getting it all here, either from my stock or from Isabelle's book." She looked me up and down. "What brought you in, by the way?"

"I need a date outfit to wear to a play in Shreveport," I said, "and I have to go to the grocery and get back at home to cook Jason's lunch. So, you got anything to show me?"

Tara's smile turned predatory. "Oh," she said, "just a few things."

5 ~

I WAS GLAD JASON WAS A LITTLE LATE. I'D FINISHED the bacon and I was putting the hamburgers in the frying pan when he arrived. I had already opened the package of buns and put two on Jason's plate, and put a bag of potato chips on the table. I'd poured him a glass of tea and set it beside his place.

Jason came in without knocking, as he always did. Jason hadn't changed that much, at least to the eyes, since he'd become a werepanther. He was still blond and attractive, and I mean attractive in the old way; he was good to look at, but he was also the kind of man that everyone looks at when he comes into a room. On top of that, he'd always had a mean streak. But since his change, he'd somehow been acting like a better person. I hadn't decided why that was. Maybe being a wild animal once a month satisfied some craving he hadn't known he had.

Since he'd been bitten, not born, he didn't change completely; he became a sort of hybrid. At first, he'd been disappointed about that. But he'd gotten over it. He'd been dating a full werepanther named Crystal for several months now. Crystal lived in a tiny community some miles out in the country—and let me tell you, out in the country from Bon Temps, Louisiana, is really *out in the country.*

We said a brief prayer and began eating. Jason didn't dig in with his usual gusto. Since the hamburger tasted good to me, I figured whatever was on his mind was important. I couldn't read it out of his brain. Since my brother had become a Were, his thoughts had not been as clear to me.

Mostly, that was a relief.

After two bites, Jason put down his hamburger, and his body posture changed. He was ready to talk. "I got something I got to tell you," he said. "Crystal doesn't want me to tell anyone, but I'm really worried about her. Yesterday, Crystal . . . she had a miscarriage."

I shut my eyes for a few seconds. I had about twenty thoughts in that brief time, and I couldn't complete a one of them. "I'm so sorry," I said. "I hope Crystal's all right?"

Jason looked at me over a plate of food he'd completely forgotten. "She won't go to the doctor."

I stared at him blankly. "But she has to," I said reasonably. "She needs a D & C." I wasn't sure what "D & C" stood for, but I knew after you'd miscarried, you went to a hospital and that's what they did there. My friend and co-worker Arlene had had a D & C after her miscarriage, and she'd told me about it several times. *Several* times. "They go in and . . ." I began, but Jason cut me off in midstream.

"Hey, I don't need to know," he said, looking very uncomfortable. "I just know that since Crystal's a werepanther, she didn't want to go to the hospital. She had to go when she got gored by that razorback, just like Calvin had to go when he got shot, but they both got well so fast that there was some comment in the doctors' lounge, she heard. So she won't go now. She's at my house, but she's . . . she's not doing well. She's getting worse, not better."

"Uh-oh," I said. "So what's happening?"

"She's bleeding too heavy, and her legs don't work right." He swallowed. "She can hardly stand up, much less walk."

"Have you called Calvin?" I asked. Calvin Norris, Crystal's uncle, is the leader of the tiny Hotshot panther community.

"She don't want me to tell Calvin. She's scared Calvin'll kill me for knocking her up. Crystal didn't want me to tell you, either, but I got to have help."

Though her mom wasn't living, Crystal had female relatives galore in Hotshot. I'd never had a baby, I'd never even been pregnant, and I wasn't a shifter. Any one of them would know more about the situation than I did. I told Jason this.

"I don't want her to sit up long enough to go back to Hotshot, specially in my truck." My brother looked as stubborn as a mule.

For an awful minute, I thought that Jason's big concern was Crystal bleeding on his upholstery. I was about to hop down his throat, when he added, "The shocks need replacing, and I'm scared the bouncing of the truck on that bad road would make Crystal worse."

Then her kin could come to Crystal. But I knew before I spoke that Jason would find a reason to veto that, too. He had some kind of plan. "Okay. What can I do?"

"Didn't you tell me that time when you got hurt, there was a special kind of doctor the vamps called to look at your back?"

I didn't like to think about that night. My back still bore the scars of the attack. The poison on the maenad's claws had nearly killed me. "Yes," I said slowly, "Dr. Ludwig." Doctor to all that was weird and strange, Dr. Ludwig was herself an oddity. She was extremely short—very, very short.

And her features were not exactly regular, either. It would come as an extreme surprise to me if Dr. Ludwig were at all human. I'd seen her a second time at the contest for packmaster. Both times, I'd been in Shreveport; so the chances were good that Dr. Ludwig actually lived there.

Since I didn't want to overlook the obvious, I fished a Shreveport directory out of the drawer below the wall-mounted telephone. There was a listing for a Doctor Amy Ludwig. Amy? I bit back a burst of laughter.

I was very nervous about approaching Dr. Ludwig on my own, but when I saw how worried Jason was, I couldn't protest over making one lousy phone call.

It rang four times. A machine picked up. A mechanical voice said, "You have reached the telephone of Dr. Amy Ludwig. Dr. Ludwig is not accepting new patients, insured or uninsured. Dr. Ludwig does not want pharmaceutical samples, and she does not need insurance of any kind. She is not interested in investing her money, or giving to charities she hasn't personally selected." There was a long silence, during which time most callers presumably hung up. I didn't. After a moment, I heard another click on the line.

"Hello?" asked a gruff little voice.

"Dr. Ludwig?" I asked cautiously.

"Yes? I don't accept new patients, you know! Too busy!" She sounded both impatient and cautious.

"I'm Sookie Stackhouse. Is this the Dr. Ludwig who treated me in Eric's office at Fangtasia?"

"You are the young woman poisoned by the maenad's claws?"

"Yes. I saw you again a few weeks ago, remember?"

"And where was that?" She remembered quite well, but she wanted another proof of my identity.

"An empty building in an industrial park."

"And who was running the show there?"

"A big bald guy named Quinn."

"Oh, all right." She sighed. "What do you want? I'm rather busy."

"I have a patient for you. Please come to see her."

"Bring her to me."

"She's too sick to travel."

I heard the doctor muttering to herself, but I couldn't make out the words.

"Pooh," the doctor said. "Oh, very well, Miss Stackhouse. Tell me what the problem is."

I explained as best I could. Jason was moving around the kitchen, because he was too worried to sit still.

"Idiots. Fools," Dr. Ludwig said. "Tell me how to get to your house. Then you can take me where the girl is."

"I may have to leave for work before you can get here," I said, after glancing at the clock and calculating how long it would take the doctor to drive from Shreveport. "My brother will be here waiting."

"Is he the responsible party?"

I didn't know if she was talking about the bill for her services, or the pregnancy. Either way, I told her that Jason definitely was the responsible party.

"She's coming," I told my brother, after I'd given the doctor directions and hung up. "I don't know how much she charges, but I told her you'd pay."

"Sure, sure. How will I know her?"

"You can't mistake her for anyone you know. She said she'd have a driver. She wouldn't be tall enough to see over the steering wheel, so I should have figured on that."

I did the dishes while Jason fidgeted. He called Crystal to check on her, seemed okay with what he'd heard. Finally, I asked him to go outside and knock old dirt-dauber nests off the tool shed. He couldn't seem to settle down, so he might as well be useful.

I thought about the situation while I started a load of laundry and put on my barmaid outfit (black pants, white boat-neck tee with *Merlotte's* embroidered over the left breast, black Adidas). I was not a happy camper. I was worried about Crystal—and I didn't like her. I was sorry she'd lost the baby because I know that's a sad experience, but I was happy because I really didn't want Jason to marry the girl, and I was pretty sure he would have if the pregnancy had continued. I cast around for something to make me feel better. I opened the closet to look at my new outfit, the one I'd bought at Tara's Togs to wear on my date. But I couldn't even get any enjoyment out of it.

Finally, I did what I'd planned on doing before I'd heard Jason's news: I got a book and settled in a chair on the front porch, reading a few sentences every now and then in between admiring the pear tree in the front yard, which was covered in white blossoms and humming with bees.

The sun was beaming, the daffodils were just past their prime, and I had a date for Friday. And I'd already done my good deed for the day, in calling Dr. Ludwig. The coil of worry in my stomach eased up a little.

From time to time, I could hear vague sounds traveling my way from the backyard; Jason had found something to keep him occupied after he'd dealt with the nests. Maybe he was pulling up weeds in the flower beds. I brightened. That would be nice, since I didn't have my grandmother's enthusiasm for gardening. I admired the results, but I didn't enjoy the whole process as she had.

After checking my watch repeatedly, I was relieved to see a rather grand pearl Cadillac pull into the front parking area. There was a tiny shape in the front passenger seat. The driver's door opened, and a Were named Amanda got out. She and I had had our differences, but we'd parted on fair terms. I was relieved to see someone I knew. Amanda, who looked exactly like a middle-class soccer mom, was in her thirties. Her red hair looked natural, quite unlike my friend Arlene's.

"Sookie, hey," she said. "When the doctor told me where we were going, I was relieved, since I knew how to get here already."

"You're not her usual driver? Hey, I like the haircut, by the way."

"Oh, thanks." Amanda's hair was newly short, cut in a careless, almost boyish style that oddly suited her. I say oddly, because Amanda's body was definitely womanly.

"Haven't got used to it yet," she admitted, running her hand over her neck. "Actually, it's usually my oldest boy that drives Dr. Ludwig, but he's in school today, of course. Is it your sister-in-law that's ailing?"

"My brother's fiancée," I said, trying to put a good face on it. "Crystal. She's a panther."

Amanda looked almost respectful. Weres often have only contempt for other shape-shifters, but something as formidable as a panther would get their attention. "I heard there was a cluster of panthers out here somewhere. Never met one before."

"I have to get to work, but my brother's going to lead you over to his place."

"So, you're not really close to your brother's fiancée?"

I was taken aback at the implication that I was less than concerned about Crystal's welfare. Maybe I should have hurried over to her bedside and left Jason here to guide the doctor? I suddenly saw my enjoyment of my moments of peace as a callous disregard for Crystal. But now was no time to wallow in guilt.

"Truthfully," I said, "no, I'm not that close to her. But Jason didn't seem to think there was anything I could do for her, and my presence wouldn't exactly be soothing since she's not any fonder of me than I am of her."

Amanda shrugged. "Okay, where is he?"

Jason came around the corner of the house just then, to my relief. "Oh, great," he said. "You're the doctor?"

"No," Amanda said. "The doctor's in the car. I'm the driver today."

"I'll lead you over there. I been on the phone with Crystal, and she's not getting any better."

I felt another wave of remorse. "Call me at work, Jason, and let me know how she's doing, okay? I can come over after work and spend the night, if you need me."

"Thanks, Sis." He gave me a quick hug and then looked awkward. "Uh, I'm glad I didn't keep it a secret like Crystal wanted me to. She didn't think you'd help her."

"I'd like to think I was at least a good enough person to help someone who needed it, no matter if we were close or not." Surely Crystal hadn't imagined that I'd be indifferent, or even pleased, that she was ailing?

Dismayed, I watched the two very different vehicles start down the driveway on their way back to Hummingbird Road. I locked up and got in my own car in no very happy mood.

Continuing the theme of an eventful day, when I walked through the back door of Merlotte's that afternoon, Sam called to me from his office.

I went in to see what he wanted, knowing ahead of time that a few other people were waiting in there. To my dismay, I found that Father Riordan had ambushed me.

There were four people in Sam's office, besides my boss. Sam was unhappy, but trying to keep a good face on. A little to my surprise, Father Riordan wasn't happy about the people that had accompanied him, either. I suspected I knew who they were. Crap. Not only did Father Riordan have the Pelts in tow, but a young woman of about seventeen, who must be Debbie's sister, Sandra.

The three new people looked at me intently. The older Pelts were tall and slim. He wore glasses and was balding, with ears that stuck out of his head like jug handles. She was attractive, if a bit overly made up. She was wearing a

Donna Karan pants set and carrying a bag with a famous logo on it. Heels, too. Sandra Pelt was more casual, her jeans and T-shirt fitting her narrow figure very tightly.

I hardly heard Father Riordan formally introduce the Pelts, I was so overwhelmed with irritation that they were intruding themselves into my life to such an extent. I'd told Father Riordan I didn't want to meet them, yet here they were. The older Pelts ate me up with their avid eyes. *Savage,* Maria-Star had termed them. *Desperate* was the word that came to my mind.

Sandra was a different kettle of fish altogether: since she was the second child, she wasn't—couldn't be—a shifter like her folks, but she wasn't altogether a regular human, either. But something caught at my brain, made me pause. Sandra Pelt *was* a shifter of some kind. I'd heard the Pelts described as much more involved with their second daughter than they'd been with Debbie. Now, getting bits of information from them, I saw why that might be. Sandra Pelt might be underage, but she was formidable. She was a full Were.

But that couldn't be, unless . . .

Okay. Debbie Pelt, werefox, had been adopted. I'd learned that the Weres were prone to fertility problems, and I assumed that the Pelts had given up on having their own little Were, and had adopted a baby that was at least some kind of shape-shifter, if not their own kind. Even a full-blooded fox must have seemed preferable to a plain human. Then the Pelts had adopted another daughter, a Were.

"Sookie," Father Riordan said, his Irish voice charming but unhappy, "Barbara and Gordon showed up on my doorstep today. When I told them you'd said all you wanted to say about Debbie's disappearance, they weren't content with that. They insisted I bring them here with me."

My intense anger at the priest receded a bit. But another emotion filled its place. I was anxious enough about the encounter to feel my nervous smile spread across my face. I beamed at the Pelts, caught the backwash of their disapproval.

"I'm sorry for your situation," I said. "I'm sorry you're left wondering what happened to Debbie. But I don't know what else I can tell you."

A tear ran down Barbara Pelt's face, and I opened my purse to remove a tissue. I handed it to the woman, who patted her face. "She thought you were stealing Alcide from her," Barbara said.

You're not supposed to speak ill of the dead, but in Debbie Pelt's case, that was just plain impossible. "Mrs. Pelt, I'm going to be frank," I told her. Just not too frank. "Debbie was engaged to someone else at the time of her disappearance, a man named Clausen, if I remember correctly." Barbara Pelt nodded, reluctantly. "That engagement left Alcide at perfect liberty to date anyone he liked, and we did spend time together briefly." No lies there. "We haven't seen each other in weeks, and he's dating someone else now. So Debbie really was mistaken in what she thought."

Sandra Pelt bit her lower lip. She was lean, with clear skin and dark brown hair. She wore little makeup, and her teeth were dazzlingly white and even. Her hoop earrings could provide a perch for a parakeet; they were that big. She had a narrow body and expensive clothes: top of the mall chain.

Her expression was angry. She didn't like what I was saying, not one little bit. She was an adolescent, and there were strong surges of emotion in the girl. I remembered what my life had been like when I'd been Sandra's age, and I pitied her.

"Since you knew both of them," Barbara Pelt said carefully, not acknowledging my words, "you must have known that they had—they have—a strong love-hate relationship, no matter what Debbie did."

"Oh, *that's* true," I said, and maybe I didn't sound respectful enough. If there was anyone I'd done a big favor to in killing Debbie Pelt, that person was Alcide Herveaux. Otherwise, he and la Pelt would have been tearing each other up for years, if not the rest of their lives.

Sam turned away when the phone rang, but I glimpsed a smile on his face.

"We just feel that there must be something you know, some tiny little thing, that would help us discover what happened to our daughter. If—if she's met her end, we want her killer to come to justice."

I looked at the Pelts for a long moment. I could hear Sam's voice in the background as he reacted with astonishment to something he was hearing over the telephone.

"Mr. and Mrs. Pelt, Sandra," I said. "I talked to the police when Debbie vanished. I cooperated with them fully. I talked to your private investigators when they came here, to my place of work, just like you've done. I let them come into my home. I answered their questions." Just not truthfully.

(I know, the whole edifice was a lie, but I was doing the best I could.)

"I am very sorry for your loss and I sympathize with your anxiety to discover what's happened to Debbie," I continued, speaking slowly so I could pick my words. I took a deep breath. "But this has got to end. Enough's enough. I can't tell you a thing other than what I've already told you."

To my surprise, Sam edged around me and went into the bar, moving fast. He didn't say a word to anyone in the room. Father Riordan glanced after him, startled. I became even more anxious for the Pelts to leave. Something was up.

"I understand what you're saying," Gordon Pelt said stiffly. It was the first time the man had spoken. He didn't sound happy to be where he was, or to be doing what he was doing. "I realize we haven't gone about this in the best way, but I'm sure you'll excuse us when you think about what we've been through."

"Oh, of course," I said, and if that wasn't a complete truth, it wasn't a complete lie, either. I shut my purse and stowed it in the drawer in Sam's desk where all the servers kept their purses, and I hurried out to the bar.

I felt the upheaval wash over me. Something was wrong; almost every brain in the bar was broadcasting a signal combining excitement with anxiety bordering on panic.

"What's up?" I asked Sam, sidling behind the bar.

"I just told Holly that the school called. Holly's little boy is missing."

I felt the chill start at the base of my spine and work up. "What happened?"

"Danielle's mom usually picks up Cody from school when she picks up Danielle's little girl, Ashley." Danielle Gray and Holly Cleary had been best friends all through high school and their friendship had continued through the failure of both their marriages. They liked to work the same shift. Danielle's mother, Mary Jane Jasper, had been a lifesaver for Danielle, and from time to time her generosity had spilled over to include Holly. Ashley must be about eight, and Danielle's son, Mark Robert, should now be four. Holly's only child, Cody, was six. He was in the first grade.

"The school let someone else pick Cody up?" I'd heard that the teachers were on the alert for unauthorized spouses picking up their kids.

"No one knows what happened to the little guy. The teacher on duty, Halleigh Robinson, was standing outside watching the kids get in their cars. She says Cody suddenly remembered he'd left a picture for his mom on his desk, and he ran back into the school to get it. She doesn't remember seeing him come out, but she couldn't find him when she went in to check."

"So Mrs. Jasper was there waiting for Cody?"

"Yes, she was the only one left, sitting there in her car with her grandchildren."

"This is very scary. I don't suppose David knows anything?" David, Holly's ex, lived in Springhill and had remarried. I registered the departure of the Pelts: one less irritant.

"Apparently not. Holly called him at his job, and he was there and had been all afternoon, no doubt about it. He called his new wife, and she had just gotten back from picking up her own kids at the Springhill school. The local police went by their house and searched, just to be sure. Now David's on his way here."

Holly was sitting at one of the tables, and though her face was dry, her eyes had the look of someone who'd seen inside Hell. Danielle was crouched on the floor beside her, holding her hand and speaking to Holly urgently and quietly. Alcee Beck, one of the local detectives, was sitting at the same table. A pad and pen were in front of him, and he was talking on his cell phone.

"They've searched the school?"

"Yeah, that's where Andy is now. And Kevin and Kenya." Kevin and Kenya were two uniformed patrol officers. "Bud Dearborn is on the phone setting up an Amber Alert."

I spared a thought for how Halleigh must be feeling right now; she was only twenty-three or so, and this was her first teaching job. She hadn't done anything wrong, at least that I could tell—but when a kid goes missing, no one escapes blame.

I tried to think how I could help. This was a unique opportunity for my little disability to work for the greater good. I'd kept my mouth shut for years about all kinds of things. People didn't want to know what I knew. People didn't want to be around someone who could do what I could do. The way I survived was keeping my mouth shut, because it was easy for the humans around me to forget or disbelieve, when the evidence of my odd talent wasn't shoved in their face.

Would you want to be around a woman who knew you were cheating on your spouse, and with whom? If you were a guy, would you want to be around a woman who knew that you secretly wanted to wear lacy underwear? Would you want to hang with a gal who knew your most secret judgments on other people and all your hidden flaws?

No, I thought not.

But if a child was involved, how could I hold back?

I looked at Sam, and he looked back at me sadly. "It's hard, isn't it, *cher*?" he said. "What are you going to do?"

"Whatever I have to. But I have to do it now," I said.

He nodded. "Go on down to the school," he said, and I left.

6 ~

I DIDN'T KNOW HOW I WAS GOING TO ACCOMPLISH this. I didn't know who would acknowledge that I could help.

There was a crowd at the elementary school, of course. A group of about thirty adults was standing on the grass on the street side of the sidewalk in front of the school, and Bud Dearborn, the sheriff, was talking to Andy on the front lawn. Betty Ford Elementary was the same school I'd attended. The building had been fairly new then, a straightforward single-level brick building with a main hall containing the offices, the kindergarten, the first-grade classrooms, and the cafeteria. There a wing to the right for the second grade, a wing to the left for the third. A small recreational building was behind the school in the large playground, attainable by a covered walkway. It was used for the children's bad-weather exercise sessions.

Of course there were flagpoles in front of the school, one for the American flag and one for the Louisiana flag. I loved driving by when they were snapping in the breeze on a day like today. I loved thinking of all the little children inside, busy being children. But the flags had been taken down for the day, and only the tied-down ropes moved in the stiff wind. The green lawn of the school was dotted with the occasional candy wrapper or crumpled notebook paper. The school custodian, Madelyn Pepper (always called "Miss Maddy"), was sitting on a plastic chair right outside the main school doors, her rolling cart beside her. Miss Maddy had been the custodian for many years. Miss Maddy was a very slow woman, mentally, but she was a hard worker, and absolutely reliable. She looked much the same as she had when I had gone to school there: tall, husky, and white, with a long fall of dyed platinum hair. She was smoking a cigarette. The principal, Mrs. Garfield, had had a running battle with Miss Maddy for years about her habit, a battle that Miss Maddy had always won. She smoked outside, but she smoked. Today, Mrs. Garfield was completely indifferent to Miss Maddy's bad habit. Mrs. Garfield, the wife of a Methodist-Episcopal minister, was dressed in a mustard-color business suit, plain hose, and black pumps. She was just as strained as Miss Maddy, and a lot less guarded about showing it.

I worked my way through the front of the little crowd, not certain how to go about doing what I had to do.

Andy saw me first, and touched Bud Dearborn on the shoulder. Bud had a cell phone to his ear. Bud turned to look at me. I nodded at them. Sheriff Dearborn was not my friend. He'd been a friend of my father's, but he'd never had the time of day for me. To the sheriff, people fell into two categories: people who broke the law and could be arrested, and people who did not break the law and could not be. And most of those were people who just hadn't been caught breaking the law yet; that was what Bud believed. I fell somewhere in between. He felt sure I was guilty of something, but he couldn't figure out what it was.

Andy didn't like me much, either, but he was a believer. He jerked his head to the left, almost imperceptibly. I couldn't see Bud Dearborn's face clearly, but his shoulders stiffened in anger, and he leaned forward a little, his whole body posture saying that he was furious with his detective.

I worked my way out of the knot of anxious and curious citizens and slipped around the third-grade wing to the back of the school. The playground, about the size of half a football field, was fenced in, and the gate was ordinarily locked with a chain secured by a padlock. It had been opened, presumably for the convenience of the searchers. I saw Kevin Pryor, a thin young patrol officer who always won the 4K race at the Azalea Festival, bending over to peer into a culvert right across the street. The grass in the ditch was high, and his dark uniform pants were dusted with yellow. His partner, Kenya, who was as buxom as Kevin was thin, was across the street on the other side of the block, and I watched her head move from side to side as she scanned the surrounding yards.

The school took up a whole block in the middle of a residential area. All the houses around were modest homes on modest lots, the kind of neighborhood where there were basketball goals and bicycles, barking dogs, and driveways brightened with sidewalk chalk.

Today every surface was dusted in a light yellow powder; it was the very beginning of pollen time. If you rinsed off your car in town in your driveway, there would be a ring of yellow around the storm drain. Cats' bellies were tinged yellow, and tall dogs had yellow paws. Every other person you talked to had red eyes and carried a cache of tissues.

I noticed several thrown down around the playground. There were patches of new green grass and patches of hard-packed dirt, in areas where the children congregated the most. A big map of the United States had been painted on the concrete apron right outside the school doors. The name of each state was painted carefully and clearly. Louisiana was the only state colored bright red, and a pelican filled up its outline. The word *Louisiana* was too long to compete with the pelican, and it had been painted on the pavement right where the Gulf of Mexico would be.

Andy emerged from the rear door, his face set and hard. He looked ten years older.

"How's Halleigh?" I asked.

"She's in the school crying her eyes out," he said. "We have to find this boy."

"What did Bud say?" I asked. I stepped inside the gate.

"Don't ask," he said. "If there's anything you can do for us, we need all the help we can get."

"You're going out on a limb."

"So are you."

"Where are the people that were in the school when he ran back in?"

"They're all in here, except for the principal and the custodian."

"I saw them outside."

"I'll bring them in. All the teachers are in the cafeteria. It has that little stage at one end. Sit behind the curtain there. See if you can get anything."

"Okay." I didn't have a better idea.

Andy set off for the front of the school to gather up the principal and the custodian.

I stepped into the end of the third-grade corridor. There were bright pictures decorating the walls outside every classroom. I stared at the drawings of rudimentary people having picnics and fishing, and tears prickled my eyes. For the first time, I wished I were psychic instead of telepathic.

Then I could envision what had happened to Cody, instead of having to wait for someone to think about it. I'd never met a real psychic, but I understood that it was a very uncertain talent to have, one that was not specific enough at times, and too specific at others. My little quirk was much more reliable, and I made myself believe I could help this child.

As I made my way to the cafeteria, the smell of the school evoked a rush of memories. Most of them were painful; some were pleasant. When I'd been this small, I'd had no control over my telepathy and no idea what was wrong with me. My parents had put me through the mental health mill to try to find out, which had further set me off from my peers. But most of my teachers had been kind. They'd understood that I was doing my best to learn—that somehow I was constantly distracted, but it wasn't through my own choice. Inhaling the scent of chalk, cleaner, paper, and books brought it all back.

I remembered all the corridors and doorways as if I'd just left. The walls were a peach color now, instead of the off-white I remembered, and the carpet was a sort of speckled gray in place of brown linoleum; but the structure of the school was unchanged. Without hesitation, I slipped through a back door to the little stage, which was at one end of the lunchroom. If I remembered correctly, the space was actually called the "multipurpose room." The serving area could be shut off with folding doors, and the picnic tables that lined the room could be folded and moved aside. Now they were taking up the floor in orderly rows, and the people sitting at them were all adults, with the exception of some teachers' children who'd been in the classrooms with their mothers when the alarm had been raised.

I found a tiny plastic chair and set it back behind the curtains on stage left. I closed my eyes and began to concentrate. I lost the awareness of my body as I shut out all stimuli and began to let my mind roam free.

It's my fault, my fault, my fault! Why didn't I notice he hadn't come back out? Or did he slip by me? Could he have gotten into a car without my noticing?

Poor Halleigh. She was sitting by herself, and the mound of tissues by her showed how she'd been spending her waiting time. She was completely innocent of anything, so I resumed my probing.

Oh my God, thank you God that it's not my son that's missing. . . .

. . . go home and have some cookies . . .

Can't go to the store and pick up some hamburger meat, maybe I can call Ralph and he can go by Sonic . . . but we ate fast food last night, not good . . .

His mom's a barmaid, how many lowlifes does she know? Probably one of them.

It went on and on, a litany of harmless thoughts. The children were thinking about snacks and television, and they were also scared. The adults, for the most part, were very frightened for their own children and worried about the effect of Cody's disappearance on their own families and their own class.

Andy Bellefleur said, "In just a minute Sheriff Dearborn will be in here, and then we'll divide you into two groups."

The teachers relaxed. These were familiar instructions, as they themselves had often given.

"We'll ask questions of each of you in turn, and then you can go. I know you're all worried, and we have patrol officers searching the area, but maybe we can get some information that will help us find Cody."

Mrs. Garfield came in. I could feel her anxiety preceding her like a dark cloud, full of thunder. Miss Maddy was right behind her. I could hear the wheels of her cart, loaded with its lined garbage can and laden with cleaning supplies. All the scents surrounding her were familiar. Of course, she started cleaning right after school. She would have been in one of the classrooms, and she probably hadn't seen anything. Mrs. Garfield might have been in her office. The principal in my day, Mr. Heffernan, had stood outside with the teacher on duty until all the children were gone, so that parents would have a chance to talk to him if they had questions about their child's progress . . . or lack thereof.

I didn't lean out from behind the dusty curtain to look, but I could follow the progress of the two easily. Mrs. Garfield was a ball of tension so dense it charged the air around her, and Miss Maddy was equally surrounded by the smell of all the cleaning products and the sounds of her cart. She was miserable, too, and above all she wanted to get back to her routine. Maddy Pepper might be a woman of limited intelligence, but she loved her job because she was good at it.

I learned a lot while I was sitting there. I learned that one of the teachers was a lesbian, though she was married and had three children. I learned that another teacher was pregnant but hadn't told anyone yet. I learned that most of the women (there were no male teachers at the elementary school) were stressed out by multiple obligations to their families, their jobs, and their churches. Cody's teacher was very unhappy, because she liked the little boy, though she thought his mother was weird. She did believe Holly was trying hard to be a good mother, and that offset her distaste for Holly's goth trappings.

But nothing I learned helped me discover Cody's whereabouts until I ventured into Maddy Pepper's head.

When Kenya came up behind me, I was doubled over, my hand over my mouth, trying to cry silently. I was not capable of getting up to look for Andy or anyone else. I knew where the boy was.

"He sent me back here to find out what you know," Kenya whispered. She was massively unhappy about her errand, and though she'd always liked me okay, she didn't think I could do anything to help the police. She thought Andy was a fool for stalling his career by asking me to sit back there, concealed.

Then I caught something else, something faint and weak.

I jumped to my feet and grabbed Kenya by the shoulder. "Look in the garbage can, the one loaded on the cart, right now!" I said, my voice low but (I hoped) urgent enough to light a fire under Kenya. "He's in the can, he's still alive!"

Kenya wasn't rash enough to leap out from behind the curtain, jump down from the stage, and dash over to the custodian's cart. She gave me a hard, hard, look. I stepped out from behind the curtain to watch as Kenya made her way down the little stairs at the front of the stage, and went over to where Maddy Pepper was sitting, her fingers tapping against her legs. Miss Maddy wanted a cigarette. Then she realized that Kenya was approaching her, and a dull alarm sounded in her brain. When the custodian saw Kenya actually touch the edge of the large garbage can, she leaped to her feet and yelled, "I didn't mean to! I didn't mean to!"

Everyone in the room turned to the commotion, and everyone's face wore identical expressions of horror. Andy strode over, his face hard. Kenya was bent over the can, rummaging, tossing a snowstorm of used tissues over her shoulder. She froze for a second when she found what she'd been looking for. She bent over, almost in danger of falling into the can.

"He's alive," she called to Andy. "Call 911!"

"She was mopping when he ran back into the school to get the picture," Andy said. We were sitting in the cafeteria all by ourselves. "I don't know if you could hear all that, there was so much noise in the room."

I nodded. I'd been able to hear her thoughts as she'd spoken. All these years on her job, and she'd never had a problem with a student that wasn't easily resolved with a few strong words on her part. Then, today, Cody had come running into the classroom, pollen all over his shoes and pants cuffs, tracking up Maddy's freshly mopped floor. She'd yelled at him, and he'd been so startled that his feet had slipped on the wet floor. The little boy had gone over backward and hit his head on the floor. The corridor had indoor-outdoor carpeting to reduce the noise, but the classrooms did not, and his head had bounced on the linoleum.

Maddy had thought she'd killed him, and she'd hastily concealed his body in the nearest receptacle. She'd realized she'd lose her job if the child was dead, and on an impulse she'd tried to hide him. She had no plan and no idea of what would happen. She hadn't figured out how she'd dispose of his body, and she hadn't counted on how miserable she'd feel about the whole thing, how guilty.

To keep my part of it silent, which the police and I both agreed was absolutely the best idea, Andy suggested to Kenya that she'd suddenly realized the only receptacle in the school she hadn't searched was Maddy Pepper's trash can. "That's exactly what I thought," Kenya said. "I should search it, at least poke around and see if an abductor had tossed something into it." Kenya's round face was unreadable. Kevin looked at her, his brows drawn together, sensing something beneath the surface of the conversation. Kevin was no fool, especially where Kenya was concerned.

Andy's thoughts were clear to me. "Don't ever ask me to do this again," I told him.

He nodded in acquiescence, but he was lying. He was seeing before him a vista of cleared cases, of malefactors locked up, of how clean Bon Temps would be when I'd told him who all the criminals were and he'd found a way to charge them with something.

"I'm not going to do it," I said. "I'm not going to help you all the time. You're a detective. You have to find things out in a legal way, so you can build a court case. If you use me all the time, you'll get sloppy. The cases will fall through. You'll get a bad reputation." I spoke desperately, helplessly. I didn't think my words would have any effect.

"She's not a Magic 8 Ball," Kevin said.

Kenya looked surprised, and Andy was more than surprised; he thought this was almost heresy. Kevin was a patrolman; Andy was a detective. And Kevin was a quiet man, listening to all his co-workers, but not often offering a comment of his own. He was notoriously mother-ridden; maybe he'd learned at his mother's knee not to offer opinions.

"You can't shake her and come up with the right answer," Kevin continued. "You have to find out the answer on your own. It's not right to take over Sookie's life so you can do your job better."

"Right," said Andy, unconvinced. "But I would think any citizen would want her town to be rid of thieves and rapists and murderers."

"What about adulterers and people who take extra papers out of the newspaper dispensers? Should I turn those in, too? What about kids who cheat on their exams?"

"Sookie, you know what I mean," he said, white-faced and furious.

"Yeah, I know what you mean. Forget it. I helped you save that child's life. Don't make me even think about regretting it." I left the same way I'd come, out the back gate and down the side of the school property to where I'd left my car. I drove back to work very carefully, because I was still shaking with the intensity of the emotions that had flowed through the school this afternoon.

At the bar, I found that Holly and Danielle had left—Holly to the hospital to be with her son, and Danielle to drive her there because she was so shaky.

"The police would have taken Holly, gladly," Sam said. "But I knew Holly didn't have anyone but Danielle here, so I thought I might as well let Danielle go, too."

"Of course, that leaves me to serve by myself," I said tartly, thinking I was getting punished doubly for helping Holly out.

He smiled at me, and for a second I couldn't help but smile back. "I've called that Tanya Grissom. She said she'd like to help out, just on a fill-in basis."

Tanya Grissom had just moved to Bon Temps, and she'd come into Merlotte's right away to put in an application. She'd put herself through college waitressing, she'd told Sam. She'd pulled down over two hundred dollars a night in tips. That wasn't going to happen in Bon Temps, and I'd told her so frankly.

"Did you call Arlene and Charlsie first?" I realized I'd overstepped my bounds, because I was only a waitress/barmaid, not the owner. It wasn't for me to remind Sam he should call the women with longer time in before he called the newcomer. The newcomer was definitely a shape-shifter, and I was afraid Sam was prejudiced in her favor.

Sam didn't look irritated, just matter-of-fact. "Yeah, I called them first. Arlene said she had a date, and Charlsie was keeping her grandbaby. She's been hinting pretty heavily that she won't be working much longer. I think she's going to keep the baby full-time when her daughter-in-law goes back to work."

"Oh," I said, disconcerted. I'd have to get used to someone new. Of course, barmaids come and barmaids go, and I'd seen quite a few pass through the employee door of Merlotte's in my—gosh, now five—years of working for Sam. Merlotte's was open until midnight on weeknights and until one on Friday and Saturday. Sam had tried opening on Sunday for a while, but it didn't pay. So now Merlotte's was closed on Sunday, unless it had been rented for a private party.

Sam tried to rotate our times so everyone got a chance to work the more lucrative night shift, so some days I worked eleven to five (or six-thirty, if we became extra busy) and sometimes I worked five to closing. He'd experimented with times and days until we'd all agreed on what worked best. He expected a little flexibility from us, and in return he was good about letting us off for funerals and weddings and other milestones.

I'd had a couple of other jobs before I'd started working for Sam. He was the easiest person to work for, by far. He'd become more than my employer somewhere along the way; he was my friend. When I'd found out he was a shapeshifter, it hadn't bothered me a bit. I'd heard rumors in the shifting community that the Weres were thinking of going public, the way the vampires had. I worried about Sam. I worried about people in Bon Temps accepting him. Would they feel he'd been deceiving them all these years, or would they take it in stride? Since the vampires had made their carefully orchestrated revelation, life as we knew it had changed, all over the world. Some countries, after the initial shock had worn off, had begun working to include vampires in the mainstream of life; others had pronounced vampires nonhuman and urged their citizens to kill vampires on sight (easier said than done).

"I'm sure Tanya will be fine," I said, but I sounded uncertain, even to my own ears. Acting on an impulse—and I can only suppose the tidal wave of emotions I'd experienced that day had something to do with this—I threw my arms around Sam and gave him a hug. I smelled clean skin and hair and the slight sweet smell of a light aftershave, an undertone of wine, a whiff of beer . . . the Sam smell. I drew it into my lungs like oxygen.

Surprised, Sam hugged me back, and for a second the warmth of his embrace made me feel almost light-headed with pleasure. Then we both backed off, because after all, this was our workplace and there were a few customers scattered around. Tanya came in, so it was good we were out of the clinch. I didn't want her to think this was routine.

Tanya was shorter than my five foot six, and she was a pleasant-looking woman in her late twenties. Her hair was short and straight and shiny, a medium brown that almost matched her eyes. She had a small mouth and a button nose and a nice figure. I had absolutely no reason to dislike her, but I wasn't happy to see her. I was ashamed of myself. I should give Tanya a fair chance to show her true character.

After all, I'd discover it sooner or later. You can't hide what you really are, not from me—not if you're a regular human person. I try not to listen in, but I can't block everything out. When I'd dated Bill, he'd helped me learn how to close my mind. Since then, life had been easier—more pleasant, more relaxed.

Tanya was a smiling woman, I'd give her that. She smiled at Sam, and she smiled at me, and she smiled at the customers. It wasn't a nervous smile, like mine, the grin that says "I'm hearing a clamor inside my head and I'm trying to look normal on the outside"; Tanya's smile was more of a "I'm really cute and perky and will endear myself to everyone" kind of smile. Before she picked up a tray and started working, Tanya asked a list of sensible questions, and I could tell she'd had experience.

"What's wrong?" Sam asked.

"Nothing," I said. "I just . . ."

"She seems nice enough," he said. "Do you think there's something wrong with her?"

"Nothing I know of," I said, trying to sound brisk and cheerful. I knew I was smiling that jittery smile. "Look, Jane Bodehouse is signaling for another round. We'll have to call her son again."

Tanya turned around and looked at me just then, as if she felt my eyes on her back. Her own smile was gone, replaced with a look so level that my estimate of her capacity for serious action instantly upgraded. We stood for a moment, regarding each other steadily, and then she beamed at me and continued to the next table, asking the man there if he was ready for another beer.

Suddenly I thought, *I wonder if Tanya is interested in Sam.* I didn't like the way I felt when I thought about that. I decided the day had been exhausting enough without creating a new worry. And no call from Jason.

After work, I went home with a lot on my mind: Father Riordan, the Pelts, Cody, Crystal's miscarriage.

I drove down my graveled driveway through the woods, and when I pulled into the clearing and drove behind the house to park at the back door, its isolation struck me all over again. Living in town for a few weeks had made the house seem even lonelier, and though I loved being back in the old place, it didn't feel the same as it had before the fire.

I'd seldom felt worried living by myself in this isolated spot, but over the past few months my vulnerability had been impressed on me. I'd had a few close calls, and twice there'd been intruders in my house waiting for me when I'd come in. Now I had installed some really good locks on my doors, I had peepholes front and back, and my brother had given me his Benelli shotgun to keep for good.

I had some big lights on the corners of the house, but I didn't like to leave them on all night. I was considering the purchase of one of those motion-detector lights. The drawback was, since I lived in a large clearing in the middle of the woods, critters often crossed my yard at night, and the light would come on when every little possum rambled across the grass.

The second point about a light coming on was . . . *So what?*

The kind of thing I was scared of wasn't going to be intimidated by a light. I'd just be able to see it better before it ate me. Furthermore, there were no neighbors that a light might startle or rouse. Strange, I reflected, that I'd seldom had a frightened moment when my grandmother had been alive. She'd been a tough little lady for a woman in her late seventies, but she couldn't have defended me against a flea. Somehow, the simple fact of not being alone had made me feel safer.

After all this thinking about danger, I was in a tense state when I got out of my car. I'd passed a truck parked in front, and I unlocked the back and went through the house to open the front door with the miserable feeling that I was about to have to go through a scene. The quiet interlude on my front porch watching the bees in the pear tree seemed a week ago, instead of hours.

Calvin Norris, leader of the Hotshot werepanthers, got out of his truck and came up the steps. He was a bearded man in his early forties, and he was a serious man whose responsibilities sat squarely on his shoulders. Evidently Calvin had just gotten off work. He was wearing the blue shirt and blue jeans all the Norcross crew leaders wore.

"Sookie," he said, nodding to me.

"Please come in," I answered, though I was reluctant. However, Calvin had never been anything but civil to me, and he had helped me rescue my brother a couple of months ago, when Jason had been held hostage. At the least, I owed him civility.

"My niece called me when the danger had passed," he said heavily, taking a seat on the couch after I'd waved my hand to show he was welcome to stay. "I think you saved her life."

"I'm real glad to hear Crystal's better. All I did was make a phone call." I sat in my favorite old chair, and I noticed

I was slumping with weariness. I forced my shoulders back. "Dr. Ludwig was able to stop her bleeding?"

Calvin nodded. He looked at me steadily, his strange eyes solemn. "She's going to be okay. Our women miscarry a lot. That's why we were hoping . . . Well."

I flinched, the weight of Calvin's hopes that I'd mate with him resting heavily on my shoulders. I'm not sure why I felt guilty; because of his disappointment, I guess. After all, it was hardly my fault that the idea had limited appeal for me.

"I guess Jason and Crystal will be getting hitched," Calvin said matter-of-factly. "I have to say, I'm not crazy about your brother, but then I'm not the one marrying him."

I was nonplussed. I didn't know if this wedding was Jason's idea, or Calvin's, or Crystal's. Jason certainly hadn't been thinking marriage this morning, unless it was something he'd neglected to mention in the turmoil of his worry about Crystal. I said, "Well, to be honest, I'm not crazy about Crystal. But I'm not the one marrying her." I took a deep breath. "I'll do my best to help them out, if they decide to . . . do that. Jason's about all I've got, as you know."

"Sookie," he said, and his voice was suddenly far less certain, "I want to talk about something else, too."

Of course he did. No way was I going to dodge this bullet.

"I know that something you got told, when you came out to the house, put you off me. I'd like to know what it was. I can't fix it, if I don't know what's broken."

I took a deep breath, while I considered my next words very carefully. "Calvin, I know that Terry is your daughter." When I'd gone to see Calvin when he'd gotten out of the hospital after being shot, I'd met Terry and her mother Maryelizabeth at Calvin's house. Though they clearly didn't live there, it was equally clear that they treated the place as an extension of their own home. Then Terry had asked me if I was going to marry her father.

"Yes," Calvin said. "I would've told you if you'd asked me."

"Do you have other children?"

"Yes. I have three other children."

"By different mothers?"

"By three different mothers."

I'd been right. "Why is that?" I asked, to be sure.

"Because I'm pure-blooded," he said, as if it were self-evident. "Since only the first child of a pureblood couple turns out to be a full panther, we have to switch off."

I was profoundly glad I'd never seriously considered marrying Calvin, because if I had, I would have thrown up right then. What I'd suspected, after witnessing the succession-to-packmaster ritual, was true. "So it's not the woman's first child, period, that turns out to be a full-blooded shape-shifter . . . it's her first child with a specific man."

"Right." Calvin looked surprised that I hadn't known that. "The first child of any given pureblood couple is the real thing. So if our population gets too small, a pure-blooded male has to mate with as many pure-blooded women as he can, to increase the pack."

"Okay." I waited for a minute, to collect myself. "Did you think that I would be okay with you impregnating other women, if we got married?"

"No, I wouldn't expect that of an outsider," he answered, in that same matter-of-fact voice. "I think it's time I settled down with one woman. I've done my duty as leader."

I tried not to roll my eyes. If it had been anyone else I would have sniggered, but Calvin was an honorable man, and he didn't deserve that reaction.

"Now I want to mate for life, and it would be good for the pack if I could bring new blood into the community. You can tell that we've bred with each other for too long. My eyes can hardly pass for human, and Crystal takes forever to change. We have to add something new to our gene pool, as the scientists call it. If you and I had a baby, which was what I was hoping, that baby wouldn't ever be a full Were; but he or she might breed into the community, bring new blood and new skills."

"Why'd you pick me?"

He said, almost shyly. "I like you. And you're real pretty." He smiled at me then, a rare and sweet expression. "I've watched you at the bar for years. You're nice to everyone, and you're a hard worker, and you don't have no one to take care of you like you deserve. And you know about us; it wouldn't be any big shock."

"Do other kinds of shape-shifters do the same thing?" I asked this so quietly, I could hardly hear myself. I stared down at my hands, clenched together in my lap, and I could hardly breathe as I waited to hear his answer. Alcide's green eyes filled my thoughts.

"When the pack begins to grow too small, it's their duty to," he said slowly. "What's on your mind, Sookie?"

"When I went to the contest for the Shreveport packmaster, the one who won—Patrick Furnan—he had sex with a young Were girl, though he was married. I began to wonder."

"Did I ever stand a chance with you?" Calvin asked. He seemed to have drawn his own conclusions.

Calvin could not be blamed for wanting to preserve his way of life. If I found the means distasteful, that was my problem.

"You definitely interested me," I said. "But I'm just too human to think of having my husband's children all around me. I'd just be too . . . it would just throw me off all the time, knowing my husband had had sex with almost every woman I saw day-to-day." Come to think of it, Jason would fit right into the Hotshot community. I paused for a second, but he remained silent. "I hope that my brother will be welcomed into your community, regardless of my answer."

"I don't know if he understands what we do," Calvin said. "But Crystal's already miscarried once before, by a full-blood. Now she's miscarried this baby of your brother's. I'm thinking this means Crystal had better not try any more to have a panther. She may not be able to have a baby of your brother's. Do you feel obliged to talk to him about that?"

"It shouldn't be up to me to discuss that with Jason . . . it should be up to Crystal." I met Calvin's eyes. I opened my mouth to remark that if all Jason wanted was babies, he shouldn't get married; but then I recognized that was a sensitive subject, and I stopped while I was ahead.

Calvin shook my hand in an odd, formal way when he left. I believed that marked the end of his courtship. I had never been deeply attracted to Calvin Norris, and I'd never seriously thought about accepting his offer. But I'd be less than honest if I didn't admit that I'd fantasized about a steady husband with a good job and benefits, a husband who came straight home after his shift and fixed broken things on his days off. There were men who did that, men who didn't change into anything other than their own form, men who were alive twenty-four/seven. I knew that from reading so many minds at the bar.

I'm afraid that what really struck me about Calvin's confession—or explanation—is what it might reveal to me about Alcide.

Alcide had sparked my affection, and my lust. Thinking of him did make me wonder what marriage to him would be like, wonder in a very personal way, as opposed to my impersonal speculation about health insurance that Calvin had inspired. I'd pretty much abandoned the secret hope Alcide had inspired in me, after I'd been forced to shoot his former fiancée; but something in me had clung to the thought, something I'd kept secret even from myself, even after I'd found out he was dating Maria-Star. As recently as this day, I'd been stoutly denying to the Pelts that Alcide had any interest in me. But something lonely inside me had nursed a hope.

I got up slowly, feeling about twice my actual age, and went into the kitchen to get something out of the freezer for my supper. I wasn't hungry, but I'd eat unwisely later if I didn't fix something now, I told myself sternly.

But I never cooked a meal for myself that night.

Instead, I leaned against the refrigerator door and cried.

7 ~

THE NEXT DAY WAS FRIDAY; NOT ONLY WAS IT MY day off this week, but I had a date, so it was practically a red-letter day. I refused to ruin it by moping. Though it was still cool for such a pastime, I did one of my favorite things: I put on a bikini, greased myself up, and went to lie in the sun on the adjustable chaise lounge I'd gotten at Wal-Mart on sale at the end of the previous summer. I took a book, a radio, and a hat into the front yard, where there were fewer trees and flowering plants to encourage bugs that bit. I read, sang along with the tunes on the radio, and painted my toenails and fingernails. Though I was goose-pimply at first, I warmed up quickly along with the sun, and there was no breeze that day to chill me.

I know sunbathing is bad and evil, and I'll pay for it

later, etc., etc., but it's one of the few free pleasures available to me.

No one came to visit, I couldn't hear the phone, and since the sun was out, the vampires weren't. I had a delightful time, all by myself. Around one o'clock, I decided to run into town for some groceries and a new bra, and I stopped at the mailbox out by Hummingbird Road to see if the mail carrier had run yet. Yes. My cable bill and my electric bill were in the mailbox, which was a downer. But lurking behind a Sears sales brochure was an invitation to a wedding shower for Halleigh. Well . . . gosh. I was surprised, but pleased. Of course, I'd lived next to Halleigh in one of Sam's duplexes for a few weeks while my house was being repaired after the fire, and we'd seen each at least once a day during that time. So it wasn't a complete stretch, her putting me on her list of invitees. Plus, maybe she was relieved that the Cody situation had been cleared up so quickly?

I didn't get many invitations, so receiving it added to my sense of well-being. Three other teachers were giving the shower, and the invitation designated kitchen gifts. How timely, since I was on my way to the Wal-Mart Supercenter in Clarice.

After a lot of thought, I bought a two-quart Corning Ware casserole dish. Those were always handy. (I also got fruit juice, sharp cheddar, bacon, gift paper, and a really pretty blue bra and matching panties, but that's beside the point.)

After I'd gotten home and unloaded my purchases, I wrapped the boxed casserole dish in some silvery paper and stuck a big white bow on it. I wrote the date and time of the shower on my calendar, and I put the invitation on top of the present. I was on top of the shower situation.

Riding high on a crest of virtue, I wiped down the inside and outside of my new refrigerator after I'd eaten lunch.

I washed a load of clothes in my new washer, wishing for the hundredth time that my cabinets were in place since I was tired of looking for things in the clutter on the floor.

I walked through the house to make sure it looked nice, since Quinn was picking me up. Not even letting myself think, I changed my sheets and cleaned my bathroom—not that I had any intention of falling into bed with Quinn, but it's better to be prepared than not, right? Besides, it just made me feel good, knowing that everything was clean and nice. Fresh towels in both bathrooms, a light dusting around the living room and bedroom, a quick circuit with the vacuum. Before I got in the shower, I even swept the porches, though I knew they would be covered again in a yellow haze before I got back from my date.

I let the sun dry my hair, probably getting it full of pollen, too. I put on my makeup carefully; I didn't wear a lot, but it was fun to apply it for something more interesting than work. A little eye shadow, a lot of mascara, some powder and lipstick. Then I put on my new date underwear. It made me feel special from the skin on out: midnight blue lace. I looked in the full-length mirror to check out the effect. I gave myself a thumbs-up. You have to cheer for yourself, right?

The outfit I'd bought from Tara's Togs was royal blue and made out of some heavy knit that hung beautifully. I zipped up the pants and put on the top. It was sleeveless and it wrapped across my breasts and tied. I experimented with the depth of cleavage, at last picking a degree of revelation I was sure toed the line between sexy and cheap.

I got my black wrap out of the closet, the one Alcide had given me to replace one Debbie Pelt had vandalized. I'd need it later in the evening. I slipped into my black sandals. I experimented with jewelry, finally settling on a plain gold chain (it had been my grandmother's) and plain ball earrings.

Hah!

There was a knock on the front door, and I glanced at the clock, a bit surprised that Quinn was fifteen minutes early. I hadn't heard his truck, either. I opened the door to find not Quinn, but Eric, standing there.

I am sure he enjoyed my gasp of surprise.

Never open your door without checking. Never assume you know who's on the other side. That's why I'd gotten the peepholes! Stupid me. Eric must have flown, since I couldn't see a car anywhere.

"May I come in?" Eric asked politely. He had looked me over. After appreciating the view, he realized it hadn't been designed with him in mind. He wasn't happy. "I suppose you're expecting company?"

"As a matter of fact I am, and actually, I'd rather you stayed on that side of the doorsill," I said. I stepped back so he couldn't reach me.

"You told Pam that you didn't want to come to Shreveport," he said. Oh yes, he was angry. "So here I am, to find out why you don't answer my call." Usually, his accent was very slight, but tonight I noticed that it was pronounced.

"I didn't have time," I said. "I'm going out tonight."

"So I see," he said, more quietly. "Who are you going out with?"

"Is that really any of your business?" I met his eyes, challengingly.

"Of course it is," he said.

I was disconcerted. "And that would be why?" I rallied a little.

"You should be mine. I have slept with you, I have cared for you, I have . . . assisted you financially."

"You paid me money you owed me, for services rendered," I answered. "You may have slept with me, but not recently, and you've shown no signs of wanting to do so again. If you care for me, you're showing it in a mighty strange way.

I never heard that 'total avoidance aside from orders coming from flunkies' was a valid way to show caring." This was a jumbled sentence, okay, but I knew he got it.

"You're calling Pam a flunky?" He had a ghost of smile on his lips. Then he got back to being miffed. I could tell because he began dropping his contractions. "I do not have to hang around you to show you. I am sheriff. You . . . you are in my retinue."

I knew my mouth was hanging open, but I couldn't help it. "Catching flies," my grandmother had called that expression, and I felt like I was catching plenty of them. "Your retinue?" I managed to splutter. "Well, *up* you and your retinue. You don't tell me what to do!"

"You are obliged to go with me to the conference," Eric said, his mouth tense and his eyes blazing. "That was why I called you to Shreveport, to talk to you about travel time and arrangements."

"I'm not obliged to go anywhere with you. You got outranked, buddy."

"Buddy? *Buddy*?"

And it would have degenerated from there, if Quinn hadn't pulled up. Instead of arriving in his truck, Quinn was in a Lincoln Continental. I felt a moment of sheer snobbish pleasure at the thought of riding in it. I'd selected the pants outfit at least partly because I thought I'd be scrambling up into a pickup, but I was just as pleased to slither into a luxurious car. Quinn came across the lawn and mounted the porch with an understated speed. He didn't look as though he was hurrying, but suddenly he was there, and I was smiling at him, and he looked wonderful. He was wearing a dark gray suit, a dark purple shirt, and a tie that blended the two colors in a paisley pattern. He was wearing one earring, a simple gold hoop.

Eric had fang showing.

"Hello, Eric," Quinn said calmly. His deep voice rumbled

along my spine. "Sookie, you look good enough to eat." He smiled at me, and the tremors along my spine spread into another area entirely. I would never have believed that in Eric's presence I could think another man was attractive. I'd have been wrong to think so.

"You look very nice, too," I said, trying not to beam like an idiot. It was not cool to drool.

Eric said, "What have you been telling Sookie, Quinn?"

The two tall men looked at each other. I didn't believe I was the source of their animosity. I was a symptom, not the disease. Something lay underneath this.

"I've been telling Sookie that the queen requires Sookie's presence at the conference as part of her party, and that the queen's summons supercedes yours," Quinn said flatly.

"Since when has the queen given orders through a shifter?" Eric said, contempt flattening his voice.

"Since this shifter performed a valuable service for her in the line of business," Quinn answered, with no hesitation. "Mr. Cataliades suggested to Her Majesty that I might be helpful in a diplomatic capacity, and my partners were glad to give me extra time to perform any duties she might give me."

I wasn't totally sure I was following this, but I got the gist of it.

Eric was incensed, to use a good entry from my Word of the Day calendar. In fact, his eyes were almost throwing sparks, he was so angry. "This woman has been mine, and she will be mine," he said, in tones so definite I thought about checking my rear end for a brand.

Quinn shifted his gaze to me. "Babe, are you his, or not?" he asked.

"Not," I said.

"Then let's go enjoy the show," Quinn said. He didn't seem frightened, or even concerned. Was this his true reaction, or was he presenting a façade? Either way, it was pretty impressive.

I had to pass by Eric on my way to Quinn's car. I looked up at him, because I couldn't help it. Being close to him while he was this angry was not a safe thing, and I needed to be on my guard. Eric was seldom crossed in serious matters, and my annexation by the Queen of Louisiana—his queen—was a serious matter. My date with Quinn was sticking in his throat, too. Eric was just going to have to swallow.

Then we were both in the car, belted in, and Quinn did an expert backing maneuver to point the Lincoln back to Hummingbird Road. I breathed out, slowly and carefully. It took a few quiet moments for me to feel calm again. Gradually my hands relaxed. I realized the silence had been building. I gave myself a mental shake. "Do you go to the theater often, as you're traveling around?" I asked socially.

He laughed, and the deep, rich sound of it filled up the car. "Yes," he said. "I go to the movies and the theater and any sporting event that's going on. I like to see people do things. I don't watch much television. I like to get out of my hotel room or my apartment and watch things happen or make them happen myself."

"So do you dance?"

He gave me a quick glance. "I do."

I smiled. "I like to dance." And I was actually pretty good at dancing, not that I got many chances to practice. "I'm no good at singing," I admitted, "but I really, really enjoy dancing."

"That sounds promising."

I thought we'd have to see how this evening went before we made any dancing dates, but at least we knew there was something we both liked to do. "I like movies," I said. "But I don't think I've ever been to any live sports besides high school games. But those, I do attend. Football, basketball, baseball . . . I go to 'em all, when my job will let me."

"Did you play a sport in school?" Quinn asked. I confessed

that I'd played softball, and he told me he'd played basketball, which, considering his height, was no surprise at all.

Quinn was easy to talk to. He listened when I spoke. He drove well; at least he didn't curse at the other drivers, like Jason did. My brother tended to be on the impatient side when he drove.

I was waiting for the other shoe to drop. I was waiting for that moment—you know the one I mean—the moment when your date suddenly confesses to something you just can't stomach: he reveals himself as a racist or homophobe, admits he'd never marry anyone but another Baptist (Southerner, brunette, marathon runner, whatever), tells you about his children by his first three wives, describes his fondness for being paddled, or relates his youthful experiences in blowing up frogs or torturing cats. After that moment, no matter how much fun you have, you know it's not going anywhere. And I didn't even have to wait for a guy to tell me this stuff verbally; I could read it right out of his head before we even dated.

Never popular with the regular guys, me. Whether they admitted it or not, they couldn't stand the idea of going out with a girl who knew exactly how often they jacked off, had a lusty thought about another woman, or wondered how their teacher looked with her clothes off.

Quinn came around and opened my door when we parked across the street from the Strand, and he took my hand as we crossed the street. I enjoyed the courtesy.

There were lots of people going into the theater, and they all seemed to look at Quinn. Of course, a bald guy as tall as Quinn is going to get some stares. I was trying not to think about his hand; it was very large and very warm and very dry.

"They're all looking at you," he said, as he pulled the tickets from his pocket, and I pressed my lips together to keep from laughing.

"Oh, I don't think so," I said.

"Why else would they be staring?"

"At you," I said, amazed.

He laughed out loud, that deep laugh that made me vibrate inside.

We had very good seats, right in the middle and toward the front of the theater. Quinn filled up his seat, no doubt about it, and I wondered if the people behind him could see. I looked at my program with some curiosity, found I didn't recognize the names of the any of the actors in the production, and decided I didn't care at all. I glanced up to find that Quinn was staring at me. I felt my face flood with color. I'd folded my black wrap and placed it in my lap, and I had the abrupt desire to pull my top higher to cover every inch of my cleavage.

"Definitely looking at you," he said, and smiled. I ducked my head, pleased but self-conscious.

Lots of people have seen *The Producers.* I don't need to describe the plot, except to say it's about gullible people and lovable rascals, and it's very funny. I enjoyed every minute. It was marvelous to watch people performing right in front of me on such a professional level. The guest star, the one whom the older people in the audience seemed to recognize, swashed through the lead role with this amazing assurance. Quinn laughed too, and after the intermission he took my hand again. My fingers closed around his quite naturally, and I didn't feel self-conscious about the contact.

Suddenly it was an hour later, and the play was over. We stood up along with everyone else, though we could tell it would take a while for the theater to clear out. Quinn took my wrap and held it for me, and I threw it around me. He was sorry I was covering myself up—I got that directly from his brain.

"Thank you," I said, tugging on his sleeve to make sure he was looking at me. I wanted him to know how much I meant it. "That was just great."

"I enjoyed it, too. You want to go get something to eat?"

"Okay," I said, after a moment.

"You had to think about it?"

I had actually sort of flash-thought about several different items. If I'd enumerated them, it'd have run something like, *He must be having a good time or he wouldn't suggest more of the evening. I have to get up and go to work tomorrow but I don't want to miss this opportunity. If we go to eat I have to be careful not to spill anything on my new clothes. Will it be okay to spend even more of his money, since the tickets cost so much?*

"Oh, I had to consider the calories," I said, patting my rear end.

"There's nothing wrong with you, front or back," Quinn said, and the warmth in his eyes made me feel like basking. I knew I was curvier than the ideal. I'd actually heard Holly tell Danielle that anything over a size eight was simply disgusting. Since a day I got into an eight was a happy day for me, I'd felt pretty forlorn for all of three minutes. I would have related this conversation to Quinn if I hadn't been sure it would sound like I was angling for a compliment.

"Let the restaurant be my treat," I said.

"With all due respect to your pride, no, I won't." Quinn looked me right in the eyes to make sure I knew he meant it.

We'd reached the sidewalk by that time. Surprised at his vehemence, I didn't know how to react. On one level, I was relieved, since I have to be careful with my money. On another level, I knew it was right for me to offer and I would have felt good if he'd said that would be fine.

"You know I'm not trying to insult you, right?" I said.

"I understand that you're being equal."

I looked up at him doubtfully, but he was serious.

Quinn said, "I believe you are absolutely as good as me in every way. But I asked you out, and I am providing the financial backup for our date."

"What if I asked you out?"

He looked grim. "Then I'd have to sit back and let you take care of the evening," he said. He said it reluctantly, but he said it. I looked away and smiled.

Cars were pulling out of the parking lot at a steady pace. Since we'd taken our time leaving the theater, Quinn's car was looking lonely in the second row. Suddenly, my mental alarm went off. Somewhere close, there was a lot of hostility and evil intent. We had left the sidewalk to cross the street to the parking lot. I gripped Quinn's arm and then let it go so we could clear for action.

"Something's wrong," I said.

Without replying, Quinn began scanning the area. He unbuttoned his suit coat with his left hand so he could move without hindrance. His fingers curled into fists. Since he was a man with a powerful protective urge, he stepped ahead of me, in front of me.

So of course, we were attacked from behind.

8

In a blur of movement that couldn't be broken down into increments my eye could clearly recognize, a beast knocked me into Quinn, who stumbled forward a step. I was on the ground underneath the snarling half man, half wolf by the time Quinn wheeled, and as soon as he did, another Were appeared, seemingly out of nowhere, to leap on Quinn's back.

The creature on top of me was a brand-new fresh half Were, so young he could only have been bitten in the past three weeks. He was in such a frenzy that he had attacked before he had finished with the partial change that a bitten Were can achieve. His face was still elongating into a muzzle, even as he tried to choke me. He would never attain the beautiful wolf form of the full-blooded Were. He was "bitten, not blood," as the Weres put it. He still had arms, he still had legs, he had a body covered with hair, and he had a wolf's head. But he was just as savage as a full-blood.

I clawed at his hands, the hands that were gripping my neck with such ferocity. I wasn't wearing my silver chain tonight. I'd decided it would be tacky, since my date was himself a shifter. Being tacky might have saved my life, I thought in a flash, though it was the last coherent thought I had for a few moments.

The Were was straddling my body, and I brought my knees up sharply, trying to give him a big enough jolt that he'd loosen his hold. There were shrieks of alarm from the few remaining pedestrians, and a higher, more piercing shriek from Quinn's attacker, whom I saw flying through the air as if he'd been launched from a cannon. Then a big hand grasped my attacker by his own neck and lifted him. Unfortunately, the half beast who had his hands wrapped around my throat didn't let me go. I began to rise from the pavement, too, my throat becoming more and more pinched by the grip he had on me.

Quinn must have seen my desperate situation, because he struck the Were on top of me with his free hand, a slap that rocked the Were's head back and simply knocked him for a loop so thoroughly that he let go of my neck.

Then Quinn grabbed the young Were by the shoulders and tossed him aside. The boy landed on the pavement and didn't move.

"Sookie," Quinn said, hardly sounding out of breath. Out of breath is what I was, struggling to get my throat to open back up so I could gulp in some oxygen. I could hear a police siren, and I was profoundly thankful. Quinn slipped his arm under my shoulders and held me up. Finally I breathed in, and the air was wonderful, blissful. "You're breathing okay?" he asked. I gathered myself enough to nod. "Any bones broken in your throat?" I tried to raise my hand to my neck, but my hand wasn't cooperating just at the moment.

His face filled my scope of vision, and in the dim light of the corner lamp I could see he was pumped. "I'll kill them if they hurt you," he growled, and just then, that was delightful news.

"Bitten," I wheezed, and he looked horrified, checking me over with hands and eyes for the bite mark. "Not me," I elaborated. "Them. Not born Weres." I sucked in a lot of air. "And maybe on drugs," I said. Awareness dawned in his eyes.

That was the only explanation for such insane behavior.

A heavyset black patrolman hurried up to me. "We need an ambulance at the Strand," he was saying to someone on his shoulder. No, it was a little radio set. I shook my head.

"You need an ambulance, ma'am," he insisted. "Girl over there says the man took you down and tried to choke you."

"I'm okay," I said, my voice raspy and my throat undeniably painful.

"Sir, you with this lady?" the patrolman asked Quinn. When he turned, the light flashed off his name pin; it said *Boling.*

"Yes, I am."

"You . . . ah, you got these punks offa her?"

"Yes."

Boling's partner, a Caucasian version of Boling, came up to us then. He looked at Quinn with some reservation. He'd been examining our assailants, who had fully changed to human form before the police had arrived. Of course, they were naked.

"The one has a broken leg," he told us. "The other is claiming his shoulder's dislocated."

Boling shrugged. "Got what was coming to 'em." It might have been my imagination, but he, too, seemed a bit more cautious when he looked at my date.

"They got more than they expected," his partner said neutrally. "Sir, do you know either of these kids?" He tilted his head toward the teenagers, who were being examined by a patrolman from another car, a younger man with a more athletic build. The boys were leaning against each other, looking stunned.

"I've never seen them before," Quinn said. "You, babe?" He looked down at me questioningly. I shook my head. I was feeling better enough that I felt at a distinct disadvantage, being on the ground. I wanted to get up, and I said so to my date. Before the police officers could tell me once again to wait for an ambulance, Quinn managed to get me to my feet with as little pain as possible.

I looked down at my beautiful new outfit. It was really dirty. "How does the back look?" I asked Quinn, and even I could hear the fear in my voice. I turned my back to Quinn and looked at him anxiously over my shoulder. Quinn seemed a little startled, but he dutifully scanned my rear view.

"No tearing," he reported. "There may be a spot or two where the material got a little scraped across the pavement."

I burst into tears. I probably would have started crying no matter what, because I was feeling a powerful reaction to the adrenaline that had surged through my body when we'd been attacked, but the timing was perfect. The police got more avuncular the more I cried, and as an extra bonus, Quinn pulled me into his arms and I rested my cheek against his chest. I listened to his heartbeat when I quit sobbing. I'd gotten rid of my nervous reaction to the attack and disarmed the police at the same time, though I knew they'd still wonder about Quinn and his strength.

Another policeman called from his place by one of the assailants, the one Quinn had thrown. Our two patrolmen went to answer the summons, and we were briefly alone.

"Smart," Quinn murmured into my ear.

"Mmmm," I said, snuggling against him.

He tightened his arms around me. "You get any closer, we're going to have to excuse ourselves and get a room," he whispered.

"Sorry." I pulled back slightly and looked up at him. "Who you reckon hired them?"

He may have been surprised I'd figured that out, but you couldn't tell by his brain. The chemical reaction that had fueled my tears had made his mental snarl extra complicated. "I'm definitely going to find out," he said. "How's your throat?"

"Hurts," I admitted, my voice raspy. "But I know there's nothing really wrong with it. And I don't have health insurance. So I don't want to go to the hospital. It would be a waste of time and money."

"Then we won't go." He bent and kissed my cheek. I turned my face up to him, and his next kiss landed in exactly the right spot. After a gentle second, it flared into something more intense. We were both feeling the aftereffects of the adrenalin rush.

The sound of a throat clearing brought me back into my right mind as effectively as if Officer Boling had thrown a bucket of cold water on us. I disengaged and buried my face against Quinn's chest again. I knew I couldn't move away for a minute or two, since his excitement was pressed right up against me. Though these weren't the best circumstances for evaluation, I was pretty sure Quinn was proportional. I had to resist the urge to rub my body against his. I knew that would make things worse for him, from a public viewpoint—but I was in a much better mood than I had been, and I guess I was feeling mischievous. And frisky. Very frisky. Going through this ordeal together had probably accelerated our relationship the equivalent of four dates.

"Did you have other questions for us, Officer?" Quinn asked, in a voice that was not perfectly calm.

"Yes, sir, if you and the lady will come down to the station, we need to take your statements. Detective Coughlin will do that while we take the prisoners to the hospital."

"All right. Does that have to be tonight? My friend

needs to rest. She's exhausted. This has been quite an ordeal for her."

"It won't take long," the officer said mendaciously. "You sure you've never seen these two punks before? Because this seems like a real personal attack, you don't mind me saying so."

"Neither of us knows them."

"And the lady still refuses medical attention?"

I nodded.

"Well, all right then, folks. Hope you don't have no more trouble."

"Thank you for coming so quickly," I said, and turned my head a little to meet Officer Boling's eyes. He looked at me in a troubled way, and I could hear in his head that he was worried about my safety with a violent man like Quinn, a man who could throw two boys several feet in the air. He didn't realize, and I hoped he never would, that the attack had been personal. It had been no random mugging.

We went to the station in a police car. I wasn't sure what their thinking was, but Boling's partner told us that we'd be returned to Quinn's vehicle, so we went along with the program. Maybe they didn't want us to have a chance to talk to each other alone. I don't know why; I think the only thing that could have aroused their suspicion was Quinn's size and expertise in fighting off attackers.

In the brief seconds we had alone before an officer climbed into the driver's seat, I told Quinn, "If you think something at me, I'll be able to hear you—if you need me to know something urgently."

"Handy," he commented. The violence seemed to have relaxed something inside him. He rubbed his thumb across the palm of my hand. He was thinking he'd like to have thirty minutes in a bed with me, right now, or even fifteen; hell, even ten, even in the backseat of a car, would be fantastic. I tried not to laugh, but I couldn't help it, and when he realized that I'd read all that clearly, he shook his head with a rueful smile.

We have somewhere to go after this, he thought deliberately. I hoped he didn't mean he was going to rent a room or take me to his place for sex, because no matter how attractive I found him, I wasn't going to do that tonight. But his brain had mostly cleared of lust, and I perceived his purpose was something different. I nodded.

So don't get too tired, he said. I nodded again. How I was supposed to prevent exhaustion, I wasn't sure, but I'd try to hoard a little energy.

The police station was much like I expected it to be. Though there's a lot to be said for Shreveport, it has more than its fair share of crime. We didn't excite much attention at all, until officers who'd been on the scene put their heads together with police in the building, and then there were a few stolen glances at Quinn, some surreptitious evaluations. He was formidable-looking enough for them to credit ordinary strength as the source of his defeat of the two muggers. But there was just enough strangeness about the incident, enough peculiar touches in the eyewitness reports . . . and then my eye caught a familiar weathered face. Uh-oh.

"Detective Coughlin," I said, remembering now why the name had sounded familiar.

"Miss Stackhouse," he responded, with about as much enthusiasm as I had shown. "What you been up to?"

"We got mugged," I explained.

"Last time I saw you, you were engaged to Alcide Herveaux, and you'd just found one of the most sickening corpses I've ever seen," he said easily. His belly seemed to have gotten even bigger in the few months since I'd met him at a murder scene here in Shreveport. Like many men with a disproportionate belly, he wore his khaki pants buttoned underneath the overhang, so to speak. Since his shirt had broad blue and white stripes, the effect was that of a tent overhanging packed dirt.

I just nodded. There was really nothing to say.

"Mr. Herveaux doing okay after the loss of his father?" Jackson Herveaux's body had been found half-in, half-out of a feed tank filled with water on an old farm belonging to the family. Though the newspaper had tap-danced around some of the injuries, it was clear wild animals had chewed at some of the bones. The theory was that the older Herveaux had fallen into the tank and broken his leg when he hit the bottom. He had managed to get to the edge and haul himself halfway out, but at that point he had passed out. Since no one knew he'd visited the farm, no one came to his rescue, the theory went, and he'd died all by himself.

Actually, a large crowd had witnessed Jackson's demise, among them the man beside me.

"I haven't talked to Alcide since his dad was found," I said truthfully.

"My goodness, I'm sure sorry that didn't work out," Detective Coughlin said, pretending he didn't see that I was standing with my date for the evening. "You two sure made a nice-looking couple."

"Sookie is pretty no matter who she's with," Quinn said.

I smiled up at him, and he smiled back. He was sure making all the right moves.

"So if you'll come with me for a minute, Miss Stackhouse, we'll get your story down on paper and you can leave."

Quinn's hand tightened on mine. He was warning me. Wait a minute, who was the mind reader around here? I squeezed right back. I was perfectly aware that Detective Coughlin thought I must be guilty of *something*, and he'd do his best to discover what. But in fact, I was not guilty.

We had been the targets, I'd picked that from the attackers' brains. But why?

Detective Coughlin led me to a desk in a roomful of desks, and he fished a form out of a drawer. The business of the room continued; some of the desks were unoccupied and had that "closed for the night" look, but others showed signs of work in progress. There were a few people coming in and out of the room, and two desks away, a younger detective with short white-blond hair was busily typing on his computer. I was being very careful, and I'd opened my mind, so I knew he was looking at me when I was looking in another direction, and I knew he'd been positioned there by Detective Coughlin, or at least prodded to get a good hard look at me while I was in the room.

I met his eyes squarely. The shock of recognition was mutual. I'd seen him at the packmaster contest. He was a Were. He'd acted as Patrick Furnan's second in the duel. I'd caught him cheating. Maria-Star had told me his punishment had been having his head shaved. Though his candidate won, this punishment had been exacted, and his hair was just now growing in. He hated me with the passion of the guilty. He half rose from his chair, his first instinct being to come over to me and beat the crap out of me, but when he absorbed the fact that someone had already tried to do that, he smirked.

"Is that your partner?" I asked Detective Coughlin.

"What?" He'd been peering at the computer through reading glasses, and he glanced over at the younger man, then back at me. "Yeah, that's my new partner. The guy I was with at the last crime scene I saw you at, he retired last month."

"What's his name? Your new partner?"

"Why, you going after him next? You can't seem to settle on one man, can you, Miss Stackhouse?"

If I'd been a vampire, I could have made him answer me, and if I were really skilled, he wouldn't even know he'd done it.

"It's more like they can't settle on me, Detective Coughlin," I said, and he gave me a curious look. He waved a finger toward the blond detective.

"That's Cal. Cal Myers." He seemed to have called up the right form, because he began to take me through the incident once again, and I answered his questions with genuine indifference. For once, I had very little to hide.

"I did wonder," I said, when we'd concluded, "if they'd taken drugs."

"You know much about drugs, Miss Stackhouse?" His little eyes went over me again.

"Not firsthand, but of course, from time to time someone comes into the bar who's taken something they shouldn't. These young men definitely seemed . . . influenced by something."

"Well, the hospital will take their blood, and we'll know."

"Will I have to come back?"

"To testify against them? Sure."

No way out of it. "Okay," I said, as firmly and neutrally as I could. "We through here?"

"I guess we are." He met my eyes, his own little brown eyes full of suspicion. There was no point in my resenting it; he was absolutely right, there was something fishy about me, something he didn't know. Coughlin was doing his best to be a good cop. I felt suddenly sorry for him, floundering through a world he only knew the half of.

"Don't trust your partner," I whispered, and I expected him to blow up and call Cal Myers over and ridicule me to him. But something in my eyes or my voice arrested that impulse. My words spoke to a warning that had been sounding surreptitiously in his brain, maybe from the moment he'd met the Were.

He didn't say anything, not one word. His mind was full of fear, fear and loathing . . . but he believed I was telling him the truth. After a second, I got up and left the squad room. To my utter relief, Quinn was waiting for me in the lobby.

A patrolman—not Boling—took us back to Quinn's car, and we were silent during the drive. Quinn's car was sitting in solitary splendor in the parking lot across from the Strand, which was closed and dark. He pulled out his keys and hit the keypad to open the doors, and we got in slowly and wearily.

"Where are we going?" I asked.

"The Hair of the Dog," he said.

9 ~

THE HAIR OF THE DOG WAS OFF KINGS HIGHWAY, not too far from Centenary College. It was an old brick storefront. The large windows facing the street were covered with opaque cream curtains, I noticed, as we turned in to the left side of the building to lurch through an alley that led to a parking area at the back. We parked in the small, weedy lot. Though it was poorly lit, I could see that the ground was littered with empty cans, broken glass, used condoms, and worse. There were several motorcycles, a few of the less expensive compact cars, and a Suburban or two. The back door had a sign on it that read NO ENTRANCE—STAFF ONLY.

Though my feet were definitely beginning to protest the unaccustomed high heels, we had to pick our way through the alley to the front entrance. The cold creeping down my spine intensified as we grew close to the door. Then it was like I'd hit a wall, the spell gripped me that suddenly. I stopped dead. I struggled to go forward, but I couldn't move. I could smell the magic. The Hair of the Dog had been warded. Someone had paid a very good witch a handsome amount of money to surround the door with a go-away spell.

I fought not to give in to a compulsion to turn and walk in another direction, any other direction.

Quinn took a few steps forward, and turned to regard me with some surprise, until he realized what was happening. "I forgot," he said, that same surprise sounding in his voice. "I actually forgot you're human."

"That sounds like a compliment," I said, with some effort. Even in the cool night, my forehead beaded with sweat. My right foot edged forward an inch.

"Here," he said, and scooped me up, until he was holding me just like Rhett carried Scarlett O'Hara. As his aura wrapped around me, the unpleasant go-away compulsion eased. I drew a deep breath of relief. The magic could no longer recognize me as human, at least not decisively. Though the bar still seemed unattractive and mildly repellent, I could enter without wanting to be sick.

Maybe it was the lingering effects of the spell, but after we'd entered it, the bar *still* seemed unattractive and mildly repellent. I wouldn't say all conversation ceased when we walked in, but there was a definite lull in the noise that filled the bar. A jukebox was playing "Bad Moon Rising," which was like the Were national anthem, and the motley collection of Weres and shifters seemed to reorient themselves.

"Humans are not allowed in this place!" A very young woman leaped across the bar in one muscular surge and strode forward. She was wearing fishnet stockings and high-heeled boots, a red leather bustier—well, a bustier that wished it was made of red leather, it was probably more like

Naugahyde—and a black band of cloth that I supposed she called a skirt. It was like she'd pulled a tube top on, and then worked it down. It was so tight I thought it might roll up all at once, like a window shade.

She didn't like my smile, correctly reading it as a comment on her ensemble.

"Get your human ass out of here," she said, and growled. Unfortunately, it didn't sound too threatening, since she hadn't had any practice at putting the menace into it, and I could feel my smile widen. The dress-challenged teen had the poor impulse control of the very new Were, and she pulled her hand back to punch me.

Then Quinn snarled.

The sound came from deep in his belly, and it was thunderous, the deep sound of it penetrating every corner of the bar. The bartender, a biker type with beard and hair of considerable length and tattoos that covered his bare arms, reached down below the bar. I knew he was pulling out a shotgun.

Not for the first time, I wondered if I shouldn't start going armed everywhere I went. In my law-abiding life, I had never seen the need until the past few months. The jukebox cut off just then, and the silence of the bar was just as deafening as the noise had been.

"Please don't get the gun out," I said, smiling brightly at the bartender. I could feel it stretching my lips, that too-bright grin that made me look a little nuts. "We come in peace," I added, on a crazy impulse, showing them my empty palms.

A shifter who'd been standing at the bar laughed, a sharp bark of startled amusement. The tension began to ratchet down a notch. The young woman's hand dropped to her side, and she took a step back. Her gaze flickered from Quinn to me and back again. Both the bartender's hands were in sight now.

"Hello, Sookie," said a familiar voice. Amanda, the red-haired Were who'd been chauffeuring Dr. Ludwig the day before, was sitting at a table in a dark corner. (Actually, the room seemed to be full of dark corners.)

With Amanda was a husky man in his late thirties. Both were supplied with drinks and a bowl of snack mix. They had company at the table, a couple sitting with their backs to me. When they turned, I recognized Alcide and Maria-Star. They turned cautiously, as if any sudden movement might trigger violence. Maria-Star's brain was a motley jumble of anxiety, pride, and tension. Alcide's was just conflicted. He didn't know how to feel.

That made two of us.

"Hey, Amanda," I said, my voice as cheerful as my smile. It wouldn't do to let the silence pile up.

"I'm honored to have the legendary Quinn in my bar," Amanda said, and I realized that, whatever other jobs she might have, she owned the Hair of the Dog. "Are you two out for an evening on the town, or is there some special reason for your visit?"

Since I had no idea why we were there, I had to defer to Quinn for an answer, which didn't make me look too good, in my opinion.

"There's a very good reason, though I've long wanted to visit your bar," Quinn said in a courtly, formal style that had come out of nowhere.

Amanda inclined her head, which seemed to be a signal for Quinn to continue.

"This evening, my date and I were attacked in a public place, with civilians all around us."

No one seemed awfully upset or astonished by this. In fact, Miss Fashion-Challenged shrugged her bare skinny shoulders.

"We were attacked by Weres," Quinn said.

Now we got the big reaction. Heads and hands jerked and

then became still. Alcide half rose to his feet and then sat down again.

"Weres of the Long Tooth pack?" Amanda asked. Her voice was incredulous.

Quinn shrugged. "The attack was a killing one, so I didn't stop to ask questions. Both were very young bitten Weres, and from their behavior, they were on drugs."

More shocked reaction. We were creating quite the sensation.

"Are you hurt?" Alcide asked me, as if Quinn weren't standing right there.

I tilted my head back so my neck would be visible. I wasn't smiling anymore. By now the bruises left by the boy's hands would be darkening nicely. And I'd been thinking hard. "As a friend of the pack, I didn't expect anything to happen to me here in Shreveport," I said.

I figured my status as friend of the pack hadn't changed with the new regime, or at least I hoped it hadn't. Anyway, it was my trump card, and I played it.

"Colonel Flood did say Sookie was a friend of the pack," Amanda said unexpectedly. The Weres all looked at each other, and the moment seemed to hang in the balance.

"What happened to the cubs?" asked the biker behind the bar.

"They lived," Quinn said, giving them the important news first. There was a general feeling that the whole bar gave a sigh; whether of relief or regret, I couldn't tell you.

"The police have them," Quinn continued. "Since the cubs attacked us in front of humans, there was no way around police involvement." We'd talked about Cal Myers on our way to the bar. Quinn had caught only a glimpse of the Were cop, but of course he'd known him for what he was. I wondered if my companion would now raise the issue of Cal Myers's presence at the station, but Quinn said nothing. And truthfully, why comment on something the Weres were sure to already know? The Were pack would stand together against outsiders, no matter how divided they were among themselves.

Police involvement in Were affairs was undesirable, obviously. Though Cal Myers's presence on the force would help, every scrutiny raised the possibility that humans would learn of the existence of creatures that preferred anonymity. I didn't know how they'd flown (or crawled, or loped) under the radar this long. I had a conviction that the cost in human lives had been considerable.

Alcide said, "You should take Sookie home. She's tired."

Quinn put his arm around me and pulled me to his side. "When we've received your assurance that the pack will get to the bottom of this unprovoked attack, we'll leave."

Neat speech. Quinn seemed to be a master of expressing himself diplomatically and firmly. He was a little overwhelming, truthfully. The power flowed from him in a steady stream, and his physical presence was undeniable.

"We'll convey all this to the packmaster," Amanda was saying. "He'll investigate, I'm sure. Someone must have hired these pups."

"Someone converted them to start with," Quinn said. "Unless your pack has degraded to biting street punks and sending them out to scavenge?"

Okay, hostile atmosphere now. I looked up at my large companion and discovered that Quinn was nearasthis to losing his temper.

"Thank you all," I said to Amanda, my bright smile again yanking at the corners of my mouth. "Alcide, Maria-Star, good to see you. We're going to go now. Long drive back to Bon Temps." I gave Biker Bartender and Fishnet Girl a little wave. He nodded, and she scowled. Probably she wouldn't be interested in becoming my best friend. I wriggled out from under Quinn's arm and linked his hand with mine.

"Come on, Quinn. Let's hit the road."

For a bad little moment, his eyes didn't recognize me. Then they cleared, and he relaxed. "Sure, babe." He said good-bye to the Weres, and we turned our backs on them to walk out. Even though the little crowd included Alcide, whom I trusted in most ways, it was an uncomfortable moment for me.

I could feel no fear, no anxiety, coming from Quinn. Either he had great focus and control, or he really wasn't scared of a bar full of werewolves, which was admirable and all, but kind of . . . unrealistic.

The correct answer turned out to be "great focus and control." I found out when we got to the dim parking lot. Moving quicker than I could track, I was against the car and his mouth was on mine. After a startled second, I was right in the moment. Shared danger does that, and it was the second time—on our first date—that we'd been in peril. Was that a bad omen? I dismissed that rational thought when Quinn's lips and teeth traveled down to find that vulnerable and sensitive place where the neck curves into the shoulder. I made an incoherent noise, because along with the arousal I always felt when kissed there, I felt undeniable pain from the bruises that circled my neck. It was an uncomfortable combination.

"Sorry, sorry," he muttered into my skin, his lips never stopping their assault. I knew if I lowered my hand, I'd be able to touch him intimately. I'm not saying I wasn't tempted. But I was learning a little caution as I went along . . . probably not enough, I reflected with the sliver of my mind that wasn't getting more and more involved with the heat that surged up from my lowest nerve bundle to meet the heat generated by Quinn's lips. Oh, geez. Oh, oh, oh.

I moved against him. It was a reflex, okay? But a mistake, because his hand slipped under my breast and his thumb began stroking. I shuddered and jerked. He was doing a little gasping, too. It was like jumping onto the running board of a car that was already speeding down the dark road.

"Okay." I breathed, pulled away a little. "Okay, let's stop this now."

"Ummm," he said in my ear, his tongue flicking. I jerked.

"I'm not doing this," I said, trying to sound definite. Then my resolve gathered. "Quinn! I'm not having sex with you in this nasty parking lot!"

"Not even a little bit of sex?"

"No. Definitely not!"

"Your mouth" (here he kissed it) "is saying one thing, but your body" (he kissed my shoulder) "is saying another."

"Listen to the mouth, buster."

"Buster?"

"Okay. Quinn."

He sighed, straightened. "All right," he said. He smiled ruefully. "Sorry. I didn't plan on jumping you like that."

"Going into a place where you're not exactly welcome, and getting out unhurt, that's some excitement," I said.

He expelled a deep breath. "Right," he said.

"I like you a lot," I said. I could read his mind fairly clearly, just at this instant. He liked me, too; right at the moment, he liked me a whole bunch. He wanted to like me right up against the wall.

I battened my hatches. "But I've had a couple of experiences that have been warnings for me to slow down. I haven't been going slow with you tonight. Even with the, ah, special circumstances." I was suddenly ready to sit down in the car. My back was aching and I felt a slight cramp. I worried for a second, then thought of my monthly cycle. That was certainly enough to wear me out, coming on top of an exciting, and bruising, evening.

Quinn was looking down at me. He was wondering

about me. I couldn't tell what his exact concern was, but suddenly he asked, "Which of us was the target of that attack outside the theater?"

Okay, his mind was definitely off sex now. Good. "You think it was just one of us?"

That gave him pause. "I had assumed so," he said.

"We also have to wonder who put them up to it. I guess they were paid, in some form—either drugs or money, or both. You think they'll talk?"

"I don't think they'll survive the night in jail."

10

THEY DIDN'T EVEN RATE THE FRONT PAGE. THEY were in the local section of the Shreveport paper, below the fold. JAILHOUSE HOMICIDES, the headline read. I sighed.

> Two juveniles awaiting transport from the holding cells to the Juvenile Facility were killed last night sometime after midnight.

The newspaper was delivered every morning to the special box at the end of my driveway, right beside my mailbox. But it was getting dark by the time I saw the article, while I was sitting in my car, about to pull out onto Hummingbird Road and go to work. I hadn't ventured out today until now. Sleeping, laundry, and a little gardening had taken up my day. No one had called, and no one had visited, just like the ads said. I'd thought Quinn might phone, just to check up on my little injuries . . . but not.

> The two juveniles, brought into the police station on charges of assault and battery, were put in one of the holding cells to wait for the morning bus to arrive from the Juvenile Facility. The holding cell for juvenile offenders is out of sight from that for adult offenders, and the two were the only juveniles incarcerated during the night. At some point, the two were strangled by a person or persons unknown. No other prisoners were harmed, and all denied seeing any suspicious activity. Both the youths had extensive juvenile records. "They had had many encounters with the police," a source close to the investigation said.
>
> "We're going to look into this thoroughly," said Detective Dan Coughlin, who had responded to the original complaint and was heading the investigation of the incident for which the youths were apprehended. "They were arrested after allegedly attacking a couple in a bizarre manner, and their deaths are equally bizarre." His partner, Cal Myers, added, "Justice will be done."

I found that especially ominous.

Tossing the paper on the seat beside me, I pulled my sheaf of mail out of the mailbox and added it to the little pile. I'd sort through it after my shift at Merlotte's.

I was in a thoughtful mood when I got to the bar. Preoccupied with the fate of the two assailants of the night before, I hardly flinched when I found that I would be working with Sam's new employee. Tanya was as bright-eyed and efficient as I'd found her previously. Sam was very happy with her; in fact, the second time he told me how pleased he was, I told him a little sharply that I'd already heard about it.

I was glad to see Bill come in and sit at a table in my section. I wanted an excuse to walk away, before I would have to respond to the question forming in Sam's head: *Why don't you like Tanya?*

I don't expect to like everyone I meet, any more than I expect everyone to like me. But I usually have a basis for disliking an individual, and it's more than an unspecified distrust and vague distaste. Though Tanya was some kind of shapeshifter, I should have been able to read her and learn enough to either confirm or disprove my instinctive suspicion. But I couldn't read Tanya. I'd get a word here and there, like a radio station that's fading out. You'd think I'd be glad to find someone my own age and sex who could perhaps become a friend. Instead, I was disturbed when I realized she was a closed book. Oddly, Sam hadn't said a word about her essential nature. He hadn't said, "Oh, she's a weremole," or "She's a true shifter, like me," or anything like that.

I was in a troubled mood when I strode over to take Bill's order. My bad mood compounded when I saw Selah Pumphrey standing in the doorway scanning the crowd, probably trying to locate Bill. I said a few bad words to myself, turned on my heel, and walked away. Very unprofessional.

Selah was staring at me when I glanced at their table after a while. Arlene had gone over to take their order. I simply listened to Selah; I was in a rude mood. She was wondering why Bill always wanted to meet her here, when the natives were obviously hostile. She couldn't believe that a discerning and sophisticated man like Bill could ever have dated a barmaid. And the way she'd heard it, I hadn't even gone to college, and furthermore, my grandmother had gotten *murdered.*

That made me sleazy, I guess.

I try to take things like this with a grain of salt. After all,

I could have shielded myself pretty effectively from these thoughts. People who eavesdrop seldom hear good about themselves, right? An old adage, and a true one. I told myself (about six times in row) that I had no business listening to her, that it would be too drastic a reaction to go slap her upside the head or snatch her baldheaded. But the anger swelled in me, and I couldn't seem to get it under control. I put three beers down on the table in front of Catfish, Dago, and Hoyt with unnecessary force. They looked up at me simultaneously in astonishment.

"We do something wrong, Sook?" Catfish said. "Or is it just your time of the month?"

"You didn't do anything," I said. And it wasn't my time of the month—oh. Yes, it was. I'd had the warning with the ache in my back, the heaviness in my stomach, and my swollen fingers. My little friend had come to visit, and I felt the sensation even as I realized what was contributing to my general irritation.

I glanced over at Bill and caught him staring at me, his nostrils flaring. He could smell the blood. A wave of acute embarrassment rolled over me, turning my face red. For a second, I glimpsed naked hunger on his face, and then he wiped his features clean of all expression.

If he wasn't weeping with unrequited love on my doorstep, at least he was suffering a little. A tiny pleased smile was on my lips when I glimpsed myself in the mirror behind the bar.

A second vampire came in an hour later. She looked at Bill for a second, nodded to him, and then sat at a table in Arlene's section. Arlene hustled over to take the vamp's order. They spoke for a minute, but I was too busy to check in on them. Besides, I'd just have heard the vamp filtered through Arlene, since vampires are silent as the grave (ho ho) to me. The next thing I knew, Arlene was wending her way through the crowd to me.

"The dead gal wants to talk to you," she said, not moderating her voice in the least, and heads turned in our direction. Arlene is not long on subtlety—or tact, for that matter.

After I made sure all my customers were happy, I went to the vamp's table. "What can I do for you?" I asked, in the lowest voice I could manage. I knew the vamp could hear me; their hearing is phenomenal, and their vision is not far behind in acuity.

"You're Sookie Stackhouse?" asked the vamp. She was very tall, just under six feet, and she was of some racial blend that had turned out awfully well. Her skin was a golden color, and her hair was thick and coarse and dark. She'd had it cornrowed, and her arms were weighed down with jewelry. Her clothes, in contrast, were simple; she wore a severely tailored white blouse with long sleeves, and black leggings with black sandals.

"Yes," I said. "Can I help you?" She was looking at me with an expression I could only identify as doubtful.

"Pam sent me here," she said. "My name is Felicia." Her voice was as lilting and exotic as her appearance. It made you think about rum drinks and beaches.

"How-de-do, Felicia," I said politely. "I hope Pam is well."

Since vampires don't have variable health, this was a stumper for Felicia. "She seems all right," the vamp said uncertainly. "She has sent me here to identify myself to you."

"Okay, I know you now," I said, just as confused as Felicia had been.

"She said you had a habit of killing the bartenders of Fangtasia," Felicia said, her lovely doe eyes wide with amazement. "She said I must come to beg your mercy. But you just seem like a human, to me."

That Pam. "She was just teasing you," I said as gently as I could. I didn't think Felicia was the sharpest tool in the shed. Super hearing and super strength do not equal super intelligence. "Pam and I are friends, sort of, and she likes to embarrass me. I guess she likes to do the same thing to you, Felicia. I have no intention of harming anyone." Felicia looked skeptical. "It's true, I have a bad history with the bartenders of Fangtasia, but that's just, ah, coincidence," I babbled on. "And I am really, truly just a human."

After chewing that over for a moment, Felicia looked relieved, which made her even prettier. Pam often had multiple reasons for doing something, and I found myself wondering if she'd sent Felicia here so I could observe her attractions—which of course would be obvious to Eric. Pam might be trying to stir up trouble. She hated a dull life.

"You go back to Shreveport and have a good time with your boss," I said, trying to sound kind.

"Eric?" the lovely vampire said. She seemed startled. "He's good to work for, but I'm not a lover of men."

I glanced over at my tables, not only checking to see if anyone urgently needed a drink, but to see who'd picked up on that line of dialogue. Hoyt's tongue was practically hanging out, and Catfish looked as though he'd been caught in the headlights. Dago was happily shocked. "So, Felicia, how'd you end up in Shreveport, if you don't mind me asking?" I turned my attention back to the new vamp.

"Oh, my friend Indira asked me to come. She said servitude with Eric is not so bad." Felicia shrugged, to show how "not so bad" it was. "He doesn't demand sexual services if the woman is not so inclined, and he asks in return only a few hours in the bar and special chores from time to time."

"So he has a reputation as a good boss?"

"Oh, yes." Felicia looked almost surprised. "He's no softie, of course."

Softie was not a word you could use in the same sentence as *Eric.*

"And you can't cross him. He doesn't forgive that," she

continued thoughtfully. "But as long as you fulfill your obligations to him, he'll do the same for you."

I nodded. That more or less fit with my impression of Eric, and I knew Eric very well in some respects . . . though not at all in others.

"This will be much better than Arkansas," Felicia said.

"Why'd you leave Arkansas?" I asked, because I just couldn't help it. Felicia was the simplest vampire I'd ever met.

"Peter Threadgill," she said. "The king. He just married your queen."

Sophie-Anne Leclerq of Louisiana was by no means *my* queen, but out of curiosity, I wanted to continue the conversation.

"What's so wrong with Peter Threadgill?"

That was a poser for Felicia. She mulled it over. "He holds grudges," she said, frowning. "He's never pleased with what he has. It's not enough that he's the oldest, strongest vampire in the state. Once he became king—and he'd schemed for years to work his way up to it—he still wasn't content. There was something wrong with the state, you see?"

"Like, 'Any state that would have me for a king isn't a good state to be king of'?"

"Exactly," Felicia said, as if I were very clever to think of such a phrase. "He negotiated with Louisiana for months and months, and even Jade Flower got tired of hearing about the queen. Then she finally agreed to the alliance. After a week of celebrating, the king grew sullen again. Suddenly, that wasn't good enough. She had to love him. She had to give up everything for him." Felicia shook her head at the vagaries of royalty.

"So it wasn't a love match?"

"That's the last thing vampire kings and queens marry for," Felicia said. "Now he is having his visit with the queen in New Orleans, and I'm glad I'm at the other end of the state."

I didn't grasp the concept of a married couple visiting, but I was sure that sooner or later I'd understand.

I would have been interested in hearing more, but it was time for me to get back to my section and work. "Thanks for visiting, Felicia, and don't worry about a thing. I'm glad you're working for Eric," I said.

Felicia smiled at me, a dazzling and toothy experience. "I'm glad you don't plan on killing me," she said.

I smiled back at her, a bit hesitantly.

"I assure you, now that I know who you are, you won't get a chance to creep up on me," Felicia continued. Suddenly, the true vampire looked out from Felicia's eyes, and I shivered. It could be fatal to underestimate Felicia. Smart, no. Savage, yes.

"I don't plan on creeping up on anyone, much less a vampire," I said.

She gave me a sharp nod, and then she glided out the door as suddenly as she'd come in.

"What was all that about?" Arlene asked me, when we happened to be at the bar waiting for orders at the same time. I noticed Sam was listening, as well.

I shrugged. "She's working at Fangtasia, in Shreveport, and she just wanted to make my acquaintance."

Arlene stared at me. "They got to check in with you, now? Sookie, you need to shun the dead and involve yourself more with the living."

I stared right back. "Where'd you get an idea like that?"

"You act like I can't think for myself."

Arlene had never worked out a thought like that in her life. Arlene's middle name was *tolerance*, mostly because she was too easygoing to take a moral stance.

"Well, I'm surprised," I said, sharply aware of how harshly I'd just evaluated someone I'd always looked on as a friend.

"Well, I been going to church with Rafe Prudhomme."

I liked Rafe Prudhomme, a very quiet man in his forties who worked for Pelican State Title Company. But I'd never had the chance to get to know him well, never listened in to his thoughts. Maybe that had been a mistake. "What kind of church does he go to?" I said.

"He's been attending that Fellowship of the Sun, that new church."

My heart sank, almost literally. I didn't bother to point out that the Fellowship was a collection of bigots who were bound together by hatred and fear. "It's not really a church, you know. There's a branch of the Fellowship close to here?"

"Minden." Arlene looked away, the very picture of guilt. "I knew you wouldn't like that. But I saw the Catholic priest, Father Riordan, there. So even the ordained people think it's okay. We've been the past two Sunday evenings."

"And you believe that stuff?"

But one of Arlene's customers yelled for her, and she was definitely glad to walk away.

My eyes met Sam's, and we looked equally troubled. The Fellowship of the Sun was an antivampire, antitolerance organization, and its influence was spreading. Some of the Fellowship enclaves were not militant, but many of them preached hatred and fear in its most extreme form. If the Fellowship had a secret underground hit list, I was surely on it. The Fellowship founders, Steve and Sarah Newlin, had been driven out of their most lucrative church in Dallas because I'd interfered with their plans. I'd survived a couple of assassination attempts since then, but there was always the chance the Fellowship would track me down and ambush me. They'd seen me in Dallas, they'd seen me in Jackson, and sooner or later they'd figure out who I was and where I lived.

I had plenty to worry about.

11 ~

THE NEXT MORNING, TANYA SHOWED UP AT MY house. It was Sunday, and I was off work, and I felt pretty cheerful. After all, Crystal was healing, Quinn seemed to like me, and I hadn't heard any more from Eric, so maybe he would leave me alone. I try to be optimistic. My gran's favorite saying from the Bible was, "Sufficient unto the day is the evil thereof." She had explained that that meant that you don't worry about tomorrow, or about things you can't change. I tried to practice that philosophy, though most days it was hard. Today it was easy.

The birds were tweeting and chirping, the bugs were buzzing, and the pollen-heavy air was full of peace as if it were yet another plant emission. I was sitting on the front porch in my pink robe, sipping my coffee, listening to *Car Talk* on Red River Radio, and feeling really good, when a little Dodge Dart chugged up my driveway. I didn't recognize the car, but I did recognize the driver. All my peacefulness vanished in a puff of suspicion. Now that I knew about the proximity of a new Fellowship conclave, Tanya's inquisitive presence seemed even more suspicious. I was not happy to see her at my home. Common courtesy forbade me from warning her off, with no more provocation than I'd had, but I wasn't giving her any welcoming smile when I lowered my feet to the porch and stood.

"Good morning, Sookie!" she called as she got out of her car.

"Tanya," I said, just to acknowledge the greeting.

She paused halfway to the steps. "Um, everything okay?"

I didn't speak.

"I should have called first, huh?" She tried to look winsome and rueful.

"That would have been better. I don't like unannounced visitors."

"Sorry, I promise I'll call next time." She resumed her progress over the stepping stones to the steps. "Got an extra cup of coffee?"

I violated one of the most basic rules of hospitality. "No, not this morning," I said. I went to stand at the top of the steps to block her way onto the porch.

"Well . . . Sookie," she said, her voice uncertain. "You really are a grump in the morning."

I looked down at her steadily.

"No wonder Bill Compton's dating someone else," Tanya said with a little laugh. She knew immediately she'd made an error. "Sorry," she added hastily, "maybe I haven't had enough coffee myself. I shouldn't have said that. That Selah Pumphrey's a bitch, huh?"

Too late now, Tanya. I said, "At least you know where you stand with Selah." That was clear enough, right? "I'll see you at work."

"Okay. I'll call next time, you hear?" She gave me a bright, empty smile.

"I hear you." I watched her get back into the little car. She gave me a cheerful wave and, with a lot of extra maneuvering, she turned the Dart around and headed back to Hummingbird Road.

I watched her go, waiting until the sound of the engine had completely died away before I resumed my seat. I left my book on the plastic table beside my lawn chair and sipped the rest of my coffee without the pleasure that had accompanied the first few mouthfuls.

Tanya was up to something.

She practically had a neon sign flashing above her head. I wished the sign would be obliging enough to tell me what she was, who she worked for, and what her goal might be, but I guessed I'd just have to find that out myself. I was going to listen to her head every chance I got, and if that didn't work—and sometimes it doesn't, because not only was she a shifter, but you can't make people think about what you need to them to, on demand—I would have to take more drastic action.

Not that I was sure what that would be.

In the past year, somehow I'd assumed the role of guardian of the weird in my little corner of our state. I was the poster girl for interspecies tolerance. I'd learned a lot about the other universe, the one that surrounded the (mostly oblivious) human race. It was kind of neat, knowing stuff that other people didn't. But it complicated my already difficult life, and it led me into dangerous byways among beings who desperately wanted to keep their existence a secret.

The phone rang inside the house, and I stirred myself from my unhappy thoughts to answer it.

"Hey, babe," said a warm voice on the other end.

"Quinn," I said, trying not to sound too happy. Not that

I was emotionally invested in this man, but I sure needed something positive to happen right now, and Quinn was both formidable and attractive.

"What are you doing?"

"Oh, sitting on my front porch drinking coffee in my bathrobe."

"I wish I was there to have a cup with you."

Hmmm. Idle wish, or serious "ask me over"?

"There's plenty in the pot," I said cautiously.

"I'm in Dallas, or I'd be there in a flash," he said.

Deflation. "When did you leave?" I asked, because that seemed the safest, least prying question.

"Yesterday. I got a call from the mother of a guy who works for me from time to time. He quit in the middle of a job we were working on in New Orleans, weeks ago. I was pretty pissed at him, but I wasn't exactly worried. He was kind of a free-floating guy, had a lot of irons in the fire that took him all over the country. But his mom says he still hasn't shown up anywhere, and she thinks something's happened to him. I'm looking around his house and going through his files to help her out, but I'm reaching a dead end. The track seems to have ended in New Orleans. I'll be driving back to Shreveport tomorrow. Are you working?"

"Yes, early shift. I'll be off around five-ish."

"So can I invite myself over for dinner? I'll bring the steaks. You got a grill?"

"As a matter of fact, I do. It's pretty old, but it works."

"Got coals?"

"I'd have to check." I hadn't cooked out since my grandmother had died.

"No problem. I'll bring some."

"Okay," I said. "I'll fix everything else."

"We have a plan."

"See you at six?"

"Six it is."

"Okay, good-bye then."

Actually, I would have liked to talk to him longer, but I wasn't sure what to say, since I'd never had the experience of much idle chitchat with boys. My dating career had begun last year, when I'd met Bill. I had a lot of catching up to do. I was not like, say, Lindsay Popken, who'd been Miss Bon Temps the year I graduated from high school. Lindsay was able to reduce boys to drooling idiots and keep them trailing after her like stunned hyenas. I'd watched her at it often and still could not understand the phenomenon. It never seemed to me she talked about anything in particular. I'd even listened to her brain, but it was mostly full of white noise. Lindsay's technique, I'd concluded, was instinctive, and it was based on never saying anything serious.

Oh well, enough of reminiscence. I went into the house to see what I needed to do to get it ready for Quinn's visit the next evening and to make a list of necessary purchases. It was a happy way to spend a Sunday afternoon. I'd go shopping. I stepped into the shower contemplating a pleasurable day.

A knock at my front door interrupted me about thirty minutes later as I was putting on some lipstick. This time I looked through the peephole. My heart sank. However, I was obliged to open the door.

A familiar long black limo was parked in my drive. My only previous experience with that limo led me to expect unpleasant news and trouble.

The man—the being—standing on my front porch was the personal representative and lawyer for the vampire queen of Louisiana, and his name was Mr. Cataliades, emphasis on the second syllable. I'd first met Mr. Cataliades when he'd come to let me know that my cousin Hadley had died, leaving her estate to me. Not only had Hadley died, she'd been murdered, and the vampire responsible had been punished right before my eyes. The night had been full of multiple shocks: discovering not only that Hadley had left this world, but she'd left it as a vampire, and she'd been the favorite of the queen, in a biblical sense.

Hadley had been one of the few remaining members of my family, and I felt her loss; at the same time, I had to admit that Hadley, in her teenage years, had been the cause of much grief to her mother and much pain to my grandmother. If she'd lived, maybe she'd have tried to make up for that—or maybe she wouldn't. She hadn't had the chance.

I took a deep breath. I opened the door. "Mr. Cataliades," I said, feeling my anxious smile stretch my lips unconvincingly. The queen's lawyer was a man composed of circles, his face round and his belly rounder, his eyes beady and circular and dark. I didn't think he was human—or perhaps not wholly human—but I wasn't sure what he could be. Not a vampire; here he was, in broad daylight. Not Were, or shifter; no red buzz surrounding his brain.

"Miss Stackhouse," he said, beaming at me. "What a pleasure to see you again."

"And you also," I said, lying through my teeth. I hesitated, suddenly feeling achy and jumpy. I was sure Cataliades, like all the other supes I encountered, would know I was having my time of the month. Just great. "Won't you come in?"

"Thank you, my dear," he said, and I stepped aside, filled with misgivings, to let this creature enter my home.

"Please, have a seat," I said, determined to be polite. "Would you care for a drink?"

"No, thank you. You seem to be on your way somewhere." He was frowning at the purse I'd tossed on my chair on my way to the door.

Okay, something I wasn't understanding, here. "Yes," I said, raising my eyebrows in query. "I had planned on going to the grocery store, but I can put that off for an hour or so."

"You're not packed to return to New Orleans with me?"

"What?"

"You received my message?"

"What message?"

We stared at each other, mutually dismayed.

"I sent a messenger to you with a letter from my law office," Mr. Cataliades said. "She should have arrived here four nights ago. The letter was sealed with magic. No one but you could open it."

I shook my head, my blank expression telling him what I needed to say.

"You are saying that Gladiola didn't get here? I expected her to arrive here Wednesday night, at the latest. She wouldn't have come in a car. She likes to run." He smiled indulgently for just a second. But then the smile vanished. If I'd blinked, I would have missed it. "Wednesday night," he prompted me.

"That was the night I heard someone outside the house," I said. I shivered, remembering how tense I'd been that night. "No one came to the door. No one tried to break in. No one called to me. There was only the sense of something moving, and all the animals fell silent."

It was impossible for someone as powerful as the supernatural lawyer to look bewildered, but he did look very thoughtful. After a moment he rose ponderously and bowed to me, gesturing toward the door. We went back outside. On the front porch, he turned to the car and beckoned.

A very lean woman slid from behind the wheel. She was younger than me, maybe in her very early twenties. Like Mr. Cataliades, she was only partly human. Her dark red hair was spiked, her makeup laid on with a trowel. Even the striking outfit of the girl in the Hair of the Dog paled in comparison to this young woman's. She wore striped stockings, alternating bands of shocking pink and black, and her ankle boots were black and extremely high-heeled. Her skirt was transparent, black, and ruffled, and her pink tank top was her sole upper garment.

She just about took my breath away.

"Hi, howareya?" she said brightly, her smile revealing very sharp white teeth a dentist would fall in love with, right before he lost a finger.

"Hello," I said. I held out my hand. "I'm Sookie Stackhouse."

She covered the ground between us very speedily, even in the ridiculous heels. Her hand was tiny and bony. "Pleasedtameetya," she said. "Diantha."

"Pretty name," I said, after I figured out it wasn't another run-on sentence.

"Thankya."

"Diantha," Mr. Cataliades said, "I need to you to conduct a search for me." '

"To find?"

"I'm very afraid we are looking for Glad's remains."

The smile fell from the girl's face.

"No shit," she said quite clearly.

"No, Diantha," the lawyer said. "No shit."

Diantha sat on the steps and pulled off her shoes and her striped tights. It didn't seem to bother her at all that without the tights, her transparent skirt left nothing to the imagination. Since Mr. Cataliades's expression didn't change in the least, I decided I could be worldly enough to ignore it, too.

As soon as she'd disencumbered herself, the girl was off, moving low to the ground, sniffing in a way that told me she was even less human than I'd estimated. But she didn't move like the Weres I'd observed, or the shape-shifting panthers. Her body seemed to bend and turn in a way that simply wasn't mammalian.

Mr. Cataliades watched her, his hands folded in front of him. He was silent, so I was, too. The girl darted around the yard like a demented hummingbird, vibrating almost visibly with an unearthly energy.

For all that movement, I couldn't hear her make a sound.

It wasn't long before she stopped at a clump of bushes at the very edge of the woods. She was bent over looking at the ground, absolutely still. Then, not looking up, she raised her hand like a schoolchild who'd discovered the correct answer.

"Let us go see," Mr. Cataliades suggested, and in his deliberate way he strode across the driveway, then the grass, to a clump of wax myrtles at the edge of the woods. Diantha didn't look up as we neared, but remained focused on something on the ground behind the bushes. Her face was streaked with tears. I took a deep breath and looked down at what held her attention.

This girl had been a little younger than Diantha, but she too was thin and slight. Her hair had been dyed bright gold, in sharp contrast with her milk chocolate skin. Her lips had drawn back in death, giving her a snarl that revealed teeth as white and sharp as Diantha's. Oddly enough, she didn't seem as worse for wear as I would have expected, given the fact that she might have been out here for several days. There were only a few ants walking over her, not at all the usual insect activity . . . and she didn't look bad at all for a person who'd been cut in two at the waist.

My head buzzed for a minute, and I was little scared I would go down on one knee. I'd seen some bad stuff, including two massacres, but I'd never seen anyone divided like this girl had been. I could see her insides. They didn't look like human insides. And it appeared the two halves had been separately seared shut. There was very little leakage.

"Cut with a steel sword," Mr. Cataliades said. "A very good sword."

"What shall we do with her remains?" I asked. "I can get an old blanket." I knew without even asking that we would not be calling the police.

"We have to burn her," Mr. Cataliades said. "Over there,

on the gravel of your parking area, Miss Stackhouse, would be safest. You're not expecting any company?"

"No," I said, shocked on many levels. "I'm sorry, why must she be . . . burned?"

"No one will eat a demon, or even a half demon like Glad or Diantha," he said, as if explaining that the sun rises in the east. "Not even the bugs, as you see. The ground will not digest her, as it does humans."

"You don't want to take her home? To her people?"

"Diantha and I are her people. It's not our custom to take the dead back to the place where they were living."

"But what killed her?"

Mr. Cataliades raised an eyebrow.

"No, of course she was killed by something cutting through her middle, I'm seeing that! But what wielded the blade?"

"Diantha, what do you think?" Mr. Cataliades said, as if he were conducting a class.

"Something real, real strong and sneaky," Diantha said. "It got close to Gladiola, and she weren't no fool. We're not easy to kill."

"I have seen no sign of the letter she was carrying, either." Mr. Cataliades leaned over and peered at the ground. Then he straightened. "Have you got firewood, Miss Stackhouse?"

"Yessir, there's a good bit of split oak in the back by the toolshed." Jason had cut up some trees the last ice storm had downed.

"Do you need to pack, my dear?"

"Yes," I said, almost too overwhelmed to answer. "What? What for?"

"The trip to New Orleans. You can go now, can't you?"

"I . . . I guess so. I'll have to ask my boss."

"Then Diantha and I will take care of this while you are getting permission and packing," Mr. Cataliades said, and I blinked.

"All right," I said. I didn't seem to be able to think very clearly.

"Then we need to leave for New Orleans," he said. "I'd thought I'd find you ready. I thought that Glad had stayed to help you."

I wrenched my gaze from the body to stare up at the lawyer. "I'm just not understanding this," I said. But I remembered something. "My friend Bill wanted to go to New Orleans when I went to clean out Hadley's apartment," I said. "If he can, if he can arrange it, would that be all right with you?"

"You want Bill to go," he said, and there was a tinge of surprise in his voice. "Bill is in favor with the queen, so I wouldn't mind if he went."

"Okay, I'll have to get in touch with him when it's full dark," I said. "I hope he's in town."

I could have called Sam, but I wanted to go somewhere away from the strange funeral on my driveway. When I drove off, Mr. Cataliades was carrying the limp small body out of the woods. He had the bottom half.

A silent Diantha was filling a wheelbarrow with wood.

12

SAM," I SAID, KEEPING MY VOICE LOW, "I NEED A FEW days off." When I'd knocked on his trailer door, I'd been surprised to find he had guests, though I'd seen the other vehicles parked by Sam's truck. JB du Rone and Andy Bellefleur were perched on Sam's couch, beer and potato chips set handily on the coffee table. Sam was engaging in a male bonding ritual. "Watching sports?" I added, trying not to sound astonished. I waved over Sam's shoulder to JB and Andy, and they waved back: JB enthusiastically, and Andy less happily. If you can be said to wave ambivalently, that was what he did.

"Uh, yeah, basketball. LSU's playing . . . oh, well. You need the time off right now?"

"Yes," I said. "There's kind of an emergency."

"Can you tell me about it?"

"I have to go to New Orleans to clean out my cousin Hadley's apartment," I said.

"And that has to be right now? You know Tanya is still new, and Charlsie just quit, she says for good. Arlene's not as reliable as she used to be, and Holly and Danielle are still pretty shaky since the school incident."

"I'm sorry," I said. "If you want to let me go and get someone else, I'll understand." It broke my heart to say that, but in fairness to Sam, I had to.

Sam shut the trailer door behind him and stepped out on the porch. He looked hurt. "Sookie," he said, after a second, "you've been completely reliable for at least five years. You've only asked for time off maybe two or three times total. I'm not going to fire you because you need a few days."

"Oh. Well, good." I could feel my face redden. I wasn't used to praise. "Liz's daughter might be able to come help."

"I'll call down the list," he said mildly. "How are you getting to New Orleans?"

"I have a ride."

"Who with?" he asked, his voice gentle. He didn't want me to get mad at his minding my business. (I could tell that much.)

"The queen's lawyer," I said, in an even quieter voice. Though tolerant of vampires in general, the citizens of Bon Temps might get a little excitable if they knew that their state had a vampire queen, and that her secret government affected them in many ways. On the other hand, given the disrepute of Louisiana politics, they might just think it was business as usual.

"You're going to clean out Hadley's apartment?"

I'd told Sam about my cousin's second, and final, death.

"Yes. And I need to find out about whatever she left me."

"This seems real sudden." Sam looked troubled. He ran a hand over his curly red-gold hair until it stood out from his head in a wild halo. He needed a haircut.

"Yes, to me, too. Mr. Cataliades tried to tell me earlier, but the messenger was killed."

I heard Andy yelling at the television as some big play roused his excitement. Strange, I'd never thought of Andy as a sports guy, or JB either, for that matter. I'd never added up all the time I'd heard men thinking about assists and three-pointers when the women with them were talking about the need for new kitchen drapes or Rudy's bad grade in algebra. When I did add it up, I wondered if the purpose of sports wasn't to give guys a safe alternative to thornier issues.

"You shouldn't go," Sam said instantly. "It sounds like it could be dangerous."

I shrugged. "I have to," I said. "Hadley left it to me; I have to do it." I was far from as calm as I was trying to look, but it didn't seem to me like it would do any good to kick and scream about it.

Sam began to speak, then reconsidered. Finally, he said, "Is this about money, Sook? Do you need the money she left you?"

"Sam, I don't know if Hadley had a penny to her name. She was my cousin, and I have to do this for her. Besides . . ." I was on the verge of telling him the trip to New Orleans had to be important in some way, since someone was trying so hard to keep me from going.

But Sam tended to be a worrier, especially if I was involved, and I didn't want to get him all worked up when nothing he could say would dissuade me from going. I don't think of myself as a stubborn person, but I figured this was the last service I could perform for my cousin.

"What about taking Jason?" Sam suggested, taking my hand. "He was Hadley's cousin, too."

"Evidently, he and Hadley were on the outs toward the end," I said. "That's why she left her stuff to me. Besides, Jason's got a lot on his plate right now."

"What, something besides bossing Hoyt around and screwing every woman who'll stand still long enough?"

I stared at Sam. I'd known he was not a big fan of my brother's, but I hadn't known his dislike went this deep.

"Yes, actually," I said, my voice as cold and frosty as a beer mug. I wasn't about to explain my brother's girlfriend's miscarriage while I was standing on a doorstep, especially given Sam's antagonism.

Sam looked away, shaking his head in disgust with himself. "I'm sorry, Sookie, I'm really sorry. I just think Jason should pay more attention to the only sister he's got. You're so loyal to him."

"Well, he wouldn't let anything happen to me," I said, bewildered. "Jason would stand up for me."

Before Sam said, "Of course," I caught the flicker of doubt in his mind.

"I have to go pack," I said. I hated to walk away. No matter his feelings about Jason, Sam was important to me, and leaving him with this unhappiness between us shook me a bit. But I could hear the men roaring at some play inside the trailer, and I knew I had to let him get back to his guests and his Sunday afternoon pleasure. He gave me a kiss on the cheek.

"Call me if you need me," he said, and he looked as if he wanted to say a lot more. I nodded, turned away, and went down the steps to my car.

"Bill, you said you wanted to go to New Orleans with me when I went to close out Hadley's estate?" Finally it was full dark, and I was able to call Bill. Selah Pumphrey had answered the phone and called Bill to talk to me in a very chilly voice.

"Yes."

"Mr. Cataliades is here, and he wants to leave real shortly."

"You could have told me earlier, when you knew he was coming." But Bill didn't sound truly angry, or even surprised.

"He sent a messenger, but she was killed in my woods."

"You found the body?"

"No, a girl who came with him did. Her name's Diantha."

"Then it was Gladiola who died."

"Yes," I said, surprised. "How did you know?"

Bill said, "When you come into a state, it's only polite to check in with the queen or king if you're staying for any length of time. I saw the girls from time to time, since they function as the queen's messengers."

I looked at the telephone in my hands with as much thoughtfulness as if it'd been Bill's face. I couldn't help but think all these thoughts in quick succession. Bill wandered in my woods . . . Gladiola had been killed in my woods. She'd been killed without noise, efficiently and accurately, by someone well versed in the lore of the supernatural, someone who'd known to use a steel sword, someone who'd been strong enough to sweep a sword through Gladiola's entire body.

These were characteristics of a vampire—but any number of supernatural creatures could do the same.

To get close enough to wield the sword, the killer had been super quick or quite innocuous-looking. Gladiola hadn't suspected she was going to be killed.

Maybe she had known the murderer.

And the way Gladiola's little body had been left, tossed in the bushes carelessly . . . the killer hadn't cared if I found her body or not, though of course the demonic lack of putrefaction had played a role there. Her *silence* was all the killer had wanted. Why had she been killed? Her message, if I was getting the whole story from the heavy lawyer, had simply been for me to prepare for my trip to New Orleans. I was going, anyway, though she hadn't had a chance to deliver it. So what had been gained by silencing her? Two or three more days of ignorance on my part? It didn't seem to me that was much motivation.

Bill was waiting for me to end the long pause in our conversation, one of the things I'd always liked about him. He didn't feel the need to fill conversational pauses.

"They burned her in the driveway," I said.

"Of course. It's the only way to dispose of anything with demon blood," Bill said, but absently, as if he'd been thinking deep thoughts about something else.

" 'Of course'? How was I supposed to know that?"

"At least you know now. Bugs won't bite them, their bodies won't corrupt, and sex with them is corrosive."

"Diantha seems so perky and obedient."

"Of course, when she's with her uncle."

"Mr. Cataliades is her uncle," I said. "Glad's uncle, too?"

"Oh, yes. Cataliades is mostly demon, but his half brother Nergal is a full demon. Nergal's had several half-human children. All by different mothers, obviously."

I wasn't sure why this was so obvious, and I wasn't about to ask him.

"You're letting Selah listen to all this?"

"No, she's in the bathroom showering."

Okay, still feeling jealous. And envious: Selah had the luxury of ignorance, while I did not. What a nicer world it was when you didn't know about the supernatural side of life.

Sure. Then you just had to worry about famine, war, serial killers, AIDS, tsunamis, old age, and the Ebola virus.

"*Can* it, Sookie," I said to myself, and Bill said, "Pardon me?"

I shook myself. "Listen, Bill, if you want to go to New Orleans with me and the lawyer, be over here in the next thirty minutes. Otherwise, I'll assume you have other fish to fry." I hung up. I would have a whole drive to the Big Easy to think about all this.

"He'll be here, or not, in the next thirty minutes," I called out the front door to the lawyer.

"Good to hear," Mr. Cataliades called back. He was standing by Diantha while she was hosing the black smudge off my gravel.

I trotted back to my room and packed my toothbrush. I ran down my mental checklist. I'd left a message on Jason's answering machine, I'd asked Tara if she'd mind running out to get my mail and my papers every day, I'd watered my few houseplants (my grandmother believed that plants, like birds and dogs, belonged outside; ironically enough, I'd gotten some houseplants when she died, and I was trying hard to keep them alive).

Quinn!

He wasn't with his cell phone, or wasn't answering it, at any rate. I left a voice mail message. Only our second date, and I had to cancel it.

I found it hard to figure out exactly how much to tell him. "I have to go to New Orleans to clean out my cousin's apartment," I said. "She lived in a place on Chloe Street, and I don't know if there's a phone or not. So I guess I'll just call you when I get back? I'm sorry our plans changed." I hoped he would at least be able to tell I was genuinely regretful that I wouldn't be able to eat dinner with him.

Bill arrived just as I was carrying my bag out to the car. He had a backpack, which struck me as funny. I suppressed my smile when I saw his face. Even for a vampire, Bill looked pale and drawn. He ignored me.

"Cataliades," he said, with a nod. "I'll hitch a ride with you, if that suits you. Sorry about your loss." He nodded to Diantha, who was alternating long, furious monologues in a language I didn't understand with the sort of frozen-faced stare I associated with deep shock.

"My niece died an untimely death," Cataliades said, in his deliberate way. "She will not go unavenged."

"Of course not," Bill said, in his cool voice. While Diantha reached in to pop the trunk, Bill moved to the back of the car to toss his backpack into its depths. I locked my front door behind me and hurried down the steps to put my bag in with his. I caught a glimpse of his face before he registered my approach, and that glimpse shook me.

Bill looked desperate.

13

THERE WERE MOMENTS ON THE DRIVE SOUTH WHEN I felt like sharing all my thoughts with my companions. Mr. Cataliades drove for a couple of hours, and then Diantha took the wheel. Bill and the lawyer didn't have a lot of small talk, and I had too many things on my mind for social chitchat, so we were a silent bunch.

I was as comfortable as I'd ever been in a vehicle. I had the rear-facing seat all to myself, while Bill and the lawyer sat opposite me. The limo was the last word in automotive luxury, at least in my eyes. Upholstered in leather and padded to the nth degree, the limo boasted lots of leg room, bottles of water and synthetic blood, and a little basket of snacks. Mr. Cataliades was real fond of Cheetos.

I closed my eyes and thought for a while. Bill's brain, naturally, was a null to me, and Mr. Cataliades's brain was very nearly so. His brain emitted a low-level buzz that was almost soothing, while the same emanation, from Diantha's brain, vibrated at a higher pitch. I'd been on the edge of a thought when I'd been talking with Sam, and I wanted to pursue it while I could still catch hold of its tail. Once I'd worked it through, I decided to share it.

"Mr. Cataliades," I said, and the big man opened his eyes. Bill was already looking at me. Something was going on in Bill's head, something weird. "You know that Wednesday, the night your girl was supposed to appear on my doorstep, I heard something in the woods."

The lawyer nodded. Bill nodded.

"So we assume that was the night she was killed."

Again with the double nods.

"But why? Whoever did it had to know that sooner or later you would contact me, or come to see me, to find out what had happened. Even if the killer didn't know the message Gladiola was bringing, they'd figure that she'd be missed sooner rather than later."

"That's reasonable," Mr. Cataliades said.

"But on Friday night, I was attacked in a parking lot in Shreveport."

I got my money's worth out of that statement, I can tell you. If I'd hooked both the men up to electroshock machines and given them a jolt, the reaction couldn't have been more dynamic.

"Why didn't you tell me?" Bill demanded. His eyes were glowing with anger, and his fangs were out.

"Why should I? We don't date any more. We don't see each other regularly."

"So this is your punishment for my dating someone else, keeping something so serious from me?"

Even in my wildest fantasies (which had included such scenes as Bill breaking up with Selah in Merlotte's, and his subsequent public confession to me that Selah had never measured up to my charms), I'd never envisioned such a reaction. Though it was very dark in the car's interior, I thought I saw Mr. Cataliades roll his eyes. Maybe he thought that was over the top, too.

"Bill, I never set out to punish you," I said. At least I didn't think I had. "We just don't share details of our lives any more. Actually, I was out on a date when the attack occurred. I believe I'm used to us not being part of the scenery."

"Who was your date?"

"Not that it's actually your business, but it is pertinent to the rest of the story. I'm dating Quinn." We'd had one date and planned another. That counted as "dating," right?

"Quinn the tiger," Bill said expressionlessly.

"Hats off to you, young lady!" Mr. Cataliades said. "You are courageous and discerning."

"I'm not really asking for approval," I said as neutrally as I could manage. "Or disapproval, for that matter." I waved my hand to show that topic was off the table. "Here's what I want you to know. The attackers were very young Weres."

"Weres," Mr. Cataliades said. As we sped through the darkness, I couldn't decipher his expression or his voice. "What kind of Weres?"

Good question. The lawyer was on the ball. "Bitten Weres," I said. "And I believe they were on drugs, as well." That gave them pause.

"What happened during the attack and afterward?" Bill said, breaking a long silence.

I described the attack and its aftermath.

"So Quinn took you to the Hair of the Dog," Bill said. "He thought that was an appropriate response?"

I could tell Bill was furious, but as usual, I didn't know why.

"It may have worked," Cataliades said. "Consider. Nothing else has happened to her, so apparently Quinn's threat took root."

I tried not to say "Huh?" but I guess Bill's vampire eyes could see it on my face.

"He challenged them," Bill said, sounding even colder than usual. "He told them you were under his protection, and that they harmed you at their peril. He accused them of being behind the attack, but at the same time reminded them that even if they didn't know of it, they were responsible for bringing the one who planned it to justice."

"I got all that on the spot," I said patiently. "And I think Quinn was warning them, not challenging them. Big difference. What I didn't get was . . . nothing should happen in the pack without Patrick Furnan's knowledge, right? Since he's the grand high poobah now. So why not go straight to Patrick? Why go to the local watering hole?"

"What a very interesting question," Cataliades said. "What would your answer be, Compton?"

"The one that springs to mind . . . Quinn might know there's a rebellion fomenting against Furnan already. He's added fuel to it by letting the rebels know that Furnan is trying to kill a friend of the pack."

We're not talking armies here. There might be thirty-five members of the pack, maybe a little more with servicemen from Barksdale Air Force Base added in. It would take only five people to make a rebellion.

"Why don't they just take him out?" I asked. I'm not politically minded, as I guess you can tell.

Mr. Cataliades was smiling at me. It was dark in the car, but I just knew it. "So direct, so classic," he said. "So American. Well, Miss Stackhouse, it's like this. The Weres can be savage, oh yes! But they do have rules. The penalty for killing the packleader, except by open challenge, is death."

"But who would, ah, enact that penalty, if the pack kept the killing secret?"

"Unless the pack is willing to kill the whole Furnan family,

I think the Furnan family would be delighted to inform the Were hierarchy of Patrick's murder. Now maybe you know the Shreveport Weres better than most. Are there ruthless killers among them who wouldn't mind slaughtering Furnan's wife and children?"

I thought about Amanda, Alcide, and Maria-Star. "That's a whole different kettle of fish. I see that."

"Now vampires, you'd find many more who were up for that kind of treachery," the lawyer said. "Don't you think so, Mr. Compton?"

There was a curious silence. "Vampires have to pay a price if they kill another vampire," Bill said stiffly.

"If they're affiliated with a clan," Mr. Cataliades said mildly.

"I didn't know vampires had clans," I said. Learning something new all the time, that was me.

"It's a fairly new concept. It's an attempt to regularize the vampire world so it looks more palatable to humans. If the American model catches on, the vampire world will resemble a huge multinational corporation more than a loosely ruled collection of vicious bloodsuckers."

"Lose some of the color and tradition, gain some of the profits," I murmured. "Like Wal-Mart versus Dad's Downtown Hardware." Mr. Cataliades laughed.

"You're right, Miss Stackhouse. Exactly. There are those in both camps, and the summit we'll attend in a few weeks will have this item high on the agenda."

"To get from what's going to take place weeks from now and get back to something a little more on topic, why would Patrick Furnan try to kill me? He doesn't like me, and he knows I'd stand with Alcide if I had to make a choice between 'em, but so what? I'm not important. Why would he plan all this—find the two boys who would do it, bite them, send them out to get me and Quinn—if there wasn't some big payoff?"

"You have a knack for asking good questions, Miss Stackhouse. I wish my answers were as good."

Well, I might as well keep my thoughts to myself if I wasn't going to get any information out of my companions.

The only reason to kill Gladiola, at least the only reason that this direct human could see, was to delay my getting the message that I needed to be ready to leave for New Orleans. Also, Gladiola would have provided some buffer between me and anything that came after me, or at the least she would have been more alert to the attack.

As it was, she'd been lying dead in the woods when I'd gone on my date with Quinn. Whoa. How had the young wolves known where to find me? Shreveport isn't that big, but you couldn't guard every road into town on the off chance I'd show up. On the other hand, if a Were had spotted Quinn and me going into the theater, they'd have known I'd be there for a couple of hours, and that was time enough to arrange something.

If this mastermind had known even earlier, it would have been even easier . . . if someone, say, had known beforehand that Quinn had asked me to go the theater. Who'd known I had a date with Quinn? Well, Tara: I'd told her when I bought my outfit. And I'd mentioned it to Jason, I thought, when I'd called him to inquire after Crystal. I'd told Pam I had a date, but I didn't remember telling her where I was going.

And then there was Quinn himself.

I was so grieved by this idea that I had to suppress tears. It was not like I knew Quinn that well or could judge his character based on the time I'd spent with him. . . . I'd learned over the past few months that you couldn't really know someone that quickly, that learning a person's true character might take years. It had shaken me profoundly, since I'm used to knowing people very well, very quickly. I know them better than they ever suspect. But making mistakes about the character of a few supernaturals had caught me flatfooted, emotionally. Used to the quick assessment my telepathy made possible, I'd been naïve and careless.

Now I was surrounded by such creatures.

I snuggled into a corner of the broad seat and shut my eyes. I had to be in my own world for a while, with no one else allowed inside. I fell asleep in the dark car, with a semidemon and a vampire sitting across from me and a half demon in the driver's seat.

When I woke up, I had my head in Bill's lap. His hand was gently stroking my hair, and the familiar touch of his fingers brought me peace and a stirring of that sensual feeling that Bill had always been able to rouse in me.

It took a second for me to remember where we were and what we were doing, and then I sat up, blinking and tousled. Mr. Cataliades was quite still on the opposite seat, and I thought he was asleep, but it was impossible to be sure. If he'd been human, I would've known.

"Where are we?" I asked.

"Almost there," Bill said. "Sookie . . ."

"Hmm?" I stretched and yawned and longed for a toothbrush.

"I'll help you go through Hadley's apartment if you want me to."

I had a feeling he'd changed his mind about what he was going to say, at the last minute.

"If I need help, I know where to go," I answered. That should be ambiguous enough. I was beginning to get a mighty bad feeling about Hadley's apartment. Maybe Hadley's legacy to me was more in the nature of a curse than a blessing. And yet she'd pointedly excluded Jason, because he had failed her when she'd needed help, so Hadley presumably had meant her bequest to be a boon. On the other hand, Hadley had been a vampire, no longer human, and that would have changed her. Oh, yeah.

Looking out the window, I could see streetlights and a few other cars moving through the gloom. It was raining, and it was four in the morning. I wondered if there was an IHOP anywhere nearby. I'd been to one, once. It had been wonderful. That had been on my only previous trip to New Orleans, when I'd been in high school. We'd been to the aquarium and the slave museum and the church on Jackson Square, the St. Louis Cathedral. It had been wonderful to see something new, to think about all the people who had passed through the same area, what they must have looked like in the clothes of their time. On the other hand, a telepath with poor shielding is not going to have a great time with a bunch of teenagers.

Now my companions were much less easy to read, and quite a bit more dangerous.

We were on a quiet residential street when the limousine pulled to a curb and stopped.

"Your cousin's apartment," Mr. Cataliades said as Diantha opened the door. I was out and on the sidewalk while Mr. Cataliades maneuvered himself into the right position to exit, and Bill was stuck behind him.

I was facing a six-foot wall with an opening for the driveway. It was hard to tell, in the uncertain glow of a streetlight, what lay within, but it seemed to be a small courtyard with a very tight circular drive. In the middle of the drive was an explosion of greenery, though I couldn't discern the individual plants. In the right front corner was a tool shed. There was a two-story building forming an L. To take advantage of the depth of the lot, the building was oriented with the L inverted. Right next door was a similar building, at least as far as I could tell. Hadley's was painted white, with dark green shutters.

"How many apartments are here, and which one is Hadley's?" I asked Mr. Cataliades, who was steaming along behind me.

"There's the bottom floor, where the owner lives, and the top floor, which is yours now for as long as you want it. The queen has been paying the rent until the estate was probated. She didn't think it fair that Hadley's estate should do so." Even for Mr. Cataliades, this was a formal speech.

My reaction was muted by my exhaustion, and I could only say, "I can't think why she didn't just put Hadley's stuff into storage. I could have gone through it all at one of the rental places."

"You'll get used to way the queen does things," he said.

Not if I had anything to say about it. "For right now, can you just show me how to get into Hadley's apartment, so I can unpack and get some sleep?"

"Of course, of course. And dawn is coming, so Mr. Compton needs to go to the queen's headquarters to gain shelter for the day." Diantha had already started up the stairs, which I could just make out. They curved up the short part of the L, which lay to the back of the lot. "Here is your key, Miss Stackhouse. As soon as Diantha comes down, we'll leave you to it. You can meet the owner tomorrow."

"Sure," I said, and trudged up the stairs, holding to the wrought-iron handrail. This wasn't what I had envisioned at all. I thought Hadley would have a place like one of the apartments at the Kingfisher Arms, the only apartment building in Bon Temps. This was like a little bitty mansion.

Diantha had put my sports bag and my big carryall by one of two doors on the second floor. There was a broad roofed gallery running below the windows and doors of the second floor, which would provide shade for people sitting inside on the ground floor. Magic trembled around all those French windows and the doors. I recognized the smell and feel of it, now. The apartment had been sealed with more than locks.

I hesitated, the key in my hand.

"It will recognize you," called the lawyer from the courtyard. So I unlocked the door with clumsy hands, and pushed the door open. Warm air rushed out to meet me. This apartment had been closed for weeks. I wondered if anyone had come in to air it out. It didn't smell actively bad, just stale, so I knew the climate control system had been left on. I fumbled around for the switch of the nearest light, a lamp on a marble-topped pedestal to the right of the door. It cast a pool of golden light on the gleaming hardwood floors and some faux antique furniture (at least I was assuming it was faux). I took another step inside the apartment, trying to imagine Hadley here, Hadley who'd worn black lipstick to have her senior picture made and bought her shoes at Payless.

"Sookie," Bill said behind me, by way of letting me know that he was standing right outside the doorway. I didn't tell him he could come in.

"I have to get to bed now, Bill. I'll see you tomorrow. Do I have the queen's phone number?"

"Cataliades stuck a card in your purse while you were sleeping."

"Oh, good. Well, night."

And I shut the door in his face. I was rude, but he was hovering, and I just wasn't up for talking to him. It had shaken me, finding my head in his lap when I woke; it was like we were still a couple.

After a minute I heard his footsteps going back down the stairs. I was never more relieved to be alone in my life. Thanks to the night spent in a car and the brief sleep I'd had, I felt disoriented, rumpled, and desperately in need of a toothbrush. Time to scope out the place, with emphasis on bathroom discovery.

I looked around carefully. The shorter segment of the upside-down L was the living room, where I now stood. Its open plan included a kitchen against the far right wall. On my left, forming the long side of the L, was a hall lined with French windows that opened directly onto the gallery. The wall that formed the other side of the hall was punctuated with doors.

Bags in hand, I started down the hall, peering into each open door. I didn't find the light switch that would illumine the hall, though there must be one, since there were fixtures at regular intervals on the ceiling.

But enough moonlight streamed through the windows of the rooms to enable me to see as much as I needed. The first room was a bathroom, thank God, though after a second I realized it wasn't Hadley's. It was very small and very clean, with a narrow shower stall, a toilet and sink; no toiletries, no personal clutter. I passed it by and glanced in the next doorway, discovering that it opened into a small room that had probably been intended as the guest bedroom. Hadley had set up a computer desk loaded with computer gear, not items of great interest to me.

In addition to a narrow daybed, there was a bookshelf crammed full with boxes and books, and I promised myself I'd go through that tomorrow. The next door was shut, but I cracked it open to peer inside for a second. It was the door to a narrow, deep, walk-in closet lined with shelves full of items that I didn't take the time to identify.

To my relief, the next door was that of the main bathroom, the one with the shower and the tub and a large sink with a dressing table built in. The surface of the surround was littered with cosmetics and an electric curler, still plugged in. Five or six bottles of perfume were lined up on a shelf, and there were crumpled towels in the hamper, spotted with dark blotches. I put my face right down to them; at that range, they emitted an alarming reek. I couldn't understand why the smell hadn't pervaded the entire apartment. I picked up the whole hamper, unlocked the French window on the other side of the hall, and set it outside. I left the light on in the bathroom, because I intended to revisit it shortly.

The last door, set at right angles to all the others and forming the end of the hall, led into Hadley's bedroom. It was big enough, though not as big as my bedroom at home. It held another large closet, crammed full with clothes. The bed was made, not a Hadley trademark, and I wondered who'd been in the apartment since Hadley had been killed. Someone had entered before the place had been sealed by magic. The bedroom, of course, was completely darkened. The windows had been covered by beautifully painted wood panels, and there were two doors to the room. There was just enough space between them for a person to stand.

I set my bags on the floor by Hadley's chest of drawers, and I rooted around until I found my cosmetics bag and my tampons. Trudging back into the bathroom, I extricated my toothbrush and toothpaste from the small bag and had the delight of brushing my teeth and washing my face. I felt a little more human after that, but not much. I switched out the bathroom light and pulled back the covers on the bed, which was low and broad. The sheets startled me so much that I stood there with my lips curled. They were disgusting: black satin, for God's sake! And not even real satin, but some synthetic. Give me percale or 100% cotton, any day. However, I wasn't going to hunt down another set of sheets at this hour of the morning. Besides, what if this was all she had?

I climbed into the king-size bed—well, I slithered into the king-size bed—and after an uneasy wiggle or two to get used to the feel of them, I managed to fall asleep between those sheets just fine.

14

Someone was pinching my toe and saying "Wake up! Wake up!" I roared back to consciousness in a terrified rush, my eyes opening on the unfamiliar room streaming with sunshine. A woman I didn't know was standing at the foot of the bed.

"Who the hell are you?" I was irritated, but not scared. She didn't look dangerous. She was about my age, and she was very tan. Her chestnut hair was short, her eyes a bright blue, and she was wearing khaki shorts and a white shirt that hung open over a coral tank top. She was rushing the season a little.

"I'm Amelia Broadway. I own the building."

"Why are you in here waking me up?"

"I heard Cataliades in the courtyard last night, and I figured he'd brought you back to clean out Hadley's apartment. I wanted to talk to you."

"And you couldn't wait until I woke up? And you used a key to get in, instead of ringing the doorbell? What's wrong with you?"

She was definitely startled. For the first time, Amelia Broadway looked as if she realized she could have handled the situation better. "Well, see, I've been worried," she said in a subdued way.

"Yeah? Me, too," I said. "Join the club. I'm plenty worried right now. Now get out of here and wait for me in the living room, okay?"

"Sure," she said. "I can do that."

I let my heart rate get back to normal before I slid out of bed. Then I made the bed quickly and pulled some clothes out of my bag. I shuffled into the bathroom, catching a quick glimpse of my uninvited guest as I went from bedroom to bath. She was dusting the living room with a cloth that looked suspiciously like a man's flannel shirt. O-kay.

I showered as quickly as I could, slapped on a little makeup, and came out barefoot but clad in jeans and a blue T-shirt.

Amelia Broadway stopped her housecleaning and stared at me. "You don't look a thing like Hadley," she said, and I couldn't decide by her tone if she thought that was a good thing or a bad thing.

"I'm not at all like Hadley, all the way through," I said flatly.

"Well, that's good. Hadley was pretty awful," Amelia said unexpectedly. "Whoops. Sorry, I'm not tactful."

"Really?" I tried to keep my voice level, but a trace of sarcasm may have leaked through. "So if you know where the coffee is, can you point me in that direction?" I was looking at the kitchen area for the first time in the daylight. It had exposed brick and copper, a stainless steel food preparation area and a matching refrigerator, and a sink with a faucet that cost more than my clothes. Small, but fancy, like the rest of the place.

All this, for a vampire who didn't really need a kitchen in the first place.

"Hadley's coffeepot is right there," Amelia said, and I spotted it. It was black and it kind of blended in. Hadley had always been a coffee freak, so I'd figured that even as a vampire she'd kept a supply of her favorite beverage. I opened the cabinet above the pot, and behold—two cans of Community Coffee and some filters. The silvery seal was intact on the first one I opened, but the second can was open and half full. I inhaled the wonderful coffee smell with quiet pleasure. It seemed amazingly fresh.

After I fixed the pot and punched a button to set it perking, I found two mugs and set them beside it. The sugar bowl was right by the pot, but when I opened it, I found only a hardened residue. I pitched the contents into the trash can, which was lined but empty. It had been cleaned out after Hadley's death. Maybe Hadley had had some powdered creamer in the refrigerator? In the South, people who don't use it constantly often keep it there.

But when I opened the gleaming stainless steel refrigerator, I found nothing but five bottles of TrueBlood.

Nothing had brought home to me so strongly the fact that my cousin Hadley had died a vamp. I'd never known anyone before and after. It was a shock. I had so many memories of Hadley, some of them happy and some of them unpleasant—but in all of those memories, my cousin was breathing and her heart was beating. I stood with my lips compressed, staring at the red bottles, until I'd recovered enough to shut the door very gently.

After a vain search in the cabinets for Cremora, I told Amelia I hoped she took her coffee black.

"Yes, that'll be fine," Amelia said primly. She was obviously trying to be on her better behavior, and I could only be grateful for that. Hadley's landlady was perched on one of Hadley's spindle-legged armchairs. The upholstery was really pretty, a yellow silky material printed with dark red and blue flowers, but I disliked the fragile style of the furniture. I like chairs that look as though they could hold big people, heavy people, without a creak or a groan. I like furniture that looks as though it won't be ruined if you spill a Coke on it, or if your dog hops up on it to take a nap. I tried to settle myself on the loveseat opposite the landlady's. Pretty, yes. Comfortable, no. Suspicion confirmed.

"So what are you, Amelia?"

"Beg pardon?"

"What are you?"

"Oh, a witch."

"Figured." I hadn't caught the sense of the supernatural that I get from creatures whose very cells have been changed by the nature of their being. Amelia had acquired her "otherness." "Did you do the spells to seal off the apartment?"

"Yes," she said rather proudly. She gave me a look of sheer evaluation. I had known the apartment was warded with spells; I had known she was a member of the other world, the hidden world. I might be a regular human, but I was in the know. I read all these thoughts as easily as if Amelia had spoken them to me. She was an exceptional broadcaster, as clear and clean as her complexion. "The night Hadley died, the queen's lawyer phoned me. Of course, I was asleep. He told me to shut this sucker up, that Hadley wouldn't be coming back, but the queen wanted her place kept intact for her heir. I came up and began cleaning early the next morning." She'd worn rubber gloves, too; I could see that in her mental picture of herself the morning after Hadley had died.

"You emptied the trash and made the bed?"

She looked embarrassed. "Yes, I did. I didn't realize 'intact' meant 'untouched.' Cataliades got here and let me have it. But I'm glad I got the trash out of here, anyway. It's strange, because someone went through the garbage bin that night, before I could put it out for pickup."

"I don't guess you know if they took anything?"

She cast me an incredulous look. "It's not like I inventory the trash," she said. She added, reluctantly, "It had been treated with a spell, but I don't know what the spell was for."

Okay, that wasn't good news. Amelia wasn't even admitting it to herself; she didn't want to think about the house being the target for supernatural assault. Amelia was proud because her wards had held, but she hadn't thought to ward the garbage bin.

"Oh, I got all her potted plants out and moved them down to my place for easier care, too. So if you want to take 'em back to Hole-in-the-Road with you, you're welcome."

"Bon Temps," I corrected. Amelia snorted. She had the born city dweller's contempt for small towns. "So you own this building, and you rented the upstairs to Hadley when?"

"About a year ago. She was a vamp already," Amelia said. "And she was the queen's girlfriend, had been for quite a while. So I figured it was good insurance, you know? No one's going to attack the queen's honeybun, right? And no one's going to break into her place, either."

I wanted to ask how come Amelia could afford such a nice place herself, but that was just too rude to get past my lips. "So the witch business supports you?" I asked instead, trying to sound only mildly interested.

She shrugged, but looked pleased I'd asked. Though her mother had left her a lot of money, Amelia was delighted to be self-supporting. I heard it as clearly as if she'd spoken it out loud. "Yeah, I make a living," she said, aiming for a modest tone and just missing. She'd worked hard to become a witch. She was proud of her power.

This was just like reading a book.

"If things get slow, I help out a friend who has a magic

shop right off Jackson Square. I read fortunes there," she admitted. "And sometimes I do a magic tour of New Orleans for the tourists. That can be fun, and if I scare 'em enough, I get big tips. So between one thing and another, I do okay."

"You perform serious magic," I said, and she nodded happily. "For who?" I asked. "Since the regular world doesn't admit it's possible."

"The supes pay real well," she said, surprised I had to ask. I didn't really need to, but it was easier to direct her thoughts to the right information if I asked her out loud. "Vamps and Weres, especially. I mean, they don't like witches, but vamps especially want every little advantage they can gain. The rest aren't as organized." With a wave of her hand she dismissed the weaker ones of the supernatural world, the werebats and the shape-shifters and so on. She discounted the power of the other supes, which was a mistake.

"What about fairies?" I asked curiously.

"They have enough of their own magic," she said, shrugging. "They don't need me. I know someone like you might have a hard time accepting that there's a talent that's invisible and natural, one that challenges everything you were taught by your family."

I stifled a snort of disbelief. She sure didn't know anything about me. I didn't know what she and Hadley had talked about, but it hadn't been Hadley's family, for sure. When that idea crossed my mind, a bell rang in the back of my head, one that said that avenue of thought should be explored. But I put it aside to think of later. Right now, I needed to deal with Amelia Broadway.

"So you would say you have a strong supernatural ability?" I said.

I could feel her stifle the rush of pride. "I have some ability," she said modestly. "For example, I laid a stasis spell on this apartment when I couldn't finish cleaning it. And though it's been shut up for months, you don't smell anything, do you?"

That explained the lack of odor wafting from the stained towels. "And you do witchcraft for supernaturals, you read fortunes off Jackson Square, and you lead tour groups sometimes. Not exactly regular office jobs," I said.

"Right." She nodded, happy and proud.

"So you make up your own schedule," I said. I could hear the relief bouncing through Amelia's mind, relief that she didn't have to go into an office any more, though she'd done a stint at the post office for three years until she'd become a full-fledged witch.

"Yes."

"So will you help me clean out Hadley's apartment? I'll be glad to pay you."

"Well, sure I'll help. The sooner all her stuff is out, the sooner I can rent the place. As for your paying me, why don't we wait to see how much time I can give it? Sometimes I get, like, emergency calls." Amelia smiled at me, a smile suitable for a toothpaste ad.

"Hasn't the queen been paying the rent since Hadley passed?"

"Yeah, she has. But it's given me the creeps, thinking of Hadley's stuff up here. And there've been a couple of break-in attempts. The last one was only a couple of days ago." I gave up any pretense of smiling.

"I thought at first," Amelia burbled on, "that it might be like when someone dies and their death notice is in the paper, you get break-ins during the funeral. Course, they don't print obituaries for vampires, I guess because they're already dead or because the other vampires just don't send one to the paper . . . that would be interesting, to see how they handled it. Why don't you try sending in a few lines about Hadley? But you know how vamps gossip, so I guess a few people heard she was definitely dead, dead for the second time. Especially after Waldo vanished from the court. Everyone knows he didn't care for Hadley. And then, too, vamps don't have funerals. So I guess the break-in wasn't related. New Orleans does have a pretty high crime rate."

"Oh, you knew Waldo," I said, to interrupt the flow. Waldo, once the queen's favorite—not in bed, but as a lackey, I thought—had resented being supplanted by my cousin Hadley. When Hadley remained in favor with the queen for an unprecedented length of time, Waldo lured her to St. Louis Cemetery Number One with the ruse of pretending they were going to raise the spirit of Marie Laveau, the notorious voodoo queen of New Orleans. Instead, he'd killed Hadley and blamed it on the Fellowship of the Sun. Mr. Cataliades had nudged me in the right direction until I'd figured out Waldo's guilt, and the queen had given me the opportunity to execute Waldo myself—that was the queen's idea of a big favor. I'd taken a pass on that. But he was finally, definitely dead, now, just like Hadley. I shuddered.

"Well, I know him better than I want to," she said, with the frankness that seemed to be Amelia Broadway's defining characteristic. "I hear you using the past tense, though. Dare I hope that Waldo has gone to his final destination?"

"You can," I said. "Dare, that is."

"Oo-wee," she said happily. "My, my, my."

At least I'd brightened someone's day. I could see in Amelia's thoughts how much she'd disliked the older vampire, and I didn't blame her. He'd been loathsome. Amelia was a single-minded kind of woman, which must make her a formidable witch. But right now she should have been thinking about other possibilities involving me, and she wasn't. There's a downside to being focused on a goal.

"So you want to clear out Hadley's apartment because you think your building won't be targeted any more? By these thieves who've learned that Hadley's dead?"

"Right," she said, taking a final gulp of her coffee. "I kind of like knowing someone else is here, too. Having the apartment empty just gives me the creeps. At least vampires can't leave ghosts behind."

"I didn't know that," I said. And I'd never thought about it, either.

"No vamp ghosts," Amelia said blithely. "Nary a one. Got to be human to leave a ghost behind. Hey, you want me to do a reading on you? I know, I know, it's kind of scary, but I promise, I'm good at it!" She was thinking that it would be fun to give me a touristy-type thrill, since I wouldn't be in New Orleans long; she also believed that the nicer she was to me, the quicker I'd clean out Hadley's place so she could have the use of it back.

"Sure," I said slowly. "You can do a reading, right now, if you want." This might be a good measure of how gifted a witch Amelia really was. She sure didn't bear any resemblance to the witch stereotype. Amelia looked scrubbed and glowing and healthy, like a happy suburban housewife with a Ford Explorer and an Irish setter. But quick as a wink, Amelia extricated a Tarot pack from a pocket of her cargo shorts and leaned over the coffee table to deal them out. She did this in a quick and professional way that didn't make a bit of sense to me.

After poring over the pictures for a minute, her gaze stopped roaming over the cards and fixed on the table. Her face reddened, and she closed her eyes as if she were feeling mortified. Of course, she was.

"Okay," she said at last, her voice calm and flat. "What are you?"

"Telepath."

"I'm always making assumptions! Why don't I learn!"

"No one thinks of me as scary," I said, trying to sound gentle, and she winced.

"Well, I won't make that mistake again," she said. "You

did seem more knowledgeable about supes than the ordinary person."

"And learning more every day." Even to myself, my voice sounded grim.

"Now I'll have to tell my advisor that I blew it," my landlady said. She looked as gloomy as it was possible for her to look. Not very.

"You have a . . . mentor?"

"Yeah, an older witch who kind of monitors our progress the first three years of being a professional."

"How do you know when you're a professional?"

"Oh, you have to pass the exam," Amelia explained, getting to her feet and going over to the sink. In a New York minute, she had washed the coffeepot and the filter apparatus, put them neatly in the drainer, and wiped out the sink.

"So we'll start packing up stuff tomorrow?" I said.

"What's wrong with right now?"

"I'd like to go through Hadley's things by myself, first," I said, trying not to sound irritated.

"Oh. Well, sure you would." She tried to look as if she'd thought of that already. "And I guess you have to go over to the queen's tonight, huh?"

"I don't know."

"Oh, I'll bet they're expecting you. Was there a tall, dark, and handsome vamp out there with you last night? He sure looked familiar."

"Bill Compton," I said. "Yes, he's lived in Louisiana for years and he's done some work for the queen."

She looked at me, her clear blue eyes surprised. "Oh, I thought he knew your cousin."

"No," I said. "Thanks for getting me up so I could start work, and thanks for being willing to help me."

She was pleased that she was leaving, because I hadn't been what she'd expected, and she wanted to think about me some and make some phone calls to sisters in the craft in the Bon Temps area. "Holly Cleary," I said. "She's the one I know best."

Amelia gasped and said a shaky good-bye. She left as unexpectedly as she'd arrived.

I felt old all of a sudden. I'd just been showing off, and I'd reduced a confident, happy young witch to an anxious woman in the space of an hour.

But as I got out a pad and pencil—right where they should be, in the drawer closest to the telephone—to figure out my plan of action, I consoled myself with the thought that Amelia had needed the mental slap in the face pretty badly. If it hadn't come from me, it might have come from someone who actually meant her harm.

15 ~

I NEEDED BOXES, THAT WAS FOR SURE. SO I'D ALSO need strapping tape, lots of it, and a Magic Marker, and probably scissors. And finally, I'd need a truck to take whatever I salvaged back to Bon Temps. I could ask Jason to drive down, or I could rent a truck, or I could ask Mr. Cataliades if he knew of a truck I could borrow. If there was a lot of stuff, maybe I would rent a car and a trailer. I'd never done such a thing, but how hard could it be? Since I didn't have a ride right now, there was no way to obtain the supplies. But I might as well start sorting, since the sooner I finished, the sooner I could get back to work and away from the New Orleans vampires. I was glad, in a corner of my mind, that Bill had come, too. As angry as I sometimes felt with him, he was familiar. After all, he'd been the first vampire I'd ever met, and it still seemed almost miraculous to me how it had happened.

He'd come into the bar, and I'd been fascinated with the discovery that I couldn't hear his thoughts. Then later the same evening, I'd rescued him from drainers. I sighed, thinking how good it had been until he'd been recalled by his maker, Lorena, now also definitely dead.

I shook myself. This wasn't the time for a trip down memory lane. This was the time for action and decision. I decided to start with the clothes.

After fifteen minutes, I realized that the clothes were going to be easy. I was going to give most of them away. Not only was my taste radically different from my cousin's, but her hips and breasts had been smaller and her coloring had been different from mine. Hadley had liked dark, dramatic clothes, and I was altogether a lower-key person. I did sort of wonder about one or two of the black wispy blouses and skirts, but when I tried them on, I looked just like one of the fangbangers who hung around Eric's bar. Not the image I was going for. I put only a handful of tank tops and a couple of pairs of shorts and sleep pants in the "keep" pile.

I found a large box of garbage bags and used those to pack the clothes away. As I finished with each bag, I set it out on the gallery to keep the apartment clear of clutter.

It was about noon when I started to work, and the hours passed quickly after I found out how to operate Hadley's CD player. A lot of the music she had was by artists who'd never been high on my list, no big surprise there—but it was interesting listening. She had a horde of CDs: No Doubt, Nine Inch Nails, Eminem, Usher.

I'd started on the drawers in the bedroom when it just began turning dark. I paused for a moment to stand on the gallery in the mild evening, and watch the city wake up for the dark hours ahead. New Orleans was a city of the night now. It had always been a place with a brawling and brazen nightlife, but now it was such a center for the undead that its entire character had changed. A lot of the jazz on Bourbon

Street was played these days by hands that had last seen sunlight decades before. I could catch a faint spatter of notes on the air, the music of faraway revels. I sat on a chair on the gallery and listened for a while, and I hoped I'd get to see some of the city while I was here. New Orleans is like no other place in America, both before the vampire influx and after it. I sighed and realized I was hungry. Of course, Hadley didn't have any food in the apartment, and I wasn't about to start drinking blood. I hated to ask Amelia for anything else. Tonight, whoever came to pick me up to go to the queen's might be willing to take me to the grocery store. Maybe I should shower and change?

As I turned to go back into the apartment, I spotted the mildewed towels I'd set out the night before. They smelled much stronger, which surprised me. I would have thought the smell would have diminished by now. Instead, my breath caught in the back of my throat in disgust as I picked up the basket to bring it inside. I intended to wash them. In a corner of the kitchen was one of those washer/dryer sets with the dryer on top. Like a tower of cleanliness.

I tried to shake out the towels, but they'd dried in a stiff crumpled mass. Exasperated, I jerked at the protruding edge of one towel, and with a little resistance, the clots of stuff binding the folds together gave, and the medium blue terrycloth spread out before my eyes.

"Oh, *shit*," I said out loud in the silent apartment. "Oh, *no.*"

The fluid that had dried and clumped on the towels was blood.

"Oh, Hadley," I said. "What did you do?"

The smell was as awful as the shock. I sat down at the small dining table in the kitchen area. Flakes of dried blood had showered onto the floor and clung to my arms. I couldn't read the thoughts of a towel, for God's sake. My condition was of no help to me whatsoever. I needed . . . a witch. Like the one I'd chastened and sent away. Yep, just like that one.

But first I needed to check the whole apartment, see if it held any more surprises.

Oh, yeah. It did.

The body was in the walk-in closet in the hall.

There was no odor at all, though the corpse, a young man, had probably been there for the whole time my cousin had been dead. Maybe this young man had been a demon? But he didn't look anything like Diantha or Gladiola, or Mr. Cataliades, for that matter. If the towels had started to smell, you would think . . . oh well, maybe I'd just gotten lucky. This was something that I would have to find the answer to, and I suspected it lay downstairs.

I knocked on Amelia's door. She answered it immediately, and I saw over her shoulder that her place, though of course laid out exactly like Hadley's, was full of light colors and energy. She liked yellow, and cream, and coral, and green. Her furniture was modern and heavily cushioned, and the wooden bits were polished to the nth degree. As I'd suspected, Amelia's place was spotless.

"Yes?" she said, in a subdued kind of way.

"Okay," I said, as if I were laying down an olive branch. "I've got a problem, and I suspect you do, too."

"Why do you say that?" she asked. Her open face was closed now, as if keeping her expression blank would keep me out of her mind.

"You put a stasis spell on the apartment, right? To keep everything exactly as it was. Before you warded it against intruders?"

"Yes," she said cautiously. "I told you that."

"No one's been in that apartment since the night Hadley died?"

"I can't give you my word on it, because I suppose a very

good witch or wizard could have breached my spell," she said. "But to the best of my knowledge, no one's been in there."

"So you don't know that you sealed a body in there?"

I don't know what I expected in the way of reaction, but Amelia was pretty cool about it. "Okay," she said steadily. She may have gulped. "Okay. Who is it?" Her eyelids fluttered up and down a few extra times.

Maybe she wasn't quite so cool.

"I really don't know," I said carefully. "You'll have to come see." As we went up the stairs, I said, "He was killed there, and the mess was cleaned up with towels. They were in the hamper." I told her about the condition of the towels.

"Holly Cleary tells me you saved her son's life," Amelia said.

That took me aback. It made me feel awkward, too. "The police would have found him," I said. "I just accelerated it a little."

"The doctor told Holly if the little boy hadn't gotten to the hospital when he did, the bleeding in his brain might not have been stopped in time," Amelia said.

"That's good then," I said, uncomfortable in the extreme. "How's Cody doing?"

"Well," the witch said. "He's going to be well."

"In the meantime, we got a problem right here," I reminded her.

"Okay, let's see the corpse." Amelia worked hard to keep her voice level.

I kind of liked this witch.

I led her to the closet. I'd left the door open. She stepped inside. She didn't make a sound. She came back out with a slightly green tinge to her glowing tan and leaned against the wall.

"He's a Were," she said, a moment later. The spell she'd put on the apartment had kept everything fresh, as part of the way it worked. The blood had begun to smell a little before the spell had been cast, and when I'd entered the apartment, the spell had been broken. Now the towels reeked of decay. The body didn't have an odor yet, which surprised me a little, but I figured it would any minute. Surely the body would decompose rapidly now that it had been released from Amelia's magic, and she was obviously trying not to point out how well that had worked.

"You know him?"

"Yes, I know him," she said. "The supernatural community, even in New Orleans, isn't that big. It's Jake Purifoy. He did security for the queen's wedding."

I had to sit down. I exited the walk-in closet and slid down the wall until I was sitting propped up, facing Amelia. She sat against the opposite wall. I hardly knew where to start asking questions.

"That's would be when she married the King of Arkansas?" I recalled what Felicia had said, and the wedding photo I'd seen in Al Cumberland's album. Had that been the queen, under that elaborate headdress? When Quinn had mentioned making the arrangements for a wedding in New Orleans, was this the wedding he'd meant?

"The queen, according to Hadley, is bi," Amelia told me. "So yes, she married a guy. Now they have an alliance."

"They can't have kids," I said. I know, that was obvious, but I wasn't getting this alliance thing.

"No, but unless someone stakes them, they'll live forever, so passing things on is not a big issue," Amelia said. "It takes months, even years, of negotiations to hammer out the rules for such a wedding. The contract can take just as long. Then they both gotta sign it. That's a big ceremony, takes place right before the wedding. They don't actually have to spend their lives together, you know, but they have to visit a couple of times a year. Conjugal-type visit."

Fascinating as this was, it was beside the point right now.

"So this guy in the closet, he was part of the security force." Had he worked for Quinn? Hadn't Quinn said that one of his workers had gone missing in New Orleans?

"Yeah, I wasn't asked to the wedding, of course, but I helped Hadley into her dress. He came to pick her up."

"Jake Purifoy came to pick Hadley up for the wedding."

"Yep. He was all dressed up that night."

"And that was the night of the wedding."

"Yeah, the night before Hadley died."

"Did you see them leave?"

"No, I just . . . No. I heard the car pull up. I looked out my living room window and saw Jake coming in. I knew him already, kind of casually. I had a friend who used to date him. I went back to whatever I was doing, watching TV I think, and I heard the car leave after a while."

"So he may not have left at all."

She stared at me, her eyes wide. "Could be," she said at last, sounding as if her mouth were dry.

"Hadley was by herself when he came to pick her up . . . right?"

"When I came down from her apartment, I left her there alone."

"All I came to do," I said, mainly to my bare feet, "was clean out my cousin's apartment. I didn't much like her anyway. Now I'm stuck with a body. The last time I got rid of a body," I told the witch, "I had a big strong helper, and we wrapped it in a shower curtain."

"You did?" Amelia said faintly. She didn't look too happy to be the recipient of this information.

"Yes." I nodded. "We didn't kill him. We just had to get rid of the body. We thought we'd be blamed for the death, and I'm sure we would have been." I stared at my toenail polish some more. It had been a good job when it started out, a nice bright pink, but now I needed to refresh the paint job or remove it. I stopped trying to think about other things and resumed my gloomy contemplation of the body. He was lying in the closet, stretched out on the floor, pushed under the lowest shelf. He'd been covered with a sheet. Jake Purifoy had been a handsome man, I suspected. He'd had dark brown hair, and a muscular build. Lots of body hair. Though he'd been dressed for a formal wedding, and Amelia had said he looked very nice, now he was naked. A minor question: where were his clothes?

"We could just call the queen," Amelia said. "After all, the body's been here, and Hadley either killed him or hid the body. No way could he have died the night she went out with Waldo to the cemetery."

"Why not?" I had a sudden, awful thought.

"You got a cell phone?" I asked, rising to my feet as I spoke. Amelia nodded. "Call the queen's place. Tell them to send someone over *right now.*"

"What?" Her eyes were confused, even as her fingers were punching in numbers.

Looking into the closet, I could see the fingers of the corpse twitch.

"He's rising," I said quietly.

It only took a second for her to get it. "This is Amelia Broadway on Chloe Street! Send an older vampire over here *right now*," she yelled into the phone. "New vamp rising!" She was on her feet now, and we were running for the door.

We didn't make it.

Jake Purifoy was after us, and he was hungry.

Since Amelia was behind me (I'd had a head start) he dove to grab her ankle. She shrieked as she went down, and I spun around to help her. I didn't think at all, because I would have kept on going out the door if I had. The new vamp's fingers were wrapped around Amelia's bare ankle like a shackle, and he was pulling her toward him across the smooth laminated-wood floor. She was clawing at the floor with her fingers, trying to find something to stop her progress toward his mouth, which was wide open with the fangs extended full length, oh God! I grabbed her wrists and began pulling. I hadn't known Jake Purifoy in life, so I didn't know what he'd been like. And I couldn't find anything human left in his face, anything I could appeal to. "Jake!" I yelled. "Jake Purifoy! Wake up!" Of course, that didn't do a damn bit of good. Jake had changed into something that was not a nightmare but a permanent otherness, and he could not be roused from it: he was it. He was making a kind of *gnarr-gnarr-gnarr* noise, the hungriest sound I'd ever heard, and then he bit down on the calf of Amelia's leg, and she screamed.

It was like a shark had hold of her. If I yanked at her any more, he might take out the bit his teeth had clamped on. He was sucking on the leg wound now, and I kicked him in the head with my heel, cursing my lack of shoes. I put everything I had behind it, and it didn't faze the new vampire in the least. He made a noise of protest, but continued sucking, and the witch kept shrieking with pain and shock. There was a candlestick on the table behind one of the loveseats, a tall glass candlestick with lots of heft to it. I plucked the candle from it, grasped it with both hands, and brought it down as hard as I could on Jake Purifoy's head. Blood began to run from his wound, very sluggishly; that's how vampires bleed. The candlestick came apart with the blow, and I was left with empty hands and a furious vampire. He raised his blood-smeared face to glare at me, and I hope I'm never on the receiving end of another look like that again in my life. His face held the mindless rage of a mad dog.

But he'd let go of Amelia's leg, and she began to scramble away. It was obvious she was hurt, and it was kind of a slow scramble, but she made the effort. Tears were streaming down her face and her breathing was all over the place, harsh in the night's silence. I could hear a siren drawing closer and

I hoped it was coming here. It would be too late, though. The vampire launched himself from the floor to knock me down, and I didn't have time to think about anything.

He bit down on my arm, and I thought the teeth would penetrate the bone. If I hadn't thrown up the arm, those teeth would have gripped my neck, and that would have been fatal. The arm might be preferable, but just at this moment the pain was so intense I nearly passed out, and I'd better not do that. Jake Purifoy's body was heavy on top of mine, and his hands were pressing my free arm to the floor, and his legs were on top of mine. Another hunger was waking in the new vampire, and I felt its evidence pressing against my thigh. He freed a hand to begin yanking at my pants.

Oh, no . . . this was so bad. I would die in the next few minutes, here in New Orleans in my cousin's apartment, far away from my friends and my family.

Blood was all over the new vampire's face and hands.

Amelia crawled awkwardly across the floor toward us, her leg trailing blood behind her. She should have run, since she couldn't save me. No more candlesticks. But Amelia had another weapon, and she reached out with a violently shaking hand to touch the vampire. *"Utinam hic sanguis in ignem commutet!"* she yelled.

The vampire reared back, screaming and clawing at his face, which was suddenly covered by tiny licking blue flames.

And the police came through the door.

They were vampires, too.

For an interesting moment, the police officers thought we had attacked Jake Purifoy. Amelia and I, bleeding and screaming, were shoved up against the wall. But in the meantime, the spell Amelia had cast on the new undead lost its efficacy and he leaped on the nearest uniformed cop, who happened to be a black woman with a proud straight back and a high-bridged nose. The cop whipped out her nightstick and used it with a reckless disregard for the new vamp's teeth. Her partner, a very short man whose skin was the color of butterscotch, fumbled to open a bottle of TrueBlood that was stuck in his belt like another tool. He bit off the tip, and stuck the rubber cap in Jake Purifoy's questing mouth. Suddenly, all was silence as the new vamp sucked down the contents of the bottle. The rest of us stood panting and bleeding.

"He will be quiet now," said the female officer, the cadence of her voice letting me know that she was far more African than American. "I think we have subdued him."

Amelia and I sank onto the floor, after the male cop gave us a nod to let us know we were off the hook. "Sorry we got confused about who was the bad guy," he said in a voice as warm as melted butter. "You ladies okay?" It was a good thing his voice was so reassuring, since his fangs were out. I guess the excitement of the blood and the violence triggered the reaction, but it was kind of disconcerting in a law enforcement officer.

"I think not," I said. "Amelia here is bleeding pretty bad, and I guess I am, too." The bite didn't hurt as badly as it was going to. The vamp's saliva secretes a tiny bit of anesthetic, along with a healing agent. But the healing agent was meant for sealing the pinpricks of fangs, not for actual large tears in human flesh. "We're going to need a doctor." I'd met a vamp in Mississippi who could heal large wounds, but it was a rare talent.

"You both human?" he asked. The female cop was crooning in a foreign language to the new vampire. I didn't know if the former werewolf, Jake Purifoy, could speak the language, but he recognized safety when he saw it. The burns on his face healed as we sat there.

"Yes," I said.

While we waited for the paramedics to come, Amelia and I leaned against each other wordlessly. Was this the second body I'd found in a closet, or the third? I wondered why I even opened closet doors any more.

"We should have known," Amelia said wearily. "When he didn't smell at all, we should have known."

"Actually, I figured that out. Since it was only thirty seconds before he woke up, it didn't do a hell of a lot of good," I said. My voice was just as limp as hers.

Everything got very confusing after that. I kept thinking it would be a good time to faint if I was ever going to, because this was really not a process I wanted to be in on, but I just couldn't pass out. The paramedics were very nice young men who seemed to think we'd been partying with a vamp and it had gotten out of hand. I guessed neither of them would be calling Amelia or me for a date any time soon.

"You don't want to be messing with no vampires, *cherie*," said the man who was working on me. His name tag read DELAGARDIE. "They supposed to be so attractive to women, but you wouldn't believe how many poor girls we've had to patch up. And that was the lucky ones," Delagardie said grimly. "What's your name, young lady?"

"Sookie," I said. "Sookie Stackhouse."

"Pleased to meet you, Miss Sookie. You and your friend seem like nice girls. You need to hang with better people, live people. This city's overrun with the dead, now. It was better when everyone here was breathing, I tell you the truth. Now let's get you to the hospital and get you stitched up. I'd shake your hand if you wasn't all bloody," he said. He gave me a sudden smile, white-toothed and charming. "I'm giving you good advice for free, pretty lady."

I smiled, but it was the last time I was going to be doing that for a while. The pain was beginning to make itself felt. Very quickly, I became preoccupied with coping.

Amelia was a real warrior. Her teeth were gritted as she fought to keep herself together, but she managed all the way to the hospital. The emergency room seemed to be packed.

By a combination of bleeding, being escorted by cops, and the friendly Delagardie and his partner putting in a word for us, Amelia and I got put in curtained cubicles right away. We weren't adjacent to each other, but we were in line to see a doctor. I was grateful. I knew that had to be quick, for an urban emergency room.

As I listened to the bustle around me, I tried not to swear at the pain in my arm. In moments when it wasn't throbbing as much, I wondered what had happened to Jake Purifoy. Had the vampire cops taken him to a vampire cell at the jail, or was everything excused since he was a brand new vamp with no guidance? There'd been a law passed about that, but I couldn't remember the terms and strictures. It was hard for me to be too concerned. I knew the young man was a victim of his new state; that the vampire who had made him should have been there to guide him through his first wakening and hunger. The vampire to blame was most likely my cousin Hadley, who had hardly expected to be murdered. Only Amelia's stasis spell on the apartment had kept Jake from rising months ago. It was a strange situation, probably unprecedented even in vampire annals. And a werewolf who'd become a vampire! I'd never heard tell of such a thing. Could he still change?

I had a while to think about that and quite a few other things, since Amelia was too far away for conversation, even if she'd been up to it. After about twenty minutes, during which time I was disturbed only by a nurse who wrote down some information, I was surprised to see Eric peer around the curtain.

"May I come in?" he asked stiffly. His eyes were wide and he was speaking carefully. I realized that to a vampire, the smell of blood in the emergency room was enchanting and pervasive. I caught a glimpse of his fangs.

"Yes," I said, puzzled by Eric's presence in New Orleans. I wasn't really in an Eric mood, but there was no point in telling the former Viking he couldn't come into the curtained area. This was a public building, and he wasn't bound by my words. Anyway, he could simply stand outside and talk to me through the cloth until he found out whatever he'd come to discover. Eric was nothing if not persistent. "What on earth are you doing here in town, Eric?"

"I drove down to bargain with the queen for your services during the summit. Also, Her Majesty and I have to negotiate how many of my people I can bring with me." He smiled at me. The effect was disconcerting, what with the fangs and all. "We've almost reached an agreement. I can bring three, but I want to bargain up to four."

"Oh, for God's sake, Eric," I snapped. "That's the lamest excuse I've ever heard. Modern invention, known as the telephone?" I moved restlessly on the narrow bed. I couldn't find a comfortable position. Every nerve in my body was jangling with the aftermath of the fear of my encounter with Jake Purifoy, new child of the night. I was hoping that when I finally saw a doctor, he or she would give me an excellent painkiller. "Leave me alone, okay? You don't have a claim on me. Or a responsibility to me."

"But I do." He had the gall to look surprised. "We have a bond. I've had your blood, when you needed strength to free Bill in Jackson. And we've made love often, according to you."

"You *made* me tell you," I protested. And if I sounded a little on the whiny said, well, dammit, I thought it was okay to whine a little. Eric had agreed to save a friend of mine from danger if I'd spill the truth to him. Is that blackmail? Yes, I think so.

But there wasn't any way to untell him. I sighed. "How'd you get here, anyway?"

"The queen monitors what happens to vampires in her city very closely, of course. I thought I'd come provide moral support. And, of course, if you need me to clean you of blood . . ." His eyes flashed as he inspected my arm. "I'd be glad to do it."

I almost smiled, very reluctantly. He never gave up.

"Eric," said Bill's cool voice, and he slipped around the curtain to join Eric at my bedside.

"Why am I not surprised to see you here?" Eric said, in a voice that made it clear he was displeased.

Eric's anger wasn't something Bill could ignore. Eric outranked Bill, and he looked down his substantial nose at the younger vampire. Bill was around one hundred thirty-five years old: Eric was perhaps over a thousand. (I had asked him once, but he honestly didn't seem to know.) Eric had the personality for leadership. Bill was happier on his own. The only thing they had in common was that they'd both made love to me: and just at the moment, they were both pains in my butt.

"I heard over the police band radio at the queen's headquarters that the vampire police had been called in to subdue a fresh vampire, and I recognized the address," Bill said by way of explanation. "Naturally, I found out where Sookie had been brought, and came here as fast as I could."

I closed my eyes.

"Eric, you're tiring her out," Bill said, his voice even colder than usual. "You should leave Sookie alone."

There was a long moment of silence. It was fraught with some big emotion. My eyes opened and went from one face to another. For once, I wished I could read vampire minds.

As much as I could read from his expression, Bill was deeply regretting his words, but why? Eric was looking at Bill with a complex expression compounded of resolve and something less definable; regret, maybe.

"I quite understand why you want to keep Sookie isolated while she's in New Orleans," Eric said. His *r*'s became more pronounced, as they did when he was angry.

Bill looked away.

Despite the pain pulsing in my arm, despite my general exasperation with the both of them, something inside me sat up and took notice. There was an unmistakable significance to Eric's tone. Bill's lack of response was curious . . . and ominous.

"What?" I said, my eyes flicking from one to the other. I tried to prop myself up on my elbows and settled for one when the other arm, the bitten one, gave a big throb of pain. I pressed the button to raise the head of the bed. "What's all the big hinting about, Eric? Bill?"

"Eric should not be agitating you when you've got a lot to handle already," Bill said, finally. Though never known for its expressiveness, Bill's face was what my grandmother would have described as "locked up tighter than a drum."

Eric folded his arms across his chest and looked down at them.

"Bill?" I said.

"Ask him why he came back to Bon Temps, Sookie," Eric said very quietly.

"Well, old Mr. Compton died, and he wanted to reclaim his . . ." I couldn't even describe the expression on Bill's face. My heart began to beat faster. Dread gathered in a knot in my stomach. "Bill?"

Eric turned to face away from me, but not before I saw a shade of pity cross his face. Nothing could have scared me more. I might not be able to read a vampire's mind, but in this case his body language said it all. Eric was turning away because he didn't want to watch the knife sliding in.

"Sookie, you would find out when you saw the queen . . . Maybe I could have kept it from you, because you won't understand . . . but Eric has taken care of that." Bill gave Eric's back a look that could have drilled a hole through Eric's heart. "When your cousin Hadley was becoming the queen's favorite . . ."

And suddenly I saw it all, knew what he was going to

say, and I rose up on the hospital bed with a gasp, one hand to my chest because I felt my heart shattering. But Bill's voice went on, even though I shook my head violently.

"Apparently, Hadley talked about you and your gift a lot, to impress the queen and keep her interest. And the queen knew I was originally from Bon Temps. On some nights, I've wondered if she sent someone to kill the last Compton and hurry things along. But maybe he truly died of old age." Bill was looking down at the floor, didn't see my left hand extended to him in a "stop" motion.

"She ordered me to return to my human home, to put myself in your way, to seduce you if I had to . . ."

I couldn't breathe. No matter how my right hand pressed to my chest, I couldn't stop the decimation of my heart, the slide of the knife deeper into my flesh.

"She wanted your gift harnessed for her own use," he said, and he opened his mouth to say more. My eyes were so blurred with tears that I couldn't see properly, couldn't see what expression was on his face and didn't care anyway. But I could not cry while he was anywhere near me. I would not.

"Get out," I said, with a terrible effort. Whatever else happened, I could not bear for him to see the pain he had caused.

He tried to look me straight in the eyes, but mine were too full. Whatever he wanted to convey, it was lost on me. "Please let me finish," he said.

"I never want to see you again, ever in my life," I whispered. "Ever."

He didn't speak. His lips moved, as if he were trying to form a word or phrase, but I shook my head. "Get out," I told him, in a voice so choked with hatred and anguish that it didn't sound like my own. Bill turned and walked past the curtain and out of the emergency room. Eric did not turn around to see my face, thank God. He reached back to pat me on the leg before he left, too.

I wanted to scream. I wanted to kill someone with my bare hands.

I had to be by myself. I could not let anyone see me suffer this much. The pain was tied up with a rage so profound that I had never felt its like. I was sick with anger and hurt. The snap of Jake Purifoy's teeth had been nothing compared to this.

I couldn't stay still. With some difficulty, I eased off the bed. My feet were still bare, of course, and I noticed with an odd detached part of my mind that they were extraordinarily dirty. I staggered out of the triage area, spotted the doors to the waiting room, and aimed myself in that direction. Walking was a problem.

A nurse bustled up to me, a clipboard in her hand. "Miss Stackhouse, a doctor's going to be with you in just a minute. I know you've had to wait, and I'm sorry, but . . ."

I turned to look at her and she flinched, took a step backward. I kept on toward the doors, my steps uncertain but my purpose clear. I wanted out of there. Beyond that, I didn't know. I made it to the doors and pushed and then I was dragging myself through the waiting room thronged with people. I blended in perfectly with the mix of patients and relatives waiting to see a doctor. Some were dirtier and bloodier than I was, and some were older—and some were way younger. I supported myself with a hand against a wall and kept moving to the doors, to the outside.

I made it.

It was much quieter outside, and it was warm. The wind was blowing, just a little. I was barefoot and penniless, standing under the glaring lights of the walk-in doors. I had no idea where I was in relation to the house, and no idea if that was where I was going, but I wasn't in the hospital any more.

A homeless man stepped in front of me. "You got any change, sister?" he asked. "I'm down on my luck, too."

"Do I *look* like I have *anything*?" I asked him, in a reasonable voice.

He looked as unnerved as the nurse had. He said, "Sorry," and backed away. I took a step after him.

I screamed, *"I HAVE NOTHING!"* And then I said, in a perfectly calm voice, "See, I never had anything to start with."

He gibbered and quavered and I ignored him. I began my walk. The ambulance had turned right coming in, so I turned left. I couldn't remember how long the ride had been. I'd been talking to Delagardie. I had been a different person. I walked and I walked. I walked under palm trees, heard the rich rhythm of music, brushed against the peeling shutters of houses set right up to the sidewalk.

On a street with a few bars, a group of young men came out just as I was passing, and one of them grabbed my arm. I turned on him with a scream, and with a galvanic effort I swung him into a wall. He stood there, dazed and rubbing his head, and his friends pulled him away.

"She crazy," one of them said softly. "Leave her be." They wandered off in the other direction.

After a time, I recovered enough to ask myself why I was doing this. But the answer was vague. When I fell on some broken pavement, scraping my knee badly enough to make it bleed, the new physical pain called me back to myself a little bit more.

"Are you doing this so they'll feel sorry they hurt you?" I asked myself out loud. "Oh my God, poor Sookie! She walked out of the hospital all by herself, driven crazy with grief, and she wandered alone through the dangerous streets of the Big Easy because Bill made her so crazy!"

I didn't want my name to cross Bill's lips ever again. When I was a little more myself—just a little—the depth of my reaction began to surprise me. If we'd still been a couple when I learned what I'd learned this evening, I'd have killed him; I knew that with crystal clarity. But the reason I'd had to get away from the hospital was equally clear; I couldn't have stood dealing with anyone in the world just then. I'd been blindsided with the most painful knowledge: the first man to ever say he loved me had never loved me at all.

His passion had been artificial.

His pursuit of me had been choreographed.

I must have seemed so easy to him, so gullible, so ready for the first man who devoted a little time and effort to winning me. Winning me! The very phrase made me hurt worse. He'd never thought of me as a prize.

Until the structure had been torn down in a single moment, I hadn't realized how much of my life in the past year had been built on the false foundation of Bill's love and regard.

"I saved his life," I said, amazed. "I went to Jackson and risked my life for his, because he loved me." One part of my brain knew that wasn't entirely accurate. I'd done it because I had loved him. And I was amazed, at the same moment, to realize that the pull of his maker, Lorena, had been even stronger than the orders of his queen. But I wasn't in the mood to split emotional hairs. When I thought of Lorena, another realization socked me in the stomach. "I killed someone for him," I said, my words floating in the thick dark night. "Oh, my God. I killed someone for *him.*"

I was covered in scrapes, bruises, blood, and dirt when I looked up to see a sign reading CHLOE STREET. That was where Hadley's apartment was, I realized slowly. I turned right, and began to walk again.

The house was dark, up and down. Maybe Amelia was still at the hospital. I had no idea what time it was or how long I had walked.

Hadley's apartment was locked. I went downstairs and picked up one of the flowerpots Amelia had put around her door. I carried it up the stairs and smashed in a glass pane on the door. I reached inside, unlocked the door, and stepped in. No alarm shrieked. I'd been pretty sure the police wouldn't have known the code to activate it when they'd left after doing whatever it was they'd done.

I walked through the apartment, which was still turned upside down by our fight with Jake Purifoy. I had some more cleaning to do in the morning, or whenever . . . whenever my life resumed. I went into the bathroom and stripped off the clothes I'd been wearing. I held them and looked at them for a minute, at the state they were in. Then I stepped across the hall, unlocked the closest French window, and threw the clothes over the railing of the gallery. I wished all problems were that easily disposed of, but at the same time my real personality was waking up enough to trigger a thread of guilt that I was leaving a mess that someone else would have to clean up. That wasn't the Stackhouse way. That thread wasn't strong enough to make me go back down the stairs to retrieve the filthy garments. Not then.

After I'd wedged a chair under the door I'd broken, and after I'd set the alarm system with the numbers Amelia had taught me, I got into the shower. The water stung my many scrapes and cuts, and the deep bite in my arm began bleeding again. Well, shit. My cousin the vampire hadn't needed any first aid supplies, of course. I finally found some circular cotton pads she'd probably used for removing makeup, and I rummaged through one of the bags of clothes until I found a ludicrously cheerful leopard-patterned scarf. Awkwardly, I bound the pads to the bite and got the scarf tight enough.

At least the vile sheets were the least of my worries. I climbed painfully into my nightgown and lay on the bed, praying for oblivion.

16

I WOKE UP UNREFRESHED, WITH THAT AWFUL FEELING that in a moment I would remember bad things.

The feeling was right on the money.

But the bad things had to take a backseat, because I had a surprise to start the day with. Claudine was lying beside me on the bed, propped up on one elbow looking down at me compassionately. And Amelia was at the end of the bed in an easy chair, her bandaged leg propped up on an ottoman. She was reading.

"How come you're here?" I asked Claudine. After seeing Eric and Bill last night, I wondered if everyone I knew followed me around. Maybe Sam would come in the door in a minute.

"I told you, I'm your fairy godmother," Claudine said. Claudine was usually the happiest fairy I knew. Claudine was just as lovely for a woman as her twin Claude was for a man; maybe lovelier, because her more agreeable personality shone through her eyes. Her coloring was the same as his; black hair, white skin. Today she was wearing pale blue capris and a coordinating black-and-blue tunic. She looked ethereally lovely, or at least as ethereal as you can look in capris.

"You can explain that to me right after I go to the bathroom," I said, remembering all the water I'd chugged down when I'd gotten to the sink the night before. All my wanderings had made me thirsty. Claudine swung gracefully from the bed, and I followed her awkwardly.

"Careful," Amelia advised, when I tried to stand up too quickly.

"How's your leg?" I asked her, when the world had righted itself. Claudine kept a grip on my arm, just in case. It felt good to see Claudine, and I was surprisingly glad to see Amelia, even limping.

"Very sore," she said. "But unlike you, I stayed at the hospital and had the wound treated properly." She closed her book and put it on the little table by the chair. She looked a little better than I suspected I did, but she was not the radiant and happy witch she'd been the day before.

"Had a learning experience, didn't we?" I said, and then my breath caught when I remembered just how much I'd learned.

Claudine helped me into the bathroom, and when I assured her I could manage, she left me alone. I did the necessary things and came out feeling better, almost human. Claudine had gotten some clothes out of my sports bag, and there was a mug on the bedside table with steam rising from it. I carefully sat against the headboard, my legs crossed in front of me, and held the mug to my face so I could breathe in the smell.

"Explain the fairy godmother thing," I said. I didn't want to talk about anything more urgent, not just yet.

"Fairies are your basic supernatural being," Claudine said. "From us come elves and brownies and angels and demons. Water sprites, green men, all the natural spirits . . . all are some form of fairy."

"So you're what?" Amelia asked. It hadn't occurred to Amelia to leave, and that seemed to be okay with Claudine, too.

"I'm trying to become an angel," Claudine said softly. Her huge brown eyes looked luminous. "After years of being . . . well, a good citizen, I guess you'd call it, I got a person to guard. The Sook, here. And she's really kept me busy." Claudine looked proud and happy.

"You're not supposed to prevent pain?" I asked. If so, Claudine was doing a lousy job.

"No, I wish I could." The expression on Claudine's oval face was downcast. "But I can help you recover from disasters, and sometimes I can prevent them."

"Things would be *worse* without you around?"

She nodded vigorously.

"I'll take your word for it," I said. "How come I rated a fairy godmother?"

"I'm not allowed to say," Claudine said, and Amelia rolled her eyes.

"We're not learning a lot, here," she said. "And in view of the problems we had last night, maybe you're not the most competent fairy godmother, huh?"

"Oh, right, Miss I-Sealed-Up-The-Apartment-So-It-Would-Be-All-Fresh," I responded, irrationally indignant at this assault on my godmother's competence.

Amelia scrambled out of her chair, her skin flushed with anger. "Well, I did seal it up! He would have risen like that no matter when he rose! I just delayed it some!"

"It would have helped if we had known he was in there!"

"It would have helped if your ho of a cousin hadn't killed him in the first place!"

We both screeched to a halt in our dialogue. "Are you sure that's what happened?" I asked. "Claudine?"

"I don't know," she said, her voice placid. "I'm not omnipotent or omniscient. I just pop in to intervene when I can. You remember that time you fell asleep at the wheel and I got there in time to save you?"

And she'd nearly given me a heart attack in the process, appearing in the front seat of the car in the blink of an eye. "Yes," I said, trying to sound grateful and humble. "I remember."

"It's really, really hard to get somewhere that fast," she said. "I can only do that in a real emergency. I mean, a life-or-death emergency. Fortunately, I had a bit more time when your house was on fire. . . ."

Claudine was not going to give us any rules, or even explain the nature of the rule maker. I'd just have to muddle through on my belief system, which had helped me out all my life. Come to think of it, if I was completely wrong, I didn't want to know.

"Interesting," said Amelia. "But we have a few more things to talk about."

Maybe she was being so hoity-toity because she didn't have her own fairy godmother.

"What do you want to talk about first?" I asked.

"Why'd you leave the hospital last night?" Her face was tight with resentment. "You should have told me. I hauled myself up these stairs last night to look for you, and there you were. And you'd barricaded the door. So I had to go back down the damn stairs again to get my keys, and let myself in the French windows, and hurry—*on this leg*—to the alarm system to turn it off. And then this doofus was sitting by your bed, and she could have done all of that."

"You couldn't open the windows with magic?" I asked.

"I was too tired," she said with dignity. "I had to recharge my magical batteries, so to speak."

"So to speak," I said, my voice dry. "Well, last night,

I found out . . ." and I stopped dead. I simply couldn't speak of it.

"Found out what?" Amelia was exasperated, and I couldn't say as I blamed her.

"Bill, her first lover, was planted in Bon Temps to seduce her and gain her trust," Claudine said. "Last night, he admitted that to her face, and in front of her only other lover, another vampire."

As a synopsis, it was flawless.

"Well . . . that sucks," Amelia said faintly.

"Yeah," I said. "It does."

"Ouch."

"Yeah."

"I can't kill him for you," Claudine said. "I'd have to take too many steps backward."

"That's okay," I told her. "He's not worth your losing any brownie points."

"Oh, I'm not a brownie," Claudine explained kindly. "I thought you understood. I'm a full-blooded fairy."

Amelia was trying not to laugh, and I glared at her. "Just let it go, witch," I said.

"Yes, telepath."

"So what next?" I asked, in general. I would not talk any more about my broken heart and my demolished self-worth.

"We figure out what happened," the witch said.

"How? Call CSI?"

Claudine looked confused, so I guessed fairies didn't watch television.

"No," Amelia said, with elaborate patience. "We do an ectoplasmic reconstruction."

I was sure that my expression matched Claudine's, now.

"Okay, let me explain," Amelia said, grinning all over. "This is what we do."

Amelia, in seventh heaven at this exhibition of her wonderful witch powers, told Claudine and me at length about the procedure. It was time- and energy-consuming, she said, which was why it wasn't done more often. And you had to gather at least four witches, she estimated, to cover the amount of square footage involved in Jake's murder.

"And I'll need real witches," Amelia said. "Quality workers, not some hedgerow Wiccan." Amelia went off on Wiccans for a good long while. She despised Wiccans (unfairly) as tree-hugging wannabes—that came out of Amelia's thoughts clearly enough. I regretted Amelia's prejudice, as I'd met some impressive Wiccans.

Claudine looked down at me, her expression doubtful. "I'm not sure we ought to be here for this," she said.

"You can go, Claudine." I was ready to experiment with anything, just to take my mind off the big hole in my heart. "I'm going to stay to watch. I have to know what happened here. There are too many mysteries in my life, right now."

"But you have to go to the queen's tonight," Claudine said. "You missed last night. Visiting the queen is a dress-up occasion. I have to take you shopping. You don't want to wear any of your cousin's clothes."

"Not that my butt could get into them," I said.

"Not that your butt should want to," she said, equally harshly. "You can cut that out right now, Sookie Stackhouse."

I looked up at her, letting her see the pain inside me.

"Yeah, I get that," she said, her hand patting me gently on the cheek. "And that sucks big-time. But you have to write it off. He's only one guy."

He'd been the first guy. "My grandmother served him lemonade," I said, and somehow that triggered the tears again.

"Hey," Amelia said. "Fuck him, right?"

I looked at the young witch. She was pretty and tough and off-the-wall nuts, I thought. She was okay. "Yeah," I said. "When can you do the ecto thing?"

She said, "I have to make some phone calls, see who I can

get together. Night's always better for magic, of course. When will you go pay your call to the queen?"

I thought for a moment. "Just at full dark," I said. "Maybe about seven."

"Should take about two hours," Amelia said, and Claudine nodded. "Okay, I'll ask them to be here at ten, to have a little wiggle room. You know, it would be great if the queen would pay for this."

"How much do you want to charge?"

"I'd do it for nothing, to have the experience and be able to say I'd done one," Amelia said frankly, "but the others will need some bucks. Say, three hundred apiece, plus materials."

"And you'll need three more witches?"

"I'd like to have three more, though whether I can get the ones I want on this short notice . . . well, I'll do the best I can. Two might do. And the materials ought to be . . ." She did some rapid mental calculations. "Somewhere in the ballpark of sixty dollars."

"What will I need to do? I mean, what's my part?"

"Observe. I'll do the heavy lifting."

"I'll ask the queen." I took a deep breath. "If she won't pay for it, I will."

"Okay, then. We're set." She limped out of the bedroom happily, counting off things on her fingers. I heard her go down the stairs.

Claudine said, "I have to treat your arm. And then we need to go find you something to wear."

"I don't want to spend money on a courtesy call to the vampire queen." Especially since I might have to foot the bill for the witches.

"You don't have to. It's my treat."

"You may be my fairy godmother, but you don't have to spend money on me." I had a sudden revelation. "It's you who paid my hospital bill in Clarice."

Claudine shrugged. "Hey, it's money that came in from the

strip club, not from my regular job." Claudine co-owned the strip club in Ruston, with Claude, who did all the day-to-day running of the place. Claudine was a customer service person at a department store. People forgot their complaints once they were confronted with Claudine's smile.

It was true that I didn't mind spending the strip club money as much as I would have hated using up Claudine's personal savings. Not logical, but true.

Claudine had parked her car in the courtyard on the circular drive, and she was sitting in it when I came down the stairs. She'd gotten a first aid kit from the car, and she'd bandaged my arm and helped me into some clothes. My arm was sore but it didn't seem to be infected. I was weak, as if I'd had the flu or some other illness involving high fever and lots of fluids. So I was moving slowly.

I was wearing blue jeans and sandals and a T-shirt, because that was what I had.

"You definitely can't call on the queen in that," she said, gently but decisively. Whether she was very familiar with New Orleans or just had good shopping karma, Claudine drove directly to a store in the Garden District. It was the kind of shop I'd dismiss as being for more sophisticated women with lots more money than I had, if I'd been shopping by myself. Claudine pulled right into the parking lot, and in forty-five minutes we had a dress. It was chiffon, short-sleeved, and it had lots of colors in it: turquoise, copper, brown, ivory. The strappy sandals that I wore with it were brown.

All I needed was a membership to the country club.

Claudine had appropriated the price tag.

"Just wear your hair loose," Claudine advised. "You don't need fancy hair with that dress."

"Yeah, there is a lot going on in it," I said. "Who's Diane von Furstenburg? Isn't it real expensive? Isn't it a little bare for the season?"

"You might be a little cool wearing it in March," Claudine conceded. "But it'll be good to wear every summer for years. You'll look great. And the queen will know you took the time to wear something special to meet her."

"You can't go with me?" I asked, feeling a little wistful. "No, of course, you can't." Vampires buzz around fairies like hummingbirds around sugar water.

"I might not survive," she said, managing to sound embarrassed that such a possibility would keep her from my side.

"Don't worry about it. After all, the worst thing has already happened, right?" I spread my hands. "They used to threaten me, you know? If I didn't do thus and such, they'd take it out on Bill. Hey, guess what? *I don't care any more.*"

"Think before you speak," Claudine advised. "You can't mouth off to the queen. Even a goblin won't mouth off to the queen."

"I promise," I said. "I really appreciate your coming all this way, Claudine."

Claudine gave me a big hug. It was like an embrace with a soft tree, since Claudine was so tall and slim. "I wish you hadn't needed me to," she said.

17~

THE QUEEN OWNED A BLOCK OF BUILDINGS IN DOWNtown New Orleans, maybe three blocks from the edge of the French Quarter. That tells you what kind of money she was pulling in, right there. We had an early dinner—I realized I was really hungry—and then Claudine dropped me off two blocks away, because the traffic and tourist congestion were intense close to the queen's headquarters. Though the general public didn't know Sophie-Anne Leclerq was a queen, they knew she was a very wealthy vampire who owned a hell of a lot of real estate and spent lots of money in the community. Plus, her bodyguards were colorful and had gotten special permits to carry arms in the city limits. This meant her office building/living quarters were on the tourist list of things to see, especially at night.

Though traffic did surround the building during the

day, at night the square of streets around it was open only to pedestrians. Buses parked a block away, and the tour guides would lead the out-of-towners past the altered building. Walking tours and gaggles of independent tourists included what the guides called "Vampire Headquarters" in their plans.

Security was very evident. This block would be a natural target for Fellowship of the Sun bombers. A few vampire-owned businesses in other cities had been attacked, and the queen was not about to lose her life-after-death in such a way.

The vampire guards were on duty, and they were scary-looking as hell. The queen had her own vampire SWAT team. Though vampires were simply lethal all on their own, the queen had found that humans paid more attention if they found the silhouettes recognizable. Not only were the guards heavily armed, but they wore black bulletproof armor over black uniforms. It was lethal-killer *chic*.

Claudine had prepared me for all this over dinner, and when she let me out, I felt fully briefed. I also felt as if I were going to the Queen of England's garden party in all my new finery. At least I didn't have to wear a hat. But my brown high heels were a risky proposition on the rough paving.

"Behold the headquarters of New Orleans's most famous and visible vampire, Sophie-Anne LeClerq," a tour guide was telling his group. He was dressed colorfully in a sort of colonial outfit: tricorn hat, knee breeches, hose, buckled shoes. My goodness. As I paused to listen, his eyes flickered over to me, took in my outfit, and sharpened with interest.

"If you're calling on Sophie-Anne, you can't go in casual," he told the group, and gestured to me. "This young lady is wearing proper dress for an interview with the vampire . . . one of America's most prominent vampires." He grinned at the group, inviting them to enjoy his reference.

There were fifty other vampires just as prominent.

Maybe not as publicly oriented or as colorful as Sophie-Anne Leclerq, but the public didn't know that.

Rather than being surrounded with the appropriate air of exotic deadliness, the queen's "castle" was more of a macabre Disneyland, thanks to the souvenir peddlers, the tour guides, and the curious gawkers. There was even a photographer. As I approached the first ring of guards, a man jumped in front of me and snapped my picture. I was frozen by the flash of light and stared after him—or in what I thought was his direction—while my eyes adjusted. When I was able to see him clearly, I found he was a small, grubby man with a big camera and a determined expression. He bustled off immediately to what I guessed was his accustomed station, a corner on the opposite side of the street. He didn't offer to sell me a picture or tell me where I could purchase one, and he didn't give me any explanation.

I had a bad feeling about this incident. When I talked to one of the guards, my suspicion was confirmed.

"He's a Fellowship spy," said the vampire, nodding in the little man's direction. He'd located my name on a checklist clamped to a clipboard. The guard himself was a sturdy man with brown skin and a nose as curved as a rainbow. He'd been born somewhere in the Middle East, once-upon a time. The name patch attached with Velcro to his helmet said RASUL.

"We're forbidden to kill him," Rasul said, as if he were explaining a slightly embarrassing folk custom. He smiled at me, which was kind of disconcerting, too. The black helmet came down low on his face and the chinstrap was the kind that actually rounded his chin, so I could see only a little bit of his face. At the moment, that bit was mostly sharp, white, teeth. "The Fellowship photographs everyone who goes in and out of this place, and there doesn't seem to be anything we can do about it, since we want to keep the goodwill of the humans."

Rasul correctly assumed I was a vampire ally, since I was on the visitors list, and was treating me with a camaraderie that I found relaxing. "It would be lovely if something happened to his camera," I suggested. "The Fellowship is hunting me already." Though I felt pretty guilty, asking a vampire to arrange an accident to another human being, I was fond enough of my own life to want it saved.

His eyes gleamed as we passed under a streetlight. The light caught them so that for a moment they shone red, like people's eyes sometimes do when the photographer is using a flash.

"Oddly enough, a few things have happened to his cameras already," Rasul said. "In fact, two of them have been smashed beyond repair. What's one more accident? I'm not guaranteeing anything, but we'll do our best, lovely lady."

"Thank you so much," I said. "Anything you can do will be much appreciated. After tonight, I can talk to a witch who could maybe take care of that problem for you. Maybe she could make all the pictures turn out overexposed, or something. You should give her a call."

"That's an excellent idea. Here is Melanie," he said, as we reached the main doors. "I'll pass you on to her, and return to my post. I'll see you when you exit, get the witch's name and address?"

"Sure," I said.

"Did anyone ever tell you that you smell enchantingly like a fairy?" Rasul said.

"Oh, I've been with my fairy godmother," I explained. "She took me shopping."

"And the result was wonderful," he said gallantly.

"You flatterer." I couldn't help but smile back at him. My ego had taken a blow to the solar plexus the night before (but I *wasn't thinking about that*), and a little thing like the guard's admiration was just what I needed, even if it was really Claudine's smell that had triggered it.

Melanie was a delicate woman, even in the SWAT gear. "Yum, yum, you do smell like fairy," she said. She consulted her own clipboard. "You are the Stackhouse woman? The queen expected you last night."

"I got hurt." I held my arm out, showing the bandage. Thanks to a lot of Advil, the pain was down to a dull throb.

"Yes, I heard about it. The new one is having a great night tonight. He received instructions, he has a mentor, and he has a volunteer donor. When he feels more like his new self, he may tell us how he came to be turned."

"Oh?" I heard my voice falter when I realized she was talking about Jake Purifoy. "He might not remember?"

"If it's a surprise attack, sometimes they don't remember for a while," she said, and shrugged. "But it always comes back, sooner or later. In the meantime, he'll have a free lunch." She laughed at my inquiring look. "They register for the privilege, you know. Stupid humans." She shrugged. "There's no fun in that, once you've gotten over the thrill of feeding, in and of itself. The fun was always in the chase." Melanie really wasn't happy with the new vampire policy of feeding only from willing humans or from the synthetic blood. She clearly felt the lack of her former diet.

I tried to look politely interested.

"When the prey makes the first advance, it's just not the same," she grumped. "People these days." She shook her little head in weary exasperation. Since she was so small that her helmet almost wobbled on her head, I could feel myself smiling.

"So, he wakes up and you all herd the volunteer in? Like dropping a live mouse into a snake's tank?" I worked to keep my face serious. I didn't want Melanie to think I was making fun of her personally.

After a suspicious moment, Melanie said, "More or less. He's been lectured. There are other vampires present."

"And the volunteer survives?"

"They sign a release beforehand," Melanie said, carefully.

I shuddered.

Rasul had escorted me from the other side of the street to the main entrance to the queen's domain. It was a three-story office building, perhaps dating from the fifties, and extending a whole city block. In other places, the basement would have been the vampires' retreat, but in New Orleans, with its high water table, that was impossible. All the windows had received a distinctive treatment. The panels that covered them were decorated in a Mardi Gras theme, so the staid brick building was pepped up with pink, purple, and green designs on a white or black background. There were iridescent patches on the shutters, too, like Mardi Gras beads. The effect was disconcerting.

"What does she do when she throws a party?" I asked. Despite the shutters, the prosaic office rectangle was simply not festive.

"Oh, she owns an old monastery," Melanie said. "You can get a brochure about it before you go. That's where all the state functions are held. Some of the old ones can't go into the former chapel, but other than that . . . it's got a high wall all around, so it's easy to patrol, and it's decorated real nice. The queen has apartments there, but it's too insecure for year-round living."

I couldn't think of anything to say. I doubted I would ever see the queen's state residence. But Melanie seemed bored and inclined to chat. "You were Hadley's cousin, I hear?" she asked.

"Yes."

"Strange, to think of having living relatives." For a moment, she looked far away, and as wistful as a vampire can look. Then she seemed to kind of shake herself mentally. "Hadley wasn't bad for one so young. But she seemed to take her vampire longevity a little too much for granted."

Melanie shook her head. "She should never have crossed someone as old and wily as Waldo."

"That's for damn sure," I said.

"Chester," Melanie called. Chester was the next guard in line, and he was standing with a familiar figure clothed in the (what I was coming to think of as) usual SWAT garb.

"Bubba!" I exclaimed, as the vampire said, "Miss Sookie!" Bubba and I hugged, to the vampires' amusement. Vampires don't shake hands, in the ordinary course of things, and hugging is just as outré in their culture.

I was glad to see they hadn't let him have a gun, just the accoutrements of the guards. He was looking fine in the military outfit, and I told him so. "Black looks real good with your hair," I said, and Bubba smiled his famous smile.

"You're mighty nice to say so," he said. "Thank you very much."

Back in the day, everyone in the world had known Bubba's face and smile. When he'd been wheeled into the morgue in Memphis, a vampire attendant had detected the tiniest flicker of life. Since the attendant was a huge fan, he had taken on the responsibility for bringing the singer over, and a legend had been born. Unfortunately, Bubba's body had been so saturated with drugs and physical woes that the conversion hadn't been entirely successful, and the vampire world passed Bubba around like the public relations nightmare he was.

"How long have you been here, Bubba?" I asked.

"Oh, a couple of weeks, but I like it real well," he said. "Lots of stray cats."

"Right," I said, trying not to think about that too graphically. I really like cats. So did Bubba, but not in the same way.

"If a human catches a glimpse of him, they think he's an impersonator," Chester said quietly. Melanie had gone back to her post, and Chester, who'd been a sandy-haired kid from the backwoods with poor dentition when he was taken, was now in charge of me. "That's fine, most often. But every so now and then, they call him by his used-to-be name. Or they ask him to sing."

Bubba very seldom sang these days, though every now and then he could be coaxed into belting out a familiar song or two. That was a memorable occasion. Most often, though, he denied he could sing a note, and he usually got very agitated when he was called by his original name.

He trailed along after us as Chester led me further into the building. We had turned, and gone up a floor, encountering more and more vampires—and a few humans—heading here or there with a purposeful air. It was like any busy office building, any weekday, except the workers were vampires and the sky outside was as dark as the New Orleans sky ever got. As we walked, I noticed that some vampires seemed more at ease than others. I observed that the wary vamps were all wearing the same pins attached to their collars, pins in the shape of the state of Arkansas. These vamps must be part of the entourage of the queen's husband, Peter Threadgill. When one of the Louisiana vampires bumped into an Arkansas vampire, the Arkansan snarled and for a second I thought there would be a fight in the corridor over a slight accident.

Jeesh, I'd be glad to get out of here. The atmosphere was tense.

Chester stopped before a door that didn't look any different from all the other closed doors, except for the two whacking big vampires outside it. The two must have been considered giants in their day, since they stood perhaps six foot three. They looked like brothers, but maybe it was just their size and mien, and the color of their chestnut hair, that sparked the comparison: big as boulders, bearded, with ponytails that trailed down their backs, the two looked like prime meat for the pro wrestling circuit. One had a huge scar across his face, acquired before death, of course. The other had had some skin disease in his original life. They weren't just display items; they were absolutely lethal.

(By the way, some promoter had had the idea for a vampire wrestling circuit a couple of years before, but it went down in flames immediately. At the first match, one vamp had ripped another's arm off, on live TV. Vamps don't get the concept of exhibition fighting.)

These two vampires were hung with knives, and each had an ax in his belt. I guess they figured if someone had penetrated this far, guns weren't going to make a difference. Plus their own bodies were weapons.

"Bert, Bert," Chester said, nodding to each one in turn. "This here's the Stackhouse woman; the queen wants to see her."

He turned and walked away, leaving me with the queen's bodyguards.

Screaming didn't seem like a good idea, so I said, "I can't believe you both have the same name. Surely he made a mistake?"

Two pairs of brown eyes focused on me intently. "I am Sigebert," the scarred one said, with a heavy accent I couldn't identify. He said his name as *See-ya-bairt.* Chester was using a very Americanized version of what must be a very old name. "Dis my brodder, Wybert."

This is my brother, Way-bairt? "Hello," I said, trying not to twitch. "I'm Sookie Stackhouse."

They seemed unimpressed. Just then, one of the pinned vampires squeezed past, casting a look of scarcely veiled contempt at the brothers, and the atmosphere in the corridor became lethal. Sigebert and Wybert watched the vamp, a tall woman in a business suit, until she rounded a corner. Then their attention switched back to me.

"The queen is . . . busy," Wybert said. "When she wants you in her room, the light, it will shine." He indicated a round light set in the wall to the right of the door.

So I was stuck here for an indefinite time—until the light, it shone. "Do your names have a meaning? I'm guessing they're, um, early English?" My voice petered out.

"We were Saxons. Our fadder went from Germany to England, you call now," Wybert said. "My name mean Bright Battle."

"And mine, Bright Victory," Sigebert added.

I remembered a program I'd seen on the History Channel. The Saxons eventually became the Anglo-Saxons and later were overwhelmed by the Normans. "So you were raised to be warriors," I said, trying to look intelligent.

They exchanged glances. "There was nothing else," Sigebert said. The end of his scar wiggled when he talked, and I tried not to stare. "We were sons of war leader."

I could think of a hundred questions to ask them about their lives as humans, but standing in the middle of a hallway in an office building in the night didn't seem the time to do it. "How'd you happen to become vampires?" I asked. "Or is that a tacky question? If it is, just forget I said anything. I don't want to step on any toes."

Sigebert actually glanced down at his feet, so I got the idea that colloquial English wasn't their strong suit. "This woman . . . very beautiful . . . she come to us the night before battle," Wybert said haltingly. "She say . . . we be stronger if she . . . have us."

They looked at me inquiringly, and I nodded to show I understood that Wybert was saying the vampire had implied her interest was in bedding them. Or had they understood she meant to bleed them? I couldn't tell. I thought it was a mighty ambitious vampire who would take on these two humans at the same time.

"She did not say we only fight at night after that," Sigebert said, shrugging to show that there had been a catch they hadn't understood. "We did not ask plenty questions. We too eager!" And he smiled. Okay, nothing so scary as a vampire left with only his fangs. It was possible Sigebert had more teeth in the back of his mouth, ones I couldn't see from my height, but Chester's plentiful-though-crooked teeth had looked super in comparison.

"That must have been a very long time ago," I said, since I couldn't think of anything else to say. "How long have you worked for the queen?"

Sigebert and Wybert looked at each other. "Since that night," Wybert said, astonished I hadn't understood. "We are hers."

My respect for the queen, and maybe my fear of the queen, escalated. Sophie-Anne, if that was her real name, had been brave, strategic, and busy in her career as a vampire leader. She'd brought them over and kept them with her, in a bond that—the one whose name I wasn't going to speak even to myself—had explained to me was stronger than any other emotional tie, for a vampire.

To my relief, the light shone green in the wall.

Sigebert said, "Go now," and pushed open the heavy door. He and Wybert gave me matching nods of farewell as I walked over the threshold and into a room that was like any executive's office anywhere.

Sophie-Anne Leclerq, Queen of Louisiana, and a male vampire were sitting at a round table piled with papers. I'd met the queen once before, when she'd come to my place to tell me about my cousin's death. I hadn't noticed then how young she must have been when she died, maybe no more than fifteen. She was an elegant woman, perhaps four inches shorter than my height of five foot six, and she was groomed down to the last eyelash. Makeup, dress, hair, stockings, jewelry—the whole nine yards.

The vampire at the table with her was her male counterpart. He wore a suit that would have paid my cable bill for a year, and he was barbered and manicured and scented until he almost wasn't a guy any more. In my neck of the woods,

I didn't often see men so groomed. I guessed this was the new king. I wondered if he'd died in such a state; actually, I wondered if the funeral home had cleaned him up like that for his funeral, not knowing that his descent below ground was only temporary. If that had been the case, he was younger than his queen. Maybe age wasn't the only requirement, if you were aiming to be royalty.

There were two other people in the room. A short man stood about three feet behind the queen's chair, his legs apart, his hands clasped in front of him. He had close-cut white-blond hair and bright blue eyes. His face lacked maturity; he looked like a large child, but with a man's shoulders. He was wearing a suit, and he was armed with a saber and a gun.

Behind the man at the table stood a woman, a vampire, dressed all in red; slacks, T-shirt, Converses. Her preference was unfortunate, because red was not her color. She was Asian, and I thought she'd come from Vietnam—though it had probably been called something else then. She had very short unpainted nails, and a terrifying sword strapped to her back. Apparently, her hair had been cut off at chin length by a pair of rusty scissors. Her face was the unenhanced one God had given her.

Since I hadn't had a briefing on the correct protocol, I dipped my head to the queen, said, "Good to see you again, ma'am," and tried to look pleasantly at the king while doing the head-dip thing again. The two standees, who must be aides or bodyguards, received smaller nods. I felt like an idiot, but I didn't want to ignore them. However, they didn't have a problem with ignoring me, once they'd given me an all-over threat assessment.

"You've had some adventures in New Orleans," the queen said, a safe lead-in. She wasn't smiling, but then I had the impression she was not a smiley kind of gal.

"Yes, ma'am."

"Sookie, this is my husband. Peter Threadgill, King of Arkansas." There was not a trace of affection on her face. She might as well have been telling me the name of her pet cockapoo.

"How-de-do," I said, and repeated my head-bob, adding, "Sir," hastily. Okay, already tired of this.

"Miss Stackhouse," he said, turning his attention back to the papers in front of him. The round table was large and completely cluttered with letters, computer printouts, and an assortment of other papers—bank statements?

While I was relieved not to be an object of interest to the king, I was wondering exactly why I was there. I found out when the queen began to question me about the night before. I told her as explicitly as I could what had happened.

She looked very serious when I talked about Amelia's stasis spell and what it had done to the body.

"You don't think the witch knew the body was there when she cast the spell?" the queen asked. I noticed that though the king's gaze was on the papers in front of him, he hadn't moved a one of them since I'd begun talking. Of course, maybe he was a very slow reader.

"No, ma'am. I know Amelia didn't know he was there."

"From your telepathic ability?"

"Yes, ma'am."

Peter Threadgill looked at me then, and I saw that his eyes were an unusual glacial gray. His face was full of sharp angles: a nose like a blade, thin straight lips, high cheekbones.

The king and the queen were both good-looking, but not in a way that struck any chord in me. I had an impression that the feeling was mutual. Thank God.

"You're the telepath that my dear Sophie wants to bring to the conference," Peter Threadgill said.

Since he was telling me something I already knew, I didn't feel the need to answer. But discretion won over sheer irritation. "Yes, I am."

"Stan has one," the queen said to her husband, as if vampires collected telepaths the way dog fanciers collected springer spaniels.

The only Stan I knew was a head vampire in Dallas, and the only other telepath I'd ever met had lived there. From the queen's few words, I guessed that Barry the Bellman's life had changed a lot since I'd met him. Apparently he worked for Stan Davis now. I didn't know if Stan was the sheriff or even a king, since at the time I hadn't been privy to the fact that vampires had such.

"So you're now trying to match your entourage to Stan's?" Peter Threadgill asked his wife, in a distinctly unfond kind of way. From the many clues thrown my way, I'd gotten the picture that this wasn't a love match. If you asked me to cast a vote, I would say it wasn't even a lust match. I knew the queen had liked my cousin Hadley in a lusty way, and the two brothers on guard had said she'd rocked their world. Peter Threadgill was nowhere near either side of that spectrum. But maybe that only proved the queen was omnisexual, if that was a word. I'd have to look it up when I went home. If I ever got home.

"If Stan can see the advantage in employing such a person, I can certainly consider it—especially since one is easily available."

I was in stock.

The king shrugged. Not that I had formed many expectations, but I would have anticipated that the king of a nice, poor, scenic state like Arkansas would be less sophisticated and folksier, with a sense of humor. Maybe Threadgill was a carpetbagger from New York City. Vampire accents tended to be all over the map—literally—so it was impossible to tell from his speech.

"So what do you think happened in Hadley's apartment?" the queen asked me, and I realized we'd reverted to the original subject.

"I don't know who attacked Jake Purifoy," I said. "But the night Hadley went to the graveyard with Waldo, Jake's drained body landed in her closet. As to how it came there, I couldn't say. That's why Amelia is having this ecto thing tonight."

The queen's expression changed; she actually looked interested. "She's having an ectoplasmic reconstruction? I've heard of those, but never witnessed one."

The king looked more than interested. For a split second, he looked extremely angry.

I forced my attention back to the queen. "Amelia wondered if you would care to, ah, fund it?" I wondered if I should add, "My lady," but I just couldn't bring myself to do it.

"That would be a good investment, since our newest vampire might have gotten us all into a great deal of trouble. If he had gotten loose on the populace . . . I will be glad to pay."

I drew a breath of sheer relief.

"And I think I'll watch, too," the queen added, before I could even exhale.

That sounded like the worst idea in the world. I thought the queen's presence would flatten Amelia until all the magic was squished out. However, there was no way I was going to tell the queen she was not welcome.

Peter Threadgill had looked up sharply when the queen had announced she'd watch. "I don't think you should go," he said, his voice smooth and authoritative. "It will be hard for the twins and Andre to guard you out in the city in a neighborhood like that."

I wondered how the King of Arkansas had any idea what Hadley's neighborhood was like. Actually, it was a quiet, middle-class area, especially compared to the zoo that was vampire central headquarters, with its constant stream of tourists and picketers and fanatics with cameras.

Sophie-Anne was already preparing to go out. That preparation consisted of glancing in a mirror to make sure the flawless façade was still flawless and sliding on her high, high heels, which had been below the edge of the table. She'd been sitting there barefoot. That detail suddenly made Sophie-Anne Leclerq much more real to me. There was a personality under that glossy exterior.

"I suppose you would like Bill to accompany us," the queen said to me.

"No," I snapped. Okay, there was a personality—and it was unpleasant and cruel.

But the queen looked genuinely startled. Her husband was outraged at my rudeness—his head shot up and his odd gray eyes fixed me with a luminous anger—but the queen was simply taken aback by my reaction. "I thought you were a couple," she said, in a perfectly even voice.

I bit back my first answer, trying to remember who I was talking to, and said, almost in a whisper, "No, we are not." I took a deep breath and made a great effort. "I apologize for being so abrupt. Please excuse me."

The queen simply looked at me for a few seconds longer, and I still could not get the slightest indication of her thoughts, emotions, or intentions. It was like looking at an antique silver tray—a shining surface, an elaborate pattern, and hard to the touch. How Hadley could have been adventurous enough to bed this woman was simply beyond my comprehension.

"You are excused," she said finally.

"You're too lenient," her husband said, and his surface, at least, began to thin somewhat. His lips curled in something closely approaching a snarl, and I discovered I didn't want to be the focus of those luminous eyes for another second. I didn't like the way the Asian gal in red was looking at me, either. And every time I looked at her haircut, it gave me the heebie-jeebies. Gosh, even the elderly lady who'd given my gran a permanent three times a year would have done a better job than the Mad Weed Whacker.

"I'll be back in an hour or two, Peter," Sophie-Anne said, very precisely, in a tone that could have sliced a diamond. The short man, his childish face blank, was by her side in a jiffy, extending his arm so she could have his assistance in rising. I guessed he was Andre.

The atmosphere was cuttable. Oh, I so wished I were somewhere else.

"I would feel more at ease if I knew Jade Flower was with you," the king said. He motioned toward the woman in red. Jade Flower, my ass: she looked more like Stone Killer. The Asian woman's face didn't change one iota at the king's offer.

"But that would leave you with no one," the queen said.

"Hardly true. The building is full of guards and loyal vampires," Peter Threadgill said.

Okay, even I caught that one. The guards, who belonged to the queen, were separate from the loyal vampires, whom I guessed were the ones Peter had brought with him.

"Then, of course, I would be proud to have a fighter like Jade Flower accompany me."

Yuck. I couldn't tell if the queen was serious, or trying to placate her new husband by accepting his offer, or laughing up her sleeve at his lame strategy to ensure that his spy was at the ectoplasmic reconstruction. The queen used the intercom to call down—or up, for all I knew—to the secure chamber where Jake Purifoy was being educated in the ways of the vampire. "Keep extra guards on Purifoy," she said. "And let me know the minute he remembers something." An obsequious voice assured Sophie-Anne that she'd be the first to know.

I wondered why Jake needed extra guards. I found it hard to get real concerned about his welfare, but obviously the queen was.

So here we went—the queen, Jade Flower, Andre, Sigebert,

Wybert, and me. I guess I've been in company just as assorted, but I couldn't tell you when. After a lot of corridor tromping, we entered a guarded garage and piled into a stretch limo. Andre jerked his thumb at one of the guards, indicating that the guard should drive. I hadn't heard the baby-faced vampire utter a word, so far. To my pleasure, the driver was Rasul, who felt like an old friend compared to the others.

Sigebert and Wybert were uncomfortable in the car. They were the most inflexible vampires I'd ever met, and I wondered if their close association with the queen hadn't been their undoing. They hadn't had to change, and changing with the times was the key vampire survival technique before the Great Revelation. It remained so in countries that hadn't accepted the existence of vampire with the tolerance America had shown. The two vampires would have been happy wearing skins and hand-woven cloth and would have looked perfectly at home in handmade leather boots, carrying shields on their arms.

"Your sheriff, Eric, came to speak to me last night," the queen told me.

"I saw him at the hospital," I said, hoping I sounded equally offhanded.

"You understand that the new vampire, the one that was a Were—he had no choice, you understand?"

"I get that a lot with vampires," I said, remembering all the times in the past when Bill had explained things by saying he couldn't help himself. I'd believed him at the time, but I wasn't so sure any more. In fact, I was so profoundly tired and miserable I hardly had the heart to continue trying to wrap up Hadley's apartment and her estate and her affairs. I realized that if I went home to Bon Temps, leaving unfinished business here, I'd just sit and brood when I got there.

I knew this, but at the moment, it was hard to face.

It was time for one of my self–pep talks. I told myself sternly I'd already enjoyed a moment or two of that very evening, and I would enjoy a few more seconds of every day until I built back to my former contented state. I'd always enjoyed life, and I knew I would again. But I was going to have to slog through a lot of bad patches to get there.

I don't think I've ever been a person with a lot of illusions. If you can read minds, you don't have many doubts about how bad even the best people can be.

But I sure hadn't seen this coming.

To my horror, tears began sliding down my face. I reached into my little purse, pulled out a Kleenex, and patted my cheeks while all the vamps stared at me, Jade Flower with the most identifiable expression I'd seen on her face: contempt.

"Are you in pain?" the queen asked, indicating my arm.

I didn't think she really cared; I was sure that she had schooled herself to give the correct human response for so long that it was a reflex.

"Pain of the heart," I said, and could have bitten my tongue off.

"Oh," she said. "Bill?"

"Yes," I said, and gulped, doing my best to stop the display of emotion.

"I grieved for Hadley," she said unexpectedly.

"It was good she had someone to care." After a minute I said, "I would have been glad to know she was dead earlier than I did," which was as cautiously as I could express it. I hadn't found out my cousin was gone until weeks after the fact.

"There were reasons I had to wait to send Cataliades down," Sophie-Anne said. Her smooth face and clear eyes were as impenetrable as a wall of ice, but I got the definite impression that she wished I hadn't raised the subject. I looked at the queen, trying to pick up on some clue, and she gave a tiny flick of the eye toward Jade Flower, who was sitting on her right. I didn't know how Jade Flower could be sitting in her relaxed position with the long sword strapped to her back. But I definitely had the feeling that behind her expressionless face and flat eyes, Jade Flower was listening to everything that transpired.

To be on the safe side, I decided I wouldn't say anything at all, and the rest of the drive passed in silence.

Rasul didn't want to take the limo into the courtyard, and I recalled that Diantha had parked on the street, too. Rasul came back to open the door for the queen, and Andre got out first, looked around for a long time, then nodded that it was safe for the queen to emerge. Rasul stood at the ready, rifle in his hands, sweeping the area visually for attackers. Andre was just as vigilant.

Jade Flower slithered out of the backseat next and added her eyes to those scanning the area. Protecting the queen with their bodies, they moved into the courtyard. Sigebert got out next, ax in hand, and waited for me. After I'd joined him on the sidewalk, he and Wybert took me through the open gateway with less ceremony than the others had taken the queen.

I'd seen the queen at my own home, unguarded by anyone but Cataliades. I'd seen the queen in her own office, guarded by one person. I guess I didn't realize until that moment how important security was for Sophie-Anne, how precarious her hold on power must be. I wanted to know against whom all these guards were protecting her. Who wanted to kill the Louisiana queen? Maybe all vampire rulers were in this much danger—or maybe it was just Sophie-Anne. Suddenly the vampire conference in the fall seemed like a much scarier proposition than it had before.

The courtyard was well lit, and Amelia was standing on the circular driveway with three friends. For the record, none of them were crones with broomsticks. One of them was a kid who looked just like a Mormon missionary: black pants, white shirt, dark tie, polished black shoes. There was a bicycle leaning up against the tree in the center of the circle. Maybe he *was* a Mormon missionary. He looked so young that I thought he might still be growing. The tall woman standing beside him was in her sixties, but she had a Bowflex body. She was wearing a tight T-shirt, knit slacks, sandals, and a pair of huge hoop earrings. The third witch was about my age, in her mid- to late twenties, and she was Hispanic. She had full cheeks, bright red lips, and rippling black hair, and she was short and had more curves than an S turn. Sigebert admired her especially (I could tell by his leer), but she ignored all the vampires as if she couldn't see them.

Amelia might have been startled by the influx of vampires, but she handled introductions with aplomb. Evidently the queen had already identified herself before I approached. "Your Majesty," Amelia was saying, "These are my co-practitioners." She swept her hand before them as if she were showing off a car to the studio audience. "Bob Jessup, Patsy Sellers, Terencia Rodriguez—Terry, we call her."

The witches glanced at each other before nodding briefly to the queen. It was hard to tell how she took that lack of deference, her face was so glass-smooth—but she nodded back, and the atmosphere remained tolerable.

"We were just preparing for our reconstruction," Amelia said. She sounded absolutely confident, but I noticed that her hands were trembling. Her thoughts were not nearly as confident as her voice, either. Amelia was running over their preparations in her head, frantically itemizing the magic stuff she'd assembled, anxiously reassessing her companions to satisfy herself they were up to the ritual, and so on. Amelia, I belatedly realized, was a perfectionist.

I wondered where Claudine was. Maybe she'd seen the vamps coming and prudently fled to some dark corner. While I was looking around for her, I had a moment when the heartache I was staving off just plain ambushed me. It was like the moments I had after my grandmother died, when I'd be doing something familiar like brushing my teeth, and all of a sudden the blackness would overwhelm me. It took a moment or two to collect myself and swim back to the surface again.

It would be like that for a while, and I'd just have to grit my teeth and bear it.

I made myself take notice of those around me. The witches had assumed their positions. Bob settled himself in a lawn chair in the courtyard, and I watched with a tiny flare of interest as he drew powdered stuff from little snack-size Ziploc bags and got a box of matches out of his chest pocket. Amelia bounded up the stairs to the apartment, Terry stationed herself halfway down the stairs, and the tall older witch, Patsy, was already standing on the gallery looking down at us.

"If you all want to watch, probably up here would be best," Amelia called, and the queen and I went up the stairs. The guards gathered in a clump by the gate so they'd be as far away from the magic as they could be; even Jade Flower seemed respectful of the power that was about to be put to use, even if she did not respect the witches as people.

As a matter of course, Andre followed the queen up the stairs, but I thought there was a less than enthusiastic droop to his shoulders.

It was nice to focus on something new instead of mulling over my miseries, and I listened with interest as Amelia, who looked like she should be out playing beach volleyball, instead gave us instructions on the magic spell she was about to cast.

"We've set the time to two hours before I saw Jake arrive," she said. "So you may see a lot of boring and extraneous stuff. If that gets old, I can try to speed up the events."

Suddenly I had a thought that blinded me by its sheer

serendipity. I would ask Amelia to return to Bon Temps with me, and there I would ask her to repeat this procedure in my yard; then I would know what had happened to poor Gladiola. I felt much better once I'd had this idea, and I made myself pay attention to the here and now.

Amelia called out "Begin!" and immediately began reciting words, I suppose in Latin. I heard a faint echo come up from the stairs and the courtyard as the other witches joined in.

We didn't know what to expect, and it was oddly boring to hear the chanting continue after a couple of minutes. I began to wonder what would happen to me if the queen got very bored.

Then my cousin Hadley walked into the living room.

I was so shocked, I almost spoke to her. When I looked for just a second longer, I could tell it wasn't really Hadley. It had the shape of her, and it moved like her, but this simulacrum was only washed with color. Her hair was not a true dark, but a glistening impression of dark. She looked like tinted water, walking. You could see the surface's shimmer. I looked at her eagerly: it had been so long since we'd seen each other. Hadley looked older, of course. She looked harder, too, with a sardonic set to her mouth and a skeptical look to her eyes.

Oblivious to the presence of anyone else in the room, the reconstruction went over to the loveseat, picked up a phantom remote control, and turned on the television. I actually glanced at the screen to see if it would show anything, but of course, it didn't.

I felt a movement beside me and I glanced at the queen. If I had been shocked, she was electrified. I had never really thought the queen could have truly loved Hadley, but I saw now that she had, as much as she was able.

We watched Hadley glance at the television from time to time while she painted her toenails, drank a phantom glass of blood, and made a phone call. We couldn't hear her. We could only see, and that within a limited range. The object she reached for would appear the minute her hand touched it, but not before, so you could be sure of what she had only when she began to use it. When she leaned forward to replace the glass of blood on the table, and her hand was still holding the glass, we'd see the glass, the table with its other objects, and Hadley, all at once, all with that glistening patina. The ghost table was imposed over the real table, which was still in almost exactly the same space as it had been that night, just to make it weirder. When Hadley let go of the glass, both glass and table winked out of existence.

Andre's eyes were wide and staring when I glanced back at him, and it was the most expression I'd seen on his face. If the queen was grieving and I was fascinated and sad, Andre was simply freaked out.

We stood through a few more minutes of this until Hadley evidently heard a knock at the door. (Her head turned toward the door, and she looked surprised.) She rose (the phantom loveseat, perhaps two inches to the right of the real one, became nonexistent) and padded across the floor. She stepped through my sneakers, which were sitting side by side next to the loveseat.

Okay, that was weird. This whole thing was weird, but fascinating.

Presumably the people in the courtyard had watched the caller come up the outside stairs, since I heard a loud curse from one of the Berts—Wybert, I thought. When Hadley opened a phantom door, Patsy, who'd been stationed outside on the gallery, pushed open the real door so we could see. From Amelia's chagrined face, I could tell she hadn't thought that one through ahead of time.

Standing at the door was (phantom) Waldo, a vampire who had been with the queen for years. He had been much punished in the years before his death, and it had left him with permanently wrinkled skin. Since Waldo had been an ultrathin albino before this punishment, he'd looked awful the one and only night I'd known him. As a watery ghost creature, he looked better, actually.

Hadley looked surprised to see him. That expression was strong enough to be easily recognizable. Then she looked disgusted. But she stepped back to let him in.

When she strolled back to the table to pick up her glass, Waldo glanced around him, as if to see if anyone else was there. The temptation to warn Hadley was so strong it was almost irresistible.

After some conversation, which of course we couldn't understand, Hadley shrugged and seemed to agree to some plan. Presumably, this was the idea Waldo had told me about the night he'd confessed to killing my cousin. He'd said it had been Hadley's idea to go to St. Louis Cemetery Number One to raise the ghost of voodooienne Marie Laveau, but from this evidence it seemed Waldo was the one who had suggested the excursion.

"What's that in his hand?" Amelia said, as quietly as she could, and Patsy stepped in from the gallery to check.

"Brochure," she called to Amelia, trying to use equally hushed tones. "About Marie Laveau."

Hadley looked at the watch on her wrist and said something to Waldo. It was something unkind, judging by Hadley's expression and the jerk of her head as she indicated the door. She was saying "No," as clearly as body language could say it.

And yet the next night she had gone with him. What had happened to change her mind?

Hadley walked back to her bedroom and we followed her. Looking back, we watched Waldo leave the apartment, putting the brochure on the table by the door as he departed.

It felt oddly voyeuristic to stand in Hadley's bedroom

with Amelia, the queen, and Andre, watching Hadley take off a bathrobe and put on a very fancy dress.

"She wore that to the party the night before the wedding," the queen said quietly. It was a skintight, cut-down-to-here red dress decked with darker red sequins and some gorgeous alligator pumps. Hadley was going to make the queen regret what she was losing, evidently.

We watched Hadley primp in the mirror, do her hair two different ways, and mull her choice of lipsticks for a very long time. The novelty was wearing off the process, and I was willing to fast-forward, but the queen just couldn't get enough of seeing her beloved again. I sure wasn't going to protest, especially since the queen was footing the bill.

Hadley turned back and forth in front of her full-length mirror, appeared satisfied with what she saw, then burst into tears.

"Oh, my dear," the queen said quietly. "I am so sorry."

I knew *exactly* how Hadley felt, and for the first time I felt the kinship with my cousin I'd lost through the years of separation. In this reconstruction, it was the night before the queen's wedding, and Hadley was going to have to go to a party and watch the queen and her fiancé be a couple. And the next night she would have to attend their wedding; or so she thought. She didn't know that she'd be dead by then; finally, definitely dead.

"Someone coming up," called Bob the witch. His voice wafted through the open French windows onto the gallery. In the phantom, ghostly world, the doorbell must have rung, because Hadley stiffened, gave herself a last look in the mirror (right through us, since we were standing in front of it) and visibly braced herself. When Hadley walked down the hall, she had a familiar sway to her hips and her watery face was set in a cold half smile.

She pulled open the door. Since the witch Patsy had left the actual door open after Waldo had "arrived," we could see this happening. Jake Purifoy was dressed in a tux, and he looked very good, as Amelia had said. I glanced at Amelia when he stepped into the apartment, and she was eyeing the phantasm regretfully.

He didn't care for being sent to pick up the queen's honeybun, you could tell, but he was too politic and too courteous to take that out on Hadley. He stood patiently while she got a tiny purse and gave her hair a final combing, and then the two were out the door.

"Coming down out there," Bob called, and we went out the door and across the gallery to look over the railing. The two phantoms were getting into a glistening car and driving out of the courtyard. That was where the area affected by the spell came to an end. As the ghost car passed through the gate area, it winked out of existence right by the group of vampires who were clustered by the opening. Sigebert and Wybert were wide-eyed and solemn, Jade Flower appeared disgruntled, and Rasul looked faintly amused, as if he were thinking of the good stories he'd have to tell in the guards' mess hall.

"Time to fast-forward," Amelia called. She was looking tired now, and I wondered how great a strain coordinating this act of witchcraft was placing on the young witch.

Patsy, Terry, Bob, and Amelia began to say another spell in unison. If there was a weak link in this team effort, it was Terry. The round-faced little witch was sweating profusely and shaking with the effort of keeping her magical end up. I felt a little worried as I saw the strain on her face.

"Take it easy, easy!" Amelia exhorted her team, having read the same signs. Then they all resumed chanting, and Terry seemed to be pacing herself a bit better; she didn't look so desperate.

Amelia said, "Slow . . . down . . . now," and the chanting eased its pace.

The car appeared again in the gate, this time running

right through Sigebert, who'd taken a step forward, the better to watch Terry, I suspected. It lurched to an abrupt stop half-in, half-out of the aperture.

Hadley threw herself out of the car. She was weeping, and from the looks of her face, she'd been weeping for some time. Jake Purifoy emerged from his side and stood there, his hands on the top of his door, talking across the roof of the car at Hadley.

For the first time, the queen's personal bodyguard spoke. Andre said, "Hadley, you have to cut this out. People will notice, and the new king will do something about it. He's the jealous kind, you know? He doesn't care about—" Here Andre lost the thread, and shook his head. "He cares about keeping face."

We all stared at him. Was he channeling?

The queen's bodyguard switched his gaze to the ectoplasmic Hadley. Andre said, "But Jake, I can't stand it. I know she has to do this politically, but she's sending me away! I can't take it."

Andre could read lips. Even ectoplasmic lips. He began speaking again.

"Hadley, go up and sleep on it. You can't go to the wedding if you're going to create a scene. You know that would embarrass the queen, and it would ruin the ceremony. My boss will kill me if that happens. This is the biggest event we've ever worked."

He was talking about Quinn, I realized. Jake Purifoy *was* the employee Quinn had told me was missing.

"I can't stand it," Hadley repeated. She was shrieking, I could tell from the way her mouth moved, but luckily Andre saw no need to imitate that. It was eerie enough hearing the words come out of his mouth. "I've done something terrible!" The melodramatic words sounded very strange in Andre's monotone.

Hadley ran up the stairs, and Terry automatically moved

out of the way to let her pass. Hadley unlocked the (already open) door and stormed into her apartment. We turned to watch Jake. Jake sighed, straightened up, and stepped away from the car, which vanished. He flipped open a cell phone and punched in a number. He spoke into the phone for less than a minute, with no pause for an answer, so it was safe to assume he'd gotten voice mail.

Andre said, "Boss, I have to tell you I think there's going to be trouble. The girlfriend won't be able to control herself on the day."

Oh my God, tell me Quinn didn't have Hadley killed! I thought, feeling absolutely sick at the thought. But even as the idea formed fully, Jake wandered over to the rear of the car, which appeared again as he brushed against it. He ran his hand lovingly along the line of the trunk, stepping closer and closer to the area outside the gate, and suddenly a hand reached out and grabbed him. The witches' area did not extend beyond the walls, so the rest of the body was absent, and the effect of a hand materializing from nowhere and seizing the unsuspecting Were was as scary as anything in a horror movie.

This was exactly like one of those dreams where you see danger approaching, but you can't speak. No warnings on our part could alter what had already happened. But we were all shocked. The brothers Bert cried out, Jade Flower drew her sword without my even seeing her hand move, and the queen's mouth fell open.

We could see only Jake's feet, thrashing. Then they lay still.

We all stood and looked at each other, even the witches, their concentration wavering until the courtyard began to fill with mist.

"Witches!" Amelia called harshly. "Back to work!" In a moment, everything had cleared up. But Jake's feet were still, and in a moment, their outline grew still more faint;

he was fading out of sight like all the other lifeless objects. In a few seconds, though, my cousin appeared on the gallery above, looking down. Her expression was cautious and worried. She'd heard something. We registered the moment when she saw the body, and she came down the stairs with vampiric speed. She leaped through the gate and was lost to sight, but in a moment she was back in, dragging the body by the feet. As long as she was touching it, the body was visible as a table or chair would have been. Then she bent over the corpse, and now we could see that Jake had a huge wound in his neck. The wound was sickening, though I have to say that the vamps watching did not look sickened, but enthralled.

Ectoplasmic Hadley looked around her, hoping for help that didn't come. She looked desperately uncertain. Her fingers never left Jake's neck as she felt for his pulse.

Finally she bent over him and said something to him.

"It's the only way," Andre translated. "You may hate me, but it's the only way." We watched Hadley tear at her wrist with her own fangs and then put her bleeding wrist to Jake's mouth, watched the blood trickle inside, watched him revive enough to grip her arms and pull her down to him. When Hadley made Jake let go of her, she looked exhausted, and he looked as if he were having convulsions.

"The Were does not make a good vampire," Sigebert said in a whisper. "I've never before seen a Were brought over."

It was sure hard for poor Jake Purifoy. I began to forgive him the horror of the evening before, seeing his suffering. My cousin Hadley gathered him up and carried him up the stairs, pausing every now and then to look around her. I followed her up one more time, the queen right behind me. We watched Hadley pull off Jake's ripped clothes, wrap a towel around his neck until the bleeding stopped, and stow him in the closet, carefully covering him and closing the door so the morning sun wouldn't burn the new vampire, who would have to lie in the dark for three days. Hadley crammed the bloody towel into her hamper. Then she stuffed another towel into the open space at the bottom of the door, to make sure Jake was safe.

Then she sat in the hall and thought. Finally she got her cell phone and called a number.

"She asks for Waldo," Andre said. When Hadley's lips began moving again, Andre said, "She makes the appointment for the next night. She says she must talk to the ghost of Marie Laveau, if the ghost will really come. She needs advice, she says." After a little more conversation, Hadley shut her phone and got up. She gathered up the former Were's torn and bloody clothing and sealed it in a bag.

"You should get the towel, too," I advised, in a whisper, but my cousin left it in the hamper for me to find when I arrived. Hadley got the car keys out of the trouser pockets, and when she went down the stairs, she got into the car and drove away with the garbage bag.

18

YOUR MAJESTY, WE HAVE TO STOP," AMELIA SAID, and the queen gave a flick of her hand that might have been agreement.

Terry was so exhausted she was leaning heavily against the railing of the stairs, and Patsy was looking almost as haggard out on the gallery. The nerdy Bob seemed unchanged, but then he'd wisely seated himself in a chair to start with. At Amelia's wordless signal, they began undoing the spell they'd cast, and gradually the eerie atmosphere lessened. We became an ill-assorted bunch of weird people in a courtyard in New Orleans, rather than helpless witnesses to a magical reenactment.

Amelia went to the corner storage shed and pulled out some folding chairs. Sigebert and Wybert did not understand the mechanism, so Amelia and Bob set the chairs out.

After the queen and the witches sat, there was one remaining seat, and I took it after a silent to and fro between me and the four vampires.

"So we know what happened the next night," I said wearily. I was feeling a little silly in my fancy dress and high-heeled sandals. It would be nice to put on my regular clothes.

"Uh, 'scuse me, you might, but the rest of us don't, and we want to know," Bob said. He seemed oblivious to the fact that he ought to be shaking in his sandals in the queen's presence.

There was something kind of likable about the geeky witch. And all four had worked so hard; if they wanted to know the rest of the story, there wasn't any reason they couldn't hear it. The queen raised no objection. Even Jade Flower, who had resheathed her sword, looked faintly interested.

"The next night, Waldo lured Hadley to the cemetery with the story of the Marie Laveau grave and the vampire tradition that the dead can raise the dead—in this case, the voodoo priestess Marie Laveau. Hadley wanted Marie Laveau to answer her questions, which Waldo had told Hadley the ghost could, if the correct ritual was followed. Though Waldo gave me a reason Hadley agreed to do this on the night I met him, now I know he was lying. But I can think of several other reasons she might have agreed to go with Waldo to St. Louis Cemetery," I said. The queen nodded silently. "I think she wanted to find out what Jake would be like when he rose," I said. "I think she wanted to find out what to do with him. She couldn't let him die, you saw that, but she didn't want to admit to anyone that she had created a vampire, especially one that had been a Were."

I had quite an audience. Sigebert and Wybert were squatting on either side of the queen, and they were wrapped up in the story. This must be like going to the movies, for them.

All the witches were interested in hearing the backstory on the events they'd just witnessed. Jade Flower had her eyes fixed on me. Only Andre seemed immune, and he was busy doing his bodyguard job, constantly scanning the courtyard and the sky for attack.

"It's possible, too, that Hadley might have believed the ghost could give her advice on how to regain the queen's affections. No offense, ma'am," I added, remembering too late that the queen was sitting three feet away from me in a folding lawn chair with the Wal-Mart price label still hanging on a plastic loop.

The queen waved her hand in a negligent gesture. She was sunk in thought, so deeply that I wasn't even sure she heard me.

"It wasn't Waldo who drained Jake Purifoy," the queen said, to my amazement. "Waldo could not have imagined that when he succeeded in killing Hadley and reported it to me, blaming it on the Fellowship of the Sun, this clever witch would obey the order to seal the apartment very literally, including a stasis spell. Waldo already had a plan. Whoever killed Jake had a separate plan—perhaps to blame Hadley for Jake's death and his rebirth . . . which would condemn her to jail in a vampire cell. Perhaps the killer thought that Jake would kill Hadley when he rose in three days . . . and possibly, he would have."

Amelia tried to look modest, but it was an uphill battle. It should have been easy, since the only reason she'd cast the spell was to prevent the apartment from smelling like garbage when it finally was reopened. She knew it, and I knew it. But it had been a pretty piece of witchcraft, and I wasn't about to burst her bubble.

Amelia burst it all by herself.

"Or maybe," she said blithely, "someone paid Waldo to get Hadley out of the picture, by one means or another."

I had to shut down my shields immediately, because all

the witches began broadcasting such strong panic signals that being around them was unbearable. They knew that what Amelia had said would upset the queen, and when the Queen of Louisiana was agitated, those around her tended to be even more agitated.

The queen shot out of her chair, so we all scrambled to our feet, hastily and clumsily. Amelia had just gotten her legs tucked underneath her, so she was especially awkward, which served her right. Jade Flower took a couple steps away from the rest of the vampires, but maybe she wanted more room in case she had to swing her sword. Andre was the only one who noticed that, besides me. He kept his gaze fixed on the king's bodyguard.

I don't know what would have happened next if Quinn hadn't driven through the gate.

He got out of the big black car, ignored the tense tableau as if it didn't even exist, and strode across the gravel to me. He casually draped an arm over my shoulders and bent to give me a light kiss. I don't know how to compare one kiss to another. Men all kiss differently, don't they? And it says something about their character. Quinn kissed me as if we were carrying on a conversation.

"Babe," he said, when I'd had the last word. "Did I get here at a good time? What happened to your arm?"

The atmosphere relaxed a bit. I introduced him to the people standing in the courtyard. He knew all the vampires, but he hadn't met the witches. He moved away from me to meet and greet. Patsy and Amelia had obviously heard of him and tried hard not to act too impressed at meeting him.

I had to get the rest of the evening's news off my chest. "My arm got bitten, Quinn," I began. Quinn waited, his eyes intent on my face. "I got bitten by a . . . I'm afraid we know what happened to your employee. His name was Jake Purifoy, wasn't it?" I said.

"What?" In the bright lights of the courtyard, I saw that

his expression was guarded. He knew something bad was coming; of course, seeing the assembled company, anyone would guess that.

"He was drained and left here in the courtyard. To save his life, Hadley turned him. He's become a vampire."

Quinn didn't comprehend, for a few seconds. I watched as realization dawned as he grasped the enormity of what had happened to Jake Purifoy. Quinn's face became stony. I found myself hoping he never looked at me like that.

"The change was without the Were's consent," the queen said. "Of course, a Were would never agree to become one of us." If she sounded a little snarky, I wasn't too surprised. Weres and vamps regarded each other with scarcely concealed disgust, and only the fact that they were united against the normal world kept that disgust from flaring into open warfare.

"I went by your house," Quinn said to me, unexpectedly. "I wanted to see if you'd gotten back from New Orleans before I drove down here to look for Jake. Who burned a demon in your driveway?"

"Someone killed Gladiola, the queen's messenger, when she came to deliver a message to me," I said. There was a stir among the vampires around me. The queen had known about Gladiola's death, of course; Mr. Cataliades would have been sure to tell her. But no one else had heard about it.

"Lots of people dying in your yard, babe," Quinn said to me, though his tone was absent, and I didn't blame him for that being on his back burner.

"Just two," I said defensively, after a quick mental rundown. "I would hardly call that a lot." Of course, if you threw in the people who'd died in the house . . . I quickly shut off that train of thought.

"You know what?" Amelia said in a high, artificially social voice. "I think we witches will just mosey on down the street to that pizza place on the corner of Chloe and Justine.

So if you need us, there we'll be. Right, guys?" Bob, Patsy, and Terry moved faster than I'd thought they were able to the gate opening, and when the vampires didn't get any signal from their queen, they stood aside and let them by. Since Amelia didn't bother retrieving her purse, I hoped she had money in one pocket and her keys in another. Oh well.

I almost wished I were trailing along behind them. Wait a minute! Why couldn't I? I looked longingly at the gate, but Jade Flower stepped into the gap and stared at me, her eyes black holes in her round face. This was a woman who didn't like me one little bit. Andre, Sigebert, and Wybert could definitely take me or leave me, and Rasul might think I wouldn't be a bad companion for an hour on the town—but Jade Flower would enjoy whacking off my head with her sword, and that was a fact. I couldn't read vampire minds (except for a tiny glimpse every now and then, which was a big secret) but I could read body language and I could read the expression in her eyes.

I didn't know the reason for this animosity, and at this point in time I didn't think it mattered a heck of a lot.

The queen had been thinking. She said, "Rasul, we shall go back to the house very shortly." He bowed and walked out to the car.

"Miss Stackhouse," she said, turning her eyes on me. They shone like dark lamps. She took my hand, and we went up the stairs to Hadley's apartment, Andre trailing behind us like something tied to Sophie-Anne's leg with string. I kept having the unwise impulse to yank my hand from the queen's, which of course was cold and dry and strong, though she was careful not to squeeze. Being so close to the ancient vampire made me vibrate like a violin string. I didn't see how Hadley had endured it.

She led me into Hadley's apartment and shut the door behind us. I didn't think even the excellent ears of the vampires below us could hear our conversation now. That had been her goal, because the first thing she said was, "You will not tell anyone what I am about to tell you."

I shook my head, mute with apprehension.

"I began my life in what became northern France, about . . . one thousand, one hundred years ago."

I gulped.

"I didn't know where I was, of course, but I think it was Lotharingia. In the last century I tried to find the place I spent my first twelve years, but I couldn't, even if my life depended on it." She gave a barking laugh at the turn of phrase. "My mother was the wife of the wealthiest man in the town, which meant he had two more pigs than anyone else. My name then was Judith."

I tried hard not to look shocked, to just look interested, but it was a struggle.

"When I was about ten or twelve, I think, a peddler came to us from down the road. We hadn't seen a new face in six months. We were excited." But she didn't smile or look as if she remembered the feeling of that excitement, only the fact of it. Her shoulders rose and fell, once. "He carried an illness that had never come to us before. I think now that it was some form of influenza. Within two weeks of his stay in our town, everyone in it was dead, excepting me and a boy somewhat older."

There was a moment of silence while we thought about that. At least I did, and I suppose the queen was remembering. Andre might have been thinking about the price of bananas in Guatemala.

"Clovis did not like me," the queen said. "I've forgotten why. Our fathers . . . I don't remember. Things might have gone differently if he had cared for me. As it was, he raped me and then he took me to the next town, where he began offering me about. For money, of course, or food. Though the influenza traveled across our region, we never got sick."

I tried to look anywhere but at her.

"Why will you not meet my eyes?" she demanded. Her phrasing and her accent had changed as she spoke, as if she'd just learned English.

"I feel so bad for you," I said.

She made a sound that involved putting her top teeth on her lower lip and making the extra effort to intake some air so she could blow it out. It sounded like *"fffft!"* "Don't bother," the queen said. "Because what happened next was, we were camped in the woods, and a vampire got him." She looked pleased at the recollection. What a trip down memory lane. "The vampire was very hungry and started on Clovis first, because he was bigger, but when he was through with Clovis, he could take a minute to look at me and think it might be nice to have a companion. His name was Alain. For three years or more I traveled with Alain. Vampires were secret then, of course. Their existence was only in stories told by old women by the fire. And Alain was good at keeping it that way. Alain had been a priest, and he was very fond of surprising priests in their beds." She smiled reminiscently.

I found my sympathy diminishing.

"Alain promised and promised to bring me over, because of course I wanted to be as he was. I wanted the strength." Her eyes flicked over to me.

I nodded heartily. I could understand that.

"But when he needed money, for clothes and food for me, he would do the same thing with me that Clovis had, sell me for money. He knew the men would notice if I was cold, and he knew I would bite them if he brought me over. I grew tired of his failing in his promise."

I nodded to show her I was paying attention. And I was, but in the back of my mind I was wondering where the hell this monologue was heading and why I was the recipient of such a fascinating and depressing story.

"Then one night we came into a village where the headman knew Alain for what he was. Stupid Alain had forgotten he had passed through before and drained the headman's wife! So the villagers bound him with a silver chain, which was amazing to find in a small village, I can tell you . . . and they threw him into a hut, planning to keep him until the village priest returned from a trip. Then they meant to put him in the sun with some church ceremony. It was a poor village, but on top of him they piled all the bits of silver and all the garlic the people possessed, in an effort to keep him subdued." The queen chuckled.

"They knew I was a human, and they knew he had abused me," she said. "So they didn't tie me up. The headman's family discussed taking me as a slave, since they had lost a woman to the vampire. I knew what that would be like."

The expression on her face was both heartbreaking and absolutely chilling. I held very still.

"That night, I pulled out some weak planks from the rear of the hut and crawled in. I told Alain that when he'd brought me over, I'd free him. We bargained for quite a time, and then he agreed. I dug a hole in the floor, big enough for my body. We planned that Alain would drain me and bury me under the pallet he lay on, smoothing the dirt floor over as best he could. He could move enough for that. On the third night, I would rise. I would break his chain and toss away the garlic, though it would burn my hands. We would flee into the darkness." She laughed out loud. "But the priest returned before three days were up. By the time I clawed my way out of the dirt, Alain was blackened ash in the wind. It was the priest's hut they'd stored Alain in. The old priest was the one who told me what had happened."

I had a feeling I knew the punch line to this story. "Okay," I said quickly, "I guess the priest was your first meal." I smiled brightly.

"Oh, no," said Sophie-Anne, formerly Judith. "I told him I was the angel of death, and that I was passing him over since he had been so virtuous."

Considering the state Jake Purifoy had been in when he'd risen for the first time, I could appreciate what a gut-wrenching effort that must have been for the new vampire.

"What did you do next?" I asked.

"After a few years, I found an orphan like me; roaming in the woods, like me," she said, and turned to look at her bodyguard. "We've been together ever since."

And I finally saw an expression in Andre's unlined face: utter devotion.

"He was being forced, like I had been," she said gently. "And I took care of that."

I felt a cold shiver run down my spine. I couldn't have picked something to say if you had paid me.

"The reason I've bored you with my ancient history," the queen said, shaking herself and sitting up even straighter, "is to tell you why I took Hadley under my wing. She, too, had been molested, by her great-uncle. Did he molest you, too?"

I nodded. I'd had no idea he'd gotten to Hadley. He hadn't progressed to actual penetration, only because my parents had died and I'd gone to live with my grandmother. My parents hadn't believed me, but I'd convinced my grandmother I was telling the truth by the time he would have felt I was ripe, when I was about nine. Of course, Hadley had been older. We'd had much more in common than I'd ever thought. "I'm sorry, I didn't know," I said. "Thanks for telling me."

"Hadley talked about you often," the queen said.

Yeah, thanks, Hadley. Thanks for setting me up for the worst . . . no, wait, that was unfair. Finding out about Bill's massive deception was *not* the worst thing that had ever happened to me. But it wasn't too far down on my personal list, either.

"That's what I've found out," I said, my voice as cold and crisp as a celery stick.

"You are upset that I sent Bill to investigate you, to find out if you could be of use to me," the queen said.

I took a deep breath, forced my teeth to unclench. "No, I'm not upset with you. You can't help being the way you are. And you didn't even know me." Another deep breath. "I'm *upset* with Bill, who *did* know me and went ahead with your whole program in a very thorough and calculated way." I had to drive away the pain. "Besides, why would you care?" My tone was bordering on insolent, which was not wise when you're dealing with a powerful vampire. She'd touched me in a very sore spot.

"Because you were dear to Hadley," Sophie-Anne said unexpectedly.

"You wouldn't have known it from the way she treated me, after she became a teenager," I said, having apparently decided that reckless honesty was the course to follow.

"She was sorry for that," the queen said, "once she became a vampire, especially, and found out what it was like to be a minority. Even here in New Orleans, there is prejudice. We talked about her life often, when we were alone."

I didn't know which made me more uncomfortable, the idea of the queen and my cousin Hadley having sex, or having pillow talk about me afterward.

I don't care if consenting adults have sex, no matter what that sex consists of, as long as both parties agree beforehand. But I don't necessarily need to hear any details, either. Any prurient interest I might have had has been flooded over the years with images from the minds of the people in the bar.

This was turning out to be a long conversation. I wanted the queen to get to the point.

"The point is," the queen said, "I am grateful that you—through the witches—gave me a better idea of how Hadley died. And also you have let me know there is a wider plot against me than just Waldo's jealous heart."

I had?

"So I am in your debt. Tell me what I can do for you now."

"Ah. Send over a lot of boxes so I can pack up Hadley's stuff and get back to Bon Temps? Get someone to take the stuff I don't want to a charity drop-off?"

The queen looked down, and I swear she was smothering a smile. "Yes, I think I can do that," she said. "I'll send some human over tomorrow to do those things."

"If someone could pack the stuff I want into a van and drive it up to Bon Temps, that would be real good," I said. "Maybe I could ride back in that van?"

"Also not a problem," she said.

Now for the big favor. "Do I actually have to go with you to this conference thing?" I asked, which I knew was kind of pushing it.

"Yes," she said.

Okay, stonewall there.

She added, "But I'll pay you handsomely."

I brightened. Some of the money I'd gotten for my previous vampire services was still in my savings account, and I'd gotten a big financial break when Tara "sold" me her car for a dollar, but I was so used to living close to the financial bone that a cushion was always welcome. I was always scared I'd break my leg, or my car would throw a rod, or my house would burn down . . . wait, that had already happened . . . well, that some disaster would happen, like a high wind would blow off the stupid tin roof my grandmother had insisted on, or something.

"Did you want something of Hadley's?" I asked her, my train of thought having veered away from money. "You know, a remembrance?"

Something flashed in her eyes, something that surprised me.

"You took the words right out of my mouth," said the queen, with an adorable hint of a French accent.

Uh-oh. It couldn't be good that she'd switched on the charm.

"I did ask Hadley to hide something for me," she said. My bullshit meter was beeping like an alarm clock. "And if you come across it in your packing, I'd like to have it back."

"What does it look like?"

"It's a jewel," she said. "My husband gave it to me as an engagement gift. I happened to leave it here before I got married."

"You're welcome to look in Hadley's jewelry box," I said immediately. "If it belongs to you, of course you have to have it back."

"That's very kind of you," she said, her face back to its regular glassy smoothness. "It's a diamond, a large diamond, and it's fixed on a platinum bracelet."

I didn't remember anything like that in Hadley's stuff, but I hadn't looked carefully. I'd planned to pack Hadley's jewelry box intact so I could pick through it at my leisure in Bon Temps.

"Please, look now," I suggested. "I know that it would be like a faux pas to lose a present from your husband."

"Oh," she said gently, "you have no idea." Sophie-Anne closed her eyes for just a second, as if she were too anxious for words. "Andre," she said, and with that word he took off for the bedroom—didn't need any directions, I noticed—and while he was gone, the queen looked oddly incomplete. I wondered why he hadn't accompanied her to Bon Temps, and on an impulse, I asked her.

She looked at me, her crystalline eyes wide and blank. "I was not supposed to be gone," she said. "I knew if Andre showed himself in New Orleans, everyone would assume I was here, too." I wondered if the reverse would be true. If the queen was here, would everyone assume Andre was, also? And that sparked a thought in me, a thought that had gone before I could quite grasp hold of it.

Andre came back at that moment, the tiniest shake of his head telling the queen he hadn't found what she wanted to reclaim. For a moment, Sophie-Anne looked quite unhappy. "Hadley did this in a minute of anger," the queen said, and I thought she was talking to herself. "But she may bring me down from beyond the veil." Then her face relaxed into its usual emotionless state.

"I'll keep an eye open for the bracelet," I said. I suspected that the value of the jewelry did not lie in its appraisal. "Would that bracelet have been left here the last night before the wedding?" I asked cautiously.

I suspected my cousin Hadley had stolen the bracelet from the queen out of sheer pique that the queen was getting married. That seemed like a Hadley thing to do. If I'd known about Hadley's concealment of the bracelet, I would have asked the witches to roll the clock back on the ectoplasmic reconstruction. We could have watched Hadley hide the thing.

The queen gave one short nod. "I must have it back," the queen said. "You understand, it's not the value of the diamond that concerns me? You understand, a wedding between vampire rulers is not a love match, where much can be forgiven? To lose a gift from your spouse, that's a very grave offense. And our spring ball is scheduled for two nights from now. The king expects to see me wearing his gifts. If I'm not . . ." Her voice trailed away, and even Andre looked almost worried.

"I'm getting your point," I said. I'd noticed the tension already rolling through the halls at Sophie's headquarters. There'd be hell to pay, and Sophie-Anne would be the one to pay it. "If it's here, you'll get it back. Okay?" I spread my hands, asking her if she believed me.

"All right," she said. "Andre, I can't spend any more

time here. Jade Flower will report the fact that I came up here with Sookie. Sookie, we must pretend to have had sex."

"Sorry, anyone who knows me knows I don't do women. I don't know who you expect Jade Flower's reporting to . . ." (Of course I did, and that would be the king, but it didn't seem tactful to say "I know your business," just then.) "But if they've done any homework, that's just a fact about me."

"Perhaps you had sex with Andre, then," she said calmly. "And you let me watch."

I thought of several questions, the first one being, "Is that the usual procedure with you?" followed by, "It's not okay to misplace a bracelet, but okay to bump pelvises with someone else?" But I clamped my mouth shut. If someone were holding a gun to my head, I'd actually have to vote for having sex with the queen rather than with Andre, no matter what my gender preference, because Andre creeped me out big-time. But if we were just pretending . . .

In a businesslike way, Andre removed his tie, folded it, put it in his pocket, and undid a few shirt buttons. He beckoned to me with a crook of his fingers. I approached him warily. He took me in his arms and held me close, pressed against him, and bent his head to my neck. For a second I thought he was going to bite, and I had a flare of absolute panic, but instead he inhaled. That's a deliberate act for a vampire.

"Put your mouth on my neck," he said, after another long whiff of me. "Your lipstick will transfer."

I did as he told me. He was cold as ice. This was like . . . well, this was just weird. I thought of the picture-taking session with Claude; I'd spent a lot of time lately *pretending* to have sex.

"I love the smell of fairy. Do you think she knows she has fairy blood?" he asked Sophie-Anne, while I was in the process of transferring my lipstick.

My head snapped back then. I stared right into his eyes,

and he stared right back at me. He was still holding me, and I understood that he was ensuring I would smell like him and he would smell like me, as if we'd actually done the deed. He definitely wasn't up for the real thing, which was a relief.

"I what?" I hadn't heard him correctly, I was sure. "I have what?"

"He has a nose for it," the queen said. "My Andre." She looked faintly proud.

"I was hanging around with my friend Claudine earlier in the day," I said. "She's a fairy. That's where the smell is coming from." I really must need to shower.

"You permit?" Andre asked, and without waiting for an answer, he jabbed my wounded arm with a fingernail, right above the bandage.

"Yow!" I said in protest.

He let a little blood trickle onto his finger, and he put it in his mouth. He rolled it around, as if it were a sip of wine, and at last he said, "No, this smell of fairy is not from association. It's in your blood." Andre looked at me in a way that was meant to tell me that his words made it a done deal. "You have a little streak of fairy. Maybe your grandmother or your grandfather was half-fey?"

"I don't know anything about it," I said, knowing I sounded stupid, but not knowing what else to say. "If any of my grandparents were other than a hundred percent human, they didn't pass that information along."

"No, they wouldn't," the queen said, matter-of-factly. "Most humans of fairy descent hide the fact, because they don't really believe it. They prefer to think their parents are mad." She shrugged. Inexplicable! "But that blood would explain why you have supernatural suitors and not human admirers."

"I don't have human admirers because I don't want 'em," I said, definitely piqued. "I can read their minds, and that just knocks them out of the running. If they're not put off from the get-go by my reputation for weirdness," I added, back into my too-much-honesty groove.

"It's a sad comment on humans that none of them are tolerable to one who can read their minds," the queen said.

I guess that was the final word on the value of mind-reading ability. I decided it would be better to stop the conversation. I had a lot to think about.

We went down the stairs, Andre leading, the queen next, and me trailing behind. Andre had insisted I take off my shoes and my earrings so it could be inferred that I had undressed and then just slipped back into the dress.

The other vampires were waiting obediently in the courtyard, and they sprang to attention when we began making our way down. Jade Flower's face didn't change at all when she read all the clues as to what we'd been up to in the past half hour, but at least she didn't look skeptical. The Berts looked knowing but uninterested, as if the scenario of Sophie-Anne watching her bodyguard engaging in sex (with a virtual stranger) were very much a matter of routine.

As he stood in the gateway waiting for further driving instructions, Rasul's face expressed a mild ruefulness, as if he wished he had been included in the action. Quinn, on the other hand, was pressing his mouth in such a grim line that you couldn't have fed him a straight pin. There was a fence to mend.

But as we'd walked out of Hadley's apartment, the queen had told me specifically not to share her story with anyone else, emphasis on the *anyone.* I would just have to think of a way to let Quinn know, without letting him *know.*

With no discussion or social chitchat, the vampires piled into their car. My brain was so crowded with ideas and conjectures and everything in between that I felt punch-drunk. I wanted to call my brother, Jason, and tell him he wasn't so irresistible after all, it was the fairy blood in him, just to see what he'd say. No, wait, Andre had implied that humans weren't affected by the nearness of fairies like vampires were. That is, humans didn't want to consume fairies, but did find them sexually attractive. (I thought of the crowd that always surrounded Claudine at Merlotte's.) And Andre had said that other supernaturals were attracted by fairy blood too, just not in the eat-'em-up way that vamps were. Wouldn't Eric be relieved? He would be so glad to know he didn't really love me! It was the fairy blood all along!

I watched the royal limo drive away. While I was fighting a wave compounded of about six different emotions, Quinn was fighting only one.

He was right in front of me, his face angry. "How'd she talk you into it, Sookie?" he asked. "If you'd yelled, I'd have been right up there. Or maybe you wanted to do that? I would have sworn you weren't the type."

"I haven't gone to bed with anyone this evening," I said. I looked him straight in the eyes. After all, this wasn't revealing anything the queen had told me, this was just . . . correcting an error. "It's fine if others think that," I said carefully. "Just not you."

He looked down at me for a long moment, his eyes searching mine as if he were reading some writing on the back of my eyeballs.

"Would you *like* to go to bed with someone this evening?" he asked. He kissed me. He kissed me for a long, long time, as we stood glued together in the courtyard. The witches did not return; the vampires stayed gone. Only the occasional car going by in the street or a siren heard in the distance reminded me we were in the middle of a city. This was as different from being held by Andre as I could imagine. Quinn was warm, and I could feel his muscles move beneath his skin. I could hear him breathe, and I could feel his heartbeat. I could sense the churn of his thoughts, which were mostly now centered on the bed he knew must be somewhere upstairs in Hadley's apartment. He loved the smell of me, the touch of me, the way my lips felt . . . and a large part of Quinn was attesting to that fact. That large part was pressed between us right at this very moment.

I'd gone to bed with two other males, and both times it hadn't worked out well. I hadn't known enough about them. I'd acted on impulse. You should learn from your mistakes. For a second, I wasn't feeling especially smart.

Luckily for my decision-making ability, Quinn's phone chose that moment to ring. God bless that phone. I'd been within an ace of chucking my good resolutions right out the window, because I'd been scared and lonely throughout the evening, and Quinn felt relatively familiar and he wanted me so much.

Quinn, however, was not following the same thought processes—far from it—and he cursed when the phone rang a second time.

"Excuse me," he said, fury in his voice, and answered the damn phone.

"All right," he said, after listening for a moment to the voice on the other end. "All right, I'll be there."

He snapped the tiny phone shut. "Jake is asking for me," he said.

I was so at sea with a strange combination of lust and relief that it took me a moment to connect the dots. Jake Purifoy, Quinn's employee, was experiencing his second night as a vampire. Having been fed some volunteer, he was enough himself to want to talk to Quinn. He'd been in suspended animation in a closet for weeks, and there was a lot he would need to catch up on.

"Then you have to go," I said, proud that my voice was practically rock steady. "Maybe he'll remember who attacked him. Tomorrow, I have to tell you about what I saw here tonight."

"Would you have said yes?" he asked. "If we'd been undisturbed for another minute?"

I considered for a minute. "If I had, I would've been sorry I did," I said. "Not because I don't want you. I do. But I had my eyes opened in the past couple of days. I know that I'm pretty easy to fool." I tried to sound matter-of-fact, not pitiful, when I said that. No one likes a whiny woman, least of all me. "I'm not interested in starting that up with someone who's just horny at the moment. I never set out to be a one-night-stand kind of woman. I want to be sure, if I have sex with you, that it's because you want to be around for a while and because you like me for who I am, not what I am."

Maybe a million women had made approximately the same speech. I meant it as sincerely as any one of those million.

And Quinn gave a perfect answer. "Who would want just one night with you?" he said, and then he left.

19

I SLEPT THE SLEEP OF THE DEAD. WELL, PROBABLY not, but as close as a human would ever come. As if in a dream, I heard the witches come carousing back into the courtyard. They were still congratulating one another with alcohol-lubricated vigor. I'd found some real, honest cotton sheets among the linens (Why are they still called linens? Have you seen a linen sheet in your life?) and I'd tossed the black silky ones into the washer, so it was very easy to slip back into sleep.

When I got up, it was after ten in the morning. There was a knocking at the door, and I stumbled down the hall to unlock it after I'd pulled on a pair of Hadley's spandex exercise pants and a hot pink tank top. I saw boxes through the peephole, and I opened the door feeling really happy.

"Miss Stackhouse?" said the young black man who was

holding the flattened boxes. When I nodded, he said, "I got orders to bring you as many boxes as you want. Will thirty do to start with?"

"Oh, yes," I said. "Oh, that'll be great."

"I also got instructions," he said precisely, "to bring you anything related to moving that you might need. I have here strapping tape, masking tape, some Magic Markers, scissors, and stick-on labels."

The queen had given me a personal shopper.

"Did you want colored dots? Some people like to put living room things in boxes with an orange dot, bedroom things in boxes with a green dot, and so on."

I had never moved, unless you counted taking a couple of bags of clothes and towels over to Sam's furnished duplex after the kitchen burned, so I didn't know the best way to go about it. I had an intoxicating vision of rows of neat boxes with colored dots on each side, so there couldn't be any mistake from any angle. Then I snapped back to reality. I wouldn't be taking that much back to Bon Temps. It was hard to form an estimate, since this was unknown territory, but I knew I didn't want much of the furniture.

"I don't think I'll need the dots, thanks anyway," I said. "I'll start working on these boxes, and then I can call you if I need any more, okay?"

"I'll assemble them for you," he said. He had very short hair and the curliest eyelashes I'd ever seen on a person. Cows had eyelashes that pretty, sometimes. He was wearing a golf-type shirt and neatly belted khakis, along with high-end sneakers.

"I'm sorry, I didn't catch your name," I said, as he whipped a roll of strapping tape from a large lumpy plastic shopping bag. He set to work.

"Oh, 'scuse me," he said, and it was the first time he'd sounded natural. "My name is Everett O'Dell Smith."

"Pleasure to meet you," I said, and he paused in his work so we could shake hands. "How did you come to be here?"

"Oh, I'm in Tulane Business School, and one of my professors got a call from Mr. Cataliades, who is, like, *the* most famous lawyer in the vampire area. My professor specializes in vampire law. Mr. Cataliades needed a day person; I mean, he can come out in the day, but he needed someone to be his gofer." He'd gotten three boxes done, already.

"And in return?"

"In return, I get to sit in court with him on his next five cases, and I get to earn some money I need real bad."

"Will you have time this afternoon to take me to my cousin's bank?"

"Sure will."

"You're not missing a class now, are you?"

"Oh, no, I got two hours before my second class."

He'd already been to a class and accumulated all this stuff before I'd even gotten up. Well, he hadn't been up half the night watching his dead cousin walk around.

"You can take these garbage bags of clothes to the nearest Goodwill or Salvation Army store." That would clear the gallery and make me feel productive all at the same time. I'd gone over the garments quite carefully to make sure Hadley hadn't hidden anything in them, and I wondered what the Salvation Army would make of them. Hadley had been into Tight and Skimpy; that was the nicest way to put it.

"Yes, ma'am," he said, whipping out a notebook and scribbling in it. Then he waited attentively. "Anything else?" he prompted me.

"Yes, there's no food in the house. When you come back this afternoon, can you bring me something to eat?" I could drink tap water, but I couldn't create food out of nothing.

Just then a call from the courtyard made me look over

the railing. Quinn was down there with a bag of something greasy. My mouth began watering.

"Looks like the food angle is covered," I told Everett, waving Quinn up.

"What can I do to help?" Quinn asked. "It struck me your cousin might not have coffee and food, so I brought some beignets and some coffee so strong it'll make you grow hair on your chest."

I'd heard that quite a few times, but it still made me smile. "Oh, that's my goal," I said. "Bring it on. There's actually coffee here, but I didn't have a chance to make it because Everett here is such a take-charge kind of guy."

Everett smiled up from his tenth box. "You know that's not true, but it's good to hear you say it," he said. I introduced the two men, and after Quinn handed me my bag, he began to help Everett assemble boxes. I sat at the glass-topped dining table and ate every crumb of the beignets that were in the bag and drank every drop of the coffee. I got powdered sugar all over me, and I didn't care a bit. Quinn turned to look at me and tried to hide his smile. "You're wearing your food, babe," he said.

I looked down at the tank top. "No hair on my chest, though," I said, and he said, "Can I check?"

I laughed and went to the back to brush my teeth and hair, both essential tasks. I checked out Hadley's clothes that I'd wriggled into. The black spandex workout pants came to midthigh. Hadley probably had never worn them, because they would have been too big, to her taste. On me, they were very snug, but not the snug Hadley liked, where you could count the . . . oh, never mind. The hot pink tank top left my pale pink bra straps showing, to say nothing of a couple of inches of my middle, but thanks to Peck's Tan-a-Lot (located inside Peck's Bunch-o-Flicks, a video rental place in Bon Temps), that middle was nice and brown. Hadley would have put a piece of jewelry in her belly button.

I looked at myself in the mirror, trying to picture myself with a gold stud or something. Nah. I slipped on some sandals decorated with crystal beads and felt quite glamorous for about thirty seconds.

I began talking to Quinn about what I planned to do that day, and rather than yell, I stepped from the bedroom into the hall with my brush and my elastic band. I bent over at the waist, brushed my hair while I was inverted, and gathered it into a ponytail on top of my head. I was sure it was centered, because the movements were just automatic after all these years. My ponytail came down past my shoulder blades now. I looped the band, ran the ponytail through, and I straightened, ponytail flying back over my shoulders to bounce in the middle. Quinn and Everett had stopped their task to stare. When I looked back at them, the two men hastily bent back to their tasks.

Okay, I didn't get that I'd done anything interesting, but apparently I had. I shrugged and vanished into the master bathroom to slap on some makeup. After another glance in the mirror, it occurred to me that maybe anything I did in that outfit was fairly interesting, if you were a fully functional guy.

When I came out, Everett had gone and Quinn gave me a slip of paper with Everett's cell number on it. "He says to call him when you need some more boxes," Quinn said. "He took all the bagged clothes. Looks like you don't need me at all."

"No comparison," I said, smiling. "Everett didn't bring me grease and caffeine this morning, and you did."

"So what's the plan, and how can I help?"

"Okay, the plan is . . ." I didn't exactly have one more specific than "go through this stuff and sort it out," and Quinn couldn't do that for me.

"How's this?" I asked. "You get everything out of the kitchen cabinets, and set it out where I can see it all, and I'll make a 'keep or toss' decision. You can pack what I want to keep, and put what I want to toss out on the gallery. I hope the rain stays away." The sunny morning was clouding over, fast. "While we work, I'll fill you in on what happened here last night."

Despite the threat of bad weather, we worked all morning, called in a pizza for lunch, and resumed work in the afternoon. The stuff I didn't want went into garbage bags, and Quinn furthered his muscular development by carrying all the garbage bags down to the courtyard and putting them in the little shed that had held the lawn chairs, still set up on the grass. I tried to admire his muscles only when he wasn't looking, and I think I was successful. Quinn was very interested to hear about the ectoplasmic reconstruction, and we talked about what it might all mean without reaching any conclusions. Jake didn't have any enemies among the vampires that Quinn knew of, and Quinn thought that Jake must have been killed for the embarrassment it would cause Hadley, rather than for any sin of Jake's own.

I saw neither hide nor hair of Amelia, and I wondered if she'd gone home with the Mormonish Bob. Or maybe he'd stayed with her, and they were having a fabulous time in Amelia's apartment. Maybe he was a real ball of fire under that white shirt and those black pants. I looked around the courtyard. Yes, Bob's bicycle was still propped against the brick wall. Since the sky was getting darker by the minute, I put the bike in the little shed, too.

Being with Quinn all day was stoking my fire a bit hotter every moment. He was down to a tank top and jeans, and I found myself wondering what he'd look like without those. And I didn't think I was the only one conjecturing about what people would look like naked. I could catch a flash from Quinn's mind every now and then as he was toting a bag down the stairs or packing pots and pans into a box, and those flashes weren't about opening his mail or doing his laundry.

I had enough practical presence of mind left to switch on a lamp when I heard the first peal of thunder in the distance. The Big Easy was about to be drenched.

Then it was back to flirting with Quinn wordlessly—making sure he had a good view when I stretched up to get a glass down from the cabinets or bent down to wrap that glass in newspaper. Maybe a quarter of me was embarrassed, but the rest of me was having fun. Fun had not been a big factor in my life recently—well, ever—and I was enjoying my little toddle on the wild side.

Downstairs, I felt Amelia's brain click on, after a fashion. I was familiar with the feel of this, from working in a bar: Amelia had a hangover. I smiled to myself as the witch thought of Bob, who was still asleep beside her. Aside from a basic, "How could I?" Amelia's most coherent thought was that she needed coffee. She needed it bad. She couldn't even turn on a light in the apartment, which was darkening steadily with the approach of the storm. A light would hurt her eyes too much.

I turned with a smile on my lips, ready to tell Quinn we might be hearing from Amelia soon, only to find he was right behind me, and his face was intent with a look I could not mistake. He was ready for something entirely different.

"Tell me you don't want me to kiss you, and I'll back off," he said, and then he was kissing me.

I didn't say a word.

When the height difference became an issue, Quinn just picked me up and put me on the edge of the kitchen counter. A clap of thunder sounded outside as I parted my knees to let him get as close to me as he could. I wrapped my legs around him. He pulled the elastic band out of my hair, not a totally pain-free process, and ran his fingers through the tangles. He crushed my hair in his hand and inhaled deeply, as if he were extracting the perfume from a flower.

"This is okay?" he asked raggedly, as his fingers found the bottom back edge of my tank top and sneaked up under it. He examined my bra tactilely and figured out how to open it in record time.

"Okay?" I said, in a daze. I wasn't sure whether I meant, "Okay? Hell, yes, hurry up!" or "Which part of this is okay, you want to know?" but Quinn naturally took it as a green light. His hands pushed the bra aside and he ran his thumbs across my nipples, which were already hard. I thought I was going to explode, and only the sure anticipation of better things to come kept me from losing it right then and there. I wriggled even further to the edge of the counter, so the big bulge in the front of Quinn's jeans was pressed against the notch in my pants. Just amazing, how they fit. He pressed against me, released, pressed again, the ridge formed by the stretch of the jeans over his penis hitting just the right spot, so easy to reach through the thin and stretchy spandex. Once more, and I cried out, holding on to him through the blind moment of orgasm when I could swear I'd been catapulted into another universe. My breathing was more like sobbing, and I wrapped myself around him like he was my hero. In that moment, he certainly was.

His breathing was still ragged, and he moved against me again, seeking his own release, since I had so loudly had mine. I sucked on his neck while my hand went down between us, and stroked him through his jeans, and suddenly he gave a cry as ragged as mine had been, and his arms tightened around me convulsively. "Oh, God," he said, "oh, God." His eyes closed tight with his release, he kissed my neck, my cheek, my lips, over and over. When his breathing—and mine—was a little more even, he said, "Babe, I haven't come like that since I was seventeen, in the backseat of my dad's car with Ellie Hopper."

"So, that's a good thing," I mumbled.

"You bet," he said.

We stayed clinched for a moment, and I became aware that the rain was beating against the windows and the doors, and the thunder was booming away. My brain was thinking of shutting down for a little nap, and I was lazily aware of Quinn's brain going equally drowsy as he rehooked my bra at my back. Downstairs, Amelia was making coffee in her dark kitchen and Bob the witch was waking up to the wonderful smell and wondering where his pants were. And in the courtyard, swarming silently up the stairs, enemies were approaching.

"Quinn!" I exclaimed, just in the moment his sharp hearing picked up the shuffle of the footsteps. Quinn went into fighting mode. Since I hadn't been home to check the calendar symbols, I'd forgotten we were close to the full moon. There were claws on Quinn's hands now, claws at least three inches long, instead of fingers. His eyes slanted and became altogether gold, with dilated black pupils. The change in the bones of his face had made him alien. I'd made a form of love with this man in the past ten minutes, and now I would hardly have known him if I'd passed him on the street.

But there wasn't time to think about anything but our best defense. I was the weak link, and I had better depend on surprise. I slid off the counter, hurried past him to the door, and lifted the lamp from its pedestal. When the first Were burst through the door, I bashed him upside the head, and he staggered, and the one coming in right after him tripped over his flailing predecessor, and Quinn was more than ready for the third one.

Unfortunately, there were six more.

20

IT TOOK JUST TWO OF THEM TO SUBDUE ME, AND I WAS kicking and screaming, biting and hitting, with every bit of energy I had. It took four for Quinn, but those four succeeded only because they used a stun gun. Otherwise, I'm sure he could have taken six or eight of them out of action, instead of the three he took care of before they got him.

I knew I would be overcome, and I knew I could save myself some bruises and maybe a broken bone if I just assented to be taken. But I have my pride. More practically, I wanted to be sure that Amelia heard what was happening above her. She'd do something. I wasn't sure what she'd do, but she'd act.

I was hustled down the stairs, my feet hardly touching them, by two husky men I'd never seen before. These same two men had bound my wrists together with duct tape. I'd done my best to arrange for a little slack, but I was afraid they'd done a fair job of it.

"Mmm, smells like sex," the shorter one said as he pinched my butt. I ignored his tacky leer and took some satisfaction in eyeing the bruise I'd given him on his cheekbone with my fist. (Which, by the way, was aching and smarting over the knuckles. You can't hit someone without paying for it yourself.)

They had to carry Quinn, and they weren't gentle about it. He got banged around against the stairs, and once they dropped him. He was a big guy. Now he was a bleeding big guy, since one of the blows had cut the skin above his left eye. He'd had the duct tape treatment, too, and I wondered how the fur would react to the tape.

We were being held side by side in the courtyard, briefly, and Quinn looked over at me as if he desperately wanted to speak to me. The blood was running down his cheek from the wound over his eyes, and he looked groggy from the stun gun. His hands were changing back to regular hands. I lunged toward him, but the Weres kept us apart.

Two vans drove into the circular drive, two vans that said BIG EASY ELECTRIC on the side. They were white and long and windowless in the back, and the logo on the side had been covered up with mud, which looked highly suspicious. A driver jumped out of the cab of each van, and the first driver threw open the doors to the rear of the first vehicle.

While our captors were hustling Quinn and me over to that van, the rest of the raiding party was being brought down the stairs. The men Quinn had managed to hurt were damaged far worse than Quinn, I'm glad to say. Claws can do an amazing amount of damage, especially wielded with the force a tiger can exert. The guy I'd hit with the lamp was unconscious, and the one who'd reached Quinn first was possibly dead. He was certainly covered with blood and there were things exposed to the light that should have been neatly packed in his belly.

I was smiling with satisfaction when the men holding me shoved me into the back of the van, which I discovered was awash with trash and absolutely filthy. This was a high-class operation. There was a wide-mesh screen between the two front seats and the open rear, and the shelves in the rear had been emptied, I supposed for our occupancy.

I was crammed into the narrow aisle between the shelves, and Quinn was jammed in after me. They had to work hard because he was still so stunned. My two escorts were slamming the rear van doors on the two of us as the hors de combat Weres were loaded into the other van. I was guessing the vans had been parked out on the street briefly so we wouldn't hear the vehicles pulling into the driveway. When they were ready to load us up, our captors had pulled into the courtyard. Even the people of a brawling city like New Orleans would notice some battered bodies being loaded into vans . . . in the pouring rain.

I hoped the Weres wouldn't think of grabbing Amelia and Bob, and I prayed that Amelia would think cleverly and hide herself, rather than do some impulsive and brave witch thing. I know it's a contradiction, right? Praying for one thing (asking God a favor) while at the same time hoping your enemies would be killed. All I can say is, I have a feeling Christians have been doing that from the get-go—at least bad ones, like me.

"Go, go, go," bellowed the shorter man, who'd hopped into the front seat. The driver obliged with a completely unnecessary squealing of tires, and we lurched out of the courtyard as if the president had just been shot and we had to get him to Walter Reed.

Quinn came to completely as we turned off Chloe Street to head for our final destination, wherever it might be. His hands were bound behind him, which is painful, and he hadn't quit bleeding from the head. I'd expected him to remain groggy and shocked. But when his eyes focused on my face, he said, "Babe, they beat you bad." I must not look too good.

"Yeah, well, you seem to be in the same boat," I said. I knew the driver and his companion could hear us, and I didn't give a damn.

With a grim attempt at a smile, he said, "Some defender I turned out to be."

In the Weres' estimation, I wasn't very dangerous, so my hands had been bound in front. I squirmed until I was able to put pressure on the cut on Quinn's forehead. That had to have hurt even more, but he didn't say a word in protest. The motion of the van, the effects of the beating, and the constant shifting and smell of the trash all around us combined to make the next ten minutes very unpleasant. If I'd been very clever, I could have told which way we were going—but I wasn't feeling very clever. I marveled that in a city with as many famed restaurants as New Orleans had, this van was awash with Burger King wrappers and Taco Bell cups. If I got a chance to rummage through the debris, I might find something useful.

"When we're together, we get attacked by Weres," Quinn said.

"It's my fault," I said. "I'm so sorry I dragged you into this."

"Oh, yeah," he said. "I'm known for hanging with a desperate crowd."

We were lying face to face, and Quinn sort of nudged me with his leg. He was trying to tell me something, and I wasn't getting it.

The two men in the front seat were talking to each other about a cute girl crossing the street at a traffic light. Just listening to the conversation was almost enough to make you swear off men, but at least they weren't listening to us.

"Remember when we talked about my mental condition?" I said carefully. "Remember what I told you about that?"

It took him a minute because he was hurting, but he got the hint. His face squinched up as if he were about to chop some boards in half, or something else requiring all his concentration, and then his thought shoved into my head. *Phone in my pocket,* he told me. The problem was, the phone was in his right pocket, and he was lying on that side. There was hardly room for him to turn over.

This called for a lot of maneuvering, and I didn't want our captors to see it. But I managed, finally, to work my fingers into Quinn's pocket, and made a mental note to advise him that, under this set of circumstances, his jeans were too tight. (Under other circumstances, no problem with the way they fit.) But extricating that phone, with the van rocking, while our Were assailants checked on us every minute or so, that was difficult.

Queen's headquarters on speed dial, he told me when he felt the phone leave his pocket. But that was lost on me. I didn't know how to access speed dial. It took me a few moments to make Quinn understand that, and I'm still not sure I how I did it, but finally he *thought* the phone number at me, and I awkwardly punched it in and pressed SEND. Maybe we hadn't thought that through all the way, because when a tiny voice said, "Hello?" the Weres heard it.

"You didn't search him?" the driver asked the passenger incredulously.

"Hell no, I was trying to get him in the back and get myself out of the rain," the man who had pinched me snarled right back. "Pull over, dammit!"

Has someone had your blood? Quinn asked me silently, though this time he could have spoken, and after a precious second, my brain kicked in. "Eric," I said, because the Weres were out their doors and running to open the rear doors of the van.

"Quinn and Sookie have been taken by some Weres," Quinn said into the phone I was holding to his mouth. "Eric the Northman can track her."

I hoped Eric was still in New Orleans, and I further hoped whoever answered the phone at the queen's headquarters was on the ball. But then the two Weres were yanking open the van doors and dragging us out, and one of them socked me while the other hit Quinn in the gut. They yanked the phone from my swollen fingers and tossed it into the thick undergrowth at the side of the road. The driver had pulled over by an empty lot, but up and down the road were widely spaced houses on stilts in a sea of grasses. The sky was too overcast for me to get a fix on our direction, but I was sure now we'd driven south into the marshes. I did manage to read our driver's watch, and was surprised to find out it was already past three in the afternoon.

"You dumb shit, Clete! Who was he calling?" yelled a voice from the second van, which had pulled over to the side of the road when we did. Our two captors looked at each other with identical expressions of consternation, and I would have been laughing if I hadn't been hurting so badly. It was as if they'd practiced looking stupid.

This time Quinn was searched very thoroughly, and I was, too, though I had no pockets or anywhere else to conceal anything, unless they wanted to do a body cavity check. I thought Clete—Mr. Pinch-Ass—was going to, just for a second, as his fingers jabbed the spandex into me. Quinn thought so, too. I made an awful noise, a choked gasp of fear, but the sound that came from Quinn's throat was beyond a snarl. It was a deep, throaty, coughing noise, and it was absolutely menacing.

"Leave the girl alone, Clete, and let's get back on the road," the tall driver said, and his voice had that "I'm done with you" edge to it. "I don't know who this guy is, but I don't think he changes into a nutria."

I wondered if Quinn would threaten them with his identity—most Weres seemed to know him, or know of him—but since he didn't volunteer his name, I didn't speak.

Clete shoved me back into the van with a lot of muttering along the lines of "Who died and made you God? You ain't the boss of me," and so on. The taller man clearly *was* the boss of Clete, which was a good thing. I wanted someone with brains and a shred of decency between me and Clete's probing fingers.

They had a very hard time getting Quinn into the van again. He didn't want to go, and finally two men from the other van came over, very reluctantly, to help Clete and the driver. They bound Quinn's legs with one of those plastic things, the kind where you run the pointed tip through a hole and then twist it. We'd used something similar to close the bag when we'd baked a turkey last Thanksgiving. The tie they used on Quinn was black and plastic and it actually locked with what looked like a handcuff key.

They didn't bind my legs.

I appreciated Quinn's getting angry at their treatment of me, angry enough to struggle to be free, but the end result was that my legs were free and his weren't—because I still didn't present a threat to them, at least in their minds.

They were probably right. I couldn't think of anything to do to prevent them from taking us wherever we were going. I didn't have a weapon, and though I worried at the duct tape binding my hands, my teeth didn't seem to be strong enough to make a weak spot. I rested for a minute, shutting my eyes wearily. The last blow had opened a cut on my cheek. A big tongue rasped over my bleeding face. Then again.

"Don't cry," said a strange, guttural voice, and I opened my eyes to check that it was, indeed, coming from Quinn.

Quinn had so much power that he could stop the change

once it had begun. I suspected he could trigger it, too, though I'd noticed that fighting could bring it on in any shape-shifter. He'd had the claws during the fight in Hadley's apartment, and they'd almost tipped the balance in our favor. Since he'd gotten so enraged at Clete during the episode by the side of the road, Quinn's nose had flattened and broadened. I had a close-up view of the teeth in his mouth, teeth that had altered into tiny daggers.

"Why didn't you change fully?" I asked, in a tiny whisper.

Because there wouldn't be enough room for you in this space, babe. After I change, I'm seven feet long and I weigh about four hundred fifty pounds.

That will make any girl gulp. I could only be grateful he'd thought that far ahead. I looked at him some more.

Not grossed out?

Clete and the driver were exchanging recriminations about the phone incident. "Why, grandpa, what big teeth you have," I whispered. The upper and lower canines were so long and sharp they were really scary. (I called them *canines;* to cats, that might be an insult.)

Sharp . . . they were sharp. I worked my hands up close to his mouth, and begged him with my eyes to understand. As much as I could tell from his altered face, Quinn was worried. Just as our situation aroused his defensive instincts, the idea I was trying to sell to him excited other instincts. *I will make your hands bleed,* he warned me, with a great effort. He was partially animal now, and the animal thought processes didn't necessarily travel the same paths as the human.

I bit my own bottom lip to keep from gasping as Quinn's teeth bit into the duct tape. He had to exert a lot of pressure to get the three-inch canines to pierce the duct tape, and that meant that those shorter, sharp incisors bit into my skin, too, no matter how much care he took. Tears began rolling down my face in an unending stream, and I felt him falter. I shook my bound hands to urge him on, and reluctantly he bent back to his task.

"Hey, George, he's biting her," Clete said from the passenger's seat. "I can see his jaw moving."

But we were so close together and the light was so poor that he couldn't see that Quinn was biting the binding on my hands. That was good. I was trying hard to find good things to cling to, because this was looking like a bleak, bleak world just at this moment, lying in the van traveling through the rain on an unknown road somewhere in southern Louisiana.

I was angry and bleeding and sore and lying on my already injured left arm. What I wanted, what would be ideal, would be to find myself clean and bandaged in a nice bed with white sheets. Okay, clean and bandaged and in a clean nightgown. And then Quinn would be in the bed, completely in his human form, and he would be clean and bandaged, too. And he'd have had some rest, and he'd be wearing nothing at all. But the pain of my cut and bleeding arms was becoming too demanding to ignore any longer, and I couldn't concentrate enough to cling to my lovely daydream. Just when I was on the verge of whimpering—or maybe just out-and-out screaming—I felt my wrists separate.

For a few seconds I just lay there and panted, trying to control my reaction to the pain. Unfortunately Quinn couldn't gnaw on the binding on his own hands, since they'd been bound behind him. He finally succeeded in turning over so I could see his wrists.

George said, "What are they doing?"

Clete glanced back at us, but I had my hands together. Since the day was dark, he couldn't see very clearly. "They're not doing anything. He quit biting her," Clete said, sounding disappointed.

Quinn succeeded in getting a claw hooked into the silvery duct tape. His claws were not sharp-edged along their curve like a scimitar; their power lay in the piercing point backed by a tiger's huge strength. But Quinn couldn't get the purchase to exercise that strength. So this was going to take time, and I suspected the tape was going to make a ripping noise when he succeeded in slicing it open.

We didn't have much time left. Any minute even an idiot like Clete would notice that all was not well.

I began the difficult maneuvering to get my hands down to Quinn's feet without giving away the fact that they weren't bound any longer. Clete glanced back when he glimpsed my movement, and I slumped against the empty shelves, my hands clasped together in my lap. I tried to look hopeless, which was awfully easy. Clete got more interested in lighting a cigarette after a second or two, giving me a chance to look at the plastic strap binding Quinn's ankles together. Though it had reminded me of the bag tie we used last Thanksgiving, this plastic was black and thick and extra tough, and I didn't have a knife to cut it or a key to unlock it. I did think Clete had made a mistake putting the restraint on, however, and I hurried to try to take advantage of it. Quinn's shoes were still on, of course, and I unlaced them and pulled them off. Then I held one foot pointed down. That foot began to slide up inside the circle of the tie. As I'd suspected, the shoes had held his feet apart and allowed for some slack.

Though my wrists and hands were bleeding onto Quinn's socks (which I left on so the plastic wouldn't scrape him) I was managing pretty well. He was being stoic about my drastic adjustments to his foot. Finally I heard his bones protest at being twisted into a strange position, but his foot slid up out of the restraint. Oh, thank God.

It had taken me longer to think about than to do. It had felt like hours.

I pulled the restraint down and shoved it into the debris, looked up at Quinn, and nodded. His claw, hooked in the duct tape, ripped at it. A hole appeared. The sound hadn't been loud at all, and I eased myself back full length beside Quinn to camouflage the activity.

I stuck my thumbs in the hole in the duct tape and yanked, achieving very little. There's a reason duct tape is so popular. It's a reliable substance.

We had to get out of that van before it reached its destination, and we had to get away before the other van could pull up behind ours. I scrabbled around through the chalupa wrappers and the cardboard french fry cartons on the floor of the van and finally, in a little gap between the floor and the side, I found an overlooked Phillips screwdriver. It was long and thin.

I looked at it and took a deep breath. I knew what I had to do. Quinn's hands were bound and he couldn't do it. Tears rolled down my face. I was being a crybaby, but I just couldn't help it. I looked at Quinn for a moment, and his features were steely. He knew as well as I did what needed to be done.

Just then the van slowed and took a turn from a parish road, reasonably well paved, onto what felt like a graveled track running into the woods. A driveway, I was sure. We were close to our destination. This was the best chance, maybe the last chance, we would have.

"Stretch your wrists," I murmured, and I plunged the Phillips head into the hole in the duct tape. It became larger. I plunged again. The two men, sensing my frantic movement, were turning as I stabbed at the duct tape a final time. While Quinn strained to part the perforated bindings, I pulled myself to my knees, gripping the latticed partition with my left hand, and I said, "Clete!"

He turned and leaned between the seats, closer to the partition, to see better. I took a deep breath and with my right hand I drove the screwdriver between the crosshatched metal. It went right into his cheek. He screamed and bled and George could hardly pull over fast enough. With a roar, Quinn separated his wrists. Then Quinn moved like lightning, and the minute the van slammed into Park, he and I were out the back doors and running through the woods. Thank God they were right by the road.

Beaded thong sandals are not good for running in the woods, I just want to say here, and Quinn was only in his socks. But we covered some ground, and by the time the startled driver of the second van could pull over and the passengers could leap out in pursuit, we were out of sight of the road. We kept running, because they were Weres, and they would track us. I'd pulled the screwdriver out of Clete's cheek and had it in my hand, and I remember thinking that it was dangerous to run with a pointed object in my hand. I thought about Clete's thick finger probing between my legs, and I didn't feel so bad about what I'd done. In the next few seconds, while I was jumping over a downed tree snagged in some thorny vines, the screwdriver slipped from my hand and I had no time to search for it.

After running for some time, we came to the swamp. Swamps and bayous abound in Louisiana, of course. The bayous and swamps are rich in wildlife, and they can be beautiful to look at and maybe tour in a canoe or something. But to plunge into on foot, in pouring rain, they suck.

Maybe from a tracking point of view this swamp was a good thing, because once we were in the water we wouldn't be leaving any scent. But from my personal point of view, the swamp was awful, because it was dirty and had snakes and alligators and God knows what else.

I had to brace myself to wade in after Quinn, and the water was dark and cool since it was still spring. In the summer, it would feel like wading through warm soup. On a day so overcast, once we were under the overhanging trees, we would be almost invisible to our pursuers, which was good; but the same conditions also meant that any lurking wildlife would be seen approximately when we stepped on it, or when it bit us. Not so good.

Quinn was smiling broadly, and I remembered that some tigers have lots of swamps in their natural habitat. At least one of us was happy.

The water got deeper and deeper, and soon we were swimming. There again, Quinn swam with a large grace that was kind of daunting to me. I was trying with all my might just to be quiet and stealthy. For a second, I was so cold and so frightened I began to think that . . . no, it wouldn't be better to still be in the van . . . but it was a near thing, just for a second.

I was so tired. My muscles were shaking with the aftermath of the adrenalin surge of our escape, and then I'd dashed through the woods, and before that there'd been the fight in the apartment, and before that . . . oh my God, I'd had sex with Quinn. Sort of. Yes, definitely sex. More or less.

We hadn't spoken since we'd gotten out of the van, and suddenly I remembered I'd seen his arm bleeding when we'd burst out of the van. I'd stabbed him with the Phillips head, at least once, while I was freeing him.

And here I was, whining. "Quinn," I said. "Let me help you."

"Help me?" he asked. I couldn't read his tone, and since he was forging through the dark water ahead of me, I couldn't read his face. But his mind, ah, that was full of snarled confusion and anger that he couldn't find a place to stuff. "Did I help you? Did I free you? Did I protect you from the fucking Weres? No, I let that son of a bitch stick his finger up you, and I watched, I couldn't do anything."

Oh. Male pride. "You got my hands free," I pointed out. "And you can help me now."

"How?" he turned to me, and he was deeply upset. I realized that he was a guy who took his protecting very seriously. It was one of God's mysterious imbalances, that men are stronger than women. My grandmother told me it was his way of balancing the scales, since women are tougher and more resilient. I'm not sure that's true, but I knew that Quinn, perhaps because he was a big, formidable guy and, perhaps because he was a weretiger who could turn into this fabulously beautiful and lethal beast, was in a funk because he hadn't killed all our attackers and saved me from being sullied by their touch.

I myself would have preferred that scenario a lot, especially considering our present predicament. But events hadn't fallen out that way. "Quinn," I said, and my voice was just as weary as the rest of me, "they have to have been heading somewhere around here. Somewhere in this swamp."

"That's why we turned off," he said in agreement. I saw a snake twined around a tree branch overhanging the water right behind him, and my face must have looked as shocked as I felt, because Quinn whipped around faster than I could think and had that snake in his hand and snapped it once, twice, and then the snake was dead and floating away in the sluggish water. He seemed to feel a lot better after that. "We don't know where we're going, but we're sure it's away from them. Right?" he asked.

"There aren't any other brains up and running in my range," I said, after a moment's checking. "But I've never defined how big my range is. That's all I can tell you. Let's try to get out of the water for a minute while we think, okay?" I was shivering all over.

Quinn slogged through the water and gathered me up. "Link your arms around my neck," he said.

Sure, if he wanted to do the man thing, that was fine. I put my arms around his neck and he began moving through the water.

"Would this be better if you turned into a tiger?" I asked.

"I might need that later, and I've already partially changed twice today. I better save my strength."

"What kind are you?"

"Bengal," he said, and just then the pattering of the rain on the water stopped.

We heard voices calling then, and we came to a stop in the water, both of our faces turned to the source of the sound. As we were standing there stock-still, I heard something large slide into the water to our right. I swung my eyes in that direction, terrified of what I'd see—but the water was almost still, as if something had just passed. I knew there were tours of the bayous south of New Orleans, and I knew locals made a good living out of taking people out on the dark water and letting them see the alligators. The good thing was, these natives made money, and out-of-staters got to see something they'd never have seen otherwise. The bad thing was, sometimes the locals threw treats to attract the gators. I figured the gators associated humans with food.

I laid my head on Quinn's shoulder and I closed my eyes. But the voices didn't get any closer, and we didn't hear the baying of wolves, and nothing bit my leg to drag me down. "That's what gators do, you know," I told Quinn. "They pull you under and drown you, and stick you somewhere so they can snack on you."

"Babe, the wolves aren't going to eat us today, and neither will the gators." He laughed, a low rumble deep in his chest. I was so glad to hear that sound. After a moment, we began moving through the water again. The trees and the bits of land became close together, the channels narrow, and finally we came up on a piece of land large enough to hold a cabin.

Quinn was half supporting me when we staggered out of the water.

As shelter, the cabin was poor stuff. Maybe the structure had once been a glorified hunting camp, three walls and a roof, no more than that. Now it was a wreck, halfway fallen. The wood had rotted and the metal roof had bent and buckled, rusting through in spots. I went over to the heap of man-tailored material and searched very carefully, but there didn't seem to be anything we could use as a weapon.

Quinn was occupied by ripping the remnants of the duct tape off his wrists, not even wincing when some skin went with it. I worked on my own more gently. Then I just gave out.

I slumped dismally to the ground, my back against a scrubby oak tree. Its bark immediately began making deep impressions in my back. I thought of all the germs in the water, germs that were doubtless speeding through my system the moment they'd gained entry through the cuts on my wrists. The unhealed bite, still covered by a now-filthy bandage, had doubtless received its share of nasty particles. My face was swelling up from the beating I'd taken. I remembered looking in the mirror the day before and seeing that the marks left by the bitten Weres in Shreveport had finally almost faded away. Fat lot of good that had done me.

"Amelia should have done something by now," I said, trying to feel optimistic. "She probably called vampire HQ. Even if our own phone call didn't reach anyone who'd do something about it, maybe someone's looking for us now."

"They'd have to send out human employees. It's still technically daylight, even though the sky's so dark."

"Well, at least the rain's over with," I said. At that moment, it began to rain again.

I thought about throwing a fit, but frankly, it didn't seem worth using up the energy. And there was nothing to do about it. The sky was going to rain, no matter how many fits I threw. "I'm sorry you got caught up in this," I said, thinking that I had a lot for which to apologize.

"Sookie, I don't know if *you* should be telling me *you're* sorry." Quinn emphasized the pronouns. "Everything has happened when we were together."

That was true, and I tried to believe all this wasn't my fault. But I was convinced that somehow, it really was.

Out of the blue, Quinn said, "What's your relationship with Alcide Herveaux? We saw him in the bar last week with some other girl. But the cop, the one in Shreveport, said you'd been engaged to him."

"That was bullshit," I said, sitting slumped in the mud. Here I was, deep inside a southern Louisiana swamp, the rain pelting down on me . . .

Hey, wait a minute. I stared at Quinn's mouth moving, realized he was saying something, but waited for the trailing end of a thought to snag on something. If there'd been a lightbulb above my head, it would have been flashing. "Jesus Christ, Shepherd of Judea," I said reverently. "That's who's doing this."

Quinn squatted in front of me. "You've picked who's been doing what? How many enemies do you have?"

"At least I know who sent the bitten Weres, and who had us kidnapped," I said, refusing to be sidetracked. Crouched together in the downpour like a couple of cave people, Quinn listened while I talked.

Then we discussed probabilities.

Then we made a plan.

21

ONCE HE KNEW WHAT HE WAS DOING, QUINN WAS relentless. Since we couldn't be any more miserable than we already were, he decided we might as well be moving. While I did little more than follow him and stay out of his way, he began to scour the area for smells. Finally he got tired of crouching, and he said, "I'm going to change." He stripped quickly and efficiently, rolling the clothes into a compact (but sopping) bundle and handing them to me to carry. Every conjecture I'd had about Quinn's body was absolutely on target, I was pleased to note. He'd begun taking off his clothes without a single hesitation, but once he noticed I was looking, he held still and let me look. Even in the dark, dripping rain, he was worth it. Quinn's body was a work of art, though a scarred work of art. He was one large block of muscle, from his calves to his neck.

"Do you like what you see?" he asked.

"Oh, *boy*," I said. "You look better than a Happy Meal to a three-year-old."

Quinn gave me a broad, pleased smile. He bent to crouch on the ground. I knew what was coming. The air around Quinn began to shimmer and tremble, and then within that envelope Quinn began to change. Muscles rippled and flowed and reformed, bones reshaped, fur rolled out of somewhere inside him—though I knew that couldn't be, that was the illusion. The sound was dreadful. It was a kind of gloppy, sticky sound, but with hard notes in it, as if someone were stirring a pot of stiff glue that was full of sticks and rocks.

At the end of it, the tiger stood across from me.

If Quinn had been a gorgeous naked man, he was an equally beautiful tiger. His fur was a deep orange slashed with black stripes, and there were touches of white on his belly and face. His eyes slanted, and they were golden. He was maybe seven feet long and at least three feet tall at the shoulder. I was amazed at how big he was. His paws were fully developed and as big as some dinner plates. His rounded ears were just plain cute. He walked over to me silently, with a grace unusual in such a massive form. He rubbed his huge head against me, almost knocking me down, and he purred. He sounded like a happy Geiger counter.

His dense fur was oily to the touch, so I figured he was pretty well waterproofed. He gave a barking cough, and the swamp went silent. You wouldn't think Louisiana wildlife would recognize the sound of a tiger, right? But it did, and it shut its mouth and hid.

We don't have the same special space requirements with animals that we do with people. I knelt beside the tiger that had been Quinn, in some magical way was still Quinn, and I put my arms around his neck, and I hugged him. It was a little disturbing that he smelled so much like an actual tiger, and I forced my mind around the fact that he was a tiger, that Quinn was inside him. And we set out through the swamp.

It was a little startling to see the tiger mark his new territory—this is not something you expect to see your boyfriend do—but I decided it would just be ridiculous to mind the display. Besides, I had enough to think about, keeping up with the tiger. He was searching for scents, and we covered a lot of ground. I was growing more and more exhausted. My sense of wonder faded, and I was simply wet and chilly, hungry and grumpy. If someone had been thinking right under my feet, I'm not sure my mind would have picked the thoughts up.

Then the tiger froze, nose testing the air. His head moved, ears twitching, to search in a particular direction. He turned to look at me. Though tigers can't smile, I got the definite wave of triumph from the huge cat. The tiger turned his head back to the east, rotated his massive head to look at me, and turned his head to the east again. *Follow me*, clear as a bell.

"Okay," I said, and put my hand on his shoulder.

Off we went. The trip through the swamp lasted an eternity, though later I estimated that "eternity," in this case, was probably about thirty minutes. Gradually the ground grew firmer, the water scarcer. Now we were in forest, not swamp.

I'd figured we'd gotten close to our abductors' destination when the van had turned off onto the side road. I'd been right. When we came to the edge of the clearing surrounding the little house, we were to the west side of the north-facing house. We could see both front and back yards. The van that had held us captive was parked in the back. In the tiny clearing at the front was a car, some kind of GMC sedan.

The little house itself was like a million other houses in

rural America. It was a box of a place: wooden, painted tan, with green shutters on the windows and green uprights to support the roof over the tiny front porch. The two men from the van, Clete and George, were huddled on the concrete square because of that bit of shelter, however inadequate it was.

The matching structure at the rear of the house was a little deck outside the back door, scarcely large enough to hold a gas grill and a mop. It was open to the elements. By the way, the elements were really going to town.

I stowed Quinn's clothes and shoes at the foot of a mimosa tree. The tiger's lips pulled back when he scented Clete. The long teeth were as frightening as a shark's.

The afternoon of rain had lowered the temperature. George and Clete were shivering in the damp cool of the evening. They were both smoking. The two Weres, in human form and smoking, would not have a better sense of smell than regular people. They showed no sign of being aware of Quinn at all. I figured they would react pretty dramatically if they caught the scent of tiger in southern Louisiana.

I worked my way through the trees around the clearing until I was very close to the van. I eased my way around it and crept up to the passenger side. The van was unlocked, and I could see the stun gun. That was my goal. I took a deep breath and opened the door, hoping the light that came on wasn't interesting to anyone who could see out the back window. I grabbed the stun gun from the jumble of stuff between the front seats. I shut the door as quietly as a van door can be shut. Luckily, the rain seemed to muffle the noise. I gave a shaky sigh of relief when nothing happened. Then I duckwalked back into the edge of the woods and knelt by Quinn.

He licked my cheek. I appreciated the affection in the gesture, if not the tiger breath, and I scratched his head.

(Somehow, kissing his fur had no appeal.) That done, I pointed to the left west window, which should belong to a living room. Quinn didn't nod or give me a high five, both of which would have been untigerlike gestures, but I guess I had expected him to give me some kind of green light. He just looked at me.

Picking up my feet carefully, I stepped out into the little open space between the forest and the house, and very carefully I made my way to the lit window.

I didn't want to pop into view like a jack-in-the-box, so I hugged the side of the house and inched sideways until I could peer in at the very corner of the glass. The older Pelts, Barbara and Gordon, were sitting on an "early American" loveseat dating from the sixties, and their body language clearly proclaimed their unhappiness. Their daughter Sandra paced back and forth in front of them, though there wasn't much room for such an exhibtion. It was a very small family room, a room that would be comfortable only if you had a family of one. The older Pelts looked as if they were going to a Lands' End photo shoot, while Sandra was more adventurously clad in skintight stretch khakis and a bright striped short-sleeved sweater. Sandra was dressed for trolling for cute guys at the mall, rather than torturing a couple of people. But torturing was what she'd been planning to do. There was a straight-backed chair crammed into the room, too, and it had straps and handcuffs already attached.

On a familiar note, there was a roll of duct tape sitting ready beside it.

I'd been pretty calm until I saw the duct tape.

I didn't know if tigers could count, but I held up three fingers in case Quinn was watching. Moving slowly and carefully, I squatted down and moved south until I was below the second window. I was feeling pretty proud of my sneaking ability, which should have alerted me to potential disaster. Pride goeth before a fall.

Though the window was dark, when I eased up into position, I was looking through the glass right into the eyes of a small swarthy man with a mustache and goatee. He was sitting at a table right by the window, and he'd been holding a cup of coffee in his hand. In his shock, he let it drop to the table and the hot backsplash hit his hands and chest and chin.

He shrieked, though I wasn't sure he was using actual words. I heard a commotion at the front door and in the front room.

Well . . . eff.

I was around the corner of the house and up the steps to the little deck faster than you could say Jack Robinson. I yanked open the screen door and pushed in the wooden door, and I leaped into the kitchen with the stun gun on. The small guy was still patting at his face with a towel while I zapped him, and he went down like a sack of bricks. Wow!

But the stun gun had to recharge, I discovered, when Sandra Pelt, who'd had the advantage of already being on her feet, charged into the kitchen, teeth bared. The stun gun didn't do a damn thing to her, and she was on me like an—well, like an enraged wolf.

However, she was still in the form of a girl, and I was desperate and desperately angry.

I've seen at least two dozen bar fights, ranging from half-hearted punches to rolling-on-the-ground biting, and I know how to fight. Right now I was willing to do whatever it took. Sandra was mean, but she was lighter and less experienced, and after some wrestling and punching and hair pulling that went by in a flash, I was on top of her and had her pinned to the floor. She snarled and snapped but she couldn't reach my neck, and I was prepared to head-butt her if I had to.

A voice in the background bellowed, "Let me in!" and I assumed it was Quinn behind some door. "Come on now!" I yelled in answer. "I need help!"

She was squirming underneath me, and I dared not let go to shift my grip. "Listen, Sandra," I panted, "hold still, dammit!"

"Fuck you," she said bitterly, and her efforts redoubled.

"This is actually kind of exciting," a familiar voice said, and I glanced up to see Eric looking down at us with wide blue eyes. He looked immaculate: neat as a pin in blue jeans that had a crease and a starched blue-and-white striped dress shirt. His blond hair was shining clean and (here was the most enviable part) dry. I hated his guts. I felt nasty to the nth degree.

"I could use some help here," I snapped, and he said, "Of course, Sookie, though I'm enjoying the wiggling around. Let go of the girl and stand up."

"Only if you're ready for action," I said, my breathing ragged with the effort of holding Sandra down.

"I'm always ready for action," Eric said, with a glowing smile. "Sandra, look at me."

She was too smart for that. Sandra squeezed her eyes shut and fought even harder. In a second, she freed one of her arms and swung it back to get momentum for her punch. But Eric dropped to his knees and caught the hand before it could fly at my head.

"That's enough," he said in an entirely different tone, and her eyes flew open in surprise. Though he still couldn't catch her with his eyes, I figured he had charge of her now. I rolled off the Were to lie on my back in what remained of the floor in the tiny kitchen. Mr. Small and Dark (and Burned and Stunned), who I figured owned this house, was crumpled by the table.

Eric, who was having almost as much trouble with Sandra as I'd had, took up a lot more of the available space. Exasperated with the Were, he adopted a simple solution. He squeezed the fist he'd caught, and she screamed. And shut up—and quit struggling.

"That's just not fair," I said, fighting a wave of weariness and pain.

"All's fair," he said quietly.

I didn't like the sound of that. "What are you talking about?" I asked. He shook his head. I tried again. "Where's Quinn?"

"The tiger has taken care of your two abductors," Eric said, with an unpleasant smile. "Would you like to go see?"

"Not particularly," I said, and closed my eyes again. "I guess they're dead?"

"I'm sure they wish they were," Eric said. "What did you do to the little man on the floor?"

"You wouldn't believe me if I told you," I said.

"Try me."

"I scared him so bad he spilled hot coffee on himself. Then I hit him with a stun gun that I got out of the van."

"Oh." There was a kind of breathy sound, and I opened my eyes to see that Eric was laughing silently.

"The Pelts?" I asked.

"Rasul has them covered," Eric said. "You have another fan, it seems."

"Oh, it's because of the fairy blood," I said irritably. "You know, it's not fair. Human guys don't like me. I know about two hundred of 'em who wouldn't want to date me if I came with a Chevy truck. But because supes are attracted to the fairy smell, I get accused of being a guy magnet. How wrong is that?"

"You have fairy blood," Eric said, as if his own lightbulb had just lit up. "That explains a lot."

That hurt my feelings. "Oh no, you couldn't just like me," I said, tired and hurting beyond coherence. "Oh no, gosh, there has to be a *reason.* And it's not gonna be my sparkling personality, oh no! It's gonna be my blood, because it's *special.* Not me, *I'm* not special . . ."

And I would have gone on and on, if Quinn hadn't said,

"I don't give a damn about fairies, myself." Any available room left in the kitchen vanished.

I scrambled to my feet. "You okay?" I asked in a wobbly voice.

"Yes," he said, in his deepest rumble. He was altogether human again, and altogether naked. I would've hugged him, but I felt a little embarrassed about embracing him in the altogether, in front of Eric.

"I left your clothes out there in the woods," I said. "I'll go get 'em."

"I can."

"No, I know where they are, and I couldn't get any wetter." Besides, I'm not sophisticated enough to be comfortable in a room with a naked guy, an unconscious guy, a real horrible girl, and another guy who's been my lover.

"Fuck you, bitch," the charming Sandra called after me, and shrieked again, as Eric made it clear he didn't care for name calling.

"Right back at you," I muttered, and trudged out into the rain.

Oh, yes, it was still raining.

I was still brooding over the fairy-blood thing as I scooped up the bundle of Quinn's sodden clothes. It would be easy to slide into a depressed trough if I thought the only reason anybody ever liked me was because I had fairy blood. Of course, there was always the odd vampire who had been ordered to seduce me . . . I was sure the fairy blood had just been a bonus, in that case . . . no, no, no, *wasn't going there.*

If I looked at it in a reasonable way, the blood was just as much a part of me as my eye color or the thickness of my hair. It hadn't done a thing for my half-fairy grandmother, assuming the gene had come to me through her and not one of my other grandparents. She'd married a human man who hadn't treated her any differently than he would have if her blood had been plain old grade A human. And she'd been killed by a human who hadn't known anything about her blood other than the color of it. Following the same assumption, fairy blood hadn't made a bit of difference to my father. He'd never in his life encountered a vampire who might be interested in him because of it—or if he had, he'd kept it mighty close. That didn't seem likely. And the fairy blood hadn't saved my father from the flash flood that had washed my parents' truck off the bridge and into the swollen stream. If the blood had come to me through my mother, well, she'd died in the truck, too. And Linda, my mother's sister, had died of cancer in her midforties, no matter what kind of heritage she had.

I didn't believe this wonderful fairy blood had done all that much for me, either. Maybe a few vampires had been a little more interested in me and friendly to me than they would have been otherwise, but I couldn't say that had been much of an advantage.

In fact, many people would say the vampire attention had been a big negative factor in my life. I might be one of those people. Especially since I was standing out here in the pouring rain holding someone else's wet clothes and wondering what the hell to do with them.

Having come full circle, I slogged back to the house. I could hear a lot of moaning coming from the front yard: Clete and George, presumably. I should have gone to check, but I couldn't muster up the energy.

Back in the kitchen, the small dark man was stirring a little, his eyes opening and shutting and his mouth twitching. His hands were tied behind him. Sandra was bound with duct tape, which cheered me up quite a bit. It seemed a neat piece of poetic justice. She even had a neat rectangle squarely over her mouth, which I presumed was Eric's work. Quinn had found a towel to secure around his waist, so he looked very . . . preppy.

"Thanks, babe," he said. He took his clothes and began

squeezing them out over the sink. I dripped on the floor. "I wonder if there's a dryer?" he asked, and I opened another door to find a little pantry/utility room with shelves on one wall and on the other a water heater and a tiny washer and dryer.

"Pass 'em in here," I called, and Quinn came in with his clothes. "Yours need to go in there, too, babe," he said, and I noticed he sounded as tired as I felt. Changing into and out of tiger form without the full moon, in such a short space of time, must have been very difficult. "Maybe you can find me a towel?" I asked, pulling off the wet pants with great effort. Without a single joke or leer, he went to see what he could find. He returned with some clothes, I assumed from the small man's bedroom: a T-shirt, shorts, socks. "This is the best I could do," he said.

"It's better than I hoped for," I said. After I'd used the towel and I had pulled on the clean, dry clothes, I almost wept with gratitude. I gave Quinn a hug and then went to find out what we were going to do with our hostages.

The Pelts were sitting on the floor, securely handcuffed, in the living room, watched by Rasul. Barbara and Gordon had looked so mild when they'd come to Merlotte's to meet with me in Sam's office. They looked mild no longer. Rage and malice sat oddly on their suburban faces.

Eric brought Sandra in, too, and dumped her by her parents. Eric stood in one doorway, Quinn in another (which a glance told me led into Small and Dark's bedroom). Rasul, gun in hand, relaxed his vigilance a little now that he had such formidable backup. "Where's the little guy?" he asked. "Sookie, I'm glad to see you looking so well, even though your ensemble falls below your usual standards."

The shorts were baggy cargo shorts, the shirt was big, and the white socks were the capper. "You really know how to make a girl feel beautiful, Rasul," I said, scraping together maybe half a smile to offer him. I sat down in the straight-backed chair and I asked Barbara Pelt, "What were you going to do with me?"

"Work on you until you told us the truth, and Sandra was satisfied," she said. "Our family couldn't be at peace until we knew the truth. And the truth lies in you, I just know it."

I was troubled. Well, beyond troubled. Because I didn't know what to say to her just yet, I looked from Eric to Rasul. "Just the two of you?" I asked.

"Any time two vampires can't handle a handful of Weres is the day I become human again," Rasul said, with an expression so snooty I was tempted to laugh. But he'd been exactly right (though of course he'd had a tiger who helped). Quinn was propped in the doorway looking picturesque, though just at the moment his great expanse of smooth skin didn't interest me at all.

"Eric," I said, "what should I do?"

I don't think I'd ever asked Eric for advice before. He was surprised. But the secret wasn't only mine.

After a moment, he nodded.

"I'll tell you what happened to Debbie," I said to the Pelts. I didn't ask Rasul and Quinn to leave the room. I was getting rid of this right now, both the lingering guilt and the hold Eric had on me.

I'd thought about that evening so often that my words came automatically. I didn't cry, because all my tears had been shed months ago, in private.

Once I'd finished the story, the Pelts sat and stared at me, and I stared back.

"That sounds like our Debbie," said Barbara Pelt. "This has the ring of truth."

"She did have a gun," said Gordon Pelt. "I gave it to her for Christmas two years ago." The two Weres looked at each other.

"She was . . . proactive," Barbara said, after a moment. She turned to Sandra. "Remember when we had to go to court, when she was in high school, because she put superglue in that cheerleader's hairbrush? The one that was dating her ex-boyfriend? That does sound like Debbie, huh?"

Sandra nodded, but the duct tape wouldn't permit her speech. Sandra had tears rolling down her cheeks.

"You still don't remember where you put her?" Gordon asked Eric.

"I would tell you if I did," Eric said. *Not that I care,* his tone implied.

"You guys hired the two kids who attacked us in Shreveport," Quinn said.

"Sandra did," Gordon admitted. "We didn't know about it until Sandra had already bitten them. She'd promised them . . ." He shook his head. "She'd sent them to Shreveport on her errand, but they would have returned home to collect their reward. Our Jackson pack would have killed them. Mississippi doesn't permit bitten Weres. They kill them on sight. The boys would have named Sandra as their maker. The pack would have abjured her. Barbara's dabbled with witchcraft, but nothing of the level that would have sealed the boys' mouths. We hired an out-of-state Were to track them when we found out. He couldn't stop them, couldn't prevent their arrest, so he had to be arrested and go into the jail system with them, to take care of the problem." He looked up at us, shook his head sternly. "He bribed Cal Myers to put him in the cell with them. Of course, we punished Sandra for that."

"Oh, did you take away her cell phone for a week?" If I sounded sarcastic, I thought I had a right to be. Even cooperative, the Pelts were pretty horrible. "We were both hurt," I said, nodding toward Quinn, "and those two kids are dead now. Because of Sandra."

"She's our daughter," Barbara said. "And she believed she was avenging her murdered sister."

"And then you hired all the Weres that were in the second

van, and the two Weres lying out in the front yard. Are they going to die, Quinn?"

"If the Pelts don't take them to a Were doctor, they may. And they sure can't go to any human hospital."

Quinn's claws would have left distinctive marks.

"Will you do that?" I asked skeptically. "Take Clete and George to a Were doctor?"

The Pelts looked at each other and shrugged. "We figured you were going to kill us," Gordon said. "Are you going to let us walk away? With what assurances?"

I'd never met anyone quite like the Pelts before, and it was easier and easier to see where Debbie had gotten her charming personality, adopted or not.

"With assurances that I never hear of this again," I said. "Neither I nor Eric."

Quinn and Rasul had been listening silently.

"Sookie is a friend of the Shreveport pack," Quinn said. "They are very upset she was attacked, in their own city, and now we know you're responsible for that attack."

"We heard she was no favorite of the new packleader." Barbara's voice held a trace of contempt. She was reverting to her own personality, since she no longer feared her own death. I liked them better when they were scared.

"He may not be packleader for long," Quinn said, his voice a quiet threat. "Even if he stays in office, he can't rescind the pack's protection, since it was guaranteed by the previous packleader. The honor of the pack would be destroyed."

"We'll make reparations to the Shreveport pack," Gordon said wearily.

"Did you send Tanya to Bon Temps?" I asked.

Barbara looked proud of herself. "Yes, I did that. You know our Debbie was adopted? She was a werefox."

I nodded. Eric looked quizzical; I didn't think he'd met Tanya.

"Tanya is a member of Debbie's birth family, and she

wanted to do something to help. She thought if she went to Bon Temps and began working with you, you might let something spill. She said you were too suspicious to warm up to her offer of friendship. I think she might stay in Bon Temps. I understand finding the bar owner so attractive was an unexpected bonus."

It was kind of gratifying to discover Tanya was as untrustworthy as I'd suspected. I wondered if I had the right to tell Sam this whole story, by way of warning. I'd have to think about that later.

"And the man who owns this house?" I could hear him groaning and moaning from the kitchen.

"He's a former high school buddy of Debbie's," Gordon said. "We asked him if we could borrow his house for the afternoon. And we paid him. He won't talk after we leave."

"What about Gladiola?" I asked. I remembered the two burning body sections on my driveway. I remembered Mr. Cataliades's face, and Diantha's grief.

They all three stared at me blankly. "Gladiola? The flower?" Barbara said, looking genuinely puzzled. "It's not even the right season for glads, now."

That was a dead end.

"Do you agree we're square on this?" I asked baldly. "I've hurt you, you've hurt me. Even?"

Sandra shook her head from side to side, but her parents ignored her. Thank God for duct tape. Gordon and Barbara nodded at each other.

Gordon said, "You killed Debbie, but we do believe that you killed her in self-defense. And our living daughter took extreme and unlawful methods to attack you. . . . It goes against my grain to say this, but I think we have to agree to leave you alone, after this day."

Sandra made a lot of weird noises.

"With these stipulations." Gordon's face suddenly looked hard as a rock. The yuppie man took a backseat to the Were. "You won't come after Sandra. And you stay out of Mississippi."

"Done," I said instantly. "Can you control Sandra enough to make her keep to this agreement?" It was a rude but valid question. Sandra had enough balls for an army, and I doubted very much if the Pelts had ever really had control over either of their daughters.

"Sandra," Gordon said to his daughter. Her eyes blazed at him from her forcibly mute face. "Sandra, this is law. We are giving our word to this woman, and our word is binding on you. If you defy me, I'll challenge you at the next full moon. I'll take you down in front of the pack."

Both mother and daughter looked shocked, Sandra more so than her mother. Sandra's eyes narrowed, and after a long moment, she nodded.

I hoped Gordon lived a long time and enjoyed good health while he lived. If he grew ill, or if he died, Sandra wouldn't feel bound by this agreement, I felt pretty darn sure. But as I walked out of the little house in the swamp, I thought I had a reasonable chance of not seeing the Pelts again in my life, and that was absolutely okay with me.

22

AMELIA WAS RUMMAGING THROUGH HER WALK-IN closet. It was just after dark the next day. Suddenly the hangers quit sliding across the rack at the very back of the closet.

"I think I have one," she called, sounding surprised. I waited for her to emerge, sitting on the edge of her bed. I'd had at least ten hours' sleep, I'd had a careful shower, I'd had some first aid, and I felt a hundred times better. Amelia was glowing with pride and happiness. Not only had Bob the Mormony witch been wonderful in bed, they'd been up in time to watch Quinn's and my abduction, and to have the brilliant idea of calling the vampire queen's mansion instead of the regular police. I hadn't told her yet that Quinn and I had made our own call, because I didn't know which one had been more effective, and I enjoyed seeing Amelia so happy.

I hadn't wanted to go to the queen's shindig at all until

after my trip to the bank with Mr. Cataliades. After I'd returned to Hadley's apartment, I'd resumed packing my cousin's stuff and heard a strange noise when I'd put the coffee into a box. Now if I wanted to avert disaster, I had to go to the queen's spring party, the supernatural event of the year. I'd tried getting in touch with Andre at the queen's headquarters, but a voice had told me he was not to be disturbed. I wondered who was answering the phones at Vampire Central that day. Could it be one of Peter Threadgill's vamps?

"Yes, I do!" Amelia exclaimed. "Ah, it's kind of daring. I was the bridesmaid at an extreme wedding." She emerged from the closet with her hair disheveled, her eyes lit with triumph. She rotated the hanger so I could get the full effect. She'd had to pin the dress to the hanger because there was so little to hang.

"Yikes," I said, uneasily. Made mostly of lime-green chiffon, it was cut in a deep V almost down to the waist. A single narrow strap ran around the neck.

"It was a movie star wedding," Amelia said, looking as if she had a lot of memories of the service. Since the dress was also backless, I was wondering how those Hollywood women kept their boobs covered. Double-sided tape? Some kind of glue? As I hadn't seen Claudine since she vanished from the courtyard before the ectoplasmic reconstruction, I had to assume she'd gone back to her job and her life in Monroe. I could have used her special services just about now. There had to be a fairy spell that would make your dress stay still.

"At least you don't need a special bra to wear under it," Amelia said helpfully. That was true; it wasn't possible to wear a bra at all. "And I've got the shoes, if you can wear a seven."

"That's a big help," I said, trying to sound pleased and grateful. "I don't suppose you can do hair?"

"Nah," Amelia said. She waved a hand at her own short 'do. "I wash it, brush it, and that's that. But I can call Bob." Her eyes glowed happily. "He's a hairdresser."

I tried not to look too astonished. *At a funeral home?* I thought, but I was smart enough to keep that to myself. Bob just looked no way like any hairdresser I'd ever seen.

After a couple of hours, I was more or less into the dress, and fully made up.

Bob had done a good job with my hair, though he'd reminded me several times to keep very still, in a way that had made me a little nervous.

And Quinn had shown up on time in his car. When Eric and Rasul had dropped me off at about two in the morning, Quinn had just gotten in his car and driven away to wherever he was staying, though he'd put a light kiss on my forehead before I started up the stairs. Amelia had come out of her apartment, all happy I was safely back, and I'd had to return a call from Mr. Cataliades, who wondered if I was quite all right, and who wanted me to go to the bank with him to finalize Hadley's financial affairs. Since I'd missed my chance to go with Everett, I'd been grateful.

But when I'd returned to Hadley's apartment after the bank trip, I'd found a message on Hadley's answering machine telling me that the queen expected to see me at the party at the old monastery tonight. "I don't want you to leave the city without seeing me again," the queen's human secretary had quoted her as saying, before informing me that the dress code was formal. After my discovery, when I realized I'd have to attend the party, I'd gone down the stairs to Amelia's in a panic.

The dress caused another kind of panic. I was better-endowed than Amelia, though a bit shorter, and I had to stand really straight.

"The suspense is killing me," said Quinn, eyeing my chest. He looked wonderful in a tux. My wrist bandages stuck out against my tan like strange bracelets; in fact, one of them was acutely uncomfortable, and I was anxious to take it off. But the wrist would have to stay covered a while, though the bite on my left arm could remain uncovered. Maybe the suspense about my boobs would distract party-goers from the fact that my face was swollen and discolored on one side.

Quinn, of course, looked as though nothing had ever happened to him. Not only did he have the quick-healing flesh of most shape-shifters, but a man's tux covers up a lot of injuries.

"Don't you make me feel any more self-conscious than I already do," I said. "For about a dime, I'd go crawl back into bed and sleep for a week."

"I'm up for that, though I'd reduce the sleep time," Quinn said sincerely. "But for our peace of mind, I think we better do this first. By the way, my suspense was about the trip to the bank, not your dress. I figure, with your dress, it's a win-win situation. If you stay in it, good. If you don't, even better."

I looked away, trying to control an involuntary smile. "The trip to the bank." That seemed like a safe topic. "Well, her bank account didn't have a lot in it, which I figured would be the case. Hadley didn't have much sense about money. Hadley didn't have much sense, period. But the safe-deposit box . . ."

The safe-deposit box had held Hadley's birth certificate, a marriage license, and a divorce decree dated more than three years ago—both naming the same man, I was glad to see—and a laminated copy of my aunt's obituary. Hadley had known when her mother had died, and she'd cared enough to keep the clipping. There were pictures from our shared childhood, too: my mother and her sister; my mother and Jason, me, and Hadley; my grandmother and her husband. There was a pretty necklace with sapphires and diamonds (which Mr. Cataliades had said the queen had given to Hadley), and a pair of matching earrings. There were a couple more things that I wanted to think about.

But the queen's bracelet was not there. That was why Mr. Cataliades had wanted to accompany me, I think; he half expected the bracelet would be there, and he seemed quite anxious when I held the lockbox out to him so he could see its contents for himself.

"I finished packing the kitchen stuff this afternoon after Cataliades took me back to Hadley's apartment," I said to Quinn, and watched his reaction. I would never again take the disinterestedness of my companions for granted. I found myself fairly convinced Quinn had not been helping me pack the day before in order to search for something, after I saw that his reaction was perfectly calm.

"That's good," he said. "Sorry I didn't make it over to help you today. I was closing out Jake's dealings with Special Events. I had to call my partners, let them know. I had to call Jake's girlfriend. He wasn't steady enough to be around her, if she even wants to see him again. She's not a vamp lover, to put it mildly."

At the moment, I wasn't either. I couldn't fathom the true reason the queen wanted me at the party, but I had found another reason to see her. Quinn smiled at me, and I smiled back at him, hoping that some good would come out of this evening. I had to admit to myself that I was a bit curious about seeing the queen's party barn, so to speak—and I was also kind of glad to dress up and be pretty after all the swamp slogging.

As we drove, I almost opened a conversation with Quinn at least three times—but on every occasion, when it got to the point, I kept my mouth shut.

"We're getting close," he told me when we'd reached one of the oldest neighborhoods in New Orleans, the Garden District. The houses, set in beautiful grounds, would cost many times what even the Bellefleur mansion would fetch. In the middle of these marvelous homes, we came to a high wall that extended for a whole block. This was the renovated monastery that the queen used for entertaining.

There might be other gates at the back of the property, but tonight all the traffic was moving through the main front entrance. It was heavily protected with the most efficient guards of all: vampires. I wondered if Sophie-Anne Leclerq was paranoid, or wise, or simply did not feel loved (or safe) in her adopted city. I was sure the queen also had the regular security provisions—cameras, infrared motion detectors, razor wire, maybe even guard dogs. There was security out the ying-yang here, where the elite vampires occasionally partied with the elite humans. Tonight the party was supes only, the first large party the newlyweds had given since they'd become a couple.

Three of the queen's vampires were at the gate, along with three of the Arkansas vampires. Peter Threadgill's vampires all wore a uniform, though I suspected the king called it livery. The Arkansas bloodsuckers, male and female, were wearing white suits with blue shirts and red vests. I didn't know if the king was ultrapatriotic or if the colors had been chosen because they were in the Arkansas state flag as well as the U.S. flag. Whichever, the suits were beyond tacky and into some fashion hall of shame, all on their own. And Threadgill had been dressed so conservatively! Was this some tradition I'd never heard of? Gosh, even I knew better than that, tastewise, and I bought most of my clothes at Wal-Mart.

Quinn had the queen's card to show to the guards at the gate, but still they called up to the main house. Quinn looked uneasy, and I hoped he was as concerned as I was about the extreme security and the fact that Threadgill's vampires had worked so hard to distinguish themselves from the queen's adherents. I was thinking hard about the queen's need to offer the king's vamps a reason she would go upstairs with me at Hadley's. I thought of the anxiety she displayed when she asked about the bracelet. I thought of the presence of both camps of vampires at the main gate. Neither monarch trusted the spouse to provide protection.

It seemed like a long time before we were given leave to pass through. Quinn was as quiet as I while we waited.

The grounds seemed to be beautifully landscaped and kept, and they were certainly well lit.

"Quinn, this is just wrong," I said. "What's going on here? Do you think they'd let us leave?" Unfortunately, it seemed as though all my suspicions were true.

Quinn didn't look any happier than I was. "They won't let us out," he said. "We have to go on now." I clutched my little evening bag closer to me, wishing there was something more lethal in it than a few small items like a compact and a lipstick, and a tampon. Quinn drove us carefully up the winding drive to the front of the monastery.

"What did you do today, besides work on your outfit?" Quinn asked.

"I made a lot of phone calls," I said. "And one of them paid off."

"Calls? Where to?"

"Gas stations, all along the route from New Orleans to Bon Temps."

He turned to stare at me, but I pointed just in time for Quinn to apply the brakes.

A lion strolled across the drive.

"Okay, what's that? Animal? Or shifter?" I was edgier by the minute.

"Animal," Quinn said.

Scratch the idea of dogs roaming the enclosure. I hoped the wall was high enough to keep the lion in.

We parked in front of the former monastery, which was a very large two-story building. It hadn't been built for beauty, but for utility, so it was a largely featureless structure. There was one small door in the middle of the façade, and small windows placed regularly. Again, fairly easy to defend.

Outside the small door stood six more vampires, three in fancy but unmatching clothes—surely Louisiana bloodsuckers—and three more from Arkansas, in their glaringly garish outfits.

"That's just butt-ugly," I said.

"But easy to see, even in the dark," Quinn said, looking as if he were thinking deep, significant thoughts.

"Duh," I said. "Isn't that the point? So they'll instantly . . . oh." I mulled it over. "Yeah," I said. "No one would wear anything close to that, on purpose or by accident. Under any circumstances. Unless it was really important to be instantly identifiable."

Quinn said, "It's possible that Peter Threadgill is not devoted to Sophie-Anne."

I gave a squawk of laughter just as two Louisiana vampires opened our car doors in a move so coordinated it must have been rehearsed. Melanie, the guard vampire I'd met at the queen's downtown headquarters, took my hand to help me from the car, and she smiled at me. She looked a lot better out of the overwhelming SWAT gear. She was wearing a pretty yellow dress with low heels. Now that she wasn't wearing a helmet, I could see her hair was short, intensely curly, and light brown.

She took a deep, dramatic breath as I passed, and then made an ecstatic face. "Oh, the odor of the fairy!" she exclaimed. "It makes my heart sing!"

I swatted at her playfully. To say I was surprised would be an understatement. Vampires, as a whole, are not noted for their sense of humor.

"Cute dress," Rasul said. "Kind of on the daring side, huh?"

Chester said, "Can't be too daring for me. You look really tasty."

I thought it couldn't be a coincidence that the three vampires I'd met at the queen's headquarters were the three vampires on door duty tonight. I couldn't figure out what that could mean, though. The three Arkansas vampires were silent, regarding the to-and-fro between us with cold eyes. They were not in the same relaxed and smiling mood as their fellows.

Something definitely off-kilter here. But with the acute vampire hearing all around, there wasn't anything to say about it.

Quinn took my arm. We walked into a long hall that seemed to run nearly the length of the building. A Threadgill vampire was standing at the door of a room that seemed to serve as a reception area.

"Would you like to check your bag?" she asked, obviously put out at being relegated to a hat-check girl.

"No, thanks," I said, and thought she was going to pull it out from under my arm.

"May I search it?" she asked. "We screen for weapons."

I stared at her, always a risky thing to do to a vampire. "Of course not. I have no weapons."

"Sookie," Quinn said, trying not to sound alarmed. "You have to let her look in your purse. It's procedure."

I glared at him. "You could have told me," I said sharply.

The door guard, who was a svelte young vamp with a figure that challenged the cut of the white pants, seized my purse with an air of triumph. She turned it out over a tray, and its few contents clattered to the metal surface: a compact, a lipstick, a tiny tube of glue, a handkerchief, a ten-dollar bill, and a tampon in a rigid plastic applicator, completely covered in plastic wrap.

Quinn was not unsophisticated enough to turn red, but he did glance discreetly away. The vampire, who had died long before women carried such items in their purses, asked me its purpose and nodded when I explained. She repacked my little evening bag and handed it to me, indicating with a hand gesture that we should proceed down the hall. She'd turned to the people who'd come in behind us, a Were couple in their sixties, before we'd even exited the room.

"What are you up to?" Quinn asked, in the quietest possible voice, as we moved along the corridor.

"Do we have to pass through any more security?" I asked, in a voice just as hushed.

"I don't know. I don't see any up ahead."

"I have to do something," I said. "Excuse me, while I find the nearest ladies' room." I tried to tell him, with my eyes, and with the pressure of my hand on his arm, that in a few minutes everything would be all right, and I sincerely hoped that was the truth. Quinn was clearly not happy with me, but he waited outside the ladies' room (God knows what that had been when the building was a monastery) while I ducked into one of the stalls and made a few adjustments. When I came out, I'd tossed the tampon container into the little bin in the stall, and one of my wrists had been rebandaged. My purse was a little heavier.

The door at the end of the corridor led into the very large room that had been the monks' refectory. Though the room was still walled with stone and large pillars supported the roof, three on the left and three on the right, the rest of the decor was considerably different now. The middle of the room was cleared for dancing, and the floor was wooden. There was a dais for musicians close to the refreshments table, and another dais at the opposite end of the room for the royalty.

Around the sides of the room were chairs in conversational groupings. The whole room was decorated in white and blue, the colors of Louisiana. One of the walls had murals depicting scenes from around the state: a swamp scene, which made me shudder; a Bourbon Street montage; a field being plowed and lumber being cut; and a fisherman hoisting up a net in the Gulf Coast. These were all scenes featuring humans, I thought, and wondered what the thinking was behind that. Then I turned to look at the wall surrounding the doorway I'd just entered, and I saw the vampire side of Louisiana life: a group of happy vampires with fiddles under their chins, playing away; a vampire police officer patrolling the French Quarter; a vampire guide leading tourists through one of the Cities of the Dead. No vamps snacking on humans, no vamps drinking anything, I noticed. This was a statement in public relations. I wondered if it really fooled anyone. All you had to do was sit down at a supper table with vampires, and you'd be reminded how different they were, all right.

Well, this wasn't what I'd come to do. I looked around for the queen, and I finally saw her standing by her husband. She was wearing a long-sleeved orange silk dress, and she looked fabulous. Long sleeves maybe seemed a little strange in the warm evening, but vampires didn't notice such things. Peter Threadgill was wearing a tux, and he looked equally impressive. Jade Flower was standing behind him, sword strapped to her back even though she was wearing a red sequined dress (in which, by the way, she looked awful). Andre, also fully armed, was at his station behind the queen. Sigebert and Wybert couldn't be far off. I spotted them on either side of a door that I assumed led to the queen's private apartments. The two vampires looked acutely uncomfortable in their tuxes; it was like watching bears who'd been made to wear shoes.

Bill was in the room. I caught a glimpse of him in the far corner, in the opposite direction from the queen, and I shivered with loathing.

"You have too many secrets," Quinn complained, following the direction of my gaze.

"I'll be glad to tell you a few of 'em, real soon," I promised, and we joined the tail end of the reception line. "When we reach the royals, you go ahead of me. While I'm talking to the queen, you distract the king, okay? Then I will tell you everything."

We reached to Mr. Cataliades first. I guess he was sort of the queen's secretary of state. Or maybe attorney general would be more appropriate?

"Good to see you again, Mr. Cataliades," I said, in my most correct social tone. "I've got a surprise for you," I added.

"You may have to save it," he said with a kind of stiff cordiality. "The queen is about to have the first dance with her new king. And we're all so looking forward to seeing the present the king gave her."

I glanced around but I didn't see Diantha. "How's your niece?" I asked.

"My surviving niece," he said grimly, "is at home with her mother."

"That's too bad," I said. "She should be here this evening."

He stared at me. Then he looked interested.

"Indeed," he said.

"I heard that someone from here stopped to get gas a week ago Wednesday, on her way to Bon Temps," I said. "Someone with a long sword. Here, let me tuck this in your pocket. I don't need it any more." When I stepped away from him and faced the queen, I had one hand over my injured wrist. The bandage had vanished.

I held out my right hand, and the queen was forced to take it in her own. I had counted on obliging the queen to follow the human custom of shaking hands, and I was mighty relieved when she did. Quinn had passed from the queen to the king, and he said, "Your Majesty, I'm sure you remember me. I was the event coordinator at your wedding. Did the flowers turn out like you wanted?"

Somewhat startled, Peter Threadgill turned his large eyes on Quinn, and Jade Flower kept her eyes on what her king did.

Trying very hard to keep my movements swift but not jerky, I pressed my left hand and what was in it onto the queen's wrist. She didn't flinch, but I think she thought about it. She glanced down at her wrist to see what I'd put on it, and her eyes closed in relief.

"Yes, my dear, our visit was lovely," she said, at random. "Andre enjoyed it very much, as did I." She glanced back over her shoulder, and Andre picked up his cue, and inclined his head to me, in tribute to my supposed talents in the sack. I was so glad to get the ordeal over with that I smiled at him radiantly, and he looked a shade amused. The queen raised her arm slightly to beckon him closer, and her sleeve rode up. Suddenly Andre was smiling as broadly as I was.

Jade Flower was distracted by Andre's movement forward, and her eyes followed his. They widened, and she was very much not smiling. In fact, she was enraged. Mr. Cataliades was looking at the sword on Jade Flower's back with a completely blank face.

Then Quinn was dismissed by the king and it was my turn to pay homage to Peter Threadgill, King of Arkansas.

"I hear that you had an adventure in the swamps yesterday," he said, his voice cool and indifferent.

"Yes, sir. But it all worked out okay, I think," I said.

"Good of you to come," he said. "Now that you have wrapped up your cousin's estate, I am sure you will be returning to your home?"

"Oh, yes, quick as can be," I said. It was the absolute truth. I would go home providing I could just survive this evening, though at the moment the chances weren't looking too good. I had counted, as well as I was able in a throng like this. There were at least twenty vampires in the room wearing the bright Arkansas outfit, and perhaps the same number of the queen's homies.

I moved away, and the Were couple that had entered after Quinn and me took my place. I thought he was the lieutenant governor of Louisiana, and I hoped he had good life insurance.

"What?" Quinn demanded.

I led him over to a place against the wall, and gently maneuvered him until his back was against it. I had to face away from any lip-readers in the room.

"Did you know the queen's bracelet was missing?" I asked.

He shook his head. "One of the diamond bracelets the king gave her as a wedding present?" he asked, his head ducked to baffle any watchers.

"Yes, missing," I said. "Since Hadley died."

"If the king knew the bracelet was missing, and if he could force the queen to acknowledge that she'd given it to a lover, then he would have grounds for divorce."

"What would he get then?"

"What *wouldn't* he get! It was a vampire hierarchal marriage, and you don't get any more binding than that. I think the wedding contract was thirty pages."

I understood much better now.

A beautifully dressed vampire woman wearing a gray-green gown strewn with gleaming silver flowers raised her arm to get the attention of the crowd. Gradually the assembled people fell silent.

"Sophie-Anne and Peter welcome you to their first joint entertainment," the vamp said, and her voice was so musical and mellow that you wanted to listen to her for hours. They should get her to do the Oscars. Or the Miss America pageant. "Sophie-Anne and Peter invite all of you to have a wonderful evening of dancing, eating, and drinking. To open the dancing, our host and hostess will waltz."

Despite his glitzy surface, I thought Peter might be more comfortable doing a square dance, but with a wife like Sophie-Anne, it was waltz or nothing. He advanced on his wife, his arms at the ready to receive her, and in his carrying vampire voice he said, "Darling, show them the bracelets."

Sophie-Anne swept the crowd with a smile and raised her own arms to make the sleeves slide back, and a matching bracelet on each wrist shone at the guests, the two huge diamonds winking and blinking in the chandelier lights.

For a moment Peter Threadgill was absolutely still, as if someone had zapped him with a freeze gun. He altered his stance as he moved forward, after that, and took one of her hands in both of his. He stared down at one bracelet, then released her hand to take the other. That bracelet, too, passed his silent test.

"Wonderful," he said, and if it was through his fangs you'd only think they'd extended because he was horny for his beautiful wife. "You're wearing both of them."

"Of course," Sophie-Anne said. "My darling." Her smile was just as sincere as his.

And away they danced, though something about the way he swung her let me know the king was letting his temper get the better of him. He'd had a big plan, and now I'd spoiled it . . . but thankfully, he didn't know my part. He just knew that somehow Sophie-Anne had managed to retrieve her bracelet and save her face, and he had nothing to justify whatever he'd plotted to do. He would have to back down. After this, he'd probably think of another way to subvert his queen, but at least I'd be out of the fray.

Quinn and I retreated to the refreshments table, located to the south side of the large room, beside one of the thick pillars. Servers were there with carving knives to shave off ham or roast beef. There were yeasty rolls to pile the meat on. It smelled wonderful, but I was too nervous to think of eating. Quinn got me a cup of ginger ale from the bar.

I stared at the dancing couple and waited for the ceiling to fall in.

"Don't they look lovely together?" a well-dressed gray-haired woman said. I realized she was the one who'd come in after me.

"Yes, they do," I agreed.

"I'm Genevieve Thrash," she said. "This is my husband, David."

"Pleased to meet you," I said. "I'm Sookie Stackhouse, and this is my friend, John Quinn." Quinn looked surprised. I wondered if that was actually his first name.

The two men, tiger and Were, shook hands while Genevieve and I watched the couple dance a bit longer.

"Your dress is so pretty," Genevieve said, giving every indication she was speaking sincerely. "It takes a young body to show off a gown like that."

"I appreciate your saying so," I said. "I'm showing a bit more of that body than I'm comfortable with, so you've made me feel better."

"I know your date appreciates it," she said. "And so does that young man over there." She nodded her head subtly, and I glanced in the direction she was indicating. Bill. He looked very good in his tuxedo, but even being in the same room made something within me twist with pain.

"I believe your husband is the lieutenant governor?" I said.

"You're absolutely correct."

"And how do you like being Mrs. Lieutenant?" I asked.

She told some amusing stories about people she'd met while she followed David's political career. "And what does your young man do?" she asked, with that eager interest that must have helped her husband up that ladder.

"He's an events coodinator," I said, after a moment's hesitation.

"How interesting," Genevieve said. "And yourself, you have a job?"

"Oh, yes ma'am," I said. "I'm a barmaid."

That was a bit startling to the politician's wife, but she grinned at me. "You're the first I've ever met," she said cheerfully.

"You're the first Mrs. Lieutenant Governor I've ever met," I said. Damn, now that I'd met her and liked her, I felt responsible for her. Quinn and David were just chatting away, and I think fishing was their topic.

"Mrs. Thrash," I said, "I know you're a Were and that means you're tough as tough can be, but I'm going to give you a piece of advice."

She looked at me quizzically.

"This advice is pure gold," I said.

Her eyebrows flew up. "Okay," she said, slowly. "I'm listening."

"Something very bad is going to happen here in the next hour or so. It's going to be so bad that it might get a lot of people killed. Now you can stay and have a good time until it happens, and then you'll wonder why you didn't listen to me, or you can leave now after acting like you've been taken ill, and you can save yourself a lot of unhappiness."

Her gaze was intent. I could hear her wondering whether to take me seriously. I didn't seem like a weirdo or a crazy person. I seemed like a normal, attractive, young woman with a heck of a handsome date.

"Are you threatening me?" she asked.

"No, ma'am. I'm trying to save your ass."

"We'll get one dance in first," Genevieve Thrash said, making up her mind. "David, honey, let's take a spin around the dance floor and then make our excuses. I've got the worst headache you ever felt." David obligingly broke off his conversation with Quinn to take his wife to the clear space and begin waltzing along with the royal vampire couple, who looked relieved to have company.

I was beginning to relax my posture again, but a glance

from Quinn reminded me to stand very straight. "I *love* the dress," he said. "Shall we dance?"

"You can waltz?" I hoped my jaw hadn't dropped too far.

"Yep," he said. He didn't ask if I could, though as a matter of fact I'd been watching the queen's steps intently. I can dance—can't sing, but I love a dance floor. I'd never waltzed, but I figured I could do it.

It was wonderful to have Quinn's arm around me, to be moving so gracefully around the floor. For a moment, I just forgot everything and enjoyed looking up at him, feeling the way a girl feels when she's dancing with a guy she expects she'll make love with, sooner or later. Quinn's fingers touching my bare back just made me tingle.

"Sooner or later," he said, "we're gonna be in a room with a bed, no phones, and a door that will lock."

I smiled up at him and spied the Thrashes easing out of the door. I hoped their car had been brought around. And that was the last normal thought I had for some time.

A head flew past Quinn's shoulder. It was moving too fast for me to pin down whose head it was, but it looked familiar. A spray of blood created a ruddy cloud in the head's wake.

I made a sound. It wasn't a scream or a gasp; more like "Eeeeep."

Quinn stopped dead, though the music didn't for a long moment. He looked in all directions, trying to analyze what was happening and how we could survive it. I'd thought one dance would be okay, but we should have gone with the Were couple. Quinn began pulling me over to the side of the ballroom, and he said, "Backs against the wall." We'd know from which direction the danger was coming: good thinking. But someone cannoned into us and Quinn's hold on my hand was broken.

There was a lot of screaming and a lot of movement. The screaming was all from the Weres and other supes who'd been invited to the party, and the movement was mostly from the vampires, who were looking for their allies amid the chaos. This was where the horrible outfits worn by the king's followers came into their own. It was instantly easy to see who belonged to the king. Of course, that made them an easy target, too, if you didn't happen to like the king and his minions.

A thin black vampire with dreadlocks had whipped a sword with a curved blade out of nowhere, apparently. The blade was bloody, and I thought Dreadlocks was the head-lopper. He was wearing the awful suit, so he was someone I wanted to dodge. If I had any allies here, it wasn't anyone working for Peter Threadgill. I'd gotten behind one of the pillars holding up the ceiling of the west end of the refectory, and I was trying to figure out the safest way from the room when my foot bumped something that shifted. I looked down to see the head. It belonged to Wybert. I wondered for a fraction of a second if it would move or speak, but decapitation is pretty final, no matter what species you are.

"Oh," I moaned, and decided I'd better get a good hold on myself, or I was gonna look just like Wybert, at least in one important respect.

Fighting had broken out throughout the room. I hadn't seen the precipitating incident, but on some pretext the black vampire had attacked Wybert and cut off his head. Since Wybert was one of the queen's bodyguards and Dreadlocks was one of Peter's attendants, the beheading was a pretty decisive act.

The queen and Andre were standing back to back in the middle of the floor. Andre was holding a gun in one hand and a long knife in the other, and the queen had acquired a carving knife from the buffet. There was a circle of white coats surrounding them, and when one fell, another would take its place. This was like Custer's last stand, with the queen standing in for Custer. Sigebert was equally besieged on the bandstand, and the orchestra, part Were or shifter and part vampire, had separated into its various components. Some were joining in the combat, while others were trying to flee. Those who were doing their best to get the hell out of there were clogging the door leading to the long corridor. The effect was a logjam.

The king was under attack from my three friends Rasul, Chester, and Melanie. I was sure I'd find Jade Flower at his back, but she was having her own problems, I was glad to see. Mr. Cataliades was doing his best to—well, it looked like he was just trying to touch her. She was parrying his attempts with her whacking big sword, the sword that had sliced Gladiola in two, but neither of them looked like they were giving up any time soon.

Just then I was knocked flat to the floor, losing my breath for a minute. I struck out, only to have my hand trapped. I was smushed under a big body. "I've got you," Eric said.

"What the hell are you doing?"

"Protecting you," he said. He was smiling with the joy of battle, and his blue eyes were glittering like sapphires. Eric loved a brawl.

"I don't see anybody coming after me," I said. "It seems to me like the queen needs you more than I do. But I appreciate it."

Carried away on a wave of excitement, Eric kissed me long and hard and then scooped up Wybert's head. "Bowling for vampires," he said happily, and flung the disgusting object at the black vampire with an accuracy and force that knocked the sword out of the vampire's hand. Eric was on it with a great leap, and the sword swung on its owner with deadly force. With a war cry that had not been heard in a thousand years, Eric attacked the circle around the queen and Andre with a savagery and abandon that was almost beautiful in its way.

A shifter trying to find another way out of the room knocked against me with enough force to dislodge me from behind my comparatively secure position. Suddenly, there were too many people between me and the pillar, and the way back was blocked. Damn! I could see the door Wybert and his brother had been guarding. The door was across the room, but it was the only empty passage. Any way out of this room was a good way. I began sidling around the walls to reach it, so I wouldn't have to cross the dangerous open spaces.

One of the whitecoats leaped in front of me.

"We're supposed to find you!" he bellowed. He was a young vampire; there were clues, even at such a moment. This vamp had known the amenities of modern life. He had all the signs—superstraight teeth that had known braces, a husky build from modern nutrition, and he was big-boned and tall.

"Look!" I said, and pulled one side of my bodice away. He did, God bless him, and I kicked him in the balls so hard I thought they'd come out through his mouth. That's gonna get a man on the floor, no matter what their nature is. This vampire was no exception. I hurried around him and reached the east wall, the one with the door.

I had maybe a yard to go when someone grabbed my foot, and down I went. I slipped in a pool of blood and landed on my knees in it. It was vamp blood, I could tell by the color.

"Bitch," said Jade Flower. "Whore." I didn't think I'd ever heard her talk before. I could have done without it now. She began dragging me, hand over hand, toward her extended fangs. She wasn't getting up to kill me, because one of her legs was missing. I almost threw up but became more concerned with getting away than with ralphing. My hands scrabbled at the smooth wood floor, and my knees tried to get purchase so I could pull away from the vampire. I didn't know if Jade Flower would die of this terrible wound or not. Vampires could survive so many things that would kill a human, which of course was a big part of the attraction . . . *Snap to, Sookie!* I told myself fiercely.

The shock must be getting to me.

I threw out my hand and managed to get a grip on the door frame. I pulled and pulled, but I couldn't break free from Jade Flower's hold, and her fingers were digging into the flesh of my ankle. Soon she would snap the bones, and then I wouldn't be able to walk.

With my free foot I kicked the little Asian woman in the face. I did it again and again. Her nose was bleeding, and her lips were, too, but she would not let go. I don't think she even felt it.

Then Bill jumped on her back, landing with enough force to break her spine, and her hold on my ankle relaxed. I scrambled away while he raised a carving knife very like the one the queen had had. He sank it into Jade Flower's neck, over and over, and then her head was off and he was looking at me.

He didn't speak, just gave me that long, dark look. Then he was up and gone, and I had to get the hell out of there.

The queen's apartments were dark. That wasn't good. Beyond where the light penetrated from the ballroom, who knew what could be lurking?

There just had to be an outside door through here. The queen wouldn't leave herself bottled up. She'd have a way to get outside. And if I was remembering the orientation of the building, I needed to walk straight ahead to reach the correct wall.

I gathered myself and decided I'd just stride right on through. No more of this skulking around the wall. The hell with it.

And to my surprise, it worked, up to a point. I went through one room—a sitting room, I figured—before I ended up in what must have been the queen's bedroom. A whisper of movement in the room retriggered my fear switch, and I fumbled along the wall for the light. When I flipped it, I found I was in the room with Peter Threadgill. He was facing Andre. A bed was between them, and on the bed was the queen, who had been badly wounded. Andre didn't have his sword, but then neither did Peter Threadgill. Andre did have a gun, and when I turned on the light, he shot the king right in the face. Twice.

There was a door beyond the body of Peter Threadgill. It had to lead to the grounds. I began to sidle around the room, my back pressed against the wall. No one paid a bit of attention to me.

"Andre, if you kill him," the queen said quite calmly, "I'll have to pay a huge fine." She had a hand pressed to her side, and her beautiful orange dress was dark and wet with her blood.

"But wouldn't it be worth it, lady?"

There was a thoughtful silence on the queen's part, while I unlocked about six locks.

"On the whole, yes," Sophie-Anne said. "After all, money isn't everything."

"Oh, *good*," Andre said happily, and raised the gun. He had a stake in the other hand, I saw. I didn't stick around to see how Andre did the deed.

I set off across the lawn in my green evening shoes. Amazingly, the evening shoes were still intact. In fact, they were in better shape than my ankle, which Jade Flower had hurt pretty badly. I was limping by the time I'd taken ten steps. "Watch out for the lion," called the queen, and I looked behind me to see that Andre was carrying her out of the building. I wondered whose side the lion was on.

Then the big cat appeared right in front of me. One minute my escape route was clear, and the next it was filled by a lion. The outside security lights were off, and in the moonlight the beast looked so beautiful and so deadly that fear pulled the air right out of my lungs.

The lion made a low, guttural sound.

"Go away," I said. I had absolutely nothing to fight a lion with, and I was at the end of my rope. "Go away!" I yelled. "Get out of here!"

And it slunk into the bushes.

I don't think that is typical lion behavior. Maybe it smelled the tiger coming, because a second or two later, Quinn appeared, moving like a huge silent dream across the grass. Quinn rubbed his big head against me, and we went over to the wall together. Andre laid down his queen and leaped up on top with grace and ease. For his queen, he pulled apart the razor wire with hands just barely cushioned with his torn coat. Then down he came and carefully lifted Sophie-Anne. He gathered himself and cleared the wall in a bound.

"Well, I can't do that," I said, and even to my own ears, I sounded grumpy. "Can I stand on your back? I'll take my heels off." Quinn snugged up to the wall, and I ran my arm through the sandal straps. I didn't want to hurt the tiger by putting a lot of weight on his back, but I also wanted to get out of there more than I've wanted anything, just about. So, trying to think light thoughts, I balanced on the tiger's back and managed to pull myself, finally, to the top of the wall. I looked down, and it seemed like a very long way to the sidewalk.

After all I'd faced this evening, it seemed stupid to balk at falling a few feet. But I sat on the wall, telling myself I was an idiot, for several long moments. Then I managed to flip over onto my stomach, let myself down as far as I could reach, and said out loud, "One, two, three!" Then I fell.

For a couple of minutes I just lay there, stunned at how the evening had turned out.

Here I was, lying on a sidewalk in historical New Orleans, with my boobs hanging out of my dress, my hair coming down, my sandals on my arm, and a large tiger licking my face. Quinn had bounded over with relative ease.

"Do you think it would be better to walk back as a tiger, or as a large naked man?" I asked the tiger. "Because either way, you might attract some attention. I think you stand a better chance of getting shot if you're a tiger, myself."

"That will not be necessary," said a voice, and Andre loomed above me. "I am here with the queen in her car, and we will take you where you need to go."

"That's mighty nice of you," I said, as Quinn began to change back.

"Her Majesty feels that she owes you," Andre said.

"I don't see it that way," I said. Why was I being so frank, now? Couldn't I just keep my mouth shut? "After all, if I hadn't found the bracelet and given it back, the king would have . . ."

"Started the war tonight anyway," Andre said, helping me to my feet. He reached out and quite impersonally pushed my right breast under the scanty lime-green fabric. "He would have accused the queen of breaking her side of the contract, which held that all gifts must be held in honor as tokens of the marriage. He would have brought suit against the queen, and she would have lost almost everything and been dishonored. He was ready to go either way, but when the queen was wearing the second bracelet, he had to go with violence. Ra Shawn set it off by beheading Wybert for bumping against him." Ra Shawn had been Dreadlock's name, I assumed.

I wasn't sure I got all that, but I was equally sure Quinn could explain it to me at a time when I had more brain cells to spare for the information.

"He was so disappointed when he saw she had the bracelet! And it was the right one!" Andre said merrily. He was turning into a babbling brook, that Andre. He helped me into the car. "Where was it?" asked the queen, who was stretched across one of the seats. Her bleeding had stopped, and only the way she was holding her lips indicated what pain she was in.

"It was in the can of coffee that looked sealed," I said. "Hadley was real good with arts and crafts, and she'd opened the can real carefully, popped the bracelet inside, and resealed it with a glue gun." There was a lot more to explain, about Mr. Cataliades and Gladiola and Jade Flower, but I was too tired to volunteer information.

"How'd you get it past the search?" the queen asked. "I'm sure the searchers were checking for it."

"I had the bracelet part on under my bandage," I said. "The diamond stood out too far, though, so I had to prize it out. I put it in a tampon holder. The vampire who did the searching didn't think of pulling out the tampon, and she didn't really know how it was supposed to look, since she hadn't had a period in centuries."

"But it was put together," the queen said.

"Oh, I went into the ladies room after I'd had my purse searched. I had a little tube of superglue in my purse, too."

The queen didn't seem to know what to say. "Thank you," she told me, after a long pause. Quinn had climbed into the back with us, quite bare, and I leaned against him. Andre got into the driver's seat, and we glided off.

He dropped us off in the courtyard. Amelia was sitting on the pavement in her lawn chair, a glass of wine in her hand.

When we emerged, she set the glass down very carefully on the ground and then looked us over from head to toe.

"Okay, don't know how to react," she said, finally. The big car glided out of the courtyard as Andre took the queen to some safe hideaway. I didn't ask, because I didn't want to know.

"I'll tell you tomorrow," I said. "The moving truck will be here tomorrow afternoon, and the queen promised me people to load it and drive it. I have to get back to Bon Temps."

The prospect of going home seemed so sweet I could taste it on my tongue.

"So you got lots to do at home?" Amelia asked, as Quinn and I began going up the stairs. I guessed Quinn could sleep in the same bed. We were both too tired to plunge into anything; tonight was not the night to begin a relationship, if I hadn't already begun one. Maybe I had.

"Well, I have a lot of weddings to go to," I said. "I have to get back to work, too."

"Got an empty guest bedroom?"

I stopped about halfway up the stairs. "I might. Would you be needing one?"

It was hard to tell in the poor light, but Amelia might be looking embarrassed. "I tried something new with Bob," she said. "And it didn't exactly work out right."

"Where is he?" I asked. "In the hospital?"

"No, right there," she said. She was pointing at a garden gnome.

"Tell me you're joking," I said.

"I'm joking," she said. "This is Bob." She picked up a big black cat with a white chest that had been curled up in an empty planter. I hadn't even noticed him. "Isn't he cute?"

"Sure, bring him along," I said. "I've always been fond of cats."

"Babe," said Quinn, "I'm glad to hear you say that. I was too tired to completely change."

For the first time, I really looked at Quinn.

Now he had a tail.

"You're definitely sleeping on the floor," I said.

"Ah, babe."

"I mean it. Tomorrow you'll be able to be all human, right?"

"Sure. I've changed too many times lately. I just need some rest."

Amelia was looking at the tail with wide eyes. "See you

tomorrow, Sookie," she said. "We'll have us a little road trip. And then I'll get to stay with you for a while!"

"We'll have such fun," I said wearily, trudging up the rest of the stairs and feeling profoundly glad I'd stuck my door key in my underwear. Quinn was too tired to watch me retrieve it. I let the remnants of the dress fall back into place while I unlocked the door. "Such fun."

Later, after I'd showered and while Quinn was in the bathroom himself, I heard a tentative knock on the door. I was decent enough in my sleep pants and tank top. Though I wanted to ignore it more than anything, I opened the door.

Bill was looking pretty good for someone who'd fought in a war. The tuxedo would never be functional again, but he wasn't bleeding, and whatever cuts he might have sustained had already healed over.

"I have to talk to you," he said, and his voice was so quiet and limp that I took a step out of the apartment. I sat down on the gallery floor, and he sat with me.

"You have to let me say this, just once," he said. "I loved you. I love you."

I raised a hand to protest, and he said, "No, let me finish. She sent me there, true. But when I met you—after I came to know you—I really . . . loved you."

How long after he'd taken me to bed had this supposed love come about? How could I possibly believe him, since he'd lied so convincingly from the very moment I'd met him—playing disinterested because he could read my fascination with the first vampire I'd ever met?

"I risked my life for you," I said, the words coming out in a halting sequence. "I gave Eric power over me forever, for your sake, when I took his blood. I killed someone for you. This is not something I take for granted, even if you do . . . even if that's everyday existence for you. It's not, for me. I don't know if I can ever not hate you."

I got up, slowly and painfully, and to my relief he didn't

make the mistake of trying to help me. "You probably saved my life tonight," I said, looking down at him. "And I thank you for that. But don't come into Merlotte's any more, don't hang around in my woods, and don't do anything else for me. I don't want to see you again."

"I love you," he said stubbornly, as if that fact were so amazing and such an undeniable truth that I should believe him. Well, I had, and look at where it had gotten me.

"Those words are not a magical formula," I said. "They're not going to open my heart to you."

Bill was over a hundred and thirty years old, but at that moment I felt I could match him. I dragged myself inside, shut the door behind me and locked it, and made myself go down the hall to the bedroom.

Quinn was drying himself off, and he turned around to show me his muscular derriere. "Fur-free," he said. "Can I share the bed?"

"Yes," I said, and crawled in. He got in the other side, and he was asleep in thirty seconds. After a minute or two, I slid over in the bed and put my head on his chest.

I listened to his heartbeat.

23 ~

WHAT WAS THE DEAL WITH JADE FLOWER?" AMELIA asked the next day. Everett was driving the U-Haul, and Amelia and I were following in her little car. Quinn had left the next morning by the time I'd gotten up, leaving me a note telling me he was going to call me after he'd hired someone to take Jake Purifoy's place and after his next job, which was in Huntsville, Alabama—a Rite of Ascension, he said, though I had no idea what that was. He ended the note with a very personal comment about the lime-green dress, which I won't repeat here.

Amelia had her bags packed by the time I'd dressed, and Everett was directing two husky men in loading up the boxes I wanted to take back to Bon Temps. When he returned, he would take the furniture I didn't want to Goodwill. I'd offered it to him, but he'd looked at the fake antiques and politely said they weren't his style. I'd tossed my own stuff in Amelia's trunk, and off we'd driven. Bob the cat was in his own cage on the backseat. It was lined with towels and also held a food and water bowl, which was kind of messy. Bob's litter box was on the floorboard.

"My mentor found out what I'd done," Amelia said gloomily. "She's very, very unhappy with me."

I wasn't surprised, but it didn't seem tactful to say so, when Amelia had been such a help to me.

"He is missing his life now," I pointed out, as mildly as I could manage.

"Well, true, but he's having a hell of an experience," Amelia said, in the voice of someone determined to look on the bright side. "I'll make it up to him. Somehow."

I wasn't sure this was something you could "make up" to someone. "I'll bet you can get him back to himself soon," I said, trying to sound confident. "There are some really nice witches in Shreveport who might help." If Amelia could conquer her prejudice against Wiccans.

"Great," the witch said, looking more cheerful. "In the meantime, what the hell happened last night? Tell me in detail."

I figured it was all over the supernatural community today, so I might as well spill the beans. I told Amelia the whole story.

"So how did Cataliades know Jade Flower had killed Gladiola?" Amelia asked.

"Um, I told him," I said, my voice small.

"How'd you know?"

"When the Pelts told me they hadn't hired anyone to watch the house, I figured the murderer was someone sent by Peter Threadgill to delay my getting the message from Cataliades. Peter Threadgill knew all along that the queen had lost the bracelet to Hadley. Maybe he had spies among the queen's own people, or maybe one of her dumber followers, like Wybert, let it slip. It wouldn't be hard to watch the movements of the two goblin girls the queen used as messengers. When one of them came to deliver the queen's message to me, Jade Flower followed her and killed her. The wound was pretty drastic, and after I saw Jade Flower's sword and watched her whip it out so fast I couldn't see it move, I figured she was a likely candidate for the designated killer. Plus, the queen had said if Andre was in New Orleans, everyone had to assume she was, too . . . so the reverse had to be true, right? If the king was in New Orleans, everyone would assume Jade Flower was, too. But she was outside my house, in the woods." I shuddered all over at the memory. "I found out for sure after calling a lot of gas stations. I talked to a guy who definitely remembered Jade Flower."

"So why did Hadley steal the bracelet?"

"Jealousy, I guess, and the desire to put the queen in a bad spot. I don't think Hadley understood the implications of what she'd done, and by the time she did, it was too late. The king had laid his plans. Jade Flower watched Hadley for a while, snatched the opportunity to take Jake Purifoy and kill him. They hoped it would be blamed on Hadley. Anything that would discredit Hadley would discredit the queen. They had no way of knowing she would turn him."

"What will happen to Jake now?" Amelia looked troubled. "I liked him. He was a nice guy."

"He still may be. He's just a vampire nice guy."

"I'm not sure there's such a thing," my companion said quietly.

"Some days, I'm not sure either." We rode for a while in silence.

"Well, tell me about Bon Temps," Amelia said, to get us out of our conversational doldrums.

I began to tell her about the town, and the bar where

I worked, and the wedding shower I'd been invited to attend, and all the upcoming weddings.

"Sounds pretty good," Amelia said. "Hey, I know I kind of asked myself along. Do you mind, I mean, really?"

"No," I said, with a speed that surprised even me. "No, it'll be nice to have company . . . for a while," I added cautiously. "What will you do about your house in New Orleans while you're gone?"

"Everett said he wouldn't mind living in the upper apartment, because his mom was getting kind of hard to take. Since he's got such a good job with Cataliades, he can afford it. He'll watch my plants and stuff until I get back. He can always e-mail me." Amelia had a laptop in her trunk, so for the first time there'd be a computer in the Stackhouse home. There was a pause, and then she said, her voice tentative, "How are you feeling now? I mean, with the ex and all?"

I considered. "I have a big hole in my heart," I said. "But it'll close over."

"I don't want to sound all Dr. Phil," she said. "But don't let the scab seal the pain in, okay?"

"That's good advice," I said. "I hope I can manage it."

I'd been gone a few days, and they'd been eventful ones. As we drew closer to Bon Temps, I wondered if Tanya had succeeded in getting Sam to ask her out. I wondered if I'd have to tell Sam about Tanya's role as spy. Eric didn't have to be confused about me any more, since our big secret was out. He didn't have a hold on me. Would the Pelts stick to their word? Maybe Bill would go on a long trip. Maybe a stake would accidentally fall on his chest while he was gone.

I hadn't heard from Jason while I was in New Orleans. I wondered if he was still planning on getting married. I hoped Crystal had recovered. I wondered if Dr. Ludwig accepted insurance payments. And the Bellefleur double wedding should be an interesting event, even if I was working while I was there.

I took a deep breath. My life was not so bad, I told myself, and I began to believe that was true. I had a new boyfriend, maybe; I had a new friend, surely; and I had events to look forward to. This was all good, and I should be grateful.

So what if I was obliged to attend a vampire conference as part of the queen's entourage? We'd stay in a fancy hotel, dress up a lot, attend long boring meetings, if everything other people had told me about conferences was true.

Gosh, how bad could that be?

Better not to think about it.

GOLLANCZ
ROMANCZ

ALL TOGETHER DEAD

Also by Charlaine Harris

SOOKIE STACKHOUSE

Dead Until Dark

Living Dead in Dallas

Club Dead

Dead to the World

Dead as a Doornail

Definitely Dead

All Together Dead

From Dead to Worse

Dead and Gone

HARPER CONNELLY

Grave Sight

Grave Surprise

An Ice Cold Grave

Grave Secret

ALL TOGETHER DEAD

CHARLAINE HARRIS

First published in Great Britain in 2008 by
Gollancz
An imprint of the Orion Publishing Group
Orion House, 5 Upper St Martin's Lane, London WC2H 9EA
An Hachette UK Company

This edition published in Great Britain in 2009 by
Gollancz

7 9 10 8

A CIP catalogue record for this book
is available from the British Library

ISBN 978 0 575 08392 9

Printed and bound in the UK by
CPI Mackays, Chatham ME5 8TD

www.orionbooks.co.uk

This book is dedicated to a few of the women I'm proud to call "friend": Jodi Dabson Bollendorf, Kate Buker, Toni Kelner, Dana Cameron, Joan Hess, Eve Sandstrom, Paula Woldan, and Betty Epley. All of you have meant something different to me, and I feel grateful to know you.

Acknowledgments

There are a few people I've thanked before and need to thank again: Robin Burcell, former cop and present writer, and FBI Agent George Fong, who were great about answering my questions about security and bomb disposal. I appreciate the input of Sam Saucedo, the former newscaster and now writer, who explained a few things about border politics to me. I also need to thank S. J. Rozan, who was happy to answer my questions about architecture, though the vampire part was a distinct shock. I may have misused the information given me, but it was in a good cause. As always, I owe a great debt to my friend Toni L. P. Kelner, who read my first draft without laughing in my face. And my new continuity person, Debi Murray, gets a tip of the hat; from now on if I make mistakes, I have someone to blame. I owe a lot to the many wonderful readers who visit my website (www.charlaineharris.com) and leave messages of encouragement and interest. Beverly Batillo, my fan club president, has given me a boost many a time when I was down in the dumps.

1

THE SHREVEPORT VAMPIRE BAR WOULD BE OPENING late tonight. I was running behind, and I'd automatically gone to the front door, the public door, only to be halted by a neatly lettered sign, red Gothic script on white cardboard: WE'LL BE READY TO GREET YOU WITH A BITE TONIGHT, AT EIGHT O'CLOCK. PLEASE EXCUSE OUR DELAYED OPENING. It was signed "The Staff of Fangtasia."

It was the third week in September, so the red neon FANGTASIA sign was already on. The sky was almost pitch-black. I stood with one foot inside my car for a minute, enjoying the mild evening and the faint, dry smell of vampire that lingered around the club. Then I drove around to the back and parked beside several other cars lined up at the employee entrance. I was only five minutes late, but it looked like everyone else had beaten me to the meeting. I rapped on the door. I waited.

I'd raised my hand to knock again when Pam, Eric's second-in-command, opened the door. Pam was based at the bar, but she had other duties in Eric's various business dealings. Though vampires had gone public five years ago and turned their best face to the world, they were still pretty secretive about their moneymaking methods, and sometimes I wondered how much of America the undead actually owned. Eric, the owner of Fangtasia, was a true vampire in the keeping-things-to-himself department. Of course, in his long, long existence he'd had to be.

"Come in, my telepathic friend," Pam said, gesturing dramatically. She was wearing her work outfit: the filmy, trailing black gown that all the tourists who came into the bar seemed to expect from female vampires. (When Pam got to pick her own clothing, she was a pastels-and-twinset kind of woman.) Pam had the palest, straightest blond hair you ever saw; in fact, she was ethereally lovely, with a kind of deadly edge. The deadly edge was what a person shouldn't forget.

"How you doing?" I asked politely.

"I am doing exceptionally well," she said. "Eric is full of happiness."

Eric Northman, the vampire sheriff of Area Five, had made Pam a vampire, and she was both obliged and compelled to do his bidding. That was part of the deal of becoming undead: you were always in sway to your maker. But Pam had told me more than once that Eric was a good boss to have, and that he would let her go her own way if and when she desired to do so. In fact, she'd been living in Minnesota until Eric had purchased Fangtasia and called her to help him run it.

Area Five was most of northwestern Louisiana, which until a month ago had been the economically weaker half of the state. Since Hurricane Katrina, the balance of power in

Louisiana had shifted dramatically, especially in the vampire community.

"How is that delicious brother of yours, Sookie? And your shape-shifting boss?" Pam said.

"My delicious brother is making noises about getting married, like everyone else in Bon Temps," I said.

"You sound a bit depressed." Pam cocked her head to one side and regarded me like a sparrow eyeing a worm.

"Well, maybe a tad wee bit," I said.

"You must keep busy," Pam said. "Then you won't have time to mope."

Pam *loved* "Dear Abby." Lots of vampires scrutinized the column daily. Their solutions to some of the writers' problems would just make you scream. Literally. Pam had already advised me that I could only be imposed on if I permitted it, and that I needed to be more selective in picking my friends. I was getting emotional-health counseling from a vampire.

"I am," I said. "Keeping busy, that is. I'm working, I've still got my roommate from New Orleans, and I'm going to a wedding shower tomorrow. Not for Jason and Crystal. Another couple."

Pam had paused, her hand on the doorknob of Eric's office. She considered my statement, her brows drawn together. "I am not remembering what a wedding shower is, though I've heard of it," she said. She brightened. "They'll get married in a bathroom? No, I've heard the term before, surely. A woman wrote to Abby that she hadn't gotten a thank-you note for a large shower gift. They get . . . presents?"

"You got it," I said. "A shower is a party for someone who's about to get married. Sometimes the shower is for the couple, and they're both there. But usually only the bride is the honoree, and all the other people at the party are women. Everyone brings a gift. The theory is that this way the couple can start life with everything they need. We do the same thing when a couple's expecting a baby. Course, then it's a baby shower."

"Baby shower," Pam repeated. She smiled in a chilly way. It was enough to put frost on your pumpkin, seeing that upcurve of the lips. "I like the term," she said. She knocked on Eric's office door and then opened it. "Eric," she said, "maybe someday one of the waitresses will get pregnant, and we can go to a *baby shower*!"

"That would be something to see," said Eric, lifting his golden head from the papers on his desk. The sheriff registered my presence, gave me a hard look, and decided to ignore me. Eric and I had issues.

Despite the fact that the room was full of people waiting for his attention, Eric lay down his pen and stood to stretch his tall and magnificent body, perhaps for my benefit. As usual, Eric was in tight jeans and a Fangtasia T-shirt, black with the white stylized fangs that the bar used as its trademark. "Fangtasia" was written in jazzy red script across the white points in the same style as the neon sign outside. If Eric turned around, the back would read "The Bar with a Bite." Pam had given me one when Fangtasia first got into marketing its own stuff.

Eric made the shirt look good, and I remembered all too well what was underneath it.

I tore my gaze away from Eric's stretch to look around the room. There were lots of other vampires crammed into the smallish space, but till you saw them you didn't know they were there, they were so still and silent. Clancy, the bar manager, had claimed one of the two visitor chairs before the desk. Clancy had just barely survived the previous year's Witch War, but he hadn't come out unscathed. The witches had drained Clancy near to the point of no return. By the time Eric discovered Clancy, tracing his smell to a Shreveport cemetery, Clancy was one Vacutainer short of dead. During his long recovery, the red-haired vamp had grown bitter and snappish. Now he grinned at me, showing some fang. "You can sit in my lap, Sookie," he said, patting his thighs.

I smiled back, but not like my heart was in it. "No, thanks, Clancy," I said politely. Clancy's flirting had always had an edge to it, and now that edge was razor sharp. He was one of those vamps I'd rather not be alone with. Though he ran the bar capably, and he had never laid a finger on me, he still set off warning bells. I can't read vampire minds, which was why I found it refreshing to hang with them, but when I felt that tingle of warning, I did find myself wishing I could just dip into Clancy's head and find out what was going on in there.

Felicia, the newest bartender, was sitting on the couch, along with Indira and Maxwell Lee. It was like the vampire Rainbow Coalition meeting. Felicia was a happy mixture of African and Caucasian, and she was almost six feet tall, so there was more loveliness to appreciate. Maxwell Lee was one of the darkest men I'd ever seen. Little Indira was the daughter of Indian immigrants.

There were four more people in the room (using the term "people" loosely), and each one of them upset me, though in varying degrees.

One of them was someone I didn't acknowledge. I'd taken a page from the Were rule book and treated him like an outlawed member of my pack: I abjured him. I didn't speak his name, I didn't speak to him, I didn't recognize his existence. (Of course, this was my ex, Bill Compton—not that I recognized that he was in the room, brooding away in a corner.)

Leaning against the wall next to him was ancient Thalia, who was possibly even older than Eric. She was as small as Indira and very pale, with tightly waving black hair—and she was extremely rude.

To my amazement, some humans found that a complete turn-on. Thalia actually had a devoted following who seemed thrilled when she used her stilted English to tell them to fuck off. I'd discovered she even had a website, established and maintained by fans. Go figure. Pam had told me that when Eric had agreed to let Thalia live in Shreveport, it was the equivalent of keeping a badly trained pit bull tethered in the yard. Pam had not approved.

These undead citizens all lived in Area Five. To live and work under Eric's protection, they'd all sworn fealty to him. So they were required to devote a certain amount of their time to doing his bidding, even if they didn't work at the bar. There were a few extra vampires in Shreveport these days, since Katrina; just like a lot of humans, they had to go somewhere. Eric hadn't decided what to do about the undead refugees, and they hadn't been invited to the meeting.

Tonight there were two visitors in Fangtasia, one of whom outranked Eric.

Andre was the personal bodyguard of Sophie-Anne Leclerq, the Queen of Louisiana. The queen, at present, was an evacuee in Baton Rouge. Andre looked very young, maybe sixteen; his face was baby smooth, his pale hair was thick and heavy. Andre had lived a long existence caring only for Sophie-Anne, his maker and savior. He was not wearing his saber tonight, because he wasn't acting as her bodyguard, but I was sure Andre was armed with something—knife or gun. Andre himself was a lethal weapon, with or without an aid.

Just as Andre was about to speak to me, from beyond his chair a deep voice said, "Hey, Sookie." Our second visitor, Jake Purifoy. I made myself hold still when every impulse I had was telling me to get out of the office. I was being an idiot. If I hadn't run screaming at the sight of Andre, Jake shouldn't make me think of bolting. I forced myself to nod to the nice-looking young man who still looked alive. But

I knew my greeting didn't look natural. He filled me with a terrible blend of pity and fear.

Jake, born a Were, had been attacked by a vampire and bled to the point of death. In what had been perhaps a mistaken gesture of mercy, my cousin Hadley (another vampire) had discovered Jake's nearly lifeless body and brought Jake over. This might have been considered a good deed; but as it turned out, no one had really appreciated Hadley's kindness . . . not even Jake himself. No one had ever heard of a turned Were before: Weres disliked and distrusted vampires, and the feeling was heartily reciprocated. The going was very rough for Jake, who occupied a lonely no-man's-land. The queen had given him a place in her service, since no one else had stepped forward.

Jake, blind with bloodlust, had gone after me as his first vampire snack. I had a still-red scar on my arm as a result.

What a wonderful evening this was turning out to be.

"Miss Stackhouse," said Andre, rising from Eric's second guest chair. He bowed. This was a true tribute, and it lifted my spirits a bit.

"Mr. Andre," I said, bowing back. Andre swept his hand to indicate his politely vacated seat, and since that solved my placement problem, I accepted.

Clancy looked chagrined. He should have given me his chair, since he was the lower-ranked vampire. Andre's action had pointed that out as clearly as a blinking neon arrow. I tried hard not to smile.

"How is Her Majesty?" I asked, trying to be just as courteous as Andre had been. It would be stretching it to say I liked Sophie-Anne, but I sure respected her.

"That's part of the reason I am here tonight," he said. "Eric, can we get started now?" A gentle chiding for Eric's time-wasting tactics, I thought. Pam folded to the floor beside my chair, crouched on the balls of her feet.

"Yes, we're all here. Go ahead, Andre. You have the floor," Eric said with a little smile at his own modern terminology. He slumped back down into his chair, extending his long legs to rest his feet on the corner of his desk.

"Your queen is living in the Area Four sheriff's house in Baton Rouge," Andre said to the little assemblage. "Gervaise was very gracious in extending his hospitality."

Pam cocked an eyebrow at me. Gervaise would have lost his head if he *hadn't* extended his hospitality.

"But staying at Gervaise's place can only be a temporary solution," Andre continued. "We've been down to New Orleans several times since the disaster. Here's a report of our property's condition."

Though none of the vampires moved, I felt their attention had heightened.

"The queen's headquarters lost most of its roof, so there was extensive water damage on the second floor and in the attic area. Furthermore, a large piece of someone else's roof landed inside the building, causing a pileup of debris and some holes in walls—problems like that. While we're drying the inside, the roof is still covered with blue plastic. One reason I came up this way is to find a contractor who will start reroofing immediately. So far, I haven't had any luck, so if any of you have personal influence with some human who does this kind of work, I need your help. On the ground floor, there was a lot of cosmetic damage. Some water came in. We had some looters, too."

"Maybe the queen should remain in Baton Rouge," Clancy said maliciously. "I'm sure Gervaise would be overwhelmed with delight at the prospect of hosting her permanently."

So Clancy was a suicidal idiot.

"A delegation of New Orleans leaders came to visit our

queen in Baton Rouge to ask that she return to the city," Andre said, ignoring Clancy completely. "The human leaders think that if the vampires will return to New Orleans, tourism will pick up again." Andre fixed Eric with a cold gaze. "In the meantime, the queen has talked to the four other sheriffs about the financial aspect of restoring the New Orleans buildings."

Eric gave an almost imperceptible inclination of the head. Impossible to say what he felt about being taxed for the queen's repairs.

New Orleans had been the place to go for vampires and those who wanted to be around them ever since Anne Rice had been proven right about their existence. The city was like Disneyland for vamps. But since Katrina, all that had gone to hell, of course, along with so much else. Even Bon Temps was feeling the storm's effect, and had been ever since Katrina had hit land. Our little town was still crowded with people who had fled from the south.

"What about the queen's entertainment estate?" asked Eric. The queen had bought an old monastery at the edge of the Garden District for entertaining large numbers of people, both vamp and non-vamp. Though surrounded by a wall, the estate was not considered easily defensible (since it was a registered building, historic and unchangeable, the windows couldn't be blocked up), so the queen couldn't actually live there. I thought of it as her party barn.

"It didn't suffer much damage," Andre said. "There were looters there, too. Of course, they left a trace of their smell." Vampires were second only to Weres in their tracking abilities. "One of them shot the lion."

I felt sorry for that. I'd liked the lion, sort of.

"Do you need help with the apprehension?" Eric asked.

Andre arched an eyebrow.

"I only ask because your numbers are low," Eric said.

"No, already taken care of," Andre said, and smiled just a tad.

I tried not to think about that.

"Aside from the lion and the looting, how was the estate?" Eric said to get the discussion of the storm damage back on track.

"The queen can stay there while she views the other properties," Andre continued, "but at the most for a night or two only."

There were tiny nods all around.

"Our loss of personnel," Andre said, moving on in his agenda. All the vampires tensed a bit, even Jake, the newbie. "Our initial assessment was modest, as you know. We assumed some would come forward after the impact of the storm was absorbed. But only ten have surfaced: five here, three in Baton Rouge, two in Monroe. It seems that we have lost thirty of our number just in Louisiana. Mississippi has lost at least ten."

There were tiny sounds and movements all over the room as the Shreveport vampires reacted to the news. The concentration of vamps, both resident and visiting, had been high in New Orleans. If Katrina had visited Tampa with that much force, the number of dead and missing would have been much lower.

I raised my hand to speak. "What about Bubba?" I asked when Andre nodded at me. I hadn't seen or heard of Bubba since Katrina. You'd know Bubba if you saw him. Anyone on earth would know him; at least, anyone over a certain age. He hadn't quite died on that bathroom floor in Memphis. Not quite. But his brain had been affected before he was brought over, and he wasn't a very good vampire.

"Bubba's alive," said Andre. "He hid in a crypt and survived on small mammals. He isn't doing too well mentally, so the queen has sent him up to Tennessee to stay with the Nashville community for a while."

"Andre has brought me a list of those that are missing," Eric said. "I'll post it after the meeting."

I'd known a few of the queen's guards, too, and I would be glad to find out how they'd fared.

I had another question, so I waved my hand.

"Yes, Sookie?" Andre asked. His empty gaze fixed me in place, and I was sorry I'd asked to speak.

"You know what I wonder, y'all? I wonder if one of the kings or queens attending this summit, or whatever you all call it, has a—like a weather predictor, or something like that on staff."

Plenty of blank stares were aimed my way, though Andre was interested.

"Because, look, the summit, or conference, or whatever, was supposed to take place in late spring originally. But—delay, delay, delay, right? And then Katrina hit. If the summit had started when it was supposed to, the queen could have gone in a powerful position. She would have had a big war chest and a full quiver of vamps, and maybe they wouldn't have been so anxious to prosecute her for the king's death. The queen would have gotten anything she asked for, probably. Instead, she's going in as"—I started to say "a beggar," but I considered Andre just in time—"much less powerful." I'd been afraid they'd laugh or maybe ridicule me, but the silence that followed was intensely thoughtful.

"That's one of the things you'll need to look for at the summit," Andre said. "Now that you've given me the idea, it seems oddly possible. Eric?"

"Yes, I think there is something in that," Eric said, staring at me. "Sookie is good at thinking outside the box."

Pam smiled up at me from beside my elbow.

"What about the suit filed by Jennifer Cater?" Clancy asked Andre. He'd been looking increasingly uncomfortable in the chair he'd thought he was so clever to snag.

You could have heard a pin drop. I didn't know what the hell the red-haired vampire was talking about, but I thought it would be better to find out from the conversation than to ask.

"It's still active," Andre said.

Pam whispered, "Jennifer Cater was in training to become Peter Threadgill's lieutenant. She was in Arkansas managing his affairs when the violence erupted."

I nodded to let Pam know I appreciated her filling me in. The Arkansas vampires, though they hadn't gone through a hurricane, had undergone quite a reduction in their own ranks, thanks to Louisiana's group.

Andre said, "The queen has responded to the suit by testifying that she had to kill Peter to save her own life. Of course, she offered reparation to the common fund."

"Why not to Arkansas?" I whispered to Pam.

"Because the queen maintains that since Peter is dead, Arkansas goes to her, according to the marriage contract," Pam murmured. "She can't make reparation to herself. If Jennifer Cater wins her suit, not only will the queen lose Arkansas, she'll have to pay Arkansas a fine. A huge one. And make other restitution."

Andre began to drift around the room soundlessly, the only indication that he was unhappy about the topic.

"Do we even have that much money after the disaster?" Clancy asked. It was an unwise question.

"The queen hopes the suit will be dismissed," Andre said, again ignoring Clancy. Andre's permanently teenage face was quite blank. "But apparently the court is prepared to hear a trial. Jennifer is charging that our queen lured Threadgill to New Orleans, away from his own territory, having planned all along to start the war and assassinate him." This time Andre's voice came from behind me.

"But that wasn't what happened at all," I said. And Sophie-Anne hadn't killed the king. I'd been present at his death. The vampire standing behind me right at this moment had killed Threadgill, and I'd thought at the time he was justified.

I felt Andre's cold fingers brush my neck as I sat there. How I knew the fingers were Andre's, I couldn't tell you; but the light touch, the second of contact, made me suddenly focus on an awful fact: I was the only witness to the death of the king, besides Andre and Sophie-Anne.

I'd never put it to myself in those terms, and for a moment, I swear, my heart stopped beating. At that skipped beat, I drew the gaze of at least half the vamps in the room. Eric's eyes widened as he looked at my face. And then my heart beat again, and the moment was over as if it never had been. But Eric's hand twitched on the desk, and I knew that he would not forget that second, and he would want to know what it meant.

"So you think the trial will be held?" Eric asked Andre.

"If the queen had been going to the summit as the ruler of New Orleans—New Orleans as it was—I believe the sitting court would have negotiated some kind of settlement between Jennifer and the queen. Maybe something involving Jennifer being raised to a position of power as the queen's deputy and getting a large bonus; something like that. But as things are now . . ." There was a long silence while we filled in the blanks. New Orleans wasn't as it had been, might never be so again. Sophie-Anne was a lame duck right now. "Now, because of Jennifer's persistence, I think the court will pursue it," Andre said, and then fell silent.

"We know there's no truth to the allegations," a clear,

cold voice said from the corner. I'd been doing a good job of ignoring the presence of my ex, Bill. But it didn't come naturally to me. "Eric was there. I was there. Sookie was there," the vampire (Nameless, I told myself) continued.

That was true. Jennifer Cater's allegation, that the queen had lured her king to her party barn in order to kill him, was completely bogus. The bloodbath had been precipitated by the decapitation of one of the queen's men by one of Peter Threadgill's.

Eric smiled reminiscently. He'd enjoyed the battle. "I accounted for the one who started it," he said. "The king did his best to trap the queen in an indiscretion, but he didn't, thanks to our Sookie. When his plot didn't work, he resorted to a simple frontal attack." Eric added, "I haven't seen Jennifer in twenty years. She's risen fast. She must be ruthless."

Andre had stepped to my right and within my line of vision, which was a relief. He nodded. Again, all the vampires in the room made a little group movement, not quite in unison but eerily close. I had seldom felt so alien: the only warmblood in a room full of animated dead creatures.

"Yes," Andre said. "Ordinarily the queen would want a full contingent there to support her. But since we're forced to practice economy, the numbers going have been cut." Again, Andre came near enough to touch me, just a brush of my cheek.

The idea triggered a kind of mini-revelation: *This was how it felt to be a normal person.* I hadn't the slightest idea of the true intentions and plans of my companions. This was how real people lived every day of their lives. It was frightening but exciting; a lot like walking through a crowded room blindfolded. How did regular people stand the suspense of day-to-day living?

"The queen wants this woman close to her in meetings, since other humans will be there," Andre continued. He was speaking strictly to Eric. The rest of us might as well not have been in the room. "She wants to know their thoughts. Stan is bringing his telepath. Do you know the man?"

"I'm sitting right here," I muttered, not that anyone paid any attention but Pam, who gave me a sunny smile. Then, with all those cold eyes fixed on me, I realized that they were waiting for me, that Andre had been addressing me directly. I'd become so used to the vamps talking over and around me that I'd been taken by surprise. I mentally replayed Andre's remarks until I understood he was asking me a question.

"I've only met one other telepath in my life, and he was living in Dallas, so I'm supposing it's the same guy—Barry the Bellboy. He was working at the vamp hotel in Dallas when I picked up on his, ah, gift."

"What do you know about him?"

"He's younger than me, and he's weaker than me—or at least he was at the time. He'd never accepted what he was, the way that I had." I shrugged. That was the sum total of my knowledge.

"Sookie will be there," Eric told Andre. "She is the best at what she does."

That was flattering, though I faintly recalled Eric saying he'd encountered only one telepath previously. It was also infuriating, since he was implying to Andre that my excellence was to Eric's credit instead of my own.

Though I was looking forward to seeing something outside of my little town, I found myself wishing I could think of a way to back out of the trip to Rhodes. But months ago I'd agreed to attend this vampire summit as a paid employee of the queen's. And for the past month, I'd been working long hours at Merlotte's Bar to bank enough time so the other barmaids wouldn't mind covering for me for a week. My boss, Sam, had been helping me keep track of my overage with a little chart.

"Clancy will stay here to run the bar," Eric said.

"This human gets to go while I have to remain?" the red-haired manager said. He was really, really unhappy with Eric's decision. "I won't get to see any of the fun."

"That's right," Eric said pleasantly. If Clancy had thought of saying something else negative, he took one look at Eric's face and clamped down on it. "Felicia will stay to help you. Bill, you will stay."

"No," said that calm, cool voice from the corner. "The queen requires me. I worked hard on that database, and she's asked me to market it at the summit to help recoup her losses."

Eric looked like a statue for a minute, and then he moved, a little lift of his eyebrows. "Yes, I'd forgotten your computer skills," he said. He might have been saying, "Oh, I'd forgotten you can spell *cat*," for all the interest or respect he showed. "I suppose you need to be with us, then. Maxwell?"

"If it's your will, I will stay." Maxwell Lee wanted to make it clear that he knew a thing or two about being a good underling. He glanced around at the assemblage to underscore his point.

Eric nodded. I guessed that Maxwell would get a nice toy for Christmas, and Bill—whoops, Nameless—would get ashes and switches. "Then you'll remain here. And you, too, Thalia. But you must promise me that you will be good in the bar." Thalia's required tour of duty in the bar, which simply consisted of sitting around being mysterious and vampiric a couple of evenings a week, did not always go by without incident.

Thalia, perpetually sullen and broody, gave a curt nod. "I don't want to go, anyway," she muttered. Her round black eyes showed nothing but contempt for the world. She had seen too much in her very long life, and she hadn't enjoyed herself in a few centuries, was the way I read it. I tried to avoid Thalia as much as possible. I was surprised she'd even hang with the other vamps; she seemed like a rogue to me.

"She has no desire to lead," Pam breathed into my ear. "She only wants to be left in peace. She was thrown out of Illinois because she was too aggressive after the Great Revelation." The Great Revelation was the vampire term for the night that they'd gone on television all over the world to let us know that they actually existed and, furthermore, that they wanted to come out of the shadows and into the economic and social flow of human society.

"Eric lets Thalia do what she wants as long as she follows the rules and shows up on time for her hours at the bar," Pam continued in her tiny whisper. Eric was ruler of this little world, and no one was forgetting it. "She knows what the punishment will be if she steps out of line. Sometimes she seems to forget how little she would like that punishment. She should read Abby, get some ideas."

If you weren't getting any joy out of your life, you needed to . . . oh, do something for others, or take up a new hobby, or something like that, right? Wasn't that the usual advice? I flashed on Thalia volunteering to take the night shift at a hospice, and I shuddered. The idea of Thalia knitting, with two long, sharp needles, gave me another frisson of horror. To heck with the therapy.

"So, the only ones attending the summit are Andre, our queen, Sookie, myself, Bill, and Pam," Eric said. "Cataliades the lawyer and his niece as his runner. Oh, yes, Gervaise from Four and his human woman, a concession since Gervaise has been hosting the queen so generously. Rasul, as driver. And Sigebert, of course. That's our party. I know some of you are disappointed, and I can only hope that next year will be a better year for Louisiana. And for Arkansas, which we now consider part of our territory."

"I think that's all that we needed to talk about with all of you present," Andre said. The rest of the stuff he and Eric had to discuss would be done in private. Andre didn't touch me again, which was a good thing. Andre scared me down to my polished pink toenails. Of course, I should feel that way about everyone in the room. If I'd had good sense, I would move to Wyoming, which had the lowest vamp population (two; there'd been an article about them in *American Vampire*). Some days I was sorely tempted.

I whipped a little notepad out of my purse as Eric went over the date of our departure, the date of our return, the time our chartered Anubis Airline plane was arriving from Baton Rouge to pick up the Shreveport contingent, and a rundown of the clothes we would need. With some dismay, I realized I would have to go borrowing from my friends again. But Eric added, "Sookie, you wouldn't need these clothes if it wasn't for the trip. I've called your friend's store and you have credit there. Use it."

I could feel my cheeks redden. I felt like the poor cousin until he added, "The staff has an account at a couple of stores here in Shreveport, but that would be inconvenient for you." My shoulders relaxed, and I hoped he was telling the truth. Not one flicker of an eyelid told me any different.

"We may have suffered a disaster, but we won't go in looking poor," Eric said, being careful to give me only a fraction of his stare.

"Don't look poor," I made a note.

"Is everyone clear? Our goals for this conference are to support the queen as she tries to clear herself of these ridiculous charges, and to let everyone know that Louisiana is still a prestigious state. None of the Arkansas vampires who came to Louisiana with their king survived to tell the tale." Eric smiled, and it wasn't a pleasant smile.

I hadn't known that before this night.

Gosh, wasn't that convenient.

2

"HALLEIGH, SINCE YOU'RE MARRYING A POLICEMAN, maybe you'll be able to tell me . . . just how big is a cop's nightstick?" Elmer Claire Vaudry asked.

I was sitting beside the bride-to-be, Halleigh Robinson, since I'd been given the all-important task of recording each gift and its giver as Halleigh opened all the white-and-silver wrapped boxes and flowered gift bags.

No one else seemed the least surprised that Mrs. Vaudry, a fortyish grade school teacher, was asking a bawdy question at this firmly middle-class, church lady event.

"Why, I wouldn't know, Elmer Claire," Halleigh said demurely, and there was a positive chorus of disbelieving sniggers.

"Well, now, what about the handcuffs?" Elmer Claire asked. "You ever use those handcuffs?"

A fluttering of southern lady voices rose in the living

room of Marcia Albanese, the hostess who'd agreed to let her house be the sacrificial lamb: the actual shower site. The other hostesses had had the lesser problems of bringing the food and the punch.

"You are just *something*, Elmer Claire," Marcia said from her spot by the refreshments table. But she was smiling. Elmer Claire had her role as the Daring One, and the others were glad to let her enjoy it.

Elmer Claire would never have been so vulgar if old Caroline Bellefleur had been present at the shower. Caroline was the social ruler of Bon Temps. Miss Caroline was about a million years old and had a back stiffer than any soldier. Only something extreme would keep Miss Caroline home from a social event of this importance to her family, and something extreme had happened. Caroline Bellefleur had suffered a heart attack, to the amazement of everyone in Bon Temps. To her family, the event had not been a tremendous surprise.

The grand Bellefleur double wedding (Halleigh and Andy's, Portia and her accountant's) had been set for the previous spring. It had been organized in a rush because of Caroline Bellefleur's sudden deterioration in health. As it happened, even before the hurried-up wedding could be held, Miss Caroline had been felled by the attack. Then she'd broken her hip.

With the agreement of Andy's sister, Portia, and her groom, Andy and Halleigh had postponed the wedding until late October. But I'd heard Miss Caroline was not recovering as her grandchildren had hoped, and it seemed unlikely she ever would be back to her former self.

Halleigh, her cheeks flushed, was struggling with the ribbon around a heavy box. I handed her a pair of scissors. There was some tradition about not cutting the ribbon, a tradition that somehow tied into predicting the number of children the bridal couple would produce, but I was willing to bet that Halleigh was ready for a quick solution. She snipped the ribbon on the side closest to her so no one would notice her callous disregard for custom. She flashed me a grateful look. We were all in our party best, of course, and Halleigh looked very cute and young in her light blue pantsuit with pink roses splashed on the jacket. She was wearing a corsage, of course, as the honoree.

I felt like I was observing an interesting tribe in another country, a tribe that just happened to speak my language. I'm a barmaid, several rungs below Halleigh on the social ladder, and I'm a telepath, though people tended to forget about it since it is hard to believe, my outside being so normal. But I'd been on the guest list, so I'd made a big effort to fit in sartorially. I was pretty sure I'd succeeded. I was wearing a sleeveless tailored white blouse, yellow slacks, and orange-and-yellow sandals, and my hair was down and flowing smoothly past my shoulder blades. Yellow earrings and a little gold chain tied me all together. It might be late September, but it was hot as the six shades of hell. All the ladies were still dressed in their hot-weather finery, though a few brave souls had donned fall colors.

I knew everyone at the shower, of course. Bon Temps is not a big place, and my family has lived in it for almost two hundred years. Knowing who people are is not the same as being comfortable with them, and I'd been glad to be given the job of recording the gifts. Marcia Albanese was sharper than I'd given her credit for being.

I was certainly learning a lot. Though I was trying hard not to listen in, and my little task helped in that, I was getting a lot of mental overflow.

Halleigh was in hog heaven. She was getting presents, she was the center of attention, and she was getting married to a great guy. I didn't think she really knew her groom that well, but I was certainly willing to believe that there were wonderful sides to Andy Bellefleur that I'd never seen or heard. Andy had more imagination than the average middle-class man in Bon Temps; I knew that. And Andy had fears and desires he'd buried deeply; I knew that, too.

Halleigh's mother had come from Mandeville to attend the shower, of course, and she was doing her smiling best to support her daughter. I thought I was the only one who realized that Halleigh's mother hated crowds, even crowds this small. Every moment she sat in Marcia's living room was very uncomfortable for Linette Robinson. At this very moment, while she was laughing at another little sally by Elmer Claire, she was wishing passionately that she was home with a good book and a glass of iced tea.

I started to whisper to her that it would all be over in (I cast a glance at my watch) another hour, hour-fifteen at the outside—but I remembered in time that I'd just freak her out worse than she already was. I jotted down "Selah Pumphrey—dish towels," and sat poised to record the next gift. Selah Pumphrey had expected me to give her a Big Reaction when she'd sailed in the door, since for weeks Selah had been dating that vampire I'd abjured. Selah was always imagining I'd jump on her and whack her in the head. Selah had a low opinion of me, not that she knew me at all. She certainly didn't realize that the vampire in question was simply off my radar now. I was guessing she'd been invited because she'd been Andy and Halleigh's real estate agent when they'd bought their little house.

"Tara Thornton—lace teddy," I wrote, and smiled at my friend Tara, who'd selected Halleigh's gift from the stock at her clothing store. Of course, Elmer Claire had a lot to say about the teddy, and a good time was had by all—at least on the face of it. Some of the assembled women weren't comfortable with Elmer Claire's broad humor, some of them were thinking that Elmer Claire's husband had a lot to put up with, and some of them just wished she would shut up. That group included me, and Linette Robinson, and Halleigh.

The principal at the school where Halleigh taught had given the couple some perfectly nice place mats, and the assistant principal had gotten napkins to match. I recorded those with a flourish and stuffed some of the torn wrapping paper into the garbage bag at my side.

"Thanks, Sookie," Halleigh said quietly, as Elmer Claire was telling another story about something that had happened at her wedding involving a chicken and the best man. "I really appreciate your help."

"No big," I said, surprised.

"Andy told me that he got you to hide the engagement ring when he proposed," she said, smiling. "And you've helped me out other times, too." Then Andy had told Halleigh *all* about me.

"Not a problem," I said, a little embarrassed.

She shot a sideways glance at Selah Pumphrey, seated two folding chairs away. "Are you still dating that beautiful man I saw at your place?" she asked rather more loudly. "The handsome one with the gorgeous black hair?"

Halleigh had seen Claude when he dropped me off at my temporary lodging in town; Claude, the brother of Claudine, my fairy godmother. Yes, really. Claude *was* gorgeous, and he could be absolutely charming (to women) for about sixty seconds. He'd made the effort when he'd met Halleigh, and I could only be thankful, since Selah's ears had pricked up just like a fox's.

"I saw him maybe three weeks ago," I said truthfully. "But we're not dating now." We never had been, actually, because Claude's idea of a good date was someone with a little beard stubble and equipment I'd never possess. But not everyone had to know that, right? "I'm seeing someone else," I added modestly.

"Oh?" Halleigh was all innocent interest. I was getting fonder of the girl (all of four years younger than me) by the second.

"Yes," I said. "A consultant from Memphis."

"You'll have to bring him to the wedding," Halleigh said. "Wouldn't that be great, Portia?"

This was another kettle of fish entirely. Portia Bellefleur, Andy's sister and the other bride-to-be in the double Bellefleur wedding, had asked me to be there to serve alcohol, along with my boss, Sam Merlotte. Now Portia was in a bind. She would never have invited me other than as a worker. (I sure hadn't been invited to any showers for *Portia*.) Now I beamed at Portia in an innocent, I'm-so-happy way.

"Of course," Portia said smoothly. She had not trained in the law for nothing. "We'd be delighted if you'd bring your boyfriend."

I had a happy mental picture of Quinn transforming into a tiger at the reception. I smiled at Portia all the more brightly. "I'll see if he can come with me," I said.

"Now, y'all," Elmer Claire said, "a little bird told me to write down what Halleigh said when she unwrapped her gifts, cause you know, that's what you'll say on your wedding night!" She waved a legal pad.

Everyone fell silent with happy anticipation. Or dread.

"This is the first thing Halleigh said: 'Oh, what pretty wrapping!'" A chorus of dutiful laughter. "Then she said, let's see: 'That's going to fit; I can hardly wait!'" Snickers. "Then she said, 'Oh, I needed one of those!'" Hilarity.

After that, it was time for cake and punch and peanuts and the cheese ball. We'd all resumed our seats, carefully balancing plates and cups, when my grandmother's friend Maxine opened a new topic of discussion.

"How's your new friend, Sookie?" Maxine Fortenberry asked. Maxine was clear across the room, but projecting was no problem for Maxine. In her late fifties, Maxine was stout and hearty, and she'd been a second mother to my brother, Jason, who was best friends with her son Hoyt. "The gal from New Orleans?"

"Amelia's doing well." I beamed nervously, all too aware I was the new center of attention.

"Is it true that she lost her house in the flooding?"

"It did sustain quite a bit of damage, her tenant said. So Amelia's waiting to hear from the insurance company, and then she'll decide what to do."

"Lucky she was here with you when the hurricane hit," Maxine said.

I guess poor Amelia had heard that a thousand times since August. I think Amelia was pretty tired of trying to feel lucky. "Oh, yes," I said agreeably. "She sure was."

Amelia Broadway's arrival in Bon Temps had been the subject of lots of gossip. That's only natural.

"So for right now, Amelia'll just stay on with you?" Halleigh asked helpfully.

"For a while," I said, smiling.

"That's just real sweet of you," Marcia Albanese said approvingly.

"Oh, Marcia, you know I got that whole upstairs that I never use. She's actually improved it for me; she got a window air conditioner put in up there, so it's much nicer. It doesn't put me out one bit."

"Still, lots of people wouldn't want someone living in their home that long. I guess I should take in one of the poor souls staying at the Days Inn, but I just can't bring myself to let someone else in my house."

"I like the company," I said, which was mostly true.

"Has she been back to check on her house?"

"Ah, only once." Amelia had to get in and out of New Orleans real quick, so none of her witch friends could track her down. Amelia was in a bit of hot water with the witch community of the Big Easy.

"She sure loves that cat of hers," Elmer Claire said. "She had that big old tom at the vet the other day when I took Powderpuff in." Powderpuff, Elmer Claire's white Persian, was about a million years old. "I asked her why she didn't get that cat neutered, and she just covered that cat's ears like he could hear me, and she asked me not to talk about it in front of Bob, just like he was a person."

"She's real fond of Bob," I said, not quite knowing whether I wanted to gag or laugh at the idea of the vet neutering Bob.

"You know that Amelia how?" Maxine asked.

"You remember my cousin Hadley?"

Everyone in the room nodded, except newcomer Halleigh and her mother.

"Well, when Hadley lived in New Orleans, she rented the upstairs of Amelia's house from her," I said. "And when Hadley passed away"—here there were solemn nods all around—"I went down to New Orleans to clean out Hadley's things. And I met Amelia, and we became friends, and she just decided she'd visit Bon Temps for a while."

All the ladies looked at me with the most expectant expressions, as if they couldn't wait to hear what would come next. Because there had to be more explanation, right?

There was indeed a lot more to the story, but I didn't think they were ready to hear that Amelia, after a night of great loving, had accidentally turned Bob into a cat during a sexual experiment. I'd never asked Amelia to describe the circumstances, because I was pretty sure I didn't want to get a visual on that scene. But they were all waiting for a little more explanation. Any explanation.

"Amelia had a bad breakup with her boyfriend," I said, keeping my tone low and confidential.

All the other ladies' faces were both titillated and sympathetic.

"He was a Mormon missionary," I told them. Well, Bob had *looked* like a Mormon missionary, in dark slacks and a white short-sleeved shirt, and he'd even arrived at Amelia's on a bicycle. He was actually a witch, like Amelia. "But he knocked on Amelia's door and they just fell in love." Actually, into bed. But you know—same thing, for the purposes of this story.

"Did his parents know?"

"Did his church find out?"

"Don't they get to have more than one wife?"

The questions crowded in too thick for me to deal with, and I waited until the attendees had subsided into their waiting mode again. I was not used to making up fabrications, and I was running out of truth to base the rest of the story on. "I really don't know much about the Mormon church," I told the last questioner, and that was the absolute truth. "Though I think modern Mormons aren't supposed to have more than one wife. But what happened to them was his relatives found out and got real mad because they didn't think Amelia was good enough for the man, and they snatched him away and made him go home. So she wanted to leave New Orleans to get a change of scene, forget about the past, you know."

They all nodded, absolutely fascinated by Amelia's big drama. I felt a twinge of guilt. For a minute or two, everyone gave her opinion about the sad story. Maxine Fortenberry summed it all up.

"Poor girl," said Maxine. "He should've stood up to them."

I passed Halleigh another present to open. "Halleigh, you know that won't happen to you," I said, diverting the conversation back to its proper topic. "Andy is just nuts about you; anyone can tell."

Halleigh blushed, and her mother said, "We all love

Andy," and the shower was back on track. The rest of the conversation veered from the wedding to the meals each church was taking in turn to cook for the evacuees. The Catholics had tomorrow night, and Maxine sounded a little relieved when she said the number to cook for had dropped to twenty-five.

As I drove home afterward, I was feeling a little frazzled from the unaccustomed sociability. I also faced the prospect of telling Amelia about her new invented background. But when I saw the pickup standing in my yard, all such thoughts flew out of my head.

Quinn was here—Quinn the weretiger, who made his living arranging and producing special events for the world of the weird—Quinn, my honey. I pulled around back and practically leaped out of my car after an anxious glance in my rearview mirror to make sure my makeup was still good.

Quinn charged out of the back door as I hurried up to the steps, and I gave a little jump. He caught me and whirled me around, and when he put me down he was kissing me, his big hands framing my face.

"You look so beautiful," he said, coming up for air. A moment later, he gasped. "You smell so good." And then he was back into the kissing.

We finally broke it off.

"Oh, I haven't seen you in so long!" I said. "I'm so glad you're here!" I hadn't seen Quinn in weeks, and then I'd been with him only briefly as he'd passed through Shreveport on his way to Florida with a load of props for the coming-of-age ceremony for a packleader's daughter.

"I've missed you, babe," he said, his big white teeth gleaming. His shaved head shone in the sunlight, which was coming at quite an angle this late in the afternoon. "I had a little time to catch up with your roomie while you were at the shower. How'd it go?"

"Like showers usually do. Lots of presents and lots of gossip. This was the second shower I've been to for this gal, plus I gave them a plate in their everyday china for a wedding present, so I've done them proud."

"You can go to more than one shower for the same person?"

"In a small town like this, yeah. And she went home to have a shower and a dinner party in Mandeville during the summer. So I guess Andy and Halleigh are set up pretty well."

"I thought they were supposed to get married last April."

I explained about Caroline Bellefleur's heart attack. "By the time she was getting over that and they were talking wedding dates again, Miss Caroline fell and broke her hip."

"Wow."

"And the doctors didn't think she'd get over *that*, but she survived that, too. So I think Halleigh and Andy and Portia and Glen are actually going to have the most-anticipated wedding of the Bon Temps year sometime next month. And you're invited."

"I am?"

We were heading inside by this time, since I wanted to take off my shoes and I also wanted to scout out what my housemate was up to. I was trying to think of some long errand I could send her off on, since I so seldom got to see Quinn, who was kind of my boyfriend, if at my age (twenty-seven), I could use that term.

That is, I thought he would be my boyfriend if he could ever slow down enough to latch on to me.

But Quinn's job, working for a subsidiary of Extreme(ly Elegant) Events, covered a lot of territory, literally and figuratively. Since we'd parted in New Orleans after our rescue from Were abductors, I'd seen Quinn three times. He'd been in Shreveport one weekend as he passed through on his way to somewhere else, and we'd gone out to dinner at

Ralph and Kacoo's, a popular restaurant. It had been a good evening, but he'd taken me home at the end of it since he had to start driving at seven the next morning. The second time, he'd dropped into Merlotte's while I was at work, and since it was a slow night, I'd taken an hour off to sit and talk to him, and we'd held hands a little. The third time, I'd kept him company while he was loading up his trailer at a U-RENT-SPACE storage shed. It had been in the middle of summer, and we'd both been sweating up a storm. Streaming sweat, lots of dust, storage sheds, the occasional vehicle trolling through the lot . . . not a romantic ambience.

And even though Amelia was now obligingly coming down the stairs with her purse over her shoulder and clearly planning to head into town to give us some privacy, it hardly seemed promising that we'd have to grab an instant to consummate a relationship that had had so little face time.

Amelia said, "Good-bye!" She had a big smile all over her face, and since Amelia has the whitest teeth in the world, she looked like the Cheshire cat. Amelia's short hair was sticking out all over (she says no one in Bon Temps can cut it right) and her tan face was bare of makeup. Amelia looks like a young suburban mom who has an infant seat strapped into the back of her minivan; the kind of mom who takes time off to run and swim and play tennis. In point of fact, Amelia did run three times a week and practiced tai chi out in my backyard, but she hated getting in the water and she thought tennis was for (and I quote) "mouth-breathing idiots." I'd always admired tennis players myself, but when Amelia had a point of view, she stuck to it.

"Going to the mall in Monroe," she said. "Shopping to do!" And with an I'm-being-a-good-roommate kind of wave, she hopped into her Mustang and vanished . . .

. . . leaving Quinn and me to stare at each other.

"That Amelia!" I said lamely.

"She's . . . one of a kind," Quinn said, just as uneasy as I was.

"The thing is—" I began, just as Quinn said, "Listen, I think we ought—" and we both floundered to a halt. He made a gesture that indicated I should go first.

"How long are you here for?" I asked.

"I have to leave tomorrow," he said. "I could stay in Monroe or Shreveport."

We did some more staring. I can't read Were minds, not like regular humans. I can get the intent, though, and the intent was . . . intent.

"So," he said. He went down on one knee. "Please," he said.

I had to smile, but then I looked away. "The only thing is," I began again. This conversation would come much more easily to Amelia, who was frank to a very extreme point. "You know that we have, uh, a lot of . . ." I gestured back and forth with my hand.

"Chemistry," he said.

"Right," I said. "But if we never get to see any more of each other than we have the past three months, I'm not really sure I want to make that next step." I hated to say it, but I had to. I didn't need to cause myself pain. "I have big lust," I said. "Big, big lust. But I'm not a one-night-stand kind of woman."

"When the summit is over, I'm taking a long time off," Quinn said, and I could tell he was absolutely sincere. "A month. I came here to ask you if I could spend it with you."

"Really?" I couldn't help sounding incredulous. "Really?"

He smiled up at me. Quinn has a smooth, shaved head, an olive complexion, a bold nose, and a smile that makes these little dimples in the corners of his mouth. His eyes are purple, like a spring pansy. He is as big as a pro wrestler, and just as scary. He held up a huge hand, as if he were swearing an oath. "On a stack of Bibles," he said.

"Yes," I said after a moment's scan of my inner qualms to make sure they were minor. And also, I may not have a built-in truth detector, but I could have told if he'd been thinking, *I'm saying that to get in her pants.* Shifters are very hard to read, their brains are all snarly and semiopaque, but I would've picked up on that. "Then . . . yes."

"Oh, boy." Quinn took a deep breath and his grin lit up the room. But in the next moment, his eyes got that focused look men get when they're thinking about sex very specifically. And then, lickety-split, Quinn was on his feet and his arms were around me as tightly as ropes tying us together.

His mouth found mine. We picked up where we'd left off with the kissing. His mouth was a very clever one and his tongue was very warm. His hands began examining my topography. Down the line of my back to the curve of my hips, back up to my shoulders to cup my face for a moment, down to brush my neck teasingly with the lightest of fingertips. Then those fingers found my breasts, and after a second he tugged my top out of my pants and began exploring territory he'd only visited briefly before. He liked what he found, if "Mmmmm" was a statement of delight. It spoke volumes to me.

"I want to see you," he said. "I want to see all of you."

I had never made love in the daytime before. It seemed very (excitingly) sinful to be struggling with buttons before the sun had even set, and I was so grateful I'd worn an extra-nice white lace bra and little bitty panties. When I dress up, I like to dress up all the way down to the skin.

"Oh," he said when he saw the bra, which contrasted nicely with my deep summer tan. "Oh, *boy*." It wasn't the words; it was the expression of deep admiration. My shoes were already off. Luckily that morning I'd dispensed with handy-but-totally-unsexy knee-high hose in favor of bare legs. Quinn spent some quality time nuzzling my neck and kissing his way down to the bra while I was struggling to undo his belt, though since he would bend while I was trying to deal with the stiff buckle, that wasn't working out fast enough.

"Take off your shirt," I said, and my voice came out as hoarse as his. "I don't have a shirt, you shouldn't have a shirt."

"Fine," he said, and presto, the shirt was off. You'd expect Quinn to be hairy, but he isn't. What he is, is muscular to the *n*th degree, and right at the moment his olive skin was summer-tan. His nipples were surprisingly dark and (not so surprisingly) very hard. Oh, boy—right at my eye level. He began dealing with his own damn belt while I began to explore one hard nub with my mouth, the other with my hand. Quinn's whole body jerked, and he stopped what he was doing. He ran his fingers into my hair to hold my head against him, and he sighed, though it came out more like a growl, vibrating through his body. My free hand yanked at his pants, and he resumed working on the belt but in an unfocused and distracted way.

"Let's move into the bedroom," I said, but it didn't come out like a calm and collected suggestion, more a ragged demand.

He swooped me up, and I latched my arms around his neck and kissed him on his beautiful mouth again.

"No fair," he muttered. "My hands are full."

"Bed," I said, and he deposited me on the bed and then simply fell on top of me.

"Clothes," I reminded him, but he had a mouthful of white lace and breast, and he didn't reply. "Oh," I said. I may have said "Oh" a few more times; and "Yes," too. A sudden thought yanked me right out of the flow of the moment.

"Quinn, do you have, you know . . ." I had never needed to have such items before, since vamps can't get a girl pregnant or give her a disease.

"Why do you think I still have my pants on?" he said, pulling a little package out of his back pocket. His smile this time was far more feral.

"Good," I said from my heart. I would have thrown myself from a window if we'd had to quit. "And you might take the pants off now."

I'd seen Quinn naked before but under decidedly stressful circumstances—in the middle of a swamp, in the rain, while we were being pursued by werewolves. Quinn stood by the bed and took off his shoes and socks and then his pants, moving slowly enough to let me watch. He stepped out of his pants, revealing boxer briefs that were suffering their own kind of stress. In one quick movement he eased them off, too. He had a tight, high butt, and the line from his hip to his thigh was just mouthwatering. He had fine, thin white scars striping him at random, but they seemed like such a natural part of him that they didn't detract from his powerful body. I was kneeling on the bed while I admired him, and he said, "Now you."

I unhooked my bra and slid it off my arms, and he said, "Oh, God. I am the luckiest man alive." After a pause, he said, "The rest."

I stood by the bed and eased the little white lacey things off.

"This is like standing in front of a buffet," he said. "I don't know where to begin."

I touched my breasts. "First course," I suggested.

I discovered that Quinn's tongue was just a bit raspier than a regular man's. I was gasping and making incoherent noises when he moved from my right breast to my left as he tried to decide which one he liked best. He couldn't make up his mind immediately, which was fine with me. By the time he settled on the right breast, I was pushing against him and making sounds that couldn't be mistaken for anything but desperate.

"I think I'll skip the second course and go right to dessert," he whispered, his voice dark and ragged. "Are you ready, babe? You sound ready. You feel ready."

"I am so ready," I said, reaching down between us to wrap my hand around his length. He quivered all over when I touched him. He rolled on the condom.

"Now," he growled. "Now!" I guided him to my entrance, thrust my hips up to meet him. "I dreamed of this," he said, and shoved inside me up to the hilt. That was the last thing either of us was able to say.

Quinn's appetite was as outstanding as his equipment.

He enjoyed dessert so much, he came back for seconds.

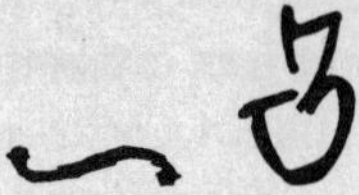

WE WERE IN THE KITCHEN WHEN AMELIA RETURNED. I'd fed Bob, her cat, since she'd been so tactful earlier and deserved some reward. Tact does not come naturally to Amelia.

Bob ignored his kibble in favor of watching Quinn fry bacon, and I was slicing tomatoes. I'd gotten out the cheese and the mayonnaise and the mustard and the pickles, anything I could imagine a man might want on a bacon sandwich. I'd pulled on some old shorts and a T-shirt, while Quinn had gotten his bag from his truck and put on his workout clothes—a tank top and worn shorts made from sweat material.

Amelia gave Quinn a top-to-bottom scan when he turned back to the stove, and then she looked at me, grinning broadly. "You guys have a good reunion?" she said, tossing her shopping bags on the kitchen table.

"Up to your room, please," I said, because otherwise Amelia would want us to admire every single thing she'd bought. With a pout, Amelia snagged the bags and carried them upstairs, returning in a minute to ask Quinn if there was enough bacon for her.

"Sure," Quinn said obligingly, taking out some strips and putting a few more in the pan.

I liked a man who could cook. While I set out plates and silverware, I was pleasantly aware of the tenderness I felt south of my belly button and of my overwhelmingly relaxed mood. I got three glasses out of the cabinet but kind of forgot what I was doing on my way to the refrigerator, since Quinn stepped away from the stove to give me a quick kiss. His lips were so warm and firm, they reminded me of something else that had been warm and firm. I flashed on my astonished moment of revelation when Quinn had slid into me for the first time. Considering that my only previous sexual encounters had been with vampires, who are definitely on the cool side, you can imagine what a startling experience a breathing lover with a heartbeat and a warm penis would be. In fact, shape-shifters tended to run a bit warmer than regular humans. Even through the condom, I'd been able to feel the heat.

"What?" Quinn asked. "Why the look?" He was smiling quizzically.

I smiled. "I was just thinking of your temperature," I said.

"Hey, you knew I was hot," he said with a grin. "What about the thought reading?" he said more seriously. "How did that work out?"

I thought it was great that he'd even wondered. "I can't call your thoughts any trouble," I said, unable to suppress a huge grin. "It might be a stretch to count 'yesyesyesyespleasepleaseplease' as a thought."

"Not a problem then," he said, totally unembarrassed.

"Not a problem. As long as you're wrapped in the moment and you're happy, I'm gonna be happy."

"Well, hot damn." Quinn turned back to the stove. "That's just *great*."

I thought it was, too.

Just great.

Amelia ate her sandwich with a good appetite and then picked Bob up to feed him little bits of bacon she'd saved. The big black-and-white cat purred up a storm.

"So," said Quinn, after his first sandwich had disappeared with amazing quickness, "this is the guy you changed by accident?"

"Yeah," said Amelia, scratching Bob's ears. "This is the guy." Amelia was sitting cross-legged in the kitchen chair, which is something I simply couldn't do, and she was focused on the cat. "The little fella," she crooned. "My fuzzy wuzzy honey, isn't he? Isn't he?" Quinn looked mildly disgusted, but I was just as guilty of talking baby talk to Bob when I was alone with him. Bob the witch had been a skinny, weird guy with a kind of geeky charm. Amelia had told me Bob had been a hairdresser; I'd decided if that were true, he'd fixed hair at a funeral parlor. Black pants, white shirt, bicycle? Have you ever known a hairdresser who presented himself that way?

"So," Quinn said. "What are you doing about it?"

"I'm studying," Amelia said. "I'm trying to figure out what I did wrong, so I can make it right. It would be easier if I could . . ." Her voice trailed off in a guilty kind of way.

"If you could talk to your mentor?" I said helpfully.

She scowled at me. "Yeah," she said. "If I could talk to my mentor."

"Why don't you?" Quinn asked.

"One, I wasn't supposed to use transformational magic. That's pretty much a no-no. Two, I've looked for her online since Katrina, on every message board witches use, and I can't find any news of her. She might have gone to a shelter somewhere, she might be staying with her kids or some friend, or she might have died in the flooding."

"I believe you had your main income from your rental property. What are your plans now? What's the state of your property?" Quinn asked, carrying his plate and mine to the sink. He wasn't being bashful with the personal questions tonight. I waited with interest to hear Amelia's answers. I'd always wanted to know a lot of things about Amelia that were just plain rude to ask: like, What was she living on now? Though she had worked part-time for my friend Tara Thornton at Tara's Togs while Tara's help was sick, Amelia's outgo far exceeded her visible income. That meant she had good credit, some savings, or another source of income besides the tarot readings she'd done in a shop off Jackson Square and her rent money, which now wasn't coming in. Her mom had left her some money. It must have been a chunk.

"Well, I've been back into New Orleans once since the storm," Amelia said. "You've met Everett, my tenant?"

Quinn nodded.

"When he could get to a phone, he reported some damage to the bottom floor, where I live. There were trees and branches down, and of course there wasn't electricity or water for a couple of weeks. But the neighborhood didn't suffer as badly as some, thank God, and when the electricity was back on, I snuck down there." Amelia took a deep breath. I could hear right from her brain that she was scared to venture into the territory she was about to reveal to us. "I, um, went to talk to my dad about fixing the roof. Right then, we had a blue roof like half the people around us." The blue plastic that covered damaged roofs was the new norm in New Orleans.

This was the first time Amelia had mentioned her family

to me, in more than a very general way. I'd learned more from her thoughts than I'd learned from her conversation, and I had to be careful not to mix the two sources when we talked. I could see her dad's presence in her head, love and resentment mixing in her thoughts to form a confused mishmash.

"Your dad is going to repair your house?" Quinn asked casually. He was excavating in my Tupperware box in which I stored any cookies that happened to cross my threshold—not a frequent occurrence, since I have a tendency to put on weight when sweets are in the house. Amelia had no such problem, and she'd stocked the box with a couple of kinds of Keebler cookies and told Quinn he was welcome to help himself.

Amelia nodded, much more fascinated by Bob's fur than she had been a moment before. "Yeah, he's got a crew on it," she said.

This was news to me.

"So who is your dad?" Quinn was keeping up the directness. So far it had worked for him.

Amelia squirmed on the kitchen chair, making Bob raise his head in protest.

"Copley Carmichael," she muttered.

We were both silent with shock. After a minute, she looked up at us. "What?" she said. "Okay, so he's famous. Okay, so he's rich. So?"

"Different last name?" I said.

"I use my mom's. I got tired of people being weird around me," Amelia said pointedly.

Quinn and I exchanged glances. Copley Carmichael was a big name in the state of Louisiana. He had fingers in all kinds of financial pies, and all those fingers were pretty dirty. But he was an old-fashioned human wheeler-dealer: no whiff of the supernatural around Copley Carmichael.

"Does he know you're a witch?" I asked.

"He doesn't believe it for a minute," Amelia said, sounding frustrated and forlorn. "He thinks I'm a deluded little wannabe, that I'm hanging with weird little people and doing weird little jobs to stick my tongue out at him. He wouldn't believe in vampires if he hadn't seen them over and over."

"What about your mom?" Quinn asked. I got myself a refill on my tea. I knew the answer to this one.

"Dead," Amelia told him. "Three years ago. That's when I moved out of my dad's house and into the bottom floor of the house on Chloe. He'd given it to me when I graduated from high school so I'd have my own income, but he made me manage it myself so I'd have the experience."

That seemed like a pretty good deal to me. Hesitantly I said, "Wasn't that the right thing to do? Get you to learn by doing?"

"Well, yeah," she admitted. "But when I moved out, he wanted to give me an allowance . . . at my age! I knew I had to make it on my own. Between the rent, and the money I picked up doing fortunes, and magic jobs I got on my own, I've been making a living." She threw up her head proudly.

Amelia didn't seem to realize the rent was income from a gift of her father's, not something she'd actually earned. Amelia was truly pleased as punch with her own self-sufficiency. My new friend, whom I'd acquired almost by accident, was a bundle of contradictions. Since she was a very clear broadcaster, I got her thoughts loud and clear. When I was alone with Amelia, I had to shield like crazy. I'd relaxed with Quinn around, but I shouldn't have. I was getting a whole mess from Amelia's head.

"So, could your dad help you find your mentor?" Quinn asked.

Amelia looked blank for a moment, as if she was considering that. "I don't see how," she said slowly. "He's a powerful guy; you know that. But he's having as much trouble in New Orleans since Katrina as the rest of the people are."

Except he had a lot more money and he could go somewhere else, returning when he pleased, which most of the inhabitants of the city could not. I closed my mouth to keep this observation to myself. Time to change the topic.

"Amelia," I said. "How well did you know Bob, anyway? Who's looking for him?"

She looked a little frightened, not Amelia's normal thing. "I'm wondering, too," she said. "I just knew Bob to speak to, before that night. But I do know that Bob had—has—great friends in the magic community. I don't think any of them know we got together. That night, the night before the queen's ball when the shit hit the fan between the Arkansas vamps and our vamps, Bob and I went back to my place after we'd left Terry and Patsy at the pizza place. Bob called in sick to work the next day, since we had celebrated so hard, and then he spent that day with me."

"So it's possible Bob's family has been looking for him for months? Wondering if he's dead or alive?"

"Hey, chill. I'm not that awful. Bob was raised by his aunt, but they don't get along at all. He hasn't had much contact with her for years. I'm sure he does have friends that are worrying, and I'm really, really sorry about that. But even if they knew what had happened, that wouldn't help Bob, right? And since Katrina, everyone in New Orleans has a lot to worry about."

At this interesting point in the discussion, the phone rang. I was closest, so I picked it up. My brother's voice was almost electric with excitement.

"Sookie, you need to come out to Hotshot in about an hour."

"Why?"

"Me and Crystal are getting married. Surprise!"

While this was not a total shock (Jason had been "dating" Crystal Norris for several months), the suddenness of the ceremony made me anxious.

"Is Crystal pregnant again?" I asked suspiciously. She'd miscarried a baby of Jason's not long ago.

"Yes!" Jason said, like that was the best news he could possibly impart. "And this time, we'll be married when the baby comes."

Jason was ignoring reality, as he was increasingly willing to do. The reality was that Crystal had been pregnant at least once before she was pregnant by Jason, and she had lost that child, too. The community at Hotshot was a victim of its own inbreeding.

"Okay, I'll be there," I said. "Can Amelia and Quinn come, too?"

"Sure," Jason said. "Crystal and me'll be proud to have them."

"Is there anything I can bring?"

"No, Calvin and them are getting ready to cook. It's all going to be outside. We got lights strung up. I think they'll have a big pot of jambalaya, some dirty rice, and coleslaw, and me and my buddies are bringing the alcohol. Just come looking pretty! See you at Hotshot in an hour. Don't be late."

I hung up and sat there for a minute, my hand still clutching the cordless phone. That was just like Jason: come in an hour to a ceremony planned at the last minute for the worst possible reason, and don't be late! At least he hadn't asked me to bring a cake.

"Sookie, you okay?" Quinn asked.

"My brother Jason's getting married tonight," I said, trying to keep my voice even. "We're invited to the wedding, and we need to be there in an hour." I'd always figured Jason wouldn't marry a woman I truly adored; he'd always shown a partiality to tough sluts. And that was Crystal, sure enough.

Crystal was also a werepanther, a member of a community that guarded its own secrets jealously. In fact, my brother was now a werepanther himself because he'd been bitten over and over by a rival for Crystal's attentions.

Jason was older than I, and God knows, he'd had his share of women. I had to assume he knew when one suited him.

I emerged from my thoughts to find that Amelia was looking startled and excited. She loved to go out and party, and the chances for that around Bon Temps were limited. Quinn, who'd met Jason when he was visiting me, looked at me with a skeptical raised eyebrow.

"Yeah, I know," I said. "It's crazy and dumb. But Crystal's pregnant again, and there's no stopping him. Do you two want to come along with me? You don't have to. I'm afraid I've got to get ready right now."

Amelia said, "Oh, goody, I can wear my new outfit," and sped upstairs to tear the tags off.

Quinn said, "Babe, do you want me to come?"

"Yes, please," I said. He came over to me and wrapped his heavy arms around me. I felt comforted, even though I knew Quinn was thinking what a fool Jason was.

I pretty much agreed with him.

4 ~

IT WAS STILL WARM AT NIGHT, BUT NOT OPPRESSIVELY so, not this late in September. I wore a sleeveless white dress with red flowers on it, one I'd worn before when I had a date with Bill (whom I *wouldn't* think about). Out of sheer vanity, I put on my high-heeled red sandals, though they were hardly practical footwear for a wedding on a roughly paved road. I put on some makeup while Quinn was showering, and I wasn't displeased with my reflection. There's nothing like great sex to give you a glow. I came out of my room and glanced at the clock. We needed to leave pretty quickly.

Amelia was wearing a short-sleeved dress, beige with a tiny navy pattern. Amelia loved to buy clothes and considered herself a snappy dresser, but her taste was strictly suburban young matron. She wore little navy sandals with flowers on the straps, much more appropriate than my heels.

Just when I was beginning to worry, Quinn came out of my room wearing a brown silk dress shirt and khakis.

"What about a tie?" he asked. "I've got some in my bag."

I thought of the rural setting and vast lack of sophistication in the little community of Hotshot. "I don't think a tie will be necessary," I said, and Quinn looked relieved.

We piled into my car and drove west and then south. On the drive, I had a chance to explain to my out-of-town guests about the isolated band of werepanthers and their small cluster of houses grouped together in rural Renard Parish. I was driving, since that was just simplest. Once out of sight of the old railroad tracks, the country became increasingly unpopulated until for two or three miles we saw no lights of any kind. Then we saw cars and lights at a crossroads ahead. We were there.

Hotshot was out in the middle of nowhere, set in a long depression in the middle of gently rolling land, swells that were too ill-defined to be called hills. Formed around an ancient crossroads, the lonely community had a powerful vibration of magic. I could tell that Amelia was feeling that power. Her face became sharper and wiser as we got closer. Even Quinn inhaled deeply. As for me, I could detect the presence of magic, but it didn't affect non-supernatural me.

I pulled over to the side of the road behind Hoyt Fortenberry's truck. Hoyt was Jason's best friend and lifelong shadow. I spied him right ahead of us, trudging down the road to a well-lit area. I'd handed Amelia and Quinn a flashlight, and I kept one aimed at my feet.

"Hoyt," I called. I hurried to catch up with him, at least as much as was practical in the red heels. "Hey, are you okay?" I asked when I saw his downcast face. Hoyt was not a very good-looking guy, or very bright, but he was steady and tended to see past the moment to its consequences, something my brother had never mastered.

"Sook," Hoyt said. "I can't believe he's getting hitched. I guess I thought me and Jason would be bachelors forever." He attempted to smile.

I gave him a pat on the shoulder. Life would've been neat 'n' tidy if I could have fallen in love with Hoyt, thus attaching him to my brother forever, but Hoyt and I had never had the slightest interest in each other.

Hoyt's mind was radiating a dull misery. He was certain that his life was changing forever this night. He expected Jason to mend his ways completely, to stay in with his wife like a husband should, and to forsake all others.

I sure hoped Hoyt's expectations were right on the money.

On the edges of the crowd, Hoyt met up with Catfish Hennessy, and they began making loud jokes about Jason's breaking down and marrying.

I hoped the male bonding would help Hoyt get through the ceremony. I didn't know if Crystal truly loved my brother—but Hoyt did.

Quinn took my hand, and with Amelia in our wake we forged through the little crowd until we reached the center.

Jason was wearing a new suit, and the blue of it was only a bit darker than the blue of his eyes. He looked great, and he was smiling to beat the band. Crystal was wearing a leopard-print dress cut as low in the front as you could get and still term the garment a dress. I didn't know if the leopard motif was an ironic statement on her part or a simple expression of her fashion sense. I suspected the latter.

The happy couple was standing in the middle of an empty space, accompanied by Calvin Norris, leader of the Hotshot community. The crowd kept respectfully back, forming an uneven circle.

Calvin, who happened to be Crystal's uncle, was holding Crystal's arm. He smiled at me. Calvin had trimmed his beard and dug out a suit for the occasion, but he and Jason were the only men wearing ties. Quinn noticed that and thought relieved thoughts.

Jason spotted me right after Calvin did, and he beckoned to me. I stepped forward, suddenly realizing that I was going to have a part in the ceremony. I hugged my brother, smelling his musky cologne . . . but no alcohol. I relaxed a fraction. I had suspected Jason had fortified himself with a drink or two, but he was quite sober.

I let go of Jason and glanced behind me to see what had become of my companions, so I knew the moment when the werepanthers realized Quinn was there. There was a sudden hush among the two-natured, and I heard his name ripple through them like a little wind.

Calvin whispered, "You brought *Quinn*?" as if I'd arrived with Santa Claus or some other mythical creature.

"Is that okay?" I said, since I'd had no clue it would create such a stir.

"Oh, yes," he said. "He's your man now?" Calvin's face held such a mixture of startled reevaluation and speculation that I immediately began wondering what I didn't know about my new lover.

"Um, well, sorta," I said with sudden caution.

"We're honored to have him here," Calvin assured me.

"Quinn," Crystal breathed. Her pupils were dilating, and I felt her brain focus on my date with a sort of groupie longing. I wanted to kick her. *Here to marry my brother, remember?*

Jason looked as puzzled as I was. Since he'd been a panther only a few months, there was a lot about the hidden world of the two-natured he hadn't picked up on yet.

Me, too.

Crystal made an effort to quell herself and get back into

the moment. She was naturally enjoying being the center of attention, but she spared a moment to reassess her prospective sister-in-law. Her respect for me (pretty much nonexistent, heretofore) had just shot off the charts.

"What's the procedure?" I asked briskly, trying to get us all back on track.

Calvin reverted to his practical self. "Since we have human guests, we've adapted the ceremony," he explained in a very low voice. "Here's how it goes . . . you vouch for Jason as his closest living relative, because he ain't got no one older than you to do it. I'm Crystal's oldest living relative, so I vouch for her. We offer to take the penalty if either of them does wrong."

Ah-oh. I didn't like the sound of that. I darted a quick look at my brother, who (naturally) didn't seem to think twice about the commitment I was making. I shouldn't have expected anything else.

"Then the minister comes forward and the service proceeds just like any other wedding," Calvin said. "If there weren't outsiders here, it would be different."

I was curious about that, but this wasn't the time to ask lots of questions. However, there were a few that had to be answered. "What penalty am I promising to pay? What constitutes 'doing wrong'?"

Jason huffed a sigh, exasperated that I wanted to find out what I was promising. Calvin's calm yellow eyes met mine, and they were full of understanding.

"Here's what you're vowing," Calvin said in a voice that was quiet but intense. We huddled around him. "Jason, you listen hard. We went over this, but I don't think you were giving me your full attention." Jason was listening now, but I could feel his impatience.

"Being married here"—and Calvin waved a hand to indicate the little Hotshot community—"means being faithful to your mate, unless the mate has to breed to keep the group up. Since Crystal's pretty much out of the running on that, Jason, that means she has to be faithful to you, and you to her. You don't have mating obligations like the purebloods do." Jason flushed at this reminder that his status was lesser since he was only a shifter because he'd been bitten by one, not because he'd been born with the gene. "So if Crystal runs around on you and a member of the community can attest to it, and if she can't pay the price for some reason—pregnancy, or illness, or a kid to raise—I have to do it. We're not talking money here, you understand?"

Jason nodded. "You're talking physical punishment," he said.

"Yes," Calvin said. "Not only are you promising to be faithful, you're also swearing to keep our secret."

Jason nodded again.

"And to help out other members of the community if they're in need."

Jason scowled.

"Example?" I said.

"If Maryelizabeth's roof needs replacing, we might all chip in a bit to buy the material and we'd all make time to do the work. If a kid needs a place to stay, your home is open to that kid. We take care of each other."

Jason nodded again. "I understand," he said. "I'm willing." He would have to give up some of his buddy time, and I felt sad for Hoyt; and I confess I felt a little sad for myself. I wasn't gaining a sister; I was losing my brother, at least to some degree.

"Mean this from the heart or call it off now," I said, keeping my voice very low. "You're committing my life to this, too. Can you keep the promises you're making to this woman and her community, or not?"

Jason looked at Crystal for a long moment, and I had no

right to be in his head, so I pulled out and instead cast through the crowd for random thoughts. They were mostly what you'd expect: a bit of excitement at being at a wedding, a bit of pleasure at seeing the parish's most notorious bachelor shackled to a wild young woman, a bit of curiosity about the odd Hotshot ritual. *Hotshot* was a byword in the parish—"as weird as a guy from Hotshot" had been a saying for years, and Hotshot kids who attended the Bon Temps school often had a hard time of it until after the first few playground fights.

"I'll keep my promises," Jason said, his voice hoarse.

"I'll keep mine," Crystal said.

The difference between the two was this: Jason was sincere, though I doubted his ability to stick to his word. Crystal had the ability, but she wasn't sincere.

"You don't mean it," I said to her.

"The hell you say," she retorted.

"I don't usually say one way or another," I said, making the effort to keep my voice low. "But this is too serious to keep silent. I can see inside your head, Crystal. Don't you ever forget I can."

"I ain't forgetting nothing," she said, making sure each word had weight. "And I'm marrying Jason tonight."

I looked at Calvin. He was troubled, but in the end, he shrugged. "We can't stop this," he said. For a second, I was tempted to struggle with his pronouncement. *Why not?* I thought. *If I hauled off and slapped her, maybe that would be enough disruption to stall the whole thing.* Then I reconsidered. They were both grown-ups, at least theoretically. They would get married if they chose, either here and now or somewhere else on some other night. I bowed my head and sucked up my misgivings.

"Of course," I said, raising my face and smiling that

bright smile I got when I was really anxious. "Let's get on with the ceremony." I caught a glimpse of Quinn's face in the crowd. He was looking at me, concerned by the low-voiced argument. Amelia, on the other hand, was happily chatting with Catfish, whom she'd met at the bar. Hoyt was by himself right under one of the portable lights rigged up for the occasion. He had his hands thrust in his pockets, and he looked more serious than I'd ever seen him. There was something strange about the sight, and after a second I figured out why.

It was one of the few times I'd ever seen Hoyt alone.

I took my brother's arm, and Calvin again gripped Crystal's. The priest stepped into the center of the circle, and the ceremony began. Though I tried hard to look happy for Jason, I had a difficult time holding back my tears while my brother became the bridegroom of a wild and willful girl who had been dangerous from birth.

There was dancing afterward, and a wedding cake, and lots of alcohol. There was food galore, and consequently there were huge trash cans that filled up with paper plates, cans, and crumpled paper napkins. Some of the men had brought cases of beer and wine, and some had hard liquor, too. No one could say that Hotshot couldn't throw a party.

While a zydeco band from Monroe played, the crowd danced in the street. The music echoed across the fields in an eerie way. I shivered and wondered what was watching from the dark.

"They're good, aren't they?" Jason asked. "The band?"

"Yeah," I said. He was flushed with happiness. His bride was dancing with one of her cousins.

"That's why we hurried this wedding up," he said. "She found out she was pregnant, and we decided to go on and do it—just do it. And her favorite band was free for tonight."

I shook my head at my brother's impulsiveness. Then I reminded myself to keep visible signs of disapproval at a minimum. The bride's family might take issue.

Quinn was a good dancer, though I had to show him some of the Cajun steps. All the Hotshot belles wanted a dance with Quinn, too, so I had a turn with Calvin, and Hoyt, and Catfish. Quinn was having a good time, I could tell, and on one level I was, too. But around two thirty a.m., we gave each other a little nod. He had to leave the next day, and I wanted to be alone with him. Plus, I was tired of smiling.

As Quinn thanked Calvin for the wonderful evening, I watched Jason and Crystal dancing together, both apparently delighted with each other. I knew right from Jason's brain that he was infatuated with the shifter girl, with the subculture that had formed her, with the newness of being a supernatural. I knew from Crystal's brain that she was exultant. She'd been determined to marry someone that hadn't grown up in Hotshot, someone who was exciting in bed, someone able to stand up to not only her but her extended family . . . and now she had.

I made my way over to the happy couple and gave each of them a kiss on the cheek. Now Crystal was family, after all, and I would have to accept her as such and leave the two to work out their own life together. I gave Calvin a hug, too, and he held me for a second before releasing me and giving me a reassuring pat on the back. Catfish danced me around in a circle, and a drunken Hoyt took up where he'd left off. I had a hard time convincing the two that I really meant to leave, but finally Quinn and I began to make our way back to my car.

As we wended through the edges of the crowd, I spotted Amelia dancing with one of her Hotshot beaux. They were both in high spirits, both literally and libation-wise. I called to Amelia that we were leaving, and she yelled, "I'll get a ride with someone later!"

Though I enjoyed seeing Amelia happy, it must have been Misgiving Night, because I worried about her a little. However, if anyone could take care of herself, it was Amelia.

We were moving slow when we let ourselves into the house. I didn't check out Quinn's head, but mine was muzzy from the noise, the clamor of all the brains around me, and the extra surges of emotion. It had been a long day. Some of it had been excellent, though. As I recalled the very best parts, I caught myself smiling down at Bob. The big cat rubbed himself against my ankles, meowing in an inquiring kind of way.

Oh, geez.

I felt like I had to explain Amelia's absence to the cat. I squatted down and scratched Bob's head, and (feeling incredibly foolish) I said, "Hey, Bob. She's going to be real late tonight; she's still dancing at the party. But don't you worry, she'll be home!" The cat turned his back on me and stalked out of the room. I was never sure how much human was lurking in Bob's little feline brain, but I hoped he'd just fall asleep and forget all about our strange conversation.

Just at that moment, I heard Quinn call to me from my bedroom, and I put thoughts about Bob on hold. After all, it was our last night together for maybe weeks.

While I brushed my teeth and washed my face, I had one last flare of worry about Jason. My brother had made his bed. I hoped he could lie comfortably in it for some time. *He's a grown-up*, I told myself over and over as I went into the bedroom in my nicest nightgown.

Quinn pulled me to him, said, "Don't worry, babe, don't worry. . . ."

I banished my brother and Bob from my thoughts and this bedroom. I brought a hand up to trace the curve of Quinn's scalp, kept those fingers going down his spine, loved it when he shivered.

5

I WAS WALKING IN MY SLEEP. IT WAS A GOOD THING I knew every inch of Merlotte's like I knew my own house, or I'd have bumped into every table and chair. I yawned widely as I took Selah Pumphrey's order. Ordinarily Selah irritated the hell out of me. She'd been dating Nameless Ex-Lover for several weeks—well, months now. No matter how invisible Ex had become, she'd never be my favorite person.

"Not getting enough rest, Sookie?" she asked, her voice sharp.

"Excuse me," I apologized. "I guess not. I was at my brother's wedding last night. What kind of dressing did you want on that salad?"

"Ranch." Selah's big dark eyes were examining me like she was thinking of etching my portrait. She really wanted to know all about Jason's wedding, but asking me would be like surrendering ground to the enemy. Silly Selah.

Come to think of it, what was Selah doing here? She'd never come in without Bill. She lived in Clarice. Not that Clarice was far; you could get there in fifteen or twenty minutes. But why would a real estate saleswoman from Clarice be . . . oh. She must be showing a house here. Yes, the brain was moving slowly today.

"Okeydokey. Coming right up," I said, and turned to go.

"Listen," Selah said. "Let me be frank."

Oh, boy. In my experience, that meant, "Let me be openly mean."

I swung around, trying to look anything but massively irritated, which was what I actually was. This was not the day to screw with me. Among my many worries, Amelia hadn't come home the night before, and when I'd gone upstairs to look for Bob, I'd found that he'd thrown up in the middle of Amelia's bed . . . which would have been okay by me, but it had been covered with my great-grandmother's quilt. It had fallen to me to clean up the mess and get the quilt to soaking in the washing machine. Quinn had left early that morning, and I was simply sad about that. And then there was Jason's marriage, which had such potential to be a disaster.

I could think of a few more items to add to the list (down to the dripping tap in my kitchen), but you get that my day was not a happy one.

"I'm here working, Selah. I'm not here to have any personal chitchats with you."

She ignored that.

"I know you're going on a trip with Bill," she said. "You're trying to steal him back from me. How long have you been scheming about this?"

I know my mouth was hanging open, because I just hadn't gotten enough warning that was coming. My telepathy was affected when I was tired—just as my reaction time and thought processes were—and I was heavily shielded when I worked, as a matter of course. So I hadn't picked up on Selah's thoughts. A flash of rage passed through me, lifting my palm and raising it to slap the shit out of her. But a warm, hard hand took mine, gripped it, brought it down to my side. Sam was there, and I hadn't even seen him coming. I was missing everything today.

"Miss Pumphrey, you'll have to get your lunch somewhere else," Sam said quietly. Of course, everyone was watching. I could feel all the brains go on alert for fresh gossip as eyes drank in every nuance of the scene. I could feel my face redden.

"I have the right to eat here," Selah said, her voice loud and arrogant. That was a huge mistake. In an instant, the sympathies of the spectators switched to me. I could feel the wave of it wash over me. I widened my eyes and looked sad like one of those abnormally big-eyed kids in the awful waif paintings. Looking pathetic was no big stretch. Sam put an arm around me as though I were a wounded child and looked at Selah with nothing on his face but a grave disappointment in her behavior.

"I have the right to tell you to go," he said. "I can't have you insulting my staff."

Selah was never likely to be rude to Arlene or Holly or Danielle. She hardly knew they existed, because she wasn't the kind of woman who really looked at a server. It had always stuck in her craw that Bill had dated me before he'd met her. ("Dated," in Selah's book, being a euphemism for "had enthusiastic and frequent sex with.")

Selah's body was jerky with anger as she threw her napkin on the floor. She got to her feet so abruptly that her chair would have fallen if Dawson, a boulder of a werewolf who ran a motorcycle repair business, hadn't caught it with one huge hand. Selah grabbed up her purse to stalk out of the door, narrowly avoiding a collision with my friend Tara, who was entering.

Dawson was highly amused by the whole scene. "All that over a vamp," he said. "Them cold-blooded things must be something, to get fine-looking women so upset."

"Who's upset?" I said, smiling and standing straighter to show Sam I was unfazed. I doubt he was fooled, since Sam knows me pretty well, but he got my emotional drift and went back behind the bar. The buzz of discussion of this juicy scene rose from the lunch crowd. I strode over to the table where Tara was sitting. She had JB du Rone in tow.

"Looking good, JB," I said brightly, pulling the menus from between the napkin box and the salt and pepper shakers in the middle of the table and handing one to him and one to Tara. My hands were shaking, but I don't think they noticed.

JB smiled up at me. "Thanks, Sookie," he said in his pleasant baritone. JB was just beautiful, but really short on the brains. However, that gave him a charming simplicity. Tara and I had watched out for him in school, because once that simplicity was observed and targeted by other, less handsome boys, JB had been in for some rough patches . . . especially in junior high. Since Tara and I also both had huge flaws in our own popularity profiles, we'd tried to protect JB as much as we were able. In return, JB had squired me to a couple of dances I'd wanted to go to very badly, and his family had given Tara a place to stay a couple of times when I couldn't.

Tara had had sex with JB somewhere along this painful road. I hadn't. It didn't seem to make any difference to either relationship.

"JB has a new job," Tara said, smiling in a self-satisfied way. So that was why she'd come in. Our relationship had been uneasy for the past few months, but she knew I'd want to share in her pride at having done a good thing for JB.

That was great news. And it helped me not think about Selah Pumphrey and her load of anger.

"Whereabouts?" I asked JB, who was looking at the menu as if he'd never seen it before.

"At the health club in Clarice," he said. He looked up and smiled. "Two days a week, I sit at the desk wearing this." He waved a hand at his clean and tight-fitting golf shirt, striped burgundy and brown, and his pressed khakis. "I get the members to sign in, I make healthy shakes, and I clean the equipment and hand out towels. Three days a week, I wear workout clothes and I spot for all the ladies."

"That sounds great," I said, awestruck at the perfection of the job for JB's limited qualifications. JB was lovely: impressive muscles, handsome face, straight white teeth. He was an ad for physical health. Also, he was naturally good-natured and neat.

Tara looked at me, expecting her due praise. "Good work," I told her. We gave each other a high five.

"Now, Sookie, the only thing that would make life perfect is you calling me some night," JB said. No one could project a wholesome, simple lust like JB.

"Thanks so much, JB, but I'm seeing someone now," I said, not troubling to keep my voice down. After Selah's little exhibition, I felt the need to brag a little.

"Oooh, that Quinn?" Tara asked. I may have mentioned him to her once or twice. I nodded, and we did another high five. "Is he in town now?" she asked in a lower voice, and I said, "Left this morning," just as quietly.

"I want the Mexican cheeseburger," JB said.

"Then I'll get you one," I said, and after Tara had ordered, I marched to the kitchen. Not only was I delighted for JB, I was happy that Tara and I seemed to have mended our fences. I had needed a little upswing to my day, and I had gotten it.

When I reached home with a couple of bags of groceries, Amelia was back and my kitchen sparkled like an exhibit in a Southern Homes show. When she was feeling stressed or bored, Amelia cleaned, which was a fantastic habit to have in a housemate—especially when you're not used to having one at all. I like a neat house myself, and I get cleaning spurts from time to time, but next to Amelia I was a slob.

I looked at the clean windows. "Feeling guilty, huh?" I said.

Amelia's shoulders slumped. She was sitting at the kitchen table with a mug of one of her weird teas, steam rising from the dark liquid.

"Yeah," she said glumly. "I saw the quilt was in the washing machine. I worked on the spot, and it's hanging out back on the line now."

Since I'd noted that when I came in, I just nodded. "Bob retaliated," I said.

"Yeah."

I started to ask her who she'd stayed with, then realized it was really none of my business. Besides, though I was very tired, Amelia was a broadcaster of the first order, and within seconds I knew she'd stayed with Calvin's cousin Derrick and the sex hadn't been good; also, Derrick's sheets had been very dirty and that had made her nuts. Plus, when Derrick had woken up this morning, he'd indicated that in his mind, a night together made them a couple. Amelia had had a hard time getting Derrick to give her a ride back to the house. He wanted her to stay with him, in Hotshot.

"Weirded out?" I asked, putting the hamburger meat in the refrigerator drawer. It was my week to cook, and we were going to have hamburger steak, baked potatoes, and green beans.

Amelia nodded, lifting her mug to take a sip. It was a homemade hangover restorative she'd concocted, and she shuddered as she experimented on herself. "Yeah, I am. Those Hotshot guys are a little strange," she said.

"Some of them." Amelia had adjusted better to my telepathy than anyone I'd ever encountered. Since she was frank and open anyway—sometimes way too much—I guess she never felt she had secrets to hide.

"What are you gonna do?" I asked. I sat down opposite her.

"See, it's not like I'd been dating Bob for a long time," she said, jumping right into the middle of the conversation without bothering with preliminaries. She knew I understood. "We'd only gotten together that one night. Believe me, it was great. He really *got* me. That's why we began, ah, experimenting."

I nodded, tried to look understanding. To me, experimenting was, well, licking a place you'd never licked before, or trying a position that gave you a cramp in your thigh. Like that. It did not involve turning your partner into an animal. I'd never worked up enough nerve to ask Amelia what their goal had been, and it was one thing her brain wasn't throwing out.

"I guess you like cats," I said, following my train of thought to its logical conclusion. "I mean, Bob is a cat, but a small one, and then you picked Derrick out of all the guys who would have been thrilled to spend the night with you."

"Oh?" Amelia said, perking up. She tried to sound casual. "More than one?"

Amelia did have the tendency to think way too well of herself as a witch, but not enough of herself as a woman.

"One or two," I said, trying not to laugh. Bob came in and wreathed himself around my legs, purring loudly. It could hardly have been more pointed, since he walked around Amelia as if she were a pile of dog poop.

Amelia sighed heavily. "Listen, Bob, you've gotta forgive me," she said to the cat. "I'm sorry. I just got carried away.

A wedding, a few beers, dancing in the street, an exotic partner . . . I'm sorry. Really, really sorry. How about I promise to be celibate until I can figure out a way to turn you back into yourself?"

This was a huge sacrifice on Amelia's part, as anyone who'd read her thoughts for a couple of days (and more) would know. Amelia was a very healthy girl and she was a very direct woman. She was also fairly diverse in her tastes. "Well," she said, on second thought, "what if I just promise not to do any guys?"

Bob's hind end sat while his front end stood, and his tail wrapped around his front paws. He looked adorable as he stared up at Amelia, his large yellow eyes unblinking. He appeared to be thinking it over. Finally, he said, "Rohr."

Amelia smiled.

"You taking that as a yes?" I said. "If so, remember . . . I just do guys, so don't go looking my way."

"Oh, I probably wouldn't try to hook up with you anyway," Amelia said.

Did I mention Amelia is a little tactless? "Why not?" I asked, insulted.

"I didn't pick Bob at random," Amelia said, looking as embarrassed as it is possible for Amelia to look. "I like 'em skinny and dark."

"I'll just have to live with that," I said, trying to look deeply disappointed. Amelia threw a tea ball at me, and I caught it in midair.

"Good reflexes," she said, startled.

I shrugged. Though it had been ages since I'd had vampire blood, a trace seemed to linger on in my system. I'd always been healthy, but now I seldom even got a headache. And I moved a little quicker than most people. I wasn't the only person to enjoy the side effects of vamp blood ingestion. Now that the effects have become common knowledge, vampires have become prey themselves. Harvesting that blood to sell on the black market is a lucrative and highly perilous profession. I'd heard on the radio that morning that a drainer had disappeared from his Texarkana apartment after he'd gotten out on parole. If you make an enemy of a vamp, he can wait it out a lot longer than you can.

"Maybe it's the fairy blood," Amelia said, staring at me thoughtfully.

I shrugged again, this time with a definite drop-this-subject air. I'd learned I had a trace of fairy in my lineage only recently, and I wasn't happy about it. I didn't even know which side of my family had bequeathed me this legacy, much less which individual. All I knew was that at some time in the past, someone in my family had gotten up close and personal with a fairy. I'd spent a couple of hours poring over the yellowing family trees and the family history my grandmother had worked so hard to compile, and I hadn't found a clue.

As if she'd been summoned by the thought, Claudine knocked at the back door. She hadn't flown on gossamer wings; she'd arrived in her car. Claudine is a full-blooded fairy, and she has other ways of getting places, but she uses those ways only in emergencies. Claudine is very tall, with a thick fall of dark hair and big, slanted dark eyes. She has to cover her ears with her hair, since unlike her twin, Claude, she hasn't had the pointy parts surgically altered.

Claudine hugged me enthusiastically but gave Amelia a distant wave. They are not nuts about each other. Amelia has acquired magic, but Claudine is magic to the bone. Neither quite trusts the other.

Claudine is normally the sunniest creature I ever met. She is very kind, and sweet, and helpful, like a supernatural Girl Scout, because it's her nature and because she's trying to work her way up the magical ladder to become an angel. Tonight, Claudine's face was unusually serious. My heart sank. I wanted to go to bed, and I wanted to miss Quinn in private, and I wanted to get over the jangling my nerves had taken at Merlotte's. I didn't want bad news.

Claudine settled at the kitchen table across from me and held my hands. She spared a look for Amelia. "Take a hike, witch," she said, and I was shocked.

"Pointy-eared bitch," muttered Amelia, getting up with her mug of tea.

"Mate killer," responded Claudine.

"He's not dead!" shrieked Amelia. "He's just—different!"

Claudine snorted, and actually that was an adequate response.

I was too tired to scold Claudine for her unprecedented rudeness, and she was holding my hands too tight for me to be pleased about her comforting presence. "What's up?" I asked. Amelia stomped out of the room, and I heard her shoes on the stairs up to the second floor.

"No vampires here?" Claudine said, her voice anxious. You know how a chocoholic feels about chunky fudge ice cream, double dipped in dark chocolate? That's how vamps feel about fairies.

"Yeah, the house is empty except for me, you, Amelia, and Bob," I said. I was not going to deny Bob his personhood, though sometimes it was pretty hard to recall, especially when his litter box needed cleaning.

"You're going to this summit?"

"Yes."

"Why?"

That was a good question. "The queen is paying me," I said.

"Do you need the money so badly?"

I started to dismiss her concern, but then I gave it some serious thought. Claudine had done a lot for me, and the least I could do for her was think about what she said.

"I can live without it," I said. After all, I still had some of the money Eric had paid me for hiding him from a group of witches. But a chunk of it had gone, as money seems to; the insurance hadn't covered everything that had been damaged or destroyed by the fire that had consumed my kitchen the winter before, and I'd upgraded my appliances, and I'd made a donation to the volunteer fire department. They'd come so quickly and tried so hard to save the kitchen and my car.

Then Jason had needed help to pay the doctor's bill for Crystal's miscarriage.

I found I missed that layer of padding between being solvent and being broke. I wanted to reinforce it, replenish it. My little boat sailed on precarious financial waters, and I wanted to have a towboat around to keep it afloat.

"I can live without it," I said, more firmly, "but I don't want to."

Claudine sighed. Her face was full of woe. "I can't go with you," she said. "You know how vampires are around us. I can't even put in an appearance."

"I understand," I said, a bit surprised. I'd never dreamed of Claudine's going.

"And I think there's going to be trouble," she said.

"What kind?" The last time I'd gone to a vampire social gathering, there had been big trouble, major trouble, the bloodiest kind of trouble.

"I don't know," Claudine said. "But I feel it coming, and I think you should stay home. Claude does, too."

Claude didn't give a rat's ass what happened to me, but Claudine was generous enough to include her brother in her kindness. As far as I could tell, Claude's benefit to the world was strictly as a decoration. He was utterly selfish, had no social skills, and was absolutely beautiful.

"I'm sorry, Claudine, and I'll miss you while I'm in Rhodes," I said. "But I've obligated myself to go."

"Going in the train of a vampire," Claudine said dismally. "It'll mark you as one of their world, for good. You'll never be an innocent bystander again. Too many creatures will know who you are and where you can be found."

It wasn't so much what Claudine said as the way she said it that made cold prickles run up my spine and crawl along my scalp. She was right. I had no defense, though I rather thought that I was already into the vamp world too deeply to opt out.

Sitting there in my kitchen with the late afternoon sun slanting through the window, I had one of those illuminations that changes you forever. Amelia was silent upstairs. Bob had come back into the room to sit by his food bowl and stare at Claudine. Claudine herself was gleaming in a beam of sunlight that hit her square in the face. Most people would be showing every unattractive skin flaw. Claudine still looked perfect.

I wasn't sure I would ever understand Claudine and her thinking about the world, and I still knew frighteningly little about her life; but I felt quite sure that she had devoted herself to my well-being, for whatever reason, and that she was really afraid for me. And yet I knew I was going to Rhodes with the queen, and Eric, and the abjured one, and the rest of the Louisiana contingent.

Was I just curious about what the agenda might be at a vampire summit? Did I want the attention of more undead members of society? Did I want to be known as a fangbanger, one of those humans who simply adored the walking dead? Did some corner of me long for a chance to be near Bill without seeking him out, still trying to make some emotional sense of his betrayal? Or was this about Eric? Unbeknownst to myself, was I in love with the flamboyant Viking who was so handsome, so good at making love, and so political, all at the same time?

This sounded like a promising set of problems for a soap opera season.

"Tune in tomorrow," I muttered. When Claudine looked at me askance, I said, "Claudine, I feel embarrassed to tell you I'm doing something that really doesn't make much sense in a lot of ways, but I want the money and I'm going to do it. I'll be back here to see you again. Don't worry, please."

Amelia clomped back into the room, began making herself some more tea. She was going to float away.

Claudine ignored her. "I'm going to worry," she said simply. "There is trouble coming, my dear friend, and it will fall right on your head."

"But you don't know how or when?"

She shook her head. "No, I just know it's coming."

"Look into my eyes," muttered Amelia. "I see a tall, dark man . . ."

"Shut up," I told her.

She turned her back to us, made a big fuss out of pinching the dead leaves off some of her plants.

Claudine left soon after. For the remainder of her visit, she didn't recover her normal happy demeanor. She never said another word about my departure.

6

On the second morning after Jason's wedding, I was feeling much more myself. Having a mission helped. I needed to be at Tara's Togs right after it opened at ten. I had to pick out the clothes Eric said I needed for the summit. I wasn't due at Merlotte's until five thirty or so that night, so I had that pleasant feeling of the whole day stretching ahead of me.

"Hey, girl!" Tara said, coming from the back of the shop to greet me. Her part-time assistant, McKenna, glanced at me and resumed moving clothes around. I assumed she was putting misplaced items back into their correct positions; clothing store employees seem to spend a lot of time doing that. McKenna didn't speak, and unless I was much mistaken, she was trying to avoid talking to me at all. That hurt, since I'd gone to see her in the hospital when she'd had her appendix out two weeks ago, and I'd taken her a little present, too.

"Mr. Northman's business associate Bobby Burnham called down here to say you needed some clothes for a trip?" Tara said. I nodded, trying to look matter of fact. "Would casual clothes be what you needed? Or suits, something of a business nature?" She gave me an utterly false bright smile, and I knew she was angry with me because she was scared for me. "McKenna, you can take that mail to the post office," Tara told McKenna with an edge to her voice. McKenna scuttled out the back door, the mail stuffed under her arm like a riding crop.

"Tara," I said, "it's not what you think."

"Sookie, it's none of my business," she said, trying hard to sound neutral.

"I think it is," I said. "You're my friend, and I don't want you thinking I'm just going traveling with a bunch of vampires for fun."

"Then why are you going?" Tara's face dropped all the false cheer. She was deadly serious.

"I'm getting paid to go with a few of the Louisiana vamps to a big meeting. I'll act as their, like, human Geiger counter. I'll tell them if a human's trying to bullshit them, and I'll know what the other vamps' humans are thinking. It's just for this one time." I couldn't explain more fully. Tara had been into the world of the vampires more heavily than she needed to be, and she'd almost gotten killed. She wanted nothing more to do with it, and I couldn't blame her. But she still couldn't tell me what to do. I'd gone through my own soul searching over this issue, even before Claudine's lecture, and I wasn't going to permit anyone else to second-guess me once I'd made up my mind. Getting the clothes was okay. Working for the vamps was okay . . . as long as I didn't turn humans over to get killed.

"We've been friends for a coon's age," Tara said quietly. "Through thick and thin. I love you, Sookie, I always will; but this is a real thin time." Tara had had so much disappointment and worry in her life that she simply wasn't willing to undertake any more. So she was cutting me loose, and she thought she would call JB that night and renew their carnal acquaintance, and she would do that almost in memory of me.

It was a strange way to write my premature epitaph.

"I need an evening dress, a cocktail-type dress, and some nice day clothes," I said, checking my list quite unnecessarily. I wasn't going to fool with Tara anymore. I was going to have fun, no matter how sour she looked. She'd come around, I told myself.

I was going to enjoy buying clothes. I started off with an evening dress and a cocktail dress. And I got two suits, like business suits (but not really, since I can't see myself in black pinstripes). And two pants outfits. And hose and knee-highs and a nightgown or two. And a bit of lingerie.

I was swinging between guilt and delight. I spent more of Eric's money than I absolutely had to, and I wondered what would happen if Eric asked to see the things he'd bought. I'd feel pretty bad then. But it was like I'd been caught up in a buying frenzy, partly out of the sheer delight of it, and partly out of anger at Tara, and partly to deny the fear I was feeling at the prospect of accompanying a group of vampires anywhere.

With another sigh, this one a very quiet and private one, I returned the lingerie and the nightgowns to their tables. Nonessentials. I felt sad to part with them, but I felt better overall. Buying clothes to suit a specific need, well, that was okay. That was a meal. But buying underthings, that was something else entirely. That was like a MoonPie. Or Ding Dongs. Sweet, but bad for you.

The local priest, who had started attending Fellowship of the Sun meetings, had suggested to me that befriending vamps, or even working for them, was a way of expressing a death wish. He'd told me this over his burger basket the week before. I thought about that now, standing at the cash register while Tara rang up all my purchases, which would be paid for with vampire money. Did I believe I wanted to die? I shook my head. No, I didn't. And I thought the Fellowship of the Sun, which was the ultra right-wing anti-vampire movement that was gaining an alarming stronghold in America, was a crock. Their condemnation of all humans who had any dealings with vampires, even down to visiting a business owned by a vamp, was ridiculous. But why was I even drawn to vamps to begin with?

Here was the truth of it: I'd had so little chance of having the kind of life my classmates had achieved—the kind of life I'd grown up thinking was the ideal—that any other life I could shape for myself seemed interesting. If I couldn't have a husband and children, worry about what I was going to take to the church potluck and if our house needed another coat of paint, then I'd worry about what three-inch heels would do to my sense of balance when I was wearing several extra pounds in sequins.

When I was ready to go, McKenna, who'd come back from the post office, carried my bags out to my car while Tara cleared the amount with Eric's day man, Bobby Burnham. She hung up the phone, looking pleased.

"Did I use it all up?" I asked, curious to find out how much Eric had invested in me.

"Not nearly," she said. "Want to buy more?"

But the fun was over. "No," I said. "I've gotten enough." I had a definite impulse to ask Tara to take every stitch back.

Then I thought what a shabby thing that would be to do to her. "Thanks for helping me, Tara."

"My pleasure," she assured me. Her smile was a little warmer and more genuine. Tara always liked making money, and she'd never been able to stay mad at me long. "You need to go to World of Shoes in Clarice to get something to go with the evening gown. They're having a sale."

I braced myself. This was the day to get things done. Next stop, World of Shoes.

I would be leaving in a week, and work that night went by in a blur as I grew more excited about the trip. I'd never been as far from home as Rhodes, which was way up there by Chicago; actually, I'd never been north of the Mason-Dixon Line. I'd flown only once, and that had been a short flight from Shreveport to Dallas. I would have to get a suitcase, one that rolled. I'd have to get . . . I thought of a long list of smaller items. I knew that some hotels had hair dryers. Would the Pyramid of Gizeh? The Pyramid was one of the most famous vampire-oriented hotels that had sprung up in major American cities.

Since I'd already arranged my time off with Sam, that night I told him when I was scheduled to leave. Sam was sitting behind his desk in the office when I knocked on the door—well, the door frame, because Sam almost never shut the door. He looked up from his bill paying. He was glad to be interrupted. When he worked on the books, he ran his hands through his reddish blond hair, and now he looked a little electrified as a result. Sam would rather be tending bar than doing this task, but he'd actually hired a substitute for tonight just for the purpose of getting his books straight.

"Come in, Sook," he said. "How's it going out there?"

"Pretty busy; I haven't got but a second. I just wanted to tell you I'll be leaving next Thursday."

Sam tried to smile, but he ended up simply looking unhappy. "You have to do this?" he asked.

"Hey, we've talked about this," I said, sounding a clear warning.

"Well, I'll miss you," he explained. "And I'll worry a little. You and lots of vamps."

"There'll be humans there, like me."

"*Not* like you. They'll be humans with a sick infatuation with the vampire culture, or deaddiggers, looking to make a buck off the undead. None of these are healthy people with long life expectancies."

"Sam, two years ago I didn't have any idea of what the world around me was really like. I didn't know what you really were; I didn't know that vampires were as different from each other as we are. I didn't know that there were real fairies. I couldn't have imagined any of that." I shook my head. "What a world this is, Sam. It's wonderful and it's scary. Each day is different. I never thought I would have any kind of life for myself, and now I do."

"I'd be the last person in the world to block your place in the sun, Sookie," Sam said, and he smiled at me. But it didn't escape my attention that his statement was a wee bit ambiguous.

Pam came to Bon Temps that night, looking bored and cool in a pale green jumpsuit with navy piping. She was wearing navy penny loafers . . . no kidding. I hadn't even realized those were still for sale. The dark leather was polished to a high shine, and the pennies were new. She got plenty of admiring looks in the bar. She perched at a table in my section and sat patiently, her hands clasped on the table in front of her. She went into the vampire state of suspension that was so unnerving to anyone who hadn't seen it yet—her eyes open but not seeing, her body totally unmoving, her expression blank. Since she was having some downtime,

I waited on a few people before I went to her table. I was sure I knew why she was there, and I wasn't looking forward to the conversation.

"Pam, can I get you a drink?"

"What's with the tiger, then?" she asked, going straight for the conversational jugular.

"Quinn is who I'm seeing now," I said. "We don't get to stay together much because of his job, but we'll see each other at the summit." Quinn had been hired to produce some of the summit's expected ceremonies and rituals. He'd be busy, but I'd catch glimpses of him, and I was already excited about the prospect. "We're spending a month together after the summit," I told Pam.

Ah-oh, maybe I'd over-shared on that one. Pam's face lost its smile.

"Sookie, I don't know what strange game you and Eric have going, but it's not good for us."

"I have nothing going! Nothing!"

"You may not, but he does. He has not been the same since the time you two spent together."

"I don't know what I can do about that," I said weakly.

Pam said, "I don't either, but I hope he can resolve his feelings for you. He doesn't enjoy having conflicts. He doesn't enjoy feeling attached. He is not the carefree vampire he used to be."

I shrugged. "Pam, I've been as straight with him as I can be. I think maybe he's worried about something else. You're exaggerating my importance in Eric's scheme of things. If he has any kind of undying love for me, then he's sure not telling me about it. And I never see him. And he knows about Quinn."

"He made Bill confess to you, didn't he?"

"Well, Eric was there," I said uncertainly.

"Do you think Bill would ever have told you if Eric hadn't commanded him to?"

I'd done my best to forget that night altogether. In the back of my mind, I'd known the strange timing of Bill's revelation was significant, but I just hadn't wanted to think about it.

"Why do you think Eric would give a flying fuck what Bill had been ordered to do, much less reveal it to a human woman, if he didn't have inappropriate feelings for you?"

I'd never put it to myself quite like that. I'd been so ripped up by Bill's confession—the queen had planted him to seduce me (if necessary) to gain my trust—that I hadn't thought of why Eric had forced Bill into the position of telling me about the plot.

"Pam, I don't know. Listen, I'm working here, and you need to order something to drink. I gotta take care of my other tables."

"O-negative, then. TrueBlood."

I hurried to get the drink out of the cooler, and I warmed it up in the microwave, shaking it gently to make sure the temperature was even. It coated the sides of the bottle in an unpleasant way, but it certainly looked and tasted like real blood. I'd poured a few drops into a glass one time at Bill's so I could have the experience. As far as I could tell, drinking synthetic blood was exactly like drinking real blood. Bill had always enjoyed it, though he'd remarked more than once that flavor wasn't the thing; it was the sensation of biting into flesh, feeling the heartbeat of the human, that made being a vampire fun. Glugging out of a bottle just didn't do the trick. I took the bottle and a wineglass to Pam's table and deposited both before her, along with a napkin, of course.

"Sookie?" I looked up to see that Amelia had come in.

My roomie had come into the bar often enough, but I was surprised to see her tonight. "What's up?" I asked.

"Um . . . hi," Amelia said to Pam. I took in Amelia's pressed khakis, her neat white golf shirt, her equally white tennis shoes. I glanced at Pam, whose pale eyes were wider than I'd ever seen them.

"This is my roommate, Amelia Broadway," I told Pam. "Amelia, this is Pam the vampire."

"I am pleased to meet you," Pam said.

"Hey, neat outfit," Amelia said.

Pam looked pleased. "You look very nice, too," she said.

"You a local vamp?" Amelia asked. Amelia was nothing if not blunt. And chatty.

Pam said, "I'm Eric's second-in-command. You do know who Eric Northman is?"

"Sure," Amelia said. "He's the blond hunk of burning love who lives in Shreveport, right?"

Pam smiled. Her fangs popped out a little. I looked from Amelia to the vampire. Geez Louise.

"Perhaps you would like to see the bar some night?" Pam said.

"Oh, sure," Amelia said, but not as if she were particularly excited. Playing hard to get. For about ten minutes, if I knew Amelia.

I left to answer a customer beckoning from another table. Out of the corner of my eye, Amelia sat down with Pam, and they talked for a few minutes before Amelia got up and stood by the bar, waiting for me to return.

"And what brings you here tonight?" I asked maybe a little too abruptly.

Amelia raised her eyebrows, but I didn't apologize.

"I just wanted to tell you, you got a phone call at the house."

"Who from?"

"From Quinn."

I felt a smile spread across my face, a real one. "What did he say?"

"He said he'd see you in Rhodes. He misses you already."

"Thanks, Amelia. But you could've just called here to tell me, or told me when I got home."

"Oh, I got a little bored."

I'd known she would be, sooner or later. Amelia needed a job, a full-time job. She missed her city and her friends, of course. Even though she'd left New Orleans before Katrina, she'd suffered a little every day since the storm's aftermath had devastated the city. Amelia missed the witchcraft, too. I'd hoped she'd pal around with Holly, another barmaid and a dedicated Wiccan. But after I'd introduced the two and they'd had some conversations, Amelia had told me glumly that she and Holly were very different sorts of witches. Amelia herself was (she considered) a true witch, while Holly was a Wiccan. Amelia had a thinly veiled contempt for the Wiccan faith. Once or twice, Amelia had met with Holly's coven, partly to keep her hand in . . . and partly because Amelia yearned for the company of other practitioners.

At the same time, my houseguest was very anxious she might be discovered by the witches of New Orleans and made to pay a high price for her mistake in changing Bob. To add yet another emotional layer, since Katrina, Amelia feared for the safety of these same former companions. She couldn't find out if they were okay without them discovering her in return.

Despite all this, I'd known the day (or night) would come when Amelia would be restless enough to look outside my house and yard and Bob.

I tried not to frown as Amelia went over to Pam's table to visit some more. I reminded my inner worrier that Amelia could take care of herself. Probably. I'd been more certain the night before in Hotshot. As I went about my work, I switched my thoughts to Quinn's call. I wished I'd had my new cell phone (thanks to Amelia's paying me a little rent, I could afford one) with me, but I didn't think it was right to carry it at work, and Quinn knew I wouldn't have it with me and turned on unless I was at liberty to answer it. I wished Quinn would be waiting at home when I left the bar in an hour. The strength of that fantasy intoxicated me.

Though it would have been pleasant to roll in that feeling, indulging myself in the flush of my new relationship, I concluded was time to back down and face a little reality. I concentrated on serving my tables, smiling and chatting as needed, and refreshing Pam's TrueBlood once or twice. Otherwise, I left Amelia and Pam to their tête-à-tête.

Finally, the last working hour was over, and the bar cleared out. Along with the other servers, I did my closing-up chores. When I was sure the napkin holders and salt shakers were full and ready for the next day, I went down the little hall into the storeroom to deposit my apron in the large laundry basket. After listening to us hint and complain for years, Sam had finally hung a mirror back there for our benefit. I found myself standing absolutely still, staring into it. I shook myself and began to untie my apron. Arlene was fluffing her own bright red hair. Arlene and I were not such good friends these days. She'd gotten involved in the Fellowship of the Sun. Though the Fellowship represented itself as an informational organization, dedicated to spreading the "truth" about vampires, its ranks were riddled with those who believed all vampires were intrinsically evil and should be eliminated, by violent means. The worst among the Fellowship took out their anger and fear on the humans who consorted with vampires.

Humans like me.

Arlene tried to meet my eyes in the mirror. She failed.

"That vamp in the bar your buddy?" she asked, putting a very unpleasant emphasis on the last word.

"Yes," I said. Even if I hadn't liked Pam, I would have said she was my buddy. Everything about the Fellowship made the hair rise up on my neck.

"You need to hang around with humans more," Arlene said. Her mouth was set in a solid line, and her heavily made-up eyes were narrow with intensity. Arlene had never been what you'd call a deep thinker, but I was astonished and dismayed by how fast she'd been sucked into the Fellowship way of thinking.

"I'm with humans ninety-five percent of the time, Arlene."

"You should make it a hundred."

"Arlene, how is this any of your business?" My patience was stretched to its breaking point.

"You been putting in all these hours because you're going with a bunch of vamps to some meeting, right?"

"Again, what business of yours?"

"You and me were friends for a long time, Sookie, until that Bill Compton walked into the bar. Now you see vamps all the time, and you have strange people staying at your house."

"I don't have to defend my life to you," I said, and my temper utterly snapped. I could see inside her head, see all the smug and satisfied righteous judgment. It hurt. It rankled. I had babysat her children, consoled her when she was left high and dry by a series of unworthy men, cleaned her trailer, tried to encourage her to date men who wouldn't walk all over her. Now she was staring at me, actually surprised at my anger.

"Obviously you have some big holes in your own life if

you have to fill them with this Fellowship crap," I said. "Look at what sterling guys you pick to date and marry." With that unchristian dig, I spun on my heel and walked out of the bar, thankful I'd already gotten my purse from Sam's office. Nothing's worse than having to stop in the middle of a righteous walkout.

Somehow Pam was beside me, having joined me so quickly that I hadn't seen her move. I looked over my shoulder. Arlene was standing with her back flat against the wall, her face distorted with pain and anger. My parting shot had been a true one. One of Arlene's boyfriends had stolen the family silverware, and her husbands . . . hard to know where to start.

Pam and I were outside before I could react to her presence.

I was rigid with the shock of Arlene's verbal attack and my own fury. "I shouldn't have said anything about him," I said. "Just because one of Arlene's husbands was a murderer is no reason for me to be ugly." I was absolutely channeling my grandmother, and I gave a shaky hoot of laughter.

Pam was a little shorter than I, and she looked up into my face curiously as I struggled to control myself.

"She's a whore, that one," Pam said.

I pulled a Kleenex out of my purse to blot my tears. I often cried when I got angry; I hated that. Crying just made you look weak, no matter what triggered it.

Pam held my hand and wiped my tears off with her thumb. The tender effect was a little weakened when she stuck the thumb in her mouth, but I figured she meant well.

"I wouldn't call her a whore, but she's truly not as careful as she might be about who she goes with," I admitted.

"Why do you defend her?"

"Habit," I said. "We were friends for years and years."

"What did she do for you, with her friendship? What benefit was there?"

"She . . ." I had to stop and think. "I guess I was just able to say I had a friend. I cared about her kids, and I helped her out with them. When she couldn't work, I'd take her hours, and if she worked for me, I'd clean her trailer in return. She'd come see me if I was sick and bring me food. Most of all, she was tolerant of my differences."

"She used you and yet you felt grateful," Pam said. Her expressionless white face gave me no clue to her feelings.

"Listen, Pam, it wasn't like that."

"How was it, Sookie?"

"She really did like me. We really did have some good times."

"She's lazy. That extends to her friendships. If it's easy to be friendly, she will be. If the wind blows the other way, her friendship will be gone. And I'm thinking the wind is blowing the other way. She has found some other way to be an important person in her own right, by hating others."

"Pam!"

"Is this not true? I've watched people for years. I know people."

"There's true stuff you should say, and true stuff that's better left unsaid."

"There's true stuff you would *rather* I left unsaid," she corrected me.

"Yes. As a matter of fact, that's . . . true."

"Then I'll leave you and go back to Shreveport." Pam turned to walk around the building to where her car was parked in front.

"Whoa!"

She turned back. "Yes?"

"Why were you here in the first place?"

Pam smiled unexpectedly. "Aside from asking you questions about your relationship with my maker? And the bonus of meeting your delectable roommate?"

"Oh. Yeah. Aside from all that."

"I want to talk to you about Bill," she said to my utter surprise. "Bill, and Eric."

7

"I don't have anything to say." I unlocked my car and tossed my purse inside. Then I turned to face Pam, though I was tempted to get in the car and go home.

"We didn't know," the vampire said. She walked slowly, so I could see her coming. Sam had left two lawn chairs out in front of his trailer, set at right angles to the rear of the bar, and I got them out of his yard and set them by the car. Pam took the hint and perched in one while I took the other.

I drew a deep, silent breath. I had wondered ever since I returned from New Orleans if all the vamps in Shreveport had known Bill's secret purpose in courting me. "I wouldn't have told you," Pam said, "even if I had known Bill had been charged with a mission, because . . . vampires first." She shrugged. "But I promise you that I didn't know."

I bobbed my head in acknowledgment, and a little pocket of tension in me finally relaxed. But I had no idea how to respond.

"I must say, Sookie, that you have caused a tremendous amount of trouble in our area." Pam didn't seem perturbed by that; she was just stating a fact. I hardly felt I could apologize. "These days Bill is full of anger, but he doesn't know who to hate. He feels guilty, and no one likes that. Eric is frustrated that he can't remember the time he was in hiding at your house, and he doesn't know what he owes you. He's angry that the queen has annexed you for her own purposes, through Bill, and thus poached on Eric's territory, as he sees it. Felicia thinks you are the bogeyman, since so many of the Fangtasia bartenders have died while you were around. Longshadow, Chow." She smiled. "Oh, and your friend, Charles Twining."

"None of that was my fault." I'd listened to Pam with growing agitation. It's so not good to have vampires angry with you. Even the current Fangtasia bartender, Felicia, was much stronger than I would ever be, and she was definitely the low vamp on the totem pole.

"I don't see that that makes any difference," Pam said, her voice curiously gentle. "Now that we know you have fairy blood, thanks to Andre, it would be easy to write all this off. But I don't think that's it, do you? I've known many humans descended from the fae, and none of them have been telepathic. I think that's just you, Sookie. Of course, knowing you have this streak of fairy makes one wonder how you would taste. I certainly enjoyed the sip I got when the maenad maimed you, though that was tainted with her poison. We love fairies, as you know."

"Love them to death," I said under my breath, but of course Pam heard.

"Sometimes," she agreed with a little smile. That Pam.

"So what's the bottom line here?" I was ready to go home and just be human, all by myself.

"When I say 'we' didn't know about Bill's agreement with the queen, that includes Eric," Pam said simply.

I looked down at my feet, struggling to keep my face under control.

"Eric feels especially angry about this," Pam said. She was picking her words now. "He is angry at Bill because Bill made an agreement with the queen that bypassed Eric. He is angry that he didn't discern Bill's plan. He is angry at you because you got under his skin. He is angry at the queen because she is more devious than he is. Of course, that's why she's the queen. Eric will never be a king, unless he can control himself better."

"You're really worried about him?" I'd never known Pam to be seriously concerned about much of anything. When she nodded, I found myself saying, "When did you meet Eric?" I'd always been curious, and tonight Pam seemed to be in a sharing mood.

"I met him in London the last night of my life." Her voice was level, coming out of the shadowy darkness. I could see half her face in the overhead security light, and she looked quite calm. "I risked everything for *love*. You'll laugh to hear this."

I wasn't remotely close to laughing.

"I was a very wild girl for my times. Young ladies weren't supposed to be alone with gentlemen, or any males, for that matter. A far cry from now." Pam's lips curved upward in a brief smile. "But I was a romantic, and bold. I slipped out of my house late at night to meet the cousin of my dearest friend, the girl who lived right next door. The cousin was visiting from Bristol, and we were very attracted to each other. My parents didn't consider him to be my equal in social class, so I knew they wouldn't let him court me. And if

I were caught alone with him at night, it would be the end of me. No marriage, unless my parents could force him to wed me. So, no future at all." Pam shook her head. "Crazy to think of now. Those were the times women didn't have choices. The ironic part is, our meeting was quite innocent. A few kisses, a lot of sentimental claptrap, undying love. Yada yada yada."

I grinned at Pam, but she didn't look up to catch the smile.

"On my way back to my house, trying to move so silently through the garden, I met Eric. There was no way to slip silently enough to avoid *him*." For a long moment, she was quiet. "And it really was the end of me."

"Why'd he turn you?" I settled lower in my chair and crossed my legs. This was an unexpected and fascinating conversation.

"I think he was lonely," she said, a faint note of surprise in her voice. "His last companion had struck out on her own, since children can't stay with their maker for long. After a few years, the child must strike out on its own, though it may come back to the maker, and must if the maker calls."

"Weren't you angry with him?"

She seemed to be trying to remember. "At first, I was shocked," Pam said. "After he'd drained me, he put me in bed in my own room, and of course my family thought I'd died of some mysterious ailment, and they buried me. Eric dug me up, so I wouldn't wake up in my coffin and have to dig my own way out. That was a great help. He held me and explained it all to me. Up until the night I died, I'd always been a very conventional woman underneath my daring tendencies. I was used to wearing layers and layers of clothes. You would be amazed at the dress I died in: the sleeves, the trim. The fabric in the skirt alone could make you three dresses!" Pam looked fondly reminiscent, nothing more.

"After I'd awakened, I discovered being a vampire freed some wild thing in me."

"After what he did, you didn't want to kill him?"

"No," she said instantly. "I wanted to have sex with him, and I did. We had sex many, many times." She grinned. "The tie between maker and child doesn't have to be sexual, but with us it was. That changed quite soon, actually, as my tastes broadened. I wanted to try everything I'd been denied in my human life."

"So you actually liked it, being a vampire? You were glad?"

Pam shrugged. "Yes, I've always loved being what I am. It took me a few days to understand my new nature. I'd never even heard of a vampire before I became one."

I couldn't imagine the shock of Pam's awakening. Her self-proclaimed quick adjustment to her new state amazed me.

"Did you ever go back to see your family?" I asked. Okay, that was tacky, and I regretted it as soon as the words passed my lips.

"I saw them from a distance, maybe ten years later. You understand, the first thing a new vampire needed to do was leave her home area. Otherwise she ran the risk of being recognized and hunted down. Now you can parade around as much as you like. But we were so secret, so careful. Eric and I headed out of London as quickly as we could go, and after spending a little time in the north of England while I became accustomed to my state, we left England for the continent."

This was gruesome but fascinating. "Did you love him?"

Pam looked a little puzzled. There was a tiny wrinkle in her smooth forehead. "Love him? No. We were good companions, and I enjoyed the sex and the hunting. But love? No." In the glare of the overhead security lights, which cast curious dark shadows in the corners of the lot, I watched

Pam's face relax into its normal smooth lines. "I owe him my loyalty," Pam said. "I have to obey him, but I do it willingly. Eric is intelligent, ambitious, and very entertaining. I would be crumbled to nothing in my grave by now if he hadn't been watching me slip back to my house from meeting that silly young man. I went my own way for many, many years, but I was glad to hear from him when he opened the bar and called me to serve him."

Was it possible for anyone in the world to be as detached as Pam over the whole "I was murdered" issue? There was no doubt Pam relished being a vampire, seemed to genuinely harbor a mild contempt for humans; in fact, she seemed to find them amusing. She had thought it was hilarious when Eric had first exhibited feelings for me. Could Pam truly be so changed from her former self?

"How old were you, Pam?"

"When I died? I was nineteen." Not a flicker of feeling crossed her face.

"Did you wear your hair up every day?"

Pam's face seemed to warm a little. "Yes, I did. I wore it in a very elaborate style; my maid had to help me. I put artificial pads underneath my hair to give it height. And the underwear! You would laugh yourself sick to see me get into it."

As interesting as this conversation had been, I realized I was tired and ready to go home. "So the bottom line is, you're really loyal to Eric, and you want me to know that neither of you knew that Bill had a hidden agenda when he came to Bon Temps." Pam nodded. "So, you came here tonight to . . . ?"

"To ask you to have mercy on Eric."

The idea of Eric needing my mercy had never crossed my mind. "That's as funny as your human underwear," I said. "Pam, I know you believe you owe Eric, even though he killed you—honey, he *killed* you—but I don't owe Eric a thing."

"You care for him," she said, and for the first time she sounded a little angry. "I know you do. He's never been so entangled in his emotions. He's never been at such a disadvantage." She seemed to gather herself, and I figured our conversation was over. We got up, and I returned Sam's chairs.

I had no idea what to say.

Fortunately, I didn't have to think of anything. Eric himself walked out of the shadows at the edge of the lot.

"Pam," he said, and that one word was loaded. "You were so late, I followed your trail to make sure all was well."

"Master," she said, which was something I'd never heard from Pam. She went down on one knee on the gravel, which must have been painful.

"Leave," Eric said, and just like that, Pam was gone.

I kept silent. Eric was giving me that vampiric fixed stare, and I couldn't read him at all. I was pretty sure he was mad—but about what, at whom, and with what intensity? That was the fun part of being with vampires, and the scary part of being with vampires, all at the same time.

Eric decided action would speak louder than words. Suddenly, he was right in front of me. He put a finger under my chin and lifted my face to his. His eyes, which looked simply dark in the irregular light, latched on to mine with an intensity that was both exciting and painful. Vampires; mixed feelings. One and the same.

Not exactly to my astonishment, he kissed me. When someone has had approximately a thousand years to practice kissing, he can become very good at it, and I would be lying if I said I was immune to such osculatory talent. My temperature zoomed up about ten degrees. It was everything I could do to keep from stepping into him, wrapping my arms around him, and stropping myself against him. For a dead guy, he had the liveliest chemistry—and apparently all my hormones were wide awake after my night with Quinn. Thinking of Quinn was like a dash of cold water.

With an almost painful reluctance, I pulled away from Eric. His face had a focused air, as if he was sampling something and deciding if it was good enough to keep.

"Eric," I said, and my voice was shaking. "I don't know why you're here, and I don't know why we're having all this drama."

"Are you Quinn's now?" His eyes narrowed.

"I'm my own," I said. "I choose."

"And have you chosen?"

"Eric, this is beyond gall. You haven't been dating me. You haven't given me any sign that was on your mind. You haven't treated me as though I had any significance in your life. I'm not saying I would have been open to those things, but I'm saying in their *absence* I've been free to find another, ah, companion. And so far, I like Quinn just fine."

"You don't know him any more than you really knew Bill."

That sliced down where it hurt.

"At least I'm pretty damn sure he wasn't ordered to get me in bed so I'd be a political asset!"

"It's better that you knew about Bill," Eric said.

"Yes, it's better," I agreed. "That doesn't mean I enjoyed the process."

"I knew that would be hard. But I had to make him tell you."

"Why?"

Eric seemed stumped. I don't know any other way to put it. He looked away, off into the darkness of the woods. "It wasn't right," he said at last.

"True. But maybe you just wanted to be sure I wouldn't ever love him again?"

"Maybe both things," he said.

There was a sharp moment of silence, as if something big was drawing in breath.

"Okay," I said slowly. This was like a therapy session. "You've been moody around me for months, Eric. Ever since you were . . . you know, not yourself. What's up with you?"

"Ever since that night I was cursed, I've wondered why I ended up running down the road to your house."

I took a step or two back and tried to pull some evidence, some indication of what he was thinking, from his white face. But it was no use.

It had never occurred to me to wonder why Eric had been there. I'd been so astounded over so many things that the circumstances of finding Eric alone, half naked, and clueless, early in the morning on the first day of the New Year, had been buried in the aftermath of the Witch War.

"Did you ever figure out the answer?" I asked, realizing after the words had left my mouth how stupid the question was.

"No," he said in a voice that was just short of a hiss. "No. And the witch who cursed me is dead, though the curse was broken. Now she can't tell me what her curse entailed. Was I supposed to look for the person I hated? Loved? Could it have been random that I found myself running out in the middle of nowhere . . . except that nowhere was on the way to your house?"

A moment of uneasy silence on my part. I had no idea what to say, and Eric was clearly waiting for a response.

"Probably the fairy blood," I said weakly, though I had spent hours telling myself that my fraction of fairy blood was not significant enough to cause more than a mild attraction on the part of the vampires I met.

"No," he said. And then he was gone.

"Well," I said out loud, unhappy with the quiver in my voice. "As exits go, that was a good one." It was pretty hard to have the last word with a vampire.

8

"MY BAGS ARE PACKED . . ." I SANG.

"Well, I'm not so lonesome I could cry," Amelia said. She'd kindly agreed to drive me to the airport, but I should have made her promise to be pleasant that morning, too. She'd been a little broody the whole time I was putting on my makeup.

"I wish I was going, too," she said, admitting what had been sticking in her craw. Of course, I'd known Amelia's problem before she'd said it out loud. But there wasn't a thing I could do.

"It's not up to me to invite or not invite," I said. "I'm the hired help."

"I know," she said grumpily. "I'll get the mail, and I'll water the plants, and I'll brush Bob. Hey, I heard that the Bayou State insurance salesman needs a receptionist, since the mom of the woman who worked for him got evacuated from New Orleans and has to have full-time care."

"Oh, do go in to apply for that job," I said. "You'll just love it." My insurance guy was a wizard who backed up his policies with spells. "You'll really like Greg Aubert, and he'll interest you." I wanted Amelia's interview at the insurance agency to be a happy surprise.

Amelia looked at me sideways with a little smile. "Oh, is he cute and single?"

"Nope. But he has other interesting attributes. And remember, you promised Bob you wouldn't do guys."

"Oh, yeah." Amelia looked gloomy. "Hey, let's look up your hotel."

Amelia was teaching me how to use my cousin Hadley's computer. I'd brought it back with me from New Orleans, thinking I'd sell it, but Amelia had coaxed me to set it up here at the house. It looked funny on a desk in the corner of the oldest part of the house, the room now used as a living room. Amelia paid for an extra phone line for the Internet, since she needed it for her laptop upstairs. I was still a nervous novice.

Amelia clicked on Google and typed in "Pyramid of Gizeh hotel." We stared at the picture that popped up on the screen. Most of the vampire hotels were in large urban centers, like Rhodes, and they were also tourist attractions. Often called simply "the Pyramid," the hotel was shaped like one, of course, and it was faced with bronze-colored reflective glass. There was one band of lighter glass around one of the floors close to the base.

"Not exactly . . . hmmm." Amelia looked at the building, her head tilted sideways.

"It needs to slant more," I said, and she nodded.

"You're right. It's like they wanted to have a pyramid, but they didn't really need enough floors to make it look right. The angle's not steep enough to make it look really grand."

"And it's sitting on a big rectangle."

"That, too. I expect those are the convention rooms."

"No parking," I said, peering at the screen.

"Oh, that'll be below the building. They can build 'em that way up there."

"It's on the lakefront," I said. "Hey, I get to see Lake Michigan. See, there's just a little park between the hotel and the lake."

"And about six lanes of traffic," Amelia pointed out.

"Okay, that, too."

"But it's close to major shopping," Amelia said.

"It's got an all-human floor," I read. "I'll bet that's this floor, the one that's lighter. I thought that was just the design, but it's so humans can go somewhere to have light during the day. People need that for their well-being."

"Translation: it's a law," Amelia said. "What else is there? Meeting rooms, blah blah blah. Opaque glass throughout except for the human floor. Exquisitely decorated suites on the highest levels, blah blah blah. Staff thoroughly trained in vampires' needs. Does that mean they're all willing to be blood donors or fuck buddies?"

Amelia was so cynical. But now that I knew who her father was, that kind of made sense.

"I'd like to see the very top room, the tip of the pyramid," I said.

"Can't. It says here that that's not a real guest floor. It's actually where all the air conditioner stuff is."

"Well, hell. Time to go," I said, glancing at my watch.

"Oh, yeah." Amelia stared gloomily at the screen.

"I'll only be gone a week," I said. Amelia was definitely a person who didn't like to be by herself. We went downstairs and carried my bags to the car.

"I got the hotel number to call in case of emergency. I got your cell phone number, too. You pack your charger?" She maneuvered down the long gravel driveway and out onto Hummingbird Road. We'd go right around Bon Temps to get to the interstate.

"Yeah." And my toothbrush and toothpaste, my razor, my deodorant, my hair dryer (just in case), my makeup, all my new clothes and some extras, lots of shoes, a sleeping outfit, Amelia's traveling alarm clock, underwear, a little jewelry, an extra purse, and two paperbacks. "Thanks for loaning me the suitcase." Amelia had contributed her bright red roller bag and a matching garment bag, plus a carry-on I'd crammed with a book, a crossword puzzle compendium, a portable CD player, and a headset, plus a small CD case.

We didn't talk much on the drive. I was thinking how strange it was going to be, leaving Amelia alone in my family home. There had been Stackhouses in residence on the site for over a hundred and seventy years.

Our sporadic conversation died by the time we neared the airport. There didn't seem to be anything else to be said. We were right by the main Shreveport terminal, but we were going to a small private hangar. If Eric hadn't booked an Anubis charter plane weeks ago, he would've been up a creek, because the summit was definitely taxing Anubis's capabilities. All the states involved were sending delegations, and a big hunk of Middle America, from the Gulf to the Canadian border, was included in the American Central division.

A few months ago, Louisiana would have needed two planes. Now one would suffice, especially since a few of the party had gone ahead. I'd read the list of missing vampires after the meeting at Fangtasia, and to my regret, Melanie and Chester had been on it. I'd met them at the queen's New Orleans headquarters, and though we hadn't had time to become bosom buddies or anything, they'd seemed like good vamps.

There was a guard at the gate in the fence enclosing the hangar, and he checked my driver's license and Amelia's before he let us in. He was a regular human off-duty cop, but he seemed competent and alert. "Turn to the right, and there's parking by the door in the east wall," he said.

Amelia leaned forward a little as she drove, but the door was easy enough to see, and there were other cars parked there. It was about ten in the morning, and there was a touch of cool in the air, just below the surface warmth. It was an early breath of fall. After the hot, hot summer, it was just blissful. It would be cooler in Rhodes, Pam had said. She'd checked the temperatures for the coming week on the Internet and called me to tell me to pack a sweater. She'd sounded almost excited, which was a big deal for Pam. I'd been getting the impression that Pam was a wee bit restless, a bit tired of Shreveport and the bar. Maybe it was just me.

Amelia helped me unload the suitcases. Amelia had had to take a number of spells off the red Samsonite before she could hand it over to me. I hadn't asked what would have happened if she'd forgotten. I pulled up the handle on the rolling bag and slung the carry-on bag across my shoulder. Amelia took the hanging bag and opened the door.

I'd never been in an airplane hangar before, but it was just like the ones in the movies: cavernous. There were a few small planes parked inside, but we proceeded as Pam had instructed to the large opening in the west wall. The Anubis Air jet was parked outside, and the coffins were being loaded onto the luggage belt by the uniformed Anubis employees. They all wore black relieved only by a stylized jackal's head on the chest of the uniform, an affectation that I found irritating. They glanced at us casually, but no one challenged us or asked to see identification until we got to the steps leading up to the plane.

Bobby Burnham was standing at the foot of the steps

with a clipboard. Of course, since it was daylight, it was obvious Bobby wasn't a vamp, but he was nearly pale and stern enough to be one. I'd never met him before, but I knew who he was, and he certainly recognized me. I plucked that right from his brain. But his certainty didn't stop him from checking my ID against his damn list, and he was giving Amelia the big glare, like she couldn't turn him into a toad. (That was what Amelia was thinking.)

"He'd have to croak," I murmured, and she smiled.

Bobby introduced himself, and when we nodded, he said, "Your name is on the list, Miss Stackhouse, but Miss Broadway's isn't. I'm afraid you'll have to get your luggage up by yourself." Bobby was loving the power.

Amelia was whispering something under her breath, and in a rush Bobby blurted, "I'll carry the heavy bag up the stairs, Miss Stackhouse. Can you handle the other bag? If that's not something you want to do, I'll be back down in a minute and take them up for you." The astonishment on his face was priceless, but I tried not to enjoy it too much. Amelia was playing a slightly mean trick.

"Thanks, I can manage," I reassured him, and took the hanging bag from Amelia while he bumped up the stairs with the heavier piece of luggage.

"Amelia, you rascal," I said, but not too angrily.

"Who's the asshole?" she asked.

"Bobby Burnham. He's Eric's daytime guy." All vamps of a certain rank had one. Bobby was a recent acquisition of Eric's.

"What does he do? Dust the coffins?"

"No, he makes business arrangements, he goes to the bank, he picks up the dry cleaning, he deals with the state offices that are open only in the day, and so forth."

"So he's a gofer."

"Well, yeah. But he's an important gofer. He's Eric's gofer."

Bobby was coming back down the steps now, still looking surprised that he'd been polite and helpful. "Don't do anything else to him," I said, knowing that she was considering it.

Amelia's eyes flashed before she got the sense of what I was saying. "Yeah, petty of me," she admitted. "I just hate power-mad jerks."

"Who doesn't? Listen, I'll see you in a week. Thanks for bringing me to the plane."

"Yeah, yeah." She gave me a forlorn smile. "You have a good time, and don't get killed or bitten or anything."

Impulsively, I hugged her, and after a second's surprise, she hugged me back.

"Take good care of Bob," I said, and up the stairs I went.

I couldn't help feeling a little anxious, since I was cutting my ties with my familiar life, at least temporarily. The Anubis Air employee in the cabin said, "Choose your seat, Miss Stackhouse." She took the hanging bag from me and put it away. The interior of the aircraft was not like that of any human plane, or at least that was what the Anubis website had alleged. The Anubis fleet had been designed and outfitted for the transportation of sleeping vamps, with human passengers coming in second. There were coffin bays around the wall, like giant luggage bins, and at the front end of the aircraft there were three rows of seats, on the right three seats, and on the left two, for people like me . . . or, at least, people who were going to be helpful to the vamps at this conference in some capacity. At present, there were only three other people sitting in the seats. Well, one other human and two part-humans.

"Hi, Mr. Cataliades," I said, and the round man rose from his seat, beaming.

"Dear Miss Stackhouse," he said warmly, because that was the way Mr. Cataliades talked, "I am so very glad to see you again."

"Pleased to see you, too, Mr. Cataliades."

His name was pronounced Ka-TAL-ee-ah-deez, and if he had a first name, I didn't know it. Sitting next to him was a very young woman with bright red spiked hair: his niece, Diantha. Diantha wore the strangest ensembles, and tonight she'd topped herself. Maybe five feet tall, bony thin, Diantha had chosen orange calf-length leggings, blue Crocs, a white ruffled skirt, and a tie-dyed tank top. She was dazzling to the eye.

Diantha didn't believe in breathing while she talked. Now she said, "Goodtoseeya."

"Right back at ya," I said, and since she didn't make any other move, I gave her a nod. Some supes shake hands, others don't, so you have to be careful. I turned to the other passenger. With another human, I thought I was on firmer ground, so I held out my right hand. As if he'd been offered a dead fish, the man extended his own hand after a perceptible pause. He pressed my palm in a limp way and withdrew his fingers as if he could just barely refrain from wiping them on his suit pants.

"Miss Stackhouse, this is Johan Glassport, a specialist in vampire law."

"Mr. Glassport," I said politely, struggling not to take offense.

"Johan, this is Sookie Stackhouse, the queen's telepath," Mr. Cataliades said in his courtly way. Mr. Cataliades's sense of humor was as abundant as his belly. There was a twinkle in his eye even now. But you had to remember that the part of him that wasn't human—the majority of Mr. Cataliades—was a demon. Diantha was half-demon; her uncle even more.

Johan gave me a brief up-and-down scan, almost audibly sniffed, and returned to the book he had in his lap.

Just then, the Anubis stewardess began giving us the usual spiel, and I buckled myself into my seat. Soon after that, we were airborne. I didn't have a twinge of anxiety, because I was so disgusted by Johan Glassport's behavior.

I didn't think I'd ever encountered such in-your-face rudeness. The people of northern Louisiana may not have much money, and there may be a high teen pregnancy rate and all kinds of other problems, but by God, we're polite.

Diantha said, "Johan'sanasshole."

Johan paid absolutely no attention to this accurate assessment but turned the page of his book.

"Thanks, dear," Mr. Cataliades said. "Miss Stackhouse, bring me up to date on your life."

I moved to sit opposite the trio. "Not much to tell, Mr. Cataliades. I got the check, as I wrote you. Thanks for tying up all the loose ends on Hadley's estate, and if you'd reconsider and send me a bill, I'd be glad to pay it." Not exactly glad, but relieved of an obligation.

"No, child. It was the least I could do. The queen was happy to express her thanks in that way, even though the evening hardly turned out like she'd planned."

"Of course, none of us imagined it would end that way." I thought of Wybert's head flying through the air surrounded by a mist of blood, and I shuddered.

"You are the witness," Johan said unexpectedly. He slipped a bookmark into his book and closed it. His pale eyes, magnified behind his glasses, were fixed on me. From being dog poop on his shoe, I had been transformed into something quite interesting and remarkable.

"Yeah. I'm the witness."

"Then we must talk, now."

"I'm a little surprised, if you're representing the queen at this very important trial, that you haven't gotten around to talking to me before," I said in as mild a voice as I could manage.

"The queen had trouble contacting me, and I had to finish with my previous client," Johan said. His unlined face didn't exactly change expression, but it did look a bit tenser.

"Johan was in jail," Diantha said very clearly and distinctly.

"Oh, my goodness," I said, truly startled.

Johan said, "Of course, the charges were completely unfounded."

"Of course, Johan," Mr. Cataliades said with absolutely no inflection in his voice.

"Ooo," I said. "What were those charges that were so false?"

Johan looked at me again, this time with less arrogance. "I was accused of striking a prostitute in Mexico."

I didn't know much about law enforcement in Mexico, but it did seem absolutely incredible to me that an American could get arrested in Mexico for hitting a prostitute, if that was the only charge. Unless he had a lot of enemies.

"Did you happen to have something in your hand when you struck her?" I asked with a bright smile.

"I believe Johan had a knife in his hand," Mr. Cataliades said gravely.

I know my smile vanished right about then. "You were in jail in Mexico for knifing a woman," I said. Who was dog poop now?

"A prostitute," he corrected. "That was the charge, but of course, I was completely innocent."

"Of course," I said.

"Mine is not the case on the table right now, Miss Stackhouse. My job is to defend the queen against the very serious charges brought against her, and you are an important witness."

"I'm the only witness."

"Of course—to the actual death."

"There were several actual deaths."

"The only death that matters at this summit is the death of Peter Threadgill."

I sighed at the image of Wybert's head, and then I said, "Yeah, I was there."

Johan may have been lower than pond scum, but he knew his stuff. We went through a long question and answer session that left the lawyer knowing more about what had happened than I did, and I'd been there. Mr. Cataliades listened with great interest, and now and then threw in a clarification or explained the layout of the queen's monastery to the lawyer.

Diantha listened for a while, sat on the floor and played jacks for half an hour, then reclined her seat and went to sleep.

The Anubis Airline attendant came through and offered drinks and snacks from time to time on the three-hour flight north, and after I'd finished my session with the trial lawyer, I got up to use the bathroom. That was an experience; I'd never been in an airplane bathroom before. Instead of resuming my seat, I walked down the plane, taking a look at each coffin. There was a luggage tag on each one, attached to the handles. With us in the plane today were Eric, Bill, the queen, Andre, and Sigebert. I also found the coffin of Gervaise, who'd been hosting the queen, and Cleo Babbitt, who was the sheriff of Area Three. The Area Two sheriff, Arla Yvonne, had been left in charge of the state while the queen was gone.

The queen's coffin was inlaid with mother-of-pearl designs, but the others were quite plain. They were all of polished wood: no modern metal for these vamps. I ran my hand over Eric's, having creepy mental pictures of him lying inside, quite lifeless.

"Gervaise's woman drove ahead by night with Rasul to make sure all the queen's preparations were in place," Mr. Cataliades's voice said from my right shoulder. I jumped and shrieked, which tickled the queen's civil lawyer pink. He chuckled and chuckled.

"Smooth move," I said, and my voice was sour as a squeezed lemon.

"You were wondering where the fifth sheriff was."

"Yes, but you were maybe a thought or two behind."

"I'm not telepathic like you, my dear. I was just following your facial expressions and body language. You counted the coffins and began reading the luggage tags."

"So the queen is not only the queen, but the sheriff of her own area."

"Yes; it eliminates confusion. Not all the rulers follow that pattern, but the queen found it irksome to constantly consult another vampire when she wanted to do something."

"Sounds like the queen." I glanced forward at our companions. Diantha and Johan were occupied: Diantha with sleep, Johan with his book. I wondered if it was a dissection book, with diagrams—or perhaps an account of the crimes of Jack the Ripper, with the crime scene photographs. That seemed about Johan's speed. "How come the queen has a lawyer like him?" I asked in as low a voice as I could manage. "He seems really . . . shoddy."

"Johan Glassport is a great lawyer, and one who will take cases other lawyers won't," said Mr. Cataliades. "And he is also a murderer. But then, we all are, are we not?" His beady dark eyes looked directly into mine.

I returned the look for a long moment. "In defense of my own life or the life of someone I loved, I would kill an attacker," I said, thinking before every word left my mouth.

"What a diplomatic way to put it, Miss Stackhouse. I

can't say the same for myself. Some things I have killed, I tore apart for the sheer joy of it."

Oh, *ick.* More than I wanted to know.

"Diantha loves to hunt deer, and she has killed people in my defense. And she and her sister even brought down a rogue vampire or two."

I reminded myself to treat Diantha with more respect. Killing a vampire was a very difficult undertaking. And she could play jacks like a fiend.

"And Johan?" I asked.

"Perhaps I'd better leave Johan's little predilections unspoken for the moment. He won't step out of line while he's with us, after all. Are you pleased with the job Johan is doing, briefing you?"

"Is that what he's doing? Well, yes, I guess so. He's been very thorough, which is what you want."

"Indeed."

"Can you tell me what to expect at the summit? What the queen will want?"

Mr. Cataliades said, "Let's sit and I'll try to explain it to you."

For the next hour, he talked, and I listened and asked questions.

By the time Diantha sat up and yawned, I felt a bit more prepared for all the new things I faced in the city of Rhodes. Johan Glassport closed his book and looked at us, as if he were now ready to talk.

"Mr. Glassport, have you been to Rhodes before?" Mr. Cataliades asked.

"Yes," the lawyer answered. "I used to practice in Rhodes. Actually, I used to commute between Rhodes and Chicago; I lived midway between."

"When did you go to Mexico?" I asked.

"Oh, a year or two ago," he answered. "I had some disagreements with business associates here, and it seemed a good time to . . ."

"Get the heck out of the city?" I supplied helpfully.

"Run like hell?" Diantha suggested.

"Take the money and vanish?" Mr. Cataliades said.

"All of the above," said Johan Glassport with the faintest trace of a smile.

9

IT WAS MIDAFTERNOON WHEN WE ARRIVED IN Rhodes. There was an Anubis truck waiting to onload the coffins and transport them to the Pyramid of Gizeh. I looked out the limo windows every second of the ride into the city, and despite the overwhelming presence of the chain stores we also saw in Shreveport, I had no doubt I was in a different place. Heavy red brick, city traffic, row houses, glimpses of the lake . . . I was trying to look in all directions at once. Then we came into view of the hotel; it was amazing. The day wasn't sunny enough for the bronze glass to glint, but the Pyramid of Gizeh looked impressive anyway. Sure enough, there was the park across the six-lane street, which was seething with traffic, and beyond it the vast lake.

While the Anubis truck pulled around to the back of the Pyramid to discharge its load of vampires and luggage, the limo swept up to the front of the hotel. As we daytime creatures scooted out of the car, I didn't know what to look at first: the broad waters or the decorations of the structure itself.

The main doors of the Pyramid were manned by a lot of maroon-and-beige uniformed men, but there were silent guardians, too. There were two elaborate reproductions of sarcophagi placed in an upright position, one on each side of the main lobby doors. They were fascinating, and I would have enjoyed the chance to examine both of them, but we were swept into the building by the staff. One man opened the car door, one examined our identification to make sure we were registered guests—not human reporters, curiosity seekers, or assorted fanatics—and another pushed open the door of the hotel to indicate we should enter.

I'd stayed in a vampire hotel before, so I expected the armed guards and the lack of ground floor windows. The Pyramid of Gizeh was making more of an effort to look a bit like a human hotel than Dallas's Silent Shore had; though the walls held murals imitating Egyptian tomb art, the lobby was bright with artificial light and horribly perky with piped-in music—"The Girl from Ipanema" in a vampire hotel.

The lobby was busier than the Silent Shore's, too.

There were lots of humans and other creatures striding around purposefully, lots of action at the check-in desk, and some milling around the hospitality booth put up by the host city's vampire nest. I'd gone with Sam to a bar supply convention in Shreveport once when he was shopping for a new pump system, and I recognized the general setup. Somewhere, I was sure, there would be a convention hall with booths, and a schedule of panels or demonstrations.

I hoped there would be a map of the hotel, with all events and locations noted, in our registration packet. Or were the vampires too snooty for such mundane aids? No, there was a hotel diagram framed and lit for the perusal of guests and scheduled tours. This hotel was numbered in reverse order. The top floor, the penthouse, was numbered 1. The bottom, largest floor—the human floor—was numbered 15. There was a mezzanine between the human floor and lobby, and there were large convention rooms in the annex to the northern side of the hotel, the rectangular windowless projection that had looked so odd in the Internet picture.

I eyed people scurrying through the lobby—maids, bodyguards, valets, bellmen. . . . Here we were, all us little human beavers, scurrying around to get things ready for the undead conventioneers. (Could you call them that, when this was billed as a summit? What was the difference?) I felt a little sour when I wondered why this was the order of things, when a few years ago, the vampires were the ones doing the scurrying, and that was back into a dark corner where they could hide. Maybe that had been the more natural way. I slapped myself mentally. I might as well go join the Fellowship, if that was how I really felt. I'd noticed the protesters in the little park across the street from the Pyramid of Gizeh, which some of the signs referred to as "The Pyramid of Geezers."

"Where are the coffins?" I asked Mr. Cataliades.

"They're coming in through a basement entrance," he said.

There had been a metal detector at the hotel door. I'd tried hard not to look when Johan Glassport had emptied his pockets. The detector had gone off like a siren when he'd passed through. "Do the coffins have to go through a metal detector, too?" I asked.

"No. Our vampires have wooden coffins, but the hardware on them is metal, and you can't empty the vampires out to search their pockets for other metal objects, so that wouldn't make any sense," Mr. Cataliades answered, for the first time sounding impatient. "Plus, some vampires have chosen the modern metal caskets."

"The demonstrators across the street," I said. "They have me spooked. They'd love to sneak in here."

Mr. Cataliades smiled, a terrifying sight. "No one will get in here, Miss Sookie. There are other guards that you can't see."

While Mr. Cataliades checked us in, I stood to his side and turned to look around at the other people. They were all dressed very nicely, and they were all talking. About us. I felt instantly anxious at the looks we were getting from the others, and the buzzing thoughts from the few live guests and staff reinforced my anxiety. We were the human entourage of the queen who had been one of the most powerful vampire rulers in America. Now she was not only weakened economically, but she was going on trial for murdering her husband. I could see why the other flunkies were interested—*I* would've found us interesting—but I was uncomfortable. All I could think about was how shiny my nose must be, and how much I wanted to have a few moments alone.

The clerk went over our reservations very slowly and deliberately, as if to keep us on exhibit in the lobby for as long as possible. Mr. Cataliades dealt with him with his usual elaborate courtesy, though even that was getting strained after ten minutes.

I'd been standing at a discreet distance during the process, but when I could tell the clerk—fortyish, recreational drug user, father of three—was just fucking us over to entertain himself, I took a step closer. I laid a hand on Mr. C's sleeve to indicate that I wanted to join in the conversation. He interrupted himself to turn an interested face toward me.

"You give us our keys and tell us where our vamps are, or I'll tell your boss that you're the one selling Pyramid of Gizeh items on eBay. And if you bribe a maid to even *touch* the queen's panties, much less steal 'em, I'll sic Diantha on you." Diantha had just returned from tracking down a bottle of water. She obligingly revealed her sharp, pointed teeth in a lethal smile.

The clerk turned white and then red in an interesting display of blood flow patterns. "Yes, ma'am," he stammered, and I wondered if he would wet himself. After my little rummage through his head, I didn't much care.

In very short order, we all had keys, we had a list of "our" vampires' resting places, and the bellman was bringing our luggage in one of those neat carts. That reminded me of something.

Barry, I said in my head. *You here?*

Yeah, said a voice that was far from the faltering one it had been the first time I'd heard it. *Sookie Stackhouse?*

It's me. We're checking in. I'm in 1538. You?

I'm in 1576. How are you doing?

Good, personally. But Louisiana . . . we've had the hurricane, and we've got the trial. I guess you know all about that?

Yeah. You saw some action.

You could say that, I told him, wondering if my smile was coming across in my head.

Got that loud and clear.

Now I had an inkling of how people must feel when they were faced with me.

I'll see you later, I told Barry. *Hey, what's your real last name?*

You started something when you brought my gift out into the open, he told me. *My real name is Barry Horowitz. Now I just call myself Barry Bellboy. That's how I'm registered, if you forget my room number.*

Okay. Looking forward to visiting with you.

Same here.

And then Barry and I both turned our attention to other

things, and that strange tickling feeling of mind-to-mind communication was gone.

Barry's the only other telepath I've ever encountered.

Mr. Cataliades had discovered that the humans—well, the non-vampires—in the party had each been put in a room with another person. Some of the vampires had roommates, too. He hadn't been pleased that he himself was sharing a room with Diantha, but the hotel was extremely crowded, the clerk had said. He may have been lying about a lot of other things, but that much was clearly true.

I was sharing a room with Gervaise's squeeze, and as I slid the card into the slot on the door, I wondered if she'd be in. She was. I'd been expecting a woman like the fangbangers who hang around at Fangtasia, but Carla Danvers was another kind of creature entirely.

"Hey, girl!" she said, as I entered. "I figured you'd be along soon when they brought your bags up. I'm Carla, Gerry's girlfriend."

"Nice to meet you," I said, shaking hands. Carla was a prom queen. Maybe she hadn't been, literally; maybe she hadn't made homecoming queen, either, but she'd surely been on the court. Carla had dark brown chin-length hair, and big brown eyes, and teeth that were so straight and white that they were an advertisement for her orthodontist. Her breasts had been enhanced, and her ears were pierced, and her belly button, too. She had a tattoo on her lower back, some black vines in a vee pattern with a couple of roses with green leaves in the middle. I could see all this because Carla was naked, and she didn't seem to have the slightest idea that her nudity was a little on the "too much information" side to suit me.

"Have you and Gervaise been going together long?" I asked to camouflage how uncomfortable I was.

"I met Gerry, let's see, seven months ago. He said it would be better for me to have a separate room because he might have to have business meetings in his, you know? Plus, I'm going shopping while I'm here—retail therapy! Big city stores! And I wanted someplace to store my shopping bags so he won't ask me how much it all costs." She gave me a wink I can only say was roguish.

"Okay," I said. "Sounds good." It really didn't, but Carla's program was hardly my business. My suitcase was waiting for me on a stand, so I opened it and started to unpack, noting that my hanging bag with my good dresses was already in the closet. Carla had left me exactly half the closet space and drawer space, which was decent. She had brought about twenty times more clothes than I had, which made her fairness all the more remarkable.

"Whose girlfriend are you?" Carla asked. She was giving herself a pedicure. When she drew up one leg, the overhead light winked on something metallic between her legs. Completely embarrassed, I turned away to straighten my evening dress on the hanger.

"I'm dating Quinn," I said.

I glanced over my shoulder, keeping my gaze high.

Carla looked blank.

"The weretiger," I said. "He's arranging the ceremonies here."

She looked marginally more responsive.

"Big guy, shaved head," I said.

Her face brightened. "Oh, yeah, I saw him this morning! He was eating breakfast in the restaurant when I was checking in."

"There's a restaurant?"

"Yeah, sure. Though of course it's tiny. And there's room service."

"You know, in vampire hotels there often isn't a restaurant," I said, just to make conversation. I'd read an article about it in *American Vampire*.

"Oh. Well, that makes no sense at all." Carla finished one set of toes and began another.

"Not from a vampire point of view."

Carla frowned. "I know they don't eat. But people do. And this is a people world, right? That's like not learning English when you emigrate to America."

I turned around to check out Carla's face, make sure she was serious. Yeah, she was.

"Carla," I said, and then stopped. I didn't have any idea what to say, how to get across to Carla that a four-hundred-year-old vamp really didn't care very much about the eating arrangements of a twenty-year-old human. But the girl was waiting for me to finish. "Well, it's good that there's a restaurant here," I said weakly.

She nodded. "Yeah, 'cause I need my coffee in the morning," she said. "I just can't get going without it. Course, when you date a vamp, your morning is liable to begin at three or four in the afternoon." She laughed.

"True," I said. I'd finished unpacking, so I went over to our window and looked out. The glass was so heavily tinted that it was hard to make out the landscape, but it was seeable. I wasn't on the Lake Michigan side of the hotel, which was a pity, but I looked at the buildings around the west side of the hotel with curiosity. I didn't see cities that often, and I'd never seen a northern city. The sky was darkening rapidly, so between that and the tinted windows I really couldn't see too much after ten minutes. The vampires would be awake soon, and my workday would begin.

Though she kept up a sporadic stream of chatter, Carla didn't ask what my role was at this summit. She assumed I was there as arm candy. For the moment, that was all right with me. Sooner or later, she'd find out what my particular talent was, and then she'd be nervous around me. On the other hand, now she was a little *too* relaxed.

Carla was getting dressed (thank God) in what I thought of as "classy whore." She was wearing a glittery green cocktail dress that almost didn't have a top to it, and fuck-me shoes, and what amounted to a see-through thong. Well, she had her working clothes, and I had mine. I wasn't too pleased with myself for being so judgmental, and maybe I was a little envious that my working clothes were so conservative.

For tonight, I had chosen a chocolate brown lace handkerchief dress. I put in my big gold earrings and slid into brown pumps, put on some lipstick, and brushed my hair really well. Sticking my keycard into my little evening purse, I headed to the front desk to find out which suite was the queen's, since Mr. Cataliades had told me to present myself there.

I had hoped to run into Quinn along the way, but I didn't see hide nor hair of him. What with me having a roommate, and Quinn being so busy all the time, this summit might not promise as much fun on the side as I'd hoped.

The desk clerk blanched when he saw me coming, and he looked around to see if Diantha was with me. While he was scrawling the queen's room number on a piece of notepaper with a shaking hand, I looked around me with more attention.

There were security cameras in a few obvious locations, pointed at the front doors and at the registration desk. And I thought I could see one at the elevators. There were the usual armed guards—usual for a vampire hotel, that is. The big selling point for any vampire hotel was the security and privacy of its guests. Otherwise, vampires could stay more cheaply and centrally in the special vampire rooms of mainstream hotels. (Even Motel 6 had one vampire room at almost every location.) When I thought about the protesters outside, I really hoped the security crew here at the Pyramid was on the ball.

I nodded at another human woman as I crossed the lobby to the central bank of elevators. The rooms got ritzier the higher up you went, I gathered, since there were fewer on the floor. The queen had one of the fourth floor suites, since she'd booked for this event a long time ago, before Katrina—and probably while her husband was still alive. There were only eight doors on her floor, and I didn't have to see the number to know which room was Sophie-Anne's. Sigebert was standing in front of it. Sigebert was a boulder of a man. He had guarded the queen for hundreds of years, as had Andre. The ancient vampire looked lonely without his brother, Wybert. Otherwise, he was the same old Anglo-Saxon warrior he'd been the first time I'd met him—shaggy beard, physique of a wild boar, missing a tooth or two in crucial places.

Sigebert grinned at me, a terrifying sight. "Miss Sookie," he said by way of greeting.

"Sigebert," I said, carefully pronouncing it "See-ya-bairt." "Are you doing okay?" I wanted to convey sympathy without dipping into too-sentimental waters.

"My brother, he died a hero," Sigebert said proudly. "In battle."

I thought of saying, "You must miss him so much after a thousand years." Then I decided that was exactly like reporters asking the parents of missing children, "How do you feel?"

"He was a great fighter," I said instead, and that was exactly what Sigebert wanted to hear. He clapped me on the shoulder, almost knocking me to the ground. Then his look got a little absent, as if he were listening to an announcement.

I'd suspected that the queen could talk to her "children" telepathically, and when Sigebert opened the door for me without another word, I knew that was true. I was glad she couldn't talk to me. Being able to communicate with Barry was kind of fun, but if we hung out together all the time I was sure it would get old in a hurry. Plus, Sophie-Anne was a heck of a lot scarier.

The queen's suite was lavish. I'd never seen anything like it. The carpet was as thick as a sheep's pelt, and it was off-white. The furniture was upholstered in shades of gold and dark blue. The slanting slab of glass that enclosed the outside wall was opaque. I have to say, the large wall of darkness made me feel twitchy.

In the midst of this splendor, Sophie-Anne sat curled on a couch. Small and extremely pale, with her shining brown hair swept up in a chignon, the queen was wearing a raspberry-colored silk suit with black piping and black alligator heels. Her jewelry was heavy, gold, and simple.

Sophie-Anne would have looked more age-appropriate wearing a Gwen Stefani L.A.M.B. outfit. She'd died as a human when she'd been maybe fifteen or sixteen. In her time, that would have made her a fully-grown woman and mother. In our time, that made her a mall rat. To modern eyes, her clothes were too old for her, but it would take an insane person to tell her so. Sophie-Anne was the world's most dangerous teenager, and the second most dangerous had her back. Andre was standing right behind Sophie-Anne, as always. When he'd given me a thorough look, and the door had closed behind me, he actually sat beside Sophie-Anne, which was some kind of signal that I was a member of the club, I guess. Andre and his queen had both been drinking TrueBlood, and they looked rosy as a result—almost human, in fact.

"How are your accommodations?" Sophie-Anne asked politely.

"Fine. I'm rooming with a . . . girlfriend of Gervaise's," I said.

"With *Carla*? Why?" Her brows rose up like dark birds in a clear sky.

"The hotel's crowded. It's no big thing. I figure she'll be with Gervaise most of the time, anyway," I said.

Sophie-Anne said, "What did you think of Johan?"

I could feel my face harden. "I think he belongs in jail."

"But he will keep me out of it."

I tried to imagine what a vampire jail would be like, gave up. I couldn't give her any positive feedback on Johan, so I just nodded.

"You are still not telling me what you picked up from him."

"He's very tense and conflicted."

"Explain."

"He's anxious. He's scared. He's fighting different loyalties. He only wants to come out alive. He doesn't care for anyone but himself."

"So how does that make him different from any other human?" Andre commented.

Sophie-Anne responded with a twitch of one side of her mouth. That Andre, what a comedian.

"Most humans don't stab women," I said as quietly and calmly as I could. "Most humans don't enjoy that."

Sophie-Anne was not completely indifferent to the violent death Johan Glassport had meted out, but naturally she was a little more concerned with her own legal defense. At least, that was how I read her, but with vampires, I had to go on subtle body language rather than the sure knowledge right out of their brains. "He'll defend me, I'll pay him, and then he's on his own," she said. "Anything might happen to him then." She gave me a clear-eyed look.

Okay, Sophie-Anne, I got the picture.

"Did he question you thoroughly? Did you feel he knew

what he was doing?" she asked, returning to the important stuff.

"Yes, ma'am," I said promptly. "He did seem to be really competent."

"Then he'll be worth the trouble."

I didn't even let my eyes flicker.

"Did Cataliades tell you what to expect?"

"Yes, ma'am, he did."

"Good. As well as your testimony at the trial, I need you to attend every meeting with me that includes humans."

This was why she was paying me the big bucks.

"Ah, do you have any schedule of meetings?" I asked. "It's just, I'd be ready and waiting if I had any idea when you needed me."

Before she could answer, there was a knock at the door. Andre rose and moved to answer it so smoothly and fluidly that you would have sworn he was part cat. His sword was in his hand, though I hadn't seen it before. The door opened a bit just as Andre reached it, and I heard Sigebert's bass rumble.

After they'd exchanged a few sentences, the door opened wider, and Andre said, "The King of Texas, my lady." There was only a hint of pleased surprise in his voice, but it was the equivalent of Andre doing cartwheels across the carpet. This visit was a show of support for Sophie-Anne, and all the other vampires would notice.

Stan Davis came in, trailing a group of vamps and humans.

Stan was a nerd's nerd. He was the kind of guy who you checked out for a pocket protector. You could see the comb marks in his sandy hair, and his glasses were heavy and thick. They were also quite unnecessary. I'd never met a vamp who didn't have excellent vision and very precise hearing. Stan was wearing a wash 'n' wear white shirt with a Sears brand logo and some navy Dockers. And brown leather moccasins. Hoo, boy. He'd been a sheriff when I'd met him, and now that he was king, he was maintaining the same low-key approach.

Behind Stan came his sergeant at arms, Joseph Velasquez. A short, burly Hispanic with spiky hair, Joseph never seemed to crack a smile. By his side was a red-haired female vamp named Rachel; I remembered her, too, from my trip to Dallas. Rachel was a savage one, and she didn't like cooperating with humans in the least. Trailing the two was Barry the Bellboy, looking good in designer jeans and a taupe silk T-shirt, a discreet gold chain around his neck. Barry had matured in an almost scary way since I'd last seen him. He'd been a handsome, gawky boy of maybe nineteen when I'd first spotted him working as a bellboy at the Silent Shore Hotel in Dallas. Now Barry had had a manicure, a very good haircut, and the wary eyes of someone who'd been swimming in the shark pool.

We smiled at each other, and Barry said, *Good to see you. Looking pretty, Sookie.*

Thanks, and likewise, Barry.

Andre was doing the proper vampire greeting thing, which did not include handshaking. "Stan, we are pleased to see you. Who have you brought to meet us?"

Stan gallantly bent to kiss Sophie-Anne's hand. "Most beautiful queen," he said. "This vampire is my second, Joseph Velasquez. And this vampire is my nest sister Rachel. This human is the telepath Barry Bellboy. Indirectly, I have you to thank for him."

Sophie-Anne actually smiled. She said, "Of course, I am always delighted to do you any sort of favor in my power, Stan." She gestured to him to sit opposite her. Rachel and Joseph took up flanking positions. "It's so good to see you here in my suite. I had been concerned that I wouldn't have any visitors at all."

("Since I'm under indictment for killing my husband, and since I've also sustained a staggering economic blow," was the subtext.)

"I extend my sympathies to you," Stan said with a completely inflectionless voice. "The losses in your country have been extreme. If we can help . . . I know the humans from my state have helped yours, and it's only right that the vampires do likewise."

"Thank you for your kindness," she said. Sophie-Anne's pride was hurting in a major way. She had to struggle to paste that smile back on her face. "I believe you know Andre," she continued. "Andre, you now know Joseph. And I believe all of you know our Sookie."

The phone rang, and since I was closest to it, I answered it.

"Am I speaking to a member of the Queen of Louisiana's party?" the gruff voice asked.

"Yes, you are."

"One of you needs to come down to the loading bay to get a suitcase that belongs to your party. We can't read the label."

"Oh . . . okay."

"Sooner the better."

"All right."

He hung up. Okay, that was a little abrupt.

Since the queen was waiting for me to tell her who had called, I relayed the request, and she looked equally puzzled for all of a millisecond. "Later," she said dismissively.

In the meantime, the light eyes of the King of Texas were focused on me like laser beams. I inclined my head to him, which I hoped was the correct response. It seemed to be adequate. I would have liked to have had time to go over the protocol with Andre before the queen began receiving guests, but truthfully, I hadn't expected there to be any, much less a powerful guy like Stan Davis. This had to mean something good for the queen, or maybe it was a subtle vampire insult. I was sure I'd find out.

I felt the tickle of Barry in my mind. *She good to work for?* Barry asked.

I just help her out from time to time, I said. *I still have a day job.*

Barry looked at me with surprise. *You kidding? You could be raking it in, if you go to a good state like Ohio or Illinois where there's real money.*

I shrugged. *I like where I live,* I said.

Then we both became aware that our vampire employers were watching our silent exchange. Our faces were changing expression, I guess, like faces do during a conversation . . . except our conversation had been silent.

"Excuse me," I said. "I didn't mean to be rude. I just don't see people like me very often, and it's kind of a treat to talk to another telepath. I beg your pardon, ma'am, sir."

"I could almost hear it," Sophie-Anne marveled. "Stan, he has been very useful?" Sophie-Anne could talk to her own children mentally, but it must be as rare an ability among vampires as it was among people.

"Very useful," Stan confirmed. "The day that your Sookie brought him to my attention was a very good day for me. He knows when the humans are lying; he knows what their ulterior motives are. It's wonderful insight."

I looked at Barry, wondering if he ever thought of himself as a traitor to humankind or just as a vendor supplying a needed good. He met my eyes, his own face hard. Sure, he was conflicted about serving a vampire, revealing human secrets to his employer. I struggled with that idea myself from time to time.

"Hmmm. Sookie only works for me on occasion." Sophie-Anne was staring at me, and if I could characterize her smooth face, I would say she was thoughtful. Andre had something going on behind his pink-tinged teenage facade, and it was something I had better watch out for. He wasn't just thoughtful, he was interested; engaged, for want of a better description.

"Bill brought her to Dallas," Stan observed, not quite asking a question.

"He was her protector at the time," Sophie-Anne said.

A brief silence. Barry leered at me hopefully, and I gave him an in-your-dreams look. Actually, I felt like hugging him, since that little exchange broke up the silence into something I could handle.

"Do you really need Barry and me here, since we're the only humans, and it might not be so productive if we just sat around and read each other's minds?"

Joseph Velasquez actually smiled before he could stop himself.

After a silent moment, Sophie-Anne nodded, and then Stan. Queen Sophie and King Stan, I reminded myself. Barry bowed in a practiced way, and I felt like sticking out my tongue at him. I did a sort of bob and then scuttled out of the suite. Sigebert eyed us with a questioning face. "The queen, she not need you?" he asked.

"Not right now," I said. I tapped a pager that Andre had handed me at the last minute. "The pager will vibrate if she needs me," I said.

Sigebert eyed the device mistrustfully. "I think it would be better if you just stayed here," he said.

"The queen, she says I can go," I told him.

And off I went, Barry trailing along behind me. We took the elevator down to the lobby, where we found a secluded corner where no one could sneak up on us to eavesdrop.

I'd never conversed with someone entirely in my head, and neither had Barry, so we played around with that for a while. Barry would tell me the story of his life while I tried to block out all the other brains around me; then I'd try to listen to everyone else *and* to Barry.

This was actually a lot of fun.

Barry turned out to be better than I was at picking out who was thinking what in a crowd. I was a bit better at hearing nuance and detail, not always easy to pick up in thoughts. But we had some common ground.

We agreed on who the best broadcasters in the room were; that is, our "hearing" was the same. He would point at someone (in this case it was my roommate, Carla) and we would both listen to her thoughts, then rate them on a scale of one to five, five being the loudest, clearest broadcast. Carla was a three. After that agreement, we rated other people, and we found ourselves reacting almost as one over that.

Okay, this was interesting.

Let's try touching, I suggested.

Barry didn't even leer. He was into this, too. Without further ado, he took my hand, and we faced in nearly opposite directions.

The voices came in so clearly, it was like having a full-voice conversation with everyone in the room, all at once. Like pumping up the volume on a DVD, with the treble and bass perfectly balanced. It was elating and terrifying, all at once. Though I was facing away from the reception desk, I clearly heard a woman inquiring about the arrival of the Louisiana vamps. I caught my own image in the brain of the clerk, who was feeling delighted at doing me a bad turn.

Here comes trouble, Barry warned me.

I swung around to see a vampire advancing on me with not a very pleasant expression on her face. She had hot hazel eyes and straight light brown hair, and she was lean and mean.

"Finally, one of the Louisiana party. Are the rest of you in hiding? Tell your bitch whore of a mistress that I'll nail her hide to the wall! She won't get away with murdering my king! I'll see her staked and exposed to the sun on the roof of this hotel!"

I said the first thing that came into my head, unfortunately. "Save the drama for your mama," I told her, just like an eleven-year-old. "And by the way, who the heck are you?"

Of course, this had to be Jennifer Cater. I started to tell her that her king's character had been really substandard, but I liked my head right where it sat on my shoulders, and it wouldn't take much to tip this gal over the edge.

She gave good glare, I'd say that for her.

"I'll drain you dry," she said, harshly. We were attracting a certain amount of attention by then.

"Ooooo," I said, exasperated beyond wisdom. "I'm so scared. Wouldn't the court love to hear you say that? Correct me if I'm wrong, but aren't vampires prevented by—oh, yes—the *law* from threatening humans with death, or did I just read that wrong?"

"As if I give a snap of my fingers for human law," Jennifer Cater said, but the fire was dying down in her eyes as she realized that the whole lobby was listening to our exchange, including many humans and possibly some vampires who'd love to see her out of the way.

"Sophie-Anne Leclerq will be tried by the laws of our people," Jennifer said as a parting shot. "And she will be found guilty. I'll hold Arkansas, and I'll make it great."

"That'll be a first," I said with some justification. Arkansas, Louisiana, and Mississippi were three poor states huddled together, much to our mutual mortification. We were all grateful for each other, because we got to take turns being at the bottom of almost every list in the United States: poverty level, teen pregnancy, cancer death, illiteracy. . . . We pretty much rotated the honors.

Jennifer marched off, not wanting to try a comeback. She was determined, and she was vicious, but I thought Sophie-Anne could outmaneuver Jennifer any day. If I were a betting woman, I'd put money on the French nag.

Barry and I gave each other a shrug. Incident over. We joined hands again.

More trouble, Barry said, sounding resigned.

I focused my brain where his was going. I heard a weretiger heading our way in a big, big hurry.

I dropped Barry's hand and turned, my arms out already and my whole face smiling. "Quinn!" I said, and after a moment where he looked very uncertain, Quinn swung me up in his arms.

I hugged him as hard as I could, and he returned the hug so emphatically that my ribs creaked. Then he kissed me, and it took all my strength of character to keep the kiss within social boundaries.

When we parted to breathe, I realized Barry was standing awkwardly a few feet away, not sure what to do.

"Quinn, this is Barry Bellboy," I said, trying not to feel embarrassed. "He's the only other telepath I know. He works for Stan Davis, the King of Texas."

Quinn extended a hand to Barry, who I now realized was standing awkwardly for a reason. We'd transmitted a bit too graphically. I felt a tide of red sweep over my cheeks. The best thing to do was pretend I hadn't noticed, of course, and that's what I did. But I could feel a little smile twitching the corners of my mouth, and Barry looked more amused than angry.

"Good to meet you, Barry," Quinn rumbled.

"You're in charge of the ceremony arrangements?" Barry asked.

"Yep, that's me."

"I've heard of you," Barry said. "The great fighter. You've got quite a rep among the vamps, man."

I cocked my head. Something I wasn't getting here. "Great fighter?" I said.

"I'll tell you about it later," Quinn said, and his mouth set in a hard line.

Barry looked from me to Quinn. His own face did some hardening, and I was surprised to see that much toughness in Barry. "He hasn't told you?" he asked, and then read the answer right from my head. "Hey, man, that's not right," he said to Quinn. "She should know."

Quinn almost snarled. "I'll tell her about it soon."

"Soon?" Quinn's thoughts were full of turmoil and violence. "Like now?"

But at that moment, a woman strode across the lobby toward us. She was one of the most frightening women I'd ever seen, and I've seen some scary women. She was probably five foot eight, with inky black curls that hugged her head, and she was holding a helmet under her arm. It matched her armor. The armor itself, black and lusterless, was very much like a rather tailored baseball catcher's outfit: a chest guard, thigh protectors, and shin guards, with the addition of thick leather braces that strapped around the forearms. She had some heavy boots on, too, and she carried a sword, a gun, and a small crossbow draped about her in appropriate holsters.

I could only gape.

"You are the one they call Quinn?" she asked, coming to a halt a yard away. She had a heavy accent, one I couldn't trace.

"I am," Quinn said. I noticed Quinn didn't seem to be as amazed as I was at the appearance of this lethal being.

"I'm Batanya. You are in charge of special events. Does

that include security? I wish to discuss my client's special needs."

"I thought security was your job," Quinn said.

Batanya smiled, and it would really make your blood run cold. "Oh, yes, that's my job. But guarding him would be easier if—"

"I'm not in charge of security," he said. "I'm only in charge of the rituals and procedures."

"All right," she said, her accent making the casual phrase into something serious. "Then whom do I talk to?"

"A guy named Todd Donati. His office is in the staff area behind the registration desk. One of the clerks can show you."

"Excuse me," I said.

"Yes?" She looked down an arrow-straight nose at me. But she didn't look hostile or snooty, just worried.

"I'm Sookie Stackhouse," I said. "Who do you work for, Miss Batanya?"

"The King of Kentucky," she said. "He has brought us here at great expense. So it's a pity there's nothing I can do to keep him from being killed, as things stand now."

"What do you mean?" I was considerably startled and alarmed.

The bodyguard looked like she was willing to give me an earful, but we were interrupted.

"Batanya!" A young vampire was hurrying across the lobby, his crew cut and all-black Goth ensemble looking all the more frivolous when he stood by the formidable woman. "The master says he needs you by his side."

"I am coming," Batanya said. "I know my place. But I had to protest the way the hotel is making my job much harder than it needs to be."

"Complain on your own dime," the youngster said curtly.

Batanya gave him a look I wouldn't have wanted to have earned. Then she bowed to us, each in turn. "Miss Stackhouse," she said, extending her hand for me to shake. I hadn't realized hands could be characterized as muscular. "Mr. Quinn." Quinn got the shake, too, while Barry got a nod, since he hadn't introduced himself. "I will call this Todd Donati. Sorry I filled your ears, when this is not your responsibility."

"Wow," I said, watching Batanya stride away. She was wearing pants like liquid leather, and you could see each buttock flex and relax with her movement. It was like an anatomy lesson. She had muscles in her butt.

"What galaxy did she come from?" Barry asked, sounding dazed.

Quinn said, "Not galaxy. Dimension. She's a Britlingen."

We waited for more enlightenment.

"She's a bodyguard, a super-bodyguard," he explained. "Britlingens are the best. You have to be really rich to hire a witch who can bring one over, and the witch has to negotiate the terms with their guild. When the job's over, the witch has to send them back. You can't leave them here. Their laws are different. Way different."

"You're telling me the King of Kentucky paid gobs of money to bring that woman to this . . . this dimension?" I'd heard plenty of unbelievable things in the past two years, but this topped them all.

"It's a very extreme action. I wonder what he's so afraid of. Kentucky isn't exactly rolling in money."

"Maybe he bet on the right horse," I said, since I had my own royalty to worry about. "And I need to talk to you."

"Babe, I gotta get back to work," Quinn said apologetically. He shot an unfriendly look at Barry. "I know we need to talk. But I've got to line up the jurors for the trial, and I've got to set up a wedding ceremony. Negotiations between the King of Indiana and the King of Mississippi have been concluded, and they want to tie the knot while everyone's here."

"Russell's getting married?" I smiled. I wondered if he'd be the bride or the groom, or a little bit of both.

"Yeah, but don't tell anyone yet. They're announcing it tonight."

"So when are we gonna talk?"

"I'll come to your room when the vamps are in bed for the day. Where are you?"

"I have a roommate." I gave him the room number anyway.

"If she's there, we'll find somewhere else to go," he said, glancing at his watch. "Listen, don't worry; everything's okay."

I wondered what I should be worrying about. I wondered where another dimension was, and how hard it would be to bring over bodyguards from it. I wondered why anyone would go to the expense. Not that Batanya hadn't seemed pretty damn effective; but the extreme effort Kentucky had gone to, that sure seemed to argue extreme fear. Who was after him?

My waist buzzed at me, and I realized I was being summoned back up to the queen's suite. Barry's pager went off, too. We looked at each other.

Back to work, he said, as we went toward the elevator. *I'm sorry if I caused trouble between you and Quinn.*

You don't mean that.

He glanced at me. He had the grace to look ashamed. *I guess I don't. I had a picture built up of how you and me would be, and Quinn kind of intruded on my fantasy life.*

Ah . . . ah.

Don't worry—you don't have to think of something to say. It was one of those fantasies. Now that I'm really with you, I have to adjust.

Ah.

But I shouldn't have let my disappointment make me a jerk.

Ah. Okay. I'm sure Quinn and I can work it out.

So, I kept the fantasy screened from you, huh?

I nodded vigorously.

Well, at least that's something.

I smiled at him. *Everyone's got to have a fantasy,* I told him. *My fantasy is finding out where Kentucky got that money, and who he hired to bring that woman here. Was she not the scariest thing you've ever seen?*

No, Barry answered, to my surprise. *The scariest thing I've ever seen . . . well, it wasn't Batanya.* And then he locked the communicating door between our brains and threw away the key. Sigebert was opening the door into the queen's suite, and we were back at work.

After Barry and his party left, I kind of waved my hand in the air to let the queen know I had something to say if she wanted to listen. She and Andre had been discussing Stan's motivation in paying the significant visit, and they paused in identical attitudes. It was just weird. Their heads were cocked at the same angle, and with their extreme pallor and stillness, it was like being regarded by works of art carved in marble: Nymph and Satyr at Rest, or something like that.

"You know what Britlingens are?" I asked, stumbling over the unfamiliar word.

The queen nodded. Andre just waited.

"I saw one," I said, and the queen's head jerked.

"Who has gone to the expense to hire a Britlingen?" Andre asked.

I told them the whole story.

The queen looked—well, it was hard to say how she looked. Maybe a little worried, maybe intrigued, since I'd garnered so much news in the lobby.

"I never knew how useful I'd find it, having a human servant," she said to Andre. "Other humans will say anything around her, and even the Britlingen spoke freely."

Andre was perhaps a tad jealous if the look on his face was any indication.

"On the other hand, I can't do a damn thing about any of this," I said. "I can just tell you what I heard, and it's hardly classified information."

"Where did Kentucky get the money?" Andre said.

The queen shook her head, as if to say she hadn't a clue and really didn't care that much. "Did you see Jennifer Cater?" she asked me.

"Yes, ma'am."

"What did she say?" asked Andre.

"She said she'd drink my blood, and she'd see you staked and exposed on the hotel roof."

There was a moment of utter silence.

Then Sophie-Anne said, "Stupid Jennifer. What's that phrase Chester used to use? She's getting too big for her britches. What to do . . . ? I wonder if she would accept a messenger from me?"

She and Andre looked at each other steadily, and I decided they were doing a little telepathic communication of their own.

"I suppose she's taken the suite Arkansas had reserved," the queen said to Andre, and he picked up the in-house phone and called the front desk. It wasn't the first time I'd heard the king or queen of a state referred to as the state itself, but it seemed a really impersonal way to refer to your former husband, no matter how violently the marriage had ended.

"Yes," he said after he'd hung up.

"Maybe we should pay her a visit," the queen said. She and Andre indulged in some of that silent to and fro that was their way of conversing. Probably like watching Barry and me, I figured. "She'll admit us, I'm sure. There'll be something she wants to say to me in person." The queen picked up the phone, but not as if that was something she did every day. She dialed the room number with her own fingers, too.

"Jennifer," she said charmingly. She listened to a torrent of words that I could hear only a bit. Jennifer didn't sound any happier than she'd been in the lobby.

"Jennifer, we need to talk." The queen sounded much more charming and a lot tougher. There was silence on the other end of the line. "The doors are not closed to discussion or negotiation, Jennifer," Sophie-Anne said. "At least, my doors aren't. What about yours?" I think Jennifer spoke again. "All right, that's wonderful, Jennifer. We'll be down in a minute or two." The queen hung up and stood silent for a long moment.

It seemed to me like going to visit Jennifer Cater, when she was bringing a lawsuit against Sophie-Anne for murdering Peter Threadgill, was a real bad idea. But Andre nodded approvingly at Sophie-Anne.

After Sophie-Anne's conversation with her archenemy, I thought we'd head to the Arkansas group's room any second. But maybe the queen wasn't as confident as she'd sounded. Instead of starting out briskly for the showdown with Jennifer Cater, Sophie-Anne dawdled. She gave herself a little extra grooming, changed her shoes, searched around for her room key, and so on. Then she got a phone call about what room service charges the humans in her group could put on the room bill. So it was more than fifteen minutes before we managed to leave the room. Sigebert was coming out of the staircase door, and he fell into place with Andre at the waiting elevator.

Jennifer Cater and her party were on floor seven. There was no one standing at Jennifer Cater's door: I guessed she didn't rate her own bodyguard. Andre did the knocking honors, and Sophie-Anne straightened expectantly. Sigebert hung back, giving me an unexpected smile. I tried not to flinch.

The door swung open. The interior of the suite was dark.

The smell that wafted from the door was unmistakable.

"Well," said the Queen of Louisiana briskly. "Jennifer's dead."

10

"Go see," the queen told me.

"What? But all y'all are stronger than I am! And less scared!"

"And we're the ones she's suing," Andre pointed out. "Our smell cannot be in there. Sigebert, you must go see."

Sigebert glided into the darkness.

A door across the landing opened, and Batanya stepped out.

"I smell death," she said. "What's happened?"

"We came calling," I said. "But the door was unlocked already. Something's wrong in there."

"You don't know what?"

"No, Sigebert is exploring," I explained. "We're waiting."

"Let me call my second. I can't leave Kentucky's door unguarded." She turned to call back into the suite, "Clovache!"

At least, I guess that was how it was spelled, it was pronounced "Kloh-VOSH."

A kind of Batanya Junior emerged—same armor, but smaller scale; younger, brown-haired, less terrifying . . . but still plenty formidable.

"Scout the place," Batanya ordered, and without a single question Clovache drew her sword and eased into the apartment like a dangerous dream.

We all waited, holding our breaths—well, I was, anyway. The vamps didn't have breath to hold, and Batanya didn't seem at all agitated. She had moved to a spot where she could watch the open door of Jennifer Cater's place and the closed door of the King of Kentucky. Her sword was drawn.

The queen's face looked almost tense, perhaps even excited; that is, slightly less blank than usual. Sigebert came out and shook his head without a word.

Clovache appeared in the doorway. "All dead," she reported to Batanya.

Batanya waited.

"By decapitation," Clovache elaborated. "The woman was, ah"—Clovache appeared to be counting mentally—"in six pieces."

"This is bad," the queen said at the same moment Andre said, "This is good." They exchanged exasperated glances.

"Any humans?" I asked, trying to keep my voice small because I didn't want their attention, but I did want to know, very badly.

"No, all vampires," Clovache said after she got a go-ahead nod from Batanya. "I saw three. They're flaking off pretty fast."

"Clovache, go in and call that Todd Donati." Clovache went silently into the Kentucky suite and placed a call, which had an electrifying effect. Within five minutes, the area in front of the elevator was crammed with people of all sorts and descriptions and degrees of living.

A man wearing a maroon jacket with *Security* on the pocket seemed to be in charge, so he must be Todd Donati. He was a policeman who'd retired from the force early because of the big money to be made guarding and aiding the undead. But that didn't mean he liked them. Now he was furious that something had happened so early in the summit, something that would cause him more work than he was able to handle. He had cancer, I heard clearly, though I wasn't able to discern what kind. Donati wanted to work as long as he could to provide for his family after he was gone, and he was resentful of the stress and strain this investigation would cause, the energy it would drain. But he was doggedly determined to do his job.

When Donati's vampire boss, the hotel manager, showed up, I recognized him. Christian Baruch had been on the cover of *Fang* (the vamp version of *People*) a few months ago. Baruch was Swiss born. As a human, he'd designed and managed a bunch of fancy hotels in Western Europe. When he'd told a vampire in the same line of business that if he was "brought over" (not only to the vampire life but to America), he could run outstanding and profitable hotels for a syndicate of vampires, he'd been obliged in both ways.

Now Christian Baruch had eternal life (if he avoided pointy wooden objects), and the vampire hotel syndicate was raking in the money. But he wasn't a security guy or a law enforcement expert, and he wasn't the police. Sure, he could decorate the hell out of the hotel and tell the architect how many suites needed a wet bar, but what good would he be in this situation? His human hireling looked at Baruch sourly. Baruch was wearing a suit that looked remarkably wonderful, even to inexperienced eyes like mine.

I was sure it had been made for him, and I was sure it had cost a bundle.

I had been pushed back by the crowd until I was pressed against the wall by one of the suite doors—Kentucky's, I realized. It hadn't opened yet. The two Britlingens would have to guard their charge extra carefully with this mob milling around. The hubbub was extraordinary. I was next to a woman in a security uniform; it was just like the ex-cop's, but she didn't have to wear a tie.

"Do you think letting all these people into this space is a good idea?" I asked. I didn't want to be telling the woman her business, but dang. Didn't she ever watch *CSI*?

Security Woman gave me a dark look. "What are *you* doing here?" she asked, as if that made some big point.

"I'm here because I was with the group that found the bodies."

"Well, you just need to keep quiet and let us do our work."

She said this in the snottiest tone possible. "What work would that be? You don't seem to be doing anything at all," I said.

Okay, maybe I shouldn't have said that, but she *wasn't* doing anything. It seemed to me that she should be—

And then she grabbed me and slammed me into the wall and handcuffed me.

I gave a kind of yelp of surprise. "That really wasn't what I meant you to do," I said with some difficulty, since my face was mashed against the door of the suite.

There was a large silence from the crowd behind us. "Chief, I got a woman here causing trouble," said Security Woman.

Maroon looked awful on her, by the way.

"Landry, what are you doing?" said an overly reasonable male voice. It was the kind of voice you use with an irrational child.

"She was telling me what to do," replied Security Woman, but I could tell her voice was deflating even as she spoke.

"What was she telling you to do, Landry?"

"She wondered what all the people were doing here, sir."

"Isn't that a valid question, Landry?"

"Sir?"

"Don't you think we should be clearing out some of these people?"

"Yes, sir, but she said she was here because she was in the party that found the bodies."

"So she shouldn't leave."

"Right. Sir."

"Was she trying to leave?"

"No, sir."

"But you handcuffed her."

"Ah."

"Take the fucking handcuffs off her, Landry."

"Yes, sir." Landry was a flat pancake by now, no air left in her at all.

The handcuffs came off, to my relief, and I was able to turn around. I was so angry I could have decked Landry. But since I would've been right back in the handcuffs, I held off. Sophie-Anne and Andre pushed through the crowd; actually, it just kind of melted in front of them. Vampires and humans alike were glad to get out of the way of the Queen of Louisiana and her bodyguard.

Sophie-Anne glanced at my wrists, saw that they really weren't hurt at all, and correctly diagnosed the fact that my worst injury was to my pride.

"This is my employee," Sophie-Anne said quietly, apparently addressing Landry but making sure everyone there heard her. "An insult or injury to this woman is an insult or injury to me."

Landry didn't know who the hell Sophie-Anne was, but

she could tell power when she saw it, and Andre was just as scary. They were the two most frightening teenagers in the world, I do believe.

"Yes, ma'am, Landry will apologize in writing. Now can you tell me what happened here just now?" Todd Donati asked in a very reasonable voice.

The crowd was silent and waiting. I looked for Batanya and Clovache and saw they were missing. Suddenly Andre said, "You are the chief of security?" in a rather loud voice, and as he did, Sophie-Anne leaned very close to me to say, "Don't mention the Britlingens."

"Yes, sir." The policeman ran a hand over his mustache. "I'm Todd Donati, and this is my boss, Mr. Christian Baruch."

"I am Andre Paul, and this is my queen, Sophie-Anne Leclerq. This young woman is our employee Sookie Stackhouse." Andre waited for the next step.

Christian Baruch ignored me. But he gave Sophie-Anne the look I'd give a roast I was thinking of buying for Sunday dinner. "Your presence is a great honor to my hotel," he murmured in heavily accented English, and I glimpsed the tips of his fangs. He was quite tall, with a large jaw and dark hair. But his small eyes were arctic gray.

Sophie-Anne took the compliment in stride, though her brows drew together for a second. Showing fang wasn't an exactly subtle way of saying, "You shake my world." No one spoke. Well, not for a long, awkward second. Then I said, "Are you all going to call the police, or what?"

"I think we must consider what we have to tell them," Baruch said, his voice smooth, sophisticated, and making fun of rural-southern-human me. "Mr. Donati, will you go see what's in the suite?"

Todd Donati pushed his way through the crowd with no subtlety at all. Sigebert, who'd been guarding the open doorway (for lack of anything better to do), stood aside to let the human enter. The huge bodyguard worked his way over to the queen, looking happier when he was in proximity to his ruler.

While Donati examined whatever was left in the Arkansas suite, Christian Baruch turned to address the crowd. "How many of you came down here after you heard something had happened?"

Maybe fifteen people raised their hands or simply nodded.

"You will please make your way to the Draft of Blood bar on the ground level, where our bartenders will have something special for all of you." The fifteen moved out pretty quickly after that. Baruch knew his thirsty people. Vamps. Whatever.

"How many of you were not here when the bodies were discovered?" Baruch said after the first group had left. Everyone raised a hand except the four of us: me, the queen, Andre, Sigebert.

"Everyone else may feel free to leave," Baruch said as civilly as if he was extending a pleasant invitation. And they did. Landry hesitated and got a look that sent her hurtling down the stairs.

The area around the central elevator seemed spacious now, since it was so much emptier.

Donati came back out. He didn't look deeply disturbed or sick, but he did look less composed.

"There's only bits of them left now. There's stuff all over the floor, though; residue, I guess you'd call it. I think there were three of them. But one of them is in so many pieces, that it might be two of them."

"Who's on the registration?"

Donati referred to a palm-held electronic device. "Jennifer Cater, of Arkansas. This room was rented to the delegation of Arkansas vampires. The remaining Arkansas vampires."

The word *remaining* possibly got a little extra emphasis. Donati definitely knew the queen's history.

Christian Baruch raised a thick, dark brow. "I do know my own people, Donati."

"Yes, sir."

Sophie-Anne's nose might have wrinkled delicately with distaste. *His own people, my ass,* that nose said. Baruch was at most four years old, as a vampire.

"Who's been in to see the bodies?" Baruch asked.

"Neither of us," Andre said promptly. "We haven't set foot in the suite."

"Who did?"

"The door was unlocked, and we smelled death. In view of the situation between my queen and the vampires of Arkansas, we thought it was unwise to go inside," Andre said. "We sent Sigebert, the queen's guard."

Andre simply omitted Clovache's exploration of the suite. So Andre and I did have something in common: we could skirt the truth with something that wasn't quite a lie. He'd done a masterful job.

As the questions continued—mostly unanswered or unanswerable—I found myself wondering if the queen would still have to go to trial now that her main accuser was dead. I wondered whom the state of Arkansas belonged to; it was reasonable to assume that the wedding contract had given the queen some rights regarding Peter Threadgill's property, and I knew Sophie-Anne needed every bit of income she could claim, since Katrina. Would she still have those rights to Arkansas, since Andre had killed Peter? I hadn't thought through how much was hanging over the queen's head at this summit.

But after I'd finished asking myself all these questions, I realized that the most immediate issue had yet to be addressed. Who'd killed Jennifer Cater and her companions? (How many Arkansas vamps could be left, after the battle in New Orleans and today's slaughter? Arkansas wasn't that big a state, and it had very few population centers.)

I was recalled to the here and now when Christian Baruch caught my eyes. "You're the human who can read minds," he said so suddenly that I jerked.

"Yes," I said, because I was tired of sirring and ma'aming everyone.

"Did you kill Jennifer Cater?"

I didn't have to fake astonishment. "That's giving me a lot of credit," I said. "Thinking I could have gotten the drop on three vampires. No, I didn't kill her. She came up to me in the lobby this evening, talking trash, but that's the only time I ever even saw her."

He looked a little taken aback, as if he'd expected another answer or maybe a humbler attitude.

The queen took a step to stand beside me, and Andre mirrored her, so that I was bracketed by ancient vampires. What a warm and cozy feeling. But I knew they were reminding the hotelier that I was their special human and not to be harassed.

At that very opportune moment, a vampire flung open the door from the stairs and hurtled toward the death suite. But Baruch was just as swift, and he barred the way so that the new vampire bounced off him and onto the floor. The small vamp was up in a movement so quick my eyes couldn't break it down and was making a desperate effort to get Baruch out of the doorway.

But the newcomer couldn't, and finally he took a step away from the hotelier. If the smaller vampire had been human, he'd have been panting, and as it was his body shook with tremors of delayed action. He had brown hair and a short beard, and he was wearing a suit, a regular old JCPenney one. He looked like an ordinary guy until you saw his wide eyes and realized that he was some kind of lunatic.

"Is it true?" he asked, his voice low and intent.

"Jennifer Cater and her companions are dead," Christian Baruch said, not without compassion.

The small man howled, literally howled, and the hair on my arms stood up. He sank to his knees, his body swaying back and forth in a transport of grief.

"I take it you are one of her party?" the queen said.

"Yes, yes!"

"Then now I am your queen. I offer you a place at my side."

The howling stopped as if it had been lopped off by a pair of scissors.

"But you had our king killed," the vampire said.

"I was the spouse of your king, and as such, I'm entitled to inherit his state in the event of his death," Sophie-Anne said, her dark eyes looking almost benevolent, almost luminous. "And he is undoubtedly dead."

"That's what the fine print said," Mr. Cataliades murmured in my ear, and I barely suppressed a yelp of astonishment. I'd always thought that what people said about big men moving lightly was total bullshit. Big people move bigly. But Mr. Cataliades walked as lightly as a butterfly, and I had no idea he was nearby until he spoke to me.

"In the queen's wedding contract?" I managed to say.

"Yes," he said. "And Peter's attorney went over it very thoroughly indeed. The same applied in the event of Sophie-Anne's death, too."

"I guess there were a lot of clauses hanging on that?"

"Oh, just a few. The death had to be witnessed."

"Oh, gosh. That's me."

"Yes, indeed it is. The queen wants you in her sight and under her thumb for a very good reason."

"And other conditions?"

"There could be no second-in-command alive to take the state over. In other words, a great catastrophe had to occur."

"And now it has."

"Yes, it seems that it has." Mr. Cataliades appeared quite pleased about that.

My mind was tumbling around like one of those wire bins they draw bingo numbers from at the fair.

"My name is Henrik Feith," the small vamp said. "And there are only five vampires left in Arkansas. I am the only one here in Rhodes, and I am only alive because I went down to complain about the towels in the bathroom."

I had to slap a hand over my own mouth to keep from laughing, which would have been, shall we say, inappropriate. Andre's gaze remained fixed on the man kneeling before us, but somehow his hand wandered over and gave me a pinch. After that it was easy to not laugh. In fact, it was hard not to shriek.

"What was wrong with the towels?" Baruch said, completely sidetracked by this slur on his hotel.

"Jennifer alone used up three," Henrik began explaining, but this fascinating byway was cut short when Sophie-Anne said, "Enough. Henrik, you come with us to my suite. Mr. Baruch, we look forward to receiving updates from you on this situation. Mr. Donati, are you intending to call the Rhodes police?"

It was polite of her to address Donati as though he actually had a say in what was done. Donati said, "No, ma'am, this seems like a vampire matter to me. There's no body to examine now, there's no film since there's no security camera in the suite, and if you'll look up . . ." We all did, of course, to the corner of the hallway. "You'll notice that someone has very accurately thrown a piece of gum over the lens of the security camera. Or perhaps, if it was a vampire, he jumped up and planted the gum on the lens. Of course I'm going to review the tapes, but as fast as vampires can jump, it may well be impossible to determine who the individual is. At the moment, there aren't any vampires on the homicide squad in the Rhodes police force, so I'm not sure there's anyone we can call. Most human cops won't investigate vampire crime, unless they have a vampire partner to get their backs."

"I can't think of anything more we can do here," Sophie-Anne said, exactly as if she could not care less. "If you don't need us any longer, we'll go to the opening ceremony." She had looked at her watch a few times during this conversation. "Master Henrik, if you are up to it, come with us. If you're not up to it, which of course we would understand, Sigebert will take you up to my suite and you may remain there."

"I would like to go somewhere quiet," Henrik Feith said. He looked like a beaten puppy.

Sophie-Anne nodded to Sigebert, who didn't look happy about getting his marching orders. But he had to obey her, of course, so off he went with the little vampire who was one-fifth of all that was left of the Arkansas undead.

I had so much to think about that my brain went into a stall. Just when I believed nothing more could happen, the elevator dinged and the doors swept open to allow Bill to leap out. He didn't arrive as dramatically as Henrik, but he made a definite entrance. He stopped dead and assessed the situation. Seeing we were all standing there calmly, he gathered his composure around him and said, "I hear there has been trouble?" He addressed this to the air in between us, so anyone could answer him.

I was tired of trying to think of him as Nameless. Hell, it was Bill. I might hate every molecule in his body, but he was undeniably there. I wondered if the Weres really managed to keep the abjured off their radar, and how they dealt with it. I wasn't managing very well.

"There is trouble," the queen said. "Though I don't understand what your presence will achieve."

I'd never seen Bill looking abashed, but he did now. "I apologize, my queen," he said. "If you need me for something, I'll have returned to my booth in the convention hall."

In icy silence, the elevator doors slid shut, blocking out my first lover's face and form. It was possible that Bill was trying to show he cared about me by showing up with such haste when he was supposed to be doing business for the queen elsewhere. If this demonstration was supposed to soften my heart, it failed.

"Is there anything I can be doing to help you in your investigation?" Andre asked Donati, though his words were really aimed at Christian Baruch. "Since the queen is the legal heir of Arkansas, we stand ready to assist."

"I would expect nothing less of such a beautiful queen, one also well-known for her business acumen and tenacity." Baruch bowed to the queen.

Even Andre blinked at the convoluted compliment, and the queen gave Baruch a narrow-eyed look. I kept my gaze fixed on the potted plant, and I kept my face absolutely blank. I was in danger of snickering. This was brownnosing on a scale I'd never encountered.

There really didn't seem to be any more to say, and in subdued silence I got on the elevator with the vampires and Mr. Cataliades, who had remained most remarkably quiet.

Once the doors shut, he said, "My queen, you must marry again immediately."

Let me tell you, Sophie-Anne and Andre had quite a reaction to this bombshell; their eyes widened for all of a second.

"Marry anyone: Kentucky, Florida, I would add even Mississippi, if he were not negotiating with Indiana. But you need an alliance, someone lethal to back you up. Otherwise jackals like this Baruch will circle around, yipping for your attention."

"Mississippi's out of the running, thankfully. I don't think I could stand all the men. Once in a while, of course, but not day in, day out, scores of them," Sophie-Anne said.

It was the most natural and unguarded thing I'd ever heard her say. She almost sounded human. Andre reached out and punched the button to stop the elevator between floors. "I wouldn't advise Kentucky," he said. "Anyone who needs Britlingens is in enough trouble of his own."

"Alabama is lovely," Sophie-Anne said. "But she enjoys some things in bed that I object to."

I was tired of being in the elevator and also of being regarded as part of the scenery. "May I ask a question?" I said.

After a moment's silence, Sophie-Anne nodded.

"How come you get to keep your children with you, and you've gone to bed with them, and most vampires aren't able to do that? Isn't it supposed to be a short-term relationship, sire and child?"

"Most vampire children don't stay with their makers after a certain time," Sophie-Anne agreed. "And there are very few cases of children staying with their maker as long as Andre and Sigebert have been with me. That closeness is my gift, my talent. Every vampire has a gift: some can fly, some have special skills with the sword. I can keep my children with me. We can talk to each other, as you and Barry can. We can love each other physically."

"If all that's so, why don't you just name Andre the King of Arkansas and marry him?"

There was a long, total silence. Sophie-Anne's lips parted a couple of times as if she was about to explain to me why that was impossible, but both times she pressed them shut again. Andre stared at me with such intensity that I expected to see two spots on my face begin smoking. Mr. Cataliades just looked shocked, as if a monkey had begun to speak to him in iambic pentameter.

"Yes," said Sophie-Anne finally. "Why don't I do that? Have as king and spouse my dearest friend and lover." In the blink of an eye, she looked positively radiant. "Andre, the only drawback is that you will have to spend some time apart from me when you return to Arkansas to take care of the state's affairs. My oldest child, are you willing?"

Andre's face was transformed with love. "For you, anything," he said.

We had us a Kodak moment going. I actually felt a little choked up.

Andre pressed the button again and down we went.

Though I am not immune to romance—far from it—in my opinion, the queen needed to focus on finding out who'd killed Jennifer Cater and the remaining Arkansas vampires. She needed to be grilling Towel Guy, the surviving vampire—Henrik Whatever. She didn't need to be trailing around meeting and greeting. But Sophie-Anne didn't ask me what I thought, and I'd volunteered enough of my ideas for the day.

The lobby was thronged. Plunged into such a crowd, my brain would normally be going into overload unless I was very careful indeed. But when the majority of the beings with brains were vampires, I got a lobby full of nothing, just a few flutters from the human flunky brains. Watching all the movement and not hearing much was strange, like watching birds' wings beating and yet not hearing the movement. I was definitely working now, so I sharpened up and scanned the individuals who had circulating blood and beating hearts.

One male witch, one female. One lover/blood donor—in

other words, a fangbanger, but a high-class one. When I tracked him down visually, I saw a very handsome young man wearing everything designer down to his tighty whities, and proud of it. Standing beside the King of Texas was Barry the Bellboy: he was doing his job as I was doing mine. I tracked a few hotel employees going about their business. People aren't always thinking about interesting stuff like, "Tonight I'm in on a plot to assassinate the hotel manager," or something like that, even if they *are.* They're thinking stuff like, "The room on eleven needs soap, the room on eight has a heater that won't work, the room service cart on four needs to be moved . . ."

Then I happened upon a whore. Now, *she* was interesting. Most of the whores I knew were of the amateur variety, but this woman was a thorough professional. I was curious enough to make eye contact. She was fairly attractive in the face department, but would never have been a candidate for Miss America or even homecoming queen—definitely not the girl next door, unless you lived in a red-light district. Her platinum hair was in a tousled, bedtime hairdo, and she had rather narrow brown eyes, an allover tan, enhanced breasts, big earrings, stiletto heels, bright lipstick, a dress that was mostly red spangles—you couldn't say she didn't advertise. She was accompanying a man who'd been made vamp when he was in his forties. She held on to his arm as if she couldn't walk without help, and I wondered if the stiletto heels were responsible for that, or if she held on because he liked it.

I was so interested in her—she was projecting her sexuality so strongly, she was so very much a prostitute—that I slipped through the crowd to track her more closely. Absorbed in my goal, I didn't think about her noticing me, but she seemed to feel my eyes on her and she looked over her shoulder to watch me approach. The man she was with was talking to another vampire, and she didn't have to kowtow to him just for the moment, so she had time to eye me with sharp suspicion. I stood a few feet away to listen to her, out of sheer ill-bred curiosity.

Freaky girl, not one of us, does she want him? She can have him; I can't stand that thing he does with his tongue, and after he does me he'll want me to do him and that other guy—geez, do I have some spare batteries? Maybe she could go away and stop staring?

"Sure, sorry," I said, ashamed of myself, and plunged back into the crowd. Next I went over the servers hired by the hotel, who were busy circulating through the crowd with trays of glasses filled with blood and a few actual drinks for the humans scattered around. The servers were all preoccupied with dodging the milling crowd, not spilling, sore backs and tender feet, things like that. Barry and I exchanged nods, and I caught a trailing thought that had Quinn's name embedded, so I followed that trail until I found it led to an employee of E(E)E. I knew this because she was wearing the company T-shirt. This gal was a young woman with a very short haircut and very long legs. She was talking to one of the servers, and it was definitely a one-sided conversation. In a crowd that was noticeably dressed up, this woman's jeans and sneakers stood out.

"—and a case of iced soft drinks," she was saying. "A tray of sandwiches, and some chips. Okay? In the ballroom, within an hour." She swung around abruptly and came face-to-face with me. She scanned me up and down and was little impressed.

"You dating one of the vamps, blondie?" she asked. Her voice was harsh to my ears, a northeastern clipped accent.

"No, I'm dating Quinn," I said. "Blondie, yourself." Though at least I was naturally blond. Well, *assisted* natural. This gal's hair looked like straw . . . if straw had dark roots.

She didn't like that at all, though I wasn't sure which

part of it displeased her most. "He didn't say he had a new woman," she said, and of course she said it in the most insulting way possible.

I felt free to dip into her skull, and I found there a deep affection for Quinn. She didn't think any other women were worthy of him. She thought I was a slow southern girl who hid behind men.

Since this was based on our conversation of less than sixty seconds, I could excuse her for being wrong. I could excuse her for loving Quinn. I couldn't forgive her overwhelming contempt.

"Quinn doesn't have to tell you his personal information," I said. What I really wanted was to ask her where Quinn was now, but that would definitely hand the advantage to her, so I was going to keep that question to myself. "If you'll excuse me, I have to get back to work, and I assume you do, too."

Her dark eyes flashed at me, and she strode off. She was at least four inches taller than me, and very slim. She hadn't bothered with a bra, and she had little plum-like boobs that jiggled in an eye-catching way. This was a gal who'd always want to be on top. I wasn't the only one who watched her cross the room. Barry had jettisoned his fantasy about me for a brand-new one.

I returned to the queen's side because she and Andre were moving into the convention hall from the lobby. The wide double doors were propped open by a really beautiful pair of urns that held huge arrangements of dried grasses.

Barry said, "Have you ever been to a real convention, a normal one?"

"No," I said, trying to keep my scan of the surrounding crowd up. I wondered how Secret Service agents coped. "Well, I went to one with Sam, a bartending supplies convention, but just for a couple of hours."

"Everyone wore a badge, right?"

"If you can call a thing on a lanyard around your neck a badge, yeah."

"That's so workers at the door can be sure you've paid your admittance, and so that unauthorized people won't come in."

"Yeah, so?"

Barry went silent. *So, you see anyone with a badge? You see anyone checking?*

No one but us. And what do we know? The whore might be an undercover spy for the northeastern vampires. Or something worse, I added more soberly.

They're used to being the strongest and scariest, Barry said. *They might fear each other, but they don't seriously fear humans, not when they're together.*

I took his point. The Britlingen had already aroused my concern, and now I was even more worried.

Then I looked back at the doors to the hotel. They were guarded, now that it was dark, by armed vampires instead of armed humans. The front desk, too, was staffed with vampires wearing the hotel uniform, and those vampires were scanning each and every person who walked in the doors. This building was not as laxly protected as it might seem. I relaxed and decided to check out the booths in the convention hall.

There was one for prosthetic fangs that you could have implanted; they came in natural ivory, silver, or gold, and the really expensive ones retracted by means of a tiny motor when your tongue pressed a tiny button in your mouth. "Undetectable from the real thing," an elderly man was assuring a vampire with a long beard and braided hair. "And sharp, oh goodness, yes!" I couldn't figure out who would want a pair. A vamp with a broken tooth? A vamp wannabe who wanted to pretend? A human looking for a little role-playing?

The next booth sold CDs of music from various historical eras, like *Russian Folk Songs of the Eighteenth Century* or *Italian Chamber Music, the Early Years.* It was doing a brisk business. People always like the music of their prime, even if that prime was centuries past.

The next booth was Bill's, and it had a large sign arching over the temporary "walls" of the enclosure. VAMPIRE IDENTIFICATION, it said simply. TRACK DOWN ANY VAMPIRE, ANYWHERE, ANYTIME. ALL YOU NEED IS A COMPUTER-SMART MINION, said a smaller sign. Bill was talking to a female vamp who was extending her credit card to him, and Pam was popping a CD case into a little bag. Pam caught my eye and winked. She was wearing a campy harem outfit, which I would have supposed she'd refuse to do. But Pam was actually smiling. Maybe she was enjoying the break in her routine.

HAPPY BIRTHDAY PRESS PRESENTS: SANGUINARY SOUP FOR THE SOUL was the sign over the next booth, at which sat a bored and lonely vampire with a stack of books in front of her.

The next exhibit took up several spaces and needed no explanation. "You should definitely upgrade," an earnest salesman was telling a black vampire whose hair was braided and tied with a thousand colored strings. She listened intently, eyeing one of the sample miniature coffins open in front of her. "Certainly, wood's biodegradable and it's traditional, but who needs that? Your coffin is your home; that's what my daddy always said."

There were others, including one for Extreme(ly Elegant) Events. That one was a large table with several price brochures and photo albums lying open to tempt the passersby. I was ready to check it out when I noticed that the booth was being "manned" by Miss Snooty Long-Legs. I didn't want to talk to her again, so I sauntered on, though I never lost sight of the queen. One of the human waiters was admiring Sophie-Anne's ass, but I figured that wasn't punishable by death, so I let it go.

By that time the queen and Andre had met with the sheriffs Gervaise and Cleo Babbitt. The broad-faced Gervaise was a small man, perhaps five foot six. He appeared to be about thirty-five, though you could easily add a hundred years to that and be closer to his true age. Gervaise had borne the burden of Sophie-Anne's maintenance and amusement for the past few weeks, and the wear and tear was showing. I'd heard he'd been renowned for his sophisticated clothing and debonair style. The only time I'd seen him before, his light hair had been combed as smooth as glass on his sleek round head. Now it was definitely disheveled. His beautiful suit needed to go to the cleaner, and his wing tips needed polishing. Cleo was a husky woman with broad shoulders and coal black hair, a wide face with a full-lipped mouth. Cleo was modern enough to want to use her last name; she'd been a vampire for only fifty years.

"Where is Eric?" Andre asked the other sheriffs.

Cleo laughed, the kind of deep-throated laugh that made men look. "He got conscripted," she said. "The priest didn't show up, and Eric's taken a course, so he's going to officiate."

Andre smiled. "That'll be something to watch. What's the occasion?"

"It'll be announced in a second," Gervaise said.

I wondered what church would have Eric as a priest. The Church of High Profits? I drifted over to Bill's booth and attracted Pam's attention.

"Eric's a priest?" I murmured

"Church of the Loving Spirit," she told me, bagging three copies of the CD and handing them to a fangbanger sent by his master to pick them up. "He got his certificate from the online course, with Bobby Burnham's help. He can perform marriage services."

A waiter somehow outmaneuvered all the guests around the queen and approached her with a tray full of wineglasses brimming with blood. In the blink of an eye Andre was between the waiter and the queen, and in the blink of another eye, the waiter swiveled and walked in another direction.

I tried to look in the waiter's mind but found it perfectly blank. Andre had grabbed control of the guy's will and sent him on his way. I hoped the waiter was okay. I followed his progress to a humble door set in a corner until I was sure that he was going back to the kitchen. Okay, incident averted.

There was a ripple in the currents of the display hall, and I turned to see what was happening. The King of Mississippi and the King of Indiana had come in together hand in hand, which seemed to be a public signal that they'd concluded their marriage negotiations. Russell Edgington was a slight, attractive vampire who liked other men—exclusively and extensively. He could be good company, and he was a good fighter, too. I liked him. I was a little anxious about seeing Russell, since a few months before I'd left a body in his pool. I tried to look on the bright side. The body was a vampire's, so it should have disintegrated before the pool covering had been removed in the spring.

Russell and Indiana stopped in front of Bill's booth. Indiana, incidentally, was a big bull-like guy with brown curly hair and a face I thought of as no-nonsense.

I drifted closer, because this could be trouble.

"Bill, you look good," Russell said. "My staff tells me you had a hard time at my place. You seem to have recovered nicely. I'm not sure how you got free, but I'm glad." If Russell was pausing for a reaction, he didn't get one. Bill's face was just as impassive as if Russell had been commenting on the weather, not Bill's torture. "Lorena was your sire, so I couldn't interfere," Russell said, his voice just as calm as Bill's face. "And here you are, selling your own little computer thing that Lorena was trying so hard to get from you. As the Bard said, 'All's well that ends well.' "

Russell had been too verbose, which was the only indication that the king was anxious about Bill's reaction. And sure enough, Bill's voice was like cold silk running over glass. But all he said was, "Think nothing of it, Russell. Congratulations are in order, I understand."

Russell smiled up at his groom.

"Yes, Mississippi and I are tying the knot," the King of Indiana said. He had a deep voice. He would look at home beating up some welsher in an alley or sitting in a bar with sawdust on the floor. But Russell did everything but blush.

Maybe this was a love match.

Then Russell spotted me. "Bart, you have to meet this young woman," he said immediately. I about had a panic attack, but there was no way out of the situation without simply turning tail and running. Russell pulled his intended over to me by their linked hands. "This young woman was staked while she was in Jackson. Some of those Fellowship thugs were in a bar, and one of them stabbed her."

Bart looked almost startled. "You survived, obviously," he said. "But how?"

"Mr. Edgington here got me some help," I said. "In fact, he saved my life."

Russell tried to look modest, and he almost succeeded. The vampire was trying to look good in front of his intended, such a human reaction that I could scarcely believe it.

"However, I believe you took something with you when you left," Russell said severely, shaking a finger at me.

I tried to glean something from his face that would tell me which way to jump with my answer. I'd taken a blanket, sure enough, and some loose clothes the young men in Russell's harem had left lying around. And I'd taken Bill, who'd been a prisoner in one of the outbuildings. Probably Russell was referring to Bill, huh?

"Yessir, but I left something behind in return," I said, since I couldn't stand this verbal cat and mouse. All right, already! I'd rescued Bill and killed the vampire Lorena, though that had been more or less by accident. And I'd dumped her evil ass in the pool.

"I did think there was some sludge at the bottom when we got the pool ready for the summer," Russell said, and his bitter chocolate eyes examined me thoughtfully. "What an enterprising young woman you are, Miss . . ."

"Stackhouse. Sookie Stackhouse."

"Yes, I remember now. Weren't you at Club Dead with Alcide Herveaux? He's a Were, honey," Russell said to Bart.

"Yessir," I said, wishing he hadn't remembered that little detail.

"Didn't I hear Herveaux's father was campaigning for packleader in Shreveport?"

"That's right. But he . . . ah, he didn't get it."

"So that was the day Papa Herveaux died?"

"It was," I said. Bart was listening intently, his hand running up and down Russell's coat sleeve all the while. It was a lusty little gesture.

Quinn appeared at my side just then and put his arm around me, and Russell's eyes widened. "Gentlemen," Quinn said to Indiana and Mississippi, "I believe we have your wedding ready and waiting."

The two kings smiled at each other. "No cold feet?" Bart asked Russell.

"Not if you keep them warm," Russell said with a smile that would have melted an iceberg. "Besides, our lawyers would kill us if we reneged on those contracts."

They both nodded at Quinn, who loped to the dais at one end of the exhibit hall. He stood at the highest level and stretched out his arms. There was a microphone up there, and his deep voice boomed out over the crowd. "Your attention, ladies and gentlemen, kings and commoners, vampires and humans! You are all requested and invited to attend the union of Russell Edgington, King of Mississippi, and Bartlett Crowe, King of Indiana, in the Ritual Room. The ceremony will begin in ten minutes. The Ritual Room is through the double doors in the east wall of the hall." Quinn pointed regally at the double doors.

I'd had time to appreciate his outfit while he spoke. He was wearing full trousers that gathered at the waist and the ankle. They were deep scarlet. He had cinched the trousers with a wide gold belt like a prizefighter's, and he was wearing black leather boots with the trouser legs tucked in. He wasn't wearing a shirt. He looked like a genie who'd just popped out of a really big bottle.

"This is your new man?" Russell said. "Quinn?"

I nodded, and he looked impressed.

"I know you got things on your mind right now," I said impulsively. "I know you're about to get married. But I just want to say I hope that we're even-steven, right? You're not mad at me, or holding a grudge at me, or anything?"

Bart was accepting the congratulations of assorted vampires, and Russell glanced his way. Then he did me the courtesy of concentrating on me, though I knew he had to turn away and enjoy his evening in a very short time, which was only right.

"I hold no grudge against you," he said. "Fortunately,

I have a sense of humor, and fortunately, I didn't like Lorena worth a damn. I lent her the room in the stable because I'd known her for a century or two, but she always was a bitch."

"Then let me ask you, since you're not mad at me," I said. "Why does everyone seem so in awe of Quinn?"

"You really don't know, and you've got the tiger by his tail?" Russell looked happily intrigued. "I don't have time to tell you the whole story, because I want to be with my husband-to-be, but I'll tell you what, Miss Sookie, your man has made a lot of people a lot of money."

"Thanks," I said, a bit bewildered, "and best wishes to you and, ah, Mr. Crowe. I hope you'll be very happy together." Since shaking hands was not a vampire custom, I bowed and tried to sort of back away quickly while we were still on such good terms with each other.

Rasul popped up at my elbow. He smiled when I jumped. Those vamps. Gotta love their sense of humor.

I'd only seen Rasul in SWAT gear, and he'd looked good in that. Tonight he was wearing another uniform, but it was also pretty military looking, in a kind of Cossack way. He wore a long-sleeved tunic and tailored pants in a deep plum with black trim and bright brass buttons. Rasul was deeply brown, quite naturally, and had the large, dark liquid eyes and black hair of someone from the Middle East.

"I knew you were supposed to be here, so it's nice to run into you," I said.

"She sent Carla and me ahead of time," he said lightly in his exotic accent. "You are looking lovelier than ever, Sookie. How are you enjoying the summit?"

I ignored his pleasantries. "What's with the uniform?"

"If you mean, whose uniform is it, it's the new house uniform of our queen," he said. "We wear this instead of the armor when we're not out on the streets. Nice, huh?"

"Oh, you're stylin'," I said, and he laughed.

"Are you going to the ceremony?" he said.

"Yeah, sure. I've never seen a vampire wedding. Listen, Rasul, I'm sorry about Chester and Melanie." They'd been on guard duty with Rasul in New Orleans.

For a second, all the humor left the vampire's face. "Yes," he said after a moment of stiff silence. "Instead of my comrades, now I have the Formerly Furred." Jake Purifoy was approaching us, and he was wearing the same uniform as Rasul. He looked lonely. He hadn't been a vampire long enough to maintain the calm face that seemed to be second nature to the undead.

"Hi, Jake," I said.

"Hi, Sookie," he said, sounding forlorn and hopeful.

Rasul bowed to both of us and set off in another direction. I was stuck with Jake. This was too much like grade school for my taste. Jake was the kid who'd come to school wearing the wrong clothes and packing a weird lunch. Being a combo vamp-Were had ruined his chances with either crowd. It was like trying to be a Goth jock.

"Have you had a chance to talk to Quinn yet?" I asked for lack of anything better to say. Jake had been Quinn's employee before his change had effectively put him out of a job.

"I said hello in passing," Jake said. "It's just not fair."

"What?"

"That he should be accepted no matter what he's done, and I should be ostracized."

I knew what *ostracized* meant, because it had been on my Word of the Day calendar. But my brain was just snagging on that word because the bigger meaning of Jake's comment was affecting my equilibrium. "No matter what he's done?" I asked. "What would that mean?"

"Well, of course, you know about Quinn," Jake said, and I thought I might jump on his back and beat him around the head with something heavy.

"The wedding begins!" came Quinn's magnified voice, and the crowd began streaming into the double doors he'd indicated earlier. Jake and I streamed right along with them. Quinn's bouncy-boobed assistant was standing just inside the doors, passing out little net bags of potpourri. Some were tied with blue and gold ribbon, some with blue and red.

"Why the different colors?" the whore asked Quinn's assistant. I appreciated her asking, because it meant I didn't have to.

"Red and blue from the Mississippi flag, blue and gold from the Indiana," the woman said with an automatic smile. She still had it pasted on her face when she handed me a red-and-blue tied bag, though it faded in an almost comical way when she realized who I was.

Jake and I worked our way to a good spot a bit to the right of center. The stage was bare except for a few props, and there were no chairs. They weren't expecting this to take very long, apparently. "Answer me," I hissed. "About Quinn."

"After the wedding," he said, trying not to smile. It had been a few months since Jake had had the upper hand on anyone, and he couldn't hide the fact that he was enjoying it. He glanced behind us, and his eyes widened. I looked in that direction to see that the opposite end of the room was set up as a buffet, though the main feature of the buffet was not food but blood. To my disgust, there were about twenty men and women standing in a line beside the synthetic blood fountain, and they all had name tags that read simply, "Willing Donor." I about gagged. Could that be legal? But they were all free and unrestrained and could walk out if they chose, and most of them looked pretty eager to begin their donation. I did a quick scan of their brains. Yep, willing.

I turned to the platform, only eighteen inches high, which Mississippi and Indiana had just mounted. They'd put on elaborate costumes, which I remembered seeing before in a photo album at the shop of a photographer who specialized in recording supernatural rituals. At least these were easy to put on. Russell was wearing a sort of heavy brocade, open-fronted robe that fit over his regular clothes. It was a splendid garment of gleaming gold cloth worked in a pattern of blue and scarlet. Bart, King of Indiana, was wearing a similar robe in a copper brown color, embroidered with a design in green and gold.

"Their formal robes," Rasul murmured. Once again, he'd drifted to my side without me noticing. I jumped and saw a little smile twitch the corners of his generous mouth. To my left, Jake sidled a little closer to me, as if he were trying to hide from Rasul by concealing himself behind my body.

But I was more interested in this ceremony than I was in vampire one-upmanship. A giant ankh was the prop at the center of the group onstage. Off to one side, there was a table bearing two thick sheaves of paper with two plumed pens arranged between them. A female vampire was standing behind the table, and she was wearing a business suit with a knee-length skirt. Mr. Cataliades stood behind her, looking benevolent, his hands clasping each other across his belly.

Standing on the opposite side of the stage from the table, Quinn, my honey (whose background I was determined to learn pretty shortly), was still in his Aladdin's genie outfit. He waited until the crowd's murmur died to nothing and then he made a great gesture to stage right. A figure came up the steps and onto the platform. He was wearing a cloak of black velvet, and it was hooded. The hood was drawn well forward. The ankh symbol was embroidered in gold on the shoulders of the cloak. The figure took its position between Mississippi and Indiana, its back to the ankh, and raised its arms.

"The ceremony begins," Quinn said. "Let all be silent and witness this joining."

When someone tells a vampire to be quiet, you can be sure the silence is absolute. Vampires don't have to fidget, sigh, sneeze, cough, or blow their nose like people do. I felt noisy just breathing.

The cloaked figure's hood fell back. I sighed. Eric. His wheat-colored hair looked beautiful against the black of the cloak, and his face was solemn and commanding, which was what you want in an officiant.

"We are here to witness the joining of two kings," he said, and every word carried to the corners of the room. "Russell and Bart have agreed, both verbally and by written covenant, to ally their states for a hundred years. For a hundred years, they may not marry any other. They may not form an alliance with any other, unless that alliance is mutually agreed and witnessed. Each must pay the other a conjugal visit at least once a year. The welfare of Russell's kingdom shall come second only to his own in Bart's sight, and the welfare of Bart's kingdom shall come second only to his own in Russell's sight. Russell Edgington, King of Mississippi, do you agree to this covenant?"

"Yes, I do," Russell said clearly. He held out his hand to Bart.

"Bartlett Crowe, King of Indiana, do you agree to this covenant?"

"I do," Bart said, and took Russell's hand. Awwww.

Then Quinn stepped forward and knelt, holding a goblet under the joined hands, and Eric whipped out a knife and cut the two wrists with two movements too quick to separate.

Oh, *ick.* As the two kings bled into the chalice, I chided myself. I might have known that a vampire ceremony would include a blood exchange.

Sure enough, when the wounds closed, Russell took a sip from the chalice, and then handed it to Bart, who drained it dry. Then they kissed, Bart holding the smaller man tenderly. And then they kissed some more. Evidently the mingled blood was a real turn-on.

I caught Jake's eye. *Get a room*, he mouthed, and I looked down to hide my smile.

Finally, the two kings moved on to the next step, a ceremonious signing of the contract they'd agreed upon. The business-suit woman turned out to be a vampire lawyer from Illinois, since a lawyer from another state had to draw up the contract. Mr. Cataliades had been a neutral lawyer, too, and he signed the documents after the kings and the vampire lawyer.

Eric stood in his black-and-gold glory while all this was done, and once the pens were back on their elaborate stands, he said, "The marriage is sacred for one hundred years!" and a cheer went up. Vampires aren't big on cheering, either, so it was mostly the humans and the other supes in the crowd who did the hurrahing, but the vampires all made an appreciative murmur—not as good, but the best they could do, I guess.

I sure wanted to find out more about how Eric had qualified as a priest, or whatever they called the officiant, but first I was going to make Jake tell me about Quinn. He was trying to wriggle away in the crowd, but I caught up with him pretty quick. He wasn't a good enough vampire yet to get away from me.

"Spill," I said, and he tried to act like he didn't know what I was talking about, but he saw from my face I wasn't buying it.

So, while the crowd eddied around us, trying not to speed toward the open bar, I waited for Quinn's story.

"I can't believe he hasn't told you this himself," Jake said, and I was tempted to slap him upside the head.

I glared at him to let him know I was *waiting.*

"Okay, okay," he said. "I heard all this when I was still a Were. Quinn is like a rock star in the shifter world, you know. He's one of the last weretigers, and he's one of the most ferocious."

I nodded. So far, that paralleled my knowledge of Quinn.

"Quinn's mom was captured one full moon when she changed. A bunch of hunters were out camping, set up a trap because they wanted a bear for their illegal dogfights. Something new to bet on, you know? A pack of dogs versus a bear. This was somewhere in Colorado, and snow was on the ground. His mom was out on her own, and somehow she fell into the trap, didn't sense it."

"Where was his dad?"

"He had died when Quinn was little. Quinn was about fifteen when this happened."

I had a feeling worse was coming, and I was right.

"He changed, of course, the same night, soon as he found she was missing. He tracked them to the camp. His mom had turned back into a woman under the stress of the capture, and one of them was raping her." Jake took a deep breath. "Quinn killed them all."

I looked down at the floor. I couldn't think of anything to say.

"The campsite had to be cleaned up. There wasn't a pack around to step in—course, tigers don't hang in packs—and his mother was hurt bad and in shock, so Quinn went to the local vampire nest. They agreed to do the job, if he'd be indebted to them for three years." Jake shrugged. "He agreed."

"What exactly did he agree to do?" I asked.

"To fight in the pits for them. For three years or until he died, whichever came first."

I began to feel cold fingers moving up my spine, and this time it wasn't creepy Andre . . . it was just fear. "The pits?" I said, but if he hadn't had vampire hearing, he wouldn't have been able to make my words out.

"There's a lot of bets placed on pit fighting," Jake said. "It's like the dogfights the hunters wanted the bear for. Humans aren't the only ones who like to watch animals kill each other. Some vamps love it. So do some other supes."

My lips curled in disgust. I felt almost nauseated.

Jake was looking at me, troubled by my reaction, but also giving me time to understand the sad story was not at an end. "Obviously Quinn survived his three years," Jake said. "He's one of the few who've lived that long." He looked at me sideways. "He kept winning and winning. He was one of the most savage fighters anyone's ever seen. He fought bears, lions, you name it."

"Aren't they all really rare?" I asked.

"Yeah, they are, but I guess even rare Were creatures need money," Jake said with a toss of his head. "And you can make big bucks pit fighting, when you've earned enough to bet on yourself."

"Why did he stop?" I asked. I regretted more than I could say that I had been curious about Quinn. I should have waited until he volunteered all this. He would have, I hoped. Jake caught a human servant walking by and snagged a glass of synthetic blood off the tray. He drained it in one gulp.

"His three years ended, and he had to take care of his sister."

"Sister?"

"Yeah, his mom got pregnant that night, and the result was the dyed blonde who gave us the potpourri bags at the door. Frannie gets into trouble from time to time, and Quinn's mother can't handle her, so she sends her to stay with Quinn for a while. Frannie turned up here last night."

I'd had as much as I could stomach. I turned in one quick movement and walked away from Jake. And to his credit, he didn't try to stop me.

11

I WAS SO ANXIOUS TO GET OUT OF THE CROWD IN THE wedding hall that I collided with a vampire, who whirled and grabbed my shoulders in a blur of darkness. He had a long Fu Manchu mustache and a mane of hair that would have done a couple of horses credit. He was wearing a solid black suit. At another time, I might have enjoyed the total package. Now I just wanted him to move.

"Why in such a hurry, my sweet maid?" he asked.

"Sir," I said politely, since he must be older than I, "I really am in a hurry. Excuse me for bumping into you, but I need to leave."

"You're not a donor, by any chance?"

"Nope, sorry."

Abruptly he let go of my shoulders and turned back to the conversation I'd interrupted. With a great wave of relief,

I continued to pick my way through the assemblage, though with more care now that I'd already had one tense moment.

"There you are!" Andre said, and he almost sounded cross. "The queen needs you."

I had to remind myself that I was there to work, and it really didn't matter how much inner drama I was experiencing. I followed Andre over to the queen, who was in conversation with a knot of vamps and humans.

"Of course I am on your side, Sophie," said a female vampire. She was wearing an evening gown of pink chiffon joined at one shoulder with a big broach sparkling with diamonds. They might be Swarovski crystals, but they looked real to me. What do I know? The pale pink looked real pretty against her chocolate skin. "Arkansas was an asshole, anyway. I was only astonished that you married him in the first place."

"So if I come to trial, you will be kind, Alabama?" Sophie-Anne asked, and you would have sworn she wasn't a day over sixteen. Her upturned face was smooth and firm, her big eyes gleamed, her makeup was subtle. Her brown hair was loose, which was unusual for Sophie-Anne.

The vamp seemed to soften visibly. "Of course," she said.

Her human companion, the designer-clad fangbanger I'd noticed earlier, thought, *That'll last ten minutes, until she turns her back on Sophie-Anne. Then they'll be plotting again. Sure, they all say they like crackling fires and long walks on the beach by moonlight, but whenever you go to a party, it's maneuver, maneuver, maneuver, and lie, lie, lie.*

Sophie-Anne's gaze just brushed mine, and I gave a tiny shake of my head. Alabama excused herself to go congratulate the newlyweds, and her human tagged along. Mindful of all the ears around us, most of which could hear far better than I could, I said, "Later," and got a nod from Andre.

Next to court Sophie-Anne was the King of Kentucky, the man who was guarded by Britlingens. Kentucky turned out to look a lot like Davy Crockett. All he needed was a ba'ar and a coonskin cap. He was actually wearing leather pants and a suede shirt and jacket, fringed suede boots, and a big silk kerchief tied around his neck. Maybe he needed the bodyguards to protect him from the fashion police.

I didn't see Batanya and Clovache anywhere, so I assumed he'd left them in his room. I didn't see what good it was to hire expensive and otherworldly bodyguards if they weren't around your body to guard it. Then, since I didn't have another human to distract me, I noticed something odd: there was a space behind Kentucky that stayed constantly empty, no matter what the flow of the crowd might be. No matter how natural it would be for someone passing behind Kentucky to step in that area, somehow no one ever did. I figured the Britlingens were on duty, after all.

"Sophie-Anne, you're a sight for sore eyes," said Kentucky. He had a drawl that was thick as honey, and he made a point of letting Sophie-Anne see his fangs were partially out. Ugh.

"Isaiah, it's always good to see you," Sophie-Anne said, her voice and face smooth and calm as always. I couldn't tell whether or not Sophie-Anne knew the bodyguards were right behind him. As I drew a little closer, I found that though I couldn't see Clovache and Batanya, I could pick up their mental signatures. The same magic that cloaked their physical presence also muffled their brain waves, but I could get a dull echo off both of them. I smiled at them, which was really dumb of me, because Isaiah, King of Kentucky, picked up on it right away. I should have known he was smarter than he looked.

"Sophie-Anne, I want to have a chat with you, but you gotta get that little blond gal out of here for the duration," Kentucky said with a broad grin. "She pure-dee gives me the willies." He nodded toward me, as if Sophie-Anne had lots of blond human women trailing her.

"Of course, Isaiah," Sophie-Anne said, giving me a very level look. "Sookie, please go down to the lower level and fetch the suitcase the staff called about earlier."

"Sure," I said. I didn't mind a humble errand. I'd almost forgotten the gruff voice on the phone earlier in the evening. I thought it was stupid that procedure required us to come down to the bowels of the hotel, rather than allowing a bellman to bring us the suitcase, but red tape is the same everywhere you go, right?

As I turned to go, Andre's face was quite blank, as usual, but when I was almost out of earshot, he said, "Excuse me, your majesty, we didn't tell the girl about your schedule for the night." In one of those disconcerting flashes of movement, he was right beside me, hand on my arm. I wondered if he'd gotten one of those telepathic communications from Sophie-Anne. Without a word, Sigebert had moved into Andre's place beside Sophie-Anne, a half step back.

"Let's talk," said Andre, and quick as a wink he guided me to an EXIT sign. We found ourselves in a blank beige service corridor that extended for maybe ten yards, then made a right-angle turn. Two laden waiters came around the corner and passed us, giving us curious glances, but when they met Andre's eyes they hurried away on their task.

"The Britlingens are there," I said, assuming that was why Andre had wanted to talk to me in private. "They're trailing right behind Kentucky. Can all Britlingens become invisible?"

Andre did another movement that was so fast it was a blur, and then his wrist was in front of me, dripping blood. "Drink," he said, and I felt him pushing at my mind.

"No," I said, outraged and shocked at the sudden movement, the demand, the blood. "Why?" I tried to back away, but there was no place to go and no help in sight.

"You have to have a stronger connection to Sophie-Anne

or me. We need you bound to us by more than a paycheck. Already you've proved more valuable than we'd imagined. This summit is critical to our survival, and we need every advantage we can get."

Talk about brutal honesty.

"I don't want you to have control over me," I told him, and it was awful to hear my voice going wavery with fear. "I don't want you to know how I'm feeling. I got hired for this job, and after it, I'm going back to my real life."

"You don't have a real life anymore," Andre said. He didn't look unkind; that was the weird, and most frightening, thing. He looked absolutely matter-of-fact.

"I do! You guys are the blip on the radar, not me!" I wasn't totally sure what I meant by that, but Andre got my drift.

"I don't care what your plans are for the rest of your human existence," he said, and shrugged. *Phooey for your life.* "Our position will be strengthened if you drink, so you must. I've explained this to you, which I wouldn't bother to do if I didn't respect your ability."

I pushed at him, but it was like shoving an elephant. It would work only if the elephant felt like moving. Andre didn't. His wrist came closer to my mouth, and I clamped my lips together, though I was sure Andre would break my teeth if he had to. And if I opened my mouth to scream, he'd have that blood in my mouth before you could say Jack Robinson.

Suddenly there was a third presence in the stark beige corridor. Eric, still wearing the black velvet cape, hood thrown back, was standing right by us, his face uncharacteristically uncertain.

"Andre," he said, his voice sounding deeper than usual. "Why are you doing this?"

"Are you questioning the will of your queen?"

Eric was in a bad place, because he was definitely interfering with the execution of the queen's orders—at least, I assumed the queen knew about this—but I could only pray he stayed to help me. I begged him with my eyes.

I could name several vamps I'd rather have a connection to than Andre. And, stupidly, I couldn't help but feel hurt. I'd given Andre and Sophie-Anne such a good idea about him being King of Arkansas, and this was the way I got repaid. That would teach me to keep my mouth shut. That would teach me to treat vampires like they were people.

"Andre, let me offer a suggestion," Eric said in a much cooler, calmer voice. Good. He was keeping his head together. One of us needed to. "She must be kept happy, or she won't cooperate anymore."

Oh, crap. Somehow I knew his suggestion wasn't going to be, "Let her go or I'll break your neck," because Eric was way too canny for that. Where was John Wayne when you needed him? Or Bruce Willis? Or even Matt Damon? I would be glad to see Jason Bourne right now.

"We've exchanged blood several times, Sookie and I," Eric said. "In fact, we've been lovers." He took a step closer. "I think she wouldn't be so balky if I were the blood giver. Would that suit your purposes? I'm under oath to you." He bowed his head respectfully. He was being careful, so careful. That made me more frightened of Andre.

Andre let me go while he pondered. His wrist had almost healed up, anyway. I took a few long, shaky breaths. My heart was racing.

Andre looked at Eric, and I thought I could detect a certain amount of distrust in his gaze. Then he looked at me.

"You look like a rabbit hiding under a bush while the fox tracks her," he said. There was a long pause. "You did do my queen and me a large service," he said. "More than once. If the end result will be the same, why not?"

I started to say, "And I'm the only witness to Peter Threadgill's death," but my guardian angel shut my mouth to seal in the words. Well, maybe it wasn't my *actual* guardian angel, but my subconscious, which told me not to speak. Whatever. I was grateful.

"All right, Eric," Andre said. "As long as she's bonded to someone in our kingdom. I've only had a drop of her blood, to find out if she was part fae. If you've exchanged blood with her more than once, the bond is already strong. Has she answered well to your call?"

What? What call? When? Eric had never called me. In fact, I'd out and out defied him before.

"Yes, she heels nicely," Eric said without a blink of an eye. I about choked, but that would have ruined the effect of Eric's words, so I looked down at my chest as if I was embarrassed by my thralldom.

"Well, then," Andre said with an impatient gesture of his hand. "Go on."

"Right here? I'd prefer somewhere more private," Eric said.

"Here and now." Andre was not going to compromise any further.

Eric said, "Sookie." He looked at me intently.

I looked right back at him. I understood what that one word was saying. There was no way out of this. No struggling or screaming or refusal would prevent this procedure. Eric might have spared me from submitting to Andre, but that was as far as he could go.

Eric raised one eyebrow.

With that arched eyebrow, Eric was telling me that this was my best bet, that he would try not to hurt me, that being tied to him was infinitely preferable to being tied to Andre.

I knew all this not only because I wasn't stupid, but because we *were* bound together. Both Eric and Bill had had my blood, and I theirs. For the first time, I understood there was a real connection. Didn't I see the two of them as more human than vampire? Didn't they have the power to wound me more than any others? It wasn't only my past relationships with the two that kept me tied to them. It was the blood exchange. Maybe because of my unusual heritage, they couldn't order me around. They didn't have mind control over me, and they couldn't read my thoughts; and I couldn't do any of those things to them. But we did share a tie. How often had I heard their lives humming away in the background, without realizing what I was listening to?

It takes way longer to tell this than it did to think it.

"Eric," I said, and tilted my head to one side. He read as much from the gesture and word as I had from his. He stepped over to me and extended his arms to hold the black cloak out as he leaned over me, so the cloak and the hood could give us some illusion of privacy. The gesture was hokey, but the idea was nice. "Eric, no sex," I said in a voice as hard as I could make it. I could tolerate this if it wasn't like a lovers' blood exchange. I *wouldn't* have sex in front of another person. Eric's mouth was in the bend of my neck and shoulder, and his body pressed against mine. My arms slid around him, because that was simply the easiest way to stand. Then he bit, and I couldn't choke back a gasp of pain.

He didn't stop, thank God, because I wanted to get this over with. One of his hands stroked my back as if he was trying to soothe me.

After a long few seconds, Eric licked my neck to be sure his coagulant-laden saliva had coated the little wounds. "Now, Sookie," he said right into my ear. I couldn't reach his neck unless we were lying down, not without him bending over awkwardly. He started to hold his wrist up to my mouth, but we'd have to rearrange ourselves for that to work. I unbuttoned his shirt and pushed it open. I hesitated. I always hated this part, because human teeth are not nearly as sharp as vampire teeth, and I knew it would be messy when I bit. Eric did something that surprised me, then; he produced the same small ceremonial knife he'd used in marrying Mississippi and Indiana. With the same quick motion he'd used on their wrists, Eric sliced a cut in his chest right below his nipple. The blood oozed out sluggishly, and I took advantage of the flow to latch on. This was embarrassingly intimate, but at least I didn't have to look at Andre, and he couldn't see me.

Eric moved restlessly, and I realized he was getting aroused. There was nothing I could do about it, and I held our bodies apart that crucial couple of inches. I sucked hard, and Eric made a small noise, but I was strictly trying to get this over with. Vampire blood is thick and almost sweet, but when you think about what you're actually doing and you're not sexually aroused, it's not pleasant at all. When I thought I'd done it long enough, I let go and rebuttoned Eric's shirt with unsteady hands, thinking this little incident was over and I could hide somewhere until my heart stopped pounding.

And then Quinn flung open the door and stepped into the corridor.

"What the hell are you doing?" he roared, and I wasn't sure if he meant me, or Eric, or Andre.

"They are obeying orders," Andre said sharply.

"My woman doesn't have to take orders from you," Quinn said.

I opened my mouth to protest, but under these circumstances, it was hard to hand Quinn the line that I could take care of myself.

There was no social guideline to cover a calamity like this, and even my grandmother's all-purpose rule of etiquette ("Do what will make everyone most comfortable") could not remotely stretch to encompass my situation. I wondered what Dear Abby would say.

"Andre," I said, trying to sound firm instead of cowed and scared, "I'll finish the job I undertook to do for the queen here, because I shook on it. But I'll never work for you two again. Eric, thank you for making that as pleasant for me as you could." (Though *pleasant* hardly seemed the right word.)

Eric had staggered a step over to lean against the wall. He'd allowed the cloak to fall open, and the stain on his pants was clearly visible. "Oh, no problem," Eric said dreamily.

That didn't help. I suspected he was doing it on purpose. I felt heat rise in my cheeks. "Quinn, I'll talk to you later, as we agreed," I snapped. Then I hesitated. "That is, if you're still willing to talk to me." I thought, but couldn't say because it would have been too grossly unfair, that it would have been more help to me if he'd come ten minutes earlier . . . or not at all.

Looking neither to the right nor the left, I made myself march down that hall, took the right-angle turn, and walked through a swinging doorway directly into the kitchen.

This clearly wasn't where I wanted to be, but at least it was away from the three men in the hall. "Where's the baggage area?" I asked the first uniformed staff person I saw. She was a server loading glasses of synthetic blood onto a huge round tray, and she didn't pause in her task but nodded her head toward a door in the south wall marked EXIT. I was taking a lot of those this evening.

This door was heavier and led to a flight of stairs descending to a lower level, which I figured was actually under the ground. We don't have basements where I come from (the water table's too high), so it gave me a little frisson to be below street level.

I'd been walking as if something was chasing me, which in a nonliteral way was absolutely true, and I'd been thinking about the damn suitcase so I wouldn't have to think about anything else. But when I reached the landing, I came a complete stop.

Now that I was out of sight and truly alone, I took a moment to stand still, one hand resting against the wall. I let myself react to what had just happened. I began shaking, and when I touched my neck, I realized my collar felt funny. I pulled the material out and away and did a sort of sideways downward squinch to have a look at it. The collar was stained with my blood. Tears began flooding my eyes, and I sank to my haunches on the landing of that bleak staircase in a city far from home.

12 ~

I SIMPLY COULDN'T PROCESS WHAT HAD JUST HAPPENED; it didn't jibe with my inner picture of myself or how I behaved. I could only think, *You had to be there.* And even then that didn't sound convincing.

Okay, Sookie, I said to myself. *What else could you have done?* It wasn't the time to do a lot of detailed thinking, but a quick scan of my options came up zero. I couldn't have fought off Andre or persuaded him to leave me alone. Eric could have fought Andre, but he chose not to because he wanted to keep his place in the Louisiana hierarchy, and also because he might have lost. Even if he'd chanced to win, the penalty would have been incredibly heavy. Vampires didn't fight over humans.

Likewise, I could have chosen to die rather than submit to the blood exchange, but I wasn't quite sure how I would have achieved that, and I was quite sure I didn't want to.

There was simply nothing I could have done, at least nothing that popped to my mind as I squatted there in the beigeness of the back stairway.

I shook myself, blotted my face with a tissue from my pocket, and smoothed my hair. I stood up straighter. I was on the right track to regaining my self-image. I would have to save the rest for later.

I pushed open the metal door and stepped into a cavernous area floored with concrete. As I'd progressed farther into the working area of the hotel (beginning with the first plain beige corridor), the decor had scaled back to minimal. This area was absolutely functional.

No one paid the least attention to me, so I had a good look around. It's not like I was anxious to hurry back to the queen, right? Across the floor, there was a huge industrial elevator. This hotel had been designed with as few openings onto the outside world as possible, to minimize the chance of intrusion, both of humans and the enemy sun. But the hotel had to have at least one large dock to load and unload coffins and supplies. This was the elevator that served that dock. The coffins entered here before they were taken to their designated rooms. Two uniformed men armed with shotguns stood facing the elevator, but I have to say that they looked remarkably bored, not at all like the alert watchdogs in the lobby.

In an area by the far wall, to the left of the huge elevator, some suitcases were slumped together in a forlorn sort of suitcase corral, an area delineated by those posts that contain retractable strips that are used to direct crowds in airports. No one appeared to be in charge of them, so I walked over—and it was a long walk—and began reading labels. There was already another lackey like me searching through the luggage, a young man with glasses and wearing a business suit.

"What are you looking for?" I asked. "If I see it while I'm looking, I can pull it out for you."

"Good idea. The desk called to say we had a suitcase down here that hadn't made it to the room, so here I am. The tag should say 'Phoebe Golden, Queen of Iowa' or something like that. You?"

"Sophie-Anne Leclerq, Louisiana."

"Wow, you work for her? Did she do it?"

"Nope, and I know because I was there," I said, and his curious face got even more curious. But he could tell I wasn't going to say any more about it, and he resumed looking.

I was surprised at the number of suitcases in the corral.

"How come," I asked the young man, "they can't just bring these up and leave them in the rooms? Like the rest of the luggage?"

He shrugged. "I was told it's some kind of liability issue. We have to identify our suitcases personally, so they can say we were the ones who picked them out. Hey, this is the one I want," he said after a moment. "I can't read the name of the owner, but it does say Iowa, so it must belong to someone in our group. Well, bye, nice to talk to you." He set off briskly with a black rolling bag.

Immediately after that, I hit luggage pay dirt. A blue leather suitcase was tagged with "Sheriff, Area"—well, that was too scribbled to make out. The vampires used all kinds of scripts, depending on the education they'd had in the age they were born. "Louisiana": the label did say that. I picked up the old suitcase and lifted it over the barrier. The writing wasn't any clearer closer to my eyes. Like my opposite number in Iowa, I decided the best course would be to take it upstairs and show it around until someone claimed it.

One of the armed guards had turned halfway from his post to figure out what I was doing. "Where you going with that, beautiful?" he called.

"I work for the Queen of Louisiana. She sent me down to get it," I said.

"Your name?"

"Sookie Stackhouse."

"Hey, Joe!" he called to a fellow employee, a heavy guy who was sitting behind a really ugly desk on which sat a battered computer. "Check out the name Stackhouse, will ya?"

"Sure thing," Joe said, wrenching his gaze from the young Iowan, who was just barely visible over on the other side of the cavernous space. Joe regarded me with the same curiosity. When he saw that I'd noticed, he looked guilty and tapped away at the keyboard. He eyed the computer screen like it could tell him everything he needed to know, and for the purposes of his job, maybe he was right.

"Okay," Joe called to the guard. "She's on the list." His was the gruff voice that I remembered from the phone conversation. He resumed staring at me, and though all the other people in the cavernous space were having blank, neutral thoughts, Joe's were not blank. They were shielded. I'd never encountered anything like it. Someone had put a metaphysical helmet on his head. I tried to get through it, around, under it, but it stayed in place. While I fumbled around, trying to get inside his thoughts, Joe was looking at me with a cross expression. I don't think he knew what I was doing. I think he was a grouch.

"Excuse me," I asked, calling so my question could reach Joe's ears. "Is my picture by my name on your list?"

"No," he said, snorting as if I'd asked a strange question. "We got a list of all the guests and who they brought with them."

"So, how do you know I'm me?"

"Huh?"

"How do you know I'm Sookie Stackhouse?"

"Aren't you?"

"Yeah."

"Then what you bitching about? Get outta here with the

damn suitcase." Joe looked down at his computer, and the guard swung around to face the elevator. *This must be the legendary Yankee rudeness,* I thought.

The bag didn't have a roller mechanism; no telling how long the owner had had it. I picked it up and marched back over to the door to the stairs. There was another elevator close to the door, I noticed, but it wasn't half as large as the huge one that had access to the outside. It could take up coffins, true, but perhaps only one at a time.

I'd already opened the stair door when I realized that if I went up that way I'd have to pass through the service corridor again. What if Eric, Andre, and Quinn were still there? What if they'd ripped each other's throats out? Though just at the moment such a scenario wouldn't have devastated me, I decided to forgo the chance of an encounter. I took the elevator instead. Okay, cowardly, but a woman can handle only so much in one night.

This elevator was definitely for the peons. It had pads on the walls to prevent cargo from being damaged. It serviced only the first four floors: basement levels, lobby, mezzanine, human floor. After that, the shape of the pyramid dictated that to rise, you had to go to the center to catch one of elevators that went all the way up. This would make taking the coffins around a slow process, I thought. The staff of the Pyramid worked hard for their money.

I decided to take the suitcase straight to the queen's suite. I didn't know what else to do with it.

When I stepped off at Sophie-Anne's floor, the lobby area around the elevator was silent and empty. Probably all the vampires and their attendants were downstairs at the soiree. Someone had left a discarded soda can lying in a large, boldly patterned urn holding some kind of small tree. The urn was positioned against the wall between the two elevators. I think the tree was supposed to be some kind of short palm tree, to maintain the Egyptian theme. The stupid soda can bothered me. Of course, there were maintenance people in the hotel whose job it was to keep everything clean, but the habit of picking up was ingrained in me. I'm no neat freak, but still. This was a nice place, and some idiot was strewing garbage around. I bent over to pick the darn thing up with my free right hand, intending to toss it into the first available garbage can.

But it was a lot heavier than it should have been.

I set down the suitcase to look at the can closely, cradling it in both my hands. The colors and the design made the cylinder look like a Dr Pepper can in almost every respect, but it just wasn't. The elevator doors whooshed open again, and Batanya stepped off, a strange-looking gun in one hand, a sword in the other. Looking over the bodyguard's shoulder into the elevator car, I saw the King of Kentucky, who looked back at me curiously.

Batanya seemed a bit surprised to see me standing there, smack-dab in front of the door. She scanned the area, then pointed her gunlike weapon carefully at the floor. The sword remained ready in her left hand. "Could you step to my left?" she asked very courteously. "The king wants to visit in that room." Her head nodded toward one of the rooms to the right.

I didn't move, couldn't think of what to say.

She took in the way I was standing and the expression on my face. She said in a sympathetic way, "I don't know why you people drink those carbonated things. They give me gas, too."

"It's not that."

"Is something wrong?"

"This isn't an empty can," I said.

Batanya's face froze. "What do you think it is?" she asked very, very calmly. That was the voice of Big Trouble.

"It might be a spy camera," I said hopefully. "Or, see, I'm thinking it might be a bomb. Because it's not a real can. It's full of something heavy, and that heaviness is not fluid." Not only was the tab top not on the can, but the innards didn't slosh.

"I understand," Batanya said. Again with the calm. She pressed a little panel on the armor over her chest, a dark blue area about the size of a credit card. "Clovache," she said. "Unknown device on four. I'm bringing the king back down."

Clovache's voice said, "How large is the device?" Her accent was sort of like Russian, at least to my untravelled ears. ("Hau larch . . . ?")

"The size of one of those cans of sweetened syrup," Batanya answered.

"Ah, the burping drinks," Clovache said. *Good memory, Clovache,* I thought.

"Yes. The Stackhouse girl noticed it, not me," Batanya said grimly. "And now she is standing with it in her hand."

"Tell her to put it down," advised the invisible Clovache with the simplicity of one who was stating an obvious fact.

Behind Batanya, the King of Kentucky was beginning to look very nervous. Batanya glanced over her shoulder at him. "Get a bomb team up here from the local policing unit," Batanya said to Clovache. "I'm bringing the king back down."

"The tiger is here, too," Clovache said. "She is his woman."

Before I could say, "For God's sake, don't send him up," Batanya pressed the rectangle again, and it went dark.

"I have to protect the king," Batanya said with an apology in her voice. She stepped back into the elevator, punched a button, and gave me a nod.

Nothing had scared me as much as that nod. It was a good-bye look. And the door swooshed shut.

There I stood, alone on the silent hotel floor, holding an instrument of death. Maybe.

Neither of the elevators gave any signs of life. No one came out of the doors on the fourth floor, and no one went into them. The stair door didn't budge. There was a long, dead time in which I did nothing but stand and hold a fake Dr Pepper can. I did a little breathing, too, but nothing too violent.

With an explosion of sound that startled me so much I nearly dropped the can, Quinn burst onto the floor. He'd taken the stairs in a huge hurry if his breathing was any indication. I couldn't spare the brainpower to find out what was going on in his head, but his face was showing nothing but the same kind of calm mask that Batanya wore. Todd Donati, the security guy, was right on Quinn's heels. They stopped dead about four feet away from me.

"The bomb squad is coming," Donati said, leading off with the good news.

"Put it down where it was, babe," Quinn said.

"Oh, yeah, I *want* to put it back where it was," I said. "I'm just scared to." I hadn't moved a muscle in what felt like a million years, and I was becoming tired already. But still I stood looking down at the can I was holding in both hands. I promised myself I would never drink another Dr Pepper as long as I lived, and I'd been real fond of them before tonight.

"Okay," Quinn said, holding out his hand. "Give it to me."

I'd never wanted to do anything more in my life.

"Not till we know what it is," I said. "Maybe it's a camera. Maybe some tabloid is trying to get insider shots of the big vampire summit." I tried to smile. "Maybe it's a little computer, counting vampires and humans as they go by. Maybe it's a bomb Jennifer Cater planted before she got offed. Maybe she wanted to blow up the queen." I'd had a couple of minutes to think about this.

"And maybe it'll take your hand off," he said. "Let me take it, babe."

"You sure you want to do that, after tonight?" I asked dismally.

"We can talk about that later. Don't worry about it. Just give me the damn can."

I noticed Todd Donati wasn't offering, and he already had a fatal disease. Didn't he want to go out as a hero? What was wrong with him? Then I was ashamed of myself for even thinking that. He had a family, and he'd want every minute with them.

Donati was sweating visibly, and he was white as a vampire. He was talking into the little headset he wore, relaying what he was seeing to . . . someone.

"No, Quinn. Someone with one of those special suits on needs to take it," I said. "I'm not moving. The can's not moving. We're okay. Till one of those special guys gets here. Or special gal," I added in the interest of fairness. I was feeling a little light-headed. The multiple shocks of the night were taking their toll on me, and I was beginning to tremble. Plus, I thought I was nuts for doing this; and yet here I was, doing it. "Anyone got X-ray vision?" I asked, trying to smile. "Where's Superman when you need him?"

"Are you trying to be a martyr for these damn things?" Quinn asked, and I figured the "damn things" were the vampires.

"Ha," I said. "Oh, ha-ha. Yeah, 'cause they *love* me. You see how many vampires are up here? Zero, right?"

"One," said Eric, stepping out of the stairwell. "We're bound a bit too tightly to suit me, Sookie." He was visibly tense; I couldn't remember ever seeing Eric so notably anxious. "I'm here to die right along with you, it seems."

"Good. To make my day absolutely effing complete, here's Eric again," I said, and if I sounded a little sarcastic, well, I was due. "Are you all completely nuts? Get the hell out of here!"

In a brisk voice, Todd Donati said, "Well, *I* will. You won't let anyone take the can, you won't put it down, and you haven't blown up yet. So I think I'll go downstairs to wait for the bomb squad."

I couldn't fault his logic. "Thanks for calling in the troops," I said, and Donati took the stairs, because the elevator was too close to me. I could read his head easily, and he felt deep shame that he hadn't actually offered to help me in any more concrete way. He planned to go down a floor to where no one could see him and then take the elevator to save his strength. The stairwell door shut behind him, and then we three stood by ourselves in a triangular tableau: Quinn, Eric, and me. Was this symbolic, or what?

My head was feeling light.

Eric began to move very slowly and carefully—I think so I wouldn't be startled. In a moment, he was at my elbow. Quinn's brain was throbbing and pulsating like a disco ball farther to my right. He didn't know how to help me, and of course, he was a bit afraid of what might happen.

Who knew, with Eric? Aside from being able to locate him and determine how he was oriented to me, I couldn't see more.

"You'll give it to me and leave," Eric said. He was pushing his vampire influence at my head with all his might.

"Won't work, never did," I muttered.

"You are a stubborn woman," he said.

"I'm *not*," I said, on the verge of tears at being first accused of nobility, then stubbornness. "I just don't want to move it! That's safest!"

"Some might think you suicidal."

"Well, 'some' can stick it up their ass."

"Babe, put it down on the urn. Just lay it down re-a-a-llll

easy," Quinn said, his voice very gentle. "Then I'll get you a big drink with lots of alcohol. You're a real strong gal, you know that? I'm proud of you, Sookie. But if you don't put that down now and get out of here, I'm gonna be real mad, hear me? I don't want anything to happen to you. That would be nuts, right?"

I was saved from further debate by the arrival of another entity on the scene. The police sent up a robot in the elevator.

When the door swooshed open we all jumped, because we'd been too wrapped up in the drama to notice the noise of the elevator. I actually giggled when the stubby robot rolled off the elevator. I started to hold the bomb out to it, but I figured the robot wasn't supposed to take it. It seemed to be operating on remote control, and it turned slightly right to face me. It remained motionless for a couple of minutes to have a good look at me and what was in my hand. After a minute or two of examination, the robot retreated onto the elevator, and its arm jerkily reached up to punch the correct button. The doors swished shut, and it left.

"I hate modern technology," Eric said quietly.

"Not true," I said. "You love what computers can do for you. I know that for a fact. Remember how happy you got when you saw the Fangtasia employee roster, with all the work hours filled in?"

"I don't like the impersonality of it. I like the knowledge it can hold."

This was just too weird a conversation for me to continue under the circumstances.

"Someone's coming up the stairs," Quinn said, and opened the stair door.

Into our little group strode the bomb disposal guy. The homicide squad might not have boasted any vampire cops, but the bomb squad did. The vampire wore one of those space suit–looking outfits. (Even if you can survive it, I guess getting blown up is not a good experience.) Someone had written "BOOM" on his chest where a name tag would normally be. Oh, that was *so funny*.

"You two civilians need to leave the floor to the lady and me," Boom said, moving slowly across the floor to me. "Take a hike, guys," he said when neither man moved.

"No," said Eric.

"Hell, no," said Quinn.

It isn't easy to shrug in one of those suits, but Boom managed. He was holding a square container. Frankly, I was in no mood to have a look at it, and all I cared about was that he opened the lid and held it out, carefully placing it under my hands.

Very, very carefully I lowered the can into the padded interior of the container. I let it go and brought my hands out of the container with a relief that I can't even describe, and Boom closed the container, still grinning merrily through his clear face guard. I shuddered all over, my hands trembling violently from the release of the position.

Boom turned, slowed by the suit, and gestured to Quinn to open the stairwell door again. Quinn did, and down the stairs the vampire went: slowly, carefully, evenly. Maybe he smiled all the way. But he didn't blow up, because I didn't hear a noise, and I've got to say we all stood frozen in our places for a good long while.

"Oh," I said, "Oh." This was not brilliant, but I was in about a thousand emotional pieces. My knees gave way.

Quinn pounced on me and wrapped his arms around me. "You idiot," he said. "You idiot." It was like he was saying, "Thank you, God." I was smothered in weretiger, and I rubbed my face against his E(E)E shirt to wipe up the tears that had leaked from my eyes.

When I peered under his arm, there was no one else in the area. Eric had vanished. So I had a moment to enjoy being held, to know that Quinn still liked me, that the thing with Andre and Eric hadn't killed all feeling he had begun to have for me. I had a moment to feel the absolute relief of escaping death.

Then the elevator and the stair door opened simultaneously, and all manner of people wanted to talk to me.

13

"It was a bomb," Todd Donati said. "A quick, crude bomb. The police will be telling me more, I hope, after they've finished their examination." The security chief was sitting in the queen's suite. I had finally gotten to stow the blue suitcase by one of her couches, and, boy, was I glad to be rid of it. Sophie-Anne hadn't bothered to thank me for its return, but I hadn't really expected her to, I guess. When you had underlings, you sent them on errands and you didn't have to thank them. That's why they were underlings. For that matter, I wasn't sure the stupid thing was even hers.

"I expect I'll get fired over it, especially after the murders," the security chief said. His voice was calm, but his thoughts were bitter. He needed the health insurance.

Andre gave the security chief one of his long, blue gazes. "And how did the can come to be on the queen's floor, in that area?" Andre couldn't have cared less about Todd Donati's job situation. Donati glared back, but it was a weary kind of glare.

"Why on earth would you be fired, just because someone was able to bring a bomb in and plant it? Maybe because you are in charge of the safety of everyone in the hotel?" Gervaise asked, definitely on the cruel side. I didn't know Gervaise very well, and I was beginning to feel that was just fine with me. Cleo slapped him on the arm hard enough to make Gervaise wince.

Donati said, "That's it in a nutshell. Obviously someone brought that bomb up and put it on the potted plant by the elevator door. It might have been meant for the queen, since it was closest to her door. Almost equally, it might have been meant for anyone else on the floor, or it might have been planted at random. So I think the bomb and the murder of the Arkansas vampires are two different cases. In our questioning, we're finding Jennifer Cater didn't have a lot of friends. Your queen isn't the only one with a grudge against her, though your queen's is the most serious. Possibly Jennifer planted the bomb, or arranged to have someone else do it, before she was murdered." I saw Henrik Feith sitting in a corner of the suite, his beard quivering with the shaking of his head. I tried to picture the one remaining member of the Arkansas contingent creeping around with a bomb, and I just couldn't feature it. The small vampire seemed convinced that he was in a nest of vipers. I was sure he was regretting his acceptance of the queen's protection, because right now that was looking like it wasn't a very reliable prospect.

"There is much to do here and now," Andre said. He sounded just a shade concerned, and he was riding his own conversational train. "It was rash of Christian Baruch to threaten to fire you now, when he needs your loyalty the most."

"The guy's got a temper on him," Todd Donati said, and I knew without a doubt that he wasn't a native of Rhodes. The more stressed he got, the more he sounded like home; not Louisiana, maybe, but northern Tennessee. "The ax hasn't fallen yet. And if we can get to the bottom of what's happening, maybe I'll get reinstated. Not too many people would cotton to this job. Lots of security people don't like—"

Working with the damn vampires, Donati completed his sentence silently to everyone but me and him. He reminded himself harshly to stick to the immediate present. "Don't like the hours it takes to run security in a big place like this," he finished out loud, for the vampires' benefit. "But I enjoy the work." *My kids will need the benefits when I die. Just two more months and coverage will stay with them after I pass.*

He'd come to the queen's suite to talk to me about the Dr Pepper incident (as had the police, and the ever-present Christian Baruch), but he was staying to chat. Though the vampires didn't seem to notice, Donati was so chatty because he had taken some heavy pain medication. I felt sorry for him, and at the same time I realized that someone with so many distractions wasn't likely to be doing a good job. What had gotten by Donati in the past couple of months, since his illness had begun affecting his daily life?

Maybe he'd hired the wrong people. Maybe he'd omitted some vital step in protecting the guests of the hotel. Maybe— I was distracted by a wave of warmth.

Eric was coming.

I'd never had such a clear sense of his presence, and my heart sank as I knew the blood exchange had been an important one. If my memory was clear, it was the third time I'd taken Eric's blood, and three is always a significant number. I felt a constant awareness of his presence when he was anywhere near me, and I had to believe it was the same for him. There might be even more to the tie now, more that I just hadn't experienced yet. I closed my eyes and leaned over to rest my forehead on my knees.

There was a knock at the door, and Sigebert answered it after a careful look through the peephole. He admitted Eric. I could scarcely bring myself to look at him or to give him a casual greeting. I should be grateful to Eric, and I knew it; and on one level I was. Sucking blood from Andre would have been intolerable. Scratch that: I would've had to tolerate it. It would have been disgusting. But exchanging blood at all had not been a choice I got to make, and I wasn't going to forget it.

Eric sat on the couch beside me. I jumped up as if I'd been poked by a cattle prod and went across the room to the bar to pour myself a glass of water. No matter where I went, I could feel Eric's presence; to make that even more unsettling, I found his nearness was somehow comforting, as if it made me more secure.

Oh, just *great.*

There wasn't anywhere else for me to sit. I settled miserably by the Viking, who now owned a piece of me. Before this night, when I'd seen Eric, I'd felt simply a casual pleasure—though I had thought of him perhaps more often than a woman ought to think about a man who would outlive her for centuries.

I reminded myself that this was not Eric's fault. Eric might be political, and he might be focused on looking out for number one (which was spelled E-R-I-C), but I didn't see how he could have surmised Andre's purpose and caught up with us to reason with Andre, with any degree of premeditation. So I owed Eric a big thank-you, no matter how you looked at it, but that wasn't going to be a conversation we had anywhere in the vicinity of the queen and the aforesaid Andre.

"Bill is still selling his little computer disk downstairs," Eric remarked to me.

"So?"

"I thought perhaps you were wondering why I showed up when you were in dire straits, and he didn't."

"It never crossed my mind," I said, wondering why Eric was bringing this up.

"I made him stay downstairs," Eric said. "After all, I'm his area sheriff."

I shrugged.

"He wanted to hit me," Eric said with only the hint of a smile on his lips. "He wanted to take the bomb from you and be your hero. Quinn would have done that, too."

"I remember that Quinn offered," I said.

"I did, too," Eric said. He seemed a bit shocked at the fact.

"I don't want to talk about it," I said, and I hoped my tone made it clear I was serious. It was getting close to dawn, and I'd had a stressful night (which was the mildest way I could put it). I managed to catch Andre's eye and give him the tiny nod toward Todd Donati. I was trying to clue him in that Donati was not entirely okay. In fact, he was as gray as a snow sky.

"If you'll excuse us, Mr. Donati. . . . We've enjoyed your company, but we have much to discuss about our plans for tomorrow night," Andre said smoothly, and Donati tensed, since he knew quite well he'd been dismissed.

"Of course, Mr. Andre," the security chief said. "I hope all of you sleep well this day, and I'll see you tomorrow night." He rose to his feet with a lot more effort than it should have taken, and he suppressed a flinch at the pain. "Miss Stackhouse, I hope you get over your bad experience real soon."

"Thank you," I said, and Sigebert opened the door for Donati to leave.

"If you'll excuse me," I said the minute he was gone, "I'll just go to my room now."

The queen gave me a sharp look. "Are you unhappy about something, Sookie?" she said, though she sounded like she didn't really want to hear my answer.

"Oh, why would I be unhappy? I *love* having things done to me without my will," I said. The pressure had built up and up, and the words came out like lava erupting from a volcano, even though my more intelligent self kept telling me to put a plug in it. "And then," I said very loudly, not listening to myself one little bit, "I like hanging around the ones responsible. That's *even better*!" I was losing coherence and gaining momentum.

There was no telling what I would have said next if Sophie-Anne hadn't held up one little white hand. She seemed a weensy bit perturbed, as my grandmother would have put it.

"You are assuming I know what you are talking about, and that I want to hear a human yelling at me," Sophie-Anne said.

Eric's eyes were glowing as if a candle burned behind them, and he was so lovely I could have drowned in him. God help me. I made myself look at Andre, who was examining me as if he was deciding where the best cut of meat was. Gervaise and Cleo just looked interested.

"Excuse me," I said, returning to the world of reality with a thud. It was so late, and I was so tired, and the night had been filled with so many incidents that I thought for a split second that I might actually faint. But the Stackhouses don't produce fainters, and neither do the fairies, I guess. It was time I gave a nod to that little percentage of my heritage. "I'm very tired." I had no fight left in me all of a sudden. I really wanted to go to bed. Not a word was spoken as I trudged to the door, which was almost a miracle. Though, as I closed it behind me, I heard the queen say, "Explain, Andre."

Quinn was waiting by the door to my room. I didn't know if I even had the energy to be glad or sad to see him. I got out the plastic rectangle and opened the door, and after I'd scanned the interior and seen that my roommate was gone (though I wondered where, since Gervaise had been by himself), I jerked my head to tell Quinn he could come in.

"I have an idea," he said quietly.

I raised my eyebrows, too exhausted to speak.

"Let's just climb in the bed and sleep."

I finally managed to smile at him. "That's the best offer I've had all day," I said. At that second, I saw how I could come to love Quinn. While he visited the bathroom, I pulled off my clothes, folded them, and slipped into my pajamas, short and pink and silky to the touch.

Quinn came out of the bathroom in his briefs, but I was just too worn out to appreciate the view. He got into the bed while I brushed my teeth and washed my face. I slid in beside him. He turned on his side and his arms opened, and I just kept on sliding right into them. We hadn't showered, but he smelled good to me: he smelled alive and vital.

"Good ceremony tonight," I remembered to say after I'd switched off the bedside lamp.

"Thanks."

"Got any more coming up?"

"Yeah, if your queen goes on trial. Now that Cater was killed, who knows if that's still on. And tomorrow night is the ball, after the trial."

"Oh, I get to wear my pretty dress." A little pleasure stirred in me at the prospect. "You got to work?"

"No, the ball's being run by the hotel," he said. "You gonna dance with me or the blond vampire?"

"Oh, hell," I said, wishing Quinn hadn't reminded me.

And right on cue, he said, "Forget it now, babe. We're here, now, in bed together like we ought to be."

Like we ought to be. That sounded good.

"You heard about me tonight, right?" he asked.

The night had contained so many incidents it took me a moment to remember that I'd learned about the things he'd had to do to survive.

And that he had a half sister. A troublesome, nutty, dependent half sister who hated me on sight.

He was a little tense, waiting for my reaction. I could feel it in his head, in his body. I tried to think of a sweet, wonderful way to put how I felt. I was too tired.

"Quinn, I've got no problem with you," I said. I kissed his cheek, kissed his mouth. "No problem at all. And I'll try to like Frannie."

"Oh," he said, sounding simply relieved. "Well, then." He kissed my forehead, and we fell asleep.

I slept like a vampire. I didn't wake to make a trip to the bathroom, even, or to turn over. I swam almost up to consciousness once to hear Quinn was snoring, just a faint ruffle of sound, and I snuggled closer to him. He stopped, murmured, and fell silent.

I looked at the bedside clock when I finally, really, woke up. It was four in the afternoon; I'd slept for twelve hours. Quinn was gone, but he'd drawn a big pair of lips (with my lipstick) on a piece of hotel stationery and laid it on his pillow. I smiled. My roommate hadn't come in. Maybe she was spending the day in Gervaise's coffin. I shuddered. "He leaves *me* cold," I said out loud, wishing Amelia was there to respond. Speaking of Amelia . . . I fished my cell phone out of my purse and called her.

"Hey," she said. "What's up?"

"What are you doing?" I asked, trying not to feel homesick.

"Brushing Bob," she said. "He had a hair ball."

"Aside from that?"

"Oh, I worked at the bar a little," Amelia said, trying to sound casual.

I was dumbfounded. "Doing what?"

"Well, serving drinks. What else is there to do?"

"How come Sam needed you?"

"The Fellowship is having a big rally in Dallas, and Arlene wanted time off to go with that asshole she's dating. Then Danielle's kid got pneumonia. So Sam was really worried, and since I happened to be in the bar, he asked me if I knew how to do the job. I said, 'Hey, how hard could it be?' "

"Thanks, Amelia."

"Oh, okay, I guess that sounded pretty disrespectful." Amelia laughed. "So, it is a little tricky. Everyone wants to talk to you, but you have to hurry, and you can't spill their drinks on 'em, and you have to remember what everyone was drinking, and who's paying for the round, and who's on a tab. And you have to stand up for hours and hours."

"Welcome to my world."

"So, how's Mr. Stripes?"

I realized she was talking about Quinn. "We're okay," I said, pretty sure that was true. "He did one big ceremony last night; it was so cool. A vampire wedding. You would've loved it."

"What's on for tonight?"

"Well, maybe a trial." I didn't feel like explaining, especially over a cell phone. "And a ball."

"Wow, like Cinderella."

"Remains to be seen."

"How's the business part of it going?"

"I'll have to tell you about that when I get back," I said, suddenly not so cheerful. "I'm glad you're busy and I'm glad everything's going okay."

"Oh, Terry Bellefleur called to ask if you wanted a puppy. You remember when Annie got out?"

Annie was Terry's very expensive and much-loved Catahoula. He'd come out to my place looking for Annie when she'd roamed away, and by the time he'd found her, she had had some close encounters.

"What do the puppies look like?"

"He said you had to see them to believe them. I told him you'd come by next week, maybe. I didn't commit you to anything."

"Okay, good."

We chatted a minute more but since I'd been gone from Bon Temps less than forty-eight hours, there really wasn't that much to say.

"So," she said in closing, "I miss you, Stackhouse."

"Yeah? I miss you, too, Broadway."

"Bye. Don't get any strange fangs on you."

Too late for that. "Bye. Don't spill any beer on the sheriff."

"If I do, it'll be on purpose."

I laughed, because I'd felt like dousing Bud Dearborn, too. I hung up feeling pretty good. I ordered room service, very tentatively. That was not something I got to do every day; even every year. Or ever. I was a little nervous about letting the waiter into my room, but Carla wandered in at just the same moment. She was decorated with hickeys and wearing last night's dress.

"That smells good," she said, and I handed her a croissant. She drank my orange juice while I had the coffee. It worked out okay. Carla did the talking for both of us, telling me all about the things I'd experienced. She didn't seem to realize I'd been with the queen when the slaughter of Jennifer Cater's group was discovered, and though she'd heard I'd found the Dr Pepper bomb, she told me all about it anyway, as though I hadn't been there. Maybe Gervaise made her keep silent, and the words just built up.

"What are you wearing to the ball tonight?" I asked, feeling impossibly hokey to even be asking such a question. She showed me her dress, which was black, spangled, and almost nonexistent above the waist, like all her other evening wear. Carla definitely believed in emphasizing her assets.

She asked to see my dress, and we both made insincere noises about what good taste the other had.

We had to take turns in the bathroom, of course, which I wasn't used to doing. I was pretty exasperated by the time Carla emerged. I hoped the entire city hadn't run out of hot water. Of course, there was plenty left, and despite the scattering of her cosmetics on the bathroom counter, I managed to get clean and get made-up on time. In honor of my beautiful dress, I tried to put my hair up, but I'm no good with anything more complex than a ponytail. The hair would be down. I went a little heavier on the makeup than I do in the daytime, and I had some big earrings that Tara had told me were just right. I turned my head experimentally and watched them swing and glitter. They were silvery and white, just like the beading on the bodice of my evening dress. *Which it is now time to put on,* I told myself with a little jolt of anticipation.

Oh, boy. My dress was ice blue, and had silver and white beads, and was cut just the right depth in the front and back. It had a built-in bra so I didn't have to wear one, and I pulled on some blue panties that would never leave a line on me. Then thigh-high hose. Then my shoes, which were high heeled and silvery.

I'd done my nails while Water Woman was in the shower, and I put on my lipstick and had a final look in the mirror.

Carla said, "You look real pretty, Sookie."

"Thanks." I knew I was smiling a big smile. There's nothing like dressing up once in a while. I felt like my prom date was picking me up with a corsage to pin to my dress. JB had taken me to my senior prom, though other girls had asked him because he would look so good in the photographs. My aunt Linda had made my dress.

No more homemade dresses for me.

A knock at the door had me looking anxiously in the mirror. But it was Gervaise, checking to see if Carla was ready. She smiled and turned around to garner the admiration due her, and Gervaise gave her a kiss on the cheek. I wasn't too impressed with Gervaise's character, and he wasn't my cup of tea physically, either, with his broad, bland face and his light mustache, but I had to hand it to him for generosity: he fastened a diamond tennis bracelet around Carla's wrist then and there, with no further ado than if he were giving her a bauble. Carla tried to restrain her excitement, but then she cast that to the winds and threw her arms around Gervaise's neck. I was embarrassed to be in the room, because some of the pet names she used while thanking him were sort of anatomically correct.

After they left, well pleased with each other, I stood in the middle of the bedroom. I didn't want to sit down in my dress until I had to, because I knew it would wrinkle and lose that perfect feeling. That left me with very little to do, other than trying not to get miffed about the chaos Carla had left on her side and feeling a bit at a loss. Surely Quinn had said he'd come by the room to get me? We hadn't been supposed to meet downstairs, right?

My purse made a noise, and I realized I'd stuck the queen's pager in there. Oh, surely not!

"Get down here," read the message. "Trial is now."

At the same moment, the room phone rang. I picked it up, trying to catch my breath.

"Babe," said Quinn. "I'm sorry. In case you hadn't heard, the council has decided that the queen will have to go on trial, right now, and you gotta hustle down here. I'm sorry," he said again, "I'm in charge of setting up. I gotta work. Maybe this won't take long."

"Okay," I said weakly, and he hung up.

So much for my glamorous evening with my new guy.

But, dammit, I wasn't going to change into anything less festive. Everyone else would have party clothes on, and even if my role in the evening had altered, I deserved to look pretty, too. I rode down on the elevator with one of the hotel employees, who couldn't tell if I was a vampire or not. I made him very nervous. It always tickles me when people can't tell. To me, vampires sort of glow, just a bit.

Andre was waiting for me when I got off the elevator. He was as flustered as I'd ever seen him; I could tell because his fingers were clenching and unclenching, and his lip was bloody where he'd bitten it, though it healed as I watched. Before last night, Andre had just made me nervous. Now I loathed him. But it was evident I had to put personal issues aside until another time.

"How could this happen?" he asked. "Sookie, you need to learn everything you can about this. We have more enemies than we knew."

"I thought there wouldn't be a trial after Jennifer got killed. Since she was the queen's chief accuser—"

"That's what we all thought. Or, if there was a trial, it would be an empty form, staged simply so the charges could be dismissed. But we got down here tonight and they were waiting for us. They've put off the start of the ball to do this. Take my arm," he said, and I was so taken by surprise that I slid my arm through his.

"Smile," he said. "Look confident."

And we walked into the convention hall with bold faces—me and my good buddy Andre.

It was lucky I'd had plenty of practice in insincere smiling, because this was like the marathon of Saving Face. All the vampires and their human entourages parted way for us. Some of them were smiling, too, though not pleasantly, and some looked concerned, and some just looked mildly anticipatory, as if they were about to watch a movie that had gotten good buzz.

And the rush of thoughts engulfed me. I smiled and walked on automatic while I listened in. *Pretty . . . Sophie-Anne'll get what's coming to her . . . maybe I can call her lawyer, see if she's open to an approach from our king . . . nice boobs . . . my man needs a telepath . . . hear she's fucking Quinn . . . hear she's fucking the queen and Baby Boy Andre . . . found her at a bar . . . Sophie-Anne's washed up, serves her right . . . hear she's fucking Cataliades . . . stupid trial, where's the band? . . . hope they have some food at the dance, people food . . .*

And on and on. Some of it pertaining to me, the queen, and/or Andre, some of it the simple thoughts of people who are tired of waiting and want to get the party started.

We strolled the gauntlet until it terminated in the room where the wedding had been held. The crowd in this room was almost 100 percent vampire. A notable absence: human servers, and any other human hotel staff. The only ones circulating with drinks trays were vampires. Things were going to happen in this room that weren't for human consumption. If it was possible for me to feel more anxious, I did.

I could see Quinn had been busy. The low platform had been rearranged. The giant ankh had been put away, and two lecterns had been added. On the spot where Mississippi and his loved one had taken their vows, about midway between the two lecterns, there sat a thronelike chair. In it was an ancient woman with wild white hair. I had never seen a vampire who had been turned when she was so old, and though I'd sworn I wasn't going to speak to him, I said as much to Andre.

"That is the Ancient Pythoness," he said absently. He was scanning the crowd, trying to find Sophie-Anne, I supposed. I spotted Johan Glassport, who was going to get his moment in the limelight after all, and the rest of the Louisiana contingent was with the murderous lawyer—all except the queen and Eric and Pam, whom I'd glimpsed standing near the stage.

Andre and I took our seats at the right front. On the left front was a clump of vampires who were no fans of ours. Chief among them was Henrik Feith. Henrik had transformed himself from a panicky scaredy-cat to a ball of wrath. He glowered at us. He did everything but throw spitballs.

"What crawled up his ass and died?" muttered Cleo Babbitt, dropping into the seat to my right. "The queen offers to take him under her wing when he's alone and defenseless, and this is the thanks she gets?" Cleo was wearing a traditional tuxedo, and she looked pretty darn good in it. The severity of it suited her. Her boy toy looked much more feminine than she did. I wondered at his inclusion in the crowd, which was all supe and overwhelmingly vampire. Diantha leaned forward from the row behind us to tap me on the shoulder. She was wearing a red bustier with black ruffles and a black taffeta skirt, also ruffled. Her bustier didn't have much bust to fill it. She was clutching a handheld computer game. "Goodtoseeya," she said, and I made the effort of smiling at her. She returned her attention to the computer game.

"What will happen to us if Sophie-Anne is found guilty?" Cleo asked, and we all fell silent.

What *would* happen to us if Sophie-Anne were convicted? With Louisiana in a weakened position, with the scandal surrounding Peter's death, we were all at risk.

I don't know why I hadn't thought this through, but I hadn't.

In a moment, I understood that I hadn't even thought about worrying because I'd grown up a free United States human citizen; I wasn't used to worrying about my fate being in question. Bill had joined the little group surrounding the queen, and as I peered across the room at them, he knelt, along with Eric and Pam. Andre leaped up from his seat to my left, and in one of his lightning moves he crossed the room to kneel with them. The queen stood before them like a Roman goddess accepting tribute. Cleo followed my gaze, and her shoulder twitched. Cleo wasn't going to go do any kneeling.

"Who's on the council?" I asked the dark-haired vamp, and she nodded to the group of five vampires seated right before the low stage, facing the Ancient Pythoness.

"The King of Kentucky, the Queen of Iowa, the King of Wisconsin, the King of Missouri, the Queen of Alabama," she said, pointing to them in order. The only one I'd met was Kentucky, though I recognized the sultry Alabama from her conversation with Sophie-Anne.

The lawyer for the other side joined Johan Glassport on the stage. Something about the Arkansans' lawyer reminded me of Mr. Cataliades, and when he nodded in our direction, I saw Mr. Cataliades nod back.

"They related?" I asked Cleo.

"Brothers-in-law," Cleo said, leaving me to imagine what a female demon would look like. Surely they didn't all look like Diantha.

Quinn leaped up on the stage. He was wearing a gray

suit, white shirt, and tie, and he carried a long staff covered with carvings. He beckoned to Isaiah, King of Kentucky, who floated onto the stage. With a flourish, Quinn handed the staff to Kentucky, who was dressed much more stylishly than he had been earlier. The vampire thudded the staff against the floor, and all conversation ceased. Quinn retreated to the back of the stage.

"I am the elected master-at-arms of this judicial session," Kentucky announced in a voice that carried easily to the corners of the room. He held the staff up so it could not be ignored. "Following the traditions of the vampire race, I call you all to witness the trial of Sophie-Anne Leclerq, Queen of Louisiana, on the charge that she murdered her signed and sealed spouse, Peter Threadgill, King of Arkansas."

It sounded very solemn, in Kentucky's deep, drawling voice.

"I call the lawyers for the two parties to be ready to present their cases."

"I am ready," said the part-demon lawyer. "I am Simon Maimonides, and I represent the bereaved state of Arkansas."

"I am ready," said our murderous lawyer, reading from a pamphlet. "I am Johan Glassport, and I represent the bereaved widow, Sophie-Anne Leclerq, *falsely* charged with the murder of her signed and sealed spouse."

"Ancient Pythoness, are you ready to hear the case?" Kentucky asked, and the crone turned her head toward him.

"Is she blind?" I whispered.

Cleo nodded. "From birth," she said.

"How come she's the judge?" I asked. But the glares of the vampires around us reminded me that their hearing hardly made whispering worthwhile, and it was only polite to shut up.

"Yes," said the Ancient Pythoness. "I am ready to hear the case." She had a very heavy accent that I couldn't begin to identify. There was a stirring of anticipation in the crowd.

Okay. Let the games begin.

Bill, Eric, and Pam went to stand against the wall, while Andre sat by me.

King Isaiah did a little staff-pounding again. "Let the accused be brought forth," he said with no small amount of drama.

Sophie-Anne, looking very delicate, walked up to the stage, escorted by two guards. Like the rest of us, she'd gotten ready for the ball, and she was wearing purple. I wondered if the royal color had been a coincidence. Probably not. I had a feeling Sophie-Anne arranged her own coincidences.

The dress was high-collared and long-sleeved, and it actually had a train.

"She is beautiful," said Andre, his voice full of reverence.

Yeah, yeah, yeah. I had more on my mind than admiring the queen. The guards were the two Britlingens, probably pressed into service by Isaiah, and they had packed some dress armor in their interdimensional trunks. It was black, too, but it gleamed dully, like slowly moving dark water. It was just as figure-hugging as the first set of armor. Clovache and Batanya lifted Sophie-Anne onto the low platform and then retreated a bit. This way, they were close to both the prisoner and their employer, so it worked out great, I suppose, from their point of view.

"Henrik Feith, state your case," Isaiah said with no further ado.

Henrik's case was long and ardent and full of accusations. Boiled down, he testified that Sophie-Anne had married his king, signed all the usual contracts, and then immediately began maneuvering Peter into his fatal fight, despite the king's angelic temperament and his adoration of his new queen. It sounded like Henrik was talking about Kevin and Britney, rather than two ancient and crafty vampires.

Blah blah blah. Henrik's lawyer let him go on and on, and Johan did not object to any of Henrik's highly colored statements. Johan thought (I checked) that Henrik would lose sympathy by being so fervent and immoderate—and boring—and he was quite right, if the slight movements and shifts in body language in the crowd were anything to go by.

"And now," Henrik concluded, faint pink tears running down his face, "there are only a handful of us left in the whole state. She, who killed my king and his lieutenant Jennifer, she has offered me a place with her. And I was almost weak enough to accept, for fear of being rogue. But she is a liar and she will kill me, too."

"Someone told him that," I murmured.

"What?" Andre's mouth was right by my ear. Keeping a conversation private in a group of vampires is not an easy thing.

I held up a hand to request his silence. No, I wasn't listening to Henrik's brain but to Henrik's lawyer's, who didn't have as much demon blood as Cataliades. Without realizing I was doing it, I was leaning forward in my seat and craning toward the stage to hear better. Hear with my head, that is.

Someone had told Henrik Feith that the queen planned to kill him. He had been willing to let the lawsuit slide, since Jennifer Cater's murder had taken out the chief complainant. He had never rated high enough in the ranks to take up the mantle of leadership; he didn't have the wit or the desire. He would rather go into the service of the queen.

But if she really meant to kill him . . . he would try to kill her first by the only means he might survive, and that was through the law.

"She doesn't want to kill you," I called, hardly knowing what I was doing.

I wasn't even aware I'd gotten to my feet until I felt the eyes of everyone in the audience on me. Henrik Feith was staring at me, his face stunned, his mouth still open. "Tell us who told you that, and we'll know who killed Jennifer Cater, because—"

"Woman," said a stentorian voice, and I was drowned out and shut up very effectively. "Be silent. Who are you and what right do you have to intrude on these solemn proceedings?" The Pythoness was surprisingly forceful for someone as frail as she appeared. She was leaning forward on her throne, glaring in my direction with her blind eyes.

Okay, standing in a roomful of vampires and interrupting their ritual was a pretty good way to get bloodstains all over my beautiful new dress.

"I don't have any right in the world, Your Majesty," I said, and from a few yards to my left, I heard Pam snicker. "But I know the truth."

"Oh, then I have no role in these proceedings, do I?" croaked the Ancient Pythoness in her heavily accented English. "Why should I have come forth from my cave to give judgment?"

Why, indeed.

"I may hear the truth, but I don't have the juice to get justice done," I said honestly.

Pam snickered again. I just knew it was her.

Eric had been standing to the side of the room with Pam and Bill, but now he moved forward. I could feel his presence, cold and steady, very near to me. He gave me some courage. I don't know how. I felt it, though, felt a rising strength where there had been only my shaking knees. A shocking suspicion hit me with the force of a Mack truck. Eric had given me enough blood now that I qualified, hemoglobin-wise, as being close to a vampire; and my strange gift had slopped over into fatal territory. I wasn't reading Henrik's lawyer's mind. I was reading *Henrik's.*

"Then come tell me what I must do," said the Ancient Pythoness with a sarcasm so sharp it could have sliced a meat loaf.

I needed a week or two to get over the shock of my terrible suspicion, and I had a renewed conviction that I really ought to kill Andre, and maybe Eric, too, even if a corner of my heart would weep for the loss.

I had all of twenty seconds to process this.

Cleo gave me a sharp pinch. "Cow," she said furiously. "You will ruin everything." I edged left out of the row, stepping over Gervaise as I did so. I ignored his glare and Cleo's pinch. The two were fleas compared to the other powers that might want a piece of me first. And Eric stepped up behind me. My back was covered.

As I moved closer to the platform, it was hard to tell what Sophie-Anne was thinking of this new turn in her unexpected trial. I concentrated on Henrik and his lawyer.

"Henrik thinks that the queen decided to have him killed. He was told that, so he would testify against her in self-defense," I said.

Now I was behind the judges' chairs on the floor, with Eric by my side.

"The queen didn't decide to have me killed?" Henrik said, looking hopeful, confused, and betrayed all at the same time. That was a tall order for a vampire, since facial expressions are not their foremost means of communication.

"No, she didn't. She was sincere in offering you a place." I kept my eyes fixed on his, trying to drill my sincerity into his frightened brain. I'd moved almost squarely in front of him now.

"You're probably lying, too. You're in her pay, after all."

"Perhaps I might have a word?" the Ancient Pythoness said, with acid sarcasm.

Oops. There was a silence that was just chilling.

"Are you a seer?" she asked, speaking very slowly so that I could understand her.

"No, ma'am, I'm a telepath." This close, the Ancient Pythoness looked even older, which I wouldn't have thought possible.

"You can read minds? Vampire minds?"

"No, ma'am, those are the only ones I can't read," I said very firmly. "I pieced all this together from the lawyer's thoughts."

Mr. Maimonides was not happy about that.

"All this was known to you?" the Ancient P. asked the lawyer.

"Yes," he said. "I did know that Mr. Feith felt he was threatened with death."

"And you knew the queen had offered to accept him into her service?"

"Yes, he told me she said so." That was said in so doubtful a tone that you didn't have to be an A.P. to read between the lines.

"And you did not believe the word of a vampire queen?"

Okay, that was a stumper for Maimonides. "I felt it my duty to protect my client, Ancient Pythoness." He struck just the right note of humble dignity.

"Hmmm," said the A.P., sounding as skeptical as I felt. "Sophie-Anne Leclerq, it is your turn to present your side of the story. Will you proceed?"

Sophie-Anne said, "What Sookie has said is true. I offered

Henrik a place with me and protection. When we get to call witnesses, Ancient One, you will hear that Sookie is my witness and was there during the final fight between Peter's people and mine. Though I knew that Peter married me with a secret agenda, I didn't lift a hand against him until his people attacked on the night of our celebratory feast. Due to many circumstances, he didn't get to pick his best moment to go after me, and as a result, his people died and most of mine lived. He actually began the attack when there were others there not of our blood." Sophie-Anne managed to look shocked and saddened. "It has taken me all these months to be sure the accounts were hushed."

I thought I'd gotten most of the humans and Weres out before the slaughter started, but apparently there'd been some around.

Probably they weren't "around" anymore.

"In the time since that night, you have suffered many other losses," the Ancient Pythoness observed. This sounded quite sympathetic.

I began to sense that the deck had been stacked in Sophie-Anne's favor. Was it significant that Kentucky, who'd been courting Sophie-Anne, was the council member in charge of the proceedings?

"As you say, I've had many losses—both in terms of my people and in terms of my income," Sophie-Anne agreed. "This is why I need my inheritance from my husband, to which I'm entitled as part of our marriage covenant. He thought he would inherit the rich kingdom of Louisiana. Now I will be glad if I can get the poor one of Arkansas."

There was a long silence.

"Shall I call our witness?" Johan Glassport said. He sounded very hesitant and uncertain, for a lawyer. But in this courtroom, it wasn't hard to understand why. "She's already right here, and she was witness to Peter's death." He held out his hand to me, and I had to mount the platform. Sophie-Anne looked relaxed, but Henrik Feith, a few inches to my left, was gripping the arms of his chair.

Another silence. The wild white hair of the ancient vampire hung forward to hide her face as she stared at her own lap. Then she looked up, and her sightless eyes went unerringly to Sophie-Anne. "Arkansas is yours by law, and now yours by right. I declare you innocent of conspiring to murder your husband," the Ancient Pythoness said, almost casually.

Well . . . *yippee.* I was close enough to see that Sophie-Anne's eyes widened with relief and surprise, and Johan Glassport gave a private little grin to his lectern. Simon Maimonides looked down at the five judges to see how they'd take the A.P.'s pronouncement, and when none of them voiced a word of protest, the lawyer shrugged.

"Now, Henrik," croaked the Ancient Pythoness, "your safety is assured. Who has told you lies?"

Henrik hardly looked assured. He looked scared witless. He rose to his feet to stand by me.

Henrik was smarter than we were. There was a flash through the air.

The next time an expression crossed his face, it was utter horror. He looked down, and we all followed his eyes. There was a thin wooden shaft protruding from his chest, and as soon as his eyes identified it, Henrik's hand rose to touch it, and he swayed. A human crowd would have erupted in chaos, but the vampires threw themselves on the floor in near silence. The only person who shrieked was the blind Ancient Pythoness, who demanded to know what had happened and why everyone was so tense. The two Britlingens leaped across the stage to Kentucky and stood in front of him, their weapons in their hands and ready. Andre literally flew out of his seat in the audience to land in front of Sophie-Anne. And Quinn leaped across the stage to knock me down, and he took the second arrow, the insurance arrow, that was meant for Henrik. It was quite unnecessary. Henrik was dead when he hit the floor.

14 ~

Batanya killed the assassin with a throwing star. She was facing the crowd, so she saw the vampire left standing after all the others had prudently hit the floor. This vampire wasn't firing the arrows from a bow; he was *throwing* them, which was why he'd managed to remain inconspicuous. Even in that group, someone carrying in a bow would have attracted a certain amount of attention.

Only a vampire could throw an arrow and kill someone. Perhaps only a Britlingen could throw a razor-sharp star in such a way as to decapitate a vampire.

I've seen vampires decapitated before, and it's not as messy as you'd think; not like cutting off the head of a human. But it's not pleasant, either, and as I watched the head topple off the shoulders, I had a moment of knee-knocking nausea from my position on the floor. I scrambled to my knees to check on Quinn.

"I'm not bad," he said instantly. "Not bad. It's in my shoulder, not my heart." He rolled over to lie on his back. The Louisiana vamps had all leaped up to the platform to circle the queen, just a second behind Andre. Once they were sure the threat was over, they clustered around us.

Cleo threw off her tuxedo jacket and ripped off the pleated white shirt. She folded it into a pad in movements so fast I could hardly follow them. "Hold this," she said, pressing it into my hand and placing my hand close to the wound. "Prepare to press hard." She didn't wait for me to nod. "Hold on," she said to Quinn. And she put her strong hands on his shoulders to hold him still while Gervaise pulled the arrow out.

Quinn bellowed, not too surprisingly. The next few minutes were pretty bad. I pressed the pad against the wound, and while Cleo pulled on the tuxedo jacket over her black lace bra, she directed Herve, her human squeeze, to donate his shirt, too. I've got to say, he whipped it right off. There was something really shocking about seeing a bare hairy chest in the middle of all this evening finery. And it was beyond weird that I would note that, after I'd just seen a guy's head separated from his body.

I knew Eric was beside me before he spoke, because I felt less terrified. He knelt down to my level. Quinn was concentrating on not yelling, so his eyes were shut as though he was unconscious and there was still lots of action going on all around me. But Eric was next to me, and I felt . . . not exactly calm, but not as upset. Because he was there.

I just hated that.

"He's going to heal," Eric said. He didn't sound especially happy about it, but not sad, either.

"Yes," I said.

"I know. I didn't see it coming."

"Oh, would you have flung yourself in front of me?"

"No," Eric said simply. "Because it might have hit me in the heart, and I would die. But I would have dived in and tackled you to take you out of the arrow's path if there had been time."

I couldn't think of a thing to say.

"I know you may come to hate me because I spared you the bite of Andre," he said quietly. "But I really am the lesser of two evils."

I glanced sideways at him. "I know that," I said, Quinn's blood staining my hands as it soaked through the makeshift pad. "I wouldn't have rather died than get bit by Andre, but it was a close thing."

He laughed, and Quinn's eyes flickered. "The weretiger is regaining consciousness," Eric said. "Do you love him?"

"Don't know yet."

"Did you love me?"

A team of stretcher bearers came over. Of course, these weren't regular paramedics. Regular paramedics wouldn't have been welcome in the Pyramid of Gizeh. These were Weres and shifters who worked for the vamps, and their leader, a young woman who looked like a honey bear, said, "We'll make sure he gets healed in record time, lady."

"I'll check on him later."

"We'll take care of him," she said. "Among us, he'll do better. It's a privilege to take care of Quinn."

Quinn nodded. "I'm ready to be moved," he said, but he was clenching the words between his teeth.

"See you later," I said, taking his hand in mine. "You're the bravest of the brave, Quinn."

"Babe," he said, biting his lower lip from the pain. "Be careful."

"Don't you be worrying about her," said a black guy with a short, clipped Afro. "She's got guardians." He gave Eric a cool look. Eric held out his hand and I took it to stand up.

My knees were aching a little after their acquaintance with the hard floor.

As they got him onto the stretcher and lifted him, Quinn seemed to lose consciousness. I started forward, but the black guy held out his arm. It looked like carved ebony, the muscles were so defined. "Sister, you just stay here," he said. "We're on the job now."

I watched them carry him off. Once he was out of sight, I looked down at my dress. Amazingly, it was all right. Not dirty, not bloody, and the wrinkles were at a minimum.

Eric waited.

"Did I love you?" I knew Eric wasn't going to give up, and I might as well figure out an answer. "Maybe. Sort of. But I knew all along that whoever was with me, it wasn't the real you. And I knew sooner or later you'd remember who you were and what you were."

"You don't seem to have yes or no answers about men," he said.

"You don't exactly seem to know how you feel about me, either," I said.

"You're a mystery," he said. "Who was your mother, and who was your father? Oh, I know, you'll say they raised you from a child and died when you were a little girl. I remember you telling me the story. But I don't know if it's exactly true. If it is, when did the fairy blood enter your family tree? Did it come in with one of your grandparents? That's what I'm supposing."

"And what business is it of yours?"

"You know it is my business. Now we are tied."

"Is this going to fade? It will, right? We won't always be like this?"

"I like being like this. You'll like it, too," he said, and he seemed mighty damn sure.

"Who was the vampire who tried to kill us?" I asked, to

change the subject. I was hoping he wasn't right, and anyway, we'd said everything there was to say on the subject, as far as I was concerned.

"Let's go find out," he said, and took my hand. I trailed along with him, simply because I wanted to know.

Batanya was standing by the vampire's body, which had begun the rapid disintegration of its kind. She'd retrieved her throwing star, and she was polishing it on her pants leg.

"Good throw," Eric said. "Who was he?"

She shrugged. "I dunno. The guy with the arrows, was all I know. All I care."

"He was the only one?"

"Yes."

"Can you tell me what he looked like?"

"I was sitting next to him," said a very small male vampire. He was perhaps five feet tall, and slim besides. His hair trailed down his back. If he went to jail, he'd have guys knocking on his cell door within thirty minutes. They'd be sorry, of course, but to the unobservant eye, he did look like the world's easiest target. "He was a rough one, and not dressed for the evening. Khakis and a striped dress shirt . . . well, you can see."

Though the body was blackening and flaking away as vamp corpses did, naturally the clothes were intact.

"Maybe he had a driver's license?" I suggested. That was almost a given with humans, but not with vampires. However, it was worth a shot.

Eric squatted and inserted his fingers into the man's front pocket. Nothing came out, or from the other front pocket, so without further ado Eric rolled him over. I took a couple of steps back to avoid the flurry of flakes of ash. There was something in the rear pocket: a regular wallet. And inside it, sure enough, was a driver's license.

It had been issued by Illinois. Under blood type was the

designation "NA." Yep, a vamp, for sure. Reading over Eric's shoulder, I could see that the vamp's name had been Kyle Perkins. Perkins had put "3V" as his age, so he had been a vamp for only three years.

"He must have been an archer before he died," I said. "Because that's not a skill you'd pick up right away, especially that young."

"I agree," Eric said. "And in the daytime, I want you to check all the local places you can practice archery. Throwing arrows is not a skill you can improvise. He trained. The arrow was specially made. We need to find out what happened to Kyle Perkins, and why this rogue accepted the job to attend this meeting and kill whomever necessary."

"So he was a . . . vampire hit man?"

"Yes, I think so," Eric said. "Someone is maneuvering us very carefully. Of course, this Perkins was simply backup in case the trial went wrong. And if it hadn't been for you, the trial might well have gone wrong. Someone went to a lot of trouble to play on Henrik Feith's fears, and stupid Henrik was about to give that someone up. This Kyle, he was planted to prevent just that."

Then the cleanup crew arrived: a group of vampires with a body bag and cleaning supplies. The human maids would not be asked to mop up Kyle. Luckily, they were all occupied in refreshing the vampire rooms, which were off-limits to them during the day.

In very short order, the residue of Kyle Perkins was bagged up and taken away, with one vampire remaining behind to wield a little handheld vacuum. Let Rhodes CSI try to get ahold of *that.*

I sensed a lot of movement and looked up to see that the service doors were open and staff was pouring into the large room to pack away the chairs. In less than fifteen minutes, Quinn's judicial paraphernalia was being stored away, his sister directing the work. Then a band set up on the platform, and the room was cleared for dancing. I'd never seen anything like it. First a trial, then a few murders, then dancing. Life goes on. Or, in this case, death continues.

Eric said, "You had better check in with the queen."

"Oh. Yeah, she might have a few words to say to me." I glanced around and spotted Sophie-Anne pretty quickly. She was surrounded by a crowd of people congratulating her on the favorable verdict. Of course, they would have been just as glad to see her executed, or whatever would have happened if the Ancient Pythoness had turned thumbs down. Speaking of the A.P. . . .

"Eric, where'd the old gal go?" I asked.

"The Ancient Pythoness is the original oracle that Alexander consulted," he said, his voice quite neutral. "She was considered so revered that even in her old age, she was converted by the very primitive vampires of her time. And now she has outlasted all of them."

I didn't want to think about how she'd fed before the advent of the synthetic blood that had changed the vampire world. How'd she hobble after her human prey? Maybe they'd brought people to her, like snake owners bring live mice to their pets?

"To answer your question, I would guess her handmaidens have removed her to her suite. She is brought out for special occasions."

"Like the good silver," I said seriously, and then burst into giggles. To my surprise, Eric smiled, too, that big smile that made multiple little arcs appear in the corners of his mouth.

We took our places behind the queen. I wasn't sure she'd even registered my presence, she was so busy being the belle of the ball. But in a momentary lull in the chitchat, she reached behind her and took my hand, squeezing it very lightly. "We'll talk later," she said, and then greeted a stout female vampire in a sequined pantsuit. "Maude," Sophie-Anne said, "how good to see you. And how are things going in Minnesota?"

Just then a tap on the music stand drew everyone's attention to the band. It was all vampire, I noticed with a start. The slick-haired guy at the podium said, "If all you hot vamps and vampesses are ready to rumble, we're ready to play! I'm Rick Clark, and this is . . . the Dead Man Dance Band!"

There was a polite smattering of applause.

"Here to open the evening are two of Rhodes's finest dancers, courtesy of Blue Moon Productions. Please welcome . . . Sean and Layla!"

The pair who stepped out into the middle of the dance floor were striking, whether you were human or vamp. They were both of the cold-blooded variety themselves, though he was very old and she was freshly turned, I thought. She was one of the most beautiful women I'd ever seen, and she was wearing a beige lace dress that drifted around her world-class legs like snow falling around trees. Her partner was maybe the only vampire I'd ever seen with freckles, and his dusty red hair was as long as hers.

They only had eyes for each other, and they danced together as if they were gliding through a dream.

I had never seen anything like it, and from the rapt attention of the audience, no one else had, either. As the music drew to a conclusion—and to this day, I can't remember what they danced to—Sean flung Layla back over his arm, bent over her, and bit. I was shocked, but the others seemed to expect it, and it turned them on no little amount. Sophie-Anne smoldered up at Andre (though she didn't have far to smolder, since he wasn't much taller than she), and Eric looked down at me with that hot light in his eyes that made me wary.

I turned my attention to the dance floor with determination and clapped like a maniac when the two took their bow and more couples began to join them as the music started up again. From habit I looked around for Bill, who was nowhere to be seen.

Then Eric said, "Let's dance," and I found I couldn't say no.

We took the floor along with the queen and her potential king, and I saw Russell Edgington and his husband, Bart, step out to dance, too. They looked almost as enthralled with each other as the two exhibition dancers.

I can't sing, but by golly, I can dance. And Eric had had a few ballroom lessons along the way, some century or other. My hand rested on his back, his on mine, our free hands clasped, and off we went. I wasn't sure exactly what the dance was, but he was a strong leader, so it was easy to follow along. More like the waltz than anything else, I decided.

"Pretty dress," said the dancer Layla as we swung by them.

"Thank you," I said, and beamed at her. From someone as lovely as she was, that was a great compliment. Then her partner leaned over to give her a kiss, and they swirled away into the crowd.

"That *is* a pretty dress," Eric said. "And you are a beautiful woman."

I was oddly embarrassed. I'd gotten compliments before—you can't be a barmaid and not get compliments—but most of them had consisted of (various degrees of drunk) guys telling me I was really cute—or, in one man's case, how impressive my "rack" was. (Somehow, JB du Rone and Hoyt Fortenberry had managed to stomp on that guy's toes and spill a drink all over him at the same time, just accidentally.)

"Eric," I said, but I couldn't finish the sentence because I couldn't think of what to say next. I had to concentrate on the speed with which my feet were moving. We were dancing so fast I felt like I was flying. Suddenly Eric dropped my hand to grip my waist, and as we turned, he swung me up, and then I was really flying, with a little help from a Viking. I laughed like a loon, my hair billowing out around my head, and then he let me go and caught me, just inches away from the floor, and then he did it again and again, until at last I was standing on the floor and the music was over.

"Thank you," I said, knowing I must look like I'd been standing in a high gale. "Excuse me while I go to the ladies' room."

I scooted off through the crowd, trying not to grin like an idiot. I should be with—oh, yeah—*my boyfriend.* Instead of dancing with another guy until I felt tingly with happiness. And it didn't do any good, excusing myself on account of our blood tie.

Sophie-Anne and Andre had stopped dancing, and they were standing with a group of other vampires. She couldn't need me, then, since there were no humans for me to "listen" to. I spotted Carla dancing with Gervaise, and they seemed happy enough. Carla was getting lots of admiring looks from other vampires, and that would make Gervaise swell with pride. Having his fellow vampires craving what he was already getting was sweet.

I knew how Gervaise felt.

I stopped in my tracks.

Had I . . . I wasn't really reading his mind, was I? No, I couldn't. The only times I'd caught a fragment of vampire thought prior to tonight, that fragment had felt cold and snaky.

But I knew how Gervaise felt, for sure, just as I'd read Henrik's thoughts. Was it just my knowledge of men and their reactions or my knowledge of vampires, or could I really follow vampire emotions better since I'd had Eric's blood for a third time? Or had my skill, or my talent, or my curse—whatever I called it—broadened to include vampires since I was closer to being one myself?

No. No, no, no. I felt like myself. I felt human. I felt warm. I was breathing. I had to use the bathroom. I was hungry, too. I thought about old Mrs. Bellefleur's famous chocolate cake. My mouth watered. Yep, human.

Okay, then, this new affinity for vamps would fade, like my extra strength would fade, in time. I'd had two drinks from Bill, I thought; maybe more. And three from Eric. And every time I'd had their blood, two or three months had seen the waning of the strength and acuity I'd gained from the intake. So that would happen this time, too, right? I shook myself briskly. Sure, it would.

Jake Purifoy was leaning against the wall, watching the couples dance. I'd glimpsed him earlier steering a young vampire woman around the floor, and she'd been laughing. So it wasn't all melancholy for Jake, and I was glad.

"Hey," I said.

"Sookie, that was quite some action at the trial."

"Yeah, it was scary."

"Where'd that guy come from?"

"Rogue, I guess. Eric's got me looking at archery ranges tomorrow to track him down, try to find out who hired him."

"Good. That was a close call for you. I'm sorry," he said awkwardly. "I know you must have been frightened."

I'd really been too worried about Quinn to think about the arrow being aimed at me. "I guess I was. You have a good time, now."

"Something's got to make up for not being able to change anymore," Jake said.

"I didn't know you'd tried." I couldn't think of anything else to say.

"Over and over," he said. We looked at each other for a long, long moment. "Well, I'm off to find another partner," he told me, and headed purposefully in the direction of a vampire who'd come with Stan Davis's group from Texas. She looked glad to see him coming.

By that time I was ducking into the ladies' room, which was small, of course; most of the females at the Pyramid of Gizeh wouldn't need to use such a facility, except to comb their hair. There was an attendant, a nicety I'd never seen before though I'd read about it in books. I was supposed to tip her. I still had my little evening purse with my room key in it, and I was relieved to recall I'd slipped a few dollars in there, along with some tissues and breath mints and a tiny brush. I nodded to the attendant, a squatty, dark-skinned woman with an unhappy face.

I took care of business in the nice clean stall and then emerged to wash my hands and to try to smooth out my hair. The attendant, wearing a name tag that read "Lena," turned on the water for me, which kind of weirded me out. I mean, I can turn a faucet. But I washed my hands and used the towel she extended to me, figuring this was the routine and I shouldn't act ignorant. I dropped two dollars in the tip bowl, and she tried to smile at me, but she looked too unhappy to manage it. She must be having a bad night.

"Thanks," I said, and turned to leave. I don't know why, but I glanced into the mirror on the inside of the door before I pulled on the handle. There Lena was, staring a hole into my back. She'd looked so unhappy because she'd been having to suppress how much she loathed me.

That's always a bad feeling, when you know someone hates you; especially when it's for no good reason. But her problems were not mine, and if she didn't want to turn on the faucet for women who dated vampires, she could find another job. I didn't want her damn faucet-turning-on, anyway, by God.

So I forged my way through the crowd, checking with the queen to see if she had any humans around who needed scanning (no), checking to see if I could find a Were or shifter to give me an update on Quinn (no).

By a stroke of luck, I did find the weather witch, the male witch I'd spotted earlier. I confess it made me a little proud to find my conjecture had actually been right. His being here tonight was his reward for good service, though I couldn't detect who his patron was. The weather witch had a drink in his hand and a middle-aged woman on his arm. Mrs. Witch, I discovered with another quick dip into his mental pool. He was hoping she hadn't observed that he was very interested in the beautiful vampire dancer and the pretty blond human coming toward him, the one who'd looked at him earlier like she knew him. Oh . . . that would be me.

I couldn't pick up his name, which would have greased the skids, and I didn't know what to say to him. But this was a person who should be brought to Sophie-Anne's attention. Someone had used him against her.

"Hello," I said, giving them my biggest smile. The wife smiled back, a little cautiously, because the sedate couple weren't normally approached by young single women (she'd glanced at my left hand) during glamorous parties. The weather witch's smile was more on the frightened side. "Are you all enjoying the party?" I asked.

"Yes, quite an evening," the wife said.

"My name is Sookie Stackhouse," I said, oozing charm.

"Olive Trout," she replied, and we shook hands. "This is my husband, Julian." She had no idea what her husband was.

"Are you all from around here?" I was scanning the crowd as unobtrusively as possible. I had no idea what to do with them now that I'd found them.

"You haven't watched our local stations," Olive said proudly. "Julian is the Channel 7 weatherman."

"How interesting," I said, with absolute sincerity. "If you two would just come with me, I know someone who'd just love to meet you." As I dragged the two through the crowd, I began to have second thoughts. What if Sophie-Anne intended retribution? But that wouldn't make sense. The important fact was not that there *was* a weather witch; the important fact was that someone had hired Julian Trout to predict the weather outlook for Louisiana and had somehow postponed the summit until Katrina had wreaked its havoc.

Julian was bright enough to figure out something was wrong with my enthusiasm, and I was afraid they'd both balk. I was mighty relieved to spot Gervaise's blond head. I called his name in a hearty voice as if I hadn't talked to him in a coon's age. By the time I reached him I was almost out of breath from herding the Trouts with such speed and anxiety.

"Gervaise, Carla," I said, depositing the Trouts in front of the sheriff as if I'd drug them out of the water. "This is Olive Trout and her husband, Julian. The queen's been anxious to meet someone like Julian. He's *really into the weather*." Okay, not subtle. But Julian's face turned white. Yeah, a little knowledge of wrongdoing definitely present in Julian's conscience.

"Honey, are you sick?" Olive asked.

"We need to go home," he said.

"No, no, no," Carla said, leaping into the conversation. "Gervaise, honey, you remember Andre said if we heard of anyone who was really a weather authority, he and the queen especially wanted to have a word with 'em?" She tucked her arms around the Trouts and beamed at them. Olive looked uncertain.

"Of course," said Gervaise, the lightbulb finally switching on above his head. "Thank you, Sookie. Please, come with us." And they guided the Trouts away.

I felt a little giddy with the pleasure of having been proved right.

Looking around, I spotted Barry sticking a little plate on an empty tray.

"You wanna dance?" I asked, because the Dead Man Dance Band was playing a great cover of an old Jennifer Lopez song. Barry looked reluctant, but I pulled him by his hand, and pretty soon we were shaking our bonbons all over the place and having a great time. Nothing's like dancing for relaxing tension and losing yourself, just for a little while. I wasn't as good as Shakira at muscle control, but maybe if I practiced once in a while . . .

"What are you doing?" Eric asked, and he wasn't being facetious. He was glacial with disapproval.

"Dancing, why?" I gave a wave to signal Eric to scoot. But Barry had stopped, already, and given me a little good-bye wave.

"I was having a good time," I protested.

"You were twitching your assets in front of every male in the room," he said. "Like a . . ."

"You hold up, buddy! You stop right there!" I held up a finger, warning him.

"Take your finger out of my face," he said.

I inhaled to say something unforgivable, welcoming the tide of anger with actual delight—I was *not* tied to him at the waist—when a strong, wiry arm clamped around me, and an unfamiliar Irish-accented voice said, "Dance, darling?" As the red-haired dancer who'd opened the night's shindig swung me off in a more sedate but complicated set of steps, I spotted his partner seizing Eric's wrist to do the same.

"Just follow while you calm down, girl. I'm Sean."

"Sookie."

"Pleased to meet you, young woman. You're a fine dancer."

"Thank you. That's a high compliment, coming from you. I really enjoyed your routine earlier." I could feel the rush of anger draining away.

"It's my partner," he said, smiling. It didn't look easy for him, that smile, but it transformed him from a thin-faced freckled man with a blade of a nose to a man with sexiness to spare. "My Layla is a dream to dance with."

"She's very beautiful."

"Oh, yes, inside and out."

"How long have you been partners?"

"In dancing, two years. In life, over a year."

"From your accent, I guess you came here in a roundabout way." I glimpsed Eric and the beautiful Layla. Layla had an easy smile on her lips, and she was talking to Eric, who was still looking sort of grim. But not angry.

"You could say so," he agreed. "Of course, I'm from Ireland, but I've been over here for . . ." His brow furrowed in thought, and it was like watching marble ripple. "Been here for a hundred years, anyway. From time to time, we think about moving back to Tennessee, where Layla's from, but we haven't made up our minds."

This was a lot of conversation from a quiet-looking guy. "You're just getting tired of living in the city?"

"Too much anti-vampire stuff going around lately. The Fellowship of the Sun, the Take the Night from the Dead movement: we seem to breed 'em here."

"The Fellowship is everywhere," I said. The very name made me feel gloomy. "And what'll happen when they get to hear about Weres?"

"Aye. And I think that'll be soon. I keep hearing from Weres that it's just around the corner."

You'd think, that out of all the supes I knew, one of them would let me know what was up. Sooner or later the Weres and the shifters would have to let the world in on their big secret, or they'd get outed by the vampires, either intentionally or unintentionally.

"There might even be a civil war," Sean said, and I forced my mind back to the topic at hand.

"Between the Fellowship and the supes?"

He nodded. "I'm thinking that could happen."

"What would you do in that case?"

"I've been through a few wars, and I don't want to go through another one," he said promptly. "Layla hasn't seen the Old World, and she would enjoy it, so we'd go to England. We could dance there, or we could just find a place to hide out."

As interesting as this was, it wasn't getting me any closer to solving the numerous problems facing me right at the moment, which I could count off on my fingers. Who had paid Julian Trout? Who had planted the Dr Pepper bomb? Who had killed the rest of the Arkansas vampires? Was it the same person who'd had Henrik killed, the employer of the rogue vamp?

"What was the result?" I said out loud, to the red-haired vamp's confusion.

"I beg your pardon?"

"Just talking to myself. It's been a pleasure to dance with you. Excuse me; I have to go find a friend."

Sean danced me to the edge of the crowd, and we parted ways. He was already looking for his mate. Vampire couples didn't stay together for long, as a rule. Even the hundred-year marriages of kings and queens required only a once-a-year nuptial visit. I hoped Sean and Layla would prove to be the exception.

I decided I should check on Quinn. That might be a lengthy process, since I had no idea where the Weres had taken him. I was so confused by the effect Eric was having on me, all mixed up with the beginnings of affection for Quinn. But I knew whom I was beholden to. Quinn had saved my life tonight. I started my search by calling his room but got no answer.

If I was a Were, where would I take a wounded tiger? Well, nowhere public, because Weres were secretive. They wouldn't want the hotel staff to catch a word or a phrase that would tip them off to the existence of the other supes. So they'd take Quinn to a private room, right? So, who had a private room and was sympathetic to the Weres?

Jake Purifoy, of course—former Were, current vamp. Quinn could be there—or he could be down in the hotel garage somewhere, or in the security chief's room, or in the infirmary, if there was such a thing. I had to start somewhere. I inquired at the front desk, where the clerk didn't seem to have any problem releasing the room number to me, though it's true Jake and I were flagged as being members of the same party. The clerk was not the one who'd been so rude when we'd checked in. She thought my dress was very pretty, and she wanted one just like it.

Jake's room was a floor up from mine, and as I raised my hand to knock on the door, I casually scanned inside to count the brains. There was the hole in the air that marked a vampire brain (that's the best way I can describe it), and a couple of human signatures. But I picked up on a thought that froze my fist before it had a chance to touch the door.

. . . *they should all die,* came the faint fragment of thought. Nothing followed it, though—no other thought that clarified or elaborated on that malign idea. So I knocked, and the pattern in the room changed instantly. Jake answered the door. He didn't look welcoming.

"Hi, Jake," I said, making my smile as bright and innocent as I could. "How you doing? I came by to check if Quinn was with you."

"With me?" Jake sounded startled. "Since I turned, I've hardly talked to Quinn, Sookie. We just don't have anything to talk about." I must have looked disbelieving, because he said in a rush, "Oh, it's not Quinn; it's me. I just can't bridge the chasm between who I was and who I am now. I'm not even sure who I am." His shoulders slumped.

That sounded honest enough. And I felt a lot of sympathy for him. "Anyway," Jake said, "I helped carry him to the infirmary, and I bet he's still there. There's a shifter called Bettina and a Were called Hondo with him."

Jake was holding the door shut. He didn't want me to see his companions. Jake didn't know that I could tell that he had people in his room.

It wasn't any of my business, of course. But it was disquieting. Even as I thanked him and turned to leave, I was thinking the situation over. The last thing in the world I wanted to do was to cause the troubled Jake any more problems, but if he was somehow involved in the plot that seemed to be snaking through the halls of the Pyramid of Gizeh, I had to find out.

First things first. I went down to my room and called the desk to get directions to the infirmary, and I carefully wrote them on the phone pad. Then I sneaked back up the stairs to stand outside Jake's door again, but in the time I'd been gone, the party had begun to disperse. I saw two humans from the rear. Strange; I couldn't be certain, but one of them looked like the surly Joe, the computer-consulting employee from the luggage area. Jake had been meeting with some of the hotel staff in his room. Maybe he still felt more at home with humans than he did with vampires. But surely Weres would have been his choice. . . .

As I stood there in the corridor, feeling sorry for him, Jake's door opened and he stepped out. I hadn't checked for blank spots, only live signatures. My bad. Jake looked a bit suspicious when he saw me, and I couldn't blame him.

"Do you want to go with me?" I asked.

"What?" He looked startled. He hadn't been a vampire long enough to get the inscrutable face down pat.

"To see Quinn?" I said. "I got directions to the infirmary, and you said you hadn't talked to him in a while, so I thought you might want to go with me if I'd kind of smooth the way?"

"That's a nice idea, Sookie," he said. "I think I'll pass. The fact is, most shifters don't want me around anymore. Quinn is better than most, I'm sure, but I make him uneasy. He knows my mom, my dad, my ex-girlfriend; all the people in my former life, the ones who don't want to hang with me now."

I said impulsively, "Jake, I'm so sorry. I'm sorry Hadley turned you if you would rather have passed on. She was fond of you, and she didn't want you to die."

"But I did die, Sookie," Jake said. "I'm not the same guy anymore. As you know." He picked up my arm and looked at the scar on it, the one he'd left with his teeth. "You won't ever be the same, either," he said, and he walked away. I'm not sure he knew where he was going, but he just wanted to get away from me.

I watched him until he was out of sight. He didn't turn to look back at me.

My mood had been fragile anyway, and that encounter pretty much started it on the downslope. I trudged to the elevators, determined to find the damn infirmary. The queen hadn't buzzed me, so presumably she was hobnobbing with other vampires, trying to find out who had hired the weather witch, and generally reveling in her relief. No more trial, a clear inheritance, the chance to put her beloved

Andre in power. Things were coming up roses for the Queen of Louisiana, and I tried not to be bitter. Or did I have a right to be? Hmmm, let's see. I'd helped stop the trial, though I hadn't counted on it stopping as finally and completely as it had for, say, the hapless Henrik. Since she'd been found innocent, she'd get the inheritance as promised in her marriage contract. And who'd had the idea about Andre? And I'd been proved right about the witch. Okay, maybe I could be a little bitter at my own unbenevolent fortune. Plus, sooner or later I'd have to choose between Quinn and Eric, through no fault of my own. I'd stood holding a bomb for a very long time. The Ancient Pythoness was not a member of my fan club, and she was an object of reverence to most of the vampires. I'd almost been killed with an arrow.

Well, I'd had worse nights.

I found the infirmary, which was easier to locate than I'd thought, because the door was open and I could hear a familiar laugh coming from the room. I stepped in to find that Quinn was talking to the honey bear–looking woman, who must be Bettina, and the black guy, who must be Hondo. Also, to my astonishment, Clovache was there. Her armor was not off, but she managed to give the impression of a guy who'd loosened his tie.

"Sookie," said Quinn. He smiled at me, but the two shapechangers didn't. I was definitely an unwelcome visitor.

But I hadn't come to see them. I'd come to see the man who'd saved my life. I walked over to him, letting him watch me, giving him a little smile. I sat on the plastic chair by the bed and took his hand.

"Tell me how you're feeling," I said.

"Like I had a real close shave," he said. "But I'm gonna be fine."

"Could you all excuse us a moment, please?" I was at my most polite as I met the eyes of the three others in the room.

Clovache said, "Back to guarding Kentucky," and took off. She might have winked at me before she vanished. Bettina looked a bit disgruntled, as if she'd been student teaching on her own and now the teacher had returned and snatched back her authority.

Hondo gave me a dark look that held more than a hint of threat. "You treat my man right," he said. "Don't give him no hard time."

"Never," I said. He couldn't think of a way to stay, since Quinn apparently wanted to talk to me, so he left.

"My fan base just gets bigger and bigger," I said, watching them go. I got up and shut the door behind them. Unless a vampire, or Barry, stood outside the door, we were reasonably private.

"Is this where you dump me for the vampire?" Quinn asked. All trace of good humor had vanished from his face, and he was holding very still.

"No. This is where I tell you what happened, and you listen, and then we talk." I said this as if I was sure he'd go along with it, but that was far from the case, and my heart was thudding in my throat as I waited for his reply. Finally he nodded, and I closed my eyes in relief, clutching his left hand in both of mine. "Okay," I said, bracing myself, and then I was off and running with my narrative, hoping that he would see that Eric really was the lesser of two evils.

Quinn didn't pull his hand away, but he didn't hold mine, either. "You're bound to Eric," he said.

"Yes."

"You've exchanged blood with him at least three times."

"Yes."

"You know he can turn you whenever he feels like it?"

"Any of us could be turned whenever the vampires feel like it, Quinn. Even you. It might take two of them to hold you down and one to take all your blood and give you his, but it still could happen."

"It wouldn't take that long if he made up his mind, now that you two have swapped so often. And this is Andre's fault."

"There's nothing I can do about that now. I wish there were. I wish I could cut Eric out of my life. But I can't."

"Unless he gets staked," Quinn said.

I felt a pang in my heart that almost had me clapping a hand to my chest.

"You don't want that to happen." Quinn's mouth was compressed in a hard line.

"No, of course not!"

"You care about him."

Oh, *crap.* "Quinn, you know Eric and I were together for a while, but he had amnesia and he doesn't remember it. I mean, he knows it's a fact, but he doesn't remember it at all."

"If anyone besides you told me that story, you know what I'd think."

"Quinn. I'm not anybody else."

"Babe, I don't know what to say. I care about you, and I love spending time with you. I love going to bed with you. I like eating at the table with you. I like cooking together. I like almost everything about you, including your gift. But I'm not good at sharing."

"I don't go with two guys at the same time."

"What are you saying?"

"I'm saying, I'm going with you, unless you tell me different."

"What will you do when Mr. Big and Blond tells you to hop in bed with him?"

"I'll tell him I'm spoken for . . . if you're going to speak."

Quinn shifted restlessly on the narrow bed. "I'm healing, but I'm hurting," he admitted. He looked very tired.

"I wouldn't trouble you with all this if it didn't seem pretty important to me," I said. "I'm trying to be honest with you. Absolutely honest. You took the arrow for me, and it's the least I can do in return."

"I know that. Sookie, I'm a man who almost always knows his own mind, but I have to tell you . . . I don't know what to say. I thought we were just about ideal for each other until this." Quinn's eyes blazed in his face suddenly. "If he died, we'd have no problems."

"If you killed him, I'd have a problem," I said. I couldn't get any plainer than that.

Quinn closed his eyes. "We have to think about this again when I'm all healed and you've had sleep and time to relax," he said. "You gotta meet Frannie, too. I'm so . . ." To my horror, I thought Quinn was going to choke up. If he cried, I would, too, and the last thing I needed was tears. I leaned over so far I thought I was going to fall on top of him, and I kissed him, just a quick pressure of my mouth on his. But then he held my shoulder and pulled me back to him, and there was much more to explore, his warmth and intensity . . . but then his gasp drew us out of the moment. He was trying not to grimace with pain.

"Oh! I'm sorry."

"Don't ever apologize for a kiss like that," he said. And he didn't look teary anymore. "We definitely have something going on, Sookie. I don't want Andre's vampire crap to ruin it."

"Me, either," I said. I didn't want to give Quinn up, not the least because of our sizzling chemistry. Andre terrified me, and who knew what his intentions were? I certainly didn't. I suspected Eric didn't know, either, but he was never averse to power.

I said good-bye to Quinn, a reluctant good-bye, and began finding my way back to the dance. I felt obliged to check in with the queen to make sure she didn't need me, but I was exhausted, and I needed to get out of my dress and collapse on my bed.

Clovache was leaning against a wall in the corridor ahead, and I had the impression she was waiting for me. The younger Britlingen was less statuesque than Batanya, and while Batanya looked like a striking hawk with dark curls, Clovache was lighter altogether, with feathery ash-brown hair that needed a good stylist and big green eyes with high, arched brows.

"He seems like a good man," she said in her harsh accent, and I got the strong feeling that Clovache was not a subtle woman.

"He seems that way to me, too."

"While a vampire, by definition, is twisty and deceptive."

"By definition? You mean, without exception?"

"I do."

I kept silent as we walked. I was too tired to figure out the warrior's purpose in telling me this. I decided to ask. "What's up, Clovache? What's the point?"

"Did you wonder why we were here, guarding the King of Kentucky? Why he had decided to pay our truly astronomical fees?"

"Yes, I did, but I figured it wasn't my business."

"It's very much your business."

"Then tell me. I'm not up to guessing."

"Isaiah caught a Fellowship spy in his entourage a month ago."

I stopped dead, and Clovache did, too. I processed her words. "That's really bad," I said, knowing the words were inadequate.

"Bad for the spy, of course. But she gave up some information before she went to the vale of shadows."

"Wow, that's a pretty way to put it."

"It's a load of crap. She died, and it *wasn't* pretty. Isaiah is an old-fashioned guy. Modern on the surface, a traditional vampire underneath. He had a wonderful time with the poor bitch before she gave it up."

"You think you can trust what she said?"

"Good point. I'd confess to anything if I thought it would spare me some of the things his cronies did to her."

I wasn't sure that was true. Clovache was made of pretty stern stuff.

"But I think she told him the truth. Her story was, a splinter group in the Fellowship got wind of this summit and decided it would be a golden opportunity to come out in the open with their fight against the vampires. Not simply protests and sermons against the vamps, but out-and-out warfare. This isn't the main body of the Fellowship . . . the leaders are always careful to say, 'Oh, gosh, no, we don't condone violence against anyone. We're only cautioning people to be aware that if they consort with vampires, they're consorting with the devil.'"

"You know a lot about things in this world," I said.

"Yes," she agreed. "I do a lot of research before we take a job."

I wanted to ask her what her world was like, how she got from one to the other, how much she charged, if all the warriors on (in?) her world were women or could the guys kick butt, too; and if so, what they looked like in the wonderful pants. But this wasn't the time or the place.

"So, what's the bottom line on this?" I asked.

"I think maybe the Fellowship is trying to mount some major offensive here."

"The bomb in the soda can?"

"Actually, that baffles me. But it was outside Louisiana's room, and the Fellowship has to know by now that their operative didn't succeed, if it was their work."

"And there are also the three murdered vampires in the Arkansas suite," I pointed out.

"Like I say, baffled," Clovache said.

"Would they have killed Jennifer Cater and the others?"

"Certainly, if they had a chance. But to tip their hand in such a small way when according to the spy they have planned something really big—that seems very unlikely. Also, how could a human get into the suite and kill three vampires?"

"So, what was the result of the Dr Pepper bomb?" I asked, trying hard to figure out the thinking behind it. We'd resumed walking, and now we were right outside the ceremonies room. I could hear the orchestra.

"Well, it gave you a few new white hairs," Clovache said, smiling.

"I can't think that was the goal," I said. "I'm not that egocentric."

Clovache had made up her mind. "You're right," she said, "because the Fellowship wouldn't have planted it. They wouldn't want to draw attention to their larger plan with the little bomb."

"So it was there for some other purpose."

"And what was that purpose?"

"The end result of the bomb, if it had gone off, would have been that the queen got a big scare," I said slowly.

Clovache looked startled. "Not killed?"

"She wasn't even in the room."

"It should have gone off earlier than it did," Clovache said.

"How do you know that?"

"Security guy. Donati. That's what the police told him.

Donati sees us as fellow professionals." Clovache grinned. "He likes women in armor."

"Hey, who doesn't?" I grinned back.

"And it was a weak bomb, if any bomb can be called weak. I'm not saying there wouldn't have been damage. There would have. Maybe even someone killed, like you could have been. But the episode seems to be ineffective and ill-planned."

"Unless it was designed only to scare. Designed to be spotted. Designed to be disarmed."

Clovache shrugged.

"I don't understand," I said. "If not the Fellowship, who? What does the Fellowship plan to do? Charge the lobby armed with sharpened baseball bats?"

"The security here is not so good," Clovache said.

"Yeah, I know. When I was down in the basement, getting a suitcase for the queen, the guards were pretty lazy, and I don't think the employees are searched as they come in, either. And they got a lot of suitcases mixed up."

"And the vampires hired these people. Unbelievable. On one level vampires realize they're not immortal. They can be killed. On another, they've survived for so long, it makes them feel omnipotent." Clovache shrugged. "Well, back to duty." We'd reached the ballroom. The Dead Man Dance Band was still playing.

The queen was standing very close to Andre, who no longer stood behind her but to her side. I knew this was significant, but it wasn't plain enough to cause Kentucky to give up hope. Christian Baruch was also in close attendance. If he'd had a tail, it would have been wagging, he was so anxious to please Sophie-Anne. I glanced around the room at the other kings and queens, recognizable by their entourages. I hadn't seen them in a room all together before, and I counted. There were only four queens. The other twelve rulers were males. Of the four queens, Minnesota appeared to be mated with the King of Wisconsin. Ohio had his arm around Iowa, so they were a couple. Besides Alabama, the only unmated queen was Sophie-Anne.

Though many vampires tend to be elastic about the gender of their sexual partner, or at least tolerant of those who prefer something different, some of them definitely aren't. No wonder Sophie-Anne was shining so brightly, even from under the lifted cloud of Peter Threadgill's death. Vampires didn't seem to be afraid of merry widows.

Alabama's boy toy scuttled his fingers up her bare back, and she shrieked in pretended fear. "You know I hate spiders," she said playfully, looking almost human, clutching him close to her. Though he'd played at frightening her, she clung closer.

Wait, I thought. *Wait just a minute.* But the idea wouldn't form.

Sophie-Anne noticed me lurking, and she beckoned. "I think most of the humans are gone for the night," she said.

A glance around the room told me that was true. "What did you think of Julian Trout?" I asked, to allay my fear that she'd do something awful to him.

"I think he doesn't understand what he did," Sophie-Anne said. "At least to some extent. But he and I will come to an understanding." She smiled. "He and his wife are quite all right. I don't need you anymore tonight. Go amuse yourself," she said, and it didn't sound condescending. Sophie-Anne really wanted me to have a good time, though, granted, she wasn't too particular about how I did it.

"Thanks," I said, and then recalled that I'd better dress that up a bit. "Thank you, ma'am, and you have a good night. See you tomorrow evening."

I was glad to get out of there. With the room chock full o' vampires, the glances I was getting were a little on the pointy-toothed side. Individual bloodsuckers had an easier time of it sticking to the artificial blood than a group did. Something about the memory of the good ole days just made them want something warm from the source, rather than a liquid created in a lab and heated up in a microwave. Right on schedule, the crowd of Willing Donors returned through a back door and lined up, more or less, against the back wall. In very short order, they were all occupied, and (I suppose) happy.

After Bill had taken my blood during lovemaking, he'd told me blood from the neck of a human—after a diet of TrueBlood, say—was like going to Ruth's Chris Steak House after many meals at McDonald's. I saw Gervaise nuzzling Carla off in a corner, and I wondered if she needed help; but when I saw her face, I decided not.

Carla didn't come in that night, either, and without the distraction of Quinn, I was kind of sorry. I had too much to think about. It seemed that trouble was looking for me in the corridors of the Pyramid of Gizeh, and no matter which turn I took, it was going to find me.

15 ~

I'D FINALLY GONE TO BED AT FOUR IN THE MORNING, and I woke at noon. That eight hours wasn't a good eight hours. I kept starting half awake, and I couldn't regulate my temperature, which might have had something to do with the blood exchange . . . or not. I had bad dreams, too, and twice I thought I heard Carla entering the room, only to open my eyes enough to see she wasn't there. The weird light that entered through the heavily colored glass of the human-only floor was not like real daylight, not at all. It was throwing me off.

I felt a tad bit better after a long shower, and I lifted the phone to call room service to get something to eat. Then I decided to go down to the little restaurant. I wanted to see other humans.

There were a few there; not my roommate, but a human playmate or two, and Barry. He gestured to the empty chair at his table, and I dropped into it, looking around for the waiter to signal for coffee. It came right away, and I shuddered with pleasure at the first sip. After I'd finished the first cup, I said—in my way—*How are you today? Were you up all night?*

No, Stan went to bed early with his new girlfriend, so I wasn't needed. They're still in the honeymoon stage. I went to the dance for a while, then I hung out with the makeup girl the Queen of Iowa brought with her. He waggled his eyebrows to tell me that the makeup girl was hot.

So, what's your program for today?

Did you get one of these slid under your door? Barry pushed a stapled sheaf of papers across the table to me just as the waiter brought my English muffin and eggs.

Yeah, I stuffed it in my purse. Wow, I could talk to Barry while I ate, the neatest answer to talking with your mouth full I could ever devise.

Take a look.

While Barry cut open a biscuit to slather it with butter, I scanned the pages. An agenda for the night, which was very helpful. Sophie-Anne's trial had been the most serious case that had to be adjudicated, the only one involving royalty. But there were a couple of others. The first session was set for 8:00, and it was a dispute over a personal injury. A Wisconsin vampire named Jodi (which seemed unlikely in and of itself) was being sued by an Illinois vampire named Michael. Michael alleged that Jodi had waited until he had dozed off for the day and then broken off one of his canines. With pliers.

Wow. That sounds . . . interesting. I raised my eyebrows. *How come the sheriffs aren't handling this?* Vampires really didn't like airing their dirty laundry.

"Interstate," Barry said succinctly. The waiter had just brought a whole pot of coffee, so Barry topped off my cup and filled his own.

I flipped over a page. The next case involved a Kansas City, Missouri, vampire named Cindy Lou Suskin, who'd turned a child. Cindy Lou claimed that the child was dying of a blood disorder anyway, and she'd always wanted a child; so now she had a perpetual vampire preteen. Furthermore, the boy had been turned with his parents' consent, gotten in writing. Kate Book, the Kansas City, Kansas, lawyer appointed by the state to supervise the child's welfare, was complaining that now the child refused to see his human parents or to have any interaction with them, which was contrary to the agreement between the parents and Cindy Lou.

Sounded like something on daytime television. *Judge Judy*, anyone?

So, tonight is court cases, I summarized after scanning the remaining sheets. "I guess we're needed?"

"Yes, I guess so. There'll be human witnesses for the second case. Stan wants me to be there, and I'm betting your queen will want you there, too. Her subject Bill is one of the appointed judges. Only kings and queens can judge other kings and queens, but for cases involving lesser vampires, the judges are picked from a pool. Bill's name came out of the hat."

"Oh, goody."

You got a history with him?

Yeah. But I think he'd probably be a good judge. I wasn't sure why I believed this; after all, Bill had shown he was capable of great deception. But I thought he would try to be fair and dispassionate.

I had noticed that the "court" cases would take up the hours between eight and eleven. After that, midnight to four a.m. was blocked out as "Commerce." Barry and I looked at each other and shrugged.

"Swap meet?" I suggested. "Flea market?"

Barry had no idea.

The fourth night of the conference was the last, and the first half of it was marked "Free Time for Everyone in Rhodes." Some of the suggested activities: seeing the Blue Moon dancers again, or their more explicit division, Black Moon. The difference wasn't spelled out, but I got the definite idea that the Black Moon employees did much more sexually oriented performances. Different dance teams from the studio were listed as appearing at different venues. The visiting vampires were also advised to visit the zoo, which would be open at night by special arrangement, or the city museum, ditto. Or they could visit a club "for the particular enjoyment of those who enjoy their pleasures on the darker side." It was called Kiss of Pain. *Remind me to walk down the other side of the street from that one,* I told Barry.

You never enjoy a little bite? Barry touched his tongue to his own blunt canines so I couldn't miss the implication.

There's lots of pleasure in that, I said, because I could hardly deny it. *But I think this place probably goes a little beyond a nip in the neck. Are you busy right now? Because I have to do some legwork for Eric, and I could use some help.*

"Sure," Barry said. "What's up?"

"We need to find archery places," I said.

"This was left for you at the desk, miss," said our waiter, who dropped a manila envelope on the table and retreated as if he suspected we had rabies. Evidently our silent exchanges had freaked someone out.

I opened the envelope to find a picture of Kyle Perkins inside. There was a note paper-clipped to it in Bill's familiar cramped handwriting. "Sookie: Eric says you need this to do some detective work, and that this picture is necessary. Please be cautious. William Compton." And just when I was thinking about asking the waiter for a phone book, I saw there was a second sheet. Bill had searched the Internet and made a list of all the archery practice places in the city.

There were only four. I tried not to be impressed by Bill's thoughtfulness and assistance. I'd done with being impressed by Bill.

I called the hotel garage to get one of the cars brought by the Arkansas contingent. The queen had assumed ownership of them, and Eric had offered me one of them.

Barry had run up to his room to get a jacket, and I was standing by the front door, waiting for the car to be brought around and wondering how much I should tip the valet when I spotted Todd Donati. He came over to me, walking slowly and somehow heavily, though he was a thin man. He looked bad today, the scalp exposed by his receding hairline gray and damp looking, even his mustache sagging.

He stood facing me for a moment, not speaking. I thought he was gathering his courage, or his hopelessness. If ever I saw death riding on a man's shoulder, it was on Todd Donati's.

"My boss is trying to interest your boss in hooking up," he said abruptly. If I'd imagined how he'd open our conversation, it had never included that line.

"Yeah, now that she's a widow, she's attracting quite a lot of interest," I said.

"He's an old-fashioned guy in a lot of ways," Todd Donati said. "Comes from an old family, doesn't like modern thinking."

"Um-hum," I said, trying to sound neutral but encouraging.

"He don't believe in women making up their own minds, being able to fend for themselves," the security chief said.

I couldn't look like I understood what Donati was talking about, because I sure didn't.

"Even vampire women," he said, and looked at me squarely and directly.

"Okay," I said.

"Think about it," Donati said. "Get your queen to ask him where the security tape is that shows that area in front of her room."

"I will," I said, having no idea why I was agreeing. Then the ailing man spun on his heel and walked away with an air of having discharged his duty.

Then the car came around, Barry hurried out of the elevator and came over to join me, and any thinking I might have done about the encounter faded in my fear of driving in the city. I don't think Eric ever considered how hard it would be for me to drive in Rhodes, because he just didn't think about stuff like that. If I hadn't had Barry with me, it would have been nearly impossible. I could cope with the driving, or I could look at the map the parking attendant loaned us, but not both.

I didn't do too bad, though the traffic was heavy and the weather was cold and raining. I hadn't been out of the hotel since we'd arrived, and it was kind of refreshing to see the outside world. Also, this was probably the only glimpse of the rest of the city I would get. I did as much looking as I could. Who knew if I'd ever come back? And this was so far north.

Barry plotted our course, and we began our archery tour of Rhodes.

We started with the farthest business, called Straight Arrow. It was a long, narrow place on a very busy avenue. It was gleaming, well-lit—and had qualified instructors behind the counter who were heavily armed. I knew this, because a big sign said so. The men there were not impressed by Barry's southern accent. They thought it made him sound stupid. Though when I talked, they thought I was cute. Okay, how insulting is that? The subtext, which I read very clearly from their minds, was: women sound stupid anyway, so a southern accent just enhances that adorable dimness. Men are supposed to sound crisp and direct, so southern men sound stupid and weak.

Anyway, aside from their built-in prejudices, these men were not helpful. They'd never seen Kyle Perkins at any of their night classes, and they didn't think he'd ever rented time to practice at their place.

Barry was fuming at the disrespect he'd endured, and he didn't even want to go in the second place. I trotted in by myself with the picture, and the one guy at work at the second archery supply store, which had no range, said, "No," immediately. He didn't discuss the picture, ask me why I wanted to know about Kyle Perkins, or wish me a nice day. He didn't have a sign to tell me how formidable he was. I figured he just ruded people to death.

The third place, housed in a building that I thought might at one time have been a bowling alley, had a few cars in the parking lot and a heavy opaque door. STOP AND BE IDENTIFIED a sign said. Barry and I could read it from the car. It seemed a little ominous.

"I'm tired of being in the car anyway," he said gallantly, and got out with me. We stood where we could be seen, and I alerted Barry when I spotted the camera above our heads. Barry and I both looked as pleasant as we could. (In Barry's case, that was pretty pleasant. He just had a way about him.) After a few seconds, we heard a loud click, and the door unlocked. I glanced at Barry, and he pulled open the heavy door while I stepped inside the room and to one side so he could enter, too.

We were faced with a long counter extending the length of the opposite wall. There was a woman about my age behind the counter, with coppery hair and skin, the product of an interesting racial blend. She'd dyed her eyebrows black, which added a touch of the bizarre to the whole uni-color effect.

She looked us over just as carefully in person as she had

over the camera, and I could read the thought that she was much happier to see Barry than she was to see me. I told Barry, *You better take this one.*

Yeah, I'm getting the idea, he answered, and while I laid Kyle's picture on the counter, he said, "Could you tell us if this guy ever came in here to buy arrows or to practice?"

She didn't even ask why we wanted to know. She bent over to look at the picture, maybe a little farther than necessary to give Barry the benefit of her neckline. She scanned Kyle's picture and immediately made a face. "Yeah, he came in here right after dark yesterday," she said. "We'd never had a vampire customer, and I didn't really want to serve him, but what are you gonna do? He had the money, and the law says we can't discriminate." She was a woman who was ready and willing to discriminate, no doubt about it.

"Was anyone with him?" Barry asked.

"Oh, let me think." She posed, her head thrown back, for Barry's benefit. *She* didn't think his southern accent sounded stupid. She thought it was adorable and sexy. "I just can't remember. Listen, I'll tell ya what I'll do. I'll get the security tape for last night; we've still got it. And I'll let you have a look at it, okay?"

"Can we do that right now?" I asked, smiling sweetly.

"Well, I can't leave the counter right now. There's no one else here to watch the store if I have to go to the back. But if you'll come to look tonight after my replacement gets here"—she cast a very pointed glance at Barry, to make sure I realized I need not come—"I'll let you have a peek."

"What time?" Barry said, rather reluctantly.

"Shall we say seven? I get off right after that."

Barry didn't touch the hint, but he agreed to be back at seven.

"Thanks, Barry," I said as we buckled up again. "You're really helping me out." I called the hotel and left a message for the queen and Andre, explaining where I was and what I was doing, so they wouldn't get mad when I wasn't at their disposal the moment they woke, which should be very soon. After all, I was following Eric's orders.

"You gotta come in with me," Barry said. "I'm not seeing that woman by myself. She'll eat me alive. That was the War of Northern Aggression, for sure."

"Okay. I'll stay out in the car, and you can yell to me from your head if she climbs on top of you."

"It's a deal."

To fill the time, we had a cup of coffee and some cake at a bakery. It was great. My grandmother had always believed that northern women couldn't cook. It was delightful to find out exactly how untrue that conviction had been. My appetite was also delightful. It was a continuing relief to find that I was just as hungry as I normally was. Nothing vampy about me, no sir!

After we filled up the tank and checked our route back to the Pyramid, it was finally time to return to the archery range to talk to Copper. The sky was full dark, and the city glowed with light. I felt sort of urban and glamorous, driving around such a large and famous city. And I'd been given a task and performed it successfully. No country mouse, me.

My feeling of happiness and superiority didn't last long.

Our first clue that all was not well at the Monteagle Archery Company was the heavy metal door hanging askew.

"Shit," said Barry, which summed up my feelings in a nutshell.

We got out—very reluctantly—and, with many glances from side to side, we went up to the door to examine it.

"Blown or ripped?" I said.

Barry knelt on the gravel to have a closer look.

"I'm no 007," he said, "but I think this was ripped off."

I looked at the door doubtfully. But when I bent over to look more closely, I saw the twisted metal of the hinges. Chalk one up for Barry.

"Okay," I said. *Here's the part where we actually have to go in.*

Barry's jaw tightened. *Yeah,* he said, but he didn't sound too sure. Barry was definitely not into violence or confrontations. Barry was into money, and he had the best-paying employer. Right now, he was wondering if any amount of money would be enough to compensate for this, and he was thinking if he weren't with a woman, he'd just get in the car and drive away.

Sometimes male pride can be a good thing. I sure didn't want to do this by myself.

I shoved the door, which responded in a spectacular way by falling off its hinges and crashing to the gravel.

"Hi, we're here," Barry said weakly. "Anyone who didn't know before . . ."

After the noise had stopped and nothing had leaped out of the building to eat us, Barry and I straightened up from our instinctive crouching positions. I took a deep breath. This was my task, since this had been my errand. I stepped into the stream of light coming from the empty doorway. I took one big step forward over the threshold of the building. A quick scan hadn't given me a brain signal, so I pretty much figured what I was going to find.

Oh, yeah, Copper was dead. She was on top of the counter, laid out in a sprawl of limbs, her head canting off to one side. There was a knife protruding from her chest. Someone had been sick about a yard to the left of my foot—not blood—so there'd been at least one human on-site. I heard Barry step into the building and pause, just as I had.

I'd noted two doors from the room on our earlier visit.

There was a door to the right, outside the counter, that would admit customers to the range. There was a door behind the counter that would allow employees to duck back for breaks and to attend customers in the range area. I was sure the tape we'd come to watch had been back there, because that would be the natural place for the security equipment. Whether it was still back there, that was the big question.

I wanted to turn around and leave without a backward glance, and I was scared out of my mind, but she'd died because of that tape, I figured, and it seemed like I'd be discarding her unwilling sacrifice if I discarded the tape. That didn't really make much sense, but that was how I felt.

I'm not finding anyone else in the area, Barry told me.

Me, either, I said, after I'd performed my second, more thorough, scan.

Barry, of course, knew exactly what I planned to do, and he said, *Do you want me to come with you?*

No, I want you to wait outside. I'll call you if I need you. In truth, it would have been nice to have him closer, but it smelled too bad in the room for anyone to stand around for more than a minute, and our minute was up.

Without protesting, Barry went back outside, and I crept down the counter to a clear area. It felt indescribably creepy to scramble over, avoiding Copper's body. I was glad her sightless eyes were not aimed in my direction as I used a tissue to wipe the area my hands had gripped.

On the employee side of the counter, there was evidence of a considerable struggle. She'd fought hard. There were smears of blood here and there, and paperwork had gotten knocked to the floor. There was a panic button clearly visible, below the top of the counter, but I guess she hadn't had time to punch it.

The lights were on in the office behind the counter, too,

as I could see through the partially open door. I pushed it with my foot, and it swung away from me with a little creak. Again, nothing leaped out at me. I took a deep breath and stepped through.

The room was a combination security room/office/breakroom. There were counters built around the walls with rolling chairs pulled up to them, and there were computers and a microwave and a little refrigerator: the usual stuff. And there were the security tapes, heaped in a pile on the floor and smoldering. All the other smells in the outer room had been so bad we simply hadn't gotten around to this one. There was another door leading out; I didn't go check to see where it led to, because there was a body blocking it. It was a man's body, and it was lying facedown, which was a blessing. I didn't need to go over to check to see if he was dead. He was surely dead. Copper's replacement, I assumed.

"Well, crap," I said out loud. And then I thought, *Thank God I can get the hell out of here.* One thing about the security tapes having been burned: any record of our earlier visit was gone, too.

On my way, I pressed the panic button with my elbow. I hoped it was ringing somewhere at a police station, and that they'd get here soon.

Barry was waiting for me outside, as I'd been 99 percent sure he would be. Though I confess I wouldn't have been completely surprised if he'd left. "Let's book! I set off the alarm," I said, and we jumped into the car and got the hell out of there.

I was driving, because Barry was looking green. We had to pull over once (and in Rhodes traffic that wasn't easy) for him to be sick. I didn't blame him one little bit. What we'd seen was awful. But I've been blessed with a strong stomach, and I'd seen worse.

We got back to the hotel in time for the judicial session.

Barry looked at me with gaping astonishment when I commented that I'd better get ready for it. He hadn't had an inkling what I'd been thinking, so I knew he was really feeling bad.

"How can you think of going?" he said. "We have to tell someone what happened."

"I called the police, or at least a security company who'll report it," I said. "What else can we do?" We were in the elevator rising from the parking garage to the lobby.

"We have to talk to them."

"Why?" The doors opened and we stepped out into the hotel lobby.

"To tell them."

"What?"

"That someone tried to kill you last night here by . . . okay, throwing an arrow at you." He fell silent.

"Right. See?" I was getting his thoughts now, and he'd come to the correct conclusion. "Would it help solve her murder? Probably not, because the guy is dead and the tapes are destroyed. And they'd come here asking questions of the master vampires of a third of the United States. Who would thank me for that? No one, that's who."

"We can't stand by and do nothing."

"This isn't perfect. I know that. But it's realistic. And practical."

"Oh, so now you're *practical*?" Barry was getting shrieky.

"And you're yelling at my—at Sookie," said Eric, earning another shriek (this one wordless) from Barry. By that time, Barry didn't care if he ever saw me again in his life. Though I didn't feel quite that drastic, I didn't think we were going to become pen pals, either.

If Eric didn't know how to pick a term for what I was to him, I was equally stumped. "Do you need something?" I asked him in a voice that warned him I wasn't in the mood for any double entendres.

"What did you find out today?" he asked, all business, and the starch ran out of me in a stream.

"You go on," I told Barry, who didn't need telling twice.

Eric looked around for a safe place to talk, didn't see one. The lobby was busy with vampires who were going to the judicial proceedings, or chatting, or flirting. "Come," he said, not as rudely as it sounds, and we went to the elevators and up to his room. Eric was on the ninth floor, which covered a much larger area than the queen's. There were twenty rooms on nine, at least. There was a lot more traffic, too; we passed quite a few vamps on the way to Eric's room, which he told me he was sharing with Pam.

I was a little curious about seeing a regular vampire room, since I'd seen only the living room of the queen's suite. I was disappointed to find that aside from the traveling coffins, it looked quite ordinary. Of course, that was kind of a big "aside." Pam's and Eric's coffins were resting on fancy trestles covered with fake hieroglyphics in gilt on black-painted wood, which gave them a neat atmospheric touch. There were two double beds, too, and a very compact bathroom. Both towels were hung up, which I could see because the door was open. Eric had never hung up his towels when he lived with me, so I was willing to bet that Pam had folded them and hung them on the rack. It seemed oddly domestic. Pam had probably picked up for Eric for over a century. Good God. I hadn't even managed two weeks.

What with the coffins and the beds, the room was a bit crowded, and I wondered what the lower echelon vamps had to put up with, say, on floor twelve. Could you arrange coffins in a bunk configuration? But I was just waffling, trying not to think about being alone with Eric. We sat down,

Eric on one bed and I on another, and he leaned forward. "Tell me," he said.

"Well, it's not good," I said, just to put him on the right track.

His face darkened, the blond brows drawing in to meet, his mouth turning down.

"We did find an archery range that Kyle Perkins visited. You were right about that. Barry went with me to be nice, and I really appreciated it," I said, getting my opening credits in. "To condense the whole afternoon, we found the right range at our third stop, and the gal behind the counter said we could look at the security tape from the night Kyle visited. I thought we might see someone we knew coming in with him. But she wanted us to come back at the end of her shift, seven o'clock." I paused to take a deep breath. Eric's face didn't change at all. "We came back at the appointed time, and she was dead, murdered, in the store. I went past her to look in the office, and the tapes had been burned."

"Killed how?"

"She'd been stabbed, and the knife was left in her chest, and the killer or someone with him had thrown up food. Also, a guy who worked at the store was killed, but I didn't check him out to see how."

"Ah." Eric considered this. "Anything else?"

"No," I said, and got to my feet to leave.

"Barry was angry with you," he observed.

"Yeah, he was, but he'll get over it."

"What's his problem?"

"He doesn't think I handled the . . . He doesn't think we should've left. Or . . . I don't know. He thinks I was unfeeling."

"I think you did exceptionally well."

"Well, *great*!" Then I clamped down on myself. "Sorry," I said. "I know you meant to compliment me. I'm not feeling all that good about her dying. Or leaving her. Even if it was the practical thing to do."

"You're second-guessing yourself."

"Yes."

A knock at the door. Since Eric didn't shift himself, I got up to answer it. I didn't think it was a sexist thing; it was a status thing. I was definitely the lower dog in the room.

Completely and totally not to my surprise, the knocker was Bill. That just made my day complete. I stood aside to let him enter. Darn if I was going to ask Eric if I should let him in.

Bill looked me up and down, I guess to check that my clothes were in order, then strode by me without a word. I rolled my eyes at his back. Then I had a brilliant idea: instead of turning back into the room for further discussion, I stepped out of the open door and shut it behind me. I marched off quite briskly and grabbed the elevator with hardly any wait. In two minutes, I was unlocking my door.

End of problem.

I felt quite proud of myself.

Carla was in our room, naked again.

"Hi," I said. "Please put on a robe."

"Well, hey, if it bothers you," she said in a fairly relaxed manner, and pulled on a robe. Wow. End of another problem. Direct action, straightforward statements; obviously, those were the keys to improving my life.

"Thanks," I said. "Not going to the judicial stuff?"

"Human dates aren't invited," she said. "It's Free Time for us. Gervaise and I are going out nightclubbing later. Some really extreme place called Kiss of Pain."

"You be careful," I said. "Bad things can happen if there are lots of vamps together and a bleeding human or two."

"I can handle Gervaise," Carla said.

"No, you can't."

"He's nuts about me."

"Until he stops being nuts. Or until a vamp older than Gervaise takes a shine to you, and Gervaise gets all conflicted."

She looked uncertain for a second, an expression I felt sure Carla didn't wear too often.

"What about you? I hear you're tied to Eric now."

"Only for a while," I said, and I meant it. "It'll wear off."

I will never go anywhere with vampires again, I promised myself. *I let the lure of the money and the excitement of the travel pull me in. But I won't do that again. As God is my witness . . .* Then I had to laugh out loud. Scarlett O'Hara, I wasn't. "I'll never be hungry again," I told Carla.

"Why, did you eat a big supper?" she asked, focused on the mirror because she was plucking her eyebrows.

I laughed. And I couldn't stop.

"What's up with you?" Carla swung around to eye me with some concern. "You're not acting like yourself, Sookie."

"Just had a bad shock," I said, gasping for breath. "I'll be okay in a minute." It was more like ten before I gathered my control back around me. I was due at the judicial meeting, and frankly, I wanted to have something to occupy my mind. I scrubbed my face and put on some makeup, changed into a bronze silk blouse and tobacco-colored pants with a matching cardigan, and put on some brown leather pumps. With my room key in my pocket and a relieved good-bye from Carla, I was off to find the judicial sessions.

~ 16

THE VAMPIRE JODI WAS PRETTY FORMIDABLE. SHE PUT me in mind of Jael, in the Bible. Jael, a determined woman of Israel, put a tent peg through the head of Sisera, an enemy captain, if I was remembering correctly. Sisera had been asleep when Jael did the deed, just as Michael had been when Jodi broke off his fang. Even though Jodi's name made me snicker, I saw in her a steely strength and resolve, and I was immediately on her side. I hoped the panel of judges could see past the vampire Michael's whining about his damn tooth.

This wasn't set up like the previous evening, though the session took place in the same room. The panel of judges, I guess you'd call them, were on the stage and seated at a long table facing the audience. There were three of them, all from different states: two men and a woman. One of the males was Bill, who was looking (as always) calm and collected. I didn't know the other guy, a blond. The female was a tiny, pretty vamp with the straightest back and longest rippling black hair I ever saw. I heard Bill address her as "Dahlia." Her round little face whipped back and forth as she listened to the testimony of first Jodi, then Michael, just as if she was watching a tennis match. Centered on the white tablecloth before the judges was a stake, which I guess was the vampire symbol of justice.

The two complaining vampires were not represented by lawyers. They said their piece, and then the judges got to ask questions before they decided the verdict by a majority vote. It was simple in form, if not in fact.

"You were torturing a human woman?" Dahlia asked Michael.

"Yes," he said without blinking an eye. I glanced around. I was the only human in the audience. No wonder there was a certain simplicity to the proceedings. The vampires weren't trying to dress it up for a warm-blooded audience. They were behaving as they would if they were by themselves. I was sitting by those of my party who'd attended—Rasul, Gervaise, Cleo—and maybe their closeness masked my scent, or maybe one tame human didn't count.

"She'd offended me, and I enjoy sex that way, so I abducted her and had a little fun," Michael said. "Then Jodi goes all ballistic on me and breaks my fang. See?" He opened wide enough to show the judges the fang's stump. (I wondered if he'd gone by the booth that was still set up out in the vendors' area, the one that had such amazing artificial fangs.)

Michael had the face of an angel, and he didn't get that what he'd done was wrong. He had wanted to do it, so he did it. Not all people who've been brought over to be vampires are mentally stable to start with, and some of them are utterly conscienceless after decades, or even centuries, of disposing of humans as they damn well please. And yet, they enjoy the openness of the new order, getting to stride around being themselves, with the right not to be staked. They don't want to pay for that privilege by adhering to the rules of common decency.

I thought breaking off one fang was a very light punishment. I couldn't believe he'd had the gall to bring a case against anyone. Apparently, neither did Jodi, who was on her feet and going for him again. Maybe she meant to snap off his other fang. This was way better than *The Peoples' Court* or *Judge Judy*.

The blond judge tackled her. He was much larger than Jodi, and she seemed to accept that she wasn't going to heave him off. I noticed Bill had moved his chair back so he could leap up if further developments required quick action.

The tiny Dahlia said, "Why did you take such exception to Michael's actions, Jodi?"

"The woman was the sister of one of my employees," Jodi said, her voice shaking with anger. "She was under my protection. And stupid Michael will cause all of us to be hunted again if he continues his ways. He can't be corrected. Nothing stops him, not even losing the fang. I warned him three times to stay away, but the young woman spoke back to him when he propositioned her yet again on the street, and his pride was more important than his intelligence or discretion."

"Is this true?" the little vamp asked Michael.

"She insulted me, Dahlia," he said smoothly. "A human publicly insulted me."

"This one's easy," said Dahlia. "Do you both agree?" The blond male restraining Jodi nodded, and so did Bill, who was still perched on the edge of his chair to Dahlia's right.

"Michael, you will bring retribution on us by your unwise

actions and your inability to control your impulses," Dahlia said. "You have ignored warnings, and you ignored the fact that the young woman was under the protection of another vampire."

"You can't mean this! Where is your pride?" Michael was yelling and on his feet.

Two men stepped forward out of the shadows at the back of the stage. They were both vampires, of course, and they were both good-sized men. They held Michael, who put up quite a fight. I was a little shocked by the noise and the violence, but in a minute they'd take Michael off to some vampire prison, and the calm proceedings would continue.

To my absolute astonishment, Dahlia nodded to the vamp sitting on Jodi, who got up and assisted her to rise. Jodi, smiling broadly, was across the stage in one leap, like a panther. She grabbed up the stake lying on the judges' table, and with one powerful swing of her lean arm, she buried the stake in Michael's chest.

I was the only one who was shocked, and I clapped both hands over my mouth to keep from squeaking.

Michael looked at her with utter rage, and he even kept struggling, I suppose to free his arms so he could pull the stake out, but in a few seconds it was all over. The two vamps holding the new corpse hauled it off, and Jodi stepped off the stage, still beaming.

"Next case," called Dahlia.

The next was the one about the vampire kid, and there were humans involved in this one. I felt less conspicuous when they came in: the hangdog parents with their vampire representative (was it possible that humans couldn't testify before this court?) and the "mother" with her "child."

This was a longer, sadder case, because the parents' suffering over the loss of their son—who was still walking and talking, but not to them—was nearly palpable. I wasn't the only one who cried, "For shame!" when Cindy Lou revealed the parents were giving her monthly payments for the boy's upkeep. The vampire Kate argued for the parents ferociously, and it was clear she thought Cindy Lou was a trailer-trash vampire and a bad mother, but the three judges—different ones this time, and I didn't know any of them—abided by the written contract the parents had signed and refused to give the boy a new guardian. However, they ruled, the contract had to be equally enforced on the parents' behalf, and the boy was required to spend time with his biological parents as long as they chose to enforce the right.

The head judge, a hawk-faced guy with dark, liquid eyes, called the boy up to stand before them. "You owe these people respect and obedience, and you signed this contract, too," he said. "You may be a minor in human law, but to us, you are as responsible as . . . *Cindy Lou.*" Boy, it just killed him, having to admit there was a vampire named Cindy Lou. "If you try to terrorize your human parents, or coerce them, or drink their blood, we will amputate your hand. And when it grows back, we'll amputate it again."

The boy could hardly be whiter than he was, and his human mother fainted. But he'd been so cocky, so sure of himself, and so dismissive of his poor parents, I thought the strong warning was necessary. I caught myself nodding.

Oh, yeah, this was fair, to threaten a kid with having his hand amputated.

But if you'd seen this kid, you might have agreed. And Cindy Lou was no prize; whoever had turned her must have been mentally and morally deficient.

I hadn't been needed after all. I was wondering about the rest of the evening when the queen came through the double doors at the end of the room, Sigebert and Andre in close attendance. She was wearing a sapphire blue silk pantsuit with a beautiful diamond necklace and small diamond earrings. She looked classy, absolutely smooth, sleek, and perfect. Andre made a beeline to me.

"I know," he said, "that is, Sophie-Anne tells me that I have done wrong to you. I'm not sorry, because I will do anything for her. Others don't mean anything to me. But I do regret that I have not been able to refrain from causing something that distresses you."

If that was an apology, it was the most half-assed one I'd ever received in my life. It left almost everything to be desired. All I could do was say, "I hear you." It was the most I'd ever get.

By then, Sophie-Anne was standing in front of me. I did my head-bob thing. "I will need you with me during the next few hours," she said, and I said, "Sure." She glanced up and down my clothes, as if wishing I had dressed up a little more, but no one had warned me that a part of the night marked off for Commerce meant fancy clothes were appropriate.

Mr. Cataliades steamed up to me, wearing a beautiful suit and a dark red-and-gold silk tie, and he said, "Good to see you, my dear. Let me brief you on the next item on the schedule."

I spread my hands to show I was ready. "Where's Diantha?" I asked.

"She is working something out with the hotel," Cataliades said. He frowned. "It's most peculiar. There was an extra coffin downstairs, apparently."

"How could that be?" Coffins belonged to somebody. It's not like a vampire was going to be traveling with a spare, like you had to have a dress coffin and an everyday coffin. "Why did they call you?"

"It had one of our tags on it," he said.

"But all of our vamps are accounted for, right?" I felt a tingle of anxiety in my chest. Just then, I saw the usual waiters moving among the crowd, and I saw one spot me and turn away. Then he saw Barry, who'd come in with the King of Texas. The waiter turned away yet again.

I actually started to call to a nearby vampire to hold the guy so I could have a look into his head, and then I realized I was acting as high-handed as the vampires themselves. The waiter vanished, and I hadn't had a close look at him, so I wasn't sure I could even identify him in a crowd of other servers in the same outfit. Mr. Cataliades was talking, but I held up a hand. "Hold it for a sec," I murmured. The waiter's quick turn had reminded me of something, something else that had seemed odd.

"Please pay attention, Miss Stackhouse," the lawyer said, and I had to stow the thread of thought away. "Here's what you need to do. The queen will be negotiating for a few favors she needs to help rebuild her state. Just do what you do best to discover if everyone dealing with her is honorable."

This was not a very specific guideline. "Do my best," I said. "But I think you should go find Diantha, Mr. C. I think there's something really strange and wrong about this extra coffin they're talking about. There was that extra suitcase, too," I said. "I carried it up to the queen's suite."

Mr. Cataliades looked at me blankly. I could see that he considered the small problem of extra items turning up in a hotel to be a small one and below his concern. "Did Eric tell you about the murdered woman?" I asked, and his attention sharpened.

"I haven't seen Master Eric this evening," he said. "I'll be sure to track him down."

"Something's up; I just don't know what," I muttered more or less to myself, and then I turned away to catch up with Sophie-Anne.

Commerce was conducted in a sort of bazaar style. Sophie-Anne positioned herself by the table where Bill was sitting, back at work selling the computer program. Pam was helping him, but she was in her regular clothes, and I was glad the harem costume was getting a rest. I wondered what the procedure was, but I adopted a wait-and-see attitude, and I found out soon enough. The first to approach Sophie-Anne was the big blond vampire who'd served as a judge earlier. "Dear madam," he said, kissing her hand. "I am charmed to see you, as always, and devastated by the destruction of your beautiful city."

"A small portion of my beautiful city," Sophie-Anne said with the sweetest of smiles.

"I am in despair at the thought of the straits you must be in," he continued after a brief pause to register her correction. "You, the ruler of such a profitable and prestigious kingdom . . . now brought so low. I hope to be able to assist you in my humble fashion."

"And what form would that assistance take?" Sophie-Anne inquired.

After much palaver, it turned out that Mr. Flowery was willing to bring a gazillion board feet of lumber to New Orleans if Sophie-Anne would give him 2 percent of her next five years' revenue. His accountant was with him. I looked into his eyes with great curiosity. I stepped back, and Andre slithered to my side. I turned so that no one could read my lips.

"Quality of the lumber," I said as quietly as a hummingbird's wings.

That took forever to hammer out, and it was boring, boring, boring. Some of the wannabe providers didn't have humans with them, and I was no help with those; but most of them did. Sometimes the human had paid the vampire a substantial sum to "sponsor" him, so he could just be in the hall and pitch his woo in a one-on-one setting. By the time vendor number eight simpered to a stop in front of the queen,

I was unable to suppress my yawns. I'd noticed Bill was doing a landmark business selling copies of his vampire database. For a reserved kind of guy, he did a good job of explaining and promoting his product, considering some of the vampires were very mistrustful of computers. If I heard about the "Yearly Update Package" one more time, I was gonna puke. There were lots of humans clustering around Bill, because they were more computer savvy than the vamps as a whole. While they were absorbed, I tried to get a scan in here and there, but they were just thinking megahertz and RAM and hard drives—stuff like that.

I didn't see Quinn. Since he was a wereanimal, I figured he'd be completely over his wound of the night before. I could only take his absence as a signal. I was heart-heavy and weary.

The queen invited Dahlia, the little, pretty vampire who'd been so direct in her judgment, up to her suite for a drink. Dahlia accepted regally, and our whole party moved up to the suite. Christian Baruch tagged along; he'd been hovering around Sophie-Anne all evening.

His courtship of Sophie-Anne was heavy-handed, to say the least. I thought again of the boy toy I'd watched the previous evening, tickling the back of his ladylove in imitation of a spider, because he knew she was frightened of them, and how he'd gotten her to snuggle closer to him. I felt a lightbulb come on over my head and wondered if it was visible to anyone else.

My opinion of the hotelier plummeted. If he thought such a strategy would work on Sophie-Anne, he had a lot of thinking to do.

I didn't see Jake Purifoy anywhere around, and I wondered what Andre had him doing. Something innocuous probably, like checking to make sure all the cars were gassed up. He wasn't really trusted to handle anything more taxing, at least not yet. Jake's youth and his Were heritage counted against him, and he'd have to bust his tail to earn points. But Jake didn't have that fire in him. He was looking to the past, to his life as a Were. He had a backlog of bitterness.

Sophie's suite had been cleaned; all the vampire suites had to be cleaned at night, of course, while the vamps were out of them. Christian Baruch started telling us about the extra help he'd had to take on to cope with the summit crowd and how nervous some of them were about cleaning rooms occupied by vampires. I could tell Sophie-Anne was not impressed by Baruch's assumption of superiority. He was so much younger than her, he must seem like a swaggering teenager to the centuries-old queen.

Jake came in just then, and after paying his respects to the queen and meeting Dahlia, he came to sit by me. I was slumping in an uncomfortable straight chair, and he pulled a matching one over.

"What's up, Jake?"

"Not much. I've been getting the queen and Andre tickets to a show for tomorrow night. It's an all-vampire production of *Hello, Dolly!*"

I tried to imagine that, found I couldn't. "What are you going to be doing? It's marked as free time on the schedule."

"I don't know," he said, a curiously remote tone in his voice. "My life has changed so much I just can't predict what will happen. Are you going out tomorrow in the day, Sookie? Shopping, maybe? There are some wonderful stores on Widewater Drive. That's down by the lake."

Even I had heard of Widewater Drive, and I said, "I guess it's possible. I'm not much of a shopper."

"You really should go. There're some great shoe stores, and a big Macy's—you'd love Macy's. Make a day of it. Get away from this place while you can."

"I'll sure think about it," I said, a little puzzled. "Um, have you seen Quinn today?"

"Glimpsed him. And I talked to Frannie for a minute. They've been busy getting props ready for the closing ceremonies."

"Oh," I said. Right. Sure. That took loads of time.

"Call him, ask him to take you out tomorrow," Jake said.

I tried to picture me asking Quinn to take me shopping. Well, it wasn't totally out of the question, but it wasn't likely, either. I shrugged. "Maybe I'll get out some."

He looked pleased.

"Sookie, you can go," Andre said. I was so tired I hadn't even noticed him glide up.

"Okay. Good night, you two," I said, and stood to stretch. I noticed the blue suitcase was still where I'd dropped it two nights ago. "Oh, Jake, you need to take that suitcase back down to the basement. They called me and told me to bring it up here, but no one's claimed it."

"I'll ask around," he said vaguely, and took off for his own room. Andre's attention had already returned to the queen, who was laughing at the description of some wedding Dahlia had attended.

"Andre," I said in a very low voice, "I gotta tell you, I think Mr. Baruch had something to do with that bomb outside the queen's door."

Andre looked as if someone had stuck a nail up his fundament. "What?"

"I'm thinking that he wanted Sophie-Anne scared," I said. "I'm thinking that he thought she'd be vulnerable and need a strong male protector if she felt threatened."

Andre was not Mr. Expressive, but I saw incredulity, disgust, and belief cross his face in quick order.

"And I'm also thinking maybe he told Henrik Feith that

Sophie-Anne was going to kill him. Because he's the hotel owner, right? And he'd have a key to get into the queen's room, where we thought Henrik was safe, right? So Henrik would continue the queen's trial, because he'd been persuaded she would do him in. Again, Christian Baruch would be there, to be her big savior. Maybe he had Henrik killed, after he'd set him up, so he could do a tah-*dah* reveal and dazzle Sophie-Anne with his wonderful care of her."

Andre had the strangest expression on his face, as if he was having trouble following me. "Is there proof?" he asked.

"Not a smidge. But when I talked to Mr. Donati in the lobby this morning, he hinted that there was a security tape I might want to watch."

"Go see," Andre said.

"If I go ask for it, he'll get fired. You need to get the queen to ask Mr. Baruch point-blank if she can see the security tape for the lobby outside during the time the bomb was planted. Gum on the camera or not, that tape will show something."

"Leave first, so he won't connect you to this." In fact, the hotelier had been absorbed in the queen and her conversation, or his vampire hearing would have tipped him off that we were talking about him.

Though I was exhausted, I had the gratifying feeling that I was earning the money they were paying me for this trip. And it was a load off my mind to feel that the Dr Pepper thing was solved. Christian Baruch would not be doing any more bomb planting now that the queen was on to him. The threat the splinter group of the Fellowship posed . . . well, I'd only heard of that from hearsay, and I didn't have any evidence of what form it would take. Despite the death of the woman at the archery place, I felt more relaxed than I had since I'd walked into the Pyramid of Gizeh, because

I was inclined to attribute the killer archer to Baruch, too. Maybe when he saw that Henrik would actually take Arkansas from the queen, he'd gotten greedy and had the assassin take out Henrik, so the queen would get everything. There was something confusing and wrong about that scenario, but I was too tired to think it through, and I was content to let the whole tangled web lie until I was rested.

I crossed the little lobby to the elevator and pressed the button. When the doors dinged open, Bill stepped out, his hands full of order forms.

"You did well this evening," I said, too tired to hate him. I nodded at the forms.

"Yes, we'll all make a lot of money from this," he said, but he didn't sound particularly excited.

I waited for him to step out of my way, but he didn't do that, either.

"I would give it all away if I could erase what happened between us," he said. "Not the times we spent loving each other, but . . ."

"The times you spent lying to me? The times you pretended you could hardly wait to date me when it turns out you were under order to? Those times?"

"Yes," he said, and his deep brown eyes didn't waver. "Those times."

"You hurt me too much. That's not ever gonna happen."

"Do you love any man? Quinn? Eric? That moron JB?"

"You don't have the right to ask me that," I said. "You don't have any rights at all where I'm concerned."

JB? Where'd that come from? I'd always been fond of the guy, and he was lovely, but his conversation was about as stimulating as a stump's. I was shaking my head as I rode down in the elevator to the human floor.

Carla was out, as usual, and since it was five in the morning the chances seemed good that she'd stay out. I put on my pink pajamas and put my slippers beside the bed so I wouldn't have to grope around for them in the darkened room in case Carla came in before I awoke.

17

MY EYES SNAPPED OPEN LIKE SHADES THAT WERE wound too tight.

Wake up, wake up, wake up! Sookie, something's wrong.

Barry, where are you?

Standing at the elevators on the human floor.

I'm coming. I pulled on last night's outfit, but without the heels. Instead, I slid my feet into my rubber-soled slippers. I grabbed the slim wallet that held my room key, driver's license, and credit card, and stuffed it in one pocket, jammed my cell phone into the other, and hurried out of the room. The door slammed behind me with an ominous thud. The hotel felt empty and silent, but my clock had read 9:50.

I had to run down a long corridor and turn right to get to the elevators. I didn't meet a soul. A moment's thought told me that was not so strange. Most humans on the floor would still be asleep, because they kept vampire hours. But there weren't even any hotel employees cleaning the halls.

All the little tracks of disquiet that had crawled through my brain, like slug tracks on your back doorstep, had coalesced into a huge throbbing mass of uneasiness.

I felt like I was on the *Titanic,* and I'd just heard the hull scrape against the iceberg.

I finally spotted someone, lying on the floor. I'd been woken so suddenly and sharply that everything I did had a dreamlike quality to it, so finding a body in the hall was not such a jolt.

I let out a cry, and Barry came bounding around the corner. He crouched down with me. I rolled over the body. It was Jake Purifoy, and he couldn't be roused.

Why isn't he in his room? What was he doing out so late? Even Barry's mental voice sounded panicked.

Look, Barry, he's lying sort of pointing toward my room. Do you think he was coming to see me?

Yes, and he didn't make it.

What could have been so important that Jake wasn't prepared for his day's sleep? I stood up, thinking furiously. I'd never, ever heard of a vampire who didn't know instinctively that the dawn was coming. I thought of the conversations I'd had with Jake, and the two men I'd seen leaving his room.

"You *bastard,*" I hissed through my teeth, and I kicked him as hard as I could.

"Jesus, Sookie!" Barry grabbed my arm, horrified. But then he got the picture from my brain.

"We need to find Mr. Cataliades and Diantha," I said. "They can get up; they're not vamps."

"I'll get Cecile. She's human, my roommate," Barry said, and we both went off in different directions, leaving Jake to lie where he was. It was all we could do.

We were back together in five minutes. It had been surprisingly easy to raise Mr. Cataliades, and Diantha had been sharing his room. Cecile proved to be a young woman with a no-nonsense haircut and a competent way about her, and I wasn't surprised when Barry introduced her as the king's new executive assistant.

I'd been a fool to discount, even for a minute, the warning that Clovache had passed along. I was so angry at myself I could hardly stand to be inside my own skin. But I had to shove that aside and we had to act now.

"Listen to what I think," I said. I'd been putting things together in my head. "Some of the waiters have been avoiding Barry and me over the past couple of days, as soon as they found out what we were."

Barry nodded. He'd noticed, too. He looked oddly guilty, but that had to wait.

"They know what we are. They didn't want us to know what they're about to do, I'm assuming. So I'm also assuming it must be something really, really bad. And Jake Purifoy was in on it."

Mr. Cataliades had been looking faintly bored, but now he began to look seriously alarmed. Diantha's big eyes went from face to face.

"What shall we do?" Cecile asked, which earned her high marks in my book.

"It's the extra coffins," I said. "And the blue suitcase in the queen's suite. Barry, you were asked to bring up a suitcase, too, right? And it didn't belong to anyone?"

Barry said, "Right. It's still sitting in the foyer of the king's suite, since everyone passes through there. We thought someone would claim it. I was going to take it back to the luggage department today."

I said, "The one I went down for is sitting in the living room of the queen's suite. I think the guy who was in on it was Joe, the manager down in the luggage and delivery area.

He's the one who called me down to get the suitcase. No one else seemed to know anything about it."

"The suitcases will blow up?" Diantha said in her shrill voice. "The unclaimed coffins in the basement, too? If the basement goes, the building will collapse!" I'd never heard Diantha sound so human.

"We have to wake them up," I said. "We have to get them out."

"The building's going to blow," said Barry, trying to process the idea.

"The vamps won't wake up." Cecile the practical. "They can't."

"Quinn!" I said. I was thinking of so many things at once that I was standing rooted in place. Fishing my phone from my pocket, I punched his number on speed dial and heard his mumble at the other end. "Get out," I said. "Quinn, get your sister and get out. There's going to be an explosion." I only waited to hear him sound more alert before I shut the phone.

"We have to save ourselves, too," Barry was saying.

Brilliantly, Cecile ran down the hall to a red fixture and flipped the fire alarm. The clamor almost split our eardrums, but the effect was wonderful on the sleeping humans on this floor. Within seconds, they began to come out of the rooms.

"Take the stairs," Cecile directed them in a bellow, and obediently, they did. I was glad to see Carla's dark head among them. But I didn't see Quinn, and he was always easy to spot.

"The queen is high up," said Mr. Cataliades.

"Can those glass panels be busted from the inside?" I asked.

"They did it on *Fear Factor*," Barry said.

"We could try sliding the coffins down."

"They'd break on impact," Cecile said.

"But the vamps would survive the explosion," I pointed out.

"To be burned up by the sun," Mr. Cataliades said. "Diantha and I will go up and try to get out the queen's party, wrapped up in blankets. We'll take them . . ." He looked at me desperately.

"Ambulances! Call 911 now! They can figure out where to take them!"

Diantha called 911 and was incoherent and desperate enough to get ambulances started to an explosion that had not happened yet. "The building's on fire," she said, which was like a future truth.

"Go," I told Mr. Cataliades, actually shoving the demon, and off he sped to the queen's suite.

"Go try to get your party out," I said to Barry, and he and Cecile ran for the elevator, though at any minute it might be unworkable.

I'd done everything about getting humans out that I could. Cataliades and Diantha could take care of the queen and Andre. Eric and Pam! I knew where Eric's room was, thank God. I took the stairs. As I ran up, I met a party coming down: the two Britlingens, both with large packs on their backs, carrying a wrapped bundle. Clovache had the feet, Batanya the head. I had no doubt that the bundle was the King of Kentucky, and that they were doing their duty. They both nodded as I hugged the wall to let them by. If they weren't as calm as if they were out for a stroll, they were close to it.

"You set off the fire alarm?" Batanya said. "Whatever the Fellowship is doing, it's today?"

"Yes," I said.

"Thanks. We're getting out now, and you should, too," Clovache said.

"We'll go back to our place after we deposit him," Batanya said. "Good-bye."

"Good luck," I told them stupidly, and then I was running

upstairs as if I'd trained for this. As a result, I was huffing like a bellows when I flung open the door to the ninth floor. I saw a lone maid pushing a cart down a long corridor. I ran up to her, frightening her even more than the fire alarm already had.

"Give me your master key," I said.

"No!" She was middle-aged and Hispanic, and she wasn't about to give in to such a crazy demand. "I'll get fired."

"Then open this door"—I pointed to Eric's—"and get out of here." I'm sure I looked like a desperate woman, and I was. "This building is going to blow up any minute."

She flung the key at me and made tracks down the hallway to the elevators. Dammit.

And then the explosions began. There was a deep, resounding quiver and a boom from way below my feet, as if some gargantuan sea creature were making its way to the surface. I staggered over to Eric's room, thrusting the plastic key into the slot and shoving open the door in a moment of utter silence. The room was in complete darkness.

"Eric, Pam!" I yelled. I fumbled for a light switch in the pitch-black room, felt the building sway. At least one of the upper charges had gone off. Oh, shit! Oh, shit! But the light came on, and I saw that Eric and Pam had gotten in the beds, not the coffins.

"Wake up!" I said, shaking Pam since she was closest. She didn't stir at all. It was exactly like shaking a doll stuffed with sawdust. "Eric!" I screamed right in his ear.

This got a bit of a reaction; he was much older than Pam. His eyes opened a slit and tried to focus. "What?" he said.

"You have to get up! You have to! You have to go out!"

"Daytime," he whispered. He began to flop over on his side.

I slapped him harder than I've ever hit anyone in my life. I screamed, "Get up!" until my voice would hardly work.

Finally Eric stirred and managed to sit up. He was wearing black silk pajama bottoms, thank God, and I spied the ceremonial black cloak tossed over his coffin. He hadn't returned it to Quinn, which was huge luck. I arranged it over him and fastened it at the neck. I pulled the hood over his face. "Cover your head!" I yelled, and I heard a burst of noise above my head: shattering glass, followed by shrieks.

Eric would drop back to sleep if I didn't keep him awake. At least he was trying. I remembered that Bill had managed to stagger, under dire circumstances, at least for a few minutes. But Pam, though roughly the same age as Bill, simply could not be roused. I even pulled her long pale hair.

"You have to help me get Pam out," I said finally, despairing. "Eric, you just have to." There was another roar and a lurch in the floor. I screamed, and Eric's eyes went wide. He staggered to his feet. As if we'd shared thoughts like Barry and I could, we both shoved his coffin off its trestle and onto the carpet. Then we slid it over to the opaque slanting glass panel forming the side of the building.

Everything around us trembled and shook. Eric's eyes were a little wider now, and he was concentrating so heavily on keeping himself moving that his strength was pulling on mine.

"Pam," I said, trying to push him into more action. I opened the coffin, after some desperate fumbling. Eric went over to his sleeping child, walking like his feet were sticking to the floor with each step. He took Pam's shoulders and I took her feet, and we picked her up, blanket and all. The floor shook again, more violently this time, and we lurched over to the coffin and tossed Pam into it. I shut the lid and latched it, though a corner of Pam's nightgown was sticking out.

I thought about Bill, and Rasul flashed across my mind, but there was nothing I could do, and there wasn't any time left. "We have to break the glass!" I shrieked at Eric. He nodded very slowly. We knelt to brace ourselves against the end of the coffin and we pushed as hard as we could till it slammed into the glass, which cracked into about a thousand pieces. They hung together, amazingly—the miracle of safety glass. I could have screamed from frustration. We needed a *hole*, not a curtain of glass. Crouching lower, digging our toes into the carpet, trying to ignore the rumbling noises in the building below us, Eric and I shoved with all our strength.

Finally! We punched the coffin all the way through. The window let go of its frame and cascaded down the side of the building.

And Eric saw sunlight for the first time in a thousand years. He screamed, a terrible, gut-wrenching noise. But in the next instant, he pulled the cloak tight around him. He grabbed me and hopped astride the coffin, and we pushed off with our feet. For just a fraction of a minute, we hung in the balance, and then we tilted forward. In the most awful moment of my life, we went out the window and began tobogganing down the building on the coffin. We would crash unless—

Suddenly we were off the coffin and kind of staggering through the air, Eric holding me to him with dogged persistence.

I exhaled with profound relief. Of course, Eric could fly.

In his light-stunned stupor, he couldn't fly very well. This was not the smooth progress I'd experienced before; we had more of a zigzag, bobbing descent.

But it was better than a free fall.

Eric could delay our descent enough to keep me from being dashed to my death on the street outside the hotel. However, the coffin with Pam inside had a bad landing, and Pam came catapulting out of the remains of the wood and into the sunlight where she lay motionless. Without making a sound, she began to burn. Eric landed on top of her and used the blanket to cover both of them. One of Pam's feet was exposed, and the flesh was smoking. I covered it up.

I also heard the sound of sirens. I flagged down the first ambulance I saw, and the medics leaped out.

I pointed to the blanketed heap. "Two vampires—get them out of the sun!" I said.

The pair of EMTs, both young women, exchanged an incredulous glance. "What do we do with them?" asked the dark one.

"You take them to a nice basement somewhere, one without any windows, and you tell the owners to keep that basement open, because there are gonna be more."

High up, a smaller explosion blew out one of the suites. A suitcase bomb, I thought, wondering how many Joe had talked us into carrying up into the rooms. A fine shower of glass sparkled in the sun as we looked up, but darker things were following the glass out of the window, and the EMTs began to move like the trained team they were. They didn't panic, but they definitely moved with haste, and they were already debating which building close at hand had a large basement.

"We'll tell everyone," said the dark woman. Pam was now in the ambulance and Eric halfway there. His face was bright red and steam was rising from his lips. Oh, my God. "What you going to do?"

"I have to go back in there," I said.

"Fool," she said, and then threw herself in the ambulance, which took off.

There was more glass raining down, and part of the bottom floor appeared to be collapsing. That would be due to some of the larger explosive-packed coffin bombs in the shipping and receiving area. Another explosion came from about the sixth floor, but on the other side of the pyramid.

My senses were so dulled by the sound and the sight that I wasn't surprised when I saw a blue suitcase flying through the air. Mr. Cataliades had succeeded in breaking the queen's window. Suddenly I realized the suitcase was intact, had not exploded, and was hurtling straight at me.

I began to run, flashing back to my softball days when I had sprinted from third to home and had to slide in. I aimed for the park across the street, where traffic had come to a stop because of the emergency vehicles: cop cars, ambulances, fire engines. There was a cop just ahead of me who was facing away, pointing something out to another cop. "Down!" I yelled. "Bomb!" and she swung around to face me and I tackled her, taking her down to the ground with me. Something hit me in the middle of the back, whoosh, and the air was shoved out of my lungs. We lay there for a long minute, until I pushed myself off of her and climbed unsteadily to my feet. It was wonderful to inhale, though the air was acrid with flames and dust. She might have said something to me, but I couldn't hear her.

I turned around to face the Pyramid of Gizeh.

Parts of the structure were crumbling, folding in and down, all the glass and concrete and steel and wood separating from the whole into discrete parts, while most of the walls that had created the spaces—of rooms and bathrooms and halls—collapsed. That collapse trapped many of the bodies that had occupied these arbitrarily divided areas. They were all one now: the structure, its parts, its inhabitants.

Here and there were still bits that had held together. The human floor, the mezzanine, and the lobby level were partially intact, though the area around the registration desk was destroyed.

I saw a shape I recognized, a coffin. The lid had popped clean off with the impact of its fall. As the sun hit the creature inside, it let out a wail, and I rushed over. There was a hunk of drywall by it, and I hauled that over the coffin. There was silence as soon as the sun was blocked from touching the vampire inside.

"Help!" I yelled. "Help!"

A few policemen moved toward me.

"There are people and vamps still alive," I said. "The vamps have to be covered."

"People first," said one beefy veteran.

"Sure," I agreed automatically, though even as I said it, I thought, *Vampires didn't set these bombs.* "But if you can cover the vamps, they can last until ambulances can take them to a safe place."

There was a chunk of hotel still standing, a bit of the south part. Looking up, I saw Mr. Cataliades standing at an empty frame where the glass had fallen away. Somehow, he had worked his way down to the human floor. He was holding a bundle wrapped in a bedspread, clutching it to his chest.

"Look!" I called, to get a fireman's attention. "Look!"

They leaped into action at seeing a live person to rescue. They were far more enthusiastic about that than about rescuing vamps who were possibly smoldering to death in the sunlight and could easily be saved by being covered. I tried to blame them, but I couldn't.

For the first time I noticed that there was a crowd of regular people who had stopped their cars and gotten out to help—or gawk. There were also people who were screaming, "Let them burn!"

I watched the firemen go up in a bucket to fetch the demon and his burden, and then I turned back to working my way through the rubble.

After a time, I was flagging. The screams of the human survivors, the smoke, the sunlight muted by the huge cloud of dust, the noise of the groaning structure settling, the hectic noise of the rescue workers and the machinery that was arriving and being employed . . . I was overwhelmed.

By that time, since I'd stolen one of the yellow jackets and one of the hard hats all the rescuers were wearing, I'd gotten close enough to find two vampires, one of whom I knew, in the ruins of the check-in area, heavily overlaid by debris from the floors above. A big piece of wood survived to identify the reception desk. One of the vampires was very burned, and I had no idea if he'd survive it or not. The other vamp had hidden beneath the largest piece of wood, and only his feet and hands had been singed and blackened. Once I yelled for help, the vamps were covered with blankets. "We got a building two blocks away; we're using it for the vampire repository," said the dark-skinned ambulance driver who took the more seriously injured one, and I realized it was the same woman who'd taken Eric and Pam.

In addition to the vampires, I uncovered a barely alive Todd Donati. I spent a few moments with him until a stretcher got there. And I found, near to him, a dead maid. She'd been crushed.

I had a smell in my nose that just wouldn't go away, and I hated it. It was coating my lungs inside, I thought, and I'd spend the rest of my life breathing it in and breathing it out. The odor was composed of burning building materials, scorched bodies, and disintegrating vampires. It was the smell of hatred.

I saw some things so awful I couldn't even think about them then.

Suddenly, I didn't feel I could search anymore. I had to sit down. I was drawn to a pile created by the chance arrangement of a large pipe and some drywall. I perched on it and wept. Then the whole pile shifted sideways, and I landed on the ground, still weeping.

I looked into the opening revealed by the shifted debris.

Bill was crouched inside, half his face burned away. He was wearing the clothes I'd last seen him in the night before. I arched myself over him to keep the sun off, and he said, "Thanks," through cracked and bloody lips. He kept slipping in and out of his comatose daytime sleep.

"Jesus God," I said. "Come help!" I called, and saw two men start toward me with a blanket.

"I knew you'd find me," Bill said, or did I imagine that?

I stayed hunched in the awkward position. There just wasn't anything near enough to grab that would cover as much of him as I did. The smell was making me gag, but I stayed. He'd lasted this long only because he'd been covered by accident.

Though one fireman threw up, they covered him and took him away.

Then I saw another yellow-jacketed figure tear off across the debris field toward the ambulances as fast as anyone could move without breaking a leg. I got the impression of a live brain, and I recognized it at once. I scrambled over piles of rubble, following the signature of the brain of the man I wanted most to find. Quinn and Frannie lay half-buried under a pile of loose rubble. Frannie was unconscious, and she'd been bleeding from the head, but it had dried. Quinn was dazed but coming to full awareness. I could see that fresh water had cut a path in the dust on his face, and I realized the man who'd just dashed away had given Quinn some water to drink and was returning with stretchers for the two.

He tried to smile at me. I fell to my knees beside him. "We might have to change our plans, babe," he said. "I may have to take care of Frannie for a week or two. Our mom's not exactly Florence Nightingale."

I tried not to cry, but it was like, once turned to "on," I

couldn't tell my tear ducts to switch off. I wasn't sobbing anymore, but I was trickling steadily. Stupid. "You do what you have to do," I said. "You call me when you can. Okay?" I hated people who said "Okay?" all the time, like they were getting permission, but I couldn't help that, either. "You're alive; that's all that matters."

"Thanks to you," he said. "If you hadn't called, we'd be dead. Even the fire alarm might not have gotten us out of the room in time."

I heard a groan from a few feet away, a breath on the air. Quinn heard it, too. I crawled away from him, pushing aside a large chunk of toilet and sink. There, covered with dust and debris, under several large bits of drywall, lay Andre, completely out of it. A quick glance told me he had several serious injuries. But none of them was bleeding. He would heal them all. Dammit.

"It's Andre," I told Quinn. "Hurt, but alive." If my voice was grim, I felt grim. There was a nice, long wood splinter right by his leg, and I was so tempted. Andre was a threat to my freedom of will, to everything I enjoyed about my life. But I'd seen so much death that day already.

I crouched there beside him, hating him, but after all . . . I knew him. That should have made it easier, but it didn't.

I duckwalked out of the little alcove where he lay, scuttled back to Quinn.

"Those guys are coming back to get us," he told me, sounding stronger every minute. "You can leave now."

"You want me to leave?"

His eyes were telling me something. I wasn't reading it.

"Okay," I said hesitantly. "I'll go."

"I've got help coming," he said gently. "You could be finding someone else."

"All right," I said, not knowing how to take this, and pushed to my feet. I'd gone maybe two yards when I heard him begin to move. But after a moment of stillness, I kept walking.

I returned to a big van that had been brought in and parked close to the rescue command center. This yellow jacket had been a magic pass, but it might run out any minute. Someone would notice I was wearing bedroom slippers, and they were ripping up, since they'd hardly been intended for ruin-scrambling. A woman handed me a bottle of water from the van, and I opened it with unsteady hands. I drank and drank, and poured the rest of the water over my face and hands. Despite the chill in the air, it felt wonderful.

By then, two (or four, or six) hours must have passed since the first explosion. There were now scores of rescuers there who had equipment, machinery, blankets. I was casting around for someone who looked authoritative, intending to find out where the other human survivors had been taken, when a voice spoke in my head.

Sookie?

Barry!

What kind of shape are you in?

Pretty rocky, but not much hurt. You?

Same. Cecile died.

I'm so sorry. I couldn't think of anything else to say.

I've thought of something we can do.

What? I probably didn't sound very interested.

We can find living people. We'll be better, together.

That's what I've been doing, I told him. *But you're right, together we'll be stronger.* At the same time, I was so tired that something inside of me cringed at the thought of making further effort. *Of course we can,* I said.

If this pile of debris had been as horrifyingly huge as the Twin Towers, we couldn't have done it. But this site was smaller and more contained, and if we could get anyone to believe us, we had a chance.

I found Barry close to the command center, and I took his grimy hand. He was younger than me, but now he didn't look it, and I didn't think he'd ever act it again. When I scanned the line of bodies on the grass of the little park, I saw Cecile, and I saw what might have been the maid I'd accosted in the hallway. There were a few flaking, vaguely manlike shapes that were disintegrating vampires. I could have known any of them, but it was impossible to tell.

Any humiliation would be a small thing to pay if we could save someone. So Barry and I prepared to be humiliated and mocked.

At first, it was hard to get anyone to listen. The professionals kept referring us to the casualty center or to one of the ambulances parked nearby ready to take survivors to one of Rhodes's hospitals.

Finally, I was face-to-face with a thin, gray-haired man who listened to me without any expression on his face at all.

"I never thought I'd be rescuing vampires, either," he said, as though that explained his decision, and maybe it did. "So, take these two men with you, and show 'em what you can do. You have fifteen minutes of these men's valuable time. If you waste it, you might be killing someone."

Barry had had the idea, but now he seemed to want me to speak for us. His face was blackened with smears of soot. We had a silent conference about the best way to go about our task, and at the end of it, I turned to the firemen and said, "Put us up in one of those bucket things."

For a wonder, they did, without further argument. We were lifted out over the debris, and yes, we knew it was dangerous, and yes, we were prepared to take the consequences. Still holding hands, Barry and I shut our eyes and *searched*, flinging our minds open and outward.

"Move us left," I said, and the fireman in the bucket with us gestured to the man in the cab of the machine. "Watch me," I said, and he looked back. "Stop," I said, and the bucket stopped. We searched again. "Directly below," I said. "Right below here. It's a woman named something Santiago."

After a few minutes, a roar went up. They'd found her alive.

We were popular after that, and there were no more questions about how we did it, as long as we kept it up. Rescue people are all about rescuing. They were bringing dogs, and they were inserting microphones, but Barry and I were quicker and more articulate than the dogs, and more precise than the microphones. We found four more live people, and we found a man who died before they could get to him, a waiter named Art who loved his wife and suffered terribly right up until the end. Art was especially heartbreaking, because they were trying like hell to dig the guy out, and I had to tell them it was no good. Of course, they didn't take my word for it; they kept excavating, but he had passed. By that time, the searchers were really excited about our ability and wanted us to work through the night, but Barry was failing and I wasn't much better. Worse, dark was closing in.

"The vampires'll be rising," I reminded the fire chief. He nodded and looked at me for further explanation. "They'll be hurt bad," I said. He still didn't get it. "They'll need blood instantly, and they won't have any control. I wouldn't send any rescue workers out on the debris alone," I said, and his face went blank with thought.

"You don't think they're all dead? Can't you find them?"

"Well, actually, no. We can't find vamps. Humans, yes. But not undead. Their brains don't give off any, ah, waves. We've got to go now. Where are the survivors?"

"They're all in the Thorne Building, right down there," he said, pointing. "In the basement." We turned to walk away. By this time, Barry had slung his arm around my shoulders, and not because he was feeling affectionate. He needed the support.

"Let me get your names and addresses, so the mayor can thank you," the gray-haired man said, holding a pen and clipboard at the ready.

No! Barry said, and my mouth snapped shut.

I shook my head. "We're going to pass on that," I said. I'd had a quick look in his head, and he was greedy for more of our help. Suddenly I understood why Barry had stopped me so abruptly, though my fellow telepath was so tired he couldn't tell me himself. My refusal didn't go over big.

"You'll work for vamps, but you don't want to stand and be counted as someone who helped on this terrible day?"

"Yes," I answered. "That's just about right."

He wasn't happy with me, and I thought for a minute he was going to force the issue: grab my wallet out of my pants, send me to jail, or something. But he reluctantly nodded his head and jerked it in the direction of the Thorne Building.

Someone will try to find out, Barry said. *Someone will want to use us.*

I sighed, and I hardly had the energy to take in more air. I nodded. *Yeah, someone will. If we go to the shelter, someone will be watching for us there, and they'll ask for our names from someone who recognizes us, and after that, it's only a matter of time.*

I couldn't think of a way to dodge going in there. We had to have help, we had to find our parties and discover how and when we could leave the city, and we had to find out who had lived and who hadn't.

I patted my back pocket, and to my amazement, my cell phone was still in it and still had bars. I called Mr. Cataliades. If anyone besides me had come out of the Pyramid of Gizeh with a cell phone, the lawyer would be the one.

"Yes," he said cautiously. "Miss St—"

"Shhh," I said. "Don't say my name out loud." It was sheer paranoia talking.

"Very well."

"We helped them out down here, and now they really want to get to know us better," I said, feeling very clever for talking so guardedly. I was very tired. "Barry and I are outside the building where you are. We need to stay somewhere else. Too many people making lists in there, right?"

"That is a popular activity," he said.

"You and Diantha okay?"

"She has not been found. We were separated."

I didn't speak for a few seconds. "I'm so sorry. Who were you holding when I saw them rescue you?"

"The queen. She is here, though badly injured. We can't find Andre."

He paused, and because I couldn't help it, I said, "Who else?"

"Gervaise is dead. Eric, Pam, Bill . . . burned, but here. Cleo Babbitt is here. I haven't seen Rasul."

"Is Jake Purifoy there?"

"I haven't seen him, either."

"Because you might want to know he's at least partially responsible if you do see him. He was in on the Fellowship plot."

"Ah." Mr. Cataliades registered that. "Oh, yes, I certainly did want to know that. Johan Glassport will be especially interested, since he has several broken ribs and a broken collarbone. He's very, very angry." It said something about Johan Glassport's viciousness, that Mr. Cataliades thought him capable of exacting as much vengeance as a vampire would. "How did you come to know there was a plot at all, Miss Sookie?"

I told the lawyer the story Clovache had told me; I figured now that she and Batanya had gone back to wherever they came from, that would be okay.

"Hiring them proved to be worth the money for King Isaiah." Cataliades sounded thoughtful rather than envious. "Isaiah is here and completely uninjured."

"We need to go find somewhere to sleep. Can you tell Barry's king that he's with me?" I asked, knowing I needed to get off the phone and make a plan.

"He is too injured to care. He is not aware."

"All right. Just someone from the Texas party."

"I see Joseph Velasquez. Rachel is dead." Mr. Cataliades couldn't help himself; he had to tell me all the bad news.

"Cecile, Stan's assistant, is dead," I told him.

"Where are you going to go?" Cataliades asked.

"I don't know what to do," I said. I felt exhausted and hopeless, and I'd had too much bad news and gotten too battered to rally one more time.

"I will send a cab for you," Mr. Cataliades offered. "I can get a number from one of the nice volunteers. Tell the driver you are rescue workers and you need a ride to the nearest inexpensive hotel. Do you have a credit card?"

"Yeah, and my debit card," I said, blessing the impulse that had led me to stuff the little wallet in my pocket.

"No, wait, they'll track you very easily if you use it. Cash?"

I checked. Thanks largely to Barry, we had a hundred ninety dollars between us. I told Mr. Cataliades we could swing it.

"Then spend the night in a hotel, and tomorrow call me again," he said, sounding unutterably weary.

"Thanks for the plan."

"Thanks for your warning," the courtly demon said. "We would all be dead if you and the Bellboy hadn't wakened us."

I ditched the yellow jacket and the hard hat. Barry and I tottered along, more or less holding each other up. We found a concrete barricade to lean against, our arms around each other. I tried to tell Barry why we were doing this, but he didn't care. I was worried that at any minute some firefighter or cop from the scene would spot us and stop to find out what we were doing, where we were going, who we were. I was so relieved that I felt sick when I spied a cab cruising slowly, the driver peering out the window. Had to be for us. I waved my free arm frantically. I had never hailed a cab before in my life. It was just like the movies.

The cab driver, a wire-thin guy from Guyana, wasn't too excited about letting filthy creatures like us get into his cab, but he couldn't turn down people as pitiful as we were. The nearest "inexpensive" hotel was a mile back into the city, away from the water. If we'd had the energy, we could have walked it. At least the cab ride wasn't too pricey.

Even at the mid-range hotel, the desk clerks were less than thrilled with our appearance; but after all, it was a day for charity to people who were involved in the blast. We got a room at a price that would have made me gasp if I hadn't seen the room rates at the Pyramid. The room itself wasn't much, but we didn't need much. A maid knocked on the door right after we got in and said she'd like to wash our clothes for us, since we didn't have any more. She looked down when she said that, so she wouldn't embarrass me. Trying not to choke up at her kindness, I looked down at my shirt and slacks and agreed. I turned to Barry to find he was absolutely out cold. I maneuvered him into the bed. It was unpleasantly like handling one of the vampires, and I held my lips pressed together in a tight line the whole time I undressed his limp body. Then I shucked my own clothes, found a plastic bag in the closet to hold them, and handed the soiled clothes out to her. I got a washcloth and wiped off Barry's face and hands and feet, and then I covered him up.

I had to shower, and I thanked God for the complimentary shampoo and soap and cream rinse and skin lotion. I also thanked God for hot and cold running water, particularly hot. The kind maid had even handed me two toothbrushes and a little packet of toothpaste, and I scrubbed my mouth clean of the flavor of ashes. I washed my panties and bra in the sink and rolled them up in a towel before I hung them up to dry. I'd given the lady every stitch of Barry's clothes.

Finally, there was nothing else to do, and I crawled into the bed beside Barry. Now that I smelled so good, I noticed that he didn't, but that was just tough for me, right? I wouldn't have woken him for anything. I turned on my side away from him, thought about how frightening that long, empty corridor had been—isn't it funny that that was what I picked out as scary, after such a horrific day?

The hotel room was so very quiet after the tumult of the scene of the explosions, and the bed was so very comfortable, and I smelled so much better and hardly hurt at all.

I slept and didn't dream.

18

I KNOW THERE ARE MANY WORSE THINGS THAN WAKing up naked in a bed with someone you don't know very well. But when my eyes fluttered open the next day, I couldn't think of any, for five long minutes. I knew Barry was awake. You can tell when a brain pops into awareness. To my relief, he slipped out of the bed and into the bathroom without speaking, and I heard the drumming of the water in the shower stall soon after.

Our clean clothes were in a bag hanging on our inside doorknob, and there was a *USA Today*, too. After hastily donning my clothes, I spread the newspaper out on the small table while I brewed a pot of the free coffee. I also extended the bag with Barry's clothes in it into the bathroom and dropped it on the floor, waving it a little first to attract his attention.

I'd looked at the room service menu, and we didn't have enough cash to get anything on it. We had to reserve some of our funds for a cab, because I didn't know what our next move would be. Barry came out, looking as refreshed as I'd been last night. To my surprise, he kissed me on the cheek, and then sat opposite me with his own insulated cup that contained something that bore a faint relationship to brewed coffee.

"I don't remember much about last night," he said. "Fill me in on why we're here."

I did.

"That was good thinking on my part," he said. "I'm in awe of myself."

I laughed. He might be feeling a little male chagrin that he had wilted before I did, but at least he could make fun of himself.

"So, I guess we need to call your demon lawyer?"

I nodded. It was eleven by then, so I called.

He answered right away. "There are many ears here," he said without preamble. "And I understand these phones aren't too secure. Cell phones."

"All right."

"So I will come to you in a while, bringing some things you'll need. You are where?"

With a twinge of misgiving, since the demon was a guy people would notice, I told him the name of the hotel and our room number, and he told me to be patient. I'd been feeling fine until Mr. Cataliades said that, and all of a sudden I began to twitch inwardly. I felt like we were on the run now, when we in no way deserved to be. I'd read the newspaper, and the story about the Pyramid said the catastrophe was due to "a series of explosions" that Dan Brewer, head of the state terrorist task force, attributed to several bombs. The fire chief was less committal: "An investigation is underway." I should damn well hope so.

Barry said, "We could have sex while we wait."

"I liked you better unconscious," I said. I knew Barry was only trying not to think about stuff, but still.

"You undress me last night?" he said with a leer.

"Yeah, that was me, lucky me," I said. I smiled at him, surprising myself.

A knock at the door had us both staring at it like startled deer.

"Your demon guy," said Barry after a second of mental checking.

"Yep," I said, and got up to answer it.

Mr. Cataliades hadn't had the kindness of a maid, so he was still in the soiled clothes of the day before. But he managed to look dignified, anyway, and his hands and face were clean.

"Please, how is everyone?" I asked.

"Sophie-Anne has lost her legs, and I don't know if they'll come back," he said.

"Oh, geez," I said, wincing.

"Sigebert fought free of the debris after dark," he continued. "He'd hidden in a safe pocket in the parking garage, where he landed after the explosions. I suspect he found someone to feed off, because he was healthier than he ought to have been. But if that's the case, he shoved the body into one of the fires, because we would have heard if a drained body had been found."

I hoped the donor had been one of the Fellowship guys.

"Your king," Mr. Cataliades said to Barry, "is so injured it may take him a decade to recover. Until the situation is clear, Joseph leads, though he'll be challenged soon. The king's child Rachel is dead; perhaps Sookie told you?"

"Sorry," I said. "I just had too much bad news to finish getting through it all."

"And Sookie has told me the human Cecile perished."

"What about Diantha?" I asked, hesitating to do so. It had to be significant that Mr.Cataliades hadn't mentioned his niece.

"Missing," he said briefly "And yet that piece of filth, Glassport, has only bruises."

"I'm sorry for both things," I said.

Barry seemed numb. All traces of his flippant mood had vanished. He looked smaller, sitting on the edge of the bed. The cocky sharp dresser I'd met in the lobby of the Pyramid had gone underground, at least for a while.

"I told you about Gervaise," Mr. Cataliades said. "I identified his woman's body this morning. What was her name?"

"Carla. I can't remember her last name. It'll come to me."

"The first name will probably be enough for them to identify her. One of the corpses in hotel uniform had a computer list in his pocket."

"They weren't all in on it," I said with some certainty.

"No, of course not," Barry said. "Only a few."

We looked at him.

"How do you know?" I asked.

"I overheard them."

"When?"

"The night before."

I bit the inside of my mouth, hard.

"What did you hear?" Mr. Cataliades asked in a level voice.

"I was with Stan in the, you know, the buy-and-sell thing. I had noticed the waiters and so on were dodging me, and then I watched to see if they were avoiding Sookie as well. So I thought, 'They know what you are, Barry, and there's something they don't want you to know. You better check it out.' I found a good place to sort of skulk behind some of those fake palm trees, close by the service door, and I could get a reading on what they were thinking inside. They didn't spell it out or anything, okay?" He had gotten an accurate reading on our thoughts, too. "It was just, like, 'Okay, we're gonna get those vamps, damn them, and if we take some of their human slaves, well, that's just too bad, we'll live with it. Damned by association.' "

I could only sit there and look at him.

"No, I didn't know when or what they were going to do! I went to bed finally kind of worrying about them, what the plan was, and when I couldn't settle into a good sleep, I finally quit trying and called you. And we tried to get everyone out," he said, and began crying.

I sat beside him and put my arm around him. I didn't know what to say. Of course, he could tell what I was thinking.

"Yes, I wish I'd said something before I did," he said in a choked voice. "Yes, I did the wrong thing. But I thought if I spoke up before I knew something for sure, the vamps would fall on them and drain them. Or they'd want me to point out who knew and who didn't. And I couldn't do that."

There was a long silence.

"Mr. Cataliades, have you seen Quinn?" I asked to break the silence.

"He's at the human hospital. He couldn't stop them from taking him."

"I have to go see him."

"How serious is your fear that the authorities will try to coerce you into doing their bidding?"

Barry raised his head and looked at me. "Pretty serious," we said simultaneously.

"It's the first time I've ever shown anyone, aside from local people, what I can do," I said.

"Me, too." Barry wiped his eyes with the back of his hand. "You should have seen that guy's face when he finally believed that we could find people. He thought we were psychics or something, and he couldn't understand that what we were doing was registering a live brain signature. Nothing mystical about it."

"He was all over the idea once he believed us," I said. "You could hear in his head that he was thinking of the hundred different ways we could be of use to rescue operations, to the government at conferences, police interrogations."

Mr. Cataliades looked at us. I couldn't pick out all his snarly demon thoughts, but he was having a lot of them.

"We'd lose control over our lives," Barry said. "I like my life."

"I guess I could be saving a lot of people," I said. I'd just never thought about it before. I'd never been faced with a situation like the one we'd faced the previous day. I hoped I never was again. How likely was it I would ever be onsite again at a disaster? Was I obligated to give up a job I liked, among people I cared about, to work for strangers in far away places? I shivered when I thought of it. I felt something harden within me when I realized that the advantage Andre had taken of me would only be the beginning, in situations like that. Like Andre, everyone would want to own me.

"No," I said. "I won't do it. Maybe I'm just being selfish and I'm damning myself, but I won't do it. I don't think we're exaggerating how bad that would be for us, not a bit."

"Then going to the hospital is not a good idea," Cataliades said.

"I know, but I have to, anyway."

"Then you can stop by on your way to the airport."

We sat up straighter.

"There's an Anubis plane flying out in three hours. It'll go to Dallas first, then Shreveport. The queen and Stan are paying for it jointly. It'll have all the survivors of both parties on it. The citizens of Rhodes have donated used coffins for the trip." Mr. Cataliades made a face, and honestly, I couldn't blame him. "Here's all the cash we can spare," he continued, handing me a short stack of bills. "Make it to the Anubis terminal in time, and you'll both go home with us. If you don't make it, I'll assume something happened to stop you and you'll have to call to make some other arrangement. We know we owe you a great debt, but we have wounded to get home ourselves, and the queen's credit cards and so on were lost in the fire. I'll have to call her credit company for emergency service, but that won't take much time."

This seemed a little cold, but after all, he wasn't our best friend, and as the daytime guy for the queen, he had a lot to do and many more problems to solve.

"Okay," I said. "Hey, listen, is Christian Baruch at the shelter?"

His face sharpened. "Yes. Though somewhat burned, he's hanging around the queen in Andre's absence as if he would take Andre's place."

"He wants to, you know. He wants to be the next Mr. Queen of Louisiana."

"Baruch?" Cataliades could not have been more scornful if a goblin had applied for the job.

"No, he's gone to extreme lengths." I already told Andre about this. Now I had to explain again. "That's why he planted that Dr Pepper bomb," I said about five minutes later.

"How do you know this?" Mr. Cataliades asked.

"I figured it out, from this and that," I said modestly. I sighed. Here came the yucky part. "I found him yesterday, hiding underneath the registration desk. There was another vampire with him, badly burned. I don't even know who that one was. And in the same area was Todd Donati, the security guy, alive but hurt, and a dead maid." I felt the exhaustion all over again, smelled the awful smell, tried to breathe the thick air. "Baruch was out of it, of course."

I was not exactly proud of this, and I looked down at my hands. "Anyway, I was trying to read Todd Donati's mind, to find out how hurt he was, and he was just hating Baruch and blaming him, too. He was willing to be frank, this time. No more job to worry about. Todd told me he'd watched all the security tapes over and over again, and he'd finally figured out what he was seeing. His boss was leaping up to block the camera with gum so he could plant the bomb. Once he'd figured that out, Donati knew that Baruch had wanted to alarm the queen, make her insecure, so she'd take a new husband. And that would be Christian Baruch. But guess why he wants to marry her?"

"I can't imagine," said Mr. Cataliades, thoroughly shocked.

"Because he wants to open a new vampire hotel in New Orleans. Blood in the Quarter got flooded and closed, and Baruch thought he could rebuild and reopen."

"But Baruch didn't have anything to do with the other bombs?"

"I sure don't think so, Mr. Cataliades. I think that was the Fellowship, just like I said yesterday."

"Then who killed the vampires from Arkansas?" Barry asked. "I guess the Fellowship did that, too? No, wait . . . why would they? Not that they'd quibble at killing some vampires, but they'd know the vampires would probably get killed in the big explosion."

"We have an overload of villains," I said. "Mr. Cataliades, you got any ideas about who might have taken out the Arkansas vampires?" I gave Mr. Cataliades a straight-in-the-eyes stare.

"No," Mr. Cataliades said. "If I did, I would *never* say those ideas out loud. I think you should be concentrating on your man's injuries and getting back to your little town, not worrying about three deaths among so many."

I wasn't exactly worried about the deaths of the three Arkansas vampires, and it seemed like a really good idea to take Mr. Cataliades's advice to heart. I'd had the odd moment to think about the murders, and I'd decided that the simplest answer was often the best.

Who'd thought she had a good chance of skipping a trial altogether, if Jennifer Cater was silenced?

Who'd prepared the way to be admitted to Jennifer's room, by the simple means of a phone call?

Who'd had a good long moment of telepathic communication with her underlings before she began the artificial flurry of primping for the impromptu visit?

Whose bodyguard had been coming out of the stairway door just as we were exiting the suite?

I knew, just as Mr. Cataliades knew, that Sophie-Anne had ensured Sigebert would be admitted to Jennifer Cater's room by calling down ahead and telling Jennifer she herself was on her way. Jennifer would look out the peephole, recognize Sigebert, and assume the queen was right behind him. Once inside, Sigebert would unsheath his sword and kill everyone in the place.

Then he would hurry back up the stairs to appear in time to escort the queen right back down to the seventh floor.

He'd enter the room again so there'd be a reason for his scent to be on the air.

And at the time I'd suspected absolutely nothing.

What a shock it must have been to Sophie-Anne when Henrik Feith had popped up alive; but then the problem had been solved when he accepted her protection.

The problem reasserted itself when someone talked him into accusing her anyway.

And then, amazingly, problem solved again: the nervous little vampire had been assassinated in front of the court.

"I do wonder how Kyle Perkins was hired," I said. "He must have known he was on a suicide mission."

"Perhaps," Mr. Cataliades said carefully, "he had decided to meet the sun anyway. Perhaps he was looking for a spectacular and interesting way to go, earning a monetary legacy for his human descendants."

"It seems strange that I was sent looking for information about him by a member of our very own party," I said, my voice neutral.

"Ah, not everyone needs to know everything," Mr. Cataliades said, his voice just as neutral.

Barry could hear my thoughts, of course, but he wasn't getting what Mr. Cataliades was saying, which was just as well. It was stupid that it made me feel better, Eric and Bill not knowing the queen's deep game. Not that they weren't capable of playing deep games themselves, but I didn't think Eric would have sent me on the wild goose chase for the archery range where Kyle Perkins had trained if Eric had known the queen herself had hired Perkins.

The poor woman behind the counter had died because the queen hadn't told her left hand what her right hand was doing. And I wondered what had happened to the human, the one who'd thrown up on the murder scene, the one who'd been hired to drive Sigebert or Andre to the range . . . after

I'd so thoughtfully left a message to tell them when Barry and I were going back to collect the evidence. I'd sealed the woman's fate myself by leaving that phone message.

Mr. Cataliades took his departure, shaking our hands with his beaming smile, almost normal. He urged us once again to get to the airport.

"Sookie?" said Barry.

"Yeah."

"I really want to be on that plane."

"I know."

"What about you?"

"I don't think I can do it. Sit on the same plane with them."

"They all got hurt," Barry said.

"Yeah, but that isn't payback."

"You took care of that, didn't you?"

I didn't ask him what he meant. I knew what he could pick up out of my head.

"As much as I could," I said.

"Maybe I don't want to be on the same plane with *you*," Barry said.

Of course it hurt, but I guess I deserved it.

I shrugged. "You gotta decide that on your own. All of us have different things we can live with."

Barry considered that. "Yeah," he said. "I know. But for right now, it's better that we go our separate ways, here. I'm leaving for the airport to hang around until I can leave. Are you going to the hospital?"

I was too wary now to tell him. "I don't know," I said. "But I'm finding a car or a bus to take me home."

He hugged me, no matter how upset he was about the choices I'd made. I could feel the affection and regret in his heart. I hugged him back. He'd made his own choices.

I left the maid ten dollars when I departed on foot about

five minutes after Barry got in a cab. I waited until I got two blocks from the hotel, and then I asked a passerby how to get to St. Cosmas. It was a long ten-block hike, but the day was beautiful, cool and crisp with a bright sun. It felt good to be by myself. I might be wearing rubber-soled slippers, but I was dressed nicely enough, and I was clean. I ate a hot dog on my way to the hospital, a hot dog I'd bought from a street vendor, and that was something else I'd never done before. I bought a shapeless hat from a street vender, too, and stuffed all my hair up under it. The same guy had some dark glasses for sale. With the sky being so bright and the wind blowing in off the lake, the combination didn't look too odd.

St. Cosmas was an old edifice, with lots of ornate architectural embellishment on the outside. It was huge, too. I asked about Quinn's condition, and one of the women stationed at the busy visitors' desk said she couldn't give out that information. But to see if he was registered at the hospital, she'd had to look up his records, and I plucked his room number from her thoughts. I waited until all three of the women were occupied with other queries, and I slipped into the elevator and rode up.

Quinn was on the tenth floor. I'd never seen a hospital so large, and I'd never seen one so bustling. It was easy to stride around like I had a purpose and knew where I was going.

There was no one on guard outside his room.

I knocked lightly, and there wasn't a sound from inside. I pushed open the door very gently and stepped inside. Quinn was asleep in the bed, and he was attached to machines and tubes. And he was a fast-healing shifter, so his injuries must have been grievous. His sister was by his side. Her bandaged head, which had been propped on her hand, jerked up as she became aware of my presence. I pulled off the sunglasses and the hat.

"You," she said.

"Yeah, me, Sookie. What's Frannie short for, anyway?"

"It's really Francine, but everyone calls me Frannie." She looked younger as she said it.

Though I was pleased at the decreased hostility, I decided I'd better stay on my side of the room. "How is he?" I asked, jerking my chin at the sleeping man.

"He fades in and out." There was a moment of silence while she took a drink from a white plastic cup on the bedside table. "When you woke him up, he got me up," she said abruptly. "We started down the stairs. But a big piece of ceiling fell on him, and the floor went out from beneath us, and the next thing I knew, some firemen are telling me some crazy woman found me while I was still alive, and they're giving me all kinds of tests, and Quinn's telling me he was going to take care of me until I was well. Then they told me he had two broken legs."

There was an extra chair, and I collapsed onto it. My legs just wouldn't hold me. "What does the doctor say?"

"Which one?" Frannie said bleakly.

"Any. All." I took one of Quinn's hands. Frannie almost reached out as if she thought I'd hurt him, but then she subsided. I had the hand that was free of tubes, and I held it for a while.

"They can't believe how much better he is already," Frannie said just when I'd decided she wasn't going to answer. "In fact, they think it's something of a miracle. Now we're gonna have to pay someone to get his records out of the system." Her dark-rooted hair was in clumps, and she was still filthy from the blast site.

"Go buy some clothes and come back and have a shower," I said. "I'll sit with him."

"Are you really his girlfriend?"

"Yes, I am."

"He said you had some conflicts."

"I do, but not with him."

"So, okay. I will. You got any money?"

"Not a lot, but here's what I can spare."

I handed her seventy-five dollars of Mr. Cataliades's money.

"Okay, I can stretch it," she said. "Thanks." She said it without enthusiasm, but she said it.

I sat in the quiet room and held Quinn's hand for almost an hour. In that time, his eyes had flickered open once, registered my presence, and closed again. A very faint smile curved his lips for a moment. I knew that while he was sleeping, his body was healing, and when he woke, he might be able to walk again. I would have found it very comforting to climb on that bed and snuggle with Quinn for a while, but it might be bad for him if I did that; I might jostle him or something.

After a while, I began talking to him. I told him why I thought the crude bomb had been left outside the queen's door, and I told him my theory about the deaths of the three Arkansas vampires. "You gotta agree, it makes sense," I said, and then I told him what I thought about the death of Henrik Feith and the execution of his murderer. I told him about the dead woman in the shop. I told him about my suspicions about the explosion.

"I'm sorry it was Jake that was in with them," I told him. "I know you used to like him. But he just couldn't stand being a vamp. I don't know if he approached the Fellowship or the Fellowship approached him. They had the guy at the computer, the one who was so rude to me. I think he called a delegate from each party to have them come pick up a suitcase. Some of them were too smart or too lazy to pick them up, and some of them returned the suitcases when no one claimed them. But not me, oh no, I put it in the queen's effing living room." I shook my head. "I guess not too many of the staff were in on it, because otherwise Barry or I would've picked up on something way before Barry did."

Then I slept for a few minutes, I think, because Frannie was there when I looked around, and she was eating from a McDonald's bag. She was clean, and her hair was wet.

"You love him?" she asked, sucking up some Coke through a straw.

"Too soon to tell."

"I'm going to have to take him home to Memphis," she said.

"Yeah, I know. I may not get to see him for a while. I've got to get home, too, somehow."

"The Greyhound station is two blocks away."

I shuddered. A long, long bus ride was not a prospect that I could look forward to.

"Or you could take my car," Frannie said.

"What?"

"Well, we got here separately. He drove here with all the props and a trailer, and I left out of my mama's in a hurry in my little sports car. So there are two cars here, and we only need one. I'm going to have to go home with him and stay for a while. You have to get back to work, right?"

"Right."

"So, drive my car home, and we'll pick it up when we're able."

"That's very nice of you," I said. I was surprised by her generosity, because I'd definitely had the impression she wasn't keen on Quinn having a girlfriend, and she wasn't keen on me, specifically.

"You seem okay. You tried to get us out of there in time. And he really cares about you."

"And you know this how?"

"He told me so."

She'd gotten part of the family directness, I could tell.

"Okay," I said. "Where are you parked?"

19

I'd been terrified the whole two-day drive: that I'd be stopped and they wouldn't believe I'd gotten permission to use the car, that Frannie would change her mind and tell the police I'd stolen it, that I'd have an accident and have to repay Quinn's sister for the vehicle. Frannie had an old red Mustang, and it was fun to drive. No one stopped me. The weather was good all the way back to Louisiana. I thought I'd see a slice of America, but along the interstate, everything looks the same. I imagined that in any small town I passed through, there was another Merlotte's, and maybe another Sookie.

I didn't sleep well on the trip, either, because I dreamed of the floor shaking under my feet and the dreadful moment we went out the hole in the glass. Or I saw Pam burning. Or other things, things I'd done and seen during the hours we patrolled the debris, looking for bodies.

When I turned into my driveway, having been gone a week, my heart began to pound as if the house was waiting for me. Amelia was sitting on the front porch with a bright blue ribbon in her hand, and Bob was sitting in front of her, batting at the dangling ribbon with a black paw. She looked up to see who it was, and when she recognized me behind the wheel, she leaped to her feet. I didn't pull around back; I stopped right there and jumped out of the driver's seat. Amelia's arms wrapped around me like vines, and she shrieked, "You're back! Oh, blessed Virgin, you're back!"

We danced around and hopped up and down like teenagers, whooping with sheer happiness.

"The paper listed you as a survivor," she said. "But no one could find you the day after. Until you called, I wasn't sure you were alive."

"It's a long story," I said. "A long, long story."

"Is it the right time to tell it to me?"

"Maybe after a few days," I said.

"Do you have anything to carry in?"

"Not a thing. All my stuff went up in smoke when the building went down."

"Oh, my God! Your new clothes!"

"Well, at least I have my driver's license and my credit card and my cell phone, though the battery's flat and I don't have the charger."

"And a new car?" She glanced back at the Mustang.

"A borrowed car."

"I don't think I have a single friend who would loan me a whole car."

"Half a car?" I asked, and she laughed.

"Guess what?" Amelia said. "Your friends got married."

I stopped dead. "Which friends?" Surely she couldn't mean the Bellefleur double wedding; surely they hadn't changed the date yet again.

"Oh, I shouldn't have said anything," Amelia said, looking guilty. "Well, speak of the devil!" There was another car coming to a stop right by the red Mustang.

Tara scrambled out. "I saw you driving by the shop," she called. "I almost didn't recognize you in the new car."

"Borrowed it from a friend," I said, looking at her askance.

"You did *not* tell her, Amelia Broadway!" Tara was righteously indignant.

"I didn't," Amelia said. "I started to, but I stopped in time!"

"Tell me what?"

"Sookie, I know this is going to sound crazy," Tara said, and I felt my brows draw together. "While you were gone, everything just clicked in a strange way, like something I'd known should happen, you know?"

I shook my head. I didn't know.

"JB and I got married!" Tara said, and the expression on her face was full of so many things: anxiety, hopefulness, guilt, wonder.

I ran that incredible sentence through my head several times before I was sure I understood the meaning of it. "You and JB? Husband and wife?" I said.

"I know, I know, it seems maybe a little strange . . ."

"It seems perfect," I said with all the sincerity I could scrape together. I wasn't really sure how I felt, but I owed my friend the happy face and cheerful voice I offered her. At the moment, this was the true stuff, and vampire fangs and blood under the bright searchlights seemed like the dream, or a scene from a movie I hadn't much enjoyed. "I'm so happy for you. What do you need for a wedding present?"

"Just your blessing, we put the announcement in the paper yesterday," she said, burbling away like a happy brook. "And the phone just hasn't stopped ringing off the wall since then. People are so nice!"

She truly believed she'd swept all her bad memories into a corner. She was in the mood to credit the world with benevolence.

I would try that, too. I would do my best to smother the memory of that moment when I'd glanced back to see Quinn pulling himself along by his elbows. He'd reached Andre, who lay mute and stricken. Quinn had propped himself on one elbow, reached out with his other hand, grabbed the piece of wood lying by Andre's leg and jammed it into Andre's chest. And, just like that, Andre's long life was over.

He'd done it for me.

How could I be the same person? I wondered. How could I be happy that Tara had gotten married and yet remember such a thing—not with horror, but with a savage sense of pleasure? I had wanted Andre to die, as much as I had wanted Tara to find someone to live with who would never tease her for her awful past, someone who would care for her and be sweet to her. And JB would do that. He might not be much on intellectual conversation, but Tara seemed to have made her peace with that.

Theoretically, then, I was delighted and hopeful for my two friends. But I couldn't feel it. I'd seen awful things, and I'd felt awful things. Now I felt like two different people trying to exist inside the same space.

If I just stay away from the vampires for a while, I told myself, smiling and nodding the whole time as Tara talked on and Amelia patted my shoulder or my arm. *If I pray every night, and hang around with humans, and leave the Weres alone, I'll be okay.*

I hugged Tara, squeezing her until she squeaked.

"What do JB's parents say?" I asked. "Where'd you get the license? Up in Arkansas?"

As Tara began to tell me all about it, I winked at Amelia,

who winked back and bent down to scoop up Bob in her arms. Bob blinked when he looked into my face, and he rubbed his head against my offered fingers and purred. We went inside with the sun bright on our backs and our shadows preceding us into the old house.